HIM

Kerry D. King

Publisher's note: Names, characters, descriptions, places, businesses, occupations, vehicles, incidents, and dog breeds are either the product of the author's imagination or are used fictitiously, and any resemblance to actual persons living or dead, or any resemblance to businesses, establishments, events, or locales is entirely coincidental.

ISBN number: 978-0-615-56949-9

Published by Unicorn Castle Books
PO Box 233
White Bluff, TN 37187
unicorncastlebooks@gmail.com

www.kerrydking.com

The publisher is not responsible for websites (or their content) that are not owned by the publisher.

Printed in the United States of America

First Edition September 2012

Cover image by the amazing Duncan Long. View his gallery at:
http://duncanlong.com/art.html

For Him

If not for your visit to my world, I would never have known about yours.

A Word from the Author

It's been almost forty years, yet I still remember it as if it were yesterday.

While *HIM* is based on actual events, it was necessary to protect the privacy of everyone who participated in this psychic drama. I have made every effort to change or disguise names, physical descriptions, occupations, vehicles, locations, and even dog breeds. Therefore, even if you believe you recognize someone within these pages, they cannot and do not exist as a participant of this story.

Restaurants have been closed or torn down and replaced with high-rises or hotels. The company workplace is no longer in business, as if someone had erected a set for this drama and dismantled it when it was over.

The people who shared this event with me were some of the most unique, remarkable, and awesome individuals ever to cross my path in this lifetime. They came together from every walk of life to play a role in a drama that would save my life and my sanity. Hopefully, as you live this experience along with Kerry, it will save or change yours.

Devin, especially, sacrificed a part of his life so that this event could occur. He was very brave to allow this to happen…very unselfish to give up what he did to help someone else…someone who could not have accomplished his mission without that agreement and participation. Devin was a generous, kind, and gregarious guy. Everyone who knew him loved and admired him. The waning hippie world, which still existed in some crowds, and the establishment world of the straight and narrow, both respected him. He managed to straddle both worlds effortlessly. He had an engaging personality and a smile that lit up every room he entered. He was a man's man and a lady's fantasy, but he chose to be just himself, and that was more than enough for everyone who had the pleasure and good fortune to know him. Of all the participants in this cosmic play, I owe him my gratitude more than anyone.

1974 was a completely different world than the one we know today. Young readers will be shocked and probably dismayed at the lack of technology and the simple life we took for granted, while older readers may look back on those years with longing and nostalgia.

Personal computers did not exist in our homes. You had to turn pages to read a book. There were no iPods, iPads, iTunes, or cell phones. For that matter, not everyone even had a landline. Ma Bell was a monopoly that made the decisions on who could get a phone and how much the deposit would cost. Some of you may remember Lily Tomlin in the *Laugh-In* series, playing the telephone operator. I still smile when I remember her famous line… "We don't care. We don't have to. We're the phone company." And that's just the way it was.

Many people relied on pay phones, which were everywhere. If you were lucky enough to afford a phone, or had a friend who would cosign for you, you had to actually dial it to reach someone. There were no speed dials, redials, or contact lists. There was no caller ID, and you had to trust your hunch as to who was calling before you picked up the phone to answer. There was no option of leaving a message. A few long-distance calls could consume your entire paycheck.

The idea of cell phones existed only in the imaginations of writers like Jules Verne and Gene Roddenberry. Once you left your house, you were unreachable until you arrived at your destination, assuming there was a phone there.

If you needed information, you visited or called the library or consulted an encyclopedia. Today you can type your question into a search engine and receive thousands of pages to review. You can read customer reviews at the click of a mouse before you purchase anything. In 1974, you either relied on a friend's referral, or you took your chances with the luck of the draw.

If you needed to understand the lyrics of your favorite song, and if you were lucky, the album jackets had the lyrics printed on them. Otherwise, you lifted the arm of your record player and set it back a few grooves over and over, or you reversed the tape on your reel-to-reel and replayed until you got it right. Sometimes you just never did. There were some cassettes and many 8-tracks, but they were more fragile than records. Compact discs were a decade away.

Today, thanks to the Internet, you can type in the title or artist, or even just a few words of a song, and not only read the full lyrics and hear the song instantly, but you will likely be directed to a YouTube video where you can often actually see the original artist perform in the year he made the song famous. Music is a very important part of this story, and if you become curious about the songs I refer to in each chapter, finding it is instantaneous and just a click away. I have included a song and album bibliography at the end of the book.

If you smoked cigarettes, and almost everybody did, they were much cheaper than today (well under 50 cents a pack), and each pack came with a book of matches. The only lighters around were the occasional Zippo, carried by people with the patience to continually refill them as they ran out of lighter fluid, often too frequently to be worth the bother.

If you wanted to see an older movie, you hoped one of the few local channels on your television would broadcast it, and if one did, it was so cut and edited for TV that you hardly recognized the movie. There were no premium channels, and no pay television. There were no videos or video stores, and certainly no DVDs or camcorders either.

If you took photographs with your 110, 126, or 135 camera, you had to deposit the film in your local store and wait several days for the developing. There were no digital options where, if you didn't like the photo, you could delete and try again.

We had to actually mail our letters, and they took several days to arrive unless you paid extra for airmail. Instant email was unimaginable.

The Civil Rights Act of 1964 did not change the general consensus that interracial relationships were taboo, and many people still frowned upon them in 1974. One of the arguments for this thinking was that it was unfair to the children born of these mixed marriages because neither race would accept them. In this day and age, of course, this logic sounds outdated, but in 1974, this was an idea that our parents had drilled into us throughout our childhoods.

Wages were lower, but rent and food were cheaper. Babysitters would keep your children while you worked, get them to school and back, feed them breakfast and sometimes dinner, all for 25 dollars a week. Working mothers could actually afford to take a job.

This was the world Kerry King lived in.

This was 1974.

About the Music

I was fourteen when they assassinated President John F. Kennedy, and on that violent day, America changed forever. The Vietnam War kicked up full scale, and young men were drafted and forced to participate in that senseless and horrifying bloodbath. This gave rise to the Hippie Movement, which in turn gave birth to the era of mind-expanding drugs.

Before and shortly after the assassination, the top forty charts consisted of, first, the Motown groups, then the English invasion of rock music, and on the charts, sandwiched between The Rolling Stones above and The Four Seasons below, would be Perry Como or another of our parents' genre. The music was teeny-bop and poppy and largely geared to teenagers.

With the advent of the war, the Hippie Movement, and the drugs, music also took an abrupt turn, and underground FM stations began to spring up. Unlike the poppy AM stations whose singers just wanted to hold your hand or order you off of their cloud, the underground music had a different message. War protest songs were of course how it started, but eventually the singers wanted to take you places you'd never been, places they'd just returned from. You didn't have to physically leave to go there. Some of the greatest bands the world has ever known arose from the ashes of the Vietnam War and the Hippie Movement.

Bands that may never have been noticed otherwise; some of them local garage types, rose to the top of the charts and became smash hits on the underground stations. Pink Floyd, The Moody Blues, Deep Purple, Led Zeppelin and Quicksilver Messenger Service were household names. Uriah Heep, Savoy Brown, Badfinger, The Who, Steppenwolf, Bob Dylan, Grand Funk Railroad, Jefferson Airplane, Creedence Clearwater Revival and Cat Stevens...all had something to say, and if you were listening close, you were learning something your parents never told you.

In his book, *UFOs: Operation Trojan Horse*, John Keel refers to an invisible force that has been influencing our world from another dimension. In 1969, he wrote that young people were more aware of these forces than any other generation before them. He said there was a mass illumination taking place that had begun in the sixties, mainly through music, although it was occurring on other levels as well. He felt that music was an important medium for this force.

This music plays an important role in these events that occurred in 1974. Because of the music bibliography I included at the end of this book, some of you early readers have run searches on the songs you encountered in each chapter, and many of you have purchased the albums after you found and heard them.

I hope that those of you who have never heard of these music groups will give them a few minutes of your time. Readers who are already familiar with these artists know exactly what I am talking about.

This music and its messages continued well into the late '70s bringing in many more groups with even more blatant lyrics, all sending the same message. Styx, Boston, Kansas, Rush, Al Stewart and many others remained on the music scene outselling many other bands and spreading the word.

I hope that word has gotten to many of you already and that it is on its way to newcomers willing to explore this genre for the first time.

Acknowledgements

I've always believed that acknowledgments are for the people who directly influenced and affected the outcome of a book. There are only a few people who fall into this category.

To my sister Pammy, who was there when it happened and who painstakingly poured over the manuscript many times searching for events that she believed I should remove from my account of what happened in 1974. Although she felt like she'd *already* read the book the first time she read it, she endured several additional readings just so she could advise me of what she insisted the reader didn't need to know—every time I took a shower, for example, and what each meal consisted of. The book was long enough as it was, she said. When Pam reads this, she will insist that I cut my word count in her section of the acknowledgment, or just remove it altogether, but that's just Pam. Without Pam's guidance and memories, this book would not be the same, so to Pammy I owe my heartfelt thanks. She refused, however, to comb the manuscript for spelling or grammar errors, so any of those you stumble across are mine.

To Debra Ice, my sister writer and friend of five years: Although we've never met, I promise I intend to remedy that shortly now that the book is finished. We've been email buddies since we met on a writers' site, and Debra has been my light at the end of the writing tunnel in more ways than one. Debra has written her own book, *Vicissitudes: the ups and downs and changes experienced in a lifetime,* and if it weren't for her diligence and determination to master the art of formatting manuscripts for publishing, this work would still be a stack of 1530 typed pages collecting dust in the closet. Period. Thanks, Debra! Debra also read this book and offered her encouragement and kind words during my long editing process. My book did not help her because her life is already perfect. Because she didn't need any help at perfecting her life, she dedicated a part of it to helping me with my manuscript. A large part, actually.

To my brother, Warren Peace, who spent many hours hunched over the computer searching and marking errors, typos, misprints, and wording that just didn't make sense: Thanks for all the hours and help. You took on the job that nobody wants to do, especially for free. Thankfully, Sue found a way to install it on your Kindle. Even then, the process of reading and marking errors was a daunting task. Thank you!

To Deneen Ansley and Sue Bowers, who took on the job of reading the entire book prior to its publication: Your feedback and honest reviews of the story meant a lot to me. And Deneen, your tedious corrections, page by page, for typos and misused words, words lost or added in the editing process, and your willingness to recheck the book again after all corrections were made was just above and beyond the call of duty and friendship. Thank you both.

And to my husband, Joe. Love of my life: No one has been more persistent in insisting this book come to fruition. Without his continual nudging, I'm not sure I'd have kept up the fight. Joe did everything he could to give me the tools and technology, the peace and quiet, and the encouragement to keep on keeping on. If it weren't for Joe, this manuscript would still be a stack of 50 notebooks of handwritten pages, written so I would never forget, collected in binders and stored in the attic. For all you've done, Joe, to help move this book forward, and for the myriad of other things too numerous to mention...*thank you!*

CONTENTS

Part One

Stairway to Heaven

Is it possible that, before we were born on this earth, we had a prior life in another dimension?

"Among the most neglected of all soft sightings are the strange purple blobs, some so faint that they can barely be seen by the naked eye.... People who see these things often dismiss them as some kind of illusion or natural phenomena, or they feel they are not worthy of being reported."

John A. Keel
UFOs: Operation Trojan Horse
© 1970 John A. Keel
Originally published by G.P. Putnam's Sons

1 The book arrived on a June afternoon in 1974.
My younger sister, Pammy, must have brought the package in and set it on the coffee table where I would spot it when I came in from work. Pam was nowhere in sight, but her car was parked out front, and an unfamiliar album was playing on the record player. Pink Floyd, according to the record label, lyrics that only reminded me of my dull days and moments ticking away. *Thanks, Pam.*

The shower was running in the bathroom. She probably had an early date, and my house and shower were closer to where she worked.

I was leafing through the book when the bathroom door opened, and Pammy darted across the hall into the bedroom, wrapped in a towel. She waved to me in transit.

"There's a package from Mom on the coffee table there."

I sighed and rolled my eyes. "I got it. How'd you get in?"

"My old house key. Hey, Kerry, we're going to a drive-in tonight. Why don't you come with us?"

I thumbed through the book absently, not looking up. "No, I'll leave that to you hippies. Besides, who'd watch the kids?"

Pam came out fully dressed, perched on the arm of the couch, and vigorously rubbed her long hair with a towel. "Bring 'em with us! Hey, where are they anyway?"

"They're still at the sitter's. And five people in one Jeep? Thanks anyway."

Pink Floyd continued to rub it in, reminding me that ten years had gotten behind me.

She shrugged. "It's better than sitting here all night by yourself again." She glanced at the book and scowled. "Good grief! Mom didn't send you *that* book!"

"Yeah. She's been pushing it for months. Probably hoping it will scare me out of my Wicca studies. I finally agreed to read it just to get her off my back." I set the book on the table.

"Oh, that'll straighten you out all right. You'll be sorry if you read *that* thing. What's she trying to do to you? Ever since *she* read it, she's been sleeping with the lights on every night. She won't mess with occult stuff anymore, and you *know* we were raised Catholic-occult. She won't read your Tarot cards anymore, either. And if that isn't bad enough, she gives the book to all her close friends and now *they're* all sleeping with the lights on."

"Oh, come on. No book is that convincing. What's this on the dust jacket? '*This book is a warning*'?"

"I'm telling you, Kerry, I remember when it was kicking around at Mom's. It's probably a bunch of bullshit, but with you living here by yourself, I wouldn't advise your reading it." She began to gather her clothes and belongings and stuff them into a paper grocery bag.

"Why don't you move back in, then?" I smiled, baiting her. "Sure is empty around here lately."

I'm thinking about it, believe me. I've had it with living with George. I'll be going up to Allentown in a few months to visit the family. That will give me an excuse to pack everything up. Then, when I come back, I'll just move back in here."

I smiled at her scheme. "Sounds like you might mean it this time. Why don't you just tell him now?"

She reached over, lifted the arm of the record player, and silenced Pink. "With George, you don't just drop a relationship like it never happened. I've tried before. But this time I'm sticking to it. Anyways, when I go, I'll take that stupid book back. You're not really going to read it, are you?" She slid the album into a black jacket with the image of a prism refracting light into rainbow colors. Then, it too, disappeared into the bag.

"I might." I picked up the book again. *UFOs: Operation Trojan Horse. John A. Keel.* "Doesn't sound like anything scary."

"Kerry, that book is not really about UFOs. That's where the Trojan Horse part comes in. According to that book, UFOs, among other things, are supposed to be a camouflage from another dimension."

"Did you read it?"

"I didn't have to." Pam screwed up her face. "The way she carried on while she was reading it? I got a blow by blow with each chapter. First, her UFO books went off the shelf. Then she threw out anything she had on possession, including *The Exorcist*. Then she put the cards away. When she started looking at her saint books with suspicion, *that's* when I left home."

"Her *saint* books too?"

"Everything. If you're going to believe in the Trojan Horse Theory, even Jesus Christ was one of *them!*"

"Now you've got my curiosity up. No book could be that scary."

"Tell that to five grown women who are all still sleeping with the lights on. Really, I think it's the idea of an invisible world around you all the time. It's creepy. I wouldn't *want* to believe in it. Not if I can't see it." She got up and went into the bathroom. "Got a comb in here?"

"Medicine cabinet."

"I found it. Come on. Come with us. You can take your own car."

"Thanks, but I think I'll just make myself a drink and kick back with this book and see what the big deal is."

Pam shrugged. "Well, okay. I'll see if I can snag you a joint if anyone has one."

"SHH, not so loud! You never know who might be on the other side of that door!"

"Good grief, you're so paranoid!"

A vehicle beeped outside, and Pam laughed. "Perceptive, but paranoid." She shook her head, still laughing, and opened the front door. "It's George. I guess I'll see you later."

"Okay, Pam. Thanks for stopping in."

"Sure. Thanks for letting me use the shower. It's a good excuse really, so I can see you without *him* on my tail." She jerked her thumb toward the idling Jeep outside. "Later. And don't drink too much."

"You just remember the joints."

"And don't read that stupid book!" Her final words were underlined by the slamming of the heavy front door. When the roar of the Jeep faded away, I was alone once again.

As usual.

I left to pick up the girls.

Thursday night. Another evening to kill. It had been better when Pam lived here. With people coming and going, the house hadn't been so quiet and empty. Now it mocked me with its silent, cold cleanliness. Not a speck of dust anywhere. Not a dish in the sink. It hadn't been so immaculate when Pam had lived here, but it had been more alive.

The TV was running in the kids' room. I sometimes let it run all night until the National Anthem played, just for the sound of life in the house. I picked up the book. At least it was something to do.

The beginning looked boring enough. Sightings. I'd read enough sighting reports over the years, so I skipped to the middle of the book where I found a detailed explanation of elementary physics. It was too technical to understand, so I decided to start at the beginning, but I'd skip the sighting reports.

After a couple of pages of background history on the UFO phenomenon, I took a break, fixed myself a drink, and lay back on the couch with my feet elevated on the coffee table. Instantly I felt blood rush to my head, and I closed my eyes, trying to regain my equilibrium. My heart began to race, and I folded the book on my chest, suddenly frightened.

Instead of my balance returning to normal, a sensation of wind and speed swept through me, as if I had been tossed onto a soaring carnival ride. My stomach plunged in the sudden surge upward. I squeezed my eyes tighter and found myself walking on a sprawling plantation-like lawn. Far up the sloping green stood a colossal, luminous, bone white, three-story mansion, one you might find on a Southern Colonial estate. Tall sturdy columns supported a second-floor balcony. A wide veranda ran the length of the manor in front, and the top floor consisted almost entirely of windows and glass. There were many people—strangers—on the lawn. They didn't appear to notice me. Eerie voices emanated from inside the house, and suddenly I was afraid of where I might be. Everything seemed to be phosphorous, glowing with its own light source. The mansion, the lawn, the shrubbery...even the sky...appeared to be plugged in.

I opened my eyes to find that I was still flying toward the ceiling in my own home, that roller-coaster sensation terrifying. Sensing an inevitable crash, I closed them again.

Now I was ascending the steps and walking across the porch, my feet ignoring my silent pleas to turn and run. I felt hypnotized...with no will of my own. Before my foot took the first step onto the veranda, I opened my eyes again.

I was back on the couch. My heart was pounding, my pulse racing, and I was struggling to breathe. Once again, I felt blood rushing to my head and blackness overtaking me. Then I had a sensation of being violently flung across the room. I tried to scream, only to find I had no voice and no lung capacity. Struggling to suck in air I closed my eyes again and realized I was unabashedly approaching a young man on the porch of that eerie white mansion. His hair was the color of autumn and flames, and his luminous eyes shone like a wolf or jackal—amber and black with a green cast that would surely glow in the dark if I hung around long enough. The sky was a queer lemon yellow, and due to the lack of sun or moon, I could not determine whether it was early morning or just before dusk. I didn't know where I was, but I was sure of one thing. I did not want to be wandering around here in the dark.

My strong desire to be home again landed me back on the couch with a painful electric jolt. Whether I'd returned on my own power or been thrown back like a fish that was too small, I couldn't be sure. It didn't matter. Though the room looked fuzzy and drab compared to the clarity of the scene I'd left behind, I was relieved to be back in my own living room again.

The book still lay folded against my chest. Realization spread through me that I could not possibly have left the couch during those terrifying moments. I sat up, groggy and disoriented. My sister's remarks must have gotten to me. I'd dreamed the whole thing, I told myself. I'd probably been asleep for hours.

A glance at my drink sent a chill through me. The ice had not even begun to melt. The clock verified the facts. Not three minutes had passed since I'd sat down with the book. I flung it across the room, feeling a feeble satisfaction that it too could be thrown against a wall, and I made sure that *it* made contact.

There had been nothing frightening about the few pages I'd read, but I no longer had any curiosity about reading that book. The sight of it lying half-open in the corner of the room repulsed me. Just looking at it brought back, too clearly, the memory of that haunting mansion and the horrible sensation of flying toward ceiling and walls. I lay back nervously on the couch again. After an hour, unable to sleep, I rolled the TV out into the living room.

The TV broadcasting had long since gone off the air before I accepted the fact that Pammy would not be stopping back tonight. I made a mental note to call my mother and tell her just what I thought of her stupid book. I would do it before work.

It was still dark when I herded the kids into the car the next morning. Every day was the same routine, awakening the kids and all of us rushing to get ready. Me, for work. Mandy, for first grade, and Michelle—for anything the babysitter could handle. Usually I dropped the girls off at Kathy's by seven, but this morning I had other plans. The anxious feelings of the night before had dissipated, and the only thing on my mind this morning was getting out of the house early. My Uncle Joe had promised to leave me some gas money on his phone table so I headed there first. I could call my mother from there.

Uncle Joe lived out near the cow pastures where there were no streetlights. The bumpy dirt road stretched for a mile past towering pines and acres of fenced farmland. A thick fog blanketed the road and fields, and it wasn't going to lift until the sun came up. I braked irritably, hating to have to crawl through this mist in the dark.

"Mommy, why are we slowing down?" My five-year-old leaned curiously over the front seat, and I leaned forward myself, wiping the fogged windows with a sheet of newspaper I'd scooped from the floorboard.

"It's fog, can't you *see?*" Mandy answered for me with six-and-a-half-year-old wisdom. "Turn on the windshield wipers, Mom!"

Good idea, I thought, and turned on both the wipers and the defroster. It didn't help. I couldn't see a foot in front of me. I stuck my head out the side window, but it made no difference. It wasn't the fog.

In front of the windshield was a dark, bluish-purple, shivering, translucent mass of cloud. Too dark to see through to the road ahead, but only obstructing the view in front of the windshield. Michelle squealed when I stopped the car abruptly, and both kids lurched forward.

"Mommy! What *is* that, Mommy?"

There was nothing behind us and nothing on either side of the car. Only in the front. I could see the left turn up ahead through my side window. That road led to Joe's parallel dirt road, and thanks to the dawn we were rapidly gaining visibility and light, but I still could not see through my windshield.

When we reached the side road, I swung left, and visibility returned. I exhaled with relief and gunned it to the next parallel dirt road. Only then did I dare to turn and look across the field to where I'd left the bluish-purple cloud. It had not followed me. Like a small thundercloud in the middle of the road, it waited, as though it knew I had to come down that same road to get back on the Interstate. I watched it in the rearview mirror. The girls watched it too, fascinated and curious about the thing that had caused their mom so much grief. Then Michelle suddenly let out an excited screech. "Mommy, Mommy, there's arrows shooting out of it all around! Orange and pink arrows!"

I didn't look back. I just gassed it all the way to Joe's and was still trembling when we parked in his dirt yard. I didn't mention it to the kids, but I'd gotten the morbid impression that whatever that thing was, it was not just a fog. I was sure it had been alive.

Nobody was up at Joe's, but as he'd promised, a worn five-dollar bill lay beside the phone with a note indicating it was for me. The clock read seven o'clock. I had wasted twenty minutes out on that road when it shouldn't have taken even five to get from the exit to Joe's house. I wasn't about to sit alone long in this house, not after what had just happened and most certainly not after last night. Still shaking, I dialed my mother's home in Allentown. She answered on the first ring.

"It's me. I got your book."

"Already? That's great, Kerry. Did you get a chance to read any of it?"

"Well, a little. But something happened when I started to."

"Uh-oh, what's the matter? You sound upset."

"Oh, I'm upset, all right. Something just happened out on the road a few minutes ago that scared the living shit out of me!"

"Not an accident, I hope." She sounded alarmed.

"No, but it could have been if I'd been going my usual speed. I don't want to talk about it until the sun comes up. It really freaked me out. And the kids saw it too."

"Kerry, what are you talking about? You didn't let that book get to you, did you?"

"No, I didn't read enough of it. This morning was something else, but I do want to tell you what happened last night when I started to read it."

I related the incident, though it seemed rather silly after this fog event. For one thing, it was easy to pass off the whole thing as a dream, even though I knew I hadn't been asleep. This morning was different, and I ended up telling her about that, too.

"I still have to drive back the same way I came," I concluded. "I'm just waiting for the sun to come up."

My mother said something about the book dealing with those same purple, foggy blobs and sounded a little disturbed.

"It's not the book, Mom. I told you. I barely read ten pages of it. UFO stuff. No mention of any bluish-purple fogs."

"You just haven't read far enough, Kerry. Those blue blobs have been sighted even more frequently than the saucers. They're called soft sightings, and *they* are your real UFOs. They've been reported breathing, breaking into smaller blobs and flying back together. They are almost transparent and are more visible at some hours and times of the year than others."

"It does sound like we're talking about the same thing," I admitted. "Michelle saw arrows coming out of it as we drove away."

"Well, do the girls seem okay?"

"They're not as shook up as I am. Seems like some kind of warning not to read the book. If the premise is about another dimension, maybe one of its denizens doesn't want me reading it."

"Were you drinking last night?

"I never drank the only one I made. And there's no weed around to blame it on either. Maybe all the hype about the book had an effect on me, but it's not as if I was reading about some purple blob attacking someone's car. And I intended to call you when I got here. Maybe something didn't want me discussing the book with you. It isn't my imagination working overtime. You can rationalize last night all you want, but the kids were with me this morning."

"You may not have seen a UFO, Kerry, but you might have seen the same energy manifesting in another of its forms."

"Well, I don't know what the UFOs would want with me! I do bookkeeping at a bottled-water plant, for Christ's sake. It's not like I'm working on the sequel to the Air Force Blue Book!"

"I'm worried about you, honey. I wish you'd just quit that job and come home for a while."

"Mother, I'm twenty-five."

"I know, but living alone can get to you. I'm divorced too, and it isn't easy with kids. Does Pam ever come by to see you?"

"I saw her just yesterday. Mom, forget it, will you?"

"Well, still. I wish you would find a boyfriend. At least go out once in a while."

"I've got all the companionship I can stand right now. Remember that kid, Scotty, the guy I bought my stereo from?"

"Is *he* still hanging around?"

"Yeah, I gave him the money, and he's been mine ever since." I laughed at the thought.

"I meant someone your own age. You're five years older than him. At least go out and try to meet someone."

"Mom, I've told you and everyone else a million times. If I ever meet a guy who isn't a liar, a cheat, and an egotist, I'll be the first to grab him, even if he's *taken*, and believe me, that kind always is."

She gave up with a sigh. "Okay, Kerry, okay."

"Stop worrying about me."

"I'll try. So how's your job going?"

"Used to be better before they hired this jerk, Perry Jason. The new district manager. Ever since he came, the whole place has changed. All socializing has been stopped during working hours. The drivers had to cut their hair if it was over an inch long. Shine their work boots. They're not allowed in the office anymore. It's a drag. We can't be late from lunch. Can't wear Levis. Just like a regular company now. The Chicago office is always down checking on us and to top it off, the work has tripled since they hired him. He's merging the Chicago accounts in with ours, so we have to post them, too."

"That sounds awful. And you want to *stay*?"

"Well, it'd be worse if we paid any attention to his new rules. Really, anyone who didn't quit makes a game out of breaking the rules. Even my boss, Lola. She's really cool. She can't stand him either, and she lets us get away with murder. We run the radio loud all day, sing, joke around and have a blast. We still keep up with the workload, though, so if anyone approaches her about her uncontrollable kindergarten, she just tells them to stick it in their ear."

"Well, at least she's on your side. How about the girls you work with?"

"There's only two. Kelly's nuts like me, but she's married. Cute girl. Shaggy blond hair and green eyes. Teeny little thing with a big sassy mouth. She thinks I'm a witch because my corner of the office is decorated with pentagrams and astrology signs. You'd think we were bitter enemies the way we fight all day over the radio stations. She bitches that she has more Ss in her section than all the A-to-Fs I'm in charge of. I tell her it's because she's full of shit, and Lola tells us both to shut up."

My mother laughed. "How about the other girl?"

"Hannah? She's an eighteen-year-old workhorse, and she isn't any fun, but Lola and Kelly make up for her. And there are a few drivers who sneak in anyway. They don't care much for the rules or the job. I guess it's easy enough to find another one in this business. There are huge bottled-water companies out there, not dinky ones like this. But I kind of liked the family atmosphere, though it's changing now. Anyway, we can't be late anymore either, so I'd better go. At least I feel better getting off those spooky subjects."

We hung up, and I motioned for the kids to follow me. They set their comic books aside and tiptoed after me. When we slammed shut the car doors, I was thankful for the sun being out, and even more relieved when I arrived at the turnoff to see that, whatever that thing on the road had been this morning, it was as gone as the fog.

The sky was blue, and today was Friday. Payday. Suddenly, I felt good.

2

"Hey, Mama!"

"Mama doesn't work here anymore."

We all recognized that exchange uttered daily whenever any route salesman brought in more work for Lola—and—consequently us, and our posting machines coasted to a halt. All the drivers called Lola "Mama" even though we girls had tagged the nickname on her. With her cascading blond hair and cobalt-blue eyes, she looked like anything but someone's mother, especially ours. Or theirs. That voice belonged to Devin Drew, and *his* conversations always turned out to be interesting.

"Hey-hey-hey." Devin was smiling, as usual, as he pointed his finger at our boss with stabbing gestures in the air. "Don't give me none of your jive now—this ain't no social call, you know."

"Certainly, Devin," Lola replied, not looking up. "That's what you all say." She was teasing him. Lola didn't mind, really, and she liked Devin. Everybody did.

"What's with this crackback, Mama?" Devin went on. "Davian's Jewelers is a *charge*, man. We've been delivering there for years. Joey Burns is freaking out. He thinks it's going to come out of his paycheck!"

"It is, Devin," Lola said wearily. "It's been delinquent for three months now, and you guys know that—Kerry, look up Davian's—and Devin, what are you doing in here anyway? This is Joey's problem, not yours. You know damn well fraternization is not allowed. Only route supervisors or assistants can come in here, so if your name isn't Tim or Pat, that excludes you."

"Heeeey…buzz off, chick." Devin leaned casually against the doorjamb. "You see these shiny shoes? You see this ultra-short hair, man? Well, that's because the commie of Sparklear Water is now a supervisor, Lola baby! The hippie of this water plant is *in charge* ! Now, if you'll excuse me, I have this account to check on. Who's got the Ds?"

Lola made a sincere effort not to smile as she pointed into our adjoining office, past his shoulder, to me.

"How many, how many, I wonder," Devin sang loudly as he stepped toward me.

I already had the account in my hand. "But you really don't want to know," I sang back, holding up the yellow ledger card—redlined, black-tabbed, balance circled—all the signs of delinquent processing, the final steps just prior to the rented water cooler being picked up.

Devin stopped dead in his tracks, barely glancing at the ledger, and stared directly at me with piercing hazel eyes. "How many months delinquent?"

"Three."

"You know, you picked up on that song pretty quick, whoever you are," he said seriously. He took the ledger without taking his eyes off me.

"Oh, Kerry knows all those hick songs," Lola called in from her own office. "Did you find Dave all right?"

"Yeah…uh…yup." He gave me an odd look, then turned to resume his original act with Lola. His tone of voice, however, was a little more humble. "Mama, look, man, you can't crack this back on Joey. He never even got a delinquent notice."

"Uh-uh-uh…let's don't start that crap, Devin. He *did* get a notice. We make them out every month."

Devin switched tactics. "Well, okay, then he *got* one, but maybe it got lost in the route room. You know what a mess it is back there lately."

"I only know what a mess it's getting to be up here!" Lola snapped. "I don't know what you route guys are telling these people to sign them up, but half the new accounts have called in thinking that water cooler they rented was free, and they only have to pay for the water. You think we have nothing to do but answer the phone all day and fight with the customers?" She snatched the ticket from his hand, glanced at it briefly, and initialed it. "All right, Devin. This time only. Now scram."

"Thank you, Mama. From the bottom of my poor, overworked heart." He thumped his chest hard with his fist. "Joey won't forget this."

"As long as he doesn't forget it's delinquent." Lola smiled and shook her head. "Are you really a supervisor now?"

"Well, assistant, temporarily. The real backup is in Bermuda trying to regain his sanity."

"Oh, I see." Lola nodded, even though she obviously didn't. Popular as he was with the rest of the plant, Tim included, everybody knew what Perry Jason thought of the hippie. Commie was one of his nicer adjectives. While Perry looked like a district attorney, Devin was a full-blooded hippie. On his father's side, he would tell us. Whatever, Perry Jason *hated* hippies.

"Hey, Mama…"

"Go away," Lola said absently, working.

"Hey, I just wanted to check on this ticket."

Lola looked up, surprised. "Joey, look…" she began.

Joey Burns bravely marched up to her desk, the ticket dangling from his fingers behind his back. Before Lola could finish her sentence Devin appeared from out of nowhere, grabbed Joey by the shoulders and pointed him toward the door.

"Don't blow it, bro," Devin told him in a loud whisper. "Me and Mama already settled it—didn't we, Lola—now just go back to the route room like a good little boy. You ain't supposed to be in here anyway. Shit, if we get caught…don't worry Mama. I'll get this sweaty, contaminated thing out of your office…"

Lola burst out laughing, and it was a signal as far as we girls were concerned. The three of us got up to greet our long-lost route cousins. I got up mostly out of curiosity. Every time that loud hippie walked in here there was a commotion of some sort. Kelly wasted no time with her usual playful harassment. "My-my-my. Don't we look like *gentlemen* today! Hey Kerry, Hannah! Come see the pretty, shiny boots!"

Meanwhile Lola was eyeing Devin suspiciously. "Devin Drew! Are you wearing a *wig* ?"

To our utter amazement, Devin yanked at his short hair, and it slid off, exposing his real hair, a black mass of curls pulled tightly into a ponytail. His real hair was the same color as his mustache, a Fu Manchu style that seemed to be the *in* thing these days. A silver earring flashed from his left ear as he shook his hair loose from the band. "Hey, man, what?" He grinned defiantly. "The man said short hair. Now he didn't say *whose* short hair…and I don't really see what difference it makes as long as it's short! You dig?"

Lola and Kelly were in hysterics. "I just don't believe it," Lola said, when she finally caught her breath. "You actually went out and bought a wig, just because they told you to cut your hair?"

"Well, it's really my wife's wig," Devin admitted, "but it does look a lot better on me. Hey, them suckers cost a lot of bread. Which reminds me, I'm off duty now. I don't have to wear it anymore."

He stuffed the wig into his back pocket. A hunk of it hung out like a dead animal, and that started another barrage of laughter.

"Gee, we sure miss you guys in here these days. This place is getting to be like a morgue." Lola, still laughing, wiped tears from her eyes.

"Yeah, well, you'll have to take that up with Mr. Jason," Devin said with a loud sigh. "Come on, Joey. Let's get you out of here before you get caught and they hang *my* ass!"

"Perry *has* been roaming around here all day," Lola agreed. "You two, vamoose. And Kerry, get off that step. You're blocking the doorway. I realize it's easier to alphabetize tickets that way, but every time that man brings his train in here from Chicago you guys are always working on the floor."

"Anyhow, Mama," Devin interrupted. "You all have a nice night, now. Just think, ten minutes, the whistle blows."

"What whistle?" Kelly grumbled, as we all watched Devin nearly collide with Perry in the lobby.

"Oh, excuse me, sir," Devin said loudly to Jason with a grin. "I almost stepped on your foot with my shiny new boots!"

I returned to my filing thinking vaguely about the strange person Devin was. He was too happy-go-lucky. Too noisy. Too friendly. Nobody liked everybody, but Devin seemed to. Nobody was liked *by* everybody, but with the exception of Jason, Devin was. Devin was the driver who customers demanded to speak to when their own routeman couldn't get a word in edgewise. Devin was the one who even Big Tim, the route manager, raved about. The superman who could take the smallest, dying, pitiful route and turn it into a five-hundred-dollar-a-day boardwalk inside of two weeks, rapping his way through the sale with whatever "trip" he sensed the customer was "into." Devin, who called our office four times a day, and who knew *how* many times he called Tim's? Devin just stood flat on his own two feet, cocksure with Scorpio confidence. Yet Devin was basically a loner, and I wondered what he did when he wasn't at work. Evidently, he was married, though he'd never mentioned his wife before today. He wasn't a girl chaser, either. At least, I never saw him give any one girl any special attention. Male or female, Devin just seemed to get off on people. He *was* funny, but how much of *that* could a wife take? That set me to wondering who would even marry a loud obnoxious hippie like that, and then it was five o'clock.

Time sort of drifted, and Devin cut his hair. It was probably the first notice of Devin Drew I'd taken that wasn't one of amusement. Not only were those black curls cut and styled to perfection, and even more shocking, mustache completely gone, but if you could make your way through the crowd gathered in the time-clock area you'd swear that this elegantly and expensively outfitted young man was a new guy. In the dirty old concrete time-clock area, right in the middle of employee traffic punching in for work, stood someone who definitely was not a driver. At least, if that was Perry's idea for a new uniform, he was going to lose the rest of the guys, too.

I didn't recognize him. I would have walked right past him if it hadn't been for Kelly, who had just entered the building. I heard her yelp, turned around, and saw her making her way over to that new guy.

"Devin! Devin! What happened to you?"

The crowd that had gathered around him was expressing its admiration, awe, shock, and in the drivers' cases, concern. Not necessarily in that order.

Devin? I looked again. *That* was *Devin* ?

"Sales," he explained. "I've switched departments to cooler sales."

Back in accounts receivable, everyone was talking about Devin's new image. In fact, the whole phone-room crew was in our tiny office, including Kim, the department's supervisor and "sister" peer to Lola. Everyone was talking and laughing with Lola when we walked in. As usual, Hannah was already there.

"Well, *I* didn't recognize him," Lola was saying. "If he hadn't spoken up and said 'Hey, Mama'…and even then I still couldn't believe it was him."

"I know," Kim said, nodding, eyes wide. "He looks like a completely different person."

"Hi, Mama," we said in unison.

"Oh, hello, kiddies—hey, did you guys see Devin Drew this morning?"

"That's the first time I ever noticed he was good-looking," Hannah piped up shyly.

"Perry's gonna faint!" Brenda, the lobby receptionist, was another employee everyone liked. She had a sense of humor and would usually go along with anything. This morning, though, she was as much in shock as the rest of us. And probably right. Perry *was* going to faint.

"Not unless someone calls Devin by name," Kim said. "Perry will walk right past him."

They were right, there, too. There was no resemblance in Devin, now, to the routeman of yesterday. He looked *that* different.

As it turned out, we never did hear of Perry's anticipated coma. In fact, it didn't take long for the whole shock thing to die down. We were just too busy to care.

I forgot about Devin Drew completely, and work went on in the routine way bookkeeping jobs always do. It was still amusing sometimes, even if only in the fun of breaking the rules. Rumor drifted in that Devin was out of sales and into the office trip again, this time as a route-realignment specialist, but nobody paid any attention.

Nobody had time to. Our own office was swamped with new accounts pouring in weekly, and Lola, who'd had enough of it all, took a vacation toward the end of August leaving Hannah, who knew the most about Lola's job, in charge.

A question arose over the status of a new account just after Lola left, and we were once again graced with a visit from Devin Drew. Joey Burns had come along, just to say hello, and with no one to throw them out, Kelly opened a large bag of Lay's potato chips, and the reunion commenced. The ticket and account were forgotten. Thirty minutes later Pat Mallard (Devin's route-realignment partner and Tim's assistant) came in. Pat's face wore a tired exasperated look as he stood in Lola's doorway, hands on his hips. Devin and Joey, backs to him, were rapping away when Pat loudly cleared his throat.

"I might have known," he said, attempting to sound stern. "Boy, anytime I need you two I know just where to look."

"Hey-hey-hey," Devin replied, smiling. "You're finally starting to see where it's at, hey Pat?"

"It ain't back there with all those routes and charts, man," Joey added.

"Oh, and just where might *it* be, then?" Pat crossed his arms smugly.

Up until now, I had been quietly listening to the other four as I filed, but Pat's entrance made it an official party, so I set my ledgers aside. "Will someone kindly define *it* ?" I asked, joining the conversation.

Pat shrugged helplessly. "I just came in," he said, "and I wasn't looking for *it*. I only get paid to find *them*."

"Don't tell us, then." Kelly turned her back, feigning annoyance. "Devin probably doesn't even know, *himself* !"

Surprisingly, even quiet Hannah was interested and spoke up. "Come on, Devin. You're the one who shot your mouth off. The least you can do is let us in on it."

Joey tapped Devin on the shoulder with raised eyebrows. "Go ahead," he urged. "They asked. You're always saying you can tell if they ask."

Joey evidently knew what Devin was hinting at. Devin, however, only smiled down at us from the step, as if he truly had the secret. "Nope," he said. "Uh...this is where the subject usually ends. You know, it isn't the kind of thing you go rapping down to some chicks in an office. It's just...there...you know...there!" And with that, he made another hand-sweeping gesture so common to his personality. Like... way out there...like...later!

"Oh, go ahead, Devin. I dare you," Pat said.

Devin now had all eyes on him.

Kelly gave him her undivided attention. "Come on! Whatever it is, we'd *really* like to *know* !"

After some hesitation, Devin finally spoke. "Well, all right. Here comes the argument, but—it's called...Wicca."

The room went silent. Devin was verbalizing my own beliefs and didn't even know it! Here I'd thought that I was the only one in the plant who was seriously interested in witchcraft! "You tell 'em, Devin!" I exclaimed excitedly, jumping to my feet.

Bewildered, Kelly looked from me to Devin and back to me again. "Wicca? Isn't that the religious name for witchcraft?"

"Hey-hey-hey," Devin answered for me.

Kelly suddenly burst into laughter. "Wait till Lola hears *this* ! I don't believe it! Hannah, we have two witches now. One in the route room and one in our very own office!"

Even Hannah was laughing. "That's all *she* talks about," she agreed.

Devin just studied me quietly until the giggling subsided, and then he said, "Are you really into the occult?"

That set Kelly and Hannah off laughing all over again. "This just can't happen," Hannah said.

"Not at the same plant!" Kelly added. She grinned widely. "What kind of witchcraft are *you* into? Kerry's a good witch."

"Kelly!" I shot her a warning look.

"No, really," Kelly continued, ignoring me. "Are you a warlock? Do you worship the Devil? Kill babies? Or what? I'm serious. I really *want* to know." She made an absolute attempt to look somber.

Devin gave me a look that said *do you get this a lot?* He turned, smiling, to Kelly. "No, Kel, killing babies just ain't my trip, you know? No sacrifices. No blood. Nothing like that."

Kelly eyed him with new respect. "Oh, so you're into white magic, huh?"

Devin shrugged. "Hey, it's all the same thing. Just depends on how you use it."

That was it. He had my attention. From there we talked about Wicca, the craft holidays, Salem, Massachusetts—where Devin was born—persecutions, and books. Devin had most of the books I owned and quite a few more that I'd never even heard of. That was because they couldn't legally be sold in America, Devin proudly explained. A bookshop in Salem imported them for him by special order. He had a personal connection with the shop owner.

"Do you celebrate the holidays too?" Kelly wanted to know.

"You mean will I be out celebrating Halloween this year? You bet your sweet ass!"

With this, even Pat and Joey joined in the laughter.

I was really interested in Halloween, and Devin told us that most of the Wiccans lived south of the city and usually headed upstate for the biggest event of the witches' year. Impulsively, I blurted out my desire to attend something like that. Kelly and Hannah were aghast.

"You'd really *go*?" Hannah gave me a disgusted *wouldn't you know it* look.

Kelly compensated for it with one of admiration. "Really, Kerry? You wouldn't be scared?"

Devin, however, took my comment most seriously. "I'm not sure if it can be arranged, but it may be…that is, if you're serious. Do you really want to come along this year?"

I nodded, too excited to speak.

"Far out. I'll have to check with my brother, but I'm sure it will be cool. I can almost guarantee it. If something's cool with me, it's usually cool with him."

When Lola returned to work, Kelly was the first to ask her if she'd heard the latest.

"If it has anything to do with *this* place, I don't want to know," Lola said emphatically. "We went all the way to the *bottom of the state*—eighty miles south of here—stopped at a gas station, and the attendant was really in a bad mood. He said he'd offer us a glass of water, but the Sparklear man hadn't shown up...*again*. Can you believe that?"

"You didn't tell him you worked here," Kelly said with a smirk.

"No, I didn't," Lola replied. "Jeez, he was really upset. Anyway, I guess I'm ready. What's the latest?"

"Devin's taking Kerry to a witchcraft meeting on Halloween night."

"Hey, Kel," I yelled in from my machine. "Don't go spreading that around. He just said he would *ask*."

Lola stepped into the doorway. "Oh, you'd go?"

"Well, if I'm allowed."

"You know Devin's married, don't you?"

"What's that got to do with it?"

"Well those things go on all night, don't they?"

"What's the big deal? I may not even be allowed to go."

Kelly started chanting. "Kerry's getting ma-ad, Kerry's getting ma-ad."

"Shut up, Kelly," I hissed, glaring. "Act your age!"

Hannah stopped typing and looked plaintively at Lola. "Mama, make them stop."

"Okay, pipe down in there, you guys. Hannah's trying to work."

I glared at Kelly again and turned back to my posting. I had just started the first ledger when I heard Devin come in.

"Where's Mama?"

"She was right in there," Kelly replied. "Hey, what happened to your arm?"

"Oh, I dropped one of those big water bottles, got a little cut. Where'd she go?"

"I don't know. We were just talking to her. If it's just a little cut, how come your whole arm's all bandaged?"

Sure enough, there was a professionally wrapped, clinical white bandage securely covering his arm, up to the elbow.

"Well, maybe it was more than a little cut."

"Oh, that must have hurt! When?"

"This morning. I was helping one of the new guys load up the truck."

"And you're still *working* today?"

"Yeah, well, the anesthetic is just starting to wear off."

Kelly reached for his hand and examined the wrap job. "Did the company pick up the bill for this?"

"Sure did. Tim sent me over to some clinic the company's tight with. Personally, I wouldn't have bothered. Doctors are such rip-offs.

But…insurance purposes…Tim made me go get stitches. Wait till they get the bill."

"It's pretty swollen," Kelly said, comparing it to his other arm. "How many stitches?"

"Sixteen."

Ironically the radio was playing a song by The Who, and they were announcing that sixteen stitches had put someone right, and Dad had said 'Don't say I didn't warn ya.'

Devin was pale, but it was hard to feel sorry for him when he seemed so unconcerned himself.

"It's no big deal," he said, yanking his arm away from Kelly. "I'll have this back to normal in a day or so."

"Like hell," Kelly retorted. "When that stuff wears off, buddy, you're gonna be hurting."

"Oh, yeah? In that case, maybe I'd better go home. If you think it's that bad. You can just give this paperwork to Mama when she comes back."

Kelly looked pleased that she had convinced him to go home. "Should I inform the route room?" she asked gravely.

"No, don't bother." Devin smiled and ruffled her hair with his good-arm hand. "I'm leaving for home now. Doctor's orders. I'm already punched out."

"You bastard."

"Just make sure Mama gets those tickets, and tell her I said welcome back and all that shit." With a wave of his good arm, he was gone.

Kelly turned to me. "He's feeling lousy, but he'd never admit it. Not Devin."

Monday was Labor Day, and nobody worked. Tuesday brought Devin into A/R bright and early with the usual ticket problems and no bandage. The radio was playing softly in Lola's office. Something about it being lovely to see someone again and inviting that someone to come along to the next bend.

"Now where's Mama?"

"In a meeting," Hannah replied. "Where's your bandage?"

Devin waved that aside with his now unwrapped arm. "Them rags were a pain in the ass. I don't need 'em anymore anyway. It's completely healed now. See?"

Kelly pushed his extended arm away without looking. "No! I can't stand to look at stitches."

"What stitches? I took them out yesterday. They were starting to annoy me. Them suckers itch like a son of a bitch."

"You took them out?" I lifted up his arm and stared in wonder. There were no stitches and not even a sign of a cut. "Wow, Devin! There isn't even a scar."

Kelly peeked cautiously, her hand ready to cover her eyes. "Hey, where's it at?"

"Here we go with the where it's *at* thing again," Devin said.

"No, I mean the cut! Where's the cut?"

"Oh, there's a scar there. See?" He stretched the skin to show the razor-thin line, just barely detectable. "I could get rid of that too but, well…why waste the energy? Anyhow, I didn't come in here to discuss my arm. Kerry, I talked to my brother about your coming with us this Halloween. It's cool. But we decided against going north with the herd this year. You're actually coming to a wedding. See, it's my brother who's getting married. In the witches' circle. It will be a private thing. Just us four. That is, if you still want to come."

"That sounds even better," I said. "A lot of strange people are hard to get used to at one time." I was suddenly conscious of the quiet in our office and beckoned Devin into Lola's. He followed.

"Anyhow, as I was saying, I had to check with Trevor." He paused and corrected himself. "Well, actually, it wasn't Trevor. His chick is kind of weird. She's not one of us."

"She isn't?"

"Well, she's not straight, now. She smokes pot and all but, well, she's only interested in astrology at this point. What can I say? She does love Trevor."

"So she's not into the religion, but she's going along with it because your brother is?"

"In a sense, yes. Because she loves him. The rest…that will all come later."

"You think so?"

"Oh, it has to. Strange things happen when my brother and I are together. She'll have to believe what she sees." He sounded positive.

"What do *you* think of her, Dev?"

"Oh, I like her. She's good for him. Sharp, too. Picks up on shit pretty fast. She's a little nervous about the wedding, but she won't back out. Anyhow, I must be getting back. Perry saw me come in here so he's probably timing me. I wanted to bring you up to date, though. Later, huh?"

We stepped back into my section, and the other two girls immediately stopped posting.

"So, you finally decided to get back to work," Kelly said teasingly. "And what's this about a wedding she's going to?"

"It's a real live witchcraft wedding, Kelly," Devin shot back. "We sacrifice my brother's wife to the Devil at midnight."

"Come on—who's going to perform the ceremony? Is it going to be legal?"

"I am. It's legal. I have a preacher's license. It's valid in Massachusetts."

"Devin, this ain't Massachusetts!"

"I know, but what's time and space really? Who's going to argue about it?" He shrugged and left.

Devin quickly gained notoriety throughout the plant when the word spread of the impossibly quick healing of the sixteen stitches, so when the Halloween rumor hit the phone-room hotwire, people really started talking. I didn't care. It was all I could do to keep my mind off Devin and that wedding and into my charges, which should have been posted by now. The other girls were already done, so I started rushing. Jeez! And Halloween wasn't even for another month.

3 By the first week in October, it was all over the plant that Kerry and Devin were attending a Black Mass together, naked, on Halloween night. I had to admit, their version sounded a lot more exciting. I would never have admitted it to myself, but I was thinking a little too much about Devin lately. I'd discovered, through Brenda, that he'd been married for several years, and she'd promised to bring me the rest of his vital statistics—age, birthday and such—as soon as she could get away from her receptionist's desk. I grabbed the typewriter seat by Lola's office doorway, which afforded a good view of Brenda.

One of the phone girls stopped by to tell us about some new ring Devin was wearing, but Lola shooed her out. When Brenda came in with my information, she dropped the folded paper on the doorway side of the typewriter where Lola couldn't see it.

"Have you guys seen Devin's new ring?" she asked as if to explain her unnecessary walk-in.

"No, we haven't," Lola replied. "But it must be something. Yours is the second announcement of it this morning. What *is* it with Devin lately?"

"That's what I'd like to know," Hannah sniffed. "What's suddenly so great about Devin? He's *been* here for *years* !"

"Well, you should go back there and see it. It's really…" She made a face depicting disgust.

Lola laughed. "That sounds like something Devin would buy."

"If he didn't buy it, he dug it out of a dead jackal. It sure looks real. He says it is." Without another word, she crossed the lobby and sat down at her desk.

I looked at Lola out of the corner of my eye. I knew she was expecting me to ask permission to run back to the route room, but I wasn't going to give her the satisfaction. Reluctantly, I remained glued to my seat, and then another phone girl pranced in.

"Heeeeey, cousins! Hi, Aunt Lola. Have any of you guys seen..."

"Devin's ring," Lola and I finished with her in unison.

She had been gleefully rubbing her hands together, as if in anticipation of our negative replies. Her face fell. "Yeah...how'd you know?"

"Yours is the third announcement of it." Lola smiled. "Jeez, Devin goes out and buys a ring, and everybody in the whole plant's talking about it. It can't be any worse than that inverted cross he wears!"

"Oh, well, he wears that *under* his shirt. You should go back and see the ring, though. That is, if you've got a strong stomach. It's the most horrible, gross, sickening, ugly, utterly repulsive thing to wear right out in public like that. And I only looked at it for a second!"

Lola laughed. "I'm glad you didn't get a better look. Boy, for driver statistics we see Brenda, but for gossip, Ethel, you hold the title." She smiled broadly at me to let me know that she'd seen Brenda drop the note.

I couldn't stand the suspense anymore. "Mama...please!"

She nodded and called after me. "But *walk* back there!"

I was already gone.

I found Devin sitting over his charts in the route office, realigning a route.

"Hi, Devin!"

He looked up and smiled. "Hey, yourself. How'd you get out of there? Dig under the floor like they do in jail?"

"No, Mama let me come back to see your ring."

"You must mean this one." He flipped the outstretched map that covered his left hand. "The jackal's eye."

His ring finger displayed an amber eye with a black pupil and an overall greenish cast when the light hit it. It looked eerily like his own hazel eyes when the light caught them the same way. Eagle talons held the eye, which peered through the claws, and the legs continued around to make up the circle of the ring. For me, it was love at first sight.

"Wow, Devin," I breathed, mesmerized. "I've never seen anything like it! I *want* it!"

He just laughed.

"No. I mean it! I'll pay you *anything* for it!"

"I can't sell it," he said with a sigh. "The vibes are just too good."

"Not even for double what you paid for it?"

"No, I can't sell the ring."

"Please..." I really didn't have any money, and my coming paycheck was allocated for the phone bill, but as I stood there, a plot was hatching on where to get some.

"No. No way, chick." He smiled and shrugged apologetically. "It's not for sale."

I didn't blame him. I took one last look at the ring. The eye stared at me through the talons. It sure did look real. Moist, even. "No way, huh? I can understand. Well, okay. I gotta get back."

I felt oddly depressed as I left.

Back in my own office, Pink Floyd's *Money* was playing on the radio. The machines were hammering furiously—the girls posting checks and charges, and the song's cash register sounds blended right in with the noise. Lola didn't hide her amused smile when I sat down across from her at the typewriter. "It's so beautiful," I told her sadly. "I wish it were mine."

She just laughed and rolled her eyes. "It figures *you'd* like it."

I didn't think about the ring again until the following morning when I punched in for work. Devin was standing in the time-clock area, and the ring again caught the light and my eye. "Let me see it again, Devin!" I called to him, jamming my time card into the machine and slamming it back in the metal rack.

He walked over to me and, with a quick glance around to make sure we were alone, said, "Remember back a couple months ago when I asked you and Kelly where I could find a good silversmith?"

Vaguely, I did. I hadn't paid much attention to the hippie back then, but I nodded anyway.

"Well, I found one. The guy's getting more rings in tonight. This was the last one like it he had. It's a little big for you anyway. Are you sure it has to be this one? This is a dude's ring, but he had some smaller owl's eye rings there. Are you sure?"

"I'm sure! It has to be that one." I didn't understand my own obsession with *that* ring, but I knew I couldn't settle for any other. "You wouldn't care if I got one like it?"

He looked at me steadily with those intense hazel eyes. "No."

"How much?" I could barely contain my excitement.

"I paid forty for this one. The dude's got ordinary rings on the top counters. You have to ask for the under-the-counter stock. Want me to go with you?"

"Well, it's liable to start more rumors. You must have heard the talk."

"Sure. I've heard some, started some, fed some, and starved some." He smiled. "Human games. I like to confuse issues. It blows their heads. Anyhow, here's the card. Call and find out what nights they're open. And I can take you. Don't give me that rumor shit. Unless *you* care!"

"No, I was thinking of you. You're the one who's married."

"Well, my attitude is: Feed the hungry. Tell them what they want to hear. Anyhow, you got the bread now?"

"No. I don't get paid till next Friday, and that's supposed to cover the phone bill. I'll come up with something before that. I'll call this place tonight and get back to you, okay?" I slipped the jeweler's card in my jacket pocket.

He smiled. "Later."

"Forty bucks for a *ring*?" Kelly backed away from me like I'd finally lost my last marble. "You're *starving* at home, and you want to spend forty bucks for a ring? Boy, wait till Mama hears *this* one!"

Hannah observed this interruption of work with her usual placidness. "Yow. I can think of a lot better things to do with forty bucks than buy an ugly thing like that."

"Oh, I *like* the ring," Kelly admitted. "It's cool. But Devin can afford it. He makes about three hundred a week. You don't."

"But I want it so bad, Kelly. Think about it. In all the time you've known me, when have you ever seen me buy myself something?"

"If Kerry spends forty dollars on a ring, I will never speak to her again." The voice of authority. Lola had returned to hear the tail end of our conversation. Lola was always looking out for my lack of financial sense.

"Mama, you keep out of this!" I laughed and stepped into the doorway. Ironically, that Pink Floyd song was playing on her radio, making cash register sounds and singing about money again. "If I do get it, it won't be with the phone bill money."

"Then how else will you buy it? You got another job we don't know about?"

"What if I can get someone to buy it for me?"

"Oh, one of your countless rich boyfriends?"

"Well, I betcha Scotty would."

"Scotty *would*," Lola agreed, laughing at the thought of the big generous ox. "I can't believe he's still hanging around."

"Ever since I bought that stereo from him. But I know he would loan me the money."

"Poor Scotty. And speaking of Scotty, are you two still going to pick up Mark this weekend?" Mark was Lola's eleven-year-old son. Often we took all three kids to the drive-in on weekends, and Mark usually stayed overnight. I'd forgotten that we'd planned on it this weekend.

"Yes, we'll pick him up tonight. We'll even take him over to that new occult shop."

Lola groaned. "Do you have to?"

"Well, he was with us when we found it, but it was closed. I did kind of promise him."

Lola sighed. "All right, but don't you go teaching him your hocus-pocus. And don't you dare mention that ring to Scotty. And if you do and he buys it for you, he's out of his mind."

"Well, will you get off my back if *anyone* buys it for me?" I persisted, back to the original subject.

"Yes, but nobody is going to buy you a forty-dollar ring either, so go back to work."

Actually, I had a better idea than that. My mother had been after me to sell her my African tapestry for, ironically, forty dollars. I had always refused. Well, here was her big chance. If she agreed to the sale, Scott could *loan* me the money, and Pammy could cover Scott's loan when she got off work tonight. Then when the money arrived from Allentown, I could pay Pammy back. That way, I could get the ring *now*. I tried to explain my devious scheme to Lola who couldn't quite see the logic in so many steps. Why not wait until the money arrived? *Wait?* Was she *nuts?* I wanted the ring *tonight*!

Lola nabbed me on my way out the door at five o'clock. "No ring tonight," she reminded me dutifully, as if she really were my mother.

"Unless my old lady goes for it," I conceded. "Fair enough? That way the phone bill will get paid, and I'll still get the ring."

"Why should Lola care about your stupid phone bill, anyway?" Kelly put in impatiently, ready to go.

"It's in *my name*, that's why!" Lola responded quickly.

"She had the deposit waived for me, but had to add her name to my bill," I explained. "Don't worry, Lo, I'll pay the phone bill, no matter what."

"Okay." She smiled. "But you don't need that damn ring."

Friday night. No work till Monday. No Devin till Monday, either. I brushed that depressing thought aside. So what? What did I care? It was the *ring* I wanted. Why the nagging thoughts of Devin?

The phone was ringing even before I had the key in the door. Damn Scotty. He never gave me time to get in the house. Well, I'd wanted to talk to him anyway. He agreed to bring the forty with him and to pick up Mark, and even to wait for the explanation about the money since I was in such a big hurry. I was, indeed, on a mission. My mother jumped at the offer and said she'd mail the money immediately. Pammy was to bring the tapestry when she came up for her visit. Even Pam was willing to front me the forty until the money arrived from Allentown. She didn't mince words, though, about what I wanted it for.

"Are you sure you want to waste money on a thing like that? It sounds so ugly," she said when I called her to ask.

"Never mind what it sounds like! Are you still with me?"

She sighed. "I'll bring the money tonight. It'll be late, though."

"That's okay. Scotty's covering it until you get here. You give yours to him."

"What the hell...do you know what you're doing?"

"Yeah, covering all angles so I'll be sure it's on my hand tonight."

Pammy laughed. "You impatient Virgos! Later."

Scotty was surprised at my uncommon enthusiasm over the purchase of a material object. And giving up the tapestry? He'd heard me refuse its sale too many times to believe that one. He was even more bewildered over the dramatic distress I displayed when I couldn't find the jeweler's card Devin had given me.

"Just look it up in the phone book," he suggested calmly. "And relax. If we don't find it tonight, we'll figure it out in the morning."

"Scott! That's it! I'll look it up!"

It turned out there were four of them. One for each direction.

"Call them all. What can you lose? Come on, I'll make you a nice stiff drink. How's that sound?"

I was already dialing. "I hope this works. I don't want it tomorrow. I want it tonight."

"But whyyyy?"

"Because. I want to go to bed with it on my hand."

"Oh brother." We both laughed. Scott knew me when I made up my mind.

The first one wasn't it, so I went on to the next one, fully prepared to call them all. Scotty lumbered his six-foot frame out to the kitchen counter, which only served as a bar when he or Uncle Joe was visiting. "You're gonna need that forty bucks to cover this phone bill," he kidded me when he returned with a couple of cocktails.

I was already half-stoned, finished with the phone, and toking on a joint. Defeated. Done. At eight o'clock. "These toll calls won't go on that bill. Why do you think I had to go through so many steps for the money? My paycheck's already spent on that one. And not *one* of those places was the right one." I kicked the phone book disgustedly.

"Well, tomorrow isn't so bad," Scott offered halfheartedly.

"Yeah, sure."

When Pam arrived, she knew the minute she saw my face. "Oh, no. Don't tell me you didn't get it. What happened?"

"She lost the card," Scotty whispered loudly. "Don't remind her. I gotta put up with her."

"Hey, you don't *gotta* put up with anything!" I snapped.

He shrugged. "See? And I'd just about got her drunk and pacified."

"Boy, I can't wait to see this ring when you *do* get it," Pam said, shaking her head at my sour mood.

"I can't wait to see it either," Scott grumbled. "For all this and forty bucks, that thing better blink and cry."

"Where's Mark?" Pammy asked, changing the subject.

"In the kids' room watching TV, last I checked."

"Oh, I guess they're all sleeping by now, huh? Do you still want this money?"

"Yeah. I had hoped to get it with Scott's loan, but I don't need his money now." I looked apologetically at Scotty. "Thanks, anyway. I'm sorry. I just really had my heart set on tonight."

"Well, here." Pam handed me the bills. "You talked to Mom, right?"

"Yeah. You'll be taking the tapestry up with you, along with that book."

"Oh, the book! I've been meaning to ask you about that. Mom told me what happened. I warned you not to read that thing. You've got too wild of an imagination."

"Imagination? It had to be mass hallucination if you're going to call it anything. The kids were witnesses to that car episode."

"Hmm, that's right. What do you think it was?"

"Beats me. But I haven't picked up that book since. You can take it with you now if you want to."

Scott lay on the couch sideways, his cheek resting on his steepled hands. I was sorry I'd snapped at him. He was only trying to help, and he hadn't even acknowledged my apology. I tried again.

"Oh, I understand. I know how hyped up you were about it. We'll get that bastard tomorrow if I have to call this Devin character myself."

Those words registered. "Scott! That's *it* ! Call Devin. I don't know why I didn't think of that myself. Damn, the place is probably closed by now."

"You still need the directions," he reminded me. "You have his number?"

"No, but I'll bet it's listed."

"Well, before you get involved in that project, I'd better get out of here," Pam interjected. "Ker, call me when you get it, okay?"

"I will, Pam. Thanks for the loan."

"No problem. Good luck."

Information only had one Devin Drew, and it had to be him. I talked Scott into getting him on the phone for me in case someone else answered. I didn't want to get him in trouble. When Scott had him on the line I took the phone, hands shaking, back into the den where I could talk in privacy.

"Devin?"

"Hey…" He sounded stoned. "What's up?"

I told him. The whole thing. The trouble I'd gone to just to get the money. The missing card. The missing jewelers. Everything. He mostly listened, interrupting only when I mentioned Lola's reaction to my buying the ring.

"Hold on a minute. Slow down," he said gently. "*Lola* doesn't want you buying the ring? Isn't that carrying the Mama bit a little too far?"

I explained about the phone and why I couldn't let the bill slide. "Lola knows how tight money is around here. She means well."

"Oh, I think I understand a little better now. Anyhow, enough of the third degree. You won't find this place in a phone book. It's too new. And all that bullshit just to get the money—look, why don't I just *give* you the ring. It means so much more to you. Damn, I should have thought of it sooner."

"What?" I nearly dropped the phone.

"Sure. If I just give it to you, it'll save you all that hassle."

"Oh, no, Devin. That's your ring. I wouldn't accept that one. I couldn't."

"But you don't understand," he protested. "If I give you the ring, well, I wouldn't really feel like I was losing it. You like it so much more than I do. Not that I don't love the ring—don't get me wrong. It's far out. But by giving it to you, I would gain so much for the gesture."

"No, Devin. That's forty dollars of your hard-earned money. And yesterday you wouldn't even consider selling it."

"Sell it. That's different than giving it away. Let's keep the money bullshit out of this. The ring is yours."

"But Devin, the forty dollars…"

"You still don't understand. If you accept the ring, then you would be doing me a favor. If you refuse, you deprive me of the energy I could have received." He sighed. "Do you at least understand that much?"

"At least let me pay you for it."

"Damn. You're really hung up on that forty bucks, aren't you? It's just a ring. A material object. That's all. Look, I wouldn't have gone to all the trouble you did. It obviously has more value for you."

"But…"

"I mean it now. Don't be jiving me. I won't take no for an answer." I didn't have an answer anymore, so he went on. "When are you planning on going to sleep? I was thinking about taking the bike out to see Trevor. Now that he's getting married, I don't see much of him. Are you anywhere near the Interstate? That's near his house."

"It's right down the road from me."

"Okay, give me your address. If I do go, I'll stop by. He may be sleeping, so it may be sooner than you think."

"Why don't you call him first?"

"He doesn't have a phone. My wife only recently had this one installed. My brother and I don't need phones. When I need him, he's usually there. And when he needs me, I end up flying out of the house on an impulse. Like tonight." He laughed softly. "Tell me how to get to your house."

I told him, adding that he should knock hard in case I fell asleep.

"Well, if it's too late, I may just put it in your mailbox. But even if it's not there in the morning, it just means I didn't go out tonight. Don't buy one. I *will* get it to you. And don't wait up."

"I hope I didn't cause you any problems with this phone call."

He told me it had not been necessary to have someone call for me. There would never be any problem. "I wouldn't allow that," he said. "I take my own calls."

I maintained my cool only until I hung up the phone. Then the pent-up excitement burst, and I raced back to the living room where Scotty was engrossed in a comic book. So close to getting the ring! "Scotty! Scotty! He's giving me *his*! He's giving me *his*!"

"When? Now?"

"Well, maybe tonight." I tried to take a deep breath and calm down.

"What? Didn't you tell him it *had* to be tonight?" He grinned, obviously glad for my change in mood.

"No, I told him I didn't want *his* ring."

"Oh. And he twisted your arm, right?"

"Scotty, he can twist anything on me he wants to," I said seriously. "I really like him. I *really* like him."

He scowled. "I thought there was a little more to all this than just the ring."

I ignored his comment. Scotty had no right or reason to be jealous. We were strictly friends.

"Do you mind if I sleep on your couch?" he asked, a little coldly. "I'm too buzzed to drive."

"Sure, it's okay with me. I'll be right here in the beanbag in case…someone comes."

"Yeah. Someone," Scott muttered under his breath.

I shut the air conditioner down, turned off the lights, lit a red bayberry candle, and tried to settle down to sleep. I didn't want to get my hopes up.

Couldn't handle any more letdowns tonight. Even in the near dark, I could imagine what the ring would look like on my hand. As I listened for the sound of a clink in my mailbox, the day's events replayed over and over in my mind. Especially that last phone call. Devin. Just what was it about Devin so suddenly? Was it really only the ring, or was it the beliefs we held in common? Not so long ago, I had observed him with distaste. It wasn't that he was bad-looking. He was rather cute since he'd cut his hair and shaved off the mustache. He was still a hippie, though, and that was something else too.

Me, conventional Kerry. Country music, straight-living Kerry. Well, I did smoke a little weed now and then, but for the most part, hippies with their long hair and repulsive beards and hairy mustaches had always turned me off. Me, the loner. Just what was it about this twenty-five-year-old, curly-headed hippie, all of a sudden? So different.

My thoughts went back to the ring, and I reached for my journal beside the stereo. Here was something I could do until I settled down enough to sleep.

"I just can't wait till tomorrow," I said aloud to an already sleeping Scotty, his huge frame draped over the small couch, fitting perfectly except for his head and his legs.

I don't know for sure what time it was. There was a quiet rap on the door, but I snapped awake like we were being raided. The house was dark, and I could hear Scotty's snores as I fumbled for the switch on the red plastic mushroom-shaped lamp. The room was instantly bathed in a soft red glow.

"Who is it?"

"Devin."

"Devin?" I crawled from the beanbag to the door, unlocked it and shoved it open, all from floor level. Devin entered carrying a helmet with a pentagram painted on it. He was geared up in U.S. Army goggles and green field jacket.

"I usually leave the helmet on the bike," he said, "but there's a pig parked out there wanting to get on my ass."

"A cop? Where? In front of my house?"

"Yeah, but don't panic. He was just looking for some hippie to get on. He told me to make sure I took the helmet in with me so I won't be reporting it stolen later."

"There has been a lot of theft in this neighborhood," I said.

"Yeah? What's wrong with this neighborhood? Looks all white to me."

I didn't understand the comment. It was the kind of thing a black guy might say if he thought someone was implying that theft only took place in a black neighborhood. He peeled off his goggles as he spoke.

"Well, that's not what I meant. It actually is pretty white, but there's still a lot of theft around here. Druggies, you know? Did you go to Trevor's?"

"I stopped, but all the lights were out, so I came up here."

The clock read 2:30.

Somewhere during this exchange, Scotty had awoken. He rubbed his eyes and stared at Devin. Devin stared back and then glanced around the rest of the house. "Nice place you have here," he remarked, though I was sure he was wondering who the guy was on my couch.

"Thanks. That's Scott. A friend of mine. We were going to take Lola's son and my two kids to a drive-in tonight, but this jewelry shop business screwed that up."

Devin nodded, smiling politely.

"Scott, this is Devin…the guy with the ring, and Devin, sit down. You're making me nervous sitting on your heels like that. You look like you're going to jump up and run."

Devin changed his position to kneeling, set down the helmet, and shrugged out of his Army jacket. Now he looked more like Devin, only dressed in Levis and a white T-shirt, again, with a pentagram on it. It was the first I'd seen him out of company uniform since his cooler-sales days. He dug around in his pockets and pulled out…the ring. "Anyhow, here it is." He handed it to me and adjusted himself to an Indian-sitting position.

I accepted the ring in awe. The huge silver claws took on an eerie glow in the blood red light, the amber eye staring at me. Suspiciously, I thought. Coldly. The pupil seemed to float around in the eyeball—an illusion, of course, but maddeningly realistic. It fixed its gaze on me, no matter how I turned the ring. I studied the etched black detail work in the talons and then the eye again.

"Watch it, it'll hypnotize you," Devin warned. "I found that out the hard way."

I moved the ring away from the light and, to my horror, the pupil seemed to dilate. I turned to Devin to see if he'd seen it too. Evidently, it was nothing new.

"Already?" He smiled. "It took at least a day before it did that to me."

I looked again, then tore my gaze away. "I can't stop looking at it, Devin. Here, check it out, Scott." I handed Scotty the ring. "Devin, what kind of an eye did you say that is?"

"A jackal, and I don't know what significance that has, if any. I just liked the ring. I had the same problem at first, staring at it all the time."

I suddenly remembered the stash box. "Hey, want to smoke?"

"No, pass, thanks," Devin said. "Not now." He seemed uneasy. Out of place maybe, or at a loss for words. Yet my face must have been glowing. I was so excited about the ring.

"So this is what all the uproar was about," Scotty said. "It's exactly how you described it." He handed it back to me. "That's been quite the subject ever since she saw it," he added to Devin.

"Now you can see why," I said happily, still trying to quell the excitement I felt when the ring was back on my hand. "Oh, Devin. Thank you."

"Don't say thanks," he replied quickly. "I'm just happy that you're so happy. You can't possibly realize what I'm getting out of this. Actually, I should be thanking you." He twisted the ring on my finger. "Yeah, I thought it would be a little big, but I can fix that."

"No, I like it the way it is now," I told him. "Don't change anything. I'll wrap something around the silver to make it smaller."

"Good." He seemed to relax, and leaned against the wall. "Your hands are shaking. Too much coffee and cigarettes. I know. I'm bad at it too."

"Yeah?"

"Too much. Sometimes I think about quitting the cigs, but I never do. I guess because the damage is so easy to heal." He looked so young and boyish sitting there in his jeans. And that curly black hair—it looked good since he'd cut it. It was so curly, though, that it was probably longer than it looked. He was so sincere. No acts or games. No wonder everybody liked him. He was just Devin.

"Lola says you wear an inverted cross," I commented, to break the silence.

He smiled. "I do." He pulled it out from under his shirt. "No one understands it though, so I don't wear it out in the open. Misunderstandings." He shook his head.

I kind of liked the cross. For one thing, it had a pentagram in the center, and its point was up, not down. White magic. "Look," I pointed out. "It contradicts the inverted cross. The point is up."

"That's what I mean. Most people don't even know there's a difference. I'd invert that sucker if it weren't welded to the silver. You know, *make* it satanic. Then there might be an excuse for throwing me out of bookstores. That has happened, but what can I say? Misunderstandings, again. They don't know what is or isn't satanic. This cross is an heirloom, handed down through the family, you know? Ancestors in Salem. I'm not going to get rid of it. It's sentimental to me."

I glanced over at Scotty to see if he was taking any of this in, but all he was taking in was air.

"He nods out fast," Devin observed, following my glance.

"Yes, he does," I agreed. "It must have been quite a scene to you when you first came in. Him there, me here." I nodded at the beanbag.

"It did look a little strange, but what the hell? It's none of my business."

"Scotty's just a good friend." I felt silly explaining, and yet I also felt it was necessary. Why, I don't know. After all, he was married. We sat in the doorway for a few more minutes, and finally he stood up.

"Well, enjoy it. Watch people's expressions. I've had it long enough to know people don't take to it. Not humans anyway."

I stood up too, wanting to hug him or…anything…to show my appreciation, but *it* was there…the distance. The distance wouldn't allow it. Instead, I took his hand and squeezed it. "Devin…thanks."

"Uh-uh-uh…don't say thanks. I did it for me."

I lay alone in the dark, long after the rumble of the cycle had died away, expecting to wake up from this dream at any moment. The ring felt good on my hand, but there was a funny chest pain starting up in my heart.

"Come *on*, Kerry…lemmee *see*!"

One thing about Saturdays. You sure couldn't sleep late around here. I buried my face deeper into the beanbag as Mark's fingers pried my hand out from under it. "Goll-ee…It's *hideous*! I wouldn't pay no forty bucks for *that*!" He looked positively fascinated.

"You're just too young to appreciate it." By now, my eyes were open and staring at the coffee Scott had set before me.

"Good morning, witch," Scotty chirped, then burst out laughing. "Conning that poor guy out of his own ring. And he's probably still wondering how you did it. Gotta hand it to you, though, you *did* go to sleep with it on your hand."

"Yeah, the *original* ring yet," I mused aloud. I felt for the ring, and a funny charge went through me. Just as I touched the silver, somewhere in my half-awake brain, memory spurts exploded. Of dreams all night. Nightmares. Could all that mayhem and tension have brought them on? And now I couldn't remember any of them.

"You were mumbling in your sleep all night," Scotty said as if to verify my thoughts. "I sat up listening for a while, but I couldn't make out a word. Too muffled." He shrugged. "Man, were you hyped up!"

"What time is it anyway?"

"Around ten. I gotta get going. You taking Mark to that occult shop?"

"Yeah, soon as I drink this coffee. Scott, thanks for everything."

"For what? I didn't have to go anywhere. Got my money back. What the hell! It was interesting anyway."

"Incidentally, Mark, you *do not* mention this ring to your mother," I warned him, just now realizing I had to break it to Lola.

Scotty left, and I piled Mark and the kids into the car.

The occult shop was a recently discovered bookstore. It was located in a sunny little shopping center across from the college. The students probably kept it in business—they and the Devins and Kerrys of the world. Inside, it was dark and musty, and it reeked of incense. The counters contained a variety of jewelry including talismans and amulets. The walls were covered with eerie posters and lined with books. Candles, hex charms, and love potions—this shop had it all.

Mark and the girls lost themselves in the candle department. I spotted an unusual talisman inside the glass cabinets. There was a description beside it that said in bold letters: **To Obtain Love**. By now I already knew where my feelings for Devin were headed, or I never would have asked the price.

"It's three dollars," the clerk told me.

I looked at it closely. A black cross on a silver medallion with a Latin inscription. I wondered whether it would be fair to Devin if I bought it, then decided all was fair in love and war. "I can't pay you any money for this," I told the clerk, "or it won't work. How about you add three dollars to that candle-making kit Mark is drooling over, and you *give* me the talisman."

Mark whooped. The clerk shrugged indifferently, rolled his eyes, and rung up the sale. "Whatever turns you people on," he said dryly.

I put the talisman on as soon as I got in the car. *Sador* the card read. *Guaranteed to attract love, especially the one intended.*

I started the engine, wishing the days weren't so hot, and looked longingly over at the A&W Root Beer stand. The kids were thirsty. I had nothing better to do, so I pulled in and was floored to find Pammy and George already parked and sipping from frosted mugs. I told her how the night had ended up and, of course, she wanted to see the ring. Her reaction was no different than when I'd first described it to her.

"Oh, Kerry, that's repulsive," she said disgustedly "Get *rid* of that thing! It looks positively evil. I don't like the vibes at all. Get it away from me."

"That's your opinion," George interrupted. "You wanna sell it, Kerry?"

We all laughed at the stupidity of his question. He examined the ring admiringly and patted my hand. "It's you," he said finally, and even the kids joined in the laughter.

After dropping Mark off, we went home. I plopped into the beanbag, rolled a joint, and went back to studying the ring. Maybe it was just the grass, but it sure seemed like the ring was glaring at me. As if it were homesick and missing its real owner. I chided myself for, once again, letting Pammy's remarks get to me. Pam's little pep talk was probably even responsible for what had happened the night that I'd tried to read the Trojan Horse book, though, realistically, I couldn't find a way to blame the purple fog on her. The phone sat beside me, silent. I looked at it, wishing Devin would call. My number was listed, so he could get it if he had any interest at all, but it remained mute. I stared at the eyeball. Devin's vibrations just emanated from it. Boy, *you* could make Devin call, I thought absently at the ring. The weed had taken its effect. Yeah, why not? It was worth a shot. Just why couldn't I channel a thought *through* the ring? It was already connected to Devin. All I needed was a link, and the link was on my hand.

With all the concentration I could muster up, I placed the ring to my forehead and dredged up an image of Devin from the depths of my memory. To my astonishment, the phone rang instantly.

"Hello?" I answered hopefully. It was only Uncle Joe. The letdown was worse than the shock of the phone ringing, and my disappointment really surprised me. Why should I be so bummed out? It was just a bad coincidence.

I tried again. Again, the phone rang immediately, but this time I wasn't so confident when I answered it. It was only Pam. A third try produced a long-distance call from my mother, and I gave up for the day. One more try the following afternoon proved even more fruitless. As hard as I concentrated, nobody called.

I *felt* like I was reaching him, so I hated to admit the only explanation left. Maybe Devin just had no *interest* in calling. And what was wrong with me anyway? Devin was married. What was I even thinking?

I reached for my journal and, after recording the day's events, thumbed through the recent entries. There wasn't a page in there that didn't have some reference to Devin. Who was I kidding? I picked up the pen, then set it back down. I wasn't in the mood to write anymore.

Instead, I put on a couple of country albums and settled back for a couple hours of daydreaming, determined to put Devin and the ring completely out of my mind. Music was my escape from a monotonous reality. Usually I could control my thinking, but tonight the forbidden thoughts kept coming anyway. What was his home life like? Who were his friends? How did he get along with his wife, and why didn't he have children? Out of nowhere, the craziest thought hit me. Devin didn't have kids because he was not meant to stay with his wife. Devin would have a child eventually, but it would be different from other kids. Devin's child would be special.

I caught myself noting these thoughts in my journal a little later, and it was then that I realized just how out of control I was letting this thing get. Devin had just done a nice thing for someone who wanted something he had and that was the extent of it. In big bold letters, I gouged into the next blank page: *Devin Drew is happily married. Forget it.*

I tossed the pen aside, resolving to forget Devin entirely, and set the alarm for work.

4

Monday, October 14, 1974

Tim Lipton, the route manager, stood by the time clock greeting the gang of employees who were, for once, arriving at the same time. Beyond his shoulder, I saw Devin sitting at his desk in the route office, already looking at me when our eyes met. Again, that clammy chest feeling. He waved almost imperceptibly, pointed to the time clock, and then resumed his attention to the route maps. I smiled at him, balled up my right hand so the ring wouldn't be seen, and reached for my time card with my left.

A note. Yellow legal tablet paper. Constructed with many staples to form a crude makeshift envelope, folded in half, and finally affixed to my time card with one lone staple. As subtle as a pine tree in a desert. It was heavy, too. Something in there rattled and rolled around. I pried it from the card, punched in, and headed straight for the ladies' lounge where I could open it in privacy. I could feel Tim's stare following me as I walked down the corridor. He'd seen. My heart was pounding. That chest feeling slithered again. Like my heart was shifting its position.

Inside the toilet stall, I pried the envelope open carefully. Heavy ink indentations told me there was writing on it, but I was not prepared for the chain that fell out, attached to something that resembled an inverted pentagram. It was a face, and I recognized it from some books I'd seen on black magic. The message read:

Things being as they are, I do not think it is advisable that you wear the ring. I do not wish the responsibility. The enclosed should help. It has been properly treated and has been through all the rites. It should ward off any problems due to the ring. Details will come on verbal contact, but you should have some idea what I am talking about. Later—Devin.

Beside the signature, a scribbled scorpion, symbol of his sun sign.

The *enclosed* referred to the pentagram, sterling silver on a sturdy gleaming silver chain. Within the pentagram was the face of the hierarchic Goat of Mendes. I'd often seen it referred to as the Sigil of Baphomet. The two top points of the star contained the horns, while the two side points made up his shaggy ears. The bottom point held its face and chin, and when I turned it over, it became a smooth inverted pentagram soldered into a metal circle. Sterling stamped on the rim. Looked expensive. But…point *down*?

I put it on and reread the note twice. My telephone attempts crossed my mind. Had I somehow gotten through to Devin this weekend? I *had* to talk to him. Back to the route room.

Devin was already on a route, but Pat promised to have him call me as soon as he called in. He hadn't been all that anxious to leave today, Pat had added, but said it was a small route and that he shouldn't be gone long.

Coward that I was, I just didn't have the guts to walk in there flashing that ring, especially when I was late. I took it off until I was settled at my posting machine. Even then, I tried to keep it hidden in my lap and began posting with one hand. I just wasn't ready for the onslaught of office jokers when they finally realized I was wearing the ring. As it was, Kelly had not forgotten about it and wasted no time in bringing the matter up.

"Well, did you buy the ring, Kerry King?" she taunted loudly, obviously hoping to get Lola in on the fun.

"No," I replied, which wasn't a lie.

"Wha-da-ya-mean no? I don't believe you. After all that noise Friday? And how come you're hiding your hand?"

I glared at her. "Shut up, Kelly. If Mama heard that, you're dead."

She obligingly lowered her voice. "Okay. Lemmee see." She let out a yelp when she looked at my hand. "You *did* buy it, huh?"

"No," I whispered, knowing Hannah's lone machine would drown us out. "But you won't believe how I really got it."

She eyed me suspiciously. "How?"

I sighed, knowing I was wasting my breath. "Devin *gave* it to me."

"Oh, sure. You just don't want Mama to know. What'd you buy it with? The phone money?"

"See, I knew you wouldn't believe me."

"Okay." She crossed her arms smugly. "*When* did Devin *give* it to you?"

"Friday night. At three o'clock in the morning."

"*What was Devin doing at your house at three o'clock in the morning?*" Kelly exploded loudly.

"Shut *up*, Kelly!"

Hannah stopped posting. "Oh. You got it? Let me see." At least she was quiet about it.

"Kerry better not have a new ring on today," Lola called in. I couldn't tell if she was kidding or not.

"Oh, it's *okay*, Mama," Kelly yelled back. "She didn't *buy* it. She claims Devin *gave* it to her." She jumped up and raced into Lola's office. "*At three o'clock in the morning!*"

"Kerry! Get *in* here."

I shot Kelly a warning look and went in.

"Kerry, what the *hell* was Devin doing at your house at that hour of the morning?" She was teasing. In fact, she obviously didn't believe it. I offered her my hand but she pushed it away. "That's gross," she said, then added with the Leo smug know-it-all smile, "Where's the tapestry?"

"Still on my wall," I admitted. "But I won't back out on the deal. I promised. I'm just forty bucks richer than I planned to be."

"Well, how come Mark didn't mention it to me?"

"He was sleeping. Besides, I told him not to."

"Why that disloyal little…"

"Ask Scotty. *He* was there."

"At three o'clock in the morning, too?"

"Yeah, too stoned to drive." I laughed at the confused look on her face.

"Well, I don't understand. Why would Devin just *give* you his ring?"

I heard Kelly's loud *ahem* from the other room, but I ignored it. What did I expect them to think, after all? I tried to brief Lola on how it happened, but I could see she still wasn't convinced.

"Well, don't you wear that thing at my house," she said finally, dismissing the issue.

"Honest, Mama, that's really how it happened."

"Oh, okay." She smiled her humoring-me smile and went back to her paperwork.

At eleven o'clock, I was notified of a phone call on line three by a smirking Ethel.

"Kerry," she called loudly from Lola's doorway. "Devin Drew is on hold for you, and I don't think it's business."

The gossipers were at it already. "You walked all the way in here to tell me that?" Usually they buzzed.

"They're going steady now," Kelly quipped.

"All of you knock it off!" Lola was standing in our doorway trying to sound stern. "Ethel, out! I have heard enough about that stupid ring. Kerry, pick up the damn phone and, Kelly, you mind your own business."

She scared Ethel, who left quickly. I smiled sweetly at Kelly, who stuck her tongue out at me, and punched three. "Hello?"

"Hey!"

"Who's this? Devin?"

"Yeah, it's me." It didn't *sound* like Devin, and I said so.

He laughed. That sounded better. "I assure you it's me. I'm calling to make sure you read my note."

"Yes, I did, but it didn't tell me much. Did something happen?"

"Well, it isn't something I wish to discuss over the phone. However, I may slip out around five or so, you know?" He sounded nervous.

"Okay, I'll meet you back there. But I wish you'd tell me now."

"Well, I'm not quite sure how to put this, but you could say I was the victim of a psychic attack. Several of them, in fact."

My telephone games crossed my mind again. "When, Devin? Over the weekend? Do you remember what times they happened?"

"Sure I remember. But what's the difference? You sound like you know something about it, which doesn't exactly surprise me."

"Well, I'm not sure, but damn! I may have caused them."

"Oh. No. No way. No human could have caused this. But I think I know what did. It all comes down to the ring. I don't know if it's safe for you to wear it. Did you put that pentagram on?"

"Yes, right away." I glanced down at the ring. It looked friendlier now. Warmer. Like it had finally accepted me. I didn't want to give it up. "Look," I said. "You're right. Let's wait till five. I've got an audience here." I looked directly at the girls. They both shifted in their seats, guilty eavesdroppers. Kelly pretended to look up an account, and Hannah started posting again.

"I have the same problem," Devin said. "I'm calling from a customer phone. Later."

Lola was standing in the doorway looking at me when I replaced the receiver. Lately, I'd been catching her with that same stare when I least expected it. She was obviously worried—trying to read into my sudden interest in Devin. She'd been long aware of my opinion of hippies and longhairs. We had been out numerous times socially, and I was a constant guest at her home on the weekends when Mark wasn't visiting mine. Our families, Pammy included, had spent Christmas together just last year. And Devin Drew just didn't jive with what she knew of me. She did know about my interest in the occult. She'd heard me argue *The Bible* with her husband numerous times, and she was probably wondering what on earth Devin was filling my head with now. Presently, they were all looking at me. Hannah was the first to speak, smiling of course.

"What was *that* all about?"

I decided to stick with the truth. So far, it was the only thing they didn't believe. "It had to do with the ring."

"You're breaking up!" Kelly screeched. "Already?" She was laughing so hard I thought she was going to fall out of her chair.

"Buzz off, Kelly," I said, using one of Devin's favorite expressions. "And now that I've hung up, you can all go back to work."

"Boy, touchy-touchy today, aren't we?" Hannah beamed. "It must be love!"

"Just think," Kelly added enthusiastically. "A father for Kerry's kids. It's about time. And a warlock, to boot. Hey Kerry, do your kids have any toys? Like dolls? I mean, what *do* witches' children play with?"

"Oh, they have a few wax images and hatpins," I retorted.

"Okay, that's enough," Lola intercepted, smiling too. "Kerry's getting punchy now." She tried to assume a professional look and, not succeeding, returned to her desk, laughing.

I wasn't sure how much of the phone conversation had been heard, but oddly enough, the harassment ended for the day. Nobody mentioned Devin again. At five o'clock I waited until they'd all left before heading for the time clock. Devin wasn't in the route office, so I punched out and hung around there for another few minutes. No Devin. The chest feeling had started up again. I cursed myself for being so disappointed. He'd probably forgotten and gone home.

I pushed the heavy door open and stepped outside where the trucks were parked, and there he was. Leaning against one of them. He looked tired, and there was no inverted cross hanging around his neck. No rings at all. Not even the big Pentagram of Solomon that he usually wore on his other hand. "Yeah, no jewelry today," he remarked, in answer to my unspoken observation. "You noticed, huh?" He held up both hands to verify the fact.

"All right, Devin, what happened? I have something to tell you, too, but I'd like to hear your story first."

"Well, actually, it's difficult to describe. But it scared me."

"You said attacks. What kind? Were they physical? Did you see something?"

"Well, physical in a sense. You'd probably call it mental because it left no marks. A better word is invisible, although I felt it physically and mentally. It sounds rather insignificant in the light of day, but it was like fighting off something I couldn't see. It hit me with electric shocks. It's really hard to put across what happened with words."

"And it scared you."

"Paralyzed me, and believe me, chick, I've seen some things, and I don't scare easily. Nothing I did stopped it. I tried every trick in the book. First three lasted for about an hour, off and on. When I was pretty sure it had quit, I went over to Trevor's. He did a Tarot reading, and it all came out the ring. Unless he misinterpreted the cards, it looks like that ring could be dangerous. I'm not telling you not to wear it. It's yours. However, I would not want to see you go through something like that. That's why I gave you the pentagram. If you're still going to wear the ring, and I think you will, at least keep that on too."

"You don't sound like you believed the pentagram would protect you. Why do you think it would protect me?"

"Well, I can't assure you of that. I was wearing the Tetragrammaton. The Ring of Solomon. The most powerful piece of psychic protection you can cover yourself with. And I never even felt like I needed protection. Against anything. That's why I took everything off. To show whatever it was that I'd meet it bare. I hate to admit it, but I was scared shitless. Nothing like that has ever happened to me. Anyhow, I'm going to put the cross back on. I would have left it on during the attacks, but then it became an ego thing."

"Do you think it's not safe for me to wear the ring, then?"

"I can't tell you one way or the other. I can say that if I were you, I'd wear it anyway."

"Even after what happened?"

"Well, admittedly that would be enough to scare your average person away from wearing it, however, I would wear the ring. Meet that sucker with my own power." His ego was showing now, but it looked good on him. "Well, you said you had something to tell me too."

That chest feeling dropped to my stomach. "Devin, after all that, I don't know if I should *ever* tell you what I have to tell you." I shuddered just to think of it. "You're going to be furious. If I do tell you, I hope you'll try to remember, if I did cause all this, that it was never done intentionally. I mean, I never meant for you to get hurt."

His eyes bored through me. "What are you talking about?"

"Look, can it wait till tonight? It's a long story, and I see now that there is more to this than I even thought. Is there any way…?" I stopped, mentally groping for words, then, "I know it's presumptuous of me, what with you being married and all, but is there any way you could come up to my house tonight? Would that cause a problem with your wife?"

"Yes and no." He laughed, breaking the sinister mood of this talk. "Yes, I can come, and no, there wouldn't be a problem. I told you before. I wouldn't allow it."

"Well, you could bring her if you want to. There's just more to this than I can explain here on company grounds."

"She wouldn't care to come. She steers clear of this sort of thing."

"You're kidding! Your wife isn't into this stuff?"

He laughed again. "I'd be happy if I could just get her into my room to clean it like she does the rest of the house."

"You have your own room?"

"Sure. I needed one. She wouldn't hang *my* paintings in her quaint, normal living room. Besides, I keep everything in there. Books, albums, sound equipment. All my magic tools. Sort of a den. Couple beanbags. Matter of fact, that's where I was when the attacks started. I was making you an eight-track tape from my collection of music."

I groaned, more sure than ever that I was responsible. He'd been attacked while doing something for me. "I did cause this."

He looked floored. "Why? What makes you think that?"

"Well, that's part of what I have to tell you."

"Okay, I'll be up then. It'll be late. I have to lock up. Pat opens up, and I close."

"Speaking of Pat..." I pointed behind Devin to the exit where Pat had appeared.

"As you can see, they're looking for me. I must get back. I'll see you tonight."

I drove home feeling very anxious about his coming up. For one thing, in order to tell him how I had used the ring, I would also have to tell him *why*. That meant admitting how much I'd been thinking about him. And since it obviously wasn't a mutual interest, tonight was going to be pretty embarrassing, not to mention uncomfortable for both of us. But if I didn't tell him, he would go on blaming the ring. Probably live in fear of some invisible entity. Then again, I *had* used the ring. Maybe it *was* the ring.

I thought of Myrna. She was a psychic friend of my family's who lived in Pennsylvania. Although she refused money for it, she would often go into trances for friends and do 'readings.' On things. And people. As far as I knew, she had never been wrong and was often unaware of the words she spoke while in trance. Claimed her answers came from spirit guides. In fact, those trance words usually contradicted the logical, conscious Myrna. She could do a reading on the ring for me. Under these circumstances, I was sure she would. But did I really want to know the answer? Or was I just afraid to admit to Devin how I was feeling about him?

I *could* just hand him the tablet and let him see for himself how this thing had grown out of nothing and nowhere, but how embarrassing would *that* be? As I contemplated the idea of giving him my journal, a song came on the radio that just couldn't be a coincidence, yet there it was, singing about an entry into a diary and asking...*what's happening to me?*

No, I was not looking forward to tonight. Not at all.

5 It was nine-thirty before the van cruised up to the chain-link gate of my fenced front yard. I had been rereading my journal while waiting and knew that, by handing him this notebook, I would be openly admitting to this crush I was developing on him. I couldn't see any other way to do it, though. At least he would see the progression day by day and know that it wasn't anything I had planned or wanted. Seeing it in print was like reading a horror novel that someone else had written. Was this really *my* journal? The knock at the door startled me out of these last minute thoughts and, with a sick feeling in my stomach, I got up to let him in.

He entered, looking as though he felt as awkward as I did. I noticed that those Pink Floyd guys were on the radio again, singing about seeing me on the dark side of the moon. That sure wasn't my country station, and I wondered if Pammy had changed it the last time she had visited.

"No motorcycle tonight, huh?" I attempted a smile.

"No, I came straight from work. I don't always get out this late but Lucky didn't show today, and I ended up doing his route. I've been working over his figures since I left you."

"Sounds like you could use a cup of coffee," I offered.

"I believe we could both use a cup," he agreed, taking a seat in my red, wide-armrests, Naugahyde armchair. "Looks like you have a head start on me, though. Your hands are shaking."

"I wish I could blame it on the coffee." I sighed. "But it hasn't helped, and neither have the cigarettes. You take cream and sugar?"

"Yeah, two. Are you going to tell me what you wouldn't down there?"

"Yes, but let me get the coffee first. It's going to take a while, and I'm not sure how to begin. Or where."

"The beginning's usually a good place," he replied. "I'm anxious to know what it had to do with those attacks."

"Well, maybe nothing. But I wish I could believe that." I threw two cups of Sunrise instant coffee together, brought them in, and sat down on the floor in front of him. "Here. And I'm still afraid you're going to be angry."

Devin lit a cigarette. "I can't imagine anything you could say that would anger me."

"We'll see. You told me the eye in the ring is real, right?"

"That's what I was told. In order to be sure, I would have to take the ring apart, you know?"

"Well, I can practically guarantee another way," I began, "but I'd better get this over with first." I handed him the notebook with a resigned sigh. "I think you'll understand better after you read this."

Devin gaped at me with astonishment. "You *write?*"

"Yeah." I felt stupid. Like a schoolgirl. Devin apparently didn't take it that way.

"Far *out*," he breathed. "I do too. In fact, a lot of communication between my brother and me is done this way." He gestured with the tablet.

"If you can't read my writing, just ask," I told him as he opened the notebook. I sat back in discomfort, freshly familiar with the contents. It was all in there. The buildup since the first day in the office. The references to the ring and how badly I wanted it. Its immediate unfriendly vibes and the nightmares I'd had the first night. Worst of all, the penned thoughts as to Devin's wife and childless state. I shuddered to think of previous tablets, now filed in my dresser, containing the episode I'd had while reading the Trojan Horse book, and the blue fog encounter the following day. But, for the one he had now, it was only a matter of time before he came to the day I had bought the Sador. The day of the attacks.

"You're probably reading about the dreams I had the night you gave me the ring. Scotty said I was mumbling in my sleep all night. Now I wish I had made more of an effort to recall them. I was just so excited about the ring. I don't know if there's a connection, but happiness doesn't usually bring on nightmares."

Devin eased back in the armchair. When he didn't comment, I went on. "Those notations about your marriage…I was just wondering about you, that's all. No harm meant."

He nodded. "This fear stuff refers to the ring?" He didn't wait for a reply. "I see you were afraid of it at first."

"I was, yes, but keep reading. Once I quit hiding it from the office today, I stopped worrying. I think I let my sister's remarks get to me too. She thinks the ring is evil. I was also smoking some pretty good grass."

"Yeah, I'm hep to what the combination of grass and fear can do to you." He smiled at last. "You aren't still afraid of it, are you? Because if you are, you shouldn't be wearing it even with the pentagram on. Fear can do funny things."

"I'm not afraid of it now. Not even after what you told me today. And I don't think you'll blame the ring when you finish that tablet."

He leaned over and pointed to a line that said *met him before*, but had been changed to *knew him before*. "Does this mean before this particular existence, or did you mean you may have met me somewhere in this life and don't remember?"

I looked away. "You were right the first time. Déjà vu. Maybe a reincarnation thing, if you believe in that. Just a sudden weird recognition of you."

I had elaborated on that quite a bit in the tablet, so I let him go back to reading. He did for a few pages, then set it aside. "Strange. I, too, experienced that same feeling of familiarity with you. The funny part is, I've seen you in that office for months and didn't feel that way before. I take it this is relatively new to you too. Say…just in the last few weeks?"

"To be honest, Devin, I could hardly stand you. No offense, I'll explain that in a minute. But…this recent…thing…was *all* of a sudden. First you changed jobs…then your appearance…and then jobs again. It was as if you became an entirely different person overnight. I've been getting some funny pains in my chest whenever I'm near you. Even if I just get a glimpse of you at your desk. And it's not comfortable either. It almost hurts. Like I'm supposed to remember something about you. Maybe that's where the dreams come in. I sure wish I could remember them now."

He nodded. I couldn't believe it. He seemed to understand. He wasn't angry, and he didn't seem to think I was some nut. Yet.

"What about this—Mama, Kelly…you didn't go into detail."

"Just the ribbing in the office. It will die down now." We looked at each other in silence. I could feel his scrutiny of me, and it was the same scrutinizing as I was doing to him. There was something extremely different about him tonight. I couldn't put my finger on it. It had been the same on the telephone with him today. A different voice…or mood. Serious. Almost sinister. Very intense. The usual clowning was gone. His face seemed older…more mature…but earnest. Like he was holding something back. As if a part of him knew what was going on, and another part was just as confused as I was. As if one part wanted to say more and dared not. He finally broke the silence.

"Okay to read the rest of it?" he asked quietly, flipping the page.

"Sure. It's actually easier for me than having to explain."

I was growing more uncomfortable by the minute. I knew what came next. I'd read it repeatedly tonight while waiting for him. The chest feeling was annoying and getting to that aching stage. I turned my back on him and started flipping through the newspaper. Somehow, I knew he realized my embarrassment, and I felt him giving me a funny glance before returning to the tablet. Super. Now he was going to read the *why him?* notations. I had gone through that for days, too, recording my puzzlement over this sudden interest in the hippie. At one point, Devin tapped the notebook with the pen, and I looked around at him.

"This…*am not in love with him…barely know him yet*…uh…I'm glad you said yet." He touched me gently on the nose with his finger. I didn't know how to answer that so I just nodded, motioned for him to continue reading, and turned back to my newspaper. I could feel his gaze boring into my back.

"It must be important," he observed aloud. "You've been through that paper twice already."

"It is, kind of. I'm looking for Sydney. You know—the guy who writes the horoscopes?"

"Who?"

"Sydney Omarr. For a long time they had him on the comic page, but he was so accurate they moved him to the births and obits. Now I've lost him again. He's the only astrologer who's got his shit halfway together..." I stopped abruptly. "Oh, here he is."

Devin glanced over my shoulder. "I probably shouldn't ask, but...where'd you find the dude?"

"Local news," I replied absently, scanning the signs for Virgo.

"I knew I shouldn't have asked." He sighed, and we both laughed. "Local news! The paper must think he's astounding." With a wink he went back to the notebook, and I got up to make more coffee. It was taking longer than I'd expected. By now, he should be reading all that stuff about his future kid being special. Shit. How was I going to explain that? I just didn't add asterisks beside the notations in the journal with explanations of where I got my ideas.

Devin flipped the page. "Are you sure you wish me to continue with this?" he asked. "If it's uncomfortable for you..."

"Finish it," I interrupted, feeling my face flush. "We have to get this over with."

He looked like he was going to reply, then went back to the notebook. "I'll take another one too," he said instead.

"Coming up." I stood by the stove waiting for the water to boil and dreaded what I was sure would come next.

When I brought the coffee in, he laid the tablet aside again and reached gratefully for the steaming cup. "I have questions," he said, sipping, "but I'll wait until I've finished it. I really don't see what all this has to do with those attacks, but then, I see there's quite a few pages left."

"I'm sorry to put you on the spot like this, Devin."

"Oh, you aren't. And even if you were, don't be sorry for anything you ever do. There is no such thing as a mistake. We learn from all our experiences. We're both learning something right now."

"Yeah, like not to keep diaries, huh?"

"No. This is enlightening. I have a couple corrections to make but, those too, later."

After what seemed like hours, Devin set the tablet aside and looked at me. Really looked at me. Well, here it comes, I thought. The lecture. How happily married he is. The whole bit.

Instead, he turned back several pages and marked certain paragraphs with little stars as he skimmed through the entries. Then he handed it to me. "Can you explain these assumptions?" he asked, still gazing at me intently. *I have a secret*, the look accused. *And I think you know it too.*

I read the marked paragraphs from the first (I'm not in love with him) to the later ones plainly contradicting that statement. "I can't explain that, Devin," I admitted, unable to look him in the eye. "I don't understand the feelings. I didn't *ask* for these feelings, and I don't know what's going on. For me, nothing's ever happened this fast or snowballed this quickly. I don't like it. It isn't *me* ! It doesn't add up or make sense." I took a deep breath, close to tears now. I just couldn't help the way I felt. "Look. I fall for very few guys. It takes me a long time to even trust someone enough to *like* him, much less all this bullshit!" I waved my hand, indicating the tablet and all its contents. "I can't *possibly* be in love with you. I barely *know* you. And yet, the feelings are there anyway. Like someone else is pushing the buttons, and I'm just reacting like I'm supposed to." I stopped talking. If he didn't understand where I was at now...the confusion I was going through...

Instead of commenting on my outburst, he turned to the many references and reminders to myself that he was happily married, circled one of them, and handed the notebook back to me. "Are you *sure* about this, and what makes you think so?"

"It's just an opinion. You're always so happy and, well, you're faithful to her. You could have had me in bed without trying...obviously...you never say anything against her, and..."

"Well, you can scratch all that," he interrupted, "because it's all wrong. She's leaving. Going back home. In February. Mutual agreement a month ago. We both decided. It seemed better to wait till after the holidays. Nobody else knows that, by the way, except Tim. That's why he's so worried about you. Haven't you noticed the look he's been giving you lately?"

"I thought so, but what the hell? We're breaking every rule Perry's made."

"Well, I don't knock my wife to anybody because there's no reason to. She's been a good wife. She tries. But we were married when we were kids. We both knew it was a mistake before the first year was up. I guess we just stayed together for lack of any real reason to split up. However, I knew I was looking for someone and that when the right time came, I'd find her. That's why you see me happy every day, doing my job, late hours, rarely home. But smiling anyway. I figured that someday I'd get back all the good I've tried to put out. When I came into your department at work, especially recently, I would see you with Kelly, joking around, rarely serious. You reminded me of myself. Always alone. You stuck out as a loner. Different from everybody. You know, the word's back in the route room that the office had a couple of chicks who were down on men, and one of them was you. But I saw through all that. I knew you couldn't be happy with a human any more than I was. I used to watch you and think...now there goes a strange chick."

"Strange? What do you mean strange?"

"Just strange, you know, meant as a compliment. I admit I've been interested lately, but I really didn't think you'd give me a chance. Especially since I'm married."

I gave that some thought. "You were right, too," I finally admitted. "Awhile back, before all this, I'd have turned you down, and not just because you're married. I...I know this sounds snobbish but, well, you aren't the type of guy I'd ordinarily go out with. I sure hope you can understand that. I'm twenty-five and, well, hippies and longhairs... biker mustaches like you used to have...all that stuff became popular after I was already married. And to a military man back from Viet Nam. So I steered clear of the whole movement. I can usually tell right off when I meet a guy whether the chemistry is there or not. Since you, all that has changed. Maybe because of you. The entire hippie world, what's left of it, is okay with me now. See what I mean? Do you really expect me to be able to explain all this?"

Devin ran a hand through his own hippie mass of curls. "Yeah, Tim's getting down on me to cut it again. I told him I would. He says Jason is having a shit fit."

"Why? It's not too long now. It's just starting to grow again."

"It's longer than you think. You just can't tell because of the curls. No, I'll cut it. It doesn't even matter anymore. At one time I would have fought it, but now, for some reason, it just doesn't matter anymore. Something else that's changed only recently." He was still watching me intently.

I had the unnerving feeling that he knew damn well what these sudden changes in both of us were about. I grew uneasy under his silent, meditative scrutiny. "Devin, why are you staring at me like that?"

"What about my child?" The question was fired like a missile. I was not prepared for it, nor for the tone of voice that launched it.

"Devin, I don't know. That's going to be the hardest to explain, but I'll try. Sometimes, when I get myself into the right mental state, and especially if I'm not looking for it—like when I'm stoned or listening to music—I see pictures. I hear voices. And I get these sudden flashes, you know, ideas out of nowhere."

His eyebrows rose almost undetectably, but I caught the interest. "And how long has *this* been going on? Flashes...pictures...the whole bit?"

"It's the only thing about all this that isn't new," I assured him. "All my life. I used to lie in bed while my brothers and sisters were out making mud pies...I was supposed to be taking a nap. I'd lie there and watch...little movies. It's fascinating. Don't you see anything when you close your eyes?"

"I don't see that way," he said, "but I'm aware that the ability exists. Perhaps I haven't been here long enough—" He stopped short, closed his eyes as if realizing he'd slipped up, shook his head, and began again. "Just what exactly did you get on my son?"

"Wait, Devin. What did you mean you haven't been here long enough? You're as old as I am."

"Slip of the tongue, believe me. Please. I asked you first. It's very important."

"Please don't be upset. I honestly don't know what it meant. And before you ask..."

"Where it came from? Another of your flashes?"

I looked at him, awed. He had an incredible ability to read minds. I was just about to tell him that I was unaware of the source, both of that flash and any of the others I'd come to take for granted. I knew most people didn't experience these things, but the ability really had been with me all my life and had long ago ceased to amaze me. I was usually very careful who I mentioned it to, but my family, Pam included, accepted its validity without question. "Look, I know you don't like kids, for one thing," I began.

"Whoa, back up, chick!" He gaped at me disbelievingly. "Don't like kids? Where did you get *that*? If that's an example of the reliability of your sources..."

"No," I said, laughing at the look on his face. "I have *human* sources, too. See, I've asked a lot about you around the plant lately. You also have a reputation among the girls. Married for years and no kids because you supposedly hate them."

"I used to feel that I would never bring a child into this world the way it is now, and is heading. I may have said that I wouldn't bring a child into this world, but it's because of the world, not the child. I don't hate kids. I very much love them. They didn't ask for what they're about to inherit. The fucked-up system. All the shit humans are saving up to dump on the next generation. Well, one day *I* had a flash. Maybe similar to the kind you get. Maybe even from the same source. It wasn't that long ago. However, I realized that it was not that I wouldn't *father* a child. Just that I hadn't found the right mother yet. At least for the kind of child I would bring into the world. His mother can't be humanly programmed. She can't be the stereotypical mother. She can't be *human*. Your flash was correct, wherever you got it. I've known this...oh, just a couple of months now. My son will be special, all right. He will be a savior to the world. He'll have to be raised differently than human children are today.

He'll never see the inside of one of *their* schools, nor will he learn to read using their textbooks."

"But you have to send him to school, Devin," I interrupted. "It's the law!"

"Yeah, *their* law! I will teach him myself. Things *they* can't possibly teach him."

I suddenly became acutely aware of the radio playing softly in the background. Pink Floyd again, singing about *us* and *them*. Between this conversation and that radio, I was starting to feel uneasy again. The intensity in his eyes and voice raised goosebumps on my arms. Again, I was seeing a marked difference in him tonight, one that the people at work had to be completely unaware of. "It's ten-thirty," I pointed out, deliberately changing the subject. "Your wife is probably calling the hospitals."

"Hey, lighten up, chick." He laughed, making a face that brought the Devin I knew back into perspective. "I'm telling you, she's used to it. If I weren't here, I would probably be at my brother's. I'll tell you where she's at right now. In Wonderworld. She goes to bed early." He picked up the notebook and resumed reading. I knew what came next. The bomb. The attempts using the ring to get him to call. That was all that was left. I just sat there nervously waiting. The attempts, the supposed failures. Everything up to the present. He read without comment until he came to the final page. I remembered the last entry well. *Devin Drew is happily married. Forget it.*

Finally, he tipped the tablet toward me. "You wrote that this morning?"

I nodded. "Well, middle of the night. I really meant it too. I came to work prepared to put you completely out of my mind. To forget about you. Just to do my job and not even look for you. Instead, your note was on my time card and, well, you know the rest. So, here you are again. Now do you see the connections between the ring and the attacks you experienced?"

Devin laid the tablet aside. "What you're saying, then, is that you *used* the ring…with enough concentrated thought…to create what I felt to be a psychic attack? Three or four times?"

I was sure he had to be controlling pure rage by now. "It wasn't intentional. I swear! If I'd had any idea that could happen, I wouldn't have done it. I…I…just wanted you to call. That's all."

"No, I'm not mad," he said, smiling reassuringly, and once again reading my thoughts and fears. "You meant well, but…whew." He shook his head in disbelief. "What a mind. Do you realize…are you even slightly aware of the force it hit me with? If it *was* you, you hit me seventy miles away, and you weren't even trying to hurt me? And those attacks, chick…I hope you never have to experience anything that physical or that terrifying. And you think you caused this with your thoughts? And that ring?"

"Well, that's the big question," I said hopefully. "Was it me? Or the ring? Would it have happened anyway if I *hadn't* used the ring?"

Devin removed the object of discussion from my hand. "Still wearing it, though," he mused, almost admiringly. "When exactly? What times were you making those projections? No...suppose I tell you!"

"I think we both know the times."

"Three times Saturday, between noon and one," Devin continued, in spite of my interjection, "and at least once late Sunday afternoon."

I shrugged helplessly. "So the times coincide."

Another long stare. "It's possible you didn't even need the ring to do that."

We both just looked at each other. Now what? Devin was twirling the ring on his thumb, deep in thought. There was still one question I had to ask.

"Devin, during the attacks...didn't you ever *once* get a notion to call? Even one you obviously ignored?"

"Of course I did." His expression told me he was surprised that I had to ask. "Especially after the Tarot reading. You had the ring. I was concerned for you. However, after the reading I feared it would look like an excuse to ask you for the ring back. When I thought to call you Sunday, the attacks started again. Another coincidence? Or does the attacker exist independently of you and it didn't want us to connect? This does shed new light on the events, I have to admit, but where are we now? We still don't know if it was you, or..."

"Or if some *it* didn't want you to call me. What were you doing when the first one hit?"

"Yet another coincidence. Like I told you, I was recording your tape. Excerpts from the music on my reel-to-reel. But I don't see what that has to do with anything. I hate to think it's the ring. I had such good vibes from it. And it seemed to show up out of nowhere."

"Yeah? Seems like a lot of things are happening from out of nowhere. Here's another kicker. Look how I reacted to the ring. You know, I don't ordinarily get excited over *things*. If you knew me better, you'd be questioning that too. I buy weed, take the kids to restaurants, and make expensive phone calls...all insubstantial things. That's where my money goes. A record, occasionally. Stuff for the kids. I don't even buy clothes like most girls do. Oh, once, when I was first hired. Because I had to. Office clothes. That's it, though."

Devin groaned. "Did you have to add that to it? I thought your desire for the ring was a normal chick's craving for jewelry. So it's a strange piece of jewelry, but for you it would be normal."

"Devin, nothing's really been normal since the day you came in to look up that delinquent account. Not that I'm complaining. Anyway, here's my idea."

I told him about my Catholic-occult upbringing and about Myrna. I explained her track record and told him that she would probably do a reading on the ring for us. Devin thought it was worth a try, so we put in a call to her, left word with the person who answered, and added that it was urgent. Then we waited.

Devin remarked that the attacks seemed too intense and painful to be only the product of a strong desire for a simple phone call. He tried his best to describe the electrifying jolts that had shuddered through his body, and his own terror and feeling of helplessness. As he talked, I was remembering a night back in June when I'd been reading a stupid book that had generated a similar terror and helplessness. I considered telling him about it—and about the blue blob that had hovered over my windshield the next morning—but decided against it. One more story added to what was already going on and Devin was likely to split before we even got our answer from Myrna.

While I was pondering my own past events, Devin continued to explore the possibilities of our current situation. He was sure there was another force involved. One that had taken advantage of my attempts and coincided them with the attacks. Well, we couldn't rule it out, but what...or who? Was this source connected to the purchase of the ring, or was the ring just a prop in an apparent mysterious production orchestrated by the source of Devin's attacks?

The phone ringing cut our wild speculations short. I glanced at Devin as I answered it. We both knew who it was. It only took a few minutes to run down the story to Myrna who listened attentively until I was finished. Then she advised me to bury it. When I protested to such a drastic solution, she asked me if I wanted the young man to go through another attack. I said I thought a reading might clarify things for us on this end. She was quiet for a minute, then asked to speak to Devin.

Devin obliged and verified all the information I had given her. He added that, as opposed to bad luck with the ring, he had had a rather drastic turn of good luck, but he did admit we were worried that the attacks might have been connected to it. She must have asked him about the nature of our relationship because he repeatedly insisted that we were just friends, that we had practically just met, and that our relationship was very casual. He then handed the phone back to me.

"All right, Kerry. I will do a reading on it. Why on earth you would want the eye of a dead jackal on your hand is beyond me. I will insist on one condition, though. Wrap the ring in something and put it in a drawer for three days. By that time, I will have your answer, and I will airmail it to you. I have to be strict about this. You are not to wear it until you hear from me. Any kind of psychic attacks are nothing to play around with."

I reluctantly agreed to her terms without mentioning aloud that there were any conditions. I was sure Devin would not go for hiding the ring for three days, and I wasn't crazy about the idea myself. I thanked her and hung up.

"She'll do it," I told him.

"And the conditions?"

I looked up, startled. How could he have known? "I'm supposed to put it away for three days until she does her thing. No condition, no reading."

"Well, then, why don't you?"

Like everything else about Devin tonight, the suggestion to go along with Myrna was a shock. I'd half expected him to demand the ring back rather than hide, bury or destroy it. "You think I *should*?"

"Three days won't kill you. Besides, my curiosity is up. I'd like to know. However, if she does say it's the ring and that bothers you, then I would like to have it back rather than bury it or destroy it. I don't fear the ring. I would wear it as a challenge."

"Do *you* think it's dangerous for me to wear it?"

"That depends. Dangerous for you or dangerous for me?"

I caught the jest in his voice and laughed. "Come on, Devin. I'm serious."

"Okay. Let's wait it out and see what she says. If she hasn't answered by Thursday, you can call her."

I wrapped the ring in cotton as Devin left for the bathroom. With a heavy sigh, I picked out an empty desk drawer and hid it way in the back. I was sorry we had called her. The ring was still too much of a novelty for me to be hiding it away for three long days.

"Speaking of conditions," Devin said as he returned to the living room, "as far as the wedding goes, don't buy a gift. It not only isn't expected, but my brother would be insulted. He picked up the notebook, found a blank page, and began to write something on it. I refilled the coffee cups without asking him, and when I returned, Devin was sitting on the floor, leaning back against the armchair, still writing.

I sat across from him, Indian style, watching him. "More comfortable down here, huh?"

He didn't answer. The pen moved across the page in a strange printing that didn't even resemble the writing on Devin's route tickets—writing I'd come to recognize at a glance over the last month. As he penned his unspoken thoughts, I noticed that his face had taken on a chiseled earnestness, as if he doubted the advisability of what he was about to give me. He abruptly stopped writing, dropped the pen, and pushed the notebook across the green shag carpet to me. He said nothing, but his eyes studied me with a wariness and concern, revealing the caution he felt about what he had written.

I looked at him questioningly. "For me?"

He nodded. "My turn," he said.

6 As I picked up the tablet to see what he'd written, the song on the unfamiliar radio station was now playing an eerie ballad with a beautiful melody and very odd lyrics. It spoke of telling tales under sleepy morning skies and said that if I asked, then I needed to know, and if I still doubted, I should be told. The artist was equally unfamiliar to me, though I would later learn that it was Uriah Heep, a rock group that would become very familiar to me in the months ahead. The haunting melody and lyrics only added to the chill that came over me as I read his words.

Things being as they are, we can only accept what we understand. We take on too much, we receive more than we understand, so why dwell on the misunderstood thoughts that we have? Together we can understand more than we can apart. However, can the union be understood by anyone but us? Or is it important to think of others? Can we be sure this is—is where, or why? Because it is already known, or I feel so. Why bother, because the need is there.

Need for intelligent union is necessary, however, how necessary, and to whom is it necessary?

The signature was unintelligible, and beside it, like the time-clock note, a hastily scribbled scorpion. The message made no sense to me. I read it twice and handed it back with a blank look. Devin glanced at the radio as the song trailed to an end, and then at me with eyes that seemed to shine like an animal's in the dark.

"As you can see," he said finally, "I have a little difficulty with the language. I'm trying to tell you something, and yet, I'm evading it." He picked up the pen again, studied me thoughtfully for a moment, and then wrote without the slightest hesitation:

The feelings we share are as hard for me to put across as for you. I wish…but that could be misunderstood. The shyness in me is afraid to ask. No—ask isn't the word I'm looking for. I just can't see myself—my feelings—being understood. Yet, I cannot say what I wish. Troublesome. However, that's me. TOGETHER. What more can I say and not actually say it? But why am I afraid of saying it? Only because I wish it to be important, and not just another thing.

I had stretched across the floor opposite him so I could read each word as it appeared. When he pushed the tablet over to me, he studied me with an expression I could not interpret as I read the paragraph in its entirety. He seemed to be searching my face for some trace of recognition or understanding. What was he trying to say? What could be so awesome that he had to keep hedging? In some ways, it seemed like a possible romantic overture, but I sensed there was something else, between the lines, that he continued to avoid in print.

I looked up at him. He was sitting cross-legged, rolling a joint from a small plastic bag he had extracted from his uniform pocket. He seemed to be doing it as a distraction, because he didn't light it.

"Devin." I sat up to face him. "Whatever it is you're avoiding, whatever you're trying to ask me or tell me, please…just go ahead and say it. Or write it if it's easier. You're not going to upset me."

He lay back against the front of the chair again, squinting, his brow furrowed. "You got any candles?"

"Of course." I pointed to the stereo where two unlit red bayberry candles sat.

He looked relieved. "This light in here…I don't know how you can stand it."

"I can't. Usually I light that candle, or use that red lamp." I nodded at the plastic mushroom-shaped lamp that sat on the floor beside the stereo. "But in view of the business you were coming up here for, I didn't want you to think I was trying to make it…romantic…or something."

He got up, lit both candles with a silver Zippo, and then blew one out. "There. That's better."

Back to the tablet. With almost a sad look, he printed in bold letters:

Respect the ones you wish to respect you. If you chase, can you handle what you catch?

My ego reacted swiftly to that one—in shock, and with a little guilt. "I wasn't aware that I was chasing you."

"I wasn't referring to you," Devin said quietly. "I was referring to me. But, you see? Misunderstandings again."

Our voices echoed in the still room. For some reason the radio had shut off while we'd been preoccupied with the tablet, and I just now noticed the quiet. The candle cast eerie, fiery-red reflections on his face and, once again, I noticed the weird effect on his shining eyes. He heaved a resigned sigh. "If you misunderstood that, how can I ever expect you to really grasp what I'm trying to tell you?"

Embarrassed, and at a loss for words, I picked up my hairbrush and ran it through my hair quickly. My own distraction. My long copper-colored hair was halfway down my back, and my bangs were almost brushing my eyelashes. They needed to be cut, I thought, and set the brush down, ready to face whatever else was to come on this strange night.

"Why cut them? Why not let your bangs grow out?"

Devin's sudden quiet question, the reply to the thought I had not voiced, startled me at first, but I quickly rationalized it. It was only natural for him to comment on the obvious. My bangs *were* too long. "I guess I could," I said, "and I actually do try once in a while, but when they get to this stage they drive me crazy, and I end up cutting them again."

"Brush them aside for a minute." Without waiting for me to do it, he reached over and did it himself. "There. That looks better."

Everybody who'd ever seen me growing them out had gone to great lengths to tell me how awful I looked. Lola and Kelly were the worst. "You think I should?"

"That's up to you. However, I think it looks better."

"Okay. I'll let them grow. They've already got a good start the way they are now." It really didn't matter to me, but all of a sudden, his opinion did. A lot.

He was back at the tablet again. Twice he lifted the pen, and twice he stopped in midair. His expression and mannerisms throughout this weird exchange of thoughts did not indicate shyness to me, but rather a skeptical fear of being misunderstood again. I would later learn that his stalling that night was a desperate search for words that he hoped I could understand on my own level. Finally, he wrote:

Misunderstandings are people's main fault. This has made me too secretive about what I know and how I really feel. Time is…but will time be at all tomorrow? Fear is what will destroy what we have already accomplished.

After reading it twice and still not getting it, I set the tablet behind me so we could try to talk. "Look, Devin. I'm getting the impression that this has something to do with more than an ordinary male-female chemistry, although I'm not excluding that altogether. Am I correct so far?"

He nodded.

"It seems like you are trying to prepare me for something."

"I guess I'm trying to feel you out on what you might already know. Perhaps it is up to me to inform you, however, with that hotline you have going for you in your mind, I thought perhaps you would tell me that you already know the things I'm afraid to bring up so soon."

I actually had to shake my head to clear it after that one. This was going nowhere. "Okay, Devin. I am going to make us some more coffee. You go ahead and smoke that joint you rolled. When I get back, you are just going to blurt it out, okay? If I could sit here while you read me inside and out for an hour, I think you owe me that same uncomfortable hour."

I left for the kitchen. He watched me as I prepared the cups. "I'm going to miss that ring for the next three days," I called in. "So is everyone in my office."

The serious edge lightened for a while as we talked about the ring and the reactions to it at the plant. *Both* ends of the plant, I discovered, as he informed me that the rumors were even wilder back in the route room. I told him I didn't care myself, but then again, I was not the one with a spouse or even a boyfriend. *His* only concern, he assured me, was what the talk might be doing to my reputation. That, in itself, was funny, considering I was supposedly known as a man-hater. That ring had stirred up an awful lot of something with its purchase, and the place was having a heyday with it. On the other hand, it was displaying capabilities other than just stirring up talk. Powers we weren't sure existed within the ring or within ourselves.

That déjà vu feeling I had experienced in the early days of our meeting was growing stronger as the hours wore on. It was like picking up from a left-off point, long ago forgotten. But was it *really* forgotten? Latent, yet buried, that spark of memory nagged at me and tried to fit my feelings into some logical category. I knew I already loved him. I had loved him before. Of this, I felt sure. He knew me already, and I knew him. Like amnesia victims, we just couldn't seem to remember *where* or *when.* Just *that. That* there was another time and place. Or *did* he remember, and was *that* what he was trying to break to me? Maybe that was where his difficulty was coming in. If that was the case, I could surely understand his hesitation. Another grass flash? I had not smoked anything.

"You don't think I'll believe you, do you, Devin," I said suddenly, even though we had been off the subject for some time.

Devin picked up immediately where we'd left off. "Whether you believe me or not doesn't matter," he replied, "because you already know. What's holding back your memories is your fear. And worse, your doubts."

He began to sketch out, in heavy detailed ink, a grotesque human eye. Its pupil glared at me with the same accusing look as the ring had done in the beginning. Beside the sketch, he printed the word *time* and above it, the symbol of eternity, a figure-eight, sideways. After a brief pause, he continued in print:

Wants…needs…desires…hopes…fears. Do we already know, and we are trying to convince each other? Or are we even on the same train of thought, however distant in our involvement levels? Can it be? Or is WHAT IT IS going to be, already? Now I feel I am drifting toward too much of the same train of thought, which to me, is. However misunderstood it may be. Perhaps my mind is tracked at this point, and it would be better not to pursue this.

He dropped the pen and looked at me. I read it to the bottom of the page and looked to see if there was more. There wasn't. When I looked up, he was staring at me. *Do you understand?* His eyes seemed to be pleading with me to recognize. To read through his faltering attempts and just *know* what he was really trying to say.

I decided to take a stab at it. "I'm not sure," I said hesitantly, "but it seems like you are trying to get me to say what you won't. You expect me to know already. Like it doesn't have anything to do with here and now, but has to do with something long past. Something to do with why you and I are on this earth at this place and time."

"Hey-hey-hey…" Devin sat back, his features a little more relaxed. Then, lighting a cigarette, he gave me a reassuring smile and proceeded to fill up another page in blazing capitals. As he wrote, he spoke. "Why *are* we here, Kerry? And for that matter, why are *they* here?"

"They?"

"Yes, they. Them." He handed me the tablet.

TO FEEL, TO TOUCH, AND TO EXPERIENCE THE WANTS OF NEED. THERE IT IS. MAN'S PATHWAY TO SOLVING ALL. FEAR AGAIN DRIFTS IN WHERE HONESTY SHOULD PLAY ITS PART IN ALL WE KNOW. PERHAPS IT IS ONLY NOW, AND WELL, BUT THE EARTH AND I KNOW, FOR WE, TOGETHER, HAVE EXPERIENCED THE WIND'S BENDING BLADES OF GRASS OR WATER CUTTING CANYONS THROUGH STONE. HOW CAN IT BE ASKED OR EXPLAINED? EXPERIENCE IS THE KEY TO THE WORLD'S DOORS OF ENLIGHTENMENT. HOWEVER, THE DOORS BEING OPENED BEFORE THEIR TIME COULD PLAY HAVOC ON YOUR MIND. HOWEVER, WAIT WE WILL, FOR WE ARE ONLY HOPING FOR

THE TIME TO COME TO PUT AWAY TROUBLING EXPERIENCES...

"*We?*" I asked. "They?"

"Us," Devin said with a finality that seemed to shake the very foundations of the room. "And them." He swept his arm in an outward gesture that obviously included an area far beyond the boundaries of the room we sat in.

The radio chose that ironic moment to burst back on, and I jumped, startled, and turned to look at it. Devin was staring intently at it as a song began, and then he gave me a knowing look as the first words...*us and them*...filled the room. This was the same song that had played while Devin had been discussing his future child and its education. The moment was so chilling that we just sat there without speaking until the song played out. When it was finished, Devin reached over and turned the main stereo button off.

"Your radio do that often?" he asked with a smile that told me he knew it didn't.

"That's the first time. Maybe there's a loose connection. Pretty weird about that song, though. Who was that anyway, and for that matter, what is that station?"

"You don't know who Pink Floyd is?"

"Them again? Those guys have been following me around lately. My sister has their album."

"I'm not surprised. That they are following you around, that is, or that your sister has the album. They are a pretty big group. That station is also very big with the underground rock people. It doesn't play teeny-bop. I *am* surprised that you listen to it, though."

"I don't. I've never heard of it. Pammy probably put it on one day and left it there."

I picked up the tablet again and reread what he'd written. This night was getting weirder and weirder. The Devin I knew would never have said anything this profound. This was not the way he talked. And what did it mean anyway? I was becoming frustrated and impatient. Devin still watched me, no doubt absorbing my feelings. He seemed to be on the verge of making a decision. Finally, he turned away.

"It's much too soon," he said. "Inwardly, I know this. I know I could make this easier on both of us but...can I take that chance this soon?"

I sighed. "I really like you Devin, if that's any help."

The pen moved swiftly.

I CAN VENTURE TO SAY THAT I LOVE US. I REALLY CAN RELATE, HOWEVER I DO NOT KNOW THE MANNERISMS IN WHICH YOU WOULD UNDERSTAND. WE IS WHAT I WISH TO DEVELOP, YET WE IS WHAT I FEAR COULD BE DESTROYED. ONLY IN MISUNDERSTANDING. EXPLAIN SOMETHING TO ME THAT YOU DON'T KNOW. I WISH VERY MUCH TO EXPLAIN, HOWEVER I DO NOT KNOW US. I WISH IT TO BE MORE THAN I HAVE KNOWN BEFORE AND WHAT I DON'T KNOW I CANNOT RELATE TO. FEAR DRIFTS BUT NEVER LEAVES. I FEAR THE ME YOU DON'T KNOW OF YET...THE ME THAT WANTS TO...

Immediately he struck a line through *wants to* and changed it to *is impulsive*.

He sighed again and closed his eyes. Tired. The pen lay loosely in his hand. I had seen the original words and the change he'd made.

"Impulsive? You've been here for five hours trying to say something and you call that impulsive?" I looked at him leaning back against the chair, his eyes closed as if in private thought. His white uniform shirt was rumpled and partially open. His hair was a mass of curls. When he finally did open his eyes, they were red and bleary. Shadows of fatigue were etched in his face.

"I'm keeping you up by being here, huh?" he said.

"You're not keeping me up, but you do have to be at work in a few hours."

"So do you."

"I don't start till eight-thirty. When was the last time you slept, Devin?"

He smiled and turned to another blank page in the notebook.

BEFORE YOU. TO SLEEP WITH THE THOUGHT OF BEING CLOSE IN SPIRIT, AS THE EARTH IS TO THE SUN. WITHOUT THIS CLOSENESS, THE EARTH WOULD DIE. DYING IS NOT MY STYLE. I DO NOT CONSIDER THINGS I HAVE HOPED FOR, BUT DARE NOT ASK. FEAR AGAIN. I KNOW MUCH OF NOTHING, YET I FEEL THIS WITHIN MY INNER SELF. TOGETHER WE CAN BE ONE WITH THE WORLD. LIVE FREE, HAPPY, AND AS ONE.

"I'm not referring to sex," Devin added verbally as he paused with the pen. "Anyway, sex is just, well, as Louise Huebner puts it..." and then he wrote *TRANSFER OF ENERGY* and underlined it. When he saw my blank expression, he explained. "Okay. Who's she? She is the Los Angeles official witch. You must have heard of her."

I shook my head, smiling at his amazing ability to pull thoughts out of my head.

He continued. "She has a couple of albums out, one of them being *Seduction Through Witchcraft*. Her albums are funny, though. She's so commercial. I'm surprised you never heard of her, just because of the Wicca connection. How about Uriah Heep?"

I shook my head. "If it's acid rock, forget it. I only listen to country western music."

"You heard Uriah Heep tonight. Moody Blues? Black Sabbath? *Any* of the occult music that's out?"

"No. Never heard of them."

"Dr. John? Savoy Brown? Grand Funk?"

"Give up, I'm telling you."

"You've never listened to FM? What about Pink Floyd, the song we heard on the radio tonight? Twice, actually."

"Dark Side of the Moon album? My sister has that one. Probably all the others, too. She's twenty, but she was a teenager when all that stuff hit the air. I've heard *of* them, just never got into that kind of music."

"Oh, Kerry. You don't know what you've missed. Country is...well, human bullshit. Self-pity…woe is me…she left me…gotta get drunk…you know. You listen to it. Well that's going to change. I made you an eight-track tape with some of these songs on it. I did manage to put some good occult stuff together before the day was over, in spite of the attacks. I would have brought it with me if I'd gone home first."

I left for the kitchen thinking about the coincidence of his recording a tape for me at the same time I was buying the Sador, and of the synchronization of the attacks in the same time span. Regardless of what was behind it all, it seemed to have some connection with whatever that Trojan Horse book was concerned with and, ultimately, whatever was happening to Devin and me. That we were getting mutual interference from the same type of thing was hardly coincidental. What Devin didn't know was that I had been at an occult shop in that same time frame purchasing a damn love talisman with *him* in mind.

That familiar chest feeling. I really only knew him this one evening. Tonight. Yet, the physical urge was there…to go in and put my arms around him. As though I had done it for years. Or was it actually eons? I didn't dare *do* it. What if it all wore off tomorrow? What if next week? What if next month? I looked in at him, writing again, but pausing a lot. What if forever?

"Hey, uh…if you're tired, you know, throw me out. I have a habit of overstaying my welcome."

"I don't want you to go. I know it's three in the morning, but…" I brought the steaming cups in and glanced at what he'd written.

MY INNER SELF HAS GAINED MUCH FROM YOUR FRIENDSHIP. PERHAPS I AM IN NEED OF THIS INNER CHANGE. YOUR CONSIDERATION AND HELP ARE GREATLY APPRECIATED. MORE THAN MORTAL MAN CAN EXPRESS. SIMPLY LOVE GROWING.

I took the pen and wrote under his words: *Devin, I wish you lived here.* Then, realizing what I had done, I dropped the pen in horror. Had I actually written that? Just what was it that was locked up inside me and only coming out tonight? Before I could change it or apologize for my own impulsive move, the answer was on its way, like a ticker tape.

MY HEART ALREADY DOES. SOON TO FOLLOW WILL BE WHAT I HOPE WE ARE BOTH WORKING TOWARD, FOR NOW I KNOW WHAT I WAS LOOKING FOR IN AN UNDERSTANDING WOMAN THAT I COULD SPEND MY LIFE WITH. FEAR NOT, FOR I HAVE ONLY MAKING YOU HAPPY IN MY THOUGHTS. I CAN DO WHAT ONLY MORTAL MAN CAN DO, YET THIS MUCH DIRECTED TOWARD YOU MIGHT EASE THE PAIN OF MY MORTAL FAULTS…

AHEAD LIES DISTURBING TIMES, YET THE PEACE WE CAN FIND TOGETHER SHOULD SEE US THROUGH. MY BEST IS ALL I CAN GIVE, AND ALL THAT I WISH FOR IS HAPPINESS TOGETHER. WE CAN LEARN MORE IN TIME, BUT FOR NOW I HAVE KNOWN, LOVED, FELT, AND TOUCHED THE REAL YOU,

AND IT'S LIKE NOTHING I HAVE EVER KNOWN BEFORE. REST NOW, FOR TOMORROW BRINGS YET GREATER LOVE.

Again, the scorpion as the signature. The final paragraph. As I read these words, the unreality of the situation hit me. In four days, we had gone from passing strangers…to this.

Not once had Devin made a physical move toward me. We had just spent seven hours together without so much as a kiss. And now we were talking about *love? Living together?*

Me? And this *stranger?* It was too preposterous.

"I'd better get trucking. It's a long haul to my house. You going to leave the ring put away for three days?"

"I guess so." I got up to walk him out. Almost four in the morning. We stepped out into the night. Cold for this time of year, but then again, it was almost winter.

"Look, uh…Kerry, you're going to have to bear with me," Devin said as he boarded the van. "I'm officially married now, but I'll get to work on that right away. I can rush things forward, maybe get things finalized by Christmas."

My head was spinning. "Hey, slow down, Devin." I laughed. "I'm not going anywhere."

"That's what you think." He started the engine. "How does a wedding on Gallows Hill in Salem sound to you?"

For the first time all night, I reached over and grasped his hand. On contact, an electric shock went through my hand, up my arm and straight to my heart.

"Devin."

He squeezed my hand. "I know," he said softly. "It feels just like I knew it would." He kissed me gently on the cheek. "See you at work in a couple hours. Oh, Kerry…better let me get out of here."

I realized I was still holding his hand. "Damn, Devin, you were trying to tell me something *else* in there, weren't you? Something I still have to become aware of."

He sighed. "Yes. We do eventually have to get to that. I just haven't found the words to tell you yet."

"What can it be, Devin? What does it have to do with?"

"Me. You'll realize it eventually. It's only a matter of time. Then, you may tell me."

"Tell you what?"

"Who I am."

A light rain had begun to sprinkle as the last sliver of moon slid behind a cloud. "Go inside," he said gently. "Before you get wet."

I nodded and stepped back so he could shut the van door.

"Well, there goes the moon," he said, watching it waver in and out of the cloud, almost gone. "We've already had one full moon this month, on the first. On Halloween, it will be full again. Two full moons in one month. What they call a blue moon. You know how often that happens?"

"Not too often," I said. "Well, there it goes. That's the last of it for a while."

"Yup, dark side from this moment on."

'Well, actually, it's not official until noon tomorrow."

He smiled. "You and your damn astrology, chick. Later…"

I watched until the van was down the road and out of sight, then turned and walked slowly back to the house.

Dark side of the moon.

It was starting to pour.

7 "More coffee?" The waitress sounded like she was speaking through a megaphone.

I opened my eyes and looked around. I'd almost fallen asleep right there in the booth of the coffee shop. This was going to be one long day. Outside, beyond the glass windows, it was still drizzling, and still dark. I pushed my cup forward gratefully.

"It's going to take a lot of these today, Jane," I said, yawning. "And the usual English muffin." I picked up the sugar jar and dumped some into my freshly refilled cup.

"You're really early today. What's the occasion?"

"Just never went to bed last night." I had spent an hour rereading all the writing in the tablet, and then awoken the kids. I had not really started to feel the lack of sleep until now. Before she could respond, another customer walked in, and she waddled off, always the waitress.

I liked the coffee shop. It was close to the plant, and I wasn't the only one from work who patronized it. It was the company hangout for both breakfast and lunch. I often stopped in at opening hour and read a book, wrote my letters, or balanced my checkbook. I drank a lot of coffee, but I always left Jane a good tip. Frequently I'd indulge Lola with an English muffin just because she loved them.

Just to keep awake, I went out to the yellow metal newspaper machine. I'd been so groggy that I'd forgotten to get my daily Sydney Omarr. I dropped in the coins, retrieved the paper and dragged myself back to the booth. I was scanning the horoscope when two shadows fell across the paper.

"What's he say for Scorpio?"

I nearly jumped out of my skin. "Devin! Pat!"

"Shh!" they both hissed loudly, obviously in a jovial mood. "We're not supposed to have left the office." They took a seat in my booth, Pat across from me and Devin beside me, both laughing. Pat snapped his fingers and waved his hand back and forth in front of my eyes. "Wow, Dev, she's asleep with her eyes open." Apparently, Pat had some idea of why I might be tired.

"Hey, check it out, Pat. So am I." True, Devin didn't look much better than I felt.

Pat looked around for Jane, but she was already heading toward us with two steaming mugs.

"How do you feel, Dev?" I asked, while Pat's attention was diverted.

"Like a million bucks." He tried to smile, but it came out a yawn.

"Yeah, I feel all wrinkled and green, too."

Jane set the mugs before them and refilled mine. "I'm glad you guys are finally teaming up," she remarked as she poured. "It saves on booths."

Pat and Devin went through an exaggerated act of ducking down in the orange-cushioned booth. "You haven't seen us today, Jane," Pat said warningly.

"Oh, snuck out, huh?"

"Naw...now, Jane..." Pat straightened up indignantly. "We're just grabbing a fast hot one before we start out in that heat, right Dev?"

"Right," Devin agreed, smiling. "We do work hard, hauling those heavy bottles on and off the trucks all day."

Jane reached over and tapped the big red *supervisor* tags sewn onto both their uniform shirts. "If it weren't for that, I might actually believe you. Your drivers look like something out of an advertisement now, ever since that lawyer-looking guy took over. I expect he's curtailing your morning coffee excursions too, huh?"

"Route salesmen, Jane. Don't let Jason catch you using the word driver."

"Jeez, he's that bad, huh?"

"He's that bad," Devin confirmed. "Like we said, you have not seen us."

"Don't worry, I won't snitch." She strolled away, laughing, shaking her head.

"Did you get the third degree when you got home?" I asked Devin.

"Well, she was up getting ready for work when I came in. She did ask where I was all night."

"What did you tell her?"

"The truth. What else?"

Pat choked on his coffee. In the midst of lighting a cigarette, my match stopped in midair. "What?" we both said in unison.

"I told her I was with a female friend," he replied with a shrug. "I didn't say who, not that it would have mattered. She wouldn't recognize your name anyway."

I couldn't believe my ears. He had not lied to her. My respect for him skyrocketed.

"I hope that was okay," he added, misreading my stunned expression. "I mean, we *are* technically separated, and she *is* leaving in a couple of months anyway."

"You told me February yesterday," Pat interrupted.

"Well, we talked about it this morning, and she's pretty much into the idea of moving the date up. That way she can be settled in with her family before Christmas. That's good for me and Kerry, because I'd like *us* to be married by February and getting settled in ourselves."

Pat looked flabbergasted. "Damn, Devin...you're really serious, aren't you!"

"Damn, Pat. No Shit!"

Pat glanced at his watch. "Drink up, Devin. Tim will be pulling into the place any minute now. I'll take care of the check." He disappeared down the aisle. Devin didn't get up.

"Hey, Devin, what time is your lunch hour anyway?" I asked.

"It's pretty flexible, why?"

"Want to go to lunch with me and Kelly?"

He smiled. "Like to live dangerously, do you? Can you see Jason's face if he caught wind of that?"

"Oh, fuck him. Lunch is not officially company time. But…you're probably right. They'd never give us permission."

Devin thought a moment. "I think I can swing it. I'll let you know before twelve. Maybe Pat likes to live dangerously, too. Well, he's waiting out there so I'd better go." He gave my hand a squeeze. "Later."

I took one last gulp of coffee after he left. Five more minutes and I would be late too. A thought hit me as I headed for my car. Devin hadn't even met the kids yet.

The sun was finally overpowering the cloudy sky as I started the engine.

I was surprised to see a note stapled to my time card when I punched in. The fact that I had just left Devin didn't detract from the excitement of seeing this note, and I couldn't believe this was happening so quickly. To me! That chest feeling was growing with the usual discomfort as I released the message from its stapled bonds. Only when I was safely hidden in a stall in the ladies' lounge did I open the note. Last night's tablet communication had pretty well given me an idea of Devin's personal style, and it surprised me that this note was written in handwriting I recognized from Devin's route tickets, unlike last night's strange lettering. And if the difference in penmanship wasn't a total shock in itself, the contents of the note were, for in striking contrast to the philosophic thoughts projected onto paper last night, this note sounded much more like something Devin would write.

Thank you for last night, babe. It meant much more to me than you can imagine. Or maybe you have the general idea. I'm going to miss the hell out of you today. There's a chance I might be in the office today, but don't count on it. If Tim gets the idea I like being in now, that will be the end of that. I'll be delivering specials all month. He is prone to dumping off the specials on me because I know the city so well. Anyhow, babe, thanks for the insight. It calmed my existence. Later…Devin.

Again, the scorpion. I reread the note, feeling an affectionate warmth spread through me. Devin must have written it before he'd left with Pat this morning. I was amused at the tone. Typical Devin. Happy-go-lucky and loose. Not at all like the strange implications of last night with the undertones of secrecy and mystery created under flickering candlelight. The sinister blanket of the night had lifted with the sun and evaporated with the light of day. Things were back to normal again. Or were they?

A loud squeak and the shuffling of feet indicated the invasion of my privacy and the entrance of people. The ladies' lounge was filling up with its usual early-morning gossipers.

One of the phone girls was arguing with two other sets of shoes about the sloppy condition of the coffee bar, and they in turn were reprimanding her on her rude phone manner. The lounge door squeaked open again.

"Grouchy, grouchy, grouchy!" Kelly, having entered at that moment, had caught the tone of the conversation, if not the words. "Jesus Christ! Every time I come in here, the whole phone room is having a meeting. Someday I'm going to hide in the stalls like Kerry's doing and listen in…see what you say about our department." She rapped on the stall door as I hastily folded the note and tucked it in my pocket. "What're you doing in there, Kerry? Taking notes?"

"How do you even know it's me?"

"Who else paints astrology signs on their shoes?"

I flushed the toilet for show and opened the stall door. "Never fear! Reporter Kerry is on the scene in war-torn Sparklear. No dice, Kelly. I heard the whole thing, including the rumor about the sloppy bar those phone girls are in charge of, but alas…not one word about accounts receivable."

The phone girls burst into laughter. Kelly was gingerly applying a new set of eyes to the ones she'd already put on this morning. "Rumor of the day, huh? Is that how bad this place is getting?"

"Yeah," I said. "You want the details? It's a juicy piece of gossip. I'll trade you for two stale rumors and one unconfirmed report."

"Oh, I don't know, Kerry. I'm not sure I'm ready for it. I'm not even awake yet."

"Poor you. I never even got to bed last night."

"Oh, partying it up, huh? On a weeknight? Hey…where's your ring?"

Washing my hands, I had forgotten Kelly's microscopic observation ability. She didn't miss a trick. "Well, it's a long story, Kel," I began. Kelly was one of the few friends I did grant the privilege of seriousness to. Occasionally. Kelly, however, did not always reciprocate.

"Aw…did you guys break up already?"

"Oh, take that down," Janet said loudly. "That's even better than the sloppy bar rumor. Kerry King and Devin Drew have broken up."

"Now *that* is how rumors get started," I said nonchalantly and walked out without a backward glance.

As usual, I didn't go straight to my office, but turned left out of the lounge and went down the hall to the phone room…first door on the right. Every morning I greeted each phone girl by name in their office, just to keep the family vibes going at the place. Since three out of five were in the lounge, it almost seemed like a wasted trip, but out of habit, I went anyway.

I never used the door designed to swing open like the lounge door. Instead, I used the little mail window, which was always open. Kim, the phone room supervisor, was almost a bigger gossip than the girls she employed, but we all just accepted that as part of her personality. I caught her engrossed in studying a route sheet of driver names, completely unaware that I was right behind her.

"Hi, Aunt Kim!" I quipped in a high childish voice, knowing I was going to startle the shit out of her.

"Whaaa…oh, hi, Kerry." She lowered her voice. "Better use the door today. Hitler *and* Mussolini are both running around here this morning."

"Mussolini?" I ducked inside.

"Yeah. That creepy little bookkeeper he hired. Maurice." She turned back to the route sheet. "What's the story on this…Devin Drew…route seven? Didn't he get a promotion?"

"Oh, I meant to tell you." Janet had just entered as the phones started cranking up. "Sparklear, please hold…Margie, take that will you?"

Kim turned to Janet again. "Isn't Devin a supervisor now?"

"Yes, he is," Janet replied, handing the phone to Margie. "But when a driver…er…route salesman is out, he subs in for them."

"Oh, that's right." Kim buried her face in her hands. "John Marshall is out sick and Lucky's *been* out. Now *Ethan*. He called in again. His car won't start. Those phones are going to be a bitch today."

"Oh, Devin's on a route today?" I asked innocently, as if I didn't care. I probably could have pulled off sounding disinterested if Kelly had not pranced in at just that moment.

"Did you hear the big news, Aunt Kim?"

"Hi Kel…no, what?"

"Devin and Kerry have broken up already!"

"What? Oh, you clown. For a minute there I thought you were serious!"

"I *am* serious. Look!" She snatched my bare hand and thrust it in Kim's face. "See? She gave him back his ring."

Kim set the route sheet aside. "Hey! You *aren't* wearing it! What happened?"

"We were getting too serious!" I cried dramatically, fist to forehead.

"Oh, get outta here, you two nuts." Kim laughed. "From the way Devin looked this morning—"

"What?" Kelly looked suspiciously at me. "Kerry, was Devin at your house again last night? You homewrecker! What time did he leave *this* time? Midnight? Or three again?"

I could see Kelly was really getting off on this. "Four-thirty." I tried to assume a serious face. "But don't worry, Kelly, now that we've broken up Devin will be getting his beauty sleep once again." I perched on the edge of Kim's desk. "Besides, I'm more tired than he is. I never even got to bed."

"Aha!" Kelly retorted. "Never even made it to the bedroom, huh? What'd you use? The beanbag?"

"Beanbag?" Kim repeated stupidly. She looked confused.

"Yeah, beanbag," Kelly repeated. "This uncivilized thing was given a queen-sized bed for her birthday. From Lola. And she *still* sleeps in that fucking beanbag!"

"Really, Ker?"

"Well, I'm adjusting to it gradually. I take the beanbag into the bedroom twice a week and practice sleeping with it on the bed." I looked at Kelly. "He was there on *business*, Kel." I made an attempt at a straight face, then laughed aloud at her nosiness.

"Oh, now you're charging him. You rat! No wonder he took his ring back."

"He didn't take it back. I had a one-cent sale, you know, bring a friend for just a penny more?"

"Boy-oh-boy! She's come a long way in a few days, hasn't she Kim?"

"She certainly has, but I wouldn't keep that sale going, Kerry." Kim laughed. "It'll take you forever to pay off that ring at that rate. Hey, where's it at, really?"

"Hidden away at home," I replied seriously.

"Oh, good place for it. I won't ask why. I'm sure it's a long story, and I don't have time for it. There are three guys out today. It's a good thing we *have* Devin."

"Well, you'd better enjoy him while he can still walk," Kelly said. "And Lola is going to destroy *Kerry!* She sent me in to get her."

"Oh, she did? I guess I'd better split, then."

"I feel sorry for your poor mother," Kim said as I hopped down from her desk. "If you two worked for me, you'd both get a good spanking once a week." She smiled affectionately. "Bye, you guys."

Hannah was already posting when we walked in.

"Good afternoon, kiddies." Lola smiled at us. "So nice of you to come! Did you plan on working today, or is this just a social call?"

I dropped the white to-go bag on her desk and shrugged. "Might as well. We're already here."

"Oh? What makes today different from yesterday?" She fished around in the bag and pulled out the muffin. "And *this*," she added, "will not get you out of trouble today!"

"Why not?" I retorted. "It worked yesterday." I set my purse down by the typewriter seat across from her.

"It's cold for one thing. And take that suitcase of yours in by your own machine. Or is that as far as you could carry it?"

Everyone smiled. My purse was the laughing stock of the plant. It contained no less than three occult books, along with numerous oddities; things that most girls don't usually carry in their purses. The irony of this was that when someone *did* need an unusual item, it was there in my purse somewhere. Guitar picks, needles with thread, tampons or light bulbs, the possibilities were endless. It had a bigger capacity than Mary Poppins's bag, and wasn't nearly as large.

Obediently I transferred it to the empty spot under my posting machine. "Oh, good morning, Horrible…" I cooed loudly to my Burroughs posting machine. "I missed you last night."

"What did you need Horrible for?" Kelly threw in. "To add up the bill Devin's running up every night?"

"That reminds me, Kelly," I said, ignoring her sarcasm. "Guess who we might be having lunch with."

"Oh, no. Now she's trying to break up *my* home, too." Kelly was sorting charge tickets into alphabetical order as she talked.

"Well, call Benny and clear it with him."

"I don't have to clear it with Benny! But thanks a lot. I get to sit by myself."

"No you don't. You get to sit with Pat."

"Oh, he's going, too? What are we celebrating, anyway? National Divorce Week?"

"Might as well include everybody," I said. "Want to ask Lola and Perry, too?"

"We'll have to. Lunch falls under fraternization, kiddo, remember? Or have you forgotten the new commandments? Lola, do you hear this shit? Do you believe this girl?"

Lola was thumbing absently through Kelly's accounts. "I don't believe these *files,* Kelly. What are you filing them under…first names? And what's all this baloney about lunch?"

There it goes, I thought. "It was just an idea. Anyway, rumor has it that Devin's on a route. He probably won't get back in time."

Lola gave me a strange look, shook her head, and said pointedly to Kelly, "She is not well."

"Oh, everyone knows that. But, just for the hell of it, *would* we be allowed?"

"Yeah, Jason can't do anything about our lunch breaks, can he?" I pushed. We both looked at Lola.

"That would be a suicide mission," Lola retorted. "You can't break two rules in one lunch. You'll get us all fired!"

Kelly and I exchanged looks hopefully. "Two rules?"

"Yes, two. You and Kelly have sinned at lunch every day since the new bulletin. I've clocked you. You always take forty-five minutes. I don't know if you're working the red-light district or what, but coming in with …men…would be, like I said…Russian roulette with six bullets."

"But are we *allowed?*" I persisted. "Devin had a small route today. I saw the list. He's doing Lucky's…"

"Lucky was always the last man in," Lola reminded me.

"But Speedy Gonzales will be back by eleven," Kelly argued. "So, can we?"

"Well," Lola conceded thoughtfully, "I guess Perry can't really stop you from going, but if you're any later than thirty minutes, I'll have to answer for you, and you know what that means."

"We'll be on time," I promised her. "Thanks, Mama."

"Why don't you come too?" Kelly squealed. "Then, if there's any problem, Perry can do it all in one firing squad!"

"No, thank you," Lola replied. "I need the money, or I would."

"Oh, come on, lunch isn't that much."

"I meant the job." Lola smiled, too sweetly, and returned to her desk.

I tried to get back to my posting, but Kelly wasn't going to let me.

"Pssst! Kerry!"

"What now, Kelly?"

"Are you sure you two don't want to be alone?"

"Kelly, it's just lunch!"

"Okay. Who's paying?"

"*We* are…damn it, Kelly. Lunch was my idea."

"Ooh, you invited *them?* You brazen hussy!"

"Oh, shut up. Hannah? You want to come?"

Hannah turned away coolly. "No, thank you." She began to post before we could say anything else. Kelly and I exchanged shrugs, and again I returned to my machine.

"You saucy wench!" Kelly hissed. "Troublemaker! That's what you are!"

"Hey, Kerry, is Devin back yet?"

The posting was going slow. I turned to see Pat standing in the doorway. It was only eleven o'clock. "I thought he was with you."

"He was, but we're back from that run. Maybe he went to do something about his tickets."

"Well, *I'd* like to do something about Devin's tickets too!" Kelly bolted from her seat in frustration, waving a company charge ticket at Lola. "Just look at this! Do you *believe* him?"

Pat looked confused. "I meant his traffic tickets. For not having a sticker on his van."

I got up to see what Kelly was bitching about. Lola looked at the ticket and cracked up laughing. "I hope the customer doesn't call asking for a copy." She handed it to Pat. "If we don't have enough trouble reading their handwriting, do we have to be subjected to this, too?"

I peered over Pat's shoulder. "Lemme see!"

On the face of the ticket, next to the number, was a vicious face, drawn quite artistically, its teeth sharp and drooling. Printed beside this neatly was *bill customer.*

"Here's another one." Hannah brushed past me and laid another on Lola's desk. This one had a smiling face and a pentagram, point down, in the corner.

"That's Devin, all right." Lola smiled and passed it over to Pat. "*He* is not well *either!*"

Hannah stood by indignantly, as if waiting for something to be done on the spot, but Lola was plainly amused. Pat just shrugged and handed them back. "Take it up with Devin."

Lola returned them to her desk. "All right, back to work, girls. It's Tim's problem, not ours." She pointed us back to our room.

"I think they're kinda cute," I said.

"You would!" Kelly retorted. "I guess you get normal ones!"

"Well, you know, I don't pay much attention," I lied. "Hey, Pat. When Devin does return, send him up here, will you? We're all going to lunch today. You too."

"We all?" The look of surprise on Pat's face was genuine. "You mean...boy-girl-boy-girl?"

"He didn't tell you?"

"No, but it's okay with me! Anyone would be a refreshing change from Tim!"

"You're Kelly's partner," I added, hoping to get a rise out of her, but for once she remained unruffled. "Benny already knows," she said, trying to sound holier-than-thou. "I just talked to him."

"Well, just holler when you're ready." Pat laughed, a depraved look on his face. "Boy, this oughta torque Jason's mind, but good!"

"That's what I'm afraid of," Lola interrupted. "In fact, these two can't be late. Tell Mr. Drew I want to see him before any of you leave this place."

"Will do, Mama. See ya."

"Kerry?"

"What'd I do now?" I left my machine to see what Lola wanted.

"Who said you did anything? You got a guilty conscience?" She smiled. " I was just wondering...just a little curious, you know—" she paused to light a cigarette—"I realize it's none of my business but...what the *hell* is going on with you and Devin Drew?"

"Nothing, Mama," I replied innocently. "Just a lunch, that's all."

"Well, I know you *know* he's married."

"Yes, Mama, you told me that last week. Come on! What's the big deal?" I kept my tone light.

"Well, okay, but would you mind telling me why Pat and Kelly are going along?"

I knew her interrogation was more concern for the talk about me than any prying intent. "Well, I always go to lunch with Kelly."

"Yes, I know that."

"And Devin and Pat usually go together too, you know, now that they're partners in the route room."

"So that still doesn't explain why the four of you all suddenly…"

"Mama, Kelly and Pat are our friends. We want them to come. It would be fun! Besides, it would look better, wouldn't it?" I raised my eyebrows challengingly.

She shrugged in defeat. "Okay. I suppose you know what you're doing." Her eyes showed warm concern.

"Don't worry, Mama. It's cool. Really."

"I hope so."

In contrast to Lola, Kelly was hardly taking any of it seriously. She found me in the lounge with my arms crossed, smoldering.

"What's bugging you? And where's Devin?"

"I don't know where Devin is, and this whole place is starting to bug me, Kelly. Lola just called me aside, all freaked out, just because we're all going to lunch. I think she may be getting some flak from some of the higher-ups."

"You think so? I don't. I think Lola is afraid there really *is* something going on between you two. She probably doesn't want to see you get hurt!" She looked at me through the mirror as she fixed her hair. "And I wouldn't give a shit what anyone else thinks."

"But what if they are? What if that new bookkeeper, what's his name…"

"Mussolini? Oh, I'm sure he's watching. But so what? Devin is a supervisor. If he wants to count the trips Devin makes into our office, he can use his calculator." She put the finishing touches on her face and turned squarely to me. "I can just imagine what Lola thinks. I was going to say something to you too. I mean, Devin's a nice guy. I've known him for years. That's a little longer than you have, Kerry. He's married! I like him, but you're my friend. I don't know if something is really going on or not, but I would hate to see you get hurt! For *your* sake, I hope this *is* just a big joke with you!"

"Kelly, look. Nobody in this plant really knows what's going on. Not even you and Lola. Devin and I are the only ones—"

Kelly's eyes widened. "You *are* starting to like him, aren't you!"

"Well, it's not just that…"

"Not just *that?* Oh, Kerry, listen. When Benny and I were separated, you would not believe the married men who approached me. They'll tell you anything, but they'll never leave their wives. And Devin…He's been married for…"

"Years. I know! If I hear that one more time I'm going to scream."

"Okay. I'll shut up. That's all I'll say about it. You're a big girl. Been through it all. I'm not telling you anything you don't already know."

"No, but I'm going to tell *you* something *you* don't know. But you have to promise to keep your mouth shut. No slip-ups. Not even kidding."

She gave me a hurt look. "I know where to draw the line."

"I know, but it's really important that you realize you can't slip up. No one else knows this yet. Oh, Tim maybe, and Pat in the last couple days..."

"Kerry, I hope you're not...don't tell me Devin's going to leave his wife for you after all these years *just* because you guys made friends last week, and he gave you his ring—"

"Not *because* of me, Kelly. It was all set up and agreed upon *before* me! She was planning to leave after the holidays anyway."

It took Kelly a few minutes to digest that. "Devin's...splitting up with his wife...and...you think you're in love with him. Is that what you're telling me?"

"I'm afraid so. And for the record, Devin has not so much as even kissed me."

"Well, what about all those nights he was—"

"Two nights, Kelly. And when I said he was there on business, I wasn't kidding. You have no idea what's happened since I got that ring, but there just hasn't been time for sex, or what everyone thinks."

"Kerry, what are you trying to tell me?"

"That Devin and I are getting married."

She looked as stunned as if I had slapped her. "In five days you decided that?"

"No. I knew five days ago. I just waited the five days out to be sure I wasn't losing my marbles. I'm not. They're already gone."

Kelly picked up her purse, still looking at me oddly. "Let's go."

It was ten after twelve. Kelly went back to round up Devin and Pat. I went to our office to let Lola know we were leaving. I found her at her desk, talking to Devin, who did not look at all like he'd been up all night. The atmosphere was friendly and informal, so I went in.

"Well, this face with the sharp teeth," Devin was saying, "is a customer who gave me a hard time. It's not even my route, but he kept yelling and screaming, and I could see there was no reasoning with him. I had to do something while he was blowing off steam." He winked at me as I entered, and Lola flashed me a smile. Then she turned back to Devin. "I guess I shouldn't ask what the other one means."

"Yeah," I interrupted. "I like your pentagrams, Devin."

Devin tried to divide his attention between the two of us. "The happy face with the pentagram—" he glanced at me, "—is a guy who tipped me for doing nothing special. Speaking of pentagrams, chick, I like yours, too."

I feigned ignorance. "*My* pentagrams?"

"On some of your ledgers. Oh, not on all of them, but..."

Lola gave me a dirty look. "You'd better not be drawing that stuff on your accounts!"

"Oh, he must mean the accounts that get duplicate tickets with the statements. Those are *stars*, Mama. To remind me while I'm posting." I said it as though it had never occurred to me to call them otherwise, but my explanation fell on deaf ears.

"Oh, okay. Stars," Lola said, with a smirk that told me I wasn't kidding anyone.

Kelly burst in just then, purse swinging, foot tapping with her usual Gemini impatience. "Come *on!* It's almost twelve-thirty. Are we going to lunch or dinner?"

"Hey, lighten up, chick. Can't you see I'm in conference?"

"Oh, you're dismissed." Lola sighed and picked up her keys and sunglasses. "I'm leaving now too, and you guys remember what I told you. If you screw up…"

"Don't worry, Mama," Devin said seriously. "I'll have them back by midnight."

"No longer than their usual forty-five minutes."

Kelly and I exchanged glances. Jason's rule clearly said thirty. I could have hugged her. "Thanks, Mama," we said gratefully.

"Just get going." She left us all standing there, still a little stunned. She had just given us permission to hang our whole department, and probably Devin and Pat's as well.

I turned to Devin. "Look, uh…in view of the scandalous affair we are about to engage in…"

"Oh, stop wasting time," Kelly broke in. "You sound like a damn lawyer, and we may need one after this. Devin, should we all walk out together, or meet at the cars or, for that matter, who's driving?"

"Well, if you mean are we going to slip out the back, Jack, no," Devin replied, grinning. "Just get Pat, and wait for me out by the van. I have to see Tim before I leave. I'll be right out. Oh, it's parked right in front of the place."

"Oh, neat!" Kelly rolled her eyes. "With Brenda's desk sitting right in front of the glass doors…if there weren't any suspicious ideas already, there will be by the time we get back."

"And if there aren't any by then," Devin added, "we'll see to it that we start some."

Twelve-thirty at the plant was not a time for an empty lobby. Even the executives are stretching their legs and liable to turn up anywhere. It took more than a little guts to parade brazenly through the lobby on either side of Pat, arm-in-arm-in-arm.

"Now if they want to talk," Pat was saying, "you've really got to give them a mouthful. Now you two have permission, and me and Dev don't need any," and as he talked, he smiled and waved at everyone in the lobby, as if we were *always* going out to lunch. Kelly and I were in hysterics by the time we reached the van, and Devin was already there unlocking it. We could see him through the glass doors like a Cinerama drive-in movie.

"Devin, you're not supposed to park here," Kelly began nervously as we all boarded.

"I know, I know. Seventeenth commandment. Office personnel only. Alphabetical order, one a week. Anderson, Benson, Caldwell…Kerry, you sit up front with me."

"Oh, we get the back, huh?" Pat leered at Kelly, wiggling his eyebrows.

"Hey! There's a damn *bed* back here!" Kelly wailed. "You expect us to sit back here with the whole plant watching?"

"Oh, just lie down and be quiet," Devin called back. "Make yourselves comfortable. There's Pepsi in the fridge, and…oh shit…" he nudged me with amusement and nodded toward the lobby. "Check it out!"

Brenda was peering out at us with disbelief, and Mussolini stood right in front of those glass doors watching, hands behind his back, his mouth set in an expression of controlled rage. Ethel and Janet smiled conspiratorially and waved from the window. Then Jason strode up and stood right beside the bookkeeper.

"Oh, my God! We might be legal for lunch, Devin, but he *can* get you for parking here."

"Hey, when I park on the street, the pigs give me a ticket. Damn! Look at them stare. What'd you do, Kelly? Strip back there?"

"I wonder who's collecting the admission," Kelly said, ignoring him. "Christ! Look at all those people!"

"What did you expect?" Devin shrugged. "We're sinning before God and everybody. Want to give them something to watch?"

"Just start the engine before someone shoots out the tires."

Pat and Kelly were peeking out the side portholes, laughing so hard I thought they would choke. Devin revved the engine as the glass doorway filled up with more wide-eyed employees. "Sorry about that," he said with a mischievous grin. "I had to warm her up."

"Sure, Devin," Pat said with a smirk. "Everybody wave, now. Don't disappoint the folks!"

And with all of us waving, the van peeled out in a cloud of dust.

We weren't even late returning, arriving at exactly one-fifteen. Lola's deadline.

"Man, we have got to do this more often," Pat said earnestly. "That was so much fun. Devin, I can't believe what you and Kerry are like together."

"I had a blast," Kelly agreed. "But I don't think my stomach could take this two days in a row. I'm literally sore from laughing."

We agreed among ourselves that, considering the scene we'd made driving away, it wouldn't be very smart to go in the same way we had gone out. Not when Lola wasn't back to protect us. We separated at the van, and the guys returned via the time-clock exit. Kelly and I went through the front lobby, unescorted, but still laughing.

Hannah was posting like a sullen robot when we walked in. Lola still had not returned, so we sat down at our machines. Hannah made a remark about the time, but we ignored it. Then Kelly looked at me and we cracked up all over again. "Never again will I go anywhere with you and Devin. You're each bad enough alone."

"Oh, you had fun, and you know it. Besides, you didn't even have to pay for it."

"Hey! That's right! Where did you say we're eating tomorrow? The Hilton dining room?"

"Yeah, right. If there *is* a tomorrow, we pay our own way. Separate checks." I turned the radio on, and my country station burst out loudly. I quickly lowered the volume.

"Do we have to listen to that shit all afternoon?" Kelly whined.

"You had your dumb oldies all morning."

"Don't you two start fighting over that radio!"

Lola was back. Kelly jumped up and raced into her office.

"Hi!" Lola smiled. "How was your lunch?"

"Oh, Lola! You wouldn't believe," Kelly began. "I was never so embarrassed in my whole life."

"Oh, I can imagine," Lola retorted. "I've been out with Kerry before. You can dress her up, but you can't take her anywhere."

"Uh-uh-uh, Lola," I called in. "She's not talking about me this time."

Lola stepped into our doorway. "Well, you and Devin would be a little much for anyone to take. How'd poor Pat come out of it?"

"Oh, poor Pat. He's so used to conservative Tim, and I doubt that Devin acts like that around either one of them."

"I'll bet he does," Lola sniffed. "But no one is used to the two of them at one table."

"Never again," Kelly swore.

"Did you make it back on time?"

"Yes, barely. But we did it."

"Good. I'm glad you had to sweat it. Now you, Kelly, back to work. Kerry, you come in here."

"Now what did I do?"

"Kerry's in trouble, Kerry's in trouble," Kelly sang.

"Goodbye, Kelly." Lola smiled, and Kelly left, glancing over her shoulder the whole way.

When she heard Kelly posting, Lola assumed a businesslike role and handed me a stack of charge tickets. "These are tickets that we either can't find accounts for, or we never had an account for…or they're misspelled…or, you know. Our suspense file."

"Okay."

"Take these back to the route room and give them to Tim, or the supervisor, or…whoever's there."

A warm feeling for Lola spread through me. She knew damn well who was back there. She was sending me straight into the lion's den. Unescorted. She could have sent Hannah, but she hadn't. "Thanks, Mama," I said.

"Okay. Don't be all day now." She gave me her best supervisor voice and a suppressed Mama smile.

"Oh, Mama?"

She looked up, as if surprised I wasn't already gone.

"I've been deliberately avoiding that route room all week, and Devin's trying to do the same with this office."

"Oh. Is that why he was only in here twenty-five times today instead of his usual fifty?"

"No, I'm serious. We're aware of what it might look like, and I just wanted you to know—"

"Well, that's ridiculous. We all have a job to do here, and Devin shouldn't feel like he can't come in here. The company pays Devin and Pat to go in and out of here. If they don't, then Tim will have to, and Tim doesn't have time for all that nonsense. Now scram."

She smiled and went back to her work.

He was alone when I tapped on the open door. He looked up from an outstretched map.

"Devin?"

"Hey-hey-hey! What brings you here?" From his smile, I could see that he was both happy and surprised to see me. I handed him the tickets, which he glanced at with instant comprehension. "Okay. More of these, huh?" He set them aside. "Tell me. How did you get out of the office?"

"Lola. She knew you were back here, too. She could have sent anyone but me."

We just looked at each other quietly, both of us still playing the friends role. There was no longer any question in my mind about how I felt, but I had no idea how to go about saying it. Finally, I turned to leave. "Well, I guess I'd better get back. She also told me to make it quick."

"Kerry?"

I turned around. "Yes?"

"You tell Mama I think she's a fine lady. A *fine lady!*"

Maybe it was the tone of voice. Something about the way he said it. It just wasn't a word I'd heard Devin use in references to females. Chick...babe...anything but lady. I studied his face, which was no longer smiling, but serious and intense. Like last night with the tablet. When Devin wasn't fooling around, he just...changed drastically. Well, everyone has a serious side, I told myself. But how many people were aware of *this* Devin that came and went? I had never seen him talk or act like this around the routemen. Was *this* what his wife had seen in him long ago, so buried under the hippie image? A side that he never displayed in public?

"I'll tell her, Dev," I said finally. "And thanks for lunch. It was super!"

"Hey, what'd I tell you about that thank-you shit?"

"Yeah, I forgot. Oh, and Devin?"

"Yeah?"

Say it! Say it now before you lose your nerve!

"Devin, I may be crazy, but...I...I think I love you."

He didn't flinch. Never changed that somber look, nor did he register surprise. "I was hoping you did. It'll help."

Another silence and, beginning to feel awkward, I again turned to leave. The radio in his office began playing *Tubular Bells*, the theme from *The Exorcist*.

"Lady?"

I looked back.

"I love you too. I'll see you at five. If not before."

I was in a mild shock when I left his office. That he had expressed the same feelings for me was more than I would have hoped for. The fact that he was radically different at certain times than others did not really concern me at that moment. I had no way of knowing that I would encounter yet another Devin, stranger still, before the day was out. Overshadowing my ordinary caution was the memory of the last twelve words he had spoken to me. Nothing else mattered.

8 Back in accounts receivable the phones were buzzing, the machines were slamming, the radio was still playing *Tubular Bells*, and Lola wasn't at her desk when I walked in. I was glad. She would have immediately noticed the daze I was in.

Kelly pointed to a line flashing on hold. "For you, Ker. I think it's your sister."

Pam never called me at work just to bullshit, and when I picked up she got right to the point. She was getting ready to leave for her family visit to Allentown, and was just rechecking on permission to move back in with me when she returned. I told her it was okay, but it was hard to keep my mind on her enthusiastic chatter. I had left most of myself back in Devin's office. Pammy quickly gathered that I wasn't exactly listening.

"Are you with me, Kerry?" she asked, midsentence.

"Huh? Oh, yeah…I was daydreaming. That's what this job'll do to you."

"Yeah, I've been talking to you. What's the matter? You sound kind of funny. Are you stoned?"

I laughed. "Here? Oh, sure. We were all just sitting around toking on a joint when you buzzed." Then, in a lower voice I whispered, "I just came from Devin's office."

"Oh. Him again. I don't know about this dude. You sure are acting funny lately. What's going on, anyway? Has something happened since I talked to you on Saturday?"

"You wouldn't believe it. Remember I told you I was concentrating on Devin to get him to call?"

"I remember. You got *me* to call. Did you ever get *him?*"

"Something did." I looked around. Both girls were posting, and Lola was still out. No one could hear with the machines going anyway, so I briefed her on the attacks and our call to Myrna, and of the conditions she had put on her reading of the ring.

"See?" Pam's triumphant smugness came through over the wire. "I told you that thing was evil. I'm starting to wonder about the idiot that gave it to you too."

"Good grief, Pam. We haven't had its…evility…evaluated yet. We're still waiting for an answer."

Pam snickered. "Evility is not a word," she corrected me.

"It is not a fact yet, either. Let's see what Myrna says, and as far as Devin goes, wait until you meet him. Then we'll see what you say."

"I might just do that. When's the next time he's coming up?"

"I hope tonight. I'm going to ask, anyway."

"Maybe George and I will stop up. Oh, by the way, Bonnie said she'd watch the kids when you go to that wedding with Devin. And my friend Lorry said she'll do it if Bonnie bombs out at the last minute."

"Why would Bonnie do that?" Bonnie was not only Pammy's very best friend since high school, but she had become, just recently, our cousin Jake's new wife.

"Well, she's pregnant, and you know how that goes."

"I forgot about that. How far along is she anyway?"

"About seven months, I guess. Give or take. She never did go to a doctor, and Jake still hasn't told his parents yet. Aunt Myrtle and Uncle Ab don't even know that they finally got married."

"What's he waiting for?"

"He's afraid to tell them. They never liked Bonnie anyway, and when they find out their son, raised sooo Catholic, had engaged in you-know-what before—"

"Okay, spare me." I laughed.

"Well, one of them will babysit if you need it. What *did* you end up doing with the ring, anyway?"

"I put it in the desk drawer."

"Devin went along with that?"

"Well, he's just as bewildered as I am about all this. And he wasn't happy about the attacks."

"I bet it *was* you." Pammy sniffed. "Maybe we *will* be up tonight."

"You'll be surprised when you do meet him."

"Does he have horns?"

"Goodbye, Pam." We were both laughing when I replaced the receiver.

Inviting Devin up really wasn't as awkward as I thought it would be.

"I've been thinking along those lines myself," he confessed, when I asked him after work.

Finding him hadn't been difficult either. I had only to follow the chest ache that seemed to increase as I neared him which, today, was toward the time-clock area. Hannah, who had been cool and quiet all afternoon, punched out without a word to Kelly or me. Kelly had two kids to pick up from a babysitter's, so she couldn't hang around either. As usual, the time-clock area was packed with drivers unloading their trucks and scurrying to the route room to do their paperwork.

Devin and Pat would be the last to leave, closing up only after the last driver had gone, so I wasn't surprised to find them both standing in the area, bullshitting with the men who went in and out. Joey Burns was another of the hang-ins, despite Jason's rule about loitering, and he was almost as fast on his route as Devin was on any of them. As I approached, I caught the tail end of the chewing out he was giving both supervisors.

"What's this I heard about lunch today? With the *girls* no less! Man, some pals you turned out to be. I mean, I appreciate the invite, but I just *couldn't* make it! Hell, I like to live a little dangerous too!"

Pat patted him sympathetically on the shoulder. "You need the job, Joey. Besides, supervisors are expected to get a few extra privileges than the ordinary driver."

"Route salesman," Joey corrected, dutifully and sarcastically.

"I forgot," Pat said humbly. "Forgive me."

"Drivers wear comfortable work boots," Joey added looking down at his shiny patent-leather boots. "There is a difference, you know."

"Yeah," Devin put in. "The difference is if you're a driver, you won't be here long. Jason only hires route salesmen."

"Of the highest breeding," Joey adding, waving to someone entering the exit beyond Devin and Pat's vision. "Hey, Ethan! Wha-da-ya-say? Thought you weren't here today!"

Ethan hadn't been with the company long, and no one was too sure about him. Devin was still considering my invitation when he realized who Joey was addressing. He leapt to the ground from the ladder rung where he had been perched.

"Hey, Jack!" The sudden change in his tone made us all turn around with a start. "Jist what're *you* doin' here, man...lak yer *car* won' start...remember? 'Er doesn' it *run* till after fahve o'clock?"

There was a heavy black accent intertwined with the words that thrust from Devin like punching jabs. I watched in shock as Devin swaggered over in a rhythmic stroll, eyes mere slits in his face.

Pat did a double take, stepped in front of me so that I was in a corner, and threw his arm across me as if suddenly braking in a car. "Ethan called in with another excuse today," he told me under his breath, but his eyes never left Devin. He looked as stunned as I felt, but he kept his arm protectively across me and did not interfere as Devin continued.

"Well?" Devin hissed between clenched teeth. "Ain't that what you told Tim?"

Pat finally found his voice. "Hey...uh...Devin," he began.

"No, Pat! He ain't lately gettin' 'way with it *this* tahm. No fuckin' way!" He circled Ethan who had frozen in his tracks. "Ya didn' even *bother* t' *call in* till nahn o'clock this mornin'! Just what kinda *jive* you tryin' t' hand us here?"

"That's right...uh...I did call in." Ethan tried to smile, but his eyes reflected the confusion we all felt as we watched. Aside from the strange black mannerisms, Devin had never displayed such temper or lack of cool on company grounds. He was well known as the most easygoing supervisor in the plant.

"An' whap that *smirk* off yer face 'for Ah do it fer ya!"

Pat's eyes really widened now, but he did not attempt to interfere again. I almost felt sorry for Ethan, but there was no stopping Devin now. He must have been saving this all day for the moment when he could confront the huge panda-looking routeman who now stood rigid in Devin's slow orbit, his eyes darting left and right behind those horn-rimmed glasses. There was a kind of crafty intelligence in those eyes, but it was hard to distinguish it from the fear they displayed now. Pat took a step forward, prepared to intercede if it turned out that he needed to, but he didn't say another word to Devin.

"Nahn o'clock yer car wuz broke down, raht, Jack? Ain't that raht?"

"That's right, Devin...I uh...didn't even know till I went to start it up this morning. It wouldn't even turn over."

"At nahn o'clock..." Devin crossed his arms. "Ah guess ya worked on it all day."

"Well, how else do you think I got it running?"

"Hey, cut the lip, Jack!" Devin grabbed him by the collar and thrust him against the ladder, just inches from Pat and me. He leaned over him, nostrils flaring. "Spose you tell me why, at nahn o'clock when Ah wuz at yer place, *you* weren' *there*, Ethan, and neither wuz yer *fuckin' car*. Did it *rain*, Jack? Possibly, ya were in yer 'partment workin' on it!"

Ethan looked down, apparently not trusting his voice, his back still pinned against the ladder. I moved back even closer to the wall. Pat remained in front of me, his arm still protectively between the ladder and me.

"Now you lissen to me, honk. You ain't lately gwin git away wit' this another tahm. Not while A'hm here. There ain't gonna be no secon' tahm, you *got that*, Jack?"

Ethan nodded.

"Then, hit it, man…an' if ya git up at nahn t'morrow, stay home. There's a lot of guys that kin use that route you lucked out on!"

The second Ethan was out of sight, Devin hopped back up on the ladder as though nothing unusual had happened. He was not breathing hard, nor did he look the slightest bit ruffled. In fact, he was perfectly composed.

"Jesus Christ, Devin!" Pat lowered his arm and scratched his head in genuine puzzlement. "What the hell—"

"Git 'em, Dev!" Joey began punching the air, darting around like a boxer, and the atmosphere of shock was broken. "Git 'em Dev!"

"Over at Ethan's at nine o'clock," Pat said. "Really, Devin. You were with *me* at nine o'clock!"

"He doesn't know that, Pat." Devin shrugged, his voice loose and casual again. "And anyhow, he didn't deny not being there, so I was right, in any case. I'm telling you, Pat, that dude is a smooth one. Like, the man has been here a month, and he's called in at least once a week with some excuse. And today? His car won't start?" Devin lit a cigarette and laughed easily. "When that mother don't show up, Devin's the one who gets stuck on the route, and *Devin* has better things to do." There was no emotion or bitterness in his words. The discussion had resumed its friendly atmosphere.

"Hey, how's he getting away with it?" Joey asked. "I could use a day off once in a while."

"That's what we're trying to figure out," Devin said, shaking his head. "He's the one who okays the excuses!" He jerked his thumb toward Tim's office. "And they're fantastic excuses, too. You have to give the guy credit. He's got one hell of an imagination."

"I think he gets them from the eleven o'clock news," Pat said.

"You know he's lying," Devin went on, but you can either let it slide or call his bluff. And, as you all saw, that's not difficult either. Tim may be the sucker, but I ain't no patsy." He jumped down from the ladder. "Anyhow, if I'm going to make it to your place, Kerry, I'd better get moving. Come on, I'll walk you to your car."

"Pretty rough on Ethan, weren't you?" I commented as we left the exit.

"Hey, it's my job, you know? What I get paid all this money for. I'll be up as soon as I can. I'm not sure what time, but I will be there."

We had reached my car. "Are you sure you should?"

"Wild horses couldn't keep me away…" His voice died off as he seemed to realize the seriousness of my question, and his features softened. "Hey, I've spent my whole life looking for you. Now that I've found you, do you really think I could go home and sleep?"

"I was just feeling guilty because you haven't *had* any sleep." In actuality, that scene I had just witnessed in the time-clock area had me a little unnerved. Maybe too many sleepless nights were catching up with him.

"Hey, you let *me* worry about when I need sleep. I'll see you tonight." He winked and slapped the top of my car and then took off jogging back toward the plant.

I had just opened the front door when Scotty's usual call came in. When I told him I couldn't hold the phone, and especially why, he sounded a little insulted, but nothing compared to when I hit him with *the bomb*.

"What do you mean *married?* You just *met* the guy!"

"Well, technically, yes, but—"

"You're crazier than I thought you were," he interrupted rudely. "Don't expect me to be around to pick up the pieces." The phone went dead in my hand.

I tried to push my conscience pangs aside. I'd never led Scotty on, and our friendship had always been purely platonic. Now someone was banging on the door, and the phone was ringing again.

"Hello? Oh, Pam?" I answered the door at the same time. "Hold on, Pam, hi Lana…Coleen…come on in, I'll be right with you."

Pam was just double-checking on the Halloween babysitting situation so one of the girls could plan to hand the candy out that night.

"It won't be on trick-or-treat night, Pam. Wiccans start on Halloween Eve. The night before."

Lana began waving wildly to get my attention. "Us! Us!" she mouthed silently, pointing fingers at herself and Colleen.

"Oh, Lana? You want to do it? Pam, never mind. Lola's daughter is here, and she says she wants to." Both teenagers nodded enthusiastically. Pam also added that she wouldn't be making it up tonight, but that she could definitely come tomorrow. George, she said, was dying to meet the guy that had caused such a stir in the past week.

When I finally hung up the phone, I dropped into the beanbag. "This day has been unbelievable. Look at me, I'm a nervous wreck."

"I noticed that," Lana agreed. She was a miniature of her mother, except her curly golden hair hung down her back, whereas Lola's was medium length.

"How'd you know about the wedding?"

"Oh, *that!*" Both girls broke into a giggling fit, and Lana answered for both. "It's *all* my mom and dad talk about. That wedding…that ring…speaking of which, we came to see the ring."

I considered my promise to Myrna, then chucked it and brought out the ring. I felt a remorseful pang at seeing it again. It didn't look angry or homesick now. It looked downright indignant.

"Ooh, how ugly," Lana breathed. "Is *this* what they've been babbling about?"

"Your dad hasn't even seen it," I reminded her. "I'd bet he'd like it."

"Well, he sure wants to go to that wedding," Colleen said. "I've been there every night for dinner this week. That's all they talk about. Devin-Devin-Devin…" She burst into giggling again. "Ring, ring, ring."

"Wedding, wedding, wedding," Lana added, giggling too.

I could hardly believe my ears. "Lana, your mom told me I couldn't even wear it at your house."

"Oh, she just does that, she says, to maintain control. But really, that *is* all they talk about. You're a hot subject all of a sudden. They really do want to go to the ceremony, but don't worry. They won't ask. Just what kind of wedding is it, anyway?"

"Beats me! I've never been to one."

"Then aren't you scared?" Colleen's eyes widened. "I would be, especially after seeing *The Exorcist* three times." She raised her arms in the classic position of Regan floating over the bed, her eyes rolling back in her head.

Lana slapped her arms playfully. "Oh, it's not *that* kind of thing."

"Are you sure you'll be allowed, Lana? I'll be gone all night."

"Oh, I asked my mom already. She *wants* me to babysit. Probably wants to hear the details when I get home."

"Well, great! It's settled then. Why don't you stick around? You can meet him."

"We can't." Colleen sounded disappointed. "We just took the car. We have to get it back. Too bad. I bet he's scary-looking."

"My mom says he's cute!" Lana corrected. "I want to meet him just to find out who pushed Kerry's button."

"Did you pick that up at home, too?" I asked, smiling.

"My dad said that. But that's because you're always sitting in the house. You never go out."

I was glad to get a little breather before the van finally pulled up to the house. I was out the door and waiting by the grass strip before he even cut the engine off. The chest ache had started up again, as if my heart was bursting at the seams. I looked up at his tired face. His own eyes were intently fixed on mine.

"Hello, lady." He swung the door open and reached for my hand.

"Devin…" As though I had always held him, the sudden need to be close to him shot the message to my brain. As though we'd done it thousands of times. Like memory responding. As natural as breathing, I was in his arms, my face pressed against his pounding heart. There was no strangeness to him now, no newness to the feel of his arms around me. As if I had held him centuries ago and somehow lost or forgotten him. "Devin, I love you so much."

He patted my shoulder, and I could hear his voice in my ear, which was pressed against his chest. "That's good. It'll help.".

Help what? I was too happy to ask. I reluctantly let him loosen his grip and hop down to the ground. "I'm sorry I'm late again," he said.

"Don't be sorry!" I countered, teasing him.

"Well, selfishly, I meant. I would have liked to have been here sooner." He followed me into the house.

Although I hated to leave his side even for a few minutes, I offered him dinner and coffee. It was cold and late, and I didn't know if he had eaten.

"Coffee sounds great, but as far as dinner goes, I was just stuffed about an hour ago. Daniel's wife makes these huge meals, and every time I get within three feet of her, she thinks she has to feed me. I must look undernourished or something. I only stopped for a few joints. I've been helping him fix his car, and they act like I'm doing them the greatest favor in the world."

I put the coffee together as he talked. "Who is Daniel?"

"You don't know Daniel? He sure knows who you are." Devin thought a minute "The other day. Before the ring. You were in my office talking to Pat and me. That big muscular guy with red hair came in. Mustache…comes down to meet a goatee like mine did? He'd be a hard one to miss."

"Wow! That was only last week?" I remembered, all right. "I thought he looked like the Devil. Lucifer himself."

"He's new at the place." Devin stirred the coffee I'd handed him. "Really far-out dude. I never thought about it, but now that you mention it, he does kind of look like the chap. Don't judge him by that, though. He's one of the nicest guys working there."

"All he needs is horns," I mused.

"You don't like old Lucifer, I take it?"

"Well, I can't say as I've ever met him," I replied. "Have you?"

"Well, I *have* met Lucifer, since you asked, and you will too." I froze, and he chuckled. "Lucifer is the name of Daniel's dog. Big malamute. Very friendly. You'll like him, I'm sure." His eyes twinkled. "Had you there for a minute, didn't I?"

I laughed too. "Well, I'm still not sure what kind of a witch you are."

"We have plenty of time for you to find out. As for Daniel, I'm sure you'll like his wife, Julie, too. They have two kids like Trevor and us. I think Daniel will be a brother too."

"Will be? Isn't Trevor your real brother?"

"Well, he is, but he isn't. He's more of a brother than my real brother is. That is, we're closer."

"How many in your actual family?"

"Mother and father, but divorced. My father, Gerald, lives with another chick up north, and then there's Brian, my real brother. He's a few years younger, and he lives with Gerald and Faye." He leaned back in the red armchair and sipped his coffee. "Sure feels good to relax."

I sat in the beanbag watching him, wishing the ache in my heart would stop throbbing. His eyes were closed, but he balanced his coffee on the wide winged arms of the chair, a cigarette between his fingers. "You asleep?"

"Sleep?" He opened one eye. "What's that? I haven't slept in days. Probably won't until I get over this hump coming up."

"The home situation?"

"Yeah, well it's a lot to organize. However, let's not get into that now. I came up here to see you." He downed the coffee and held up the cup. "Got any more? Man, I never drank coffee like I've been doing lately, but then, I used to sleep at night."

I made two more cups and remembered Lana's visit on my way back in. "I almost forgot. Lola's daughter was here tonight." I briefed him on the visit and told him what Lana had disclosed about her family's interest in the upcoming wedding. He was surprised that Lola could have a teenage daughter and an eleven-year-old son. She looked much too young. He was even more surprised at the interest Lola was apparently taking in our budding relationship.

"You're probably really blowing their minds." Devin smiled. "How long have you known the family?"

"I met them at a party at my Uncle Joe's about five years ago. Only been working for Lola about a year, though."

He sighed. "That *is* a long time. She'll probably notice any drastic changes in you now that you're with me. Kerry, I sure hope you can roll with all this. It's only the beginning. The talk at the place is hot and heavy, and in their eyes I'm a married man. Very few people know that's being changed soon. And if either one of us tries to tell them otherwise…not that it's any of their business—"

"I know. Who would believe it? You can't blame them, Devin. I can hardly believe it myself."

"I can." He finished his coffee and leaned forward, continuing. "What I mean is there are going to be a lot of strange things going down. Many curious people…like Mama. We won't be sneaking around like they expect us to, and I can't guarantee you'll hear as much about yourself as I will, and vice-versa." He laughed wryly and went on. "And the talk about us will be rather amusing compared to what is to come."

That comment went right over my head. "I know. Did you see the faces on all those people in the lobby today? Freaking out!"

"I'm hep. No one has approached me directly, but they're doing it in other ways." He ran a hand through his curls. "Like this. Tim's really hassling me about cutting it. We're losing a good driver a week over Jason's rules and getting idiots like Ethan."

I shuddered at the memory of that scene this afternoon. I could never have imagined Devin so mean and harsh. Such burning, slitted eyes and flared nostrils. That black accent. Not from the peace-and-love hippie I thought I knew. Before I could comment, he pointed to the hallway.

"Someone's up," he said. "Think it's about time I finally meet my kids. Our kids now, right?"

I turned as the bathroom light flashed on and saw Michelle sleepily rubbing her eyes, staring at Devin.

"Mommy, can I get a drink?" Her eyes never left Devin. I nodded.

I heard the sound of running water, and then the bedroom door creaked. I smiled at Devin. "Here comes the other one."

Mandy was groggy, but more awake than Michelle was. "Mom, did Devin ever get here yet—?" She stopped at the edge of the living room and stared the way Michelle had. "Hi."

"Hi," Devin echoed.

Her face broke into a shy smile. Michelle came up behind her, a little more awake and obviously curious as hell.

"Mandy and Michelle," I told Devin, pointing to them respectively.

Michelle marched up to Devin boldly. "Are you Devin?"

"Yes, I'm Devin." He smiled warmly at her, and she grinned back.

"I'm Kerry's daughter, and that's my sister, Mandy."

"Are you the one who gave Mother the ring?" Mandy asked.

Devin and I exploded with laughter. It seemed no one could mention Devin without referring to that damn ring.

"I'm the culprit," he admitted, shaking his head with a smile.

"Mandy, you guys better get back to bed. School tomorrow."

She yawned. "How come you didn't wake us up?"

"He didn't get here till late. Now scoot."

"Are you going to come back?" Michelle asked.

"Until you're sick of me," he promised, smiling at her boldness.

They both planted a quick kiss on me, and then to my surprise, walked over to Devin. Michelle, especially, was staring at him in the most captivated way. She climbed up on Devin's lap and kissed him smack on the forehead. "Goodnight, Devin. I'm glad Mom finally met you."

Devin looked at me and raised his eyebrows. Mandy, not as dramatic, kissed his cheek and murmured, "Thanks for giving Mother the ring. Goodnight, Devin." Then they both galloped back to their room.

Devin looked thoughtful. "They don't seem surprised to see me. I presume you told them I was coming, but still, you would think they were in on all this. Especially Michelle."

"I know. Did you catch that *finally*?"

"Yes, but it doesn't really surprise me. Your kids seem to know me like you do. As different entities other than as their current roles. Right now they're your kids."

"You mean, wherever I'm supposed to recognize you from, they know you too?"

"Perhaps, but I'm not talking about another reincarnation on this planet, like you are. This isn't the only world in the cosmos."

"Oh, another planet, you mean? I guess that's possible. Who knows how many other worlds are inhabited?"

"I didn't mean that either," Devin said quietly. "Anyhow, it's not important at the moment. What grade is Mandy in?"

I knew he was deliberately changing the subject, but I let it pass. "She's in first grade, but already they want to jump her to second. I know that isn't always the best thing socially, so I said no. Michelle's just gone into kindergarten."

"I don't doubt they're intelligent. Do they take after you?"

"Oddly enough, they don't seem to take after anybody."

"Yeah, the kids being born today...well, whatever. You've done a good job with them."

"Thanks, but if they were boys, they might have turned out differently. Imagine me trying to raise two boys alone."

"You're not alone anymore," he reminded me, "so we could have a boy now."

"Well, I've had a little practice with one boy. Lola's son, Mark. He's at that age where cars and vans are all he thinks about. He saw your van parked down at the plant one Saturday when Lola took him to work, and that's all he talks about now."

Devin smiled. "Yeah, sometimes we never outgrow it." He glanced over at the desk, and I suddenly remembered the ring. "You know, I'd like to get the ring back out again," I said wistfully. "It seems so stupid hiding it away."

"Are you still afraid of it?"

"No. I feel sorry for it. It looks insulted."

"Oh, you checked on it, did you?"

"Just to show Lana and Colleen."

"I'd like to see you wearing it again myself." Without waiting for a response, he walked over to the desk. He studied the drawers, then opened the correct one and reached into the rear without any hesitation. It appeared, cotton and all.

"Hey, how'd you do that?"

"Do what?"

"How'd you know where it was? You weren't even in the room when I put it there."

He didn't answer, just unwrapped it and held it up. "Give me your hand."

I held up my left.

"Which finger?"

I couldn't resist. I formed my hand into a bird with the middle finger sticking up, and he laughed. "That's gratitude for you. You sure you want to do this now? We can still wait for Myrna, you know."

"Oh, Devin." He slid the ring on, and I felt instantly better. "It's finally starting to like me. I'll take my chances."

"Far out. I was hoping you would."

"But what if...it...happens again?"

"It won't. I really didn't think it was the ring. Not after what you told me. It might have been you...or something else. *What* else, I'm still working on. I will find out. Meanwhile, if you want to talk to me, call me yourself. Don't need whatever that was to deliver the message." He laughed, showing his real lack of concern.

I went back to my bedroom and brought out a pillow. "Here. You can't afford to stay awake all night again. You're getting on that couch, and *I* am going to rub your back."

With a grateful look, he transferred his body to the couch, and I started to massage his tense muscles. He looked so tired. I could relate, having been up most of the past few days myself.

"That feels so good. Would you consider doing this for a living?"

"Depends on who the boss is."

"Hey!" He raised his head suddenly. "I just realized what's missing in this house! You don't have a refrigerator."

"Sure do." I pointed to the den, extended from the kitchen, paneled like the living room, and one step down just like at the office. "Back there. In the corner behind the archway."

"And you keep that *six-foot desk* in the kitchen? Shit, you know, that's not even a whole kitchen. And with that monster in it you barely have an aisle to walk through."

"Oh, you sound like Lola. She's been trying to get me to switch them for months."

"Well, why haven't you? The fridge would take up less space, and that's a big den. It would easily handle the desk."

"Well, I use the desk to eat dinner. There is no table, if you haven't noticed. The kids eat at their own little table and chairs in the den, but I'm a bit big for them."

"Hey, it's okay." He shrugged as I continued squeezing his tight muscles. "There are probably lots of people that keep their desk in the kitchen. And yours does fit in there so compactly."

I gave him a gentle punch. "You are being sarcastic, and if Lola couldn't civilize me, you won't be able to either."

He laughed. "Well, they did warn me that you were strange."

"They said the same thing about you. See…that backrub was just what you needed. You're finally starting to loosen up."

"Yup." He rolled over on his back and reached for me. "Just what I needed."

"And you'd probably be a lot more comfortable if you stretched out on the bed," I added. He pulled me down on his chest and hugged me tightly.

"You still going to rub my back if we move in there?" He smiled, and I nodded.

Backrub my ass.

It was somewhere around three when I started awake. It was dim in the bedroom, but I could see Devin lying there awake, pillow propped up against the wall. He rubbed my shoulder, his arm still around me.

"How come you're still up?" I moved closer to him.

"Oh, I slept a little."

"Are you going to stay the night?"

"Shh, lady, yes. Of course. Go back to sleep. You have to work tomorrow too."

"Can you sleep here every night?"

I could feel his smile in the dark. "After that, I may never go back to my apartment again."

I lay back, face against his bare chest. The warmth and rhythm of his body and heart were my last conscious memory.

The next time I opened my eyes, Devin was sitting on the edge of the bed, dressed for work. One look at the clock told me he was late. I bolted upright. "Devin…I'm sorry! The alarm! I didn't set it!"

"Shh, it's okay," he whispered, kissing me gently. It's way too early for you to get up. I was just going to say goodbye before I left."

I swung my legs over the side of the bed and got up to pull a long T-shirt from the closet. I felt achy from head to foot. "Ow…what's the matter with me? I feel like I've been run over by a truck." I put the shirt on slowly.

"Not used to so much exercise?" he offered, smiling. "Why don't you stay home? I can get the kids to the sitter's and tell Lola you're not feeling good today."

I shook my head. "No, she'd blame it on…us. Besides, I want to go in. You'll be there. Devin, how late are you?"

"Don't worry. Pat's there. I've already called him. Everything's cool."

I walked him to the door, and he took me in his arms. "You stay home. I hate to leave…I really do." He kissed me and then gently eased away from me. "Careful. Watch that stuff, or I'll never get out of here."

The kidding suddenly stopped, and he looked deep into my eyes for what seemed like forever. "I love you, Kerry."

I hugged him again. "I love you too."

He touched a finger to my nose and smiled. "That's good," he said. "It'll help."

He left me pondering that remark, but I was too happy to give it too much thought. I should have.

It was the third time he'd said it to me.

9 After dropping the kids off, I went directly to work and straight to my office. *Easy Living*, a current Uriah Heep hit, was playing on Lola's radio when I walked in.

"Hi, Mama. No muffin today."

"Oh, that's okay. How are you feeling?"

Somehow, I knew the small talk was leading to something else. "Okay. A little tired, maybe. How'd you know?"

"Devin popped in this morning. He thought you might at least be a little late, but I see he was wrong."

The song was talking about someone having walked behind me, day after day, and now it was easy living. I decided not to point out to Lola that she was playing that acid-rock station. "Oh, Mama," I said instead. "You know I wouldn't let a few aches and pains let me miss even one minute of this glorious place."

"Well, not now that you and Devin have this little…thing…going. But you got fooled. Tim sent him out on specials. But. He did ask about lunch again today."

I waited without comment and she continued briskly. "I said it was okay with me as long as you girls are back here on time. You *are* aware of the talk going around now, I presume?"

"Yes, Mama." I laughed, in spite of her worried look. "We know."

"Oh, Devin does too?"

"Yes. He says he doesn't care."

"He'll care when his wife shows up here with a forty-five."

"She's not going to do that. Mama, we're getting married."

"That," Lola said casually, "is illegal. Devin is already married."

"*Now* he is," I replied, and she really gave me a wild look.

"Oh? He's divorcing his wife after all these years so you and he can…" Her tone of voice plainly indicated that she wouldn't swallow that one so easily if she were me.

"Not because of me, Lo. She's leaving anyway. In February. Devin's the one who's pushing it up to the holidays, and apparently she's all for it. I'm not in that big of a hurry."

"Christmas?"

"That's what he said."

"Well, I hope you two know what you're doing."

"Please don't tell anyone. I don't think he wants that all over the plant just yet."

"Well, it would certainly help to make the situation look better. He's not exactly trying to hide anything from what I can see. He was flying around here this morning like he was on cloud nine, jumping around as if the world changed overnight. Just how long has it been since he gave you that ring anyway? It hasn't even been a week. Don't you think you're rushing things a little?"

"Kerry's wearing her ring again," Kelly called in.

Damn Kelly. Why would she even notice? "Kelly, you never mind what I'm wearing," I called back.

"Bet you weren't wearing anything last night!" she responded, and then poked her head in Lola's doorway. "Little tired, are we?"

"All right, you guys...please. Not so early in the morning. Well anyway, since you two aren't making any effort to hide it, I guess I can stop covering for you, huh?"

"Mama, I'm so happy, I don't want to hide it."

Hannah walked in at that moment, brushing past me as though I'd suddenly contacted the most contagious venereal disease. "Good morning, Mama." She went straight to her station, not waiting for a reply, and began to post. Kelly, Lola, and I exchanged shrugs.

"What's with her?" Lola asked.

"Beats me," Kelly retorted. "She hasn't spoken a friendly word to us since lunch yesterday. I figure she's mad about Kerry and Devin, but I didn't do anything to her."

"You're an accomplice, I guess," Lola said. "Well, it's none of her business. She'd better get off that high horse or—"

"Let her be, Lola," I said. "You know how moral she is."

"That's beside the point."

"Well, she better not pull that shit with me," Kelly said hotly. "Not only is it none of her business, but Benny knows about our lunch yesterday, besides."

"Well, anyway," Lola said with a sigh, "If you do go to lunch today, no more than forty-five minutes, okay?"

"Okay, Mama. We watch it. Especially now."

Kelly followed me into our office, not even trying to shield Hannah from the immoral facts. "So! Lunch again, huh?"

"Yes, and we pay our own way. Got it?" We took our places at the machines.

Pat came in around eleven-thirty looking for Devin. It was so close to lunchtime that I had stopped posting and started dividing the tickets so that Kelly and I could put them in alphabetical order. Kelly grabbed her half gratefully. We were both tired of the machine noise.

"Why don't you ask Kerry," Lola advised Pat. "She usually knows where he is. And since you're all running around loose today, I was wondering if you could stop in at the print shop and pick up our statements."

"We're going out again today?" Pat looked baffled. "I really thought that would have been stopped by now."

"Well, it's Devin's harem, and he's agreed to take the responsibility. The printer's is over by the Walgreens. Why don't you just eat there?"

"Boy, that figures. Nobody tells me nothin' these days."

"Well, you're going, aren't you?"

"Long as you don't care. You're our bodyguard, you know."

"I'll get the statements for you, Lola," Kelly hollered in. "I've been there before."

"Why don't you go find Devin and get an early start? Or, you girls go ahead and the guys can meet you over there. That place gets kind of crowded at twelve. It's already fifteen to."

"Oh, no crowds, Mama, please!" Kelly wailed. "They are *so* embarrassing."

"That's your tough luck, kiddo. Get going. I'm letting you leave in plenty of time so my errand won't infringe on your…uh…social activities."

"Let's go, Kelly."

"You are going to wreck my marriage," Kelly grumbled, but she followed me out through the lobby and we headed for her car, the closer one.

"Are you eating?" Kelly demanded, once we'd found a table for four. " 'Cause I have money, if that's the problem."

"I never eat lunch, Kelly, you know that."

"Look, Kerry. You have to eat if you intend to keep all these late hours with Devin. You look like hell! You have black circles under your eyes, and you must have lost ten pounds this week. Go look in the mirror. You're supposed to look like you're in love, not going through a divorce."

"In love? With Devin?" I covered my mouth with exaggerated awe. "Is *that* what's going around?"

"Kerry, I'm not kidding you. You should hear the plant. Take Hannah, just for an example in our own department. You look like shit. Oh, there's a waitress. Grab her!"

We gave the waitress our order, sandwich for Kelly and coffee for me. By the time it arrived, we began to wonder where the guys were. "Maybe they're sitting at that corner waiting to get across that line of traffic?" Kelly offered.

"Sitting at what corner?"

I recognized that voice, chest ache assisting. Sure enough, Pat and Devin were approaching the table.

"What took you so long?" Kelly demanded. "It's twenty-five after already. I don't know what time we're being clocked from, but Lola let us leave early, remember?"

"Don't yell at me," Devin protested, palms up and forward innocently. "Pat had to do Tim a favor. I'm just the driver."

"Let's speed things up," Pat urged. "I'm starving."

"I'll get the waitress," I said, getting up. The last thing I wanted to do was take advantage of Lola.

"No, I'll get her." Pat motioned for me to sit down. "If push comes to shove, you girls take off. No sense in getting in trouble because of us."

"You," Devin corrected. "Don't worry, Kerry. I'll explain to Mama. Get me a burger, Pat." He turned back to us. "Anyone got a Sydney?"

"I do." I was using today's horoscope for a bookmark.

"That figures," Kelly remarked dryly. "I don't suppose you have any Scotch

Tape in there too."

"Actually, I do." I handed it to her and she accepted it with a sigh. "Figures. It figures."

"Hey, Ker," Pat said, looking into the murky blackness of my purse. "How about a spare tire. Devin's feels a little wobbly. What do you need Scotch Tape for, Kelly?"

"I have to tape up this letter to Benny."

"You still write notes to Benny?"

"Only when we're not speaking, like now. This way, he can't interrupt." She taped up the homemade envelope and returned the tape to my purse.

"How's it going in accounts receivable?" Pat asked, and then added, "Oh, here comes our lunch, Dev."

"It's boring. We're doing cooler rent. Every damn account. I hate it!" Kelly answered for both of us.

The waitress set Devin's hamburger in front of him and turned to go.

"Hey! What about me?" Pat called after her.

"Oh, did you order something too?"

Devin buried his face in his hands. "Wonder how long the line is at unemployment this time of year. Make it a cold sandwich, Pat."

By the time it arrived, everyone else was finished and lighting up the after-lunch smoke. Devin was studying the horoscope. After some scrutiny, he tossed it on the table in mock disgust. "Now, you tell me how Sydney can know all that! Talk about company rumors. They made it all the way to the syndicated press."

"They're guaranteed." Pat stuffed the last of his sandwich down. "Does your wife get the paper, Devin?"

"Not any more. That dude gets fucking personal, you know. Speaking of rumors, Kel, how are Kerry and I doing at the plant? You loaf with those phone-room gossips, don't you?"

"Don't you *dare* link me with them," Kelly retorted, glancing around quickly. "But here's how it stands. Hannah isn't speaking to either one of us. Lola is amused, but confused. Tim's watching you like a hawk and Mussolini has hash marks on his desk for each trip you make into our department. The phone room is behind the times. They're still gawking about the Halloween wedding, and the latest rumor on you, Devin, is that you used to run a church in Salem before you turned evil. Also, they notice you call in more A to Fs than any other letter."

"Whew! All that in a few short days?"

"I'm not finished yet. As far as the drivers go..."

"Please, Kelly," Pat broke in. "As authority back there, allow me."

We all looked at Pat and he cleared his throat importantly. "Okay, most of them, especially the older ones, are outwardly ignoring it, but behind the scenes they're discussing how Devin could have lucked out with that piece of ass...sorry, Kerry."

I smiled. "And the others?"

"Well, me, Joey, Daniel...even Ethan," he added, glancing at Devin, "We all like you both, so you can exclude us."

"*Oh my God!*" Kelly's expression turned horrified. "It's fifteen to *one* ! The *printers!"*

We all looked at each other. We had forgotten all about the statements. "That's it," I said with a sigh. "We're dead."

"We'll get the check paid. You girls go get the statements."

Everyone bolted and Kelly and I took off. The print shop was directly over the Walgreens, so I waited outside while Kelly raced in. Devin and Pat were on their way up the stairs when Kelly came tearing out of the shop and down the steps. "Let's go! There was a line. With luck, we won't hit any lights."

All four of us took off running toward the cars.

"Hey…slow down." I grabbed Kelly by the elbow. "Running in this heat isn't going to make that much difference."

Everyone slowed to a fast walk. Pat went straight to Devin's van, which was parked directly behind Kelly's car. He stood waiting for Devin to come and unlock it.

Devin, who had been silent through the rush to the printers and to the cars, followed me to Kelly's car and stood quietly beside it. I jumped in the car, slammed the door, and rolled down the window as Kelly sat impatiently racing the engine. Still, Devin did not move out of the way. Instead, he leaned into the car slightly and searched my face for a full minute. I looked at him in alarm. He seemed to be in some kind of a trance. The chest ache hit a full-blown peaking throb, and it was then, of all the most inconvenient times, that he hit me with the question.

"Do you wish to have my child?"

Kelly, who had been anxiously waiting for him to step away, froze in her seat. The engine, no longer racing, fell to idle, suddenly silent in the afternoon heat. Devin repeated the question, making no effort to conceal his words or the volume. He spoke as if there were no one there but the two of us. A chill went through me as he echoed the question. Kelly looked nervously at her watch, and back at Pat.

"Should I assume your silence means no?" He was obviously waiting for my answer…here…now. I swallowed uneasily.

"You mean …now…Devin? I mean, what brought this…I don't…"

"Do you wish to be the mother of my son?"

Kelly sat there gripping the steering wheel, her knuckles white. I glanced at her apologetically, but she refused to look at me. Even Pat stood silent, watching, as though they were both somehow drawn into this absurd conversation as mute, unwilling witnesses.

Neither of us mentioned the time, or how late we were, or the pending trouble because of it. The fooling around, the panic, the rushing…everything had abruptly ceased. Like a scene from *The Twilight Zone*, the world seemed to have frozen.

I rolled the window back up and opened the door. Pat might as well have been miles away, rather than a few feet. Upon the slam of the car door, *all sound stopped,* and so did all of my fear and concern about the time. An isolated feeling crept over me and an inner serenity began to take hold. I wondered if Devin knew anything about hypnotism.

We faced each other in the blinding sunlight, unspoken questions hanging in the air, both of us unsure of what to do next. Devin blinked for a second, as though he was struggling to maintain his awareness of what was going on. I seized that moment to speak.

"Devin, what made you suddenly ask me that?"

"I...I don't know...I wasn't thinking about anything like that..." His mouth was moving. He was speaking the words, but his eyes—almond-shaped slits—lizard eyes, but amber with a green cast...those eyes bored into mine and they were not the eyes of Devin Drew. The sun seemed to catch his black hair and swirl it into the color of autumn and flames. It was as if there were two faces, one superimposed over the other. The body and uniform were Devin's, but the eyes and the face...belonged to someone or something else.

Please don't make me play these games!

Devin's lips never moved, but it didn't alarm me when I heard the voice speak these words. It seemed only natural because the voice did not belong to Devin either. The tranquility that had swept over me remained within and I felt no fear when I verbally responded to the unspoken thought.

"Who are you? What games do you think you are playing?"

At my sudden reply, Devin seemed to snap out of it. His entire mannerism and expression returned to normal. He looked around. He glanced over at Pat and then at Kelly, as if trying to piece together the last few minutes. That vacant silence began to fill with sounds of traffic and voices and the living world grew louder and louder, as if someone was turning up a volume dial. Devin suddenly raised his hand, shielding his eyes from the brilliant sun, which seemed magnified by the macadamized blacktop of the huge parking lot.

"Kerry—uh—what are we standing here for? Hey, Pat, that door is unlocked...uh...Kerry, listen...I don't know what...look...you get going. You're really late. I shouldn't have...held you up like...I apparently did." He took me by the shoulders. "Kerry, I didn't mean to put you on the spot like that. I...I had no right. I told you I was impulsive."

The world seemed ordinary again. I was back with it and Devin but felt somewhat dazed. "Devin. Did you mean...right now?"

"I meant after you were my wife."

"Devin, the answer's yes. You know the answer's yes. But you hit me so fast—"

"Don't give me an answer now, Kerry. I don't know what...came over me. Go on—get in the car. I've held you up as it is." He kissed me quickly and turned toward the van.

When I pulled the door shut this time, it was as if I had all the time in the world. Kelly hit the gas and peeled out, only to brake suddenly as we reached the corner and the light turned red. "*You* are going to get us *both* killed!" she hissed. The light changed and she screeched out again. "Do you *know* what time it is?"

"No." I was still in too much of a daze to care. We were so outrageously late that nothing could excuse it, but I did not know what time it was, no.

"Well, it's *one-thirty*, Juliette! We left almost *two hours ago!* What is wrong with you anyway? You seem like you're in some kind of a trance!"

I was vaguely aware of flying around corners and speeding through alleys and finally pulling up to another red light.

"Kerry, what's the *matter* with you? Kerry? Did he say what I think he said?"

"What do you think you heard?" I was barely conscious of my reply.

"Something about having a kid. Kerry, *please* don't do anything stupid! It…it didn't sound like he meant…a regular…kid, you know?"

The light changed, but she didn't peel out this time. We both knew we were dead anyway. When I didn't respond she added, "You'd better snap out of it before Lola adds smoking pot to the list of charges today. We still have to walk in there and she's probably going to fire us both on the spot."

"Kel…" I didn't care about Lola. My mind was back in that parking lot and my heart was pounding so hard. That sinking feeling of not knowing…but knowing. "Kel, do you see what I meant about Devin now?"

"He's not fucking around, is he?"

"But don't you see? That isn't the old routeman, Devin, that you knew."

"Kerry, can't you get it through your head, or those rose-colored glasses, that you don't even *know* Devin?"

"Oh, yes I do. I'm finally piecing it all together. I think." I was no longer talking to Kelly and she knew it.

"Okay, Kerry, I give up. I absolutely give up! I've tried to warn you. I don't know what's gotten into him lately. He isn't even the same person anymore, but—"

"But Kelly…" I finally found my voice and looked at her as we glided up to the plant and she switched off the engine. "Was *that* who you saw and heard back there? The Devin you know…or knew? The same Devin that you *know* I couldn't stand at one time?"

She ripped the keys from the ignition and threw the door open. "Come to think of it, Kerry, I have never seen Devin, in all the time I've known him, behave like this. Anyway, who knows what the hell he's messing with. Now let's go!"

We still had to face Lola.

She was not looking very happy when we walked in, and the sound of Hannah's lone machine died at the same time.

"Do you know…*either* of you…what time it is?"

I had to hand it to Lola. She wasn't smiling, but she wasn't fuming either.

For sure, she wasn't kidding. She went on, too calmly, "It's fifteen to…uh…" she picked up her desk clock…"two."

"Can we explain?" Kelly asked humbly.

Lola gave us a daring smile. "You can certainly *try!*"

Kelly shot me a warning look. *Let me do it.* "First of all, we sat for ten minutes trying to get across traffic…you know, that corner?"

"Okay, that's ten minutes."

"And it was twelve-thirty before anyone even took our order. It's crowded at lunchtime. And she forgot Pat's."

"So you're up to a quarter of one. Quarter after by the time you all ate."

"And from there we had to wait at the printers. I *asked* you not to send us where there was a lunch crowd."

"Hold it, kid. What was to wait about? The statements should have been ready."

"There was a long line in there and even then I had to wait at the counter for them to find them."

"Honest to God, Lola, that's how it happened," I added. It was the truth.

Lola sighed. "All right. Go in and start posting. I don't think I can stand to listen to any more of this."

We exhaled with relief. "Thanks, Mama," we began.

"Uh-uh...don't get all mushy. I should have known better than to send the four of you on an errand for me at lunchtime. We'll just count the extra time as working since you were picking up things for the office. Did anyone see you come in?"

"Nobody. Brenda wasn't even at her desk. Go look."

"I can see from here, thank you."

"I'm going to work," I said. Kelly followed me. She waited until the posting had started, and feeling it safe enough, finally turned and grinned at me.

"The next time you and Devin decide to have a hot love affair in the parking lot, will you remember to leave me here?"

Lola walked in, hands on her hips, both filled with statements. "Kerry and Devin did *what?*" She was smiling incredulously, as if she was sure she hadn't heard right.

"Oh," Kelly shrugged. "Just some stuff Devin was saying at the last minute."

"Kelly!"

She checked herself and shut up. Thankfully, Lola didn't pursue it. I wasn't mad at Kelly. I could hardly blame her, but she just didn't realize how serious the subject was that she was joking about. More disturbing than Kelly's comment was the inner battle going on inside me as I tried to post.

I had been happier in the past six days than I had ever been in my entire life. In five of those days, not even counting today, I had seen many sides of Devin. Sides that had always seemed to disappear when most people were around. Act or real, it had always seemed to be under his control. But this afternoon, people *had* been there. *Right* there. It had not stopped the change that had come over him so suddenly. There were just too many secrets surrounding Devin, and all of them appeared to have come along with recent drastic changes in him. Even Kelly, who had known Devin for years, admitted she was unfamiliar with the Devin who had held us up in the lot.

Something was very wrong here, and I knew it. Love does not happen overnight. Marriage proposals do not occur in a few hours of acquaintance. Certainly not before the first kiss. The ring wasn't even in my possession one full week.

That was another thing. The time factors. Was it really only six days ago that I had lain awake listening for the sound of a motorcycle and the subsequent clink of a silver ring in my mailbox? What had happened to my natural sense of time? I stopped posting and actually counted on my fingers. In six days, we had gone from total strangers to this? And of those six days, two of them were the weekend when Devin wasn't even around. It seemed to me that normal life would have required at least a month of daily togetherness to bring us to where we were now. Yet, entire weeks of progress had been made in single evenings. Four days, and even Lola was accepting the situation as though we had been together for months.

Devin had admitted to a deep dark secret from the very first night, but he had not even been able to put on paper just what that was. And now, out of the clear blue sky, he had to *father* a *son*, and he needed an answer *right now?*

Moods were not the explanation. There was more to Devin than just moods, and this afternoon's event had proven that to me. Devin had more sense than to pull something like that in front of Pat and Kelly. Yet, Devin had not really seemed in control at the time. Which one was the real Devin? The one I'd had lunch with, or the one who had walked me to the car?

Just who the hell was Devin anyway?

As I sat there automatically posting, the memory of the interchange remained fixed in my mind. Of those piercing lizard eyes that didn't belong to the original face I had been looking at. Of a strange voice that didn't need lips to speak. And of the baby. The son that I had received flashes of even before a child had ever been mentioned by Devin. There was a clue in that alone. Whatever was happening, it was happening to the two of us.

And I had the strangest feeling that Devin Drew knew what it was.

Something uncanny started happening with the radio that afternoon, and it was far beyond the realm of coincidence. Although Kelly had not elaborated on her statement that Lola had overheard, she might as well have. Having gotten her way with the radio station, she used its lyrics to tease me about that tail end of what had started out as a carefree lunch. When Paul Anka began the afternoon with his current hit, *Having my Baby*, she couldn't contain her mirth any longer.

"What a lovely way of saying that you love me," she sang along loudly, and then burst into a fit of laughter.

I tried to ignore her, but the few times I did laugh only fed her mischievous glee. She seemed to take great delight in the sharing of our 'secret', one that she obviously refused to take seriously. The radio played one baby song after the other. By three-thirty, the song lyrics and her comments were beginning to correlate with something out of the script of *Rosemary's Baby*.

"Hey, uh, shlucko…" She tossed a new account ledger my way. "This is one of Devin's new charges. Remind you of anything?"

I glanced at it and threw it back. "Knock it off, Kel," I began, but she was having another rolling fit on the floor. The name of the account was Gazillion-Dollar Babies.

A loud *ahem* told us Lola was getting fed up with the carrying on. Phone girl Janet had been sent in to help with the phone calls and she spent most of the afternoon going from Kelly to me asking what the joke was. Kelly apologized for her lack of control but said she couldn't help it, what with the radio playing such appropriate songs. To back up her excuse, the disc jockey selected *Watching Scotty Grow* as the oldie of the hour.

"See? See? This is a sign. Is the maternity ward of some hospital calling in these requests?" Kelly squealed, giggling uncontrollably, "Or is *Devin* making the devil do it?" Then, remembering the firing we had barely missed, clamped her hand over her mouth.

"Come on, you guys!" Janet wailed. "Tell me what you're laughing about."

"Oh, something Pat said today," Kelly lied. "Strictly A/R stuff."

"Well, in that case," Lola said, stepping into our office, "suppose you let the boss in on it."

"You have to ask Kerry," Kelly retorted smugly, crossing her arms over her chest. "If I tell you, she'll be mad at me."

Lola turned to me. "Will you be mad at Kelly if she tells me what the hell you two have wasted this entire afternoon over?" she demanded crossly.

I sighed. "She can't work with all the baby records they're playing," I replied disgustedly. "Maybe she's pregnant."

"*Me*, pregnant?" Kelly was out of her seat instantly, mouth open, finger pointed at herself. "Me? Me?"

"Who's pregnant?" Kim had just entered, unaware that she'd just stumbled onto a running joke.

"That's what *we're* trying to figure out," Lola replied, trying not to smile.

"I am," I told Kim with a straight face.

"Well, Lola? There goes another one. How come my girls only quit and yours go out on maternity leave? You ought to have this office sprayed. It might be in the air. Either that or try hiring a lesbian." She chuckled at her own joke.

"Do you mind if I change this station, Kelly?" I interrupted, already turning the dial to my country station.

"Yes, I do! All they play is those same old dragged-out, mournful songs over and over and it depresses me."

"Good," Lola spoke up. "Leave it there, Kerry. Maybe you two will get depressed enough to cut the fooling around and get some work done."

"I beg your pardon," I corrected her. "I have been posting cooler rent all day and I am in the Fs now."

Lola sighed. "It figures. Kim, did you want something?"

The country station was just clearing off its four o'clock newscast and the DJ started the next record without the usual announcement. If Kelly had ever had a case that afternoon, she rested it with another burst of laughter as the female singer, Arlene Harden, clearly began the opening line.

I was far enough along to feel the baby kicking...

Even I had to burst out laughing at that one. It was *too* much.

"What on earth is so funny?" Kim asked in total bewilderment. "That's a sad song."

"You got me," Lola shrugged. "Whatever it is, they've been at it steady since lunch. I guess we won't know until the shower. Anyway, did you come in here for something, or did you just want to pull Jan out of here before she catches something?"

"Well, I came in to get some envelopes, but maybe I'd better take Janet with me." She watched, horrified, as Kelly and I doubled over hysterically, tears streaming down our cheeks. Arlene wailed to a close, telling the father that she wasn't asking him to stay with her forever, but just long enough to hear their child's first cry.

"Are they always this bad?" Kim asked Lola.

"No. Usually they're worse. Knock it off, you two. Kerry, get Kim some envelopes."

I wiped my eyes and tried to answer seriously. "There's no more. I used the last batch an hour ago."

"Great! That means a trip to the warehouse. Come on, Ker, I'll show you. Lo, I'll bring her right back."

"No, keep her. Maybe Kelly will get something done while she's gone."

"Hey, Rosemary!" Kelly called after me. "Don't take any wooden nickels!"

Kim chatted all the way to the warehouse in the rear of the building, commenting about all the extra work and the pressure the entire plant was under, and how it was affecting everyone's sanity, not just mine and Kelly's. When we arrived, she piled me up with several boxes and asked, "You're not really pregnant, are you, Kerry?"

"Yeah, sure, Kim. In less than a week, I would know that."

"Oh, it's been longer than that!"

"Seven days tomorrow," I insisted, and then at the sight of her baffled expression I added, "But you can't rule it out. Nothing would surprise me after *this* week."

We started back to the office. "I think the whole thing was a little quick," Kim said, "but it's fantastic the way you two are going about it. I mean…it's all out in the open. You're not slipping around like a couple of sneaks. It's really cool."

"Well, what's there to sneak about?"

"Oh, nothing," she said quickly. "But you know how rumors spread around here."

"Yeah, people do talk." I laughed to myself, knowing Kim was one of the worst offenders.

"Well, Devin's not exactly helping matters any," Kim said, lowering her voice. "He was in here this morning looking so tired. I felt sorry for him, but you know how my girls are. They tried to harass him, but it's a little hard to get the last word in on Devin."

"Really? What did he say?"

"I was surprised. He really laid into them. His exact words were…uh... 'hey, I love the chick and that's where it's at.'" She smiled. "You know Devin."

"Yeah," I said, stifling a yawn. "At least a little better than I did last week."

"I hear you two are getting married."

"Who told you that?"

"I got that straight from the horse's mouth," she replied proudly. "Devin isn't trying to conceal anything. He's flaunting it. And wound up? I thought he was crazy before."

I yawned again. "Oh, well, here we are. Back to hell and my once placid office."

"Kerry, that office wasn't placid five years ago when I worked in there. But it *is* worse, for you girls especially."

Back in A/R, the clock read 4:10. Not even an hour until Devin.

"Lola, I can't *post* anymore," Kelly wailed. "Can I do something else?"

"Something else? What, pray tell, have you done all day?" Lola was distributing the print shop statements. Kelly wasn't even pretending to work, concentrating on a design she was coloring in with red and blue ink. The radio was back on her oldies station.

"How far did you get, Kerry?" Lola asked.

"I'm done."

"Hannah?"

"I'm caught up."

"Kelly?"

"I'm filing in the Ss. S is for shitty which is the way I feel." She set the design aside and Lola laughed.

"Okay, kiddies. Put your toys away. I'm going home now. Can you three look busy for the next...uh..." she glanced at her watch..."thirty-five minutes?"

"Oh, Mama, you know we can."

"I know *you* can, Kelly. You've been pretending all day. But Kerry...she's been off in some dream world all week."

"I'll be good," I said, yawning again. "I'm too tired to be anything else."

"Okay, see you tomorrow." She put her sunglasses on and looked at me. "I don't know what's happening, kid, but for the sake of the office, go to bed tonight, will you?"

"Oh, she'll do *that* all right," Kelly quipped.

"That's what I'm afraid of."

"No, I'm sleeping tonight," I mumbled, rubbing my eyes. "And Devin is going home. He hasn't been there since Monday morning."

"You mean to tell me that he hasn't been home for *three* days?" Lola shook her head. "He's lucky he's not married to me. See you tomorrow."

We spent the next ten minutes tidying up the office and filing accounts away. Hannah started posting the next day's work and Kelly went back to coloring her design. If there was anything I didn't need, it was another baby song, but the radio continued with its weird antics by hitting off the next record with Sunday Sharpe's version of *Having His Baby*, the female version of the song that had started it all off early in the afternoon.

"Hey, Rosemary," Kelly started in again.

"Kelly...I really don't want to hear it," I said tiredly.

The radio wailed on. Sunday could feel it. Wasn't it showing? Her face was glowing. Wasn't it obvious in her eyes?

"Can I ask who the father's going to be, or should I say *what?*" Kelly smirked.

"No, you can't."

Sunday was now reminding us that she didn't have to keep the baby and Kelly jerked a thumb at the radio. "Now, there's an out." She went back to coloring her design.

"That does it." I exploded, bursting into laughter. "That station is going off and Lola isn't here to back you up."

"You change that station and I won't give you this pretty design I made you." She held it up proudly, a heart with the initials DD + KK in red and blue shades.

My impatience with her vanished. "Aw, Kelly, that's really sweet. I didn't realize that's what you've been doing."

"But of course not. You were too busy thinking about making babies."

"Yeah, babies." I laughed, and couldn't have picked a worse time.

"Having his baby," Kelly sang out, then stopped. Too abruptly. "Hey, uh…Kerry…"

"Keep singing. And start designing the kid. Now it has to be a boy, 'cause I already have two girls—"

"Ker-reee!" she hissed, and this time there was a sharpness to her voice that made me turn around.

There was Devin, sitting quietly on the step, a ticket loosely dangling in his fingers. There was no way of knowing how long he'd been sitting there. His eyes reflected hurt and confusion.

"Devin!" My face must have lit up at the unexpected surprise, but he didn't smile.

Kelly lit a cigarette nervously, and I could see that she, like me, was mentally retracing the remarks we'd made in the last few minutes.

Hannah turned her back and began to file. Devin's eyes fixed on me. The radio was the only sound in the room. A current song was now playing, but instead of baby songs, it had switched to the present…a hit about a woman in love with a married man, of all things. No one spoke as the lyrics droned on about how she honestly loved him but shouldn't be hanging around him. I'd never really listened to the words before, but with Devin sitting there staring intently, I sure noticed them now. The hurt was still glistening in his eyes.

"That's a nice song," he said finally. I could only nod in agreement.

"You know, for a minute there, I thought you and Kelly—"

"No, Devin."

"Well, I'm off work now. Early for a change. I guess I'll wait for you outside."

For the second time today, I found myself at a loss for words. My feelings for Devin were getting stronger and stronger, but so was the icy fear. This afternoon's episode flashed through my mind and my stomach churned. Through it all, that throbbing chest pain. "Okay," I said quietly. I was in no position to explain now.

"Okay," he echoed, and left. Just got up and tossed the ticket on Lola's desk. Kelly and I exchanged sick glances.

"I feel so bad," Kelly began.

"He thinks we were making fun of him, Kelly."

"But we weren't, really, Ker. And anyway, you just don't pull a question like that out of thin air and expect it to be taken seriously."

"It was dead serious to him, Kel."

"Will you be able to explain what was really going on?"

"I hope so. I sure hope so." I couldn't stand the memory of that look on his face.

Silently we put the trays away, engrossed in our own private thoughts.

The chest feeling that I usually had to contend with was nothing compared to the knotted up tightness in my stomach as we approached the time clock.

Kelly was quiet as we walked and when we reached the door I said, "I sure hope he understands."

"Well, he should." Kelly sounded tired of the whole thing. "We were just kidding around."

"Yeah, but Kelly. Put yourself in his place. What would you think?"

"I would have *thought* before I asked a stupid question like that. That's what I would think."

"Kelly, I don't think you were supposed to hear that question."

"Not supposed to? How could I help it? Shit, he stuck his head in the damn window. Even *Pat* heard him and he was eight feet away."

What was the use? "Let's drop it," I said with a sigh.

When we reached the clock, Kelly pulled both of our cards. Devin wasn't standing out by the trucks. In fact, he was nowhere in sight. My heart sank.

"Maybe he's in his office?" Kelly offered hopefully. "The door's shut."

"He always has it open at five. He might have just gone home."

"Well, were you going to see him tonight?"

"I don't know. I doubt it. I hope so."

"Well, I think sleep would be a little more practical. Ker, you've got bags under your eyes."

I barely heard her. I looked over in the direction of the warehouse. No sign of him anywhere.

"Kerry, did you hear what I said?"

"Yeah, look, Kel...you go ahead. I'm going to look around the plant. I'll see you tomorrow, okay?"

"Okay, but if you're half dead tomorrow, I don't want to hear it. Not eating. Not sleeping. Shit! You can't live on love. See ya."

I watched her cross the truck lot and disappear around the corner. I didn't know what to do. There were voices coming from Tim's office, but Devin's wasn't among them. Maybe he had just left, angry and hurt. I wouldn't have blamed him. There didn't seem to be anything to do but go home too.

With a sick resignation I started walking, oblivious to the cars or people I passed. Devin didn't just magically appear at the side of the plant and I tried to accept the fact that we weren't going to get this straightened out today.

If it wasn't for the stop sign on the corner, I'd have missed him altogether, but having to stop gave me another chance to glance over at the plant. I saw Pat waving wildly at me with both arms from the truck lot and then, from out of nowhere, he was there, running towards me.

With tears of relief, I motioned for the car behind me to pass, and then pulled over to the curb. Devin broke into a hard run, not even checking to see if the street was clear. The plant was emptying now and many of the employees were milling around on the sidewalk. Executives were visible through the glass front doors and other workers were headed for their cars. Devin reached mine in a matter of seconds.

"Hey, where you going?" he panted breathlessly. "I've been looking all over the plant!"

"Devin! I thought you'd gone home. I thought you were too mad to wait." I reached out the open window to hug him, not giving a thought to where we were or who might be watching. He responded with a gripping hug of his own that told me that he too had panicked at the thought of my leaving without seeing him.

"Why didn't you *wait?*" he murmured, kissing me right there in front of the whole damn plant.

"I *did* wait! I looked everywhere. I couldn't find you and I was sure you were upset at the joking Kelly and I were doing. You can't even imagine what it's been like in there all day."

He released his hold on me and stepped back from the window to shake his hair out of his eyes. "Oh, well…I guess it doesn't matter, anyhow." He gave me a relieved smile. "I caught you in time. I wouldn't normally panic but, well…it's the third day for the ring, and you might have an answer from Myrna by now."

"Devin, about this afternoon—"

He held up a hand to silence me. "No. It isn't necessary. Really. I thought you were mocking me at first, but then I realized what was going down. With Kelly and all that shit. I put you in a hell of a position today, but you didn't get down on me for it. So it's cool. I realize that now."

"But Devin, she heard you. And she doesn't understand. All she knows is something is happening awfully fast this week and…for that matter, she isn't the only one. Turn around and look."

In front of the plant, our entire audience consisted of executives and route salesman. The office employees were long gone.

"Hey! Eat your hearts out!" Devin called loudly, and turned back to me. "Fuck them. Listen, babe. You go ahead home." He leaned inside the window and kissed me again, a good long kiss that must have added another ulcer to Perry's collection. "There. Now they all know for sure. I *love* you, Kerry."

I hugged him through the open window again, not wanting to drive away and he knew it.

"I almost got out early, as you know, but Pat asked me to stay a while. I'll be up tonight. For sure. The minute they cut me loose. Okay?"

"Okay, Devin. I love you too."

"No you don't. You're just infatuated. Get going. I can't leave till you drive off."

I glanced in the rearview mirror as I pulled up to the red light. Pat waved again as I passed, and so did some of the less important executives. No one seemed to be sporting any sour grapes, and for the first time since lunch, I felt good.

10

Pammy settled back in my red armchair with impatience. "Are you sure he's coming? 'Cause if you are, we'll skip the drive-in tonight. I've got to meet this weirdo, once and for all."

I walked outside and looked down the street trying to pick van headlights out of the procession of yellow eyes coming at me out of the blackness. It was already nine-thirty.

He said for sure," I replied when I reentered the house. "I'm starting to wonder, though."

"Well, sit down and relax. Your running out there every five minutes isn't going to get him here one way or the other." She nodded at the beanbag and I sank into it.

"I don't know what she's watching for," George said. "It's so damn dark out there. You can't see anything until it's right on top of you anyway."

"Van lights are bigger," I argued.

"Oh, come on, Ker…not when they're glaring like that!"

"Okay, okay," Pam intercepted. "If he's a boss now, he's probably working late."

"Where's your ashtrays, Ker?" George wandered out to the kitchen, not expecting an answer, found one, and returned to the couch. "So. We finally get to meet this guy! Let me see that ring again."

"Oh. You're wearing it again?" Pam looked at me, a touch of concern in her expression. "You must really like him, Ker. I've never seen you like this."

"You'll understand completely when you meet him, Pam," I told her, flashing five spread fingers at George but not removing the ring. "And Devin put it back on me last night."

"He was here last night too?" George frowned at Pam. "I thought you said he was married."

"Well, he is, sort of. Kerry says they're splitting up."

An unexpected knock made us all jump.

"What's the password?" George called out.

"Uh…sex…no, pervert…" someone stammered through the closed door. "Hell, I can't keep up with your damn passwords."

"That's Uncle Joe!" Pam jumped up to unlock the door and greeted him with a big hug.

As usual, Joe was laden down with cigarettes, booze, soda pop and ice. He was always welcome. Even though he was a city fireman and we were a weed-smoking crowd, he ignored it. Sometimes he even bought it for us, in fact. He was that cool. He waved through Pam's bear hug with a wide grin. "Boy, I'm coming up here more often. Anyone for a drink?"

We rarely drank when there was weed around, but we indulged when Joe came to visit. Mainly because it was free.

"I'll take one, Joe," George said. "You here to meet the great Devin too?"

Joe busied himself at the kitchen counter. "No. I didn't know he was coming. He was here last night, wasn't he? I think that's what Lola told me."

"Yes, but he's supposed to be coming tonight, too."

"Well, anyways," Pam said, "back to what you were saying. Are you'ns gonna call Myrna or what?"

"No. We'll probably get the answer tomorrow. You know the mail."

"What if she says it *is* the ring?"

"I don't know. I don't think it is."

"Are you still wearing that pentagram, and is the wedding still on with his brother?"

"What is this?" I laughed. "You writing a book?"

"No, but *you* should. Come on, now. This is the best soap opera I've seen in a long time."

I tugged the pentagram out to show her. "See? Nice, huh?"

Joe peered over my shoulder and rolled his eyes. "That's gorgeous." He sighed and shook his head.

George arched his neck over Joe's head. "Hey! What's that for?"

"To counteract the ring."

Joe downed his glass and went back for a refill. "I don't think I want to know, so I won't ask." Joe was both conservative *and* Catholic, so this visit was probably a double whammy for him.

"Make me one too, Uncle Joe," Pammy piped up. "Devin should be here any minute now. We should keep that bar open."

"I don't think he drinks," I said.

"I meant for us. We're skipping the drive-in for this, you know."

Joe and George got to arguing *The Bible* out in the kitchen, nothing unusual for the two Taurus men. It gave me a chance to fill Pam in on the weird events of the day. The lunch. The question. And finally...the *bomb*. Pam listened wide-eyed, unbelieving that I could be discussing wedding plans and babies so soon.

"Really serious, huh, Ker?"

"Well, I realize it's fast, but...well, there are some things it doesn't take long to be sure of. Devin is just one of those things. I know you're skeptical now, but just wait till you meet him."

"Wow. Tell Joe," Pam said. "I've got to see his expression. George too, for that matter."

"Now?"

"Sure. Joe. George...stop fighting for a minute. Kerry has an announcement to make."

Well, I had the floor, and it did seem better to get it over with so people would start taking *us* seriously. "Devin and I are getting married."

George nearly choked on his drink, and Joe looked dumbfounded.

"Oh, swell," Joe said.

"It must be the grass," George added. "Ask her when she comes down."

"Uh-uh. Married. Maybe by January or February."

"One of those love at first sight things, huh, Ker?" Pam asked.

"No. More of a 'there you are, I've been looking all over.'"

Joe looked like the uncle responsible for his brother's crazy kid, gone speechless. I could see he didn't know whether to lecture me or just leave before he stuck his nose in where it didn't belong. His usual do-your-own-thing attitude won out, apparently, because suddenly he didn't have time to wait for the great Devin. He had to get home to the kids, and five minutes after my announcement, he was long gone.

"Nothing like clearing a room," Pam noted. "Ker, I don't think we'll be seeing Joe for a while. He looked a little green."

"Well, it was your idea. Anyway, that makes you guys, Lola, Pat, Kim, and Kelly who know."

"That's enough," George said. "By tomorrow, they'll know about it in Russia."

"Well, what-da-ya-know?" Pam nodded at the window. "Is that van lights?"

"Damn sure is," George confirmed.

I was already gone. Out the door, across the yard and through the gate as the van cruised to a halt in the dirt. I was in his arms in seconds, as though he'd been away for days instead of hours. This afternoon had been the first step in a drastic turn in our relationship, and it was going too fast for me to jump off now. He was crushing me against him, and the world was fading away. All I was aware of, or cared about, was the warmth of his chest pressed against my face in the chilliness of the late October air, the hammering of his heart in my ear.

"Devin, I love you."

"That's good," he said, gripping me tighter. "You're my lady now."

I pulled away from him, awed at the change in his voice, so different from the one I was used to at the plant. He didn't *look* any different, though. He was smiling, and everything was all right.

"Here's my excuse," he said, now free to reach into his pocket. "Joints. Lots of them."

"Oh, Devin, we've got that stuff here." I laughed, so happy that he'd made it at all. "Come on in! I've got someone who's dying to meet you, and someone else who thinks I made you up. Daniel give you those?"

"Who else?" The curtain could be seen moving from where we stood. "Who *is* in there?"

"My little sister and her future ex-boyfriend."

"Far out! Let's go in. They seem a little impatient."

A radiant glow of pride swept over me as he took my hand and walked beside me up to the door. "Is your sister anything like you?"

"Yes and no. She's twenty, and we don't really look alike, but she's a lot like me in other ways."

George was at the window, checking out the van with envy. Pammy's face held the same envious expression when we walked in, though it wasn't the van she was looking at.

"Man, that's really far out," George exclaimed, extending his hand. "I'm George. This is Pam."

"Devin." He gripped George's outstretched hand, hippie-style, palm to palm, thumbs gripping each other. Then, smiling, he turned to Pam. "Kerry's right." His voice was soft and gentle. "You two *don't* look alike."

I could read Pam's thoughts. I hadn't warned her about Devin's good looks, nor had I mentioned his hippie status.

"You don't look anything like I thought *you* would either." She was still staring at him as she then addressed me. "Kerry, you didn't tell me he was *cute*, too."

"Man, I dig that van," George broke in, stepping between Pam and Devin.

Devin sat down on the floor and extracted the bag of ready-rolled joints. "You wouldn't like that sucker so much if you had to make the payments on it, George."

"What's that run you a month?"

"Two hundred and some." He tossed George the keys. "Go ahead. Take it for a spin."

"Naw...I can't do that." George was visibly taken aback by Devin's open friendliness and trust. "I wouldn't want the responsibility."

I could see that neither of them had imagined Devin to be so perfect. Pam elbowed George. "Come on, you know you want to see the inside, and I think they'd like to say hello in private."

"We did that out in the yard," Devin assured her, "but go ahead and take it around the block."

Pam flashed me the thumbs up and an okay sign as they left for the van.

Devin reached for me the instant they exited, hugging me like I was going to evaporate any second. "We won't see them for a while. Not when George discovers the bed."

"They better not. We haven't even christened it yet."

They returned a few minutes later, and George handed Devin back his keys. "Man, you're all set up in there. Fridge, couch bed, closets. Man, you could live in there if you had to."

"Hey, we really *do* gotta go," Pam said. "We were headed for the drive-in, but I'm sure we've missed the first movie. We might make the second. Devin, it was a real shock meeting you, I'll say. Kerry really didn't do you justice when she told me about you. You're just *nothing* like I'd expect *her* to come up with."

We walked them to George's Jeep, waved them off, and returned to the house. Alone, finally.

"I like your sister," Devin told me. "I mean, I like George too, but I figured you'd be more interested in my opinion of Pammy."

"Frankly, I was more interested in her opinion of *you*. She's been shaky about you ever since she saw the ring. I don't know what she was expecting, but obviously, you sure passed her approval. The last thing she expected, from her conventional sister, I mean, was a hippie." I busied myself at the stove, making coffee, while Devin sat down in the beanbag.

"How much does she know anyway?" He gratefully accepted the steaming mug I handed him.

"Well, I broke the news tonight. To them, and to my Uncle Joe. I hope that was okay. I wanted to get the shocks over with. I also had to tell Lola and Kelly, for the same reasons. Everyone acts like they've been elected my guardian or something. I was getting tired of their lectures about you married men and your wiles. Pam's the only one who's casually accepted it. Probably because anyone who could flip *me* out this much couldn't be all bad. I could see that she's very impressed."

He smiled. "How'd your uncle take it?"

I made a dumbstruck, horrified expression and mimicked him. "*Huhhhhh?*"

We both laughed. Nobody seemed to be grasping what was going on. Not even us.

"By the way, nothing from Myrna. You're probably wondering."

"I *was* wondering. Think she will? Answer at all, I mean?"

"I thought she would have by now. I don't care about calling her anymore, anyway. I don't think it was the ring. It was just convenient to blame. If we do hear back from her, we'll just deal with it then." I suddenly remembered the Sador I'd purchased Saturday during the time frame that he'd been making me the tape. "I'm not sure if you're ready for this, but I've been putting off telling you about *my* little hand in this." I pulled out the medallion and set it in Devin's hand. "See if you can read the Latin words on it."

"Oh, this." He smiled. "I noticed it last night when everything else was off, but I wasn't thinking much about jewelry at the time. I don't read Latin anyway. What is it?"

"It's a...uh...love talisman. I feel kind of guilty about it now."

"It's a *what?*"

"You heard me. Talk about timing, huh? While you were making a tape for me."

"No, when I *suddenly* thought to make a tape for you," Devin corrected. His eyes twinkled as he examined the Sador. "So. You think *this* is what brought us together?"

"Oh, no," I replied quickly. "It was an impulsive thing, buying it." I stopped when I realized he was openly laughing now, trying to muffle his face in the beanbag. "I just thought the timing was a little coinciden—hey...what's so funny?"

"Oh, nothing. It's just that...well...how do you know it wasn't me playing with the full moon on the first of the month, before I even *saw* the ring?"

The thought hadn't occurred to me that *he* might have had something to do with the suddenness of us. Here, I'd blamed the ring, the Sador, myself. "Devin! Did you really?"

In reply, he pulled me down to him, still chuckling, trying to evade the answer with a kiss. I resisted. "Oh, no you don't. Devin. Tell me. Did you?"

"Come on, chick. Think I'd stoop to that?" He grinned. "And if I did, you think I'm stupid enough to admit it?"

"Well, then tell me one thing. *If* you did, was it before or after you bought the ring?"

Devin seemed to ponder the question seriously. The smile vanished, as he appeared to honestly search his memory. "Well, the full moon was on the first, so I'd have to say it was before I got the ring."

"Aha! Then you *did*."

"No, I said *if* I did, it *would* have been." His reply was smooth and casual as he moved over in the beanbag and punched a cubbyhole in it. Room for me to join him. The beanbag looked more like a brown felt lily pad with most of the beans having escaped to the base of my green shag carpet.

"Well, anyways," I said, moving closer to him, "If you *did*, I'm *glad* you did. So there."

"Don't give *me* all the credit," he reminded me with a smug look. "I'm not the one who went running to the occult shop for a love charm." He squeezed my shoulder affectionately. "Not that I *mind* your sneaky, underhanded, unscrupulous tactics..."

The smile faded, and he suddenly looked deep into my eyes, now very serious. "The main thing is you're here now, no matter what it took. And *I'm* here now, which was actually more of a project than you know. We've got to adjust the present to our needs, and a wife here will only slow things down. She's got to go a lot sooner than Christmas. That's my first order of business."

That fast, the happy-go-lucky hippie had vanished. There didn't seem to be any sympathy or emotion in his voice but then, just as suddenly, his face began to take on a mature, kind expression. The transformation actually took place *as* he was speaking, the way a radio station might be tuned in and out. For once, I was close enough to watch it happen right before my eyes. It wasn't Devin that continued on.

"I'll have to do something about that marriage situation. Christmas is too far away. I don't want it to seem like she's being pushed out of the house, however, there doesn't seem to be any painless way to suggest a sooner date. It's not like she isn't looking forward to being with her family, and maybe Thanksgiving would be more practical for everybody. It may seem like I'm rushing things and that I should just stick to the plan, but then again, there are other factors. If it were up to me..."

His voice trailed off, leaving me to study him in the silence, his face so changed and looking much older than twenty-five under the candlelight. The candle was burning out, and the room almost plunged into darkness, but he showed no sign of noticing. In the now low-lighted room, something else was visibly different too. Something that could not be rationalized as my imagination or his moods.

I was pretty good at auras, the colors that people radiate, visible to those who can see them. Everybody had them, some more distinct than others, and green and yellow were pretty common on most people. Tonight, from my vantage point in the beanbag, I had the white ceiling for a neutral background and the scant flickering of the candle for lighting. The color radiating from Devin was a smoky bluish white. A haze brighter than anything I had ever seen coming off anybody. It was so new that I didn't even know what it meant, as all colors signify the thoughts, mood, or character of the person they radiate from. I knew any blue wasn't bad, though. I couldn't very well get up and look up the color on an aura chart, so I remained where I was, watching and saying nothing to him about it.

"Something wrong?" he asked softly.

"No, uh, well, it's just that you said...if it were up to you. What did you mean? Who else would it be up to?"

The haze surrounding him made it difficult to keep from staring at him, and the instant I asked the question, the color deepened to a purple band...yet another color I had never seen on a person. It was almost ultraviolet, and I knew from my studies that that shade was pretty much linked to cosmic consciousness. The next step after that was white, and nobody radiated white unless they were on their deathbed, just seconds before departure from this world. Not that I'd ever seen that either, but that's what the books said. Yet, here was Devin, beaming out this almost blacklight shade, completely oblivious to the mental changes I was going through. He took my hand gently as he tried to answer my question.

"I can't explain that at the present, lady. I would be getting ahead of myself if I did. But in time, you will know everything. For now, I can only ask you to trust me. The situation will be handled in the best possible way. Can you accept that for now?"

"Well, she is your wife, Devin, and that is totally up to you how you handle it. You don't owe me any explanations." His color remained purple. I couldn't take my eyes off it. He didn't reply. Just gave me a long steady gaze.

"Devin?"

"I would prefer that you forget this afternoon's episode. Forget the question you were asked." The change of subject was so abrupt that it startled me into a sitting position. Quickly. The voice made the hair at the back of my neck stand on end. He continued on as though this conversation were perfectly normal. "I'm aware that it's easy for me to say and difficult for you to forget, however I have given the matter considerable thought and, as usual, my timing was completely off."

"Devin, how *can* I forget it? It wasn't just some random remark. An issue was made in front of witnesses. If nothing else, Kelly will never let me forget it. You should have heard *her* today. And anyway, I already told you. The answer is yes. No matter when you feel the time is right. I don't understand what *is* going on, but I love you and I *do* trust you."

"Lady." He silenced me with a gentle finger to my lips. "You *don't* yet understand, therefore I cannot hold you to a promise you so willingly and trustingly pledge. It wouldn't be fair. You don't yet know the conditions under which this child will enter this dimension. You must know everything about my son before I will accept a yes so blindly offered."

My blood froze. Scenes of *Rosemary's Baby* flashed through my mind again, and the horror of the image made my stomach lurch. "Devin...what kind of conditions?" I tried to sound nonchalant, but Devin could see that my fear and sudden mistrust were very evident. "Devin, do you mean a *Rosemary's Baby* type of thing?"

"Sort of." He was watching me intently, his words carefully chosen and cautious. "Only, nothing to be afraid of. No drugs, no blood, but along those lines, yes. The doctor would be one of us, in case that's troubling you. We wouldn't put a project like this in the hands of a human doctor."

"You already have a doctor in *mind*?"

He nodded. "Is your answer still yes?" He seemed to be peering at me through a mask, his eyes and voice totally incompatible with the routeman I thought I knew. That purplish band deepened and lightened as he watched me.

"Well, it's still yes, Devin, but...I'd want to know a little more about it, you know?"

"I understand. You can't conceive until you *do* totally understand. That isn't my requirement either, so you have no reason to fear something unexpected. Nothing will develop unless we have your full cooperation. It can't be any other way. You mentioned *Rosemary's Baby*. A fictional story. Did you see the movie or read the book?"

"Yes, both."

"Remember how they described the child?"

Now I did have an impulse to throw up. "Yes," I said weakly. "I remember."

"Good. Then we have an idea we can work with. Like the child in the story, the physical attributes of my child will be apparent to the...uh...race here. Now I don't mean claws, a tail, or horns...though knobs will probably develop like these here—" He pulled my hands to his temple areas. "See, they're here...the knobby lumps that humans have somehow turned into horns over the centuries."

I recoiled my hands quickly. There *was* a lumpy knot on both sides of his head, buried under his black curly hair.

"The eyes will be the most obvious," he went on, ignoring my horrified reaction. He paused and looked me dead in the eyes. "No one will be able to look into my son's eyes this way." The candlelight flashed in his own eyes, and once again I saw hazel turn to amber and flash a green sheen the way a dog's eyes will do when caught in a flashlight beam.

By now, the chest feeling had grown to an intolerable throb. I didn't want him to pick up on the thoughts and feelings this discussion was generating, or on the fear throbbing inside me, keeping time with my pounding, rapid heartbeat. I tried to keep my voice steady. "Devin, are you telling me that your intention is to bring a child into this world that you know will be of an evil nature?"

"Evil?" A puzzled look crossed his face. "Evil? Kerry, where did you get that idea?" He heaved a frustrated sigh. "Kerry, do *I* come off as *evil* to you?" His features softened, and that purple band melted into a pink and yellow hue. Colors I was more familiar with. I knew that pink denoted warmth, love, and sincerity, and I felt myself relax with relief. He didn't wait for a reply. "No, Kerry, not evil. But I can see where this kind of discussion is making you nervous. You're trying to absorb too much, too soon, right now. Can you just trust me? As I've told you, nothing can or will happen that you don't willingly agree to." He kissed me gently and the fear began to melt away.

I was suddenly flooded with love, and with relief for his denial of any evil intent. Of *course* there was nothing to be afraid of. I was letting spooky movies and worried friends get to me. I gave him a feeble smile. "How about some coffee?"

"If you think it will get rid of those goosebumps." He smiled and winked. "Damn, lady, you are going to be a real project, I can see that."

"Well, this whole day has been eerie. Not just lunch today, but you should have heard the radio all afternoon. I was beginning to suspect that you had some deejay friend, except that changing the station didn't help."

"I know what must have happened." He sighed and got up to put the water on. "Kerry, there's a connection with me and the radio. I can't, or won't, explain tonight, not after the talk we just had. I don't wish to frighten you away because of misunderstandings. Don't be afraid of it, though."

"Well, I wasn't afraid. Are you sure we're talking about the same thing?"

"Yes. The radio started playing songs appropriate to the question you were asked at lunch today."

"Yeah. How'd you know?"

"I have smart-aleck friends. Let's let it go at that, for now. Okay? No, matter of fact, let's not." He walked over to the stereo and pushed the button. A song by the Moody Blues was in progress, singing about the eyes of a child and asking what was real. He returned to the stove as the song played out. "Is this what happened this afternoon?"

"Yeah," I said, feeling awed. "That's exactly what happened."

He came in with the coffee cups and sat down in the armchair. "Like I said, I have smart-aleck friends. Anyway, let's get off that subject. Man, Kelly really laid it out about the rumors circulating the plant, huh?"

"It didn't end there." I laughed, glad to be on a lighter subject but still wondering what he meant about the radio. "Kim mentioned how you told off the whole phone room."

"I guess they'll put my calls through without their bullshit now," he said with a smile. "But Mama kind of worries me. I realize now how close you two are. I'd kind of like to have her approval of us, too. In fact, I'd *like* to invite her to our wedding."

I burst into laughter. The thought of Lola agreeing to fly to Salem to stand on a snowy Gallows Hill was too much. "I'd like to ask her to be matron of honor, Devin, but don't hold your breath. She *definitely* is not one of us." A feeling of devotion swept through me as I thought of her.

"You really do love her, don't you," Devin said. "Okay. Matron of honor it is. I'll ask her myself, first thing in the morning."

"Well, I don't know about Gallows Hill, clear up in Salem. We'd probably have to do it a little more local. Hard to say, though. She has family in Boston, and she's about due up there for a visit. She goes every year. And she *is* very interested in the Halloween thing coming up."

"*That* I can't offer her."

"I know. She does too. It's cool."

"It's only curiosity on her part anyway. And everyone else's, too." Devin sighed. "But that's all right. The curious will always find their way. Even religious fanatics have a path that leads to the center. It's the people who don't care about anything at all that I worry about. People who aren't into *any* frame of reference. Whether it's Christian or occult or even UFOs…all those people have somewhere to grow *from*." He glanced at his watch. "I've got to get going. If I don't show tonight, my wife will have the dogs after me. Actually, she said she wanted to have a talk, and the sooner we do that, the sooner she can get packing. I get more impatient every day. We've already agreed that this is what we both want, and for that reason, before the holidays is sounding better and better."

"You called her today?"

"*She called *me.*" He screwed up his face to imitate a sarcastic expression. "You know, *do you think you can stop by tonight if you're not too busy?*"

"Yeah, wives can be like that," I agreed, feeling a little guilty.

"Hey, don't *you* feel responsible," he said quickly. "It's good! She wants this as much as I do. We've outgrown each other. It's just that it might be a little rude to go this many days without stopping home. If there's something we need to talk about, this would be the time to do it."

"I wish you'd just stay here tonight. If you do go home, you might be up fighting until morning. You haven't slept in days. I could set the alarm for earlier than normal."

"I guess I could," he mused. "But it would *have* to be early. My uniforms are there, but I guess it doesn't matter when I make the drive. It's probably too late for any kind of talk now, anyway."

"I'll rub your back."

"That's bribery."

"True, but I will."

He grinned. "Okay, babe. But let's hit it, then. Pat won't be in till late morning, and I have the only keys to the truck yard. Be a lot of pissed-off guys if they can't get in the gate to load up tomorrow."

The lack of sleep had finally caught up with Devin. As I sat on the edge of the bed, rubbing his back, I was lost in my own thoughts. Scenes of the past week kept flashing through my mind. A Devin on his knees in motorcycle attire, giving me a ring. Another Devin bent earnestly over a notebook, writing. A Devin waving at me from a blue-and-white parked truck and a Devin facing me in the parking lot of a crowded mall. Just what was I getting myself into?

I looked down at Devin, stretched out on the bed, clothes rumpled, barely breathing. Looking so innocent when he was asleep. The image of a baby in a black bassinet with red trim formed in my mind, and I angrily pushed the thought away. Worrying wasn't going to help anything now, and I had to work tomorrow too. I looked at Devin again. He didn't even look like he was breathing. I placed my hand on his back, and then my ear, amazed that he could sleep that way. Without breathing. I made a mental note to ask him about that in the morning and lay down on the other side of him, pulling the covers up around us both. Nights were getting cold, and Devin's warm back made a good pillow.

11

I don't know what woke me up so suddenly, but a frantic glance at the clock told me one thing for sure. Devin wasn't just late. He was downright in trouble. It was daylight. The drivers should be loaded up and gone, and Devin had the only keys to the gate.

"Oh, shit! Devin, it's six-thirty!"

"What?" Devin was instantly on his feet and grabbing for his shirt and boots. He couldn't have been awake as he laced up his left boot while I worked frantically with the right. Neither of us spoke. Devin headed for the bathroom and I sat on the bed, filled with dread. My fault. I should have let him go home.

"Hey, Ker? You got a hairbrush?"

I scooped one up from the dresser and hurried it in to him. He was just rinsing out the razor and smiled at my sudden appearance in the mirror. "Thanks." He winked at me and started brushing his hair with brisk fast strokes. "You could use a sharper razor."

"Devin, I'm so sorry."

"For what?" He stopped long enough to kiss me on the forehead and then resumed.

"Well, you're late and it's my fault."

He handed me the brush and looked at me curiously. "*Your* fault? Hey, ol' Devin's a big boy now. Been getting himself up for years."

"What's going to happen?" I was worried about his job, even if he wasn't.

"I don't know. I'll see when I get there." He kissed me quickly and headed for the front door. "Later, babe."

That sick feeling didn't lessen any as I mechanically went through the motions of getting myself and the kids ready to go. Nor had it subsided by the time I reached the restaurant. What if he'd been fired?

I shifted the car into park, shut it off, and scanned the restaurant parking lot across the boulevard. No company truck. It was 7:30. I myself was no earlier or later than usual. I crossed the four lanes on foot, entered the restaurant and dropped into the booth with the widest range of visibility. I could see my car and any other vehicle approaching from that street. If Devin did show up, it would be from that street. Jane brought my coffee, apparently too busy to notice my mood.

"Anything else, hon?"

"No, that's good."

I didn't feel like reading. Something else was bugging me. Something I couldn't put my finger on. Something Devin had said...or something I had dreamed, maybe. A flash of Devin...that sinister side of Devin. The Devin with those burning eyes looking out through the holes in his face...*and the child's eyes*... Now that computed. I had dreamed about the baby. And Devin. The memory came flooding back now. In the dream, I had asked Devin to clarify the circumstances of the son he wanted. Devin had replied that I must first realize who he was. Not so different from real life, though the feeling now was more frightening. The child would be conceived when he was ready to deal with the physical dimension, or better yet, he'd added, when the physical dimension was ready for him. In the dream, I had been very afraid, and sitting here now, that fear was creeping into my *real* life. The feelings of awe and fright were beginning to overwhelm me.

I had to get out. Back to the plant where at least Lola would be her normal, friendly self, and everything was real and usual. I shoved a buck at the girl behind the register. "Coffee," I told her. "Jane gets the change."

No notes greeted me on my time card when I punched in, although I had hoped he'd had time to let me know what had happened. Devin was nowhere in sight, nor was there a crowd of late drivers frantically fighting to get loaded up and out as I had feared. No way of knowing exactly what had transpired. I didn't dare show my face in the phone room and went straight down the hall, past the lounge on the right, made a sharp left across the lobby, then into Lola's office. *Shit*. In the confusion of everything, I had forgotten Lola's muffin. The thought didn't strike me until I caught sight of her. She greeted me with her usual early-morning humor.

"Hello, little girl. That's okay...I wasn't hungry anyway."

That last part added as I held up my empty hands apologetically. "I forgot. Where is everybody?"

"They're on strike. And I think I'll join them."

"Really?"

She gave me a 'you'd believe anything' look. "Hannah's not coming in today, and Kelly is always late."

Kelly picked that exact moment to enter, looking cocky as usual, having caught Lola's remark. "Kelly is *not* always late, *Mother*, and it's Friday...eight-thirty...and I am here. So *there!*"

"Oh, I knew you'd show up," Lola retorted. "Your check's small enough with the late deductions every morning. But it's Thursday, not Friday."

"Oh, no! I thought today was payday! They're gonna shut my power off. I gotta call them." She plopped down on the forbidden step beside me. "What's this about Hannah?"

"Her husband called in. He said she was up sick all night, and there was no way he was going to let her work today." Lola didn't sound like she cared much.

Kelly nudged me with her elbow. "Did you get any sleep last night?" She smirked, as if just now remembering Devin.

"Yeah, a little. Couple hours."

Kelly turned to Lola. "I bet Devin was there and didn't go home again last night."

"I hope he did," Lola said, "before his wife files a missing persons with the police, and then we'll have *them* running in and out of here all day, and Devin's bad enough."

"Mama, Devin was late! Real late. He had to open up this morning, and it was daylight when he left."

Lola's smile vanished. "Oh, no. Was Tim in?"

"I don't know. I haven't seen or heard from him since he left the house."

Lola could see I was really worried and said halfheartedly, "Well, if Pat was there you'll probably be okay. I don't know about Tim, though."

"Well, Tim loves Devin. And Devin's never late."

"That's one thing in your favor," Lola agreed and picked up the phone. She punched local. "Hi Janet, will you put me through to Tim's office?"

I waited while the call was connected, my heart in my throat.

"Hello, Pat? Is your...uh...partner-in-crime around today?" She glanced at me. "Oh, he's out on the truck? I see. Well, when he gets back will you send him up here? Uh-huh. Thanks." She replaced the receiver and shrugged. "He's still an employee. Now will you get to work? You're just going to have to wait till he calls."

"I *am* working!" Kelly said, moving from the step to the carpet in our office. "I'm putting the tickets in order...hey...where are we going to lunch today?"

As if I didn't have enough problems, Kelly was trying to rile Lola up already. I gave her a dirty look as the answer came calmly from the other room.

"Yes, where *is* Devin taking us today?"

Kelly and I exchanged looks of shock. After yesterday, neither of us expected to be allowed out of the building, much less with Devin. "You mean we're allowed?" Kelly squealed. We both jumped up and raced to her desk. "Really, Mama? You'll go with us?"

"I should, just to ruin your lunch. You ruined mine yesterday."

"You wouldn't ruin it. Come on..."

"No. I have errands to do at lunch. Maybe another time. And speaking of time..."

"We promise, Mama," I said. "We'll go to a fast empty place. It wasn't our idea to go to a crowded mall yesterday."

"*Or* to pick up something for me," Lola added, "luckily for the four of you."

"Well, will you at least come to Gallows Hill and be matron of honor at our wedding?"

"What?" Lola and Kelly burst into laughter together. "Spit that out again?"

Lola said.

"I mean it. We talked about it last night."

"What on earth does that have to do with lunch today?"

"Journey of a thousand miles begins with a single lunch," Kelly said dryly.

"Would you?" I persisted.

"Well, I don't know. Is it going to be out in some lonely woods like his brother's?"

"No. It'll be on Gallows Hill in Salem...where all the witches were tortured, burned and hung."

"Oh, that sounds romantic."

"I'm serious, Mama! Would you?"

"How can you be serious? Devin is still married, or...were you just going to overlook that tiny little detail?"

"He won't be by January or February, though. It'll be perfectly legal."

"What *is* the rush?" Lola asked.

I shrugged. "Ask Devin."

"Come on, Kerry," Kelly called in. "Are you going to work today or what?"

I gave Lola one last look.

"Ask me later," she said, and I went in to my machine.

Kelly was grinning as she sorted the tickets with expert speed. "Did you gain any weight over the night," she asked as she sorted, "or are you still awaiting mothership?" She stopped to examine a ticket closely and then said seriously, "Kerry, does Devin mark his deliveries with an initial D and then circle it? This is Lucky's route, but it sure doesn't look like a ticket Devin wrote. I mean, I *know* it's his writing, but..."

"Let's see." I leaned over, and sure enough, there was a circled D on one of the sloppiest tickets I'd seen in a long while. "That's Devin's, I guess, but it's not his usual handwriting. "I can't read the company name at all. What's it say?"

"I'll be damned if I know. Let's go ask Lola."

Lola studied the ticket with amusement. "Devin wrote this? Well, that *is* his mark."

"What's it say?" Kelly was positive Lola would know. Lola always knew.

Lola was positive, all right. "I have no idea. Take it back to Pat or Tim, Kelly. And Kerry, what are *you* mixed up with this for? Does it take two of you to carry a ticket in here?"

"Kerry's feeling guilty 'cause it's Devin's ticket," Kelly explained.

"He must have been asleep when he wrote it," Lola said.

Kelly looked at me. "Kerry, you take it back. You like to go back there, and I hate to. Mussolini's laying for me."

"I don't like to go back there when I know Devin's out. Besides, Devin was late today. Tim's probably pissed off at me."

"Well *someone* get it back there, and *someone* get those tickets in order or—"

I volunteered quickly.

Tim was surprisingly nice to me when I walked in.

"Good morning, Kerry." He greeted me with a wide smile. "What can I do for you?"

"Lola said to give this to you. We can't read it." I handed him the ticket. As he reached over, his glance fell to the pentagram, and then back up to my face. Checking me out, obviously.

"What's wrong with it?" He put his glasses on and frowned. There was absolutely no way of decoding it. "Devin wrote this?"

I felt my face flush at the mention of Devin's name. "Presumably. That's his mark."

"Okay, Kerry," he said finally. "Tell Lola I'll get back to her." He pocketed the ticket, dismissing me.

Kelly was on the phone when I walked in, and a line was blinking on hold. "It's about time! Devin's on twenty-two."

I snatched the other phone from its cradle. "Hello, Devin?"

"Hey!" There was a funny drawl in that 'hey.'

"Devin?"

"Hey, it's me. How's everything going?"

Devin and his damn voices. "Well, it's fine in here, but what about you? What happened this morning?"

"I'm not sure." He laughed and sounded more normal. "I was asleep when I got there. Tim wasn't supposed to be in this morning, but for some reason he went in anyway. He opened up."

"Then he knew you were late."

"I guess so. I damn sure wasn't going to argue with him with Baby Ben sitting on his desk."

"Well, what did he say?"

"Oh, he gave me the father talk. How I'd always been the best man he had…the old pep-talk routine."

"What did you give him for a reason?"

"The *truth*," came the answer quickly, back in that funny drawl. "Tha' Ah hadn' been *home* in three fuckin' days, an' Ah haven' slept much, an' that mah *body* jis didn' git up this mornin'."

"Did he know that you were at my place?"

"He's stupid if he doesn', th' way Ah looked when Ah walked in. Th' uniforms are delivered Thursdays, though, so Ah lucked out. Oh, an' Tim knows we're gettin' married. Ah *told* him what was goin' on."

I sighed. Everybody, it seemed, had to know what was going on. Devin's sudden change in tone must have meant that he was getting tired of it. Or just plain tired. "What did you tell Tim about us exactly?"

"That Ah waz taking mah wife home to her muther's," he replied, the black accent thicker now, as though he was deliberately putting on a drawl. "An' that Ah didn' wan' no shee-it from *him* or anyone *else* back there. That it'll be nas an' legal, an' that when Ah didn' need to be in three places at one tahm, jis maybe Ah'll get somethin' done around here."

"Do any good?"

He chuckled. "Must've. He gave me his attorney's number. Said he's been through this married shee-it fo tahms."

"Oh, sounds like he's a good one to advise you," I said sarcastically.

"Gotta a'mitt, tho, ladee…he's 'speriance. Anyhow, I figgered you'd be worried, so Ah didn' wait till Ah got in to tell you. Ah'm on mah way in now."

"Already?"

"Yeah. Ah'm jist doin' specials t'day. Ah'll be in yer office before lunch. Ah kin always fin' a reason."

"Tim's got one in his shirt pocket, Dev. A ticket of yours that none of us can read."

"Ya sure it's mahn?" The accent was even thicker now. I couldn't distinguish him from Jay Jackson, the only black driver we *did* have. It just didn't make sense to me that he would deliberately want to sound like that.

"Does any other driver put a circled D on their tickets?"

"No…tha' mahn. Ah'll see it when Ah get in."

"Okay. Want me to put you through to the phone room?"

"Shee-it, no. Jist ring Tim fer me."

True to his word, Devin cruised in to our office, quietly, at 11:30 and bored a hole in my back until I felt someone behind me. When I turned around, there he was on the forbidden step, head resting on his crossed arms, the ticket in question poking out of his shirt pocket. "Hey, lady," he said in a perfectly normal Devin voice. "And Kelly, of course."

"Oh, good morning, your highness," Kelly quipped cheerfully. "What graces us with your presence so early this morning…Devin…what *is* this?" She handed him three more tickets. "They're all *yours.* Lola says you'd better get your act together."

Devin took the tickets, plus the one in his pocket, and after a super-quick glance at the other three, carefully printed a name neatly above the scribbled abbreviated one on each of them. "Is that better?"

"Thank you. Hey, get off that step, Devin. Lola is getting pissed 'cause she has to keep telling everyone. I got yelled at this morning."

"That's *you.*" Devin said. "I'm comfortable right where I'm at."

"Well, don't fall asleep there. You look like you're about to."

"Yeah, well, you know how it is." He shrugged.

"*Devin, get the hell off that step!*" Lola, having returned, didn't waste any time with Devin. He looked up at her, chin resting on his arms, and smiled. "Hey-hey-hey!"

"Don't you hey-hey-hey *me* !Up, now…come on…"

He stood up and stretched. "I was getting up anyway," he told a smirking Kelly.

"Are you taking them out again today, or what?"

"You're paroling them already?"

"Don't give me a hard time," Lola snapped. "There better *not* be another yesterday."

"Yes, Mama. I hear you." He made an attempt to look humble.

"I mean it. If they're *one* minute late, that's the end of lunch for the gang of you."

"Okay, Mama, we'll watch it. What happened yesterday…"

"Spare me. I've heard your sad tale."

"I want to go to Lums!" Kelly said. "They're giving away these neat Disney glasses with the drinks and this week it's Daffy Duck!"

"Kerry and Kelly take separate cars," Lola interjected. "That way I'll know who to yell at."

"Then let's go now," Kelly said. "It's five to."

"Where we gonna sit?"

Kelly and I had entered through the rear entrance, relieved to see that Lums didn't have the noon-rush crowd that even the coffee shop had every day.

"Over here, against the wall," Kelly replied. "We'll see them when they drive up."

Behind us, Devin and Pat were already making their way to our table as she spoke.

"Hi, girls!" Pat said cheerfully, sitting beside Kelly and waving exaggeratedly at me. I returned it as Devin took his seat beside me and flashed a peace sign to Kelly. Then he kissed me on the cheek.

"Hey, lady."

Kelly burst out laughing. She gestured at Devin dramatically. "It's no wonder they're the talk of the town."

"Hey…buzz off, chick." Devin wrapped both his arms around me. Kelly turned to Pat.

"Would you say there was anything between these two?"

"Nah…anybody can see they're just friends." Pat shrugged and smiled.

Kelly rolled her eyes. "Well, let's get off *them* for a while. It seems to be *the* subject these days. I have an announcement to make. I have a new favorite song."

Kelly had a new favorite song every week.

"I know, Kelly. You told me. It's *Angie Baby*."

"No, that was last week. But now there's this new one out…*When Will I See You Again?* It reminds me of you two. Actually, I think the title is *Precious Moments*."

"It reminds me of your wife," Pat said to Devin, then turned to Kelly. "I'm all up on that rock and roll, you know."

"Speaking of favorite songs," Devin said, "I have a new one, too."

Everyone looked at him expectantly.

"It's by Uriah Heep, and it's called *Sunrise*. Actually, it's not my *favorite* song. It's *one* of my favorites."

"I never heard of it," Kelly said, looking at me. "Have you?"

"No. How's it go?"

Devin took out a red route pen and began to print the lyrics on a napkin. Something about another day without someone. He passed it over for me to read. "There."

"Lemmee see!" Kelly demanded, then, "Aw, that's really pretty. How come you can't write your route tickets that neat and pretty?"

"That's *one* of my favorites," Devin told her, ignoring the sarcasm. He turned to me. "It's on that tape I made for you." He printed the word *US* underneath, and gave me an intense look, then glanced around for a waitress. "What time is it anyway?"

"Don't worry, Dev," Pat said calmly. "Believe me, I'm watching."

"This is new to me," Devin said, shaking his head. "I'm not used to such a rigid time schedule…and Kerry, you *are* eating today."

After the waitress left with our orders, Devin went back to doodling on the napkin with the red felt-tip pen. Strange, disjointed lines that didn't appear to have any connection with one another. I thought of my dream and grabbed a pen, writing quickly. I filled up my napkin, cupping my hand so it couldn't be read by others, and jotted down the dream. Then I wrote *what*, if anything, did the dream mean to him?

"Well, it looks like these two are going to write love letters all through lunch," Kelly said sardonically to Pat. "Do you get the feeling we're invading their privacy?"

"Yeah, Devin. Are you sure you two wouldn't rather sit alone? We can move, you know."

Devin shoved his napkin over to Kelly and Pat. "If you two had any perception at all, you'd know what that is."

Pat glanced at the squiggly and angular symbols Devin had drawn. "Now, what the hell, Devin?"

"I don't know either," Kelly said lamely. "I think *that* one is an eye. At least it looks like it was going to be."

Devin slid it over to me. "I'll bet you'll know."

When it had been in front of Kelly, I hadn't known what it was either, but now it seemed obvious that it was only half a picture. By duplicating the same symbols across from Devin's, a devilish face began to emerge, with fiery eyes, horns, and little pointed ears. Devin watched, unflinching, as though he'd expected me to do just exactly that. The idea to copy his side of the napkin had come in a flash, so quickly that even I was astonished that it had been correct.

"Right *on*, lady." There was pride in Devin's voice.

"Wow…it was just…good grief. It just worked out like that," I stammered.

"Yeah?"

The waitress was coming with the food, so we moved the cigarettes and pens to make room on the table.

"Oh, *now* I see!" Kelly said, gaping at Devin's napkin. "Hey, that was pretty quick, Ker."

"Well, it surprised me too," I assured her, dumping mustard on my steak sandwich. "Really. I didn't know what I was going to do until I had the pen in my hand. Honest. What time is it?"

"We've got ten minutes before our usual five minutes late, unless we're going the whole forty-five minutes."

"Over my dead body," Devin said.

"Which it will be if they're late." Pat reminded him.

"Look, you girls *can't* be late," Devin said. "I gave my word."

"I'm *watching*, Devin," Pat said. "Will you relax? Let's change the subject. Let's talk about danger. Have you been home yet?"

"Nope. Tonight for sure. I have to pick up something at the house."

Kelly laughed. "Aren't you afraid to go home? If I was your wife, I'd kill you."

"Come on, Kel," Devin said, smiling. "It's only been four days."

"I hope you get some *sleep* tonight," I said, nudging his knee with mine and passing the napkin note under the table. He took it, held it below the table and scanned my words.

"I think Devin will be satisfied with some *peace* if he's lucky enough to have her not speaking to him by now," Pat said.

"Hey." Devin nodded at the note. "This was *last* night?"

I nodded. He took his red pen out and, using my same napkin, printed one word. Yes.

"Yes, what?" I asked, that clammy feeling coming over me. I had plainly mentioned the baby and a ceremony.

With a serious look, he wrote in that neat red print:

A-your position
B-No ceremony
C-our son
D-Us

I read it, forgetting Kelly, Pat, the time and everything else. Then I looked at Devin. Rapidly he wrote:

Perhaps you do not realize…but of course you do. You know not how perceptive you are. Fear not, for your rank is about to become known. The world needs a prince of peace. I will do my best to provide the world with what it needs.

He pushed the napkin into my hand and signaled the waitress for the check. "You two, split. We'll take care of this. We have more time." He kissed me. "I'll see you at five."

We drove back to the plant in silence, Kelly not speaking until we'd parked the car and were on our way into the building. "Devin's still on that baby kick, huh?" she said finally.

"You could read that?" I walked fast to keep up.

"How could I help it? Bold red capitals. Neat clear print. Even upside down, I could see what it was about. What the hell is *with* him? What's going on?"

"Never mind, Kelly. You really don't want to know."

We were approaching our office, but Lola wasn't back yet.

"Well, we made it on time," Kelly announced proudly. Then, with a worried look at me, went in to her machine and the office was relatively quiet for the rest of the day.

12   The four o'clock groan went off, as usual, by Kelly, protesting that enough was enough.
"Lolaaaaa…I can't take it anymore!"
Lola stepped into our room.

"My back hurts," Kelly said, now quietly. "Can I take tomorrow off?"

"Well, sure," Lola replied. "And…uh…what should we do with your paycheck?"

"Shit. Tomorrow's payday. I forgot."

Lola gave me a disgusted look. "And *you*. I don't even feel sorry for you. You *could* try going to bed tonight."

"Shh, Lola. " Kelly pulled out a nail file. "You'll wake her up."

There was the sound of approaching footsteps. A loud hey-hey-hey.

"Just what we needed," Kelly quipped. "Top off the old day."

"Hey, Mama, what's happening?" As usual, he made no attempt to conceal the volume of his voice. Lola waved him into our office.

"Shh…Devin, will you pipe down? Maurice turns on the intercom every day at four and broadcasts us."

"Hey, Lola baby, I'm off work now. Prince Maurice can't say zilch-point-shit to me right now. If he does, I'll just—" He assumed a fighter's stance and popped an imaginary Mussolini in the nose.

"Well, *she's* not off yet. At least as far as the company is concerned. Kerry, can you at least sit up?"

"Hey, lighten up on her, Mama. She's tired." He plopped down on the step.

"Look at that poor, huddled heap of fatigue," Kelly cooed.

Lola looked from me to Devin. "Which one, Kelly? I wonder if they liven up any when they leave here at night."

"I don't know, Lola. They sure don't look like rumor material right now."

The phone buzzed on local and Kelly grabbed it. "Yeah, what now? Oh. For Lola?" She nodded at Lola. "It's Mark."

"I'll take it on my phone," she said, gently kicking Devin. "At least move over."

After she'd left the room, Devin sat down in Hannah's empty chair and caught my hand in mid-filing. "Hey…"

I looked at him through bloodshot eyes. "I'm okay. Just exhausted, like you."

"I guess it's good I *am* going home tonight. At least you'll sleep."

I gave him a tired smile, but it really was an effort. "I guess."

"Well, I can hang around for a while. I'll wait for you so I can walk you to your car."

"No, Devin. That's forty minutes away. Just go home and crash if you can. You look like I feel."

"Well, okay, lady." He squeezed my hand and then leaned over and kissed me.

"Oh my God, our department is rated X," Kelly said with a sigh.

"Oh, buzz off, Kelly." Devin swatted her playfully on the back and stood up. Then to me: "I love you, Kerry."

"I love you too, Devin. I'm going to miss you tonight."

"Look," Kelly interrupted disgustedly. "Can't you go home with her and just *sleep*? Or is that impossible?"

"*Devin!*" Lola's warning from the other room.

"Okay, okay…*later* !" He stomped into Lola's office and pointed to his watch. "Write down five minutes. I'll pay you for your time tomorrow."

Lola called me in when she'd hung up the phone.

"Okay, Lola, I'll tell him."

"You'll tell who what?"

"Devin. You don't want him in here without a reason, right?"

"Well, that sounds good for starters, but you could also tell him to quit parking in front of the building like he's been doing all week. Charlie saw his van out there today and blew his stack."

"He says he's getting tickets when he parks on the street."

"He can take that up with Tim, but in the meantime, tell him to keep his ass out of that spot tomorrow…or…don't say I didn't warn you. Now here's what I called you in for. That was Mark on the phone. He wants to come over tomorrow after work, you know, his usual weekend visit. I didn't want to ask you with Devin in there. I figure you guys don't need an eleven-year-old around right now."

"No, it's okay. Is that all you wanted?"

"Uh-huh."

"No problem. Tell Mark I'll pick him up after work tomorrow."

"You sure, now?"

"Yes. Devin would love to meet Mark and I *know* Mark wants to meet *him*."

That evening I had nothing on my mind but sleep. Exhaustion had finally caught up with me and the second I had the girls in bed I crashed, sleeping from eight-thirty until I awoke naturally at six. There were no dreams that I could remember, and only that dull thud of a chest pain to remind me of the week's events when I first opened my eyes.

Tim saw me when I punched in Friday morning, but he ignored my greeting when I passed his office. Devin was nowhere around, nor did he call all day. Even Kelly stayed pretty much to the charges postings, running off day after day of tickets, matching me until we were finally caught up at five. Still no word from Devin. I wondered how his night had gone at home and if he'd gotten any sleep.

I walked to the exit, punched out, and looked around the drivers' room and back offices. Not finding him, I concluded that he must be waiting for me outside.

He was. The truck yard seemed to be the hangout at the moment. Most of the drivers were standing around bullshitting, and Devin walked right over to me as I stepped out into the lot.

"Hey…it's about time." He took me by the hand and looked around for Pat.

"Hey, Devin!" Joey yelled from the hood of his fleet truck. "Kiss her one time for me!"

I looked up at him, his legs dangling from his absurd bleachers, and smiled. "Hi, Joey."

"Whatdayasay, Ker?"

"Hey, Dev." Pat climbed up beside Joey. "Don't forget one for me. Lucky stiff."

Devin hugged me tighter with one arm and started walking. "You're all jealous!" he yelled back, and we made the run across the street. He seemed to be in an exceptionally good mood, and completely recharged as if he, too, had finally slept.

"Boy, I missed you, Devin," I told him and he hugged me affectionately, unmindful of the employees scattered all over the sidewalks, in cars, and even passing us in company trucks.

"Hey, I missed you too. All night *and* all day. When I got home last night, it was pretty late. Around nine. I stayed to help Pat get the paperwork finished so we could both get out of here, so of course there was no dinner waiting. But that's cool. Apparently, she'd made dinner every night this week when I didn't show, so I'm not blaming her there. Besides, I was too damn tired to eat. I just went to my room and crashed."

"Thank God. You got some sleep. I thought she might try to keep you up."

"She was already in bed. But she *was* up early this morning wanting to talk while I was trying to get ready for work. I told her to save it for tonight and we'd talk then. We do need to actually. A lot of details we have to work out for who's keeping what and how she's going to go back." He slipped his arm around me.

"You're pretty wound up. How come?"

"This is *Friday*." He beamed happily. "I just get off on Fridays, especially payday Fridays. Everybody is so hyped up and glad 'cause it's the weekend, and besides, I haven't seen you all day and won't see you tonight, so yeah, I'm pretty happy right now, even if it won't last more than a few minutes." He squeezed my shoulder. "I just wish I could be packing up to move in with you instead of going home to pack for this trip up north. Thanksgiving just feels so far away. Oh, by the way, is Tim acting strange towards you?"

"Funny you should ask. He didn't even answer me when I greeted him this morning. And up until today, he's been surprisingly nice towards me, even on all those days when you were late. It would have been more logical for him to be pissed at me then. But today, when you'd been home last night and probably on time this morning, I thought it was safe to say hello and he gave me the cold shoulder."

"Yeah, I figured," he replied. We'd reached my car, but I didn't make a move to get in. I was in no hurry to leave. Devin ran a hand through his curls. "Me and Tim had a long rap just a few minutes ago. About *everything*."

I looked at him. "Yeah?"

"Yeah. It was good, too. You know this supervisor job of mine?"

"I was beginning to wonder if you still were, what with all the routes you've been on lately."

"Well, it's not important, the routes I'm doing. I still get my salary, and I did agree to do the vacations and stand-ins, but guess who's getting transferred to the Chicago office as soon as Johnny retires from the route room there."

The blood must have drained out of my face. "Not you."

"No, *Tim*. And guess who takes over here."

"You?"

"No." He gave me an exasperated look. "Pat!"

"And you get Pat's job?"

"Yup." He waved to a driver whizzing past in a company truck.

"Permanently?"

"That's what he said. That's why he called me in today. There I was, prepared for a big fight about how it's been all week, me being late and all, and he and Pat are just sitting there grinning. That's why the guys were so hopped up tonight when we were leaving. You know, that's at least forty a week more for us, and I'll be in the office *all* the time, like Pat is now. Money's something that never used to mean a great deal to me, but now, since I've found *you*...well, I've been thinking of getting rid of the van. That's a couple hundred a month I don't need to waste on payments." He hopped up on the hood of my car and pulled me closer to him. "Now there's a reason to make money and cut expenses. More for you and the kids. Damn, I'm going to miss you so much tonight. What time will you get home?"

"Well, I'm picking up Mark, so I'll be at Lola's for a while. I never get *right* out of there."

"Okay, babe. Man, I love you. I wish I didn't have to divide myself up in threes like this. Pretty soon, I'll only be here at the plant, or with you. I wish it was already that way but—" He kissed me long and hard, then jumped to the ground to open my car door. "*Now* I'll really hear about it. I just broke a sacred rule, and look who's watching us."

I glanced toward the plant. The three musketeers. Not just Charlie and Maurice, but Perry Jason himself stood on the sidewalk in front of the place. Devin smiled as another truck went by, and the driver, seeing our kiss, blasted the horn as if cheering us on.

"There goes Ethan," Devin observed aloud. "Well, even *he* can't ruin this day for me. Come on. Let's get you going. Pat's being a nice guy, but I can't hang out here much longer, much as I'd like to. I'll be here till we lock up, but I will call you before I punch out."

He ruffled my hair and took off at a trot down the street, saluted the three bosses as he passed, and continued on into the truck yard. I sighed, started my car and gunned the engine, glad it was Friday too. By Monday, hopefully, they'd have forgotten all about our little street scene.

When I glided into Lola's driveway, the front door opened and Mark ran out, reaching my car door before I could even shut the engine off.

"Can you wait till I eat? My mom's just putting supper on now." He followed me to the front door, his cheeks flushed, ruddy with excitement. With those ocean-blue eyes and platinum-blond hair, he looked like the poster boy for the Aryan race. I could never understand why he enjoyed these weekends so much, but we sure enjoyed having him.

"Come on in, Kerry," Lola called from the kitchen which was just to the left after you entered. The aroma of ham and scalloped potatoes made my mouth water.

I poked my head in. "Do I have to take my ring off?"

She laughed. "Oh, come on."

I ended up eating dinner with them, and it was no surprise when Elwood, her husband, brought up Halloween night, as close as we were getting to the end of the month.

"So, you're going to a witchcraft wedding, are you?" he asked. "What *is* that exactly? What takes place at something like that?"

I shrugged. "I really don't know, Elwood. I've never been to one and

Devin hasn't really told me anything."

"Not even what to wear?"

"Oh, well, that, yes. But I had to ask him. I didn't think I really had, as the old saying goes, a thing to wear."

"Well, that sounds about right from what I hear," he replied, buttering a slice of corn bread. "Nothing. Witches don't wear anything at their meetings. Or at least, that's what I've heard."

Lola raised her eyebrows. "And you guys want *me* to be matron of honor at your wedding?"

"That's bullshit, Mama. I do know *that* much about it."

"Well, I've *also* heard they don't wear clothes. What is the point, then?"

"Clothes supposedly hamper the aura…which they say needs freedom, but look how stupid that is. Power that's supposed to go clear across the universe stopped short by somebody's shirt. It's bullshit. Just an excuse to strip for the sake of exhibition."

"Oh. Then you'll be dressed."

I laughed. "In something dark. Hey, your fridge *does* look pretty good in the kitchen. It matches the stove, huh?"

"Don't change the subject," Lana put in, as she joined us at the dinner table. "It was just getting good."

"Too bad. I gotta go," I said, pushing my plate away and rising. "He said he'd call, and I still have to pick up the kids."

Pammy and George came right over when they heard I had Mark for the weekend, and the house began filling up like it did every Friday night. We had a couple hours to talk before the stampede started, and Pam wanted to hear everything. I caught her up on the events of the past few days, the referrals to the baby, and all that had happened since the lunch at Walgreens. When I showed her the napkin with Devin's red printed message, she said dubiously, "Gee, I don't know, Ker. I'd find out a little more about this baby thing."

"Well, I was really worried at first, but Devin…you know…he's just too good for it to be anything bad."

"I'll go along with *that* one," she said, laughing suddenly. "Really, Ker. You never told me. I never expected—"

"Pam thought Devin would be some older straight dude," George explained. "She couldn't believe you'd come up with some hippie-looking dude that smokes pot and everything."

"But I've smoked pot for the last two years," I objected.

"Yeah, but let's face it Ker. If it wasn't for that, well, you're a straight chick."

"Yeah," Pammy agreed. "Remember how me and Bonnie hid her stash from you when we first came here to live with you? *We* didn't know you had switched to grass. We just assumed you were still on that juice trip. The last time we'd seen you in Allentown, you were drinking all the time and *hated* pot."

"Pam. That was four years ago."

"You still *look* straight," George insisted, "so we didn't expect you to come up with someone like Devin. Don't get me wrong. You guys make a great pair, and he's really far out, but…it was still a shock."

"You'ns *are* a perfect match," Pam agreed quickly. "Really. Now, I can't even imagine you with anyone else. It's so weird. Like you've always been with him. After meeting him, it didn't even surprise me that you two are getting married. It's just seems that natural."

"Just think. If it weren't for the ring, how different this week would have been," I mused aloud. "I might never have gotten to know him."

Pam and George stared at me, as if stunned. "It's only been a *week?*" Pam asked.

"One week tonight."

"God *damn*, Ker," George breathed. "That don't sound right."

Pam counted on her fingers. "Holy shit. She's right. It was *last* Friday."

The personal talk ended as new people came and went. Lana stopped by to say hello, on her way to visit my young landlord, Chris, who resided on the other side of the duplex. Bonnie and Jake stopped in, as did Coleen who was looking for Lana. By the time everyone was gone, I was ready for bed, exhausted again. It was only then that I realized that Devin had not called.

Mark was good company for me Saturday, keeping me occupied as his personal chauffeur. The girls had adopted him as an honorary big brother, and we spent Saturday exploring the occult shop again, dining at the A&W Root Beer stand, and taking in a drive-in movie that evening. On Sunday, we combed the streets and malls looking for a bike shop that sold bicycle handle grips, to no avail. Through it all, Devin...always Devin...where was he, and what was happening? By four o'clock, I gave up any hope of seeing him before Monday morning at work, and Kelly's warning about the shackles of the married thing occurred to me occasionally. I stubbornly pushed the worry aside. After all, Devin was nearly seventy miles away.

When Mark burst into the house, wild with excitement that a van was driving up, it was with no expectations that I checked the front yard, only to stare in disbelief that it really *was* Devin.

We were both there before he could even shut the engine off. He jumped to the ground, opened the side sliding door for Mark whose eyes were now bugging, and introduced himself quickly, all the while hugging me close to him. Mark charged into the interior and Devin laughed, still crushing me tightly as if I were going to follow Mark into the van.

I was so happy I couldn't see straight. "I can't believe you made it," I whispered.

"I told you I'd try, didn't I?"

"Yes, but you also said you'd call Friday and you didn't, remember?"

He looked at me sheepishly. "I did once, but you weren't home yet. No one answered, and I never did try back. I haven't stopped thinking of you, though, and trying to get up here. I've been busy working on my neighbor's car...well, it all sounds like excuses, really."

"No, it's okay," I assured him. "I just meant I missed you, not where were you."

"I felt like I was away from home. Visiting someone else's apartment. I'll be glad when I really am living in one place. Here." He nodded at my duplex, then turned to Mark who was emerging from the van. "Come on, dude, let's go in the house. I'll let you steer it later."

Mark was jabbering a mile a minute, rattling off the features the van was equipped with in manufacturer's terms, hero-worship shining in his eyes when he looked at Devin. Meanwhile, the girls burst from the house, apparently just realizing Devin was here, and came running towards us. Mandy tripped on the sidewalk and went sprawling on the concrete. Instantly she was in tears, and Devin reached her before I could. He picked her up, dusted her off and dried her eyes with his fingers.

"Shh, Mandy…be quiet a minute, and I'll show you how to make it stop hurting."

Mandy took a breath, her sniffles subsiding, and Devin took her forefinger and placed it end to end with his own. I glanced at Mark, who was watching intently.

"Now," Devin said gently. "Look up at the sky."

Mandy looked at me.

"Can we be alone, Mom?" Devin asked, looking at me too.

"Sure. Come on, Mark…Michelle…"

"I want to watch," Mark said. Michelle crossed her arms in agreement.

I went into the house, and when I looked outside minutes later, Devin had them all playing Frisbee in the yard. I wondered what he'd said to calm her. Minutes later we were all ushered into the van with Mark as copilot and sometimes steer-man for a hair-raising run to McDonald's, the treat on Devin.

When we called Lola to tell her we were bringing Mark home, she asked to speak to Devin.

"Mama needs a bottle of water put on her cooler," he informed me when he'd hung up. "Let's get that done so we can get back here and get some sleep."

I gaped at him. "You're going to *stay* tonight?"

"I can't go back there, Kerry. The weekend was too long as it was. I want to be here with *you*. This is where it's at for me now, you know?"

I knew. For me, too. There would never be any turning back now.

Monday, needless to say, Devin started out on the wrong foot. Late again.

13

Kelly met me at the time clock at eight-thirty. For once, we had practically arrived together.

"Where were *you*, Miss King?"

I grinned at her. "Why? Where were you? Up at the coffee shop?"

"Since eight o'clock. Boy, you're never there when you say you're going to be."

"I usually am, but we got up late again."

"What? Devin still hasn't gone home yet?"

"Well, he did, but he came back."

"Kerry, you are going to get him fired or killed or both. Devin never used to come in late all the time. Never. Okay, maybe it's not your fault, but you're getting blamed for it, I bet."

We punched in and headed for our office. Kelly pointed silently to Tim's open office door. When we passed, Tim looked up, but there was no morning greeting.

"Good morning, Tim," Kelly said and when there was no response as we walked away she added, "See what I mean?"

"He did the same thing on Friday, and Devin had been home the night before. At work on time. Early, if I know Devin."

"Doesn't matter, Ker. Tim needs a blamee, and he doesn't want it to be his big star, Devin. So you're automatically responsible now if he screws up. That's why it should be a little more discrete, but no…you two have to parade arm-in-arm, necking in Lums—oh, hi Aunt Kim!"

Kim had just stepped into the hallway. "Hi Kel…Ker…say, Ker, what did you do to poor Devin last night? He literally dragged himself in here this morning."

"He shouldn't have," Kelly said. "I heard he got plenty of sleep." We continued down the hall and Kelly added, "You getting the point, Kerry?"

"Yeah," I said disgustedly. "I'm starting to see what you mean."

When we reached our office, Mama was there with her coffee, smiling as usual.

I held up my empty hands apologetically, remembering I had no muffin today.

"That's okay. You're fired."

Kelly cracked up, and Lola went on unemotionally, "Oh, and Devin said to tell you he will be gone most of the day. He's on a route."

"You *saw* Devin?"

"He left about an hour ago."

"Did he look upset?"

Lola looked at me curiously. "Why, should he have?"

"He was late again. What else did he say?"

"Just that. And Charlie saw his van parked in front of the building again this morning and he is *hot*. Why can't he just park in the street like everyone else?"

He says his plates are illegal and he has no inspection sticker. He's been getting tickets, and Tim won't give him time off to take care of it. He's here till dark every night."

She sighed. "I just wish he would take it up with Tim."

Pat walked in at that moment and caught the gist of the conversation. "Kerry, if you have a set of keys, I'll move it for him. Perry Jason just mentioned it to Maurice. Everyone's trying to figure out what the hell Devin's doing. It's like he's daring someone, or something."

"What would I be doing with his keys? All I can do is tell him again if he calls."

At eleven o'clock Ethel poked her head into our office and beamed dramatically. "Devin's on twenty-two, and he wants to speak to Kerry."

"Thank you, Ethel," Lola said irritably, and motioned for me to hit it. I snatched the phone and punched the blinking button.

"Hello, Devin?"

"Yeah, what's up?"

"What're you doing on a route today?"

"Well, I almost stayed in, but I made a big mistake with Tim. I let him know I liked staying in."

"How'd you manage *that?*"

'First he said 'Devin, I'm keeping you here today,' and I said 'Far out'...then he immediately said, 'On second thought, I just thought of something you can do.' So here I am, practically south of the border."

I laughed. "Of all the dumb things to say."

Lola was motioning to me and making steering motions with her hands and I nodded. "Oh, Dev...it's becoming this big deal about your parking up front. You're going to get in trouble if you keep doing it."

"What do you mean?"

"Only office people are allowed to park there."

"So...everywhere else I park, the cops slap a fuckin' ticket on it. I've got three already. And Ah ain't lately goin' t' git another one. If the company can't give me jist an hour to take care of it, then they're just goin' t' have t' put up wit' mah unsightly van, and jist let one of them suckers say somethin' t' me!"

That heavy southern drawl was back...midsentence. Lately Devin was sounding black over the phone, especially when he was irritated. It was hard to match up the voice with the face I knew.

"Calm down, Dev...just talk to Tim and explain what's going on."

"Well, the point is," he went on in that same slurry drawl, "Ah've already explained it to Mistah Tim, an' Ah waz under the impression he waz lettin' it rahd."

"He apparently hasn't passed the word on to anyone else."

He was quiet for a minute, then finally, "Okay, I see what's going down now."

The drawl was suddenly gone. He sighed. "It took awhile, but I'm not stupid. Tim's playing this route game with me, all the while he's patting me on the back and saying what a good dog I've been. Like, go ahead, fraternize, and every time you do we'll send you out on the truck. And every time I'm on a route I can't take the time to legalize the van."

"Is it really as bad as all that, Devin?"

"I'm here, ain't I? And you're *there*. And my job is supposed to be there too, so I ought to take that fancy salary and tell Tim to shove it. You having any problems in your department because of us?"

"No, but with Mama here, there wouldn't be."

"Yeah, Mama *has* been cool. What gets me is that there was no mention of this on Friday when I thought our talk had everything straightened out. Well, that's cool. I don't need this job."

"Yeah, but Devin, you were late again. Would that have had any bearing on all this?"

"It shouldn't. We talked about that *before* he said he was keeping me in. In fact we spent a good half hour on the Why Devin Is Late subject."

"Jesus. You're getting it from all angles, aren't you?"

"Tim had every opportunity to mention the parking thing this morning. But he was too busy wanting to know what was going on with *us*. I have to keep reminding him that it may *be* this way until he gives me time off to drive my wife up north and get her settled there. First he starts out with, 'What happened, Devin?, you can tell me,' and when I did, twenty minutes later he's agreeing to stop down and take some of the furniture off my hands. He may give me six hundred for it, and that's enough to rent a trailer and get the rest of it packed for the move."

I was stunned. "Are you kidding me?"

"No. See, babe, Tim really *does* like me. I'm sure he was thinking 'oh no, Devin's running around till all hours with a shack job and I'm losing a good man because of it.' I finally got it through his head that this ain't no temporary fling. I told him you're *it*, and if he doesn't like my choice in a wife that I'd just take my services elsewhere. So now he's going to help me disassemble that apartment down south and even agreed to give me two extra days off besides the weekend to make the trip. He thinks Thanksgiving break might be slow enough to let me go. So, everything was cool, or so I thought."

"He's still not responding to me when I pass in the morning," I said.

He was quiet for another long moment. "Okay. I'm putting it together, and this shit is going to stop. You know, technically Pat's supposed to open up, and I wouldn't even be considered late by my official hours. Look how late I'm here at night, route or no route. The only way they can make me late is to schedule me for a route. See the game?"

"Yeah, I think so."

"Well, don't you get upset," he said. "This is my problem and I will take care of it. I believe Mr. Jason is at the root of all this, and he ain't lately going to be hard to get rid of. And I guess it's getting to be about that time."

"What do you mean?"

"You'll see. Halloween's coming, remember? There's only one day that's more powerful than Halloween, and that's a birthday, and I happen to have both of them coming up on the same day. You know, I've never been this happy…not in all the years of my existence…and for once in my life I feel like climbing up on the roof of the plant and shouting *'Hey, everybody…that chick in the billing office…Kerry King…I love her'*…and you know something, babe, they'd just punish me by scheduling me for the next open route. So…it looks like ol' Devin is just going to have to take matters into his own hands. I love you, babe. They aren't going to get away with this. That sucker Jason's time has come, and he has to go. That's it."

I was too choked up to speak. Lola poked her head around the doorway, signaling a powwow, and I reluctantly told him I had to go. "I wish I could…talk…" I began.

"Hey, it's cool. I know you can't. I'll see you when I get in."

Lola looked at me with raised eyebrows when I entered her office. "Everything okay?"

"Oh, sure," I said unconvincingly with a sigh. "It always is."

Lunch was quiet without Devin, and even Pat had bowed out, apologizing that Tim had requested his company for lunch. The day itself felt like the worst since the whole thing had started only ten days ago. Kelly seized the rare opportunity of privacy to talk to me while we were out.

"So. You're really getting married, huh? It sure is hard to believe. And what's even weirder is that now it seems like you two have always been a thing since I've known you."

"That's how *we* feel," I told her. "It's everyone *else* that seems to resent it."

"I know. But I've never seen you this way, Kerry. Like you're moonstruck. And after all that talk about having no use for men."

"Oh, that was just a standing joke, Kel. I thought you knew that."

"No. You had me fooled. Is Devin *really* driving his wife up north in November?"

"You doubt it?"

"Well, now I don't. It's all over the phone room, so Devin must be the one telling everyone. *You* never tell them anything."

"Have *you?*"

"What do *I* know? It's Devin, I'm telling you. He sure is going out of his way to let everyone know how he feels about you. Take Kim…when I passed the phone room today she says 'Oh, hi, Kelly…tell Kerry that Devin called and said to tell her he loves her.' Now what other way is the phone room supposed to take that?"

My depression deepened. This uncontrollable thing that was growing by the day in leaps and bounds was fouling up Devin's whole job. I picked up the check. "I guess we'd better get going. No sense in being late today."

"I wouldn't worry about it," Kelly said, picking up her purse. "With Devin and Pat gone, they wouldn't say anything anyway."

"I really missed them today."

She gave me a sideways glance. "I know you did."

Lola nabbed me when we returned and beckoned me to her desk. "Did Devin promise Mark a set of bike handle grips?"

"Jeez…he might have. They were quite an issue over the weekend, and when Devin got there, the malls were all closed. Sunday, you know. He mentioned he had a set at home. Maybe that's what Mark was talking about. He'll be going home tonight. I'll remind him."

"Oh, he's going home? What's the occasion?"

"He has to get his house unorganized. Pack. Talk to the wife. You know."

"I'd say it was unorganized enough." She laughed. "Well, okay. I just didn't know what Mark was talking about. I'll tell him Devin might bring them tomorrow."

For once, we finished posting early, and it was blessedly quiet without the machines for the rest of the afternoon. With the quiet came the opportunity to talk and kid around a little about the plant. Even Lola set her own work aside to help us file and to tease me about Devin and the upcoming Halloween wedding. Through it all, I kept a constant ear out for Devin's voice. He made it by four o'clock.

"Hey, Mama! Where you hiding?"

"In here, little boy."

Devin entered with an indignant look. "Hey, get off that little boy shit."

Lola motioned for him to sit down on the forbidden step. It was the only seat available. Devin flatly refused.

"Yeah, sure," he said. "I ain't allowed to sit there any other day, so that leads me to conclude it's another trap to—"

"Oh, hush. Sit down will you?"

He crossed his arms belligerently and remained leaning against the doorjamb. "And if it's business, you'll have to see me in the morning. Today, I'm just a route salesman, and officially off work."

"Where does he get his energy?" Kelly asked, smirking.

"Look, if you expect my daughter's hand in marriage, you'd better learn a little respect around here." Lola gave him a wide smile. "Now. Sit down."

"You know, there's such a thing as carrying this *mama* bit a little too far."

"Okay, stand up then, Clyde. I just want to know when you're bringing her to work after your wedding."

"By eight-thirty. Just when the plant starts working. *If* you're lucky. And I may just tell her to stay home that day. So don't push your luck." He returned her wide smile.

"Oh? And who's going to take her to the unemployment office, or are *you* staying out that day, too?"

"I'll definitely be out that day. Tim already knows. It's the second day I've *ever* asked for off, and he's okayed it. Religious freedom, you know?"

"Yeah? Well you'd better remind him before you leave *here* that night."

"I will." He eased himself down on the step at last. "You're sure it's okay to sit here, now…"

"No. It's too late. You had your chance," Lola said, getting up. "Get off that step."

"Oh, hell, I'm leaving." Devin motioned to me that he'd meet me at the exit. "Later, Mama. Jeez. I couldn't ask for a more affable mother-in-law." He blew Lola a kiss and ducked out.

Lola looked at me and laughed. "He," she said, "is not well."

Janet came by seconds after his departure. "Hi, Aunt Lola! Got any extra typing for all your little nieces in the phone room?"

"Scads of it." She handed Janet a big stack of ledgers. Jan poked her head into our room.

"Hi Kerry…Kelly…Hannah! Hey, Ker, my dad and me saw you walking with Devin to your car on Friday. My dad said first you just walked together, and the next time he was holding your hand, and then on Friday he had his arm around you, and then—"

"Better stay home tomorrow," Kelly interjected. "You know what their next step is."

"Out, Janet," Lola spoke up. "We don't know anything about those crazy rumors."

Janet gave Lola a puzzled look and left.

14 The next three days were a complete swing in the opposite direction. Devin remained on the route Tuesday, Wednesday and Thursday, and left for home immediately after he walked me to my car. His home, not mine.

Neither of us said it, but silently we agreed to the way things had to be, at least until the end of November. Devin was on time every day, and although I didn't see him much, he called in often during his routes. If I was at lunch, he left messages for me with the phone girls, and they drooled as they delivered them. He walked me to my car every day at five and called me nights before he locked up and left the plant. But he was never late for work, and he never gave anyone a reason to blame our relationship for anything at the water plant. I knew he was being cool because of the friction between himself and Perry Jason, but sometimes I wondered about what he had said to me. Sometimes, when he passed Jason in the hall, he seemed to smile smugly at him, as though he knew Perry's time was getting short. As if he was betting on something he had right in his pocket and knew he couldn't lose.

On our walks to the car each day, Devin filled me in on everything that was going on. The packing was tedious as was the separating of items that each was to keep. The departure date was set for Thanksgiving break, the last four days of November, which was still quite a ways off to suit me. I kept my opinions to myself.

In spite of our own separation this week, Devin told me that his brother, Trevor, had noticed a change in Devin's moods since he'd met me, and that Trevor had said that he didn't have to meet me to know I was good for him. That he could see that Devin was finally happy. This made me feel a little better.

Devin's brother wasn't the only one to notice a change in him, but it wasn't in our favor. The routemen were whispering about Devin's sudden change in where he was spending his nights. The plant in general was never one to keep its group opinion to itself, and the latest vibe was quickly becoming evident. If Devin was so serious about Kerry, then why was he spending this week at home with his wife?

Kelly voiced that one bluntly at lunch on Wednesday, and I tried to sound confident as I explained it to her. Devin was trying to keep peace and help pack up the house. Kelly listened politely but she didn't comment. I was glad she didn't because I was having enough trouble quieting my own disturbed feelings and rumblings of doubt. I was almost starting to wonder myself.

Thursday was Kelly's day to ride with a route salesman. This was Perry's latest brainstorm, the idea being to give each office person a chance to see what the routeman went through every day. All the phone girls had had their turns. Today was Kelly's turn, and Bill Whippet, an older driver, was the lucky man. Devin had come in miraculously early, in time for lunch, so Pat and Devin took me to Lums where we spent forty minutes talking about Devin's packing progress. It was all on a serious note, and I missed Kelly's interjections and smart remarks.

Friday morning, to my surprise, Devin showed up at the coffee shop and slid into the booth opposite me.

"Am I detecting a little doubt?" he asked in greeting. "You seemed a little down at lunch yesterday."

I shrugged and reached for the sugar. "Not really. It's just that everyone's wondering if we're really serious. It's all over the plant that you've been home all week."

Devin added some cream to my coffee and tipped my chin gently until I was looking into his eyes. "I hope *you* understand," he said quietly, and I looked away toward an approaching Jane, who had Devin's coffee balanced on her tray with someone else's breakfast.

"I'll be right with you kids," she told us, setting the mug on the table and hurrying down the aisle.

I looked back at Devin. His eyes were closed, and a lit cigarette was burning its way down to the filter between his fingers. A wave of sympathy rippled through me. Devin seemed to have aged a year in the past week, and I wondered if he was sleeping very much at home. Black hollow bags smoldered under reddened eyes, and there were fatigue lines now that I'd never noticed before. I nudged his hand holding the cigarette and he shook his head and blinked. Then he stubbed out the cigarette.

"Sleeping?" I smiled.

"Yeah, I guess I was." He rubbed his eyes and took my hand. "Sorry."

"For what? Hey, Dev, did you know you don't breathe when you're asleep?"

He smiled. "Yeah? You been ethereally projecting down to my apartment at night?"

I laughed. "If I knew how to do that, you'd *really* be tired." I squeezed his hand tightly. "It must really be rough on you right now, huh?"

His grip tightened over mine. "Not rough on me, Kerry, but not very fair to you. If I were in your place, I'd be wondering too."

"Well, maybe I'm just a little too concerned about what everyone thinks. And that's not fair to you. I do know what's going on and why you have to be there now."

"Thank you. I guess I needed to hear that."

I glanced out the large window to the route truck parked in the lot. "You going to be in or out today?"

"Out for a while. But I'll be back today before noon. Tim's actually giving me some time off to get the van inspected. *Then* I'll be able to get the plates. You know what an issue *that's* been."

"Oh, you got that settled. Thank God. Where did you park today?"

"Same place I've been parking, and will be until I get the van up-to-date." He glanced at his watch. "I've gotta split. I'll order Mama's muffin and pay for it on this check. Don't forget it when you leave."

I started to down the last of my cup, wanting to walk him out, but he gestured for me to stay put.

"There's no reason for you to get up yet. It's only seven-thirty."

"Kelly's back. Do you think you guys might make it for lunch today?"

In answer, he leaned over and kissed me. "I'll call you."

I was so used to the chest feeling by now that I barely noticed it anymore. I watched him with mixed feelings as he crossed the lot to his truck.

With so much free time at night I was losing more sleep reading and listening to my country albums than I did when Devin was there, but when I laid those distractions aside, there was no getting away from my own doubts.

With all the changes I had seen in Devin's 'moods,' voices, and that *something* he couldn't tell me yet, I was almost taking a deep breath from the strange week before. There was still that worry about the future innocent life he was planning to bring into the world, and things had been going too fast for me to process. But my love for him was growing at such a rapid rate each day that I knew it was now too serious to walk away from, even if I wanted to. The mere thought of life without Devin was now unimaginable, yet the fear of that mysterious *something* was gaining equal audience within my inner self. I had a little too much time on my hands not to be replaying the conversations and incidents.

At least the week of separation from Devin had helped to lessen the worry of Devin's many sides. With so much focus on the plant, Devin was just Devin. Laughing, smiling, teasing and loud, he made no attempt to conceal his feelings for me during the workday. Daring the mass mind of the plant to approach him for an explanation of just what he thought he was doing.

Sitting in the booth of the restaurant this morning, I found my coffee had grown cold, and my thoughts were still uneasy. My sympathies were with Devin, though. Here he was trying to disassemble a house and juggle the remainder of his time between me and the plant. I wondered how long he could keep this up and still maintain that uncanny cool, despite his fatigue. I finally gathered up my purse and keys. Work went on, no matter what.

I picked up the muffin and took my time crossing the boulevard. It was still early.

The sight of Kelly sitting there on our forbidden step at 8:15 in the morning was cold shock therapy. Kelly was never early.

"Here comes Rosemary now," Lola said, grinning as she spotted the white to-go bag I was toting. "Oh, *super*, I didn't eat breakfast this morning."

I grinned back and tossed the bag to her. "Am I seeing things, or is that our Kelly here before she has to be? Or is my watch wrong?"

"I would have met you at the coffee shop, but you're never there when I go. Besides, I don't even know what I'm doing *here.*"

"You should have gone, Kelly," Lola said, wiping her hands on a napkin. "Maybe you could have conned breakfast out of Devin."

I looked at Lola suspiciously. "How do you know whether Devin was there or not?"

"I saw him just before he left. He said that's where he was going. Unless you two sit in separate booths now."

"He admitted he was going to stop there?"

"Well, Devin knows I wouldn't say anything. You forget. Devin and I practically started work at this place on the same day."

I was glad that everyone really liked Devin. It helped to still the uncertainties that were always churning inside me. But I couldn't dwell on them now. Already Lola and Kelly were back on the subject of Kelly's expedition yesterday, a subject my arrival this morning had apparently interrupted.

"You can't believe all the shit I walked through, Lola," Kelly wailed. "Ugh. Mud and slime and puddles! This construction site was huge. All the water cooler sites were scattered all over thirty different locations, and that Bill

Whippet...he made me walk with him while he delivered the water. He kept saying he wanted to make sure we girls knew what they went through every day, and I saw enough, believe me."

"Oh, I know," Lola said, laughing. "I spent the entire day at Maude Industries trying to straighten out their accounts. It *is* about thirty locations too."

"Thirty spread-*out* ones. Oh, Lola, I'm so worn out. Can I go home?"

"Was it fun, Kelly?" I asked.

"Yeah, but I kept wondering if you guys went to lunch. I really missed our big lunch date."

"Okay you guys." Lola sighed. "Don't get all...mushy. Jeez, you fight all day when you're together. I would think you'd have enjoyed the break."

"Well, she's lucky she didn't go," I said. "They figured out it was her turn to buy."

"That'll be the day." Kelly laughed. "We haven't been faster than Devin with those lunch checks yet. Hey, when do *you* get to go on a route, Kerry?"

"Yeah, Mama, that's right. Can I go with—"

"No way. Don't even think about it. Even if *I* were to okay it, Tim would never—"

"Okay, okay." I was laughing hard now. "I didn't really want to go anyway."

"Why not? You could go with any other driver."

"Yeah, but Joey already had his turn, and there's no good ones left."

"That's the way I feel," Lola agreed. "Charlie told me I should go too, but like you say, the drivers we really know well are...already used."

"Hey, Lola!" Kelly said brightly. "*You* could go with Devin!"

"That's true." Lola leered at me. "I wouldn't mind *Devin* at all."

"*Mama!*"

"Okay, look. You two get to work. Hannah's entitled to be late once in a while."

At eleven-thirty Devin buzzed us on the local line. "Would you ladies care to ride in a legal vehicle for lunch today?"

"You finally did it?"

"Yup. What time can you break out of there?"

"You name it, Dev. We're clear whenever you are."

"Far out. I'll buzz you when we're ready."

"So what's happening, Kelly?" Pat asked. "How was your field trip?" He sounded like he'd really missed her presence yesterday.

"Unbelievable. You guys go through that every day?"

"We did," Devin replied seriously, then added, "What am I saying? With all the routes I've been on, I still do."

"Well, whose fault is *that?*" Pat retorted. "Really, Devin. Of all people, *you* should know better than to let your hair down in front of Tim. When I heard you say *far out*, I just rolled my eyes. I knew what was coming."

Devin laughed. "That's cool. At least I have the system down now. You watch Monday and see if I'm on a route. When he says 'Devin, I have a route for you today,' I'll say *far out!* Then he'll say 'on second thought, Devin…'"

Everybody laughed. As dense as the big route manager was, it probably would work.

"While you're at it, Dev," I said innocently, "would you ask Tim if you can take me out on a route like all the other girls went on?"

Devin, Pat and Kelly roared.

"I wouldn't touch that with a ten-foot pole," Pat said.

"Babe." Devin, still laughing, lit a cigarette and looked at me. "There is no way in royal infrared *hell* that Tim would let me and you out of his sight on a company truck."

"Or on company time," Pat added.

"He'd know the water wouldn't get delivered." Devin hugged me, then added seriously, "Not that I wouldn't dig the hell out of it."

"Damn that Tim," I said, just as seriously.

"Actually, it's not Tim anyway," Devin said, now really serious. "If Perry Jason wasn't around, it probably *would* be okayed. Perry is the problem that needs to be eliminated. We get *him* out of the picture and the whole plant can go back to breathing."

"How're you planning to rub him out, you…commie?" Pat grinned. "He really hates you, you know."

"Well, he sure has made a lot of enemies," Kelly put in. "I'm surprised he has the guts to roam the halls back there in the wee small hours of the morning."

Devin stubbed his cigarette out, glanced at me, and smiled. "I wouldn't worry too much longer about Jason," he said.

"Oh yeah?" Pat crossed his arms smugly. "You got an assassination plot going?"

"In a sense. Just hang loose here for a couple of weeks. Halloween's not so far away, and…speaking of hanging, let's get out of here."

"We've got time, Devin. Shit, the girls aren't as paranoid as you are these days."

"What's going on with the wedding?" Kelly asked.

"Well, tonight's the legal ceremony. Oh, hey…" He turned to me suddenly. "I forgot to tell you. My father is moving here. He's going to be looking for a house to rent. I want you to meet him."

A picture of Samantha's regal warlock father from the TV Bewitched series flashed through my mind. "Is he anything like you, Devin?"

"He's my father."

"Enough said," Pat said with a sigh, downed his coffee and stood up. "Time to go."

Devin appeared in our office around 4:30, and he seemed anxious to get home. Trevor had stopped by the route room to remind Devin that he only had six days to come up with a suitable ceremony for the only wedding that *he* felt counted. Devin told us that he'd exhausted his supply of Wicca books searching for a ceremony, to no avail. None of his own books contained a wedding chapter, and he'd finally concluded that Wicca just didn't have one. This meant more work, because now he'd have to write one from scratch. He heaved a tired sigh as he related all this to me Friday afternoon.

"Well, I'm sure I have one," I told him. "But whether it's one you could use or not, I don't know."

"Wow. Don't say that. I've looked *everywhere*. And I can't wait till Monday, anyway, even if you do have one at home. I want to work on it over this weekend."

"Oh, Kerry probably has it in her purse," Kelly said. "I mean, why not? She carries everything else in there."

"It wouldn't surprise *me*," Lola agreed.

I began to fish through my purse as Kelly turned around to watch. "Lola, if she really has one, I'll…I'll die!"

"When's the funeral, Kel?" My hand located the little pocketbook that I knew contained the wedding chapter.

"Oh my God," Hannah murmured, her first non-business words of the day. "I don't believe it. She's *got* it."

I thumbed through it until I found the page and handed it to Devin. "Will this do?"

He scanned it over quickly and looked up at me gratefully. "Do you realize how much time and trouble you just saved me? This is *perfect*. I may have to change a few *thees* and *thous*, but otherwise, it's exactly what I've been looking for." He hugged me and tucked the book under his arm. "I'll call you," he promised, and bowed out for the day.

15 Friday night produced its usual stampede of visitors, all regulars who found their way to my house every weekend at one time or another. First, Lana and Colleen. They cruised in with Mark who had been invited for the weekend. Pammy arrived with George around nine. Even pregnant Bonnie and her husband Jake stopped by in hopes of meeting…the warlock. Everyone was in an upbeat mood, and the reefer was making the rounds when my young landlord Chris and his roommate Steve stopped over, packing the small living room like a sardine can. In one form or another, everyone had a question about Devin.

Chris wanted to know whose van he'd seen parked here off and on lately.

"That's Devin's," I told him.

"That tells me a lot," he said loudly, looking at Steve. "Like…you've noticed…she's got *so* many dudes around here every night."

Steve seemed a little wasted on something, and his eyes tried to focus in on his roommate, me and the conversation. "I've seen that van around. Does this Devin have black…sort of…bushy hair and…he's kinda tall?"

"That's him," George said.

"Yeah, I talked to him…outside…the other day. I haven't seen him around for a few days, though. Didn't he move in?"

"Not yet, but he will be, pretty soon."

Chris looked from me to Steve and back to me again. "Want to tell *me* what's going on? I'm only the *landlord*, I know but—"

"Devin is Kerry's…uh…new friend," Steve said slowly, his eyes half closed. "I came over to bum a joint, and Devin was here. You were in the shower, Ker, I guess. Anyway, he gave me a few. I thought that was pretty cool since I only asked for one. He seems to have a pretty good head on him."

"Devin never even mentioned it," I said, glad that Devin had made a good impression with the hippie next door.

Steve shrugged. "So he *is* moving in, huh?"

"It won't be for a while."

"Where's he at now?"

"At his brother's wedding."

"I gotta see *this* dude with my own eyes," Chris said, getting up. "I've never seen *any* dude over here that wasn't just a friend. You coming, Steve?"

Lana and Colleen rose to go with them. "See ya later, Ker," Lana said, offering a peace sign.

The house felt much roomier after they left. Pammy brought up her upcoming trip to Allentown. Evidently, she'd already informed George of her plans since she was speaking about right in front of him. "I'm leaving on Tuesday, and I'll be there visiting two weeks and, oh…Kerry…" she paused and looked at me. "If Devin's moving in soon, will it still be okay—?"

"Yes, it's still okay," I assured her, though I'd completely forgotten to mention to Devin that she'd been invited to move back in long before he'd come into the picture. Now, in my stoned state, I wondered how he *would* feel about that.

"Are you *sure*, Kerry? Things are different than when—"

"Than *last* week," George supplied with a touch of sarcasm. "What a difference a day makes," he added with a little melody.

"Don't worry about it, Pam. He won't care. He likes you."

"Stop and see my mom while you're there," Bonnie broke in. "I'd go with you, but…" she gestured to her swollen belly. "I haven't told *my* mom yet either."

"I know two mothers that are going to have a lynching when they read about that kid in the births section of the paper," Pam said, laughing. "I'll stop in, Bonnie. Want *me* to break the news to her?"

"No way. Not till Jake tells *his* mother."

"Oh, and give me that tapestry, Ker. Right now. Before I forget."

I looked up sadly at the tapestry, then at my ring, and decided it had been worth it. I got up with my sister, and together we removed it from the wall and folded it up.

"Wow, looks empty now," I said.

"It does," Pam agreed. "But if I don't bring it I'll never hear the end of it. I swear she reminds me every time she calls. Oh, and the Trojan Horse book. She's obsessed with me bringing that back."

"I believe it." I picked up the book from my desk and handed it to her. "Please. Gladly, get it out of here." My thoughts weren't on the tapestry or the book anymore. I turned to my cousin. "Jake, why *haven't* you told your mom yet?"

"Well, uh…" he began sheepishly. "I've made several attempts, but, well, it's never the right time, you know."

"It won't be the right time when it's born either," Bonnie snapped.

"You're a fine one to talk. What about *your* mother?"

I was sorry I'd brought it up. While they argued, I settled down in the beanbag and let my thoughts drift back to Devin. Mark and the rest of the group engaged in a memory game, and I tuned the whole crowd out altogether. I was half asleep when Bonnie and Jake got up to leave, and Mark nagged Pam and George until they agreed to stay the night. Pam was off for the weekend anyway. It was the last thing I remember thinking.

Though I had a vague hope that Devin might stop up for the weekend, I wasn't counting on it. George, on the other hand, was out of pot, and I knew Devin could get it for him.

"Dial the number for me, and if you'll make me some coffee," he said, yawning, "I'll talk to him."

Devin answered the phone, and after George explained the reason for his call, he listened for a few minutes and then handed the phone to me. "He'll be up pretty soon. He wants to talk to you."

I took the phone. "Hey, Devin, I hope this isn't a big hassle."

"No way. I was just telling George, I'm working on my neighbor's car, but I'm almost finished. Soon as I get done, I'll be up."

He arrived at two, wearing a white T-shirt with a large marijuana leaf on the front, and faded Levis. He tossed the bag to George as he knelt down to kiss me hello, and then joined me in the beanbag.

"Guess what I remembered." He held up what looked like a blank eight-track tape. "Remember the one I made for you?"

As he spoke, he flipped the "on" button of my amp beside the beanbag and pushed the tape in.

Sunrise. The first song burst on…the very song Devin had printed out the lyrics of on the Lums napkin. The room fell silent as Uriah Heep wailed out the words that had, up till now, been only red printing to me. And now, the full-blown song that I could see the printed words simply had not done justice to.

Spellbound. That's the way we all sat as the track changed and the group gave way to Louise Huebner, Los Angeles's official witch. We all laughed at the comic relief of her chanting and lecturing the listeners, all in grave serious tones. Track Three and Uriah Heep again. Their freaky song, *Tales*, and Devin really gave me some meaningful looks throughout this one. I knew we were both thinking the same thing. This song had come on the radio that first night while we were writing in the tablet. This song absolutely described that first night, and it gave me goosebumps. Next came *Paradise/The Spell*, more Heep but this time with thrusting spellcasting in contrast to the slow eerie ballad we'd just heard. Only the magicians of the world could relate to these lyrics, but Devin explained that these songs came from two very popular albums…*The Magician's Birthday* and *Demons and Wizards*, and that they were only two of the many occult albums he had in his collection. I didn't think I could ever listen to country music again. It was a perfect Halloween sample, gifted only four days before the holiday itself.

"That music's really a trip," Pam commented when the track changed again and Devin ejected it from the stereo.

"It's just a few selections from several albums," he said. "I recorded these from my reel-to-reel. You'll hear all the rest of them when I move in. There are too many to bring up just on weekends."

Pammy apparently couldn't contain her curiosity about Devin's religious beliefs any longer. She asked him bluntly if he would answer a few questions for her, and I watched with my own curiosity, wondering how he would handle this. He told her to ask anything she wanted to.

I knew Pam was a God believer all the way, but I had no idea what Devin thought of the Old Man. Of course, her first question was whether or not he believed in God.

Devin talked, and Pam asked, and he answered every question she hit him with. There was an odd neutrality in his answers that plainly indicated a parallel system of belief. When Pam tried to describe her feeling for God, he agreed that they both respected the same Supreme Being, but perhaps with a different name. In all of Devin's answers he never once downgraded, criticized or mocked her beliefs in any way, primitive though they may have seemed to him. Then she asked him about Jesus.

Even *I* wanted to hear what he had to say about *Him*.

"Jesus?" There was sadness in his voice when he finally replied. "Jesus was a beautiful, beautiful man...centuries ahead of his time and grossly misunderstood. That is a prime example of the barbaric human race and how it deals with that which it cannot understand. They killed Jesus because of misunderstandings." He reached for the stash box and began to roll a joint. "Could we talk about anything else?" He glanced up at Pammy as he rolled. "Religion is a personal thing for everybody. If I think too hard about it, it'll just get me down."

He lit the joint and handed it to Pam. "Peace pipe. We'll talk about it another time."

"Sure, I understand." Pammy, who preferred meditation to pot, passed the joint to George, who took it and nodded at the eight-track tape Devin had made.

"That's some pretty cool stuff you brought," he said, supplying Devin with the perfect change of subject.

"Thanks. I'm anxious for you all to hear the rest of it. I flipped through your albums and I noticed a lot of country. There were a few, though, that I also have in my collection." He thumbed quickly through the stack leaning against the wall and extracted two albums, both by the same artist. "This dude."

"Well, he's not country," I agreed, "but I do love his music. I can't imagine who wouldn't." The album cover showed a large close-up of Cat Stevens, who was constantly played on the radio.

"This dude is not only nonhuman, but he is also black." Devin said.

Pam's brow creased with apparent confusion. Everyone knew this singer was Brazilian. I wondered how Devin could know if the man had any black blood in him.

Devin caught her expression and turned to her. "What constitutes a man's color, Pam? His skin or his soul? It doesn't matter what he is biologically. He has a black soul."

"But how do you know?" Pammy asked.

He looked at her quietly for a minute and finally closed the subject with one simple sentence.

"Because *I* am black."

The room fell silent. Nobody asked Devin what he meant. Not even me. I decided to wait for a more private moment to ask him to explain. He couldn't have meant it literally. No possible way. He must have meant it symbolically.

In any case, it obviously didn't change Pam's adoration of Devin, which seemed to be growing by the minute. He had managed to win her heart and George's respect, and as for me, I was just becoming more baffled by these little things Devin threw out without explanation.

The rest of the day and evening passed without much incident. Devin and George made a run to Burger King. After dinner, everyone sacked out early.

Devin's decision to stay the night was a happy surprise for me, but later, when the house was asleep and Devin was stretched out beside me sleeping in that lifeless, no-breathing way of his, my mind would not settle down.

Other than Devin's remark about his *color*, the day had almost been ordinary. There was one other minor thing, though, and it hardly seemed worth losing sleep over, yet it was there, keeping me awake. Another clue to Devin's mysterious secret.

It had occurred early in the afternoon. Mark had followed Devin into my bedroom where I'd later found them trading sketches on the tablet we'd once used for our communications. Devin was showing Mark a way of drawing faces, and there was something very odd about the face they were working on. It looked like a satanic version of the one he'd drawn in Lums with the red pen…the one I had completed, only this one was much more detailed. I watched with interest as he added pointed ears and mournful eyes, and I waited for what I was sure would be next. The horns. As he sketched, I was reminded of the baby and felt that queasiness stirring inside me. Finally, I felt compelled to make a comment on the drawing.

"Boy, you sure do have a thing for that guy, don't you." I tried to keep my voice light.

Mark and Devin both looked up as if just noticing me. "What guy?" Devin asked.

"Satan. Isn't that who you're drawing?" I nodded at the picture.

His response was to hurriedly finish the sketch in brisk rapid strokes, adding hair where I expected the horns to appear.

"That should teach you not to jump to conclusions," he said quietly. He laid the pen down and leaned back against the wall. "Even if it was, the Devil's not such a bad fellow. Not a bad-looking chap either. I've seen drawings of him, and in some of them he's a pretty handsome dude."

I didn't feel qualified to debate Satan's physical attributes, so I seized upon his reputation. "His looks don't make him what he is."

Devin's eyes contained a sort of amusement held in check. "Oh? And…uh, just what *is* he?"

I was getting uncomfortable. "Hey, how'd we get into this anyway? I don't even believe in the Devil, and I thought you didn't either."

Devin laughed, breaking the tension. "It's true that I don't believe in *their*

Devil."

"Their?"

"Yes, them," he said, getting up. "The ones who invented him."

It was then that George tapped on the door, ready for the supper run, and the conversation was abruptly terminated.

It hardly seemed important now, as I lay awake in the darkness. I believed that if I had not interrupted their session, the picture would have been completed in the manner I had expected. And that brought my thoughts back to wondering who or what was going to father this son he was planning to bring into the world. And if neither of us believed in the Christian Devil, why was I so disturbed?

The following morning, while the others had their heads bent over a game of Monopoly, I went in to lie down with Devin. He had been quiet all morning. Unusually quiet. He had declined participation in the game, so I had declined too, wanting to spend as much time with him as I could.

I found him deep in thought, his mood melancholy, and other than that incident with the drawing, I couldn't think of any reason for his sudden turn in mood. And that incident seemed to have been forgotten with the burger run. When I rapped on the partially open door, he waved me inside and I shut it behind me.

"Hi, lady."

I sat down on the bed. "Is anything wrong? Did I do something?"

He pulled me down to him and held me tightly. "No, lady. It's many things that I can do little about, but you're the one good thing that makes it all worthwhile."

As close as I was to him, I could really pick up his depressed feelings and I couldn't understand them. "Is it...the situation at home?"

"No."

"Is it work, then? Or should I shut up and mind my own business?" I pulled away from him and sat up.

His response was a long sorrowful look. Then he turned over on his stomach and buried his face in his arms. I sensed that he was trying hard to hold back tears, or some very heavy emotion. Whatever it was, he'd turned his face away, his eyes hidden in his crossed arms.

"Can't tell me, huh?"

His reply was a shrug. Well, we had been through this before. I looked at the nightstand where the white tablet lay open, the pen beside it.

"Would it be easier if you write?" I handed him the tablet and set the pen beside it.

He looked up, nodded, and turned over on his side. "I can never seem to find words when I need them." He sighed. "I'm not trying to shut you out." He picked up the pen and moved over to make room for me on the bed. He started a sketch, a grotesque eye with veins detailed through the white like a road map. "It would be easier if you would just ask questions, explicit questions...that I suppose I expect you to know the answers to anyway...hardly fair...however...that's how it is. You just trust me to the point where you take my word for everything, and you never ask any questions."

I swallowed uneasily. Devin wasn't making sense again. "Well, you *asked* me to trust you and not to question your way of doing things. If it's about the home situation…"

"It's *not* that."

"Well, what am I supposed to ask? If it isn't that, and I didn't do anything to bring this on, and nothing's happened since yesterday that I know of…what am I supposed to think? Is it that serious? Because if it is, Devin, we'd better get it out in the open right now. All this secrecy stuff is starting to scare me."

"Hey…it's nothing to bring *fear* into," he said quietly, trailing his fingers on my arm. "It's just…where do I start? How can I explain "C" to you when you don't understand "A" or "B"? As he spoke he wrote the words *One Question,* and under that, in outline form, the letters A and B. Beside A, after giving me a hard, searching look, he wrote: *Who I Am.*

I motioned for the pen. "Devin, do you even know, yourself?" I asked.

He nodded.

"And you'll tell me?"

"Haven't I always answered the few questions you *have* asked?"

Personally, I felt the answer to that question was open to debate, but I took the pen and, beside B, wrote: *Who Are You?*

Devin took the pen from me with what seemed like dread. Without another word, he began to write, nonstop, no pauses even to think, not even once.

ALL THE HATE. ALL THE LIES. ALL THE EVIL. ALL THE POWER. ALL THE SUFFERING, BITTERNESS AND SIN. ALL THE WARS. ALL THE DEATH AND PAIN. ALL THE SICKNESS, FAMINE AND KILLING.

NO, I AM NOT. BUT I AM. FOR THEY HAVE SURMISED. I AM THE SNAKE, BUT EVEN A SNAKE NEEDS A PURPOSE. AND YET, SURMISE THEY WILL, FOR HUMANS LIE. WHY DO THEY LIE? BECAUSE HUMANS ARE CRUEL. PITY THEIR CHILDREN FOR THEY HAVE ONLY INNOCENCE.

FEAR NOT, FOR I HAVE THE MEANS TO CHANGE. YOUR LOVE AND UNDERSTANDING ARE GREATLY APPRECIATED. PERHAPS I AM VERY MUCH IN NEED OF THIS COMING INNER CHANGE.

He dropped the pen suddenly and looked at me. I didn't pick it up. I was too stunned by the horrible list of adjectives and words he had used to describe himself. I rubbed my eyes with my thumb and forefinger and then looked him directly in the eyes.

"Devin! Why do you have that opinion of yourself? *None* of that is true. *None of it* !"

He shook his head wearily. "You *still* don't know who I am."

I picked up the pen and wrote: *You're Devin. I love Devin. I don't WANT Devin to change.*

The answer came in clear, sharp unhesitant printing.

HOWEVER, DEVIN WILL CHANGE. HE WILL BECOME PART

OF ONE LOVE. OUR LOVE.

The tears did well up in his eyes now, but they never fell. He had too much control. It wasn't even healthy to hold back such emotion.

"Devin," I said. "It would help a lot if you could let go of whatever is bottled up inside you."

"What good would that do? Would you understand any better? Would you then recognize me? Remember me? And do you really think you would be able to grasp...to feel the weight I must carry always? Do you think *you* could handle the feelings? Even for *one earthly minute?*" He reached up and held me firmly by the shoulders and stared into my eyes.

As if he'd pressed a button, a gradual wave of despondency and desperate hopelessness began to creep over me and grow inside me. His eyes remained locked with mine, as the heavy oppressiveness grew larger and larger. It felt like a volume dial was being increased and increased until I finally exploded into hysterical tears, *feeling* the weight...actually *feeling* the weight as he held me firmly by my shoulders. When I hit the breaking point he released me and sat watching as I struggled to regain control, sobbing so hard I could barely talk and having no idea what had come over me so fast...and was now fading...gradually...all in the span of approximately sixty seconds.

"I'm sor...sorry," I sobbed over and over. "I can't...can't...stop..."

Still he did not make a move to touch me or even take me in his arms to comfort me. He just sat there watching until I could speak without the tears or emotion. The feeling ebbed away gradually, but quickly, and then suddenly died. As quickly as it had come over me.

"I'm sorry," I said finally, wiping my eyes, now fully in control.

"What for? It's all right to cry for the world. No one else will do it for her. Do you realize *now* how I feel? I must carry these feelings inside me constantly. It was a rather cruel way to explain, but as you now know, there are no words for that kind of feeling. You had to experience it too. Some days it's worse than others. Some days, like today, it's unbearable."

In the bedroom, a slice of sun was barely detectable behind the heavy drapes. I stared at him in awe. How could he turn those feelings on and off in me like a faucet? What kind of control did he have over me? It was uncanny, and yet, now that the gloom had dissipated, I realized suddenly that it was not with either of us. Not even Devin.

"Are you...do you still feel the way you did when I came in here?"

He looked puzzled but shook his head. "For some reason it is gone now. Perhaps, for once, my fathers heard me. For once, perhaps, something has been granted."

He stood up. "I have to go. Your sister asked me to drop her and George off at the hospital. I guess he's having some minor surgery?"

"Yeah, I forgot about that."

"Do you want me to drop Mark off for you too?"

I nodded. "If it's not out of your way."

The radio was playing softly when we emerged from the room, a song by a melodious rock group, singing about being lost in a lost world, a group I would later learn was the Moody Blues. The words reflected just exactly what had gone on in that bedroom.

Pam looked up in surprise when we came out of the bedroom. My eyes were still red and swollen, but she never mentioned it or asked why. Instead, she talked cheerfully about her upcoming trip to Allentown and how she couldn't wait to tell the family how far out Devin was.

"He's so beautiful, Kerry," she told me as she gathered up her things. "You really got yourself a gem. I mean it."

They all boarded, and I climbed up on the running board to kiss Devin…one final goodbye before he drove away. I waved them off that Sunday afternoon with a lot of confusion swirling in my brain, and…no conclusions. The only thing I was sure of was that I *did* love Devin. No matter who he was.

16 Amusing myself while Devin wasn't around was no problem at all. Not only did I have plenty of books to read, but now I had a new tape to play too. It was so entirely different from country western that I was sure it was throwing Steve and Chris into total confusion as it wailed out my window and into theirs. Uriah Heep was the predominant group with the lyrics running along the lines of a black magician, although a highly esteemed one. Every time *Tales* came on, it took me back to the night of the tablet. The night we had called Myrna.

Myrna. Strange we hadn't heard from her. She hadn't written and by now the ring and the attacks were practically forgotten. I looked at the ring now. So familiar and friendly looking. It was the bond between Devin and me that linked our thoughts, even in his absence. The ring, the phone call…everything that had seemed so dramatically important thirteen days ago, had quietly died and a new phase had entered. *Us.* Had Myrna even bothered to do a reading on it?

The track changed, startling me out of my thoughts, and Uriah Heep was at it again, chanting their mysterious spellcasting and challenging some unknown person, by all the powers of darkness, promising they would steal what was theirs. His. The nameless black magician.

I fell asleep Sunday with the tape playing over and over through the night, my dreams undoubtedly being programmed by the strange lyrics that appeared to be written personally for Devin and me.

Monday morning marked the beginning of what promised to be an even bigger mind-blowing week. Devin hadn't met me at the coffee shop, so I had no way of knowing what had gone on at home since he'd left me. I'd even forgotten about the legal wedding that he'd attended Friday, and hadn't thought to ask him about it on Saturday. It was as though that part of his personal life didn't exist when he was at work or with me. I was happily surprised to find a note stapled to my time card this morning and took off for the lounge where I could read it in privacy.

Tricks—missed you last night…got home—wife in bed…house quiet. Damn I missed you. May be in the office all day if he doesn't get an idea to send me out. Lunch today, Love?

Yours, Erick

It was the handwriting that floored me…and the signature. The penmanship was large, like a grade-schooler, and there was no scribbled scorpion sketch. There *was* an eternity symbol, the figure 8 sideways, beside the name. And *who* the hell was *Erick?*

The explanation came upon immediate telephone contact. The phone was blinking on hold when I walked into the office, so I picked it up.

"Hey…"

"Devin? Hey, I got your note. Devin, who is Erick?"

There was silence for a few seconds, then, "Oh, did I sign that note? I could have sworn I forgot to."

"No, but you signed it 'Erick'. And for that matter, it doesn't even look like you wrote it."

Devin ignored any reference to the script itself. "Man, you know Halloween's coming if I signed it Erick." He chuckled. "Erick is my craft name. It's on all my tools of the trade. My chalice and Athame, you know? It's not usually given up to any but the members of the coven, but in your case I'd say it's a little different."

He'd never mentioned it before. "You *really* were a member of an actual *coven?* I thought you and your brother were just joining a herd of Wiccans for a big get-together."

"Well, I *was* a member, but I dropped out right after I started seeing you. Trevor convinced me that the private wedding ceremony was the more important way to spend Halloween night. And besides, the coven had really gotten down on me…told me my ego was really blown up because I'd done so much talking about you. I *did* examine my reasons for wanting to bring you— their suggestion—and they were right. It was mostly to show off. So I admitted I was wrong. Well, they wouldn't let up and that's when I had a talk with my brother about it. It was *his* idea to drop them. He felt that you would do me more good than they…hey, you still there, babe?"

"Yeah. Damn, Devin. I learn more about you by telephone." I smiled to myself and shook my head. "Are you sorry you broke with them?"

"No. Trevor was right. We both pulled out and I've never looked back. I've been much happier the way things are now. I'm not *there* and that should tell you something."

Lola stepped into our room and pointed to me and the phone. "Is that Devin she's talking to?"

"Who *else?* " Kelly quipped.

"Kerry, ask Devin if he remembered those bike handle grips. Mark is driving me crazy. He's called three times already from a school pay phone."

"I hear," Devin said with a groan. "Shit. I forgot to look. Put Mama on."

I tried to give the phone to Lola but she shook her head. "No. Just tell him Mark's not going to forget. If he promised him—"

"Tell Mama I'll buy him a pair while I'm out today."

I relayed the message.

"No, he doesn't have to do that. I'll just tell Mark he forgot them."

"Tell Mama I'll call Mark myself when I come in."

Lola looked at me curiously when I hung up. "Is he on a *route* again?"

"Tim's been sending him out every day. Because of me, I guess."

Lola laughed. "Oh, that's not the reason, Kerry. Tim isn't like that."

Devin called Mark at four from Lola's desk, just before he left for home. "Hey, turkey, I forgot again. Tell you what. If I forget them tomorrow, I'll buy you a new set. Fair enough? You'll have them one way or the other by tomorrow."

"Getting close to the family is he, Lola?" Kelly teased.

Lola shrugged. "I don't know what this is all about, but Devin, don't promise him anything, please."

Devin motioned for her to hush, and covered one ear with his hand. "Okay, Mark. See you tomorrow then, huh?" He hung up and held both palms up at Lola. "Tomorrow for sure, Mama. I'll drop them off in the morning."

"Not at *my* house you won't. Just bring them here." She smiled with affection, knowing damn well there wasn't much room in Devin's head these days to remember such trivia as a pair of bike handle grips for an eleven-year-old.

Myself, I wondered that he cared enough to try. Devin, who supposedly didn't like kids.

Tuesday morning I found another note stapled to my time card. In the same large childlike writing, this one really blew my mind.

As the sun coming up from a hole in the earth, so too is my spirit emerging to the dawning of a new day. You have brought inner peace to this existence. Simply love growing.
Erick Erick Erick

I pocketed the note and went in to find Lola. Smiling as usual, she'd apparently already seen Devin.

"He couldn't find them," she said, by way of greeting.

"He did remember to look though, huh?"

"Yup. I told him to forget about them. I'll get Mark a set and don't let him promise him anything else."

She didn't seem angry and it would have been pointless anyway, for Devin walked in at four o'clock with a paper bag and a card.

"Hey…lighten up ladies," he announced loudly. "Tomorrow's Halloween Eve!"

"Big deal." Kelly shrugged disinterestedly.

"Yeah. So what?" Lola agreed. "What'd you bring me?"

Devin dropped the bag on her desk. "For Mark, Mama."

I was already out of my seat. Kelly and Hannah quit posting, too.

"What time is the sacrifice?" Kelly quipped.

"At midnight, Kelly," Devin shot back, obviously in high spirits. "We need a victim. What're you doing tomorrow?"

"Aw, what's the matter, Devin? Couldn't you find any babies?"

Devin strolled into our office and over to my rolling stand that held four trays of ledgers. He stooped down, dropped the white envelope in between the trays, and thumbed innocently through my D accounts. "Is Davian's Jewelers still delinquent?"

"It most certainly *is*," Lola called in. "Why…did Joey charge it again?"

"No. He refused them delivery," Devin called back to her. "And they insisted they paid."

I flipped through the Ds until I came to the account.

"Okay," Devin said aloud, and then whispered with a smile, "Who gives a shit anyway?" Then back in a normal tone, "Get all the sleep you can tonight. You'll need it." He gave my hand a warm squeeze.

"Are you going home tonight?"

"Eventually. I still lock up, so I'll be late getting out of here. I *still* haven't written up that ceremony you gave me. I also have to finish sewing my ceremonial robe I started a while ago."

"You know how to sew?"

"And cook, *and* iron *and* everything else. Completely self-sustaining. Don't need anyone to wait on me. Anyhow, let me get out of here. I don't want to push my luck with Mama."

"It's already pushed to the limit, you two," Lola said loudly from the other room.

Devin smiled, kissed me hastily, and left.

His office door was shut when Kelly and I passed at five, so we kept on walking. Tim's voice could be heard rising and falling, and occasionally Pat's, and I knew Devin was in there by the chest feeling that pulsed stronger as I approached and faded as I punched out and left. We separated at our cars and I was glad to be alone with my thoughts and feelings through the long drive home. The moon would be coming out at dusk. Nearly full.

When I arrived home with the kids, I found a large pumpkin sitting on my front step, which Steve verified was a gift from Chris, a Halloween extra from my landlord this year. He found me carving it out, not with the usual face and toothy smile, but with Devin's name.

"Jesus Christ! You're really gonzo on that dude, aren't you?"

I agreed and poked a candle in the center. "There. Got a match?"

"Jesus Christ," he repeated, shaking his head. "I don't fuckin' believe it."

I lit the candle myself and Steve left. The pumpkin looked pretty neat if I did say so myself, flashing the name that had become a household word. Well, tomorrow was the big day.

Chris appeared around seven to drop off a message. A written note. "Some dude was here looking for you or Devin. He left this.

Devin, I was here and you weren't. Now, you're here and I'm not. But I love you anyway. Later—T

"I don't know who that could be, Chris," I said. "What'd he look like?"

"Oh, tall, skinny, long black hair…hey, what the fuck did you do to my pumpkin?"

"Well, you *gave* it to me," I retorted. "What did this guy say?"

"Not much, just looking for you. I guess he couldn't wait, so he left the note." With a disgusted glance at the pumpkin, he left.

Devin called just as I was shuffling the kids off to bed.

"Yeah, what's up?" he greeted me when I answered.

"Nothing much. Where are you?"

"Still at the plant. My brother's with me. He said he stopped by there today."

"Oh, he must have been the one who left the note." I read it to him.

"Yeah. That was him. Hey, could you use some company for a while?"

"You?" My heart skipped a beat.

"And Trevor. He wants to meet you. It might be a little late."

"I'd love it, Devin. I want to meet him, too."

"Far out. I guess we'll see you a little later. Oh, by the way…put the radio on. That station I showed you. Listen to it till we get there."

"Oh, okay. Some Halloween thing going on?"

He laughed. "You could say that. Just put it on. It's doing strange things. A little radio…activity, you could say. It usually does when my brother's with me."

"Okay," I agreed, wondering why. I didn't usually play that station, but it kept turning up on the radio, tuned in when I didn't even know the dial numbers. Tonight was no different. It was already tuned in, so I sat back to listen.

Nothing so far but unfamiliar music, and a few songs I had just learned over the weekend. Now it was playing a beautiful song called *Watching and Waiting*. The singer was waiting for someone to understand him, and he was hoping it wouldn't be very long. I later learned this was the Moody Blues, but at the time, it was just another new weird song. I remained in front of the radio, still puzzled, waiting for a message of some sort, until they arrived an hour later, two tall streamlined figures approaching the house. I put the porch light on and opened the door for them.

Trevor was exactly as Chris had described him. He was kind of quiet, but I liked him instantly. He treated me as though he'd known me all my life. I asked them what the radio business was all about and they exchanged secretive smiles.

"Did you put it on that underground station I showed you?"

"Yes, but all they played was music."

My answer really seemed to break them up. Devin took me in his arms, laughing. "Well, what did you expect it to play? Did you listen to the words at all?"

"I tried to, but I don't know FM music very well. Why?"

"Well, that particular station has a way of doing what Trevor and I want it to. It was playing Uriah Heep and Moody Blues when I called you. Pink Floyd, too. *Dark Side of the Moon*."

I shrugged. "I recognized a few from the tape you made me. I see your point, now. I just was waiting for some message."

"There was, babe, believe me. Well, I guess we'd better split. Got a lot to do tonight. And *you*, lady, try to get a lot of sleep."

He was really impressed with the pumpkin, assuring me that no one had ever monumented him in such a way.

"If you only knew what you do to my ego," he said with a sigh, and then kissed me goodbye before slamming the door of the van. "Later, lady."

When I returned to the house that same Moody Blues song was on, telling me that I'd see him soon, but he couldn't tell me where he came from. The pumpkin glowed eerily at me. I turned the radio off and turned in. There wasn't much more time left to sleep.

17 Halloween Eve. At midnight, Halloween, October 31st, 1974, would officially begin. I was a little nervous while waiting for Devin to arrive. He had told me to wear dark clothing, so I was surprised to see him wearing a cream-colored canvas shirt with pentagrams and eternity signs embroidered on it. It was, at least, appropriate to the occasion. He seemed pretty quiet and reserved.

"You about ready?"

"Yeah. We have to pick up Lana, though. She's watching the kids."

He nodded. "Might as well do that now."

On our way to the van, Devin looked up at the sky and frowned. There was a gloomy, cloudy overcast, and it looked like it was going to rain. He sighed. "You can't even *see* the full moon."

"Oh, it'll clear up by midnight," I assured him. "Don't let that bother you." I don't know why I said that as I had no way of knowing, and the radio obliged by playing Pink Floyd's *Dark Side Of The Moon* all the way to Lana's, as if to mock me.

Once Lana was situated at my house, we headed for Trevor's. Devin's unusually quiet behavior had me a little worried, but it ended abruptly when we pulled up to his brother's house.

Trevor lived out in the country, way off the main road. Inside it was dimly lit and a tape recorder ran softly in the background, music that resembled the songs that Devin had put on the tape for me. Mia was dressed in black, like me, and the introductions were dispensed with.

Mia was as quiet as Devin had been when he'd picked me up, but I could understand *her* behavior. It didn't take a genius to see she was more nervous than the rest of us. She made some tea and we sat waiting on their couch while Trevor and Devin made several trips to the van loading up tapes, bags, books and fire materials. Mia mentioned that she had two little girls like I did and she asked me about mine. She also commented on the happy mood she'd noticed in Devin these past few weeks.

"He used to be so...down all the time," she confided, shaking her short blond hair out of her eyes. "He's been different since he met you."

Mia seemed very settled and mature for her twenty-five years. She carried an air of resignation about her as though the school of hard knocks may have dented her faith in people a little. I could relate. I liked her a lot.

Devin and Trevor came in and motioned to us. "You chicks ready?" Devin asked.

"We've *been* ready," Mia replied. "Trevor, did you feed Titan yet?"

Trevor looked at Devin. "Got a minute?"

"Sure, bro."

Titan. A huge, strapping, muscular Doberman. He was released from the children's room and bounded up to Trevor and Devin in ecstatic leaps, his uncropped tail nearly a weapon in the tiny house.

"Hey…*giddown!*"

Instantly the dog dropped to the floor, gazing at Trevor with small beady eyes.

"Yeah, you'd *better* drop," Trevor murmured affectionately, scratching behind his huge pointed ears. "Now *stay* there." Trevor strode to the kitchen and only Titan's gaze followed him.

"Pretty well trained," I observed aloud to Mia, who nodded in agreement.

"Attack trained," she said. "Trevor raised him from a pup."

Trevor set out his food and picked up a heavy black leather jacket. "Think I'll need this?"

"You'd better bring it," Devin said with a smile. "You know how those deep dark woods are at night."

"Aw, cool it, Devin," I whispered. "Can't you see she's nervous enough as it is?"

"Okay." He looked seriously at Mia. "There's nothing to be nervous about. It'll be over in no time."

When we boarded the van, I nudged Mia just before she crawled back to the rear with Trevor. "Don't feel alone, Mia. I don't know what's going to happen tonight either."

She looked at me gratefully. "Oh, you've never…"

"Never. First time for me, too."

She nodded, and I took the passenger seat up front. Devin slammed up and climbed aboard from the driver's side and we were finally on our way.

Devin shoved an eight-track tape in—*Tea for the Tillerman.* Cat Stevens was *Miles from Nowhere* and *On the Road to Find Out*— and nothing was said until we were well underway on the highway and heading southwest. My own thoughts were on Titan and his obvious devotion to Trevor. Devin and Trevor began to call back and forth, joking comments to ease the tension that was steadily mounting. The moon had finally appeared and between the music, the lull of the van, the warmth, and the joint that had made its way up front, all of us were becoming less tense about the night ahead.

"Hey, bro!" Trevor called over the music. "You know where you're going?"

The joint was on its way back again. Devin glanced in the rearview mirror as he answered. "Yeah. I may need a little help with the turn."

I had moved down to the divider on the floor between us, my back to the dashboard. Now I glanced up and out the van window. Nothing but darkness. The heat radiating from the floor was warm and cozy as it wafted from the engine through the gold carpet. I was closer to Devin from this position and it felt good with his hand on my knee. He glanced down at me every mile or so and winked, and from where I sat his features looked different. Really different. His lips seemed large and swollen and hung a little. His eyes were like slits, a lot like Titan's, and there was a strange glint in them. I finally concluded that it must be distortions from the weed and moved back up into the passenger seat beside him.

An hour passed with the *Tea for the Tillerman* tape playing over and over, and we must have turned off somewhere because the bumps would have jolted awake anybody who might have been dozing. Devin cut the music and Trevor moved forward and positioned himself behind Devin, watching over his shoulder as Devin slowed the van. Both were watching for landmarks.

"It's past that radio tower," Trevor said suddenly, his voice clipped and loud in the silence.

Devin jerked a thumb back and grinned at Trevor. "Ya mean th' one we jist passed 'bout a mile ago?"

The sudden change in Devin's voice made me look up with a start. He had resumed his attention on the road and Trevor was watching closely too.

"There it is," he said. "Now, bro."

The van swung off the isolated dirt road and began a lumpy crawl through a not-so-beaten path into the actual woods.

"Thompson's Station is right down the road here," Trevor called back to Mia. "Me and Devin have had many a breakfast in that greasy spoon back there."

"Yep...frad taters n' cheeken," Devin agreed, his accent exaggerated profusely. He grinned at me as if to say *what're you staring at* ? I guess I must have been. His gaze turned back to the path ahead.

That voice. Unmistakably Negro, put on or not.

Now, as I stared at him, it was all suddenly coming together. Who Devin *was*. His fear of telling me. The dread of misunderstanding. The panic of loss. Even the adjectives he'd used to describe himself in the tablet that afternoon. *Of course*. The black race was one of the most misunderstood races in the world.

In the darkness, Devin's silhouette and curly hair were now a dead giveaway. How could I have not noticed before? The flared nostrils, the full lips...even those slitted eyes. Devin's big secret...was...that he was *black!*

My stomach churned.

Mia made her way up to Trevor and peered out the window. The van was jolting and bumping over wild ground now, no longer a path, and my stomach became even queasier.

"Are you sure you know where you're going?" Mia asked.

As she spoke, we moved into a clearing and Devin began a slow circle with the van.

"This is *way* too open, bro," Trevor said. "We'd be a dead ringer for anyone who might chance upon this place tonight."

"Well, th' lake's over there," Devin replied, pointing, "so why don' we park here and look 'round for a spot."

I saw Mia shiver as the motor died. The landscape was utterly still and breezeless, the silence broken only by the crickets and frogs chirping and croaking almost in unison. I was pretty sure there were also a few snake rattles going out there somewhere, and I could understand Mia's reluctance to leave the warm comfort and safety of the van. At least it wasn't so dark in the open area. The full moon had come through, illuminating the landscape like a spotlight, and it only added to the weird setting, considering a wedding was about to take place.

Devin glanced down at my feet when we touched ground. "Those sandals going to be okay out here?" The slang accent had vanished.

"They're all I've got. They'll be fine."

He turned to Trevor. "Let's walk down this path a ways."

"You're not leaving *us* here," Mia said quickly. "We're coming too."

Devin shrugged. "Come on, then. Follow us."

Mia and I kept the guys in sight, but we gave up trying to keep up with them.

"As long as I can *see* them, I don't care," Mia told me.

"You're not nervous anymore, are you?" I asked as we walked.

"Well, let's put it this way. I'll be glad when this is over with."

I thought she must love Trevor very much to go along with this. She was being a pretty good sport, considering.

Devin waved to us from a stand of trees and bushes. "This is pretty good. What do you two think?"

The area was wide enough for a full-sized nine-foot circle, and was surrounded by the brush.

"It'll have to do," Trevor said. "It's almost midnight."

Devin and Trevor exchanged a few private words and then Trevor walked over to Mia.

"Come on. I'll show you the lake while he's getting things ready. He'll call us."

They started walking toward the sound of the frogs and I looked questioningly at Devin.

"You too," he said.

"Okay. I wasn't sure if they wanted to be alone or not."

"No. T's gotta calm her down. Go ahead with them. I'm just setting things up."

Down at the lake I found Mia with Trevor's jacket wrapped tightly around her. Trevor was skipping rocks across the water's glassy surface, which was surprisingly visible under the moon's illumination. He turned around at the sound of my approach.

"I got kicked out too," I told them.

"He doesn't even want *me* around while he's charging that circle. It's cool. He'll call us when he's ready."

Twenty minutes went by and Trevor left to see what the holdup was. Mia and I waited together, looking at each other apprehensively. Finally, Trevor returned.

"He's ready. Let's go."

I followed a few feet behind them, thinking about Devin's big secret. Would it be obvious all the time, now that I knew? I could see now why he'd hesitated in telling me. I almost didn't blame him, but it still seemed unfair that he'd not been honest about it from the beginning.

On the other hand, if he had been, I would have run like a scared rabbit. I knew that. I was a white girl from a white family, raised with white friends in the fifties and sixties. Went to white schools. The dividing line was ingrained in me. Not that I didn't have black friends, but to cross that invisible line when it came to love…it had always been unthinkable… socially unacceptable.

Now I had a whole new problem. In spite of the shock, it had not altered my feelings for Devin one bit. I didn't love him any less than I had before it had all come together for me.

And it was really coming together now. Little things were coming to mind, things he'd said that had confused me at the time. Like the first night he had brought the ring to me and his comment that a cop had told him to take the helmet in with him, or he'd be reporting it stolen later. When I'd agreed that there was a lot of theft in the neighborhood he'd replied, *what's wrong with this neighborhood? Looks all white to me.* He'd sounded defensive. So Devin was not only black, he was defensive about it. Now I understood the changes in his voice when his guard was down, and his over-the-top brotherly treatment of the black workers in the chemical division of the plant.

I was still deep in thought when I realized we were back in the clearing again. Devin was on his knees trying to get the charcoal to burn. Trevor disappeared into the van and returned with lighter fluid. The van had been moved in to block the area where Devin would stand and there were four rocks designating the boundaries of the circle and where each of us would stand during the ceremony.

"Oh, no! Look!" Mia pointed to the can Devin was using to sprinkle fluid over the coals. "They even use Wizard lighter fluid."

I appreciated her attempt at humor.

"Yup," Devin said lightly. "And Trevor smokes Salem cigarettes too, in case you haven't noticed."

Trevor laughed. "Even *I* never noticed *that*," he assured Mia, winking at Devin, who made a face that clearly said *sure you didn't.*

The fire suddenly caught and Devin stood back. "There it goes. Ready whenever you are."

An hour later, the ceremony over, we were all back in the van for a celebratory drink. Trevor passed the cup to Mia and looked contentedly at Devin. "This is pretty good wine, bro. Where did you get it?" The wine had mellowed the newlyweds considerably.

"One of my customers," Devin said. "It's homemade. How do you like it, Mia?"

She nodded her approval and passed the cup to me. "It's really *strong.*"

"Yeah, I'm hep. Well, let's drink up and get the hell out of this van. It's too nice a night to sit in here."

I couldn't understand it. Once that ceremony had begun, I'd watched Devin like a hawk and…nothing. Not a slurred word. Not an accent of any kind except straight American hippie. No black facial features that I'd seen so clearly earlier. He had struggled with the reading, trying to pull the words out in the dark. He'd even apologized in his own humble way for the faltering and had given them both a bashful Devin smile when he was finished.

In the van, it was the same. Just Devin boasting of his gift from his favorite customer. And now… nature. Only Mia didn't think it was such a nice night to be roaming around in the dark and she gripped the jacket tighter around her.

"You two go ahead," Trevor told us. "We'll stay here."

Devin turned to me with a lusty grin. "Okay…me and my lady here…we kin fahn somethin' t' do… over yonder."

The drawl was back. "Le's go, lady. These two ain' jivin' me…not lately. It's honeymoon tahm." He tapped me gently on the shoulder and slid the side door open. We stepped to the ground. "Jis give th' horn a toot when you want us back."

He took my hand and we started walking, carefully avoiding the rocks and pits in the path that led to the lake.

Confusion was swirling in my brain but my love for him was no less than before. Whether it was to convince myself or to assure him, I felt the need to express that.

"I love you, Devin."

"Tha's good," he said quietly, squeezing my hand. "Ah dig you pretty much mahself." He stopped and glanced around the shoreline for a semiprivate area. A wind had blown up, both damp and cold, and he seemed to realize that, took off his jacket and wrapped it around my shoulders. "There. I don' need it." He then steered me over to a beach with large boulders and motioned for me to sit in front of them. When I did, he sat down beside me and reached into his jacket pocket for a joint.

"Yer pretty good out here in them sandals," he said suddenly, his accent thicker now. "You dodge them rocks lak a cat." He struck a match and when the flame flared, it illuminated his face and magnified those Negro features even more.

I could feel the blood drain from my face. Why hadn't he told me? While it hadn't changed my feelings for him, the cold realization that I was with a black man was more than I could handle right now. Was *this* what he had expected me to realize and tell *him*?

There was now another gnawing concern needling at me that I couldn't ignore anymore. The baby. What if I was already pregnant? And if I was…would the child be black? Was *that* what Devin had meant when he'd said no one would be able to look into the child's eyes? On and on the thoughts rambled, the grass magnifying the situation in my mind. It *had* to be brought out in the open. With a sick dread, I wondered if he'd *ever* intended to tell me.

"Ah love you, lady."

I looked at him. I loved him so much. Why did it have to be so complicated? I gave in to the warm feeling that spread through me with his words and wrapped my arms around him. Did it matter? Did this really matter? I had to come to terms with this within myself and I just needed some time. If Devin was black, the worst thing I could do was let him know it was upsetting me. Tonight there was no time to think. I closed my eyes and tightened my grip on him. Damn. I loved him so much.

The full moon flitted in and out of hazy clouds somewhere up there in the blackness. I watched it, hypnotized, as it faded and reappeared. The overcast had finally dissipated and the moon had a fairly consistent black and starry background, like holes pricked in a black sky with a backlight shining through.

For what seemed like an hour, he didn't speak, and it didn't seem strange to me at all. I had the gut feeling that he sensed a change in me…in my thoughts…and had somehow pinpointed the reason for it. Not trusting myself to speak either, we remained like that for some time, not speaking. It couldn't last forever, though, and Devin was the first to break the silence.

"Nice out here, isn't it?"

I sat up, more in surprise than anything. No accent. "What?"

"I said, it's nice out tonight. Not too cold, you know?" The drawl was definitely gone. Not a trace of slang or Negro accent.

"Yeah, it is." My eyes must have given me away. I was never good at hiding reaction to surprises.

"Something is bothering you. What's wrong?"

I accepted the cigarette he handed me and clutched the jacket tighter around me. It may have been a nice night, but it damn sure was a nice *cold* night. When he flared the match to light my cigarette, and then his, I couldn't help but steal a glance at his features. He looked worried, but…white worried. Not black worried. His nose and lips looked as straight and ordinary as Pat's or Trevor's. There was no slit to his eyes and that cocky look was gone now too. I was beginning to wonder if I'd manufactured the whole idea out of nothing.

"Nothing's wrong," I said quietly, reaching for his hand. And all of a sudden, nothing was.

"I like to get out here every now and then. It would be nice to get some mescaline and come out here ourselves some weekend. You can open up your mind and really get into it." He looked up at the sky. "There it is. See? Scorpio."

"That's Scorpio?" I looked up to where he was pointing. "Really? I don't think I've ever seen it."

He smiled. "That's better, lady. I don't want you unhappy. Especially tonight."

"I'm happy. Really I am."

"Good. Then I'm happy, which means *they're* happy, which guarantees that *we'll* be happy." He pitched his cigarette into the lake and looked at me. "Just one big happy universe." He raised his eyebrows, as though expecting me to challenge him.

He knew. No matter what I said, he always knew what was going on in my head. I looked away.

"Okay. I guess I can wait. However, if you want to talk about it…"

How could I?

"What time is it?" I asked, instead of taking him up on his offer. Not that I really cared about the time. It seemed to be the one thing we had plenty of tonight.

"I don't know. I didn't bring a watch."

I was starting to feel guilty as I watched him closely. There was nothing. Had I imagined the whole thing? And now he seemed to be patiently waiting for me to tell him why I'd been upset, and as normal as he appeared to be now, I didn't know how I could even begin.

"Devin, I love you," I said, knowing, at least, that *that* much was true.

"I love you too, lady. Soon we will be able to come out here alone with better things to do than just look at the moon. I look forward to the day."

What things? I just looked at him, trying to keep my expression neutral.

He smiled. "So worried, lady. You're going to have to learn not to let unimportant things get you down. Not to jump to what seems to be the obvious conclusion. I was only speaking of things you will soon become aware of. Things we will do together. I wasn't trying to frighten you, but it's much too soon to be dwelling on the future. Still, I look forward to the day. This is the second full moon this month. It's my birthday in more ways than one."

"Oh my God, that's right! I'm so sorry! Happy Birthday, Devin. I can't believe I forgot."

"Lot going on tonight so that's understandable. However I meant that this moon is another kind of birthday for me...in a strange way." He leaned back against the boulder and sighed.

"What do you mean?" I swallowed uneasily. Even if I was wrong about the black thing, there was still this baby thing.

He looked at me. "Even *I* have things I'm not comfortable discussing tonight."

He obviously knew I was harboring thoughts I wasn't sharing, so I tried to get back to the original subject. "What did you mean about coming out here to do things? Are you going to teach me those things?"

"Not exactly. For a while, we can kick back and enjoy life, love, and sex. Just like everybody else. But it won't be all play. There is much you will learn, but I won't be teaching you anything. I'm not a teacher."

"But how will I learn, then?"

"You will experience, not learn. Through experience, the knowledge will flow...like truth. You can only experience what is true. Some people come to this existence over and over and still they do not experience. Well, they do, but they view those experiences from the standpoint of a program some human put into them. Parents are notorious for doing that. We won't be coming back on any repeat voyages, lady. Not when it can all be done now...here...at one time, in this present existence."

I didn't know how to respond to that and time seemed to pass with the only sound coming from the lake. The frogs were getting louder and the crickets kept a steady rhythm as we sat in silence. Finally, I spoke.

"Devin, does any of this have to do with our future son?"

"In part. But this is much too soon. Please don't question me further. I have no wish to rush you. You have to be ready." He looked away, in the direction of the van. "I thought I heard a honk. Must be getting late for the newlyweds."

The horn sounded again and this time I heard it too.

"That's them." He sighed. "I'd hoped they wouldn't want to leave this soon."

He stood and stretched out his arm to help me up and we walked towards the sound of the horn. When we reached the van, Devin ducked his head inside, said something to Trevor, then turned to me. "I guess they *are* ready to go. Damn. I would have liked to stay out here all night. Oh, well." He shrugged. "I guess we'd better board up."

Nobody spoke until the van was started, warmed up and moving. I was still thinking about the things Devin had said down by the lake, and was totally unprepared for the sudden booming voice that I didn't need to look up to recognize.

"Ah'll tell ya *one* thing, Jack! We better git 'r asses *truckin'* to a gas station…and Ah do mean pee-dee-que!"

The drawl was back— louder, thicker and heavier than ever. And so were the facial features. Trevor never even blinked at the change.

"You mean you didn't put gas in this thing, bro?" he said disgustedly.

Devin glanced at him in the rearview mirror as the van crawled out of the muddy path and onto the paved road. There was a mischievous glint in his eyes and he grinned at Trevor mockingly. "Hey, Jack! We've only done…lahk…a hunert mahls with this thing. It don't run on piss, y'know!" He had to yell over the engine noise to even be heard in the rear and it only punctuated the slurred words even more.

"Hey, Devin," Mia called up. "If you're stopping for gas, make sure it has a bathroom."

"Yeah, me too," I added in a small voice, dread back in my heart so soon after I had dismissed the whole possibility.

"At yer service, ladies…there's one fahve minutes down the road here."

Five minutes later, there it was, brightly lit and larger than life. Devin pulled in and cut the engine. "Ah'll be rat outside here watchin', lady. This ain't th' best in terms of modern."

The warm vibrations of the motor fell to a halt as the engine died, and light flooded into the van from the two-pump center of the station. The gas station was an old, wooden two-story job, ancient with rotting boards and chipped paint. I glanced at Devin before heading in to get the key to the ladies' room. There was a look on his face as he stood, half in and half out of the van, watching me. A worried look that I'd seen at the lake less than an hour ago, only the nostrils were flared and his lips…full and hung. No resemblance to the Devin I'd been with then. Just the same worried expression.

He knew. He'd known then and he knew *now*. So now, we both knew.

18 It was a long ride to Trevor's with Devin driving and the newlyweds sleeping. I remained awake and thinking. Devin had switched on the radio and it was doing its weird thing again. The Moody Blues were singing, telling me to leave my body behind somewhere and view things with my mind. They said now that we were out there we should open our hearts to the universe and then admonished us that if all we wanted to do was play then we could just stay on earth and wait for rebirth. I could feel goosebumps erupting as I followed the lyrics, and wondered *how* this song could have just happened to come on. They were pleasant to listen to, though, and had beautiful harmonies and symphonies and I was learning to recognize them whenever a song of theirs came on. Devin made no comment on the words to the song, but he squeezed my knee from time to time as if to emphasize some phrases, like I wouldn't notice them myself.

When we were back in civilization and stopped at a light, he leaned over and kissed me. It was a sweet gesture…kind of an *'I know you're worried and I understand'* kiss. It made me feel a little better.

Mia was glad when we woke her up to tell her she was home. She thanked Devin for the evening with a sisterly kiss and mumbled something about getting some sleep before she had to pick her kids up in the morning. After they'd gone in, Devin looked at me questioningly.

"'s only two-thirty. We still have a couple of hours."

"I know where we can go. It's not as cool as the lake, but with Lana back at my house, we can't go there. My Uncle Joe, though, he's got a pretty overgrown backyard, and he's at the fire station tonight. He works every third day and tonight he's on duty."

"Le's go, then. You kin direct me from here."

I was trying to adjust to this new Devin so that I could bring up the subject when we got to Joe's. It was a crash course since I'd only discovered this tonight, and I knew it was going to have to be handled with tact.

It wasn't long before we were really, *really* in the deep woods. Joe's country house sat in front of a two-acre lot that greatly resembled the Amazon. Devin whistled as he parked in the maze of overgrown bushes, trees and hanging vines.

"Whew. Ya sure it's safe t' git out? Or is there wild animals out there?"

Without waiting for an answer, he walked back to the couch, still warm from the newlyweds, and patted the cushions in invitation for me to join him. I followed.

"Som'thin's on yer mahnd, lady. Ah wish you'd tell me what it is." He pulled me close to him.

I still couldn't find the words. I tried, but they kept choking up in my throat. There just wasn't a right way to bring it up. Not without hurting him and ruining the whole night.

"Not gonna tell me now, huh." He opened the porthole window and fired up a joint.

His features were so prominent now, so black. I wondered how I *ever* could have overlooked them. For that matter, I wondered just how many people at the water plant knew. Why had no one told me? Surely, Kelly would be aware of it as many years as she had known Devin. I decided to start with a different subject and try to work my way around to it.

"Devin, how long have you been into the occult?"

"Well…lessee…Ah waz born in Salem Hospital…" He grinned, a wide black grin, as though Salem explained everything. "But…ya mean…really heavy into it. Oh, 'bout maybe fahv 'er six years."

When I didn't comment, he went on. "There waz a turnin' point where it *became* mah life. A rather drastic one, Ah maht add." He handed me the joint and lay back against the side of the van, a small cushion propped behind him. "Jist pitch that out th' window."

I did. "When was that? The turning point?"

"Few years back. Up till then Ah had never really *used* it on anybody. Then mah brother was shot to death…rat in his own house." His voice had a bitter twinge as he talked. His eyes, slits again and glistening, gazed off into the nothingness of the murky black shadows outside.

"Shot? You mean an execution thing? Like the Mafia?"

"In a way, yeah. Only mah brother hadn' done nothin' to warrant no killin'. No matter *what* the issue waz."

"And they got away with it?"

"Ah didn' *say* they got 'way wit' it."

There was a tone of deadliness to his whispered drawl that made the hair stand up on the back of my neck. I sat up and reached into his jacket pocket for a couple cigarettes. "Tell me the story, Devin." I lit them both and handed him one.

"Not much t' tell. Mah brother opened th' door one naht and they jist blew him to pieces. An' his wahf...she waz pregnant. Kin you dig that? Three weeks to the day of his funeral she gave birth t' their firstborn." His voice trailed off as he paused to draw on the cigarette, his face suddenly glowing a fiery orange, his eyes glistening like an animal's in the dark. "Th' law couldn' prove a thing. They claimed *he* pulled a gun at th' door, an mah brother didn' even *own* a gun. Since there wuz no witnesses, it was *their* word against nobody's. Legally, they got off scot-free."

"Legally?"

"Yeah, legally. Tha's when Ah took matters inta mah own hands. One of them choked to death alone in his sleep. The other went berserk...for no 'parent reason. He's still in an institution today. An' *his* wahf? Three weeks later *she* gave birth to *their* firstborn, too." He took a final drag off the cigarette and flicked it out the window.

A hush had settled over the van. I didn't know what to say and he misunderstood my silence.

"Oh, Ah've justified th' incident many tahms over since then, but Ah do realize justifications don't make a wrong a raht."

"You didn't do anything they could *pin* on you, did you?"

He glanced at the clock on the dashboard as he replied. "Ah never even had t' dirty mah hands. Anyhow, how'd we git on *that* grizzly subject? It's years past an' talkin' 'bout it won't bring mah brother back. An' it's gittin' on four o'clock. We still have t' run Lana home."

I nodded but didn't move to get up. My opportunity to change the subject was gone.

He yawned and nudged me gently. "Com'on, lazy. Hey, Ah wish you'd tell me wha's bothering ya." He titled my chin up and looked into my eyes, frowning. "Ah didn' upset ya more wit what Ah jist told ya, did Ah?"

I shook my head. "No. Just tired, I guess. We might as well get going."

The house was warm and quiet when we walked in. I put some coffee on and woke up Lana. My kids were used to the early rising hour and, apparently, so was Lana. Within minutes, I had the kids ready to leave with no need for breakfast. Breakfasts were included in Kathy's babysitting fees. Through it all, Devin sat watching me with that same worried expression.

By the time we arrived at the coffee shop, dawn was breaking on the city and I became aware of a beaten fatigue spreading throughout my whole body. If problems were magnified when you were tired, it sure wasn't the right time to be analyzing them, but looking across the orange-and-white booth at Devin, it was impossible not to think about them. One in particular. It was just going to have to come out in the open.

Devin waited until Jane had taken his coffee order before he went outside to the phone booth to call Tim. I watched him walk away, feeling sicker by the minute. If he was black, why didn't he just say so?

On the other hand, what if I was wrong? If so, would he be insulted at such a speculation? Since there didn't seem to be any easy answer I was just doing nothing, but now, as I sat here contemplating our future child, it was a black child in a black bassinet and that's where my thoughts were when Devin slid back into the booth.

"Tim told me to go home and sleep," he said, doctoring his coffee. "I offered to go in, but I didn't tell him I was calling from a couple blocks away. Hey, lady…I wish you'd lighten up. Or tell me what's eating at you."

I managed a feeble smile. "I'm just tired."

"Will you at least admit that something is?"

I nodded wordlessly. It was a start, at least. Devin must have thought so too.

"Kerry, if there's a problem between us, the only time to solve it is now. Is it my home situation? Because if it is, I thought you understood that."

"It isn't that."

"Well, is it something I've said or—"

"Devin!" Fatigue was making me react with irritation, something that wasn't going to help anything. "Devin, it's not that you've done anything. You've been perfect. *Perfect*, you know? You treat me like a hunk of gold that fell out of the sky."

"Well, if it's not something I've done—"

"It's…it's just that…"

"Say it, Kerry."

His tone of voice stopped me cold. The look on his face was ash-gray alarm.

"It's just that…well, I shouldn't have kept it in all night. I know. I guess I should have told you right off."

The alarmed expression was now frozen on his face and like a bolt of lightning, I realized what was going through his mind.

"No, Devin, not *that*. Look, I *do* love you, okay? No matter what, nothing will change that. But—"

His face changed from relief back to frowning confusion. "But what, Kerry? What do you want to hear? My family history? Let's see. I'm Scottish, Irish, English and my grandmother was black."

My spoon fell from my hand and clattered on the booth table. The shock of what he'd said…pulling my thoughts out of my head like a public grab bag. He picked up the spoon and casually handed it back to me.

"Hey, I was just kidding, Kerry," he said, seemingly amused at my reaction. "Christ, I shouldn't tell you a thing like that, even joking. Next you'll be worrying about having a black baby."

So now he was letting me know that my thoughts were very open to him.

Well, I wasn't about to drop it now that he'd brought it up.

"So what if you have a black heritage, Devin!" I hissed, trying to keep my voice down. "Are you ashamed of it? And even if you are black, did you have to wait till I fucking *loved* you to tell me? Or weren't you ever going to?"

Devin watched this outburst with a curious expression. "I *told* you I was just kidding," he said quietly, reaching for the sugar jar as Jane approached with fresh coffee. "I didn't *expect* you to take me literally. Look, you're tired as hell. Why don't you call Lola and come home with me. Your house."

"I can't." I slumped in the booth. "She'd hit the ceiling if I called off after being up all night with you. It's okay. I'll be all right once I get up and move around." I yawned and added, "I think."

"Well, okay then. I'm gonna split. I can't stay awake much longer myself. But if you change your mind, I'll come and get you. Just call me."

"Here, take my house key. It's closer." I peeled one of my keys off my ring and handed it to him.

"Okay, lady. I guess I'll see you in a few hours. Call around four and get me up, okay? That'll give me time to get here a little early. Do you want me to drop you off at the plant?"

"No. Tim might see the van and have a change of heart about your day off. I'll walk down."

He leaned over the booth and kissed me. "Later, babe."

"I *do* love you, Devin."

He sighed. "I know. I love you too, whether you believe it or not."

I almost hated myself for the feelings that were churning around inside me now. How could he be so perceptive anyway? I wished like hell that the day was already over. What I needed was sleep. The kids were spending the night at Kathy's for their trick-or-treat night so tonight I could go home and straight to bed. Maybe after a good night's sleep things wouldn't look so bad. The walk to work would help clear my head and I was going to need my wits about me today as it was. The entire plant would be laying for me, wanting to hear the details of last night's sacrifice.

It wasn't until I reached for my time card that the startling thought occurred to me. The last half hour, every sentence Devin had spoken to me had been normal. He had walked out to the phone booth one person, and returned as another. No slang. No drawl. Just Devin. A tired Devin. A worried Devin.

But most definitely not a black Devin.

19 Something was different about the plant. I could sense it the second I entered the exit. There was just something in the air.

For one thing, Tim gave me a loud, friendly morning greeting, and Pat actually *winked* at me without looking around for superiors first. There were *two* phone girls in the route room...*in* it, not near it, and they were actually *conversing* with the route salesmen. Somewhere a radio was playing loudly, a song by the Association lamenting that it was no fair at all, that they'd never seen that side of someone until now, even after all the time they'd spent together. At the time, it didn't occur to me that the radio was still at its game of describing what was happening in my life.

The lobby was deserted. No Brenda sitting rigidly at her desk at the sound of the eight-thirty tone, and no Maurice or Perry patrolling to see that she stayed there. Lola wasn't at her desk either, but Kelly and Hannah were there, waiting for the ambush.

"Here she comes now," Kelly said, smirking. "Hey, Kerry, are you pregnant yet?"

Today, I just wasn't in the mood for her baby jokes. "I don't know, Kelly. You'll just have to wait till the test results come back," I said tiredly. I reached into the safe and removed the stack of checks marked A to F. "What the fuck's going on around here anyway? I just saw phone females talking to driver *males* in the Dee-em-Zee."

"What's the matter? You got something against socializing around here?" Kelly said, giggling and glancing at Hannah.

"All right, Kelly. What's the big joke?"

"Ain't telling you."

"All *right*, you two." Lola had arrived just before it got to the squabbling stage. "Let's...*don't*...you guys, this early in the morning. How was the wedding, Kerry?"

I had my answer rehearsed. "I'm not allowed to tell anyone anything."

"Aw, come on," Kelly wailed. "We don't get to hear the details?"

"Uh-uh. Especially not till someone tells me what's going on around this place. Tim actually smiled at me when I punched in."

Lola raised her eyebrows, her smile barely contained. "Oh, you haven't seen Brenda's little memo to the company this morning?"

"No, she hasn't," Kelly said. "Hey, Ker...wake up! We're doing *charges* first."

"Oh. Okay." I put the checks back and took out the route tickets. "What haven't I seen?"

"Is he really *gone*, Lola?" Hannah spoke up, "Or is this just a temporary argument."

"No, he's really gone, Hannah. I imagine the drivers are having a party back there. I heard some of them were even here at quitting time yesterday when it happened. I'm surprised *any* of them showed up today at all."

"Devin didn't," Kelly said tauntingly.

"Devin's got the day off," I snapped. "Come on, what the hell's going on?" I looked from Kelly to Hannah to Lola. All smirking faces, radiating glee.

Kelly gave me a playful shove. "Perry Jason was *fired* yesterday. He's *gone!* He's not *God* anymore. He no longer *works* here. Is that plain enough?"

I stared at them. For one fleeting second a memory flashed of Devin in the Lums Restaurant...his knowing words concerning Perry. But...that was ridiculous. Wasn't it? "When did this happen?"

"Around five last night." Lola shrugged. "There are a lot of rumors but nobody really knows. I heard it was done long-distance by telephone."

"He got the axe right from Ralph in Chicago?"

"Well, it had to be Ralph. Who else was higher than Perry?"

At that moment, Brenda waltzed in with a batch of brand-new yellow ledgers, and she literally *was* waltzing, humming that Association song in a voice grossly off key. "Heeeey, cousins. Did you all hear there's a meeting in the conference room today and we're *all* invited?"

Lola looked sickly at the ledgers. "Get those things outta here."

Brenda set the ledgers on Lola's desk and did a stiff turn, like a robot model. "I got the news last night. How do you like my new ragged jeans?"

We all burst into laughter.

"You're really pushing your luck, Brenda," Lola said. "Are there any holes in them?"

"Well, only one," Brenda said with a sigh, "but that's only because they're just a year old. By the way, how did you guys like my new commandments? Is everyone glad Pee-Jay got canned?"

"*Brenda!*" In spite of her attempt at an authoritative reprimand, Lola couldn't help but laugh. "I *loved* your new rules, Brenda. That was pure genius, really."

Brenda beamed. "The drivers love them too. I gave everyone a copy except Perry's wife. She's still here, but she's on her way out too. If he runs his house the way he ran this place, no way will he let her stay."

"Here, Ker." Kelly handed me a neatly photocopied company memo. "So you know what's happening, dummy."

"Oh, no. I'm still not used to the old ones."

"Well, you didn't pay attention to them anyway, but you'll like these. Read 'em out loud."

The new rules were typed on the same type of memo as Perry's, but there was a slight informality in the heading.

To: All personnel
Subject: Employee rights
From: New administration
Effective: Today

1) Effective Thursday, October 31, 1974, fraternization will be allowed in all offices providing you do not take advantage of this privilege and socialize for less than fifteen minutes a sitting."

2) Girls in the front offices will now be allowed to wear jeans to work providing at least three holes or patches are visible.

3) Phone room personnel will be permitted to visit with route salesmen providing not less than two girls at a time visit with drivers...er...route salesmen, excuse me.

4) Accounts Receivable girls will be allowed one hour a day to sit on the floor in Lola's office and discuss work of the day, and two hours on Friday. The forbidden step is included.

5) Lola Baker will be allowed to come in late every day providing she does not sneak a parking space behind Devin's van or whoever's turn it is out front.

6) Mrs. Perry Jason will be permitted to take a forty-five minute lunch so she won't be different than anyone else.

7) And Kim. You can take work home if you wish, but unfortunately, you will not be paid for this privilege.

8) If every one of us stick together and follow the new system I am sure our morale will rise and each of us will be a little less weary of walking through the

doors at 8:45…I mean 8:15 a.m.

By the time I'd almost finished the memo, our small office had filled up with daring passers-by, all eager to join in the laughter. Lola must have felt we were carrying things a little too far and shooed most of them out, telling me to finish it to myself, that everybody had already read them.

"Just because he's gone doesn't mean you don't have to work anymore. Now if you can all just cool it for a while…aw, jeez. Here come Pat and Joey. Are we going to get *anything* done today?"

Joey heard her just as they reached the doorway. "Hey, Mama. Buzz off." He was trying to imitate Devin and failing miserably, I noted.

"Don't you buzz *me* off, kiddo," Lola retorted. "I live here. Who do you think you are, anyway?"

"Devin's replacement today…hey-hey-hey!" Joey was grinning in his bratty way as he fluttered fingers of greeting at us in our room. "Hi, cousins!"

Pat glanced around the office approvingly. "Place looks pretty good, Lola. Uh, don't mind us, now. We're just touring the company, making our rounds, exercising our fraternization rights. How many *other* drivers have been in here?"

Lola smiled. "You're the first men. Maybe the word hasn't gotten around yet?"

"Are you *kidding?*" Kelly called in from her machine. "Even Kerry and Devin are old hat since this morning. I just think the drivers are still afraid to come up here."

"Well, Maurice is still here," Joey agreed, "and going past *his* office still gives me the heebie-jeebies. But I'm sure that will wear off in time. Speaking of the prince…did you hear about the big meeting today?"

"We know," Lola said. "The entire office crew. Were you guys invited?"

"No," Pat said, "but most of the guys will be out on routes. Joey here's only helping out with Devin's dirty jobs until tomorrow."

Joey scratched his back against the doorjamb. "Yeah, this is pretty neat. I may refuse to go back to the truck."

"Well, if you guys will excuse me," Lola said, "I have work to do. And they do too." She jerked her thumb towards our office.

Pat ducked his head in and waved. "How was it, Kerry?"

"Good."

Kelly looked at me suspiciously. "How was *what?*"

"The wedding, he means," Lola said.

Pat turned to Lola and bowed mockingly. "Well, thank you for your hospitality. We'll drop by later to see how your meeting went. Come on, Joey. Who can we visit now?"

"Well, how about Rina in accounts payable," Joey suggested.

"You *know* Charlie's right upstairs, don't you?" Lola reminded them warningly.

"Yeah, but he gets lots of company and phone calls. Rina's been holed up in there for months. She probably hasn't even heard the news about Pee-Jay yet. Charlie will just have to wait his turn."

They went out snickering and Lola shook her head. We then began to prepare for the meeting, setting things up to post for whenever it was over.

If nothing else, Maurice's meeting was an interesting diversion from work. It turned out to be more of a pep talk than anything else, with Maurice assuring everyone that Perry was indeed gone for good, though he couldn't say why either. As Lola had suggested, it appeared that nobody really knew. He did assure us all that our own jobs were secure and that everyone was welcome to come talk to him if they had any questions.

Kelly's hand shot up. She was sitting beside me and across from Lola at the huge, round conference table and Maurice nodded at her to go ahead before Lola could stop her.

"Are we really allowed to talk to the drivers now?"

Everyone waited for the standard correction…route salesmen, you boob, but it never came. Instead, Maurice looked at both Kelly and me shrewdly. "Within *reason*, Kelly, but there's no reason for them to be trooping in and out like they've *been* doing."

Tim spoke up. "I believe that's all been stopped," he said with a glance in my direction that everybody caught.

"Right," Maurice agreed heartily. "Only the supervisors have any reason to be up here in the offices.

I raised *my* eyebrows at Tim and everyone, including Lola, caught *that*.

"*Kerry…*" she hissed.

"Anything else?" Maurice looked over the silent room like a lost little boy. "Come on. Talk to me."

"How about the dress code?" Brenda asked in a low voice.

"Ah, yes…the…uh…dress code." Maurice rubbed his hands together with enthusiasm, obviously hoping to get some humor into the room. "That's a good question, Brenda, and I'm glad you brought it up. I know with Perry things were a little straight-laced even though I still see jeans around here now and then. Now, though, we'll accept anything as long as it's topless."

He paused for the roomful of laughter that never came. Sober faces watched him from every seat at the huge table. "Uh, as long as you don't do it every day?" he added hopefully.

"What about lunches?" Hannah asked, glancing coldly at Kelly and me. Kelly stuck out her tongue at Hannah and Lola kicked Kelly under the table.

"Uh…we won't *fire* you for taking a little longer lunch than we allow…as long as you don't do *that* every day, either." Again, his gaze focused on Kelly and me. We were sure getting a lot of looks this morning.

Margie interrupted with a question concerning pickups of delinquent water coolers, her department, and I leaned in to whisper to Kelly.

"Ask him if we're really allowed to sit on the floor now."

This time it was Lola who shot me the look, and I shrugged and smiled innocently at her.

Evidently, there were no more questions, so Maurice sighed loudly and held up both hands, palms up. "All right. I'll be in my office in case you change your mind and want to talk. I guess that's about it, then. I…uh…hope I don't get any voodoo dolls in the mail."

This time the whole room looked over at me and Kelly burst into her loud cackling. "Oh, nooooo, that's Kerry's specialty," she howled as the employees began to file out of the room.

"Kelly, that wasn't necessary," I said coldly.

"Kerry, *must* you wear that…*thing*…out in the open like that?" Lola was looking at the pentagram Devin had given me. I wore it exposed over my blouse and the silver caught the light, flashing that goat face at this most awkward time.

"I have to. It gets tangled up with the Sador if I wear it under my blouse."

"Well, can't you switch them?"

"Forget it, Lola," Kelly said. "The Sador's just as bad only it's bigger."

Lola turned to Hannah, who remained in her seat several feet away from us. Lately, it seemed, Hannah stayed as far away from us as she could manage.

"Hannah, can I…uh…speak to you in private?" Lola asked.

"Me?"

"Yes, you. Kerry, go make some coffee. And Kelly, go comb your hair."

"Okay," Kelly said. "I'll go to the lounge. I haven't heard a word about Kerry and Devin all day."

"Don't worry." Lola smiled sweetly at her. "You'll catch up. I'm *sure* the circulation will be better now that Perry's gone."

Hannah was sitting on the step when we returned and Lola beckoned for us to join the party.

"What's this?" Kelly asked. "Another meeting? Not to sound hopeful but, are we fired?"

We seated ourselves at random on empty floor spots and Lola cleared her throat.

"All right, you guys. Since the air's being cleared all over this place today, I think we ought to try to clean up our own garbage too. Hannah and I have already discussed it and I know you two are aware of the cold war that's been going on in here the past week or so. Now, we've never had any infighting before. Not speaking is just as bad. Kerry, Hannah isn't mad at you and she says she doesn't *care* what you and Devin do."

I looked at Hannah and Lola went on. "I thought that was the reason too, and I told her it was none of her business, but she said Devin wasn't the problem."

"It *is* your business, Kerry," Hannah said in a quiet voice.

"Then, what *has* been wrong? And how come you quit speaking to Kelly, too?"

"I'm *getting* to that," Lola interrupted. "Hannah feels that she's been doing all the extra work in this office since they've added all the Chicago accounts. And she *does* have more in her trays. You both have to admit that. And Kerry…you could answer the phone a little more."

"Yeah!" Kelly said. "Kerry *never* takes *her* turn. She gave me a playful shove and I shoved her back.

"That goes for you too, Kelly," I snapped. "Benny's calls, plus your mother's and your sister-in-law…none of those count."

"Look," Lola interjected. "Let's get this cleared up. What do you all think we should do about the accounts problem?"

"Redivide them!" Kelly said enthusiastically. "I want to get rid of some too!

Hannah, why didn't you say so sooner?"

"You know Hannah," Lola said, glancing at her like an understanding referee. "She never talks."

The next twenty minutes included a squabble over the letters of the alphabet. I made out like a bandit, actually losing my Fs to Hannah and now commanding the alphabet from A to E. Kelly appeared to get the worst of it, gaining several letters from Hannah, making her P to Z.

"You don't really have any more than anyone else," I consoled Kelly. "You just never had many to begin with."

"You're full of shit! What about all those fuckin' Ss, huh? And you *lose* a letter?"

"That's because every business in the world tries to start with an A," I said. "To be first in the Yellow Pages."

"All *right*, you two!"

"I was just trying to make her feel better, Mama."

"You're provoking her."

"Yeah, yeah." Kelly shot a rubber band at me. "You're provoking me."

"Lola, shut her up!" I wailed.

No answer came from Lola's office. It was lunchtime and she was gone.

With the friendly atmosphere back in our office, Hannah actually agreed to come to lunch with us. I'd tried to dial my own house before we left, but the phone just rang and rang. Devin was either in a deep sleep or at his own apartment, and I couldn't call there.

Kelly and Hannah were still wound up over Perry's dismissal, but I didn't have much to say at lunch. My mind was still back at the coffee shop when I'd last talked to Devin. I wondered if he knew about Perry. How could he, but then, how could he know any of the things he sometimes came up with?

"Hey, Ker...snap out of it." Kelly's voice dragged me back to the present and the booth we sat in at the local McDonald's. "You really look tired. Are you going to make it?"

"Yeah. It's just the being up all night."

"That's not *our* fault. Drink some more coffee. You're gonna need it. I *know* you won't have enough sense to go to bed tonight, and if I know Devin, he'll sleep all day just so he can keep you up all night. That boy...he belongs in a nuthouse if you ask me."

"Kelly. I'm not in the mood, okay?"

Back in the office, I tried to call again. I'd decided to go home if he did answer. It was only one o'clock, but at least I'd put in most of the day.

"Why don't you just let him sleep?" Kelly said as I dialed.

"What's with her?" Lola asked when no smart retort came from me, which would have been the usual.

"Oh, she's sulking because I intimated that Devin isn't all *there*, if you know what I mean."

"Why would she get upset about that?" Lola said in a reasonable tone. "He *isn't*. Everyone knows *that*!"

I slammed the phone down in frustration. "Knock it off, all of you. I really don't think you're funny."

"Aw, poor Kerry. She's so grouchy." Kelly poured it on thick. Pat walked in at that moment, though, so I ignored her and went back to the telephone.

"Here are those tickets of Devin's, Lola. Tim decoded them." He waved to me but I barely acknowledged him. Even raising my hand was becoming an effort. I wished I'd taken Devin's advice and gone home with him.

Pat looked surprised. "What's the matter with her?" he asked.

"She's sulking because Lola and I told her that Devin was demented." Kelly yawned, as if bored with the subject by now.

Pat grinned and jumped in with both feet. "Well, someone should tell her. She has a right to know. In fact, I'd have thought Devin would've had the decency to tell her. Kerry, come on. Devin didn't tell you about all those years he spent in the institution?"

"Oh, yes, the institution," Lola said, trying to keep a straight face. "I forgot about that."

"Look, I don't want to hear it!" My nerves were frayed and I could feel the breaking point looming ahead. Here they were, joking about something that was anything but funny to me. Especially after last night and this morning. "If you all have something to say about Devin, say it to his face."

"Hey, come on, Ker." Pat's face fell and his voice was wounded.

"I'm sorry, Pat. I'm just dead tired. That's all."

"Well, don't take it out on *us,*" Kelly said, flipping casually through the tickets that Pat had brought in. "It's not *our* fault your boyfriend's crazy."

"All right, Kelly," Lola said, laughing. "Don't tell her any more. Devin can tell her if he wants her to know."

"Yeah, guess you're right, Lola," Kelly said. "Some people just have to find out the hard way. Boy, just look at these tickets, will ya? Who would know this said ABC Motors?" She held up a ticket so illegible that even the run-together ABC couldn't be deciphered.

"Well, Tim looked up the addresses," Pat explained. "That's the decoding secret in the route room. Tim just goes to the address directory and it lists the current resident. We *should* keep one with Devin's route book."

"Well, it's only *his* tickets we can't read," Lola agreed. "At least *these* days. Devin used to print pretty clear."

"Tell *him* about it, not me." I tried the phone one more time and still no answer. By four o'clock, I gave up for good and resigned myself to finishing out the day.

Lola offered to take me home at five but I declined, sure that Devin would not forget to pick me up. If he wasn't out there at five, I was supposed to walk to the coffee shop and wait there. When five o'clock hit, I started walking.

I was almost glad he wasn't waiting for me in front of the plant. The air was cold and nippy enough to wake me up a little and the walk gave me a chance to think.

The biggest shock of the day had been Perry's dismissal. Devin had predicted it to the day. Devin had said that Halloween wasn't so far away. He couldn't have known, yet just yesterday he'd stated that he'd had about all he could take from Mr. Jaoon. What kind of coincidence was that?

Not that it was necessarily a bad thing Devin had done, if somehow he'd done it. I remembered the story about his murdered brother and shivered. If *that* was true, Perry had gotten off easy.

Then again, we had been losing good employees due to Perry's relentless dictatorship. Now the exit was jammed with phone girls and drivers, all in fearless reunion. Just watching the plant empty tonight would have been sheer pleasure had I not been so tired. If Devin *had* somehow initiated this, was it so bad a thing he'd done?

Another thing on my mind was the teasing in the office today…the bit about Devin being a little…crazy. Could there be any truth to the remarks about Devin having spent time in an institution? It was possible that there were a lot of things about Devin that others knew and just took for granted. I knew if I confronted him with what they'd said today, he would tell me the truth. If I'd learned anything about Devin in our time together, it was that he placed a high value on honesty and truth.

But Devin…in an institution?"

20 I took my time walking. I had been up more than 35 hours and between last night's realization and this morning's shock at the changes in the plant, I'd had enough. I wasn't going to stay up all night worrying about any of it. I kept an eye out for the van as I walked, but the only vehicle headed my way was a loud motorcycle.

As it cruised up to the curb, I realized that the funny-looking driver, face covered with goggles, was Devin. Obviously, he hadn't gone to *my* house to sleep.

I was almost too tired to be glad to see him.

"You're not afraid of these things, are you?" He indicated with his hand that I should climb aboard.

"No." I climbed on behind him and shoved my hands inside the pockets of his black leather jacket.

"Perry Jason was tired last night," I said loudly as he zoomed away from the curb, the engine drowning me out almost altogether.

Devin shifted gears, his attention on the road, but I knew that he'd heard me. I'd yelled right in his ear.

"Yeah? What for?" He'd pulled up to the five o'clock, red-light lineup and the motor idling made it easier to hear and talk.

"Nobody knows why. Not even Maurice. You don't seem surprised."

"Should I be?"

The light turned green then, and I made no further attempts to speak during the ride home.

When we arrived at my house Devin helped me down and all but carried me inside, pushing me down on the couch and shoving a nearby pillow under my head.

"You stay down. You've got to be exhausted. Where's the kids?"

"They're staying overnight at Kathy's. Their turn for Halloween tonight."

"Far out." He went to the kitchen and filled a pot with water. "I'm going to make us some coffee, and then I'm going to split so you can sleep."

When it was ready, he brought the cups to the coffee table and pulled it closer to the couch. I moved over to make room for him to sit and he began rubbing my shoulders.

"You'll feel better after you get a good night's sleep," he said.

I nodded and lay back against the pillow, so glad to be home and wishing there wasn't that invisible wall between us. Nothing had changed since this morning. That very thought seemed to trigger a reaction from Devin.

"I wish I could interpret these feelings I'm picking up from you," he said. "Better yet, I wish you'd just tell me. I realize you're exhausted but, well, I think there's something else. A question, perhaps, but something that's worrying you about *us*."

I didn't comment. He was right and there was no use denying it, but I also knew better than to get into this conversation with the mental state I was in.

"Lady, I know when something is wrong or when someone is upset, especially if I happen to love her."

As he talked, all the worries and fatigue, all the fears, doubts and uncertainties began to well up inside me and surface in a wave of despondency…in much the same way as that Sunday morning when he had listed himself as a series of terrible words…the same hopelessness *he* had made me feel that morning. But this time nobody was pushing invisible buttons to create these feelings. This time it was something inside me that just couldn't contain the pent-up feelings any longer. The pressure hit the breaking point when Devin began to talk and I could feel the tears coming. I opened my mouth to try to explain, but the words choked up and I could no longer hold the tears back.

When the dam broke, I buried my face in my sleeves. Through all this, Devin sat watching me quietly, as he had done before.

"You might as well get it all out, lady," he said with sadness and resignation. "Get it all out now so we won't have this human bullshit between us."

I wiped my eyes and looked at him in bewilderment. "What do you mean, human bullshit?"

"Just what I said." There was a quiet finality in his voice as he picked up his jacket and slung it over his shoulder. Hurt glistened in his eyes. "I guess I'll call you. Unless you'd rather I didn't."

So *this* was his solution to it, I thought, feeling just as hurt at his seeming indifference. Just get pissed off and leave. Well, *let him go*. *Let him go while you can still let him walk away*. Let him go before you're in something so deep you can never get out.

My ego had all the answers. All the advice I knew I should follow while I still could, but I didn't want him to go. I lay there, panic building as he turned to leave. He stood there for a minute as if waiting for me to say something to stop him, but I was just too exhausted and upset to find the words. Then, without another word, he turned and walked out, closing the door quietly behind him.

Let him go!

I didn't move to get up, the hard sobs coming openly now for there was nobody to care if I cried or not. Nobody, now, but me. I was better off, I told myself. In a month, it would all be forgotten and life would be boring and monotonous and sane again. There would be no more wondering about Devin or unborn children or secrets as yet unrevealed, and the sobs came harder as these thoughts emerged. I cried until there was no more emotion or tears left in me.

It was at least a half hour before I sat up and looked around me. Numb. The coffee sat, cold and untouched, still on the table. The house felt morbidly empty and I was no longer tired and irritable. There was no feeling left in me at all. Devin was gone and nothing else mattered. Inside there was a dull empty ache. A lack of feeling I had never experienced before.

I walked over to the radio and turned it on. It was still set to that acid-rock station. A song blasted out and I turned the volume down. Quicksilver Messenger Service. It was a song I had never heard before even though I was getting to know the artists and songs that rotated on this station. Quicksilver was singing *Out of My mind* and I froze as the lyrics continued from those first four words. She had accused him of being out of his mind, crazy. He thought it was cruel since she didn't even know him well. He wanted to know what he could do when someone told him he was insane. She had heard the news about him. She thought he was just too strange and that she'd be better off without him. He admitted that it made him crazy when someone told him he was insane. He tried not to cry, but it just made him crazy to be accused of being insane.

How?

How could this song just have come on after a day like this? It was beyond coincidence, a song like this. I had not even told Devin of the remarks that had flown around the office today. I sat paralyzed until the song ended, and then turned the radio off. I did not want to hear anything else it had to say.

I washed my face and blew my nose and, now awake, went outside through the back door. It opened on the unfenced side yard where my Rambler was parked in the driveway and the kids' swing set sat. The air was icy and the moon was still full, only now there was no Devin to share it with and there never again would be. It was over.

I looked around at the moon-illuminated yard and went over to sit on one of the swings. My mind was a blank. I anchored myself to the ground with my feet and held the cold chains with both hands, swaying back and forth without actually going anywhere.

A few kids were out in costume, dressed for trick-or-treat, but none of them approached my door. It was as if this awful feeling permeated the air so badly that even the kids didn't want to be anywhere near it. Dully I watched a man cross the street, heading for the fence that surrounded my front yard. It never occurred to me that it might be Devin even though, I now noticed, the motorcycle was still parked in the front yard. As he opened the gate and approached, I saw that it *was* Devin, but as he neared, I realized why I had not recognized him from a distance. The walk was different. *Completely different.* It was not a young active stride but rather the gait of an older man. He crossed the yard and ambled toward me. I half expected him to board the cycle and drive away, but he continued in my direction, strode up to the back gate, leaned over it and looked at me.

My eyes met his but I said nothing. What was there to say?

He remained watching me and we stayed that way, staring at each other, locked in time, for several minutes. He seemed to be either thinking hard or listening to my thoughts…which must have been deafening for *him*.

Go away, damn you. Can't you see that I can't take this anymore? Can't you see how much I love you?

My mind screamed at him silently and he continued to watch me. There was a different feeling in the air now…as there had been at work this morning…a change in the breeze. As I studied him I realized the illusion, for the change was actually in *him*.

Not just that his lips no longer hung, or that his nose and nostrils were as straight and narrow as mine. Not just that he'd walked up to the fence with a different stride. There was something else.

He was glowing a soft, pale blue. There was a nobility to his stance, even in the way he leaned on the fence. A calm maturity was etched in his facial features…a look of wisdom that only age can chisel into an expression. Nothing like the cocky young black, and certainly not like the hippie I'd grown so used to either. Without understanding the differences, I knew that I had never seen this man before.

He opened the gate and came to stand in front of me. My eyes were still locked with his, now in wonder and awe. I didn't know who it was, but I wasn't afraid. I knew for sure it wasn't Devin. And it wasn't that other one, the black. This gentleman standing before me had no confusion or hesitation in his eyes when he stooped down and took my face in both his hands, never once blinking or losing eye contact.

"Kerry, listen to me," he said in a voice I didn't recognize. He removed my gripping hands from the swing chains and sighed. "I…as a man…love *you*…as a woman."

I looked away but he turned my face gently back to his. "Can't we just go from there?"

Gladness and relief swept over me as I wrapped my arms around his neck and hugged him tightly. "Devin…I love you so much."

"I know you do."

Heaviness weighed on me as I buried my face in his shoulder, his breathing loud in my ear. "I'm not perfect like you are," I whispered. "I'm emotional. Sometimes I c-c-cry…"

"Shh, lady, you *are* like me. You have no idea how much you are…what you are…even *who* you are. And it's all right to cry. It's a release and it's meant to lead you to understanding."

"But you said…you get upset when I cry…"

"Over *me*, I meant." He squeezed me tighter as an icy breeze swept over us. "I never meant to cause you unhappiness. If you cry because of me, then I have no business in your life. You've been unhappy and frightened and it was never meant to be that way. I wish only happiness for you, even if it's not with me."

I pulled away and looked into his face. For all the problems I'd contemplated concerning Devin, not one of them applied here. Not to this man. He was almost blinding in his radiance. The streetlights behind him silhouetted his hair and shoulders in a kind of pale bluish-white halo. If there were tears of grief and confusion shining in my eyes, his eyes, locked with mine, reflected back only understanding and patience.

"Devin," I whispered desperately. "Who *are* you? Please *tell* me. I know it's our whole problem. Why can't you just *tell* me? Who *are* you?"

"If I told you who I am, you not only wouldn't believe me but it might frighten you away completely. You wouldn't understand. If I can wait, and you can wait, you'll know eventually without my having to tell you. And then you *will* understand. I can't risk losing you, Kerry. You've got to become aware of this on your own. Nobody can do it for you. Not even me." He kissed me tenderly on the forehead and stood up. "We'll talk about this another time. For now, let's get you in to bed. You're about ready to collapse."

Once settled back on the couch, Devin-but-not-Devin turned the radio back on, and Uriah Heep burst out singing of sweet freedom, a song that assured me that he just wanted me to be happy, even if it wasn't with him. He returned to my side and sat on the floor, leaning against the couch.

"I realize this is hard on you, Kerry," he said, "but it won't be much longer. All this will be behind us soon. When you finally *know*, you'll look back on this day and everything will make sense to you."

"Know *what*, Devin?"

"About us."

"If you won't tell me what you expect me to understand, then how will I ever find out? What other way *is* there?"

He nodded towards the speakers. "That's one way. Listen to the music. Listen to the words. It's saying very definite things. It's asking if you're sure you'll be all right without me. It's us. We've put these lyrics on the radio frequencies."

"We?"

"Others like us…*for* us. Music is a bridge between worlds, don't you see? It's the means of communication the mortal world so desperately needed. Just listen to the words of this song that comes on next."

As if he'd cued up the record, a song began with swelling symphonies that only the Moody Blues could pull off. It was beautiful.

The song was called *Watching and Waiting*. The singer wanted someone to look at him. He said he'd been waiting and watching for his friend and hoped it wouldn't be too long. He sang that he'd been alone for so very long.

The beauty of the song was indescribable. Soft and slow with violins and cellos following the lyrics, the singer went on to say that soon I would see him, because he'd be everywhere, but he couldn't tell me where he came from.

I looked at Devin who nodded at the radio and leaned back against the couch from his seat on the floor. He didn't speak while the song was playing, but he did give me several hard looks at some of the words, especially the line about not being able to tell where he came from.

I listened until it was over, realizing that, like his writing, music was a convenient form of communication for him. As I listened though, I had no way of knowing that those lyrics were pieces of a puzzle that I had yet to learn existed. Small pieces of a very *big* puzzle with Devin holding all the other pieces. When the song ended, he got up, lowered the volume and dropped into the beanbag beside the stereo, seemingly lost in thought.

I was thinking too. About the words to that song, about the one before it that had repeated what Devin had said verbatim… and about the one that had played before I went outside. Thinking about Devin and more explicitly, about all *three* Devin's. How different they all were from one another. It had taken me this long to realize that there *was* more than one Devin. I wondered about the hidden meaning in the song we had just heard, and how he seemed to feel that it would somehow explain who he was.

He spoke and startled me out of my thoughts. "Tonight would be a good night for you to conceive," he said suddenly. "Halloween night."

I got up and knelt beside him. "Is *that* what you were just thinking about?"

"Yes. Well, I told you I was impulsive about blurting things out. Rest assured, lady, it was just wishful thinking. It won't be tonight. It would actually be better to have him *born* on Halloween, not conceived."

"Then it would have to be conceived in January," I said. "It would be kind of hard to call it to the day, though, wouldn't it?"

"Not for me, it wouldn't," he replied without hesitation. "Not for *our* son."

"Oh, you have control over that?"

"The same control that keeps your womb empty now, lady. Or did you think that was an accident, too?"

I stared at him mutely. There was no way he could know whether or not I used any birth control.

"I guess that's my ego talking," he said, smiling, and reached for me. "I like to think I have that kind of control…however…"

"However?"

"However, since that idea is out of the question, take a guess at what my second idea for Halloween is." Humor and teasing sparkled in his eyes.

I smiled too. I'd had the same idea, not necessarily because it was Halloween. "Think we can wrap it up before Halloween ends?"

"Who knows? It's ten to eleven. Should we cut it short at twelve?"

He didn't wait for a reply, and I suppose it is noteworthy to lay claim to the achievement of the goal, at exactly midnight, Halloween's final moment.

Our problem remained, for the moment, unsettled, and there was an unsettled feeling in the air when he finally did leave, a weight that was almost visible on his shoulders as he boarded the bike.

"I love you," I told him and he just ruffled my hair good-naturedly.

"No, you don't. You're just infatuated."

I watched him until the bike was out of sight, its roar a muffled buzz in the distance. When I went back in, it wasn't to sleep. The problem was still between us and there was nothing to do but bring it out in the open…talk it out…straighten it out. I would tell him everything. About the black part of him that was so obvious at certain times. About the side of him I'd seen tonight for the first time. About how I loved him in spite of all these things.

And then I would ask him which one of these people he really was. He had to know. It had to be what he'd hinted at from the first night.

A multiple personality. Something I'd heard of but had never thought to consider. Devin wasn't just one person. He was at least three. It had taken me so long to realize it.

The question now was did Devin Drew himself realize it?

And if he did…

Of course he did. He *had* to.

2 1 The next morning I arrived at the coffee shop even earlier than usual. The kids had gone straight to school from the sitter's, so I had time on my hands, and time just gave me more to think about. It had been another long sleepless night and I had the whole day to beat through again. Nursing my coffee, I was deep in thought.

I'd made up my mind last night. Today would be the day. Today I was going to ask Devin to come up after work and we were finally going to clear the air once and for all. I had imagined the scene over and over, preparing for whatever denials he might have. I was so engrossed in the plan that I didn't see the big blue-and-white company truck pull into the parking lot, or Devin, until he slid into the booth opposite me. I looked up from my coffee, startled.

"Devin!"

"Hey-hey-hey." There was no enthusiasm in the greeting today. "What's up?"

"I didn't expect you here today. You've already been to the plant, huh?"

He nodded toward the truck outside, laden with bottles of water. "Does that answer your question?"

"Route again?"

"No, specials. Those one-time delivery things. They *are* part of my job though. There's no getting out of them." He sighed and reached for my hand. "Did you ever get any sleep last night?"

"Not much," I admitted.

"Why not?" He raised his eyebrows. "I'd have thought you'd have been out like a light after I left."

"Lot on my mind, Devin, but—"

Jane passed by with a tray of coffees, one of which she deposited in front of Devin. He looked at me expectantly after she'd disappeared down the aisle.

"Yes?"

"Devin, we have to talk. You know it and I know it. I've been holding in a lot of things that I should have admitted to you last night. Even before last night. And especially before—"

"Before Erick stepped in?"

My jaw dropped. He was doing the mind-reading thing again but putting a name to the man who'd returned to repair the damage last night. "Erick?"

He released my hand and busied himself with the coffee, adding cream to both our cups. He didn't look at me. "It's still there, isn't it Kerry. The wall. Right down the middle of this booth. You know, I kind of hoped I'd come in here today and all the bullshit would be gone. But it's still there. I picked up on it the minute I sat down."

"That's what I'm trying to tell you. We need to talk."

"Hold it." He paused in stirring his coffee and looked up. "Are you just referring to last night, or does this date back any further?"

"Since the wedding night, I guess. But other things, even further." I took his hand again. "I just didn't know how to say it that night. I was a little in shock, but I've had some time to think about it and I'm seeing things a little differently now. Well, maybe a *lot* differently. It's still not going to be easy for me to…"

"Your feelings have changed," he interrupted. "Is that it?"

"Well, let's just say I've gone through a lot of changes but—"

He pulled his hand away and reached for a cigarette. His expression was tenser than I'd seen it in days. "Well, that's a lot for someone who wouldn't even talk to me last night."

"I was too tired. I'd been up all day and all night and all day again. But tired or not, we really need to sit down and put all the cards on the table. I just can't live like we're doing right now. Too many secrets and too much worrying."

"You don't love me, Kerry. Is that what you're saying?"

Boy, I was really blowing this. "No, Devin, that's *not* what I'm saying but, well…I just can't start it here. It's too involved. I'd have to leave you hanging in the middle of it and go to work."

"Okay. I guess I'll be up tonight after work, then."

"Devin, please don't worry. It isn't bad. It's just that, well, I guess it's my turn to ask you to trust *me*. Just until tonight."

He nodded and looked up at the wall clock. "I guess I'd better split if I want to get back early. Maybe we can take in a legal lunch today. Probably won't be as exciting."

"That's *right*! Perry's gone. Wow…did the plant feel different when you went in?"

He smiled almost imperceptibly as he gathered up his keys and the check. "Oh, 'bout what I expected, I guess."

"Devin, did you have anything to do with that Jason business?"

"Would it make any difference to you?"

"Not really. I'm just curious."

"No. I didn't have to. He got what was coming to him."

"Did…anyone *else* do it for you? You seemed to know what day it was going to happen, and you weren't surprised when I told you."

He leaned over and kissed me. "He was an obstacle. He got his just due, that's all. I'll call you if I get near a booth."

"Wait, Devin. What did you mean about Erick stepping in?"

"Later, babe. We'll discuss it later. I love you."

I hugged him quickly. "I love you too, Devin. Please don't worry. This will be a good thing."

He nodded and left. He didn't look like he believed me as he pushed the glass door open and walked to the truck.

Gloomily, I watched him walk away. If he could just keep his cool until tonight.

I was glad for a busy morning. For once, there was only the sound of machinery to interfere with my thoughts. A schizophrenic, a split personality, a multiple personality…I knew virtually nothing about these things, although I'd seen a couple movies that dealt with the subjects and it was beginning to look like that was what I was dealing with. I could use those movies to bring the subject up.

"Kerr...phone." Kelly laid the receiver beside its counterpart and went back to her posting. I hadn't even heard the buzz.

"Hello?"

"Hey." Devin's entire mood reflected in that one hey.

"Hi. Where are you?"

"On my way in. Everything all right?"

"Sure. Think you'll be around for lunch?"

"If I can make it back in time."

"Is that why you called?"

"No. I guess I didn't have a reason. I just wanted to hear you say something. Maybe I just wanted to tell you I love you. I know that's probably hard for you to believe sometimes but, well, that's all I have to say, really. I'll see you when I get in."

I went back to my machine more heavyhearted than ever. Devin sounded like he was preparing himself for a goodbye speech. There had been no drawl in his voice and I wondered which Devin *that* was.

At noon, Devin came in, not noisily as he usually did, but somberly. As though Perry's replacement had arrived, more vicious than Perry had ever been. He went straight to Lola and I stopped posting to listen.

"Hey, Mama."

"Devin! You look terrible. What's your problem? Haven't you slept since Wednesday?"

Devin plopped into the chair beside her desk. "Buzz off, Mama."

"I wish I could. What can I do for you, sir?" She set her work aside with a fond smile.

"Okay these." He handed her two tickets.

"Oh, just *okay* these, huh? Just like that?" She looked the tickets over with amusement. "They're already okayed. What more would you like?"

"One small favor."

"You don't have to ask about lunch now," she reminded him.

"Don't have time for that. I have to go right back out. I just need one minute."

Without waiting for permission, he stepped into our office, reached into his pocket and handed me a wad of folded up papers.

Lola walked out, evidently to lunch herself, and I looked at Devin with disappointment. "I heard. You can't go, huh?"

"No, Tim's sending me somewhere else now. But I'll meet you outside at five if I'm back here on time."

After he left, I opened up the folded pages and looked down at the message. Devin's handwriting with that scribbled scorpion on top. He always found time to sketch that scorpion. There was no salutation.

How is it that we don't understand yet? Last night could have been the beginning or the end. My spirit is vexed beyond my own comprehension. That US could be doomed to failure. I can't say where this letter is going, for energy alone knows where energy is headed. I fear to say anything to you, as I tend to influence others along my way of thinking. I may have influenced you too much as it is.

Myrna! But no. You would have told me. Or would you wait until I asked? She has written, perhaps, advised you in some way of my selfish interests in you. Perhaps it would be better if I know, if that is the case. No matter what your answer may be.

My spirit is heavy. I have grown used to your love and understanding and cannot continue to live in this existence if your support is withdrawn. Yet, go on I must, no matter what the situation holds for me or where the answers lie...

There was no signature. Just a large X with a bar drawn through it across the center. Three intersecting lines. Six points. Numbers one through six written on each point. Under that was printed:

Can't decide so I won't.

Couldn't decide what? Couldn't decide which one was writing the note? Couldn't decide who he was today? And did this mean he had a choice of six names to sign? This could be even worse than I thought.

I pocketed the note with a worried frown and signaled for Kelly. It was past twelve and she had patiently waited until I'd read the note so we could leave. From the sympathetic look on her face, it seemed that I was surrounded in misunderstanding today. Devin seemed convinced that I had lost my feelings for him, and Kelly apparently thought we were fighting.

"First lover's quarrel, huh?" she commented when I folded up the note.

"Worse," I told her. "A fight would be healthier. It's not something I should discuss with anyone but him, though. It's just a misunderstanding. It'll be okay by tonight when I can sit down and really talk to him. If he doesn't do something stupid between now and then."

"Sounds *heavy*."

"Kelly, he thinks I don't love him anymore."

Kelly laughed out loud. "Don't *love* him? Jesus Christ, Kerry. You *moon* over him. What's he *want*?"

"I'm not kidding."

"Is that what was in the note he gave you?"

"Between the lines, yeah."

At three-thirty Devin walked into our department and literally shoved another note in my hand with a desperate thrust, then turned and walked out without a word to me or, for that matter, Lola. I sat there stupefied, staring at the note. Lola poked her head in.

"What the devil was *that*?"

I held the tiny paper open, the back of a small company pickup form, and Kelly stared at it too, as floored as I was.

I'll either live with you...or not at all

"I see what you mean now, Ker," Kelly breathed, her eyes wide. "What's wrong with him anyway? What'd you do to make him think like that?"

"I don't know, Kelly. Lola, I've *got* to go see him. *Please!* It'll just take a minute."

Lola hadn't seen the note, but she could see my desperation and nodded.

I grabbed an identical pickup form from my station and quickly printed in dark, bold, red print:

I love you, stupid!

I underlined the sentence so many times that it tore a line right through the paper.

I found him in the drivers' room and shoved the note into his hand. I was oblivious to the routemen who must have turned, startled, to survey the whirlwind that had hurtled in. I grabbed him by the shoulders with both hands.

"Devin," I said loudly and clearly. "I *love* you. You hear me? I *love* you. Do you understand what that *means?*"

He looked at me, then over to the audience of men that stood watching, mouths agape, then down at the crumpled note in his hand. His eyes softened and began to water.

"Look, Dev," I continued. "I'll be back here at five. Okay? Lola only gave me a minute." I kissed him then, not giving a shit what the route men thought and he nodded, squeezing me into his arms tightly.

"Just trust me, Devin. I've trusted you. Wait for me."

I pulled out of his arms and turned to leave. Devin looked over at the gawking crew.

"What are you all staring at?" he demanded. "Fraternization's legal now, remember?"

I found Devin outside at five, sitting on the hood of one of the trucks. He hopped down as I emerged into the cold November air. He looked like a young kid in his uniform and route cap and there wasn't any question in my mind that I was dealing only with *Devin*. I'd come a long way in a couple of days. I had accepted the duality of Devin, or the triple possibility, even the potential for six. That I had accepted it and was willing to deal with it was even stranger than the situation itself.

"I guess I should apologize for my lack of faith," he began, slipping his arm around me.

"Don't apologize," I said, hugging him. "That's what you always tell me."

"Well, I guess I panicked or something. I was writing you that note and the thought came out of nowhere...I was *sure* you had heard from Myrna."

"I would have told you, Devin. And besides, she couldn't say *anything* to talk me out of you now. It's a little late for that, you know? She had a three-day period to respond, and by the end of those three days, I was already flat on my face. I don't know what happened to Myrna and I couldn't care less. Are you doing better now?"

"Sure, I mean...I guess so." We had reached my car. "Until tonight, anyway. I guess I can handle anything as long as you're not leaving me."

"I'm *not*." I hugged him tightly before getting into the car. "What time are you off work?"

"It'll be late, probably."

"About eight?"

"If I stay away from Daniel's. I've already told him I can't work on his car tonight."

"Okay, Devin. Later, then. And I *do* love you."

He gave me an awkward smile. "I hope so. Later."

As I pulled up into the red-light lineup that only let one or two cars out at a time, I switched on the radio and was surprised to hear those Pink Floyd guys on the AM station. Apparently, some of their hits crossed over into pop radio. This time Pink was telling me to take a deep breath of air, and not to be afraid to care. To leave, but not to leave him.

This radio shit was beginning to get on my nerves.

Part Two

Faster Than the Speed of Life

"....I also believe that this same phenomenon is flexible to an unbelievable degree. It can create and manipulate matter through electromagnetic fields above and below the range of our perceptions and our own technical equipment."

John A. Keel
UFOs: Operation Trojan Horse
© 1970 John A. Keel
Originally published by G.P. Putnam's Sons

1 Waiting anxiously for Devin that evening, it occurred to me that we'd done all this before, like a scene we were doomed to play over and over. This time there would be no tablet to hide behind. I'd long since abandoned the journal I'd once kept. This time I would level with him face-to-face, looking him straight in the eye.

I switched on the radio to pass the time. The acid-rock station was now a permanent fixture on the dial, and Pink Floyd, once again, was beginning a song. Pink was saying there was a lunatic in his head, and that I was rearranging him until he was sane. Someone was in his head and it wasn't him. I recognized that song from Pammy's album, *Dark Side of the Moon*, but familiarity didn't stop the goosebumps from erupting as the song wailed on. Considering the conversation we were about to get into, it was a little too close for comfort.

He was at my door by nine, tired and late, but ready. Neither of us mentioned the talk we had agreed to have tonight…the purpose of his visit, but once the coffee was made and there were no more excuses to stall, I just took the plunge.

"Devin, have you ever seen the movie *The Three Faces of Eve?*"

It was a movie from the fifties about the case of a woman who had shared her body with two other personalities. I'd seen it years ago and in my rehearsals of how I would approach this delicate subject, it seemed an apt way to begin. Ideal, actually, assuming he'd ever heard of it.

He eyed me curiously at the question, but I couldn't read anything behind his serious expression. "It sounds familiar. Wasn't that a chick with a split personality or something?"

"Well, you're close. There were at least three personalities, but one didn't chow up till later. And the personalities weren't just moods either. They were actual—"

"Wait…hang loose a minute, chick." Devin whistled loudly. "Are you about to tell me that you think I'm schizoid?"

"No, let me finish. The shrinks thought *she* was, that's true, but in actuality that woman left herself wide open for other…uh…personalities to borrow her body. She drove her husband up the wall doing things totally alien to her nature. Half the time she didn't know when one would step in and she never remembered it later. Her life was a series of blank spots…"

"There's nothing wrong with my memory and I'm completely aware of what I'm doing at any given time," Devin interrupted, a slightly amused smile on his face. "So it's of no relevance to me what this Eve chick—"

"Devin, it's the same thing. I don't know if you realize it or not, but—"

"I just said. I don't have any memory blackouts and you just said *she* did. This is sounding a little more like Sybil anyway." *Sybil* was published last year. I hadn't read it myself but I'd heard of it.

"Let's keep Sybil out of this, man." I smiled too, hoping to keep it light and casual. "She had sixteen…come on, Devin, let me finish."

"Okay." He smiled agreeably and sat back leisurely in the red armchair. "*We* can wait until you're finished."

I looked at him in exasperation. "Okay, Devin. If you're going to make fun of me…"

"No, go ahead." He made a sincere effort to wipe the amused look from his face. "I am listening. You're a little closer to home than I expected but, go on."

"Okay anyway, in the movie, two personalities took turns coming out for a while and when she was Eve White she was meek and good and incapable of purposely doing anything bad. She just didn't have any backbone. But when she was Eve Black she started going on shopping sprees, spending money they didn't have on sleazy clothes, going to clubs to dance and flirt and was pretty rough on Eve's daughter. Naturally her husband had enough of it and decided she was nuts and took her to a shrink."

"Here we go with the shrink bit." Devin was plainly amused.

"Come on. The shrink found the second one, told the first one and even encouraged the third one—" I stopped abruptly as Devin broke into open laughter.

"You watch too many movies, chick," he said, attempting to compose himself.

"Devin, you can laugh if you want to, but up to Halloween night I'd seen two of you, maybe even three or four. And since that night, well, you said yourself that Erick stepped in. And I'd never met Erick until that night."

"Well, this is an entirely different thing," Devin said, suddenly serious as he lit a cigarette. "*None* of *us* tries to do any taking over. We have a little more courtesy than that."

My mouth dropped open. "You *know* about them?"

Devin's eyes twinkled. "Well, if you say so."

I pulled the beanbag closer to the couch and slumped into it, ready to give up. "Devin, if you're just humoring me…"

"Well, hold on now. Let me get this straight," Devin said, counting on his fingers. "You're proposing that there are two…no three…other guys here besides me. Three? Or four. Right?"

"*Possibly* a fourth. I've heard a voice come out of you that doesn't sound like any of the three I'm sure of."

"No, that's out. I can digest three, but not four. Lady, really. Even Eve didn't take on more than she could handle." Still that amused smile.

I sighed. "All right, Devin. Just forget it. I'm sorry I brought it up."

"You should be. I'm telling you the guys wouldn't take to someone implying that they butt each other out."

"Damn it, Devin, I'm serious."

"So am I, lady, believe me. But there's only three. Let's not make the issue more complicated than it is." He joined me in the beanbag so that we were eye level with each other.

"Then you *do* know."

"Well, I didn't say that, but *if* you're right, there are only three."

"Devin, don't you understand? If this is the case, it's not a problem. I love all three of you. There's no reason for any more secrets. I've been into the occult far too long. I don't buy that shrink explanation either. If anything, I'd call it possession before I'd call it schizoid. But the point is that I didn't realize it at first, and that is what's been creating the misunderstandings which were driving *you* up the wall and, in my ignorance, me too. I wasn't sure if you were aware of the others or not, but there isn't any real difference in my feelings no matter who you are at any given time. I love you, but I love *them* just as much."

This time his reply was deadly serious. "As a matter of fact, you *don't* yet. Two of us, maybe, but you don't dig the shit out of...*him*. And I hope you will eventually because whether you like it or not, *he* loves you, too. And I'll tell you something else, Kerry. *None* of us are going anywhere."

Theorizing about it was one thing, but to suddenly hear him talking as though it had *always* been out in the open was a little too much for me. Not only was he not *denying* it, but now he was acknowledging it and admitting it with an air of relief. I stared at him mutely, trying to absorb and adjust to this brand-new situation.

"I'm glad it's finally out in the open," Devin said suddenly, once again plucking my thoughts out of my head. He looked over at me from the joint he'd begun to roll. "Now we can deal with things as they *are*. It takes the pressure off, you know?"

"So that was *it* ? The secret you wouldn't tell me and said I had to figure out for myself?"

He gave me a long searching look before he replied. "No. That's a different thing entirely. Let's not drag that into *this* right now. I'm just adjusting to the idea of being able to discuss *this* with you after all this time."

"Then there *are* four."

He lit the joint, drew on it and passed it to me. "Try one."

I waved the joint away, thoroughly confused now. "But...you just said you knew...well, *who are you*, then?"

He sighed. "Well, I don't know *who* or *what* Erick is, to be frank. But he's handy as hell. Well, he gets me out of a lot of shit...no, he gets *him* out of a lot of shit. You know what I mean?"

I shook my head. "Who do you mean by *him?*"

"I'm referring to the one you don't like."

"Erick has a name and *he* doesn't?"

"Not that I know of. He doesn't need one, really."

"Well, why do you say I don't like him?"

"Let's not get into that right now. He brings a lot of the problem down on himself. He comes off like an egotistical wiseass, but you just have to understand him, that's all."

"And *you* do?"

"Well, for the most part. Erick keeps him in line. In fact, I'm surprised it took this long for you and Erick to meet face-to-face. It was just as well, though. I was wondering how long it would take before one of us fucked up."

"You didn't *want* me to find out?"

"About them. At least, not for a while. It's a selfish motivation, but well...*I* found you, after all. And *they* approve, too. In fact, *he's* been trying to get a little *too* friendly with you to suit *me*. For a dude who doesn't even know you that well, and especially the way you back off from him right now. But I'll clue you,

Ker, he *does* love you, same as I do. Try to remember that, no matter how you think you feel about him right now. His ego's, well, way out, you know? He gets his feelings hurt easily."

"Well, how do *you* feel about him, Devin?"

The admiring glow in Devin's eyes, as he pondered the question, answered for me. Devin hero-worshipped *him*, *whoever* he was. "He's okay, I think. He gets a little carried away at times, but then…don't we all."

I looked at Devin for a long time, taking in his black, wind-blown curls and the white uniform shirt. The way he was attaching the joint to a split paper match to hold the roach. The youthful ways he had of talking and laughing and living. I wondered now if this were possibly a game he was playing with me, or a performance. Or if he was still humoring me if, in fact, he had *ever* been. *Would* he put on such an act just to see how far it would go? Well, if so, maybe it would be good for me to see just how far he would carry it.

"How long have you known about this, Devin?"

He rubbed his eyes with his thumb and forefinger. "Oh, roughly, six or seven years. Well, it's difficult to gauge the time element exactly. Things are so contingent on the space-time continuum here. Perhaps it is longer than seven years depending on when we became aware of our brotherhood. In *this* system…"

I looked at him oddly. Not only was that a peculiar string of words to come out of Devin, but there was something else I couldn't put my finger on. Something was…missing.

"*This* system?"

"Yes, well the…uh…material world as they call it. The physical system, I meant. Time is one of the basic rules of the game here, in case you haven't noticed."

It dawned on me then what was missing in him. His youth. And he was glowing that bluish-white haze again, like last night, but there were no streetlights to blame the effect on.

"What makes you think I don't like *him?*" I asked, watching him closely.

He held both palms up and forward defensively. "Don't pin *that* one on *me*. I'm aware that you will be needing a little more time to adjust to him than you needed for Devin or me. But Devin's the only one who feels like he has to defend him. Well, you know, Devin's kind of…to use his own words…a patsy anyway. And he's always looked up to *him* as something to admire."

I felt myself bristle as he spoke. "Devin is *not* a patsy."

"What would *you* call it then? He would get walked on all day at work if it weren't for *him* and *his* lack of patience with the human bullshit. He'll take the blame for everything. Maybe the word is scapegoat. At least *he'll* stick up for his rights, whereas Devin is all love and buddy-buddy. I'm telling you, Devin would move a *bed* into his office, as dedicated to that job as he is."

My expression must have softened some. Erick tipped my chin gently and smiled. "Woman, don't get me wrong. I love Devin, of course. But he *is* a patsy for humans. And…" he touched my nose gently with his finger…"*you're* a pushover for Devin."

Already I could feel the difference in my feelings for these two "acts" of Devin's, if indeed that's what they were. "I don't think you *do* like Devin." I felt a strong, emotional, defensive love for Devin as I faced this…stranger…who now inhabited the body of the individual he appeared to be insulting.

He chuckled at the accusation, rolled his eyes and shook his head patiently. "How could I *not* like Devin, Kerry? *He's* the one who found you. We've got to give him credit for *that.*"

"Okay, so you like him," I said dryly. I resented the holier-than-Devin attitude that this Erick character radiated, complete with fucking halo. "And how does this *him* guy feel about Devin?"

"Him?" An amused smile tugged at the corners of his mouth. He clasped his hands behind his head and leaned back against the couch. "You really want to know?"

I nodded.

"Patsy. Or scapegoat." He laughed, then wrapped an arm around me, squeezing my shoulder. "We like Devin. You'll realize that as time goes on. None of us really want to exist without the others here. Believe me, woman, Devin has his personal opinions about *us*, too. Like any friends do with each other. But we also know how he *really* feels. He needs us…just as we need him."

"Then nothing's going on behind his back and he knows everything that's going on right now?"

"Of course he does. Look. Why don't you *ask* Devin how he feels? He'll tell you. Devin wouldn't have it any other way, believe me."

"So Devin knows you are talking to me right now, and he knows what you're saying about him?"

"He certainly does. He'll remember this entire conversation as he would any other memory of his own. He stepped aside voluntarily to allow me to talk to you. There *are* no secrets. And absolutely *no* conflicts. How could there be, really? Devin has the right to call it quits if he wishes. But that isn't his wish. He is concerned with *your* reactions to us and who can blame him? Perhaps he felt incapable of admitting the facts to you and thought that I could better explain than he. It was my pleasure, by the way."

I looked at him in exasperation. "See? This is what I mean. You make it sound like there's no communication between Devin and me. Well, there is. And I did figure it out before *you* verified it anyway. In fact, I had figured it out before *Devin* finally admitted it tonight."

"Well, Devin has a big heart, and he doesn't want to hurt anybody. You know that. Why do you think he's having such a hard time breaking away from his marriage?"

"*His* marriage. Oh, you're not married to her, I guess, huh?" If this was on the level, then who was *he* to put the entire burden of the marriage decision on Devin? If he'd been around for six or seven years, he certainly could have stopped the damn marriage from happening to begin with.

"Devin married her," he replied simply. "What right do I have to step into his personal life? He never agreed to relinquish his right to his own life and decisions concerning it. What kind of deal would that have been?"

"Deal? *Deal?* What do you mean deal? Just what kind of deal *was* it?"

"All right, it wasn't actually a deal like you are interpreting the word. There was no trade or bargain. It was just something Devin was honored to provide. And as for his wife, I tend to stay completely out of that situation and away from Devin. She's *his* wife and *his* responsibility, not mine. It may come to where I have to step in, but I'd prefer to avoid it. That's something Devin has to do himself."

I was still trying to figure out if this was a big act, but he seemed so serious. Still acting as if I really believed it I asked, "Are you saying she doesn't know you at *all?*" This, in itself, seemed suspicious to me. If *I* had noticed something amiss over the course of about a month, how could she not have seen the same signs over the years?

"She knows only the man she believes to be Devin. She *has* had a few near encounters with *him*. He's not quite as patient as Devin is, but she only reacted to those instances as though Devin was just in one of his moods. So basically, she is aware of only Devin."

I thought a moment. "In other words, the three of you work together in *who* does *what*…where and with *whom?*"

"In other words, where no preference is indicated, she would have Devin *all* the time, for she knows no other than Devin. Or, at least, who she believes to be Devin. *You* would be with *whom* you preferred to be with. It is *always* your choice for we bend to your desires, unless of course there is an actual *need* for one of the others. You can request one of us and we'll be here. And regardless of what you believe from looking over the past few weeks, you have encountered your expectations, if not your preference."

"Erick…" For some reason it didn't seem strange to address him this way. "What about the references, by both you and Devin, to your stepping in when Devin or *he* fucks up? Where do *you* come in?"

"Well, you have to have a comprehensive understanding about the situation among us. It isn't that Devin would foul his own job up. In fact, left alone, the only obstacle Devin might encounter at work would be *him*. In that respect, Devin is right. *He* is the one I have to keep tabs on. Devin's only problem is his *over-the-top* good-heartedness." He smiled and added teasingly, "His tendency to be the patsy. You know, take the blame for everything. With *him*, well, there's where the ego gets involved…the black magic…the eye for an eye bit. Perry Jason is a perfect example. Devin told you the truth when he didn't take credit for Perry's dismissal. That was *him*. Further verification that nothing is done behind Devin's back. He knew what was happening. He just didn't *stop him*."

"So when he sees that Devin is being taken advantage of, he steps in to balance the justice?"

"It's not that he goes out of his way to interfere. He just thinks he needs to stand up for Devin at the plant if he thinks Devin's being a little too agreeable, especially on an issue where Devin is in the right. We know Devin is too good-hearted to stand up for himself. I believe Devin *should* handle things himself, and I do try to let him, but *him*, that's a different thing altogether. He's the…uh…least human of us all."

That last sentence really threw me. "Least human? Are you saying that you and Devin are human, but *he* isn't? Just what constitutes *human* to you anyway?"

"You aren't," he replied quickly. "Nor is *he*, nor is Devin. Well, none of us are, really, but I guess Devin is the most physical of us all."

"And your role is?"

"I try to maintain balance. I see where those two can contradict each other, and too suddenly for where *you* are at, especially at this particular point in time. I usually step in to make sure you're fairly absorbing facts that you *can* handle. Sort of your guardian angel, if you can eliminate the connotations of your pre-established programs concerning celestial intelligence."

I wasn't too sure about all this. This was getting a little out there. I was prepared to deal with a split personality, even more than two. But when Erick started claiming, unabashedly, to be nonhuman, then it spawned a whole new set of questions. If they weren't human, then just what *were* they? Aliens from outer space? Divisions of Devin's subconscious?

Or was Devin just that good at acting?

Even if he was, how was he pulling off the performance of speaking in a 45-year-old voice? Where was he getting this middle-aged wisdom and this odd vocabulary?

A multiple personality was rare enough, but three personalities that claimed to be nonhuman? It was carrying things a little too far. On the other hand, Devin himself had not made this claim. Only Erick, and I could at least sense now, their absolute individuality, in spite of the general physical characteristics of the body of Devin Drew.

I needed a few minutes to adjust to this new unexpected thing, so I got up to make more coffee. My mind frantically tried to fit this new influx of information into an acceptable frame of reference. As I stood waiting for the water to boil, I mentally went over what I'd learned tonight.

Devin was at least four different people, no matter what he said. I remembered all too well that first night with the tablet. That one was none of the three I'd grown to recognize in the last couple days. And *that* one was the most misunderstood and least seen of all. He was the only one who caused the eruption of those creepy feelings in me. The fear.

Devin didn't, and neither did the black one. Most certainly not the steady, wise, infallible Erick who seemed to be more *saintly* in his glowing, bluish-white aura. If nothing else alerted me to the presence of Erick, this color frequency of his did. I was beginning to see the value of my second sight, though it really didn't change anything. Love me, love my brothers. Well, I did, didn't I?

"The word's out that you don't think too highly of us Scorpios," he said suddenly from the living room.

I brought the cups in and set them on the coffee table. "Where did you hear that?"

"Oh, Kelly, I guess. She and a couple phone girls were discussing the various traits of the sun signs, and that remark was made in reference to how you felt about us, the sex-crazed Scorpios. I don't know much about astrology, myself…charts and things like that."

"Well, it's true that I didn't use to like that sign, based on my experience with a few I knew. But then again, I didn't use to like hippies either. Besides, who knows how accurate all that is anyway?"

He smiled. "While I don't know much about how astrology purports to work, I have my own theory on why it seems to. It could be because of the belief that's placed in it, although I'd be more inclined to go with the scientific realization just lately that…well, you've heard of the Big Bang theory, haven't you?"

"That's where all creation was supposed to have exploded in one flash…like…let there be light? And it *is* called light, right?"

"Yes, except that there's much more to that theory than even your scientists realize, at least in *this* century, which is what I have to keep remembering you selected for this particular existence. Actually, it's more accurate to say that the electromagnetic spectrum includes far more than the range of visible light. Light is only the portion of the spectrum that the human race, as a whole, is confined to here in your so-called third dimension. If you look at the spectrum chart, it's commonly laid flat like a ruler and it shows light being right in the center of the known limits of the spectrum. Am I getting too technical for you?"

"Well, yeah, a little. I've seen the chart in books and I think I remember infrared as being on one side of light and that light itself is broken up into colors, red being near the infrared side and it goes from red to violet and then it leaves light and goes to ultraviolet and a bunch of others. But that's about all I know about it."

"All right, so we have the ultraviolet, x-rays, gammas, all the shorter wavelength rays on one end. These are high frequency and high energy. On the other side of visible light are, as you say, infrared, and a few even longer wavelengths, lower-frequency rays. Energy radiates throughout this spectrum and oscillates at different rates. It isn't really laid out in a straight line, but rather the oscillations overlap each other all in the same space. You've got some that are one or two cycles per second, and some a hundred billion *detected* cycles per second. Now, as a resident, temporarily, of this physical world of light and matter, you've been programmed to the idea of beginnings and endings from the day you were born here. However, this energy doesn't stop where all the charts show them stopping. They actually oscillate beyond and into infinity from both ends of visible light. You can *see* what is vibrating within the range of light, and you *don't* see what is vibrating out of that range."

"But what does all that have to do with astrology and planet influences, which do seem to work? Is that just belief?"

"Belief may be what makes it true for the believers and false for the skeptics. But that doesn't just apply to the feasibility of astrology. To explain more clearly, you are living in a world that absolutely draws to your physical experience exactly what you believe or concentrate on. If your beliefs are false, those, too, will materialize in your physical environment and even seem to reinforce the false belief. So mortals, believing in something, experience it as true. And it *will* be true for them. This should explain why so many contradictory beliefs are materialized in the physical space of people's lives."

"And what about this spectrum you brought up. Where does *this* come in?"

He glanced at the ceiling and then smiled at me. "I have to be really careful here. What I'm about to explain to you is most important and relevant to your present situation with Devin and us. You may not understand it now, but I think you will remember it later when things make a little more sense to you."

The radio, which had been playing softly in the background, suddenly began a Moody Blues song that started with the lyrics being spoken. The speaker talked of the universe and God vibrating completely, and vibrations that reached up and became light and then went on through gamma, and out of the sight of visible light. Erick looked at me and then pointed to the radio. We both knew this was no coincidence, so we sat quietly until the speech came to the final lines, which mentioned those various rays and compared them to a chord in music. It gave the chord a name—OM. The song then changed to the beautiful music that the Moody's were so talented at and Erick went back to our conversation.

"Taking a tip from the song there," he said, "try to remember that nothing is really solid and everything vibrates. All vibrations are sound, they materialize and either become solid here in visible light, or they continue on, out of the range of light. Gamma rays are located on the high frequency end of the spectrum, blending with x-rays and ultraviolet, cosmic rays...all high frequency rays. If you could get past the gamma and secondary cosmic rays, the cycles per second change from one or two cycles per second to trillions of a second apart. Some a million, or a thousandth of a second apart. Now, the waves that are beyond the cosmic, gamma and x-rays are *not* measurable by scientific instruments. They don't *know* what is beyond those. So everything beyond, on both ends of light, can only be measured or detected indirectly by observing their cycles of influence on mortal history as it is materialized here in this world. Far back in history there were some highly advanced civilizations and astrology was probably born by observing these electromagnetic waves as they coincided with solar activity. By taking that, plus the planetary positions and constellations, and putting it together, you have a new science that appears to tell you what's going to happen."

"Then these frequencies...gamma, x-rays...they are all shorter wavelengths than the range of light that people are tuned into? Higher frequencies?"

"Exactly. But remember, that's only one end of the known spectrum. Light is the world of action and slow-motion thought materialization. There are also lower frequencies accepted by the scientific community. Heat. Infrared...*radio waves...*" he glanced at the radio which was still playing the Moody's melodious song, "and these, lady, are the ones you should be *very* familiar with. VLF...very *low* frequencies. Long wavelengths. Microwaves. Radio being the longest. These are your home stomping grounds, lady, and I come a very long way to tell you this. Science knows about them, of course, even uses them, but it doesn't know *everything* about them. Other realities...other beings and existences...all reside in the electromagnetic atmosphere, as valid a part of the earth as the human race. Nothing materializes here without the idea or the essence of an idea originating in these higher or lower realms. Machines aren't really invented here. The idea is tapped from the wealth of information already there, waiting to be taken, either consciously, or collected in what people *call* dreams. But, Kerry, dreams are actual events materialized in these other realms. The majority of the human race confines itself to total physical existence because, as the song just said, it can't fathom stepping out of the one note they are focused in. A few enlightened ones spend their entire physical existence trying to experience the whole chord. It *can* be done. You will know this very soon, for you will experience this yourself. This is why we must be so cautious with what is presented to you just now. There is so much for you to realize and learn."

I shook my head trying to clear all this information. Too much to take in at one time. I think Erick realized it too, and let me change the subject back to what we were talking about to begin with.

"If Devin isn't human, then what *is* he?"

"Oh, the body's human all right," he said with a chuckle and shrugged, glancing at his upturned palms in a manner of a customer considering a purchase once he was sure it fit. "However, I'm satisfied with it. It functions quite adequately. It's healthy and streamlined…for quick action, you know?"

His reply was so genuine and serious that it gave rise to doubts that this was an act or fantasy. No man in his right mind would be caught dead in a discussion such as this one.

"I kind of like it too," I said with a smile. Erick no longer felt like a stranger and I wondered how I could ever address him as Devin when he was around. "Come on. Lie down and I'll rub your back."

"You're going to spoil me." The body didn't argue, though, and adjusted quite agreeably to the new position. "That feels good. You're going to put me to sleep."

He turned his face so that his left cheek lay against the beanbag and closed his eyes. It gave me the opportunity, as I massaged, to study the facial features and physical differences between Devin and Erick. There was just no way I could imagine this dude with a wig on, jumping around the office the way Devin had. This reminded me of this afternoon and the doubts that had overwhelmed Devin, as he believed he had lost my love somehow.

"You shook me up with your note today. Both of them. Especially the second one. I'm surprised that Lola let me go back there to see you. Personal requests to settle personal misunderstandings are unheard of on company time."

He opened his eyes and looked up at me and this time I actually witnessed the physical change take place right before my eyes. His features seemed to melt and reshape and I realized that I had brought this change on, myself, by my remark about the notes that Devin had given me. Erick had vanished in the wake of a comment not directed to him.

"I'm glad she did let you. I wouldn't normally jump to the conclusion that I could be losing you. I guess my human conditioning played a large part in that but, then again, babe, that's me. Emotions sometimes get the better of my judgment, especially where you are concerned. Having no idea that you had finally put it all together, I naturally jumped on the human explanation. I was afraid you'd come to grips with a reevaluation of *us*…you and me. I've spent so much of my life looking for you, knowing you were on the planet somewhere and having no idea where. And now that I've found you, I just couldn't deal with the possibility of losing you. I'm glad I was wrong."

As he talked, I realized that while Devin was the one who had panicked today, it was Erick who had stepped in tonight to undo the damage that Devin believed to be irreparable. Outwardly, I ignored the switch and went on rubbing his back as though nothing unusual had happened. The room was quiet for a while except for the radio, which continued with its weird lyrics as we changed from subject to subject. This time it was another ballad by the Moody Blues singing that the day never came for his love and him. That I was sighing as the night slipped away but if only I knew what was inside him right now, that somehow I wouldn't want to know him. The song then assured me that all would be all right in the end. It told me that this conversation had barely scratched the surface of Devin's mysteries, and that there was much more to come.

I paused in the massage. "Devin, look at me."

He rolled over on his back, his arms automatically reaching to embrace me.

"No, listen." I pushed him down gently. "I don't know *who* you really are, or *what* you are, but I do love you. From now on, if we have a problem, let's at least not bring any doubts about my feelings for you into it. No matter what, I *love* you. Please don't ever doubt that again."

Devin squeezed me lovingly. "I won't. I know you love me, Kerry. At least, I'm sure now."

"Good. That's all that matters. Everything else we can work through. But you took one problem and turned it into something that didn't even exist."

He released me, got up and went into the kitchen. "What are we going to do with the one that *does*, Kerry?" He filled the saucepan with water and set it on the burner. "I think we should both be giving that a little priority, because it *is* a problem."

I could hear the gas flame as it scorched the wet bottom of the pan. He leaned casually against the desk. "Are you going to be able to live with this?"

I thought about it for a minute before answering. "I assume you're referring to your partners in crime. Is that what you consider it? A problem?"

"Well, don't forget who you're asking." He threw the coffee together and brought it in, setting a steaming cup before me on the table.

I looked searchingly into his face, trying to decide once and for all if this was for real. "Devin, is this some kind of game?"

"Now who's having doubts?"

We looked at each other mutely. The traffic swished by outside and somewhere in the distance a siren screamed, setting off forty dogs in the neighborhood with their piercing howls. If this *was* a performance, I thought, the special effects were terrific.

Devin broke the stare and lit a cigarette. "Anyhow, I hate to be the one to break this little party up, but I'm gonna down this coffee and get going. My father's in town and he's temporarily staying with us. My father is looking forward to meeting you."

"Your *father?* You told your father about *me?*"

"Well, actually, I didn't have to volunteer it. He picked up on something immediately when he first called about coming. I told him we'd discuss it when he arrived. He said 'It's a girl, isn't it.' What could I say?"

"You get along good with your father?"

"Well, we didn't used to but, now, well, he's changed. Or I have. Now, even though we are on different paths, he's a brother."

He finished his coffee and took his empty cup to the kitchen. I heard the kitchen faucet running, and then silence.

"Devin, I wish you didn't have to go."

He came in and stretched out his hand to help me up. "I wish I could stay too. Better yet, I wish I could take you there with me. That would be the grand announcement, but it would be cruel to my wife and an ego trip on my part." He hoisted me up and I landed in his arms.

"Now I'll never get out of here," he said with a groan, pressing against me. Then kiddingly he pushed me away. "Cut that out. I *have* to get going. I'm already hours later than I said I'd be."

"I know." I sighed and opened the front door. "Go ahead. I won't keep you here anymore."

"I wish you wouldn't put it that way."

When we reached the van, Devin gave me a long searching look before he started the engine. "Damn, I love you, lady."

"Damn, I love you too." I reached up and smoothed back his hair. "All four of you."

"Three." He smiled.

At least we could kid about it.

2 Saturday, November the 2nd, began with a long-distance call from Pammy, who had arrived in Allentown for her family visit. Far from awake, I reached for the phone with a queasy feeling in my stomach, a throbbing headache and an overall flu feeling. The operator was a cheerful bitch who obviously didn't give a damn who she woke up.

"Collect from Pammy. Will you accept charges?"

"Oh, yeah, yeah, sure."

"Hello, Kerry?"

"Hey, wild thing. How's it going up there?"

"It's *cold*. How're you doing, yourself?"

"Oh, good. How's George?"

Pam laughed. "George is in *your* neighborhood and you're asking *me?*"

"Well, he hasn't been around and I figured he's called *you* forty times by now."

"He has. He's still in the hospital but he's fine. They're just running some tests. Anyway, that's not why I called. Did you ever ask Devin about me moving in with you'ns?"

The very utterance of his name caused a chemical reaction in me. Last night's revelation came back in a flash. "I...forgot to, Pam," I said guiltily. "But I know he won't care. I'll mention it Monday when I see him."

"Oh." She sounded surprised. "He's not coming up this weekend?"

"I doubt it. His father's in town with his new wife and brother, so he's got a houseful. He's moving here and looking for a house, so Devin's putting him up for a while."

"Is this going to change the plans with Devin's wife?"

"I don't know. It was pretty unexpected. It might. I just don't know yet."

"That's a shame. He's such a far-out guy, but I'll tell you, Ker, there were some pretty wild stories going around up here about Devin when I arrived. Especially with Mom. What the hell did you tell her about Devin anyway?"

"Are you kidding? I barely said anything to her…oh, maybe the ring. I did tell her about that, of course. When I was selling her the tapestry, so I could buy it."

"Well, it was all blown out of proportion but I straightened everybody out. She was convinced that you were involved in some satanic cult. I don't know where she got that if you haven't talked to her. So, of course, the rest of the family believed it too. She wouldn't shut up about the tapestry versus the evil ring bit. She said you were involved in something that will possess your mind and attack your children and—"

"Okay…enough, Pammy. I'm not awake yet. Really, ask her whose fault it is that we were raised so occult anyway?"

"I mentioned that but she says she quit messing with that stuff after she read that stupid book …that *UFOs:…Operation Trojan Horse* book. She thinks I should bring it back with me again and make sure you read it this time."

"Oh, jeez…" I really wasn't in the mood for this.

"Well anyways, I straightened everybody out. I told her I met Devin, so she's a little less freaked out now. Don't worry, I gave him a good report."

"Gee, thanks." I laughed, in spite of the way I felt. Dramatics ran in the family all right, but my mother got the Oscar every year for sure. "Ask her, if I'm in such a dangerous situation, how come her friend Myrna didn't pick up on it and warn me? She never did send us a reading on the ring."

"She never answered?"

"No, but it doesn't matter. I'm wearing the ring. She had her three days."

"Aren't you worried that Devin might have more attacks?"

"Well, I just pick up the telephone now if I want to talk to Devin."

Pammy laughed. "Hey, Ker, it probably *is* you. Even Mom goes around saying, 'I'm really worried about Kerry. She's always had this peculiar kind of power.' Anyways, speaking of that ring, I had her look up the jackal in one of her books. This'll blow your head. Guess what the Egyptians wore the eye of the jackal for?"

"I can hardly wait."

"To signify their devotion to their god Anubis."

"Who the hell is Anubis?"

"He's this black dude with a jackal's head and a man's body. I think the black skin signified the dead. Anubis was the guardian of the dead and the graveyards…you know, the pharaohs and the pyramids. I guess he was the dude who helped the dead cross over to the next world. He was pretty well thought of around there."

My stomach turned over. Part jackal, part man *and* black. I wondered how many personalities this Anubis had.

"Yeah, Pam, that is…enlightening. Is that all it said?"

"Just that and that the jackal was a symbol of good luck. Hey, at least it was for *good* luck. I guess that made the old lady feel a little better. Then she got off on a tangent about how you had an almost perverted interest in archeology when you were a kid. Want to talk to her?"

"No, I'll pass. I don't feel like getting into it about any incarnations she thinks I had back in the old country. Lord knows, we had enough of Edgar Cayce when we were kids, too."

I hung up with more important things on my mind than the history of the jackal's eye. Pammy would be coming home to a situation totally different than the one she'd put so much energy into defending. I had a few misgivings about what her reaction would be to what I'd learned last night. There wasn't going to be any way of hiding it. She was going to be living here. Devin had tried hard enough to keep it from me and I'd realized it without him even living here. Surely, he'd be more apt to let his guard down when he was at home. I wondered if his brother Trevor knew anything about Devin's cosmic hitchhikers.

The weekend went by slowly. The hangover feeling I'd awoken with hung in all day and for no apparent reason. I didn't feel up to leaving the house or picking up Mark, and the phone remained silent all day. I found myself looking forward to work on Monday and flinched with the chest pain that grew increasingly worse when I thought about the water plant or Devin.

To kill time, I tried to divert my mind to other things. I caught up on my reading. Smoked some weed. Played my country music albums. I didn't dare play the radio.

I still thought an awful lot about Devin.

Friday night replayed over and over in my head. At best, Devin was 'getting over,' using an act at the expense of a very gullible schmuck. At worst, he was a split or multiple personality, possibly in need of psychiatric treatment. The memory of the conversation in the office about Devin having been in an institution would creep in then, and I wondered if there was really something to it.

When I stopped trying to look at it logically, my gut feeling told me that it was no act. That Devin was very much aware of Erick and the black one.

The cooperation of the three was hard enough to believe, but needling me way back in the recesses of my mind was even another mystery. One that both Erick and Devin refused to admit to. I was sure there was another one who wasn't any of the three I knew about.

Regardless of what the answers were, it was pretty evident that Devin was clearly Devin on Monday morning as he slid into the booth across from me at the coffee shop.

"Hey-hey-hey. How's my girl?"

Jane passed by and set a cup of coffee in front of Devin who saluted her cheerfully in thanks. He was in a great mood. He doctored his coffee and then peered curiously at the book I had been reading.

"Sydney Omarr's weekly guide for Virgo…nineteen seventy-four," he read aloud, an amused smile tugging at the corners of his mouth. "You're really into that joker, aren't you. Oh, excuse me, Sydney, I shouldn't call you a joker."

"Read this," I told him seriously, pushing this week's page in front of him. "I know you don't buy astrology, but this'll freak you out."

I had just been a little freaked out myself. According to Sydney, the matter of a "ring" would be settled to my satisfaction this week, and in the "answer to a probable question" section was a one-line piece of advice. *Do take in a relative that is in need of a home.*

"That relative is my sister Pammy," I told Devin. "I've been meaning to ask you about this but so much has been going on, I kept forgetting." I gave him a briefing on Pam's plan to move in with me after her return from Pennsylvania. I explained that I'd agreed to this before he and I had gotten together.

"No problem," Devin said emphatically. "You tell your sister she's more than welcome. We'd *love* to have her."

"Well, we wouldn't see her that much. She works nights so we'd be like ships passing in the night."

"That's too bad," Devin replied. "I like Pammy. It would be nice to see more of her."

"Well, how'd it go Friday night?" My mind was racing from one subject to another to keep from thinking about what was really on my mind.

"It was a lot of catching up on old times. Been years since I've seen my father and it's strange to have him and his wife *and* my brother all staying in my apartment. He'll find a place pretty quick, though. It's crowded for them too."

"You going to be on a route all day again?" I glanced outside at the truck, laden with water bottles.

"All morning," he corrected. "You know me. Hey, lighten up. Don't look so down. You're not worried about this houseful of people messing things up are you?"

"It does seem kind of weird. Your dad, his family, your wife…all in the same house with you."

Devin tapped me on the nose playfully. "Now who's having doubts?"

The doubts stuck with me even as I punched in and headed for my department. That flu-like queasy feeling also stuck with me, as it had all weekend.

Inside our own office, Mama was her usual Monday-morning self.

"I want to go *home*," she announced with a stifled yawn. "Oh, good, you brought breakfast."

"Yeah, you can thank Devin. He's the one ordering them lately."

"That's nice of him. I guess I'll let him marry you after all."

"Gee, thanks, Mama."

"They make a good pair, don't they, Lola?" Kelly announced as she arrived for the day. "Kerry and her crazy boyfriend that everyone's talking about."

"Oh, buzz off, Kelly."

"Boy, you sure are touchy these days." She whipped out a nail file and seated herself at her machine. "Course," she added casually, "I would be too if I were engaged to a crazy person."

"Anybody that works *here* has got to be crazy," I replied, tossing her the stack of charges for the morning. "Including you."

In truth, any mention of Devin's mental stability made me especially nervous this morning, but the subject was dropped for the moment and the machines started up with their ungodly roar for the next few hours.

Around eleven, they died at the approach of Devin, Pat, and Joey, each supporting a section of a long office table. Joey walked in backwards while

Devin and Pat handled the support and steering from the other end.

"Good morning, Mama." All three greeted Lola in unison.

"Hello, little boys. Are you bringing me a present?"

Devin and Pat set their end down first, then Joey did likewise. Devin caught my eye and winked, but other than that he kept pretty much to the job at hand.

"Tim says you might be able to use this desk," Joey said.

"Desk?" Lola laughed and lit a cigarette. "It takes up the whole wall."

"Well, I ain't taking that sucker back." Devin grinned, leaned against the wall, and crossed his arms.

Kelly, spotting Devin, plunged immediately in with her usual mischief. "Hey, Devin! How come you never told Kerry about the institution?"

"Yeah, Devin." Pat elbowed him. "How come you didn't tell her? Heck of a way to start off a relationship."

"Hey, you *all* better lighten up," Devin warned them, never once wiping the grin from his face.

Lola burst into laughter. "Oh, go ahead, Devin. Tell her. She doesn't *believe* us."

I was the only one who wasn't laughing. Meanwhile Devin had managed to slip a blue bandana out of his pocket and purposefully began to twist it, as if nervous, as he continued.

"You people think this is all a big joke you invented but, you know, one of these days I'm gonna *really* tell you the title that the shrink tacked on me." He continued to twist the bandana and gazed off into empty space, ignoring their faces as they froze in stunned surprise.

"Title?" Lola gulped, her smile drooping. "Shrink?"

"Yup…title…let's see if I can remember…the shock treatments, you know. They erase parts here and there, but I believe it was…oh yes…a paranoid schizophrenic with homicidal tendencies." With that, he lunged at Lola's neck with the grossly twisted cloth and slowly tightened it as he continued. "There's more. I alternate periods of manic depression with delusions of grandeur."

Everyone broke into hysterics and in spite of my irritation with them, even I had to smile. Lola had jumped a mile and Devin had pulled that off with no warning whatsoever.

"Shrink?" I whispered to Devin. He had never mentioned any shrink to me. Not even during our discussion on Friday.

"Hey…come on, babe." He gave me a look that there was no need to question. He was apparently playing along with them for the sport of it.

"Okay, that's enough, you guys," Lola told them, still laughing as Devin released her gently from her bondage. "Settle down, now. All we need is Charlie down here. Am I supposed to keep this…this thing?"

"Can you use it?" Pat asked.

"Well, yes, if it's permanent. We do have an extra posting machine but no place to set it up."

Devin winked at me again. I acknowledged him with a smile, wondering if he'd make any changes in the office like he did when no one was around but me, but Devin seemed to be making a point of sticking around today. I took advantage of the situation at lunchtime.

Kelly had a date with her bank, and Pat was obligated to Tim, so for once I found myself alone with Devin at Lums. Devin had insisted on Lums because it didn't have the lunchtime overcrowding problem, and besides, he'd pointed out, we'd already begun to collect the Disney glasses they gave away with the cokes. Neither of us was hungry, so we just ordered coffee and the Disney cokes to go.

"So how did the rest of your weekend go?" I asked after the waitress left. "I mean with your wife, your dad and all that?"

"You mean how did they all get along?"

"Well, I guess I mean with your family there, is she still the wife that wants to leave, or is she falling into the everything's-fine wife role?"

Devin took both of my hands in his. "I was afraid of this…that you'd start worrying about that. The truth is, I can't really tell. She doesn't act like a wife that's separating from her husband when she's around him. She does seem to be falling into the role, as you call it, of a wife interacting with her father-in-law. I don't know if this is for show, or if it's her pride. I wish I could give you better news than that, but it isn't going to change anything. We made our decision a long time before my father showed up, and it's definitely going down."

I pulled my hands away and began to doctor my coffee.

"My father's pretty psychic," he added. "Always has been. But even if he wasn't, I was smiling and happy and it was probably pretty obvious to him that it's because of a girl."

I looked up at him. "Maybe it's pretty obvious to your wife, too."

He shrugged. "I think she's always suspected that anyway. If you were a wife, wouldn't you wonder if your husband was gone all weekend and most nights? I haven't lied to her and she hasn't asked, but I can sense it." He paused to light a cigarette.

I didn't know how to respond to all this. Something seemed to be changing at home. I realized that Devin was trying to be patient with her, but sometimes it seemed like he was avoiding any confrontations with her at all.

"Like I said," Devin added, "It could just be a show she's putting on while we have the family living with us. I'm not into making any waves about it right now, but she knows we didn't really have a marriage these past few years, and well, Vietnam fucked Devin up, you know?"

I had been stirring my coffee when he startled me with that remark. I looked up surprised to find Erick distastefully butting out the cigarette that Devin had just lit.

"Those things are poison," he said, making a face. "How *anyone* can smoke them! It's bad enough Devin does. I wish *you* didn't."

"Welcome to Lums," I replied cautiously, removing the cigarette from the ashtray and relighting it. "If you won't smoke it, I will. And anyway, I *was* having lunch with Devin, and *both* of us smoke."

"Devin's out to lunch all right," Erick said with a sigh, then smiled at the annoyed look that must have crossed my face. "Just teasing you."

"Well, don't tell me *you* don't smoke."

"I don't. But I can repair the damage on these lungs as fast as Devin fucks them up. And…Devin's the druggie of us, too. You ought to keep that in mind since you're so adamantly against them."

I glared at him. "How would you know that?"

"I know all about you, lady. All about you. That's good, though. I certainly wasn't criticizing your opinion of drugs. I'm happy you *aren't* involved with them. You don't need them. Devin doesn't either, but he certainly likes them."

"Oh, so I can take it that you don't like drugs either."

"I can take them or leave them. Preferably, leave them. They aren't necessary, you know, but Devin's always been hung up on them. Oh, not seriously anymore." He made an exasperated face, like an older brother discussing the problems of one of the kids in the family. "It started back in Vietnam and that's what I meant when I said the war fucked Devin up. I had to get a little involved in his personal life at that point. And I'll tell you who's worse than Devin. *He's* worse. *He'd* drop acid in a heartbeat if Devin were to take a notion to getting some."

"If Devin *were?*"

"Yes, well Devin sticks pretty much to organics now, but if Devin were ever to decide on the chemicals again, *he'd* be right there, fully enthusiastic. And why not, really? It's not *his* body."

I heaved a frustrated sigh. I had to be nuts carrying on a conversation like this, and today I'd been hoping to avoid any of them but the Devin I'd fallen in love with. Erick, it seemed, wasn't going to be avoided.

"Why are you so hung up on Devin anyway?"

"Devin's the one I fell in love with, remember?" I fired without hesitation. "Devin's the one I met. Not you, or anyone else."

I knew that sounded sarcastic and cutting but I didn't care. If Devin was playing some kind of game or putting on an act, the least he could do is speak in the first person.

Erick only smiled. "Think over your statement," he suggested amiably, leaning back in the chair. "Are you sure about that?"

That stopped me cold. I wasn't sure about anything. The appearance, speech, and mannerisms of this gentleman weren't anything like Devin's. Apparently, neither were his opinions. I felt like I was talking to a twin brother who looked a lot like his other half physically, yet there the resemblance stopped. They were as different as night and day. And in this case, I was actually dealing with triplets and possibly quadruplets, since there was a fourth one I was sure of that I could detect, even over the telephone.

"Well, if he's so crazy about drugs, this him character," I began, changing the subject back to the original, "then how come Devin's the one you pick on?"

Erick gave my hand a tolerant squeeze and sighed. "You don't seem to understand. I'm not picking on Devin. I'm simply presenting you with the facts."

"Sure," I muttered. "All the bad ones."

"Neither good nor bad. A fact is what it is. Absolute."

"You still didn't answer my question," I said, feeling resentful.

"And you still haven't answered mine."

He waited until the waitress refilled our coffee and then went on, still patiently. "Devin likes the drugs and *he* will go along with anything Devin comes up with. Devin has slacked off, though. All he does these days is grass. Sometimes a little peyote or mushrooms, but those are still organics. At least he sticks to the natural stuff now." He sighed and poured creamer into my coffee. "When he gets into any of that other shit, I split. That's Devin's trip. I don't need any drugs to get where I'm going."

"Oh? And where do you go, then?" I had to admit this guy was beginning to fascinate me. I'd already given him plenty of reason to split these past few minutes, but he'd held his ground without once losing his temper at my coolness towards him.

Now he only chuckled and glanced up at the ceiling of the restaurant before he replied. "Where I go, love, you've already been."

"So what you're telling me is that all I have to do to get rid of you is to force-feed Devin some drugs?"

I was kidding now. I was actually starting to like him in spite of my determination not to.

"Guaranteed you wouldn't have to force-feed drugs to Devin, and yes, that's true, you could get rid of me that way." His reply was genuine and sincere. "But be careful because you *could* end up with *him,* and you don't like him, remember?"

I remembered. "He doesn't like me either," I retorted in self-defense. "He hasn't been around since Halloween."

"That's where you're wrong. He's *been* around. He just doesn't *hang* around where he's not welcome. There must be some good in him, therefore, for him to respect your feelings like that."

I felt a flush of guilt at his reply. "Hey, it's not really that I don't like him. It's just that I don't *know* him, you know? He was kind of a shock."

"Because he's black?" The accusation was sudden and there was no point in lying about it.

"That was a shock, yes. You *know* it was."

"He loves you too, Kerry. He's a little dramatic, I know, but he does love you. We all do." Erick glanced at his watch and then checked it against the one on the wall. "I'd better get you back before your mother starts looking for you. I'll be…uh…home tonight. However, I'd like to try something with you if you feel up to an experiment."

"What did you have in mind?"

"Tonight. At ten o'clock. Can you be alone somewhere where you can just be receptive? No interruptions or visitors?"

"That sounds like my house on any weekday unless *you're* there."

"Okay. Don't try to *do* anything. Just sit there and listen. And write down any thoughts you pick up. No matter how trivial you think they are."

"I don't know. Remember what happened last time."

"Yes, but *you* have the ring, not me. And I'm not going to send you impulses to call me."

"Are *you* going to call me?"

"If I can. If not, we'll get together in the morning."

"How are you going to do this with the family and wife around?"

He leaned over and kissed me. "They aren't my problem. And I don't know why you're worrying about that anyway. Devin and she have already made the arrangements with her parents. She knows she's going back. Regardless of how it is playing out at the apartment, she is resigned to it. That's only three weeks away. How does that sound to you?"

"Too good to be true."

"The sooner the better, lady. The only hassle we have to deal with is the time between now and Thanksgiving. Devin did at least accomplish that much considering the original date was set for February, and then for the Christmas holidays. But he still has to spend time with his father, sell the furniture, and pack up the apartment. Quite a load. And he needs to be sure his wife is okay with everything. He wants her to be happy about this. It's in his nature to worry about people feeling hurt and he doesn't want to be the cause of it. Anyhow, if we don't move, we'll never get back on time. We'll get back to this later. Don't forget, now. Ten o'clock."

I didn't light another cigarette until I sat down at my machine.

If anyone noticed my silence in the office after lunch, it was politely and thankfully ignored. Erick walked me to the car at five and sounded like he really meant it when he said he'd rather be going home with me than to what awaited him back at his apartment. At this point, I was almost relieved that he wasn't. I needed time to sort things out and Devin needed time with the family.

While it was Erick who waved me off that afternoon, it was not Erick who *called* at six-thirty. At first, I assumed it was. It definitely wasn't Devin, and certainly wasn't the black, but there was something about the way he put his words together and the voice that reminded me of that first night with the tablet. My own voice must have reflected my uneasiness and *whoever* he was, he picked up on it right away.

"Lady, I have been giving matters some thought tonight," he said after I'd assured him that I wasn't upset about anything, just simply not feeling so hot. "Perhaps things have been going a little too rapidly for you. Perhaps too much is being expected of your progress too soon."

The voice frustrated me. It was calculating and coarse. I'd heard it before. I couldn't place it, thus the frustration. It was, however, proof enough for me that there was indeed a fourth person lobbying it up with Devin. A chill went through me, causing a rash of goosebumps on my flesh. I knew virtually nothing about this one and none of the others would admit to his existence.

"It's not that you're going too fast for me," I replied cautiously. "I'm not sure what it is. It's just that there's…uh…more to you than meets the eye. You know what I mean? Something's missing. Something I haven't been told. And on top of everything, I've been kind of sick since Saturday. Me, who never gets sick."

There was a void at the other end of the line. I was beginning to think we'd been disconnected. Then, that alien voice…like a cosmic whisper.

"Sickness in the body is purely a reflection of the contents of the mind. Evidently something is *seriously* troubling you."

"That's what I mean. You aren't telling me everything and—"

"I see. And you feel that you should know everything right now. You're that impatient."

"I guess I am. How would *you* like it if I played hopscotch with *my* personality and left *you* in the dark?"

Silence, then a tired resigned sigh over the wire. "Lady, I don't think you're ready for this yet. Your physical condition at the moment is a result of your uncertainties. You have so much to *realize*. I'm not trying to play games with your mind." His voice trailed off and I returned the silence, patiently waiting for him to resume.

"I'll tell you if you really think you're ready to hear it. If knowing means that much to you I won't keep you in limbo any longer. Devin would *like* to tell you, but he's not about to risk losing you. And that's just what might happen."

"Doesn't sound like any of you have much faith in me," I countered.

"Lady...*he*...as you call him, would take *great* pleasure in enlightening you and you can thank Erick for the fact that he hasn't. Believe me, you don't need it coming from *him*. And it would only give rise to more fears and doubts."

"What does Erick have to do with it?"

"Erick understands your semihuman need for time. I say that, not because you *are* human, but you've been *raised* human, and that's just as bad. Erick tries to be sure that nothing is going down that your ego can't handle. Sort of a guardian angel for your welfare. Erick is satisfied if you're kept up-to-date on what's happening, where *he* would prefer to drop the whole bomb on you all at once, just to get it over with."

"What about Devin?"

"For once, he's no schmuck."

I winced at his use of my word, evidently plucked from my thoughts when I was questioning the validity of what had really gone on Friday night.

He continued when I didn't respond. "He's staying out of it. And who can blame him? He'd like to keep you all to himself, but that wasn't the agreement."

"What do you mean agreement? Erick calls it a deal. What is going *on?*"

He ignored the question and then something hit me.

"Well, that's really neat," I said finally. This one had just stuck his foot in his mouth. "Here you are on the phone, talking about Devin this and Erick that and *him* the other, so Devin, or whatever you call yourself, who in the *hell* are *you?*"

There was a chilling silence for a moment, then, "Perhaps you are more ready than I've given you credit for. But damn. What if I'm wrong?"

"Well, damn it, what am I supposed to call *you?*" My voice was on the edge of hysteria.

He laughed softly, as though he'd been asked that question *so* many times. "I have a million names. Devin is good enough."

"There's no comparison! Tell me something. Which one of you do I get to *marry*, huh?"

"That's a little low, coming from you, lady."

"Oh, no, *hell* no. I'm so dead serious I could cry! *Who's* got Devin's *soul?* Who's got his *spirit?* Or have you split that four ways too?"

There was deep resignation in his voice when he quietly replied.

"There is only one."

"Yeah, seems like I've heard *that* one before, too. Is this all a big ploy to confuse me?"

"That was never our intention. Look, this is going to have to wait till later. I'm on the plant telephone and someone is paging Devin. You *are* going to be home at ten, as you prearranged, aren't you?"

"Yes, but I wish I knew what this was all about." I was grateful the subject had been abruptly changed. I really didn't know what to make of this fourth Devin at all.

"Well, I don't wish to involve myself in what's going on this evening. That's between you and Erick and I could damage the experiment by even discussing it with you. I believe he wants to see how strong your mind really is."

"Well, I'll make a point of it. Ten o'clock."

"Right. Now, I have to go."

"Later…Devin."

The phone went dead in my ear. Puzzled more now than before, I replaced the receiver. Who was *this* Devin and where did he come from?

I was willing to bet that Devin Drew knew. And wasn't saying.

3   I had plenty of time to think before the ten o'clock experiment. I turned the radio on and Steppenwolf was singing that if he could show me where he'd been, then I'd know and never ask him again. He couldn't return to where I was going and what he'd learned couldn't be undone. He couldn't believe my world was still the same now that he'd seen me again.

Right.

I just wished that Devin would tell me what was going on, and I tried to think of ways to ask that would produce an answer that made sense. The radio seemed to be trying to tell me, but I wasn't able to make sense of the messages. I reached for the stash box and rolled a small joint. I never should have smoked it, but I was trying to kill time until ten o'clock. It only increased my paranoia and exaggerated my fears to such an extreme that my imagination went wild with the what-ifs?

What if he *was* crazy? What if he was from another planet? What if he was possessed?

In my stoned state, the alien possibility frightened me even more than the others. I had read of cases where UFOs had touched down and conveniently borrowed the bodies of even Air Force officers. Well, Devin *had* spent a lot of time in remote areas, and I couldn't really rule out the possibility. And what if he was actually *possessed* by four individuals? What if—

Now there was just a raging fear. I glanced down at the ring and its stare was more accusing than ever. I yanked it off and dropped it onto the carpet as though it were poisoned, then remembered the pentagram. Given to me for protection. Protection against *what?* I tore that off too, but the absence of both articles increased the fear even worse. Within seconds I put them both back on again. The feeling of total helplessness without them was far worse than the fear of wearing them. I didn't know if it was the pot or just plain fear of fear itself, and I didn't care. When I cautiously slid the ring back on, nothing happened, and my panic started to subside. I pulled the chain over my head and glanced at the digital clock radio. The bright red electronic numbers blazed with the exact time of the appointment. 10:00.

Ten o'clock and here I sat on the verge of insanity. Was this the kind of fear that Devin had experienced prior to and during his attacks, too? Well, if so, nothing had hurt me. Yet.

I had promised to be receptive at ten, but this panic wasn't helping. Then something began to happen. The fear was ebbing away and slowly being replaced by an unmistakable serenity. I sat in awe as the calm spread through me like warmth, and then seemed to trickle in a warm wave up my foot. It was as if someone was holding an iron close enough to my flesh that I could feel the heat, but far away enough that it wouldn't burn. I felt myself drop into a state that meditators probably called alpha, and thoughts drifted in and out concerning Devin's attacks. Except now they weren't frightening thoughts, but objective. It was as if I were monitoring someone else's brain.

I wondered if the fear I had just experienced was a byproduct of Erick's thoughts just before ten, or if this soothing tranquility was the result he was aiming for. I was glad it was Erick who had set up the appointment. He was the one personality that didn't evoke fear of any kind. He seemed to be the steadiest of them all, and the most patient and tolerant.

Then I found myself thinking that maybe it was only the grass and my own fears that had created my heart hammering and spontaneous panic in the first place. The grass and my very vivid imagination.

I tried to imagine the body of Devin Drew sitting lotus-fashion in his apartment, sending thoughts to me and picturing me sitting here in this moment of time. Such a long distance for a first experiment. I was even beginning to feel that the experiment was failing. I sat there on the beanbag feeling foolish and wondering what to expect to happen.

Don' 'xpect nothin' t' happen.

The blackish drawl, intertwined with those words came out of nowhere, suddenly, though I knew I hadn't heard the voice with my physical ears. It seemed to come from inside my own head and become a memory before I even realized what I'd heard. The speed of thought. Over before I could realize just what *did* happen. I had never heard a memory before, so I listened to see if any more words would go by.

Nothing.

The fear was completely gone now and the only change that seemed to be taking place within me now was physical. Thinking of Devin was causing sexual arousal. Well, Erick had told me to be receptive to my impulses but these weren't impulses to write anything down. The urge I was getting was to take my clothes off.

I glanced at the front door. It was locked and I was alone, so against any logical reasoning, I followed the urge and removed everything. Just the *idea* of it increased the sexual desire and added the discomfort of knowing Devin was not here now to relieve it, at least not physically.

Still nothing else. I remained there, sitting in that absurd manner until the strong sexual feelings had passed. A cooling off to the point where the idea of what I'd done seemed ridiculous.

After a time, I got up and put on a warm flannel nightgown and turned off the lamp, sure that the experiment had been a failure. I hoped Erick wouldn't be too disappointed. It was only when I settled back in the beanbag that I thought to look up at the digital clock again.

Eleven o'clock.

An entire hour had actually passed.

A bright yellow note on legal paper was stapled to my time card when I walked into the exit the following morning. I knew it was concerning the experiment last night, but for some reason I was feeling pretty good this morning, regardless of whether it had or hadn't worked. With the light of new day, I was even getting used to the idea of my triplets, or quadruplets, or whatever. Now I wondered *who* the note was from. I disentangled it and headed for the lounge.

It was packed. Lola walked out as I entered and the phone girls had all the mirrors occupied. The stalls were empty, though, and a stall was all I needed to read in privacy.

Nothing happened last night, did it, love? Perhaps it wasn't the right time. Hopefully I'm wrong, but I don't feel so. You seemed so disturbed at first. Do not let the trials and tribulations of physical existence get to your inner peace. As the sun is to the earth, and the gentle rain is to the flowers…as the wind whispering among blades of grass…I love you. Another ten o'clock, perhaps?

It was signed *Erick, Erick, Erick.*

I felt a warmth wash over me as I gazed in awe at the neatly printed note. So unlike the tablet writing and so totally different than Devin's writing on the company charge tickets. Erick was a poet. A comfort. But…I missed Devin. I wondered where he'd been since our lunch at Lums, then remembered he hadn't even stayed through that. That made me wonder if the others would eventually run the hippie out altogether. And then I remembered Devin's own words. *Nobody's out to take over anybody. We all depend on one another.*

Or, had Erick told me that?

And did it matter since the words had still come from the lips of Devin Drew?

Still, did Devin *really* know what the others said about him? And did he feel any hurt at some of their statements? I decided to ask him the next time I saw him. Dismally, I considered that there might not *be* a next time but quickly pushed that thought away. Devin had a job here all day long. A job that none of the others seemed to relish.

Luck was with me, and true to company form, it *was* Devin who ushered me into his waiting van at lunchtime, calling loud jokes to his coworkers and grinning like a sweepstakes winner.

"Hey-hey-hey," he said loudly, hugging me in front of everyone watching us prepare to board. "Got some *good* fucking news for a change!"

"Yeah?" I returned the hug and he lifted me up and spun me around. Feelings of love and joy swept through me and I sent up a silent prayer of thanks to whoever had returned Devin to me.

"Yeah, first of all, don't worry about that flop last night. There's plenty of time for other experiments and besides, Tim came by my apartment a little earlier to check out my furniture. He laid a price of six hundred dollars on me. *Six hundred*, chick, can you dig that one?"

I was too happy to see him to even talk, so I just nodded happily as he went on.

"Do you realize that *that* will pay for the airfare *and* the personal stuff can be shipped up and...wow, it's just too good to be true."

His elation carried into his driving as he wheeled across the railroad tracks and headed for Lums. It was *so* good to have Devin back. He was more hopped up than I'd seen him in days and I just basked in the happiness of watching him, laughing, happy myself *without* all this good news. He pulled to a screeching halt in front of the restaurant. I hoped he'd stick around through the entire lunch, and at least long enough to answer some questions. I *wished* he'd stick around forever.

"Whoa, slow down on me, Dev..."

He hopped out and steadied my hand while I jumped to the ground.

"What do you mean the experiment was a flop? You didn't even ask me what happened, and I thought you were going to *drive* your wife up there—"

"Wait a minute...one thing at a time, chick," he said, laughing. "My head's spinning as it is. You're right. A lot's happened overnight. First Tim came by and that kept me occupied for an hour or so. And then my little brother wants to take over the van payments. He's looking for a job and even if he doesn't find one he'll be turning eighteen soon and could get a job at the water plant. So either way he'll be able to afford it."

"But why would you *sell* it? You *love* this thing!"

"I know, but I love you, too...more...and the van's two hundred a month that I could be spending on you and the kids. I've got a family now, remember?" He flashed me that bashful Devin-like grin, so typically Devin.

"Stick to one thing, now. Never mind the van. That's not important."

"You're right! What *matters* is that Thanksgiving is getting closer and closer. The plant is in for the shock of its little Peyton Place career 'cause when I send my wife home they are all gonna freak. Old Devin wasn't just bullshitting after all. I can just hear 'em now. They all think you're some sleazy affair I've got going on the side. Well, they'll see." He paused to light a cigarette and then looked up at me. "Damn, I love you so much. I can't remember being this happy in all the twenty-six years of my life."

"Me, too." I was, too. I wasn't afraid of our situation anymore. He *loved* me. That was all I cared about. "Now, what about the trip? Wouldn't driving me cheaper than flying?"

Devin thought a moment. "No, probably about the same. Hauling a trailer and all."

"I bet it wouldn't, Devin. Shipping boxes is really expensive, plus the airfare. I think driving would be cheaper."

"You may be right. I'll have to weigh it all out. Then again, three days cooped up in the van…whew… I don't know."

"Well, you make the decision, Devin and don't…let…uh…anyone *else* decide for you either."

He laughed. "Who else would want to be involved in this mess?"

"Yeah, who else *would?*" I countered, knowing he knew the trio I was referring to.

"No," he said, sobering. "That's the one thing they *do* stay out of. Neither of them wants anything to do with my marriage."

"*Neither* of them?" So he still wouldn't admit to the fourth.

"Any of them…all of them," he corrected, watching me carefully.

"Yeah, but Erick said that if—"

"Oh, Erick's *ass*." He began to scribble on a napkin, another strange-looking face.

"Well, I was only going to tell you what he said about—"

Devin looked up at me with the most sincere expression, mixed with his usual awkward shyness. "Hey, I know what the guys say about me but, it's cool, you know? They just worry about me. They're always looking out for me. That's all."

"You're aware of what they call you?"

"Sure. Nothing gets by me. And I understand what they mean, too. For one thing, they're impatient. I'm not moving out of the apartment fast enough to suit them. But I have responsibilities, you know? My wife is a good chick. And she *is* my wife at the moment, so I'll decide how it's gonna be done and how soon. Not any of *them*. Anyhow, I don't really think they'd interfere. It's just that everybody has an opinion."

"But to hear them talk, you can't bring yourself to do it. To *hurt* her. And I'm not saying you should. It's just what they say."

"Well, if they don't butt out I'll just pick up some mescaline. That will take care of Erick, at least."

I covered my eyes with my left hand, elbow on the table, shook my head and sighed. This was crazy.

"Think I should?" Devin was clearly teasing and I smiled.

"He really splits, huh?"

Devin made a bug-eyed expression. "Man, does he ever. He goes…like *way* out. I think he gets disgusted as hell with me sometimes."

"So, you *do* like the drugs, huh?"

"Well…" He blushed and looked down at his work boots, then back up at me. "I've pretty much quit most of them anyway. If it bothers you, I won't do anything but grass. I take it you're on Erick's side of the drug issue."

"I'm afraid of them, I guess. I've never done anything *but* grass, and even that's relatively new in the last couple years. From everything I've read and heard about acid I'd be afraid to even try it, and just the idea of shooting something…jeez, the thought of the needle alone…I won't even get a flu shot."

"Well, I have done some coke in the past, snorting it, not shooting it, but I gave that up years ago. Anyhow, I didn't realize how you felt about drugs, so I'll quit everything but pot. That's still okay, right? You smoke."

"Oh, Devin." I felt guilty laying this trip on him. He was so willing. "You don't have to give up anything for me, really. I won't do any drugs *with* you, but I'm not going to tell you what you can and can't do.. It's none of my business."

"It *is* your business. I want you to be happy. Happy with me. It's been a long time since I did coke, and I guess I don't need the peyote or mushrooms either. If the grass is okay, I'm fine with that."

"Look, Devin, I'm not asking you to give up the organics. Really, even Erick didn't seem too worried about those. And he's worse about drugs than I'll ever be. Even cigarettes, for Christ's sake."

"Yeah, I hear you, but lung repair is so easy."

"That's what *he* says, but he still acts like they're poison."

"Well, they *are*, really, but, well…one of these days, maybe. I don't know, though. It's the belief that causes the cancer anyway. If you can believe they're okay, then they won't hurt you." He paused and looked at the burning cigarette in his own hand. "I think, anyway," he added and butted it out in the ashtray. "Anyhow, no more drugs, and—"

"Devin," I began again. "Don't quit because of—"

"No. Don't talk me out of it now. It's cool, really. As Erick would say, I think it's about time Devin grew up. The other shit was just a pastime. A way to kill time. But now there's…us. That changes everything, okay?"

I smiled. "Okay, but I'm not holding you to anything. If you change your mind, well, you know."

He squeezed my hand. "I won't. I don't need them."

Wednesday, November the sixth. Another night alone. I picked up the kids at the sitter's, wondering how I was going to occupy myself tonight. Devin's dad and entourage had really thrown a wrinkle into the routine. I was still feeling that on-again-off-again flu feeling and I just wasn't one to even *get* sick, much less *stay* sick. It had been years since I'd even had a mild cold. Call it psychosomatic, that consciously I was forcing myself to accept a situation that just didn't fit in with any of my neat, orderly reality patterns. With the problems pushed below surface, they were now manifesting themselves physically.

"Oh, bullshit," I said aloud as the kids piled into the car. Kathy followed them out, adding her cheerful news to my day.

"Michelle's been acting a little funny all day," she informed me with a frown. "For one thing she's been sleeping a lot which is unusual for her. She was running a fever this morning so I kept her home from school, but it seems to be gone now."

"She was okay *last* night." I shrugged, checking Michelle over as I spoke. "You say this started today?"

"Just this morning. Well, it's probably nothing. I just wanted you to know she missed school today."

Michelle was awfully quiet on the way home, but she did ask about Devin.

"Is he really going to be our daddy?" She smiled hopefully in the rearview mirror, looking more pale than I'd ever seen her. *This* was my hyperactive daughter? She was usually so full of energy that I practically had to tie her down in the car. Now she sat in the back seat without moving a muscle.

"He sure is, honey," I replied, wondering if we had a thermometer at home. "Do you like him?"

"We *love* him," Mandy answered for her sister. "Don't we, Michelle."

"Uh-hum." Michelle leaned back against the seat and said nothing more for the remainder of the drive.

When we got home, I looked for and found a thermometer and took her temperature. Sure enough, she was slightly over a hundred. I gave her some aspirin and put her to bed with a new worry. Why the sudden sickness in the house?

When Devin called at nine, I told him of the latest development, adding that I didn't feel much better than Michelle looked. On top of my dizzy, weak feeling, there was a sharp pain in my heart area and it was getting worse by the minute.

"This is too much," he said. "We just can't seem to get on an even keel. How long has this heart pain been going on?"

"It just started tonight, but I've been feeling lousy since last weekend. It's weird that it's been hanging in for about five days. The heart pain isn't the same thing as the chest ache I've had since we started seeing each other. Shit. It all sounds like a bunch of excuses to get you to come up."

"I think I will, man. I want to check Michelle out. Fevers are nothing to play around with, especially with kids. Let me see what I can do here. It's late, but if I bring some clothes with me I could just go to work from there in the morning."

He was at my door at eleven, tired and looking worn out, but anxious to see Michelle. I ushered him into her bedroom where he laid the back of his hand against her face and looked at me with alarm.

"She *is* hot. Get the phone, Ker, and bring it into your bedroom. I'm going to call my father."

I brought him the phone and he dialed his own apartment.

"Yeah, it's me. Hey, Gerald, can you give us a hand here? My kid's sick. No, I probably *could* do it, but I don't know much about this kid stuff, and I'd hate to fuck up, you know? I thought maybe with your knowledge of healing…yeah, she's hurting too. How'd you know that?" He glanced at me with raised eyebrows and then back at the phone. Another pause, then, "Well, that's odd that you should ask. She's been having a pain in her heart area, among other things and Michelle's running a temp of, oh, roughly a hundred…it's hard to say without a thermometer."

I motioned to get his attention, pointed to Michelle's room and nodded.

"It is a hundred," he confirmed to Gerald. "Okay, thanks. Sure appreciate it. I'll call you if there's no change. I'll just stay here tonight. Yeah, bro, later."

He hung up and looked at me, then put both his arms around me. "He's going to see what he can do. Damn, babe, I love you so much."

"Is Michelle going to be okay, Devin? She's never had a fever this high."

"My father is excellent at healing. It's all part of this spiritual group he and Faye are into. It's not my trip, but whatever works, right? Anyhow, why don't you lie down and stop worrying about Michelle. She's in good hands now and you've got to get better before *you* start up with a fever. First things first, you know? How *do* you feel now?"

In my panic over Michelle's more serious condition, I'd forgotten my own pain. Now, as Devin called attention to it, I realized that the pain in my heart was gone. The only feeling remaining was that familiar chest ache that I'd learned to live with.

"It's gone."

"Good." There was no surprise in his voice. "Let's go check Michelle now."

As with me, Michelle's temperature seemed to be back to normal, but her breathing was strained, her nose struggling to pull in air through the clogged passages.

"She'll be okay, I hope," I whispered.

"At least her temperature's down. She's cool now."

Devin stood watching Michelle for a few minutes with the concern of a biological father. I studied his face in the semidark room, the only light shining through the window from the streetlamps outside, and I suddenly realized what he was trying to do and that it definitely wasn't Devin doing it.

His lips were moving and his eyes were closed. He held his hands about six inches from her body and passed them lengthwise over her. A radio-dial green glow streamed from them even though his aura maintained that bluish white I was familiar with now. I didn't dare interrupt, so I sat in stunned silence and amazement, watching Michelle's strained breathing return to normal in a matter of a few seconds. Her nostril passages seemed to enlarge under the energy he appeared to be expelling from his hands, allowing more air flow. It occurred to me now just how handy Erick could be to have around the house.

Beads of perspiration began to pop out near Michelle's hairline and he wiped them away gently with his fingertips. Then he drew a blanket around her, tucking her in firmly.

"She seems to be okay now," he whispered and stood up. "Let's get out of here."

We tiptoed back to my room and he fell, exhausted, onto the bed.

The bluish-white glow was not as visible in the light as it had been in the semidarkness of the girls' room.

For once, we woke up on time. Michelle bounded out of bed and Mandy was right behind her, both talking a mile a minute about the school day ahead. They were both surprised and excited to find Devin stretched out on the queen-sized bed and the change in Michelle was unbelievable. Devin smiled at me in relief. Michelle didn't look, sound or feel like she had *ever* been sick. Her forehead was cool to the touch.

"Come here, kid." Devin double-checked her forehead, not quite trusting my first check, hugged her, and winked over her head at me. "You were a pretty sick little girl last night," he told her.

Mandy crawled up beside him, trying to get an equal amount of affection from this novel new daddy they'd both suddenly acquired.

"I know," Michelle replied, nodding her head against his chest. "My nose was all stuffed up, but an angel fixed it last night."

I looked up at Devin, floored. "So Erick *is* an angel," I said, smiling. "I didn't think she was awake."

"She wasn't." Devin sat up and set Michelle gently on her feet. "Move it, kid. Devin has to go to work."

He went into the bathroom and I heard the faucet running.

"So. An angel fixed you up last night, huh Michelle?" I kept my voice casual. "What did he look like?"

"Michelle dreamed it," Mandy put in. "There's no such thing as angels."

"Uh-*huh*!" Michelle wheeled on her sister defensively. "He was *too* an angel and he had big white wings and one of those light bulbs in his hair. A blue one."

"Okay, you two. Let's get ready for school now."

They looked at each other, then trotted off to their room.

I went to the bathroom where the door was slightly ajar. Devin was rinsing out the razor and he winked at me when I entered.

"How can I thank you—?" I began.

"Hey, don't give me that thank-you shit. You know how I feel about words. Besides, it wasn't me who did it."

"I know." I sighed. "It was an angel."

He sure was a strange one, light bulbs in his hair and all.

I told Kathy that Michelle seemed fine this morning and could be sent to school today unless, of course, she noticed anything unusual in the next hour or so. Michelle was already back to normal as she raced around Kathy's house, her usual hyperactive self.

"*What happened?*" Kathy asked, obviously bewildered. "That was a *quick* recovery!"

"Don't ask," I said. "See you later."

Things were smooth and quiet at the office all morning. I didn't mention the night's events to anyone, not wanting the magical feeling ridiculed away by skeptical remarks. Devin was on a route, so Kelly and I had a quiet lunch together, the talk more on her husband and their latest quarrel than anything going on in my life. The plant had pretty much accepted our 'affair' and it was no longer an object of gossip. We returned to find Kim sorting checks in the phone room for our later postings.

"Say, Ker!" She looked up as we walked past. "You had two phone calls."

"Two? From who?"

"Well, one was from Devin who said it wasn't important but to tell you he loves you." Kim loved to relay those messages. "That's so sweet of him. And the other one was from the school your little girl goes to."

I tensed. The school had no reason to call me at work unless there was an emergency and Kathy wasn't home to answer her phone. I knew something was wrong, even before I dialed the number Kim had taken for me.

The call was quick and to the point. I was transferred to the nurse's office and told to pick up my daughter immediately at the clinic. She was running a fever of one hundred three and climbing. Her advice was the emergency room. I didn't ask for details, just grabbed my purse and keys.

"Lola, Michelle's running a fever of a hundred and three."

Lola pointed to the door. "Get going."

"Tell Devin I'll be at the emergency room at—"

"I know where it's at. I'll tell him as soon as he shows up here. You call me first chance you get. Let me know what's happening."

The period of time between reaching the school and up until I saw Erick was a nightmare. Michelle was lying flat on her back in the nurse's office, whiter than the sheet that covered her, her small frame trembling on the cot. Her lips were parched and blue, but she smiled when she saw me. It must have been an effort.

I thought of Erick and last night and felt the familiar chest feeling drop to the pit of my stomach like a chunk of ice. Something had fucked up. Michelle was worse.

4 Erick didn't waste any time with telephones. He walked into the hospital room at three-thirty and straight over to Michelle.

"How is she? What happened?" He touched Michelle's forehead and looked up to me for an explanation. He looked calm, but puzzled.

"I don't know what happened. The school called me. They couldn't reach Kathy, but I've talked to her since. She's going to keep Mandy until whenever I leave here. Even if it's tomorrow."

"You're going to stay here with her all night?"

"Yes. She's almost a hundred and four. And they're not *doing* anything. I know there isn't much I can do either, but I need to stay here with her."

Erick took a clean washcloth from the bedside nightstand and went into the bathroom. He emerged with it wet and began to sponge Michelle's body.

"Call Lola. She's worried."

"I'll call her after you leave." For once, I was glad that it was Erick instead of Devin. "Can you do anything?"

He frowned. "I thought I *did* do something. Last night. However, a fever is a sign of infection. Do the doctors say what's wrong?"

"No. They don't know for sure. They say possible bronchial pneumonia. They took all these tests and x-rays and gave her shots, but they still don't know for sure. And I don't understand all this medical terminology anyway. They talk over my head."

"I'll talk to them," Erick said. "I know medical terminology."

"How did you get away so quickly? Are you off work already?"

"Not officially. When I walked into your office, Lola told me what was happening. As I said, she's pretty worried. Temps over a hundred are dangerous, but children can handle them better than adults can. Still, at a hundred and four...anyway, you try to relax, or she'll never get better. When I got the message I dropped in on Tim long enough to tell him where I was going and why."

He slipped his arm around me and Michelle opened her eyes for the first time in hours. She looked a little dazed at the image of Devin sitting there with me.

"Hi, Devin," she whispered hoarsely, struggling to sit up. She was still white...ghastly white...and her bluish-purple lips were beginning to crack.

"Can you get me a drink? Where's Mommy?"

"Hi, Michelle. She's right here beside you." He raised his eyebrows to me as if to say *she doesn't see you?*

Michelle looked at me blankly, struggled to focus her vision. Erick placed her on his lap and reached for the hospital thermometer.

"She's so hot her skin is burning me. I'll bet she's higher than a hundred and four right now." He tilted Michelle's head up. "Let's see if you can keep still with this under your tongue, Michelle. It's very important."

Michelle opened her mouth obediently, accepted the thermometer, and leaned against Devin's body. Still white as a sheet. I carried the water pitcher into the bathroom, already filled with ice, and added fresh water.

"Is it okay to give her a drink?"

"Yes, but tap water will go down faster and she'll drink more if it's not cold. She needs all the fluid you can pump into her. She's dehydrated as hell. Has *anyone* been in here? Doctors? Nurses? Anyone checked her at all?"

"Since we checked in, just a nurse once in a while. She just takes her temperature, but she never does anything else. I think they may have given her aspirin and are waiting to see if that brings the temp down."

Erick removed the thermometer and whistled, then handed it to me while he helped Michelle with the water glass. "At *that* high temp you'd *better* leave her in here. At least they have emergency equipment whereas at home you'd kill her with worry. She's a hundred and five."

"I see that." I slipped the glass tube back in the alcohol.

"Have you eaten anything?"

"I can't."

He glanced at his watch, then reached into his pocket. "Here. Ten bucks. When you *do* get hungry, go down to the cafeteria."

I pushed the bill away. "Thanks, but I won't want anything but coffee, and I can get all the free coffee I want down at the nurses' station. I've been down there every ten minutes asking for a doctor before you got here."

"Look, lady. There's no point in *two* of my girls getting sick and you were well on your way last night. And don't forget, you have another daughter who needs you just as much as this one. Imagine how *she'd* feel if you land in the next bed here. And if you don't eat, you just might. Now, I'm going down to that nurses' station, see if I can kick some action into one of these doctors around here, and then I have to take the truck back to the plant. I'll try to stop back after work, but there's a sign in the lobby that says no visitors after eight. How are you getting away with staying overnight?"

"I'm already here and I'm refusing to leave. They didn't have a problem with that. Guess 'cause I'm her mother."

"So maybe I can tell them I'm her father? If that doesn't work, Devin does have a preacher's license. If you feel this child needs a few prayers…"

He was trying to cheer me up. It wasn't working.

"Okay, I give up. Here. Take this money. Eat something. Call Lola. Don't worry. And call me anytime, either at the plant or at the apartment. They may stop me at the desk tonight. You know how late I get out of there."

That made me smile. He was turning into a family man fast. "Anything else, sir?"

"Yes. Take care of yourself...*please*. I *love* you. I can't have two of you down on me. I don't know much about this daddy stuff." He hugged me and I wrapped my arms around him, not wanting him to leave, worried about Michelle, and still not feeling so hot myself.

I called Lola as soon as he walked out the door. She picked up on the first buzz.

"How is she?"

"Mama. She's hot. Her fever's a hundred and five."

"My *God*. What are they doing about it?"

"Nothing. She's been going steadily higher since I picked her up from school."

There wasn't much Lola could do or say. I hung up, promising to call her at home later, and turned my attention back to Michelle, who was evidently going to sleep through the clatter of a hospital supper round.

She was still sleeping at seven-thirty when Erick called, still at the plant, and it *was* still Erick. I recognized his easygoing, soft-spoken voice.

"It's me. Did you ever eat anything?"

"No. I still have your money. Are you off work yet?"

"No. Devin has to stick around here until the last route man is in and gone, so you know how *that* goes. How's Michelle?"

"Still sleeping, still hot."

"Same temp?"

"I don't know. I'm afraid to wake her up, but even sponging her off while she sleeps doesn't stir her. No one's been in here for a couple of hours. The nurses say a doctor will be around soon. The holdup is down in the operating room. Apparently, there was a pretty bad accident and all the doctors on duty are involved. That's what the nurses say anyway."

He was silent for a minute. I could hear drivers yelling goodnight to Devin and one sure way to get Devin was to address him by name.

"Yeah, good-night, Pat. Have a good one."

"Devin?" I asked. *Was Devin back?*

"Yeah, I'm still here," Devin replied. "Just trying to get everyone out of here. Daniel won't leave, though...Hey, Dan...don't point that sucker at me!"

"It's too late, man," I heard Daniel respond. "I already *got* it. Took it five minutes ago while you were occupied with the phone."

"Yeah, well I hope the hell you don't get attached to it. Hang on, Kerr..."

There was muffled laughter and the sounds of wrestling before Devin came back on the line. I heard him pick up the receiver, but he was still talking to Daniel.

"Hey, man, come on. Don't be fucking with me now. You ain't lately gonna keep that. At least, over my dead body—"

"It's not even a good picture of you, Dev," came the reply and Devin laughed audibly into the phone.

"Come on, man, hand it over."

I waited quietly through all this. Daniel sounded a little closer the next time I heard him.

"Oh, you can have the *goddamn* thing. Don't get pissed off at me, man."

"You bet your ass I'm keeping it. Hey, Kerry? You still here?"

"Yeah, what's going on?"

"Oh, Daniel. Thought he'd pull a fast one on me while I was tied up on the phone here."

I heard Daniel still laughing in the background. "Good-night, Devin," he called.

"Later, bro…hey, I won't be dropping by tonight. I'm heading straight for the hospital."

I waited patiently until Devin could resume his full attention to me.

"That's it, Ker. They're all gone now. I just saw Lucky go out the door and Daniel was the last one."

"What was all that commotion about?"

"Daniel snapped a Polaroid of me. I don't like anyone taking pictures of me, you know? It's cool, though. He gave it to me. I'm getting ready to feed the wastebasket."

"Hey, *no*, Devin, *don't*. Please! Let me have it."

For a moment he seemed to consider it, then, "No, I just can't have any pictures of me around."

"But *why?*"

No answer.

"Devin?"

"Yeah, I'm here. You really want it that bad? It's a bad picture of me, really. I don't even *like* it."

"I don't care. I don't have *any* pictures of you."

"You don't *need* any. You've got *me*."

"Yeah? Not *all* the time. Who is it a picture of anyway? You? Or Erick?"

"Me…no… now that you mention it…damn, chick, I'm not sure."

"Well, I know who I was talking to first, and I'll know when I see it. Bring it with you."

"Okay," he agreed, sounding reluctant. "I don't know, though. Pictures."

"Oh, big deal. One picture."

It *was* Erick. And obviously Devin who deposited the picture in my hand that next half hour.

"I just want you to know that this is against better judgment."

"Yeah? Whose better judgment?" I kissed him in greeting. "Let's see…aw, Devin, it *is* Erick. Well, I'll be damned."

"You will be if you keep it," Devin retorted, already at Michelle's bedside, the picture momentarily forgotten. "How's my girl, Michelle? You finally woke *up*, huh?"

Michelle sat up and gave him a weak smile. Still white, and unbelievably lethargic compared to the way I was used to seeing her.

"Fine," she answered Devin.

He ruffled her hair. "You'd better get better. Quit scaring your mommy and me."

Michelle giggled weakly and Devin reached for the thermometer. "Guess we'd better start with your temperature, wouldn't you say, kid?"

Michelle cooperated, nodding while Devin inserted the glass tube under her tongue.

"Still a hundred and five?" I asked after he removed it and read it.

He looked at me and sighed. "Still."

"Isn't there some way to get the temperature down?"

He nodded. "Yeah. You could do it better than I could."

"Me?"

"Yep. You, chick. You underestimate yourself. And you do that all the time."

"Well, this is no time to be experimenting, Devin. She can't go much higher than this without being dead."

A nurse finally picked that moment to stop into the room with a small paper cup of antibiotics. "Did she eat?" she asked me, shaking the thermometer down.

"It's still a hundred and five," Devin spoke up.

"Well, I still have to take it for the record," she replied crisply, inserting the thermometer. She turned to me again. "Did she eat?"

"No. I couldn't wake her up."

"That's all right. She probably isn't hungry with the high temp anyway."

After a couple of minutes, she removed the thermometer and studied it. "You're right, though. It is that high. We may have to resort to an ice bath. That's pretty rough. Let's wait and see if these antibiotics do anything first."

"She's sleeping a lot," I said. The nurse had no sooner removed the glass tube when Michelle closed her eyes against the cool pillow. Asleep in a matter of seconds.

Devin looked at his watch. "I've got to get going. Look. I'll call you from home. Soon as I touch ground. And if you need me, *call* me. If anyone else answers, just ask for me."

"I don't like that idea," I said.

"I'll be near the phone all night anyway. And I will call you."

"What about this picture?"

He walked over to the nightstand and picked it up. "I told you it was bad. Hey, why don't we get rid of this one and you can take another one. A better one."

"I like this one. What's the difference?" I didn't understand his reluctance to let me have this one but offer me another one.

"Well, for one thing, it's the only picture of Erick in existence."

I looked closely at the picture. The camera had captured the age, the wisdom and the kindness of our friendly Saint Erick with remarkable accuracy. The picture didn't even remotely resemble Devin. "That's the only reason?"

Devin shrugged. "Hey, it's okay with *me* if you keep it. I'm not the one who *cares*. It's not a picture of *me.*"

I sighed. This was preposterous, but better to take it while it was still okay with…Devin…anyway. Well, it *was* the image of Devin, wasn't it? His body? His face? Another look at the picture. Like hell. It was Erick.

Devin smiled. "Keep it. He'll get over it."

With Michelle still asleep, I walked him out to the van, waved him off, and returned to my vigil with nothing to do now but worry and wait. Devin had told me I could do something for her, and better than he could. But *what?*

As time went by, I began to realize just how badly help *was* needed. Her temperature had not gone down one degree by ten o'clock and all I could do was sit helplessly by with dread. Devin had not called, and I couldn't understand why. Didn't he even *care?*

Then, out of the blue, a thought hit me. The switchboard! Like the visiting hours, maybe it too closed at some point for incoming calls. Devin must have tried and had no way of even letting me know he'd tried. I picked up the phone. There was a dial tone. Apparently, you could dial *out* all night. I immediately called Lola's house.

She had been in touch with Devin all evening and, as I figured, his calls had not been put through.

"Call Devin right away," Lola told me. "He said not to worry about who answers."

"Okay, Mama, thanks."

"Uh-huh. I'll come out there and sit with you, Kerry, if they'll let me," Lola offered.

"No, that's okay, Mama. She's still sleeping. I'm scared. No one acts like it's serious enough to have a doctor in, but you coming over to sit…really, you have to work tomorrow, and I probably won't be in. I will call Devin, though."

"Well, even though they wouldn't ring the room, I did get through to the nurses' station. They will have a doctor in soon. And of *course* you won't be at work tomorrow. Right now, your place is with her."

"Thanks, Mama."

He must have been sitting on the phone. He answered it before it actually rang.

"Ah wuz jist pickin' up th' phone t' trah again. How's 'r keed?"

I was so preoccupied with Michelle's condition that at first I didn't even notice the drawl. "Devin. She's not getting better. She's still hot and her lips are blue and—" My voice broke. Michelle could *die* tonight if somebody didn't get that fever down soon. The antibiotics weren't working any better than the cold water sponging I'd been doing. I'd hoped Erick would answer the phone, but instead…my hopes were dashed before they even got off the ground. Erick stayed the hell out of Devin's marriage, so who did I really *expect* to answer the phone? Everything snapped in me then and I broke down sobbing.

"Hey, ladee, now you *stop* it! Ya hear?" His voice was raspy but it wasn't quiet. In fact, he sounded fed up. Apparently, he had no qualms about being around the marriage or the wife. No sympathy for my sensitive feelings either.

"You knock it the fuck *off.*" The black drawl went on with a deadly warning tone. "Ya gotta *pool* that fever out of her. You *hear* me? Them tears ain't gon' help her rat now. You rat *there*. Not *me*. There's no one better that kin do it rat now, but you."

"But Erick could…" I tried to stifle my sobs and bring myself under control.

"Oh, we kin *try*, lady, but *yer* her *mother*. Her flesh-'n-blood mother. And *yer* th' one tha's there. Do you un'erstan?"

So lost in the emotion of what he was saying to me, the black drawl had launched into full reign. Evidently, our differences didn't make one bit of difference to him tonight. He sounded like a slave straight out of *Gone with the Wind*. There was no patience with the hysterical, worried mother, as Erick might have had, nor was there any carefree Devin here to kid me out of my desperate worrying. I was stopped short in shock at this one's seeming lack of caring about the way I felt.

"Hey! Ya steel *there*, ladee, or are ya gonna cop out completely?" He was even louder now.

"I'm..." I wiped my eyes on my jacket sleeve and tried to get some control over the wavering in my voice. "I'm here."

"Now. Ya gotta *draw* it outa her. Don' ask me how. You jist *do it*. Ya *will it*. Ya *order it*. But you get that damn fever down."

"But I don't know how..."

"Ah tol' ya...don' worry 'bout *how*, ladee. Ah 'xpect ya done too much of that worrying shit already. Are ya gonna let 'er *lay* there lak that 'n not even *try?*"

I didn't dare speak. I had no reply for this impatient black voice. Nor did he seem to expect one.

"Now, go 'head. Erick's there with ya if ya think ya need that sucker so bad, but Ah ain't lately carin' whether ya got the 'bility to hear him rat now. You fix her and you call me rat on this here phone when she's better. *When* she's better, not if. Ah'll be rat here poolin' for ya, lady, for all tha's worth to *you*. Ah know Ah ain't no healer man an' Ah ain't no Devin ya think ya need either, but Ah'll be here and Ah'll be helpin' ya...whether ya want mah help or not. That keed ain't lately gonna leave 'er sister on this planet by 'erself...or her *mother* either. Not if Ah got any say-so 'bout it."

When I hung up, I looked at Michelle, my eyes filling up again. He was right. Self-pity wasn't going to help my little girl right now. Nor was any resentment at how I'd just been spoken to.

In the semidarkness of the room, I could see the lily-white glow of innocence radiating from her body. According to the aura color charts, white was reserved for the almost dead or the spirit after death. It was enough to scare me into trying. One more degree or two and there might not be *any* color streaming from her lifeless form. How she had escaped convulsions or coma thus far I didn't know, but I thanked God for miracles with a silent prayer.

As I sat there wondering how to start, a nurse walked in, checked her temperature by hand and looked at me with ash-gray alarm.

"No doctor's been *in* yet?"

I shook my head, too choked with frightened tears to speak.

"Well, I was hoping to avoid this as long as possible, but it's too dangerous now to put off any longer. Fevers rise at night and she's liable to go higher than this by morning. I'll make arrangements for her to get an ice bath. It works sometimes. It's very painful on the hot skin, but—"

"A *what*?"

"An ice bath. We have to shock her body temperature back to normal."

An hour later the equipment was brought in. The nurse ordered me to stand back and I cringed as I watched, gritting my teeth in horror while Michelle screamed for me over and over. Her little body trembled with pain and terror while the stinging ice was applied, sprinkled in chunks with ice water-dipped cloths. I could do nothing but watch helplessly and in shock. When the nurse finally stopped, Michelle had lost consciousness again. Her temperature was taken and she was still 105 and still pale with blue, cracked lips.

"Why hasn't a doctor been in?" I practically screamed.

"There was a several car pileup this afternoon and a lot of people are critical. The doctors have their hands full, but it wouldn't matter. We're doing everything the doctor would instruct us to do. We can only hope the antibiotics and the ice will bring this temperature down. All we can do is wait." She gave me a sympathetic look and turned to leave. "Ring the station if there is any change, or if you need me."

I lifted Michelle's limp hand. Where *was* Erick, damn it, and just who did this black character think he was to suddenly jump into the act when it was none of his business? Where had he been the whole time she was sick today and Jesus Christ, where the hell was Erick when I needed him so badly now?

Draw it out of her. That's what he'd said. *How?*

As I sat there in misery and desperation, I suddenly remembered that little Sybil Leek pocketbook in my purse. The one with the wedding ceremony. It had, if I remembered correctly, an entire chapter on healing.

I grabbed my purse and pulled out the book. In minutes, for the first time, I had a rough idea of *how*. I inserted the thermometer into my sleeping daughter's mouth and waited a couple minutes before I checked it. There was no change. The ice bath had accomplished nothing.

I took a deep breath and attempted to work out the healing technique outlined in the book. I placed my hand on her forehead, but before I could even begin another idea came to me that had nothing to do with what I'd just read. An impulse to take the fever away from her and give it to my own body cells to destroy. I could handle that fever. Michelle couldn't.

As these thoughts were occurring to me, I felt Michelle's face getting warmer under my hands, warmer than before. Hotter. Beads of perspiration began to break out on her already damp forehead and hair. I closed my eyes and remained that way with one hand on her head and one on her stomach, thinking directly *to* the fever now…inviting it through my arms and into my own body.

After a few minutes, to my amazement, Michelle opened her eyes and smiled. Her little hands reached up to my face and her fingers were *cool*.

Impossible. With shaking hands, I took her temperature again, easier now that she was awake. My eyes had to accept what they saw. Her temperature was ninety-nine. It had dropped six degrees in the span of a few minutes. She began to shiver and I pulled the covers up around her, adding an extra blanket from the other empty bed.

"Think about snow," I whispered to her and she smiled at me again. It was a chant we'd done during the few minutes she'd been awake today.

She nodded and whispered hoarsely, "And popsicles and icicles."

Then her eyes closed again.

I picked up the phone and dialed Devin's apartment. "It's me," I said when I heard his "Yeah?"

I realized now that I was shivering too.

"How is she?" The same black voice.

"It just dropped to ninety-nine."

"Oh, ladee…" He heaved a heavy sigh of relief and I waited, too tired and drained to say anything else. I was feeling hot and dizzy now too.

"Y' see? *You* did tha'." He sounded proud. Proud of me. Myself, I was too dizzy and weak to care how he sounded or what he thought.

"An' she's fine now, our daughter. She *is mah* daughter too, y'know."

In spite of the way I felt, his relief was contagious. "I know. You must have helped me or—"

"Helped? Ladee, Ah haven' *stopped* thinkin' of you 'n her since Ah last talked t' ya. Not even *once* t'night. Ah've been rat there in tha' room wit' ya. But *you* did it. An' Ah'm proud of you. Ya jist don' realize *what* ya are, yet. But ya *will*. Ah'll see t' tha'. *Ya* proved yerself t'night, ladee. If *they* can't see now that yer more than ready…"

Now that Michelle was improving, and my continuous checking of her reassured me of that, I had more room in my head to give full attention to this gentleman on the line right now. Half of me was still leery of him. The other half could see that he was the only one of the four *here*. The only one who had remained vigilantly available against my seeming dislike for him and preference for one of his brothers. *He* had been there when I needed someone. Not Erick and not Devin. And now, he was still here. He'd waited for the outcome.

"How do *you* feel, babe?"

"Not too good," I admitted. "I'm pretty tired now."

"Yeah, well that's because of the amount of energy you burned."

"Yeah." I touched my hand to my forehead. "I think *I've* got the fever now."

He laughed. "No doubt. That *can* happen if you set it up that way. But you can handle that, can't you, Ker?"

That voice. Young. No slang. Devin. He actually had the nerve to butt the other one out now that Michelle was getting better. Devin. Couldn't be there when I needed him. Well, as far as I was concerned, Devin was not just a patsy. He was a cop-out. And he was totally unaware of my resentment of him at this minute.

"Hey, Ker. You *can*, can't you?"

"Of course," I said coolly. "I'll talk to you in the morning."

He picked up on the coldness in my voice but misinterpreted it. "Hey, babe. You don't sound good. Get some sleep tonight, and I'll stop there first thing in the morning."

"Okay, Devin."

"Hey…I love you."

"I love you too."

It was hard to put any feeling into the words. Sure, I guessed I meant them, but maybe not quite as much tonight. My eyes were beginning to burn and now the heat was radiating from *my* face. I reached for the blue pitcher and drank from it without bothering with the plastic glass. Then I lay down in the bed with Michelle. Maybe she felt so cool to me now because I was so hot and shivery. I pulled the covers around both of us, thankful that she was still okay and I tried not to think about Erick or Devin or *him*.

5   Devin was the first call of the morning and the first visitor of the day. The call came from the route room at 7:30 a.m. and it was Devin. His first question was for Michelle's well-being, his second for mine.

"I feel pretty good this morning," I told him, suddenly realizing in surprise that I did. I wasn't even mad at Devin anymore and was now in awe of the teamwork amongst the four of them.

"I'm doing specials today, babe, so I'll come over to the hospital first. Tim already knows. Man, is he ever being cool. And Mama, she wants to talk to you, so I'll transfer you in a minute. Anything else I have to tell you can wait till I get there. Man, am I ever proud of you and what you did last night."

"Well, don't give me all the credit." I glanced at Michelle who was now sitting up and eating from her hospital tray. The first interest she'd shown in food since yesterday morning. "I had a little help from your end of town." I deliberately refrained from using names, especially since the black didn't appear to have one.

"Well, it doesn't matter who or how. You're both doing pretty good today and that's all I care about."

He was there when the doors opened to visitors.

"Hello, love."

"Erick!" I hugged him in grateful relief. Now I was *sure* everything was going to be all right. "Where *were* you last night?"

He looked at Michelle, smiled, and winked at her, as if they shared some secret. "Hello, Michelle," he greeted her, then to me, "Does it matter?" He pointed to Michelle's evident well-being.

"You're dodging the question."

"Well, Devin decided to get into a long rap about his future child, you know? Our future child." He transferred Michelle's now empty tray to the other bed and sat on the edge of hers.

"A rap with his *wife* ?"

Erick lifted Michelle up onto his lap, tickling her gently. "No, with his father." He looked at me with a tolerant *boy, did I split from that one* expression, then resumed playing with a giggling Michelle.

"About *what?*"

"About our future son."

"And?"

"And I split. Have you had breakfast?"

"No, and what do you mean you split? In spite of Michelle's being sick? You just split?"

He shrugged. "I knew you were in good hands. Besides, I split from Devin's, not from you. You may not realize it, but I am always nearby. Don't forget, time and space are not my hang-ups. Now, come on. Let's go get some breakfast. Michelle, your mommy and I are going down to the cafeteria. It's just right down the hall. Think you can be a good girl till we get back? We didn't have a nice breakfast like you did."

Michelle nodded and picked up the remote control for the television overhead. She had mastered it this morning while we waited for our visitor. We didn't even have a remote at home, so it was a big novelty for her.

"Erick, what about work?"

He waved that off with indifference. "Tim knows where I am. It was *his* suggestion that I stop here first."

He steered me down the hall as we talked.

"Can we get a Sydney?"

"Yep. Can't see leaving Sydney out today." He picked up today's newspaper from a stack and put it on the tray as we moved into the cafeteria line. I snatched a cup for coffee but didn't add a plate to the tray.

"Is that all you're having? Coffee?"

"That's all I want."

He shook his head. "You don't like eggs, okay. Bacon and toast, at least, and orange juice."

I gaped at him, too surprised to argue. How in the hell could he possibly know I didn't eat eggs? His suggestion did sound pretty good, though. "Okay."

"What's today, November eighth? Getting closer."

"What is?"

He smiled. "Thanksgiving."

"Oh. That's right. Just a couple more weeks, huh?"

"Yep. Time's getting short for the final packing stuff. I probably won't see you at all tonight."

"That's right. This is Friday. You'll be seventy miles away all weekend."

He looked at me with feigned dismay. "Who will?"

"Excuse me. Devin will be. But that automatically includes you, too."

"It does, huh?" He proceeded to season his breakfast and smiled as if to himself.

"Well, it's true," I insisted.

He set the shaker aside. "Oh, you could look at it that way, or you could take a different perspective. As long as I'm not needed there, I could be anywhere else. Even with you." He tapped me affectionately on the nose.

"If that's true, where were you *last* night?"

"That," he replied, "is a perfect example."

"Of what?"

"Of Devin."

I took a sip of my coffee. "*That* was not Devin."

"Oh, not by the time *you* called. Don't forget, a lot could have happened before you ever *thought* to pick up the phone."

His emphasizing of the word *thought* made me consider how suddenly I had gotten the idea. *Had* he been around, after all?

"For example," Erick went on. "Devin was saying that if he ever had a kid that he'd never send him to a regular school, public or private."

"Yeah, he's told me that too."

"Right. He tells anyone who will listen. In this case, it was his father and you know how parents are. They're programmed to the system and can't fathom their kids breaking the law like that. So, sure enough, a lively conversation ensued."

"So you didn't stick around."

"Oh, I did for a while. Human bullshit can be entertaining."

"Well, when I called, it was the black one who answered the phone. How could that be if—"

"Well, somewhere during that colorful conversation, he did get into the act. He started throwing some really wild child-rearing ideas at the old man, poor soul. Gerald was trying to be reasonable, but there's no reasoning with that troublemaker. At the point you called he was already there, so he took the call and then waited it out until you called to say she was doing better. I know he was worried, and I hoped you'd be big enough to give him a chance."

"He *was* worried. He was also *mad.* Mad at me, and looking back, I don't blame him." I considered the black on the other end of the line last night, how he had hung in, concerned, until I'd called back, and how he'd relinquished his hold after hearing the good news, allowing time for Devin to say a few words to me. Why did I back off from him? Because he was black? Or because he came off like the brat of the outfit? He did seem to love the kids. He'd proven that last night.

Erick tapped his spoon against his now empty plate. "Earth to Kerry."

I pulled out of my reminiscing. "Sorry."

"You know, he can't believe you're for real," Erick said. "He's never seen anything like you. And Devin…he's still running around going…'like wow, man.' You've got to make certain allowances for them. For what they are, and for what they aren't. Devin, if you haven't noticed, gets too wrapped up in the home situation to be dependable. He *means* to call you when he says he will and he *does* try to be on time. But how many times have you sat by the phone waiting for that call? How often does he arrive when he says he will? And our *him*, as you call him, he doesn't trust humans. Me? I may not be as much fun to be around, but I make a good leaning post and sounding board. And *I* don't mind if you cry once in a while. I know how easy it is to become involved in material living. Caught up in your own symbols. It's hard to remember that events and things *are* just symbols. Especially when it's the rule of this world that you experience them with such realism. You feel them, see them, hear them, smell and taste them. You have to realize and remember that you can't trust your physical senses to give you a true picture of what reality is. These physical senses will only convince you all the more that the only tangible and real world is *this* one. And nothing could be further from the truth." He stopped abruptly and looked at me. My eyes must have been glazing over. "I'm going entirely too fast for you, aren't I? I keep forgetting."

I continued to stir my coffee. It was going to be a long rest of my life.

Michelle's temperature fluctuated between 99 and 100 all day long, but it didn't go any higher. Erick went back to the plant and I called Lola to let her know how Michelle was doing. By 4:30, I'd had it. I needed to get clean clothes and a shower, and Mandy was still stuck at Kathy's, so I explained to Michelle that I was going to have to leave for a while. She seemed content with the hospital, her meals in bed, and remote-control television. She kissed me goodbye and told me to tell Mandy she missed her.

It was 7:00 when I finally parked my car in front of my duplex. At 9:30, the van pulled up in the side yard, and a very stoned "Devin" sauntered up to the door.

"What happened to *you*?" I opened the front door for him and he stumbled in, collapsing into the big red armchair.

He began to untie his boots. "Do you mind?" he asked.

"Of course not. Want some coffee?"

"Yes, I'd better. I'd have been here sooner, but I stopped by Daniel's and they had this surprise belated birthday party for me. They said they wanted to do it on my actual birthday, but that was the wedding night, and uh…I couldn't very well leave. It was pretty nice of them, really. They had a cake and, damn, Daniel gave me a keychain with a Scorpio insignia on it."

I watched him with amusement. It definitely wasn't Devin, but…Erick…stoned? He was talking slower than normal and seemed out of it. "It must have been some pretty powerful weed, man," I said, laughing "You can't even talk straight, much less walk. Did you bring a joint with you? Personally, I could *use* a good joint after the last twenty-four hours."

He looked at me, his face a total blank. I had never seen him so dazed. Then suddenly he snapped his fingers, or tried to. It came out in slow motion.

"Oh, you mean marijuana. Yes. How could I forget?" He pulled a plastic bag out of his uniform top pocket and dropped it at my feet. "Go ahead. Dive for 'em. You like that stuff. There's a bunch of them. Already rolled." He laughed, a lopsided laugh.

"*You* sure can't handle it," I said, smiling. I didn't make a move for the baggie. "You're kinda funny stoned. Where's Devin?"

He raised a hand in a *who-knows* fashion and it flopped back down on the arm of the chair. "Am I my brother's keeper?"

"You aren't stoned. You're *drunk!*"

He looked up at me with a serious expression. "Well, about as drunk as three glasses of wine can get me considering I have no tolerance for alcohol." He raised his eyes heavenward. "Forgive me, Fathers. How much can one be taxed in this dimension?"

He turned back to me. "Three glasses of wine and as far as Devin goes, you can have him back. All you have to do is say the word."

I got up to get the water, now boiling on the stove. I did kind of want Devin back. It seemed that all I ever saw of him anymore was spurts, but I didn't want to hurt Erick's feelings.

"How's Michelle?" he asked, changing the subject.

"She seemed fine when I left. Ninety-nine and acting normal. I was having a hard time just keeping her in bed now that she's feeling better."

He was sitting on the floor when I came back in with the coffee, more awake and sober-looking.

"This coffee should bring you down."

"Thanks. Oh, I called Mandy from the plant today. She misses her sister and you. Maybe you can take her over to visit Michelle at the hospital tomorrow. I wish I could go with you."

"I was hoping the doctors would let me bring her home tomorrow. I did stop by and see Mandy on my way home tonight, but she wanted to stay overnight. Kathy has a couple teenage daughters, so I'm sure that's more exciting to her than coming home to this empty house. If Michelle feels as good as she did when I left…"

He gave me a hopeful glance and picked up the steaming mug. "I should be going after this. There's so much packing to do and only a couple more weeks before the departure date."

"So it's really official that you're leaving around Thanksgiving?"

He ran his hand through his curly hair, nodded and yawned. "Will I ever be glad when that's over with."

I felt sorry for him. He looked tired and worried. I don't think he was used to the feeling of substances. "Are you sure you're okay to drive?"

"Well, I made it up here…but, you may be right. I could stay here tonight. I doubt anyone back at the house will miss me as late as it is now."

In the morning, we parted in separate vehicles. Before he took off, he stuffed another ten-dollar bill in my hand, insisting I pick up a few things to amuse both girls. Mandy was still at Kathy's and Michelle was cooped up in the hospital room by herself.

I didn't hear from Devin again until Sunday night. By then Michelle had been released with antibiotics and was finally home, almost her old self.

Devin's call came late and was mainly to ask about Michelle's condition. I assured him she seemed fine. He apologized for having to be away from me and wanted me to meet him at the coffee shop in the morning. In fact, he sounded pretty insistent about it.

I set the alarm for extra early and hit the beanbag, exhausted, when the thought suddenly occurred to me that I hadn't checked the mail in days.

It was no surprise then upon checking, that something was *in* the box, but the return address gave me pause. Ohio. Only one person I knew of that lived in Ohio. My mother's psychic friend who had promised to do a reading on the ring.

Myrna.

6 He was already waiting for me when I walked in and spotted him in the booth. The aroma of sizzling bacon and hot buttered toast was tempting as I made my way down the aisle and took a seat across from him, but I had a feeling there had been another reason he'd wanted to meet me here this early. It kind of put a damper on the appetite. I tossed the letter to him and began doctoring the coffee sitting before me, taking my time as he read. I could almost hear a drum roll and it didn't have anything to do with what he was reading.

Dear Kerry,

The reading has disclosed that the eye in the ring we discussed is not real, therefore it has no magical properties. Wear it as a conversation piece and have fun. Your boyfriend is very psychic and should not be mixed up in witchcraft or any similar frames of reference along demonic lines. He should instead direct his powers and energies into something positive and good, such as Zen or Yoga, or other matters of the spirit.

Fondly, Myrna

"Boyfriend?" Erick handed the letter back to me with a puzzled look. Didn't you tell her that night that we'd just met? That we were barely acquainted?"

I sighed. Of course, it wouldn't be Devin this morning. No wonder I'd felt uneasy throughout the drive in. Something was up. I could sense it.

I slipped my jacket off and laid it beside me on the orange-cushioned bench. "We both did. I remember specifically emphasizing that there were no love-type emotions that could have triggered the attacks. Even though," I lowered my eyes and sighed again, "that wasn't exactly true. But anyway, Myrna's letter, and Sydney's remark about the matter of a ring being settled to our satisfaction this week...this is all a mindblower to me. Remember that page I showed you when I asked you about Pammy moving in?"

Erick nodded. "It has been about a week, hasn't it? Well, are you satisfied with Myrna's answer? That is, are you taking her word that the eye is not real?"

We both looked down at my hand. "It looks real to me," I said.

"Well, I could settle it once and for all. Take the ring apart and see," Erick offered. "But perhaps we don't need to know. You say she's never been wrong, and I've always had such good vibes from it anyway. It was what got your attention."

"I can't see ruining the ring just to find out."

"Does it matter, really? It has served its purpose as far as *we* are concerned. Look at it this way, real or not, it's harmless."

I thought of how everything had changed since we'd first called Myrna. Now, if I were to answer this letter, I would have all new questions for her and none of them would have anything to do with the damn ring. Like, for example, who this Erick really was, borrowing Devin's body at the moment.

"I love you, woman."

He sure had a way of making such questions insignificant. "I love *you*, too."

He smiled. "No, you don't. You're just infatuated."

"Damn it! Why do you always *say* that? Is that what you *really* think?"

He shrugged. "Well, I don't know. I guess it's just that I really don't know what to say. Expressing emotion is so new to me."

I refolded Myrna's letter and returned it to its envelope and then to my purse. "So. Not to change the subject, but how come our experiment flopped? You never *did* tell me what that was all about."

"Well, basically, I wanted to see how good a receiver you are. Since we know you...uh...transmit so well?"

"But what were you trying to transmit?"

He shrugged again. "It doesn't matter. If you had responded, I'm sure you'd have mentioned it by now. Can you remember any unusual feelings that might have come over you, like a craving or an inclination toward any one third-dimensional thing?"

I smiled. Erick had the oddest way of referring to this planet as though it were a training center, and only one of many that he dealt with during my 24-hour day. "No, not really. I sat there, though, like I promised I would, from ten until about eleven."

"Yeah? That's interesting. Eleven was about when I quit. That's all you did was *wait*? Nothing else?"

"Waited and waited. Then, at eleven, I gave up. So I put my clothes back on and—" I suddenly remembered the early incidents of fright with the ring and the pentagram just prior to ten o'clock. "Oh, but the ring! I forgot about this!"

"Hold it. Back up. Did you say you put your clothes *back* on?"

"Well, yeah," I said, anxious to get on with what had happened when the fear had hit me about the jewelry. "I got dressed and…oh, wait a minute. I see what you're getting at. What was I doing with them off?"

He was staring at me intently. "Were you dressed when you started at ten?"

"Of course I was. Well, I'd better start from the beginning."

"Okay." Erick leaned back against the booth, arms crossed, with a tiny smirk, as though *this* was going to be greatly amusing.

"First of all, the ring." I ran down the events of that particular hour, starting with the scare fit and finishing with the sexual urge that had come over me. When I realized that Erick was really trying hard not to laugh, I stopped talking abruptly. He really was trying, too. Had his fist to his mouth as though it took a dam to hold back the laughter.

"What's so damn funny?" I demanded.

"You," he said. "Did it ever occur to you *what* I might have been projecting up to you?"

I looked at him suspiciously. "Did it have anything to do with my stripping like that?"

He tried to sober his expression and failed miserably. "Love, let's forget it, really. Why don't we get Lola's muffin…uh…ordered."

"Don't you *dare* change the subject. Did you *really?*"

"Now, take it easy, Kerry. It *worked.* Damn, woman. Why do you wait a week to tell me these things? I figured *sex* would be the last thing you'd expect from such a psychic venture. I thought if it *had* come across, you'd have *told* me about it by now."

"And…you thought it was a failure. Well, so did I. But…it wasn't…was it?" I looked up at him, suddenly serious. Just what kind of bond *did* I have with this being? Worse…what kind of control did he have over me that he could inject thoughts without my being able to tell what was *his* and what was *my* idea? Just how far could this kind of mind manipulation go?

All of a sudden, I had to get off this subject. To anything else. I thought of Devin and how long it had been since I'd really seen him. "Are you going to let Devin work today, or isn't he ever coming back?"

"You know, love, I'm a little disappointed. I thought you'd be happy to know that our experiment was a success." He sighed. "Sometimes I think you're being sarcastic just for the sake of it, and then I look at you…really look at you. Your aura is shooting off these little pink waves when you mention him. You're really hung up on Devin, aren't you? Or, you *think* you are."

"Well…" His honesty made me feel a little remorse for my tone of voice. "It's just that…well, it's nothing personal. I've just been wondering how things are going down there at the apartment, and no offense, but surely *you* aren't there. I don't know how to explain it. I *miss* Devin sometimes. You were a godsend when Michelle was sick. I don't know how I would have made it without you and…that other one, but…well, I haven't really spent any *real* time with Devin in so long."

He picked up his cup, took a sip and set it back down. "Please, lady. Don't look at me that way. I really don't have all that emotion bred into me. But I can understand how you think you feel, so I'll try, here and now, to explain the best way I can about this Devin, me and him business. Now, *I* spent the whole weekend at the apartment by my*self.*"

He seemed to be stressing the pronouns to trigger a reaction in me. He got it.

"What do you mean *I?* Who the *hell* is *I?* How am I supposed to know who you mean by *I?*"

As I fired these questions at him, Erick seemed to vanish before my eyes. Christ, he sure could split with no warning. A chill fell over me as I realized I was no longer talking to Erick.

"I should think you might have figured that out by now."

There was no drawl either and it was out of the question to even consider Devin. This face was timeless. There was no broadened nose, nor any full, hung lips. I was face-to-face, finally, with the *real* him. The one nobody would discuss or admit existed. Well, in broad daylight, here in the brightly lit restaurant, *I* could. The uneasiness I had felt earlier was gone.

"Why don't you just *tell* me." It wasn't a question.

He chuckled. "And risk losing you? Ah, no, lady. In time you will tell *me.*"

That chest feeling did a swan dive as he spoke. I looked into his serious eyes and once again got that sensation that they were just using Devin Drew's head like a facemask, peering out of the holes that humans used for eyes.

"So, how come I don't see you around more often? Or is that a little risky for you?"

He raised his eyebrows, amused. "Do you *always* greet old friends with such sarcasm?"

"Hey, I just asked a question," I countered defensively. "You can interpret it as sarcasm if you want to."

"Easy, easy." He held up both hands, palms forward. "You can't *blame* me for treading carefully where ice is thin."

I studied him for a moment. "You're not Devin."

He glanced up at the ceiling and looked back at me. "No. Sorry to disappoint you. I'm not Devin."

"No, you aren't. And you're not Erick."

He sighed. "No."

"Well, you're not that *black* one either."

"No."

"But you'll tell me who you are if I ask?"

"If I *must* play this game with you."

We both looked at each other wordlessly. Stalemated, or so it seemed. Myself, I'd run out of names in the hat.

"Look," I began again, careful not to address him by any name. "I *asked* you. Why don't you just admit there are four of you and tell me who *you* are. I *asked.*"

"Just because you *asked* doesn't mean I *must* answer." His smile was kind. "Don't take those *Grimoires* and that *Satanic Bible*—or any of that other *crap* available to you—too seriously. Contact is *my* choice…always. And I have already told you. There is only *one*."

"That's bullshit and you know it."

"Is it? How about five? Can you handle five?"

"I've only seen four of you."

"Have you? You're obviously not counting the original Devin Drew in this mix."

"What do you mean?"

"Well, the four you refer to are all part of me and you. Therefore, there is only one."

"What about the original Devin Drew? What did you mean by that?"

"The Devin Drew who works at your plant. The married one. The one you couldn't stand at one time. The one who was gallant enough to let us in so we could interact with you. That Devin Drew."

My head was swimming. "So…Devin…isn't really Devin?"

"Lady, trust me. There is only one you need to be concerned with. Us."

Revulsion was beginning to churn through me. I knew who he was implying he was. He wasn't beating around the bush anymore. Excerpts of *The Exorcist* flashed through my mind. I had to grip the tabletop to keep from blacking out. Fear washed over me and I struggled to keep my awareness. Gradually the room swam back into focus. Grimoires and Black Magic. How stupid did he think I was? I tried to go back to the personalities I was familiar with.

"How can there be three distinct *yous* in one—?"

He shook his head patiently and leaned closer towards me. "The idea isn't *new* to you, lady. The Catholics believe in three persons in one God, don't they? You were raised Catholic. However, at that time, the idea wasn't conceivable to you." He was whispering, maybe because of the audience around us. Still, that stubborn smile. "I'm willing to bet that you understand that idea very well now."

"Devin, you're scaring me." I lit a cigarette, my fingers trembling as they fumbled with the match. I turned around to check the clock on the wall, praying it was time for me to go. Anything to keep from looking into those burning, pensive eyes. Anything to change the subject.

"Turn around, lady. You've got plenty of time. That's why I requested that you meet me here early. Please, turn around and listen to me. Please." His hand reached for mine and gripped it firmly.

I turned back to him, my eyes downcast on the table, my lips pursed. It was all making sense to me now just *who* had requested this early-morning meeting. How could I have not known? I looked away and took a drag off my cigarette.

"Look at me," he insisted, tipping my chin so that I had to look him in the eyes. "Look at me. Can't you see that I *love* you? Have *I* hurt you in any way? Don't you realize yet who you *are?*"

I took a deep breath and tried to calm myself. After all, I was in a public place in broad daylight and surrounded by people. I had asked for this and it was only fair that I followed it through.

"Devin, look. I *know* what you're implying about yourself. What you *have* implied about yourself. But…but the *Devil*. The Devil is so evil, so—"

"Is he?" He cut me off midsentence, a tone of self-defense too obvious for comfort. "Where, may I ask, do you get your information?"

"Well, from books and, well, everyone knows…"

He sighed and released my hand, reaching for a cigarette too. "You believe everything you read?"

I swallowed uneasily. "What do you mean?"

"Don't you *know* who invented the so-called Devil, as *you* know him?"

I didn't answer. At this point, I didn't dare. It was beginning to look like I had an even bigger problem on my hands than I had ever imagined. Evidently he wasn't expecting any replies as he continued on, answering his own question.

"The very same religions that *you* laugh at for their ridiculous *God* image they've set up. You know the one. God with a long white beard, sitting up on a fluffy white cloud with a long, royal-blue robe on, checking for the calendar date when he gets to pick his so-called good sheep from the flock and damn the rest. Come on, lady. You have more intelligence than that."

I felt lame. "So, you actually don't believe in *God* either."

He turned away impatiently, throwing one arm up across the top of the booth. "Which one? I mean, we've got Allah, Jesus, Buddha, Hare Krishna, the American dollar…would you mind specifying which one?"

I glared at him. "I don't have to sit here and listen to this."

Jane brought a coffee pot over and refilled our cups, while he watched me silently. Pensively. He drummed his fingertips on the table until she left, obviously deep in thought.

"I feel defeated before I've even begun," he said at last.

I sighed. "Can we just change the subject? I didn't come here to fight with you."

"Okay." He reached for the cream and began to doctor both of our cups. "I…uh…notice your bangs are growing out."

"Yeah, they are, I guess." I pulled at them to see if they touched my nose yet. Not quite.

"They look better now than they did that night *we* first discussed your letting them grow out."

"So far, you're the only one of the four who's expressed an opinion." I paused as I caught his implication. "And that was *Devin's* idea."

"Was it?"

"Look, whoever you are—"

"Kerry."

I looked up at him.

"All you have to do is say the word. I'll be gone. And you and Devin Drew can live happily ever after. Just you and him. And I mean that."

As he spoke, I was overwhelmed with an awareness of what he was offering me. He was giving me an *out*.

"I just want you to be happy during the short span of…uh…time you'll be here. And it really is short from another perspective. I'll step out of the picture, right now, if you desire it. All you have to do is say the word."

In that instant, a series of thoughts flashed through my mind.

Having been raised Catholic the early years of my childhood, I knew that what he'd said was true. Catholicism, the religion that claimed to be the one true church, founded by Christ himself so they claimed, did indeed accept the belief that there was but one God, yet within that one God dwelt two others. The Father, the Son, and the Holy Spirit. The catch was that they were allegedly all one and the same person. Preposterous, of course, unless you brought that theme right smack into your own personal life.

Well, there was no denying any of the Devins when face-to-face with them individually. But Devin wasn't God. In fact, he was out-and-out insinuating that he was, instead, the archenemy of God! Of course, he hadn't actually *said* this.

"Well, Kerry? Does it take so much time to decide if I've been good *to* you or *for* you?"

There was a hurt tone in his voice and that tone set me to another reevaluation. If I didn't want anything to do with this being, and for lack of a better word I could only think of him as a *being*, then all I had to do was say so. Now. In this booth with the brilliant sunlight blazing through the restaurant windows as the dawn broke, just say so and I knew I would never see him again. I don't know how I knew. I just *did*.

I thought of Erick and his understanding ways, and of the black who had risked God knows what kind of reaction from me just to be assured of Michelle's recovery, and Devin, the one I rarely encountered for any length of time these days. Then I looked across the booth at him.

He, who had been shrouded in mystery and fear from the very beginning. He, who shone with the radiance and the nobility of a royal lord and carried himself with confidence, dignity and self-respect. Not like the slimy snake he had once assured me he was. Well, no matter *who* he was, he wasn't *Devin* and that was who and what he was willingly offering me. The chance for an ordinary one-on-one relationship. A full-time lifetime shift with Devin Drew.

"You love *me*," he said suddenly. "Not just Devin. Not just Erick. And, our Magick Christian, you will soon learn to appreciate. But you *love me*. You and I are *we*. It is all *us*. *We* are *one*. We always were, you and I. Is *that* so hard to understand?"

Today, no matter who he was, there was no lack of words from this one. This was obviously an all-out, cards-on-the-table, chips-fall-where-they-may, attempt to introduce himself, at apparently whatever the cost. Here he was, finally willing to take the chance and talk about himself. The one fear that he'd displayed all along. Even the others had not dared disclose his presence. He must have known full well the probable outcome that would or could result from these facts now emerging.

"Can you exist without Devin?" I finally asked after a long silence.

"Rather you should ask, lady," he said, smiling, "can Devin exist without *me*? Well, I always have. I've managed without Devin throughout all of my existence. Now, could *he* exist without me? Well, of course he could. Would he want to? Perhaps. But perhaps not. Who knows? I haven't exactly been entertaining the idea of departure, so I don't know what he'd want to do."

I glared at him. "Just what do you mean perhaps not? What do you mean departure? *You* get to decide on Devin's right to live?"

"Take it easy, lady. Devin's not going anywhere. But he doesn't want *me* going anywhere either. Whether you know it or like it is irrelevant as far as Devin is concerned. All I meant was that if I were to leave, it might be better for Devin if I offered him the opportunity to go with me, rather than withdraw and leave him here alone after he has become accustomed to this…united effort, let's call it. Right now, Devin's got it made. Don't think for one moment that he doesn't know it."

"And you…you *like* Devin?"

"I *love* Devin. He is now part of *me*."

"But what about Erick and…who did you…what did you—"

"The Magick Christian. He may not have a name, but he's always given himself a title."

"Well, whoever he is, do they all like Devin, really?"

"Of course they do. I realize they appear to look down on him at times. No more than they would a little brother. And in a sense, that's just what he is to them. Lady, they're *all* competing for your attention. Just how else would you expect them to talk? Look, those three are as thick as thieves. Take my word for it. You think you've got problems now? Going to bed…you know, sex as you know it, it's going to be like a three-ring circus. They're going to have to do it in shifts."

For a second my temper stirred. "Oh. I see. So you're saying I get to *fuck* whoever's there at the time I go to bed?" I wasn't even making an effort to keep my voice down. A few customers glanced up from their breakfast, obviously startled.

He ignored them and answered me as though this were a perfectly normal question. "You would automatically get your preference, as with everything else. You forget, lady. *They* always know how *you* feel. And where we come from, the priority is happiness for the other in a *real* love relationship. *True* love isn't common here, but egotistical love is prevalent everywhere. However, I was aware of what it was going to be like here even before I made the decision to come. Don't look so shocked. So were you. And *I* wouldn't *be* here if it weren't for *your* decision, so *now* what's fair? You tell *me*. I'm having a hard enough time accepting that you don't even *recognize* me, but then, I was *warned* about *that*, too. What's wrong? You can take all this. You're ready, remember?"

A flush of shame crept through me. I certainly *had* asked for this.

"As for me," he went on, "getting back to more familiar subjects to you, sex has never *been* a part of my normal existence. It's *new* to me, but then a lot of things are new to me, experience-wise, these past few weeks. That doesn't mean I'm going to pass on any of the rides of this…earthship, shall we call it? I have to say, sex is one of the fringe benefits and I can't say I don't understand why. Oh, back *home* I didn't, but this is here, now, and well, I just never had the interest I have in it all of a sudden."

Quite a revealing speech, I thought. Whether this was for real or whether it was just that *he* believed it, I was in it for the long haul. So *this* was *him*. I'd had the wrong him mixed up with the *real* him. Or was *that* even right?

There was Erick…mature, wise and saintly. Seemingly incapable of human error. A little like Spock in the Star Trek series, only with the qualities and gallantry of the archangel, Michael.

And the Magick Christian? Christian. There was just no description for the little brat. But, did I love him, too? A flash of his fury in the face of Michelle's raging fever. How could I *not* love him too?

And then there was Devin. Well, that went without saying or thinking. At least the Devin I was in love with. Whether *that Devin* was in any way the *real* Devin Drew was obviously open for debate now.

But what about this one? How was it that he seemed to stand out as such a main, controlling force, of such importance as far as the others were concerned, and yet he was barely spoken of and had been seen the least?

The posse of personalities fell into the background as I sat watching him. The angles at both sides of his head were now so obvious, even under that disguise of curls. Those alien protruding lizard's eyes. Such complete knowing in them. Such honesty.

He endured the waiting under my scrutiny. Finally, he spoke. "Take your time. I've got eons. I can even stop back in another century if you need more time."

"It was *you* all along, wasn't it?" I said slowly as the memories of the last few weeks unfolded almost in slow motion. "You, the ring. You with the tablet...both times. You on the phone before the experiment with Erick. You in the parking lot at Walgreens. You were always there...weren't you."

He knew that none of these statements were questions. "Lady, I have walked behind you for a long, long time. Since the moment you chose to be born among all this twentieth-century earth chaos. Of course, it's only recently that I now have the mobility of a vehicle. For *that*, we can thank our mutual friend, Devin Drew. If you want my opinion, lady, this dimension could use a few more open-minded people like him. Devin's participation is, well, unusual. It is the *extreme* in generosity and we don't and won't abuse the privilege."

"Then...you're really *it*. Is *that* what you're saying? *Not* Devin?" A wave of disappointment washed over me for a second. "I just can't believe it. I *love* Devin."

"Think about that, lady. Of course you do. But, you love *us* as a *unit*. Unless I bored you with the tablet that first night. And unless my selection of Devin's ring that he found *ever* so suddenly..."

"Okay. I see what you're saying." He was right, I thought. He *had* been there all along. I'd just been too blind to see it. "But it's going to take some getting used to. This is a lot to process."

My main inner conflict now wasn't accepting the four of them. It was getting over my lifelong belief that the heart was only capable of loving one. And in this situation, that idea was impossible.

He rested his chin in his hand, elbow on the table, and smiled at me. "You can ask me any questions that have been bothering you. I'm ready and willing, if you are. I know this is a lot to hit you with, but it had to be done, and done now."

"Well, what am I supposed to call you? *Devin* sounds ridiculous. It really does."

"I've told you before. While I really don't have a name...a label... as those are human things, I also have a million names. I mentioned a few a while ago, although I threw in the American dollar as an attempt at humor. And all right, I deliberately left out Satan and other such stupid interconnected associates of *his*. I also left out the earth and the trees and the wind and, what can I say, lady? Labels *are* a human thing. I know you're programmed to them, but it's almost too much for my old man to hear some of the labels and stories circulating about us. From where he is, it's almost like watching a damn comedy…to observe this kindergarten your scientists call physical reality. But where I came from not too long ago, it's still fresh in my conscious awareness. I do realize it is not so with you, and I'll try to be patient."

I glanced at the clock again. Still plenty of time. "But what you're saying is that *I'm* just visiting here too. Like the only difference between us is that you just got here."

"That's true. I am just recently amidst the race and walking among them. There are others from other realms trying a shot at the dice here. Evolution is in the process of change and, well, you had as much right to get involved as anyone else. So. Here you are, and here I am. Just because *you* did. You already know all this that I'm telling you, but it was necessary for you to forget. Still, lady, you were born, not of *their* frequency, but of *ours*. You're using their mode of vehicle, just as I am. Neither of us would keep our privacy long if we'd entered in our true form…which can be anything we want, by the way. But you've been *raised* human. You've been brainwashed and programmed and I have to admit, lady, they've done a good job with you. From what I've seen of your beliefs, I'd say it's going to *take* an army of us to break through what they've done to that mind of yours. That's why I stepped in when I did. Do you realize where you were heading?" He paused and shook his head in disdain. "Witchcraft. Really, lady, how primitive."

"Hey, wait a minute. *Devin* was into witchcraft. I was just studying it."

"Look, I'm not criticizing Wicca any more than any of the other frames of reference. Sure, they all work. Pray to the Virgin Mary, while Satanists pray to Lucifer, while the Buddhists acknowledge Brahma, and give your kid a Ouija board, or go to a séance and let me clue you, lady. They all tap the same source. Now if you prefer to stop and hole up in one frame of reference, you're missing the point of any and all of the others, and you'll never grow, you'll never realize what really *is*. Well, they've done a job on you, all right, but they can't take away your natural birthright. You can *still* see what's going to happen tomorrow if you close your eyes now. You can *still* lie in bed and listen to the voices that speak to you from every reality in the cosmos. They couldn't take that away, lady. Only *you* can. And practically *have*. So, as for names, well, let's be fair, lady. To Devin, who was good enough to understand my plight and provide the vehicle and allow me its unconditional use…that's trust. So let's be fair. As name's go, Devin is a fine name."

He pointed to the wall clock and added, "And Devin has to get to work. Come on, walk me to the truck."

We started across the boulevard where both my car and the big company truck were parked. He boarded and slammed up. I hopped up on the running board to kiss him goodbye.

"Damn, you're getting *cute*," he said with a twinkle in his eye. A gust of wind had blown up, throwing my bangs more to the side than ever. "I love you so much, lady. I hope I can just relax and be myself now that we've got all the introductions over with."

I hugged him tightly around the neck through the window. "It *is* going to take some getting used to," I said, kissing him lightly on the cheek. "Will you be getting in early today?"

"Why do you think I'm rushing to get out of here?"

I hopped down to the ground as he revved the engine, and waved as he pulled out. Our eyes met in the side mirror until the truck turned the corner and was out of sight. Then I opened my own car door and rolled down the window to let some of the heat escape before getting in. Erick's picture smiled up at me from the dashboard and I transferred it to my purse.

Some getting used to. What an understatement. Would I *ever* get used to it?

7 Tim barely acknowledged my greeting as I passed him in the hall, but I had bigger things to think about than Tim's opinion of me.

When I sat down at my machine, I noted that Kelly already had the radio playing on whatever station she'd chosen today. Oddly, though, Uriah Heep was singing a song from their *Sweet Freedom* album but Kelly didn't appear to notice. As we passed out the charges and checks, I listened to the lyrics, and once again, there just couldn't be a coincidence here. The singer was asking me to look around and decide if I liked what I saw, and though I might get lonely, did I really think I'd like to be free? Was I sure I'd be okay without his company? He just wanted me to be happy, even if it wasn't with him. It was the same song I'd heard the night I'd officially met Erick and now it was basically summing up some of the conversation I had just had with *him.*

I shook off the goosebumps and pulled my trays over. Then I fished around in my purse, found Erick's picture and leaned it against my pencil box. I supported it with my staple gun. Kelly watched me curiously.

"Oh! Lemmee see! You got a picture of Devin, huh? I heard he don't like his picture taken."

I smiled to myself. Well, just how observant *was* Kelly? What if I just flat out told her the truth? I couldn't resist. "That's not Devin."

"Well, it *is* a lousy picture of him. Gee, he looks so *old.* Lola, come see this picture of Devin."

"I'm telling you. It isn't Devin," I repeated, removing the rubber band from the stack of charges I was preparing to post.

"It doesn't even *look* like Devin," Kelly agreed.

"It isn't."

It was as if she'd just heard me for the first time. "What do you *mean* it's not Devin? I can *see* it's Devin, but God, what an ugly picture of him."

"It's not a bad picture," I persisted calmly. "I like it. It just isn't Devin, that's all."

"Oh, sure. I guess he's got a twin brother…oh wait a minute. You *did* say his father is in town with the family. Is that his father?"

"No. Never mind, it's just not Devin. That's all."

Kelly picked up the picture and really examined it. Then she took it in to Lola. A few seconds later, she returned and set it back against the pencil box.

"Lola says that's Devin."

"Oh, okay." I shrugged. "Lola should know."

"By the way, how's your kid?"

"She's okay, thanks. She's out of the hospital."

"Yeah? Did Devin come visit her while she was there?"

"He did, but mostly he's been home with the family."

Lola stepped into the doorway. "He's home with the family? His wife, too?"

"Well, uh, yes. She does live there." I felt uneasy answering, knowing what was coming.

"Yup, that sure is *one* way to get rid of a wife. Bring the family down and move them in. I thought she was supposed to be packing to *leave*."

"Look, she *is* leaving over Thanksgiving. He has to be there more now, what with his father and brother living there. It isn't changing anything."

Kelly rolled her eyes. "Yeah, sure. You *swallowed* that, Kerry?"

I glared at her and Lola stepped in, telling Kelly to mind her own business and both of us to get to work.

The day went by slowly without the hope of Devin popping into our office unexpectedly. Tim really knew how to hit below the belt. I couldn't understand his unfriendliness towards me, yet he was buying Devin's furniture, patting *him* on the back, giving him his own attorney's number, but then sending him out on a route all day. I wondered what Devin had to say about it all. It seemed like ages since I'd spent *any* time alone with him. And if I thought *I* wasn't seeing him enough, evidently his customers weren't either.

"He's doing it again...Lolaaaaa!" Kelly's wail stopped all the machines in mid-posting.

Lola looked in on us. "Who's doing what again?"

"Devin." She held up the ticket. "What in the hell's this supposed to say?"

Lola took the ticket from Kelly and frowned. She held it far away, then close, then turned it upside down. Then she laughed. "I'll be damned if I know."

"Well, it's *Devin's*. I *thought* we had him squared away. Just because he's routing it, it isn't *our* fault." She feigned a pouty look.

Lola held the ticket up to me. "Would you ask Devin to write in English from now on? Here, Kelly, put it in the suspense file."

During the day, it was easy to forget the strange relationship I had with Devin Drew, at least as long as incidents like these didn't occur too often. While *they* were discussing Devin's terrible penmanship, I was trying to think of a way to tell that Christian character to either let Devin write his own tickets or to print more clearly. I knew Devin's writing, and Erick's childlike, oversized script, and the bizarre hieroglyphic-style printing of the main *him*, so who else's scribble could it be?

The rest of the day dragged until five and I found Devin, as usual, hanging around the exit, waiting for me. Except one glance at his face told me it was not Devin and here was my opportunity to mention the tickets.

"Lo, ladee." He wasn't smiling or even his usual cocky self. "Okay 'f Ah walk someone *else's* lady to her chariot?"

My heart went out to him. He was trying so hard to be accepted. "Sure."

He took my hand and we started walking. "How's 'r daughter?"

"She's fine. Thanks to you." A cold gust of wind blew up and I pulled my jacket around me tighter and gave him a grateful glance.

Where in the hell was Devin?

"Oh, by the way." I knew I was going to have to be careful here. "Lola has been asking me to tell you something."

He stopped midstride and turned me towards him. "Ya jist can't stop thinkin' 'bout him, kin ya."

I didn't reply and he turned to keep walking. "She-it. *That* sucker. What's he got that Ah ain't?"

It was difficult not to smile at his pride and arrogance. "A *route* to keep up when he has one. A *job*. You know? And our department has *got* to be able to read the tickets. It's making Devin look bad."

He looked like he'd just been slapped. "Wha's that supposed t' mean?"

"Your tickets. We can't read them. Could you…"

"Could Ah what?" He spat on the ground as we walked. "Could Ah let Devin write his *own* tickets? Is *that* what dear Mama wants you to say?"

I didn't answer.

"Well, *is* it?"

I nodded.

He seemed to try to adjust his attitude. "Okay. No sweat. That'll be a *pleasure*. Ah never *did* lahk writin' them suckers anyway…no way."

We'd reached my car. I knew I'd hurt his feelings, but he'd *had* to be told. I reached for my car's door handle, but he beat me to it.

"Ah don' forgit th' manners bit." He laid a cautious hand on my shoulder. "Wha's wrong?"

I sighed. "You wouldn't understand. You'd take it personal."

"Hey." He forced a smile. "Ah kin understan' *anything*. Even things wrong that ya won' a'mit. Ah *know* what your problem is. It's Devin, ain't it?"

He could sure say that again. The more I watched him, his actions and expressions, the more I missed the youth and carefree energy of Devin's. "Yeah, I miss him," I admitted with a bitter tone. "Did you *all* think I wouldn't?"

"Devin hasn' deserted ya." He lit a cigarette and handed it to me. I looked at him in surprise. I was about to reach for one. "Well, ya *were* thinkin' of lightin' one up." He shrugged. "Jist doin' th' manners thing again."

He stopped abruptly as tears began welling up in my eyes, and he pulled me hard against him. "Oh, ladee…please don' cry."

I couldn't hold the emotion back any longer. I turned away from him and leaned against my car, hands to my eyes. People from the plant were scattered everywhere and here I was, visibly upset, while "Devin" just looked on helplessly. I wished the hell it *was* Devin. I felt strong hands grip my shoulders, so unlike Devin's gentleness, and felt his warm breath as his lips hung close to my ear.

"Ah *do* understan' how ya feel. Ah don' blame ya fer lovin' Devin, ladee, but if ya'd jist…give me as much chance…" He turned me around earnestly and held me tightly against him. "Can' ya see Ah loves ya *too*? Don' Ah count fer *anythin'*?"

I buried my face against his chest, really fighting the tears now. I knew I was doing even more damage by reacting this way, but I was so confused, and I wanted *Devin*. I had just been through too much today to be tactful. Where was my safe, solid, reliable *Devin?*

He finally released me in defeat and stepped back into the street. He looked beaten. "Go 'head home, Kerry. Ah'll...call ya. Later. Please. Don' cry anymore."

"I *do* love you too. It's just...Devin—"

"Ah know."

I got in and turned the ignition, wiping my eyes on my sleeve, and started driving slowly down the street. He watched until I reached the corner. I could see him in my rearview mirror and I felt terrible as I watched him trudge, not with the gallop gait that powered Devin, but with the resigned walk of a condemned prisoner on death row. As I drove, I had the awful feeling that I was just never going to see the Devin I knew and loved ever again.

I went through the mechanics of driving as if the car were on autopilot, thinking hard. In the last ten hours I had spoken to at least three separate "people," all using the body of Devin Drew and not one of them seemed to give a damn *where* Devin was. Devin the hippie. Devin the patsy. Devin the druggie, the pushover, the sucker.

I thought of all the people in my office and throughout the plant. Lola, Kelly...even Maurice and Tim. Just what would *they* think if they knew what was *really* going on? For that matter, I wondered if *I* even really knew what was going on.

Kathy followed the girls out to the car. "Michelle's been fine all day. I kept her here anyway so I could keep an eye on her, but she's been acting normal. Should I send her to school tomorrow?"

I looked at Michelle, bouncing against the back seat to the car radio, and managed a laugh. "You can if she's anything like *that.*"

It was always difficult to drive away each night without engaging in some adult conversation the poor woman desperately needed, but tonight there just wasn't time for it. Devin was my main hope for the evening and I didn't want to blow it by not being home for his call. Apparently, I'd done some damage to Christian's pride, but I'd had to do it. I'd at least been honest, I told myself.

I was relieved to get dinner over with, the house straightened up, and the kids in bed. Finally, I was able to sit down in peace with my troubled thoughts again. Peace and troubled thoughts. What an oxymoron. It seemed that I'd only been sitting a few minutes when the knock came at the door. I hadn't even *heard* the van and it damn sure wasn't Devin. I knew the second I opened the door to him.

"Oh. Come on in." I was surprised to see him and disappointed that it wasn't who I'd hoped it would be.

He walked past me, dropped into the easy chair and closed his eyes. As though the world out there had just been too much for him today. I watched him unconsciously loosen his work shirt, unbutton a couple buttons, and I was a little curious at his lack of greeting. He had never walked in here without kissing me, or a hello, or something. Finally, I broke the silence.

"You okay?"

He nodded and opened his eyes. "Sure," he said quietly.

"Are you stoned?"

"No. Tired. I really put in a long day."

"Are you hungry?"

"No. I stopped at Burger King on the way up here."

"I didn't know you were coming. Want some coffee?"

He smiled, as though it was inevitable that I'd get around to *that* question. "No...well, okay. Maybe it'll help. Damn, I've consumed more of that damn stuff in the last two months than I have my whole existence here."

"Yeah?" It seemed I was graced with Saint Erick tonight, and evidently, tonight's vice was coffee. Well, I didn't *dare* offer him a joint, so instead I went to the kitchen to make the coffee.

"How's Michelle?" he called to me.

"So far, so good."

I brought the coffee in and set it before him on the coffee table. "I wish you'd tell me what's on your mind. I *know* it's not just work."

He flashed me a swift glance, then picked up his steaming cup. "The whole situation, I guess."

"You mean you and ...uh...the rest of you?"

"No. That unit of cooperation was something we...us guys...all worked out quite some time ago. The problem is more with *us*. However, I feel that I have to take the blame for any misunderstandings. It was my responsibility to see that the information divulged was handled better."

"Which situation are you referring to?" I thought of Christian this afternoon and the morning's eye-opener in the coffee shop. Quite honestly, I wasn't sure which instance he meant.

He sighed. "For the sake of words, let's just say that if there is any...facet...of myself that you don't care for...*dislike* to be more blunt, then we *do* have a problem and for once, I don't have a solution."

"If you're referring to that black dude...Christian or whatever you call him—"

"The Magick Christian. Yes. That's a pretty sore spot in our relationship."

"Christian." I mused over the latest name. "Is that *really* what he calls himself?"

"Well, I think he got it from something to do with the Beatles. Anyhow, when he draws something he does put that name at the bottom of the picture. It's an irony thing. He is *anything* but Christian."

A knock sounded at the front door. I glanced at Erick. I hadn't been expecting company.

"Who is it?" I called.

"It's me. George."

"Shit." I looked at Erick again. "He must have just gotten out of the hospital."

"Come on in, George. It's unlocked." Erick issued the invite and as the door opened, he turned his attention back to me. "Anyhow, as I was saying..."

George waved and found a spot on the couch. I waved back, but I was still looking at Erick, waiting for him to continue. Erick nodded towards George.

"George," I said. "This is kind of important. Why don't you help yourself to some coffee?" I then turned back to Erick, not wanting to break the momentum. We might actually get this straightened out. "Uh…Devin…I know what you're trying to say, and it isn't that I don't like Christian. It's just that…"

"What's the matter?" George came in with his coffee and sat again. "You two getting hassles from work?"

Both of us ignored his question.

"It's just that," I went on, "I haven't *seen* someone in so long and *he* was the one that all this started with. How can I make you understand that I'm just not used to dividing my love among…well, I've just always been monogamous, that's all."

"Then perhaps Devin has dropped away so that one of *us* must bear the full weight of your complete and final enlightenment."

I rubbed my eyes with thumb and forefinger, thought a minute and then looked at him. "Okay, then, if that's the case, let's just get it over with right now. Then Devin can have an equal time thing, too." I'd forgotten George was taking this whole conversation in and must surely be getting more confused by the second.

"I do not have the *authority* to take this matter into my own hands. It doesn't mean I couldn't, lady. It just means this is a matter that only *he* can decide as to *getting it over with right now,* as you so gracefully put it. You need to ask *him.* Not any of us. Not even Devin."

"Him. Now, which him do you mean?"

George cleared his throat and set his empty cup down loudly on the coffee table. "What's going *on?*" He looked from me to Erick and back to me. "I guess I'll get some more coffee." He left for the kitchen.

"You don't mean to ask Christian," I said, knowing the answer.

"No. Christian would tell you what I've just told you. The answers you're looking for can't come from any of us, including, as I've already said, Devin."

"Well, this morning, at the coffee shop, *you* were there at first. Right?"

"At first."

"Then, the…uh…gentleman who replaced you is the one I'm supposed to be pushing for answers." I shuddered at the thought of it.

Erick smiled. He must have known what a shock I was in for when he'd stepped aside. "Pushing won't work. From what I know of him, he isn't one who *can* be pushed. When he feels you are ready…well, you *might* ask him, but if I were you, I'd be really sure I was ready for the answer. He's just liable to *tell* you."

I thought back to the morning's conversation with that inhuman being, the one who had dove to the defense of the legendary Devil. "I don't know if I *want* to ask *him.* I'm a little leery of him. But that is the one, huh?"

A look of solid respect crossed Erick's face. "Yes. Him."

George returned from the kitchen with his coffee, but this time he didn't sit down. "Hey, is this personal? Should I leave?"

Erick reached into his uniform pocket with a deep sigh, shook a cigarette from his pack, and lit it. And literally blew my mind.

"You don't smoke," I said.

"You want Devin back, don't you?"

"Oh, *now* I get it," George said. "There's another Devin and that's what's been throwing me off."

I looked at George as if noticing his presence for the first time. He was actually getting warmer than he realized. "George, don't try to figure it out, okay? Really. We're having enough problems with it."

Erick stubbed the cigarette out immediately after lighting it and my hopes for Devin fell.

George downed his coffee quickly. "Well, I'm gonna bug on out of here. You two seem like you're pretty involved."

"Okay, George," Erick said. "Sorry if it seems rude, but this is something that has to be settled." Erick stood and the two shook hands.

George shrugged and said to me, "Well, I don't *care*. It's just confusing to listen to when I can't figure out who you're talking about."

Erick and I exchanged glances. Hiding a thing like this at the office was hard enough. Close friends were bound to notice something.

"Look, George," Erick said. "It's pretty complicated, okay? We're having enough trouble adjusting to it ourselves."

"Adjusting to *what?*" George scratched his head in confusion. "I mean, I *kind* of got the idea. You and Ker are talking about three guys, near as I can figure, and there's one guy that you'd rather not discuss, and Kerry, *you* don't like him, but I can't figure out who the other Devin is. I never heard you mention no other Devin. I guess he's at the plant, huh?"

I sighed. "Not quite."

"Well, anyways." George stretched and jingled his keys. "Pammy will be home in about a week."

"Yeah, we know. She called," I said.

He nodded. "Okay. Catch ya'll later. Hope you get your problem worked out."

Tuesday started off on the wrong foot. The clock radio we'd set never went off and the darkness had sneakily lifted outside the heavy drapes in the bedroom.

Devin was late again.

8 When I reached the time clock, I caught sight of Daniel, Devin's satanic-looking friend. He greeted me even though we hadn't officially met.

"Hey, Kerry." Daniel had an unusually soft voice for someone who looked so much like the Devil. I considered the irony of one looking like the Devil and one who actually claimed to *be* him.

"Hey, Daniel."

"How's your little girl?"

"So far, so good, thanks. Hey, that was really nice what you did for Devin with that birthday party and all."

"What *we* did for Devin? Ker, man, what about all the things Devin did for *us*? He's been working on my car for weeks trying to get the thing running."

Ethan walked into the area and reached for his time card. "Daniel, Tim's looking for you. Hi, Kerry." He dropped his card into the slot and punched it.

"Hi, Ethan." I knew Devin didn't like this guy, but he didn't seem so bad to me.

"Okay, thanks Ethan," Daniel said. "Kerry, my wife really wants to meet you. When's Devin going to bring you over? We just live right around the corner."

"I know. I park my car at the top of your street when I go to the coffee shop. Devin pointed out your house."

"See? Then there's no excuse. How about tonight? My wife makes some pretty decent dinners. You can ask Devin."

"I know." I smiled. "I've heard about them. I live about forty-five minutes from here and I have to get the kids from the sitter after work. And Devin gets out so late. We will be over, but it'll have to be on a weekend when we're all off work. And Michelle is still getting over her…whatever it was."

"Yeah, well, glad she's okay. We were worried. So was Devin. You know, *we* have two kids too, just like you two."

"And just like Trevor and Mia. So many similarities. Anyway, you'd better get going. I know Tim and you're new here, so…"

"Yeah, dig it. Devin's warned me already. Later, huh?"

"Yeah. Oh, Daniel. Is Devin on a route today?"

"I don't think so. If I see him, I'll tell him you're looking for him."

We parted and I headed for my office, wondering where Devin was. Shit. It was still early enough that he *could* be at the coffee shop and I'd passed that up this morning. Tim wasn't anywhere to be seen either. Devin had been *super* late today, yet no one was mentioning it, not even Kim, who stopped me as I passed the phone room.

"I won't hold you, but I missed Devin this morning so I guess I have to ask you. Is Devin going to be moving into your house like I've been hearing, and if so, is it going to be by Christmas? We're making up the Christmas card address list for the employees."

Kim sure had a way of verifying gossip using company excuses. Christ, it wasn't even Thanksgiving yet. I told her to ask Devin, not me. Such a list would be available to anyone, including Devin's wife.

"Well, I *would* ask him," she said, "But I can't catch him. You'll probably hear from him today before I do. There's no real hurry, but if you could just leave me a company memo so I know how to list you guys."

A smile crossed my face at the mention of a company memo. She sure *would* get a company memo. I was going to personally see to that.

As I entered my office, I saw that I was the only one there. I knew I was early, but I also knew Devin had been very, very late. When the phone buzzed, I snatched it hopefully.

"Hey!"

"Devin! Christ. I've been looking all over for you."

"Yeah? Well, you won't find me there. I'm calling from a customer phone."

"I've been so worried. I know you were late and—"

"Late?" He laughed over the wire. "It's a wonder I've got a job right now. I had the keys to the gate, you know? The *only* keys. Man, when I drove up today every driver we have was lined up outside that gate. Soon as they saw me the whole gang of them cut loose with this loud cheer…you know…yaaaaay, he made it…clapping and jumping up and down. I'll tell you, I felt like an ass."

"And you still have a job, obviously."

"Yes, fortunately, for two reasons. One, Tim wasn't in yet. Two, I guess I never really knew how much these guys like me. I never appreciated them like I did this morning. They jumped into high gear…haul ass, you know? Everyone pitched in to help each other get those trucks loaded before any of the bosses showed up. Kerry, I was later than I *ever* was, and those guys should have already been loaded and gone by the time I arrived. And not one guy turned me in or mentioned it. Not even Ethan. It really made my day. Man, to have so many real friends pulling for you…"

"Devin, maybe Ethan isn't that bad of a guy."

"Maybe not. He sure didn't run to Tim this morning. He could have."

"Maybe you being the way you are, helping people out like you do, that paid off this morning after all."

"Yeah. Me. *Devin.* That patsy shit sure paid off today. Anyhow, I'd better hit it. At least when I'm there I can usually find an excuse to slip up there and see you. Hell, there are usually excuses waiting on Tim's desk. Oh…my father called the plant this morning. He found a house already. Damn, I don't see how he pulls these deals out of nowhere. Three bedrooms and only two hundred a month."

"Wow. I'm paying over two hundred and it's only half a duplex. And only two bedrooms. Well, and a den."

"Well, Gerald got the whole bit. Patio. Fenced-in backyard. Even a hammock already set up on the back deck."

"What does he need three bedrooms for?"

"Well, he's got my younger brother, Brian, and his chick, Faye. And they're both into painting and creative arts. That's where the third bedroom comes in."

"So you're going to have your apartment back to normal then?"

"What do you call normal? The place is in chaos with all the boxing up that's going on. My wife is still talking about flying up."

"Oh, is that what you decided?"

"I'm still not sure which would be cheaper. It sounds like driving would be, but I wouldn't want to do that by myself. Perhaps if Trevor could come along to help…"

"How about me?" I volunteered brightly.

He laughed. "I wish you *could*. Now *that* would change the whole atmosphere of the trip."

Lola walked in at that moment and waved. I returned it and told Devin she'd arrived, that it was work time.

"For me, too. I should be back in about an hour or so."

"Really? That soon?"

"I'm not on a route. Just a quick cooler delivery. Tim just realized how fucked up the route alignments are. When he jumped on me about it I just told him I can't be in two places at once and that he's already forbidden any ethereal projections and astral separations during working hours."

"What?" I laughed.

"You know, splitting my physical form into two separate bodies so I can do everything he expects of me. That falls under witchcraft as far as he's concerned. He's been getting down on me lately about the cross I wear and, well, my beliefs in general. I don't know *why* all of a sudden. He's known for years where I'm at. Anyhow, it got me out of a route today and back at my desk where I'm supposed to be. I don't know what's eating him lately. He's even been on me about my hair again."

"What's wrong with your hair?"

"Well, that's not new, actually. It only takes one driver to say 'Well, look at Devin's hair, and he's a supervisor. Why should I cut mine?'"

"Do you think someone complained?"

"I really don't know, Kerry. After this morning, my first impulse is to say no, but there *are* a couple of die-hard Christians back there that don't like me. Anyhow, this isn't the time to be discussing it. Later, huh?"

"Okay, Dev. Thanks for calling. I love you."

"Hey, I know the feeling."

Kelly was bullshitting with Lola when I replaced the receiver. Lola was laughing when I joined them.

"What's so funny?" I asked.

Lola beckoned me closer to her desk. "I was on my way in here. You know how Devin's got that Mama stuff started all over the route room? Well, this morning, some new driver I don't even know walked past me and said, 'hello, Mama.' It felt so weird. Like that's the only name I've got now." She burst into laughter again and we joined her.

"Boy, Mama. You sure have a lot of kids."

"I know. It's getting ridiculous. Kerry, how's Michelle?"

"Okay, so far. I sent her to school today. Her first day back."

"That's good. Oh, and did you talk to Devin about his gorgeous penmanship?"

"Yeah. He said he'll watch it."

I was in the mood to work. On days when Devin was at the plant, just knowing he could walk in at any moment was enough to elate me. My mind was on him as I posted. At some point, I had to look at the button I was pushing and my heart almost stopped. The eye was missing from the claws of the ring.

I stopped and began frantically tearing through my files, but it had not fallen into any of the four trays. I rolled my chair away from my machine and saw the eyeball on the floor.

"Well, I'll be damned!"

Kelly turned around. "I thought you already were."

"No, really, Kelly. Look." I picked up the eye, the obviously *glass* piece that had once been so tightly encased in the claws. Myrna had been correct. The eye *wasn't* real.

All the machines were stopped now.

"I thought it was real," Hannah said.

"We thought so too. Devin's gonna freak when he sees this."

"Why?" Kelly took the eye from me, examined it, and handed it back. "He can fix that, can't he? It doesn't look like it would be too hard to put back in."

"That's not the point. Remember that lady in Ohio that we called? The one we were waiting for an answer about the ring?"

"Yeah, but she never did answer, did she?"

"She *did*. We just got the answer a few days ago. I forgot to show it to you. Here."

I reached into the side pocket of my purse and handed her the blue envelope. "Go ahead. Read it."

She scanned it quickly and handed it back. "Wow, that's weird. How in the hell could she know without even seeing it?"

Lola poked her head in. "Can you guys discuss this at lunch?"

Kelly gave me one last glance before resuming her posting. "You're right, Ker. Devin *is* gonna freak."

Devin didn't make it back in time for lunch, but he rolled in shortly after. His first stop was our office. And it *was* Devin.

"Hey, Mama."

"Oh, hello, little boy," Lola said, without looking up.

He handed her a stack of corrected charge tickets. "These are okay to post now."

Lola took the tickets and flipped through them, trying to keep a straight face. They were nearly all his. "That's *much* better." She set the tickets aside. "What else brings you in here, or dare I ask? What's that in your hand?"

By now, the three of us were watching. Work always halted when Devin came in.

"Hey, Devin," Kelly piped up. "What are you gonna do about Christmas? Witches don't celebrate Christmas, do they?"

Devin laid a white envelope, the object Lola had questioned him about, beside my machine. "Oh, well." He shrugged at Kelly. "You know how it is."

The worst thing he could have said to Kelly.

"No, I don't either. Tell us, Devin. Now that you're inheriting two little girls that are used to the big day, how are you gonna get out of *that* one?"

"Same way I got out of it all these years. I just ignore it."

Kelly burst out laughing. "How can you ignore those innocent, excited, upturned faces, anxious for their annual visit from Santa?"

"How can you ignore all the Christmas trees and decorations?" Hannah asked.

"That's what I should be asking you Christians," Devin retorted. "How can *you* ignore all those slaughtered trees?"

"Devin is just too cheap to buy presents on any holiday," Lola said from our doorway. She was taking it all in and didn't look amused.

"Now, wait a minute!" Kelly, full of glee, wasn't about to have the subject changed. "What was that…uh… little religiously prejudiced remark?"

"That little religiously prejudiced remark meant how can you Christians torture and murder millions of trees every year just for the sake of a lousy one-day, human-invented holiday?" Devin wasn't smiling either. "And then scream for conservation? Seems a little hypocritical to me."

Kelly's mouth dropped open. "Murder? Torture?"

"And," he went on, "as for Christmas carols and other such irritating noises, wet cotton in the ears does wonders."

"Scrooge! Scrooge!" Kelly howled, nearly rolling out of her chair with laughter.

Kelly was obviously the only one having fun with this. Lola's next tone of voice was void of any trace of mirth. There was even an icy irritation as she spoke.

"Oh, then, uh...I guess Kerry's kids don't *get* a tree this year, huh? Well, she's had one every year I've known her. In fact, she used *my* decorations and lights for her tree last year. How's she supposed to tell these kids that just because of you—?"

I watched this unusual interchange with mixed feelings, and a lump where my chest usually ached when Devin was nearby. The envelope with obviously a thoughtful card lay loosely in my hand, still unopened. Such consideration from a supposed atheist for no occasion while an argument was ensuing over the intimated obligations of the Christmas season. And the argument *was* raging.

"I haven't ever had a tree in my house during that...uh...holiday season," Devin said quietly.

"Wow. Didn't your wife kick up a fuss?" Kelly asked curiously. "She's not into...what you are, is she?"

"She knew how I felt about it. Last year she picked up a little plastic tree, a toy imitation, oh, about eight inches high. For a joke. Ha." He added that sick laugh dryly.

"Oh, and you didn't think that was funny, huh?" Kelly crossed her arms and looked up at him.

"No, I didn't. I wouldn't have thought it funny if she'd brought in a statue of a little slaughtered lamb either." He glanced at me and raised his eyebrows.

Lola stood, hands on her hips, glaring at him in the doorway. She seemed to be in a state of controlled rage. "Well, I don't care *what* you think. Those kids had a tree last year and it's not fair. I can't see Kerry, as well as I know her, cheating those children out of the spirit of Christmas just because *you* don't believe in it!"

I finally intervened. "Look, Devin. I know you don't want to kill a tree, but—"

"A *tree*? A tree? Lady, there's not just *a* tree being destroyed around this stupid time of year! There are thousands and thousands..." Now he turned those piercing eyes on me. The eyes that gave *him* away. And right now, they were smoldering. "What gives humans the right to murder those helpless trees? Cut them right out of their peaceful existence and haul them into some overheated house, dehydrating the last fucking little bit of life there is left in them and put them through a long, slow, tortured, painful death? Fucking wasted life. Death now. Death everywhere. Millions of trees."

"But...you're talking about *live* trees," I said gently.

"You call that live?"

I flinched. "I meant, real...formerly alive trees."

"They're all alive until the human takes the axe to them."

"Well, what's wrong with the plastic trees, Devin?" Kelly interrupted. "Really, a plastic tree isn't murdering anything. And they've got some pretty realistic trees out on the market now." Kelly sounded like she was sorry she had started this whole thing.

Devin rubbed his eyes in resignation and sat down on the forbidden step. "Kerry can have a plastic tree if she wants. It's all so plastic anyway."

"Scrooge," Lola said, and stalked back to her desk.

"Devin, hear me out," I said. "I used to work in a nursery. I still have friends there."

He looked at me but said nothing, so I took a breath and continued. "They have live trees…*living* trees, still in the pot, you know? The very pot they were planted in and grew up in. In fact, their roots are bagged in fertilizer…"

"You're suggesting a compromise?" Devin looked at me with interest. "I think I see what you mean. You're talking about a tree that will still be alive on Christmas Day. One that the girls and I can plant on the same morning that all the other trees will be laying out in trash piles." There was a smile in his faraway gaze as though he was momentarily lost in his own thoughts. Then he looked back at me. "Yes. That would be a different thing altogether. A *completely* different thing."

"I can call my friend, Jamie. She can bring a good-sized potted tree home for about ten bucks if I remember employee prices right."

"Oh, how nice," Kelly chanted. "Kerry's kids are getting a real Christmas tree after all."

Devin ignored her. "Call this Jamie. I'll pick the tree up myself. Meanwhile, I'd better get back to the route room."

"Good riddance," Kelly mumbled. "Scrooge."

I waited until he was gone before I left for the ladies' lounge, the card hidden under my blouse and tucked into the waistband of my slacks. It was in the solitude and coolness of the stall that I tore open the envelope to find the strange printing I had seen only twice before. The card was of an expensive variety, the glossy front a photograph of a nature scene. A man and woman walked through a wooded forest of…Christmas trees…the man carrying a guitar. The front of the card read: *Now and forever, I love you.* Inside the card it continued, *May all your dreams of yesterday manifest in your reality tomorrow. I love you today.*

In ink, under the print, was an infinity symbol, the figure 8 sideways, and it was signed simply *Us.*

Lola beckoned me when I returned to the office and I walked over with a resigned gait, bracing myself for the lecture I knew was coming. The *don't ruin Christmas because of him* speech. Instead, she only pointed out a blemish on the corner of my chin. "Lean over," she said. "Uh, it's okay if I squeeze this for you, isn't it?"

I looked at her curiously. "It's okay. Why wouldn't it be?"

I heard Kelly cackle from the other room as Lola replied. "Well, I thought I might be violating nature or something…*must* you wear that atrocious thing outside your blouse?"

As I had leaned over, the pentagram that I wore had begun to swing obviously. "I have to, yes, because if I don't it gets tangled up with the other one." I pulled out the Sador, so much larger and more obvious. "See?"

"Oh, what a tangled web we weave," Kelly sang melodiously as she stepped into Lola's office. "Lemme see. *That's* the one I like. See Lola? It even has a cross on it. How do you explain *that* to your friends, Ker?"

"Crosses are pre-Christian, Kelly," I began. "In fact the Christians adopted the cross from the Pagans—"

"That's enough," Lola interrupted. "I am *really* getting sick of hearing about all this witchcraft baloney. Kerry, I want the subject dropped from this office. I mean it. It is now a forbidden subject around here."

I looked at Lola numbly. "I don't usually bring it up unless someone asks."

"Well, I want it dropped, and you can tell Devin Scrooge Drew that I said he is to do likewise while he's in here. Now both of you get back to work."

Lola was still smarting from the anti-Christian conversation. Well, I had always known how she felt about the Christmas season. It was her favorite time of year.

Devin was apparently having his own problems back in the route room. I discovered this at five when he met me at the time-clock exit. He looked upset and, as was becoming habitual these days, it wasn't *Devin* who was upset.

"Let's go, Kerry." He took me by the arm and we started for my car, my legs taking two steps to keep up with his one. He didn't slow his pace until we were across the street and out of earshot of the plant altogether. I noticed furrows of worry in his face, and a little impatience in his tone. Erick. He usually didn't display either of those human emotions.

"Hey, what's the rush?" I asked, panting, tired of the race. "What's wrong? Come on, slow down."

"Those...*people* get me so fed up with their ignorance day after day." He exhaled and slowed to a normal walk. "I really have to say I don't know how you've lived with it for twenty-five years and still maintained your basic home attributes. I really don't."

"What? *Who* gets you fed up?" I stopped at my car and looked at him. "What brought this on? This morning they were the greatest friends you ever had."

He jerked a thumb in the direction of the plant. "They probably *are* the greatest friends *Devin* will ever have, if indeed a human can really qualify for the high title of friend. But Devin got into it with a couple drivers back there today. I had to do something. I couldn't just stand back and let him sink."

A small sliver of hope raced through me. "Devin?"

"Yes, Devin. Can't keep his mouth shut in the workplace."

I groaned. This sounded like real trouble and we didn't need any more of that. At least not today. "Shit. Now what? What'd he do?"

"Well, it started with Tim. He started in again about the length of his hair and, well, we've been over this before, so Devin told him he was cutting it on Wednesday. That's the only evening that the shop he uses is open."

"The fight was over your hair?"

"No, I'd have let that slide. Even Devin doesn't really care if he has to cut it. But there's a driver back there…Norman Simon…you may not know him. He's a straight guy who's been brown-nosing Tim for the past couple of years. Very conventional and company-oriented. Like a miniature Perry Jason. He's been after Pat's job for years, and anti-Devin from the day they first met. He's a card-carrying Christian, for one thing. And anti-longhaired hippie, weed, and so forth. They actually came close to reaching a compromise once. You *know* Devin would try. They agreed to a swap of religious books. Devin agreed to try to read his with an open mind and Norman took one of Devin's with the same promise." He paused with a sigh. "Devin would turn the whole plant on to the knowledge if he could. Anyway, the results were a stalemate. Norman never even tried. Devin did attempt to keep his end of the bargain, but he couldn't stomach the garbage and I can't say I blame him. It's a funny thing, but when you know what *is*, then all the distortions are plain and distinct."

"I think I know the guy you're talking about. He's *super* straight. I doubt he'd recognize the smell of pot if it was blown in his face."

"Yep. Goody-two-shoes all the way. Well, today Devin was working on a route sheet and the cross he wears, the inverted one, was outside his shirt. Ordinarily he wears it inside, and how it got outside the shirt today is beyond me. Anyway, Norman comes in wearing *his* stupid death symbol—"

"Death symbol? What death symbol?"

"*You* know. That figure of Christ nailed to a cross, blood streaming down his face, agony etched in detail that only humans and the third dimension are capable of. *That's* the thing that's okay to display during working hours. Those sadistic, sick bastards. Well, Norman sees Devin's cross and has the audacity to say something about it to Devin. You can guess what happened."

I hopped up on the hood of my car with a sinking sensation. Why was everything suddenly going wrong? This wasn't even like Erick to be so emotional. He was usually so tolerant of human ways, but I guessed Norman's crucifix being considered the norm had been too much for even him.

"At first he tried to brush it off," Erick continued. "He just said 'Hey, Norman, lighten up,' you know, 'Do your own thing.' But Norman kept at him and before you know it Norman's yelling that our people are evil and that God was going to strike us all down." There was more than just disgust in his voice. "*Our* people. That little sucker hasn't any inkling of who our people really are. Or that all that garbage he so thoroughly believes was perpetrated by *our* people to begin with."

"Your people?"

"*Our* people. Those inferiors haven't any idea we're here on the planet at all. We're so disguised that we're even wearing their robot forms, but I guess they think that *they're* the ones who designed the human body with all its miraculous functions anyway." He paused, as if waiting for a reaction, but I just motioned for him to go on. Frankly, I didn't know what he was talking about. He'd lost me a couple of sentences ago.

"Anyway, getting back to this afternoon, if Norman wants to start fucking with my beliefs, that's one thing. What I know, I know, and I only feel sorry for people who don't know. But when he starts on my people…" He paused and lit two cigarettes, his hands now trembling. "I hope I'm not freaking you out with my petty work hassles."

Once again, hope glimmered in me. Erick was the only one who *didn't* smoke, so I didn't know who was coming next. Luck was with me, though. When he handed me one of the cigarettes and took a long deep drag off the other one, I wanted to scream for joy, but I somehow managed to maintain, and motioned for him to continue.

"Anyhow, babe," he went on, his voice radically different from the annoyed Erick of only seconds ago, "before you know it all the drivers were in on it. I found myself defending the religion to a whole *squad* of Christians. Christ, I can't believe how many of them there still are. I ended up losing my cool completely. Grabbed Norman by the shirt and told him if my people were so evil then how come we didn't stamp them out back during the Salem days when they thought they were exterminating us? If we're so fucking powerful, how come we didn't crush them all back then? You know, Ker, Wicca is the only religion that has never persecuted another religion." He half laughed and added wryly, "Fear that you're wrong in what you believe will drive anyone, including the government, to begin extermination of the so-called threat. The funny part is, if they didn't believe deep down that we might be right, they wouldn't have wasted so much energy trying to get rid of us. They don't realize how much more powerful we are when we aren't handicapped by the limitations of the physical body. We can do more damage unseen than we ever could in the flesh. They didn't exterminate anybody. They just added more strength to what power we already had. I told the whole route room that they didn't realize it, but Christians just did those witches a favor and in doing so handicapped themselves badly. Then I laid the clincher on them."

Devin's eyes were glistening with excitement now. "I turned to Leroy, the only black driver we've got, and to Juan, the Cuban and I asked them outright, 'Have I hurt you guys in any way? Have I ever displayed any negative or evil or shown one bit of prejudice towards you? No. But *humans* hate you, Leroy, because you're black. And they hate you, Juan…Ah don' come in here every mornin' thinkin' that if it wasn't fer yer people takin' over our jobs and cities fer yer lower wages…Ah don' lay claim to any ownership of *any* country, not when Ah kin see it's jist all one big piece of real estate an' nobody has th' raht to call any of it mahn…it's all ours, an' Ah don' carry a color code t' see what color gits t' be *us*…'"

I watched in awe as Devin really struggled to maintain his hold on his own body. I could *see* where Christian would have stepped in this afternoon. Now, in his relating the story to me, I saw where Devin must have come to a point where he'd lost hold in the route room and Christian was now obligingly filling in the gaps where Devin must have succumbed for a brief minute. Christian could certainly do better relating to Leroy because of his own race, and that must have been what happened, just as it was almost happening now. Devin, however seemed determined to remain and Christian's few words were lost to the wind. Tears of happiness were welling up in my eyes and I no longer cared *what* had happened, only that Devin was here with me now. I threw my arms around him.

"Devin, oh Devin, I can't believe it." I probably crushed every rib in his chest. He returned the hug just as tightly. "Hey-hey-hey! What the hell got into *you*, chick? *I* was the one that had the argument. It shouldn't really affect *you*."

He gave me his sweet hippie Devin smile and pulled me even tighter against him. "Actually, there wasn't much any of them could say after that. Of course, Norman had to run to Tim, practically crying. I guess I fingered his shirt or something, and then Tim comes in." He screwed up his face in imitation, "'Devin, can I see you in the office, please?'"

I burst out laughing. Devin was so cute when he imitated Tim. I was so outrageously happy to sit and just *look* at him that I'd have sat there on that hood until Christmas if I thought it would keep Devin here. It was as if he'd returned from a long vacation. Even though I was sure I'd spoken to him on the phone today, that wasn't the same as being *with* him.

He hopped up beside me and snapped up my jacket as the wind gusted again. Lola passed us in her car and waved. Kelly was just unlocking hers directly across from us.

"Merry Christmas, Devin!" she yelled over.

"Hey, buzz off, Kelly," he yelled back, smiling at last, his arm still tightly gripping me. Then he returned his attention to me. "Now, you didn't look so cheerful yourself when you punched out. That was a long face that emerged from the exit. Did something happen to you, too?"

"Well, I had a very similar experience in the office today with *my* friends. Too similar, in fact, to be a coincidence. It wasn't as dramatic, but the issue, the effect, and the bottom line were the same."

I related the conversation with Lola and Kelly, pointing out that it had begun with remarkable similarity. Devin's cross and my pentagram. If they had both been quietly hidden under our clothes, today might have been different.

On the other hand, the timing was too coincidental. I'd worn that pentagram out in the open for weeks. Devin's...well, maybe he was usually a little more discrete, but why *today* was the same issue brought into clear focus? It seemed engineered by someone's design. I pointed this all out to Devin.

He seemed perplexed. "Kerry, what can I say? If it's *him* you're thinking of, perhaps, but there would have to be some reason for it. Maybe we're both supposed to cool it in there. Hell, I know they don't have the right to tell us to shut up, and yet still allow the Christians to talk about their Lord and wear their death symbols but, well, is it really that important? Is it worth the hassle we both went through today and over a material object at that? I mean, we're not going to ever change their minds, and why try? Just because the witchcraft laws were repealed doesn't stop the harassment any more than the anti-discrimination laws stopped most people from hating the black race. So if Mama doesn't want it mentioned, then go along with her request. You've been friends with her for too long."

"That's what's bothering me, Dev. She *is* my friend, so why did she—"

"Just be a friend to her. Do as she asks."

"But they're the ones who bring it up. Make little jokes and ask questions. *They* start it. Like Kelly today with the Christmas thing. That led to the big argument, which eventually led to what happened to me today."

Devin watched me closely as I talked. "Have you always been so touchy about the religion?"

"No," I admitted. "I was never really attacked for it before."

"Well, now that you've experienced attack, ask yourself why it bothers you. Look, we aren't *really* into witchcraft anyway. It's just as close as the human race will ever come to being, well, close to the way it is. There isn't any one book that has us or *his* world right. Hell, we've been called demons and gods and, shit...you know none of them are capable of understanding. It's like trying to explain basic physics to a kindergartener. You can't. They aren't capable of understanding. You see where I'm coming from?"

"Sort of. I think there are a few things I'd better get straight, though. Some of the things you and Erick said about what we are. Even *he* insinuated it. And I'm a little confused."

He smiled. "You'll understand better as time goes on. Come on, now. Don't look so down. None of it is worth this human bullshit, and I'd rather see you smile."

I did. It was easy now that Devin was back. My one prayer had been answered.

"Oh, by the way. I forgot to tell you. Trevor was in today."

"Oh, yeah?"

"I wanted to ask you if he and I could, well, sort of borrow your house tonight. He's getting some peyote, and we were talking about where we could do it. My place is out. A guaranteed bad trip. Trevor was the one who thought about your place."

"Peyote? I heard about that. From Erick. What is it exactly?"

"Oh, it's organic. Don't worry. In fact, you can try it too if you want. It won't hurt you."

"What's it made of?" There it was, that sinking feeling in my gut. Drugs, now. Well, I had wanted Devin back. Erick *had* warned me. I could hear Erick's words ringing in my head. *I'm glad you don't take them. You don't need them.* Well, did Erick really understand my love or need for Devin? Because here was Devin with his own ideas on the stuff.

"Peyote is a natural product of the earth. I wouldn't turn you on to anything..." he stopped dead as he realized what I was thinking. "Hey, you don't have to do it. Not if you don't want to."

"Yeah, I'll pass. You two go ahead, though."

The faint rumblings of doubt and worry. *Devin is the druggie of us.*

Devin jumped to the ground and reached into his back pocket for his wallet. "Here. Pick up something for dinner on the way home. Not the cooking bit. Some fried chicken or something. Whatever the kids like. I have to go back in and finish up, wait for Trevor and lock up. That'll give you time to pick up the kids and feed them, and I guess I'll see you between eight and nine."

"Okay. Oh, what *did* Tim say when he got you alone in the office?"

"Well, first he asked me to sit down, and then he tells me that he likes me, but he'd appreciate it if I kept my philosophies to myself. I told him it wouldn't happen again as long as I wasn't provoked. Anyhow, babe, don't let it get you down. It's all just human bullshit."

"Yeah, just like with Lola today," I agreed halfheartedly.

"Oh, another thing. Tonight. When my brother comes up." He tipped my face towards him watching me anxiously. "It...uh...probably won't be me...uh...with him. You know?"

I returned his gaze, trying not to display any inner reactions of any kind. "Who would it be?"

"Well, *him*. That's okay, isn't it?"

"Christian?"

"No. Him." There was a tension in the air as he waited for my answer.

I turned away to open the car door, not wanting him to see my disappointment that it wouldn't be Devin, or my fear of who *he* was and where *he* came from.

"Sure," I said finally. "Whatever."

He nodded and, with a wave, took off for the plant at his usual gallop, as carefree as Devin always was.

Problems sure did seem to be mounting. Not just between us, but now they had leaked into the office. Even Lola was irritated with us. I wasn't sure about Kelly, but I fervently hoped that today wasn't the beginning of a conflict over something as stupid as...religion.

The radio stayed true to its warnings, playing Crosby, Stills, Nash and Young's *Teach Your Children* except when I turned it on, the song was playing in the middle, so the verse was saying to teach your *parents* well. Apropos, as usual. I was supposed to look at them and sigh, and just know that they loved me.

Right.

9 Waiting for Devin and Trevor that evening, I was filled with misgivings about the night ahead. I really didn't know what peyote was, much less how it would affect a normal human being. I wasn't really worried about Devin. By now, he certainly would know what his system could handle, but he had made it clear that it would be *him* coming, and *he* was definitely no ordinary human being. Cigarettes didn't seem to bother him, nor did any other human vices. He seemed to be beyond any negatives attached to substances, but still...he was strange enough when he *wasn't* on anything.

When I answered the knock on the door, I was surprised to see Devin standing there. *Devin*. And alone.

"Hey." I opened the door to admit him. "Where's Trevor?"

Devin sat down to unlace his boots. "Okay to take these off? Trevor will be here around ten or so. He had to go get the stuff."

"Okay." I was bewildered. Devin seemed unaware that I was expecting anyone else, and I wasn't about to bring a change on by mentioning it. "Did you eat?"

"No. You get off better on an empty stomach. Oh, I keep forgetting you aren't familiar with peyote."

"Okay, but the chicken's out there if you change your mind."

Devin loosened his shirt and shook a cigarette from his pack. "Pat and I pinned down Tim today, finally."

"Oh really? About what?"

"About Lucky."

"What's Lucky done wrong?"

He laughed. "What's Lucky done right? That sucker ain't been out delivering water. We had so many complaints from the customers while I was doing his route, and none of them had seen him. Turned out he was selling his own line of shit door-to-door instead." He glanced at his watch. Nine o'clock. "Hey, Kerry, we have about an hour. I can fill you in on what the stuff actually is. In case you want to do it with us."

"No, I can't. Even if I wanted to. Michelle was complaining that her back hurt, and if that means she's getting sick again I have to be able to drive."

"Her back hurts? Man, when did that start?" He looked at me with alarm. "You know what that could mean, don't you?"

"Yeah. The doctors warned me to watch for it. It could mean that the virus is still in her system and gaining hold again."

"Right. I think I'll go look in on her."

We went into the girls' room and he knelt beside her bed. She was sleeping peacefully. He touched her forehead and looked at me. "No fever," he whispered.

"I know. I've been checking."

"Well, a backache could mean anything," he said, getting up, "but keep checking. You just never know with kids."

We returned to the living room, and I put on the tape that Devin had made for me. Devin still hadn't lapsed into the strange voice I was watching for. I couldn't possibly imagine why *he* would be interested in a drug trip unless he had something in mind that would help me to understand what he'd been trying so hard to get me to remember. Devin joined me in the beanbag, his hands rubbing the length of my arm gently, then paused as his fingers passed over my hand.

"Hey. You're not wearing the ring."

I sat up abruptly. "Oh my God. That's right! Of all the things to forget." I reached into my pocket and pulled out the eye and the empty claws. "This is going to freak you out. Remember that letter Myrna sent us?" I dropped the two pieces into his hand. "Check it out."

He examined them quietly, glancing at me once. He held the eye up to the light. Without the ring's backing to block the light the eye looked mockingly deceitful. He handed them both back to me.

"Actually it doesn't matter. I can fix it. When did it happen?"

"Today, at work. Good thing, too. If I'd lost it outside I never would have found it."

"So. She was right." Devin raked his fingers absently through his black curls. "You know, I'd have argued to the end that she was wrong."

"Well, at least we know."

"Okay. I'll pick up the stuff while I'm out tomorrow and get that fixed for you. Perhaps we can make it smaller so it will fit you better."

"It is pretty big. My hand feels naked without it."

He smiled. "Well, the office should be happy for a couple of hours. They were getting kind of touchy anyway." He looked at his watch again. "It's only a quarter after."

The track changed and Uriah Heep was back, reminding me of Lums and paper napkins and unique printing with red felt-tip pens. *Sunrise*. Probably be about when we'd catch a couple hours of sleep before work if this night went as planned.

"I've pretty much decided to drive up," Devin said suddenly.

"Drive up…oh, you mean…what brought that on? I thought you were leaning toward flying."

"I was, and then I was on a fence, but I did some calculations and you were right. It'll be much cheaper to drive and tow a U-Haul. Trevor's going along to help with the driving. It will be much faster that way."

A knock interrupted and George opened the door slightly. "Hey, Ker…"

"Come on in, George. What's up?"

"Well, I saw the van, and I wanted to ask Devin something. Sorry to barge in, but I don't have a phone, as you know."

Devin looked at George expectantly so George went on. "Are you gonna be around this weekend?"

"I plan to be."

"Can you show me where you got that ring you gave Kerry? That thing's neat as shit. I want to get one."

"I think we can arrange that." Devin looked at me with interest. "Perhaps we can pick up Mark and take the girls with us. Make it a family outing."

"I *have* been promising them zodiac rings," I admitted. "Sounds good to me."

"Far out!" George beamed. There was no mistaking the admiration in his eyes and voice. He absolutely worshipped Devin. "Thanks…I'll stop by Friday night and see when you want to go. By the way, did you two get your problem worked out?"

"What problem?"

"You know, the one you two were knee-deep in discussing yesterday. About the other Devin and the one Kerry don't like."

Devin and I exchanged glances. George wasn't the only one who was going to be around us quite a bit in the upcoming future. Devin must have made a snap decision.

"George, I promise you, I will explain everything to you when we go to the jeweler's. We're kind of expecting company tonight, so this isn't the time to get into it, but I will fill you in on what that was all about." He turned to me. "And by the way, Kerry, on the subject of telling people, I told Daniel today. Or rather, I tried to."

My mouth dropped open, George temporarily forgotten. "You told Daniel…what exactly?"

"About me. And the others."

I stared at him. "That wasn't too smart. Don't forget, Daniel just met you, and he works there now."

"I realize that, but it wasn't really a matter of choice. I've been around him so often lately, and it's pretty difficult to be…uh…myself around him. I had to say something. The dude's not stupid, you know."

I'd been afraid of that myself. "How'd Daniel take it?" I almost felt sorry for poor Daniel. He'd thought so much of his new friend. "Did he even believe you?"

Devin shrugged awkwardly and glanced at George. "Well, he *had* to, actually. What choice did he have when he looked back on things. Like the day he snapped the Polaroid in the route office. And he was there when I lit into Norman today. He turned a little green when Leroy was brought into it. He's been looking at me oddly ever since. I knew he was confused, and I couldn't just leave him to draw his own conclusions. Really, babe. A wild guess could be worse than the actual truth."

"You mean confused like me?" George interrupted.

"Wait a minute, George. Devin, what *did* Daniel say?"

"Believe it or not, he took me seriously. He admitted that he had to, considering he'd noticed changes in me, uh…now and then. It seems that Erick and Christian don't necessarily share the same opinions regarding the diagnosis on Daniel's clunker. And Erick…well, he phrases his opinions in…uh…college-educated words whereas Christian can be rather crude. Especially when there's a clash of opinion on the diagnosis itself. Now, if they would both just leave the mechanics to me…"

I buried my face in my hands. I knew exactly how Daniel had felt. I, too, had experienced those same conflicting opinions among them. That photo, for example. Erick had wanted it destroyed while Devin didn't seem to care that I kept it.

"Well, who *is* the mechanic, Devin?" I watched him attempt a modest reply.

"Well, naturally I would have to say myself," he said with a smile. "But then again, schedules being what they are, I'm not always available for counsel, and Christian knows it *all* of course."

"Aw, come on, you guys!" George protested. "Let me in on this so I can at least follow you!"

"George, I told you. This weekend. I promise. Anyhow, getting back to Daniel, he admitted he'd noticed the others…he figured it could be a split personality. He said he first noticed it while I was working on his car, and today, during the Norman argument, he said he'd seen an inner struggle. He never really witnessed a real change because I fought to hang in through it. I could feel Christian trying to get his two cents in, especially with Leroy, and he almost made it. Damn good thing he didn't. You know, I gotta work there."

Realization was dawning on George's face. "Oh, now I see," he said slowly, his voice a little awed. "You've got a split personality. Is that it?"

"Not exactly," I put in quickly before Devin had a chance to go too far with his own version. "But Devin, it's probably better if we *do* let a few people know, people we're going to be around a lot. George, for example, is around as much as Pammy's going to be. She's bound to notice something. She's going to be living right here *with* us."

Devin couldn't argue with that logic. He turned to George with a resigned sigh. "Okay. She's right, George. I guess there are some things that are going to be a little obvious. It's a little more complicated than a 'split personality,' but you're almost half right. And there's actually more to it than even Kerry knows, although she doesn't realize that yet. I've been trying to get her to realize it herself, rather than have to tell her." He gave me an apologetic glance. "She knows, really, but she keeps waiting for me to tell her anyway, and I've told her so many times that she should go right to the source of the matter."

George sat patiently waiting for him to continue and didn't notice what I was now noticing myself. Something that was actually verifying Devin's explanation, and I wasn't sure I was *happy* that it was happening. By now, I'd learned to distinguish all four of them at a second's glance. Now a booth in the coffee shop was flashing like a strobe in my memory of the day we'd officially met. *He* had come tonight after all. Devin had disappeared without any warning. The very proof of Devin's explanation to George was right before George's eyes. A hopeless disappointment slivered through me. I'd been so happy to see Devin tonight.

His eyes bored into George's, and George suddenly stood up and snatched his keys from the table.

"Well, uh…I haven't been around you enough to say one way or the other, Dev, so…look, uh, I think I'm going to be taking off now. See ya Friday."

Devin smiled at me as the door shut behind George's sudden exit.

Now I was really wondering. A minute ago, George had been all ears with no intention of going anywhere. Then *he* appears and manages to mentally persuade George that he'd really rather be *anywhere* else. It occurred to me then that Devin seemed to have *too* damn much control over his shift changes. Almost as if he knew when to stage these appearances. The act theory was poking at the back of my mind, but that didn't explain George's sudden exit. Devin didn't give me time to dwell on it, though.

"It *looked* like he was going to be around for a while, and I don't know how much Trevor is getting," he explained, as if he knew what I was thinking.

"Well, how much do those things run?" I was obviously back with Devin again and, though relieved for that fact, I was becoming suspicious that maybe Devin's acting ability could be far more valid an explanation than the one he was rapping down to me and other people. I didn't like the feeling, but at least it *was* Devin now, regardless of the flash entrance of the personality who, real or not, frightened me the most.

If it was real, it must have been a short entrance, meant to eliminate George from our evening to ourselves, for after George's exit Devin seemed to have regained control and was steadily maintaining it.

"Oh, where T gets it, about eighty cents a hit."

I was determined to keep the subject on the drug. Drugs were Devin's trip. "Okay. Tell me exactly what peyote is, Devin."

"Sure." The smile told me that Devin was only too happy to display his knowledge of the drug. "According to Aldous Huxley…that's a dude who did some pretty open-minded experiments with mescaline in some very hairy doses…mesc is the chemical equivalent of Peyote. Peyote comes from the cactus which *is* a natural gift of the earth. And organic. They take the dried flower, known as a button, and extract what they need to chemically manufacture the same identical thing that grew in the cactus. Well, not exactly, but a molecular similarity." He took a drag off his cigarette and added, "It's a mind-expanding thing. Science calls things like this hallucinogens and it says you'll see things that aren't really there, according to Huxley."

"What kind of brain damage does it cause?"

"Well, remember, coffee and cigarettes are proven causes of brain damage in their own ways. Alcohol too. And all three of those are legal, so keep that in mind. Huxley already knew a little about physics and reality structures, so he wanted to give mescaline a fair analysis based on what he understood about the cosmic influences on things. I'll try to simplify Huxley's explanation. You know what adrenaline is, right?"

"Of course."

"Good. You also know that the body is pretty much water and chemicals, right? Carbon-based chemicals."

"Yes."

"Well, recently they've discovered that there is a waste from adrenaline, what's left after the adrenaline is burned up. They gave it the name adrenachrome, at least that's what Huxley says. The chemical composition of adrenochrome is similar to the chemical composition of mescaline. It's practically the same thing as mescaline which is the same thing as peyote. Adrenochrome causes the same symptoms you'd get if you were high on mescaline."

"So what you're saying is the body naturally makes adrenochrome from adrenaline and that it's almost the same thing as mescaline?"

"Hey-hey-hey." Devin butted his cigarette out. "You catch on pretty quick, chick."

"So you're telling me that the body *makes* mescaline, and mesc is *illegal?*"

"Yup. What a bitch, right? People are actually *producing* the chemical *inside* their bodies that will land them in jail if they are caught with it anywhere *outside* of their bodies. The body manufactures small doses of a chemical that alters consciousness drastically. Huxley says that the changes that occur while you're on mesc are similar to what they call schizophrenia, and I *know* you know what *that* is."

"Yeah, we've been through that conversation once tonight." I stopped abruptly as the obvious hit me. Split personality, and here Devin had four of them. Just how much mescaline or peyote had Devin ingested over his lifetime, and how recently? It could be a key to the entire personality mystery. I thought it might be worth mentioning.

"Devin, do you realize what you just told me? Apparently, you've taken this shit pretty often. At least, you sure know enough about it. You have these four people in you. Devin, this is a little scary."

He smiled. "Hey, I'm a Scorpio and everyone knows they're dual."

"Devin, you're not dual, you're quad."

"Well, the more the merrier." He smiled and shrugged. "Come on. Do you want to hear this or not?"

I sighed. "Go ahead. I thought you *were* finished."

"Well, you asked what mesc does to the brain."

"Yeah, but now you're connecting a chemical change with a mental illness."

"That depends on how you define illness. Here's the conclusion that Huxley came to. He claimed that everyone in the world was capable of knowing everything that's going on everywhere in the universe. What they say about God. That's why we have a brain and nervous system. Their jobs are to keep us from being overwhelmed with too much information, things we don't need to be aware of while we're here on this planet. Anything that isn't necessary to our life and to our survival."

"Who is this Huxley, anyway?" I asked.

"He wrote a book called *The Doors to Perception*. Just about everything I've told you came from what he learned and wrote about. I could not recommend this book enough to anyone who reads. He said you will only receive what your ego can handle, but that some people want to know more. He said there's kind of a reducing valve that allows humans to perceive a little, just what filters through. People receive a small amount of information and think it is the only reality when there are others that just don't get through that filter."

Something told me that there was a connection here between what he was telling me now and whatever he hinted at when Devin had vanished and others took his place. I'd been so absorbed in what he was explaining that I hadn't noticed that Devin had, once again, done just that, leaving Erick to continue past the point of what Devin knew about the drug. I didn't comment on the switch, just continued as though Erick had always been there.

"What other realities are you talking about? What do you mean by other realities?"

"I have to admit that Huxley's explanations are clearer than even I can explain," Erick said. "And I intend to use his clear explanations. He says humans are always making contact with other worlds. There are documentations everywhere of automatic writing, trance states, Ouija boards. UFO contacts. Religious miracles and manifestations. People have died on operating tables and come back to describe heavens and hells. No matter what frame of reference people are into, there is a connection that weaves all those together. They are all tapping *source*. If you tell someone that you've seen or heard something that isn't usually seen and heard, they'll think you're crazy. So the more you perceive, with or without drugs, the crazier you'll be considered by society. The majority of people are so limited perception-wise that anyone a little more advanced, anyone who *does* perceive a little more than what usually gets through, is considered mentally disturbed. '*They're seeing things.*' It's only ignorance that says these things seen and heard are not real when they absolutely *are* in their own reality structures and have just been tuned in on from *this* world. This is what Huxley said in his book and he's right."

I was fascinated. "Who are the people who aren't as limited as the majority?"

He smiled. "Even *I* don't think I could explain that better than Huxley did. He said certain people are born with a built-in bypass that tricks that reducing valve...I believe he used the word *circumvents*. It has been bypassed accidentally, or through a whole variety of techniques such as yoga, meditation...prayer from one who devoutly believes he or she is contacting God. Any explorations into deeper levels than alpha, such as theta or delta. And...uh...certain drugs will bring about this temporary bypass as well."

"Like mescaline." So this is what he'd been leading up to.

"Like mescaline, peyote, acid and psilocybin and so forth. They all produce the same effect. However, the ones *born* with this built-in bypass don't *need* to resort to drugs. And the ones that *do* use them actually believe they need them to repeat the experience. They don't know that the brain is capable of storing the technique in its memory banks and that the drug is no longer necessary. You, love, were born with the more advanced equipment, and actually so was

Devin Drew, so why he persists in the belief in drugs I'll never understand. Entertainment, perhaps, or just a lack of faith that he *can* do it without drugs. *You've* never taken any of these drugs, yet you admit to visions, voices, the whole shot."

"Is that why you guys keep insisting I'm not human? Is *that* what constitutes human and nonhuman?"

"Well, it's close, basically, but with you that natural ability was there the day you were born, and that puts you in a different category than everyone else you know. That's one clue that you're not human."

"Erick, if I *did* take this mescaline or peyote, would I actually perceive everything there is to perceive?"

He roared with laughter. "No, love," he said gently, sobering somewhat to answer my question. "It doesn't eliminate the reducing valve. It just *widens* it a little to allow more of other realities to slip in. If you, or anyone for that matter, were to receive the *total* content of the mind at large, you *would* be crazy in no time at all. Huxley guarantees it. No ego could handle that vast amount of knowledge, and no ego was *meant* to. That's *why* you have this little guard in your head that lets some things in and stops the others at the door. The nuthouses are full of humans who've attempted to handle more than their little ego-guard would accept. No, the valve only expands a little. Lets in just a little more than normal. *You* don't need the drug, or any other drugs for that matter. Huxley was pretty clear on this. You, love, do these things naturally, and you actually are capable of letting in *much* more and still handling it. You see little movies on walls and in your mind, and you have since you were a small child. Religious people call those visions, and saints who had them were proud to be singled out by God. When you throw these experiences in the face of science, mention other realities, they'll blame them on the drug, if one was used. And if no drug was used…if it's done through meditation or yoga, it's called enlightenment or cosmic consciousness. But done with no drug or method…it's call schizophrenia or crazy. I believe that was exactly how Huxley summed it up."

"Wow. I think I need to find this book." The whole picture was starting to make a little more sense. "How exactly does mescaline work to cause these things?"

"Well, Devin has the book. Now Huxley's explanation was that your brain is full of enzymes, those little buggers that allow the brain to work. Some of those enzymes regulate the glucose that's doled out to the brain cells. Mescaline slows down the enzyme production and in doing so, lowers the necessary amount of sugar to your brain. The insufficient supply of brain sugar is what allows mescaline to do what it does."

"What do you feel like when you take it?"

"You mean what are the symptoms that it's working?"

"Yeah. How I would know the drug was taking effect."

"Well, it's different than acid in that it's more of a physical drug than a mental one."

Once again, I watched his facial features undergo a melting down and reshaping as Devin took over in the area that only he was qualified to describe.

"Have you *ever* taken acid? Even just once?"

I smiled. It was Devin all right. Erick seemed to know that I never had while Devin had to ask. "No," I said.

"How about mushrooms? Christ, they're all over this damn state, and it rains enough here too. You must have been turned on to the mushrooms over by your uncle's house in that cow field."

I shook my head. "No. Too scared of them, I guess," I admitted, feeling like a square. Apparently, everyone else in the state had at least *tried* them, the way he made it sound.

"Shit. Well, I'll try to tell you, but that's no good, really. If you ever did decide to try mesc, I'll have already programmed your experience. And it really is different for everyone. It's a very personal experience."

"Well, there must be *some* common signals that tell you that you're *on* the stuff."

"That's true. You lose all perception of time and space. Everything you see will be intensified like crazy. If you stare at something long enough, you might actually see through to the molecular level. And if you hang in through that, you'll see past the point where the object is even there. You'll notice trails immediately after the drug kicks in." He attempted to demonstrate by using his hand to show several images of hand following hand. "And the drug lasts about eight hours…sometimes longer. If Trevor would get his ass over here it would pretty much be worn off by five in the morning."

"You mean it keeps you up all night?"

"Oh, you wouldn't *want* to sleep on it. It would be difficult to anyway. You're too alert and aware. And the far out thing about peyote is that it enhances understanding. It's easier to understand things and you remember it all later. You know how grass seems to enlighten you in some ways, but then you forget that brilliant revelation a minute after it hits you? Not so with mesc. Everything that happens is remembered to the most minute detail. You're just *too* aware if there is such a thing."

"How often do *you* do it, Dev?"

"Me? Oh, it's been almost a year. You don't do it every day like weed."

"And…it makes you see things that aren't there, huh?"

"No." He took a deep breath. "It allows you to perceive things as they really are."

I contemplated my next question, then plunged in. "Would it help *us*, Devin? If I took it, would it help *me* to understand *you?*"

He kissed me and smiled. "Babe, you understand me the way no other chick ever has. I'm still waiting for you to tell me to give up the drugs like other chicks would. You just haven't made a mistake with me yet."

"But, I mean would it help me to understand all the *other* stuff we're having problems with? Devin, it's hard to share you with three other people. I *miss* you when you're not here. Even when it's obviously necessary that one of the others be present, like when Michelle was in the hospital."

Devin leaned back against the padding of the beanbag and gave me a long look before he replied. "Look, uh…I realize I haven't been around much. It might seem like I don't want to be, or worse, that the guys aren't *letting* me, and neither is true. As crazy as this sounds, I've missed you too. It's funny how I know you can understand that."

"Well…I expected…him tonight."

"And…" he glanced at the clock. "I expected Trevor. I guess *he* knew that T wasn't going to show. I can't figure out what happened to him." He glanced out the window to the street outside. "Oh, well. I guess it doesn't matter. It's getting too late to take it now anyway, and I'm kind of glad T didn't show. I think I needed to spend some time with you."

I pulled myself closer to him so that I could hear his heart beating. With my head against his chest, his voice buzzed so loud in my ear.

"You know, Ker, I should go home tonight anyway. I keep meaning to bring extra uniforms up with me just for those nights I stay here. I didn't even think about it when I left the plant."

I patted him quietly on the back to let him know I understood, that it was okay for him to go. Then, I regretfully pulled away and sat up. Devin pulled his boots on, strapped them up, and winked at me.

"Keep an eye on our kid tonight."

I nodded.

He ruffled my hair gently and stood up. "Gonna walk me out?"

"You bet."

Outside, the stars were winking, the sky was black, and the air was like ice. Once he'd boarded the van, I stepped up on the running board to kiss him. He paused before he pulled the door shut. "You know, I really thought it would be *him* tonight. It was all set up that way." He almost sounded like he was musing to himself, not understanding why it hadn't been the one that both of us had expected. He turned to me for that final goodnight kiss. "I guess I just knew you needed me. It doesn't matter. I'm glad it was me instead of him."

"Me too. I was beginning to think I was never going to see you again except at work. Hey, Dev, these other worlds you were talking about. How do you know all that stuff about them? Have you ever been into one yourself? I mean, have you ever actually *been* there?"

"I don't think so," he replied, his eyes reflecting the illumination of the streetlights beyond the van. "But *they* have. And Erick for sure. And the way we've got this set up, it's practically the same thing as *me* going, you know?" He looked at me for reassurance that that *had* to be true, and I nodded.

"Okay, Dev. I'll put it together eventually. You helped a lot with your info on the mescaline. I know Erick filled in what you apparently didn't know yourself. You sure do know a lot about it, though."

He grinned. "You can thank Huxley for the info, but you don't think I'd take something or offer you something without thoroughly learning the facts about it, do you?"

"I guess not."

"Good night. Again." A final hug and he was gone and, once again, I went in to an empty beanbag.

Just before I turned out the light, I decided to switch on the radio just to see what kind of message I would receive this time. It was Uriah Heep again, asking me if I'd like to take this magic potion with him, to take a trip to a cosmic playground far away, and then he reminded me that I understood, that

I'd been there before. It was in my hands to find the door.

I switched the radio off and then the lights.

Too close for comfort.

10 Wednesday morning I was at the coffee shop early, looking at the horoscopes when Devin slid into the booth across from me. I hadn't been expecting him.

"Whatcha reading?" He leaned across the booth and kissed me.

"Sydney. What happened to your brother?"

"He couldn't get the stuff. I stopped by on the way home last night. He and Mia might be up tonight with the kids."

"Oh, really? Great."

"Yeah, it'll be good to see them. It's been a while what with them getting settled and all. By the way, how's Michelle?"

"No fever, but she says her back still hurts."

Devin frowned. "You sent her to school?"

"Yeah, she really wanted to go. It's just kindergarten."

Devin hailed Jane as she passed, ordered breakfast for both of us and a muffin for Lola, then turned back to me. "You know what you're doing, I guess."

After breakfast, I walked him to the truck outside and he reminded me to keep it cool in the office.

"You kidding? Just thinking about yesterday depresses me. I hope Lola is over it by now."

I kissed him goodbye and headed for my own car.

"Keep it cool," I reminded myself as I punched in. I hadn't been forbidden to wear my pentagram on the outside, just forbidden to discuss my so-called religion in the office. I decided I would avoid the subject, even if someone asked me, but the pentagram was staying right where it was.

Lola didn't mention it when I walked in. In fact, she seemed to have forgotten the entire episode. I set the muffin on her desk.

"Apple, Mother."

"Oh! Thank you! I *was* hungry today. You're early, aren't you?"

"Yeah, I didn't stick around the restaurant this morning."

"How's Michelle?"

"She went to school today, but she says her back still hurts. I think I'm going to run her over to the clinic after work."

We got into a discussion about fevers and backaches, and before long Kelly bounced in, noisy, but on time for once. Lola sent us both to our machines.

At four o'clock Devin made an appearance carrying a wooden plaque and a book. Due to the wind outside, his hair was one big curly bush.

"Jeez, Devin," Lola greeted him. "Go brush your hair. You look like a Ubangi."

"Buzz off, Mama," Devin retorted. "I won't take up more than a few minutes of your happy hour. I just wanted to make sure that both you and

Kelly *see* me do this. Hannah, you can watch too." With a mock bow, he stepped into our office and presented me with the gifts. "Merry Christmas, Kerry."

Kelly smirked. "It's not even Thanksgiving yet, Devin."

"Lemmee see." Hannah leaned over to look at the large stained picture. A Virgo poster varnished onto a wooden oak backing. And the book…

"Oh, we might have known," Kelly said, then read the title aloud. "*The History and Practice of Magic.*"

"Now." Devin turned to them, raising both arms in an stick-'em-up position. "I don't want to hear *any* of you say that I didn't give Kerry a Christmas present." He turned to me and pointed to the five on his watch.

"Kerry? Later."

Devin walked me to the car and reminded me that Trevor and family were coming to visit tonight. When I picked up the kids, I was relieved to find that Michelle's back didn't hurt anymore. That also left me free to get the house ready for company.

.

Wednesday night marked a turning point of sorts in our relationship. I found Trevor to be quite a bit like Devin in his thinking, manner and personality. The eye-to-eye communication was used frequently between them. Devin seemed to fight Christian all evening long to remain in his brother's company. It was apparent that Christian just dug the shit out of Trevor. This turned out to be helpful to me because with those two interacting so much, I was able to watch Christian in action without getting involved with him myself. It was plain that they were as thick as thieves, and it was encouraging to watch Trevor take his black companion for granted without seeming to notice Devin's absence, yet he always greeted Devin's reappearances with a sudden warm, recognizing smile. With Trevor treating the situation so casually, I began to relax and accept the appearances of Christian as natural. As a result, Christian sensed my warming to him and began to act like he felt more welcome around the house.

And what a character he was. All evening I watched his shifty, mischievous eyes sparkle and glint as he spouted off the way *he'd* do things if he was in charge. The wife would be outta here, and Tim would learn a little respect. The complete other side of Devin's virtues, and the total opposite of Erick who wasn't around at all tonight.

Mia was much more confident than she'd been on Halloween night. More talkative than the last time I'd seen her, she told me of the books she'd read and the numerous discussions that she and Trevor had had about the *beyond*. On human matters, she remarked again about how happy Devin seemed now since he'd become involved with me.

The kids were adorable. Mickey was Mandy's age, and Trixie was very mobile for a two-year-old. All the girls hit it off immediately and within an hour, Michelle emerged from the bedroom flashing a fancy new ring.

"Michelle!" I grabbed her as she dashed by, heading for the kitchen. "Where did you get that ring?"

"I traded it with Mickey."

"For what?"

"For my snake ring."

I looked at Mia who simply shrugged her indifference.

"Look," I said. "It's okay with *me,* but that snake ring wasn't worth that much. That looks like an expensive ring Mickey traded."

Devin removed the ring from Michelle's finger and examined it with curiosity. Then he looked at me. "Do you realize what this ring is?"

"Yes. It's a miniature of your Tetragrammaton. The ring of Solomon."

"Well, it's Michelle's ring now," Mia spoke up. "If they want to trade, they're both old enough to make that decision."

Devin seemed to think a point was being missed here. "Yeah," he said, "but *this* ring. Isn't it a little heavy for *any* child to be wearing?"

Trevor shook his head. "It's okay, Devin. It's just a ring to the kids. They don't know what it stands for."

I had to agree with Trevor. It *was* just a ring to the kids.

The girls resumed their tag game, and the ring was forgotten for the time being.

When they left for home that evening, I felt like our two families had become close friends. Real friends.

I awoke Thursday morning comfortably happy with my life and Devin, including all of his hitchhikers, and Lola burst my first bubble of the day.

"Kerry. Cut your bangs."

"I can't. Devin wants me to grow them out."

"The hell with Devin. You look awful. You should cut *his,* too, while you're at it."

I laughed. "Tim's making him cut his."

"And I'm going to make you cut *yours.*"

I was happy to have Lola back to normal. Maybe everything *had* blown over.

Kelly burst in, sized up the conversation, and sided with Lola. "You look just plain ugly with your hair parted down the middle. Hey, did you guys hear that Ethan got fired?"

"I did," Lola confirmed. "I think he just didn't show up for work a lot."

"That should make Devin happy," Kelly said, "since he was the one who had to do his routes."

The day had started to proceed normally. Lola let us argue over the radio station for several minutes before she intervened and picked a neutral station, and even then she was pretty good-natured about it.

As I posted, I contemplated my life and this weirdly unimaginable happiness that I could never have imagined before Devin. He was magic. Everything was perfect. I barely noticed the song, *Stairway to Heaven* playing in the background. It sang of a lady who was sure everything glittering was gold, but she was mistaken.

And then Ethel burst my second bubble of the day.

My babysitter had just called. Our lines had been tied up in our offices, so Ethel had taken the message for me and it was very concise.

Come to the school. Michelle's temp 103 again.

It was 3:30.

11 Michelle's readmittance into the hospital Thursday afternoon was the decision of her doctor at the attached clinic. Erick met me in the hospital parking lot just as I was parking. He was driving the company truck. I didn't express any surprise at his arrival, and he approached me as if this had all been prearranged.

"How is she?"

"Hot."

He took her in his arms and carried her in. When we got to the desk, he took complete charge while I stood mutely by. He was using medical terms with the nurses I'd never heard of, dictating which types of tests Michelle could take and which ones she'd already been through. When Michelle was settled in her new room, he headed me straight for the hospital cafeteria.

"We *have* to talk," he said, pushing the swinging doors open with his shoulder.

I was exhausted with it all and just followed him.

"Don't you see what she's doing?" He steered me to the cafeteria line, ordered for both of us, and didn't say another word about her until we were seated.

"You think Michelle is doing this for attention," I said.

"I can't say for sure. Could be." He gave me one of those humoring Saint Erick looks.

"Well, you just took her temperature before we came down here. What was it?"

"Almost normal."

"Then what's she doing in that room?"

Erick took the cigarette I'd started to light and butted it out in the ashtray on the table. "You don't need that now. You've had a cigarette in your hand since you drove up here. I've been watching."

"I'll bet you have." Still, I stubbed the smoldering butt out the rest of the way. I was in no mood to argue.

"Michelle's playing ping-pong with that thermometer, love."

"She's *registering* on it, Erick," I reminded him. "And what can I do about it even if she *is* doing it on purpose? It was a hundred and three when I brought her here."

He smiled. "For one thing, don't make the hospital so comfortable. Think about it. She's got a private room with remote-control television. Her own phone. Meals delivered to her bed. She doesn't have to go to school *and* Mommy comes to visit her." He tapped my nose affectionately.

"But how could a five-year-old do this on purpose, and why?"

"How? Love, we keep trying to tell you. Have you ever stopped to think that if *you* aren't human, maybe *they* aren't either?"

"Christ, you keep saying that."

He sat back indulgently and motioned with his hand for me to talk. "Go ahead. Tell me all about how human you are."

"Okay, if I'm not human like you keep insisting, then what am I?"

He looked at me with mock exasperation. "You mean you *still* really don't know?"

"Come on, Erick."

"Okay, love. Have it your way." He put sugar in my cup and stirred in the cream. "Oh, go ahead. Smoke your cigarette. I *know* you're dying for one. It's been at least five minutes."

I reached for the one he had butted out, but he slapped my hand gently. "Not that one. Damn, if you've got to smoke, at least get a clean one. In fact, here. Have one of Devin's."

The seriousness with which he offered Devin's pack caused me to burst into laughter. He was so self-righteous about the subject that they were only *Devin's* cigarettes. I brushed the pack away. "Never mind that. Back to Michelle. What would you suggest I do?"

"For starters, go home tonight. Don't sleep here again. There are good doctors here. She's in good hands."

"I was going to go home, anyway. She's not as serious as she was the first time."

"Well, give the kid a chance to get homesick."

"You mean don't visit her at *all?*"

He smiled. "Lady, I visit Trevor, but I don't live there."

"Big deal. You visit Devin, but you don't live here, either."

"Right you are." He stood up and picked up the trays. "Love, there's hope for you yet."

Much as I hated to admit it, Erick's theory turned out to be right. Michelle's fever rose when I was around, and hospital charts showed its normalcy when I wasn't. I must have surprised the hell out of Michelle when I told her I had to go to work on Friday morning. I definitely surprised the plant.

I explained to Lola that I wasn't needed as much at the hospital as I was at work and that Devin and I would stop and visit Michelle on our way home. As backed up as the work was in the office, this explanation was gladly accepted, but I privately wondered about the outcome of Erick's suggestion.

Devin was out all morning and didn't make it back in time for lunch, so Kelly and I headed for the restaurant alone. On the way back in, after parking the car, I saw a cluster of flowered weeds growing alongside the sidewalk.

"I'm going to pick those for Mama," I said, and plucked the weeds out of the ground.

Kelly shook her head. "You give that to Lola and she'll fire you on the spot."

"No, she'll laugh."

Kelly rolled her eyes. "Maybe you should have just gone to the hospital today. How come you didn't?"

"Well, it's a long story, but Devin thinks Michelle is doing it on purpose for attention. I'm giving his…uh…wisdom…the benefit of a doubt."

"Some wisdom. Did he get that from the herd of kids he's raised?"

"Sarcasm will get you nowhere."

I presented the flowered weeds to Lola who really tried to keep a straight face as she tucked them into her pencil box. "Oh, how lovely," she murmured.

"Yeah?" Kelly said, working absently with an emery board on her already perfect nails. "I shoulda told you, Kerry. Devin isn't going to think it's so cute. You should have heard him the day Kim got a dozen roses from the phone-room girls."

"A rose is a rose is a rose," I retorted. "And *that* is a weed."

I went in to my machine.

Devin cruised in about one, and the weed was the first thing he noticed.

"Where'd ya get the flower?" He nodded at the pencil box as he spoke to Lola, a pained look on his face.

"Kerry gave it to me. Isn't it lovely?"

"It was *lovely* growing in the ground."

I felt an uncomfortable stirring in my chest. Apparently, Kelly hadn't been kidding. It had never occurred to me to examine my little joke from Devin's point of view. Or the weed's...for that matter.

Kelly rescued me before it launched into a full-blown discussion. "So where've *you* been?"

Devin just stared at her stonily. "You writing a book?" Then he turned to me with sudden seriousness. "Oh, Kerry. I stopped in to see how Michelle's doing, and I called Mandy, but I forgot she's in school this time of day. I'll call her around five before you punch out. I don't want her to feel dumped off at the babysitter day and night."

"Okay, thanks. How *was* Michelle?"

"She's in great shape. They're having trouble keeping her in bed. She calls all the doctors and nurses by first names, and if she can hold a normal temp for twenty-four hours they'll release her."

"You think she will?"

He smiled. "She can if you stay away from her until Sunday."

"*Devin!*" Kelly said sharply.

"Hey, man, it's true. The kid's got it down pat now. Normal temp from nine-to-five. Ninety-nine from six-to-nine, and standby from two-to-four on weekends depending on when Mom's coming."

Everybody laughed, including Hannah and me.

"Are you trying to say I make my own daughter sick?"

"In a manner of speaking, yes."

"Okay, guys," Lola called in patiently.

"I'm leaving, Mama. Lighten up. Ker, if I get done early I'll just head straight for the hospital. You can meet me there when you get out. Pat offered to lock up for me tonight."

Before I could answer, Lola cleared her throat loudly from the other room. Devin kissed me quickly and Nazi-saluted Lola on his way out the door.

Lola left a little before five, and as I passed her darkened desk on my way out I saw the flowered weeds, dried out and limp, still in the pencil box. A wave of guilt washed over me and I dropped them into Lola's wastebasket, sickened. I'd learned something important about Devin today, and I promised those dead weeds that they would be the last ever snuffed out by my hand. It wasn't just Christmas trees that Devin concerned himself with. It was about all life, even weeds.

Devin was already there when I arrived, playing with Michelle and hungry as hell. Michelle's appetite was actually pretty healthy today too, and when the supper cart arrived we stayed long enough to see that she was involved in her meal and the television above her.

"Let's hit it," Devin said. "Michelle, your mom and I are going to go eat now. And after that, we're going to visit Mandy. She's all by herself at Kathy's, and she really misses you and your mom."

Michelle nodded understandingly and kissed us both goodbye. "I'll *call* Mandy," she said brightly, setting her milk on the tray and reaching for the bedside phone.

"Jesus," Devin remarked when we were out of earshot. "She's having a blast in there. Oh, by the way, her temperature is ninety-nine again." He gave me a smug smile. "Woman, you've got superkids. I'm not sure I can handle this."

I knew that smile and I'd never seen it on Devin, although I was well familiar with it. To further verify himself, Erick slipped his arm around me with his usual audible sigh, winked at me and picked up two trays as we stepped into the cafeteria line. "You *are* eating tonight, by the way."

I could smell the roast beef and gravy special and didn't argue.

Erick was talkative through supper, discussing Ethan's dismissal and the plant in general. He had his own ideas on how the routes should be managed, but he was especially interested in Devin's relationship with Tim.

"Devin's a good route man, better than most," he stated with no emotion in his voice. "He loves the job, he loves the people, and he works hard. He's earned that supervisor tag on his shirt." He absentmindedly touched the red label added above Devin's name. "He's a good supervisor, and he knows the routes inside and out. All of them. Tim likes Devin, and as long as Devin doesn't screw up he'll eventually make it up there where Tim's at."

"You seem pretty interested in Devin's promotion," I said.

"Of course, I'd have a personal interest in it, so Devin *won't* fuck up." He winked as though we shared a secret. "Big brother is watching."

"Yeah?"

"Devin does pretty well on his own," Erick added. "He knows the job. He just lets people…carry him away a little, I think."

"He sure knows his drugs, doesn't he?"

Another loud sigh. "Inside and out. I don't know why he persists with them, though. He can reach his goals better without them. Drugs only take you so far in, and then they stop you."

"Does Devin *have* a goal?"

"Well, last night it was mescaline." He laughed, then added seriously, "If you're considering experimenting with it, I'll be close by."

I felt my face flush. Erick knew I was considering it, but he didn't lecture me or do anything else to cause this guilt I felt. I did that all by myself.

"Thanks," I said.

"Ready to go?"

"Yup."

He cleared the table, dropped off the orange plastic trays and walked with me to the parking lot. "Leave your car here. I'll drop you off in the morning to get it. We'll be coming by to see Michelle anyway."

"But—" I started to protest, knowing the ratio of car theft, but he ushered me, unconcerned, into his van. "Who would steal a Rambler, anyway?" he kidded me. "Tonight you ride with me, love."

Mandy was actually having fun and wanted to spend the night with Kathy's teenagers, so we agreed, explaining that we'd be going straight to the hospital in the morning anyway and could pick her up then. Mandy reminded me about the astrology rings I'd promised them both, and Erick told her it was definitely on the agenda tomorrow.

I was looking forward to a long private evening with Erick, of whom I'd grown especially fond, but as it turned out, Erick had other plans. When we arrived home and were situated in the living room, I recognized the now familiar alien voice, and along with it, that purple-ultraviolet haze that waxed and waned as he spoke. I wasn't really afraid of him as I had been, but I also wasn't at ease enough with him to be able to relax as I now could with the other three.

"I picked up the items we needed to fix the ring today."

I eyed him cautiously. "You did?" Sure enough, that purple band was streaming from his head and shoulders the way I'd seen it the few times he'd been present.

"Yes, but I don't think I have the right epoxy resin, so I'm not going to get involved with it tonight."

The word *ring* set off a small reminder in my head. Michelle had mentioned something about the little ring Mickey had traded with her. When I'd picked her up to take her to the hospital she'd complained that it was too tight and said she didn't want it anymore. I had shown her how to adjust the band, which was just a wraparound, to make it larger, but she said she had tried that and it just...got tight again. I had pocketed the ring in the nurse's office at school, carried her to the car and forgotten about it till now. I briefed him on the story and fished the ring from my jacket pocket.

He raised his eyebrows. "The Tetragrammaton? That's strange. Have you tried it yourself?"

I admitted I hadn't. My mind had only been on Michelle, but I had seen the marks on her finger and decided against giving it back to her. She didn't want it anymore, anyway.

"Let me see it." He slipped it on his smallest finger where it stopped at the knuckle. "Let's see what happens when I wear it."

We went to bed early, both of us physically exhausted. For once talking didn't matter, at least not as much as the lovemaking did at the time, and I got a good display of yet another of the differences in Devin's many sides. They each had their own individual way of making love, and *he* was more intense than the other three put together, as though he didn't get much opportunity these days for such luxurious activities.

When morning came, so did Trevor.

The knocking woke us out of a sound sleep, and Devin went to the door. I heard Trevor's voice and Devin's welcoming greeting and hastily threw some clothes on. Trevor had the kids with him and seemed like he'd been up for hours.

"Hey, man, slow down," Devin protested, rubbing the sleep out of his eyes. "I just got up. Shit, I haven't even shaved yet. Ker, can you throw us some coffee on?"

It was nine o'clock before plans were finally settled. George pulled up out front, ready for the flea market adventure, anxious to get a copy of the ring. I felt like I needed to spend time with Michelle today, so Devin dropped me off at the hospital and then chauffeured Trevor, George and the kids to the jewelers, which was on site at the indoor flea market. I gave Devin the extra key to the house, and he promised to check on the rings for Mandy and Michelle too.

Michelle was in exceptionally good spirits, but the novelty of the hospital was growing old. Her temperature was even normal when I arrived, but the nurses informed me that until she held it for twenty-four hours she had to stay.

Devin and George arrived at the hospital around one to show Michelle and me what they'd bought. George had found a owl's eye ring and settled for that since the original jackal eye wasn't available anymore. George seemed pretty happy with his purchase. Devin gave me a rundown on how the afternoon had gone. He'd picked up Mandy at the sitter's and brought her along, and then had taken Trevor back to my house to pick up his car. He'd dropped Mandy back off at Kathy's until he knew what I wanted to do.

"Did you have any luck with the astrology rings?" I asked.

"No, but something better. Mandy picked out her own, and I selected one for Michelle."

Michelle's necklace was a single silver star on a sterling silver chain. She fell in love with it on sight.

"Mandy has a star and a moon on hers," Devin said. "Now, Michelle, you have to be very gentle with this. Keep it on and don't tug on the chain."

"I won't," she promised as she leaned forward. Devin clasped it behind her neck, and it fell to glitter against the whiteness of her hospital gown.

When visiting hours were over, Michelle wanted to go home with us. We promised her that if all went well, we would pick her up the following afternoon. Devin dropped me off at home, and George left for his from there. Then Devin left for his apartment, promising to join me at the hospital when it was time to pick Michelle up.

When we arrived the following morning, Michelle was allowed to go home. The ordeal was finally over, and after a quick thrown-together dinner and both girls snug in their beds, Devin and I collapsed together on the couch.

"Oh, this daddy business," he said with a groan.

I laughed at him. "You'll get used to it. Trevor did."

"Oh, by the way, Michelle's ring does do just exactly what she said it did." He slid the ring on my smallest finger. "Give it about a half hour. See how it's comfortable now?"

I nodded.

"Okay. It will get tighter as time goes by. Don't ask me why or how."

"Jesus, that could have stopped the flow of blood in her finger, right?"

"It probably did. Don't give it back to her under any circumstances. I'll replace it with something else, but like I said before, it's not really a child's ring."

"Well, can I keep it myself? I kind of like it."

Devin shook his head and smiled. "We do seem to have problems with rings around here. One won't let me sleep, and the other won't let Michelle. If you insist on keeping this one you'd better let me charge it first." He thought a moment, mentally calculating. "It has to be during a full moon, and there won't be one until I'm on the road."

"On the road?"

He looked at me with a surprised and amused expression. "Up north, remember? Or have you changed your mind?"

"Oh my God! But the full moon's only in about ten days!"

"Right. Time is flying. I told you we're getting close. Just don't forget to give me the ring when I leave."

I hugged him, elated. "I just can't wait!"

He returned my hug and I could hear the smile in his voice. "What? For me to leave?"

"No! For you to be living here."

"Well, it won't be long. Less than two weeks. This is the seventeenth. We've pretty much got everything packed. Your sister will be here Tuesday. You know, there are a lot of drastic changes taking place in the next couple weeks with a lot of people. And there has been already, for that matter. Everyone has changed residence, or is changing residence, except you. It's like a stage is being set, and the characters have all moved into place or are in the process."

I thought about it. "You're right. It *is* uncanny. Your dad moved from Salem to your apartment, and then into a house. Your wife's leaving the apartment and the state. Pammy's moving in here. Daniel just moved here. And you're moving from your apartment to here. The only one who isn't moving is me. Even Trevor just moved."

"That's what I mean. A stage is being set, and it all seems to be revolving around you."

"It's so hard to believe. Two more weeks and you'll really be living here."

He looked around the living room, surveying the space. "*We* may have to move anyway. I don't see how my stuff is going to fit."

"Well, you sold the furniture, right?"

"Yes. There are only a few pieces I kept. But the books, the paintings…you know, all the personal shit."

"Oh, I think we'll get it all in here okay."

"That's what you say *now*. Wait'll you see it. My dad set a whole room aside after *he* saw it. I've been slowly moving it all to that room, but as it grows, I wonder more every day how in the hell I ever accumulated so much material bullshit."

"You've been moving? How long have you been doing *that?*" Devin hadn't mentioned he'd been doing any moving. But then, Devin was only now coming around as often as Erick and the other two.

"What did you think I was doing down there all those nights I wasn't here, chick? Anyhow, this is a small place, getting back to the subject."

"Well, what exactly do you have?"

"Paintings, records, tapes. Books. My stereo equipment alone will take up that whole entire wall."

I looked at the paneled wall he indicated, the one to the right of the front door as you entered the house. It was bare now except for my own stereo sitting on the floor, a small speaker in each corner. "That pole lamp can go," I said, "and you can throw out my stereo if it's in the way. It's just a cheap component set anyway. I just use it for…well…thinking. You know."

"Yeah, I'm hep. But you can use mine now. It's got better sound and I'll show you how to operate it. It's all buttons, really. What about that armchair?"

"Pitch it. That's what my neighbor was doing when I grabbed it. Really, you're the only one who ever sat in it anyway."

Devin shook his head. "No, this is bullshit. I'm not going to move my stuff in here at the expense of yours. What won't fit, I'll just leave at my dad's."

"Well, like what?"

"I have a leather lounge chair…gold. It's about the only piece of furniture I kept. But I'll just leave it—"

I could have hit him. "You're going to leave a good expensive leather chair so we can keep this old thing?"

He smiled. "Okay. Whatever. Oh, I have an altar too, but that doesn't have to come. I just use it to store supplies. Candles, incense, all the Wicca shit, which I don't need anymore. Oh, and your walls. I'll be able to cover them with paintings. You won't believe the paintings."

"That's right! You had your own room for your stuff. I forgot. Are these paintings that *you* painted?"

"Yeah, me and there's one that Christian did. It's a self-portrait. Oh, is he ever proud of that one." Devin shook his head. "I don't really think we should hang it in the living room, but he'd be insulted if—"

"Insulted?"

"Well, the way it looks. *People* get insulted, actually. I don't know why. It's *his* self-portrait, not theirs, but they still get insulted. Anyhow, we'll worry about that later. As soon as I get settled in here, I'd like to get back to working with jewelry. Silver. If I made you a silver crown…a hairband, would you wear it?"

"Of course."

"That's future. Someday I'll have a shop, but I'll probably never make any profits. I have a hard time letting go of anything I make. And there's something else I want to make you. I have some dirt at home, from Gallows Hill in Salem. Real earth from the very ground that so many of our people's blood was spilt over. I'm going to make you a locket and place the earth inside it." He glanced at me. "But I'm only going to be able to use half the dirt I have."

"Sounds like you have plans for the other half."

He lay back against the couch, hands clasped behind his head, and smiled a distant smile. "Yes. My son."

"You have a son?"

"Well, *our* son. You know. Yours and mine. Remember?"

My chest tightened at the word. It had been entirely dropped these past few days. "What if it's a girl?" I said weakly.

"Oh, it won't be. No way."

"But Devin. What if it is?"

He sighed. "You still don't understand."

"Be that as it may, whichever one of you does it, it could still be a girl."

"Babe, nothing about this child is going to be an accident. Not even his sex."

Something about his tone of voice closed the subject for the night. The cycles of change, that had been stepped up to begin with, were moving too fast now to keep up with.

12 Pammy's return on Tuesday only added more confusion to the changes we were already trying to adjust to. She called me at the office, back in town at last, to warn me that she and George might come up tonight. George wanted to have a talk with her first, and I wasn't sure if it was personal between them or if George couldn't wait to break the news about Devin to her. He'd spent enough time with Devin, Christian and Trevor over the weekend to see what was going on. Devin had assured me that George had adjusted to the phenomenon easily, possibly because it didn't seem to faze Trevor. By now, George had already had ample time to mention it, so I decided to feel her out when she asked about Devin.

"He's fine. He's supposed to be stopping in tonight, too. Has George made any comments about Devin? He was with him this weekend."

"What about him? He *likes* him if that's what you mean. He showed me that ring he bought. Ugh. But at least it isn't as hideous as yours. Hey, I heard it broke."

"Yeah, and the eye is not real, so everyone can relax. It's safe."

"Wow, that Myrna's pretty good, huh? Anyway, I'll see ya tonight. It might be late. I don't know how long this talk is gonna take."

"That's okay. Devin's always late too."

"Well, it's nice to know he does *something* wrong. Perfect people make me nervous."

"I'd better get off before Lola sticks her head in here."

The day dragged, but finally it was quitting time. Once again, hasty plans were made outside the time-clock exit.

"I'm stopping at Daniel's first, and then I'll be up," Devin told me. "Your sister's back, isn't she?"

He'd pulled that one right out of my head. I was just thinking of tonight when they would both be in the same room together, where secrets might no longer be secrets. Lately Christian just didn't seem to care who was around or where Devin was when he made his appearances.

"She is, but she's only coming up to visit tonight. She won't move in for a few days. I think she's just wrapping things up with George so they can stay friends, but no longer live together."

"I hope that goes well. I like George, but he does seem to be attached to her. I don't think he's going to let go so easy."

There were other things that weren't going to be so easy. While George was a little familiar with two of the Devins, Pam knew of only one. And she was the one who would be living with us.

Pam and George arrived first and, as usual, Devin was late. I had tossed some barbecued chicken in the oven for the kids' dinner. They were long since in bed, and the remaining chicken pieces had turned black in the oven.

"Save some of whatever that is that smells good for me and Daniel." Devin's voice came in loud through the open windows from the still night air outside. "Julie copped out on dinner tonight."

Pammy helped to dish out the vegetables and potatoes, but she was stumped as to what to do about the blackened chicken.

"Don't worry about it," I told her. "It was done perfect, and if Devin had been on time it wouldn't be black. I've already warned them."

Daniel smiled his thanks as I handed him a plate, apologizing again for the chicken's appearance, but he assured me that as hungry as he was, he didn't care if it was green.

After dinner was over I made some coffee, and we all got to know Daniel a little better. George fell right in with him too and seemed quite comfortable with his new friends. After the second round of coffee, Devin announced that he had to get Daniel home and take off himself. Daniel just raved about the chicken and Devin agreed. Black on the outside but very tender and juicy under the burnt skin.

"Kerry," Daniel said, "thanks for dinner. It really was great. You *have* to come to our house now. Maybe on Julie's day off. We'll return the favor and have a big dinner. I owe you one."

"Okay, thanks, Daniel. It was great to finally get to know the guy Devin talks so much about."

"Ain't that strange," Daniel said with a smile. "When he's with us, he talks about *you.*"

I really liked Daniel, I decided, as they drove away, waving and flashing the headlights. He was gentle and soft-spoken, and he looked you right in the eyes when he spoke to you. Even after Devin had broken the news to him about himself, Daniel had accepted it even though he didn't understand it completely. He must have felt that the friendship with Devin was worth retaining. Anyone else might have labeled us both nuts, and split. Daniel's response was to invite us both to dinner.

Things seemed to be getting better and better. Every day I was even happier than I was the day before, and Thanksgiving was getting closer and closer.

Pam and George also had to leave, so I began to clean up the dinner mess and wash the dishes. I still had to make room for Pammy. Things seemed okay between them so I assumed their talk had gone well.

The following morning Lola called Kelly and me into her office. She looked a little upset and I wondered what we'd done now. Lola got right to the point. She had been called into Maurice's office and reprimanded for the loud joking and singing coming from our department.

"Kerry, Maurice said if he hears your mouth one more time he's going to fire you himself. And Kelly, you're no better, so don't look at Kerry like that. It's probably only because of Devin that he singled her out. I told him I didn't need anyone telling me how to handle my employees, but I'd appreciate it if you both could work on being a little quieter."

Kelly and I worked in uncomfortable silence for the rest of the day, feeling bad that Lola had had to take it on the chin for our fooling around. I was thankful that Devin didn't come in. It might have fanned the flames a little more.

I was still posting at four o'clock, and even with the clamor of my lone machine going, loud voices drifted in through the air conditioner vent into our office from the truck yard directly outside. The voices sounded familiar…two drivers yelling at each other…then suddenly the angry voices seemed to turn more into what sounded like a serious argument. The language was unbelievable. I stopped posting, but it was loud enough to hear even with my machine going.

"I ain' pickin' that fuckin' thing up. *You* pick it up."

"Yeah? You can shove that motherfucker right up your ass, you cocksucker!"

"Hey, fuck you, sonofabitch!"

Lola appeared in the doorway. "What the hell's going *on* out there? Maurice was complaining about *us?*"

"Shh…it sounds like Manny and one of the black workers…listen!" Hannah whispered, her face red from the language.

The argument was muffled now as if they were no longer at the yelling stage and had resorted to fists and cement wrestling. Two calmer voices broke it up and then there was abrupt silence.

Lola blinked in amusement at the cutoff of all sound. Then we all burst into laughter.

"That was a sudden ending," Kelly said, giggling. "Who did you say it was?"

"One was Manny," Hannah stated with surety. "He's always in an argumentative mood."

"Well, I'm going to find out," Lola said, turning to leave. "It sounded like one killed the other. Jeez! Maurice was bitching about *you two?*"

I zeroed out my machine and wrapped up the charges I'd been working on. At least *that* grind was over with.

"Did you balance?" Kelly asked me as I tossed the tickets onto the desk with everyone else's.

"Of course. Don't I always?"

"Like hell. You have to put half of Devin's in suspense anyway since no one can read them."

"You're full of shit! His writing's been fine," I whispered, reminding her to lower her voice.

It was fun, the few brief minutes of old-time kidding. It seemed like it had been days instead of hours. I dared not let it get out of hand though. I picked up the typing I'd accumulated. "I'll be out here in Lola's office at the typewriter. Got any statements you need typed? I'm so tired of posting, typing sounds like a blast right now."

"You'll *do* it?" Kelly quickly dumped a stack onto my own pile, happy to get rid of it. Unlike me, Kelly found typing to be one of the more boring aspects of this exciting job we shared.

"I know why *you* like to do it," Kelly said smugly. "You can see the lobby from that seat. You might even get a glimpse of Devin."

"I don't believe that fight out there. At least *our* language…"

"Oh, I've heard you say worse than that. Lola is always shushing you."

"Not in *that* volume, though."

Lola cruised in and grabbed her cigarettes. She looked amused as she lit up, then unable to contain herself, laughed out loud. "*That* was *your* boyfriend fighting with Manny outside."

"Devin?" Kelly's mouth dropped open in obvious disbelief. "No way! Devin doesn't use that language…does he?" She looked to me for verification, but I was a little stunned myself.

"Does he?" Lola mimicked, although I could see she didn't quite believe it either. Both sets of eyes were on me now.

"That's not even Devin's temperament, much less language," I said with a baffled shrug. "Are you sure it was him? What was the fight over anyway?" A creeping suspicion nagged at me. Christian wouldn't jeopardize Devin's job like that…would he? Worse, had Devin allowed it? Or was that control factor all bullshit too?

"That wasn't Devin's voice," Kelly declared. "Are you positive it was him, Lola?"

"Look," Lola said. "I couldn't believe it either, but Tim says it was him. I don't know what it was all about, but I'm going to ask him."

She took off through the lobby at a clipped pace, and I went back to my typing. After a few minutes, I suddenly felt that achy chest pain and the urge to look up.

Out in the lobby, Devin leaned casually against the hallway wall, calmly sipping water from a company disposable cone water cup. He was rapping easily with a driver who was making coffee at the bar beside the hot water cooler at the entrance to the hall. Devin appeared to be cool and unruffled. There was no sign of excitement, flushed cheeks, or anger. Not even a hair out of place after the alleged fistfight, and that made me doubt his involvement even more. Any red-blooded Scorpio…or black-blooded to stretch a point, would be overheated and fuming, even sweating and dirty after such a fight as we'd heard. I was confused.

Furthermore, it was not Christian at the helm now either. I could *see* that, and it most definitely wasn't Devin. That left two others, one I was sure would not stoop to such human bullshit behavior, nor hang around afterwards to get Devin off the hook.

I'd just answered my own question.

Thank God for you, Erick I thought as Tim approached. If Lola was correct, only Erick could pull Devin out of this one. Supervisors just don't fight with employees, especially physically.

I held my breath and went through the motions of typing, my eye on the two of them in the lobby hallway. A few quiet words were exchanged between them, and then Tim nodded and walked back down the hall towards the route office. Erick remained where he was, obviously knowing better than to step one foot in the direction of our office.

Joey Burns emerged from the conference room and, seeing Devin, assumed a boxer's stance, punching into empty air. I saw Devin flash in at once with a wide, carefree grin.

"Don't say it, Jack!"

"No sir, Mister Cassius Clay…I wouldn't *think* of it!"

Lola appeared out of nowhere and said something to Devin that was beyond my earshot. I couldn't make out Devin's answer either because Lola's sudden laughter drowned it out. I was even beginning to think Lola's accusation that it had *been* Devin was all wrong, that Devin hadn't been anywhere near Manny when it happened. When I looked up again, Devin was gone.

"Well," Lola said, when she sat back down at her desk. "It was your boyfriend, all right."

"He was just out in the hall."

"I know that. I just asked him. He admitted it was."

"Well, good grief," Kelly exclaimed. "Don't keep us in suspense. What happened?"

"Really," Hannah put in. "I've never seen Devin lose his temper. Never."

"Well, Devin said it wasn't much."

"Wasn't *much*!" The three of us in unison.

"Well, Tim gave Devin something to give to Manny. Manny wouldn't take it, so Devin threw it on the ground. That's how it started. I'm just glad someone broke it up."

"What else?" I asked.

"That's all I know. Guess you'll have to wait till five to get the sordid details from Devin."

Devin wasn't around at five to give any. Erick must have felt the need to hold the fort because that's who was waiting for me at the exit.

"Yeah, I know." He laughed easily when he saw the expression on my face. "You want to know what happened."

"Well, I'm a *little* curious, sure, but I'm more curious about whose fault it was. And I'm not talking about Manny."

We started walking. After we'd crossed the street, he let out his infamous sigh. "He really screwed up today. It's a damn good thing I had an eye on things."

"Who, Devin?"

"No. Christian. He can be a feisty little cock. One of these days, he's really going to blow it for Devin. Especially now that he's getting more comfortable."

"He's going to cost Devin his *job*," I said, feeling a wave of panic. "We heard most of it through the air conditioner. Everyone's blaming Devin."

"Not anymore they aren't," Erick said. "Devin wouldn't just sit back and let Tim jump all over him without a reasonable, justifiable explanation. He would at least argue his case."

"Argument is no answer with Tim, Erick. Nobody wins with Tim."

"I do." He kissed me on the cheek as we reached my car. "A little logic and reason. That's all. Tim listened."

"So. You bailed Devin out."

"I had to. Christian surely wasn't going to march in there and take the blame. Hell, we'll be lucky if we see *him* until after this blows over."

"Wow. Devin must have freaked out."

"Well, I never should have let it go as far as it did." There was a wistful sound in his voice, as though he was finally having to face up to a few facts about his colleagues.

"Don't blame Christian, Erick. Everyone on this planet gets mad once in a while."

He leaned against the door of my car and crossed his arms. "No. I should have been more alert. I should have taken control. I can't let these guys keep this shit up…one causing trouble and one getting me out of it. It's getting out of hand, and you know who has to stand up and face the music in the end."

I gave him a suspicious sideways glance. "What more could you have done? If it wasn't for…"

"No, you don't understand what I'm saying." He gestured humbly, almost sadly. In fact, more Devin-like humble. Hope stirred in my heart.

"You know," he went on. "I don't *need* big brother babysitting me all the time. I should have handled it myself. Just like now, for instance." He shook his curly head and scowled. "*Now* where is he? The great Erick. And *who's* left holding the bag?" He lit a cigarette.

I did a double take. The youthful mannerisms. The humble, worried expression. The cigarette.

"*Devin?*"

We both beamed at each other.

"Welcome back, man…" I was trying to sound casual and was too exhilarated to pull it off. "Oh, Devin, I'm so happy to see you." I threw my arms around him, elation mingling with sympathy for him. "What happened out there, Devin? *You* tell me. Your side of it. It *was* you that started out there with that package for Manny, wasn't it? It *had* to be."

He returned my strangling hug, then released me gently. "I'll tell you, Ker. I'm going to be hearing about today all day tomorrow."

"But what started it?"

He shrugged, took a drag off his cigarette and gazed out towards the plant. "I guess the truth, ego set aside, is that I get too used to letting someone else take over for me when I *do* fuck up. And actually, it wasn't *me* that screwed up."

A deep breath, another drag. I lit one too, just to keep him there.

"I was off work," he continued. "You know, punched out. I was only doing Tim a favor. I didn't have to but, well, it was just a short walk and I was going that way anyway. Tim had a report that Manny needed. Not that Manny couldn't have walked in and gotten it himself but, as I said, I was just trying to save them both a trip. I saw Manny by his truck and tried to hand it to him, but Manny was, well, you know *Manny*...in one of his moods. I don't know why, but he wouldn't take it. Whatever his problem was today, he decided to take it out on me. I didn't feel like walking all the way back in and telling Tim he wouldn't take it because I was on my way *out*, you know? But I still didn't get mad. I just said, 'Okay Manny, there it is,' and I pitched it on the ground. I didn't throw it...just...here...you know?"

I nodded. "So..."

"Well, that's when Manny just went apeshit and well, you probably heard it."

"Yeah. Loud and clear. Our whole office heard it, including Lola, who'd gotten a little peeved because she had to take some flak for me and Kelly fooling around while the drivers are getting away with that language and volume. But Devin, that wasn't you. Everyone in my office thought it was one of the black guys from the chemical division."

"I know." He sighed. "See, Christian won't take no shit from...whitey, you know? He thinks I'm the ass for letting Manny jump in my shit, and before you know it..."

"Okay," I interrupted. "I see what happened. But after it ended, I was at the typewriter in Lola's office and I saw Erick for a brief second. Then Joey showed up, teasing you and Erick split."

"I know. But I only jumped in for a second to give Joey the knock-it-off bit, and he did. People love a good fight. Personally, I don't, and Christian *knows* that. I know he meant well, but everyone in the route room knows me and...Devin *fighting?* It was embarrassing. How in the hell was I going to explain that?"

"That's my next question. How *did* you?"

"I never had the chance to. Erick stepped in, and while I'm grateful for the assistance, I resent the fact that Erick never gave me the chance to talk to Tim myself. Erick didn't give Tim any other explanation than I would have, but for some reason, Erick has a way with words. He's calmer. But it's *my* job, not his. Not Christian's. I realize both of them were looking out for me in their own ways. I see that, and I don't down them for it. I just, well, feel like an incompetent ass now, that's all. I *wasn't* in the wrong, and I should have just stood my ground and handled it myself, but I guess I just get so used to letting them take over when things get sticky. And once Erick stepped in, he didn't give me any further chance to correct it or explain myself." He sighed a frustrated sigh.

Poor Devin. He was so sincere, so willing to excuse Erick's lack of confidence in him. He must have realized that he was indeed the younger brother of the trio, so there he stood, defending his cosmic big brothers, yet insisting at the same time that they should have more faith and trust in him. He also added a few more Devin-like comments about Manny. Manny had apologized to him so, therefore, Manny was now *okay* in his book. Manny had just been *tired* or maybe *on edge*, and he was certain that Manny wasn't mad at him. At least he *hoped* not. He didn't want *any* enemies among his own men. That enemy shit was Perry Jason's trip, not his.

Devin looked so humiliated and down that I hastily changed the subject to something I'd been wondering about all day.

"I never saw Pat today. Where was he during all this?"

Devin looked relieved to drop the unpleasant subject. "Oh, didn't you know? Pat called in sick today. Can you believe it? Pat has *never* taken a sick day in all the years he's worked here."

"Boy, it must be serious," I said. "I guess he won't be here tomorrow either."

"Probably not. I think it's just the flu, but we really ought to do something to let him know how much he's missed. Maybe we can get him a card or something." He paused and glanced at his watch. "Hey, I'd better get back. Pat's not here to cover for me, so that means I'm late man tonight."

"You opened up and now you have to close too?"

"Yeah, well, someone has to. Look, I'll call you. Around six-thirty or so."

"Okay, hop in. I'll drive you to the gate."

Pammy was already home when I got there, surrounded by a skyline of boxes.

"Hey, wild thing!"

"Oh, hi Kerry. I'm just going through these boxes. I'm throwing out a lot of stuff I don't need anymore. No sense in crowding your house up."

"Oh, we've got plenty of storage room. Just put everything in the water heater closet. That room is huge."

"I did," Pammy said. "This is what wouldn't fit."

"Well, that's not the only closet in the house. Just mix your shit up with mine. Put the towels in the hall closet, your bathroom stuff in the medicine cabinet and your albums in with mine. Will that do it?"

"I think so. If that's all right. I see you still have the desk in the kitchen. I thought Devin would have moved it by now."

"Why, was he bitching about it again?"

"No, not bitching, but when he went to put the chicken away last night he couldn't find the refrigerator. He forgot it was in the den."

"Well, don't worry. We'll probably get rid of the desk anyway. Devin has a lot of stuff too, so we'll eventually put the fridge in the kitchen like normal people do. That way the den will be a real bedroom for you. No doors, but maybe we can rig up a drape in the archway. I think that room was once a back patio and Chris turned it into a den."

"Don't bother. My hours are so crazy. I'll be sacking out on the couch more than anything while you two are at work. I won't see much of you'ns except on my days off. Anyway, I hope Devin has a cabinet for his albums. Man, I'll bet he has some neat ones if that eight-track he made you was a sample of them. I know Uriah Heep. Bonnie's even got some of their stuff."

"I think most of his music is on big reels. That's what it sounded like."

"It's getting close isn't it? Man, your office must be freaking out."

"Yeah, the whole plant, actually. I can hardly believe it myself. I think everyone thought this was a brief fling, but they're not acting like that anymore."

Pam looked thoughtful. "What's weird to me is how *fast* this all happened. You really just met him, and now you'ns are moving in together. Oh, Kerry, I'm so happy for you, but it's still so hard to believe. You finding *anyone* just like you is weird enough. I remember when you first called me about the money for that ring. That seems like a year ago, and it's only been about a month. And Devin's so far out, man, if I were to tell this story to anyone they'd never believe it. It seems to me like you guys have been together for years. Like you've always been together. He's so perfect, too. I can't imagine you with anyone else."

"Pammy, I really believe we *have* been together for years and years *somewhere* before. I don't mean like in reincarnation or anything, but I just know that I know him from somewhere. Maybe in my dreams. And then again, what are dreams, really? What is reality? I don't know what's really going on. All I can say is I've never been this happy before in my life. It's too good to be true. It's too perfect. I'm so afraid something this good can't last forever."

"I know what you mean. He doesn't seem to have a flaw in him. When is he moving in?"

"Well, his boss gave him extra days off to make the trip, so if all goes well, he should be moved in by the end of the Thanksgiving weekend."

I switched on the radio, now permanently tuned to the acid-rock station, and Steppenwolf burst on with *Born to Be Wild*. Pammy and I looked at each other and smiled. Their motor was running and they were heading out on the highway. They were gonna make it happen.

I shook my head in disbelief. "This is happening a lot, lately," I told her.

13 Pat wasn't in the following day, as we had expected, so other than our usual work routine Kelly and I picked up a huge three-by-five-foot, get-well card and spent much of the day securing signatures. While more than a few remarked that he only had the flu and not a terminal illness as the size of the card suggested, no one refused to sign, including Tim, Maurice, and Charlie. Most everyone added a personal message. Even Mama signed when she saw that all her peers had done so, although she rolled her eyes at our foolishness.

The card had to be hand-delivered and since Pat lived more in my direction, I volunteered to drop it off on my way home.

I was a little later than usual getting home because of the side trip. Had I been home at my usual hour a lot of unnecessary trouble could have been averted, and Pammy might have held on to her sanity for another day or two.

I drove up after dark and immediately saw that there wasn't a light on in the house. George and Pammy's vehicles were parked out front and I wondered what was going on. I found Pammy sitting in dismay, supper already started, and a lone candle flickering on the edge of the kitchen counter.

"What's this?"

"Kerry! Finally. Hey, did you get any cutoff notices on the electric bill?"

I pulled my jacket off and tossed it on the couch. "No, but I got a warning a few days ago. Devin gave me the money to send in since payday was a few days away. They'd better *not* have…goddamn it. They did, huh?"

I found a few more candles and set the kids up in their room with some books and flashlights until we could get this straightened out. Then Pammy explained what had happened.

The electric man had come, asked for payment or proof of payment, and of course Pammy had no idea where I kept my bills. She'd tried to call me at work but I was already gone, so the man had done his job and cut off the power.

"Jeez. Devin's going to blow his stack," I groaned, "especially since it was his money."

Pammy looked at the half-cooked mess on the stove and laughed. "I know it's not funny, but that candle's just not cutting it for light here. Poor Devin's going to think we're lousy cooks."

I laughed too, remembering yesterday's chicken. "I guess I'd better call and see if they ever received the payment."

Of course, the records office was closed until morning, and the night man was no help. He told me I had to go to a pay station and pay it again if I wanted the power on tonight. That wasn't an option since I didn't have the money. All we could do now was wait for Devin.

In the meantime, we talked. George brought up Christian's name several times during the conversation, and I couldn't figure out if he sincerely forgot Pammy's ignorance of the situation and was just trying to confuse her, or if he was just bursting with pride at being in on a secret.

After looking from George to me in confusion several times, Pammy finally asked what the hell we were talking about. I figured there was no time like the present to break the news to her. With the candles casting long shadows up to the ceiling, it was surely the right atmosphere for such a strange story.

I did my best to explain the situation to her, and George interrupted more than once to color my own explanation with his recent experiences with Devin and Christian. He proudly told her how he'd been in the dark for a while too, until he had figured it out for himself.

Pam looked unsurely at both of us, and then the van drove up, nipping the conversation in the bud.

Devin wasn't stupid. Three vehicles parked outside of a blacked-out home told its own story. He walked in the front door and surveyed the obvious.

"When did *this* happen?"

"This afternoon." I gave him a brief rundown and, just as I expected, an explosion occurred.

The transformation was so swift that I don't think Devin could have stopped the sudden switch, even if he'd seen it coming.

"Gimmee that *motherfuckin'* phone, those dirty bastards! Where's th' number?"

I froze. Here we had just been breaking the news about Christian to Pammy who had never seen him, much less seen him in action. I glanced at George, whose eyes were on Pam, and there was no surprise in his smug expression. I sat down to watch. There was no reasoning with this character once he got started. Erick would have been so much more tactful.

"Yeah, thiz iz Mistah King. Put yer supervisor on, th' one that okayed mah power cutoff...what you *mean* yer office is closed...hey look, man, don' give me none of yer jive-assed excuses. Jist git a man out here rat now...hey Jack, if your funk office is closed, tha's *yer* problem. Mah bill's *paid* an' Ah got two little keeds here. If they so much as stub their *toe*, yer fuckin' closed office is gonna be in fer a law—"

He paused, as if he'd suddenly been put on hold, and he gestured for me to light him a cigarette.

"Yeah, who's *this* ?"Another pause, then, "Thiz iz *Mister* King, no Jack, you lissin t' me! If mah lights ain't on in twenty minutes, Ah'll turn the sonofabitches on mahself, an' then Ah don't want no knockin' at mah door if you *do* git yer lazy asses out here after that. Ah'll blow the balls offa th' first cocksucker that steps foot on mah property, ya hear *that*? Yeah, you try me, that iz if ya lately got th' men t' spare. You ain't fuckin' with mah keeds' safety, not when Ah know damn well that sixty bucks waz mailed to you over three days ago. An' don' give me that 'no record of jive' neither, honk, Ah'm warnin' you. You won't be the first joint that blew up in th' middle of th' naht fer no 'pparent cause..."

Christian slammed the phone down, nostrils flared, eyes squinted. Pam looked stunned, and I buried my face in my hands, sure it would be the cops or the FBI rather than the power company if *anyone* showed up. He then turned to George in a calm, Caucasian, perfect English voice with no trace of anger at all.

"Come on, George. Let's go see what it looks like out there. You ever turn power on before?"

"Sure, Devin," George said, glancing triumphantly at Pammy who seemed to be stunned into stone. "I *was* going to do it before you got here, but—" His voice trailed off as they exited the back door.

Pam finally looked at me. "What was...wow...was that...?"

It was pretty obvious that Pammy hadn't recovered from her sudden introduction to Christian or to the swift change back to Devin once Christian had taken care of business. She shook her head and tried again. "Was *that* what you and George were just trying to tell me?"

"That," I said with a sigh, "was Christian."

Pammy leaned slowly back against the couch. "Wow."

The house suddenly blazed with light.

It was still Devin who returned with George after restoring the power, and it was Devin who left with him for the Burger King. Pammy and I stayed behind with the kids and began to clean up the supper she had started. I took that opportunity to explain as much as I could in the short time I had to do it. Explaining Devin was not an easy job.

"This is all so unbelievable," Pammy said. "As unreal as that was, even I could see that it wasn't Devin who made that call."

"No, but it *was* Devin who turned the power on with George, and Devin who just walked out that door. I didn't want you to find out this way, but at least George and I had a chance to brief you a little before he arrived, so it wasn't a *total* shock. If you watch close tonight, you may even get a glimpse of Erick."

"Yeah? I'd *love* to see this Erick dude. He sounds weirder than the other two."

The front door opened, interrupting us, and George entered carrying the drinks, Devin right behind him with the white burger bags.

"Did anyone come by?" Devin asked, setting the bags on the coffee table.

"Nobody did. I don't know what we could have said if they had come and saw all the lights were back on." I started setting the small table for the girls.

"What's there to say? The power's *on*, isn't it? Never went off as far as I know. How are they going to prove it was actually off? Maybe they sent out some green dude that didn't know what he was doing."

Pam dug around in her cigarette pack. "Oh, there it is. Hey, Kerr, Bonnie gave me something to give to you. You could probably use it now. I've been waiting for this power thing to get over with. We still don't know if they might show up."

"*Fuck* them." Christian zoomed in, snapping open his Zippo. "'Jis' let one of them suckers step foot on this propertee."

Pammy did a double take, then gave me a look that I read as *I see what you mean.*

By the end of the evening Pammy had a good idea of who Christian was, though the only knowledge she had of Erick was what I had told her. As usual, Erick stayed away from human bullshit. She still knew nothing of the fourth's existence. For that matter, neither did George. *He* didn't do anything by accident, including uncontrolled appearances in front of people. And when he wasn't around, Erick and Christian seemed to be allowed free rein, darting in and out of Devin Drew's existence like a network of radio stations all operating on the same band. In more cases than one, *he* had proven, with his very existence, that the whole was indeed more than the sum of its parts.

I couldn't imagine *him* lowering himself to stoop to violence of any kind, even verbal, much as Erick wouldn't. Whether Devin met his van payment or whether Christian succeeded in winning over another black Jesus freak at the plant didn't seem to matter to him. And unlike Erick, he was more than content to light a joint or a cigarette and relax in the beanbag with me. When I'd mentioned Erick's aversion to cigarettes, he said that it was all in the belief, and that belief was what made some warnings true for some and untrue for others.

Pammy left for work at nine that evening, George peeling out behind her. When Devin closed the door, *He* turned to me with that all-knowing smile, as though he'd been there all along. He reached for me and suddenly there *was* nobody but him. I didn't see the transformation, but when he turned from the front door, I saw his eyes and that purple fluctuating band streaming from him.

"Hello, lady." He indicated I should join him in the beanbag. We lay facing each other, and he looked intently at me. I felt that royal gaze clear down to my stomach. It was a feeling I hadn't experienced so intensely since that day in the Walgreen's parking lot. The day the child had been mentioned.

I didn't look away this time. His eyes glistened in the candlelight. As I returned his gaze, I felt a sudden rushing, pulsing, magnetic pull that seemed to originate from his glowing amber eyes. The hypnotic effect was as powerful as it might have been if I'd been staring into a strobe light.

"That's it," he whispered, piercing the silence. "Go inside my head. You can do it, lady. You know you can."

"How?"

"Go *inside.*"

It didn't take any effort. I couldn't pull my eyes away now if I tried. We were locked together. I felt his hand on my shoulder as the room started to fade into dark, swirly, colorless motion before it disappeared completely. I felt my consciousness streaming into his, and then I started to black out. At the last minute, I panicked and pulled…no, wrenched away from his probing piercing eyes.

He released me at that same moment and looked away himself.

"Whew, lady. If you only realized."

"Realized what?" I took a couple deep breaths to clear my head.

"Realized," he said with a sigh. "Another Webster's special. What was going on in your head just then? Do you realize what you almost did?"

I looked at him blankly. "I felt like I was going under."

"Have you ever been hypnotized?"

"No."

"And you never got into meditation."

"No, not unless listening to music and daydreaming falls into that category."

"Meditation is in a category of its own. It's personal for everybody."

"What would you call what I'm doing when I'm listening to music? I spend hours with that stereo, and I couldn't tell you where the time goes. I practically go into a trance, and that's when I start seeing things. That's where I first got the flash about you and a child."

"Lady, that music is you…me…*us*. You've been doing what comes natural to any nonhuman."

"Nonhuman?"

"Let's leave it at that for now, but it is time you learn a few *conscious* moves. Maybe it wouldn't hurt you to experience Transcendental Meditation."

"Actually, Pammy's already into that, and she swears by it. She claims that anyone who signs up for it goes into the alpha state in the first class, but she couldn't really describe it to me so I lost interest."

"Ever hear the expression *if it can be described, it's not the way?*" He smiled. "Come on. Sit up." He tugged at my elbow.

I pulled myself into a sitting position and a feeling of dread washed over me. The dread of failure. What if whatever he had in mind didn't work? What if he discovered now that I really didn't have that natural ability that he claimed I did. He saw my fear and touched my cheek gently.

"Look. You're not afraid of *me* anymore, are you?"

I didn't trust my voice. Even a no would have come out like a quivering child, but I wasn't afraid of him so I shook my head.

"Good. Just trust me. Cross your legs. Indian-sitting style. Place the palms of your hands on your knees."

I did.

Curious now, I watched him work with my fingers, arranging them in a strange position. The thumb and first two fingers of each hand formed a circle or a kind of okay sign, the other two fingers balanced my hands on my knees. It wasn't uncomfortable. "What are you doing?"

He didn't answer, but continued with his instruction. "Close your eyes now. Trust me. All I'm going to do is place my hand a few inches from the top of your head. Try to reach my hand with your head, but don't move physically."

He anchored my shoulder down with one steady hand as I strained upward with all my muscles. "No, not with your physical body. It must stay put."

I opened my eyes in frustration, feeling failure along with that now familiar chest pain, but he closed them gently with his fingertips. A wave of coolness radiated from his hands. I didn't need my eyes to feel *that*.

"Don't give up so easily," he said, apparently sensing my frustration. "Just imagine yourself floating upwards…imagine what my hand would feel like on top of your head, and it will happen."

I tried again. And again, feeling more inadequate with each attempt. I could still feel that chilly wave of air emanating from his hand which still hovered over my head. It was like a soft icy breeze, cooling my scalp. I strained again but didn't make the contact he was striving for, and this time he didn't push the issue. When my head bumped his hand physically, failure again, he patted it reassuringly.

"There's no rush, lady. You could practice in other ways. You're just trying too hard, and you expect to fail, so you do." He glanced around the room until his gaze rested on the large desk in the kitchen. The books I owned were lined up on it against the wall, with bookends holding them in place. "There," he said. "Start with something like that desk. Close your eyes. Sit in the position I just showed you, or lay down if you're more comfortable, but just don't fall asleep."

"Why are you doing this?"

"Do you know what ethereal projection is?"

I shook my head.

"How about astral? Ever hear of that?"

"Oh, sure." My curiosity was up again. What did wandering around on some other plane of existence have to do with what he was trying to show me now? I *had* read about the astral plane, enough to know I wasn't ready for anything like that. At least on this solid planet of matter, I was sure of where my feet were planted.

"No, this isn't the same thing," he said quickly, once again displaying that uncanny ability of answering my unspoken questions and reading my private thoughts. "In fact, what you'll be mastering shortly hasn't a thing to do with the astral kingdom or the after-death realm, or whatever name you know it by. But you've got to start somewhere and I already know you have the ability. Lady, can't you get it through your head that the only difference between you and me is that you were *born* here. You have a birthright to this world. I don't.

It took a lot of persuasion on my part to get here. You have no idea. And it will take a lot more talking to get back."

I looked up in alarm. "Get back? What do you mean? You're not leaving, are you?"

He pulled me closer to him. "Hopefully, not without you, lady. I want you back at my side where you belong. Not separated from me by these two worlds. Really, I don't know how you've lasted this long."

"Devin, for God's sake, what *are* you talking about? You're not trying to tell me you're from another planet, are you?" I had the lurking suspicion that he wasn't referring to any distance in miles, but that would make his world out of the range of matter. Another dimension. Beyond the physical limits of this one. It just couldn't be possible.

"No, I wasn't referring to any planet in the physical universe, except maybe this one. It's right here, lady, though you don't perceive anything but this world at the moment. It's on a different vibration than what your body is tuned for. You won't read about it in any book, at least with any accuracy. You *will* find distortions and variations concerning it. Hell is only one of them, and when they speak of its leader..." he paused and shook his head. "It's too soon. Suffice it to say we are both from the same home world. You chose to come here twenty-five years ago. My decision was much more recent, and it required the willing services and participation of an inhabitant here. Devin Drew is more than just willing. He was honored to provide the stepping-stone. We both do owe him our appreciation and thanks. We at least owe him that much."

I tried to digest his words. "Devin, I know you believe what you're saying, but I really don't think we *are* from the same place."

"No? You think not, huh? Well, for one thing, lady, I have total recall of both the here and now, and also the before, at least in terms of your linear time. My memory has not been blotted out with twenty-five years of a time structure or programmed by the world you've grown to know. I haven't been fed *their* lies and ignorance from infancy, and even though you have, your senses try to tell you all the time that you're not one of them. Really, do you know anyone else that watches movies on the wall instead of television? You don't even *have* a television."

"Well, the kids do. But I've done that all my life, Devin. If I am the same...species as you...then why don't you do that, too?"

"Because my awareness of why I am here now is more important. You agreed to forget, but you kept your natural abilities. I agreed to certain limitations in lieu of retaining my memory. I too must follow the rules of this system while I'm here, and as for you, I think I can eliminate a few doubts of yours as to whether we are the same. You'll have to work with your abilities to remember and eventually be able to return home—at least for visits—from this dimension."

He walked over to the kitchen wall and flooded the living room with two hundred watts of bright white light. It had the effect of a flashbulb going off in my face and I turned away quickly at the sudden illumination. Then he walked over to the air conditioner and turned it off.

I shaded my eyes and turned to him, squinting. "Did you have to do that?"

He shrugged. "Light hurts your eyes, doesn't it? Ever notice how dark you keep this place? How dark you've kept every place you've ever lived?"

"I've always kept my homes dark and cool, now that you mention it. Even back when I was a kid. I've always kept the drapes drawn in my room until the sun went down."

"That thing you call the sun…what you see of it here is just the tip of the iceberg. There's a far greater reality to it. Same with the earth, and to everything else material that you know. You can only perceive portions of everything here. The parts you see, hear, feel, touch and smell are what your senses are only tuned to. I keep telling you, lady, that you aren't human. Visible light may be what you're focused in, but light really is alien to you. That's why you've always avoided it. At home everything glows from within."

By now, the room was becoming stuffy and warm.

"Could we put the air back on now?" Sweat was beading up on my forehead.

Devin opened the front door. "It's at least sixty degrees out there, but that kind of cold feels warm to you, doesn't it? Even your sister complains that the house is always air-conditioned…humidity removed, all the time. Day and night. That's a different kind of sixty degrees, isn't it? A refreshing dry ice kind of cold. Do you see what I'm getting at, lady? You're sensitive to light because there *is* no sun *as you know it* at home. There *is* no damp chilling cold. Just a refreshing coolness. Instinctively you know the difference. Your ego may not, but *you* do."

He walked around the house switching off lights, switching on the air as he talked and then returned to my side. "And you think you're human. Always preferred the dark and cold. Never wondered why."

"What about the kids? Aren't they normal…human?"

"I can't answer that. They're not your kids back home, I can tell you that. We all wear the same costume here. The only thing that stands in the way of your perception is your programming and your belief that everyone here is human, therefore *you* must be. Lady, your heritage isn't here in this country or any other country or continent or planet or galaxy or universe. How can I ever possibly make you understand who I am when you don't even know who *you* are?"

"But Devin, how can I just accept all this blindly? How? Sure, I can take your word for it in blind faith, but I just can't be a hypocrite and sit here discussing the human race as if I was better than them or different from them when I don't know it to be a fact. I assumed everyone on earth was from the same origin."

"I don't want your blind faith, lady. I'm trying to give you methods to work with while I'm on the road. Maybe when I'm not around you'll give it a fair shot. How can I even consider my son's birth until you are ready? Oh, lady." His voice softened. "You don't know how damned near ready you are. You're so close."

"Okay, Devin. Let's get back to the desk." Anything to avoid that baby subject.

"Once again, close your eyes. Don't look over at it."

I did as he instructed, still unsure and afraid of failure. "Go ahead."

"Now, reach your hand out in the air towards the desk. Keep your eyes closed. Try to forget I'm even in the room with you. Listen to my voice but, don't attach it to any physical body. Move your hand across what you would imagine to be the length of the desktop. Eyes closed. Just use your imagination."

I tried to forget his presence and ran my hand over an imaginary desktop. "I can't feel anything," I said.

"Shh...you're not supposed to. This is a mental exercise. Can you remember what the top of the desk looks like? Remember what it feels like?"

"Yes." My physical fingers moved as I strained my hand outward. A smooth finish with little scratches beneath my fingertips. Dark mahogany wood with even smoother areas than the finished wood. I trailed my fingers across the smoother wood. Devin's name. Sandpapered into the top of the desk. I smiled as my fingers traced the letters and remembered the night I had done that. A night I'd been alone hoping Devin would come.

"Hey! Where you at?"

I went from the top of the desk to the beanbag with a slightly painful click. There was a jolt of reconnection. Devin was smiling when my eyes flew open.

"Sorry if I startled you. Where'd you go?"

"Did I go somewhere?"

He shook his head with both disbelief and pride. I could read both in his expression. "You don't remember? Lady, you're not supposed to fall asleep."

"I wasn't asleep. Why do you think I was asleep?"

He sighed and looked at me wearily. "Why do you fight me so hard? Is that a Virgo trait or something?"

I smiled. "I wish you'd tell me what I'm supposed to be doing."

He returned my smile. "Well, at least you *are* doing it. If you didn't hear those desk instructions of mine, then you must be doing it."

"Doing what?"

"The whole time you had your eyes closed I was describing the objects on the desk. The titles of the books, the pen and notebook, and everything else you can walk over and look at now. The idea is to do it first without looking, then check to see how accurate you were. In time, and with enough practice, you could mentally walk into other rooms, or you can just imagine yourself there and describe them."

"Did you mention anything about the name sandpapered into the wood?"

"No, I didn't. I wanted to see if you'd feel it without my describing it."

I was surprised that he didn't have a comment about the name even *being* there, but then, it was Devin's name, and probably of no importance to *him*.

"Eventually you won't need your eyes at all. It will all be here." He tapped his temple with his index finger. "It's important that you stay awake and alert though, lady. This exercise is to train yourself to ethereally project...you can master it to where time and space are meaningless. Your body remains here, and you go to your destination in a different body...a less dense body. It's still yours, but it can move through walls and hard objects. It's the same body you use when you go to sleep and think you're dreaming, but your consciousness is very alert during dreams. Your body is physically alert back here, but you're not aware of it. All your attention is focused on where you've gone. It's the same body you will use after you die, but this doesn't have anything to do with going *home*. In fact, at home, forms are just a toy or convenience. You are totally aware of who you are with *no* form there. We use them, but we don't need them like you do here."

"Why are you telling me all this, Devin? If it hasn't anything to do with this going home, as you put it, why do I need to do this at all?"

He studied me for a full minute before he replied. "Lady, you have to realize who you are and who I am before we can bring our son into this physical world. You have to go home at least once before you'll really remember who *we* are. I think that will be important for his development. As for ethereal projection, it can be convenient if you want to check on a friend in another state or city but you don't want to physically travel there. Some humans are so obsessed with learning this that after thirteen years of trying, they accidently make it out of the body and think they've mastered the universe. They have no idea that *that* kind of projection is child's play. But once you've mastered this, then the next step won't seem so alien."

My mind had stopped registering everything beyond the mention of our son. I'd heard everything he said, but my attention really stopped at that word. I knew I was going to have to face the music eventually, so I might as well face it now.

"Is this child going to be so different from…human children, Devin?"

His eyes narrowed. "He can't be raised human like you're thinking. I told you that. There won't be any human conditioning or programs built into him when he arrives. And he's got to have the right mother. You, lady."

"Devin, you know I'm not ready now," I began hesitantly. "I'm not sure what you have in mind for this child, but I might not be the right mother for him either. You just told me that I've been programmed since birth to the human ways. I may not be capable of going along with whatever you have planned with this baby."

Something beyond recognition flickered in his eyes. "If you have misgivings or second thoughts about this, I'd like to know what they are."

"School, for one," I replied quickly. "It's the law. He'll have to go to school. You can't get out of that so easily in this country."

"I told you, I will teach him. They will never get the chance to brainwash him with their lies and ignorance about reality, Kerry. This won't be an ordinary child. Don't you understand that? If Devin were to impregnate you you'd have a cute, curly-headed kid, but he'd be no different than any other child on this planet, except maybe with a higher degree of awareness. *Our* son, that's an entirely different thing. If you want out, it would be better if you say so now. Don't you understand? There can't be any changing your mind once it goes down."

I looked at him sharply. "What will happen to us if I say no?"

"You won't. What you don't realize is that you have already unconsciously agreed to it, whether you remember or not. Where do you think you go when you're sleeping? And where do you think I am when my breathing seems to have stopped when I'm asleep? Can you answer either of these questions?"

"Okay, no I can't. But the baby, Devin. Could I be pregnant already? Is that possible? What if I'm already pregnant with a child I'm not ready to handle yet? What then?"

"You aren't. Devin would never challenge me like that. He is willing to provide what is necessary to bring my son in. He feels honored to be involved. You are the one that has misgivings. I can't say I blame you at this time, but then, we do have time. A lifetime here in this world, if necessary." He paused, then added, "It shouldn't be necessary. At least, I hope not."

"What shouldn't be necessary?"

"An entire lifetime in this world."

I pondered that one for a while. It didn't compute with everything else he'd said, but I dared not ask for an explanation. He seemed to be growing weary of my arguments and denials.

"Go to sleep, lady. I'll see you in the morning. And be happy. You and Devin only have six days left."

I buried my face in his shoulder, sorry that he was leaving, but at the same time, happy that Thanksgiving was getting closer. *This* Devin could stay forever.

14 I hadn't really expected to see Devin over the weekend. I knew he was in the final stages of packing, so when I awoke to pounding on the front door I was surprised to see him standing there. I must have really been out cold. Behind him were Trevor and Mia with their two children, and behind them, Daniel and a woman I'd never met. Behind *them* were two small boys I assumed belonged to Daniel.

Still half asleep, I rubbed my eyes and let them in, then went to the kitchen to make coffee. Daniel introduced me to his wife and children, and the group in general seemed to be in high spirits.

The plan, Devin told me over coffee, was to go to breakfast and then head down to the flea market where he'd purchased my ring. He seemed pleased to have everyone together. I hastily got the kids up and dressed and, we headed out.

After a hearty spread at the Ranch House restaurant, Devin piloted us all to the jewelers at the flea market. We spent a long day window shopping and picking up small odds and ends at the various stores. Devin bought me a necklace, a tiny Tarot card replica of *The Magician*, the card he personally identified with. He chose *The Devil* card for his own necklace. I was glad he'd given me The Magician. Finally, we headed for home.

Devin, still Devin, dropped me and the kids off, promising to return later that evening. He kissed me in the doorway before returning to the van.

"I won't be around much next week because of the loose ends I'll be tying up before departure."

"You sure you don't want to stay down there and get it done this weekend?"

In answer, Devin just hugged me. "Later," he said.

Pammy was gone when I went in, and when Devin returned I had him all to myself. The girls were asleep, exhausted from their day at the flea market, and we were finally alone.

Devin pushed the eight-track in and Uriah Heep burst out loudly. He quickly adjusted the volume, noting aloud that the amp was already set on *tape*. "You've been playing it, huh? I wasn't sure how you'd take to it after listening to country music for so long."

"I love it," I assured him. "I can't wait to hear the whole album."

"Album?" He laughed. "There are five of just Uriah Heep *alone*. And many, many more recording artists. The music world is our *best* means of infiltration, and rock music is geared towards youth. *They* are the ones we want to reach. They're the ones who will be bringing the new breed into this dimension. Not their parents. It's too late for them. The kids today…they've got to be conscious because they'll be raising the nonhumans."

He switched the track, skipping over the Los Angeles's official witch cuts. "I never should have wasted the tape on her album," he said. "It's stupid."

"Her album, or witchcraft in general?" For some reason my interest in the religion had dwindled in the last couple months. It had happened so gradually that I hadn't really noticed or thought about it until now.

"Well, the real Wicca's okay. I mean, they're a little closer to the facts than some of the other religions. With Wicca, it's all about the mind focusing on creating reality, but it's very primitive. Perhaps I should say elementary. They're a little too religious for me, but Wicca has many good points. They don't believe in the Christian Devil, they preach tolerance of all other religions, and they even require their people to learn two or three religions so they *can* be tolerant of them. And don't confuse them with the Satanists, who really have it *all* fucked up. They're on one big drug and orgy trip, worshipping some *thing* the churches invented. The so-called Devil." He reached for the stash and began to roll a joint.

"What *don't* you like about Wicca?" I asked.

"It's kindergarten for awareness, for one thing, but that's not necessarily a bad thing. Everyone has to start somewhere. It's the secrecy thing bothers me. I can see their point from back in the days when it was dangerous to go against the church *or* the state back then, and both were pretty much tied together. But this is the twentieth century, and the time for fairy tales is over. The human race doesn't have time for parables. The truth has got to come out in the open."

He paused long enough to moisten the paper and light the joint. "If the human race doesn't become aware of how this world really works they're going to blow it over and over, continue to create negativity with their thoughts, and we can't just sit back and let them upset the balance. The earth doesn't solely belong to the *human* race, and they need to wake up to that fact pretty damn quick." He handed the joint to me.

"Well, do you believe in witchcraft or not?" I took a hit and handed it back.

He shrugged. "It works. So does electricity and radar and radio. There's nothing really magic about magic. Science just doesn't understand it and hasn't found a way to explain why it works."

"But you must have *some* faith in Wicca. It was the first subject we ever discussed when I first got to know you. You were into it then. You even belonged to a coven. And you're still wearing the inverted cross." My glance fell to the chain around his neck. "I still can't figure out why the cross is inverted while the pentagram points up. That seems to be a contradiction."

He smiled and looked down at the necklace. "It's up to you, but it's down to me. From where I'm looking from anyway."

"You like that better? Down is the symbol of black magic. You know that."

"So?"

"So, you're not into devil worship. You just *said* so."

He scoffed. "I don't believe in the devil. Not the one you're referring to anyway."

"But you do believe in God, right? You *have* acknowledged His existence."

"*His?* Don't tell me you denote a sex with the Great Almighty."

"Well, you know what I mean. I'm aware that God isn't really an old white-bearded man up in the clouds, but—"

"Up in the clouds?" He laughed again, struck a match and relit the joint. "Babe, are you aware that if God is really the *only* ruler of creation, then he'd have to make sense to *all* realities. There are some worlds that don't have the male-female principle, and other worlds where up and down wouldn't make sense to the inhabitants. Maybe God modifies and adjusts its image to each world as a different idea...one that would make sense to each individual world. Wouldn't that make a lot more sense? Doesn't make it any less God. If God is everywhere and is everything, then it can be anything it wants to be."

"That does make more sense than the drivel I've been force-fed in all the Catholic schools."

"Babe, we've got to work on some things together. Really, there's so much for you to learn. But, then again, there really isn't any rush. We have an entire lifetime together."

It was unusual for Devin to devote so much conversation to his philosophy...Devin who seemed to care more about cars and routes and friends. Since he was on a roll, I seized the opportunity to question him about our mutual friend, *Him*.

"*He* didn't sound too happy about spending an entire lifetime here, now that you mention it." I said.

A look of serious concern crossed his features. "I know. This is a strange, unfriendly place for him. He can't really come out in the daylight. He wouldn't be received too well, but he's pretty big about that, I think."

"Do you mean that literally? That he can't come out in daylight, meaning the *sun?*" I was remembering the previous evening and *his* explanation of why the inhabitants of his world were light sensitive.

"Why don't we let Uriah Heep answer that." He pushed the button that switched the stereo from tape to radio and pressed the on button. The radio was just opening with a song by Uriah Heep, and if that wasn't enough to erupt goosebumps over my entire body, the lyrics just about drained the blood from my face.

The singer said that he had to look at the sun every day to remember where he'd come from. He had a feeling that he might be able to go home someday. He was tired of being here all alone. He sang that he was a traveler in time and just wanted to go back the same way he'd gotten here...to see all his loved ones again. He thought that once he could do that he'd be able to find an answer for me, but he had to wait until he himself was free first. He had no idea how long it would take.

As the song ended, Devin hit the off button and looked at me with a worried expression. "Are you all right, babe?"

I rubbed my arms to smooth out the bumps. This had just about knocked the breath out of me. "Devin, how do you do that?"

He smiled. "Not without a lot of help, believe me. The sun is really foreign to him. He does come out in it, though. What I meant is that he can't really let people know he's here or who he is. People in general, I mean. His old man doesn't really have a good name here, and dealing with that would really hurt him, I think. He seems to be getting used to this dimension, though. For us, who were born and started from scratch, well, this world kind of grows on you, but his home and his people are so nonphysical that although they can look in on this place anytime they choose to, they can't really relate to emotions or misunderstandings. Now, when *he* goes there, he can project these feelings he's experienced by pure thought transference, and they get an idea of what it feels like to feel. They'll never experience it like he does and it's probably lucky for the human race that he *does* that, although, to be truthful, those at his home are far more concerned with this personal project of his than the human race in general. The old man is aware of human hatred of him, or hatred of who they *believe* he is, but he has too much class to care."

I had just about recovered from the shock of the radio. It had happened before but this one was pretty blunt, and Devin had seemed to know it was coming on, or else he had somehow gotten the disc jockey to *put* it on. I remembered all the baby songs that had played in the office a while back, but even then, no one had said *'well, let's let the radio tell you.'*

"That helps me a lot, Devin, really. Thanks. The more I can understand him, the sooner I can stop disappointing him. I hope he doesn't give up on me."

"He knew the obstacles he'd be facing when he left to come here, so don't worry about that. He'll never give up on you. He loves you. He always has. And we all do. Come on, this is getting a little heavy, even for me. Let's go to bed. I'm beat."

He stood up and pulled me up beside him, hugging me when I was on my feet.

"And *I* love you, too, so let's not talk about *him* anymore."

"Gee," I kidded him. "You mean I actually get to sleep with *you* tonight, Dev?"

He blushed. "I doubt you'll get any sleep, chick, but you get me…Devin…tonight. I can guarantee you that. Let me roll a couple joints to take in with us."

I slid the stash over to him. "Hurry up. I don't get to roll around with *you* too often."

We spent Sunday at home, talking and adding up the things that were left to do. Taking stock told us exactly where we were at this point.

Our soap opera was still the talk of the plant, especially since Devin was actually carrying through his intentions with action. We were too happy to care what they thought. I was basking in the happiness of just being with Devin. There was no trace of *him* on Sunday, and I didn't wonder where the other two were. All I cared about was that I was with Devin.

Christian didn't stay completely out of the picture that final weekend before Devin's trip up north. He made a sneaky appearance Sunday afternoon when the weather had warmed up and we'd opened the drapes and windows to let in the fresh air.

Devin reached for the tablet when I noticed a car pulling up outside. Pammy had spent the night with George to hash out the reasons why she couldn't live with him anymore and was now returning home. With her were my Cousin Jake's pregnant wife Bonnie, and another girl I knew as Rhoda. George pulled in several dust piles behind Pam's car. With the windows and drapes open, it was easy to see them disbanding from the vehicles, laughing, talking, and walking up to the front door.

"Hey, wild thing," I called to her. "Finally made it home, huh?"

Pammy made quick introductions to Devin, adding that Rhoda's mother had nine kids, and that Bonnie was conveniently stashed among them awaiting the birth of her child and the news from our cousin that the grandparents were awaiting as well.

Pam told me that today was as good a day as any for them all to meet, and Bonnie and Rhoda expressed their pleasure at finally meeting the magic Devin they'd heard so much about.

Devin wasn't really listening. In fact, he had momentarily disappeared, and Christian was erratically engaged in swift, bold pencil strokes, sketching out a detailed white-and-black shaded figure. An eye first, then a cross.

I watched with both curiosity and revulsion as the sketch progressed. The room also fell silent as the meaning of the sketch began to become clear. There was now a black, agonized figure nailed to the cross in much the biblical pose of the last final breaths of the crucified Jesus. Two obvious points on his head near the crown of thorns indicated that it was not Jesus at all, but rather His archenemy, the Devil.

I was so engrossed in watching the sketch to its completion that I didn't notice who the artist was until I looked up from the drawing to his face.

"Nailed to a *cross?*" I asked, and at that moment I saw the flared nostrils and the mischievous glint sparkling in his eyes, the hung lips. I froze. There were too many guests. *Not now, Christian!*

He finished up the final shadings and detail in seconds, then commenced to print in that funny, sharp, illegible print of his.

Time is…But will Time be at All, Tomorrow?

He then glanced at me before he added his signature at the bottom.

The Magick Christian

Then he placed the picture in my hands for…approval? Inspection? Or reaction. I studied the picture without comment, determined not to react, and he shrugged a normal Devin shrug and smiled a regular Devin smile. Christian was long gone.

"It's just a drawing," he said, seemingly amused at my embarrassment for my human guests.

Kelly noticed the jewelry addition to my neck at lunchtime on Monday. We'd already ordered, and her nose was buried in the sun sign astrology book I'd loaned her days before. When she finally did look up she spotted the Tarot medal and grinned.

"What in the hell do you have hanging on your neck now, Kerry? I swear, you're going to strangle yourself. Do you sleep with all that junk on?" She reached for the medal and nodded approvingly. "That's nice, really. It looks just like Devin."

"I thought so too."

"Oh, everything reminds you of Devin. So. You're really going to do it, huh? Tie the knot. He's leaving any day, isn't he?"

"Yeah. Two days, Kelly. I can hardly believe it." The reality of it hit me as I sat there, incredulous. I had waited so long for this.

Kelly laughed and sat back as the food and coffee arrived. "You're not the only one who can't believe it."

The plant seemed to be in a stupor. Everywhere I turned someone was talking about Devin's upcoming trip. Kim met me in the hallway to tell me how lucky we both were, to wish us luck, and to remind me to put a note on her desk changing Devin's address officially to mine.

Ah, yes. The company Christmas list.

The phone girls winked and whispered whenever I ran into Devin at the coffee machine in the hall, which, unfortunately, was right outside Maurice's office door. For three days he was subjected to the gossip drifting in from the phone room, and then living proof of it meeting just outside his door, three times a day or better.

Devin buzzed into our department often these last few days, not always with a good business reason. Usually it was last minute reminders and damn-I-love-yous. I had never been so happy. So perfectly happy.

And yet, there was still one small cloud over all this elation. The empty days coming up when he would be gone. Not just Devin, but Erick and Christian, too. I mentioned my sadness to Devin who only shrugged his helplessness at his body being only capable of existing in one place at a time.

Christian came up with a solution on Monday night when I was explaining the way I felt to him.

"What Ah *kin* do, ladee," he told me seriously, "is t' ask him t' leave one of us here with you. Ah can't stay mahself, ol' Devin, shee-it...Ah just can't see that sucker getting all the way up th' country, cooped up in tha' van, without blowin' it, ya know?"

I had no idea what he was leading up to, but I nodded anyway.

"Anyways, Ah'd be needed. Tha's a definite." His face glowed with ego. "But, now Erick, Ah don' see where *he'd* be any use on th' trip. He damn sure wouldn' be any fun. Shee-it. Erick don' lak t' do *nothing.*"

I laughed. I had to admit I was really getting attached to the little black rogue, cocky as he was. Now, as he laid out the solution to my upcoming loneliness problem I felt the sudden urge to hug him, to let him know how I felt about him now. He'd tried so hard to earn the same love I'd bestowed on the other three.

"Hey. I love you," I said, touching his arm which was posed in midair describing this master plan of his to eliminate Erick from the trip. He stopped in midsentence at my words.

"You love...who?" he asked cautiously, as if afraid to believe I might have meant himself.

"You, you nut."

Now he really looked suspicious, but I saw a glimmer of hope in his sparkling eyes.

"Ya know who yer saying that to?"

I tried not to smile at his earnestness. He was so cute. "Well, let's see. Devin's not around, and Erick would have taken my cigarette from me by now and...*him*...well, no offense, but there's no resemblance to—"

Something stronger than relief flooded his black features and he crushed me against his chest. "Oh, lad-ee," he murmured. "Damn, lad-ee. Ah didn' ever think ya would."

"Christian, I think I always have. You just took a little getting used to."

"Christian," he mused, releasing his grip and smiling slightly. "Ah kin' of lak that name."

"Well, you do sign your artwork that way. Erick had already told me that, but I never saw you do it until Sunday. You really freaked out the Christians in the room, so it really does suit you."

"Christian. Yeah, Ah lak that. Th' Magick Christian."

I laughed again at his overblown ego.

Sex with Christian wasn't anything like the others, either. I found *that* out Monday night, too.

"Lad-ee, you ain't never been loved lak yer gonna git loved t'nat," he warned me, leering as he tossed Devin's shirt onto the bed. "Ya'd better set tha' alarm now, cuz we ain't gonna be payin' too much 'ttention to tha' thang fer th' next few hours."

Christian had such a sense of cosmic humor about everything. Even sex. He fluffed up the pillows, mumbling to himself.

"So, ya thought *you* were gonna git in t'naht, ha, fuck *you*, Jack." He seemed to be talking to the very air as though the air he addressed understood him perfectly.

"Who, Devin, you mean?"

"No, Erick. He thinks it's *his* shift t'naht, and there ain't lately gonna be no Erick, no-how t'naht an' fer tha' reason you kin safely set yer cigarettes on *mah* side of th' bed."

"Your side? I thought you didn't like the edge."

"Oh, tha's *Devin* that sleeps where *yer* at now. Pussy. Mus' be 'fraid he'll fall out. This way, Ah'm on th' outside to pertect you from danger."

"Hey, now don't start knocking Devin," I began.

"Okay...le's not talk 'bout him at *all*."

He flicked off the light and I stubbed my cigarette out. A new sex partner now, huh?

Well, Christian hadn't been kidding about his warning.

Devin heard the alarm first and nailed it before I could get to it. "Hey-hey-hey." He sat up and smiled at me, his hair a mass of unkempt curls.

"Well, hello stranger," I greeted him, smiling back. Even in the dark, I could see it was Devin.

He mumbled something else and climbed out of bed.

"What'd you say?"

"I *said*," he repeated, loudly now, "that motherfucking sneaky *son of a bitch*." He disappeared into the bathroom.

15 Daniel came up with the interesting question of where I was going to spend Thanksgiving, and his wife, Julie, offered a solution. As a waitress at a posh restaurant where she was scheduled to work that day, Daniel and the boys planned on having Thanksgiving there. Julie suggested that I join them. Devin relayed all this to me at lunchtime the day before his departure Tuesday, November 26th.

"That's really nice of them," I said, "but I don't know them very well. I've only met them that one time, so it might be a little uncomfortable."

"Well, why don't you meet me at his house after work, and we can spend a little time with them. Then you won't feel so out of place. They really want you to accept."

"Okay," I reluctantly agreed. "It'll kill the day anyway. It's going to be lonely as hell when you leave."

"Hell's not lonely. Watch that. And don't worry while I'm gone. I'm doing this so I can come home permanently to you. Home to *you!* No more of this running between three counties. No more lying at home there and wishing like hell, and that *is* the proper use of the word, that you were lying there beside me. But anyhow, that'll all be behind us soon. Meanwhile, I'll tell Daniel you said okay, and I'll lay some bucks on him ahead of time for you and the kids. Man, I'm glad you're going with them. It's a load off my mind. You've never even met my father and Faye, so you'd have been even more uncomfortable there, even though you are welcome. I didn't want you and the kids to be alone that day, especially when we have so much to be thankful for."

Kelly tugged at my purse. "Let's go!"

I looked at Devin. "You can't go with us, huh?"

"I wish I could. Too behind in the route room, and I have to get everything caught up since I'm leaving tomorrow."

Kelly left ahead of me so we could do our goodbye without an audience. Devin glanced at his watch. "I gotta split, too. I'll see you down at Daniel's around five. At least we'll have a little time together, even though I do have to head south shortly after. There's just too much last-minute shit to do, and I have to haul the last of my things over to my dad's. It's going to be a busy night."

"Okay, see you there, then. His house is the one on the corner right?"

"Yeah. You'll see the van out there. Probably a few trucks, too. It's become the local hangout for the drivers.

Devin must have been watching for me when I pulled into Daniel's driveway. He was outside before I even shut the engine off, followed by little Danny and Timmy, who obviously hero-worshipped him. He had to peel them off his back just to kiss me hello, and then they were on *me*.

"Jeez, you guys," I said, laughing. I hugged each one of them, then muttered to Devin, "Affectionate, aren't they?"

"Yes, they are." He put his arm around me, and the boys took off for the house. "Come on in and get acquainted. They're really looking forward to it."

Daniel greeted me enthusiastically when we entered, winking conspiratorially at Devin. "So you finally got her over here, huh?"

"Yup." Devin squeezed my shoulder and looked around. "Where's Julie?"

"She's outside with Lucifer," Daniel said, then, noting my startled expression, added, "Our...dog. He's a malamute and he's never met you, so we thought it'd be better if we kept him out back. He's fine with Devin since he's been around so much."

"That's right. Devin did tell me his name, but I forgot."

The back door creaked open and Julie came in. "Kerry! You made it! Oh, I'm so glad. It's about time!"

"Hi, Julie. Good to see you again."

"Well, come on in to the dining room where we can talk. Daniel's getting the coffee on. Oh, this is great!"

I was a little taken aback by her enthusiasm, but it helped me to relax and feel more at ease. I took a seat at the table. "So, is Ethan still living here?"

Julie lowered her voice. "He is, but he's not here now. I know he's kind of got a bad rap, but he's really an okay guy. He just started out on the wrong foot, shot his mouth off and turned a bunch of people against him, but once he dropped the act he turned out to be all right. Plus, we need his rent." She looked into the living room. "Timmy, Dan, why don't you guys go outside and keep Luke company."

Devin and Daniel entered the dining room with cups, coffee, cream and sugar. They passed the cups around and then sat down with us. Daniel commenced to pouring the coffee.

"I may have been a little hard on him," Devin admitted, having caught the tail end of the comments about Ethan. "He wasn't that great of an employee, so that had a lot to do with how I felt about him."

"He's not as bad as you thought, though," Daniel said. "Anyway, so how about Thanksgiving, Ker? Did Devin talk to you?"

"Yes, and thank you, I'd be honored to join you guys."

"Far out," Daniel said. "It's going to be weird enough sitting there with the kids while my wife serves me in uniform."

We spent about a half hour just shooting the shit, and then Julie looked at the clock. "Can you guys stay for dinner tonight?" she asked.

Devin downed his coffee and stood up. "I wish we could, Julie. I hate to be a party pooper, but I do gotta split. I've told Kerry what a great cook you are, but she has to go pick up the kids, and I've got a trailer to finish loading."

"Boy, that's a hell of a lot to do after working all day," I told Devin, getting up with him. "I wish I could help you."

"You are helping," Devin replied, hugging me. "Whether you know it or not."

I returned the hug and picked up my purse. Julie was just beaming.

"Thanks for the coffee, you guys," I said. "We'll definitely take a rain check on dinner after everything settles down."

Daniel and Julie were treating me with such respect that it made me wonder what Devin had told them about me. He must have given me one hell of a buildup.

At the door, Devin gave Daniel the demonic high sign, a joke we'd started in the office when words couldn't be used. The two outer fingers up while the thumb held the two middle fingers down. An old sign against the evil eye. It was a joke with us, but Daniel took it seriously and proudly flashed it back to us.

"Gotta split," Devin repeated. "Later."

Devin managed to squeeze a call in from home that evening, making no attempt to conceal or lower his voice. I could hear a television in the background. He told me all was quiet and everything was finished. All his things had been carted to his dad's, and everything going north was loaded. He was exhausted, but relieved to have it all done.

"I'm really going to miss you, Devin," I told him. "It'll be weird going to work when you won't be there."

He tried to kid me out of my gloomy mood. "Hey, now don't make me feel bad. Not after all this. Besides, I'm leaving Erick with you. He really isn't needed on the trip."

"It still won't be the same." I sighed.

"No, it could be better if you let it. Don't block it like you're doing now. Stay aware. Pay attention, and listen to what might pop into your head. He *can* talk to you. You just have to train your inner ears to pick up his frequency. With the body out of town, he can't just drive up in the van like usual, you know?"

I laughed. Devin seldom made references to the ethereal substances his partners were actually made of.

"Oh, by the way," he added seriously. "Don't forget to give me that little ring of Michelle's. How is it behaving now, anyway?"

"It still tightens up and I can't figure out how. I've stretched the metal to the point where it's too big on any of my fingers, and it slowly closes while I'm wearing it."

"Weird," Devin said. "Hopefully the charge will help. Oh, stop by and see Julie if you get bored. She really wants to rap with you. Daniel and I are always around, and I guess she wants some girl talk, whatever that consists of. Maybe even on Thanksgiving."

"I don't know. She'll be busy working, serving food."

"Well, I'm glad you'll be with them. Anyhow, I've got to hit the rack here. Big day tomorrow. You know, this living three lives has been hell on my job and everything. I have to keep reminding myself that it's almost over, or I don't think I'd hold up. With Trevor helping me drive, it'll be nonstop, and we might even make it back by Sunday. My father's chick, Faye, will be going along for the ride so my wife will have someone to talk to."

"Just be safe, Devin. I guess I'd better let you go."

He told me he'd see me at work in the morning and we hung up.

Lola smiled when I walked in Wednesday, but I didn't smile back.

"Devin's leaving today," I said, by way of greeting.

Lola shrugged. "So? What are you depressed about, dumbo? You're supposed to be happy."

"I am. It's just that I don't know what I'll do with myself for the next few days."

"Well, he's coming back. You should be happy he's not staying."

"Oh, Lola, why'd you even say that? Christ, now I'll be worrying about that, too."

The morning went slow. At noon I was hesitant about leaving the premises for fear of missing Devin's last few minutes before he drove away. Kelly pushed until I relented. She pointed out that Devin's van was still parked out there and that he'd have to come back to the plant just to get it. We made it a fast food run, but even so, as we turned the final corner, I caught sight of the van, this time in motion, barreling up to the front of the plant. It passed the glass front doors and screeched to a halt.

"Kelly! He's leaving. Hurry up!"

"Oh, shit! That *is* him." Kelly floored it to the corner and skidded to the curb. "Go ahead. I'll go in and—"

I flung the door open. "Tell Lola!"

"I will. Go!"

Devin stepped out of the van just as I reached it. In seconds, I was in his arms, all my repressed tears now cutting loose. Devin's grip crushed me.

"Thank God," he whispered. "Where have you *been?* I went to Lums, the coffee shop, Burger King...I tore this fucking plant apart until someone finally told me you were at McDonald's...and when I got there..."

"We just did the drive-through. Oh, man, Devin if you had left..."

"I should have gone thirty minutes ago. I must have just pulled in when you drove away with Kelly. I'm already punched out. I've just been looking for you."

Several employees passed us on their way in from their own lunches, but Devin kissed me anyway, one long last later, and then gently eased me away.

"I love you so much, dammit. You'd better go in before Maurice or Mama comes out after you. Kelly already went in, so they'll know you're out here with me."

"Fuck Maurice, and Mama will understand." I squeezed him harder.

"I have to go, babe, really. You go ahead inside. Don't you realize I can't drive away from you? Please. Let me go and get this bullshit over with so I can come home for good. Oh, Kerry..."

"I know. I'm gonna miss you too."

He kissed me again. "Erick will be here. I'll try to call you before I actually leave the state."

"When *are* you leaving?"

"Around four, I hope. I have to stop at Gerald's to pick up Faye. Trevor is there now waiting for me. And I've been waiting on *you*. Hey! The ring. You got it?"

I tugged it off my finger and handed it to him. "I guess I'll see you, then."

"Man, Kerr…" He hugged me again. "I knew it was going to be hard but, shit! Go in. I can't leave until you've walked away."

After one final hug, I finally turned away. "Go ahead." I squeezed his hand. "I won't even look back. And watch that Christian," I added, trying to smile. "He's a brat."

He returned my smile. "I love you, Kerry. I'll call you."

I lied. As soon as I heard him pull away, I did look back. The spot where the van had stood was vacant. Silent. Empty. Up the street, my own car was parked where I would walk to it at five…alone. I'd been out here at least twenty minutes, probably in trouble, and didn't care. I dried my eyes and went inside. It would be no secret to anyone who saw me that I'd been crying.

I returned to my office, prepared for the lecture Mama was sure to have in store for me, but she only smiled when I walked in, her usual understanding in her eyes.

"Did you find Devin?" she whispered.

I nodded.

"Okay. Cheer up. You'll live."

16 True to form, the radio chided me all the way to the sitter's with song after song reflecting where Devin and I were at up till now. Some songs I was familiar with, and some I'd never heard, but all of them had something to say about this level of our relationship, and most of them were pretty blunt. The Eagles sang about the witchy woman, and then Led Zeppelin warned me that I was buying a stairway to heaven. They cautioned that when I got there the stores would all be closed. Not exactly comforting I thought as I reflected on those lyrics. Then Crosby, Stills, Nash and Young came to my rescue. The singer said that he wouldn't be back till later on, but he assured me that I knew him, and that he missed me now.

He went on to say that he'd seen himself as I *had* known him, and that when he'd changed I'd had the opportunity to see through him. He assured me that the other side was just the same, just as real, and that he loved me. Could I feel it now?

And this was the AM radio in my car. Not the FM station I was becoming accustomed to.

The days following Devin's departure were anything but mentally inactive for me. When I thought everything was perfect, the radio seemed to warn me of unknown events to come. It made me realize that I had to come to grips with the fact that our relationship was anything but normal, and that Devin was unlike anyone I had ever known. I knew I had to sit down and face some hard facts about Devin, and I knew I had only a few days to research the many facets of Devin's personality.

In spite of the case study, *The Three Faces of Eve* example I had used to bring the subject up, I knew that I was woefully ignorant of any real facts about multiple personality and schizophrenia. I knew nothing about how to handle, much less live with, either. And if Devin wasn't in one of these categories then there was only one other left to consider. Possession.

Since I had enough occult books on hand to research possession immediately I began there, even though the only similarities between Devin's situation and possession were the common denominator of the possessor...the Devil himself. *If* he was actually the Devil, as he'd implied a few times, he was a far cry from the descriptions I'd read of him. If *this* was an example of the Devil, then maybe it was time to take a look at the authors of *The Bible* and consider the influence of personal opinion during its creation.

All of the common symptoms of historically recorded possession had no similarity to Devin or his behavior. He hadn't lapsed into any strange languages, nor had he complained of any blank spots or losses of time. There was no violent reaction to the mention of the name or subject of God. On the contrary, Devin had amazed me with his diplomacy in discussing God with people. I'd listened to him answer Pammy's questions, and never once had he spoken with any disrespect for the Universal Intelligence, whatever *that* was.

No, the common exorcist-type possession was out of the question. If Devin *was* possessed, he was well aware of the fact that he was, and if *that* was a bad point, then what was I to think of his obvious pride, love, and respect for his possessor, or possessors?

Devin was aware of every second of his time. He was in full control of his mental faculties. He displayed enough leadership and intelligence to warrant himself a supervisory position at his job, along with the respect of almost every coworker in the plant, including Tim.

He'd more than proven to me his capacity for love, generosity and understanding. He'd never gotten angry with me when I'd given him plenty of reason to lose patience. He always treated me like a priceless treasure. No, Devin was not possessed, I finally decided. At least, not against his will.

Upon finer checking, that is, getting beyond the major legendary symptoms, I uncovered some disturbing, little known, and rarely published symptoms of possession.

It seemed that dissociation of personality was one of the first symptoms, followed by unexplained powers of perception, intuition, healing, clairvoyance and telepathy. These were all listed under a *different* kind of possession. One major sign of this type of possession struck a familiar chord. Unusual physical changes in the body and facial features, including voice changes.

Delving further into the first symptom, I discovered that dissociation of personality was exactly what it sounded like. That seemingly two or more personalities occupy *one* body, but never at the same time. Each personality has its own habits, expressions, voices, handwriting and opinions, and those traits can oppose the traits of the original personality. However, and this was a big however, the possessed of *this* nature should be physically deteriorated and totally drained of energy.

Devin was the picture of health.

Not only was he in perfect health, but he seemed to stay that way quite deliberately, in spite of heavy water bottles slashing flesh deep enough to require stitches. And energy? I still was not sure what all he could do with it. His source, or supply, was evidently inexhaustible. No, Devin was not that kind of possessed either.

I was about to close the door on the whole possibility when I found one last detail that didn't help much in favor of Devin's *not* being possessed. It seemed that investigators were discovering that any experimentation with drugs, regardless of the nature of the drug, weakened the defense system of the main ego and allowed other nonphysical personalities to take over the body.

But nobody had taken *over* Devin. He was the first to admit his total willingness to cooperate with his possessor...if it was fair to call any of them possessors. It seemed to me that it was more of a joint venture than anyone possessing anyone else.

I shelved the idea on possession for a while and began to look into what facts I had on hand concerning schizophrenia. I already knew the disorder was supposed to be chemical and that it involved a split personality. However, according to the experts, again, in such known cases the ego split from what it felt to be the *bad* side of itself, and evolved an opposite. A docile, loving person in one personality, while the second displayed all the vices.

There again, I was stumped. None of Devin's partners were either all perfect or all bad. They *all* contained both types of traits, so there was no good, bad or medium Devin.

And what would explain *him* and the strange references to this other world of his? A world outside the space-time continuum as we all know it here in this dimension? A place of peace and beauty that supposedly coexisted in the same space as our physical world?

And, to be fair, if he really *was* from another dimension, wouldn't it be at least conceivable that the little-known facts and legends of such a world could cause it to be *erroneously* labeled Hell and its superior intelligence Satan?

If Satan had the lordly dignity that *he* had, then why would he waste his time with such unimportant trivia as a system called *visible light*, where the inhabitants were considerably more barbaric than the world that *he* was accustomed to?

He had defined some pretty clear differences between this world and the one he claimed to be from. He'd insisted that there was no sun like ours at *home*, and that everything shimmered with its own phosphorous light. He'd said that our sun was entirely too bright and blinding for him.

I wondered if Christian and Erick came to sub in for him while he quietly went about whatever mission he'd come here to accomplish.

The more I read, the more I began to realize that there just wasn't anything on record or in print, at least that I had access to, that could give me any insight into my situation.

Pragmatic as I was, I had not entirely discarded the possibility of a deliberately engineered act at this point. When I was with him and witness to the different personalities, it was easy to believe, but when I was away from him, the doubts seeped in. All things considered, time would tell if it was real or not. In the meantime, I had to admit the one thing I was sure of.

I loved Devin. I loved Erick, and I did finally love Christian. I loved the personality I called *Him.* Whether they were all aspects of one, or four separate intelligences, I loved them all with the same equality as I had for my two children.

There wasn't one of them I would want to leave Devin Drew. Not one that wouldn't be horribly missed, not just by me but, I was sure, by Devin himself. As long as I was going to love Devin, I was going to love all of him, or them, and nothing was going to change that. It was too late to decide now that I couldn't cope with it. There was no breaking it off, and as long as things were the way they were, they would have to be normal for me in spite of what friends, family or society would label it.

The only day I didn't hole up with my books while Devin was gone was Thanksgiving Day. After Julie served the courses and left the table, I had the opportunity to bring up the subject with Daniel. Since Devin had told me he'd explained the situation to him, I was curious as to why he hadn't run like any normal human would have when his friend began to casually discuss other people living inside himself. Daniel's response was simple, genuine and sincere.

"Kerry," he said, "I know that Devin is…uh…different than other friends of mine, and I realize that you aren't the same as…uh…other people are either. I've seen a lot of things since I met Devin that I don't understand, and I *want* to…and maybe someday I will. But in the meantime, I love Devin like a brother. I can't explain it. And you're like a sister to me too. Both of you are my friends. Whoever or whatever Devin really is, he's okay in my book. He's helped me out a lot. I wish everybody was like Devin. We could use a *world* full of Devins."

I just nodded. I knew a reply wasn't necessary. Daniel wasn't concerned with who we were or who we weren't.

He also had enough sense, I noticed, to stop talking whenever Julie approached the table. It was apparent that Daniel had not passed any of this on to his wife.

Devin called Thanksgiving night, long after I'd settled the kids in bed. It was late, about eleven. He sounded strangely different, almost hollow. Oddly enough, his first question was in regards to Erick. Had anything gone down, he asked.

I told him no, that it was empty and quiet and lonely around the house, and if Erick was around he was hiding somewhere.

Devin only laughed, an empty laugh, and assured me that if an occasion arose where I needed Erick, that I would find him hospitably available and that there would be no need to look for him.

I had to admit, Erick did seem to have a built-in emergency alarm that alerted him without any help from either Devin or me.

The trip was going fast, he said. Upon arrival, the family had invited him to dinner, but he'd been hell-bent on unloading the trailer and dropping it off at a U-Haul station. He'd been anxious to get back on the road. He asked how dinner had gone for me and I told him it had been great, that the swanky restaurant served top-notch food and the day had gone all right considering he wasn't there to make it perfect.

He asked what I thought of Daniel and Julie. I said they were great people even though Daniel might be a little baffled by us since Devin had broken the news.

"Yeah, I know," he replied, "but he'll get used to it. He won't have much of a choice if he continues to hang around us. Anyhow, babe, I don't know about Erick. He hasn't been with *us*, so listen for him and keep your eyes peeled. Well, let me get off this phone. I probably won't call again. I think you'll see me before you talk to me. We drove straight through going up, but we aren't pushing so hard on the way back. Now that the trailer is gone, it's actually going even faster without the wind drag. We'll see you, more than likely, sometime Sunday. I wouldn't expect us before that."

"Be careful, Devin. I love you."

"I love you too. Later, babe."

I hung up with vague stirrings of uneasiness. He sounded as cool and distant as if he were calling from a customer phone. Almost formal. If that was an example of Devin without Erick...

I turned out the lights, leaving only one red flickering candle, and picked up my old journal.

Day two of five without Devin.

The hours dragged through work the following day, and Kelly and Lola pretty much left me alone. They must have sensed that I had a lot on my mind. At five o'clock, I dropped by Daniel's to let them know that Devin was on his way back. Julie rolled a joint and passed it to me. A car door slammed outside, and a young man with blond hair appeared at the screen door.

"That's Brian," Daniel whispered. "Devin's brother. Have you met him yet?"

"No."

"We've only met him once. Come on in, Brian."

Brian entered, banging the screen door behind him, and waved to the three of us. Daniel introduced us and he politely nodded to me.

"Hey, Kerry. Heard a lot about you." He seemed embarrassed when he realized who I was, as though he didn't quite know what to say to his brother's girlfriend. He looked about eighteen and was tall and slender in build, like Devin.

He wanted to know about the ounce Ethan had for his dad. Daniel took him into the dining room where they spoke quietly and then Brian left, but not before he told me that it was nice to have finally met me. He seemed like a sweet kid.

Daniel invited me to stay for dinner but I bowed out. I had to pick up the kids, and Devin might call. He hadn't said so, but there was always that chance. They understood.

When I arrived home with the girls, Pammy told me that Devin *had* called. I peeled off my jacket. "Damn it. I *knew* I should have come straight home. What did he say?"

"He just said he'd call back. I guess he didn't want to waste the money if you weren't here."

"Probably. Well, how was *your* Thanksgiving?"

"I'd rather have gone with you'ns, but George's mother would have been hurt. She thinks I was so good for him."

"He's having a hard time letting go, huh?"

"Yeah." Pammy sighed. "I feel kind of sorry for him. He needs a buddy to run around with. Well, at least I got him into meditation. It's helped him a lot. He doesn't blow up anywhere near the amount of times he used to."

I perked up at the word meditation. "I told Devin you were into that, and he thinks I ought to try it," I said. "What exactly *is* it?"

"Oh, Ker, it's so neat. They give you a mantra, a word to say over and over, and then they show you how to use it to go into yourself. It's great when you're in alpha. I just love it."

"But what's it feel like? Drugs? Grass? What?"

"Like I said before, I can't explain it. It's a weird high, but natural. You feel like you're underwater, or something close. You face things to yourself that you normally wouldn't admit. It all comes out in alpha. That's about all I can tell you. It burns off tension, and you feel really relaxed when you come out of it."

The phone rang then and I grabbed it with high hopes.

Well, right family, wrong man.

"Hello, is this Kerry?" The voice was deep. Unfamiliar and slowly paced.

"Speaking. Who's this?"

"Oh, hello, Kerry. This is Gerald Drew. Devin's father?"

It took a second to compute. Devin's father? "Oh, hi, Gerald." I wondered what he was calling me for.

"Yes, I hope I'm not disturbing you. I feel like I already know you, but that's not so strange. Devin does his share of bragging around here."

"Oh, you're not disturbing me. I just thought this call might be Devin."

"That's what I'm calling *you* about. I have a phone too, but I haven't heard a word from him. Of course you know that Faye is with them."

I promised to remind Devin to call him, wondering why this Faye didn't just do it herself. There certainly was more than one phone booth out there in America. He thanked me and added that he was looking forward to meeting me.

I hung up thinking that this call might have been more to satisfy curiosity than any message for Devin. Maybe Brian had said something about meeting me this afternoon.

I returned the phone to the desk and put on some hot water.

"Making coffee?" Pam asked.

"Yeah. Want some?"

"No, well, okay. Hey Ker, why *don't* you take Transcendental Meditation?"

"Oh, I've been kicking the idea around."

Pammy left for work at 9:30, and I went back to my research. There had to be an explanation for Devin somewhere in the world. I read until late, poring over everything from *The Black Arts* to books written by parapsychologists on the rare cases of multiple personalities.

Nothing I could match up to Devin.

I finally hit the lights and dropped into the beanbag, the phone close by. I closed my eyes and tried to sense Erick, with no success. While I didn't hear from Erick, the phone rang instantly as it had rung the times I tried to use the ring to make Devin call me.

This time it was him.

He kept the call short, but admitted he'd just remembered to call again. It was pretty much the same hollow, listless Devin I'd spoken with yesterday. He sounded both tired and strained, as though the emotional portion of the trip was more than even *he* had the nerves for. He was a third of the way back, tired, and he wished like hell he was already here. He had the same distance in his voice when he asked about Erick.

"If he's been around, Devin, I guess I just don't know how to sense him."

"Well, he's been here once since I last talked to you. I guess big brother didn't have any confidence in my ability to follow through with this whole trip."

I laughed. Sometimes Devin couldn't hide his aggravation with Erick.

"I miss you, Devin."

"Hey, I know the feeling."

"Are you sure you're okay, Devin? You don't sound so good."

"You wouldn't sound so good with part of *you* missing. And for nothing, it looks like. Well, I know he's there. He'll look out for you and the kids whether you believe he's there or not."

I told him his dad had called and he sounded surprised. "Wonder what that was all about."

"He said he just wanted to know about Faye. Apparently she hasn't called him."

"I'll pass the message on. Later."

I hung up with the same uncertainties that I'd had the night before. If Erick's being missing put *that* much of a strain on his psyche, then what would happen to Devin if Erick were to split permanently? Just get fed up with the drugs and cigarettes and human bullshit. That thought was so disquieting that I dismissed it from my mind immediately. Erick wasn't going anywhere. He wouldn't.

Still, the idea of that possibility, combined with what Devin sounded like now, was more than just scary. To lose Erick, or any one of them for that matter, would be to lose Devin, too. Somehow, I just knew that.

Devin, all of him, was getting to be my whole world.

Unable to sleep now, I found myself taping a message of greeting for him with a roll of adhesive tape on the cupboards in the kitchen, just over the stove. He'd be sure to see it when he went for the first cup of coffee. In small white letters, it read: *welcome home,* and in large letters beneath, *Devin.*

I refused to put the other names in print, as if labeling them would be carrying it too far. Yet, Devin wasn't the only one I was welcoming back. There just wasn't anything normal about this relationship, but I wouldn't have changed things now for anything. A far cry from the attitude I'd had back when I'd first suspected something off-the-wall about Devin. It had frightened me then. Now, the thought of losing any of them was even more frightening. And if I wasn't scaring myself enough with little thoughts of things that *could* happen, my mother's phone call, an hour after Devin's, finished me off.

I was surprised to hear from her at this hour, but I was thankful for someone to talk to. She thanked me for the tapestry and told me how nice it looked over her fireplace.

"I'm glad you like it." I glanced at my now empty wall where the tapestry had once hung. "I guess Devin was worth the loss of it."

"How is he anyway? Pam just raved about him while she was here. He sounds like an unusual person."

"Persons," I corrected her. "I guess you haven't talked to Pam recently, have you? She could really run up your bill if you called her now."

"What do you mean?"

"Remember *The Three Faces of Eve* ?"

"Of course. I saw the movie with you, remember?"

"Well, this is the four faces of Devin, complete with superhuman abilities and you wouldn't believe what else. I wish I had time to tell you about it. It would cost you a fortune."

"Well, go ahead. I'm paying for it."

It took about a half hour to summarize my situation to her…just the bare-bones version. She was quiet, unusual for my mother, until I was finished.

So quiet that I had to ask if she was still there.

"Yeah, honey, I'm here. Look. I'm going to send that book back down to you. I think you should read it. In fact, from what you've just told me, I think you'd *better* read it."

"Oh, no, Mom, please. Don't send me any books, especially that one. Devin will be moving in here Sunday or Monday, and I'll have about two hundred of *his* to read."

"Kerry, listen to me. I don't care what kind of books he has. You'd better read *this* one. I'm not trying to scare you, honey, but I think you're being exploited. Will you promise me you'll read it if I send it?"

"You're talking about John Keel's book, that UFO thing…*Operation Trojan Horse* book? Mom, whatever the answer to Devin is, believe me it's not flying saucers. Devin drives a van, and I have never seen it take off in any direction but straight forward and occasionally backwards."

"Kerry, you're joking about something that not only isn't funny but could be downright dangerous. Do you want to end up in a mental institution?"

"Mom, don't be so dramatic. You don't even know him. He hasn't got an evil bone in his body."

"Will you *read* the book?"

I exhaled loudly, now sorry I'd told her about Devin. There was just no arguing with my mother. "Go ahead and send it. If I can get to it and have time, I'll try to read it again. Don't forget, I didn't get too far with it the *last* time."

"You'd better make time, Kerry. Do you think it was an accident that you didn't get through it last time? Think back a little. You were *contacted* by that purple fog the day after you tried to read it. You called me, scared out of your wits. And never mind what happened during the time you were trying to read it. You forget already? It wasn't two months later this whole thing broke wide open with Devin. You say he's totally different than he was before he cut his hair, shaved off his mustache, switched positions at work and bought that ring. I remember when you couldn't stand him. The whole thing makes a lot more sense to me than it does to you, Kerry, but I'm on the outside viewing this objectively. You're so blindly caught up in this…thing…you can't see what's happening. You weren't supposed to read that book back then because whatever is in Devin *now* knew back then that if you had read it you'd have run from him like nobody's business. And if you're not afraid for yourself, at least think about those two innocent little girls. Do you want them possessed or harassed or even killed? Because they do that too, you know. If they can't get to you, they'll get at you through your loved ones."

"Who're *they*? Christ, you and Devin and your *theys*. Us, you, them…who are *they*?"

"Look, I'll mail you the book. You do what you want, but I'd advise you to read it."

"Mom, I just told you. Devin is not from outer space. You are being—"

"I know he isn't from outer space, Kerry. Neither are the UFOs. They're from other dimensions."

I gave up, tired of the losing battle. "Okay, okay. Mail the damn book."

"You'll read it?"

"I'll try."

"Kerry, I'm very worried about you."

"Mom, believe me, I couldn't be in safer hands. But mail the book. It might just be the one I've been looking for."

17 Saturday evening. November 30th. The closer it got to Sunday, the slower time crawled.

I took a long, leisurely bath and dressed for bed. Pammy had her nose in a book when I entered the living room, and my intention was to do the same. I didn't have much more time to continue my research, and I hoped to come up with some answers before Devin got home. The last person I expected to see was Mia, but when the knock came at the door and I opened it, there she stood.

"Well, Mia! Damn! Come on in. How've you *been*?"

Pam looked up with curiosity as I ushered her into the house. "Hi, Mia. Can't take it huh? House getting to you?"

"I'll say," Mia said, smiling. "It's the sitting and wondering that drives you crazy. Have you heard from them, Kerry?"

"Yes, Devin called Thanksgiving and yesterday. They're actually on their way back. Want some coffee?"

"That sounds heavenly. They're making good time, then?"

"I guess. It still seems like forever to me. Where are the kids?"

"At my mom's. It feels so good just to get out of the house. I almost came up yesterday."

"I'm really sorry. I would have stopped at your house to let you know, but I didn't think I'd have been able to find it. I know what it's like not to have a phone."

"What all did Devin say? Did he mention Trevor?"

"Not much of anything, really. He didn't sound so good. Both calls he sounded like he couldn't talk, but he admitted he was alone in the phone booth. He sounds...cold, or formal...or sorry he did it, or—"

"Oh, no," she said. "Don't worry about Devin. Remember he's been under a strain, but he'll handle it okay. I have a lot of faith in Devin. He's good people. That's a hell of a drive, you know. If they're on their way back, it doesn't sound like they rested at all. Just turned around and headed back. That's enough to put anyone on edge."

"He wasn't exactly on edge." I got up to put the coffee on. "But, you're probably right. Tired and stressed."

The phone rang and Pam, closest to it, answered it.

"Hello...*Devin?* Hey! Where you *at?*"

At the sound of his name, I all but leapt to the phone from the kitchen.

"Yeah, she's right here. I think you'd *better*. Here, Kerry, calm down...good grief."

I snatched the receiver. "Devin?"

"Hey, lady." His voice sounded much more back to normal.

"Where *are* you?"

"Not far. We're about an hour away. We stopped at this truck stop for coffee, and I decided to call and warn you that we'll be there pretty soon. I was going to surprise you, but Trevor hasn't talked to Mia and you might not have been home and—"

"Mia's here, Devin! She *knew*, or something. She just stopped up here."

"Mia's there? Far out! Trevor will be happy to hear that!"

Excitement was welling up inside me as he talked. Devin was home! *Home!*

"Oh, Devin, man, I love you. Hurry up and get here!"

"That's along the lines I was working towards." He laughed. "I won't be able to stay there long, though. I've got to take Faye back to my dad's, and I might as well load up some of my shit while I'm down there. I hope I can do it all in one vanload...bring it all home in one trip, you know? At least I know where home is now."

"How'd you get here so fast? It's barely been three days!"

"Yeah, I'm hep!" He yawned. "We just haven't stopped, that's all."

Mia was looking at me with excitement shining in her eyes, but patiently waiting for the phone. I realized how selfish I was being.

"Hey, Devin, can you put Trevor on for a minute? Mia hasn't talked to him since he left."

"Right on! I can dig it. Here, say hello to him first."

A switch was made and I heard Trevor before he took the receiver. "Thanks, bro. Hey, Kerry!"

"Trevor! Damn, this is so exciting. How's it going?"

"Not bad. Glad it's over with. You been okay?"

"Living. Here, Mia wants to talk to you. Hurry up and get here, huh?"

I was almost glad to turn the phone over to her. I was in my gown and robe, and my hair was still wet.

Pammy laughed as I raced for the bedroom muttering, "*oh shit...an hour...my hair will never dry!"*

"Calm down, Ker! He ain't gonna care if your hair's wet. I'll finish making the coffee."

Apparently, they had misjudged the distance. It wasn't even a half hour before the van drove up. I looked out the window and felt a surge of elation.

"It's them, Mia!" I was out the door, and already had one foot on the running board when the engine died. Devin jumped to the ground, and for five minutes I wasn't even aware that Trevor and Faye had trooped into the house, or that George's loud Jeep had parked and he was close behind them now, too.

"Lady..." He looked like death warmed over, but he also seemed so relieved to be home.

"Devin...oh, Devin. It's so good to see you."

"Devin!" Trevor waved from the front door. "There's coffee in here!"

When we entered the house, Trevor was deep in an explanation of how rude they'd been, how hungry he'd been, and how impatient Devin had been to get back on the road.

"They wanted us to stay the rest of the day and Devin just refused. Here I was starving, the smell of turkey dinner just wafting throughout the house, and Devin's practically insulting. Just unloaded the van and then we had to split."

"Hey-hey-hey!" Devin said, taking a seat in the red armchair, motioning for me to join him. He hugged me for the hundredth time. "I *love* you! I suppose introductions are in order. Kerry, this is Faye. Faye, Kerry."

"Hi, Faye." I waved to her from Devin's lap.

"And that's Pam and George," Devin began, but Faye smiled a quiet smile. "We've already met," she said. "While you two were out there."

"Yeah, okay," Devin said, shrugging. "Whatever."

Faye was a good-looking girl. Long brown hair and kind eyes. She looked to be about my age or younger. Sweet.

"You about ready?" Devin looked over at Trevor who was kissing Mia again. "Hey, come on!"

Negotiations began. Devin wanted me to come along for the ride. Pammy offered to stay with the kids. George volunteered to replace Trevor so that he could go home with Mia, but Trevor insisted on seeing the trip to the end. Mia had to get back to her mom's to pick up the kids, and Devin agreed to drop Trevor off at home on the return trip back up. George asked if he could drive, a task neither Devin nor Trevor was much interested in now.

Devin made his way to the rear of the van and dropped onto the couch, motioning for me to join him. "Come on, lady. It's been too long."

I lay down with him, as close as I could possibly get, and he drew the rear curtains concealing us from the other passengers. It was so hard to believe he was really back, and even harder to believe he was free to move in now. There would be no more driving back and forth from one county to another unless I was with him or the company ordered it.

"We spent so much money," he said with a sigh and a gripping hug. "But I still have about two fifty left." He pulled me even closer to him. "Damn, have

I ever missed you." He kissed me then and the trip, his absence, money…everything was forgotten. There was just Devin and the rolling motion of the van. "I may just nod off until we get closer," he said. "It's a good forty-minute ride."

It didn't seem like forty minutes. One minute we were on a bright traffic-infested highway, and the next minute we were veering off into a neighborhood illuminated by street lamps posted along winding roads, houses scattered here and there.

"Hey! Devin!" Trevor called back to us.

Devin pulled the curtain aside. "Already? Okay, I figured it was about that time." He raised up on his elbow and peered out the back window as the van passed a long driveway, stopped, then backed into it. It continued down the driveway in reverse as we approached a western red cedar house. The front porch was enclosed in rails and held two wooden rockers. George braked and cut the engine.

"Hey, Devin!" Trevor's voice again.

"Yeah, I see, bro. Time to get up."

There were a couple of cars in the driveway. Suddenly I felt very self-conscious. "Maybe it would be better if I wait out here."

"No way." Devin straightened his shirt and tucked it in. "You're walking in there with me."

"I don't know." I was still dubious.

"Here comes Gerald now," Trevor said. "Open the back window, Devin."

"Up, Ker." Devin nudged me gently and opened the rear window. Then he made his way to the van's passenger's side sliding door and sauntered out into the front yard which was flooded by the porch light and the motion sensor light shining from the roof peak. Together the two lights made it almost appear to be sunshine. I caught sight of Brian and waved. Faye had joined them in the yard and they all stood in a huddle. Brian returned my wave, and then a slight man with longish hippie-style hair headed towards the rear of the van.

I wondered if this was another brother I hadn't heard about. There was no sign of age in his face, and he wore a wide, friendly smile as he reached into the open back window.

"Hello, Kerry. So we finally meet."

I reached to take his outstretched hand, but he put both arms around me in a fatherly fashion. "Welcome to the family, Kerry. Step back, boys. Let this young lady get out."

He opened the rear doors and I went straight into Devin's waiting arms.

Gerald seemed to sense my nervousness. "That poor kid," he said to Devin. "She's scared to death. Kerry, come on into the house. Devin, you stay with her until she's more comfortable. Kerry, welcome to our home."

Faye had already gone in, and now she met us at the front door as we approached. "Is anyone hungry?"

Devin remained glued to my side. "Thanks, Faye, but Trevor and I grabbed a burger a couple hours ago. We can't stay long. We're just going to load up the van and get Trevor back to his family." He glanced at Brian. "Will you tell George and Trevor to come in? The more hands we've got, the quicker we'll be on our way."

Brian rose to get them. Gerald sat alone in a massive, black, wood-carved, red velvet-upholstered throne. He proceeded to roll a joint.

"Well, sit down and we'll celebrate your safe return."

Devin was eyeing the chair with interest. "Still won't part with that sucker, huh?"

Gerald looked at Devin with an exasperated expression. "You're not going to con me out of it, I told you. Now, sit."

"Hey, Gerald, we can't, really." Devin jerked a thumb in the direction of the back of the house. "Okay if I start clearing out my shit?"

Gerald smiled. "Please do. We can use the space. That's supposed to be Brian's room, but he's been using the one with your waterbed set up in the back. I hope that's all right. We filled it up so the kid could have a bed until you empty *his* room."

"Yeah, you can leave that waterbed set up," Devin said. "We ain't lately got room for it up at our house."

"Can I help?" I asked, following Devin down the hall to a room across from the bathroom.

Devin opened the door. "Sure, if you feel like it."

My eyes surveyed the contents of the room in disbelief. "Wow! Devin, is all this stuff yours?"

"I don't know. It looks like more...yeah, this isn't mine." He kicked a small box out of the way, looked at me and laughed. "But everything else is."

"It looks like more than one van load."

"We'll see. Here, you can take the beanbags out. And send those suckers in here."

A huge Great Dane lumbered up to Devin at a lope that appeared to be a form of slow motion. Devin's face lit up and he stooped to roughhouse a little with him, petting him first, then grabbing his head in an affectionate hold. "Thor, old boy. I missed you, too."

Thor laid a ten-inch tongue on Devin, then hopped up on his shoulders with his massive legs and paws. Devin stood up and the dog matched his six-foot height exactly. "Hey-hey-hey, Thor. You know better than that. Come on, down." He gently pushed the gentle giant to the floor. "Maybe I'll romp with you tomorrow. We'll be back."

I reached out tentatively to pet him. "He's really gentle."

"I know. All Great Danes are, really. They just look intimidating. He gets a little rough playing, but he can't help that. He doesn't realize his own strength."

At that moment George, Trevor and Brian entered the room.

"Well, come on, Devin," Brian said. "Let's go! We turned the van around and have the sliding doors open. Look at all the help you've got."

"Fast getaway," Devin said with a smile. "Two of you can catch it at the van and pack it, and we'll get the boxes out to you. How's that sound?"

"I'll pack," George volunteered, looking uncomfortable among so many strangers.

"Okay. I'll help George," Trevor said. "Get a move on." Trevor was obviously anxious to get home.

We began to shuffle the boxes out to the van. With two packing the van and three of us hustling the boxes out to them, we eventually got ahead of the packers long enough to take a smoke break after fifteen minutes of steady hauling. As the room dwindled down to a few items, Brian abandoned the project, leaving me and Devin alone in the room.

"Aw, Devin, what *is* this?"

An adorable dragon, appearing to be a youngster, green with white bulging eyes, was positioned on his back, frolicking on a piece of shiny, glassed board, his four baby feet waving wildly in the air. It was made of papier-mâché and was among the last of the few remaining items in the room.

"These are all my books." Devin pushed out two large boxes with his foot. "And that's ours. I forgot to tell you about that."

"Damn, he's so cute. Does he have a name? Did you make him?"

"No name. And no, I didn't make him. Faye and Gerald made him for me. Cool, huh?"

"I *love* him. No name?"

"Well, I never asked." He grinned and wiped a bead of sweat from his forehead with his sleeve.

"Let's call him Puff. You know, the magic dragon?"

"Okay, but there's more to Puff. He's actually a lamp. There's a globe full of Christmas lights that sits on his feet. It's probably out in the van right now. You'll see it tomorrow, probably, or whenever we get everything out of these boxes. Come on. Let's speed this up. Trevor has got to be getting impatient."

He piled me up with a few small items, records and things, while he took the larger boxes filled with books.

"I suppose we're going to have to go in and smoke the peace pipe," he commented as he shoved the last box in to George. Gerald had followed us out and watched as Devin helped George finagle the last box in to fit.

"You sure you're gonna fit all that into your new house?" he asked.

"No, I'm not sure. What we can't fit, we'll bring back." Devin stood up. "Come on. Trade me that chair of yours. This is your last chance now."

"Humph." Gerald lit a cigarette and started walking towards the warmth of the house. We followed.

"It won't work, Devin. You might as well give up."

"I'll keep bugging you."

"You do that."

Once inside, I took a closer look at the carvings on the arms and legs of the throne. It was completely handcrafted, glazed ebony wood, huge claws where the arms curled and finely chiseled dragon's feet where the legs sat on the floor. It was high-backed, seat and back covered in plush red velvet. It was a lord's throne all right.

Devin shook his head and looked at me. "He just can't see it. That's *my* throne."

Gerald, who'd been sitting in it, got up. "What the hell could you possibly give me to equal it anyway?"

"That gold leather chair of mine. That's *leather*, Jack. I paid nine hundred dollars for that sucker."

"That plastic-covered shit…"

"Plastic, your ass." Devin glanced at his watch. "Well, we gotta split. There's still my chair and a few loose odds and ends we'll come by for tomorrow. I want to see how much space is left after we unload this."

"When are you moving down here out of that foreign country up there?" Gerald asked.

Devin shrugged. "I don't know. If we could run across deals like you do. Really, Gerald. I don't know how..."

"You know I always fall into 'em. Okay, Devin, I see you aren't going to sit down, so you might as well get going. Kerry, it's been a pleasure."

"Nice to have you back," Brian said, extending his hand to Devin. "Nice to see you again too, Kerry."

"Thanks, Brian. We'll see you soon. Probably tomorrow."

Nobody felt like unloading the van at 11:30 at night, so after George left, Devin headed for the shower. "Don't fall asleep," he said, smiling.

"What? Sitting on the toilet seat?"

"Oh, you're coming in to talk to me? Far out."

Devin was *home!* At last, I could get a good night's rest. We had all day to be together tomorrow and maybe Monday too. In my total happiness at Devin's return, I lost myself in the nearness of him, with no thoughts of babies or rituals or even Christian, Erick or Him. Devin was home!

I drifted off, secure in Devin's arms, to what should have been the most peaceful night of our relationship. There was no earthly reason for the dream.

The last thing I remember was the hole. A hole at the top of a vertical, cone-shaped tunnel, like the sky peeking through the top of a volcano.

A blue and purple sky.

18 Devin told me later that I screamed.
All I know is that I got out of there quickly.
One minute I was running toward my destination, a gate of some sort. The sentry didn't appear to recognize me at first. I tried to slow down and casually slip by him, but he stopped me with one question.

"You *do* realize you're being watched, don't you?"

I froze in blind panic, unsure of what to do next. Then suddenly, I found myself at the entrance of a huge purple cave-like hole which seemed to stretch, like a tunnel through a hillside, for a mile or more. Staring into it, I saw that it appeared to end at the base of something, like the bottom of a well. At least how the bottom of a well might look to someone standing or leaning over it to draw water.

The conflicting contradiction confused me. I had been running in a straight line from east to west. How, then, could the *end* of west be at the *bottom* of a well?

I floated over to the edge of the tunnel. One thing about this strange place was the convenient manner one could get about. I could walk and stand and run, just like I did back there in my *real* life, but I could do other things as well.

I could fly and bounce high from a dead standstill, and any abstract thought of a different location just landed me there with a single thud. I had to watch my thoughts carefully for fear of losing sight of the tunnel. Attempting to find it had been almost impossible, but when the sentry asked me that question it had terrified me so much that the first mental picture that came to my mind was the hole, the way I had entered to begin with, and now, here I was. But now it was a tunnel.

I looked into the darkness and then behind me. No one was coming. My arm hurt. My right arm. I couldn't remember why. But the hole...*that* I remembered.

It was from watching the hole back in my *real* world that I'd found myself drifting up closer and closer to the top, and then suddenly floating though, over the rim, where it was no longer the *top* at all, but a tunnel coming out of a hillside in a horizontal direction.

But I had entered here *vertically*, through that small hole at the top. And why did I keep forgetting things that happened earlier than this immediate moment.

The tunnel looked inviting now. All I had to do was close my eyes and imagine myself through the entrance.

The two opposing directions screwed up my perspective. I no sooner willed myself straight ahead into the tunnel, through that purplish-blue rocky tunnel, when I found myself in relatively the same position as I had been *before* I'd floated up and through the opening at the top and over the rim.

Everything I saw was through the perspective of my own eyes.

From my view I was floating and slowly drifting down, and from *this* side of the hole, that entrance into the tunnel was now the bluish-purple sky at the top of the volcano-like cone.

This meant that once I'd entered through the top, that world lay beyond the rim of that hole *sideways*.

Now that I was through the hole, I found it impossible to look away from it, and every time I tried I saw the same hole, always appearing to be at the top, even if I looked down. How was I going to get to the bottom where I had started from?

I finally deduced that direction was obviously not a working part of that world and that it only seemed to matter from the bottom when you had that hole up there in your line of vision.

To me this meant that once you went through that opening, you were *sideways* according to physical reality. From that other world's point of view, the *bottom* was the beginning journey to straight *across*. I wondered if that tunnel was also neutral to direction and which world it belonged to. My real world or *that* one.

All I was sure of was that I *had* to get back to my *real* world. Devin was home, and he was *there*, sleeping in my bed. How to get down to the bottom and home?

It seemed logical to try to descend, so I looked up for a point of reference and that's when I saw them.

Giant, shady, moving silhouettes as purple as the tunnel itself. They were hanging...*over the hole*. That was odd. From where *they* were, they should have been visible to me head to toe. Instead, only the upper portions of them were visible.

How could they hang over the entrance of a horizontal tunnel?

From my viewpoint, they were looking down at me from an opening that went straight down. I knew better. Those shadowy things needed only to march in a straight line to get to me. Panic seized me and I pulled all of my terrified concentration into going *down* to the bottom.

To my horror, trying to back up only surfaced me...*closer to the rim*. Closer to *them!*

That must have been when I screamed, and Devin dove from the bed to the wall switch in one leap.

"What's the matter, Kerry, Christ...what *happened?*"

I sat there in trembling horror, thankful to be back in my own bed, unable to shake the lucidity of what I could remember. Whole blocks of time or events were missing, but what I could remember was clearer than my memories of yesterday.

"I don't know. I guess I had a nightmare," I managed to say.

"You're shaking." Devin took both my hands in his. "Do you want to talk about it?"

I shook my head and drew a Winston from his pack on the nightstand. I didn't even want to *think* about it.

The clock read 3:30. Devin turned on the lamp and switched the overhead off. He then propped up pillows, lay back against them, and motioned for me to join him. With the room illuminated with a softer, dimmer light it was easier for me to shake off the dream. I pulled the covers around me and moved closer to Devin. He was warm.

He slid his arm around me and moved the ashtray to his stomach area. "You sure you're okay?"

"Yeah. It was just a bad dream. Real bad."

"Yeah?"

His questioning reply only mirrored my doubts. I had *not* been asleep when I first noticed the hole. I'd been awake and watching it shimmering in my mind. I'd been entranced with it as I'd never seen such a thing with my eyes closed, but I'd been awake. It just didn't make sense.

Devin reached for my cigarette, took a drag, then stubbed it out and set the ashtray back on the nightstand.

"You're still shaking, Kerry."

"I know. It was pretty scary."

"Well, if you don't want to talk about it now...is it okay to turn this lamp off?"

"Sure. I'm awake now. You're here. I'll be okay. You need to get some sleep after that run you just came in from."

He squeezed my shoulder and drew me even closer to him. "Wake me up if you need to, but there's nothing to be afraid of."

He switched off the lamp with his other hand and I lay there counting his heartbeats. I was afraid to go back to sleep, if sleep had, in fact, been where I had been.

Counting his heartbeats was better...anything was better than thinking about what lay beyond that hole.

19 It was daylight when I opened my eyes. Daylight and chilly. Devin must have opened a window last night. Pulling the heavy curtains aside confirmed this and sunlight flooded the room. Everything came together in a sudden flash. Devin was *home.* What the hell was I still doing in bed?

When I entered the living room, the aroma of brewed coffee permeated the air. The reel-to-reel was playing softly, a song by Styx called *You Need Love.* It was welcoming me to a disturbing and unnerving place. What was unnerving to *me* was the similarity of the lyrics to the dream I'd had last night. They sang about flying to a place where there was no tomorrow, and advised me to listen close if I wanted directions to get there…and they said that I *knew* where. At least it talked about how the inhabitants there knew how to laugh and love, and that *that* was all I really needed. Love.

Devin didn't seem to notice the song. I found him amid boxes in the kitchen sorting them into kitchen and bathroom categories. That is, what few boxes that were left. He'd apparently unloaded the van while I'd slept in.

He looked up when I stumbled out, and I tried to focus him into my still sleepy vision. I had an overall feeling of what it must be like to be drugged.

"Hey-hey-hey," he greeted me with a smile. "There's coffee on the stove. I found my percolator. No more of that instant stuff around here anymore."

"Cool." A wave of love and appreciation washed over me. I hugged him and he gave me a chaste kiss on my forehead. "I *still* can't believe it! You're home!" I said.

He pointed to the adhesive-taped message on the cupboards above us. "That was a surprise. I guess I missed it altogether last night." He grinned. "Still had highway hypno, you know?"

"Where's the kids?"

"In their room watching cartoons. I asked them to stay clear until these boxes are out of the way. I'm glad you woke up. I'm not sure where to put some of this stuff." He nodded at a box of pots, pans and silverware.

"I just went through this with Pam. Mix them up with my stuff."

"That's what I did with the sheets and towels. Looks like you could use these. You don't have a lot of pots and pans."

He left for the living room and I began to put the kitchen things away.

"Hey, Ker!" He reappeared in the doorway. "Come in and see Puff!"

"Oh, yeah? He's together?" I got up to follow him.

Puff was indeed all set up. Positioned on his back, white globe resting in his little paws, he looked like he was frolicking in the grass of my green shag carpet holding a world full of flashing twinkle lights.

"Oh, Devin! He's beautiful!"

"Yeah, he *is* cute. I'm gonna turn him off, though. We need groceries. Why don't you and your sister run to the store. I'll stay here with the kids and get this mess organized. We still have to drive back to Gerald's for the rest of the stuff."

"Yeah, and I have to clean up the house and take a shower."

Devin waved that aside with indifference. "I'll clean the house. Go get us some chow, babe. The money's in the drawer in the bedroom."

I surveyed the mess he was surrounded by doubtfully. "I can help you first and then go."

"No, I can do it faster alone. I know what's in these boxes. I packed them, remember?"

When Pam and I returned with the groceries, I didn't recognize the house.

Where my little stereo had once sat on the floor against the paneled wall, an entire fortress of stereo equipment now covered it. The speakers were at least four feet high. The components rested on shelving balanced on black enamel-painted cinderblocks. Expensive turntable and state of the art amplifier...built-in tape decks, both eight-track and cassette, record cabinet full of albums and a stack of reel-to-reel tapes.

To the right of the amp, closer to the floor, was his obvious pride and joy. The large stereo reel-to-reel tape recorder that had introduced me to the first song of many on his recorded reels...the Styx song that had been playing this morning. Apparently, the machine had its own self-contained speakers.

Several paintings leaned against the wall, and four boxes of books were still unpacked. The living room was clear, the house was clean and Devin was ready for the final load.

Pam and the kids put the groceries away while I attacked the books. I couldn't believe anyone could have so many hardcover books. As I sifted through them, I was impressed with the variety. He had everything from Heinlein's fiction, *Stranger in a Strange Land,* to *The Witches' Bible.*

In two other boxes were paperbacks, all subjects dealing with every religion on the planet, and every aspect of the occult. Wicca, demonology, astral projection, astrology, moon phases and books of the dead, both Tibetan and Egyptian. We were definitely going to need some bookshelves.

Meanwhile Devin was dealing out cards from the colorful Tarot deck and frowning. "Come here, lady. Let's see if your future looks any better than mine."

I was well acquainted with the cards as I had my own deck. I shuffled the oversized cards while concentrating on Devin and our future, broke the cards into three stacks, and then, moving to the left, restacked them together again.

Using the Queen of Pentacles as *my* card, Devin dealt out my future reading and scowled again. Then he quickly scattered the cards, grabbed them up and mixed them into the deck again before I could even see what the reading had predicted.

"You don't want to see this, Kerry," he said. "Besides, you can't put too much belief in anything."

"Was it that bad? Why'd you mess them up?"

"Well, mine wasn't so hot either. Maybe just a bad day to be doing them. Probably too much confusion right now. Why don't you take your shower and then we'll take off for Gerald's."

"Okay." Reluctantly I got up, still wondering what had been so bad that he hadn't wanted me to see it. "I think Uncle Joe has a couple of bookcases he isn't using," I added. "Maybe I can talk him out of them."

Trevor and Mia arrived while I was in the shower. I could hear coffee rounds starting up as I reached for the towel. Damn, my arm was sore for some reason. I wrapped the towel around me and, with my left hand, tried to pull the upper part of my right arm towards me so I could see if I had somehow bruised it. The tenderness was in the rear of my right arm, out of my sight and reach. I traced the soreness to the most sensitive spot and opened the bathroom door slightly.

"Devin?"

"Yeah, babe?" All talk ceased in the living room.

"Can you come in here for a minute?"

Devin was there instantly, closing the bathroom door behind him.

"What's up—" He stopped abruptly and frowned. "What's wrong with your arm?"

"It hurts…feels bruised…but it's way behind where I can't see. Could you look?"

Devin touched the spot where I had my fingers. "Move your hand."

I couldn't tell what he was examining so closely. Finally, he released my arm.

"Well, what is it? What does it look like?"

Devin gave me an odd, serious look. "Did you go to a doctor while I was gone?"

"No, of course not. Why would I?"

"Well, that looks like a needle mark," Devin replied. "A hypodermic. But that's hardly a vein area. It's muscle. You can probably see it in the mirror. Look."

He adjusted his shaving mirror and wiped the steam from the magnified side. Then he focused it on the area where the pain was.

It did look like a puncture all right, but it looked like it had been done days ago, the way it would look after a flu shot, but a week later.

"See how the edges are kind of white where the needle went in and the center is red?"

"Devin, there was no *needle.*"

It almost seemed like he wasn't listening. He turned my shoulder closer to the light. "You've got a bruise, babe. A bruise right below the puncture. It looks like a thumb mark. Has anyone grabbed you by the arm, even playing around?"

I twisted my arm around to try to get a real look at the flesh and flinched when I touched the bruise near the prick mark. When I looked up at Devin, our eyes met. He looked really concerned. He turned my arm over in the opposite direction.

On the underside of my arm were four incredibly long impressions of fingermarks. Without a word, Devin rested his thumb over the thumb mark and wrapped his fingers around my arm, taking care not to exert any pressure.

"My thumb isn't as large as this mark on your arm, Kerry, and my fingers don't fit around your arm like those fingermarks do. Look…they don't even point in the direction they should if I'd done this accidently. It looks like two separate hands were involved in this…whatever it is."

He was right. The position of the thumb mark compared to the position of the fingermarks didn't add up to one hand. As if one person had grabbed my arm, thus the fingermarks, and another had positioned their hand over the other's hand and held me firmly for the…shot? The fingermarks were pointed towards my armpit, not straight across as they should have been, and the thumb mark was pointed away from my shoulder, towards my elbow.

He tried his left hand and still found it impossible to fit it over the bright red impressions without changing position of his hand for each mark.

"Well, I couldn't have done it either, Devin. I can't reach around like that with my left hand and get my fingers pointed that way. I haven't been to a doctor, and I'm afraid of needles anyway. You said yourself that it's not a vein area, and no one has grabbed me either. Don't you think I'd remember an exertion with that kind of pressure?"

"Take it easy, lady. We'll figure it out. Hold still." He ran his fingers lightly over the area where I might have had a vaccination mark.

"What's this? Did you have this before?"

I don't know how either of us missed it the first time except that it was above the area of pain and red marks. It almost looked like an outbreak of veins, red against my white skin…like a brand…or a tattoo. It had apparently appeared overnight along with the red marks and the aged needle mark. Four inches diagonal to the prick hole and about an inch below where any vaccination mark might have been. I looked at Devin in horror.

"Devin, that wasn't there before either. I'm sure. I never was vaccinated. At the time I was supposed to be taken in for one, a kid had died from some complications of the vaccination, so the hospital stopped them and conducted an investigation. My parents just never took me back after that. I've won bets with people that I don't have a vaccination mark, and I've shown both arms with other people present. I would have seen something that obvious and they would have too."

Devin dropped my arm and gave me a hard look. "Get dressed. Let Trevor take a look at it. It almost looks like one of those demonic signatures I've seen in some of my books. But it's those red fingermarks that worry me. And the puncture mark."

Those red impressions, instead of fading, were getting darker by the minute. Fear was sprouting roots in my heart. Why didn't *they* hurt, and why wouldn't they just fade away?

I thought of the nightmare and the hole. My arm had hurt while I was there. Could there possibly be a connection?

I heard Devin talking to Trevor and reached for my clothes.

Trevor didn't know what it was either, although he agreed with Devin that the red-veined outbreak did look suspiciously familiar. The pattern was unusual, as though someone had drawn it on my skin with a red pen.

Pammy didn't have any ideas, nor did George, who had arrived while I was in the shower. None of us could come up with a theory that could explain the weird positioning of the thumb and fingermarks other than it being the work of two separate individuals.

For the hell of it, George and Devin applied what pressure they could each muster up of an equal or stronger grip on my left arm. Devin examined it first and there were no puncture, vaccination marks, thumbprints or long fingermarks. Neither of them could apply enough pressure to leave any lasting impressions. Devin had gripped my arm using both hands until his knuckles were white and he could no longer maintain the hold. When he finally released it, there was a similar print as the one on my right arm, but the fingerprints went straight across my inner arm and the thumb pointed towards my shoulder.

By the time we reached Gerald's house, Devin's marks had faded away while the ones on my right arm were beginning to take on a vague purple cast. I pointed out the differences in my two arms to Devin.

"Beats the hell out of me, chick," he said, sliding open the side door of the van, "but I know one thing. We're going to sit down later and see what you can recall of that nightmare."

I was still a little nervous accompanying him to his dad's, especially bringing the kids. When we pulled into his driveway, I was relieved to see that his father's car wasn't there.

"My old man said he'd be here," Devin called back to Trevor. "Let's get out."

Faye opened the door for us. "He just ran to the store. Come on in."

Thor bounded up at the sound of Devin's voice, his undocked tail almost knocking Faye over in the doorway. Devin ordered him back, then stooped to play roughly with him on the hardwood floor.

While he did that, I had an opportunity to really look at the inside of the house. It was as wooden as the outside cedar, not only the walls, but all of the furniture.

The rumble of an approaching motorcycle drifted in through the open windows. Devin and Trevor went outside to greet Brian who'd been test-driving it for Devin that morning. The kids went out to the covered back deck to swing in the hammock, and I lost myself in the bookshelf. Faye began to roll up some joints, seated in Gerald's throne.

"So, like books, do you," she observed aloud with a smile.

"Yeah. I do. What's this one? *Seth Speaks* ? It says...by Jane Roberts."

"Oh, that one's kind of hard to narrow down," Faye replied thoughtfully. "It's a book written by a personality no longer focused in physical reality, though he was at one time."

"You mean a ghost?"

She smiled. "That's one name people call them. Gerald and I don't like the term. The book's interesting, though, and it may answer a few questions regarding Devin's...uh...problem, if that's...uh...what it is."

I looked at her, startled. "Devin told you about it?"

She nodded. We had plenty of time to talk on the way back from up north. He almost had to, really. I've noticed drastic changes in him lately, but I never thought to link it up to a multiple personality or whatever Devin might think it is. He tried to explain."

Apparently, he hadn't explained *everything*. He obviously hadn't mentioned *him*.

I set the book back on the shelf. "Does Devin have that one?"

"He might. I think if you read it, you'd understand the many divisions of the main self a little better, and maybe you could find a category to fit Devin's problem into. I wouldn't worry, though. He seems to be handling it."

Gerald returned a few minutes after that and went out back to meet the kids. When he came back in, he commented on how much they looked like me.

Devin finished the van loading himself, as there wasn't much left to load. Although it didn't look like a lot in the spare room, the van was once again full despite efforts to pack it with consideration for passengers. The leather chair took up a lot of the room.

I was glad when we finally pulled up to our own house…*our* house now, and Devin hopped lightly to the ground.

"We're home, lady." He extended his hand to me. "Watch your sore arm."

I yawned. "I'm too tired to unload this van right now."

"Don't you give it any thought. I can handle everything."

By ten o'clock that night, the house had undergone plastic surgery. The desk was gone, carted away by George's Jeep and his utility trailer, along with the red armchair. The fridge was now in the kitchen.

I had salvaged the heavy desktop, a solid piece of oak, wood so heavy it almost needed two people to lift it. I told Devin I wanted to paint a picture on it someday…maybe the Tarot card version of *The Magician*. We stored it in the rear of the water heater closet where Pam had packed away a lot of her unneeded things.

I had even gotten hold of Uncle Joe, and George picked up the bookshelves for me. I was anxious to get through some of Devin's books. I hadn't forgotten that dream and the by now purple bruises on my arm that were not disappearing rapidly as Devin's attempts on my other arm had. Nor had I forgotten that crazy sideways world at the rim of the hole. Other than the sentry and the shadowy figures, I didn't remember any other living things during that dream state, so I didn't really attribute it to having any connection to the world *he* spoke of. Somewhere in Devin's books, even the ones on possession, there had to be some explanations.

While I arranged the books into their proper categories, I took the time to scan through them before I put them in place. Devin even took time out of his stereo wiring and hookups to explain some of the books, and I asked his opinion on which one I should read first.

"Which one you *should* read first, or which one would I like to *see* you read first?"

"Well?" What kind of a choice was that?

"*Journeys out of the Body* might be a good one for you to start with." He then nodded to the pile of paintings stacked against the shelves. "Have you seen any of these yet? Here's the one I told you about." He placed a framed pastel chalk picture in my hands. "Guess who?"

Artwise, the picture was a masterpiece. The subject matter could have grown hair on a nun's chest. It vaguely resembled a black man of the future although it was dated 1973. This large-headed figure was clearly a demon, his horns a dead giveaway. He had long slender fingers and exaggeratedly pointed ears. It was a profile, and in his long black fingers was a gray rock. He had one arm raised in the air, as if in allegiance to something or someone. He appeared to be demanding admittance…but admittance to what?

"Christian?" I raised my eyebrows and he nodded.

"I don't know if the living room is a good place for it," he said.

"The living room is a perfect place for it."

"But you have friends…human friends who might not understand it. Christian did it and he's proud of it. Oh, he knows it's an exaggerated statement of what people here think we are or look like. And you know his sense of humor. People wouldn't understand if—"

"If what? Look. There's already a nail up there." I placed the picture up on the left side of the paneled wall over the stereo equipment. "See?"

Devin shrugged. "As long as you don't mind."

He had another one he wanted to hang tonight, the big Witches' Wheel that he had painted himself. We hung it over the stereo equipment in the center above the plank that held Puff. The couch wall was decidedly bare though.

"I have a little Scorpio plaque that matches the Virgo one I got you," Devin said. "We can hang those two opposite each other and that would balance out that wall a little."

The Virgo plaque was already on the wall where the tapestry had once hung, so it was easy to hang the Scorpio to balance. "The thing is, now…where we gonna put the altar?" Devin asked.

The altar was a marble-topped, octagon-shaped cabinet with a classy bone handle. It opened to store things.

"What's in it right now?" I asked him.

"Oh, all the working tools of the trade. Cup, Athame, The Book of Shadows, you know. All the props."

"Oh, full moon supplies, huh?"

"Yeah. That reminds me." He reached into his pocket and extracted the tiny ring I'd given him to charge. "All set. I charged it on the road and it doesn't tighten up anymore. Unless you want to test it yourself, I think it's safe to give back to Michelle."

"She doesn't want it."

"Whatever. You keep it then. It's safe for anybody. We'll have matching rings."

"Hey, let's leave the rest of this mess until tomorrow. There's nothing left in the van, and you've got to go to work tomorrow. Or are you really thinking about taking Monday off, too. I know you're cleared for it. They aren't expecting you."

"I don't know. I haven't decided yet. I should just not go in, however…"

"However?"

"Yeah, we'll see. Let's see if I've got this wired right. I've been at it for hours. There's a lot to hook up." He switched on the radio and it powered right up, already set on the station we usually listened to. "Far out," he said with a smile. "It's good to have that music back. Tomorrow I'll introduce you to my reel- to-reels. Now…how about that dream?"

I sighed. I was so tired and didn't really want to talk about it, but I supposed it had to be dealt with in light of the marks that had turned up on me this morning. I told him everything and he listened quietly, showing concern when I told him of the sentry's remark that I was being watched. He was quiet for a long time after I finished. Then he reached for the radio dial. "Let's see what *they* have to say."

The volume had been low and the deejay was just announcing the next song. Of course, a Uriah Heep song, and it burst forth with a fast rock beat that didn't mince words, once again. The song was called *Look at Yourself,* and the first words silenced us both. They saw me running and didn't know what I was running away from. Nobody was coming. What had I done that was so wrong? I needed to know that I had a friend, and that friend was myself. They said not to be afraid…just to look at my*self.* They said there was no reason to hide and that if I needed help, or only just love, to just look at my*self.* As if the singers had been there in the dream with me and, even more eerie, as if Devin had known what song would be next. As usual, the radio was right on. As usual, Devin didn't seem surprised.

"I kind of like that idea of going to bed," he said, ignoring what the radio had played. He winked and motioned for the back room.

"That means you're planning on sticking around tonight?" I teased him.

"What you see is what you get, chick," he retorted, shutting the radio down and rising to head towards the bedroom.

I followed, closing the bedroom door behind us.

There weren't any more holes or nightmares that night. There was only Devin.

But my arm was still sore.

Part Three

Welcome to My Nightmare

"Radio beams are waves of electromagnetic energy. They vibrate at various frequencies, and we separate them or tune them by adjusting the length of the waves with coils and condensers. Your local radio station is broadcasting a signal of electrical pulses, each pulse adjusted to a specific length. When you tune your radio to the station, you move a series of metal plates which sort out the various wavelengths and enable your radio to pick up and amplify only the signal coming in at a certain point—or frequency—of the electromagnetic spectrum.

Your eyes are also receivers tuned to very specific wavelengths of the spectrum, and they turn the signals from those wavelengths into pulses which are fed to your brain. Your brain, in turn, is also a very sophisticated, little-understood receiver, and it is tuned to wavelengths far beyond the receiving capabilities of manufactured electronic instruments. Most people are running around with crude biological "crystal sets" in their heads and are not consciously receiving any of the sophisticated signals. However, about one-third of the world's population possesses a more finely tuned instrument. These people experience telepathy, prophetic dreams, and other bizarre signals from some central source. If you are one of that 30 percent, you know precisely what I mean. If you belong to the larger, ungifted two-thirds, you probably regard all this as nonsense, and we may never be able to convince you otherwise."

John A. Keel
UFOs: Operation Trojan Horse
Copyright 1970 by John A. Keel
Originally published by G.P. Putnam's Son

1 "What the hell is this?"
Lola stood in the doorway, a company memo in hand, and surveyed the contents of the room, namely Kelly and me.

"That, Mother, is the change of address that nosy Kim keeps asking me for," I said.

"*This* is a change of address?" She burst into laughter and began to read it aloud.

This is to notify you to make an adjustment on your 1974 Christmas card list.

As of December 1, 1974, Devin Drew has moved out of his previous residence and is now sinfully residing in the home of Kerry King at 666 Crowley Lane, and they are brazenly carrying on their scandalous behavior. Please adjust your Christmas address list as such.

Also, at their housewarming party, you are all invited over for coffee (before it clots), and chocolate mousse, (laced with tannis root.) Please be careful, as you enter their home, not to knock over the tombstone just inside the door. Don't be alarmed by the altar in the middle of the room, but I would advise you to come after midnight because, by then, all the sacrifices will have ended.

Also, I want to respectfully add that when and if they send out a wedding announcement, it will be in the form of a rumor, to assure that it reaches everybody's ears.

P.S. The parties involved will be sending out voodoo dolls for Christmas. Let's hope you don't get one with pins stuck in it.

Merry Christmas to all and to all a good night!

Lola had a hard time reading it without cracking up, and when she was finished she had to wipe tears from her eyes. "Does Kim have a copy of this?"

"She has the original." Kelly and I exchanged mischievous looks. It had only taken fifteen minutes for us to put it together. "Well, she *did* ask for it in writing," I said, holding both palms out and up in a *what?* position.

Lola turned towards her office, still shaking her head. "You're both nuts. I gather Devin is home now?"

"Yup!" I knew my face was shining. I was in elation mode.

"When did he get in?"

"Saturday. Early evening."

"He must have *flown* that van," Kelly added. "Up north and back in three days."

"Well, they had two driving, though," Lola said with a shrug. "Apparently, it can be done."

"Look at her, Lola. She's all radiant today."

"So I see. Where's Hannah?"

"I don't know. Late, I guess."

Punching in that morning had been fun. I knew Devin had blown their minds by walking in Monday morning when he was technically still off, and my arrival shortly after his was blessed with the friendliest greeting I had ever received from Tim. I'd never seen him so jubilant, and when I poked my head in for a quick "good morning," Pat beamed warmly at me.

"Hey, Ker! How are ya'?"

"Great," I replied.

"Man, did Devin ever do some trucking, huh?"

I managed to contain my swelling pride in Devin. People just couldn't seem to grasp how he had made that trip in three days and then shown up Monday when no one could have known he'd returned early.

"He does get on with it," I agreed. "Where's he at now?"

"Where else? On a route for a no-show."

"Good thing *he* showed, but I guess that means I won't see him all day."

"Aw…poor kid! It could be hours, you know?"

Tim turned to me. "Kerry, I really do appreciate Devin's coming in today. We're two men short on the trucks and two more are on vacation. I don't know what we would have done without Devin today. I know he could have stayed out and we'd have never known he was back."

I laughed. "You know Devin. He can't stay away. Besides…" I added, feigning false modesty, "how could he stay home with *me* here all day?"

Tim raised his eyebrows and looked at Pat, who nodded in agreement. "We can certainly understand *that*," Pat said kindly.

And so it went for the rest of the day. I was bombarded by congratulations from romantic office girls and stunned routemen. Even Charlie, the general manager, acknowledged Devin's new residence verbally. It was as if we'd eloped over the weekend.

To look at me would seem to confirm such a rumor. My happiness was so obvious that Kelly remarked on it at lunchtime.

"So! How's it feel kid?"

I thought a moment, just to give her pause, then grinned. "Good!"

"Good? That's all? And get that smirk off your face."

"You ought to see Devin."

"Yeah," she retorted good-naturedly. "He oughta be happy. He's getting laid again."

I just laughed at her.

"I see you got your ring back," Kelly remarked between spoonfuls of soup. "Did he remember to hocus-pocus it?"

"Yeah, he did. It fits fine now. Boy, Kelly, you think *I've* got weird books. You should see his. And boxes and boxes of them."

"Oh, I can imagine. If you combined them, you could probably both quit the water hole and open up your own library. I've got to stop by and see your house! Were you kidding about the altar?"

"No, but it's not in the middle of the room. You've got to see the dragon, though. And he's still looking for the tombstone. He's had it packed away for so many years that he can't remember what he did with it."

Kelly shook her head. "Dragons, tombstones and altars. Why don't you charge for tours through there? You've got *my* admission." She pushed her chair back to get up and slapped me playfully on the arm.

It was the wrong arm to swat.

"Owww…hey," I howled as my left hand moved to cover the sore part of my right arm.

"Well, Jeez! I'm sorry! I barely touched you."

"Oh, that's okay, Kel…It's just, well, look."

It only hurt when I bumped it or when someone like Kelly had a good aim. I unbuttoned my sleeve and pulled it up over the funny-looking mark, my finger covering the needle mark without having to look at it. I carefully prodded for soreness around it. "See that?"

Kelly eyed me with alarm. "Kerry, will you pull your sleeve down before we get arrested? You look like you're getting ready to shoot up."

"No, look!"

She stopped short. "Jesus Christ, Kerry! Did Devin do that to you?"

I shook my head. "First of all, why would he, and secondly he couldn't have. He was gone."

"How long have you had this?" Kelly sounded genuinely concerned.

The thumb and finger bruises were now completely black-and-blue. In twenty-four hours, they had gone from red welts to this.

"Yesterday they were as red as a beet. And I don't know what *this* is, but Devin says it looks like a needle mark."

Kelly didn't say anything. She knew how I felt about needles.

"What does it look like to you, Kelly?"

"I don't know. It does look like a puncture, but you said it just turned up yesterday? That looks more like an old puncture mark that never quite healed over. And, holy cow, what's *that?*" She pointed to the tiny red veinlike marking. "*That* wasn't there before!"

At one time, Kelly had been one of the bettors that I had to have a vaccination mark. I pulled my sleeve down. "We both know it wasn't. This all showed up yesterday morning, right after I took a shower. At least that's when I noticed them. Devin had come in Saturday night but we just picked up some of his things from his dad's, came home and went to bed. No one grabbed my arm."

"Well, from the looks of those bruises, it looks like whoever did this knew how you felt about needles. It looks like two hands had to hold your arm to give you that shot."

"Kelly, there *was* no *shot!*"

"Are you sure Devin didn't give you the fingermarks by accident? Like excited to see you, grab you a little too rough?"

"Kel, I was wide awake when he arrived, I was wide awake during the trip to his dad's and all through the packing of the van. I was wide awake when we went to bed. He was exhausted, as you can well imagine. And when I showed this to him after my shower, he tried to make those same marks on my other arm on purpose, and so did George. And they used two hands to apply the pressure. That hurt, but those marks faded away in an hour. These didn't, obviously."

"Well, what *did* Devin think it was?"

"He doesn't know what to make of it. He asked me if I'd been to a doctor while he was gone."

"I'd show Lola."

Lola's reaction was pretty much the same as Kelly's initial one. If Devin hadn't done it, then who had?

The funny part was that only the "needle" mark hurt. The rest just looked bad.

The drivers' area was packed. I pushed through the swinging doors and made my way to the time clock. It had been a hectic day, and I knew we had an even more hectic night to look forward to.

"Hey, Ker…Devin's waiting outside for you," Daniel called as I passed.

"Hey, Ker!" That voice came from my left. I poked my head in the route room. It was a mass of confusion. At least nine drivers were still racing against time to balance their sheets so they could punch out. I was surprised to see Joey Burns among them. He was usually one of the first ones done, and I suspected that more guys than Devin had picked up the extra load today. "If you're looking for Devin, he's in the office with Tim." Joey wiggled his eyebrows to indicate an important meeting. "He told me to hold you here until he's done." He made a playful grab for me and I wriggled out of his grasp, laughing.

"Yeah, I'll bet. Tell him I'll be outside."

"Well, he's the big superstar just because he came to work today. Shit, I came to work today but nobody's giving *me* any medals."

"Well, it's too crowded in here. Tell him I'll be out there."

"Okay, but don't leave. He said he wouldn't be long."

Minutes later Devin and Pat emerged, laughing and shoving each other.

"You just give me a couple days to get settled, Jack," Devin was saying. "There's going to be some drastic changes in this place pretty soon."

"Why don't you start with a haircut, Dev?" Pat teased, then ducked. "Hi, Kerry!"

"Hi, Pat!" I watched with amusement. Whatever that meeting was about, it wasn't bad. Devin wrapped his arms around me with exhilaration and lifted me up for a kiss as the wind blew up, sweeping his Sparklear cap to the ground. Pat bent to retrieve it.

"Wait till you hear the news, babe. Thanks, Pat. Hey, I'll catch you tomorrow. We gotta split."

"Don't forget the haircut, Devin."

"Oh, buzz off!" He slammed the cap back on his head, and it settled comfortably in his wind-blown curls. "Come on, babe." He reached for my hand. "Oh, you gotta pick up the kids, huh?"

"Yeah. You go ahead home. I'll be right behind you. What's the good news?"

He pulled my jacket collar up to shield me from the wind, and put his arm around me as we walked. "Well, this is unofficial but, man, Tim's so freaked out that I showed up today that he called me and Pat in to discuss the new positions after he leaves. Pat's pretty excited too, 'cause it must be getting close, and we do work pretty well together. Man, do I ever feel good! Do you realize the money I'll be making?"

"Whoa, slow down. Is that why you were in there so long?"

Devin's face was glowing. "Yeah. He must have thanked me thirty times for coming to work today. I can't believe it meant that much to him."

"When is all this supposed to happen?"

"Well, he says rumor has it that it'll be within the next couple months. Tim goes to Chicago, and Pat and I take over here. I'm *in*. Pretty cool, huh?"

I hugged him tightly, that elated feeling only increasing as he talked.

He returned the hug, then gently eased away. "Damn, chick, you are going to spoil me. Hey, let's get moving so we can go home and do this. *Home*."

We parted at the vehicles, and I left to pick up the kids. When I finally pulled up to the house, I wasn't prepared for the scene that greeted me. The windows were all open and the drapes were drawn, something I rarely did. Every light in the house seemed to be on, and light flooded the yard as I shut off the engine.

"Hey, Mommy! Devin's here. Devin's here!" Michelle squealed as she spotted the van.

"He *lives* here now, Mommy said," Mandy said, a huge smile on her face.

As soon as the car stopped, Michelle bolted from it, Mandy close at her heels. I followed at a somewhat slower pace, entered the house, and stopped dead in my tracks.

The house was immaculate. The aroma of gravy simmering on the stove filled the house, and from those huge speakers came that weird music I was always hearing on the radio. The reel-to-reel was running, and the tape moved at a crawl. Such a huge tape. At the pace it was moving, it must have contained eight hours of music or more. The song playing was a Crosby, Stills, Nash and Young song, singing about our house being a very fine house, and said that life used to be hard, but now everything was easy because of me. Once again, Devin couldn't have known when I was going to pull in.

Pammy waved at me from the couch.

"Hi, Pam. Where's Devin?"

"He went up to get some potatoes. I told him the kids wouldn't eat rice."

"What's with all the lights on?" I flipped a couple overheads off. Apparently, Devin didn't have any problem with bright lights and fresh air.

"I don't know. It was like this when I woke up. Kind of a refreshing change, huh?"

"I guess."

I went into the bedroom to change. It too was completely in order. I opened a drawer in the dresser. Devin's socks and T-shirts were folded neatly there, and his dress shirts hung in the closet. There were crisp clean sheets on the bed, folded down for the night.

I heard the front door shut as I pulled off my blouse to examine the marks on my arm. The muscles were sore and the marks were a deep purple. I tried to position myself in front of the mirror so I could get a better look at them when I heard a light tap at the door.

"Devin?"

"Yeah, it's me." The door opened and he entered, caught sight of what I was trying to do and laid his hand on my shoulder. "Hey! How's your arm today?"

I turned it towards him. "Sore. I can't figure out what that little red thing is."

"Yeah, we'll have to look that up. Maybe we'll get some time tonight. Once all the books are on the shelves, I'll show you where to look. Oh, Pam says the kids won't eat rice."

"No, but they do love potatoes."

"There's pork chops in the oven." He sat down on the bed and propped a pillow up against the wall. "Come here a second. I haven't seen you all day."

His eyes had that intense gleam in them, and I didn't need a program to realize that Devin had finally, after two days, taken a stage break. I tugged a T-shirt from its hanger in the closet and slipped it over my head... a little uncomfortable under his scrutiny. I wasn't *that* used to him.

He smiled. "What'd you do that for?"

"Well, Pam's out there. I think I need to get dressed."

"She's keeping an eye on the dinner. We have a few minutes." He lit a cigarette, took a drag, and handed it to me. "Your sister and I met this afternoon, although she wasn't aware of *me*. I am home now and, of all places, I should be able to relax and be myself here."

"But Pammy *will* notice the difference eventually. Try to be easy on her. She's really into the Jesus thing, and if you try to tell her who *you* really are..."

His features softened. "She's a good kid, really, but she is sharp. I wouldn't be able to pull the wool over her eyes for very long, not that I'd want to. We're all going to be together in this house, so don't worry. By the time Pammy really realizes who I am, she will already...uh...be used to me." He extended his hand. "Fair enough?"

We shook on it and went out to relieve Pammy of the stove duties.

I set up the kids' little table for their dinner, and Devin set the coffee table for three. The song currently playing on the large reel-to-reel was George Harrison's *Beware of Darkness*, and I didn't get a chance to listen to the lyrics because Devin got up to change the song, he said, to a more dinner table selection. He moved the tape ahead to a song performed by Styx. *Lady*, an easy ballad about love. I thought that was probably better than the one telling me to beware of darkness.

"I'd like to see what all you have on those tapes of yours," Pammy said.

"Oh, you'll hear enough of them, most assuredly. Those tapes have been a project of mine for several years. I'm putting the songs together in a special order for a special reason. By the way, how's the rice?"

"Great," she said. "I think me and Ker will let you do all the cooking from now on."

"Devin makes good lumpy mashed potatoes too," Michelle announced loudly from the den, and we all smiled.

"I like to cook," Devin said. "It gives me a chance to be creative. Besides, I've always been self-sustaining. I can also sew and clean a house and wash and iron, just like you ladies do, so let's keep it equal around here. No one waits on me."

Pam laughed. "Devin, you doing *everything* around here is not keeping it equal." She turned to me. "Kerry, even after I woke up and saw him doing all the work, he wouldn't let me help him."

I watched her for signs of recognition of *his* presence, but she just seemed to be enjoying the conversation.

"You've got some pretty neat albums," she added. "I was going through some of them while you were at work today."

"Did you play any of them? You can, you know, anytime."

"Me and George couldn't figure out how to work that set of yours. Too many buttons."

"It's very simple, really." He pushed away his plate and got up. "Kerry, you pay attention too. You might want to play it someday when I'm not here. Especially after the promotion. No telling how late I'll be coming home, then."

He went through a simple demonstration so we'd all know how to run the stereo. It was all in the buttons and didn't look too difficult.

"I usually use the tape recorder here," he said, touching the reel-to-reel. "Most of my music is on those tapes. In fact, Kerry, I want to play a couple things for you tonight. One in particular."

"Which one is that?"

"It's called *War of the Gods*, by an artist named Billy Paul. I hope I can find it. Not many of those reel boxes are marked."

"How do you know where anything is, then?"

"I know the boxes, that's all. Anyhow, this Billy Paul usually does nightclub music, such as *Me and Mrs. Jones*. More of a blues thing, but one day he came out with this one and blew everyone away. It isn't anything like nightclub music, and it takes up most of one side of the album. It's probably ten minutes long. Compared with the rest of the album, the song just sticks out like a sore thumb."

"Wow, it sounds *neat*," Pam said. "I hope you can find it."

"I'll see if I can dig it up. One thing you have to do, though, is really listen to what the man is saying. It's not what it appears to be on the surface. A lot of people mistake the meaning of the song if they aren't really listening. There's a message there to anyone who believes in *anything*—God, or the Devil, or any of the religions."

After the dinner dishes were cleared away and the kids bathed and watching television in their room, I went back to the bookshelf to finish arranging the books.

"It's going to take her all night if she keeps trying to read them first," Pammy observed with amusement.

Someone knocked at the door.

"That's Trevor, I hope," Devin said, looking up. "Come on in. It's open."

"Hey, bro." Trevor entered with Mia. "We left the kids at the sitter's to see if you can use some help getting settled. Looks like you're almost finished, though."

"Yeah, thanks, man, but I'm pretty much in. Kerry's just anxious to look through all the books. Hey, lady, take a break."

I pushed the box aside reluctantly, a book still in my hand. "Hi, guys. Boy, this is like Christmas to me."

Mia smiled. "I can imagine. He's got some good ones, huh?" Mia seemed to be more open and less shy than she'd been the first couple times I'd seen her. Apparently, she was adjusting to the unconventional life even as I was trying to, but I doubted she had as much to adjust to. She definitely didn't seem timid or afraid of the occult now.

"I wish I could read them all at once. Hey, Dev…that big painting…the *Witches' Wheel*…did you paint that?"

"About three or four times. I change it every six months or so."

"It's got some weird writing on it. Where'd that come from?"

"It's in one of the books there on the shelf. *Mastering Witchcraft*. It's got a black jacket…by Paul Huson, I believe." He gave Trevor a knowing look, as if they were both familiar with the book's content. "Now, *there's* a good one for you to start with," Devin added dryly. "*The Catholic Digest* calls it a do-it-yourself book on witchcraft."

Trevor laughed. "Ain't that a crock of shit."

I looked over the books on the shelf and found it. "This it?"

Devin nodded. "The witches' wheel drawing is in the front of the book. That weird writing you asked about is called Theban Script, and you'll find that alphabet in there too."

I did. I looked over the alphabet and then up at Devin. "I'm going to learn this alphabet," I told him. "I bet you I know it by tomorrow."

Devin gave me an indulgent smile. "I don't doubt it." He picked up a tablet from the stereo shelf. "Here. Try it."

I busied myself with practicing the letters, and Pam waved to get Devin's attention.

"Devin, have you actually read all those books?"

"No. Some of them I just use for reference. Most of those books aren't like a novel that you'd read cover to cover."

"Do you *have* any novels in there?"

"A few. *The Exorcist* is one, but I don't recommend it. Too negative. Puts too many fear programs in people. Ever read *Stranger in a Strange Land*?"

"I've heard of it," I said, looking up.

"Grok," Devin said, grinning. "That one's in there too. *Supposedly* Science Fiction."

"Grok!" Trevor repeated, returning Devin's grin, as though the word was the most hilarious joke in the world.

"That's a Martian word," Devin explained. "You have to read the book to understand the word."

"Oh," I said. They'd lost me.

Devin took the trouble to explain. "That book is about a human that was taken to Mars and raised Martian until he actually became one. Then he was brought back to earth years later, you know, whacked out, if you like Martian survival stories."

With that, he and Trevor exchanged smiles as though they truly knew something that the rest of the world was ignorant of.

"All right. What's the big secret?" I asked.

"Well, how would you like to be the only earthling on Mars? People staring at you because you're different? Shit!"

"I grok that," Trevor added. "Or the only Martian on earth."

Devin was busy with his reel-to-reel, determined to find that song. "I know it's here. Well, it will come on soon enough if I just keep playing the tapes in order. They all get played eventually."

"How many tapes do you have?" I asked.

"Reels? There will be ten when I'm finished. I believe there are eight or nine now. This music goes back to the late sixties…early seventies, up to the present. All these songs were scattered over the years, recorded by various artists from all over the world. No one really got the messages in them because they were so scattered among regular pop music. I'm putting them all together so that there will be a volume of ten tapes. If the human race can't see a thread of messages running through all this music after it's completed, then there's no hope for the planet. Shit. That reminds me. I promised to make George an eight-track tape. *And* I've got to fix your ring. I think I'll do that right now."

"Oh, you got the stuff to fix it?"

"Yes. I picked it up today." He reached for the ring and eye sitting alone on the stereo speaker.

Pammy made us a round of coffee, and we all settled back to listen to the music. Currently playing was a Moody Blues tune, singing that they were just singers in a rock and roll band and not to tell them that's all they were. They'd found the key, they'd broken the language barriers, and if we wanted the winds of change to blow about us we'd better not tell them they were mere singers in a rock and roll band. The melody was catchy and the words were clear. We all found something to do as we listened to the song.

Mia was looking through one of Devin's books, I was practicing the alphabet, Pammy was bringing in the coffee and Trevor was sketching something on another tablet. Devin was fixing my ring.

I stopped my practicing to see what Trevor was drawing. It was just a sketch of an ordinary tree standing alone on the ground. I wondered why anyone would draw just a lone tree. Devin also looked up from the ring repair to observe the sketch and the two locked eyes for a minute.

"My brother used to be a tree," Devin told me, reading my mind as usual. "At one time, I mean."

"Yeah? Were *you* a tree at one time, too?"

He handed me the ring. "Me? I don't stick to one form long, lady. You should know that."

I felt a twist in my gut at his words. "How long do you think you'll stick to this one?" I ventured to ask.

"Oh, I might be around a little longer than I intended," he replied. "We've got a son to bring in, remember?"

I didn't answer. I'd been hoping *that* subject wouldn't be brought up so soon. Erick and Christian hadn't even popped in tonight, so I supposed it was inevitable that it would come up sooner or later.

Trevor stood up. "We've got to split. When are you two coming down to our place?"

"Soon." Devin followed them to the door. "I'm still tying up loose ends here from the moving."

"You did all right," Trevor said with a sweeping glance over the room. "Place looks pretty good."

"Yeah, but there are still a few boxes to go through. Oh, Kerry, that reminds me. My notebooks and stuff…remember I told you I kept journals too? They're all in the altar with the craft supplies. Feel free to go through them anytime you want. I don't have any secrets from you."

We walked them to the car and waved them off. Devin put his arm around me carefully, taking care not to brush against the sore spot.

"It's cold out here for you," he said. "Let's go inside."

2 Pammy didn't have time to wait around for Billy Paul. She had to get to work, so she told us to save it for her if we found it. After her car pulled away, *He* walked over to the couch and patted it for me to join him.

"I'm kind of glad it's you tonight," I told him, following him to the couch. "I have questions for you. Questions that Devin and Erick and Christian won't or can't answer. And I *have* asked them."

"That doesn't surprise me—listen!" He held up a hand to silence me. The tape was emitting a weird sound that wasn't too far from what I'd expect a landing flying saucer to emit.

"Hey-hey-hey!"

So different from the way Devin said it. With Devin, it actually meant hey-hey-hey, but when *he* said it, it seemed to mean something like *there it is,* or *so, you figured it out.*

He got up to adjust the knobs on the set and returned to me, that UFO sound still vibrating throughout the house. Then other instruments followed, accompanied by some wailing voices that sounded like the chanting of a distant coven. He motioned for me to listen. That music went on for at least a minute or two before the lyrics began.

"The words, lady. Listen to the words."

I nodded and he stretched out on the couch across my lap so that he could reach the ashtray on the floor. His back to me, most of his weight rested on his left elbow which he propped up near the arm of the couch. My hand automatically reached down to rub his shoulder as the song's lyric began.

The first words claimed that the time had come for bad things to end and for life to begin. It was time for a war of the Gods.

A feeling of awe began to creep over me. Billy sang in a soulful voice, pleasant to listen to. I knew there was a reason Devin wanted me to hear this song, so I turned my full attention to it.

The next words were talking directly to Lucifer, calling him a god of hate and evil.

I glanced down at Devin, whose attention seemed to be attracted to something in the corner of the room, so I closed my eyes to try to understand the full message of the song.

Now Billy was telling Lucifer that he was seen every day, and called him the father of the lie. He accused him of being the master of tricks and having no shame.

When I opened my eyes, I saw that Devin was still intently watching that corner. The song droned on. Most of the words were crystal clear.

Now Billy was asking Lucifer if he had time to get his army ready, reminding him that love conquers all and wondering if he would stand or fall. He was telling Lucifer that Satan the Devil was his name.

I couldn't tell if he was for or against Lucifer. A picture of a noble lord came to my mind. A fiery god with a sword hanging loosely in his hand, not beaten so much as merely resigned. If the song was against the Devil, why would Devin have wanted me to hear it, and why put so much emphasis on really listening to the lyrics, to really understand what the song was actually saying? I tried to consider this fallen angel's point of view—his side of the story—as the song continued. Devin remained still, gaze fixed on that corner, every once in a while glancing up at the ceiling as though following a light or the path of a spider. I closed my eyes again.

Now Billy seemed to have shifted his thinking, saying that God was merely a title, and it was no different than calling someone president or general, preacher or father.

My interest really picked up now. Was Billy saying that God and Satan could be one and the same? It sounded like he was implying that there was one Supreme Being with many names, and he just wanted to be on the side of the real God.

Now he was listing all the names of all the gods people worshipped, from Allah to Hare Krishna and stating that they were all men, and now added that people even called Jesus "God" as well.

The room seemed to take a sudden drop in temperature. Maybe it was only the lyrics making my flesh crawl, but I could feel goosebumps erupting on my bare skin. I continued rubbing Devin's shoulder, my eyes closed. Devin remained motionless throughout the song.

Now Billy was telling Lucifer that there were rewards to those who knocked on his door…peace, eternal life and love. He declared that it was true that there was only one God, but the names were all not the same, and he seemed to be saying that one day the world would know Lucifer's great name.

A finger poked me sharply in the sore arm and I jumped. My first thought was that Devin had done it to emphasize the words I had just heard and to make sure I was paying attention. But how could he have poked me? His back was to me, one hand was on my knee and his head rested in his other hand, still propped up with his elbow.

Devin felt me jump and turned around quickly. "What's wrong?"

Fear washed over me. "You didn't do that, did you, Devin."

"Do what?" He got up and stopped the song. I sat there frozen in place, my left hand covering my sore arm, afraid it might happen again.

"I felt you jump! What happened? Lady, you're white as a sheet."

"Devin, something just poked me hard…in the arm. My sore arm. It was a definite finger poke!"

He sat down and took me in his arms. "Hey, lighten up. I figured *something* happened, but whatever it was, I'm sure it's nothing to be afraid of. Believe me, lady, fear will produce the very results that bred it to begin with. Look at you. You're shaking."

"Well, how would you like to be sitting there listening to a song and have some…some…"

"Spirit?" Devin supplied the word with a smile. "You're afraid of a mischievous little spirit?"

"How do you know that's what it was?"

"Well, it couldn't have been me unless I have three arms. No one else is here and, besides, I felt it too. Not the poke, but the presence of something. In fact, I've been aware of it since the song began." He nodded towards the corner where the left speaker sat. I looked over to see what had kept him so motionless during the song.

A mass of purplish-blue light vibrated in that corner, like a tiny flashing light. It seemed to be made of the same stuff auras were, and the color was pretty close to what radiated from *him*. A memory flashed through my mind and a feeling of déjà vu…a similar bluish-purple cloud that had enveloped my windshield one morning a few months ago. A larger version of this one, but still the same.

"Can you *see* that?" I didn't take my eyes off it, but it floated over Christian's self-portrait, casting a shadow of blue, and then returned to the corner, waxing and waning as if breathing. It was mobile. It had direction. It seemed to be alive.

"No, I can't see it," he replied, "but I know he's there…even when he moves away…like now!"

I watched the bluish cloud float from the corner out towards the kitchen. Devin's eyes seemed to follow it. Pretty good for someone who can't see him, I thought. Then aloud I said, "That's okay, as long as he stays out there."

Devin lit a cigarette and took a drag. "I don't understand why you're so upset. So a *spirit* touches you. Big deal. Can you imagine what an accomplishment that must be to him, or it, or any nonphysical personality?"

I shuddered. The floating ball of blue had disappeared.

"Watch it," Devin said with a smile. "The last time I lost track of him was when *you* jumped."

I looked around the room. I'd lost track of it too. "Well, he'd better not do it again."

Devin sighed and went into the bedroom. I followed him. "Hey! You're not leaving me out here alone with that thing!"

"What are you *afraid* of? Hell, I wish he'd touch *me* !" Devin turned to me. "Lady, he can't want to hurt you. I was trying to establish some kind of communication with him during the song, but he doesn't appear to dig my presence too much. Why don't you sit out there and see what he wants?"

I shivered. "Devin, it feels weird. I don't…want…to."

"Okay. It's your body, and certainly your prerogative, but I wish you'd give him a chance. Maybe he wants something. Maybe he's trying to tell you something. Personally, I think he *loves* you."

"Loves me? Fine way to show it, by scaring me out of my wits."

"Well, why else would he want to touch you? It can't be sex! What would he need with *sex* ?"

"Okay." I took a deep breath. "I'll try."

I returned to the couch and sat there nervously. Devin restarted the tape and then went back in the bedroom.

He had no sooner shut the bedroom door when a crawly feeling inched its way up my arm, towards the bruises. It had warmth and weight...like a hand touching as lightly as it could. It felt like a feather. Terror began to build inside me, but I was more afraid to try to move away from it than to just sit there.

The tickly sensation stopped at the top of my shoulder and suddenly began to trail across my cheek gently, like a cobweb brushing my face.

That did it!

I shot into the bedroom where Devin looked up as the door burst open, sighed and shook his head. "Okay. Stay in here with me. He won't come near me anyway. I can't blame you, I guess."

Billy Paul continued in the living room, singing that he wanted to be with God when they started the fighting, and that God had kicked Lucifer out of Heaven for not paying his rent. Damn, that was one long song.

"Jesus, Devin. It's easy for *you* to tell me to sit there and take it. I just don't like him...touching me." I shuddered visibly. "What right does he have..."

"Does he touch you in any...improper places?" Devin asked with a smile.

"No. Just my arm...and...my face."

"See what I mean? He loves you. How long has he been hanging around here?"

"I've never seen him before now."

"Maybe there was no reason for it before. Now *I'm* here. Maybe he's jealous!"

"Oh, come on."

"You have a better explanation?"

I admitted I didn't.

Devin propped up a pillow and motioned for me to lie back and relax. "You don't mind *me* touching you, do you?"

"You're being sarcastic now."

He laughed. "Well, I just wanted to be sure." He swung a fist in the air. "Hear that, Jack? I'm allowed to touch her and *you* aren't!" He rolled over playfully as if to attack when the bedroom door suddenly slammed shut. Devin sat up, instantly serious, and stared at the door. Then he looked at me. "Aren't you going to tell me the wind did that?"

"Not a chance."

"Okay." Devin turned to the closed door. "Ah waz jist jivin' with ya. Now either ya go *in* or *out*, but yer bustin' up mah act here."

I looked up, startled at the sudden change in his voice. Christian didn't seem to notice my staring at him. The bedroom door, incredibly, creaked open slowly, then stopped halfway.

"Fuck you, then. *Thiz* is *mah* room! Now *split!*"

The door slammed shut again.

"Christian!"

"Shee-it! That sucker! You jist gotta know how t' handle him, ladee. Don' be takin' no shit from him now."

"Aw, Christian!" I'd missed the little renegade, and I hugged him fiercely. "Where in the *hell* have you been?"

His white teeth flashed in the semidarkness. "Yup. Tha's where, all rat. But rat now Ah'm here 'n Ah don' like spectators. Shee-it. Well, he kin *watch* if that turns 'im on, but Ah don' need no participa-shun. That sucker thinks he's playing with th' keeds in th' alley!"

I laughed at him. Even when he was trying to be serious, he was so funny.

"Now...le's git down t' th' bizness at hand...that iz...if it's 'greeable wit' you."

"Just be careful of my arm," I said, sobering. "It's hurting like hell."

"Oh, ladee, don' you believe that. Hell's one place you wouldn' ever 'xperience pain. 'Les, of course, you *wanted* to 'xperience it."

I looked at him quizzically. "What do *you* know about it?"

He laughed. "Ever'thing *he* does. Erick knows too. *He's* been there. Damn, ladee...*we* don' have no trouble gettin' in."

"But Devin does?"

He shrugged. "Far az Ah know he has'n been. But tha's *his* fault! An' do we *have* t' spend th' night talkin' 'bout Devin?" He thrust his lower lip out belligerently and crossed his arms. "'Cause Ah got better things t' do than talk 'bout *Devin!*"

"You're jealous," I teased him.

"Well, what d' ya 'spect? Ya sound lak ya'd rather have Devin here than *me.*"

"Christian, that's not true."

His face almost crumpled for a minute, then brightened, as though nothing was going to ruin this night for him.

"Ladee...you come out in the livin' room. Old Christian has a song fer ya, too."

3 I don't know what woke me up. I had lain awake long after Devin had fallen into that motionless sleep any undertaker would have taken for dead. My mind just wouldn't shut down.

The words to the song Christian had played for me had weighed heavily on my mind. Another Moody Blues song called *New Horizons*. The lyrics spoke of having dreams enough for one but love enough for three. It also asked about the place that we had found...asked where it was. It spoke of being out of mind and far from anyone's view...beyond the reach of nightmares coming true. Eventually I'd fallen into a troubled sleep. The last thing I remembered thinking was: *just what WAS beyond the reach of a nightmare come true?*

But something had awakened me.

Nothing seemed any different in the bedroom. The clock was ticking steadily, and there was the faint sound of the television running in the girls' room. I got up to turn it off.

Then I noticed the bedroom door. It was wide open. A glance at Devin's body told me that he was dead to *this* world, his chest barely moving, and I wondered again how he managed to sleep like that, with such shallow breathing.

I tiptoed into the kids' room. They too were dead asleep. Well, maybe they'd gotten up and come into our room for some reason. I was sure we'd closed our door when we had finally shut off the tape and returned to the bedroom. Christian seemed to have the same talent *he* had for fast-forwarding the reel to some unregistered point and hitting the play button. Somehow, the song had come on, from the beginning, not in the middle, in spite of how random the selection had been.

Love enough for three. Christian seemed to want to make that point.

I wandered out into the living room, surprised at my own bravery after last night. Well, as long as Devin was within yelling distance. It had been easy to see that Christian was gone. Devin's facial features were his own, but expressionless, and there was really no way of telling who or what occupied the body. If anyone.

I found myself drawn to the altar, knelt down, and opened the door. A strong odor of bayberry and sandalwood wafted out into the darkened room. The altar looked downright sinister in the dim light of the flickering candles. It was octagon-shaped and marble-topped, and when I opened the first two sections, four of them opened wide, exposing candles and full moon supplies neatly laid out amid herbs, powders and tools of the trade. A damp, musty smell of fresh earth overrode the sweeter smells of the bayberry. I reached into the back where the notebooks and papers were stashed. Devin had given me permission to look at the journals. Maybe an answer to Devin lay in these personal journals he'd kept before we'd gotten together.

I opened the first notebook, dated January of 1972. Almost three years ago.

The notations didn't make much sense at first. It was Devin's handwriting, exactly like his route tickets used to look before Christian started horning in on the routes. But it didn't sound like the happy-go-lucky Devin I'd come to know and love. The words seemed brooding...desolate. Lonely.

I flipped through the pages, scanning. Some of his penned thoughts were pertaining to drug trips. Acid...mescaline. He seemed to be concerned that his sanity might have been affected by some of them. LSD was a big concern as far as possible brain damage went. These thoughts didn't sound like the Devin I knew at all. The Devin I knew never gave the subject of drugs any serious thought.

This journal was apparently the work of the original Devin Drew, an individual who did not seem to be part of this posse of personalities I was interacting with. Was this material pre-*him* and pre-*them*? I wondered if the original Devin Drew was still there, buried under the convoy of personalities I took for granted now. I also wondered what the original Devin had been like.

A typical young hippie from the looks of this notebook.

I turned another page. Theban script. I didn't know it well enough to transcribe, so I tiptoed to the bookshelf for the decoder.

E...R...I...*Erick.*

Erick in 1972?

Hope rose as I turned to the next page. Could there be an explanation for all this somewhere in these notebooks after all?

The next few pages were devoted to full moon dates with sentence fragments that I could glean no sense from. The mood had picked up, though. The brooding, lonely words had changed to expressions of hope and excitement. Something he was looking forward to. Two dates that were specific were October 1ˢᵗ of 1974, and October 31ˢᵗ of that same month and year. This, in a notebook from 1972. What had he been planning so far in advance?

I turned another page. The name Asmodeus was coming up a lot here, and descriptions of attempts to contact him, whoever that was. Apparently, he'd had some success as the mood of the writing stayed uplifted and ecstatic. It looked like he'd made an agreement with him and had set a future date for something to take place.

The tone of *this* Devin sounded more like the Devin I'd fallen in love with. Happy, positive and loving. What had lifted him up and out of his depression?

There were many more pages, but I was starting to feel very uncomfortable about reading them. This was Devin's private life, and I felt like I was snooping. This might be something we should read and talk about together.

I was about to close the book when a sketch caught my eye.

A small, but detailed, sketch of a glowing city skyline. It reminded me of what OZ looked like in the movie as it was viewed from a distance by Dorothy and her caravan. Underneath the sketch, in that strange print I recognized from our first night together with my own tablet, were four words written in English.

BAEL...CITY OF LOVE

It smacked of automatic writing. Had *he* been putting these ideas into Devin's head long before he had come here? Had he been, in fact, preparing Devin for *his* eventual arrival and entrance?

If so, Devin sure seemed to have been looking forward to it.

Was I actually starting to believe this?

I closed the book. Either Devin had forgotten this was all here, or he'd known it was and hoped I'd stumble across it. That would explain why he'd mentioned it at all and given me permission to look.

I returned the notebook to its original resting place. Nothing I'd read bothered me like that last page. That detailed sketch of a city skyline. Something told me this was none of my business and to leave it alone for now.

Bael. That name rang a familiar bell somewhere deep in my subconscious. Bael. City of Love.

Oz. There's no place like home.

Home.

More worried than ever, I blew out the candles, closed up the altar, and returned to my pillow at Devin's side. He hadn't changed position, and there was still no visible rise and fall of his chest.

Dismally, I wondered if it were just a shell I was sleeping with.

The room was cold. I pulled up the blanket around us and snuggled against his bare chest where it was warm. At least he was alive.

Devin offered to drive me to work the following morning. His logic was that we could drop off the girls at the sitter's, continue on to work together, and meet back up at five at Daniel's house. I loved the idea of going to work with

Devin. It felt so…together.

Work ticked by slowly with no break from the monotony except when it came time to fight with Kelly over the radio station. Kelly said that she refused to listen to those mournful hick songs all day, no matter whose turn it was to pick the station, and I turned her to stone when I agreed. I didn't want to hear that sad country stuff either. When I told her which station I *did* want today, she went howling to Lola, who promptly took the jukebox into her own office.

"No acid rock," she said, in her most authoritative voice, and we ended up working in silence.

Kelly stuck her tongue out at me every few minutes and then broke into laughter.

"Acid rock! What's gotten *into* you?"

Lola kept the radio in her office all day.

As if we'd been serious.

"How's your arm?" *He* ushered me out the exit at five and into his warm idling van out front. Daniel sat in the area behind Devin's seat. They'd both dropped Julie off at work prior to returning for me.

"It's still sore. I haven't actually looked at it all day. You know how Mama's been getting when weird things are brought up these days. Hi, Daniel. Where's the kids?"

"At home. Danny's old enough to supervise for the few minutes we've been gone."

It felt strange to be in *his* company instead of one of the other three, but I had the feeling that *he* was going to be around more now that Devin's time wasn't as divided as it had been before Thanksgiving.

When we reached Daniel's house, he turned off the engine and gestured for me to roll up my sleeve. Daniel moved up closer to see, and I turned my arm for their scrutiny.

No change at all on the "tattoo" or the needle mark, which still looked days old and exactly like it did when I'd first found it. The purple fingermarks, however, were the darkest they'd been since they first appeared.

"Unbelievable," Daniel said, looking at Devin. "You don't know how, huh?"

"I have an idea." Devin looked at me. "Kerry had a strange dream that night. She woke up with this. I'd rather not expound on the connection I think there is."

Daniel shook his head. "I don't know anything about that stuff. You two are the experts there."

"Daniel," he said, "the sad part about being an expert is that the smarter you get, the more you realize how much you *don't* know."

Danny and Timmy burst from the house, nearly knocking us over on our way up the sidewalk to the front door. Lucifer, Daniel's huge white malamute, could be seen wagging his tail slowly from the picture window as Daniel reached for the doorknob. Devin trailed behind me, Timmy riding gleefully on his shoulders, Danny's small arm curled proudly around his waist.

For a split second I flashed on the posture of the dog, whose ears were pricked, nostrils quivering and straining in Devin's direction. His nose was working overtime. I assumed Daniel's dog was used to Devin wrestling with the kids, but I also knew that it wasn't Devin that Timmy was atop of.

Devin swung Timmy to the ground as Daniel opened the door, and the boy raced to the kitchen to make Devin his tea, a ritual that had obviously started long before me.

Lucifer wheeled from the window, leapt from the couch and bounded up to Daniel, tail wagging excitedly. Then suddenly he stopped dead in his tracks. He stared at Devin and his fur bristled. I knew from Devin's expression that we both realized what was coming.

"Hey, Daniel! Better call your dog."

Daniel paused in the center of the room and turned to see the family pet, fur spiked, showing fangs as he crouched between his master and us. His head was low and ears flattened back. From his throat came a continuous menacing low growl. Devin stooped to a crouch which immediately turned the low growl into a louder snarl.

"Hey, Lukie…what gives? You know me." Devin stretched a balled-up fist out toward the dog in a friendly gesture and slowly opened it to a flat palm.

With no further warning, Luke lunged.

The next motion happened so fast that I never saw Devin take action. Luke's muzzle was trapped in Devin's closed hand before his teeth could even make contact or before Daniel could reach the dog.

"Luke! What the fuck do you think you're doing?" Daniel backhanded Luke with a force that knocked the dog clear across the room. Luke leapt to his feet, alternately glaring at Devin and lowering his tail to Daniel and whimpering. Daniel went to Devin and grabbed his hand to examine it.

"I don't believe this! Are you all right, bro?"

"Fine, Daniel. He never made contact."

"I just can't believe this! That dog's greeted you like one of the family for…" He turned to Lucifer who stood watching, total confusion in the dog's eyes. "Git out back! Go on! Git!" He turned to Devin and me. "I'm going to put him outside. Be right back."

He grabbed the dog by the collar and disappeared into the hall that led to the kitchen. We could hear him still yelling at the dog all the way to the back door.

I felt so sorry for Luke. It wasn't his fault. I looked at Devin. "Do you usually have that problem?"

He stood up from the crouch. "Occasionally. First time with Daniel's dog, though. The poor dog's just reacting the way his instincts tell him to react in the presence of a stranger. He just doesn't understand. He recognizes that it isn't Devin and, for that matter, he's used to dealing with humans. He knows I'm not. It could become a problem around here."

"I had a bad feeling when I saw him staring through the window."

"So did I, lady. Perhaps our expectations created the problem to begin with." He motioned for me to sit down and went out to the kitchen.

"I'll make the salad, Daniel," I heard him say as he entered the kitchen.

"What for?" came Daniel's joking reply. "You never eat with us anymore.

It's just me and the kids, I guess. Sure you can't stay?"

"Wish we could, man. We have to pick our kids up, and Gerald invited us to dinner tonight."

"Yeah? Cool. You gonna go?"

"Maybe. Depends on how Kerry feels."

Devin returned to my side with a steaming cup of tea. "Here, lady. Compliments of Danny and Timmy."

"Are we really going down to Gerald's tonight?" I asked him, once underway and headed for the sitter's.

"We were invited last night, but I told him it was out of the question. Too soon after the trip, you know?"

"And you changed your mind? You feel up to it now?"

"It doesn't matter to me. I guess we could go if you want to. It *is* a long drive."

"Oh, I'm okay. What're they having?"

"Spaghetti, I think. Faye's a damn good cook. I had dinner with them a few times while I was moving my stuff over there."

"Well, we can leave the kids with Pam. She's off work tonight, and they've got school tomorrow."

Devin and Gerald seemed to have a strange relationship. In his own way Gerald was as weird as, or weirder than, Devin. In a good way. He had a dry sense of humor that made it difficult to tell whether he was serious or not.

As Faye set out the plates and silverware, I noticed a new addition to the living room. In the corner sat some monstrosity that hadn't been there on our last visit.

"You've got your tree up early this year," Devin remarked as we seated ourselves around the throne. "What's the big rush?" He nodded in the direction of the contraption, shaped sort of like a tree. It was a conglomeration of wire coat hangers, beer cans, tin vegetable cans, and assorted balls and lights.

"That was Faye's idea," Gerald answered in his gravelly voice. "And changing the subject the minute you walk in the door, for Christ's sake, Devin, you haven't changed a bit. I suppose you're aware that it's nine-thirty and supper was at seven-thirty, so there's no guarantee on what the food's going to be like." He glanced down at the Great Dane that had shifted his massive body to his feet as Devin entered. "Thor...will you lay down," Gerald added, addressing the dog.

"Hey, dry up, old man," Devin retorted. "Shit. When have I ever been on time? Faye, sorry, really. We had to line up the babysitter. It was pretty last minute for her."

"That's okay, Devin," Faye replied, teasing. "We're used to it. Like Gerald says, you'll be late for your own funeral. Are you hungry now?"

"Starved." Devin motioned for me to follow him to the table. "Have a seat, Ker. I'll get the goods."

Thor rambled in from the hallway, stirred by the aroma of meat sauce simmering on the stove. Devin came out with a dishtowel over his arm, teasing

Faye about crowding him out of the kitchen. Gerald and I were watching with amusement from the table, when Thor entered the dining room, his tail going from a slow cautious wag to a stop.

It was almost a rerun of this afternoon, only with a much bigger dog. And one that knew Devin much better.

Grrrrrr…woof!

There was no friendliness to his bark, and Devin looked at me with a bewildered look. It really *was* Devin, and there was no reason for Thor to react the way Luke had. Devin tried to diffuse the situation before it could turn into a problem.

"Woof? Wha-da-ya-mean woof? Lighten up, Thor!" He dove on the animal he'd known since he was a puppy, playfully swishing the dishtowel around to entice him to play. Thor jerked his huge head away, whined, and then, with confusion in his eyes, tried to lay a sloppy tongue on Devin's hand.

"Aw, puppy, what's wrong?" Devin dropped the towel and took Thor's big head in his hands. "You don't feel like playing, huh?"

Thor continued to lick his hand, his eyes sad and mournful.

I watched this interchange between them with mixed feelings. Devin had told me that he'd first held Thor when he was only a few weeks old. Yet, Thor wasn't acting like a normal dog that hadn't seen his old friend in days. Devin remarked on the dog's depression when he joined us at the table.

"I don't know what his problem is," Gerald said. "Brian had him going in the backyard this afternoon. He nearly tore the clothesline down." He glanced disgustedly at the dog. "That overgrown ape."

"Maybe he's just worn out," I offered to Devin, whose attention was fixed on the dog. Thor had dropped back to his hallway retreat with a sigh, though he still watched Devin with a serious, fixed stare.

Devin shook his head. "No. I've seen that dog tired before. There's something else going on in his head. He acts like I've deserted him or something."

"Maybe it's because he knows you've moved away," Faye speculated. "He did see you move all your stuff out of that room and into your van the other night."

"Yeah, maybe," Devin said doubtfully. "If dogs actually reason like that. I'll have to take him up to see my new place so he'll know that I haven't gone far." He pulled the salad bowl over. "Here, Ker. Eat. None of that coffee-only shit tonight."

I was too hungry to argue, and the subject of Thor fell into the background of other topics.

Devin and Gerald got into a strange discussion after dinner. Brian had joined us late, flashing me a bashful hello smile, and then heaped up a big plate of spaghetti as the conversation continued.

"Now, I know Kerry won't understand this, Devin, but when you let go…when that little trap at the base of your neck opens and shuts, you just—" Gerald demonstrated by spiraling his finger upwards in a screw-like motion.

He was right. I had no idea what he was talking about, so I just listened politely.

Gerald went on, "Around and around and around and then—bang...out! It's all over and you're free of your body."

Devin smiled and shrugged. "If you say so. I haven't experienced it myself, but from what you tell me..."

"Hell! Faye's done it!" Gerald turned to her for confirmation. "Haven't you! Tell them."

"Well, I have," Faye began meekly. "But it's only when I'm smoking weed."

"Done what?" I finally asked.

Gerald looked over at me. "We're Spiritual Frontierists, Kerry. We're into something entirely different than what you and Devin are into. I doubt that Devin would appreciate my enlightening you otherwise."

"Let's change the subject," Brian said casually, reaching for a slice of garlic bread. "Devin, I don't suppose you could loan me the van for about an hour?"

Devin looked at his watch. "We've got to split soon. Can you really be back in an hour?"

"Sure. I just have to pick something up."

Gerald reached for the stash box. "You can stay and smoke a number with us, Devin. Faye went to the trouble of making fresh coffee."

I found Faye in the kitchen, already headed out with four cups balanced on a tray, the perfect hostess. "Need any help, Faye?" I asked.

"No, you just sit with Devin. It's nice to see him so happy."

"He doesn't sound so happy now," I said. "Listen to him and Gerald. What are they arguing about now?"

"Oh, they aren't arguing. They do this every time they get together."

The voices became louder as we approached the table, and now the subject seemed to be survival.

"What you don't realize, Devin, is that the body is nothing more than a robot. A vehicle. Even if a bomb is dropped, you can still be aware and conscious after everything is wiped out."

"I *do* realize that," Devin said. "But it's so useless. All that destruction. All that death. Wasted, useless life."

"So it's a waste. It's the human way. You're too goddamned concerned about death, Devin. Think about *life* a little. Think about Kerry, here. It's not easy to find a good woman..."

"I still say I'd survive *in* the flesh. I'd live out in the woods or up on a mountain. I'd live off the land. I don't need the security of a job."

"And what would you do with Kerry and the two kids?"

"Three."

"Okay, three children, should you two combine forces there..."

"They'd be with me, of course."

Faye cleared her throat loudly. "Can't we talk about something less morbid?"

"Well, Devin's entirely too concerned with death. Life goes on. It all goes on, and nothing dies, really. That's what I can't seem to get through to him."

"But while you're *in* this world it has to be dealt with as death. I realize you don't *really* die, but in *this* world, it has to be reckoned with as a reality. Like actors in a play. If a character dies in the script, of course he doesn't really die on that stage, but for the purposes of the play and the script, he *is* dead in the story."

"You just can't stop them," Faye said with a sigh.

"Yes, you can." Devin stood up. "I hear my van returning and therefore, Gerald, you'll have to save the rest of it for—"

"Later," Gerald finished for him.

Devin turned to Faye. "Thanks for dinner, Faye. It was great, as usual."

Faye bowed graciously. "Glad you guys could make it tonight. Hey do you like our tree?"

"That's a *tree?*" Devin kidded her.

"It's an ecology tree." She smiled at Gerald. "He has a thing about killing trees."

"Oh, is *that* where Devin got that?" I said.

"Well, it doesn't sound like it, but I think Devin and Gerald are both on the same road," she whispered. "Just taking slightly different paths, that's all."

Devin was quiet as we pulled away, and I was too tired to strike up any conversation either. It wasn't until we'd reached the highway that Devin broke the silence.

"My old man's got a lot to learn."

"About what?" I moved to the warm floor of the van and rested my head against his knee. I felt his hand on my shoulder.

"About me. He thinks he understands me. He's so sure." He rolled down the window an inch, lit two cigarettes and handed me one. "Humans are always so sure."

I blinked at the sudden switch. Devin had done a vanishing act. "Is Thor so sure too, Devin?"

A frown crossed his features in the darkened van, visible as the highway lights strobe-flashed on his face at intermittent intervals.

"Thor. I'm afraid of just how much Thor *does* understand."

"That was a little hairy tonight," I said. "First Luke this afternoon, and then Thor. Why, all of a sudden?"

"I'm around more. And I'm going to *be* around more. I didn't come all this way to stay in the shadows."

One downward glance from his luminous eyes gave me a sharp idea of how it must have been for Thor to experience one of those electric glances.

"You weren't around all night, though. In fact, I thought Devin held his ground pretty well."

"He did, and around Gerald, Devin will. I have no reason to waste my time with Devin's father. But I'm never far, lady. I'm always there. A split second away. And that's all it takes for an animal to detect my presence. Daniel's dog…well, no one thought too much of that incident, and there was no reason for anyone to question his behavior. I don't *know* the dog that well. It would be *very* noticeable if Thor was to suddenly turn on me."

"Do you really think he *might* ?"

"Didn't you catch that first bark? Thor knew. I hadn't anticipated this kind of a problem, not with Luke, and certainly not with the dog Devin has known since he was a puppy." He glanced at me again, raised his eyebrows, and then resumed his attention to the road.

The house was asleep when we arrived home. Pam had crashed on the bed in the den, so we pretty much had the rest of the night to ourselves. I started the coffee percolating, a new experience for me after all the instant coffees we'd shared in the early days. Devin began to thread a new reel into the recorder.

I recognized Uriah Heep from the tape he'd made for me and gestured towards the machine. "That's from *Demons and Wizards*?"

"The whole album is on these tapes, but certain cuts are further on in another section of the reel. Recognize it?"

"That one I do. It's about all I've been playing around here anymore. That song...*The Spell*... they really have some weird lyrics to the songs I've heard so far."

Devin lit a joint, drew on it, and passed it to me. "Listen to this next song. It'll give you a little insight as to who I am, if the description were to come from Devin."

Guitars began the song and I lay back in the beanbag to listen. *Really* listen. Nowadays, any clue to Devin's strange personality was never overlooked.

4 The song told of someone who'd met a wizard, by chance, during his wandering. The wizard had shared his wine and told him tales that made the singer want to help free the world of pain and fear. The wizard had fiery eyes and wore a golden cloak.

As the song ended and faded away, he looked at me with an eyebrow raised. "Devin's point of view?"

"Actually, I think it sounds more like the way Christian sees you."

There were a couple seconds of empty tape before the next song burst forth. Unlike the quiet ballad we'd just heard, this time strong guitars and keyboards burst out at a fast rhythm, happy and upbeat. Still Uriah Heep. *Easy Living*. This one was a radio hit so I recognized it. This time, though, the words took on special meaning, especially when the singer sang of trying to find me somewhere along a winding road. He said he had walked behind me day after day. I'd heard this song more than once, and every time I listened, it seemed to say and mean something else.

"*That's* Devin's song there," I said.

He nodded. "Perhaps you're right. Although I, too, have been looking for you on that same winding road. But remember now, these songs and their order on the ten tapes were recorded long before we reconnected, you and I. So pay attention to the words. I think you'll find them...educational."

The third song was one that Devin had also put on my eight-track tape, so I knew the lyric well. This time, though, as the singer spoke of travelling in time, looking to the sun to realize his origins and home, and trying to get back, I now knew who the song was about.

"Erick!" we said together after the first line of the song.

"Erick really *is* a traveler in time," he remarked, lowering the volume. "But then again, aren't we all."

"Where *does* Erick really come from, Devin?" I asked, feeling weird at calling him Devin but not knowing how else to address him. "He really does seem so far removed from the rest of you."

He lifted his shoulders. "Erick's really up there, or *out* there, or something. You can find a pretty accurate description of him in *The Bible*, if you have the stomach to use that source for a reference."

"Where in *The Bible*?"

"Michael was mentioned three times in Daniel, once in Jude and once in Revelations. However, you must remember what *The Bible* really is…one long parable. Written by men, and inaccurate."

"Wow, who'd have ever guessed? Michael, the Archangel." I laughed and he rolled me over playfully and planted a chaste kiss on my cheek.

"Who'd have ever guessed that *The Bible* would become what it is today? So misinterpreted and so misunderstood. So *changed* for that matter. It's not even complete. Many books of *The Bible* were removed and omitted from the final draft. Anything that contradicted what the churches wanted you to believe was omitted."

"What was the point, then?"

"I think the original energy that inspired the writers probably meant well. I believe it was meant to uplift the consciousness of the barbarians back then, but what a prime example of what a waste of time that was. Take the story of Jesus, for example. *He* tried it, and look what they did to *him*."

"So you *do* believe Jesus existed, huh?"

"The way they couched everything in stories back then, it's hard to be sure. But if he did exist, he was a good man, a very *aware* and very *nonhuman* individual. It sounds like he really tried to help people and teach them, but he found out…we *all* find out once we get here. It looks so *easy* from *there*."

"But now *you* want to try it," I reminded him. "What makes you think *your* son would fare any differently?"

He didn't answer. His eyes were following a bluish-purple light which was hovering, once again, in the corner near Christian's self-portrait.

"Devin?"

"Yeah, your friend's back."

"I thought you couldn't see him."

Devin stood up and headed towards the bathroom door. "I can't. But I can *feel* him, so I know when he's here and where he is. Like now…he's *there*."

The bluish light flickered into the hallway where it blended into the darkness. Devin came out of the bathroom with a frazzled old toothbrush.

"Okay to use this to work on your ring?"

"Yeah, that's an old one. I hope the ring's dry enough to wear tonight."

"I'd like to see you wearing it again. You're wearing the pentagram and it seems like they belong together. The ring, without the pentagram, caused attacks, and the pentagram without the ring seems to cause a nightmare…which reminds me. Let me see your arm."

The marks were still bluish purple, but now there were traces of tan around the edges.

"It's beginning to fade," he said, turning my arm over. "Here, too. Blue and tan. And your needle mark…if that's what it is…it looks like tiny veins are spreading out from the puncture. You can barely see them, they're so small and faint." He released my arm, reached for the ring, and spent a few minutes smoothing off the edges with the toothbrush. "Here you go." He handed the ring back to me. "You're in business again. Should fit you now. I loaded up filler on the back behind the eye."

I slipped the ring on my finger. "Feels better. Thanks."

"Good. Now, where were we?"

"We were talking about our son, and why you think he might do this world any good if Jesus couldn't even get the point across."

"Well, for one thing, Jesus picked the wrong century. Everything was interpreted in the language of the times back then."

"I'm aware of *The Bible's* distortions, Devin. I think the King James Version is in the seven-thousandth printing. I heard that somewhere. But I don't think our son is going to have any easier of a time than Jesus did. Back then, they put you to death. Today, they'll put you *away*."

When he didn't reply I added, "Besides, where did you ever get the idea to bring in a savior to begin with?"

"The child was an afterthought of mine, I admit. It wasn't my original intention when I started pushing for permission to come here. *You* were. For that matter, it wasn't even my idea."

"Then whose idea was it?"

"My old man's…no, not Devin's old man…*mine*. At *home*. Lady, back where we come from, there is no one with as much power and respect as *He*. Some have called him God since time began…others have called him Lucifer. Like the song says…all the names are not the same. When you get down to the real facts, though, there's no male sex involved, and no father-son relationship. And no permanent form. I'm using the terms *you* are accustomed to, lady, and *here* the old man would be experienced as a male, and in relation to me…my father. He isn't one that I would casually refuse a request either, so I imagine it was quite an affair back home when I did. A son…just wasn't part of the original deal, that's all."

"He…your old man back home…*he* wanted the child to be born here?"

"Well, suffice it to say, that's how it began. During one of Devin's full moon contacts."

Something was happening to his face as he spoke. The masklike features were melting, beginning to soften and reshape as I'd seen happen so many times before. When he paused to light us a couple of cigarettes, his warm glance told me that *he* was gone, and in his place was Devin, the only one who really *could* relate to that night in the distant past. Devin seemed oblivious to the fact that *anyone* else but him had ever been here with me tonight.

"Communications went down like usual that month. It was October…the first full moon was October first, and I knew he was going to enter me soon. We had been planning it for some time. I'd never had any trouble contacting him, but I'd never gotten involved with his old man. I think the old man was against the whole idea anyway, right from the first—about his coming here, I mean. And it was *one* thing to plan this sojourn with him, and quite another to realize he would be inside me…using my body as a vehicle. Anyway, he experimented a little with coming and going until I got a feel for it before his actual stabilizing inside me on the second full moon, which was the thirty-first of October. That was the first night I *felt* him operating inside me. I could think his thoughts and feel his feelings, and if I had had any doubt about going through with it before that night, I was completely sure it was cool after I felt him so deep within me. But that's when I sensed this turmoil between him and his old man."

"Over his coming here?"

"Not just that. His old man kept intimating that he needed a son to…well, follow in his footsteps is the human way of putting it. *He* firmly refused. He told the old man that if there was going to be *any* son born here, it would be *his* son, raised *his* way, and maybe that's what put the idea in *his* head to begin with."

"Devin, when you talk about this baby, you do realize it isn't going to be *your* baby, don't you? Allowing *him* to use your body…that's one thing, but—"

"Granted, I know it would be *his* kid. I realize that. But it's going to take my physical participation to bring the child into this world. And no matter how powerful and respected his old man is, he can't override *his* decisions. After all, *he's* next in line at home, if you were to go by rank there. There actually *are* no positions of rank, from what I gather, and I realize this might not be making a lot of sense to you, Kerry. It barely makes sense to me."

"But, if he's *got* an old man, wouldn't that, in itself, imply seniority or superiority?"

"I don't think so. Not there. These terms are all purely allegorical to the physical symbols of Mama, Papa, and offspring. It seems like everything is basically equal there. Unified. It's not like someone *has* to be in charge. I think *that* idea is a human one."

"Then how can the old man be so high in power there?"

"By the choice of the world, the way a group will single out a leader in this world and look up to him. His old man needs a rest, from what I gather from *his* thoughts. *He* seems to think the old man is weary of the weight he has carried in parable after parable, story after story, and lie after lie. This world, Kerry…it *hates* the old man. It created a story about an evil being and then hung the title on the old man. The human race has spread lies about him and his world, and I *know* you are aware of what they call his world and the reputation it now has."

I nodded. More and more I was beginning to understand what he'd been trying to tell me all along. "Devin, are you really willing to play the role of father for that type of child?"

He smiled. "I don't think that's what *he* has in mind. I think he'd be around constantly but, sure, I'm prepared for him. I was getting flashes on the child before *he* actually stabilized in me, and *you* were getting flashes on *my* flashes."

"I remember. Those thoughts just came out of nowhere when I was writing in my journal or listening to music. But you do trust him and have that much faith in him, huh?"

He stubbed his cigarette out. "Whatever he wants, Kerry. He may be equal *there,* but as long as he's here, he's a lord…a king…and if he couldn't bring his throne here, then at least he can lay his royal mark on this world…what better way to do it than through the flesh?"

"It would have been nice to have *your* baby, Devin," I said wistfully. "You know how I feel about *you.*"

"Kerry, we can have a kid someday, too." He touched my cheek and tipped my face to his. "You know, my interest in this was solely to accommodate *him*, and *his* interest was solely in *you*. I didn't plan to fall in love with you, but it happened along the way. If you want to have *our* baby someday, we could do that. A cute little curly-headed kid, maybe with your copper-colored hair. But that just never was the idea he had in mind once he decided he wanted a son."

I looked at Devin for a long time, contemplating my next sentence. "Devin, just for the logic of it, I've been here in this world for twenty-five years…a quarter of a century. And so have you. We both know the ways of this planet and its breed of people. We both know better than *he* does."

"Right. So you doubt that it would do any good to bring in a full-blooded child of his? You don't think they'll listen?"

"Not to one individual, no."

He closed his eyes and hugged me in the darkness. "Everything *he* can do, everything *you* can do…is nothing compared to what the *child* will be able to do. They'll listen, Kerry. Believe me, they'll have to listen."

I could about imagine the reaction of the earth.

5 "My brother found some peyote."

It was a statement made casually over our second cup of coffee at the coffee shop. I was practicing the Theban script, inking out *I love yous* to Devin and watching his face soften as he decoded them. As I digested those words, I realized that my attitude towards the drug was changing. I didn't freak or anything.

I looked up. "So he finally got it, huh? When'd you see him?"

"He dropped in at the plant this morning."

I laughed, picturing Trevor slinking through the back hallways of the water plant wearing a spy trench coat and high boots, carrying a briefcase stocked with peyote buttons.

"What's so funny?"

"Trevor dropping in with drugs at your workplace. How much did he get?"

He eyed my interest with curiosity. "Enough for a couple of people for a couple of nights. I was thinking of doing some tonight."

I mopped up some spilt coffee with my napkin and set it beside the sugar jar against the wall of the booth. Devin lit a cigarette and handed it to me. He always seemed to know when I was going to smoke.

"No comments, babe?"

"Just one. I think I *would* like to try it."

With all his super mindreading ability, he plainly wasn't prepared for that. He didn't lose his cool, though. "You sure that's what you want to do? I mean, you don't have to just because—"

"No, I want to. From everything I've learned about it, it sounds okay. Safe, anyway. Not like LSD. So…is it okay with you?"

"Sure. It could prove to be interesting. Trevor won't be joining us. He's just going to drop it off this afternoon before I leave there, so it'll just be me and you tonight."

"Me and…who?"

"Think you can stand me for an entire evening?" He smiled. He knew how attached to him I was. To be in Devin's company was never something I took for granted. I never knew when the next appearance would be.

"I could stand you for the rest of my life," I assured him.

"Okay! Tonight, then. You're sure now?"

"Positive. You'll be with me, and I never worry when you're around."

"That's good. I'll try not to frighten you tonight. Well, I'd better get going. I'm late now."

I watched from the window as he trotted across the boulevard to where his truck was parked, pondering that last remark. I finally decided he was kidding me.

"Lola! There's nothing to do!" Hannah rummaged through the safe, checking for stacks of charges and checks. "There's nothing to post."

"Really? We're caught up with the drivers? At one in the afternoon?" Lola fished through the safe quickly and laughed. "Jeez! We are! Don't let that leak out of this office."

Kelly hopped up on the desk and pulled the radio over. "Does that mean we can do anything we want, today?"

"Oh sure, Kelly!" I quipped. "Let's go see a movie."

"All right, you two. How about the delinquents?"

"They're done too," Hannah replied, propping her feet under her roller tray. "Everything is done."

"Can we write a poem?" Kelly turned to Lola. "Can we?"

"A what?"

"A poem…called…The Night before Christmas."

Lola smiled indulgently. "I believe that's already been done."

"No…this one would be…the night before Christmas and all through the plant."

Lola shook her head and gestured a *get-outta-here* wave of her hand. "I don't care what you do. Just do it quietly."

"Come on, Kerry! Hannah…you want to help?"

"No, thank you," Hannah murmured, smiling and rolling her eyes. "I'm sure I can put my files in order."

"Well, shit. So could I." Kelly shrugged. "But for something to do, that's really reaching. Piss on the files. We can do that any other boring day."

"Which don't come often," Hannah reminded her, still smiling.

"I'll help you, Kelly," I offered, "but first we need to know the original poem. Otherwise, we can't butcher it."

"Well, I *sort* of know it. Listen. It was the night before Christmas and all through the plant…"

"We were asking for raises and they said they can't," I supplied.

"Yeah! That's the idea," Kelly squealed, grabbing a pen. "The paychecks were hung on the time clock with care…"

"No, how 'bout this, Kelly. The customers' tongues hung with dehydrated despair…in hopes that their Sparklear man soon would be there."

"That's it…*great*…keep going, Ker!" Kelly's pen moved swiftly across the scratch pad.

Hannah laughed. "Now you're getting right down to the drivers' service insults."

"Well, we get so many drips calling in about where the truck is," I explained.

"Drips?"

"Yeah. Dehydrated, rasping, irate, phone callers."

"That's right," Kelly backed me. "Look at all the complaints we get from lack of water service. Now...shit...what's the next real line?"

"Go ask Kim how the real poem goes," I said.

"I'll go," Hannah said, getting up. "I'm tired of filing."

"What are you guys doing in there?" Lola called in.

"Hannah's going to get the real words to this poem we're aborting."

"Oh, *I* know a line," Lola said brightly. "On Cupid, on Donner..."

"Hey! Yeah, Kelly. We can use the drivers. How about...on Devin, on Joey..."

Hannah returned from the phone room and plopped down in her chair.

"What'd you get, Hannah?"

She blushed. "She didn't even ask why. She knows this one...'I rose to my window and heard such a clatter'...something like that."

"You mean, nobody knows this whole poem, really?" I turned around and saw Devin lounging comfortably on the forbidden step.

"No wonder this department is always behind." He scanned what Kelly had already written, and his eyes widened in mock horror. "What's this shit...On Devin...on Joey..." He gave Kelly a disgusted look. "I guess children must play."

"Devin, did you *want* something?" Lola asked, trying to sound stern.

"Yeah, I just dropped in to tell Kerry—"

"For Pete's sake! You live there now. Won't you see her tonight?"

He winked at me. "I may not, Mama. Kerry, would Kathy keep the kids overnight? I'll pay her extra."

"Probably."

"Okay, see what you can do." He blew me a kiss and waved to Lola on the way out, his step light and quick.

"What was *that* all about?" Lola asked.

"Oh, just a new toy me and Devin got to play with."

"Oh. I see." She gave me a weird look and went back to her paperwork. Apparently, nothing I said or did surprised her anymore.

"So, that's what it looks like."

Before us was an unfolded magazine page with a large pile of brown powder in the center creases. Devin studied me quietly for a minute, then drew out a small penknife.

"This is even better than mescaline, Kerry. This is the real McCoy. Peyote. Straight from the cactus. Originally, it was in hard dried balls...like walnuts...called peyote buttons. It's ground into this powder. Better than mescaline. No chemicals. Totally organic."

He divided the pile into two smaller ones and then divided one of the smaller piles into two again. "I'm only going to give you half of this now until I see how it affects you. The best way to take this is with a glass of milk. Just take the powder in your mouth and heave-ho the milk. That'll keep you from getting nauseated. Remember, this isn't so much a mind drug as a physical one. If you should *see* something, and you will, no matter how frightening it is, don't be afraid of it. That's imperative."

I nodded and went out to the kitchen for the milk. "You want milk, too?"

"No, I won't need it."

When I returned, I saw that he had transferred my smaller pile to another piece of paper and curled that into a small funnel. "Remember, Kerry. If you *do* see something, just remind yourself that it's your perception producing the pictures to tell you something. You may step into another reality, but don't be afraid. If it gets too squeamish, turn your attention away from it and find something else to concentrate on. Don't feed anything that scares you any energy."

This kind of talk was making me nervous, but I wasn't going to back out now. I'd made up my mind I was going to go through with it.

"Okay, I guess I'm ready." I took the funneled paper and the milk. "Just make sure you stick with me, Devin, until I see what it's going to do." With one gulp, I took the plunge, before those second thoughts had a chance to weaken my resolve.

"You'll be in excellent hands, Kerry. I won't worry about you." He watched me with a cautious expression.

"I guess you took yours already," I said, and he nodded.

"Just sit back and relax. There's nothing to be afraid of."

Why did he keep saying that?

He hit some buttons and the music started again. Puff flashed in all his colorful strobe-like glory, but reality didn't look any different than it had before I'd taken the stuff.

"How long's it supposed to take?"

"It could be twenty minutes or it could be an hour. Do you feel any different?"

"No. Are you waiting until I do before you leave me, Devin?" He hadn't said he was leaving, but an inner feeling told me that Devin would soon vanish, and in his place…who knew?

He lit a cigarette, took a drag, then handed it to me. "Why worry about what might happen later? Just pay attention to right now."

I could feel tears stinging my eyes. I didn't want Devin to abandon me on some strange drug, but I didn't dare let Devin see the tears. Casually, I laid my sleeve against my eyes to blot the tears. When I looked up again, my vision was no longer blurred, and Devin was already gone.

"What time is it?" *He* glanced at his watch. "Ten o'clock. Want the rest of the powder?"

"Sure, why not? I didn't feel this half at all."

"I'm not surprised. You probably *do* have a high tolerance to any of this stuff Devin takes. It's your frequency, lady. Remember, drugs are a material substance, and much lower in frequency than you. That shouldn't surprise you, either. I keep telling you that you're not one of *them*."

"*You* don't object to the peyote, do you?" I was glad it wasn't Erick or Christian who had taken Devin's place. Somehow, I already felt safer in the company of *him*.

"No, I don't." He walked over to the gold leather chair and sat back, looking more like a king on his throne than Gerald ever had when he was seated in his hand-carved, red velvet one.

The lights were beginning to take on a luminous glow. He caught that and turned off the small red mushroom-shaped lamp, leaving only Puff and a few low-burning candles for the scant illumination in the room.

"You don't need any help," he said, as the room dropped to a quarter of its original brightness. "Ready for the rest of it?"

I nodded. After swallowing the last of my pile, I turned back to him. "Got anything to tell me while I'm still making sense?"

"Well, I have to hand it to Devin. He did well explaining the drug's background, but he didn't complete it. That's going to hit you hard pretty soon. I'm already feeling it. Just remember the one thing that Devin did tell you. Your brain is going to be crying for sugar soon. Your ego will begin to weaken, and your ego has one primary function in this world. That's to shoot down anything that doesn't conform to physical reality. Lately, that's been plenty. Your ego's been pretty confused. When you start feeling that sugar deficiency, your ego will be too weak to give a damn about its own reality here. It'll be much more interested in alternate reality. Other worlds. That's what I was hoping to speed up tonight."

"Speed up…you mean…my going…there?"

He nodded. "Home. With me. You do it in your sleep anyway, but with no awareness or memory, lady. Since your ego is hell bent on getting you through *this* system, it's going to buck me hard. That's its job. I hope tonight will even things out a bit."

"Devin, you know I love you, don't you?"

He gazed at me. "You always have. And you know I've always loved you." He pulled me into his arms. "You should be feeling something now. Describe to me what you see."

"Not much different." It felt good to be so close to him. He was always one big electrifying charge on contact. "The lights are blurring into all kinds of colors now. I feel a little high…but alert."

"Good. It's taking effect. Let me show you something now." He pressed his fingers against my eyelids, closing them. "Now, relax. Lie back in the beanbag."

My blood felt like it was racing. I was becoming extremely alert.

"Just keep your eyes closed, and pay attention to the words." He hit the radio button, already tuned to the acid-rock station. He seemed to think that the song just beginning would somehow tell me something about himself that I needed to know. The peyote made it difficult to tune out the music…in fact, it amplified it and forced me to tune out everything else.

"I'm hoping that this might ring a familiar note for you. It wasn't easy for me to come here. With you, it was only a question of making the decision to enter the reincarnational cycle on the physical plane. As I've said before, you were born here."

As the instruments began the song, I settled back to listen, although with apprehension of the future of the evening, now magnified by the rapidly escalating effects of the drug.

It sounded like Uriah Heep. The beat was jaunty and midtempo, and the singer started right out talking about walking on a dusty road without shoes, saying he was paying his dues in spite of his troubles. It wasn't easy, but he had too much to lose…he'd wandered alone many times looking for some unknown thing. He wondered if there was anybody it was easy to be…he noted that he was still on his own, even though the moon was rising. He wondered where a good king went without his throne.

The song filled the room and flowed into my head like I was wearing earphones. I opened my eyes and saw him watching me intently. His eyes flashed amber and green like a wolf caught in the headlights, but his expression was pure love. The king who was without his throne, who was paying his dues but still found himself on his own. A feeling that I had betrayed him swept over me and I reached for his hand. I wanted to believe and trust so much. I already loved.

"Devin…that's about you, isn't it."

"Hey-hey-hey," he said quietly in that not-Devin way. *There it is. Now you're getting it.*

"Is this drug making me imagine the song is talking to me?"

"The song? Surely you don't think this is a coincidence."

"I just thought the drug…"

"You want drug songs…okay…hang in there for the next one."

The *King Without a Throne* song faded away, and with no deejay or announcement of what was to come, the next record began.

I knew this one well. One of the most famous songs ever to hit the radio. Jefferson Airplane…*White Rabbit.*

The metaphor of Alice in Wonderland, sung by Grace Slick went through the scale of notes, rising higher and higher as Alice took one pill after another, getting larger and smaller, chasing rabbits and talking to smoking caterpillars. I'd never noticed before that the song started low and continued to rise, going higher and higher until that famous last line…*feed your head.*

"It *could* be a coincidence," I said as the song ended with a drumbeat.

"I can play you drug songs all night if that's what you want, but I didn't think that was what we were here for tonight."

Before I could respond, another song began without announcement. *Magic Carpet Ride*…Steppenwolf…also drug-oriented. *Close your eyes and come with me on a magic carpet ride.*

I sat up and shook my head. He could not have known the radio's playlist, could not have known what was going to turn up on the radio, yet he seemed as sure as if he'd cued up the record himself.

"Had enough?" he asked with a smile.

I nodded.

"Good. Now, how about one that might mean something to both of us."

6 The next song was no drug song. Blind Faith's *Can't Find My Way Home* began, and I finally accepted that Devin was somehow able to play whatever he wanted on this station. Was it only this station?

Not if I was remembering correctly about the baby songs in the office that day.

The singer, Eric Clapton, said to come down off my throne and leave my body…that someone must change, that I was the reason he'd been waiting so long and that someone held the key. He couldn't find his way home. He was close to the end.

And so was I. "Okay, Devin. I know you can do that with the radio. How, I don't know…"

"Lady, we *are* radio, don't you understand that? We *are* radio…when we aren't—this." He stretched out his arms to indicate the body he was using. Then suddenly he got up and disappeared down the hall, returning with a blanket.

"How do you feel?"

"Okay." I felt the bone chill just seconds before he stooped to encase me in the blanket. And just as suddenly, my teeth began chattering violently.

"Now *that's* the drug," he said quietly, "and you *were* cold."

"Thanks," I said, feeling grateful as the warmth of the blanket took immediate effect over my back and shoulders. The bone chill, however, remained. He was still watching me intently, maybe for an adverse reaction to the drug.

"It's physical," he reminded me. "I sort of *felt* you had one coming on. Look…" He raised his hands over my head and made a downward sweeping motion slowly over the length of my body, but maintaining a distance of six inches from the blanket. "You were cold. Now…you're *warm*."

As he spoke, a strange unmistakable flow of radiant heat crept down and along my body as his hands passed, as though it were originating underneath my skin but controlled remotely from the outside.

It's the drug, I told myself, although the heat he expelled from his hands had the comforting effect of a heat lamp travelling the length of my body.

"Are you still cold?"

I didn't trust myself to speak although my eyes must have reflected my wonder and confusion. I shook my head.

"Are you okay?"

I nodded and he smiled. "Peyote…will bring about definite temperature changes, and I merely anticipated the reaction, that's all."

Sure, I thought. *At the exact moment. And how did you warm me up so easily?*

I began to wonder just what was in store for me tonight, so blithely planned by these four friends that I'd grown to trust so much. Four…or was it really only *one?*

"That heat…" I began. "How did you…what happened with the radio, Devin? How are you doing that…these songs?"

"Shh." He half laughed and pressed the reel-to-reel button, and the tape promptly started up.

"Radio waves and heat waves are in the same vicinity of the

electromagnetic spectrum. It's a cinch…really." He took my face in his hands and as he did so, that same warmth radiated my cheeks. "See? It's a natural trait, to raise or lower the temps on these robots. Even your daughter can do it…remember? But I just don't want to push you any further or faster than you are ready for, or can handle. Especially on peyote. The point I'm trying to make is that it's natural. Any consciousness can do it. It's only magic *now*. Couple hundred years from now science will have figured out what the Tibetans and Yogis have known since the beginning of time. And then, it won't be considered magic, lady. It'll be science. And maybe by then, we won't be seen as the evil we are seen as now."

I looked into the sincerity of his eyes and nodded. The strength of the drug was overwhelming me. The only light in the room was the globe Puff balanced on his frolicking legs, flashing gay Christmas colors—and one lone candle. It seemed to be creating bizarre effects on my normal perspective of the room.

The room had, in fact, grown very small and grubby feeling. I suddenly had a claustrophobic need for breathing room and wide-open space, followed by a blind panic that somehow I was losing my mind. What was left of it.

Now I felt too large to be contained in this small body of mine. On the verge of hysteria, I looked to Devin, but his face was no longer the *him* I knew, disguised in Devin Drew's fleshy face. This began the mechanics of a panic I had never before experienced in my life. A million thoughts shot through my mind in a flash.

I was crazy.

Devin was an actor.

I was trying my damnedest to believe what was just too science fiction for my ego to accept.

My mother's warning crept in then, as the room faded in and out, and my cigarette trailed fifteen cigarettes with every motion of my hand.

UFOs: Operation Trojan Horse

I was losing control of my mind.

Instinctively, I buried my face in the beanbag, only to discover, to my escalating terror, that those needling thoughts and doubts would not stop…if anything they were magnified.

I felt his hands on my shoulders as I struggled to regain control. While on one hand I ached with appreciation for his care and concern, the flooding of doubts and suspicion would not stop. This was twentieth-century earth…the real world. And *nobody* stops in from other realities just for short vacations.

The peyote was backfiring. It had only driven the doubts to the surface. Doubts as to even the validity of this being who dared to defy the laws of this normal everyday world of mine.

"Turn it off, Devin, *turn it off*!"

"Turn what off? The music?" The room silenced before he'd even finished the question.

I sat up, desperately trying to regain control of myself.

"It's not stopping!" My eyes must have been bulging in terror. "Devin…Devin!"

"Hey now, it's all right, lady. It's just the drug and your program about it. Don't blame your mind. You're okay. Don't let your fear conquer you…or your doubts, which is your real problem. Come on. Stand up."

"Can we go outside...*please* ?"

Somehow, in my panic, I realized that the room was not closing in on me, just that I was seeing it in a different way. I knew that the openness of the yard and the clear black and starry sky would bring things back into perspective.

Devin must have been alert for these signs of my freaking out, and in the next instant I found myself in the refreshing, icy December air. My equilibrium began to stabilize under those glittering diamonds that I'd expected to see. He was at my side with warm concern etched in his now unfamiliar face. I was torn between the need for a familiar Devin and the cold realization that the guessing games had to be over for me and him. Nobody had to tell me now that tonight was the night. That if I could understand our situation and *accept* it, that I *would* be able to handle it.

I could sense how much he wanted to just come out and say it...who he was, and in so doing...who *I* was. His thoughts were so clear tonight. Could that, I wondered, be the drug too?

With this reasoning, my panic was subsiding and my clarity of thought was returning. The stars weren't any less diamonds, and Scorpio blazed across the sky, complete with stinger. I could feel rationality returning to me.

"I'm not going to apologize," I began, knowing an apology would fall on deaf ears.

"There's no need to, lady. Just look up at the sky."

The stars had lost their three dimensions. The sky was now a four-dimensional pool of jewels, and when I closed one eye and stared up at them, they quickly showed themselves to be a mockery of an illusion...separated by...what? What veil separated these worlds this lordly king spoke so longingly of?

The sky looked like a blackboard with pinprick holes in it, a back light shining though the holes and shooting magnifying rays of brilliance down towards the earth.

I began to regain my sanity.

Nobody could fake that kind of homesickness he plunged into sometimes. Wherever *home* was, he believed strongly in its source, vitality and reality. Just who *was* he anyway?

The Devil had been mentioned more than once, but never in the biblical way. If the Devil was a church's fictional character, created to frighten the masses into submission, and if *Hell* was misinterpreted in translations from the word Sheol, which literally meant *invisible world* in Hebrew, or *abode of the dead,* then just who *was* he? *What* were *we?*

His voice brought me back to reality. "Okay now, lady? Ready to go back in?"

"Yes."

I really was ready. The near mental disaster was now a thing of the past. The worst was over. I was sure I could handle the rest of the night from this point on.

"Come on," I said with a sigh, and we went back into the house.

I sat down quietly and looked at him. "I guess I'm ready now."

He looked at me doubtfully. "Perhaps we should take a little more time. We have all night. Maybe you should relax a little first."

I could see that there wasn't even a question in his mind as to what I was ready *for*.

"No. We have to get this behind us once and for all. I mean it. I can't take the strain of what's been said and not been said any longer. It has to be now. Or never."

"But can you take whatever might come with it? Can you handle the knowledge yet, lady? Or will you just listen, and then let your fears and programs and human-bullshit training destroy what we have accomplished so far? Lady, your knowing could ruin everything if this goes badly. It could ruin…*us*."

"Look, Devin. We've gone around in circles with this. You've hinted to the point where, yes, there *is* a sick fear of what it's going to turn out to be. But, let's get it *out*. I know what you've implied so many times, but I have to deal with my program concerning it, and it's *my* program…my stupid Catholic program."

"You know who I've implied that I am." The eyes behind the face watched me with pure electricity as I struggled to put into words the cancer that had begun to eat at the roots of my very soul.

His implications were too obvious to ignore anymore. Some were out-and-out statements that could only be taken one way. I could no longer pretend to be deaf and ignorant. Pretending they didn't exist was not making them go away.

"Devin, I know who you've insinuated you are. And I also know that in here…" I tapped my heart, "deep inside me, I'm fighting it. Yes, it's programming. Lifelong Catholic programming. But it's partially because you, yourself, haven't come right out and said it. Put it in one clear word, Devin. But please. No more hints, implications or insinuations. Put it in absolute *There it is, take it or leave it*, and then let me accept it or reject it."

Surprised at my own alertness, clarity and bravery, I watched the mental struggle within him. It was *his* move now. *His* decision. I had done the only thing required in cosmic matters.

I had asked.

Our eyes locked for one long moment, and on a drug like peyote, a minute was too damn long. I had surprised myself with my own calm and resignation. I really was ready for anything. Or so I thought.

One second I was staring intently into the eyes of the mask that I'd grown to accept as his face, distorted from Devin's but intermingled with those same familiar features. The next second an incredible thing happened.

His physical face blinked entirely off, like a strobe, and in its place…an entirely different nonhuman face was staring back at me.

The face was angular, the eyes like a lizard, but amber and black with a green cast that shone in the candlelight. His hair was no longer black curls but the color of autumn and flames.

Then, like a strobe again, that fleshy mask of *his* again.

A wave of horror and revulsion wrenched at my guts, and I turned away from him quickly. I certainly had not been ready for *that!*

It's the drug, my brain screamed. *Don't believe anything tonight.*

Wrong again. His hand gently reached out and guided my face back to his now normal one.

"Look at me now, Kerry. Can you love *this* too? Can you love me in another form? Can you love me in any form but Devin Drew's?"

As if on cue, the alien face, reptilian eyes slanted like a wolf, flashed on and off in that uncanny strobe effect. Unconsciously, I pulled the blanket around me, feeling close to shock. "Devin…please…please don't do that again. Not yet. Please…"

"All right." He stood up and walked over to the front door, rubbing his eyes wearily with his thumb and forefinger. I wished I had the ability to tap his brain the way he did mine. To know what was going on in his mind. Even in the world of peyote, I was fully aware of my too-human reaction…horror…and that it had won out over the love and trust I'd sworn I'd placed in him. It was not the reaction he should have received. But where had I had time to prepare for such a shock?

And if it were a hallucination brought on by the drug, how, then, had he known exactly what my horror had stemmed from?

The worst of it was that I had recognized him. From where, I didn't know. The face was not unfamiliar to me. It just wasn't Devin's face and thus, my reaction.

He had known what he was doing when he strobed that face at me. It was not the drug.

I was, I realized, a victim of the now moment, and there could be no more pretenses. He had seen my reaction, had felt my fright, and it had not denoted readiness for anything, truth or otherwise. It was too late to take back my reaction or my words. It was too late to take back anything.

It was too late to do anything but wait.

It was, for sure, his move now.

Time didn't seem to matter a whole hell of a lot tonight, so I have no idea how long the wait was. Finally, seated at the gold leather footstool of his own throne, without looking at me, he spoke.

There was a sad resignation in his voice, and his shoulders hunched in dejection. "You can't even look at me."

I didn't reply. There was nothing to say for it was true. After those couple glimpses of the face with the reptilian eyes, it was true.

"Kerry, are you afraid of me?"

"No."

"That's a start. Are you afraid to be in the room with me?"

"No." At least that much was true. The peyote had long since peaked and was now in a low valley of sorts.

"Do you love me?"

I sighed. "Yes." That, too, was most emphatically true. Another long silence, and then, when he turned back to face me, I was relieved to see that his face was *his* face again, intermingled with Devin's features.

"All right. It might as well be now."

The little gold footstool was the point of action, I guessed, because before he wearily sat down, he turned so that his back was to me and he was facing the front door.

"Are you sure you want to do this? It's going to be harsh, like you requested. One clear word."

"I'm sure, Devin. I can't go on with hints and double-talk anymore."

"Okay." He sighed. "I did say to ask when you thought you were ready."

"Should I sit here?" I motioned toward the beanbag.

"No. Go over and stand by the cupboard where your masking tape…welcome home Devin…is."

I walked over to where the refrigerator now stood, not quite understanding what he was up to, but sure that he knew what he was doing. He still had not turned around to look at me, as though this now moment was surely going to blow up everything he had worked to build. All the love. All the trust. And an unknown degree of understanding.

"What does it say?" he asked finally, his back still to me.

There was nothing wrong with my vision, and even if there was, I still knew what the taped message said. After all, I had put it up.

"It says…welcome home Devin." I glanced into the living room where he still sat, face buried in both hands as if in concentrative thought. The picture of dread and desolation.

"Now, read it. Not the small letters, but the big word."

"Devin," I read aloud. I still didn't understand, but I could hear and follow instructions.

"Spell it."

"D-E-V-I-N." As I called out the letters, they began to blur and fade in and out.

"Anything happening?"

A chill went through me as the word *Devin* faded away before my eyes, then fragments reappeared and letters disappeared. He again asked me to spell only what I could clearly see. At that moment, the D had disappeared and the N had distorted. The word left was…*EVIL*. I blinked and the word was Devin again. Then the D appeared to reshape into an L and the N disappeared. Now all it said was *Levi*. Oddly enough, the structures my ego was apparently creating, the letters that were and weren't there, didn't concern me as much as trying to reassemble the original word…Devin. He couldn't possibly have had anything to do with what was going on fourteen feet away, couldn't possibly have seen through my eyes, but I heard him chuckle and I momentarily turned away from the cupboard.

"They won't stay still. Why are you laughing?"

"Levi," he called back over his shoulder. "Wasn't exactly the name I was striving for. He was a little loose with some of his paintings, the *Sabbatic Goat* in particular, but he didn't really mean anything demonic by it. But at least you're getting warm. It's working. Try again."

By this time, even his telepathy tonight didn't faze me. I was more than willing to place all the blame on the drug as I turned again to the word that I knew read Devin. Now the D had disappeared again, and the N was beginning to reform into the letter L.

"Now it says evil." I felt my eyes burning with the strain, and I longed to be able to sit down, once again, in that comfortable beanbag with my security blanket.

Apparently, he'd had enough too.

He walked over to the cupboard and yanked off the two strips of tape that had formed the crude taped N, tossed one in the sink, and re-taped the other to form the letter L.

The word now clearly said DEVIL.

There was no room or time for any more games, implications, hints, regrets, misgivings, or misunderstandings. At least, there were none of those things in his eyes as he gave me that final look, arms crossed, waiting.

No more running away. No more pretending he didn't *mean* what I hoped he didn't mean. What was…was. I looked up at the cupboard.

WELCOME HOME…DEVIL.

I looked back at Devin, the cautious look he now held, waiting, and…my turn.

"Okay, Devin. Thanks. It was necessary."

I turned to walk away, fatigued from just the strain of anticipation, and still digesting that gnawing fear that, to me, was still associated with the word *devil*. I sat down on the edge of the couch, the cold bone chill starting up again, when I felt a warm hand touch me gently on the shoulder.

"Do you *still* love me?"

The anguished pride of his very being permeated that border between the kitchen and the living room. Surrounding him, so obvious in the darkened room, was that purple blacklight color, defying the doubts and fears that I still had concerning his claim. If he *was* the Devil, of all people on the planet….why *me*?

I looked up at him again.

There was no smallness to his posture, no shame for the word *devil* now blazed so brazenly on the cupboard door.

The question had stopped me cold.

Our eyes met, and for a minute I was only aware of the love radiating from his eyes into mine. Aware, not of his name or title, nor of his reputation. Just his love. I glanced up at the cupboard and then back to him again. There was no evil there. No fear. No hatred. No ugliness. Even that strobe face he had reflected at me for those few seconds had held no features to be feared. It had merely been different. Different eyes, and different color of hair, and totally different from the Devin I thought I knew.

"Of course I love you," I said finally. "Did you really think that *that* would change anything?"

"Knowing what they say I am? Seeing me…as I really am? You still feel the same love for me?"

I reached out for him and pulled his warm chest against my face. I felt his arms tighten around me, with uncertainty at first, then stronger and tighter, in acceptance of my acceptance.

"Oh, lady," I barely heard his whisper. "I could have lost you tonight."

"Don't you bet on it Devin." I told him, my voice muffled against him. "Not on your life."

"That's what I was betting on, Kerry. Not just mine, but yours. And ours. I won't stay here without you, lady. I won't cope with this world. Not without you."

With a last glance at the cupboard, we returned to the beanbag where I was handed a freshly lit cigarette, and a new viewpoint on *him* in the form of another song on the reel-to-reel. He didn't have to point it out this time. I had finally realized that those tapes were following a pattern. A prearranged orderly pattern that had been following our story from the very beginning. The songs could be taken either of two ways. Universally, for anyone who happened to listen, or very, very personally.

How had he known back during those early recording years that *we* would be coming together now to live what he couldn't possibly have had any conscious knowledge of *then?*

And how could he have known then that the timing of these songs would correlate with what was going on...

Now?

7 It was a relief to be able to sit back now and finally relax, listen to the music, and just watch. Christian's self-portrait was visible every third flash of Puff's globe. The atmosphere in the room was perfectly attuned to Devin's music, and the peyote was beginning to peak again. Apparently, there would be a few more peaks and valleys of this drug before the night ended, but this time I was not afraid of the stepped-up awareness that the substance brought about.

The song was a beautiful ballad by the Moody Blues. *Never Comes the Day.*

The singer could feel me sighing as the night went on. If only I knew what was inside of him now...somehow I wouldn't want to know him. He said I would still love him this night, and that everything would be all right in the end if I'd just admit what I was feeling and...more importantly, see what was before my eyes. He assured me that we both knew it was true, that the truth was never out of our sight.

Thoughts entered my head and slipped beyond into the invisible windows of my mind.

He seemed intent on getting me to really *listen* to the message in the song. Under the influence of this drug, there was no way I could do anything *but* listen. I wondered if those songs could ever mean anything other than what they seemed to be saying, and if I would feel the same about them tomorrow after the peyote had worn off. Watching him from the closeness and security of his lap, my cheek resting against his thigh, I struggled to resist the sudden impulse to drift off to sleep.

Devin picked up on that thought immediately. "Don't succumb to it, lady. It's not impossible to fall asleep on this stuff."

I nodded and raised myself to a sitting position. He reached for the stash box.

"This will wake you up."

"No, I'll really fall asleep then, Devin. Am I still free to ask you questions...now that we've got *that* out of the way?" I glanced in the direction of the cupboard.

"I wish you would." He smiled at me. "I've been waiting for them. You see, you can't always—" he nodded in the same direction—"take words at face value."

"Okay." I rubbed my eyes and discovered that, in sitting up, I was more nearly back to normal than I'd realized. "This...uh...place you keep talking about...this world that you say you're...we're...from, whatever, you've mentioned it more than once, and I was wondering if it had a name."

"No. No name and, well, I'm not trying to confuse you, Kerry, but it's not exactly a *place*. Those are physical concepts...human terms. Another term is *space*, but there again, we're getting into space-time, which doesn't exist. The universe is completely contained in this room. Not just the physical universe, but all worlds. You've got to broaden your perception of space and time, and then you would realize that using the term *place* puts it in the physical universe, and this *place* I speak of is totally nonphysical. But back to your original question...its name. People have *tried* to label it, yes. It's picked up quite an assortment of names, and any one of them would do, yet all of them are incorrect. Humans just have to label everything."

I swallowed uneasily, remembering that word on the cupboard. That name...that label that he himself had actively constructed with his own two hands. That seemed to contradict the statement he'd just made. I had to force myself to ask the questions if I expected to get any answers.

"Is Hell one of the names?"

A look of deep concern crossed his features before he sighed and responded to the question.

"For one. Perhaps it is only the most widely used. People get off on horror and fear, and believe me, those people create their own hell. Heaven, to be fair, is another name but, well, that's because people haven't fully comprehended the meaning and reality of opposites in this world. If there is a heaven, and there's *got* to be one because *God* said so in his autobiography..." he paused and smiled, probably to assure me that his sarcasm was only meant teasingly..."then there *must* be a hell. If there is good, then there must be bad as well. One is said to be *up*, so the other must be *down*. There again, misconception of the term *space*. There actually *isn't* any up and down although the term is also used to describe frequencies that worlds oscillate at, such as faster and slower." He paused to light a cigarette, took a couple drags, and handed it to me as he continued.

"What people don't yet realize is that things only *seem* to be opposites of each other because opposites are things they must deal with in this physical world of matter. Two individual opposites are actually one same thing. If you follow *love* through its various gradations and degrees, it would lessen to *like* and eventually end at *hate*. It's all one thing. He who loves God must also love the Devil as well, for they are actually opposites of the same idea."

I went over to the bookshelf. Only one of my personal books was devoted to the history of the Devil. It was barely a pamphlet. The Devil had never been my trip, and everything he'd implied about himself actually *being* the Devil caused my ego to revolt. He was no devil. I had always *hated* the Devil. I looked at the pamphlet entitled *Exorcism and the Devil*. On its tiny cover was a picture of a fiery-haired being suspended on a cross in the classic position of crucifixion. I handed it wordlessly to him.

He studied the picture with faraway thoughts reflected in his eyes.

"I can remember hanging like that once." He leafed through the booklet, scanning the text. It wasn't really demeaning of the Devil. In fact, from what I could remember of it, most of it was devoted to the concept that the Devil had originally been an angel. An angel with dignity and pride, who might indeed be at least the equivalent of the legendary God, and it even depicted Satan as a god in his own right, who had no need to call down the original God whose very greed and dictatorship, according to this booklet, was said to be the reason for Satan's very fall.

As Devin came to the last few pages, his frown reappeared again, and he handed the booklet back to me. "Strange that they'd write a book about the feasible good in the Devil, and then end it with warnings about him from the New Testament. Did you read that thing from beginning to end?"

"No. I quit when I came to the biblical quotations. But did you notice that the picture on the cover looks so much *like* you? Fiery hair. *Your* eyes. Not Devin's, but *yours*. The face I saw tonight. But back to the content, I've never been able to stand those quotes from *The Bible*. It really disgusts me that people take what's in it literally word for word when you and I both know it isn't the complete Bible, and it's been changed to suit the person's beliefs who is revising it. People pushing their version on other people. I'm sure most of it was meant symbolically anyway. Entire religions were born based on four guys who couldn't agree on their own stories."

He smiled. "It had its purpose back then." He reached over, took the cigarette from me, drew on it, and exhaled. "Don't get hung up in *any* religious dogmas, good *or* evil. They especially aren't worth your hatred which, itself, feeds the dogma and spreads it. Take the fairy tales for what they're worth, but accept and believe only what you experience. You can believe in your *Self*. Other than that, why believe anything?"

"But aren't you asking me, essentially, to believe who you say you are, and to believe that a beautiful hell exists all around us now at a different vibratory level? Isn't that asking for blind faith?"

"No," he replied quickly. "Rather, I wish you *not* to take my word for it. My entire point has been, and still is, for you to experience it yourself. Only then will you come to me with full awareness and recollection. When you realize who *you* are, then you'll remember who *I* am. You will *know*, not just believe, because you will have experienced it. Blind faith, of all things, I do not want from you, lady."

"Well, how can I *do* it, then? How will I ever experience this world?"

"You're not familiar with *technical* alpha. I wish you were."

"No. Pam talks about meditation all the time. That's not what you mean, though, is it?"

"No." He stubbed the cigarette out. "Meditation's not my trip. But your sister is due for a talking to. Does that kid have any idea what meditation can *lead* to? For that matter, do *you*? Because alpha, when entered into with negative beliefs, such as *the Devil's going to get you*, can produce a thought form of that very fear. If she isn't aware that meditation will eventually lead to other realities, voids, worlds, whatever her label for it is, she could get, quite literally, the *hell* scared out of her."

"Oh, Pam's the one person who doesn't see evil in anything. She did have a scare once during one of her classes, though, and they whisked her out of the room and had a talk with her. I think it was along the lines of what you just said."

"Okay, that's good. Now you, lady. I've noticed a tendency to negative thinking. Worrying. You know what I mean. You've got to realize that worry *can* manifest exactly what you're worrying about. But then," he paused and tapped me affectionately on the nose, "so can positive thoughts. Anyhow, I keep getting sidetracked. Your question was regarding whether it was meditation, and I believe I've clarified that for you. Alpha is a leaping-off point. You're in alpha when you daydream, and daydreaming is, well, that's another question."

"Well, if it's not meditation, is it what they call astral projection?"

"No. Well…" he paused in thought for a minute, "it's a *form* of projection, in a sense. That is, you *do* leave your physical body behind. But it's not the astral plane, as they call it. Anyone has access to that anytime. That, again, is yet another question. But it's not what you need to learn now. Remember that distance isn't measured in miles or space. It's *here*. Right now. Wherever you are. You only have to realize it to perceive it. You've already worked with perception using your physical senses to lift you off, and I know you *have* used your natural abilities, but you don't use them enough. Practice alone would get you there faster than all these questions, but I understand your need to ask them. If only for the process of elimination of what it's *not*. Realizing is not the same thing as knowing. You can *know* a pot of boiling water will burn you if you watch enough people stick their hand in it and scream with pain, but you won't realize it until you stick your *own* hand in and feel it yourself. Realization is the end result of experience, which is the goal of life here. Experience is the key to it all, and you will only experience as much as your ego can handle and accept. The trick is to become aware of *what* you are, and know you can handle much more than you think you can."

"How do I do this?"

"Come *with* me. Now is as good a time as any."

"I can do that? Now? With you?"

He sighed. "Not with that kind of doubt ringing in your voice. Come here. Sit like I showed you…for balance, not because the Orientals like that position. Over here. Now. Look at Puff."

Puff had three different scenes flashing in the globe. With the Christmas lights and balls of crunched up tinfoil inside, pictures formed. Some were landscapes and some seemed to be figures of people. One scene resembled the blue and purple hole I'd gone through on the night I'd had the dream. Every once in a while a black-and-white scene of a shadowy, caped figure would appear, then flash away to another scene.

"The doors are in there, lady. See them?"

"The doors? In there?"

"They're in there for you if you wish them to be. Come *with* me."

"I *can't*, Devin. I don't know *how*. I don't have any *idea* what to do."

My frustration must have been apparent to him because he reached for my hand. That gesture alone had a calming effect on me.

"All right, lady. There's no rush. Stay this time. But I must go." He looked at me inquisitively. "That won't hurt your feelings, will it? If I go without you?"

"No. Of course not." I felt ashamed that I was not equal enough to him to be able to follow where he led, but I knew that whatever he felt he had to do, he *had* to do. "Go ahead. I'll be all right."

I don't know if he heard the entire sentence. Sitting across from me, without even closing his eyes, he was gone. His body was like a wax figure, his chest motionless. I was familiar with this as it was exactly how he slept. A song began about Timothy Leary flying his astral plane, taking trips, but it assured me that he brought you back the same day.

I sat watching the globe flash, change, and then change again. Whether the peyote had hit another temporary valley, or whether it was simply wearing off, I had no experience to compare it to. Pure feedback on what he'd just told me. Experience was something one could relate to.

Sleep became harder to resist while Devin's body remained in that corpselike position. I don't know when, but I fell asleep.

I awoke to find Erick leaning over me with concern and I looked around. I was no longer in the beanbag but lying up on the couch, my face against a cool pillow and my body securely tucked in with blanket and quilt. There was an aroma of coffee in the room.

"How do you feel?"

"Okay." I shifted my weight to my elbow. "I guess I fell asleep."

"I guess you did." He kissed me and sat down on the edge of the couch. "Is your stomach upset?"

"No."

"Hungry?"

"No. I feel worn out, but I'm not sleepy anymore. As if I slept for eight hours but my body's just tired."

"Just lie back and relax. There's coffee here on the table if you want it."

I could see the two mugs steaming on the coffee table. It suddenly occurred to me that the music was shut down. Finally. The silence was beautiful. I looked back to Erick, who was watching me with concern.

"Why do you look so worried?" I asked him, touching his hand.

He looked away as if he was embarrassed for displaying a human emotion on my behalf, or anybody's for that matter.

"Well, no drug affects everybody the same way. You didn't need it, love, but I told you I'd be nearby."

I patted his hand and lay back against the pillow, glad for the peaceful quiet darkness and scant red bayberry candlelight. The room was filled with the scent, and I felt unusually content and happy that it was Erick whose company I was in now. He smoothed my hair back away from my face, and I gave in to the blackness again.

When I opened my eyes for the second time that morning, it was to the sound of water running in the bathroom.

December fifth. Thursday. I was back in the real world.

I followed the sound and found Devin shaving, dressed for work, and showing no sign of having been up all night.

"Hey-hey-hey!" He paused to kiss me in greeting, then resumed his attention to the mirror and the razor. "How do you feel?"

"Okay, I guess. Is it all worn off now?"

"Yes. You're probably tired as hell. Why don't you stay home today and get some sleep. I can tell Mama."

"No. It's Christmas, or I would."

"Christmas?" He laughed. "Hey, uh, I hate to break it to you, but it's only the fifth."

I laughed with him. "No, I meant the season. You'd be surprised how many people give bottled water setups for Christmas gifts. The office would get backed up in the posting of new orders, and if *one* girl doesn't show up, Lola ends up doing the work. Otherwise, the offer is tempting." I yawned.

"Learn anything last night?" he asked, suddenly serious.

"Matter of fact, I did." I handed him a clean towel after he splashed on aftershave lotion, then kissed his cold cheek. "Old Spice. I love that stuff."

"Don't divert my attention with my vanity." He grinned. "I just wondered if you got anything straightened out last night."

"The way you read minds? Come on, Devin."

He shrugged. "So it's useful now and then, but I wasn't around last night, and I'd kind of like to hear it from you."

"Well, I guess I know who our...mutual friend is."

"You've known all along, Kerry."

"Okay, maybe so, but my suspicion was confirmed."

"Keep talking." He motioned for me to follow him into the kitchen where coffee was already perking, leaned against the counter and crossed his arms. "So, at least you've met formally, then."

I nodded. "He never did come back from wherever he went, though."

"He did. You were probably asleep. And, whether you realize it or not, you were never alone."

"What do you mean?"

"Your friend. That spirit, or whatever he...it is. Buzzing around last night. And Erick. Poor Erick. Got a planet-earth blast of what it feels to feel real concern for somebody. Oh, not because of your little friend...just, man, *you* on a drug. The dude was totally freaking out."

"Wait a minute. Back to that spirit thing. You mean that blue pokey thing?"

He laughed at my description. "Why don't you give him a chance? I'm telling you, the dude loves you."

"Get outta here, Devin. Where do you get he *loves* me? And...if that is the case, how come you're not jealous?" I smirked at him, defying him to explain that one.

His answer was an exaggerated leer. "*I* don't have any problems touching you. I kind of feel sorry for the chap. Playing childish little games like slamming doors and...hey, what's his name anyway?"

"How would *I* know? I'm glad he *didn't* bother me last night. On that drug, I probably would have *really* freaked out."

"Well, he was around you constantly while I was there. It's hard to believe he's a sudden guest. However, I suppose if he'd been around before, you'd have picked up on it."

"He wasn't." Something flashed through my mind and was gone before I could put my finger on it. "The first night I ever felt him, or even knew of his existence, was the night you put that *War of the Gods* song on." Again, something slithered in my memory, then vanished. Like trying to remember a dream as you were waking.

"And never before that?" Devin looked genuinely disbelieving.

"No. I think he got in through the same door all your friends use."

Devin poured the steaming coffee into two mugs as he replied. "Could be. I don't particularly *like* the dude, but...that's my ego, I guess. That he's avoiding me. But you have no beef with him, Kerry. Find out if he goes by a name. Like Casper or Spooky, or..." The glint in his eye was an unmistakable twinkle.

"Sure, Devin. I'll do that. Next time I see him."

"No really. No kidding, now. Ask him." He lit a cigarette, took a short drag off it and handed it to me, then took a sip of his coffee. "Any personality that's worked that hard to get *that* physical must have a heavy purpose." He furrowed his eyebrows menacingly. "Maybe he's trying to warn you not to get hooked up with me."

"Oh, that'll do it, all right. I'd take the word of anything that can poke *that* convincingly without a finger."

"To get your attention. That's pretty strong measures. He must want to tell you something pretty important. Or maybe it isn't important, but he wants to say it pretty badly, don't you think?" He downed the last of his coffee. "I guess I'd better split. You going to be at the coffee shop?"

"Maybe. Depends on how the traffic is. I don't have to drop the kids off since they're already there."

"Okay, I'll look for your car. And...uh, maybe we should start thinking about a closer school. You know, there's one right down the street, here."

With a quick kiss, he left.

Once on the road, driving became a pretty automatic process, and my mind was free to wander back to last night again. A memory of a face was permanently imprinted on my brain that I would never forget. There was no rational explanation for what he'd done. If I had been merely hallucinating, then how had he known what my eyes had seen? It had been deliberate, I was sure. A test, maybe, but not accidental in any case.

I was surprised at myself. How easily I had accepted that ugly title as part of him. As I drove, I began to examine my conflicting concepts and by now fucked-up beliefs. God was beginning to look more like an *idea,* and yet he *had* acknowledged *some* idea of God with obvious respect. He'd even hinted at a connection with himself somewhere.

And the *Devil.* Someone I'd really held no previous belief in, was now allegedly living in my house, sleeping in my bed, and defying all the rumors of Hades, behaving in no way like any devil I'd ever read about.

A child was being considered that would require an upbringing of the highest caliber. A job I wasn't sure I was equipped to handle.

A world, coexisting with this one, vibrating at a different rate than ordinary matter, was not just being hinted at anymore. It was out in the open now.

Instructions had begun, both subliminally and openly, on the discovery and use of dimensional doorways that I'd never heard of before. My secure belief system had been shaken like dice in a rolling cone and spilt violently out over my ordinary sense of right and wrong, good and evil, God and the Devil…beauty and ugliness.

Doubts in my ability to learn to transcend this everyday world of logic were seeping into places where trust should have been. Devin repeatedly insisted that I, like he, belonged to this invisible world. What proof did I have of such a world at all?

And if Devin Drew was really sharing space with a higher being, who identified with a title that literally translated into *little god*, then what the hell did that make me?

No, I just couldn't buy it. Devin wasn't any devil, no matter *what* he said. There had to be more to this.

As I parked my car, I made a mental note to shelve that blind faith that Devin had not asked for and do some serious checking on the history of the Devil with whatever sources there were at home.

Lola presented me with a new job today, one I was grateful for. Instead of posting the monthly bottled-water cooler rents, I was positioned at the addressograph machine and given a crash course in running it. The job consisted of inserting metal plates the size of a military identification dog tag, several at a time, into the machine and then stamping the customer name and address onto blank statements. The job was monotonous and automatic once I got the hang of it, and left my mind free to wander back to last night.

The day went by fast with even Kelly too busy posting rents in our office to call in any remarks to me. My new machine sat directly behind Lola's chair and was too loud to invite any kind of conversation with anybody.

Devin dropped in briefly around 3:30, quietly laid a white envelope beside my cigarettes and gestured a question with eyebrows raised and a thumbs up.

I nodded. So far I was okay, drugs, no sleep and all else considered.

Devin's excuse for his unnecessary walk-in was a small Polaroid camera he toted. He had to get Lola's picture for an upcoming circular the plant was putting together for the sales department. Lola obliged wearily and he snapped his one picture, winked at me, and left.

I smiled to myself and looked down at the white envelope. Another card. I tore it open to find a *no reason except I love you* inscription inside, and signed simply *Us*.

Last night washed over me in a slow-motion ripple that brought goosebumps to my arms. The peyote. The cupboard and the face he'd revealed. The face behind the face of Devin Drew. Well, of course I'd hallucinate on peyote, I reminded myself. The drug could make me think I saw anything. That icy ripple went through me again as I realized that already my stubborn ego was hammering away with rationalizations to justify last night's events. Easy enough. Just link it all together and blame it on the drug.

I returned the card to its envelope and set it aside. I had to try to get back to the job at hand.

Yellow dots were beginning to trail across the white statements, but when I looked away from the paper, they trailed across the air as well. Great, I thought, trying not to panic. Aftereffects. All I needed *now* was to get paranoid *after* the drug had supposedly worn off. I closed my eyes to see if resting them would help, but instead was startled to see the bluish-purple hole of my dream floating in front of my closed eyes, inside my mind. A bright red circle was buzzing around inside the blue hole, which was surrounded by the spiraling walls of what appeared to be the inside of a volcano. It was clear and sharp and almost seemed like an animated cartoon.

I watched the red circle until I mentally flashed on the fact that Lola was watching me, and I took my fingers away from the sockets of my closed eyes. The room was one big blur for a minute and, sure enough, when my vision did adjust, I saw that Lola *was* watching me intently.

"Are you okay?"

I nodded. "I'm fine. I just started seeing spots, that's all."

"From the camera?"

I hadn't been snapped, but that was as good an excuse as any. "I guess so."

"That's odd. I'm the one it flashed at, and I'm not seeing any spots. You sure you're okay?"

I assured her that I was, although I wasn't so sure myself.

Devin finished up early and stopped in long enough to tell me he was heading home. Pat had offered to lock up and he'd accepted the offer.

"I'll pick up the kids," he said. "Anything special you want for supper?"

Kelly burst into laughter. "Oh! Are you the cook now too? Hey, Lola, do you hear this? Devin's cooking supper now. Boy, does she have you trained."

"Well, it can't be too difficult," Lola said with a smile and a shrug. "I think Kerry's kids only eat raviolis."

"That's *Kelly's* kids," I corrected her. "They're the tin-can eaters."

"Oh, that's right. Your kids are the Burger King eaters."

"Hey!" Devin interrupted. "You ladies can fight about all that later. Kerry, anything special?"

"Oh no, Devin. Please don't you bother with supper. The kids are used to eating later. Just go home and kick back. I'll pick up the kids."

He gave me a wink and leaned over to kiss me. "Don't let *them* get to you. They're just jealous because I happen to dig cooking. *They* have to go home and do it themselves."

"Yeah, right, Devin," Kelly retorted. "Benny *never* opens the cans at our house."

"He's usually *in* it from what I hear," Devin countered, laughing. He knew Kelly's husband well, and of Benny's penchant for attracting police with his drug deals. Even Kelly had to laugh at that one.

"Touché," she said with a sigh. "I walked right into that one."

Devin was thoroughly enjoying this repartee. "Why don't you go play in traffic?"

"What traffic?" Kelly shot back, quicker than I'd have given her mind credit for. "The traffic outside, or the traffic in and out of this office since you got back from your trip?"

Lola cleared her throat loudly from the other room. Devin took the hint.

"Anyhow, lady…later." He kissed me again. "And I *will* get the kids."

After he was gone, I excused myself and headed for the lounge. It was only 4:30. I couldn't bring myself to go back in to work. Once inside the cool restroom, I sat down on the double-sink vanity to give my dizzy head a rest and covered my face with my hands again. Maybe this was just aftereffects, but hadn't Devin said there wouldn't be any? I couldn't remember.

Kelly found me in that position some five minutes later. I heard the door swing open and distant shuffling out in the hall, the creaking of the door closing…then silence. I didn't bother to look up. It was dark and cool in my mind, and clear colorful circles were swimming around inside that purple hole, no doubt intensified by my lack of sleep. In contrast, the lounge was brightly lit, so I remained with my hands over my eyes.

"Hey, kid!" I could *feel* Kelly looking at me. In fact, from inside my head, I could almost *see* her. Just like with Lola earlier, the drug seemed to have added another inner talent I'd previously had no inclination towards. Seeing without eyes. Was it permanent, I wondered, or would I be back to normal with the last trace of the peyote finally out of my system?

"Are you all right, Ker?"

"Yeah, Kelly, really. It's my own fault. I stayed up all night with Devin doing peyote, and I'm kind of seeing trails today. It's just a little freaky."

"Aw, Jesus Christ, Kerry! Peyote! Are you going to start with that drug shit now like Benny? I thought Devin didn't *do*—"

"He *doesn't*, usually," I interrupted. "It was an annual for *him* last night."

"On a work night? What's wrong with you? Some of those things take eight hours to wear off. I know. Benny scares me when he gets on them."

"Don't worry. I'm okay. I'm sure it's just a combination of the shit still in my system and being up all night."

"Well…okay. You just stay in here for a while. I'll make you some coffee and tell Lola…"

"No, *shit*. Don't worry her. She'd freak out if she knew I took any drugs. I'll be okay in a minute."

"Well…" She sounded dubious. "Okay. If you aren't back in five or ten minutes, I'm coming after you. All right?"

"I'm fine, Kelly, really. It's cool."

"Are you sure you're okay to drive?"

"Sure," I replied, more confidently than I felt. She just *had* to bring that up when it had never crossed my mind.

I heard the lounge door swing shut and went back to watching the bizarre things going on in my mind. Never had it been so clear and colorful and sharp. Among the images that came and went were smoky-white letters, floating up like cigarette smoke rings against the deep purple and blue background.

For no reason at all, I thought of that spirit that Devin had encouraged me to talk to. That bluish whatchamacallit. The latest addition to my new family. Well, if space meant nothing, the simple addressing of it should get its attention, no matter where I was.

Who are you? I thought to the screen of colors and letters in my head. *Do you have a name?*

Immediately, four letters floated up and arranged themselves into a word.

B—L—U—E

I shrugged it off and tried again. "Blue? I didn't ask you what color you are. Do you go by a name?"

I looked into my mind again, watching for anything. Again, the same letters floated up, this time prearranged into the same word.

B—L—U—E

Hell with it, I decided. I'd been gone from the office much too long.

When I returned to my station, I found my worktable already cleared, coffee standing lukewarm. I'd been gone even longer than I'd thought.

"It's ten to," Lola said when I walked in. Hang around another five minutes before you guys split."

"You're letting us out early?" I managed a smile. "How come?"

She laughed and put her sunglasses on. " 'Cause I'm going home and I just can't see Devin cooking supper when he's not even used to kids."

"Oh, that five minutes is really going to make a difference," I said.

"Well, that's all the time it takes to open a can, right?"

"That's *Kelly.*"

"Oh, that's right. Kelly's the tin-can girl." She smiled. "You're hamburgers."

She left, and we started bolting down coffee, covering machines and jacketing up.

"It's really starting to get cold out there," Kelly commented. "Oh, gee. We get to walk to the cars together without Mister Drew."

"Yeah! Just like old times."

I wish Devin had warned me who would be cooking supper because I wasn't prepared for Christian, and I'm sure Pammy wasn't either. When I walked in, Christian was in the process of entertaining her with whatever antics he could invent while making pancakes for the household. Pammy, who was laughing hysterically, looked up at me with raised eyebrows and pointed to Christian, who also looked up when the front door opened.

"Heyyyyy, ladee!" He reached for a dishtowel first, then for me. "Th' keeds'r 'n th' tub an' Ah already checked…they eat pancakes so long's Ah promised to go git sirrup."

I laughed, remembering the rice incident. He was just now adjusting to the pickiness of children. "I'll go get the syrup," I said.

"Nope! Ah'll go. *You* sit down here an' talk t' yer sister. *You* jist got done drivin'."

"No, that's okay. I still have my jacket on and it's just up the street."

"No way, ladee. You two don' see 'nuff of each other as it iz!" He removed the tall white b-b-q chef's hat he'd been jiving Pam with and replaced it with a black felt Greek fisherman's cap. Devin had worn it once to Lola's house, insisting that it was one of only two in the United States, Trevor of course happening to have the only other one. I was surprised that Christian would have the balls to wear Devin's cherished hat, but when I commented, he countered with indignation.

"Shee-it, Devin's hat hiz *ass!* Tha's mah hat an' Devin *knows* it. Ah jist don' beef when *he* wears it. Share 'n share alahk, tha's mah trip."

The door slammed behind him.

"Wow, Ker, I see what you mean. What a freak-out!" Pammy exploded. "Aw, he's so cute. I think I like *him* the best! He's been joking and showing off ever since he got home. Boy, remember you told me how black his features are when he's around? Well, that's the first time I really got a good look at him, and you weren't kidding."

"I know." I took off my jacket and laid it on the arm of Devin's gold leather chair. "He does take a little getting used to. I was just raised to believe white stays with white and black stays with black. Christian is the one that Devin and I were apprehensive about *you* meeting. He can be a little rough sometimes, like when they shut the power off."

"You and Devin were worried about *me* meeting him?"

"Well, actually, it was more like me and *him.*"

"Oh. Well, I don't think I've ever *met* him. I only know Devin and Christian. And I *love* Christian. He's so funny."

"Yeah, he tries harder, I think," I mused. "He's so sure the world will hate him just because of the very reason I reacted so badly in the beginning. Because he's black. I mean, I love him to death now, but it didn't help his ego in the beginning when I wasn't sure what to think about him. It did take some mental adjusting."

She pointed to the door he'd just exited. "Well, I don't think I met Erick or...him as you'ns call him, or have I? Are you sure Erick isn't just Devin being serious?"

"No, Devin can definitely get serious, but once you know the two of them the differences are glaringly obvious. But that was *my* first explanation for all this too. Moods. I'm still trying to understand it all, but now I'm leaning toward the idea that these guys are a series of different levels of awareness of which *him* is completely nonphysical. Out of this world, you know?"

The *mood* thing had crossed my mind more than once, but how a *mood* could take on black features, lingo, and even the rhythm of the black gait was beyond me. "You'll meet Erick, I'm sure. He doesn't show up that often. Almost like he's too good for this wicked world. Or, beyond the human bullshit Devin gets himself into, and Erick has to get him out of. Watch him when we've got company visiting. That seems to be when all three pop in and out. Except for *him.* He is, well, he doesn't seem to feel a need to be recognized. I see *him* when there *aren't* people around. You have too, but you just wouldn't recognize it as fast as I would. When you get to know *him,* you will."

"Wait a minute. You're confusing me. Are there three or four?"

"Counting Devin, there are four. And that's assuming that the Devin I fell in love with is the same Devin Drew that I met when I took the job. I'm not sure about that."

"How did you find out Christian's name?"

"He signs his artwork that way." I pointed to the self-portrait. "But I don't think he really had that as a name until we tagged it on him."

"What about Erick? Did you'ns name him too?"

"No. Devin used that for his craft name. In Wicca, they pick a second name, and Erick just adopted it. I...*think*."

The sound of tires hitting gravel announced that one of them was home.

"Let's talk about this later," I said, and she agreed. We didn't want to hurt anyone's feelings.

I went out to the van to greet him. Christian was grinning widely, white teeth flashing, as the motor died. He held up a brown paper bag.

"Hey, ladee...sirrup!"

I stepped back so he could hop down, but when he opened the door he pulled me into his arms from where he sat. "Don' be in such a huree."

I didn't need any coaxing. "Hey, watch it now. Don't break my ribs, man."

He released his grip and then looked down suddenly at my arm. "How's that sore arm comin' 'long?"

I traced my finger up to where the "puncture" mark was. When I encountered soreness, I stopped. "Is the mark...here?"

He had to actually lift my finger to verify that it was right on the mark. "Mus' still hurt, huh?" He looked at me with sympathetic eyes. Christian, whatever he was, wasn't ashamed to show concern or emotion. Maybe that was what had finally gotten to me about him. His warmheartedness. Maybe that's what had gotten to Pam, too.

"It's only sore if I touch it," I assured him. "The other marks must be gone by now."

"Well, le's take a look." He turned my arm closer to the overhead light and shook his curly head. "See fer yerself."

I strained my neck to see the rear of my arm. The purple thumb mark was now only half purple and half tan. Just like any bruise in the process of healing and fading. The fingermarks were fading too, but they were closer to tan than purple. The outbreak of veins...my "tattoo"...was as clear as the day it arrived. It didn't look like it would ever fade away.

"Y' know, ladee, *somebody* waz gonna look up tha' mark fer ya. We maht try doin' tha' later. Maybe after supper if ya feel up t' it. Ah have seen that before, but Ah jist can' remember where. An' how'r ya feelin' after th' shit las' naht? Any weird aftereffects?"

"A few." I ran down the dots episode and the crazy visualization that had picked up since I'd taken the drug. I told him about the reappearance of the hole in my dream and the clarity and depth involved within minutes of shutting my eyes.

"Ah don' think that hole *is* gonna go away. Ah think it maht stan' fer somethin' but Ah can' say as yet, what. Ah think it's connected somehow t' yer goin' home." He sighed. "Well, come on, ladee. Le's go in before yer sister gits t' wonderin'."

He alit to the ground, and we went in to find the kids dressed in their pajamas, seated at their little play table already set with dishes and...napkins?

"Napkins?" I asked Pammy. "What's with this class all of a sudden?"

"I didn't do it. *He* did."

I turned to Christian with awe. "You got napkins? What do you think this is? The Nixon residence?"

He grinned sheepishly.

"And who do I thank for the house being so clean?"

Pam pointed at him and he wagged his head, looking embarrassed.

"He wouldn't let me help him. He never does. Neither of them ever does."

Our table was also set for three, but I just wasn't hungry. It was coffee as usual for me.

"Ah don' know how she stays healthy," he told Pammy as he piled up another plate of pancakes. "On coffee day after day. She's not normal."

"Big deal," Pam retorted. "What *is* around here?"

I went in to pour myself a second cup of coffee.

"I just can't get over the perked stuff," I said as I returned to the coffee table.

"Onlee th' bes' fer *you*, ladee." He added sugar and milk for me, beaming proudly. "If all Ah gotta feed ya iz coffee, it maht as well be the real shee-it...lahk th' coffee shop."

Christian's drawl seemed to be more Southern than Harlem Black. Sometimes he did slur his words, but it seemed to only be when he lost his temper, like the day he chastised Ethan or the day of the now infamous electric company incident.

I watched Christian that evening after the supper dishes had been cleared away. Pam was showering for work. The kids had fallen asleep watching television in their room, and Christian had taken it upon himself to mess with the wiring of the stereo system, rearranging all Erick's hard work. Erick had literally spent hours last Sunday, hooking up that equipment.

My thoughts weren't as private as I figured. Christian's sudden reply to them came verbally, even though I hadn't said a word and his back had been to me as he worked.

"Don' ya be worryin' 'bout th' wirin' system, ladee. There's a rat way an' a wrong way."

"And then there's *your* way, right?" I finished for him. I wasn't really worried about it. It was just that Erick was going to have a shit fit.

"Oh, Erick kin hang it in his ass," Christian said aloud, taking his black felt cap off and placing it on my head. "Hey, that looks good on you, ladee."

"Erick's stereo and Devin's hat," I teased him.

"Tha's shee-it Devin's hat," he said. "Tha's mah hat an' he fuckin' *knows* it too."

"Okay. Don't get huffy about it."

He smiled agreeably. "Who's gettin' huffy?"

"You are."

"Huffy...shee-it. Ah let Devin wear it all the time. You call that huffy? Oh, an' Ah jist remembered..."

He got up and walked out the front door. When he returned he was carrying a small brown paper bag. He looked suspiciously different.

"I forgot I had rolling papers and cigarettes in the van. See what you do to me, chick? You scramble my brains up."

Pammy and I exchanged glances. She was out of the shower, dressed, with a towel wrapped around her wet hair.

Christian was gone. All physical, facial and verbal trace of Christian had walked out that door, and in his place was Devin, as usual, behaving as though he'd been there all along.

"Well, let's light one up! Everybody's straight here. That's what's wrong with this joint…did you catch that? Joint…little play on words for you girls."

Pam looked at me, and we both burst into laughter. The change was so obvious.

"Hey, Devin," Pam said. "Do you do that at work, too?"

"Do what?" he asked innocently, winking at me. "Smoke? Well, not in the office anyway."

"Wow," Pam said. "He must freak everybody out at that place."

"Well, we have a tendency to keep him away from the plant," Devin said with a shrug, busying himself with the rolling. "He's not wild about the place anyway." He tossed me another wink.

"I think I'm getting outta here." Pam picked up her car keys. "I might as well go in early. I can use the money. Besides that, you'ns are blowing my head."

It was all good-natured on Pam's part. Devin told her jokingly to stop back in and see us once in a while, and she assured him that she'd seen enough of us for one day.

"I'll be around more on my days off," she added seriously, as if an afterthought.

"Man, it's like she doesn't even live here," Devin commented when the sound of her engine faded off down the road. "I like her a lot. She has a natural awareness about her that you don't find in many people."

"Yeah, she's great," I agreed. "But look at the bright side. She still lives here, but look at the privacy we all have, including her. Her shift is opposite ours."

"By the way, are you still seeing things like you were at work today?"

"Well, only when I close my eyes."

"Close them now."

I shut them and waited. The hole floated into view, that purple sky through the funnel-like blackness.

"Same thing?" Devin asked, lighting the joint and handing it to me.

"Same thing." I opened my eyes and accepted the joint he extended. "Wonder what *this* will do."

"Get you good and stoned, probably." Devin laughed. "You're okay. It's just new to you, that's all. Everything's cool between you and him? No misunderstandings?"

"No misunderstandings. At least not about who he says he is. He didn't try to soft-pedal it."

He nodded. "That reminds me. We'd better get that tape off the cupboard. I don't see how your sister could have missed it. Did she mention it?"

"No, but I guess it's easy enough to overlook. He only had to change one letter."

"Did you mention the peyote to her?"

"No."

"How about your friend?" Devin worked to remove the tape as he talked.

"Find out who *he* is?"

"Who…oh, Blue?" I'd completely forgotten about him. Or it.

"Blue?" Devin echoed with a smile.

"Blue. That's what it spelled. Twice. I asked twice."

"You asked it?"

"Well, whatever. Male or female or neither. Hell, I don't know. I did as you suggested, and that's what came up."

"And his name is *Blue?*"

"Yeah. How Hollywood, huh?"

"Well, whatever. Seems to me *you're* the one who should be called Blue. Everything you wear is blue. Even your jacket and shoes are blue. Christ, your goddamned *aura* is blue. I wonder what his trip is. He's been in the back room since I got home. Maybe even before that. Why don't you go back there and deal with him face-to-face?"

"Now?"

"Why not? Good a time as any. Go ahead back there and try to talk to him. And listen for his way of talking. I'll be right out here."

"Well, okay," I said reluctantly. "But since you like him so much, why don't *you* do it?"

He smiled. "I don't think he digs guys. But for the record, I did try. When I was getting changed after work. I called him on. I invited him. I even dared him. He just ignores me. I'm not the one he's interested in."

"Okay, I'll go. Anything I can do to make it easier on him?"

"Just sit still. Think to him. And wait. Try getting undressed. You don't need all that material bullshit in the way. Nobody's here, and I won't come back there either."

I nodded and went, however hesitantly, into the bedroom. I thought about the marks on my arm and wondered if Blue had had anything to do with them. The music could be heard through the closed bedroom door, and it dawned on me that it had been running since I'd come home. Those tapes had to contain hours and hours on a single reel.

I slipped out of my clothes and sat quietly in the corner where the bed hugged the wall. Maybe it was the grass that made it so easy. Or maybe it was the music coming through the door, sounding so much louder than I knew it was.

Devin's tapes were so damned appropriate to the situations.

9 It was a few minutes before I sensed Blue's presence. While I waited, there was nothing to do but listen to the lyrics of the song. It made me wonder about the coincidences surrounding those tapes. The song was by Badfinger, and the title was Baby Blue.

Devin had just now learned Blue's "name" so he couldn't have cued that song up. The tape had already been running when the song came on. There had been no pause or fast-forward to it, and he couldn't have known exactly where the song was on the huge reel.

If I took the lyrics literally, they were a little disquieting. They placed Blue's origin right smack in Devin's world. *His* world. The words seem to confirm *his* statement that I'd left such a world twenty-five years ago, and left him behind.

The singer said he'd gotten what he deserved for keeping me waiting so long, had gone too long without a word to me, and now he was sure that I thought he had forgotten me. He wanted me to show him how to show me the way, said he'd tried so many times himself, and he wanted me by his side.

It practically tied Blue and *him* together, and the final verse really gave me pause. He wanted to tell me something before he left, and that was to take good care and to let him know that my love for him was special and to let it grow.

Where was he going? I didn't like that last verse.

I didn't have time to ponder it, though. Blue appeared out of nowhere just as the song ended. The quivering mass seemed to hover, first over me, and then I felt a sensation of something passing *through* me. I didn't have to open my eyes. I could feel it begin at the top of my head and ripple through the length of my body from the inside. I wondered if the peyote had permanently stepped up my awareness more of things like Blue, or if the reducing valve in my brain had ever shrunk back down to normal size, limiting my perception to what it had been before last night.

NO

Well, the letters were still there, but spelling out a negative reply to what? I tried to remember what I was thinking about at the second the word floated up, but stoned on grass, there was no telling. The way my mind was jumping around, I wished now that I had never taken that hit off the weed.

"Blue!" I whispered aloud. "Is *that* who you are? Are you *him*? Are you *part* of him, or some kind of extension of him?"

A maze of letters swarmed in and out, none of which I could keep my attention on, for the coolness of the vibrating mass was distracting. I knew I should be inviting him to make physical contact again. There was no question in my mind that somebody or something was here in the room with me, and it was that last thought, that I wasn't alone, that spurred me to leap from the corner and back into my clothes. I didn't care how nice the thing might be. I wasn't accustomed to things.

"It's too creepy," I told Devin when I was back with him again. I found him in his gold throne, sketching pictures, faces again, and a scorpion of some magnificent detail. He looked up when I appeared, and I was relieved to see that it was still Devin.

"Backed out, did you?" He smiled.

I nodded sheepishly. "It's easy to tell someone else to do it, Devin, but it's a creepy feeling to know you're not alone and that you can't see who else is with you."

"Well, why do you need to *see* him? The poor dude probably doesn't *have* a regular form and that blueness is the best he could come up with for you. I'm sure *one* of us would have perceived something other than that blue mist by now."

"I don't understand," I said. "I thought everything here had to have a form."

"He travels here through the use of energy." Devin set his sketch aside. "Don't feel bad. If you *did* see him, it would just be your mind supplying you with the form you saw, and even *that* would be based upon what he or it put across telepathically. It's your own symbol that you'd see."

"Well, whatever he is, he's here and I guess I'll just have to get used to him." Once again, I was surprised at my new acceptance of something that just yesterday had scared the living daylights out of me. Before the peyote.

Devin shrugged. "You'll get used to him, or, he'll give up. Anyway, have you tried to work with some of the things *he* tried to show you?"

I admitted that I hadn't found much time for practicing anything. I'd been pretty occupied with life lately. I hadn't even found time to sit down with my old record albums like I used to. That alone had been a *form* of meditation or alpha.

"Want me to go out some nights and give you some solitude?" Devin offered. "I could just get out of your way, you know."

"If you want to go out somewhere, I wouldn't want you to feel like you couldn't, but I don't need any solitude. I'd rather be with you."

"And I wouldn't enjoy myself out anywhere if you weren't with me, so I guess we agree on that. But I could get lost in the back room or something. If either one of us felt the need to be alone I'm sure we could work it out, but although I *used* to feel the need for solitude, I don't anymore." He began to thread another reel into the machine. "That doesn't solve the exercise problems, though. You need to learn to go, and you need to somehow be able to concentrate on some of the exercises to get anywhere close to that kind of projection. I suppose we'll just have to play it by ear. Meanwhile, I'm going back there to have another round with Blue. Now that I know his name, perhaps I can get his attention."

He disappeared down the hall and I heard the bedroom door shut.

A lone red bayberry candle kept me company in the now empty living room. I removed it from Devin's stereo shelves and placed it in front of me on the coffee table. I didn't understand why it was so damn important for me to practice anything. Wasn't it enough that we were finally together? Why and what was he so hell-bent on getting me to learn?

I supposed now was as good a time as any.

"Hello, candle."

A Moody Blues song began, and when I realized what song it was, I could only sigh. Of course. *The Candle of Life.* Mellow, soft, melodic and mesmerizing, it couldn't have been more appropriate. The candle of life was burning slowly, they told me, and it was there so that we'd know we could go, as long as we went with love.

Devin had once told me of his early experiments with candles. He'd said they were good to start with because they were so easy. The candle actually flickered at my greeting, as if it could hear me. I put my index finger close to the flame and, like a magnet, the flame leaned in toward it. Startled, I drew my finger back and glanced suspiciously around for Blue.

Nothing. I was alone.

I returned my attention to the candle. It must be my aura that attracts it, I thought. I'll just step back about a foot or two and then try it.

I retreated a couple feet and put my hand below the level of the coffee table so that any moving air could be ruled out.

"Dance," I said, moving my finger up and down. To my shock, the flame began to flicker in perfect sync to the rhythm of my finger. When I spread my palm out with a calm gesture, it instantly went back to a passive flame. I tried a few more experiments and found that I could raise and lower it and call it from all directions, but I could not raise it off the wick as Devin had claimed to have done. Nor could I extinguish it altogether.

The phone rang and I picked up the receiver, still excited with my success, however trivial. I had proved to myself that inanimate matter could be controlled.

"Hello?"

It was Pam. I told her what had happened with the candle and she listened quietly. Then she said quite seriously, "Boy, you're really getting into some heavy stuff, Kerry. I hope it's all okay. If Devin wasn't so cool, and if I didn't know him, from the sounds of this…well, let's put it this way. I don't know if I'd have what it took to live under the circumstances you're living under. I don't know if I could even *be* in the situation you're in."

"I guess I'm pretty used to it now, Pam. At first, I was as leery as you sound, but now, well, I know now that I wouldn't want any of them to leave. I can't explain it, but I love all of them equally."

"You mean there isn't even a preference for just Devin anymore?"

"Pam, the best example I can give you is my love for the kids. I don't love one more or less than the other. This is the same thing, but a different kind of love. Devin becomes different when one cuts out…when one is actually missing. When he went up north, Erick wasn't with him and he was withdrawn, listless…not the same. It's kind of hard to explain."

"Kerry, you realize that you're saying you don't want Devin back to normal now."

"Pam, as far as I'm concerned, he *is* normal and always was. So are Erick and Christian and the only difference between them and triplets is that they all take turns with one body. That's all."

"Well, I guess it's normal for you'ns. I always did say you weren't normal anyway." Pam laughed. "It figures you'd come up with someone as weird as yourself, but on the other hand, Ker, you and Devin are perfect for each other. Anyway, the reason I called is to let you know I won't be coming home tonight. I get off at two, and George asked me to stop by after work. I feel sorry for him. He's home all alone and he doesn't have a girl now. Like I said, he needs a buddy…someone to go out drinking with, or something. Not me, but at least he understands we can't go back to what we were."

Devin was just coming out of the bedroom, so I hurriedly said goodbye to Pam and excitedly turned to tell him of my success with the candle.

"That's good," he said calmly. "I'm glad to see you're working with things like that. And don't stop with the candle either. Did you get it off the wick?"

"No, but everything else. I guess I had too much doubt about lifting it."

"You'll find that type of thing easy enough. If fact, you'll soon be bored with it. It's too easy, and it only depletes energy that you could be using for something important, such as repairing those lungs you continue to assault every day. Put the cigarette out, Kerry."

I looked up from the candle to find Erick, his bluish-white aura lighting up the room. He took the cigarette from my hand, stubbed it out, and smiled. "Parlor tricks are a waste of energy although I suppose it's good for the ego to assure itself of its own ability. I wouldn't advise performance for curiosity seekers, though. The biggest waste is not in the ones you don't convince, but in the ones you *do*. And for what? Why a need to convince *anybody*?"

"Okay, easy, man. I wasn't going to perform for anybody. How in the hell *are* you, Erick?" I hugged him and he laughed softly to himself.

"In the hell…really, love. Your choice of words." He returned my hug tightly.

"What else is a good exercise?" My success with the candle had me anxious to learn more.

"All right, stare at a light bulb. Here. Use this one." He hit the red lamp switch and suggested that I stare at it for about sixty seconds. Directly at the bulb.

I did, and when I looked away, there was a dark blue ball floating in front of everything I looked at.

"Now, close your eyes," he said, "and you'll still see it. This exercise is good for learning to control what you see in your mind. Make it stand still. Don't allow it to float away. And here's another option. It's blue now. Change it to red. Again, it's so easy it's ridiculous."

I found the ball behaving exactly as he described, not only holding still at his words, but flashing a blazing red as the word was spoken. Apparently, I was highly suggestible.

"Okay, that was pretty easy too. What else?" When I looked up at his face, I realized that due to that floating red dot now covering it, his pale blue aura had extended even further. Or, had my aura vision merely improved?

He didn't wait to be asked. By now, I pretty much took the telepathy for granted with these guys.

"The bulb blasts the retina of your eye…bombards the pupil with sudden excess light. You are forced to rely on your peripheral vision which is the vision with which you see auras anyway," he explained.

"Peripheral vision?"

"Yes. You see *me* when you look directly at me, but it is your peripheral vision that takes in the rest of the room, even though you aren't looking directly at it. I wouldn't use that red bulb for auras, though. That shade of red will become its opposite, in this case, blue, and it will distort aura colors. A white bulb is best for that, even though *you* seem to be aware of them without the aid of the props. However, you might remember it if someone asks you what an aura *is*. Rather than trying to explain, you can simply show them how to see them for themselves. Everyone sees them at the onset of birth, but they are conditioned from that day forward to believe that they aren't there until the brain finally says, *okay, I don't see that…cut !*"

"Well, who would even ask?"

"People will. And it's your responsibility to pass knowledge along. We're working towards a better world here, and awareness is what will improve it, and eventually perfect it. Auras are normal, natural, and a fine measurement for the degree of awareness and character in an individual. You know you've mastered them when you don't *have* to look for them, and eventually you'll see them all the time, twenty-four hours a day, just as it was the day you were born. The colors will become *part* of the person you're looking at."

"Okay, well…I can see them pretty well anyway. What else?"

He looked at me with amusement. "Impatient, are you? Well, I must admit, you *do* catch on fast. By the way, how are you doing with that Theban script?"

I laughed. "Oh, you've noticed my little notes on Devin's van, huh?"

He nodded. "You know the whole alphabet now, don't you?"

"Yes. I practiced it up at the coffee shop and at work, but it really only took me a day to memorize the alphabet."

"Do you ever wonder what attracted you to it at all, or why you learned it so quickly?"

"Not really. I've always been good at memorizing. Why? Is it something important?"

"No. It just isn't something that most people in this world would have any interest in. I suppose it's good that your interests tend towards the occult. There *is* some truth among the distortions there."

"Are you saying that you'd recommend the occult as *the* answer? The road to awareness?"

"No. There is some good in all the belief systems. You have to look for the good in everything."

"Is there good in *The Bible*?" I stifled a laugh and added, "Here I'm asking *you*, the one with all the makings of an archangel."

"Hey, now," he said gruffly, but with a tone of affection. "There are no wings."

"And no *horns* either," I countered.

"Well, as for the occult, no, I don't just recommend it. All the religions have their basis in fact. Anyone who's ever studied the roots of any of the major religions finds that they are all saying the same thing, but the information is cloaked in the language of the individual dogmas. *The Bible*, the Kabala, or the Books of the Dead. God or the Devil. Good and bad. Light and dark. Does it ever end, lady?"

"It doesn't *seem* to. Not in this world anyway."

"And it won't. Don't expect it to. But work to understand the nature of opposites, as they are key to understanding how this system operates. You following me?"

"I think so. But what about books? Can *they* be believed?"

"No, not if they ask for blind belief in their content. Unless you've already experienced something you read, it's questionable. Half the books on astral projection are written by people who have done too much reading themselves, and no actual *doing*. It isn't always the writer's experience, but you'd have no way of knowing that without that edge of experience."

"Experience is pretty important to you, isn't it?"

"It's all you're here for. Someday you'll realize it."

"But I thought I did realize it."

"No. You know things intellectually. Realizing it will be quite different. You'll see. And in the meantime…" He sat behind me, wrapped an arm around my front and pulled me close enough so that he could whisper in my ear. "You busy tonight, baby? What do you say me and you get together and perform some human activities?"

I burst into laughter in his arms. "Like what?"

"Like…let's go to bed." The leer he deliberately exaggerated made me laugh even harder.

"You? Erick? Interested in some low animal desire like *sex?*"

He picked up two sets of headphones with extra-long cords, plugged them into the stereo, and stood up. "Follow me," he said with a knowing smile and extended his hand.

"With pleasure." I clutched his hand and let him pull me up, then followed him down the hall, wondering what he was up to.

When we crossed the threshold of the bedroom, the door shut. We both turned to see the cause of it.

"Your friend?" he asked, with raised eyebrows.

I looked at the door and thought directly at it.

Blue. Open it up and go away. This isn't the time for your tricks.

The door wasn't shut tightly and my thought was more of a prayer than anything, but the door creaked slowly back until it was against the wall again. I turned back to Erick, who nodded approvingly.

"He listens to you, lady, whoever he is. That's good."

He placed the headphones on my head and then put his own set on. The tape recorder wasn't running now so I could still hear him.

"Ever made love this way?"

I admitted I hadn't.

"Be right back," he said. "See how you like this."

I moved the headphones away from my ears, sure it would come blasting on, but as it turned out, the volume was already perfect. I eased them back over my ears. He returned seconds later, smiling.

"I knew I'd find a good use for those tapes of his. *Now* we can close the door."

"Hey, this is *all right*," I told him, lying back on the bed.

"Now. What was that you were saying about lower animal passions? Or haven't you experienced the other side of physical love?"

There were no further interruptions from Blue.

It was much later that I went out and returned the headphones to the shelf and shut down the music for the night. We seemed to be going through a reel a week when we were home together. Every day, the music seemed to follow us in our personal lives as though Devin had known, when he'd recorded those tapes, what would be happening right now. Some of these reels had been recorded two or three years ago.

The eerie thing about the lyrics was their dual meaning. In spite of their very literal and personal words, there were intertwined little messages, hinting at something as yet undiscovered by the human race at large. As a network, it was almost impossible *not* to get the point these tapes were making about life in other worlds—not in this physical universe—but in some other undetected dimension.

I was still a little awed by the nonsexual sex of Erick's. That mind probing that had accompanied the body language with that strange music. It had been like having sex on the most sensitive of touch levels in an entirely different world of music. It amazed me, the perfection. Could anything or anyone so perfect last forever?

I went back to bed with a sick feeling that to lose him now would be to lose my mind, my very sanity.

I severely reprimanded myself for entertaining such thoughts.

I returned to his side, loving him more now than ever.

10 Unlike the day before, I didn't feel so much like I'd been run over by a truck on Friday morning. I was still astonished at my newfound awareness, though, and still wondering if it was permanent or temporary.

During the drive to work, I found myself anticipating the lights seconds before they changed. The radio, which had stopped working for some reason, now blasted on, and my elation was boosted by one good song after the other until I pulled up to the plant.

I parked behind Devin's van and waved to Kelly, who was parking on the other side of the street.

I gestured to his van and my car. "Don't they make a good couple?" I yelled over to her as I rolled up my windows.

"Adorable," she assured me as she joined me, and we headed toward the plant. "How're you guys doing?"

"Too good, Kelly. Too perfect, you know? I've never been this happy all the time in my whole life."

She laughed. "Sounds like love, all right."

Pat was standing by the time clock when we walked in. "Hey, Ker. Devin said he'll call you at lunchtime, so hang around if you can."

"Okay…where is he anyway?" I was disappointed to see the route office empty.

"He's on a route."

"On a route?" Kelly and I echoed together. "Why?"

"I thought he was through with all that," Kelly said.

Pat shrugged. "So did Devin. He wasn't too happy about it either. And Tim was on him about his hair again, too."

"Were they fighting?"

"Well, Tim was just in one of his moods, and you know that head of Devin's when he's out loading up a truck. All curls."

"Devin's going to cut it," I said defensively. "He said he was."

"Yeah, a month ago. That's why Tim's mad."

"So now they're both mad?"

"I don't know. You know Devin. He's usually pretty reasonable, but Tim wasn't being reasonable this morning."

There was an ominous feeling in the air as Kelly and I made our way to our own office. Kelly must have felt it too, for neither of us said much until noon when Devin's promised call came through.

At first, there was no anger or bitterness in his voice. "Hey, babe. What's goin' down?" It *was* Devin.

"Not much here, but how come you're on a route?"

"That was *my* question. I couldn't seem to get any answers out of Tim today. I don't know *what* his problem is. He even got personal, asking if I'd gotten a lawyer yet."

"I don't see where your marriage situation is any business of his."

"Yeah, I'm hep. I told him that, and that I can handle my own personal affairs, and to never cross that line with me again."

"But you don't know why you're on a route?"

"Well, I didn't have time to argue with him this morning, but I should have a better idea after I get in and pin that sucker down to an explanation. This is starting to look like it's permanent." Now the bitterness was creeping into his voice.

"Take it easy, Devin. I know you're upset, but you can make more on a route anyway, can't you? And you'd get home earlier instead of having to stay and lock up every night."

"It's the principle of the thing. First Tim said it was only for today, and then when I was pulling out, he said he'd give me the route of my choice."

"What route are you on right now?"

"This one? It's pretty small. I'll be in soon. I'm still on my supervisor salary, or I'd have refused to go out on this one. It wouldn't bring in shit if it was permanent and commissioned. It's the same route Lucky screwed up and now that he's gone, instead of hiring someone else they say 'Oh, *just give it to Devin.*' They know I can take any route in this place and have it making money in two weeks. I've built all these routes up from nothing, and now that they're good thriving runs, who gets to keep them? Not *Devin!* And while I'm working my ass off, adding sales, building it up, it doesn't pay shit. Soon as it's a moneymaker, Tim assigns it to someone else and gives me another lemon to fix up. I'm getting a little tired of it. I'm not supposed to be on *any* routes. Well, sorry you had to hear it. Stick around after five. It'll be interesting. Tim's going to hear it from *me!* Not Erick. Or anyone else."

"Well, it *should* be you. It's *your* job."

"Yeah, well, like I said, babe, if I'm still in there with Tim at five, stick around. Oh, but that's not why I called, though. I almost forgot. I stopped in at Trevor's, and they're leaving for vacation on Saturday. They'll be gone until next Thursday, and he asked if we could keep the dog for him. I told him I had to check with you. Your landlord might have something to say about that, right?"

"You mean Titan? That huge Doberman?"

"That's the one. He's well trained, but I'm the only other one the dog would obey anyhow, so he can't really leave him with anyone else. It's up to you, though, and, of course, your landlord. That kid next door...Chris...he does own the place, doesn't he?"

"Yes, but what could he say if we just brought the dog home? It's only for a few days."

"Then you don't mind?"

"Of course not. No problem. I'll tell the landlord. You tell Trevor, okay?"

"Okay, babe. Hey, I love you."

"I love you too. Try not to be upset...okay?"

"I'm not. Same old cool-as-a-cucumber Devin. But I can walk off this job as fast as any other."

"That's right. You can get a job anywhere. Just keep reminding yourself of that."

He laughed. "I've already had two offers. One up north and one here, but the one here's a little shaky. I'll tell you about it later."

"Are you anywhere near here now?"

"No, I'm down south. I'm going to stop in and see Gerald while I'm in the neighborhood, and then I'll be in. And how I'm supposed to get to a barber when I'm clear down here, I don't know. Every time I try, the shop is closed."

"Yeah, Pat mentioned that."

"Pat was there. He heard me and Tim from outside the door. So did most of the guys, I guess. Well, anyhow…later."

I didn't like the direction the wind was blowing.

If Devin did return shortly after that phone call, he didn't make any appearances in our office, so I could only wonder. I did mention the situation to Lola and told her how upset he was. She didn't have any encouraging words, and I wondered if she knew more about it than she was letting on. She did agree that it didn't seem fair to use him for bad routes until they were making money and then pass them on to someone else.

At five o'clock, I found Devin, still Devin, quietly waiting for me just outside the time-clock exit. He put his arm around me and didn't speak until we'd reached my car, still parked behind his van. He looked beaten.

"Technically, I'm still a supervisor…at present," he said finally, when I let go of him to get my keys out of my jacket pocket.

I was almost afraid to ask him any details about the meeting with Tim. He wasn't registering any outward emotion, but I could still feel it wasn't good news. That ominous feeling of earlier this morning swept over me again. "So…what's the verdict?"

"The verdict…" Devin ran his hand through his curls and looked at me. "The verdict is that Tim claims that certain jobs are being cut, unnecessary to the operation of the plant, and one of them is mine. He says the route room doesn't need two supervisors now because they've transferred Janet from the phone rooms to do the paperwork and handle the phone calls. Tim's full of shit, but he'll find out the hard way. Janet is lucky she can keep up with the phone calls alone, much less anything else."

"So does this mean you're out of a job?"

"Yes and no. He offered me a position in sales again, or I can go back to a route. That's the two choices he gave me." He sighed. "Great, huh?"

I searched his face for the anger or contempt he had every right to feel, but all I could see was hurt pride. "Devin, what does it mean to *you?*"

He was quiet for a minute as if thinking. Finally, "It doesn't really, I guess. You and the kids matter. And trust in people *did*. But now, it's a choice, like any other job. Tim swore it wasn't him. He put all the blame on the Chicago office. He claims *they* cut the position, and I don't know whether to believe him or not. What difference does it make? Look, you go ahead home. I'm going back in to finish this."

"You mean you're still hashing this out?"

"Yeah. It's just me, Pat, and Tim. I'll be a little late, so take this." He handed me a ten. "Get some chicken, or something the kids'll eat. Something we don't have to bother cooking. And your gas tank is empty...I *know.*"

I tried to protest but he added a credit card to the cash. "Please, Kerry. Don't give me a hassle. I've got enough hassles waiting for me back there."

I started the engine and the gas needle barely moved. Reluctantly I took the card and reached out the window to hug him. "I'm sorry everything's going so wrong for you, Devin."

He smiled. "What are *you* sorry for? You're the bright side of my life. You still love me?"

"You know it."

"That's good. It'll help." He ruffled my hair and then leaned in to kiss me. "That's all I care about. Go on home. No point in both of us camping out here all night."

With a final squeeze of my shoulder, he turned and headed back towards the plant. When he was out of sight, I turned towards home, heartsick for him.

11 "Bad day, huh?"

Pam's awareness was picking up too. She only needed one glance at me, when I walked in the door, to know something was wrong.

"Kind of. For Devin, anyway." I turned the water on and began filling up the pot. "Want some coffee?"

"Yeah. What's happening?"

I gave her a rundown on the day's events as I measured the coffee into the basket. "We should have seen it coming," I concluded. "They started dropping him on routes here and there ever since he got back from his trip. They used the excuse they were short of help. Now they're saying it's permanent." I plopped down in the beanbag.

"Where's Devin now?"

"Still down there hashing it out. He's pretty bummed out."

"Who is?"

We both jumped as the door opened and Devin entered, his red supervisor's tag a mockery on his white uniform shirt. He didn't look upset, but he wasn't smiling either.

"What's up? How'd it go?"

He shrugged and pointed to the coffee pot. "Nothing's changed. That ready yet?"

"Coming right up." I started to rise but he anchored me with his hands, and then sat down next to me.

"What's this, chick? Now that I'm a routeman again, I don't get a kiss hello?" There was a slight smile under the veil of gloom as he pulled me into his arms.

"Aw, Devin. I feel so bad for you. I wish I—"

"Hey, don't, you know? I don't *have* to accept their consolation prize. This isn't the only water company in the city. Problem is I'd have to work my way up again from a route, so not much point in that. Now, how about that coffee."

Pam already had the cups poured and doctored with milk and sugar. She turned off the gas. "It's ready. Hey, Devin, are you going to take their route? Kerry says you'd be home earlier and make about the same money once you got the route built up." She placed the steaming cups in front of us on the coffee table.

"Well, I guess I already *have.*" He laughed wryly. "I just didn't know that this bullshit was permanent until today. Technically, I'm still on supervisor salary, but that's only because the company holds back your first two weeks on the job, so I'll just be getting the last pay period's check."

I looked at him, worried, and he took me in his arms again, squeezing hard, and then made a face imitating my frown. "You look like *you're* the one who got demoted." He released me with a squeeze on my shoulder and went over to the tape recorder. "Okay to put this on? Or were you chicks enjoying your solitude?"

"No, go ahead. Devin, what *did* you tell Tim?"

He hit the switch and the reel-to-reel cranked to life. Devin lowered the volume, and it continued to grind away, playing, to my amazement, a Cat Stevens tune, and the song was about working hard and someday having *a job like mine.*

Pam's mouth dropped open. We both knew the song. *Tea for the Tillerman* was one of the few albums I owned that was similar to the songs on Devin's tapes. In this case, one of them. And it just happened to be the next song on the reel.

Devin ignored any similarity to the song and the real world going on around us. "Well, Tim told me I could have my choice, eventually, of any of the routes, but right now I'm stuck with this one of Lucky's. The worst one on the list, and even *that's* twice the size it was last week. I've been adding accounts to it, and I know I can build it up, but I don't know if I want to. Tim told me to take my time thinking about it and then let him know. He *acts* sincere and apologetic, and granted, it could be true, but I just don't know. He swears it was out of his hands."

"I'll ask Lola, Dev. If it was the Chicago office, Charlie would know."

He looked at me curiously. "You think so? What makes you think Charlie would tell *her?*"

"She's one of the executives. She should be privy to all that information. Charlie would have no reason *not* to tell her."

He downed the last of his coffee. "Go ahead. Ask her. It can't hurt. I keep forgetting you two are age-old friends."

"What are you going to do in the meantime? Look for another job?"

"No. Just bide my time. My check will be normal next payday. The guys are all being cool about it. They'd rather me take the route than quit altogether. Like old times, they said." He glanced at his watch. "Daniel said something about leaving the kids with a sitter and coming up to visit tonight. Think you're up for it?"

"Sure. It's Friday, and maybe that will get your mind off that place for a while. You don't have to work tomorrow, do you?"

He gave me a look and laughed. "It'd be a hot day in hell, chick. Devin may be doing a lot of things tomorrow, but working is not one of them. By the way, has anyone eaten?"

"No, not yet. I just picked up the kids and came home, and I've been talking to Pam ever since. I can run out, though. I still have your money."

"No, I'll go. I have to pick up a few cards anyway. Daniel and Julie have an anniversary coming up this week, and Julie also has a birthday pretty soon too. Now, according to your Mama, the kids like hamburgers, so how about McDonald's or something along those lines?"

I laughed. "They *love* McDonald's. Boy, hand it to Mama, she's got me and Kelly pegged."

Devin stood and scooped up his keys. "Pammy, want a burger?"

"No, thanks."

"Kerry?"

I handed him back his cash. "No, not me."

"Boy, you chicks are *cheap*. Later."

"Well, he doesn't seem to be taking it too hard," Pam said after the van roared off.

"Yeah, but Devin seems to take everything cool. I'm worried about Christian. He could blow his stack at any time…anywhere."

"Yeah, I hear ya," Pam said quietly. "I feel so sorry for Devin."

"So do I. Well, at least I can ask Lola about it. I think she'd tell me."

Pam was gone by the time Devin returned with dinner. I set the kids up at their little table while Devin filled out the cards he'd bought.

By the time Daniel and Julie arrived, the house was cleaned, the showers over with, and the kids were in bed for the night.

For once, we were having a typical human evening. No magic. No tricks, and no baby discussions or deep talks about the *old country*, namely *home*.

At least it was normal until Daniel mentioned the drugs.

"You two ever do that peyote?"

"Yeah, we did," Devin said. "A couple days ago."

Daniel smiled knowingly at me. "What'd ya think? Devin said you never did anything like that."

I wasn't sure what response he was looking for. Groovy? Far out? I went with the honest answer. "Well, I was a little afraid of it at first, but it turned out all right."

Daniel turned to Devin. "That reminds me, bro. There's some acid coming down the pike. Think you might be interested in any?"

Devin smiled and shook his head. "I've got plenty of peyote left. What do I look like? I can't face reality the way it is?" He glanced at me, and I knew instantly what was in that glance. Devin only needed a second to feel out what I was thinking, and he already knew how I felt about LSD. He then returned his attention to Daniel. "Why don't we smoke one. Kerry, you feel like putting more coffee on?"

I knew there was still plenty of coffee in the pot, so I got up and poured a round while Devin rolled us all something to smoke. On my way back to the living room, I had to feel my way slowly. The only light in the living room was Puff's flashing globe and one lone bayberry candle that continually filled the room with its scent. I set the coffee before them, and Devin lit the joint.

"You really have this place looking good, Devin." Daniel glanced around with admiration at the pictures and the dragon. The whole setting in the house was indeed drastically different than it had been the last time the couple had visited.

Julie visibly shuddered. "It is…nice," she said, although I could see that it wasn't her idea of a normal home. "Hey, how about some music. Do you guys have any Cat Stevens?" She nodded towards our album collection.

"It's on the reel but it's back a ways. I believe Kerry has the eight-track, though."

I found it and put it on for her. "He doesn't have any of the reels labeled. I don't know how he finds anything."

Devin shrugged good-naturedly. "Those tapes are in some kind of order. One of these days, I'll go through them and title them, but for now I figure what comes on, comes on for a reason. I never had any need for titles, myself."

"Anyway," Daniel said. "Back to the acid. You're sure you don't want in on this? Ethan has pretty good connections, and he claims he can get it."

"No, I think we don't need anything like that around here," Devin said.

"You never even asked Kerry," Daniel said. "Kerr…that go for you, too?"

I was only half listening. The little red candle on the altar had me intrigued once again, entrancing me with its playful antics in response to my fingered commands. To me, the most amazing thing about it was not the *dancing* to the rhythm of my finger, but its immediate response to motionless when I passed my hand over it with the mental command to cease. I hadn't wanted to be involved in the acid discussion, trusting Devin to handle that for both of us, so I'd turned my attention to the candle. It was at that precise moment that Julie, the closest to me, turned to hear my response to Daniel's question, and she let out a startled scream.

"Oh my God, Daniel, do you see what she's doing?"

I dropped my hand quickly to my lap and looked up guiltily at Devin while Julie continued her blubbering to Daniel.

"Daniel, she was…she was…that candle…did you see what she did?"

Daniel looked at me with curiosity, and I could also feel Devin's eyes piercing me. Just the night before, Erick had made certain that I'd understood his opinion of showing off with a particular ability, and I was sure now that Devin probably felt that I was doing just that.

"It's okay, Julie," I said, trying to calm her down. "It's just a little candle. You could do that, too. Anyone can."

Julie took a deep breath, regained her composure, and was now immensely interested. "Do it again. Can you? Show Daniel."

I glanced at Devin, who continued quietly watching. I couldn't read his expression. "Devin, is this what Erick meant about not wasting energy trying to impress people? That's not what I was doing, but—"

His only reply was an almost undetectable smile. "Go ahead," he said finally. "I'm kind of curious myself, now. You've already started this, and I'm always interested in your progress. We're…uh…among friends, I believe."

At first, I thought he was baiting me. A closer and second look explained everything. *Erick.*

Now I was really uncomfortable. "No, it feels awkward now," I said, unwilling to try again with an audience watching. "I probably can't do it again anyway."

"Ah, the age-old obstacle to progress." He smiled. "Fear of failure, or worse, fear of success. If you succeed, you might be asked to repeat it, thus reinforcing your fear of failure." He gave me a hard look that clearly acknowledged that *he* knew that *I* knew that he was present, and that neither of our guests was aware of the switch.

I pushed the candle back and went over to sit by him in the beanbag, which had been moved from in front of the stereo equipment to under the window beside his gold leather chair where he now sat. When I settled into the beanbag, he placed an arm around me.

"At least you're practicing," he said quietly.

I couldn't help but marvel at the bluish-white haze that streamed from him, so visible in the darkened room against the one wall that wasn't paneled.

Julie picked up her purse and laid it in her lap. Daniel took the cue.

"You about ready, babe?"

"Yes. I don't think we should be gone too long. The sitter, you know."

They didn't need to explain their sudden exit, and neither of us tried to stop them. Julie had finally seen what she'd sometimes overheard Daniel discussing with Devin, and she didn't understand. We walked them to their car. I tried to engage Julie in small talk while Devin made tentative arrangements with Daniel for tomorrow. It sounded like another trip to the flea market, and once I heard Trevor's dog, Titan, mentioned.

Julie was no longer in a conversational mood, and I got the feeling that I made her a little nervous now. I stepped away from the passenger side so she could roll up her window. It was bitterly cold out tonight anyway, so I waved goodbye and signaled Erick that I'd see him back in the house.

The windows were open, ventilation Devin preferred to air-conditioning during the winter, and it did help air out some of the smoke. I began to close up the house.

I had just closed the last window when he came back in, seemingly oblivious to the temperature outside. He shook his head with an amused smile when he looked at me, and I knew what that headshake meant.

"I didn't realize anyone was watching," I said contritely. "Really. I didn't do it on purpose. I'm sorry."

"Don't apologize." He turned the fire on under the coffee pot and came in to where I was sitting, chin on my knees, in the beanbag. "Want some coffee?" He stooped down and tilted my chin up towards his face.

"Sure, I'll get it." I started to get up but he stopped me gently with the palm of his hand. "Sit. Damn, I'm already up! Now I see where Michelle gets her hyperactivity."

"Okay. Thanks."

"And don't worry about Julie. It's time she realizes we aren't ordinary…uh…people. That little demonstration with the candle was nothing. As you correctly told her, she can do that herself. And no doubt, those two will be bent over one of their candles at home for the rest of the evening. Julie will also be seeing things she *can't* do, so she might as well start getting used to it. Daniel will probably try to talk to her tonight. Up till now she's only caught snatches of our conversations, so she really is confused."

"Did he say he would?"

He nodded. "While you were trying to unfreeze her. She'll be okay. She's just been in the dark all this time. Daniel thinks she should be let in on everything that's been going on."

"Are you sure Daniel should be the one to try to explain anything to her?"

"Well, he would know what wording she will accept, but you're right. Daniel himself is just barely coming around to understanding. He *did* think that you and I were into traditional devil worship, of all things. And you *know* the human reaction to the word *devil*. Fire, brimstone and all that shit. *You* know the stories."

I nodded. "How did these stories even get started anyway? From *The Bible?*"

"Sort of. Indirectly. *The Bible* was written by men, and then the interpreters got hold of it. The translators. We've talked about this before. Hebrew words became entirely different English words, for example the way Sheol became Hell."

"Maybe because it was handwritten?"

"Yes, on scrolls and eventually transferred to what we call *The Bible* today, except it's been changed with every version. By the time it was translated into actual print with the Gutenberg edition it wasn't anything like the original scrolls. That's when a word that meant *invisible world* became *hell*, and then the stories really began. And that's not to mention the parts that were deliberately left out of the finished product."

"Well, where *did* the fire and brimstone and eternal punishment stories come from? If they weren't true, then how did they get started?"

He leaned back and turned the volume down on the music, then pressed another button and the tape gave way to FM music. He seemed not to have heard me.

"Tell me. What is this *hell* really like, if not fire and brimstone?"

For Erick, I had asked the wrong question. When he turned away from the equipment, the pale-blue aura was gone, and so was Erick. The ultraviolet haze was a dead giveaway, but I would have known from his eyes, even before he spoke. As usual, there was no verbal mention of the switch.

"Your first question was in regards to how the stories got started to begin with," he said.

I lit a cigarette and pushed the stash box towards him. I usually refrained from smoking around Erick. After all, Erick let Devin's cigarettes sit in *his* pocket, even if it was for hours. "Here, roll one. Make yourself useful."

He smiled as I touched the flame to my cigarette. "You go through withdrawals when you're with Erick? Come on. Lighten up, lady. He's not *that* far away."

"Don't change the subject. How *did* the stories get started?"

"Organized religion."

"That's the answer? Organized religion?"

"Well, that's where the punishment stories began. To control the masses. Don't forget, church and state were once united. If anyone broke the laws of the church, the state could come in and take their property. And, as you know, many landowners were accused of witchcraft just because the land was there for the taking." He put the finishing touches on the joint he was rolling. "What's amazing is that in all these centuries, and as evolved as people are supposed to be now compared to then, the Good Book is still accepted as the word of God, verbatim, with all its distortions and omissions. Don't people ever think for themselves? Do they all just follow blindly?"

"Lot of politics involved, huh?"

"Politics is right, all in the name of milking and bilking the public. Come to church once a week and give us your money...otherwise...fire and brimstone. Wicca cults don't even *have* churches. They use their money to feed their people or to help others. They *don't* put hexes on people, as is so commonly believed. *That* is against their religion. They *do* realize the process of materialization by use of direct thought, and they learn to master concentration. If they conjure up money, it's put to useful purposes, not a ton of gold statues and stained-glass windows."

"What do you think of that book of Devin's...the *Witches' Bible*?"

"It's...sincere. That's about all I can say for it. Not that there's anything wrong with Wicca. Check it out sometime. You already know Wicca forbids the use of drugs, doesn't believe in *any* devil, and yet it does respect a creator...a delegating authority similar to the Christian god. But I'm not advocating Wicca as the place to stop growing. You must never make the mistake of thinking you have *the* answer, for all the knowledge printed doesn't scratch the surface of what *really* is. Wicca is a little *too* religious for my taste, and you'll probably find it the same. It's actually better to be open to experience and have *no* ties to any organized religion. To choose any one religion both limits and stagnates you. Once you've decided that *this* is the answer, then it can't be *that* or anything else, and you stop growing."

I had to think about that one. I passed him the joint and went out to pour us some coffee. The radio provided background music, and I wondered why the tapes weren't running tonight as they usually were.

When I returned with the coffee, I went back to my questions. Looking back on them now, they must have seemed very juvenile, but he never once inferred that they were.

"So...what's this *hell*, or Sheol, really like, Devin?"

"It's cold," he said quickly. "Not the kind of cold you know here, but brisk...refreshing. Not stifling. And beautiful. Not that this world isn't beautiful in its own way, but the colors there...well, there is a difference in landscapes, auras, lighting...everything glows with its own light."

"You said landscapes. Does that mean it looks like *these* physical surroundings? Like grass and trees...houses and rooms?"

"Well, it *can*, if you *wish*. This is difficult to explain, but when you enter our world from another one, a sort of symbolic translation takes place, and you construct your surroundings to look like the world you came from." He paused, closed his eyes and rubbed them with his thumb and ring finger, and then looked up and continued. "Look, maybe this will make it easier for you to understand. Take the English language. Take the word *book*. If you went to France and mentioned a book to a native, he might not know what you were talking about, but if you pulled out your little translation book and said *livre* he would immediately comprehend. It's kind of like that, only in reverse, where you would produce the word *livre,* and he would comprehend and show you a book. Here, though, we are talking about visual symbols, not language. Someone from any other world but this physical one would construct it of things *you* can't even imagine, but it would make perfect sense to that entity."

"But why would you have to go through all that? Why wouldn't it just be like here where everything just is what it is?"

He smiled. "Like here? Kerry, humans do the same thing here. All that you see here *isn't* what it is. Any physicist can tell you that you are actually surrounded by a whirling, pulsating maze of atoms and molecules that look nothing like what you see and touch. You only perceive what you do because you are tuned to this frequency, and your senses are tuned to this world within a certain range of frequency. Nothing is even solid. It only seems to be. Basically, humans also construct their surroundings to look like the things they see and take for granted. As in my world, everything is done with thought, but at home it's quicker." He snapped his fingers. "Like that. But here everything's done in slow motion. Let's say you wanted to build a machine that no one else ever dreamed of. You'd get the idea out of what you call your imagination, or the mind at large, and then you'd slowly put parts together to make the thing shape into what you had *in mind.* People here do this with everything. Houses, roads, everything you can see. It happens so slowly that you don't even notice how the landscape changes. If you could see your world speeded up here, you'd see buildings go up and down, mountains rise and fall, lakes dry up and become pasture. Now, in our world, there is no time lag. There is no series of events that take *time.* You decide or imagine what you wish your surroundings to be and..." he snapped his fingers again. "it's quicker than that."

"So your world doesn't look like this one...normally."

"It *can* if you want it to," he repeated. "But it needn't, though, and usually doesn't."

"And humans can't get in?"

He chuckled. "Humans are *always* falling in. They amuse us. They're easily recognized by their clumsiness and their total lack of awareness of us. They don't see us if we don't want them to, for *we* have no need to be encased in a form. They usually aren't aware of where they're at. Think they're either dreaming or daydreaming. Too numb." He tapped my forehead with his finger and for a split second I wondered if I too were included in that category of numbies.

"I'm referring to *humans,"* he added quickly, catching my thought. "but I keep forgetting, you think *you're* human, don't you." He hugged me affectionately, but I struggled loose, determined to keep him talking.

"Assuming you're right, that I'm not human, are we the only ones here? And everyone *else* is human?"

He lit a pair of cigarettes before he replied. "There are others, I'm sure. I would not be so egotistical as to say we are the only ones. People are here from everywhere. This is nothing but a school. One big school of matter and experience. However, I personally don't know of any others. I've barely been here two and a half months of your time structure, but I'm sure there are. There'd have to be."

"Would they be here for the same reason as you and me?"

"I'm here only because *you* are, and no other reason. You're here because you wanted to *play* in matter…to create things in slow motion. I didn't mind that you felt the need to experience this, but I couldn't take your forgetting me, and *us* back there. I'd have been happy to see you step in once in a while and say hello, but I didn't realize, until I got here myself, how total your amnesia would be upon arrival. If I'd have followed you and entered this world the same way *you* did—through birth—you and I could have lived next door to each other our whole lives and never recognized each other."

I sighed. This was so hard to accept. "If I *am* from where you came from, why can't I remember it like you do? Was amnesia part of the conditions of entry?"

"It is a rule of this dimension when you enter by normal methods and join this world as a native. With me it was different."

"Well, *you've* been into *magic* of sorts. Isn't that the same thing as Wicca?"

"*Devin* was into that. Don't confuse us. And Devin is drifting away from it. But don't get Wicca confused with that nightmare the Satanists have concocted. Wicca is harmless. It's fairly close to natural law…primitive, but the principles are right. It *works*, but it's the long hard way. You don't need those props, candles, and incantations. They only serve as aids in concentration. They help you to focus your attention on the matter at hand, be it crops, fertility…even love spells. You can do it mentally and achieve the same results once you master the art of concentration. Eventually, even Wiccans dispense with the props, realizing they are unnecessary. However, it's a good thing for me that Devin *was* into that stuff, or I'd have never gotten his attention."

I shook my head. "At one time I would have *sworn* witches worshipped the Devil. What about that horned thing they talk about?"

"They worship male and female principles, symbolized by Diana, the moon, and a male figure that resembles a goat. But no devil. I told you…that was a *church* creation, and the Satanists actually worship the figure that the churches *invented*. So nobody's got it right."

"Then there aren't any books in this world that I could read and believe?"

"None that I would recommend. People believe what they've been told over the centuries, and they always add things to what they've been told. What they've written about us is another source of amusement to us."

I buried my face in my hands. "So you're only here because *I'm* here, and to try to remind me of where I came from?"

"Yes. I was able to come, and I wanted to. But it looked a lot different from where I was. Memories or dreams, which is all this is to me, seemed different from that standpoint."

I looked him in the eyes. "So you are telling me that I'm *really*, not hypothetically, related to you and this world. And you're saying that *we* are related to the stories of Hell and Satan? That means if anyone who knows us and was aware of that and believed it would *hate* us. I don't know, Devin. It doesn't make sense. The Devil...the Devil is known for evil...lying...bad things. I don't feel like I'm evil and I *know* you're not."

"Of course I'm not. *I'm* not the one who put that *evil* shit into people's heads. You can thank the churches for that one. And anyhow, if you're going to go by *The Bible*, Lucifer wasn't such a bad fellow according to the accounts of the original *fall*. But forget that, because it isn't true, and just accept me as you *know* me. The rest will fall into place. The *last* concept I'm trying to give you is that anything outside of physical reality is evil. Evil exists here, as an opposite of good."

"Well, how did you manage to skip the birth requirements?"

"Through Devin. He had a suitable frame of reference, and he wasn't afraid. The timing was perfect. There are certain electromagnetic conditions that make entrance possible. A condition where worlds sort of overlap. I told you once that it was during October, a month that happened to have two full moons. That's not a common occurrence, and I used it to my advantage. The moon is a strong influence for us, and that *also* has to do with electromagnetism. However, none of those ripe conditions would have meant anything if Devin had refused. I had to have his full, willing cooperation and absolutely no fear or doubts. He had to totally trust me. Devin didn't know who I was, but he trusted who he *thought* I was...implicitly. I didn't deceive him or misrepresent myself. I can answer to any name and still be myself. He knows me now just as you do. He just started out thinking I was someone else."

"He thought you were the Devil himself?"

"In a way, he wasn't too far off."

I shuddered. Why did it keep coming back to this *devil* thing? "What about Erick and Christian? Where do *they* come in?"

"They are various aspects of Devin who reside in other realities but are directly connected to Devin the way I am directly connected to you. But understand me now, I am an aspect of you, and yet I am a separate consciousness, even though I understand the oneness of *us*."

"Then they *are* separate individuals. Devin *isn't* crazy...or schizophrenic."

He laughed heartily, then sobered and responded. "No, Devin isn't crazy. Those guys are interloping, just as I am. Devin happens to be a very amiable host. Oh, your psychiatrists might label him as such, because this isn't a common thing, and that's the only category they would know to put him in. However, it is in my best interests to make sure that Devin never finds himself in the hands of a psychiatrist, and you can rest assured that as long as I'm here, he won't."

The door opened and Pammy walked in, George right behind her. I waved to them, and when I turned back to him, he was no longer there. The aura had returned to that bluish-white haze, once again with no announcement of exit or reenter. No goodbyes and no hello. I was determined not to allow the change to stop the flow of conversation.

When Erick did not respond to George's greeting to the guy he believed to be Devin, Pam tugged at his sleeve and whispered, "George, I don't think that *is* Devin. Let me get my jacket and we'll go out to the lake."

I looked at Erick and ignored the activity, glad they were leaving quickly. "How did *you* wind up with Devin?"

Pam and George waved quietly and left.

Erick sat up and stretched. "Does it matter, really?"

"I guess not. I love all four of you. I'm just trying to understand."

"By the way. How's your arm?"

The change in subject brought me to a sitting position too. "You never *have* expressed an opinion." It was true. Devin, Christian, and even *he* had all examined my arm, and none of them had offered a plausible explanation for the marks and especially that veined tattoo thing. Would Erick be any different?

He scanned the marks wordlessly, gently touching my needle mark, now set permanently in my flesh, and the…insignia. "You ever look that up?"

I shook my head. "I wouldn't know where to look. You have any ideas?"

He turned my arm to inspect the now brownish finger and thumb marks, which were fading closer to tan with each passing day. "You had a dreamlike experience the night before these turned up, didn't you?"

"Yes, I did. It was the night Devin got back from his trip. We were both pretty tired from all the moving and excitement. Devin especially was exhausted and fell asleep almost the minute his head hit the pillow." I related what I could remember of the dream to him.

"Looks like you put up quite a struggle. I'll tell you what I think, though. I believe that you made your first trip *home* from which you brought back some snippets of memory. That is, you go more frequently than you are aware of, and have been since he's been trying to refresh your memory, but this is the first time you brought back any recollection of where you went. If you could pull out the rest of that…*dream*… I believe you'd have your explanation for those marks. I wouldn't worry about it, though, even if you never remember. Where you were, the last thing anyone there would do is hurt you. Whatever these marks are, they were probably put there in the process of trying to *help* you. Have you noticed any difference in your perceptions and abilities since that night?"

"Nothing that I can't blame on the peyote."

"That's exactly why I didn't want you involved with any drugs. It's too easy to blame them for any altered states of consciousness you experience. All it did was step up your awareness for a short while, let you see a little more than your eyes and senses are normally tuned for." He sighed. "Oh, well." He released my arm. "Does it still hurt?"

"No. There isn't even any pain at the prick mark, or whatever it is."

"And no changes in your perception since the night of that dream? When *was* the last time you checked out those words and pictures you get in your mind? Or attempted to communicate with Blue? Or even tried to meditate?"

"When have I had *time* ?" I countered. "Think about it."

"Okay, you've been busy. Overwhelmed, even. Try it now."

Erick was lying on his side, elbow to floor, left hand supporting his head. I positioned myself the same way so that we were now facing each other. I gazed vacantly at the carpet and waited for the familiar blur that preceded my "visions."

Erick watched silently.

The objects in the space around me, including his body, began to melt together into one neutral, whitish slate, as though I were wiping a canvas clean of a very colorful, sharp picture and preparing to paint another. This was not new since the drug. This was normal procedure for as long as I could remember. I began to feel the sinking sensation within seconds, an ethereal elevator ride into the recesses of my mind. I kept my eyes fixed on the same spot and watched as a new blur focused in. This was one exercise I'd played with all my life. It was familiar, nonthreatening, and easy to do, though I had never known what actually brought about the changes in scenery.

This one was a room.

"Where you at?" I heard him ask, a voice on the other side of the physical veil.

I maintained the position and the scene. "A room."

"Where?"

"I don't know. In my imagination, I guess."

"Do you just imagine a room, or do you actually *see* it?"

"Oh, I'm *in* it, practically." I laughed and broke the light trance state, and the new room merged into my living room again.

"In your imagination. Hmm. You think so, huh?" He wasn't smiling. "What did it look like?"

The serious set of his features sobered me. "Shit. I never remember to take in the details. But I can find that same room and describe it while I'm in it. In general, it looked kind of like an office."

"At work?"

"No, more plush. Like an expensive shrink's office. There was a white couch…maybe a green carpet. I don't think it was shag like this one." I tapped our own carpet. "But I'm not sure."

"Get it again," he said.

It took all of three seconds. "Okay. I've got it. There's a mahogany desk, a white leather couch, and the carpet *is* green. It's a regular carpet, though, not shag, and it has designs…like swirly things, cut into the carpet. All the same color. It's a lighter green than our carpet is there."

"Any signs or people?"

"No. Just an empty room. I usually don't recognize what I see." I pulled myself out of it and sat up. "Don't tell me *you* can't do that."

"I don't. Why don't you work with it more? You *could* be tapping futures, you know. It's hard to believe that, with a gift like that, you don't use it more. You just take it for granted instead of developing it."

"Well, before Devin, I used to do it a lot. But I did it more for entertainment. I never attached any significance to it. One thing I've got to admit, though. Regardless of whether it's the drug or that dream, it's been easier, clearer, and there's been more depth since I took that peyote. That doesn't mean it didn't start after that dream, but I was too involved with Devin's homecoming to try during those first few days he was moving in and getting settled. And other things are starting to happen now."

"Like what?"

"Oh, little stuff. I'll think it's a certain time and look at a clock and find it's to the minute. The letters and words are sharper now. I seem to anticipate people's thoughts just before they verbalize them, and I know when they're staring at me, even if my eyes are shut or I'm turned away from them. Maybe all this is just from hanging around you guys so much."

"You think so? You're doing things that Devin, Christian, and I don't do, so how do you figure? And I might remind you that you've been doing this all your life. The visions...the pictures...the words. But you're wasting your ability. You don't really use it. You're more advanced than you realize. You know that, lady?"

"But...just all of a sudden?"

"Not all of a sudden. The drug may have raised you in frequency, but you know it's not all of a sudden. These realities that you tap so casually for sport...instead of television...you know, you *could* go where he wants you to go, and consciously, like you just did with this room. You *could* go there. You have the ability, but you won't. Don't you realize that if you can see and enter the others so easily, you can do the same thing with the only one that matters to *him?*"

"Then why don't I know how to do it? What is holding me back?"

"Your fears. Your doubts. You look upon things like that room as a figment of your imagination, but when he suggests to you that *home* is a real tangible place, you become afraid."

I hung my head in shame. This wasn't a sign that I was even worthy of him, much less an equal.

Erick tipped my face towards his and raised his eyebrows when our eyes met. "Something else you might want to keep in mind, love. In the beginning, only *he* had any interest in what you were doing here. Now that *he's* here, there are others who are interested in your progress. Others from *there*. They didn't think you were ready for this, and each time that you balk at going *home*, you just verify to them that this sojourn of his is a waste of time and energy. I think you *are* ready, and I *know* you can do it. You're not one of these inhabitants here, lady, but you have their hang-ups and doubts. The sooner you realize *who* you are, the faster the veil will lift and the quicker that door will open for you. Go *with* him next time."

"But I don't know *how!*"

"You won't learn by repeating *that* like a broken record. Go. It's that simple." He drummed his knuckles on the coffee table. "Just like that."

"Do I have to try to lower my vibrations to slow myself down?"

"No. You raise them, and the body will automatically slow down. Just direct all your energy to your head. *Want* it to. Will it. Decide you are *going* to go."

I sighed deeply. "I guess I'm just not ready, then."

"I guess not. Not if you give up that easily."

"There *must* be some books on how to do this...this phasing out of this reality."

"There *are* some out there, but some books can hurt you. They'll add more fears to the ones that you already have. Come on, love. It's getting late. Let's go to bed. We have plenty of time for you to become comfortable with the idea, and I can see you're getting frustrated and impatient. I wasn't trying to disturb your piece of mind." He kissed me gently. "Come on. We can find something less frustrating than *this* to do."

I followed him into the bedroom, suddenly realizing just how tired I was.

12 We got an early start on Saturday, and I was surprised to find *him* at the wheel that morning instead of Devin. Daylight didn't seem to be his favorite time of day, but then again, things and conditions changed every day anymore.

He was also in an unusually talkative mood, and I took advantage of that on the ride down to Daniel's.

The music seemed to never stop. We had fallen asleep to it last night, and the last song I remembered was another Moody Blues tune singing of making the journey out and in, and talking about wonders of a lifetime right in front of our eyes…presumably if we *made* that journey out and in. The last words the singer sang was that he'd said what he had to say, and now it was up to me.

When we weren't home with the reel-to-reel, the tape deck in the van took over. Pink Floyd's *Dark Side of the Moon* was ironic background for the discussion that began with my happy comment that it wasn't often that I got to spend a day in *his* company, instead of random spot visits during the evening hours.

"You'll see me around more and more," he said as we pulled onto the ramp of the Interstate. His reply was accompanied by one of those penetrating glances of his, eliminating any question of whether or not Devin would take over before we arrived at Daniel's. "I need to be around more, judging from Daniel's misinterpretations of what he thinks we are *into*. Daniel has a rough idea of who I am. If I'm careful, Julie won't notice. I'm sure I don't have to worry about *your* awareness of me, lady."

"I'm glad," I told him, removing his black cap from his head and transferring it to mine. "There. How's that look?" I was quite at ease in his company now. I'd come a long way in that respect.

He glanced at me and smiled. "Looks good on you. And that reminds me…" he casually retrieved his hat. "I'd better find a place to get this hair cut. That's all Tim needs for fuel on Monday."

"Why bother? Tim's putting Devin back on the routes, isn't he?"

"Well, it's not official yet, and anyway, Tim gave Devin the story that if he takes the route and demotion now, it will only be until Johnny retires in Chicago. Tim still plans to take over up there, and allegedly Devin goes back to the supervisor position, and Janet goes back to the phone room. I don't know how much of that is fact, but since he probably will accept the route, he may as well comply with the rules. He'll still be a supervisor for the next couple weeks and will be in and out of the office until things *do* become official."

"But he's only going to be a supervisor for a couple more weeks, so why should he have to cut his hair? Oh, because of the other drivers, right?"

"It's all right. It should be cut anyway. *I* think it's getting too long. Don't you?"

"No, I like it the way it is."

He reached over and squeezed my hand. "Tim doesn't think so, and Devin is still working there at present, for however long *that* will be."

He resumed his attention to the road.

"We picking up Titan today?"

"Yes, but we'll do that on the way home. We'll be down at the flea market, and we can't just leave him in the van while we're in there. Besides, once we pack Daniel's family in here with ours, it's going to be really crowded." He frowned when he said Daniel's name. "He's been pressuring me with a lot of questions lately."

"I've been afraid of that," I said with a sigh.

"Well, there's nothing wrong with asking questions but I'm a little concerned with where he's at, judging by the kind of questions he's asking."

"Like what?" I didn't like the idea of feeding Daniel's fascination with us. "What does he ask?"

"About me...you...a lot about the occult. Witchcraft, demonology...all the misguided questions. He seems to have a serious interest in it, but I'm not sure how far I should go with Daniel. He really wants to *know*, and he has a right to ask and a right to an answer, but I'm still not sure how much I should divulge. I know he's really gotten the wrong impression of us."

"Like what?"

"Well, he's convinced that we're into that stupid traditional Satanism. I can't seem to make him understand the difference, and sometimes it seems like he doesn't *want* to understand the difference. I keep saying, 'no, Daniel, you're misunderstanding,' and he just doesn't hear me. He still thinks of *the Devil* as having horns and a tail, and he probably would have started sacrificing *chickens* for dinner if I hadn't put the brakes on *that* misconception. Now he says he knows he's confused, and he's asked me to teach him."

"Are you going to?"

"I don't know yet. I hate to leave anybody hanging with the wrong concept. I feel that it's my responsibility to enlighten anyone who asks, but I don't think Daniel is going to be happy with the answers. The trouble is, things have been a secret on this physical plane for far too long. People should *know* why they're here and how to use energy constructively. They *are* manifesting their thoughts and beliefs but, unfortunately, it's easier to believe something can go wrong than it is to believe it will go right. Most people aren't using this power to materialize *consciously*, and as a result, there is a lot of negativity manifested by people's doubts, fears, and worries. And, of course, when the general populace *sees* the results, they become convinced that the negative predominates here. If it weren't so secret, people would have realized by now that they create their own problems, demons and obstacles, and they might start thinking differently." He paused to pass a slow-moving car, then continued.

"If everyone thought positively, there would be no negative physical results and feedback to reinforce the belief that negativity reigns. And we can thank the churches, and even the philosophers who took it upon themselves to cover up the real facts, cloaking them in allegories which were soon lost in the translations, until the garbage built up to what it is today. I think people *should* be told the truth."

I heartily disagreed with him.

"There are people who would misuse it if they realized the facts," I said.

"You know, people have egos, and egos tend to get overblown at times. Power in the hands of the wrong people...even governments...could be dangerous. And Daniel. What is the real reason *he* wants to know? Fascination with power? I just don't think the world is ready for that kind of open knowledge. Not all of the people anyway."

"But don't you understand? People *are* the way they *are* because they don't *know* any better. They believe everything they read, and there is so much bullshit added to the small grains of truth and so much real fact omitted. And people won't *get* the power, as you call it, until their awareness is in balance. The ones who learn half of it, without the awareness of misuse, don't last long here. You can see that by the Mansons and Hitlers and all the others who got carried away with *the power* and swept off the path by their egotistical thinking. They either land in jail, or die, or go insane, but the main self sees to it that they don't get very far."

"Yeah, but those people you just mentioned did a hell of a lot of damage before they were stopped."

"I know. But they *were* eventually stopped. My point is that if people knew the truth, they wouldn't even *begin* to use that knowledge to try to hurt each other. They'd fully understand universal law and that they can't escape the consequences of that law. It's about the only thing that operates here that doesn't depend on you believing in it. That secrecy was understandable back in the dark ages when people were tortured and killed for what they knew, but it's different now. The witchcraft laws were repealed, and it's time now for those of us who are here and know, to begin informing the people, but with instructions on what happens if it *is* abused. This planet is so preoccupied with selfishness and greed, and starving for love and trust in one another. Someone's got to do it. I guess that's where our son will come in, and believe me, he'll have the abilities to make people listen."

"Well, we have a little ways to go before we're ready to bring him into the world," I said.

"Do we? Are you keeping track of your periods?"

I mentally added up the days since my last cycle. "Actually, it's due today but I don't have any cramps or anything. Why? You don't think I could be pregnant already, do you?"

He frowned. "It's a little soon for the child yet. I wanted you to be ready."

"You don't sound too happy about it if I am. Damn, Devin, I should have been more careful. Took some precautions."

He shrugged. "Well, don't take all the blame. I had a hand in it somewhere...if you are. Anyhow, it's a little soon to be assuming anything. And even if you are, it's all right. It's just a little sooner than we planned, that's all."

"I know. Devin, I'm sorry. I never even considered the possibility of getting pregnant this soon. So much has happened—"

"Yes, it's been rough on you, I realize. But I hope *you* realize that if you *are,* it kind of forces acceleration, and I wanted you to be able to take your time."

"I guess I'd better start practicing to meditate more. If I only knew what to learn."

"Learn to *go,* lady, not just to meditate. *You* are the only one who can get you out of that body and into our world. Once you've accepted it as *being* there, then you'll see a huge difference in your abilities and awareness. At the moment, you still aren't sure it's even *there*. Look at it this way. If a human can do it by accident, you should be able to do it easily with just a little effort."

"I just wish I knew exactly *where* it is that you want me to go."

"I want you to go to *hell*, lady. Go see this terrible place for yourself." He smiled and winked at me.

"But *how?* I don't know where it *is*!"

"I've told you. It's right here. Around the corner. Down the block. You don't need to move to go there. It's all around you *now*. It's here. Everywhere."

"This is all just confusing me," I said.

"That's why I shouldn't be telling you anything. You've got to find out for yourself. You don't realize how much you are being watched right now. No one believed this would work. Particularly my old man."

"And, of course, you don't mean Gerald."

"No," he said bluntly, as we pulled into Daniel's driveway. "Gerald is not my father. My old man is not physical and never has been. You're the first one from our world who ever even *wanted* to be. My little sojourn has become pretty big time in our own reality, and it wasn't easy for me to get permission to come here. I really had to do some talking." He shut off the engine. "Coming?"

I didn't make a move to get out of the van. "Wait a minute, Devin. Your old man, as you call him...and this permission thing. All this really has nothing to do with Devin, does it?"

He drummed his fingers patiently on the steering wheel. "I wouldn't be here if it weren't for Devin."

"I know. But the world itself..."

"No. That's me. Us. Not Devin's imagination, if that's what you're asking."

I sighed. That wasn't the question, but I let it drop. "Okay. Let's go in."

Julie greeted us at the door with a welcoming smile, hanging tightly to Lucifer's choke collar. "Come on in, you guys. You're early!"

Luke sniffed the air in our direction, and when we stepped into the house, he emitted a low growl and his fur bristled.

"Luke!" Daniel's voice was sharp, and he rose from the couch to reprimand the dog. Luke lowered his hair and his tail at the sound of his master's voice.

"I don't know what *his* problem is all of a sudden, Dev," Daniel said, snapping Luke's chain collar roughly. "He never *used* to give you any problem."

"Put him outside," Julie interceded. "I think his fleas are just making him irritable. All he does is scratch."

Devin and I exchanged glances as Daniel transferred Luke to their fenced backyard. Devin handed Julie the card he'd purchased. "Here, Julie. Happy birthday."

She beamed with delight that he'd remembered. "Yeah, twenty-eight today. I'm getting ancient."

"Oh, you don't look or act twenty-eight," I offered, and she beamed even brighter.

"We've got some good Columbian," she said. "You guys up for it?"

"And some acid coming," Daniel added, rejoining the group.

"Yeah?" Devin sat down at the dining room table and I sat next to him. Mandy and Michelle took off for the backyard with Daniel's boys, and Daniel began to roll up some of that Columbian.

"Where'd you cop *this* ?" Devin asked, examining the quality of the grass, obviously impressed.

"Ethan."

"So that's why you guys keep him around," Devin said. "Although I never see him when I come."

"Working," Daniel explained, handing Devin the joint. "The *main* reason we keep him around, actually. The rent is a big help, and as you can see, he isn't here that much."

As Devin reached for the joint, his eye caught sight of the one thing I'd hoped he wouldn't notice. A bouquet of freshly cut roses.

"What…is *that?*" He nodded toward the vase, then looked at Julie.

Julie, of course, was caught off guard. "Oh, aren't they lovely? Daniel gave me those for my birthday."

Devin didn't reply, just reached for the stash box, his lips pursed tightly. He glanced at me with a defeated expression and began to roll, as if to keep his hands busy. He finally turned to Daniel, unable to hold himself in check.

"Why do you people *do* that?"

"Oh, come on, Devin. We didn't *pick* them. They were already *cut!*"

"And now you want to watch them die."

Daniel reddened, obviously embarrassed. "I *told* you, Julie. Devin doesn't *like* it. Hell, he says he can hear the grass crying when people mow."

"Well, *I* can't," Julie retorted, "so it doesn't bother me. Besides, you eat vegetables, Devin, and *they* grow. What's the difference?"

"Yeah, Devin." Daniel looked at him. "Where *do* you draw the line?"

"Perhaps I'm wrong, Daniel, but at least there's a purpose to vegetables. They're food. I'm sure the vegetable knows that before it decides to become one. But killing *flowers* and *trees* unnecessarily…I just can't see it."

"Well, this should cheer you up," Daniel said. "Julie and I aren't getting a real tree this year. *That's* because of you. That's progress for you, isn't it?"

"Don't remind me," Devin said with a weary sigh, picking up his keys. "We still have to pass all those murdered pine trees from here to the flea market. It makes me *sick!* Hundreds of thousands of trees wasted every damn year on their Christian bullshit. Come on. You two ready?"

Julie glanced at the flowers and then at Daniel. "Okay, Devin. I won't keep live flowers anymore."

"Get fake ones. They look just as good."

"But they don't smell as nice."

"Well, spray 'em with hairspray or something. Or burn incense. Come on. Let's go."

"Okay, okay." Daniel handed Devin three more joints. "For the road, bro. Hey, you're not really upset with us, are you?"

"Disappointed, that's all. It's okay, Daniel. You aren't the only ones." He turned to me. "See? This is just a demonstration of what we were talking about. The people don't know any better. It's plain ignorance."

"Well, how are you and Kerry going to do it with the kids this year? You're not getting a tree at *all?*"

"We ordered one from a nursery. Still in the pot. Alive. One that will stay alive for the kids until Christmas, and one that we will plant on that same ridiculous day."

There was no dropping the subject. Every block we passed had trees lined up for sale. Looking at so much waste and so many dead trees was even beginning to get to me. I could feel his silent shudder, even when we passed some of them without his comments. At times, he would point out some of the bragging advertising signs.

"Check it out, Daniel," he said, when we passed a lot overstocked with far more trees than it could possibly sell before the trees were too dried out to be of any service. "*We have the largest selection of live trees,*" he read aloud in a voice dripping with sarcasm. "See them? They call that *live?* Half of those poor trees are so dehydrated by now that they won't even have any *needles* left by Christmas Day. The least the sick bastards could do is wait until the twentieth or something. Well, what difference does it make? They're dead now, or dead later. It's all so senseless and cruel."

"You can't change the world, Dev," Daniel offered halfheartedly.

"You think not, huh, Daniel?"

We finally arrived at the flea market, and the subject was thankfully dropped. As everyone piled out of the van into the bright sunshine, Devin called me aside and asked me to keep Julie occupied while he and Daniel cased the joint for a birthday present.

For an hour, we canvassed the many shops and finally ended up at the jewelers where Devin had purchased my ring. Julie wanted matching rings for their anniversary, and the guys walked in just in time for Daniel to help her choose. Then they motioned for us to follow them.

They led us to a huge art gallery where a stack of velvet paintings was leaning against a wall. Daniel flipped through them and extracted a large framed one with black being the primary background color. Painted on the black velvet were a stereotypical horned devil's face, a fanned deck of cards, a set of dice, and a cocktail glass.

"I found it," Daniel said proudly. "What do *you* think, Kerry?"

Obviously, the game was to have Daniel believe that Devin was buying it for us, thus the question. "Oh, I've seen that one before in the commercial malls," I said, hedging. I really didn't want to give my opinion of it. To me it was gaudy, and its message stated that the devil was responsible for people's vices, as if they had no free will of their own.

I wandered over to another stack and flipped through them. There were no copies of these hanging on the gallery walls. I paused at the third picture.

Now here was *another* picture of Satan, but this one was completely different. Painted in black on rich blood-red velvet, Satan was featured, full-length, seated in an elaborate throne, much like the one Gerald owned. A nude woman, tastily positioned, sat submissively at his feet. Satan's face was entirely blacked out except for two fiery eyes…eyes that matched licks of flaming hair. His hand was raised in the sign of the evil eye…two outside fingers up, and the two middle fingers down and secured by the thumb.

The picture had an air of royalty, dignity and class. Not the usual trashy way people portrayed the fallen angel. I signaled to Devin, and he walked over to me.

"Look!"

He whistled. "Hey, Daniel. Look what Kerry found."

Daniel and Julie approached and stared, transfixed. "Ooh, I *like* this one," Julie breathed. "Much better than the other one."

"This one, bro," Daniel said with a nod.

Devin stuffed some money in my hand. "There's a snack bar just around the corner to the right. Go feed the kids, and order us a couple burgers. We'll meet you there in a few minutes."

When we finally returned to the van, it was much later, and now we had a new problem. Space.

"Julie, happy anniversary," Devin announced. "Or Birthday. We wanted to surprise you with it later, but I didn't think you'd dig riding home on the roof."

Julie gaped at him. "For *us?*"

"For you," Devin said, moving things in the van to make room for the picture.

"Oh, Devin…Kerry, I thought this was for *your* house! It cost so much…at least let us—"

"What, pay for half of it?" Devin grinned as he finished her sentence for her. "Sure, Julie. Catch you on payday."

Everyone laughed.

When we arrived at Trevor's, Devin insisted he come out and see the picture.

Trevor was in the midst of packing, but he followed Devin to the van. When he glimpsed the picture, he let out a low whistle. "Did you say it was Daniel's?"

"It is," Devin said with a sigh. "But I'm getting more attached to it by the minute. It was the only one, too. We tried to get a second one, but not only was it their only one, they didn't want to sell it because it was going to be their display. They called all their other warehouses, and this one was it until the next shipment. So, at least they let this one go."

"Weird, man. Like it just appeared here out of the ether, huh? I can see why you'd want this picture."

"Well," Devin said, grinning. "You gotta admit. It *is* a nice likeness."

"Well, come on in," Trevor said. "You're not going to leave them all sitting out here, are you? At least have some coffee." He opened the front door and glanced back at the van. "How many are there?"

"The entire of Devin's coven," I said.

"We can't, Trevor," Devin said. "We gotta get these guys back. Is Titan ready to go? I thought I'd save you a trip and pick him up now."

"Wow, man, I appreciate that."

We may have been ready for Titan, but for some reason, Titan didn't seem ready for us. Although he greeted me like an old friend, surprising in itself for our brief acquaintance, he balked when Devin called him. He crouched at Trevor's side, bristling, ears back, watching Devin, who looked at Trevor in genuine astonishment.

"What's with *him*?"

"Beats me," Trevor said in his quiet manner. He seemed equally amazed. "Titan! What the hell's *wrong* with ya? *Stop that*!"

Titan's body slumped, and he licked his lips as he glanced guiltily at Trevor. He then resumed his stance, glaring at Devin.

"Well, I'll be damned, Trevor. He's never done *that* before. What the hell are you teaching him?" He stooped and offered his hand. "Come here, boy."

Titan made no move to leave Trevor's side. He just maintained his unfriendly warning glare.

"Hey, Jack...lighten up!" Devin stood up, looking embarrassed.

"Why is he *doing* this?" I asked Trevor, as if I didn't have any idea.

"I don't know. Maybe he just knows we're leaving tonight."

"Well, that's no reason to take it out on Devin."

"True, but tell *him* that." With a smile, he handed Devin a bag of dog food. "He eats table scraps too. Well, hell, you know. You've known the dog as long as I have."

"Yeah, well I *thought* I did." Devin returned the smile, but it was an uneasy smile. Enough dogs could blow his cover if this continued.

The farewells over with, Devin closed the front door behind us and turned to me. We were out of earshot of the passengers in the van. "Well, let's get him in there, lady. Shit. We do have more than one problem. The van is packed as it is, and that's a big picture. If this dog so much as wags his tail..."

"Wags his tail?" I looked dubiously at Titan who obviously was not anxious to board. Trevor had leashed him for the ride home, and Titan sat where the leash range ended, some feet from both of us. He looked first at the van, then back at the house, and finally at Devin. Trevor's explanation seemed plausible until Titan lowered his head and flattened his ears menacingly. "We'll be lucky if he *only* wags his tail. What are we going to do?"

Devin sighed. "Well, we've *got* to get him in there." He handed me the leash and walked past the dog without glancing at him. Titan's eyes followed him, but at least he wasn't growling now. Devin opened the van from the passenger side.

"Daniel. I think you'd better put that picture over by the side wall and sit in front of it. We're boarding Titan." He looked at me. "Go ahead, lady. He doesn't seem to object to you."

Trying to keep Titan lying down was a problem relieved only by our arrival at Daniel's house which, fortunately, wasn't far from Trevor's place. There we unloaded everything and everyone but the dog.

Devin and Daniel immediately set to erecting the picture, and when it was finally hung, a hush fell over the room.

"Man, what a good-looking dude," Devin said approvingly, stepping back with crossed arms, his gaze sweeping the picture.

"Yeah, bro," Daniel agreed. "That is the most far-out gift. We're going to have to get a light for it. Maybe a blacklight."

"You wouldn't want to sell it, would you?" Devin joked.

Daniel glanced from Devin to the picture, and then an understanding look crossed his features. "I see it now, Dev. The resemblance. That's *you*, isn't it, bro."

"Yeah, I'm hep. I was just jiving you, Daniel, but if you ever get tired of it—"

"Don't hold your breath," Julie shot at him. "I'm in love with it now."

"Oh, well. Can't win 'em all. So, did you say there was some birthday cake out there?"

Julie said, "Let's set the kids up first."

"Yeah, and while you're doing that, I'm going to get the dog out of the van," Devin said. "He's got a bug up his ass for some reason, and I need to find out what it is. You know, I have to control that sucker for the next few days, and I don't need any misunderstandings about who the boss is."

"Titan, *too?*" Daniel looked up. "Man, Dev, what *is* it with you and *dogs* all of a sudden?"

"Well, I've known Titan since he was about this big." He gestured with his hands cupped together and then reached for the front door. "As for *your* dog, well, there's no accounting for taste."

"Yeah, but my dog never wanted to taste you before." Daniel grinned at his own joke, but Devin never heard it. He was already visible through the picture window, walking towards the van.

I wondered if Trevor's dog had ever reacted to Devin this way before he…was him. He had told me that his final entry into Devin was at Halloween, and we hadn't seen Titan since. If this was a first, it only validated to me more that Devin was who he said he was.

"Come on out here while I cut the cake," Julie said suddenly. "I never see you without Devin glued to your side. Gives us a chance to talk."

Daniel went out to see what Devin was up to, and I followed Julie to the kitchen, glancing back the whole way. Titan was loose in the front yard, sniffing and marking boundaries. I was glad that Luke was fenced up in the rear.

Julie chattered on as she served cake to the kids, about their recent move to this state and how they happened upon this house. It was hard to keep my mind on what she was saying. I kept wondering how Titan and Devin were doing. I didn't have to wonder long.

A flurry of snarls and yelling and commotion suddenly drifted piercingly through the open screen door in the living room. It sounded like a one-dog dogfight. Before we could get up, Daniel burst into the kitchen, one hand covering his wrist, and turned the cold water on.

"Man, that dog don't like Devin," he said, plunging his arm into the cold stream. "He bit *me* for Chrissake."

"Why'd he bite *you* if he doesn't like Devin?" Julie wailed, jumping up to examine the slashed wrist.

"I don't think he was aiming for me. He went after Devin, and I instinctively jumped in to pull him off. Figures. Devin didn't get a scratch. He says he wants to run the kids and the dog home and then come back. Are they done with their cake?" He pulled his wrist out and threw a clean dishtowel over it. "It's okay, Julie. It's not that bad."

I was relieved to get out of there. I grabbed the kids and took off for the van, calling see-you-laters to them on my way out.

The yard was empty. I wondered what I would find when I opened the van door.

"Devin, what's going on…" Before the entire sentence was out of my mouth I saw that Titan was lying calmly beside Devin, one paw on his knee, the bulk of his body sprawled across the bucket seats up front.

Devin's smile of greeting, as I climbed aboard and scooted the kids to the rear, was all I needed to completely understand. Christian was what was going on. I saw that broad grin and flattened nose and grinned back.

"Hey, man." I felt that old chest feeling ripple through me and pointed to Titan.

Christian nodded, rubbing the dog's large head with affectionate hands. "Tha's all thiz dog needed, la-dee. A f'miliar face."

"Is *that* how you calmed him down?" I couldn't get over the change in the dog.

"La-dee, Ah don' *need* t' calm 'im down. He lahks me. An' he even lahks *Devin*. But *him*? Well, tha's a puzzle to 'im, raht, Jack?" He scratched Titan's head. "Well, don' feel 'lone, boy. He's a puzzle t' a lot of *people*, too."

Titan thumped his tail at Christian's words, and I glanced back at the kids. They had collapsed happily into the beanbags and seemed content.

"I have to admit, that's a little closer to the way he treated you on Halloween."

Christian grinned, flashing his white teeth. "Hell, this here dog cut his teeth on mah skin. Besides Trevor, he don' take no orders from anyone *but* me."

I laughed. Christian was so dramatic. "You're so cute," I told him, reaching across the furry body to kiss him. His shoulder was all I could reach so I kissed it. "Well, I'll be. Something finally came between us." I shut the passenger door carefully and boarded from the side sliding door. You two can have the front. I'll ride back here with the girls."

Pammy was appalled when we entered the house with Titan and didn't make any bones about it.

"What…is *that*? That…that *horse!* Has *Chris* seen that?"

"Don't panic, Pam. He's just visiting for a few days," I assured her.

"Oh." She eyed him warily. "Is he friendly?"

Christian was only too proud to demonstrate, engaging the dog in a playful wrestle that quickly ended with a crash. Titan had only to wag his undocked tail in our overcrowded house to send something flying off the coffee table.

"Okay! All *right!* I believe you." Pam shook her head. "Watch *out!*"

Titan's tail had swung again, but before it could hit anything Christian dove on him and anchored him to the ground.

"Now, mutt. You *stay!*"

Titan lay, panting happily, actually smiling in his Doberman way, unintentionally displaying a set of gleaming white daggers. Christian sat up and straightened his shirt.

"See? Perfec'ly trained. All hand signals, y' notice? Hey lad-ee, does yer sister know she's sittin' t'naht?"

"Aw, waitaminute," Pam wailed. "The kids, all right, but you're not leaving me alone with *that* thing!" She pointed emphatically to the monster.

"Oh, come on, Pam. He's friendly as hell."

We hung out for another hour or so, with Christian cracking Pam and the kids up with his antics and jokes. Finally, when it began to get dark and Pam had given in, we headed out.

"What if Chris hears him over here?" Pam called out as Christian started the engine.

His reply was quickly shot back. "Jis sen' Titan to th' door. Ah guarantee he won' argue with *him.*"

"Yeah, well, he can do whatever he wants while you'ns are gone, 'cause *I'm* not going to argue with him *either.*"

Pam's last call regarding the dog was almost lost in the roar of departure.

Alone, finally, we had the chance to talk, but neither of us took advantage of it. Each of us was lost in our own private thoughts although he kept his hand on my knee as he drove and squeezed it from time to time.

Luke's behavior was understandable, I found myself rationalizing, for neither of us was that familiar with Daniel's dog. Deep inside, though, I knew I was ignoring the fact that Devin had been in and out of Daniel's house for weeks. Evidently, this was a new problem.

But Titan. Devin had held Titan when he was six weeks old and had been around him constantly as he'd grown up. And what about Thor? Devin *had* raised *him* from a pup. Yet all three dogs were definitely reacting to something in *him. Him*...the one I was so sure was not evil.

"You start yet?"

His voice startled me out of my musing about the dogs. Evidently, he'd been musing about something else entirely. It took a second to register what he meant. My period was the last thing on my mind tonight.

"Oh...oh, no, I haven't."

He nodded, his eyes still on the road. "You could be."

"If I do start, believe me, you'll be the first to know." Even as I spoke, I knew that Christian had vacated and that *he* was back. "Have you decided what you're going to do about Daniel?"

"Play it by ear. Just like I have to do with the canines."

"Bust in the ass, huh?" I kidded him, and he tossed me a wink as we glided into Daniel's driveway.

Fortunately, Luke was still out back, and Danny and Timmy buried Devin, as usual, smothering him with kisses and hugs the minute we walked in. Well, at least the children didn't growl. Julie tried to call them off, but Devin motioned for her to lighten up.

"I like 'em," he told her, swinging Timmy up on his shoulder.

I went into the kitchen where I could hear the clatter of cups and plates. "Hi. Need any help?"

"No, thanks. I'm just putting coffee on. The kids already ate, so I'm just setting up cake for us big people."

"How's Daniel's hand?"

"Oh, it's all right. All that blood made it look worse than it was."

From the sudden set of her face, I could see that she didn't want to discuss it, so I changed the subject. "Well at least let me help set up the table." I picked up some cake plates and went into the dining room.

During the cake and coffee, the discussion around the table centered more on the plant than anything supernatural or otherworldly. Devin and Daniel seemed to have an unspoken agreement to keep such subjects away from Julie.

After the table was cleared, we moved the party into the living room where the remainder of the evening was spent in sketching pictures. Daniel proudly produced a drawing he'd attempted of the big red velvet picture, crude and out of perspective, but it was the subject matter itself that aroused Devin's interest and concern. I could tell by the expression on his face, but he didn't mention it until we were halfway home that night.

"See what I mean about Daniel? You were drawing horses, Julie was drawing flowers, and I drew a scorpion. Look what Daniel draws."

I nodded. "Yeah. We may have created a monster with that painting."

"Perhaps it is a little too heavy for Daniel right now."

"If it is, it's too late to do anything about it."

Pam was already asleep when we got home, so we just headed straight for the bedroom.

Devin went to sleep almost immediately. For once the house was blessedly quiet with no tapes running, no lyrics to pick at my brain or answer my unvoiced questions. Lying there quietly in the dark, I almost wished there were. The music's uncanny ability to zero in on exactly what was going on might have been beneficial to me tonight.

I had a lot of unvoiced questions.

The baby was one. If I *was* pregnant, well, it was useless to worry about it now. I could look forward to a regular baby, but I knew too little about the nature of the child *he* wanted.

My mind ran back through the day's events and then examined the entire relationship as a whole. I was happy. Happier than I'd ever been in my whole life. Every minute of living meant something now, and Devin was at the core of my thoughts every waking second. So what was keeping me awake now?

Titan shifted his weight on the floor beside the bed and heaved a heavy sigh in the darkness. The dog hadn't been any problem tonight, but I'd noticed he'd roamed from room to room, watching Devin like a hawk. Pacing in this strange house before he'd finally settled on a place to sleep. Beside *me*. It brought to mind my first question. What did dogs have against *him*? People loved *him*, but people were so much more easily deceived than animals.

A twinge of guilt slivered through me as I lay there, quietly rubbing his back in the dark. Even though I loved him, I was still worried.

By day, I was enormously happy just living in such constant loving, understanding surroundings, counting my blessings and wondering what deity to thank for this perfect relationship and constant joy. But by night, when I had time to think and consider this way of life from a human social standpoint, the old fears and doubts would dig and prick and needle at me, reminding me of facts I didn't want to face.

There wasn't anyone I could discuss it with, not even Pammy. She seemed to love Devin, and I didn't want to say anything to her that might set off any alarm bells and cause her to suspect him of anything. Which left only me to decide what to do.

I could be pregnant, and I knew I wasn't prepared for this child. I knew it and *he* knew it. In spite of all I'd seen Devin do—his telepathy, his perceptions, even his seeming perfection, there still hung this doubt. What if Devin was mentally unstable? What if all these things were happening just because I *wanted* to believe in him? What if he *were* a paranoid schizophrenic with latent homicidal tendencies?

Could *anyone* stay so good-natured, so understanding, so tolerant, so considerate, so patient…so fucking *perfect*…without cracking sooner or later?

He never left my side unless he had to. Work, for instance. He cooked supper, cleaned the house, played with and supervised the kids, maintained the home entertainment, showered me with cards and gifts and notes, and let me know in every way that he loved me.

He never spoke of God in any negative way, and he'd never given me any reason to believe that there was an evil side to him, hidden or otherwise. Yet dogs backed up in fear and mistrust when *he* was around.

And then there was that illness that had prevailed in both Michelle and me upon early exposure to his presence. My mother's words surfaced now, her warnings that I could be being duped or exploited, but *what* or *who* had she been trying to warn me about? Flying saucers? Evil spirits? I couldn't remember exactly now. *She* had referred to them as *them*.

That book she'd wanted me to read, arriving just before I'd gotten to know Devin. I'd tried to read it that night and—

Blue

Something had happened that evening that was almost a blank in my mind now. There had been an episode of—

Blue

—a drug-like trip, only I hadn't been *on* anything that night, hadn't even drank that one drink I'd made, and somehow I'd found myself in an eerie world with a big white mansion that glowed in the dark, as did every tree and shrub and blade of glass, all phosphorescent and glowing of their own accord, almost as if they were plugged in.

Someone had been on that big, wide, columned veranda, someone who looked just like…just like that *face* I'd seen the night of the peyote, when *he* had forced me to look at him. I *had* seen that face before. He had been standing on that wide veranda, and I had been walking toward him as though I had every right in the world to be at that party, and that wasn't all, oh my god, that wasn't all, because the very next morning I had been driving down a familiar dirt road, enroute to my uncle's house, and something had been in the road that scared the shit out of me and the girls and—

Blue
Blue!

I had inadvertently lied to Devin. I *had* seen that bluish-purple cloud before! I had told Devin I'd never seen it before the night I'd been listening to the *War of the Gods* for the first time. I'd never connected it to that morning in June, just two months before Devin and I...

What had *happened* to me?

As much as I now loved Devin and Erick and Christian and *Him*, wasn't it a little absurd that I'd accepted this bizarre situation as normal? Me, Kerry! The Virgo. The doubter, the pragmatic. The demander of proof!

This wasn't *me!* Yet I'd accepted Devin's situation as though *everybody* had four or five separate personalities and names.

But when I was around them, it *was* normal!

I didn't have to wonder what a shrink would have to say about all this, much less Kelly and Lola.

Was Devin who he claimed to be?

In light of the disturbing memories that had just surfaced, there didn't seem to be any doubt of it now. It was a little too late to turn tail and run.

I was already in love with him.

And suppose he *wasn't?* Did it really matter? As long as I was this happy, did it really matter? Devin did no wrong to any living thing. While he *claimed* to be the most evil personage the world had ever known of, he lived the *opposite* of the reputation of the Devil. He never lied, he surrounded himself with scores of admiring friends and treated each friend as though he were the *only* friend. He was generous. He'd once given his last dollar to a friend for gas, and then run out of gas himself. So did it really matter *what* he was?

Hell, yes, it matters, my stubborn subconscious argued. I could be carrying a child straight out of the plot of *Rosemary's Baby*. Of *course* the Devil would convince me of his love and sincerity before implanting such a seed within me! The Devil was known for his lies and deceit and cunning. And Devin had come right out and admitted that that was who he was. Well, in so many words.

Was I just another schmuck in history, being taken in by the very thing I wasn't even sure *existed?*

Whether Devin *was* the Devil in the traditional Christian sense, or a being from another dimension *mislabeled* Hell, or whether Devin Drew was merely a victim of schizophrenic delusion—and who knew what the hell *that* was—I loved him. I didn't want to lose him, not ever. No matter what the truth was. That put me, decidedly, right where *he* was. There were only three choices... evil, divine, or crazy.

Fatigue began to overtake me, and I pulled myself closer to him, where I could feel his warm chest, though, as usual, it was barely moving. I finally fell off into what should have been, as exhausted as I was, a dead, dreamless sleep.

But if dreams are any form of communication from the subconscious or higher self, I got my answer that night, however bluntly it was put.

13

I have no recollection of how I got there, but sometime during the night, I found myself at an elaborate marina...the kind frequented by the very wealthy. It was broad daylight.

Standing on a rickety wooden pier, overlooking the bluest,

most dazzling, sparkling ocean I had ever seen, I observed the clubhouse for some time before it occurred to me that this marina had a name.

Scheherazade Yachting Club

It was then that I realized I was dreaming for I knew I had never seen nor heard such a name in the twenty-five years I'd lived on earth. I made a supreme effort to memorize the long unfamiliar name, determined to remember it when I woke up.

There was something else unfamiliar, yet familiar, about this yachting club, and it took me a few minutes to put my finger on it.

The sky was a queer lemon yellow. Not a sunrise or sunset—the whole sky was a solid yellow, and it met that cobalt-blue ocean at the horizon like a scene straight out of Oz…after the movie had turned from black-and-white to color. I forced myself to pull my dazzled gaze away and went in search of Devin. He was here somewhere, I was sure. I just had to find him.

I walked toward the clubhouse, shielding my eyes from the brilliance with my hand. There was no visible sun to *cause* the brilliance. The brightness radiated from everything that I looked at. Things back at home seemed drab, washed out, and pale by comparison.

I couldn't get over the sense of familiarity of my surroundings, but even as I knew I was dreaming, I recognized that it was not the first dream I'd ever had where things had been familiar right up till the moment I woke up. The streets were immaculate and glittering, as though pinprick diamonds had been embedded into the asphalt at the time of paving.

How I found Devin, I don't recall either. There didn't seem to be any continuity between events in this dream. One minute I was walking towards the clubhouse, and the next thing I knew, I was already with him. Nude, no less, *inside* the stateroom of one of those yachts.

It was actually much more than a yacht. It was a huge ship the size of a passenger ocean liner, and there were quite a few people aboard, but nobody I recognized.

They were quite interested in *us*, however, for many of them were peering through our cabin porthole, staring at us.

Surprisingly, the fact that we were both naked didn't embarrass me at all. It felt natural enough to be that way, but the attitudes of the observers annoyed me. They crowded around the portholes, laughing and pointing, and I looked towards Devin, expecting him to send them away from the view. Devin didn't seem concerned.

Suddenly one member of the mob rammed the door with his shoulder, burst into the stateroom, and the crowd surged in. My annoyance turned to fear then, but Devin still remained calm as he reasonably pointed out to them that they were invading his lady's privacy. I began to sense that *we* were the ones in trouble or trapped, and as it turned out, we were both.

A policeman in a brown khaki uniform arrived and began to question Devin, repeating over and over the question of who he was. Devin only looked sadly towards me, as if expecting *me* to tell them. Accusations began to fly at us, and then someone seized Devin from behind and held him while a terrifying chaos ensued. Words were flung at us like four-letter filth…all coming from the mob.

Satan...Hell...evil...destroy...eliminate

"Devin!" I screamed. "Don't just *stand* there! You can send them away! You're *stronger* than they are! It's all *lies...lies!*"

Devin only continued to look sadly at me as the crowd surged forward, obviously intent on destroying him, pulling at his limbs and hair until Devin finally nodded his intention to speak.

"No, lady, it is true. It is as I told you. Yet, is there *any* evil in me?" And with that gentle statement, huge tears began to fall from his anguished eyes. He didn't seem to believe that either of us would be harmed. The pain and hurt in those crying eyes was for me...his lady...who still did not understand or believe.

Amazingly, at his first word, the crowd became subdued, and Devin raised his arm, as if to command silence. The man who had been holding him released his blood-stopping grip, unnecessary as it had been, for Devin had not fought him, had not struggled, had made no move to defend or protect either of us.

Frantic with terror for both of us, knowing this could be the calm before the storm and chaos could again erupt at any second, I glanced around to see if there was any escape, but we were encircled by the mob. Devin was still being held, though not with any pressure.

"Please go away," I begged the policeman, but he only looked at me with cold revulsion and scorn.

"Satan's whore," he sneered. "You're the same as *he* is."

I looked at my accuser with stark horror. "We're not doing anything *wrong!* You've got it all *wrong!* You've got *him* all wrong!"

"Don't tell me you don't *know* who he is!"

"I *know* who he is," I screamed at him, unable to understand why these people didn't know him as I did. "If he was so *fucking evil* he would destroy *all of you!* Devin..." I turned to Devin now, whose head had suddenly become another face. A very familiar one. The same exact face that I'd seen on the night of the peyote. It strobe-flashed at me now, as it had done that night, on and off like a bulb, and it spoke to me in the same voice *he* used when he was with me in my regular reality. Not Devin's happy-go-lucky slang...but clear implicit echo-like whispers.

"Face it, lady. It is *true.* I am...I am..."

"You are...what?"

He suddenly spread his arms, and the people fell away like dead flies. They'd had no hold on him after all. I found myself facing him, the *him* that I knew and loved, now clad in a pair of new blue Levis and luminous, brilliant white shirt. He pointed emphatically to the pentagram around my neck.

"Don't you realize that you wear the ring of Solomon on your finger and the pentagram around your neck? You wear *my* ring. The pentagram is a symbol of Satanism and black magic. You'll find that pentagram you wear on every other page of the Satanic Bible!"

"But we're not *evil*, Devin." Horror washed over me as I faced those facts of symbolism in the jewelry that I wore. I did wear the seal of Solomon on my finger, and I *did* wear the goat-faced pentagram against my heart, and it *was* black magic. The point on the pentagram was even *down*, not up. "Then you are…"

"Yes, lady, as I have already told you. I am…and so are you."

The crowd started to close in on us then, but suddenly we vanished from the cabin and rematerialized on the deck of the ship. I looked around in astonishment and clung tightly to his hand. We were both dressed now, and the deck had a shaded blue awning over us that eased the brilliance of the day around us. The azure ocean sparkled and glistened and lapped gently against the sides of the ship. Devin still maintained that same unconcerned attitude as he pointed out various amenities of the luxury liner, and I was dimly aware that the uniformed officer was escorting us, even though no one physically held Devin now.

"How did we *get* here?" I whispered.

Devin squeezed my hand reassuringly. "Remember what I told you? Here, the thought manifests instantly. We are here now so that others who are looking for us can find us. Thinking is the way we get around here." With a wink, he pointed to a group of four people who, again, seemed oddly familiar to me, although I didn't know them from my third-dimensional experience on earth. They really appeared to be put out with *him* and with his manner of crash-course educating me, and although no words were spoken to indicate this, I knew it as clearly as if they had comic-strip clouds over their heads with tiny bubbles leading to their brains. I was reading their thoughts.

As they approached, I noted that there were three men and a woman, the latter slight in build and tall in stature. She clearly was the authority in the group, and this was evident from the way she carried herself and from the fixed looks she was giving Devin. I'd looked at Mandy and Michelle the same way when I'd caught them up to some mischief. In a flash, I knew who she was in relation to Devin. Her hair was the color of the Golden Fleece but more golden than Lola's, and she shook it away from her eyes as she gazed disquietly at him.

Was all this necessary to prove a point?

The three men watched with interest, especially the older one who maintained his place at the woman's side. Looking at him, I suddenly realized the "flash" I'd had that day at lunch, back in the third dimension, when Devin had mentioned that his father was moving to the state. Samantha, of television's *Bewitched*, had a father who resembled this man. Not so much in looks as in the air of confidence he carried about himself.

No words were spoken. The woman signed something at the main window of the deck, and then the four vanished as quickly as they'd appeared.

"We *are* evil, Devin," I whispered fearfully, shame now washing over me. I was finally accepting the fact that he was *the Devil*, for what else could he have been trying to tell me?

His good-natured smile for the impatience of those who had not necessarily approved of his methods vanished, and he closed his eyes for a minute, as if thinking. Finally, he turned to me with a tired sigh.

"What I thought you would understand was once again misunderstood. Evil and good are opposites. Good *is* evil. Evil *is* good. They are the extreme ends of the same thing. One is the extreme of the other. I am good and I am evil, but do you fear me? We have no opposites here."

"I don't fear you," I answered truthfully.

"Lady, do you love me?"

"Yes."

The deck seemed to melt away, and we were outside again, walking toward the pier, the only rickety thing in the entire marina. It extended to the wooden-structured frame of a large high-rise, still under construction and surrounded by scaffolding. No walls had been added yet. Suddenly I spotted Mandy and Michelle making their way across the high beams of the unsound structure. They seemed oblivious to the height and appeared to balance themselves with no apparent concern for their own safety.

"The *kids!*" I screamed, pointing, but Devin merely laid an arm over my shoulder, sighing impatiently again.

"The kids are all right. They have no fear such as you do, lady. They walk with surety across those high beams, and they do not fear falling. If they did, they know enough to ascend in midair. So should you."

The scenery changed again, and now we were back in my physical living room. Devin, still clad in his Levis but wearing no shirt, stood in the center of the room. I was sitting on our couch with Trevor and Mia on either side of me. I looked pleadingly at those familiar faces for understanding and explanation. They too had to be the same as us, and yet they were as calm and confident and unconcerned as Devin had been throughout this experience. Evidently, they knew something that I didn't.

I sobbed, unable to process this the way everyone else seemed to be doing. "It's true, isn't it?" I said.

Mia quietly patted my hand in her calm, placid way. "Yes, Kerry," she said gravely. "It is true."

"But why aren't *you* afraid, Mia? Why?"

"Because Trevor is his brother," Mia said simply. "And because I know Devin. And I know, not think, that no matter what *they* say, he is good." She gazed off into space with a smile of radiance, and she actually seemed to glow in the knowledge that she possessed. Her eyes shone with wisdom as she took both my hands and continued. "What *we* know is truer than what *they* say."

I looked up to Devin who still stood in the middle of the room, as if awaiting my final judgment. Rejection or acceptance.

"Devin!" I cried. "I love you!" I burst into tears then, wanting to be in his arms, not sitting on this couch, the target of his piercing gaze.

Instead of walking toward me, he strolled over to the front door and stooped down, kneeling on one knee. He pointed in the direction of the kitchen. "I didn't want to have to do this, Kerry. You know how I feel about proof. But I suppose this is necessary." He closed his eyes and, finger still pointing, said one word.

"Watch."

I looked over to where he was pointing, and that's when I awoke, screaming. Screaming...until I realized I was in my own bed and that a very disturbed Devin was shaking me gently and searching my face.

I tried to sit up and found myself quivering all over...head to foot. Vibrating with fear.

He turned the bedroom lamp on, and I buried my face in my hands, the memory still too clear of where I had just been and what had taken place. The clock on the bedside stand read 3:15. Even in my waking state, I was crying.

He sat on the edge of the bed, watching me carefully. Then he took me by the shoulders with both hands. "You're trembling," he said gently. "It must have been very real."

"Could...could you get me a glass of water?" My throat was parched and I could barely swallow. Like something had dehydrated the very moisture from my physical body.

"Sure. Ice water?"

I nodded. He rose to get it, and I saw the inverted cross swing. When he was out of the room, I looked down at my own pentagram which now looked more sinister than it ever had. I yanked it off and ripped the rings from my hands, depositing them all in a mound on the dresser. I didn't shake any less than when I'd had them on.

When Devin returned with the water he looked angry, an expression he had not left the room with.

Titan, who had apparently made his way into the kitchen during the night to sleep on the cool floor, followed him in, and it struck me odd that his tail was wagging slowly as if he too was unsure of Devin's anger.

"Here." He handed me the glass, a paper tablet, and a pen. "Write down what you can remember."

I shook my head. My hands were shaking too much to write, and I knew that I remembered it all too clearly anyway. I didn't need to write it down. I was much more concerned with Devin's obviously worried and angry expression. Even Titan, as angry as Devin was, did not bark, growl, or show any hostility toward his lifelong friend. It was Devin, all right.

Why, when *he* had been with me all day yesterday, and had even climbed into this bed we both sat on now?

Devin looked hurt that I'd refused the tablet. "You'll forget," he said quietly.

"No I won't. Never." I was still shaking, even though the initial fear had somewhat dissipated.

"Well, then tell me about it," he said, taking me in his arms and removing the glass from my unsteady hands. "I can kind of understand your not wanting to talk about it right now, but—"

"It was about *him*, Devin, and *who* he *is*, and he kept telling me that he was evil, and he pointed to those things I wear—" I indicated the jewelry on the dresser with a shaking, trembling finger.

He released me, walked over to the dresser and picked up the pentagram. "I was afraid of this. Damn. He had no *right!*" Devin was now smoldering. He looked at me in the mirror. "You *sure* you want to take these off? I mean, not that jewelry is important one way or the other but to succumb to that kind of tactic..."

"I...I don't know...after that dream..."

"Are you *sure* it was a dream?" He walked over to me and reached for my arm. "Let's see."

No new marks. He examined them both, released me, and opened his palm which held the rings and the pentagram. I placed the rings back on my fingers and pulled the chain over my head.

He looked at me questioningly.

"I'm sure," I said.

"He had no *right* to invade your…dreams…like that," Devin said furiously. "No right at all. Your dreams are your own private reality, and he had no right. It wasn't necessary!" He drew the covers up around us and pulled me against him. "Do you think you can sleep now?"

"I think so. You're here."

It was somewhat later, maybe an hour, that I sat up, carefully untwined myself from his protective hold, and got out of bed. The pen and tablet still lay on the dresser, the tablet already open to a blank page.

I turned the dimmer up so I could see what I was writing. I was no longer shaking or afraid.

I began to write down the dream.

14 Neither of us mentioned the dream in the morning. Devin put the reel-to-reel on, and the blunt, point-blank lyrics of Pink Floyd did the rest.

Pink was singing about me shouting in my sleep, asking if my conscience was at rest, because it had been put to a test. He reminded me that I'd been startled awake suddenly with my heart beating frantically. I had sailed across an ocean, and my fantasies had merged with harsh reality. While my fears hadn't been voiced, I had a final choice to make. There wasn't much left to say that the song wasn't already saying. No way could it be a coincidence. Devin had simply gotten out of bed and hit the play button. As usual, the song had started at the beginning.

I knew both of us were thinking about it because, if nothing else, the dream had given our future son a definite brand or label.

When Pam suggested a trip to the grocery store, Devin agreed. We needed food in the house, and shopping wasn't one of Devin's favorite things, so I left the tablet on the dresser for him to hash through, and we left.

When we returned, Devin helped us unload the car. As the last of the bags were brought in, he commented on the contents of the tablet, which now lay on the coffee table.

I had related the dream to Pammy as we shopped, and she'd told me of a frightening experience that she'd had during a nap one afternoon in that back bedroom that was now ours. I knew Devin would have a comment about my dream, and he did.

"That was pretty *heavy*," he told me. "Did your sister read it?"

"I just told her about it," I said.

"I still don't understand why he did it, man. What could have been the reason? That was shock therapy if I ever saw it."

Pam scanned the tablet hastily and set it down. "Yeah, she told me all this. Want to hear about *my* experience in that room?"

"Yeah, tell Devin," I said. "That *was* a weird thing."

"Yeah, I'll say." She turned to Devin. "You guys were at work, and Kerry said I could use the bed if you'ns weren't here. I was taking a nap. I dreamed this monkey thing with long, spidery arms and legs was trying to smother me. Man, I'll never forget that dream. I wanted to wake up so bad. I knew I was dreaming, just like Kerry did, and I was scared shitless that I'd smother before I could wake myself up. And when I *did* finally wake up, the covers were all tangled and wrapped around me, and I mean they were twisted around my head and neck like someone had deliberately tried to strangle me. I'll never sleep back there again."

Devin and I exchanged looks.

"Any idea what *hers* was all about?" I asked him.

He looked thoughtful for a minute before he shrugged. "Hmm, I don't know, Pammy. I really don't know."

We put away the groceries, laughing that we would finally have a night at home alone with each other. Pammy had refused to babysit Titan, insisting that she was not going to be the one having to face Chris at the door when he discovered that we were keeping a dog. Chris had long ago put the kibosh on any kind of pets, especially dogs.

When Pam left for the shower, Devin walked up behind me and wrapped both arms around my waist as I stood at the stove. I didn't need to turn around to know that my hippie Devin was gone. It was going to be nice to spend the evening together without our well-meaning friends taking up our time.

"What do you think about Devin's job situation?" I asked him, reaching behind myself to encircle his waist with my arms.

"What do *I* think?"

I nodded and turned to face him.

"I don't know. I think Devin can handle it."

"You think it will work out?"

"It always does. Tell you the truth, I'm a bit more worried about Daniel than I am about Devin. And a few other more important things. Did you start yet?"

"No."

He shook his head. "No, of course you didn't. You'd have mentioned it."

I swallowed uneasily. "You're really worried about it, aren't you."

"Worried? Strong word. Perhaps concerned. For the time factor, mainly. However, it only speeds things up, and I didn't want that kind of pressure on you until you're sure you're ready for it. And then again, you just might be late."

"You know, I just don't think I am pregnant. I don't *feel* pregnant. I've been there twice, and I think I'd recognize some signs."

"I don't think you are either, lady, but it is better to be prepared for the possibility."

"You won't be upset if I am?"

He smiled. "How could I be? It was all part of the plan. A little sooner than I expected, but…in fact…I'm beginning to like the idea."

I kissed him and turned back to the stove. "Want some coffee before we start supper? I've got potatoes baking right now."

"Sounds good. I'll roll us a number. Oh, speaking of supper, how does steak sound? I saw that you girls picked some up, and I didn't put them in the freezer."

"Yeah, that was an impulsive decision when I passed them. I haven't had steak in I don't know how long." I filled up the coffee pot and reached for the can. Devin left for the stash box.

"Oh, by the way," Devin called in. "Gerald phoned. Brian's going to bring my bike up for me one day this week. Gerald and Faye thought they'd come too, so they can see the house. Brian's been working on the cycle and says it should be ready in a day or two. I've been thinking about taking it down to Thompson's Station…just to get away from all the human bullshit for a night."

"This weekend? You mean you want to go alone?"

"Alone? What gave you that idea? No, I meant *us*. We could spend the night. Trevor's picking up Titan on Thursday, so we'd be free if Pam will stay with the kids. What do you think?"

Titan thumped his tail from the back room and we both laughed.

"Sounds like that sucker thinks he's invited," Devin said with a smile, glancing at the dog.

"More likely he heard the part about Daddy picking him up," I said. "Anyway, It sounds too good to be true! Pam would stay with the kids. I *know* she would. Let's make it official."

"You're on. Friday it is."

Throughout his visit, Titan had chosen the back den as his usual sleeping spot. It was the coolest room in the house, but tonight he was sprawled across the kitchen floor, no doubt lured by the aroma of the raw meat on the plate. I prodded him gently to his feet using my foot. He rose obediently, glanced at the steaks longingly, then at me, and then lumbered into the living room where Devin was sitting in the beanbag, rolling a joint.

Titan stopped in front of the beanbag, looked at Devin darkly, and laid his ears back.

Grrrr…Roof!

Devin did a double take, caught off guard, and I could see from the kitchen that the dog was aware of *him*.

Here we go again, I thought.

Devin glanced casually at the dog and continued rolling. Titan lifted his lip in a menacing snarl. Devin paused to lightly tap the dog on the nose with his index finger. "Lighten up!"

What happened next happened so fast that it was over before I could figure out what *did* happen. Titan lunged without further warning, and Devin nailed him to the floor in one motion with his right hand, the rolled joint intact in the other.

"Hey…Titan! You can't anticipate me, dog, so don't try."

He released Titan and reached for the matches, lighting the joint as if nothing had happened. Titan licked his lips and dropped back to the carpet, resuming his penetrating stare at Devin. When I came in with the coffee, he glanced at me and wagged his tail feebly.

"Damn, Titan." I reached down cautiously to pet him. He responded affectionately and licked my hand. "What's the matter with you, boy? He never did anything to you."

In response, Titan licked his lips again and returned to staring at Devin.

"Don't push your luck, Jack," Devin said, handing me the joint and standing up.

Titan watched him with eyes that virtually promised trouble.

Devin glared at the dog. "Get out in the kitchen." The command was quiet but firm. Titan turned and looked to where Devin pointed, and then back at Devin. There was a long silence that seemed like a draw. They locked eyes for a long moment. Finally, Titan rose and strolled out to the den, deliberately overshooting his commanded destination.

"Hey! That's not the kitchen. How 'bout it?"

Titan remained where he was and glared back at Devin.

"Let it go, Devin," I pleaded. "At least he's not in your way. What started this anyway? It seems like he hates you."

"He doesn't hate me. He's testing me. He knows Trevor isn't here to give the orders, and he doesn't feel that he owes me any obedience. But we'll have him for a few days, so I have to have the last word now, or he may get it later."

"But he likes *Devin*. Why doesn't he like *you*? Why do *all* these dogs act like they hate you?"

"He *doesn't* hate me, Kerry. He recognizes that I'm not the Devin he knows, and he *does* know the difference. I told you this. As long as I don't show him any fear we may get through the next few days without any hassles."

"Devin, the dog doesn't *like* you. Look at how he stares at you."

"He doesn't know whether to like me or not. He isn't sure he can trust me. I look like his friend, but he knows that I'm not. Maybe it's a scent or something. He just needs time. I'm a stranger right now, but he'll get used to me. It's not unusual for animals to react this way when they first sense my presence." He nodded in Titan's direction. "Thor's done the same thing. Snapped at me. With Thor's jaws, that's a hell of a snap. Titan, here, after he learns to respect me like I'm trying to respect *him*...you'll see a difference."

From the looks of Titan right now, I doubted it.

"Oh, by the way," Devin said. "We still have some peyote. We can take it with us on Friday." He talked as he seasoned the steaks and prepared them for the broiler. "There's nothing like doing that stuff in a nature environment."

"You think we should do it so soon after the last time?"

He nodded toward my belly. "I think it's imperative."

"But if I'm pregnant, won't that hurt the baby?"

He sighed. "If you *are* pregnant, nothing can touch that baby."

I forgot. Junior evidently wouldn't be subject to human substances, but I let the matter drop. What was going to be was going to be. Guiltily I realized that I wasn't disappointed by the idea of pregnancy at all. I loved Devin and I trusted him, but his feelings mattered too. Just what did he *really* feel about a baby this soon?

"Abortion is legal now, Devin."

He glanced at me as he slid the first steak into the broiler. "As I said, I'm beginning to like the idea myself, and you don't appear to be that upset about it either. However, I want you to be *sure* of me before our son is born. And if you question the dog's reaction to me, I suspect you're going to worry about the baby. That's where the need for understanding is imperative. Peyote just may help us cross you over that bridge of understanding. The Indians use it in their rituals, and I can see why. It opens doors."

I thought about last night's dream. It had made my understanding of who he was crystal clear. "What else do I need to understand? Where does the bridge lead?" I tossed the salad and buttered the garlic bread as we talked.

"Oh, philosophers have called it the bridge to the subconscious. I kind of like the term *Styx* myself." He smiled as I pictured the river Styx, the supposed separation of the living from the dead. "I'm just teasing you. Come on, lady. Lighten up. So serious." He flipped the steak, waited a few minutes, then removed it.

The bathroom door opened and Pammy came out, wet hair turbaned in a towel.

"What do I smell? Aw, man, *steaks!* We're having the steaks? You'ns are kidding. Do you know how long it's been since I've had a real live steak?"

Devin laughed. "Yours is done, Pammy. It's cooling on the plate."

"Yeah? Is *that* it? 'Cause I don't like the way Titan's staring at it."

"That sucker can look all he wants," Devin retorted. "He's got his own dog food. There's baked potatoes, too. And garlic bread. And salad."

"There's also coffee," I added.

Pam sat down on the couch. "Steak, man. I can't believe it. Hey, are you'ns going to be home tonight?"

"Yes, for once. Why?"

"Because Uncle Joe called and…oh, oh *no…stop him!*"

Devin moved at her sudden wail, but not fast enough. Titan had strolled over to the plate and before anything alive could have stopped him, tugged at the meat with his teeth, and then bolted it down, almost whole. Devin stared at the dog in disbelief as the last of the meat lumped in his throat, then stomach. I thought Pammy was going to cry.

"Never mind, Pam," Devin said. "There are other steaks. You can have the one that's cooking now."

"That's okay," Pam sniffed. "I didn't want it anyway…*Get outta here!*"

Titan actually had the brazen balls to walk over to her after that juicy snack for a pat on the head. Devin pointed to the back room, and this time there was no hesitation in his about-face and exit. He dropped at the back door with a heavy, resigned sigh.

"Like I was saying," Pam continued. "Joe called today, and he might come up tonight."

"Well," I said, looking at Devin apologetically. "There goes our quiet night at home."

Devin shrugged. "Oh, well. Good thing no one knows where Thompson's Station is. It looks like Friday's going to be the only night we can count on for no human interference."

"I'm really sorry, Devin. Joe's been wanting to meet you."

"Hey, it's cool. Any other night it would be my brother, or Daniel, and don't forget, Gerald has an appointment with us this week, too."

There was no hope for us. Not only did Uncle Joe come, but Chris stopped in to find out what was barking periodically, and no less than ten drop-ins also showed up that night, including George and two of his friends. Unfortunately, one of those friends was Henry, a conceited egotist and a guy I'd never cared for. Henry seemed to be on his best behavior, though, and I suspected that there were just too many people in the room for him to play center stage. The other friend was Henry's brother, Eddie, a guy who did not share his brother's obnoxious attributes.

Several of those drop-ins didn't stay long due to various Sunday night plans. When Lana and Colleen left with Chris for the other side of the duplex, it became easier to move and breathe.

Uncle Joe insisted on the overhead light remaining on, explaining that he just couldn't see in the dark like we did. Devin obliged politely, hitting the light switch on behind him, and I took a seat on the floor beside the gold leather chair that Devin had chosen to sit in. Joe, having secured drinks for anyone drinking, struck up a conversation with Devin about his philosophy and beliefs.

"I'm a Taurus and an arguer," he told Devin in advance. "And I'm a Roman Catholic, so tell me, are you really a witch? Or wizard, like I've been hearing?"

Pam grinned over at me from the couch as Devin replied.

"Well, I'm not an argumentative person, but I try to answer any question that's put to me." He glanced at me, and I wondered if he felt like he was on display. Everyone looked up for the great debate, and somewhere in the interim, *he* disappeared leaving a very jovial Devin and company to host our guests.

Pam smiled proudly as Devin went through his own concept of love of all mankind and giving to expect nothing in return. Listening to him talk, we were all proud to know Devin, and just when I was feeling especially proud of him, and as Joe was also beaming with approval, Christian threw in one of his contradictory remarks.

At one point, Erick, a good one to answer the question of violence, spent a good ten minutes discussing the total senselessness of brutality in *any* form, when Christian, not five seconds after Erick's last word, picked up one of Devin's ceremonial knives with a bratty, mischievous glint in his eyes. That look, I knew, told me he knew exactly what he was doing for the roomful of spectators.

Well, can't disappoint the folks, he might as well have said.

He examined every detail of the dagger while the room waited awkwardly in confused silence. This Devin character didn't *look* like he avoided violence.

I glanced at Pam, who was giggling into one of the couch pillows, and at George, who also had a look that told me he recognized Christian. George had an expectant smile plastered on his face.

Christian's features deepened as his face took on his own squat nose and hung lips. He held his position in Devin's body for a minute. "Ah'd lahk t' have tha' knife," he said finally, in his unmistakable drawl. "Man, *nobody'd* mess wit' ya with a boss blade lahk that!"

Eddie and Henry almost swallowed their tongues. Joe looked a little stunned. Christian's obvious fascination with the knife just didn't jive with

Erick's spiel about violence. Just as they all probably thought they'd heard wrong to begin with, Erick contradicted Christian's words in the next second. The black features melted abruptly, and Erick handed me the knife. In a tone of pure disgust he said, "Put that *thing* away, will you Kerry?"

"Oh," Joe said, relief flooding his voice.

All of us burst into laughter, although Joe and Erick obviously failed to see any humor in Christian's preceding statement.

"What's so funny?" Erick asked, looking around innocently.

"Oh," Henry spoke up. "Just the way you were…uh…studying that knife a minute ago."

"Yeah, well tha's disgusting, really," came Christian's swift reply. The switch happened so fast that even *I* did a double take, and I was prepared for *anything* this strange night. "Why use a sloppy thing lahk *that* when a *tire iron* in th' front seat is all ya need! Bash them motherfuckers over their fuckin' heads, Ah always say. Don' trust *nobody!*"

This time, everybody in the room was sure that Devin was just fucking with their heads, and he was indeed. When no one could take any more of it, they excused themselves one by one, for it *was* Sunday, and tomorrow *was* a workday. Before long, only Pam and George remained, and all of us were laughing.

"Aw, Devin," I teased him. "Now Joe doesn't know *what* to think. Did you do that on purpose?"

"Well, let's just say that it was a joint display that none of me could resist. I hope your uncle wasn't too upset, but, let's face it…he started it."

"He's probably just a little bit confused," Pam said.

"Christian does that a lot at the office, doesn't he?" I remarked when we were finally alone and setting the alarm for work.

"Yes, he does," Devin admitted. "However, the office just thinks it's me fucking around, so we get away with it. Hey, I'll shower and shave now so we'll have time for a little love in the morning. It's looking like about the only time we won't have company coming." He ruffled my hair and went into the bathroom.

When Devin finished shaving, he came in and bent to kiss me. I pulled him down on the bed. The aroma of Old Spice permeated the room.

"Do you really want to wait until morning?" I kidded him.

"Did you really think I would?" He grinned, rolled me over, and pinned me underneath him. "Besides, it *is* morning. Check out the time."

"I can't see the clock with you on top of me." I laughed and playfully pushed him off. "Yeah, you're right. It's after midnight. Too bad. It's past my bedtime."

Devin's face turned suddenly serious. "Speaking of bedtime, babe. I've been thinking about your dream a lot today, and there's one thing that just doesn't make any sense to me."

"What's that? The whole thing seemed pretty blunt to me." I lit a cigarette, took a drag, and handed it to him.

"Well, you said the name of the marina was Scheherazade. You even *spelled* it right. Do you know who Scheherazade *was?*"

"Who? You mean it's a person?"

He drew on the cigarette, exhaled, and stubbed it out. "It was a person all right, but fictional. I had to call Faye and ask her to look it up in the encyclopedia. It's not exactly a household word. She was the wife of a king who had murdered his previous wives, and she suspected that she was the next to go. So what she did, and it was pretty shrewd, was tell him a story every night and not finish it. He would get so involved in her story that he couldn't kill her without knowing how it ended. The next night she would finish the story and start another one. She kept him going night after night, and eventually he fell in love with her, and she didn't have to worry about it anymore."

"How grizzly. Why would she want someone who was a murderer anyway?"

"Well, I don't know, but that's beside the point. Her stories were all collected together in a book you would know as *Arabian Nights*. I think the original title was *One Thousand and One Nights,* supposedly because she kept this storytelling going on for that long."

I was beginning to get his point now, and I bolted upright. "Devin, I *have* heard about that book, only because a lot of the stories were made into movies. Ali Baba, Sinbad, Aladdin's lamp…that stuff. But I've never even *seen* a copy of the book, much less read it. Really! I don't remember ever hearing the name Scheherazade in any of those stories."

"Oh, I don't doubt that, babe. She wasn't in the stories, she was telling them. Even if you *had* read it, it's highly unlikely that you'd remember the spelling of that name."

"Well, when I realized I was dreaming, I made a point of memorizing the spelling because everything means something in dreams."

"But how did your dreaming self know how to spell it at all if you never saw it in print? Babe, I don't think you *were* dreaming. I didn't think so when I saw you shaking like that, and I don't think so now. I think he got impatient and *dragged* you into his world, and I think that sign showing the name of the yacht club was there to tell you something. Like a clue, you know? Maybe he felt a need to really speed things up since there's a possibility of you being pregnant."

"But none of this makes sense, Devin. What would that book have to do with *any* of this?"

He rose, turned off the bedroom lamp, and turned up the wall dimmer switch. His silhouette was barely a dark outline as he returned to the bed and began to undress. "I don't know. I'd have to think about that one. But there's one thing about it that we can't dispute…come on, get undressed."

I started to peel my clothes off. "What's that?"

"It was a book." He handed me my sleep shirt that was hanging on the closet door.

"So?" I slipped it over my head.

"It's a name you can't connect with anything else. You never saw that name before anywhere because it was a character in a *book*. You probably never knew anyone with that name because it's Arabic or Persian, so the symbolism can only be pointing to a book. For instance, if you'd dreamed about Tom's yacht club, you might be thinking of every Tom you ever knew trying to figure out the symbol in the dream."

I lay back down and moved over so he could join me. "I still don't see the connection. Am I supposed to read some book? That book?"

"I don't know either, babe. Yet. But I know there's something to it. He doesn't do things for no reason."

His lips found mine, and there was no further discussion.

Devin wasn't around when I punched in Monday morning. He had left the house in good spirits in spite of the bullshit going on at work. I couldn't understand why he was taking it so well. I wondered what the real reason for his demotion was. Could it be because of me?

"No, it's on the level."

Pat sat casually at his desk and looked me directly in the eyes. "Devin's one of the best, Kerry. You know that. But seven's the only route open right now. Devin will get his choice the minute another one becomes available and, well, I hope you understand the position—"

"Oh, I do, Pat. It just surprises me that he's taking it so well."

"Surprises me too, Ker. There's a little friction between Tim and him, but he's getting along great with the guys, as usual. In fact, between you and me, it's a pleasure to have him back *in* the route room again. Devin cheers people up."

Lola grabbed me when I walked into my office and pulled me out of earshot of the girls. She too had heard rumors of Devin possibly leaving the company, or having been fired due to an argument with Tim on Friday. Both stories were circulating, and who would know better than me?

"He didn't get fired," I told her, pulling up a chair. I summed up for her what Devin had been told and of the position he was in now. She agreed that it was a dirty trick to pull the supervisor status from him but said it probably *was* the main office in Chicago that had cut the position. She promised to see what she could find out and to let me know at five.

Devin finished his small route by two and came straight back to our little cubbyhole office. Lola was at her desk, and I knew who it was by her tone of voice and greeting, even before he spoke.

"Yes, sir. What can I do for you?"

"Guess."

"Do I really *have* to? Look. I'll give her a message. She'll be off in three hours."

"Hey, Mama, don't be pulling rank on me now." He poked his head into our suddenly quiet office. As usual, all work had ceased. "Hey, Ker, I'll be out of here in an hour. I just wanted to tell you that I'll pick up the girls. At least I'll be able to do *that* for you from now on."

"No, Devin," I protested. "Just go home and don't do *anything*. Please. You're making me feel guilty."

"You dummy," Lola said, smiling. "Don't you know when you've got a good thing?"

"But he does *everything!*" I turned back to Devin. "Please! Go hang around Daniel's."

"Hey, it's cool. If I can get off *this* early every day, I'd rather get them and see you home before six every night."

"Devin, what happened to your job?" Kelly interrupted, serious for once. "Why are you back on a route?"

" 'Cause it beats all hell out of unemployment, Kelly."

"What?" Hannah perked up, interested. "You're not a supervisor anymore?"

"Well, officially I am right now," he said. "But I won't be after the next payday."

Lola stepped into the doorway. "You're going to be doing *this* route until then?"

"It sure looks that way, don't it, Mama." He slung his jacket over his shoulder and leaned over to kiss me goodbye. "Ker, don't forget now. I'll get the kids."

"Wait a minute," Lola said. "Did you find out why?"

He paused in the doorway. "Well, Mama, if you want to know, you can do one of two things. You can ask Ralph, Charlie, Tim or Maurice, or…you can wait until tomorrow and see if it makes the…uh…what do you chicks call it…rumor of the day."

Kelly looked at Devin sympathetically. "That's not fair, Devin. They're really taking that new job away from you?"

"Hey-hey-hey. Anyhow, I'm checked out, paperwork's done, and I'm through. So if you chicks have any more questions, ask me tomorrow after eight."

"How are we gonna do that if you're on a route all day?" Lola reminded him, trying to kid him out of his mood.

"Take it up with Tim," Devin tossed back over his shoulder. "I don't get paid to ask why or how anymore. Later, Mama."

"Okay, Devin. Try to cheer up, huh?"

Lola's report, just before five, was a parrot of what Devin had been told. She had gone to the highest executive at the plant—the general manager, Charlie. He'd run off identical phrases of what Tim had stated. Too identical. It was almost too pat, but I thanked Lola for the effort anyway.

Christian was at the stove flipping hamburgers when I walked in. Titan lay quietly on the floor, ears pricked with interest, nostrils quivering in the direction of the frying pan.

"Oh, no you don't, Jack," Christian was saying, nudging him playfully with his foot. "Ol' Christian is *on* to you, mo' fucker. Ya think this is steak night again, but Ah got news for you. Don' hold yer breath. Hey, lad-ee. Welcome home."

I went straight into his arms. "Hi. What're you doing, you nut! Making supper! And the house is all cleaned up. You're going to give me a complex."

"Hey, you jist go git yer shower, la-dee," he retorted. "Ever'thing's under control."

I hugged him gratefully. "What'd I ever do to deserve you?"

Nothing could be depended on to remain consistent from one minute to the next. When I came out of the shower, cleaned up and ready for the evening, I found Erick holding Titan by the choke chain while Pam entered the house, feigning fear, but over-exaggerating as she was pretty well acquainted with the dog by now.

"Just don't let him jump on me," she was saying. "Hey, Ker! You're home early, huh?"

"Yeah, thanks to Devin. He picked up the kids."

"He did? That's really cool. He must have gotten off early too, huh?"

"Well, it appears that I'll be getting off early from now on," Erick said with a yawn, as though the subject of Devin's job just bored the hell out of him. "Everybody hungry? Supper's ready. Table's set. Kerry, you can call the kids anytime."

"All *right! You* made it, huh?" Pammy looked at the coffee table, set up like a regular dining room table, and beamed with admiration. "Oh, man, I'll never get used to this napkin shit! *Class*, I'll tell ya. Well, as good of a cook as *you* are…"

"Well, I'm not really responsible for the meal," Erick began with a smile.

"He just dishes it out," I added, knowing that Pam wouldn't need much of an explanation. "I believe we're having soul burgers."

We settled the kids at their little table and then all sat down to eat.

"I have to be in by seven tonight," Pam said. "Don't you wish you had a job with my hours?"

I looked at the clock. "I haven't figured out what your hours are. You don't seem to be on any kind of a schedule, but you'll never make it by seven. You'd better eat fast."

"Oh, they're lucky if I come in at all tonight. I'm supposed to be off but they called this afternoon and begged. I figure I'll leave here around eight and—"

"Eight?" Erick smiled. "You *do* have it made, little girl."

"I know. I make my own hours. I won't let them put me on a schedule, or Mr. Johns will get spoiled and expect it. Next thing I know, he'll have me punching in like everyone else."

Erick looked amused. "What makes you so privileged?"

"I'm the only *color* printer they have. That's what." Pam grinned. "And I'm *good* at it. They could hire another printer, but not one like me that takes pride in how the photos come out. Oh, Mister Johns won't hire anyone else. He loves me."

"He must," Erick agreed. "Does the pay go with it?"

"Are you kidding?" Pam almost busted a gut laughing at that one. "Ten or twelve hours a day at two bucks an hour? Why do you think I go in whenever I feel like it? Shit! I *should* ask for a raise! How about *you*, man? What kind of a day did you have? You're back on a route?"

"Yeah, Tim don't fuck around. Oh, by the way, Kerry. I believe our next paycheck's going to be pretty small, that is, when the pay goes from what it was to commission. This route's pretty small."

"Oh, money is no problem," Pam interrupted quickly. "Me and Kerry are both working, too. We can swing everything all right. I just feel so bad for you. They're really putting the screws to you down there. Wow, you have to go back on commission, huh?"

"I guess I already have. What I'm earning *now* is actually on commission already. Next paycheck after this one. Mighty Christmassy of them, don't you think?"

"Oh God, that's *right!* Christmas *is* this month! Well, don't worry. I have a lot of overtime in and—"

"That's not your problem, Pammy," Erick said gently, "and the money isn't either. I have plenty of credit cards for the girls' toys, and really, what is Christmas but for the kids?"

"Yeah, I guess. Are you going to stay working there after they've pulled this shit on you?"

"Well, that's up to Devin, really," Erick replied thoughtfully, and Pam burst into laughter.

"I'll *never* get used to this shit…*never* !" She picked up her purse and keys. "I gotta get outta here. I'll see you'ns later. Tell Christian that was a *great* hamburger."

"An' we maht be eatin' *grits* next week," Christian flashed in, grinning his wide clowning grin. "Ya never know *what* that Devin maht do, th' way *that* job's going!"

Pammy shook her head, waved and left, still laughing.

I began to clear the coffee table, carrying the plates into the kitchen and pouring coffee for the two of us. Christian's remark, however brief his entrance, worried me. It was the first time one of them had seriously implied that Devin was disturbed enough by the plant's tactics to actually quit the job.

"I've talked it over with Pat," Erick said, following me into the kitchen with his own plate. "He really wants Devin to stay on. So do the guys in the route room." He set his plate on the kitchen floor in front of Titan, his hamburger barely touched. The dog leapt to his feet, tail wagging. "Hey, easy, boy. Don't take my arm off now." He scratched Titan affectionately on the head and was rewarded by a hasty lick on the hand as the dog abandoned the plate for a second.

Apparently, the dog got along well with Erick, too.

It occurred to me then, as I watched them, that maybe Devin's absence tonight was due to the job problem to begin with.

It was also the first time I realized that Devin's supervisory status had come along during a period after Devin had gone through other drastic changes as well. A short story, *Flowers for Algernon*, crossed my mind. It had been required reading in high school. I had loved that story of Charlie the moron who had participated in an experiment that had increased his IQ a little at a time, until he reached the point of genius. A tiny mouse named Algernon had been tested first, and Charlie's progress had run concurrent with that of the mouse's. When Algernon started showing signs of slipping backwards, Charlie had worked even harder with his new intelligence to find a way to keep from slipping backwards too, but to no avail. Eventually Algernon died, and the story ended with Charlie as he was in the beginning, a moron again.

Now, watching Erick lovingly stroking Titan, I remembered a longhaired hippie in a ponytail wearing a silver earring, whose only job had been delivering bottled water to the Sparklear customers. The elevation to supervisor status had run concurrent with the newly styled hair, the loss of hippie status at work, and in short, the change in personality.

Was Devin's job an Algernon, an indication of things to come?

A black wave of ominous foreboding slithered through me.

When Erick put the reel-to-reel on, the music seemed to confirm it as Creedence Clearwater Revival sang of a bad moon rising and trouble on the way. Earthquakes, lightning and bad times coming. The end was coming soon. The voice of rage and ruin.

Literally.

15 Lola was waiting for me when I walked into the office on Tuesday.

"It's official, Kerry," she told me. Tim had nothing to do with what's going on with Devin's job. I just got off the phone with the Chicago office."

"Really? Well, I guess that *does* make it official."

"Gee, poor guy. How's he taking it?" Lola sounded genuinely concerned.

"Just between you and me, I think he's thinking of leaving the company. Just my opinion, though."

"Why doesn't he just stay where he's at? He'll clear about the same money once he gets a good route, and it's not easy to find a decent job these days."

"I don't know, Mama. That route he's got now is pretty screwed up. And Christmas is coming. Not that money's the main issue. I think this has been pretty embarrassing for him. Humiliating. I don't know if I even want to be around when he gets that first commission check. It's really going to be small. A real slap in the face."

"Well, I wish I had better news, but Ralph just called me, and *he* isn't in cahoots with *anyone*. He claims they're just cutting back positions."

When Kelly and Hannah arrived, Lola gave Hannah some paperwork to tackle, and we were given about four hundred tickets to put in alphabetical order for later posting. Kelly and I just grinned at each other. This meant no machines would be running for a while, and that we'd actually be able to *hear* the radio and talk as we worked. Lola had the radio now, and Kelly wanted me to go get it.

"You go get it, brave one. Lola took it because she's sick of arguments over the stations. We're supposed to settle on one and leave it there."

"Okay," Kelly said agreeably. "Pick one besides country and western."

"No problem. I've already switched. The acid-rock station."

"No way! Hey, I know an easier way to alphabetize these tickets, and it will be more fun. We have to put all the duplicates together first, right? Well, ever hear of Fish?"

"The card game?"

"Yeah. Watch." Kelly grabbed a stack of about ten tickets each, handed my pile to me, and turned all the other tickets facedown. "Got any McDonald's?"

I organized my pile into a fan. "Yeah, matter of fact."

I handed Kelly the ticket, and she put mine and hers facedown on the carpet. Kelly scanned her fanned-out tickets. "Got any Burger Kings?"

I looked over my tickets. "No....go...fish?"

"You got it!" Kelly pulled a facedown ticket out and glanced at it, shrugged, and put it in her fan. "Your turn."

"Got any…"

"What the *hell* are you doing?" Lola stood in the doorway, hands on her hips.

"Well, we don't have a radio, so we're just trying to make this job a little more fun."

"Is that working?" Lola burst into laughter.

"It will. We've already had one match, and we just started."

"Oh, Jeez… I don't believe you guys! Well, whatever works." She went back to her office.

"Got any…hey, Ker, did you know it's all over the plant that Devin and Tim had a fight and he's fired?"

"Got any what, and that was yesterday, Kelly, and he's not fired. But he might quit before they even get the idea to."

"Any…Ranch House Restaurant…so he *is* thinking about quitting?"

"Go fish, and yeah, I think he is. Nothing's official yet. He just makes little remarks, that's all."

Kelly fished a facedown ticket out of the pile, looked at it and squealed with glee. "Yay, I got a Ranch House. Is it still my turn?" She paired the two tickets, snatched another out of the pool, and inserted it into her fanned tickets. This was fun and efficient and was grouping our tickets together rapidly. The radio was forgotten.

When Devin came in at 2:30, he informed us all loudly that, due to his newly elevated position to route man, he was now a free agent and officially off work. He added his condolences to Lola with a sympathetic pat on the shoulder.

"Gee, Mama. Too bad. You've got to stay till five, huh?"

"Yes, and so does *she*."

"Yeah? Well, you won't mind us exchanging a few words before I split, will you?" Without waiting for her reply, he stepped into our office, but not before Lola nailed him by the belt.

"Not so fast, Clyde. I'm not done with you…*son*."

"Well." Devin straightened his shirt and belt indignantly. "I'm glad you people are finally beginning to recognize that indisputable fact…*Mama* ! Oh, and I like your new taste in music," he added with a mischievous grin.

Leave it to Devin, with all his own bad luck at work, to come into our office to cheer *it* up. He took a seat comfortably beside Lola's desk and stretched his long legs out.

"Oh, Devin. You sit in here and she'll never get anything done…Jeez! What the hell is that song? *That's* not my station!"

"You don't recognize it? Gee, Mama, I had no idea you were getting so *hip!* I'll bet Kerry knows what it is."

The radio was loud enough for all of us to hear in our own office. The words were crystal clear. Uriah Heep, a magician challenging someone using the powers of darkness to steal what belonged to him. That someone had to surrender now or face the magician's spite…it was Friday night, the thirteenth.

Lola flicked off the radio and I cracked up laughing. I had set the dial on my acid-rock station just before Lola had retrieved the jukebox from our romper room, and she was just now realizing that she'd been listening to the dreaded acid-rock station all day instead of her usual neutral one.

"Hey, *speaking* of Friday the thirteenth," Devin began.

"That's *this* Friday!" Kelly squealed, then covered her mouth quickly. We were both still under orders to keep it down.

"No *shit!*" Devin smiled. "They're playing that song for us. Kerry and I are camping out Friday night."

"In *this* weather?" Lola looked appalled.

"Well, they'll keep each other warm, right Devin?" Kelly winked at him.

"You got that right," Devin agreed.

"Hey, I hear you guys got a horse living with you now," Kelly went on, trying to get him talking and out of his gloomy mood. "How are you going to feed that thing?"

"On *my* salary, it would be impossible," Devin admitted. "However, the dog is just visiting until my brother returns from vacation."

"Has Chris seen it yet?" Kelly knew all about my pot-smoking, hippie landlord.

"Sure. We told him to take it up with Titan. Needless to say, he left without a word to the dog. Titan wasn't in a talkative mood that day."

"Look, buster," Lola interrupted. "If it was even after four I'd invite you to stay a while, but—"

"Oh, I *couldn't,* Mama." Devin held his hands up in mock horror. "I wouldn't *think* of imposing."

Lola smirked. "Yeah, right."

"No, really. In fact, I'm on my way back to say goodbye to Pat and to wish him a nice rest of the long day."

"Out!" Lola's outstretched arm clearly indicated the exit.

"Okay, okay…hey, Kerry, I've got a haircut appointment later. I'll wait for you at Daniel's, okay?"

"Oh, are we going in your van?"

"Yes. Just lock your car, and I'll bring you in tomorrow morning."

After he left, Lola looked at me with an amused smile. "Good grief. You go through that all the time now?"

"No, Mama," I replied with a straight face. "When we're at home, Devin's an entirely different person."

Devin's haircut turned out to be quite an emotional experience for me. I couldn't believe those black curls were falling to the floor for the sake of a job he might not even keep. When it was over, he still looked like Devin but with much less bushy hair. Once again, I was struck with the feeling that it was another change taking place that might be a sign of reversal in our situation, just like in *Flowers for Algernon*.

"What do you think, babe?" He opened the van door for me, and I climbed aboard and unlocked his side.

"It looks…well…okay. I just hated to see you cut it, that's all. It wasn't too long."

"Well, anyway, it's done with. Should make Tim happy. At least he'll see that *I* don't back out on *my* word."

"Yeah, I guess. Devin, did you ever read the story *Flowers for Algernon*? It was a short story under that name, and later they made a whole movie out of it and called it *Charly*."

"No." He looked at me quizzically. "Why?"

"Oh, no real reason, I guess. It keeps popping into my head lately. Just wondered if you'd heard of it."

"No, can't say I have. Well, I guess we better go get the kids. Your sister may be home alone with Titan unless she's at work."

"Which would be worse because I'd hate to see that dog get bored and start teething on one of your stereo cords."

"Maybe we'll finally have a peaceful night to ourselves. Let's go."

That dark feeling hung with me as we boarded the van. The radio didn't help. Uriah Heep was singing about a place we might be looking for where we could fly together. They told us to take the easiest road, especially if we were worried about what we were going to leave behind. We would never find peace with troubled minds, they admonished. There was one line that really underlined how I felt.

They said it was better to love each other, than to worry about looking back at a love we'd never have again.

We'd never have again.

16 By morning I'd shaken that dark feeling and was in a good mood in spite of everything I'd felt the day before. I loved going in to work with Devin. I felt so proud to be sitting in the passenger seat when we pulled up to the plant. Devin didn't have time to join me at the coffee shop because as a route man now he had to contend with loading up the truck with water bottles. I opted for going in early with him.

Kelly arrived toting an astrology magazine she wanted me to look at. This issue featured an article about auras and how to see them, and how to tell what the colors meant. Since she'd heard me mention them on occasion, she thought it would be great fun to line up the employees against the white walls and see what their colors meant. There was a color chart provided in the article.

I was happy to oblige, but it was frustrating to find that everyone we stood against the wall seemed to be putting off that same glaring yellow.

"It says here," Kelly said, "that yellow is the color of thinking and intelligence. Now I can't see where you've failed in accuracy by seeing yellow on everyone." We had just returned from lunch. "What other color would you expect to see in an office where people use their intelligence and think?"

"What color is bull?" Hannah threw in. She'd been listening to our conversation about the results of the plant's aura test. "And how come *you're* yellow, Kelly? If yellow is the color of thinking…"

Lola laughed out loud at that one. "Yeah, Kelly. You putting off yellow? I don't know how accurate all this is if *you're* yellow."

"You're not yellow, Lola," I said. She wasn't. She was radiating more of a rosy red. She caught me staring at her and smiled.

"I'll bite. What color *am* I?"

"You look kind of…Lola, according to this chart you're stoned or drunk or—"

Lola looked indignant. "Well, I did have a cocktail at lunch. Let me see that thing!" She snatched it and scanned it quickly. "Red has a lot of meanings, huh? Love, hate, action, affection, sorrow…uh, just how *do* you know which meaning applies to *my* red?"

At that moment Devin walked in, obviously in a hurry. "Kerry, I'll be over at Daniel's when you get off. Pat said he got into it with Tim and quit. I'm going over to get the straight scoop on what happened." Devin, holding both doorjambs as he talked, suddenly caught sight of Lola sitting over by our phones. "Oh, hey, Mama. Didn't see you there."

"Devin, can *you* see auras?" Kelly demanded as Lola ducked under Devin's arms to return to her own desk.

"Sure, why?"

"Well, what color am I?"

Devin gazed at her for a few seconds. "Yellow."

"Aha! Kerry was right!"

"Well, I don't doubt that. She *can* see them. That's not all she sees either. You ought to ask her sometime."

"Oh, I don't know," Kelly said, laughing. "I think all she sees these days is you. And yellow."

"Hey, look, chicks. I could dig sitting here shooting the shit, but I really do gotta split." He blew me a kiss but didn't make it out of Lola's office before she called him back.

"Wait just a minute, you clown," she said. "This is too much. Devin, what color am I?"

"Pink," he said without hesitation. "Did you have a drink a little while ago?"

Everyone burst into laughter. Devin stuck his head in our doorway. "Rose pink. Mama's always pink."

I grinned triumphantly at Kelly and then looked at my watch and back at Devin. "You're done already, huh?"

Devin rolled his eyes. "Wednesday on Lucky's route means delivering only to one account. Well, almost. Later."

He dashed off and I looked at Kelly. "Why, you yellow little…"

"Well, what color are *you?*"

"I'm blue. I checked in the mirror when we came back from lunch."

"So what's blue?"

"Deeply spiritual, Kelly, you know. Holy. Like a nun?"

Kelly, sipping her coffee, nearly choked. "Well. So much for auras. You can't go by them."

I noticed several company trucks sparkling in the sun when I walked up to Daniel's yard. My car was still parked where I'd left it. I smiled to myself. Daniel's house had quickly become the local hangout for the routemen.

It was hard to believe Daniel had quit. I could hear conversation as I reached the screen door, and Daniel's situation was the main topic. Devin held the screen door open as I entered.

"Boy, no wonder the route room's empty. Everyone's here," I said to the room full of routemen.

"Did you hear that I quit?" Daniel asked me as I took a seat beside Devin on the floor.

"I guess everyone knows by now considering most of them are here," I said.

"I don't blame you, bro," Devin said. "I may split myself. Too much human bullshit. And Tim sticking you with cooler pickups instead of the route he promised you...I'd have quit, too. Who needs to deal with pissed-off customers all day long?"

The talk then turned to the company in general. Ethan came out of his room to join in, always ready to knock the plant since he had actually been fired. Joey Burns, still happily employed, kept his opinions to himself until Devin's position came up.

"It's bullshit what they're doing to you, man," he said. "I'm surprised you even stayed on. It's too bad Tim won't let us team up on the trucks like we used to in the good old days."

"Yeah, fat chance. No, Tim wants me to fix up Lucky's route, and it's in pretty bad shape. Hardly worth the gas to make the few deliveries that route has."

"If you just weren't so fuckin' *good* at it."

"Yeah? Well, watch closely, 'cause Devin's sales are going to take a drastic drop."

"You'd only be hurting yourself," Joey said. "They won't care. It's *your* commission."

"Maybe they won't care, but they'll notice." Devin nudged me that it was time to go and turned to Daniel. "We'll stop by tomorrow. Sorry about your job, man."

"I'm not," Daniel said. "Julie still has her job and Ethan's working, so I ain't gonna sweat it. I'll find another one. If I ain't good enough for a route, I'd just as soon not work there."

It was ironic to me that the route was what Daniel really wanted, while it was an insult to Devin.

Halfway through the drive home Devin turned to me with a smile.

"I hope you enjoyed our night alone last night."

I returned the smile, remembering. With Pam at work, we'd thrown Titan out of the room and shut ourselves in. "I did. Why?"

"Oh, because you're gonna hate me when I tell you this. Gerald called today, and tonight's the night that he and Brian are bringing up my cycle."

We both laughed.

"Well, it's not like we weren't expecting it," I said. "And at least we'll have it for Thompson's Station on Friday."

"Yeah. Friday the thirteenth. No one *else* will be there. *And* we've got the peyote."

"That will make the night really special. Besides, I like your family, Devin. I don't mind them coming."

The visit was pleasant, and the conversation centered around Devin's job and the advisability of Brian even applying for work there considering all the changes going down. Titan remained quietly in the background, occasionally wandering up to Devin for attention. It was amazing how the dog was so suspicious of *him*, yet was constantly in Devin's lap like an overgrown pup whenever Devin was around.

After they left, Devin rummaged through one of his boxes and pulled out a toy kaleidoscope. "Here, Ker. Check this out."

I took it with a wave of nostalgia. "Wow. I haven't seen one of these things since I was a kid."

"Look inside it."

I put the object up to my eye. "What's so unusual about it?"

"Turn it."

As I slowly turned the end ring, star after star fell in complete circles.

"See the pentagrams?"

"Damn, Devin. That's weird. Does it do anything else?"

"That's all I've seen. That's why I kept it. But keep turning it. I think you'll be surprised at what else *is* in there...for someone like you. Turn it *really* slow."

"For something besides the stars?"

"Well, that'll be up to you. It *can* work like a crystal ball."

"Oh." I set it down quickly. "No thanks. I don't like to do that shit."

"Yeah, you're right. You don't need *that* thing. You've got so many walls."

When Devin took Titan out for his nightly yard exercise I picked up the toy again, feeling like I'd hurt Devin by rejecting his idea. When I held it up to my eye, I saw that the pattern was no longer any kind of star. Instead, it was a picture.

It was a woman, and she was holding a black bundle. It could have been an infant wrapped in black blankets. The woman was dressed completely in black as well, and the background clearly showed a cemetery out in the country with a stone wall surrounding it. That wall obstructed the view of the woman from the waist down.

When Devin and Titan came back in, overheated and breathing hard, I looked away for a minute, but when I returned to the tiny hole, the scene had changed a little. The woman in black was now standing *on* the wall, holding the black bundle over her head. I dropped the toy in horror, sickened that she might actually *throw* it. Devin, having sent the dog to the back room, returned to my side to find out what I'd seen. When I told him, he frowned.

"Think it might mean anything in relation to your period?"

"Like what? But speaking of that, I've been getting a few cramps tonight, so I think that's one burden that may be lifted from your shoulders."

"Oh?" He raised his eyebrows. "I wasn't aware that it was a burden."

On Thursday, December 12, the following day, I found that I wasn't pregnant after all, or if I had been, I wasn't anymore. The symbolism of what I'd seen in the kaleidoscope, exactly what Devin had suggested, had been correct after all.

Work went by quickly, and late in the afternoon Lola came in to tell me I had a visitor in the lobby. I was surprised to see Julie standing there at the front desk with a long brown paper bag.

She made it quick. They had been to the flea market that morning and had picked up a little gift for us. She handed me the bag and asked me not to open it until I was with Devin.

Kelly was more curious about the contents of the bag than I was, and she begged me to open it now.

"I don't know, Kelly. She asked me to wait until Devin was there."

"Oh, come on. Just let me peek at it. It feels like a rolled-up kite."

"Kelly, why would they give us a kite?"

"Yeah, really. You two are high enough as it is. Come on. Can *I* unroll it? Hey! Maybe it's a poster."

"I doubt it. We don't collect posters. Oh, go ahead and look."

Kelly tore at the plastic the roll was wrapped in and began to unravel it slowly, without actually removing it from the bag. "Oh my God! You won't believe…well, maybe you would. It's…oh…man, I can't describe it. You're just going to have to come look for yourself. It's the Devil."

"What? It better *not* be!" I looked in and closed my eyes in disbelief. "Oh, Jeez…on purple silk, no less. Just how big *is* that thing? This bag is three feet long!"

Kelly smirked. "That must be the width. If I kept unwinding it I think it would be about five or six feet long. Are you going to hang it in your living room?"

"Not if I have anything to say about it. We're not into this crap! Devin's going to *shit!*"

At five o'clock I gathered up my purse, jacket, and the brown bag. Devin was waiting outside the time clock for me, just like old times, and he told me about his day as we walked to the van.

Tim was just unnecessarily antagonistic these days, probably due to the Chicago executives now visiting the plant. The only remark he had made about Devin's haircut was that it was about time.

When we reached the van, Devin noticed the bag for the first time.

"Whatcha got there?" He nodded casually at it.

I walked around to my side, got in, and set it on the floor, leaning it against the center console. "Oh, it's something that Daniel and Julie gave us and told me not to open it till we were together. Julie dropped it off today. But Kelly just *had* to see what it was, so I did get a glimpse of part of it. I don't think you're going to like it, but since it's rolled up, we might as well wait till we get home. Oh, and I have other news for you, too."

He started the engine. "Your period started."

"Yeah. I don't know if that's good or bad news for you."

A slight frown crossed his face, but it vanished quickly, as if he'd processed this knowledge and accepted it. Then his features returned to the composed set that they'd been before my announcement. We'd arrived at Daniel's. He shut the engine down and looked at me for a long minute. "Well," he said finally. "I guess it just wasn't the right time."

"I guess not. You're not disappointed, are you?"

"I don't know. The idea was becoming a reality, but that's okay. I'll just have to get used to the idea now that you aren't." He sighed. "I don't feel like going in there now, but we can't just drive away. The boys are looking out the window, so everyone knows we're here."

"We have to pick up my car anyway, so let's just drop in for a couple minutes. We don't have to stay."

A few minutes it was. We thanked them for their gift, told them we'd open it when we got home, and bowed out quickly.

Titan greeted us like old friends when we walked in. Devin had followed me to the sitter's, waited for the kids to board, and then followed me home. Devin roughhoused a little with the dog while I went in to change, and the kids took off to watch TV. When I returned to the living room, Devin gave Titan a final pat and then picked up the paper bag.

"So you saw this already?"

"Well, Kelly saw more of it than I did. She unwound it enough that I recognized it."

Devin began to unravel the silk banner from the bamboo stick it hung from. As the image became clearer to Devin, he glanced at me, and I knew he wasn't thrilled about it either. It was the famous *Sabbatic Goat*, originally created by Levi, and picked up later by all the black magicians for its evil appearance. Ironically, Levi was one of the names I'd seen on the cupboard that peyote night. Levi had not meant for the painting to signify evil, but the goat with the sharp horns sitting atop the world looked downright sinister. A snake encircled the world below, seeming to suggest that the Devil ruled the world. Devin rolled his eyes and I laughed. He then dropped the banner on top of the bag with a loud sigh.

"My feelings exactly," I said.

"How can we hang that thing up? If we don't, Daniel will get his feelings hurt, and if we do, everyone else will." He picked it up again and held it at arm's length, studying it. "It's actually a rip-off of Levi's original portrayal of Baphomet, which was a temple icon. His depiction actually meant harmony, redemption and union, but this version is modified and appears to be satanic. Perhaps we can hang it in the bedroom."

"Oh, Devin, do you really want that thing staring down at us all night?"

"You're right. It would be better off here in the living room." He looked at the Witches' Wheel hanging over the stereo next to Christian's self-portrait and then at the bare wall opposite them. "Well," he said finally. "Let's try it."

He hung it between our zodiac plaques, and then we both laughed.

"We can't leave that thing up there," I said. "Isn't there some way we can just explain to Daniel?"

"Right. Are Daniel and Julie's well-meant intentions worth having *this* in our living room?"

"Well, it kind of confirms where Daniel thinks we're at." I shrugged. "Anyway, let's get some coffee on and supper going, and maybe we'll come up with something before Pam comes in from work tonight. Sometimes she sleeps on the couch when she's doing these overtime runs, and I don't want her to have a coronary."

I started the coffee, took out the garbage, and went in to take my shower. When I came out, I found Devin missing and *him* standing in the living room literally glowering at Titan.

The dog stood, hackles raised, lips curled in a snarl, baring razor-sharp fangs. From his throat came a growl that hummed and stopped, hummed and stopped. Titan was returning *his* glare with pure contempt.

I stopped abruptly in the hallway, immediately grasping what was going on, afraid that any motion would cause the dog to spring.

The tension hung like that for a few seconds, and then, without further warning, Titan leapt straight for his throat.

He was too quick for the dog, and he flipped Titan into the air where he landed on his feet and sprung again with no hesitation. Again, he flipped him, taking care not to hurt him but letting the dog know that he *was* going to defend himself. This time, when Titan struggled back on all fours he remained motionless, belly low to the carpet, hair still standing on end like a huge, black porcupine. His lips still bared fangs, gleaming and white.

Devin's arm was bleeding.

"What happened?" I asked in a low tone, watching Titan as I cautiously entered the living room.

Titan still lay, breathing hard, eyes fixed only on *him*.

"He attacked. For no reason. I wasn't even playing with him." He walked past Titan to the kitchen sink, and Titan didn't miss the opportunity to snarl again.

"I told you to lighten *up*," he said coldly, washing his arm where the bite was. "Now I'm afraid we're done with your little games. You and I are going to settle this outside. Once and for all. Right now." He reached for a clean dishtowel and threw it over his arm.

Titan laid his pointed ears back against his head, fur still bristled.

"Devin," I pleaded. "Please don't. You could get hurt. Trevor's picking him up tonight."

"And put up with this all night? Uh-uh, lady. This has gone far enough. He and I are going to have to come to an agreement about who's running the show. And it isn't *him*. I don't care how attack trained he is, he's got to learn some respect for the hand that feeds him."

I knew I couldn't stop it so I waited in the house, listening to the snarls and growls and barks which turned into more snarls and growls. I really was afraid that Devin would come out the loser in this battle of egos, but I was also afraid of what Devin might inadvertently do to Trevor's dog.

Suddenly all sound stopped. I looked out the window. Titan lay, panting hard, his sides heaving, but his fur was down. Devin stood over him, arms crossed, looking down at him. Then he crouched and patted the dog gently on the head. Titan laid a paw on his knee, and I breathed a sigh of relief. It appeared to be settled, and neither of them was hurt.

I went back to the stove and started supper.

A bark, now friendly and excited, came through the windows now and then. After I'd seated the girls at their table to eat, I went to the window again.

They were just playing now, and the difference was obvious. Titan's ears were up now, alert with interest, as Devin ran him through several commands that he knew the dog understood. Then they were wrestling, but in friendly fashion. I wondered if Devin had returned long enough to calm the dog, but when they came back in, it was still *him* who opened the front door for Titan.

"Settle it?" I asked, handing him a plate of pork chops, rice, and peas.

"I knew we would. I told you, lady, the dog doesn't understand me. Or...he didn't. I don't think I'll have any further problems with him now." He tossed Titan a chunk of pork chop. He caught it midair, gulped it down, and wagged his tail for more. "He's pretty good with his commands," Devin added. "Trevor did a good job of training him. I doubt that anyone else would get away with what I just did."

"I'm surprised you took the chance," I said. "I didn't know who was going to come out the victor. Dobermans can be...dangerous...especially one this size. I mean, Titan isn't really vicious, but still...he *is* going home tonight."

After supper, Devin began rolling us a joint, and the kids went in to take turns at their baths and the television. Just as he put the final touches on the joint, there was a knock at the door. I looked out the window and groaned audibly.

"Who is it?" Devin asked.

"George, Eddie, and his brother Henry. I really wish they wouldn't bring Henry over here. He's so obnoxious."

"Well, we can't leave them standing outside," Devin said, getting up to unlock the door.

Another night shot? Not for long. George admitted that they'd only stopped by to bum some weed, and Devin generously pushed the cigar box over to him. "Roll yourself a couple, man. There's plenty there."

"Man, that dog is *big!*" Henry commented.

"Yes, he is. Mean, too." Devin smiled. "Don't mess with him. He's not crazy about strangers, and he's very protective."

"Shit. He don't look mean." Henry extended his fist cautiously, slowly opened it and looked at Devin defiantly. "See? I can handle dogs. *Any* dog. See how mean your big dog is?" He began to snicker, and Devin looked at him curiously.

"Any dog, Henry?"

Titan thumped his tail at the sound of Devin's voice, and Henry took it as a gesture of friendliness towards himself. He launched into a story about the attack dogs he had taken on in his life. I knew Henry well enough to know it was all bullshit, and even Devin rolled his eyes when I looked at him.

As much as I disliked Henry, his bullshit and his bragging, I almost wished Titan wasn't as played out as he was. Devin, however, caught my thought and must have decided to have some fun.

"Just how did you manage to keep all those vicious dogs at bay?" Devin asked him, feigning interest.

"Judo. I tell you, there isn't a dog alive that I'm afraid of, or one that has ever got the best of me."

"Any dog? You use judo on *any* dog? And it *works?*"

"Well, I only use it as a last resort. My hands are registered weapons, you know. I can usually kick a dog and pin him down without actually *hurting* him."

Devin's face held amusement in check. He stood up and snapped his fingers, and Titan leapt to his feet, eager to play again. Henry noted the wagging tail and made the mistake of commenting that *this* dog would be a cinch.

"This one would, huh?" Devin had a twinkle in his eyes. "Well, perhaps he would be to someone as expert as yourself. Come on. Let's all go outside. I must see this for myself."

"Oh, well…" Henry hedged. "He looks kinda pooped. I don't think we should bother him now."

"Oh, it's no bother. Titan loves to…well, he *loves* humans, that's all. I think he'd enjoy it. Besides, I might learn something. Why, the dog just attacked *me* a short while ago." He held up his arm to prove it. The slash caught Henry's eye and he turned white. He gulped, trapped.

He'd stuck his foot in his mouth, and George wasn't about to let him walk away now. "Let's *go,* Henry! We have to listen to your goddamn bullshit all the time, but we've never had the chance to watch you kill the goddamn dogs. So let's go."

"Yeah, Henry," his brother said, smirking. "Let's see some of that judo."

Devin clapped his hands together to stir Titan to action. "Come on, boy. Outside!"

"Hey, Devin…" Henry tried again. "I'm really not up to—"

"Oh, don't be modest, Henry," Devin interrupted. "I think you can give us all a few pointers."

I turned my back so that Henry wouldn't see my laughter as they all trooped out the door, Henry lagging behind. Devin held the door until they were outside and then turned to me with a wink. "Going to watch?"

"No. I can't stand the sight of blood. Hey, don't let the jerk really get hurt. We don't need any lawsuits."

"Oh, I won't. I think he just needs to be taught a lesson."

I watched from the curtains as Devin signaled Titan to sit. Then he handed Henry the ultimate no-no for use around a dog as trained in weapons as Titan was. A long stick.

Titan's ears dropped from their interested prick to the flattened position on his head, and he growled.

"Well, looks like you might *need* that stick, Henry. Better hang on to it. I guess I'm the referee. Henry, you swing that stick at him so we can get him started." Then he turned to Titan. "Alert!"

I couldn't continue to watch. I hoped that Devin would stop it before it got too out of control, but what was coming through the open window sounded like murder on Titan's part. It only lasted a few seconds, and I didn't know exactly what had transpired until the door opened and Devin brought a foaming Titan in. He took the dogs head in his hands and gently shook it with pride and affection. George was laughing so hard I thought he would fall off the stool he'd dropped onto.

"No match, huh?" I said, smiling.

"No match," George agreed. "Poor Henry. He'll never live this down. Look. He didn't even stick around for these joints I rolled."

"Oh, he'll be back," I said with a sigh.

"I don't think so, Ker. You know, the only reason he's coming around lately is because he's out of grass. He thinks he's got the polish to get over on Devin 'cause Devin's so cool about giving away shit. Like these joints…they weren't my idea. When I run out, I'm out."

"That's cool, George. Keep them for yourself. Eddie leave too?"

"Yeah, he was Henry's ride. I can walk home from here. I think Henry's a couple inches shorter than he was when he came in, though."

"He didn't get hurt, right?" I probed.

"Naw…with Devin there?" George looked at Devin with admiration. "No, he *should* have. He's lucky that dog obeys that hand command to *cease* 'cause there was too much noise for Titan to have heard a verbal command. Between Henry screaming and…" He burst into laughter again. "Naw, he just got a little embarrassed, is all. Hey! You got a new thing up on the wall!"

"*Thing* is the word for it all right," Devin said.

"That's really far out!"

"I might give it to you. It was a gift, so we're really in an awkward position about what to do with it."

"What's wrong with leaving it where it's at?"

"Its location, for one thing. However…" Devin's voice trailed off and he looked at me. "We'll go by your sister's reaction."

"I wouldn't do *that*," George said, getting up. "I *know* that chick. When she sees that, she'll climb into bed with you two."

"That's what we figured too," I admitted.

Trevor showed up late that night, to Titan's purely delighted and ecstatic greeting. After an affectionate reunion, he asked how the dog had behaved.

"Oh, we had our moments," Devin said, "but, all in all, he listens pretty well. Hey, are you guys in the mood for a night at Thompson's station tomorrow night?"

"No, man. Mia's tired. So am I. I think we'll just be kicking back at home tomorrow. You staying overnight?"

"Yeah. Come on. We've got plenty of peyote left."

"Can't do it. Make it next week?"

"Nope. Kerry and I are going crazy with all the human bullshit. We need to get out of here. Our sanity depends on it. By the way, Brian brought my bike up yesterday."

"Oh, it's here?" Trevor's interest perked up.

"Check it out, bro." Devin beamed proudly. "It's in the back room."

"Well." Trevor's gaze swept lovingly over the cycle, parked in our paneled den. "I dig your garage. It would be nice to go with you, but...another weekend, perhaps. Well thanks for taking care of this big sucker for me. I really appreciate it." Trevor leashed Titan up. Titan was panting, grinning his Doberman grin, and he watched Trevor until he was signaled to follow. With hardly a backward glance, Titan trotted to the door.

"He's anxious," Devin said with a smile.

"Yeah. Too anxious," Trevor agreed, scratching his head. "What'd ya do to my dog, bro?"

Devin shrugged, and with a wave and a *later*, Trevor left.

Later I asked him why he hadn't told Trevor about the dog's erratic behavior.

"What would have been the point?" he replied. "Titan won't ever bother Devin, and I really believe the dog and I have come to an understanding of sorts."

"So it's just between you and the dog?"

"Something like that. Come on, lady. Let's get to sleep early tonight. We'll be up all night tomorrow. It'll be nice. We haven't been out there in a while. This full moon I'll have to go alone, so I'm glad you're going with me tomorrow. Too bad it's the dark side."

"Oh, I guess the full moon is when you have to check in?" I kidded him.

"As a matter of fact, it is," he answered seriously. "Someday you'll be going with me, but this time it'll be progress reports and, as you call it, checking in. It doesn't really *have* to be the full moon to do that. I do it all the time anyway, but there's something about the electromagnetic conditions being better for me and easier for them, too."

"Devin, why does everything seem to be falling apart at work?"

"Test, maybe? Endurance? I don't know. Who cares, really? We've got *us*. The rest...it's all just human bullshit." He reached over and switched on the reel-to-reel.

"Maybe so, but it's causing Devin problems. Don't you even care? Can't you do anything to make it easier for him?"

"Devin's cool. He can handle it. He's got *us* too."

"I hope so. Anyway, tomorrow should be really interesting. It's Friday the thirteenth. Everyone will be avoiding ladders and black cats."

"Isn't that a prime example of the distortions in this world? The thirteenth is the luckiest day of the month, and everybody loves Fridays. Damn, I sure hope your sister doesn't freak out with that purple monstrosity staring at her all night."

"Yeah. She's probably going to wonder about *us.*"

"I'm afraid it's going to have to come down," Devin mused. "I just can't have people thinking that that's the sort of thing we're into. I'm going to have to level with Daniel. It might even do some good. We've *been* wondering how to demonstrate that it's just not where we're at. This might just be the opportunity we needed."

I couldn't wait to get into bed. I was tired of people. It was heaven to finally be alone with no sound in the house except the music floating in from the living room. And no people.

When Devin reached for me that night, neither of us suggested shutting down the music. If there was one thing he didn't pass up while he was here in Devin's body, it was sex. I didn't want to get up and shut it off either.

It wasn't until later, as I was drifting off to sleep, that I realized that the songs on those tapes had somehow moved from the subject of magic and wizards to…vibrations. I fell asleep wondering about the connection between the two, and thinking about how the shift had been so gradual that I was just now noticing. It had been so magic-oriented two weeks ago, and now it was off on some kind of Eastern philosophy. Devin wasn't into that…was he? Well, he'd recorded those tapes before we'd even met, and he was definitely into magic when we first got together. Devin had not been into this kind of philosophy then, *had he?*

I listened to the words playing on the tape. They were singing about mantras and chanting a word…OM. They were referring to trips out of the body and places to go. Some even referred to *home.*

Was Devin more advanced then he'd let on in the beginning? Magic was seldom mentioned anymore, and there were no longer songs about demons and wizards coming on. Had he just chosen that magic frame of reference to get my interest because that had been where I was at the time? Uriah Heep's *Demons and Wizards* had been one of the first albums on the reel, and on the tape he'd made for me.

Beyond in the living room the tape crawled on, telling me I could fly high as a kite if I wanted to. I could speed through the universe faster than light. All by thinking. It was the best way to travel.

That was my last conscious thought.

17

Pam was predictable. When Devin and I found her, half-awake the next morning, sitting on the couch with her arms crossed, we both laughed. She was laying for us.

"Where in *God's* name did you get that…that…I don't believe you'ns, I really don't!"

"Don't get excited, Pam," I consoled her, still laughing. "It's coming down tonight. That was a little present from Daniel and Julie."

"I should *hope* it's coming down. Things are weird enough around here. I hope you'ns know that that *repulsive* thing scared the shit out of me when I came in last night. I almost woke you'ns up. You'd a deserved it, too. Instead, I had nightmares all night, that big ol' thing staring down at me!"

"So you *did* sleep on the couch?" There was a total absence of pillows or blankets.

"Of *course* not! I slept with Devin's motorcycle." She yawned and rubbed her eyes. "There's coffee made out there."

"Thanks, Pam." I poured cups for Devin and me. Pam was exaggerating her mania as usual. Nothing really scared her.

"We gotta hurry," Devin reminded me, "if you're going in with me."

"You aren't taking your own car?" Pam asked.

"Well, today we're picking up our Christmas tree, so it makes sense to just take the van."

"We're getting a *tree?*" Pam looked astonished. She knew how Devin felt about the tree season. "Oh...one like Gerald and Faye, huh?"

"No, better," Devin said. "You'll see it tonight."

Lola mentioned that morning that there was a partial eclipse of the sun at around eleven and seemed surprised that I didn't know about it. I told her we didn't have a television in the living room so I had missed any announcements of it.

"Well, it's on all the radio stations, too. The way you two are about music, I'd have thought you'd have caught it on one of the news broadcasts. You *do* listen to the radio don't you?"

"Well, mostly at work. At home Devin runs his tape recorder all day and most of the night. The only time he puts the radio on is when he gets tired of answering my stupid questions. Then he just puts the acid-rock station on, and the first song they play answers the question for him."

"Oh, get out of here," Kelly wailed. "You're so full of shit!"

"Am I? Remember that day they played all those baby records the whole afternoon? Remember the question Devin asked me after lunch?"

That sobered Kelly for a minute, and then she seemed to have thought of a rebuttal. "Yeah, but that was *my* station, and even *yours,* so you can't give the credit to that acid-rock station."

"Well, maybe it works on any station, but the kind of questions I ask wouldn't normally be answered by a country station. Devin's station plays a lot of the songs he already has on the reel, so it's really more likely to have answers to the kind of questions I ask."

"Uh...I won't pursue that," Kelly said quickly. "How can you stand that tape recorder running all day and all night anyway?"

"I don't mind, really. I *like* the music. But I just don't hear much of the radio these days. Therefore I wouldn't know about the eclipse." I switched on the office radio, and Kelly made a dive for it.

"Oh, no you don't! It's *my* turn to pick! Lolaaaaa!"

"I guess I take the juke box again," Lola said, smiling. She unplugged it and transferred it to her own desk. "I keep telling you guys to be quiet, and that's one of the things you get noisy with."

"But the eclipse..."

"I'll let you know. I'll be listening for the announcement."

Around eleven, Lola cut us loose to watch the eclipse, and at noon I called Jamie to verify that the tree would be ready for pickup. It was, and it was adorable, she informed me. Four feet tall and still in the pot. I told her we'd be by after work to pick it up.

Our camping trip never got off the ground. By the time we'd picked up the tree and the kids, it was long past sunset. By the time we got home it was too late to start out. Devin seemed to have lost interest in the trip anyway, and I thought the tree had a lot to do with it.

When he had seen it sitting there in Jamie's backyard, a look of reverence had spread over his features. The tree was green, moist and healthy, and beautifully...alive. We could smell the aroma of pine from Jamie's back porch.

Devin stooped down to caress one of the branches, and when he looked up at me, he smiled.

"This is the best idea you've ever had, lady," he said in an awed tone. "Come on. Let's get her home and get her used to the house. Do we have to hang a bunch of balls and shit all over her?"

"No, Devin. I'll leave the decorating to you. If you only want to put one string of lights on it...or her, as you say, that's fine with me."

"Oh, no. Not this beauty. She isn't going to go through Christmas with just one string of lights. I just didn't want to put too much weight on her branches. She's just a baby."

"How do you know it's a she?" I asked as Devin positioned the tree under the window for maximum light.

"Well, just the vibes I get from her." He picked up his keys and jacket. "I'll be right back."

"What's *he* up to?" Pam asked as the van roared away.

"He didn't say, but I bet it has something to do with special decorations for the tree."

"Boy, he's really getting off on this, isn't he?"

"You can say that again. Thompson Station is off the schedule, and that's all he talked about all week. I haven't heard a word about it since he laid eyes on this tree. I think Christmas is upon us at last."

When the tree was finished and decorated, it looked more beautiful in its simplicity than any gaudily decorated dead tree in the city. Devin had insisted on decorating her himself, wouldn't let anyone else near *his* tree until he was finished.

Throughout the process, he had explained everything he was doing to her as he gently padded the bark with angel hair from roots to top. He even explained why. When he spiraled the tiny flashing colored lights over the angel hair, he told her it would not hurt and that she was the most beautiful Christmas tree he had ever seen. It sounded like he was talking to a new puppy. He had picked up some lightweight blue balls and only hung them on the strongest branches. Then, when he was finished, he turned to Mandy and Michelle, who'd been enrapt with wonder as they'd watched him.

He explained to the girls that the reason he'd been so gentle with the tree was because she was as alive as Mandy's parakeet. He told them that while the human kids were at church on Christmas Day, they could help him plant our tree, either in the front yard, or somewhere out in the woods.

He had given the girls an entirely different meaning of Christmas.

Along with the tree and Devin's sudden Christmas spirit came a new problem. Devin wanted to know if the girls believed in Santa Claus. I told him Mandy didn't, but that Michelle still did.

"Do you mind if I tell Michelle the truth? I really don't believe in lying to children. It makes it hard to teach them not to lie to us or anyone else."

I thought about it for a minute. He had a good point, but it was liable to break Michelle's heart. Finally, I considered that she would be going into first grade soon and would find out the hard way anyway, so I consented. "But *please* be gentle about it," I added.

"I will. I just think it's better to be honest with them."

After the kids had been tucked in for the night, Devin looked up at the purple banner on the wall and smiled wryly. "Too bad, old chap, but when you gotta go, you gotta go."

Down it came. Pictures were rearranged, and the banner was rolled up to be given to George as a Christmas present.

We spent Saturday in leisure, talking and listening to the tapes on the reel-to-reel, and even engaged the kids in a game of Monopoly. On Sunday, Devin took the motorcycle out for a test run. It gave me a chance to clean the house and browse through some of his books.

Later that evening, Pammy brought up the subject of meditation and mentioned that she had actually gotten George interested into it.

I myself got lost after the word *alpha*. "Can't someone recommend a book to read…one that starts you from scratch?" I asked both of them, feeling left out.

"Well, you know how I feel about books compared to experiencing things yourself," Devin said. "But I understand your feelings since you won't know when you're *in* alpha, much less anything else. You, lady, of all people, should understand what it is that you're already doing and don't even realize it. There is that one book I mentioned before that might help you. It's called *Journeys Out of the Body*. Written by Paul A. Monroe, and it takes you much further than alpha. It's right there on the bookshelf and has been since you unpacked the books."

Later that evening I found Devin resting on the bed in our bedroom. On the nightstand was a book.

"Take a look at *this* one," he suggested.

I scanned the jacket, front and back. This one was against *everything*. The author was a skeptic of astrology, magic, and any kind of meditation, claiming it was a dangerous practice. As far as *this* author was concerned, magic was bullshit, ghosts only existed in the imagination of the viewer, and all *ESP* was hogwash. Thumbing through the book, I saw that he'd gone to great lengths to prove his viewpoint, and some of his arguments could have set doubts into a practicing yogi. I set the book aside, confused. "Why would you want me to read *this*, Devin?"

"For another viewpoint, that's all."

"But none of it's true!"

"How would you know that? Have you experienced any or all of the subjects he's so sure aren't real? I just wanted to give you an idea of what kind of influence books can have and how they can sway you with words. Even convince you of the author's point, which goes to show you how much damage books can do. I keep stressing experience, and if you really want to learn to *go*, I'd suggest you forget the books other than to check their contents against what you have already experienced."

The one thing that remained constant all through the weekend was those reel-to-reel tapes. Devin used them for everything. Background, meditation, and even to stress certain points he was making during his continual instructions on learning how to *go*.

As with the radio, Devin would simply hit the switch when an explanation was required to my statements or questions, or just to emphasize the moment in time. The most phenomenal thing to me was how the questions were *precisely* answered no matter how odd the question was and how the tapes were always positioned to the answer within a song that, oddly, always started at the beginning.

While the early reels had consisted of Uriah Heep and other magic and sorcery-oriented songs, the middle segments...the later reels...were more along the lines of philosophy and astral travelling. The lyrics always followed the continuity of our personal life, but at the same time, they offered a dual meaning for others who could benefit from the order of the songs on the reels and the songs themselves.

If denizens of other dimensions had the ability to send messages through the ether to the human race, they certainly seemed to have mastered the use of radio waves. If there was any one way of reaching *all* the masses, it would make sense to use music to do it, for music *was* a universal thing. If they *were* electromagnetic in origin it just made sense that radio, being a small segment of the spectrum, would be convenient and easy for them, especially the ones who resided in that portion of the spectrum.

There seemed to be many stages with those tapes, from the magic, mysticism and demon stage to the philosophical stage, songs that spoke of the beliefs of Eastern religions. Now they seemed to be moving beyond religion itself to no frame of reference at all except one message. *There is life in other worlds. Close your eyes and find it.* When I used this theme against every frame of reference I could think of, it fit with all of them. An interdimensional category. Just where did the ideas of Heaven, Hell and Limbo come from? They weren't physical; therefore, they must be realities that resided in different dimensions beyond this range of visible light where we existed now.

It must have been a lot of work for Devin to have selected and blended these songs from certain albums, and sometimes only certain *cuts* from these albums. His selections caused the themes to switch frames of reference so gradually that I had only recently noticed that the magic, mysticism and wizards were rarely mentioned anymore. The songs were international too, with contributions from countries all over the planet. England, Canada, America and South America...even Africa. And all of them said basically the same thing using their own frames of reference.

The beats vacillated from hard, heavy acid rock to easy folk, from mellow electronic music to thrusting voodoo, but the group I felt most at peace with was the Moody Blues.

This music group sang of meditation, astral trips, even the use of LSD as a gateway to awareness. Their music was filled with mentions of mantras, voices in the sky and visions of paradise, floating in inner and outer space while the body remained fixed in trance on earth and even a little science behind the mass of beliefs. Vibrations, rays and waves included in the electromagnetic spectrum, light itself, and finally the universal mantra *OM*, meant to take anyone to these invisible but very real worlds such as the one Devin spoke about.

I asked Devin what the remaining reels contained, the ones we hadn't played yet, but he passed off the question casually, assuring me that we'd get to them eventually. He said he really wasn't sure himself, as he'd recorded some of them years ago.

"I hope you're paying attention to what they're saying," he said, "because there isn't a song on them by chance or coincidence."

At that time I had been so astounded by the similarities between the lyrics and our life that it had not occurred to me until months later that had I insisted on hearing those tapes at that particular time, I would have been better prepared for what happened later.

As it was, I was content with listening to lyrics that reflected what was going on in the here and now, and *that* was uncanny enough. Equally amazing was how those lyrics also applied to every human being on the planet from every walk of life, every religion, every road of philosophy, and every avenue of belief. Those tapes of his could convert the most hard-core skeptic into a believer of some form of God, spirit, or Creator.

In some of those songs, the musicians made no bones about what they were doing, how they were using the media of music, and who they intended to reach.

Wasn't anyone aware of what was going on with the music today?

Was anyone, anywhere in the world, really *listening* to the music?

18 On Sunday evening, December 15th, we decided to take a run down to Daniel's. Pam agreed to sit with the kids and we took off. The Moody Blues entertained us during the drive, singing that we shouldn't think they were just singers in a rock and roll band because they were bridging seas and breaking language barriers with their music. Not unlike what I'd been thinking earlier.

The evening marked a turning point for me because it was that night that I finally began to realize just what kind of powers I was tapping into through my association with Devin.

It started out innocently enough. Sitting around Daniel's big dining room table with coffee and cake, the conversation pretty much centered on the company. Since Daniel no longer worked for them, he could now lampoon his job without any guilt feelings. There was a lot of laughter and jokes about his water cooler pickup instructions, which he read aloud to us, and it did seem like the instructions were written for imbeciles. Then Daniel asked Devin some serious questions about what *he* was going to do as far as leaving or staying on the route. Devin ran down the whole story from the promise of a bigger promotion and more money to what it had become—a route or nothing.

Daniel and Julie were appalled.

"This is what they do to loyal employees after all the years of service?" Daniel said, shaking his head. "Shit. You know, Devin, you should just put a hex on Tim." He gave Devin a knowing look.

Devin just appraised him coolly. I raised my eyebrows at Devin and silently rested my former case…that some people should *not* be taught anything. I looked towards the living room where the red velvet picture hung and wished for the tenth time that we had selected any other picture than that one. The noble lord with the fiery eyes just flashed me that high sign as if to assure me that all was okay anyway.

Daniel misread Devin's lack of response and continued. "No really, Devin. Maybe you and Kerry could teach me a little…" he made a circular motion with his finger…"candle control, maybe?"

Again, that expressionless glance from Devin. I looked down into my coffee cup, refusing to get involved in this conversation. Finally, Devin picked up one of the silver teaspoons and handed it to Daniel.

"Here, bro. This'll impress your friends more than that candle thing. Why not bend this spoon with pure thought? It *can* be done, you know. Candles are boring, really."

Daniel's eyes glistened. He obviously thought he was going to get a lesson or two, and he eagerly grasped the spoon by the handle. "Okay, Devin. Now what?"

Devin glanced at me a little sadly, and this time both Daniel and Julie caught the look.

"Hey, Devin, what's *wrong?* You look so—"

"Put the spoon down, Daniel." Devin sighed. "I was just jiving you. You can't learn *magic* over a dining room table, Dan." He picked up the spoon again. "There's a lot of awareness and understanding that goes *with* that kind of power and ability. And using it to *hex* someone isn't part of the deal. If you really want to learn and understand, you've got to get inside your own head."

"Oh." Daniel looked confused, but determined. "How do I do that?"

"Well, think about it, bro. How *would* you?"

"Tell me how *you* did it, man."

I almost choked on my coffee at the hidden humor in the real answer. He had brought his knowledge and awareness *with* him, and Devin Drew simply used that which belonged to *him.* I looked at *him* now, curious as to how he would explain.

Daniel, however, had asked *Devin* the question, and *he* didn't attempt to respond. He simply let Devin answer it.

"By hanging upside down with every opening in my head except my nostrils taped up. Wet cotton in the ears kills sound, and when all your physical senses are cut off, man, you can't even yell for help. You don't have anywhere to go *but* inside your own head."

Daniel whistled. "That's pretty extreme, Dev. How about Kerry?" He turned to me with sincere interest. "You too? Is that how *you* learned?"

"Kerry was born with it," Devin said quietly. I noticed the voice was *his* voice again and breathed a sigh of relief at the ultraviolet permeating the room. It was better to have *him* handle this kind of thing.

"She's got abilities that I haven't had the time to develop. I haven't been here long enough. But I've been trying to get her to work with her abilities more…however…" He looked at me and back at Daniel. "You know how it is."

"Okay. What other things *are* there…I mean…outside of hexing someone, of course." Daniel's voice was sheepish, as if realizing he was asking the wrong questions.

"It's not about things you can *do* to someone, Dan. I was referring to more beneficial things." He paused and glanced at me. "Any objections if I explain?"

I shook my head, but reluctantly, and he proceeded, with Daniel and Julie eagerly waiting, possibly, for me to demonstrate by levitating the dining room table.

Devin didn't really disappoint them. "Kerry has a peculiar ability to see into those other worlds I was telling you about, Daniel. She's been doing it all her life, and she is of a frequency that enables her to communicate from here to there with almost anything. I believe she even has the ability to see into future events. However, that does remain to be seen. We know she sees *something*, but whether it's related to futures here on this planet, we haven't discerned yet."

"That right, Kerry?" Daniel asked respectfully. "You were born able to do that?"

I shrunk down in my seat feeling a little embarrassed.

"Yes, but so were *you*, Daniel," Devin answered for me. "And Julie *and* everyone else in this world. The ability is latent in *everybody*. Kerry, here, was just born with a little higher degree of it. That, coupled with the fact that she's different from most of the people here anyway. She doesn't belong to this world any more than I do."

"Yeah, I think I can see that," Daniel admitted.

"But Kerry doesn't," Devin went on, and I shrank a little more into my chair. Devin was looking at me directly. I could see them all in my peripheral vision but I was tuning out, trying not to listen.

I knew Devin truly believed what he was saying, and I also knew that I didn't, and that he *knew* I didn't. I had decided to succumb to daydreaming and let Devin spend his energy trying to enlighten Daniel. The lights from the dining room were shining through the full-length walls of glass, passing directly through, and reflecting on, the cluster of fruit trees and shrubbery in the backyard beyond. I knew Luke was out there, and my mind drifted to the recent behavior of the dogs in Devin's life. How could I assist in explaining anything to Daniel when I had so many doubts and unanswered questions myself?

"Hey!" Devin nudged me playfully. "You still with us? Don't go phasing out on us now."

"Wait a minute, Dev." I remained motionless, one eye closed, arresting his gentle shove with one hand. The light, blurred by staring out of focus with one eye, had ceased to be a reflection, and the dining room began to blur around me the way physical surroundings did when I *looked* this way. I knew what would come next, so I tore my gaze away from the hypnotic light. "Wow. That peyote effect again." I blinked a couple times to refocus my vision.

"What'd ya *see* ?" Daniel asked, stealing a glance at Julie.

"Man, this is too spooky," Julie said. "Can we change the subject?"

Daniel started to protest, and Devin turned to me as though we were the only two in the room.

"There. Don't look away. That's what you're doing wrong, lady." His eyes pierced mine intently.

"It was just the reflection of the lights, Devin," I began weakly. "And letting it blur out. That's all."

"Yeah? And what happens when it blurs out?"

"Well, uh…" I stammered, wishing we *were* alone. "It usually refocuses back into something…uh… different. I started to let it, but, well, it looked like movement, and I guess I just freaked out again. I don't know what was coming."

"And you turned away. Lady, there's your fear again. You have a gift that you won't even *use*. Do you know how many people would give their right arm to be able to tune in on things like that?"

"But isn't that dangerous, Devin?" By now I didn't care who was there and listening. "I used to do it when I was a kid, and my mother told me not to watch them. She said I was leaving myself open to possession and other shit. Even Myrna said it was dangerous, and that it opens doors you can't always close again."

Devin's fist closed on the table. "Them. They say! And who are *they*? That, lady, is one of the biggest lies on the planet. The scare tactics. The secrecy trip."

"So you really think it's safe." I looked at him, feeling defeated. I wasn't going to change *his* mind.

"Well, who or what are you afraid of? Why *wouldn't* it be safe? It's safe to use your *physical* eyes, isn't it?"

Julie opened her mouth to say something, but Daniel issued her a look that warned her to stay out of it.

"Physical eyes were given to you as part of your physical equipment to focus *here*," Devin explained quietly. "But these *other* eyes of yours were intended for just *that* sort of thing." He nodded toward the glass windows.

"Kerry always sees things on glass?" Daniel asked curiously. "Just like that? No trance or nothing?"

"On glass and walls, and in coffee, and on the moon, or wherever else she chooses to look. She picks up the picture subjectively and projects it out here objectively. She could go a step further, *leave* here, and *enter* the damn picture *there*, but…I can't even get her to *watch* it."

"Okay, Devin." I sighed at his persistence. "I'll try."

"Don't just *try*! Do it. Close one eye if it's easier for you."

"Yeah. It *is* easier to blur one eye out than to use both focused together. Okay, just go on talking. I'll tell you if anything happens."

"Well, what kind of movement were you seeing before?"

"It's still blurry right now. But it looks like people. Actually, it *is* people."

The scene faded in and out as though I was trying to tune in a radio station, but visually. At times, it seemed to be just a lot of trees and blurred light, and then the focus would sharpen for a second. "It's definitely people. And it looks like there's a campfire going…wait…it just blurred out again. They're moving around. Wow. The scene keeps changing."

Devin glanced at the dining room light switch, and Daniel caught the look. Closest to it, he reached behind and hit it off. The darkness was relieving to my eye which had begun to water and sting. The picture came into sharp focus now while Daniel, Devin and Julie became blurs themselves. I could hear my pulse beating in my ears as my heart rate began to slow down to a rhythm with my shallow breathing. I could maintain the scene this way without losing touch with the room I sat in now.

"Thanks, whoever did that," I said gratefully. "The people...they're still moving around...moving a *lot*, and they're clearer now."

"And she said it was only the *light* reflecting," Devin said with a sigh. "Can you count them?"

"I'm trying, but they're walking around, back and forth, so it's hard to...well, it's obviously nighttime, and that little fire is the only light I have to go on. Wow! Are they ever moving! It's like a damn movie in miniature."

"How many, roughly?" Devin asked. "Thirteen?"

I laughed, almost breaking the focus. "No, Dev. It's not a coven, but that was my first thought too, because of the fire. No, I get the impression it's more of a survival group...you know...like a group lost in what seems to be...a jungle."

"You see any planes?" Devin prompted.

"No. Nothing like that. Just those people and a few small ones, too. Maybe kids. I'm not sure, though. It's as dark as if I was actually there. There are no movie set lights to illuminate the jungle."

"Jungle, huh?"

"It sure looks like it from what is visible in the firelight. Thick and vine-infested and swampy-looking. Not like a woods."

"Kerry, try to count the people."

I'd already begun. They had momentarily stopped moving. A log partially blocked my view of the fire, but the light made outlines of the people who were visible now as silhouettes. One approached the flames, and I could make out tattered khaki clothing. "One...two...three..."

"Not thirteen." Devin said.

"No. No way...four...five...six..."

"Seven, then."

"Seven, yes. That's more like it. There *are* seven." I double counted just to be sure.

The scene changed abruptly to an overhead view, something that had never ever happened in all my wall-staring of little movies. I still thought this was all somehow linked to traces of peyote in my system, but I didn't dare say that.

"What happened? It *quit?*" Devin asked anxiously.

"No, believe it or not, the, uh, perspective changed. Now it's an aerial view, and it's definitely a jungle. I wasn't sure before, but it's really obvious now. I see vines and strange trees and marsh...really swampy. The fire's still going so I'm in the same area, but just looking down on it...and them. They seem to be all huddled together in a circle."

"Ritual, maybe?" Devin suggested. "See any planes yet? Or wreckage?"

"No...it's blurring out again...shit. Now I'm back where I was...on the ground again. I don't see the fire in view anymore and...now they're all walking. Man, you should see how they're dressed. All brownish-looking rags. Like military or something. Rotten-looking clothes. And they're carrying something. One on each end of something long."

"Stretcher?" Devin's voice was the only other one in the darkened room besides mine.

"I don't know what. It looks too high to actually *be* a stretcher. It's like a long high box. Not a coffin, I don't think, but it looks like one. It's too dark to be sure. They're kind of walking single file now. Ugh…it really does look like there are little kids there. I don't like the feeling around this." I broke my stare and rubbed my eyes. "It's sickening. I really don't want to watch this anymore."

"Yes!" Julie's voice was loud and abrupt. "Let's do *anything* else."

The lamplight from the living room reflected on Devin's face, which was expressionless.

"Okay. Whatever."

I knew he was disappointed. We had gone this far already. Why wouldn't I finish it? "No, it's not okay, Devin. I'll try to get the picture back."

It was crazy how it could go on and off like that. I didn't believe I'd be able to get the same little movie again, but there it was when I looked again toward the glass walls.

"Well, it could be something you could report…or help out in some way. What if it *is* a survival group and some human has a rescue party looking for them in the mountains somewhere?"

"Okay, but there are no signs or anything, so I don't see how doing this is going to help anyone. They're facing me now…four abreast…they're hacking as if, well, maybe it's bushes or marsh. It's hard as to make out what they're using, but it looks like some kind of large blade. Oh, Jeez. Maybe a prop from a small plane."

"Well, if it's a jungle, they'd *need* something like that to clear a path," Devin said. "There are four of them?"

"Well, there were. Now it's blurring and changing again."

The room fell silent as I waited for something stable to refocus in.

The scene took another perspective, and we were back at the campfire again. It was still partially obscured by that log. I could make out three figures a few feet from the fire, and they all appeared to be gripping a one-handled object. It resembled a shovel. Three people holding and lunging with one shovel. It had to be symbolic.

"They're digging, it looks like, Devin. I think it's a shovel or something they're using for a shovel. I can't see the bottom of the device…that log and fire cover it. It's weird that it's taking three of them to dig like that."

"Can you still see that box they were carrying?"

"Yes, but it's lying in the background now."

"What are they digging?"

"I don't know."

"A burial, perhaps?"

"I don't know. Maybe. I can't see it anymore."

"Could it be a grave?"

"Devin, I don't *know!* All I can tell you is what I *see.*"

I was glad to get out of that dopey state, even if just to lose patience. The whole thing was making me uncomfortable. "Can I quit now?"

"If you wish."

I rubbed my eyes and shielded them. Both of them were stinging. When I looked again, the lights were back on, and everybody's auras were more visible than usual. His remained ultraviolet and the other two were glowing a yellowish green. I didn't see auras that well unless I was trying to.

"What are you staring at?" I was used to Devin giving me that brain-picking stare, but Daniel and Julie appeared nervous and somewhat in awe.

"Am I ever glad to have the lights back on," Julie said finally. "Look at me. I have goosebumps."

Daniel fumbled for a cigarette and had quite a time trying to light it with any kind of steady hand. "That's...uh...all right, Kerry. So...you think it might have been some kind of a plane crash, huh?"

"Well, that was Devin's suggestion. But like I said, there was no plane wreckage around. No remains of any plane."

Devin rubbed his eyes with his thumb and forefinger, then looked up at me. "Ever check the papers to see if any of these things ever actually happen?"

"What for? There aren't any signs indicating that these places are real existing places. There's no way of knowing *which* jungle that was. No remains of any plane. And even if there *was* a plane crash, Devin, planes crash every day. You can't just go grab any old plane crash and claim it as the one you saw."

"But on the *front page*, Kerry? Humor me. Let's get a paper tomorrow and look."

"Sure. Fine. But don't be disappointed, Devin."

He lifted his shoulders and then clasped his hands behind his head, leaning back in his chair. "It can't hurt to check."

The subject was dropped, to Julie's obvious relief, and the talk drifted to more everyday subjects. Eventually Devin stood up, and I took that as our cue to go. Daniel rolled us a joint for the road, rising to see us out the door. Julie rose too. Three of us had to work tomorrow.

"What time *was* it while Kerry was window-watching?" Devin asked.

"It was either ten, or five after," Julie said. I looked at the clock because I could hear the boys fooling around in their bedroom, and they need to be in bed. I just didn't want to get up while she was...you know."

"Ten o'clock seems to be our big hour," Devin remarked once we were underway. "You notice that? Wasn't that the time Erick chose for your experiment?"

I thought about it. That seemed so long ago now. "I guess so," I replied. "Hey, Devin? Are you sure that doing that isn't dangerous? Can't that leave you open to possession?"

"Well, I've heard of that regarding astral projection, not scrying, which is what you're doing, only minus the crystal ball. You're only looking. But on the astral? Sure, I've heard of that. I don't know how true it is. You're talking about some form of consciousness taking over your body and leaving *you* bodiless? To roam around whatever? Well, I suppose that could happen, but then, would that be so bad, really? It's exactly what you were doing before you were born here."

"Well, what would you call that?"

"Beats me. Dying, probably." He tossed me a wink and wheeled onto the ramp of the Interstate, headed home.

We were both exhausted.

That night I lay in bed waiting for him to return from the shower. The fresh, clean pillowcase looked so inviting. I pressed my face against its white coolness, thinking about the "movie" I'd seen down at Daniel's. And of the period I was having now. It wasn't a normal period. It was so light, it seemed like it could quit any time. What if I were pregnant anyway? I'd heard of such things.

I let my mind explore that one, including the probable reaction of the water plant, when I suddenly noticed something glowing on Devin's pillow. A white, glowing skull. An unmistakably detailed image of a skull.

My startled scream brought Devin to my side quickly. He was damp, and his waist was wrapped with a large blue towel.

"Devin...Devin..."

"Kerry, what in the name of—"

"On...on your pillow...there was—"

"Was *what?* Kerry! Was *what?* Calm down, now. What did you see?"

"A skull, Devin. It was as plain as..." I started to cry. Two unpleasant episodes in one night. "What's happening to me, Devin?"

He held me close to him and I felt, more than heard, his deep sigh. "I don't know, Kerry. But whatever it is, we can handle it. Don't be afraid. Look at yourself. You're freaking out. That skull could have meant *anything*."

"But it was so ugly...Devin, it *felt* ugly."

"Only because you associate a skull with death, and you've been taught to fear and recoil from death. Kerry, don't you see? That symbol wasn't necessarily bad. You can *make* it bad, or *take* it bad, but it's just your interpretation of it."

"No, Devin. It was a warning," I insisted, wiping my eyes. "I could *feel* it." I made an effort to get my emotions under control.

"Okay, babe." He loosened his grip on me and looked into my eyes. "Perhaps it was. Let's analyze it. A skull *does* mean death to you, right?"

I nodded. "And it was on *your* pillow."

"Okay, first of all, what's so terrible about death?"

"I'd lose you."

"You would, huh? Well, I don't see it that way. We might be separated for a short while, but we would never lose each other. I wish you wouldn't try to interpret these symbols because you attach negative things to them. Don't you realize that everything you think and everything you put any force into thinking, will happen? Especially *you*. I mean, even *humans* build their life with their thoughts. It's the way this dimension *operates*. You're fucking dangerous when you throw negativity around."

"But Devin...even Gerald...that day at dinner...even *he* said it was dangerous to watch that stuff."

Devin scoffed. "What does *he* know? Kerry, listen to me. There's *nothing* that can hurt you. Nothing would *dare!* Shit, you still don't understand, do you?

Who you are…you know who *he* is, so think about what that makes *you.* "

I did stop and think about it, then said, "But I don't *feel* that important."

"That's because you're *here*. You've been here for a long time, Kerry. Look, somehow I've got to make you understand that I mean this *literally*. Kerry, Christian and Erick and me…that's one thing, okay? We aren't human either. But *him. Him,* Kerry. *He* didn't just *select* you. You and he always *were*. You just feel so inferior to him because you've got him up on a pedestal when actually he's *level* with you. Equal. You don't realize it. I know you don't, even though you're trying to, and trying to believe. You are the *same* as he is, and you have the same abilities that he does."

"You make us sound…dangerous."

"We all can be. But, Kerry, the point isn't to use what we can do against anyone. It's to show them another way."

"Them?"

"The people. They're caught up in their wars and their hatred. Hell, look how it is just at work. Look at all the human bullshit *there*. It isn't necessary, but that's how it is. Look how they *are*. Oh, sure, there are a few good people, like Mama, but the majorities are prejudiced, some are malicious, out for themselves and all because they don't understand how it really *is* here. That's what *we're* here for. It's a thankless task, sure, but you bring fear into it and—"

"Devin," I interrupted. Do you think *he* tried to stop me from coming here? From being *born* here?"

"I can't answer that, babe. But I know one thing. No one can stop you from doing anything."

"Not even him?"

"Not anyone. And he wouldn't try. But he did care enough to come all the way here *for* you, and we're all in this together right now. Do you understand?"

I sank back against the pillow. What on earth was happening?

19 On Monday morning I approached the coffee shop's paper machine with change in hand. Admittedly, I *was* curious, and more than a little apprehensive, but as I fed the coins into the metal mustard-yellow machine I could see the headlines on the folded top half of the paper. They were rather dull and in no way connected to an accident of any kind, at least not the plane-crashing kind. I breathed a sigh of relief. There was always Sydney.

I didn't actually open the paper until I was seated in the booth. The bottom half of the front page had an article outlined in black with a bold black headline almost as large as the main headlines.

My heart must have stopped. I felt the blood drain from my face.

Seven Survive Crash. Week's Ordeal in Amazon

My heart began to triphammer. I was almost afraid to read the article that continued on page two. I couldn't predict a small filler, oh no. I had to hit one that made, to use Devin's exact words, the front page. Seven survivors. The exact number Devin had guessed, before I could actually tally what I saw. Even the fact that it was a plane crash. I had not summed it up as a plane crash. Devin had.

Just whose damn vision was it anyway?

"You getting an English muffin today?" Jane glanced down at the paper. "What's this? Something more important than the horoscope?" She filled my cup and waddled off, chuckling.

She had no idea how right on she was.

I doctored my coffee, picked up the paper, and took the plunge.

The first information was the location. La Merced, Peru. UPI. So it *was* a jungle.

The story went on to describe the events of a December seventh light plane crash that had happened to ten young family members on their way home from Christmas vacation. They had told their story on Sunday night, *last* night, at about ten o'clock in the evening. They described a harrowing week's trek through the Amazon Jungle and had finally made it to safety. They were plagued with cold, hunger, cuts and bruises, had lost their sense of direction, and were besieged by mosquitoes, maggots and insects that resembled leeches.

The pilot's name was Oscar, and even though he was only twenty-four, he was considered an ace pilot. He and six other relatives were recuperating in a La Merced hospital. All were young, ages between nine and sixteen. Three members of the party had died, one only a day away from rescue and safety. They had hacked their way through thick, spiny underbrush using machetes until they'd reached the banks of a river where a raftsman had picked them up and taken them to a village called Iscocasin. By this time some were barefoot, and they all were in tattered rags.

After a reunion there with their families, they were then transported to La Merced's hospital.

The hospital had refused to let reporters interview the pilot who was recuperating with cracked ribs and was very depressed. His sixteen-year-old sister, Gladys, was also depressed, but reportedly, all the younger kids were in pretty good spirits and had been thrilled by their adventure.

When the pilot finally told his story, he explained that the plane had begun to have engine problems halfway through the flight, and he'd been forced to crash-land in the middle of the jungle. He'd gotten rid of all the fuel so there would be no explosion. The plane had eventually crashed into some trees, and all of them were knocked unconscious. One by one, they'd begun to awaken.

They had blankets and sheets from their luggage, and they spent the night there, shivering in heavy rain. Then the pilot and his sister had set out with machetes cutting a brush path for the group. They were gone for two days. They returned on the third day and led the others through the path they had cut.

Three had died. One seven-year-old suffered a head injury in the crash and died almost immediately. Three hours later, a fourteen-year-old died, his body crushed by the engine.

The third had internal bleeding and broken legs and the group took turns carrying her on a makeshift stretcher. She had died one day before the party had reached the river.

They had eaten palm hearts and fruit they found along the way, and their cuts were maggot-infested.

I set the paper down and glanced out at the streets beyond the glass windows for some sign of Devin. Route or not, he usually found time to meet me in the morning, even if it meant leaving the supervisory duties to Pat. If he'd been here to read this with me this morning, he would probably have been speechless.

I was.

I looked back down at the paper. It had listed the names and ages of the survivors. The paragraph about the girl who had died along the way, but had been carried on a *makeshift stretcher* while she was alive, was more than a little disturbing.

Three people on a shovel in my little movie, burying something. Three had died. Symbolic or literal?

Jungles, marshes and swamps…hacking with machetes in tattered rags.

Just what bizarre source had I tapped into?

The story had not even come out until last night, around the time we were at Daniel's, and I was describing the scene to them. It was as if I was seeing what *they* were describing to officials after their rescue, as though I was picking up their story as they talked and projecting it onto the glass.

This being the case, I knew I could have been no help to them as they were already rescued. This made me feel a little better.

There was no feeling of triumph as I left the restaurant. When I arrived at work, the story was being aired on the radio's morning news, and Devin was already out on a route. I felt so alone.

Daniel called from a phone booth shortly after I arrived at work. I was in a mild shock as I picked up the phone, the paper still in my hand.

"Hello, Daniel?"

"Hey…Kerry." Daniel's voice was almost an awed hush. "Kerry, did you see the paper this morning? The front page?"

I could feel tears of depression springing to my eyes. "Yeah, I did, Daniel."

"Man, Kerry! The *front* page! The whole story…just like you told us last night."

His obvious excitement irritated me. "Yeah, Daniel. It's just *super* isn't it? Three people died. Wasn't that fun? Wonder how I missed the other two."

"Hey—" Daniel interrupted. "It wasn't your fault, Ker. Man, Devin *said* this was going to happen."

"What would?"

"That you'd feel guilty. That's why I called. It's not your fault, and you couldn't have prevented it."

"You *saw* Devin this morning?"

"He stopped by with the paper before he took off for his route. And he *said* you'd take this personal, like you could have reported it or something, but Kerry, it was too *late*, man. *Too* late."

I sighed. "I know, Daniel, but if I had to do something like that, why couldn't it have been a week ago when it might have done some good?"

"Well, you can't change that now, Kerry, and if you put your radio on you'll see that they were just telling reporters about it last night, about the same time you were describing it. Devin says the reason you saw three people with a shovel burying something was because it was just symbolic of the three people who died."

"Or maybe they *did* bury the bodies out there and it was more literal." I glanced over at Kelly and Hannah who were posting. The machines drowned out most of my end of the conversation. "Look, Daniel. I gotta go. I'm supposed to be working, and I don't feel so good right now."

"Okay, Ker. Stay cool, huh. Don't let this get you down."

"I'm trying. And please don't tell anyone about last night."

"I won't. But, of course, Julie knows, right?"

"I guess so," I said with a half laugh. "She was there. Look, later, huh?"

Dully I replaced the receiver and went over to my machine. Kelly stopped posting and looked at me.

"Are you all right? You're white as a sheet."

"I'm okay, Kel. What day are we posting?"

"We're doing checks. They're already out for you."

"Thanks, amigo."

When lunchtime rolled around I begged out of it, and Kelly finally left with Hannah for Burger King. Devin returned from his route at 12:30 and found me in the office, posting alone. He paused at the step with both hands on the doorjambs, then came straight over to me and took me in his arms.

"Lady!" It was all he could say and all he had to say. The guilt and depression that had begun at 7:10 this morning burst, and I buried my face in his chest, struggling not to cry. Trying not to care. He held me tighter, then tilted my chin up to look him in his concerned eyes. "Don't give me none of that fault shit, you hear? There was no way you could have helped. No way. Don't try to play God, babe. And don't feel responsible. Did Daniel call you?"

I nodded.

"Good. I stopped in there early this morning. That was decent of him."

I was more composed now and wiped my eyes as Kelly and Hannah came trooping in from lunch.

At the sight of Devin, Kelly was instantly her normal, noisy, playful self. "All right, break it up, break it up! What's going on in here? Devin, you ain't allowed to be in here necking with her. Just you wait till I tell Mama about this."

"Really, Kerry." Hannah was smiling. "You see him all day and all night."

"She saw him *all weekend!*" Kelly interjected.

"Hey, buzz off, Kelly," Devin retorted, dodging her swinging purse, his arm still around me. "And watch that arm! You might put me out of commission—" He lunged at Kelly who scrambled over to a buzzing phone and punched the button, stopping him cold in his tracks. You didn't fool around while business was going on. Unwritten law.

It was Tim, looking for Devin.

He took the phone, listened for a minute and gave me an exasperated look as he responded. "Man, Tim, I just got *in*. And I'm officially on my lunch hour right now, so I think I can spend that time here if I want to." Another pause.

"I'll be right there."

He hung up with a sigh. "More human bullshit. I'm really starting to rethink keeping this job. Ker, I'll be back. It seems I have to straighten a few things out with Tim. He wants to know why I can't work on realigning these routes when I get in this early. He's got a surprise coming. I'll do one or the other but I'll be damned if I'm doing both."

Devin called me from home at five to remind me that he'd picked up the kids. If ever I needed to get right home, today was the day. It cut an hour's drive to thirty minutes, and I was home by five-thirty.

Since Devin had moved in he'd relieved me of most of the *home* work, and tonight was no exception. When I walked in, the house was immaculate.

The tape was running and the dishes were done. Mandy's white shoes sat, newly polished, on a newspaper on the counter beside a bottle of shoe polish, and Christian stood at the stove, clad in chef's apron and black cap, several pots going at once. He gave me a big smile of greeting as I walked in.

"Hey, la-dee, welcome home." He held out his arms and I went straight to them.

"What're you doing, making *supper* again?"

"Shee-it, la-dee. Cookin's mah specialty, you know that! Jis wait till you taste this gravy...hey, don't feel guilty. If Ah kin git off earlier than you, the *least* Ah kin do iz make the meal 'n have *that* out of th' way. There's coffee made. See? Th' table's set, an' *this* is *done*." He turned off the burner and tossed the wooden spoon in the sink. "Hmmph. An' Devin thinks *he* kin cook."

The house was filled with the aroma of roast beef, onions, carrots and potatoes. I opened the oven, peeked inside, and shook my head. "I don't believe you. You know, that apron suits you to a tee, but don't you think a white hat would go better with it than that one?"

"La-dee." He planted a whopping kiss on my cheek as he took me in his arms again. "Nothin' iz better than mah black one. Go 'head. Get changed and call the kids so we kin siddown an' eat."

When I entered the darkened bedroom, I saw that the bed was made up with fresh sheets turned down for the night. I noticed a card, sealed in a white envelope, propped up against the dresser mirror. My name was printed on it.

I sat down to open it, a wave of love flooding over me. He was so considerate.

On the card were two simple words. *Thank you.* A color photo of a girl holding a flower. Inside the message continued...*for yesterday, today, and my dreams of tomorrow.*

Underneath in ink, in Devin's own route ticket handwriting, it said *Love, Devin.*

Thank you. Something Devin never said. And for no reason. As I sat there, ready to burst into tears of sentiment, the door opened, and Christian walked in with another card in his hand.

"Ah fergot," he said, a mischievous glint in his eyes. "Ah got somethin' for ya, too." He dropped the card in my hand, winked, and left the bedroom.

This one pictured a man and woman running through a wooded area.

Inside it read: *I feel safe and warm...in the circle of our love.*

Just like Devin's card, it was signed *love* in Devin's handwriting, then more boldly in Christian's heavy print was the best effort I'd seen him make to print legibly...*The Magick Christian.*

I changed quickly and went back out to the kitchen where he was putting our coffees together. I hugged him tightly, the two cards in my hand. "Thank you so much."

"See? Devin ain't th' only one that kin give you cards," he whispered in my ear, squeezing me tightly.

"But what's the occasion? I didn't do anything to deserve this."

"Fer bein' you," he replied. "C'mon. You ready t' eat?"

I went in to make sure the girls were in pajamas and ready for supper. When I returned with them, I found Erick setting up their table. I was immediately aware of his entrance. The black hat was gone. Erick never wore that hat. He looked up at me, smiled, and handed me another card.

"Before I forget." He leaned casually against the kitchen sink and crossed his arms. "This *is* a united effort, you know."

This card had a photo of a man whose silhouette looked identical to Erick's. He was sitting on a seashore, a guitar loosely in his arms. Inside, the inscription read: *Together we're a song.*

Below, in Erick's super-large handwriting was *Love, Erick.*

I didn't know what to say. I just hugged him, now more choked up than ever.

"Hey!" He patted me gently on the shoulder. "I'm going to do this more often."

"I love you so much."

"Good. That's what we're all striving for." He released me and smacked me gently on the rear. "Now, will you *eat?*"

I still had one more to thank for one of those cards, but Devin didn't show up for any displays of gratitude on my part. After supper, I went in to take a shower while Erick began to tear apart the stereo wiring again. When I returned I found *him*, hat cocked to one side, lounging in his golden throne and smoking a cigarette.

I was glad to see him. "I was wondering when you'd show up."

"I don't have a card for you," he began.

"You don't need one." I sat down on the matching footstool, and he reached over and drew me into his arms.

"Lady, you really let that plane crash get to you."

"Well, this is all so new to me, that's all. And what's worse, it makes me wonder what all those other things I've seen are. If this turned out to be so exact, but out of a time frame and *you* knew it..."

"Not consciously, I didn't," he corrected. "I guessed on the number of people, and even my first guess was wrong. Same with the plane. It was merely the obvious. When you hear of a survival group roaming around in an uninhabited area...well, I just drew the first conclusion. These things shouldn't be new to you, lady. Seeing is more first nature for you than you realize."

I didn't answer. Just being in his arms was the most comforting thing that had happened all day.

"Daniel and Julie are a little more shook than they're letting on," he went on.

"I was afraid of that. I don't want them glorifying us or being afraid of us."

"Well, I spoke to both of them this morning. I didn't ask you to watch that to frighten or impress anyone. I just wanted to show you that there *is* something to what you see. The rescue had already happened so you didn't see anything to cause you to curse the gift that you have. Yet, you reacted anyway."

"Devin, that's never happened before."

"That you *know* of. The point was for you to see that you see real things."

"If that was the point, then you made it last night." I sighed. "And if it proves I'm not entirely human, it would be nice to know exactly what I *am*."

"You am…" he smiled, "one of us."

I shrugged. "That still doesn't answer my question."

"It's not supposed to. Once you get *there*, you'll remember who you are. Unless I've got this dimension pegged all wrong."

"What do you mean?"

"Well, it would be a real blow to find out that as long as you're alive in this world, you aren't allowed to connect with your origins. I don't believe that, though. I don't accept it. And when you get to where *that* stuff—" he nodded at the newspaper on the bookshelf, "doesn't get to you like it did today, I think you'll be ready to find out who you are."

"But what about the other things? That lady all dressed in black. That bundle she was holding that looked like a baby. What about that?"

"Symbolic. I'm fairly certain that's how you pick up a lot of these things. I believe your period may have answered the question of what that little scene was all about. While you may not be consciously aware of it, inside you were rejecting the child that you may have been, or thought you were, developing. Not knowing as much as you need to about this child, you quite symbolically took it, mentally, to a graveyard and pitched it. You aren't ready yet, and we both know that."

"What about the skull on your pillow, then?"

"That, lady, I can't answer for you." He got up and hit the button assigned to the reel-to-reel. "We still haven't gone through all these tapes. By the way, your little friend hasn't been around."

"Blue?" I'd completely forgotten about our little blue thought-form or whatever he…it…was. "You're right. I haven't seen or thought about him either."

"Well, he'll turn up. Maybe he waits until we aren't looking for him."

"You got me. What's on that tape you're threading?"

"I don't know. I guess we'll find out."

He finished the prewinding, turned it on and walked over to the couch. "Come on, lady." He stretched out lengthwise and patted the space in front of his body that he'd made for me to join him. "It's been a long day. Maybe this song will explain what you need to know."

I lay with him and closed my eyes. That tape better answer something, I thought. I was tired of being in the dark.

2 Devin was up, dressed, and shaved before I was even out of bed.

I barely remembered going to bed. We'd mostly listened to his tapes all evening and while the Moody Blues were still peaceful, beautiful and mesmerizing, they seemed to be telling me that my visions were perfectly okay to watch and perfectly natural. I'd heard one of the songs before, either on the radio or on these reels, but the lyrics did reinforce the question of whether it was dangerous to watch or not. They asked if I was sitting comfortably, and told me to let Merlin cast his spell so that I could ride the winds of time and see where we've been.

Listening to the Moody Blues with their soft harmonies, beautiful symphonies and flutes, I felt foolish for ever entertaining fear of what I had done at Daniel's, and hearing these beautiful songs in the magical setting of our living room to the scents of bayberry and sandalwood, and the mystical flickering of candlelight, my bizarre lifestyle seemed normal.

Towards the end of the evening, however, the music on the reels took a turn in another direction…one that worried me. Up until yesterday the songs had been positive, at least for the most part, but last night certain songs began to creep in that sounded to me to be some kind of warning. There was no time to dwell on it as I sat up in bed and glanced at the clock. At least he wasn't late.

I found him in the kitchen, coffee in hand, and another mug sitting on the counter already doctored with milk and sugar. Steam wafted from the mug.

"I figured you'd be up soon, babe." He nodded towards the mug.

"How come you didn't get me up?"

"Well, we were up so late last night, and it's been a hectic week. You didn't seem to be sleeping very well, so I wanted you to sleep in a little. I don't have to open up anymore, so I can go in later now."

"You turned the keys in already?"

"Hell, yeah. *This* sucker ain't lately getting blamed if anything gets ripped off." He laughed and took me in his arms. "Oh, well. Easy come, easy go. Looks like we'll be getting that extra time together we've been needing. How about a kiss goodbye. I've got to split."

"I appreciate the card, Devin," I whispered, before I kissed him.

"Well, I knew you were feeling down about that plane wreck and, well, shit, I just love you, that's all."

"It's not bothering me now."

Devin downed the last of his coffee. "Practice," he said, picking up his keys. "That's all you need to do. You've always had the ability. You just never put it to the test before. You didn't acquire it suddenly through peyote or anything else. Well, I wish you could ride in with me again, but I suppose that doesn't make any sense. I'll be done by two or so and I can pick up the kids." He kissed me again, and after a long look he sighed and turned toward the door. "See you at work, babe."

"I love you, Devin."

"That's good." He pursed his lips. "It'll help."

For a brief second I flashed on that same feeling I'd picked up from the last of the songs on the reel last night. Then it was gone.

"Kerry, did you guys ever get a tree?"

Kelly was late as usual, and I was already posting when she came in. After a few words with Lola, she fired that question at me.

"Well, good morning to you too, Kelly."

"No, come on. Did you?"

"Who wants to know?"

"I do." Lola's reply brought me out to her office to join them. Hannah didn't leave her seat, but she did stop posting to listen.

"Sure. We got a tree. Friday. Why?"

"Well." Kelly tossed her purse in by her machine. "Me and Benny put ours up this weekend too, matter of fact. And Lola told me that *she* put *hers* up. So we were wondering…"

"Well, we did." I helped myself to one of Lola's cigarettes.

"There, Lola. See? I *told* you Kerry wouldn't let those kids go without a tree, Devin or no Devin."

I grinned at Lola. "What's the matter, Mama? You thought your grandchildren were going to be deprived this year?"

"Well, at least Devin let them have their tree. I *was* a little worried there for a while."

"We got a live tree."

Lola looked at me blankly. "A what?"

"A live tree."

"That's what I thought you said. Big deal. So did we."

"So did *we!*" Kelly squealed.

I glared at her. "You traitor. I thought you said you were putting up a fake tree."

"Well, I'm sorry…but me and Benny found this huge tree by accident."

"Wait a minute," Lola interrupted. "May I ask what difference your tree has from mine and Kelly's, or would I be looking ignorant?"

"Yes, you may ask," I replied, "and yes, you will be looking ignorant. *I* have a *living* tree. You and Kelly have *dead* trees, but you just call them live to appease your consciences."

Kelly rolled her eyes. "So. You *did* get one from that nursery, huh? I really didn't think you'd go through with it. How much of a fortune did you pay for the point you're both trying to make?"

"Oh, ten bucks. How much was your dead one?"

Kelly covered her face. "I'm embarrassed to admit it."

"Mine was about ten too," Lola said. "But I still don't understand the difference."

"Well, wait until the twenty-fifth, and you'll see a big difference in the trees," I told her. "Ours will still have all its needles and smell like a pine tree, and it might even be around *next* Christmas."

"See, Lola," Kelly said, attempting to explain. "The whole point of Devin's not wanting a tree was because you have to cut them *down*."

"Well, what does he expect? For everyone to move to the forest once a year?"

"No." Kelly stifled a yawn. "He just thinks Christmas should be abolished, and Halloween should be the day the kids get presents."

"Hold it, Kelly." Lola looked thoroughly confused. "Kerry, didn't you just get done telling us that yours was a live tree, too?"

I grinned smugly. "Yes."

"She means that hers is still planted in the pot, Lola," Kelly said. "Those nurseries don't sell dead trees."

"Oh." Lola feigned a disappointed look. "I thought the nursery was having a special on the ones that didn't make it." Then she smiled widely at me.

"Go ahead, laugh, you murderers," I retorted. "Your sarcasm will get you nowhere. What's a little extra trouble compared to the life of the tree?"

"Look, I didn't chop down the damn cherry...I mean Christmas tree," Kelly sputtered. "So there."

"Well, George," Lola interrupted. "If you and Martha would like to start work sometime this morning..."

"What?" Kelly feigned horror.

"Before *lunch?*" I added.

"Well, I realize it's a little *early*, but since we are busier at Christmastime—"

"Don't waste your breath, Lola," Kelly said, going in to her machine. "Even if you reconvinced her of Christmas, it would only last until Devin walked in here."

"You should talk," Lola's voice followed her in. "The only two who didn't sign up for the plant gift exchange are you and Kerry."

"Hmmph," Kelly shot back quickly. "I'll bet Devin didn't. And on my salary, I'm lucky I can afford my kids, much less anyone down here."

"Yeah," I agreed. "Mandy's birthday is tonight, and a couple of our friends have kids with birthdays this week too."

Lola stepped into the doorway. "Well, good grief! You're going to buy all these extra presents, plus Christmas, on the money you guys are bringing in? Kerry, is he embezzling?"

"He just conjures the money up."

"Oh, I see." She suddenly became serious. "Are you guys going to make it this year? I know Devin's pay's taking a big drop."

"It has, but Devin says we'll just use his credit cards."

Outside it was pouring. The gutters in this city were sadly insufficient when it rained hard. It did make working easier since it was too wet to do anything else, but it was a bummer to try to get to your car at lunchtime. Kelly got up to make some iced tea, and I was ready for some coffee myself. Lola glanced up when we passed her, and Kelly pointed toward the cooler in the main hallway.

"Want anything from the bar?"

"Well, I don't know." Lola laughed. "What did you have in mind?"

"Coffee, tea...what else *is* there?"

"Oh, no thanks. I did that already." She glanced at her watch. "Stay out of trouble," she added, as if an afterthought. "And whisper. Maurice is in his office, and Kerry, I know this is going to upset you, but the little dead Christmas tree that Kim put up in the lobby is there to stay. So just remember, we put up with you all day Halloween. Try to give us Christians the same courtesy."

"Well, I wasn't going to bring this up," I countered, "but Brenda has hexagrams up all over the lobby walls to counteract the Christmas stuff."

"Brenda is Jewish, Kerry. Those are Stars of David."

"Oh, is *that* what they are?" I asked innocently.

When we passed the lobby glass doors, we saw that the sky was black. We stood to watch the lightning and winced at the earsplitting cracks and booms as the thunder followed the flashes.

Kelly heaved a heavy sigh. "Look at it come down."

Brenda yawned as she doodled on her desk pad disinterestedly. As the main receptionist, in weather like this, there was no one to receive. "Tell Kerry to stop the rain," she suggested. "That's what you've got an office witch for, isn't it?"

"Yeah, *any* witch can do *that*," Kelly agreed. "Make it stop raining, Kerry."

I laughed. "Okay. Just let me stand here and talk to the sun for a minute."

Kelly patted my shoulder. "You *do* that. I'll let Mama know you're fixing the weather for us."

I followed Kelly a couple of minutes later, carefully carrying my Styrofoam cup to avoid spilling.

"Well, did you stop the rain for us?" Lola asked as I passed her desk.

"No problem," I replied confidently. "It'll be dry and sunny by noon."

As if to underline my response, a loud thunderbolt cracked, shaking the building.

Kelly nodded at Lola with surety. "See? It's slowing down already."

Devin walked into our office at noon, and he was dry when he entered, hair and all.

"What the *hell* are you doing back so early?" Lola demanded with an affectionate smile. "And isn't it raining out there?"

"Well, Mama, you know how it is. Such a big route and all. And no, it isn't raining now. Why do you ask, grasshopper?"

"Just…uh…curious." Lola's voice trailed off for a minute. It clearly wasn't the answer she expected. Even the forecast had predicted rain for the entire day. "Well, never mind that. Are you taking your harem out to lunch today?"

"That *would* be cool, but this route's commission matches its size, you know, like, you want to shell out some bread, I'll take your brats off your hands."

"Oh, listen to this," Kelly muttered, then louder, "Hey, one of these *brats* is *yours*!" She reached up to pat his head. "I just *love* your poodle cut, Devin."

"Oh, is *that* what it's called?" Hannah smiled. "I thought you just put a bowl on your head and—"

"Hey, buzz off, you dizzy broads. Get off my case."

"Devin, have you seen Tim yet?" Lola broke in.

"No way. No sooner than I have to."

"He called here looking for you. He said you haven't called in your usual four times today."

"Hey, every dime counts," Devin retorted.

Lola changed the subject. "Mister, are you aware that Kerry didn't sign up for the gift exchange this year?"

"I didn't either. I would have gotten Daniel something, perhaps, but he quit, so…"

"You're terrible, Devin," Kelly accused. "Santa Claus isn't going to bring you nothin'. He'd probably be too scared to come down *your* chimney anyway."

"We don't have a chimney, Kelly."

"Well, down the air vents then. I don't know. However Santa handles houses with no chimneys."

"Let's get this straight now," Devin said seriously. "Santa doesn't come to our house."

"Well, he'd have to make a special trip just for you since all those rotten peanuts would fill up his whole sack," Kelly replied, "but I'll bite. *Why* doesn't Santa come to your house?"

"Think about it, Kelly. On the birthday of Jay Cee? Or was that in May, sometime. Seems I remember reading about these three wise guys and the gift of a newborn lamb. Except that December twenty-fifth doesn't jive with the breeding season of sheep."

"So they're not sure of the date. What's that got to do with Santa Claus?"

"That's what *I* want to know. Just how did this Santa get hooked up with Jay Cee anyway?"

"Hey, gizmo," Lola said irritably. "I don't have to listen to your sacrilegious—"

Devin held up his palms innocently. "Hey, Mama. I'm just asking. I thought Santa was related to Jay Cee in some way. He'd almost *have* to be to make it all over the world in one night, and besides that, I moved, and I never thought to send the North Pole a change of address. And as far as being sacrilegious, I thought *everyone* knew that the Star of Bethlehem was actually a flying saucer."

"*What?*"

"Sure, and those three wise guys…ever wonder about *them?*"

"Devin, if you don't stop calling them wise guys—"

"Well, okay, whatever. But they say they came from the East. India, wasn't it? From India to Jerusalem. Some distance. A long walk unless you had a good mule. Depending on their route, they might have even needed a boat. It would have taken *years*, so therefore, the logical deduction is that they had some *prior* knowledge of the stable story."

"Well, everyone knows they did," Kelly protested, serious for once. "They had divine guidance."

"Divine guidance, my ass," Devin replied. "They were *led* by a moving star, and my dear, stars don't move. This one was quite amazing. It not only moved, but it changed directions and even disappeared when the dudes arrived at the stable. Then, these same dudes…uh, sorry, Mama…these men ran to the biggest gossip in the Middle East…Herod, was it? Then they started all those rumors and got *him* all fired up enough to do more baby-killing than Viet Nam, and *then*…they disappeared."

Lola pointed indignantly to the exit. "*Out*, Devin."

"Merry Christmas, Mama." He blew her a kiss, winked at me, and left.

"You know, he *does* have a few logical points there," Kelly admitted. "I never really thought about it before, but…"

"Well, Round John Virgin is the one I've always wondered about myself," I said.

"Who?"

"Round John Virgin."

"Kerry, who in the hell is Round John Virgin?"

"Oh, come on. You've heard of him. He's in that song, *Silent Night*. Remember?" I stood up to sing her a few bars. "Round John Virgin, mother and child, holy—"

"That is *enough* out of you, Kerry," Lola said. I decided to cool it before I got deported too.

"We should be thinking about what we're going to give Trevor and Mia for Christmas."

Devin's voice was muffled from the storage closet in our den. He emerged with a plastic gallon milk carton, the top cut off and filled with brushes and painting supplies. "These yours?"

"Yes, but I don't have any canvas."

"I do. It's been a while since I painted anything. Maybe I'll do some painting tonight."

Pam looked up with interest from the couch in the living room. "Oh, you guys are going to paint?"

Devin set the supplies on the coffee table. "Yeah. Care to join us?"

"Yes! I'd love to make up some Christmas cards."

Devin looked at me. "We could use a few ourselves. You feel up to that?"

"Devin…you're actually wanting to send out Christmas cards? You?"

"Sure. Well, not Christmas cards…but holiday cards."

"Speaking of cards!" Pam jumped up and snatched a stack of mail from the stereo speakers. "I forgot. You'ns got some cards today. In the mail."

Devin shuffled through them and smiled. "Like I said. We do have to send a few." He handed the stack to me.

There was one from Gerald and Faye (a simple holiday greeting), and one from my mother (a nativity scene). I was surprised that Devin didn't comment on that one after that conversation in the office today. There were a few from friends at the water plant (all tactfully unreligious—Santa Claus or general holiday wishes). But the card that intrigued Devin the most was the exorcist-green envelope with a large black pentagram drawn in the corner. Like most of the cards, it was addressed to both of us, but no one else had made any effort to draw a pentagram on the envelope.

"Who in the hell?" Pam peered over my shoulder. "Oh! I know who that's from."

"Who?" I opened the envelope carefully. Whoever it was, the gesture was pretty considerate, I thought. Inside was another religious card, and the inscription was equally religious. Angels adorned the blue cover, hovering over puffy clouds in an obvious scene in Heaven. Inside the printed religious message was blocked off in heavy black ink brackets, and another personal message was printed by hand underneath.

Devin and Kerry, please ignore the above. Mandy and Michelle may endure the entire message. Send the Devil back to Hell for the holidays. Love, Bonnie and Jake

I burst into laughter and handed the card to Devin. "It's from my *super* Catholic cousin, Jake, and his wife…Pam's best friend."

"I thought I recognized Bonnie's handwriting on the envelope," Pam said.

"That was really cute of them," I said. "It looks like Jake wrote the message inside. He's always rolled his eyes at what he thinks I'm into, but his sense of humor makes up for it. You're right, Devin. We do have a few cards to make."

Devin read the message inside with an amused smile. "Bonnie and Jake. I remember their names. Have I met them?"

"I don't think so."

"Jake's your cousin. Isn't Bonnie the one who was pregnant?"

"That's them. Jake hadn't told his parents about the baby back then."

"The parents still don't know about the baby," Pam added.

"Oh, sure. I remember that. Shit, that was back in October. How far along is she now?"

"I guess about eight months," Pam replied. "They don't have a lot of time left."

"Yeah," Devin said, laughing. "That's some Christmas present they've got planned for your aunt and uncle."

"And those two will *shit* when they find out," Pam said. "Our aunt has some pretty stiff moral ideas."

Devin set aside the canvas he'd been sketching on. "I think I'll paint them up a Devin Drew special. What the hell? Even *Gerald* didn't bother to put a pentagram on his envelope." He went to the closet and brought out a package of colored construction paper. "I'm surprised the mailman even delivered it. Here, Pam. Do your cards on this stuff. It's stiff and easy to fold when you're done."

"Well, I'll be using water colors."

"Those work great on this paper. Kerry, how's your Theban script coming along?"

"I know the whole alphabet, why?"

"Good, when I get done with this, you can address it."

He sketched the Scorpio and Virgo signs, folded the paper into a card and printed on the front: *Merry Whatchamacall it.* Inside the card finished: *And a happy whatever.*

The painting part only took twenty minutes, and it dried quickly. I addressed the card in the witches' runes, and Pam volunteered to deliver it.

"Poor Jake," I told Devin. "He's so human, he's a riot. He has absolutely no belief in the occult, but I know he'll get a kick out of this."

"Here you go, Pam. All ready," Devin said, handing it to her.

After Pam left, Devin turned to me. "Do you feel like painting up some cards, or do you want me to do it?"

"You seem to be pretty quick at it," I said.

Devin snapped his fingers. "I know what you can do."

He went out to the van and returned with a vinyl spare-tire cover.

"If I draw the twelve divisions, you think you could put the twelve zodiac signs on this for me?"

"Sure. Now *that* I could get into."

"Okay." He brought me some acrylic paints. "You do that and I'll handle the cards."

I was just finishing up the scorpion when Pam returned. The phone rang just as she walked in. It was Bonnie. They had both flipped over the card and wanted to know what those weird letters spelled out, adding that we sure knew how to make a great holiday out of a plain old Christmas season. She then asked to speak to Devin.

Devin told Bonnie about our tree and insisted she get over to see it soon. Bonnie said maybe Sunday, and that due to her pregnancy she'd stayed in the house most of the time, afraid someone might spot her and beat Jake to the announcement.

"And when do you plan to do that?" Devin teased her.

"Oh, either Christmas day, or we'll wait till the kid's born and leave it on their doorstep."

"Or, you could say it's ours until they get attached to it," Devin said, glancing at me with a twinkle in his eyes.

He was still laughing when he hung up the phone. "She sounds like a cool chick. I'm going out for cigarettes and some rolling papers. You need anything?"

"Nope."

While he was gone, Chris's roommate, Steve, came over from the other side of the duplex. He had something in a blue Maxwell House coffee can, something he thought Devin might like to see.

"He's up at the store, but he should be right back," I told him. "Whatcha got there?" I peered into the can.

Inside, the largest scorpion I had ever seen in my life was literally freaking out, circling the can in panic. Its tail waved wildly, stinger thrusting at the air in little stabs.

"Damn, that's a big one. Where'd you get it?"

"The twin lakes…you know, the rock quarry?"

"Oh, okay. Pammy and George go down there all the time. I didn't know there were scorpions there."

"I just figured Devin might like to see him since he's a Scorpio, but I can't hang around. I'll come back when I see the van out there."

Pam and I busied ourselves with setting up Mandy's birthday cake. We'd had it decorated with a Sagittarius sign, and when Devin returned from the store we sang the normal birthday song to her and let her blow out the candles. Then Devin put on the Uriah Heep version of *The Magician's Birthday*. During the 9 minutes and 36 seconds song, the Christmas tree sparkled and twinkled, and Puff the dragon flashed his tri-colored globe amidst the eerie lighting and candle effects, Mandy glowed in her own special way. Both of the girls worshipped Devin, and it was a birthday she would never forget.

As it turned out, Devin was never going to forget this day either.

When Steve returned to show Devin the scorpion, it was no longer alive. Its panic and terror had been justified for it had been drowned in a sea of alcohol. Its body floated motionless in the small can where it had fought so hard for an escape route only a short time ago.

Devin's reaction was one of obvious horror as he stared into the can. Then he turned icily to Steve.

"That's real cute," he said coldly, his voice pure stone. "What'd you kill him for?"

Steve, taken aback, looked flustered. "Well, I'm…I'm making a jewelry box for someone as a Christmas present. I can put some varnish on it and preserve it on the lid forever."

Devin reached into the alcohol and lifted the insect's body up to eye level. "How long's he been dead?"

"Almost an hour. Why?"

Devin wheeled on him in fury. "You *had* to do this for your goddamn Christmas present! You couldn't paint a scorpion on the lid or buy a rubber one? What the fuck did you need a scorpion on your jewelry box for anyhow? Do you even know the lengths of torture and suffering you put this through?"

Everybody in the room froze. Mandy and Michelle looked up from their cake with alarm. Pam stood against the stove immobilized.

Devin dropped the scorpion back into the can in disgust and shoved that can into Steve's hands with so much force that alcohol splashed up into his eyes.

"How's it *feel* dude?" Devin turned away from Steve, offering no apology.

"Hey! What the fuck's the matter with *you?*" Steve screamed, wiping his eyes with his sleeve. "You like scorpions or something?"

Devin appeared to be in shock. His face was white and he looked positively nauseated, but he lowered his voice, probably for the sake of the kids, and said, "Get out of my house."

He then turned and left the room. We heard the bedroom door slam.

Pammy and I exchanged looks. Steve left in a huff, obviously insulted and furious, and I went back to the bedroom to see what Devin was doing.

I opened the door a crack and looked in. He was lying on his back staring vacantly at the ceiling.

"Devin?"

"Yeah. Come on in."

"Hey." I sat down on the edge of the bed. "I'm really sorry. I had no idea he was going to kill that scorpion. He was here earlier but it was alive in that can."

"Why do humans *kill* ?" His eyes nearly bulged when he asked the question. There was almost a look of insanity in them. "Why senselessly torture and kill that scorpion? It wasn't bothering anyone! It was snatched right out of its home and brought here to be killed…*painfully and agonizingly* killed." His voice began to rise. "How would that asshole like it if I dropped *him* in a barrel of *acid?* Because that's just what he did to that scorpion." He started to sit up, as if considering doing just that.

"Devin, take it easy." I put my hands on his arms and he broke away, rolled over on his stomach and buried his face in his arms. His voice was muffled as he continued.

"If I had been here, I would have taken that scorpion while he was alive and held him in my hand. I'd have shown Steve that there was no reason to hate it or fear it or…kill it. I would have proven to him how harmless it was. I would have…set it free."

"Devin, I'm so sorry."

"Why should *you* be sorry? *I'm* sorry." He looked up at me. "You talk about your bad symbols, Kerry. This is worse than that skull on my pillow. That little scorpion was *me*… It was *us*, Kerry."

There was no talking to Devin for the remainder of the evening. The new tree, the Christmas cards, the vinyl tire cover…all forgotten. Devin remained in the bedroom until very late in the evening. Only after Pammy was gone and the girls were in bed and the darkened living room was empty did he return to the couch. He flipped on the reel-to-reel and resumed his glazed-eyed staring, oblivious to even me.

Once again, the tapes seemed to be trying to tell me something. Something ominous. Something bad.

Since I couldn't engage Devin in any kind of conversation, I had no choice but to sit there and listen.

There was no describing the look in Devin's eyes when we finally went to bed, and when we awoke the following morning his eyes still held that same anguished stare.

"I dreamed I was drowning last night," he said, sitting up in bed.

"Drowning in alcohol."

21 By the time both of us had arrived home from work that afternoon, Devin appeared to have put the scorpion incident behind him. Tonight there was a birthday party at Trevor's house for little Mickey, and of course we had been invited.

It quickly became evident how *he* had solved the problem of switching gears from the horror of the scorpion to a festive birthday party. *He* had cut out entirely leaving Devin to do the honors with his brother's family.

It was almost a relief to be with Devin again after that emotional scene last night.

Mickey's party was a big affair, and most of the family and guests were already there when we arrived.

I looked over to make sure it was still Devin with me. He picked up on my thought and smiled. "It's still me, babe," he said, as he cut the girls loose from the side of the van. "No chances with Titan tonight. Don't worry."

"Jesus Christ, Devin. How do you always know what I'm thinking?"

"Same way you do. Come on. Let's go in."

"Well, besides Titan, from the looks of all these cars…"

"I know." He put his arm around me, and we walked to the front door.

As I figured, Titan was the first to the door, and he greeted Devin the way he always did. Quivering with excitement, he had to be ordered down by

Trevor before he tore Devin's shirt off with his ecstatic, welcoming leaps. His tail was just missing every glass on the coffee table, and I heaved a sigh of relief. Titan loved Devin. As long as Devin remained, there would be no problems.

The room was crowded with Mickey's relatives. She sat in the center of a group of children, and when Titan was ordered into the kitchen, it left just enough room for my girls to sit in with them.

Devin and Trevor immediately tented into a private huddle, so I went out to the kitchen where Mia was cutting the cake. We'd apparently missed the birthday song.

"Hey, that's a nice big one," I observed approvingly. "Bakery job, huh?"

"We *had* to," she explained. "All these people...Come on, Titan...move." She nudged Titan gently with her foot, her hands full with the large tray. "Come on, I'm going to have to lock you in the bedroom again."

"Here, Titan!"

The call came from Devin. He was sitting on the floor just outside the kitchen doorway with Trevor, and they had been talking in low tones away from the conversations of the more conventional relatives. At the sound of his name, Titan lumbered to his feet, ears pricked, and I had a weird premonition of trouble.

"Mia," I began. "There are a lot of kids out there..."

"Oh, it's okay," she interrupted. "He's just a little jumpy tonight." She changed her tone to the way you'd talk to a baby. "So many people, huh, Titan."

He seemed to relax at her soothing voice as she passed with the tray of cakes, and he looked up at her, then moved toward Devin and practically dropped into his lap.

Devin unconsciously scratched his head and ears, totally engrossed in whatever Trevor was saying. I almost dismissed that feeling of trouble coming when Titan's eyes met mine for a second. When I looked back at Devin, I saw *he* had come to continue this mysterious conversation Devin had been having with his brother.

There was nothing I could do. Worried, I returned to the kitchen to get the second tray containing the beverages, and it erupted within seconds. It sounded like it started with a minor squabble among the children that, unfortunately, Devin had chosen to break up. Apparently, it was one of ours that had started it.

"Hey, Michelle," I heard him say, and then...the sound of confusion, the snarls, the chaos as Titan was hauled roughly into the bedroom, and then the sound of the master's discipline. Then Trevor returning, with a hasty apology to the guests. He then turned to Devin.

"You okay, bro?"

"Yeah, man, that sucker's protective, ain't he?"

"Dig it. He's that way with our kids, too."

Devin obviously back. Conveniently returning as Trevor apologized to the guests for the disturbance. Everything okay. Nobody hurt. No cause for alarm. Just a high-strung dog in a house full of excited people.

I watched from the kitchen as Trevor performed a cursory examination on a protesting Devin for signs of broken skin. Devin's shirt was torn slightly, but *he* was gone, and Trevor showed no signs of surprise, no reaction whatsoever, at the dog's unusual behavior towards his friend. It almost seemed like Trevor was *very* aware of the dog's mistrust of *him* and was assisting Devin in a hasty cover-up. As though this incident *had* occurred before, and the only important thing now was the brainwashing of the startled guests.

If Trevor *was* aware of changes in the dog's behavior when *he* was around, did he and Devin simply work telepathically to smooth things over, as they seemed to be doing now? A lot of personal looks were being exchanged between them, and I wondered just *what* they'd been huddled together about to begin with. It had seemed like a very serious conversation.

I was still holding the tray of beverages.

"Go ahead, Kerry." Trevor gestured for me to continue with the tray as though nothing out the ordinary had happened. "He's locked up."

I could almost see Titan bristling behind the door. I could hear him pacing and growling and no wonder. Devin had momentarily skipped again.

"I think we'd best be leaving," *he* was telling Trevor. "The kids have school tomorrow. We should get them home." He glanced at me so I wouldn't object, not that I would have, and a wave of pity rippled through me for Titan. It wasn't the poor dog's fault. What punishment had been inflicted on him for an attack, in defense of children, towards someone he had no reason to trust?

"I'm going in to see Titan first," I told Devin, who shrugged and gestured toward the closed door.

"Don't let him out, though."

"I won't." *Believe me, I won't.*

Once inside the room, I sat down on the side of the bed, and a shaking Titan acknowledged me with a huge paw on my knee...trembling.

"Aw, come here, boy."

He glanced nervously at the door as voices rose and fell, among them, *his*. Irritably I wondered why *he* couldn't just stay away, at least for the sake of the dog, but apparently that business about control was getting less and less reliable. Each time Titan heard *his* voice, he growled and his fur bristled. I took the big dog's head in my hands and looked into his confused brown eyes.

"Titan, I thought you guys had this all straightened out...I guess you did as long as he didn't holler at the kids, huh?"

Titan's response was a wet affectionate tongue on my wrist, then he resumed his attention to the sounds beyond the door.

"Titan, come here." I patted the bed. It sounded like other people were leaving too, and Devin was helping Trevor to send them off. *Devin!* The goodnights and laters were definitely Devin's easy-going voice, and Titan's response to the sound of it was a rerun of the greeting at the front door when we'd first arrived.

His ears pricked with interest and joy, and he wriggled ecstatically from head to tail with excitement. He began to pace from me to the door with anxious eyes, not understanding why I dared not release him.

"Yeah! That's *Devin*, huh, boy?"

"Woof!" Titan responded, as a rap sounded on the door, and it opened a crack.

"Hey, Kerry!" It was Devin. "Time to go. You want me to get the kids in the van?"

"Is everyone gone?" I asked, struggling to hold Titan, who strained for the partially open door. "This dog's going bananas in here."

"Oh." Devin glanced at Titan. "You can let him out. Everyone's gone now."

He stepped back so I could open the door completely. I released Titan's choke chain, and the dog bounded out to Devin, this time in joy and welcome. Trevor shook his head in disgust as the two of them set to wrestling on the now roomier floor.

"Damn dog. Wish he'd pick a side and stay on it."

During the trip home, the girls dozed in the back on the couch, and Devin drove in silence, his hand on my knee. He seemed to be in deep thought.

"Thinking?" I asked. We'd pulled up to a red light.

"Yeah, matter of fact, I was." He glanced at me briefly, then resumed his attention to the road as the light changed. "About that argument the kids got into tonight. I've been watching them. They really do compete with each other."

"Well, they're tired. It's way past their bedtime."

"I know, but there seems to be something more to it than that. It's like there's a jealousy there. Especially Michelle, you know?"

I looked at him curiously. He seemed to be choosing his words carefully, and I knew there was more to this than his notice of the squabbling of two overtired kids. "Devin, what are you getting at?"

"Well, just that maybe we ought to wait a while on that son of ours, that's all. Perhaps the girls wouldn't accept him if they're already competing with each other as it is. Perhaps…"

As he talked, the feeling went through me the same way it had earlier with the dog, just before Devin's exits and returns. Devin was deliberately avoiding the mention of the incident with Titan and, instead, pointing out a normal overtired children problem as a reason to cancel the birth of the son *he'd* planned for and spoken of from the very beginning.

"I didn't say *cancel*, now," Devin added, as if hearing my thoughts. "I just think maybe it should wait for a while."

"Don't you think that should be *his* decision?" I asked hesitantly, afraid of what his reply might be.

He lit a couple cigarettes from the lighter in the van and handed one to me before he responded. "You're right. Let's drop it for now." He squeezed my knee, shoved a tape into the deck, and closed the subject for the night. At least, it was closed between Devin and me, and the tape just picked up the conversation where'd we'd just left off.

Uriah Heep seemed to know what was happening, even if I didn't.

The lyrics were blatant and concise. The singer talked of waking up every day with no new songs to play. He felt like he needed to pack his bags. Needed to run. His mind flew to another time when he had felt free, and his time had been his own. He didn't mind some trouble, but when dark clouds blocked my beauty from his eyes, he just couldn't stand here alone.

And he needed to be free.

Neither of us spoke again until the van pulled up to the house. When Devin cut the engine, he turned and looked at me. I must have looked crestfallen because he ruffled my hair and then pulled me into his arms.

"Don't worry," he said. "It's cool."

I wanted to believe him.

Part Four

Three or Four Feet From Home

"That while it may be that some operators of UFO are normally the paraphysical denizens of a planet other than Earth, there is no logical need for this to be so. For if the materiality of UFO is paraphysical (and consequently normally invisible,) UFO could more plausibly be creations of an invisible world coincident with the space of our physical Earth than creations in the paraphysical realms of any other physical planet in the solar system...

RAF Air Marshall, Sir Victor Goddard
KCB, CBE, MA.

Excerpt from a speech in a public lecture at
Caxton Hall in London
May 3, 1969

1 When we awoke the following morning, Devin seemed his normal and cheerful self. As if last night had never happened. I tried to chalk it up to the changes coming into our life and tried even harder to shake off the lyrics to that song that had played on the tape last night.

When I arrived at work, the atmosphere was festive, probably because it was so close to Christmas. Lola called me into her office and handed me a folder of route tickets.

"Take these to the phone room and look up the addresses in the address directory. It's just like a phone book only backwards. When you find the addresses, it'll give you the names we can't read."

"The *phone room!*" I gasped. "Isn't that all decorated for Christmas?"

"Look, Kerry, we can't stop them from decorating in there."

"Well, can I hang up that poem we wrote?"

"No way," Lola said emphatically. "You trying to get us all fired?"

"Well, okay, but Devin isn't on a route for some reason. If there's any I can't find in the book, can I go back and ask Devin?" I teased.

Lola pointed to the doorway and smiled. "Do you two have some communication system we don't know about?"

"Hey-hey-hey."

"Devin, what the hell do you want?"

"Don't ask him that," Kelly said. "He'll think of a ton of things he wants just to hang around in here. Hey, Devin. What are you giving Kerry for Christmas?"

"Kelly, Christmas is every day," he retorted. "I don't need to use someone else's birthday to give her something."

"Someone *else's* birthday?"

"Alleged birthday," he corrected.

"Did you two ever make that camping trip?" Lola spoke up quickly, changing the subject.

"Tomorrow night. Cycle's ready and so am I. Believe me, so am I."

"Me too," I chimed in.

"You're both out of your minds. Do you have any idea what the temperatures are out there at night? Or don't you break apart long enough to find out?"

"Mama," Devin said slowly. "I came in here to invite you all out to lunch, not to discuss the weather."

"Oh how exciting!" Kelly squealed. "A whole afternoon off!"

"A whole afternoon?" Lola smiled.

"Well, of course, Mama." Devin picked up on Kelly's thread. "If you come, it doesn't matter when we get back."

"Well," Lola said, laughing, "at least you're honest about it."

"Come on, Mama. You too, Hannah. I don't make this offer twice in the same year. Hey, it's Christmas!"

"So what?" Hannah said. "You don't even celebrate Christmas."

"I beg your pardon. *We* have a *tree.*"

Lola interrupted to decline the invitation, thanked him anyway and told him that if there was any way in hell she *could* keep us from going to lunch, she would do her best to stop it.

We went to the coffee shop like old times. Pat and Kelly, Devin and me. I had the weirdest feeling that time was running backwards. These lunches, lately a thing of the past, were how we'd started out. The mood was carefree with the usual joking around, and the general topic was work. Pat commented that the last time we had all gone to lunch together, Devin had only been talking about moving in with me, and now he *was* living with me.

"Brazenly," Kelly added impishly. "By the way, when are you two getting married?"

"Yeah, what *is* happening, Dev? You ever talk to a lawyer?"

"Oh, I've got the lawyer's name," Devin answered seriously. "I just need the jing, you know? Lawyers want your right arm nowadays."

"So what," Pat said with a shrug, just as serious as he stood up with the check. "Knowing you, you'd just grow another one."

Thursday evening was another blessed night alone. For once, nobody came by and I'd hoped that, judging by Devin's mood this morning and at lunch today, everything might be more back to normal, but he was unusually quiet and thoughtful all evening, letting the tapes do more talking than he did. Once the kids were settled in bed, I joined him on the couch. He took me in his arms and held me tightly against him.

"Hey, Dev."

"Hey, yourself, lady." He pulled away and took my face in his hands and searched it, as though looking for some sign in my eyes. Finally, he let me go and I looked at him, puzzled.

"What's wrong?"

"Wrong? Nothing. Should there be?"

"You're just so quiet tonight."

He smiled. "I've been watching your friend buzzing around here all night. You know, Blue?"

"He's back?" I looked around but didn't see anything.

"Maybe he never went away. I still don't understand how you can treat it as if he's nothing."

"I don't even know he's there half the time. It just scares me a little…and I don't like that physical contact thing."

"But why? Electricity goes right through you. So do radio waves. They're invisible, but they still touch you. Like Blue."

"I can't feel *them.*"

"I know it's just the human conditioning thing. I won't mention it anymore."

"Devin, are you sure nothing's wrong?"

"Don't you think if there was I'd discuss it with you?"

"I guess. You just seem so quiet. What are you thinking about?"

"Just that I have to leave tonight. Immediately, to be more explicit, however I don't like to leave you sitting here by yourself while I'm gone."

"Leave? Now?"

"Not the house. But I have to do something. I have to go home. It's business, and it can't wait."

"Oh. You mean…oh, yeah. I see."

"You know, I was actually considering…but…I know better."

"Considering what?"

"Taking you with me. Now. But…you'd have to want to go, and you'd have to know you are able to. I can't drag you through."

I nodded. I couldn't argue with that. I assumed he was referring to my going with him *tonight*, for an hour or so. He corrected that misassumption quickly.

"I meant permanently." He watched my face closely as he spoke, and if it was shock he was striving for, he got it.

"Leave *here*? Physical existence? *Now?*" I could feel the nausea that had intermittently swept through me the past couple days churn in me now. Something was *not right*. It hung in the air like a hungry vulture circling us in the room. I swallowed uneasily, determined to choose my words carefully and not blow it this time. "Devin…do you mean…*die?*" I managed to keep my voice steady.

He smiled wryly. "Well, how else would you expect to get out of here permanently?"

"Me…and you?"

"Yes." He seemed to be waiting, or at least curious about my reaction to the idea.

Unfortunately, I didn't absorb things that fast. "Devin, what in God's name brought this on?"

"Well, it was just wishful thinking. Just a thought. You asked me what I've been thinking about tonight. That's what. Sorry. Considering your response, I assume the idea isn't very appealing at the moment."

I found my voice and tried to keep it as calm as possible. "Suicide, you mean."

"I hardly think that would be necessary. It needn't be that dramatic."

"But *what*, all of a sudden, *what* brought all this on? First it's our son…we need to wait on that for a while, according to Devin, and now you want to leave. Something had to have initiated this. I could *see* you've been in some heavy thought, but I never *dreamed* it was as drastic as this." My hands were shaking. I tried twice to light a match to my cigarette. He took out his Zippo, lit it for me, and continued, obviously weighing his words carefully.

"What's the matter? All this talking of death scare you?"

I exhaled slowly. "No. I'd just like to know what brought this on."

The weird thing was that I wasn't afraid at all. It just sounded too science fiction to take seriously. It was one thing to accept the fact that he wasn't always Devin, and that I didn't have to voice my thoughts for him to know what I was thinking. It was quite another to sit here and discuss dying the way other people discussed where they were going to take their next vacation.

"I don't know, lady. Or maybe I do. This place…it just isn't what it's cracked up to be."

"And by this place…you mean…living?"

"Physical existence, yes. This world," he said, not sounding like Devin at all.

"So…you've been thinking seriously about going back…back there…where you come from."

"Where *we* come from." He pulled me closer to him. "So serious, lady. It was just an abstract thought. That's all. I didn't mean to cause that frown."

"But what about the kids? What would happen to the kids?"

"I've considered the kids," he said quietly. "I thought maybe Pam…but let's not talk about this anymore. I can see the whole idea is upsetting you."

"Devin, I still don't even know how to go…there."

"I know, and I wish you did. Why don't you set aside that Witches' Bible and read the only book I *did* suggest." He pointed to *Journeys out of the Body*, still sitting on top of the shelf where I'd left it.

"Why? What's so important in that book that would help me learn to go? You said yourself that what you're talking about isn't the astral plane, and I think that's what that book is all about. But then again, I guess getting out of the body is probably the only way I *can* leave here, isn't it?"

"Well, you can't take your body with you." Devin smiled and added, "As much as I'd like to."

I had to smile too, in spite of the way this insane conversation was going.

"Look," he said finally. "You asked what I was thinking about, and I told you. I didn't mean to jolt you, lady. You know how impulsive I can be. My impulsiveness is what got me here in the first place. It was just wishful thinking on my part that you might be a little tired of the human bullshit after twenty-five years. Forget I even mentioned it. However, I *do* have a few things to straighten out, and they can't wait till the full moon. I really *do* have to go *now*."

"You will be back, though?"

"Yes. I will be back."

"Want me to go in the back bedroom and wait for you? You can be alone here with your tapes."

"No. You stay here. I'll go back there."

"So you're leaving me alone out here with Blue," I said, trying to lighten the mood.

"He's your friend, not mine," Devin retorted, already on his way down the hall. "Catch up on your reading."

I went to the bookshelf. Sitting up on the shelf, out of the bookcase, was another book lying alongside *Journeys*. I had not removed that one for later perusing. I felt that sinking feeling in my stomach again. Something wasn't right, and I couldn't put my finger on it. I picked up that book. *Mastering Witchcraft*. Paul Huson's book. The one that contained the witches runes I'd felt so compelled to learn.

I began thumbing through it, wondering what was in it that had caused Devin to pull it out. There was a segment about a legend that told of giants, watchers of the earth…even implied that they were the actual *creators* of the earth. I'd never heard of them before, but the descriptions of them reminded me too much of the shadowy forms that hung over that hole I'd recently acquired in my mind.

Hole in my head, I thought, snapping the book shut. As much as I loved Devin and wanted to believe him, a very large part of me wasn't buying this story. It was just too farfetched.

I tucked the book back into the shelf and picked up *Journeys*. It looked like very interesting reading, in plain terms and with simple explanations, but I noticed that as I scanned further into the chapters that there were some descriptions of what sounded like bad trips in these out-of-body excursions. I was surprised that Devin would recommend a book that would put fear into my head if he really wanted me to learn to go.

When I looked up at the clock I saw that an hour had gone by, so I went back to see if Devin had…returned.

I found him awake, lounging back against pillows that were propped up against the wall.

"Hi. Okay to come in?"

"Might as well. Everybody else is." He jerked a thumb toward the wall behind him. "Damn corner. I think that's where he comes in and goes out."

"Who, Blue?" Regardless of my skepticism about where Devin was from, I couldn't discount the reality of Blue, whatever he was. I looked up to where he was pointing. The southeast corner of our room.

Our bed tucked neatly into that corner, and up near the ceiling hovered that purplish mass of energy, never before so clear and bright. Surprisingly, I felt no fear, but it was probably Devin's presence that afforded my ego such bravery. Devin didn't seem to rank him very high and looked upon him as little more than a friendly pest. He certainly didn't act like Blue was anything to be afraid of.

"How long has he been in here?" I asked, sitting on the bed.

"Oh, about as long as I have. He was here when I left and still here when I returned. I'm really beginning to wonder about old Blue. I wonder if he isn't just an extension of myself. I know that sounds egotistical, but I really do wonder. In any event, he comes and goes, and that's his door."

Once again, a memory flickered in my mind when Devin mentioned the possibility of Blue being somehow connected to himself. The memory wasn't hazy or vague. It was crystal clear, as if it had just happened yesterday. It was the memory of that bluish-purple fog that had hovered over my windshield back in June. It was time for me to face up to the fact that Blue was not really a sudden guest in our house these past few weeks. And it was time to tell Devin what I was finally realizing.

"Devin, I think there's something you should know. Something I should have told you a long time ago."

He looked at me expectantly.

"You know how you keep saying that Blue can't just be a new thing to me? That he had to have been around before this? Well, please let me just tell you the whole story before you venture an opinion, okay?"

He looked interested. "Okay."

I told him everything I could remember about the night I'd sat down with the book my mother had sent me, everything I could remember about that crazy world that I'd tripped into every time I'd closed my eyes, and I gave him a detailed account of the car incident that had occurred on my way to Uncle

Joe's house the following day.

Devin kept his word. He did not interrupt me and waited until I was finished.

When I stopped talking he rubbed his chin with his fingers and thumb as if musing about what he was about to say. Finally he spoke.

"Kerry, what you've just told me coincides with a story of my own. You know how I've repeatedly told you that to describe home to you would be to program your visit, tailor it to any descriptions I gave you so that the experience wouldn't be your own if you ever consciously made it through? Well, you've told me enough that I can tell you a few things myself. That big white mansion you described just now…the wide porch and sweeping lawn? That's *my* house. That yellow sky you described both now and when you had that strange dream about the marina…that's our sky. Oh, it's not always yellow, any more than *this* sky is always blue, but yes, I know that sky. I know it well. The man you were approaching on the porch with the flaming hair and luminous eyes? That must have been me, though I don't remember seeing you.

"Now we come to your blue cloud. You say this was back in June. I arrived here, not all at once in one thud, but gradually. I had to ease in and out a little at a time. For Devin's sake as much as mine. He had to acclimate to me, and I had to acclimate to this world. I had to wait four moon cycles for a month with two full moons, and as we both know, October had one on the first and one on the thirty-first…Halloween. What they call a *blue* moon, ironically. But from the moment I was granted my request to come, I was around you constantly, watching you, feeling you out, looking for ways to bring you and Devin together. Trying to figure out what would get you to notice him. I *was* around that morning you drove to your uncle's house, but I didn't realize I was visible…or in that form."

"Devin, Blue puts off…it's… the same color as the aura you put off when you're here. I don't understand how it could be any part of you if it's here now and so are you."

"Is it possible I can project a part of myself and still be whole, here in Devin's body?"

"You're asking *me?*" I was as perplexed as he seemed to be.

"It's something to think about," he said. "Blue could be something akin to a psychic shadow of mine."

"I guess it's possible." I looked up at the corner again but Blue was gone. "Well, whatever he is, I hope he doesn't mind me curling up with you now." I sighed.

"Tired, huh?" He moved over to the edge and twisted the light switch, dimming the room. "Me too, and we have quite a day ahead of us tomorrow."

"And night," I added. "We're still going to Thompson's Station, aren't we?"

"Yes. It should be a nice night together. The bike's running good, and it's really not even that cold out."

"Pam said she'd watch the kids."

"That's good." He pulled me closer to him and was asleep almost instantly, his heart beating against my ear, normally at first, then slower and slower until it seemed there were long lapses between the thumps. I lay there in the darkness for a long time, listening for the automatic shutoff of the reel-to-reel.

It was the first night Devin had ever fallen asleep without making love.

I untangled myself from his arms, sat up, and looked down at his sleeping body. Poor Devin. Even in his sleep…especially in his sleep…he looked worried. Even though he seemed to have relaxed a little after I'd told him about those two incidents in June, the new knowledge hadn't erased that crease in his brow.

I thought about the route and its possible physical effects on him. He had to be exhausted, and for that reason alone, I decided to let him sleep. His sleep was more important than missing one night of lovemaking, so I kissed him gently on the cheek and lay back down beside him. I wished I knew the reason for that worried frown that seemed to have arrived the past couple of days and now seemed to be permanently settled in his face, even in his sleep.

Out in the living room, the tape rolled on. Bob Dylan telling someone that he must leave now, to take what was needed or what he wanted to keep, grab those things fast because those saints were coming through, and it was now all over. He addressed the person as Baby Blue. He mentioned that a painter was drawing crazy patterns on our sheets and that the sky was folding under us.

And it was all over now, Baby Blue.

2 Driving to work the next morning, I discovered that I still had a lot of the old Christmas spirit in me. It was hard not to get caught up in the feeling. Everywhere I looked was decorated for Christmas. Stores, gas stations, homes and shopping centers. The lights and the Santa figures with reindeer and sleigh were great, but along with those were the dead trees…everywhere. Before Devin, I had never realized what a massive waste it was.

Even the coffee shop had a decorated tree, I saw, as I took my usual booth near the window where I could see the streets. It was only 7:00.

Once situated with my coffee, I pulled out the *Journeys* book. I'd grabbed it on the way out the door. Something instinctively told me that Devin wouldn't push a book for no reason, any more than he did his music.

I was so engrossed in it that I didn't hear or see the company truck pull up across the boulevard, nor did I notice Devin approaching until he had almost reached this side of it. I don't even know what made me look up. There had been nothing to alert me except a kind of mental alarm.

There was something disturbingly heavy about his walk. We'd crossed those four lanes together a few times, making a game of skirting the traffic, but today his walk was slow. He almost seemed to be daring the cars to hit him.

I closed up the book as he came in and signaled to Jane for another coffee.

"Hey. Whatcha reading?" He kissed me and sat down across from me. "Oh, decided to get into it, huh?"

I nodded. "I can kind of understand why you'd suggest I read this one now that I've had a chance to go through it a little, but I saw that you'd pulled out the *Mastering Witchcraft* book too, and as far as I can tell, it's pretty much like all the other dumb black magic books out on the market."

"Yeah, but it has a pretty good chapter on psychic self-defense. Better than most."

Before I had a chance to question him on that confusing reply, Jane interrupted to take Devin's breakfast order, and after she left, he gestured for me to hand him the Huson Book. How he knew I had it with me I don't know, but I extracted it from my purse and gave it to him.

He thumbed through it until he found what he was looking for. "See? Here. And the next chapter too."

He pushed the book toward me and began to doctor his coffee, stirring disinterestedly as though his mind was anywhere but the coffee shop.

I closed both books and marked Devin's chapter with the cover of a match pack. "Are you feeling okay?"

He smiled. "Why? Do I look sick? Already? Damn. And I haven't even *seen* my paycheck yet."

"Oh, that's right. This *is* payday."

"Hey-hey-hey." That without his usual enthusiasm.

"Route today, huh?"

"Yep. Won't be out long, though."

Breakfast arrived and Devin ate hurriedly, then picked up the check and rose. "I guess I'll see you later." He squeezed my hand and left for the cash register. I watched him cross the boulevard at the same pace he had approached. I had no idea how to reach him, how to find an answer to what seemed to weigh so heavily on his mind, but asking him was getting me nowhere, and probably getting on his nerves.

I was still thinking about Devin as I finished up my day's posting at 4:00 when he buzzed me on local. He'd just received his paycheck and was on his way into our office. There was no describing his tone of voice.

I warned Kelly not to harass Devin today and told her he wasn't in the best of moods because of his check. She was too appalled to even joke about it when he finally came in.

"Where's Mama?"

"In the conference room," Kelly replied. "Devin, come in here a minute."

"Forget it, Kelly. I'm in no mood."

"Come on. So Maurice won't see you."

"Yeah? Fuck Maurice, too."

I saw the startled look cross Hannah's face, and she let her machine coast to a stop. "Such language, Devin. I think you need a vacation."

"So you got a shitty paycheck," Kelly said. "After everything you've done for them."

He shrugged. "Hey, it's a small route, you know? I knew that when I accepted it, so what the hell?"

"How bad was it?"

He laughed bitterly. "I'll give you a hint. Kerry made more than I did this week."

I gaped at him. "You're kidding."

"Am I?" He reached into his pocket and handed it to me. "Expensive joke, wouldn't you say?"

I looked at it and handed it back mutely. He wasn't exaggerating.

"Devin, you ought to quit," Kelly said hotly. "They have a lot of balls. Now that you've got two kids to support—"

"Kelly, this place doesn't care about that," Hannah put in sympathetically. "Gee, Devin…"

He repocketed the check. "If I save this one and add my next one to it, I might have enough to get gas to make it to the unemployment office."

"If that was *my* check, Devin, I wouldn't even wait around for the second one."

"Well, the place *is* getting worse. There are other jobs out there, but it's such a hassle to change. Especially when it's just a matter of building up a route. It's only money, you know?"

"I know you better than that," Kelly said, shaking her head. "If it's only money then how come you're so damn depressed? I've never seen you so down before."

"It's not the check," Devin said. "It's the human bullshit. I'm tired of it, that's all. *Real* tired of it. And I'm sick of the shit I have to pass on the route all day."

"What shit?"

"For example, have you driven down the main drag? Over by that massive parking lot? It's nothing but warehouses and warehouses of dead pine trees. There must be a million of them."

"Oh, I know the one you mean," Hannah said. "They're advertising that they have the largest selection of Christmas trees in the *world.*"

"That's the one. Talk about a *total* waste of life."

"Devin," I began, hoping to nip this subject in the bud before it went too far, but he continued anyway.

"Take a little ride down there," he told Kelly. "But then again, it probably wouldn't bother *you* anyway. What the hell, it's just a few dead trees, right? Kerry, I'm heading home. I'll get the kids."

He blew me a kiss and left.

When he was gone, Kelly turned to me with a frown. "He's *that* upset about the *trees* ?"

"You've got me, Kelly. He's been like this for a couple of days. I don't really know what's wrong. When I ask, he says nothing."

"And you're not fighting."

"No." I resented the insinuation. "We don't fight."

"Yeah, I didn't think so. Well, I guess the relationship you two have is worth a lousy paycheck. At least you have each other. Money just shouldn't make that big of a difference."

"He says it isn't the money, and I believe him. He was like this *before* he saw his check. Besides, we don't need the money."

Kelly sniffed. "Well, I just don't see how it could all be over the dead trees. On the other hand, though, we *are* talking about Devin, and with him, anything's possible. But I'm just not used to seeing him like this. He's usually so happy and carefree."

I covered my machine and picked up my purse. "If I find out anything, I'll let you know. I'm going to take off now, okay?"

"Sure, go ahead. We'll put the trays away. Maybe you can get home about the same time he does and find out what's really bothering him."

As I pulled away from the curb that afternoon, Kelly's last words echoed in my ear. *What's really bothering him.*

When I turned the radio on I was shocked to hear the exact same song I had last heard on the tape last night as I fell asleep. Bob Dylan again, continuing his warning.

It was still all over for Baby Blue. Seasick sailors were rowing home, and empty-handed armies were going home. My lover had just walked out the door taking all his blankets from my floor.

The next lines seemed to be for Devin himself. Dylan told him something was calling for him and reminded him that the one knocking at his door was standing in the clothes he used to wear. Go start anew, Dylan advised.

'Cause it was all over for Baby Blue now.

I turned the radio off. I didn't need this right now. Tonight we were going camping, and maybe we would have a chance to really talk.

3 Devin was out in the yard making some adjustments to the bike when I drove up.

I could hear the reel-to-reel running even before I shut the engine off. He looked up and waved, and I saw instantly that whatever had been bothering him still was. He didn't smile at all. He was still in his work clothes.

"Hey, your sister's feeding the kids right now," he said when I was within earshot. "Why don't you go grab something too. We'll be leaving in about an hour." There was no enthusiasm in his voice. I wondered if he were out of the mood to go but felt some obligation to go through with the promised camping trip for my sake. I dismissed that idea quickly. Devin had been looking forward to this night for too long.

I knelt down to kiss him hello. "How's it going?"

He shrugged. "This day seems to be working against me. Now the bike's acting up. I mean, it was. It's a good thing I decided to check it before takeoff." He stood up and gave me a hoist so that we were both standing. "Come on, lady. Let's go inside."

Pam and George looked up from the couch when we entered. I saw that they were both working on hand-painted Christmas cards, and I could also see, by the looks they exchanged, that they too were puzzled by Devin's mood. Pam waited until he was in the shower, though, to mention it.

"Hey! You'ns have a bad day or something?"

"Who, both of us?"

"Well, neither of you'ns look too happy, but Devin's blowing my mind. He's been out working on that bike since he got home, and he's hardly said a word to either of us. Are you guys still going?"

"I think so. I hope so. I think we *both* need to get the hell out of here. Things aren't so hot at work, and he got a bad check today, but he's been like this since before that check."

"Well, he did mention the check, but he kind of laughed about that. Matter of fact, that's the *only* time he laughed. I don't think that's the problem, Ker. You know him. Money don't mean shit to him. Whatever it is, I doubt it has anything to do with money."

"Did he say *anything* to indicate what *is* wrong?"

"Well, a lot of sarcastic remarks about Christmas and stuff. Kind of joking. Not at anyone in particular. He might have just been thinking out loud."

"Anything else?"

"Just regular stuff. You know, he came in, put the tape recorder on, kind of nodded to me, that's when he mentioned the check, and then he said the tree was thirsty and he watered that. Come to think of it, he said more to the tree than he did to me or George."

I could feel tears stinging my eyes as she talked. I knew it wasn't because of the trees or the money. It had something to do with why he'd decided to postpone the child, and why he had to *go* the other night to take care of business. But that was about all I knew.

"Hey, I wouldn't worry about it, Ker. He'll be okay once you'ns get away from here."

"I hope you're right."

I couldn't ask him anymore. Every time I did he just squeezed my hand, shook his head, and reiterated that I'd done nothing wrong and to please stop asking.

When I came out of the shower Pam told me that Devin was waiting outside for me on the bike. I ran a brush through my hair quickly, feeling myself slip into the same mood he was in, and tried to shake it off. We didn't need two of us like this.

"Okay, well the kids are watching TV, so I guess we'll get going." I sat down on the bed and tossed the brush aside. "I don't even *feel* like going anymore."

"Hey, just *go*, Ker. Forget everything and just go. It'll work itself out over the course of the night."

"Yeah. Thanks, Pam."

Devin was sitting out on the bike, head bent over the handlebars in his crossed arms. He looked up when the door slammed behind me and watched me until I reached the bike.

"Ready?"

"Yeah. Devin, are you sure you even feel up to this?"

"Sure." He didn't sound sure. He started the engine, making any further conversation impossible. I climbed up on the back, and he turned the bike around, glancing briefly up and down the street before heading out on the road. We hadn't gone two blocks when he pulled over to the side of the road and turned the bike back in the direction of the house.

"What's the matter?" I yelled over the noise.

"Helmets," he yelled back. "We forgot them. And I think we're going to need goggles too. This wind will sting your eyes. It's a long damn ride on a bike."

Pam looked up in surprise when I walked in.

"That was fast."

"We forgot helmets. And I'm supposed to get goggles too. Can you believe this? Maybe we *weren't* meant to go."

"Oh, don't start thinking like that," she warned. "And don't change your mind. Let *him* call it off, if it's gonna get called off."

I had just boarded the bike again when Devin glanced down at my sandals and sighed. "Do you have any other shoes? Those aren't the best thing to wear on a bike."

"These are the only shoes I have."

"Well, think you could fit into a pair of my boots? They'll be big, but if they'll stay on your feet, at least till we get down there...shit...the mud will eat those suckers alive."

"I could wear a couple of heavy socks. We got time?"

"Sure."

Once again, I returned to the house, the hour getting later and later. When we finally did get started again, Devin asked *me* if *I* was sure I wanted to go. I guess he was picking up on my frustration.

"Devin," I said wearily. "I just want to be with you. It doesn't matter if it's Thompson's Station, here or Mars. If *you* want to go, let's go. If not, well, that's okay, too."

He shut the engine off. "Come on. Hop down. You can get a bad burn if your leg hits those exhaust pipes." He got off the bike and held out a hand to me. I accepted it and hopped to the ground.

"It seems like *something* doesn't think we should go," he observed aloud. "Doesn't it?"

"It sure does."

He wrapped his arms around me and rested his chin on the top of my head. "We didn't make it last Friday either. I'll be damned if I'm going to try to plan it for next week."

"Maybe we should wait until after the holidays. You didn't seem like you were really into it anyway."

"Well, perhaps I did unconsciously create all these obstacles, although I don't know why I'd do that. I was really looking forward to this."

"Well, we know everything happens for a reason, right? So let's just go back in."

"You go ahead. Explain to Pam, and tell her she's free to go if she wants to." He loosened his hold on me. "I'm going to wind this thing out on the Interstate, and then I'll be back. I just want to make sure it's working all right. The mechanical problems might have been the *first* sign, but I adjusted all that. Need anything while I'm out?"

I shook my head and he nodded, mounted the bike, turned the key and zoomed away.

Fifteen minutes later I heard the back door open. I looked up to see the front end of the cycle rolling in followed by Devin, then Trevor. I hadn't heard either bike or car pull up.

"Hey, catch that front door will you, lady?" Devin called to me. "Mia and the kids are coming in. Damn, we'd better close a few of these windows. It's really getting cold out there."

"I'll get 'em. How was the bike running?" I opened the door to let Trevor's family in and began shutting the windows. It *was* cold out there. Probably wasn't the best weather for camping anyway.

"Lady, this is going to blow your mind. I made it two blocks again, to the *same spot* we stopped on the first delay, and the brakes locked up on me. The brake line had broken and all the fluid had drained out. If it weren't for those delays…if we hadn't gone back, we'd probably have been on the Interstate doing sixty when the last of the fluid leaked out. We'd be *gone*…out of here…like dead, you know? Remind me never to question the reasons why things happen."

"Yeah, really, bro," Trevor appeared in the archway between the kitchen and the back den. "That was a pretty close call. You two were going to Thompson's tonight, huh? I thought that was last week."

Mia set her purse down and pulled out her cigarette pack. Devin tossed her a rolled joint.

"Don't smoke that. Smoke this. Anyone want coffee?"

"Oh, I'd love some," Mia said. "It's freezing out."

"Me too," I said, getting up. "Anyone else?"

"Make it four, one black for Trevor," Devin said, walking over to the reel-to-reel. "Well, home sweet home. We couldn't take the reels to the station anyway."

I was thinking about the conversation Devin had initiated about leaving here for good while I put the coffee together. It seemed pretty coincidental that this close call tonight could have been the end of physical existence for both of us, and so soon after he'd mentioned it to me. It was a disturbing thought.

Devin took a seat in his gold leather chair, and I brought his coffee to him. He took it without speaking as the music was pretty loud, but appreciation was evident in his eyes. I pulled the beanbag over so that I could sit beside him, but he was off in his own little world again. For all I knew, maybe literally, staring into nothingness, seemingly oblivious to my presence beside him. I felt a little embarrassed, so I finally got up and went over to the bookshelf where we kept the writing tablets. At least I could *look* busy until Devin came around again.

I hadn't written anything in a long time. Trevor and Mia politely ignored the fact that something didn't seem normal and sipped their coffee, talking to each other. Their kids had taken off to play with Michelle and Mandy, and Devin continued to stare off into space. I brought the tablet back to the beanbag and picked up a pen.

To keep my hands busy I began to write out words in the Theban runes. First, I tried Devin to see if I remembered the alphabet, and then Erick. At that moment, I felt his eyes on me, so under those two names I printed in the runes: *I love you.* Then I handed the tablet to him.

His eyes decoded the print, and then he glanced over at me, motioning for the pen. When he returned the tablet, his reply was boldly printed in Christian's own unique print.

Why the fuck leave him out?

He'd underlined *him* so heavily that the paper had partially ripped from the pen's gouging.

As I read his words, I felt that ominous sinking feeling go through me again. I looked up to find Christian boring a hole through me. Christian, someone I hadn't seen in days. I looked down at the tablet, then back at him again, hurt. I hadn't deliberately selected names, so in the same harsh print he'd used, I wrote in English under his words:

I was just practicing the runes. First Devin's name, then Erick's. And then I felt you watching me, so I added the other line. I have never left you out! *I'm sorry you took it the wrong way.*

My feelings were really hurt now. Sure, he had things on his mind, but it wasn't like him to take it out on me or anybody. Then to make things worse, he took the tablet and swiftly penned: *fuck being sorry*.

He then tossed the pen to me and turned to Trevor. "Kill that recorder, will you? Put the radio on."

Tears were welling in my eyes, but rather than let anyone see how humiliated I felt, I got up to make another round of coffee. The radio, as usual, was tuned to the acid-rock station, and it blared out with a song already in progress. That in itself was unusual for us since most of the time the songs weirdly started from the beginning when the radio was put on. As I put the cups together, I noticed that the lyrics were right on target.

It was the Moody Blues, singing about looking out a window watching the world passing by, about having one more time to live, and advising to leave the wise to write, for the one who wanted to fight began the end of time.

I guessed this was kind of our first fight.

Nobody spoke while the song played out, but Trevor and Devin exchanged a lot of looks. I felt completely left out.

The song switched direction from the harmonious melody to a series of words all ending in *T-I-O-N*. Desolation first, then word after word including degradation and humiliation (the way I was feeling) while background voices begged for someone to tell them why all the confusion was happening, praying that it was only an illusion and then as the words continued in the foreground, more positive now, *contemplation, inspiration, communication,* and finally rounding out to *compassion,* and, to my relief, *solution.* Throughout these final words, the background chanted the words *changes in my life* over and over.

After I passed out the new round of coffee, I went back to the tablet, encouraged by the song, and tried to explain on paper what was upsetting me. The unspoken problem he would not admit to having and how I felt so helpless because I didn't know what it was. He watched over my shoulder as I wrote out my feelings.

Trevor and Mia watched the transaction without getting involved. The tension in the room was tight, but they didn't ask what was going on. When I was finished, I gave the tablet and pen to Devin and went back to the bedroom where I could think. We had never had a cross word or argument before, and even though this wasn't a fight, it still felt very uncomfortable and I felt ignored and insignificant, as though how I felt didn't matter in his grand scheme of private things.

He followed me in some five minutes later and sat down on the bed beside me.

"Hey, lady." He touched my cheek lightly.

That was all it took. I was in his arms, the tears fighting to be free, and me fighting to stop them.

"Didn't I already tell you that you haven't done anything?"

I nodded against his chest.

"And if I say it one more time, will you take my word for it and believe me? Will you believe that my problem has nothing to do with *you?*"

Gently he pushed me to a sitting position and peered into my eyes. "Go ahead and cry if it makes you feel better. I have things on my mind, decisions that have to be made, things that have to be worked out. They are extremely important, but they have *nothing* to do with you. You haven't done anything but love me. Why would I be mad at you for that? You're the one *good* thing I *do* have going for me right now."

"Then, Devin…does it have anything to do with your wife? Did she write or call or—"

"No. First of all, I'd have *told* you if it was something that simple. I wish it *were* something that trivial."

"Devin, I don't understand, but I love you."

"Don't *try* to understand. You *can't*. But please, take my word for it. You didn't do anything. This isn't your problem. It's mine."

"But the tablet…you *jumped* on me—"

"*Christian* jumped on you. You know how sensitive he is about me."

"I thought he was referring to himself…that I'd left *him* out."

"No, apparently he didn't mind being omitted. He's just defensive about me. It was just a misunderstanding, that's all. Come on. We can't just leave Trevor and Mia sitting out there by themselves."

We both got up and he hugged me again. "Trust me, lady, will you? Please just trust me."

When we returned to the front room, Trevor and Mia were ready to go. Devin walked them out to the car, waved them off, and when he came back in, the chill from the night air clung to him.

"Come on, lady." He stretched a hand out to me. "It's been a hectic day. I don't know about you, but I'm tired."

I could still feel the gloom from that unknown something radiating from him as I followed him to our room. When he reached for me that night it almost seemed to be in desperation, as though he was afraid I might evaporate in his arms. Awake, he clung to me for a long time, his eyes focused on that distant nothing, even in the dim room.

"You awake, Dev?"

"Yeah." He squeezed my shoulder. "You?"

"I guess so." We both laughed at the inanity of both his question and my answer. It felt good to hear him laugh after so sober a last couple of days. It almost seemed like this had been going on for weeks instead of days. I rose up on my elbow and looked at him. He still looked so worried.

"I love you," I whispered.

In response, he pulled me back down next to him and kissed me. "I love you, too." He was silent for a minute, just lay there rubbing my back, lost in his own private thoughts. Finally, he spoke.

"You know…we went to sleep last night…without making love. It was the first time since…us."

"I know. You went to sleep so fast. Almost in the middle of a sentence. I didn't want to wake you up."

"I wish you had. I didn't really want to miss a day of anything while I'm here. I hope that never happens again."

"Well, it was just one day. I thought you needed the sleep more."

He interrupted me with a finger to my lips, then a kiss that told me clearly that it wasn't going to be two days in a row.

There was even a desperation to his lovemaking, as though it *were* the last time. Afterwards I lay awake until dawn, unable to sleep, unable to put my finger on that mysterious *something*. Unable to trace it to any remark, event, or source. Devin had made it clear that it was his own problem, and my ego was a little hurt. He had never shut me out like this and I didn't know what to make of this sudden clamming up.

Asking was useless. It only seemed to aggravate him.

Trust me, he'd said.

It was asking a lot.

Beyond, though, in the living room, the tapes seemed to know.

4 In the morning, Devin seemed almost normal.

He was already up, watering the tree and telling her how beautiful she was. Christmas was only five days away, and she still looked fresh and healthy.

Compared to yesterday he seemed to be downright chipper. I knew *his* problems were not necessarily Devin's, and I should have been used to that by now, but I wasn't. Any problem with any one of them was still a problem between us, and I was relieved to see Devin this morning. Maybe he could shed some light on what was wrong, on what so worried *him* these past couple of days.

The lyrics to the last song that had played last night had been, once again, a warning of some kind. It was the Moody Blues, singing of a gypsy from a distant time, who was travelling in a panic, blind to which direction to go, and had no hope of going home. He was frightened and screaming for a future that would never happen. If I took the music literally, *he* was apparently trying to make a decision as to whether to stay or go home, and if he'd already chosen to go, he was possibly having some problems getting permission to return. Either one was bad news for me, and Devin wouldn't be exactly jumping for joy either.

Which possibly explained why he seemed *almost* normal.

At the moment, Devin's focus was on the tree. He had unplugged her and moved her away from the wall and was now removing the cotton from the base of the trunk.

"Hey, Ker. I'm going to take her outside and give her some sun and fresh air. She's been lacking the direct sun in here, and trees can't just get up and walk out like we do."

His sudden speaking jerked me out of my thoughts. "That's a good idea. Need some help?"

"No, I've got it." He gestured to the kids. "Come on, guys, let's back up and make some room here."

The girls cleared the area where they'd been watching with interest, just as they had when he first decorated the tree and throughout the process of his caring for it. They'd never seen anyone treat a tree like a person, and it intrigued them.

We followed Devin outside.

"It's pretty chilly out here," I observed aloud. "Even with the sun shining."

He nodded, glancing up at the sun. "Yeah, but it's still healthier for her. Too bad we can't just leave her outside."

"Well, it's only a few more days," I said.

"Yeah, I think she'll make it. In fact, I get the feeling that she's actually getting off on this whole thing."

I smiled. "You think she likes being a Christmas tree, huh?"

"I'm serious. Look how her branches are reaching toward the sun. She knows she's a special tree." He motioned for us to follow him back in. "Come on. Let's leave her out here for a few hours anyway."

The kids took off to watch TV, and we whipped up some coffee. I was waiting for an opportune moment to bring up *the subject*, but Devin was plainly in physical reality this morning.

"Do you know what the girls want for Christmas?"

"Yeah. They made lists. It's all Barbie doll stuff. Damn, I can't believe Christmas is almost on top of us."

"Mind if I break the news to Michelle about Santa Claus today? The sooner she knows the truth, the better I'll feel."

"No, go ahead. I take it you want to be the bearer of bad tidings."

"Well, I'm not the one that fibbed to her to begin with. Don't worry. I'll be gentle. While I'm doing that, you and your sister can run over to the mall and pick up the presents."

"When *is* Christmas anyway?"

"Wednesday, but it's better to get this over with tonight. I have to take a run down to Gerald and Faye's. I haven't called or dropped by in I don't know how long. They probably think I've kicked the bucket."

"Well, I have to straighten up the house, so while you're down there I can take care of business here."

"Cool. And when I get back, you'll go with Pammy to get the toys? I'll lay some credit cards on you."

"Sure. I know you hate shopping."

What I was really wondering was why he wasn't asking me if I wanted to go with him. We usually went everywhere together, and Pam was home this morning. Maybe he just wanted to take the bike out. I knew he and Trevor had fixed the brake line last night, and I chastised myself for being so paranoid.

"Far out. I guess the sooner I get going, the sooner I'll be back. Will you remember to bring the tree in later?"

"Sure."

He wheeled the cycle out of the den through the back door and around to the front where he started it up. I thought he was leaving without even a goodbye.

He ducked in at the last minute to kiss me. "Damn, I almost forgot," he said sheepishly. "Later, babe."

It was one of the rare smiles I would receive that weekend. So much for asking Devin anything. Even *he* had a foreboding air about him as he walked out to the idling bike which purred steadily now in the bright sunshine.

Pam awoke two hours later and emerged from the girls' room where she occasionally slept. Apparently, the cartoon noise didn't bother her.

"Morning, Ker. Where's Devin?"

"Went to his dad's."

"Without you? I could have stayed with the kids."

"Yeah, I wasn't invited. I wish I knew what's bothering him. He's trying not to show it, but he barely says much and hardly ever smiles anymore."

"I noticed. I've been picking up on the vibes, too. You still don't have any idea, huh?"

"No. I've run down every reason from the job to money to Christmas and dead trees. Nothing seems to fit."

"Well, try to trace it back. When did it start? When was everything fine?"

I thought a minute, backtracking the days. "Everything seemed fine on Mandy's birthday…no…wait a minute…no, it wasn't. This whole thing seemed to have started when Steve brought that damn scorpion over. That was the first obvious thing that set him off. Then, the next day, at Mickey's birthday party, on the way home…out of the blue…he mentioned that maybe we ought to put off the idea of having his child for a while."

"The *kid?* The son *he* wants? Who, now…*Devin*, or was it *him* that told you that."

"Devin. Definitely Devin. But *Him* and Trevor were huddled together that night talking about something, and then Devin was pretty quiet on the way home, but I assumed it was because of the dog."

"What about the dog? Titan, you mean?"

"Yeah. Oh, that's right. You don't know about Titan…or for that matter, about Lucifer and Thor."

"Okay, you lost me." Pam sighed. "If you expect me to keep up with your soap operas, you'll have to keep me up to date on the serials. What *about* the dogs?"

Briefly, I ran down an account of Titan's behavior whenever *he* was present that night and of previous tangles while we'd kept the dog. *And* of Luke's mistrust of *him* and *that* dog's attacks whenever *he* was present. Even Thor, his father's dog, seemed to react to *his* presence in a similar fashion.

"Wow," Pam breathed. "I haven't been around for that stuff, but it doesn't really surprise me what with *him* being *him*. I doubt that his problem has anything to do with dogs, though."

"I don't think so either. I'm just trying to pinpoint when things started changing."

"Why don't you just *ask* him? Wouldn't that be simpler than all this speculating?"

"I *have*, Pam. I've asked him fifty times."

She interrupted with a laugh she tried to suppress. "I'm sorry, Ker. I know it isn't funny, but if you've asked him that many times it's no wonder he's getting aggravated."

"He doesn't say that nothing's wrong. He admits something is, but he won't tell me anything other than that it has nothing to do with me."

"Well, if he told you it isn't you, I'd take his word for it and lay off. You know, that sounds to me like a polite *none of your business.*"

"He's practically *said* that. He says it's his problem, he can't discuss it and to trust him."

"Well, I can sympathize with what you must feel like, Kerry, but I'd lay off. Don't push it. When he's ready, he'll tell you. If not, there's nothing you can do."

"The tension's just so unbearable. He stares off into empty space, whether we're alone or with company. At least, I assume it's empty. According to *him,* it isn't. Half the time he's not even mentally in the same room with me."

"Well, try to keep it cool. He isn't your ordinary human, so maybe his problems aren't so ordinary either. I'd leave him alone."

I sometimes wonder if I'd heeded my younger sister's advice that this story might not have had a different ending.

When Devin walked in at three, he barely acknowledged my greeting.

"Want to unlock the back door so I can bring the bike in?"

"Okay." With a glance at Pam, I got up and helped him coast the cycle into the den.

He caught sight of Pam and smiled. "How do you like sleeping with a motorcycle?" he asked her.

"It's different, I'll say that much." She returned his smile.

"Well, it may not be in there too much longer. I've been thinking about how much Trevor loves it." He glanced at me. "I'm thinking about giving it to him. I mean, it's almost paid off. Just a few payments left, and he can keep what I've already paid into it. He's asked to buy it more than once."

"But Devin! You *love* that bike."

"Yeah, but it's just another material hassle. I've got you and the kids now. I don't need a motorcycle anymore. For that matter, we don't need the van payments either. I can find a cheap car to run around in."

"But why? We can afford both of them."

"Yeah?" He looked up at me. "If yesterday was a sample of my future paychecks, we'd be better off unloading the bulk of money that's going out."

Briefly, I wondered if this was a sign that he'd decided to stay, but my hope was short-lived.

"It's a little cool for the bike now anyway." He hit the switch cranking up the reel-to-reel. "Cold, actually. Just like home." That last added more like an afterthought to himself.

"Devin, you're not getting homesick for Salem, are you?" Pam asked.

"No," he said, a piercing glance my way. He knew that I knew what he meant by home.

The music kicked in making any further conversation difficult. He glanced at the tree. I'd brought it in just minutes before Pam had arisen. Its Christmas simplicity and beauty mocked me on this cold Saturday. Though it was bare of the yuletide junk and presents below, it was gorgeously alive.

Devin looked over at the ball balanced on Puff's frisky feet and then sat down in an Indian-sitting position. Without another word, he was gone. A mere statue in front of the stereo.

Pam nodded in the direction of his back. "It's serious, huh?"

That nauseous feeling swept through me at her words. "It sure looks that way."

We left at six that evening, laden with charge cards. I'd tried to refuse them, but Devin's logic was indisputable, as usual.

"Look, we need the cash for the rent. Just use these and have fun," he'd said.

"How much are we supposed to spend?" Pam asked as we pulled into the mall parking lot.

"I don't know that either," I replied. "I asked him, but he just gave me one of those looks and said '*Whatever you need*.'"

"Oh, great. So we don't even know if there's a limit on them?"

"Well, I have the kids' lists and he looked at them. He said to get it all, so…here goes nothing."

Nothing turned out to be three separate columns of charges amounting to a hundred and thirty dollars.

"Hope we didn't spend too much," Pam said.

"He didn't seem to care about the cost. He's miserable, Pam. You know, Erick disappears when there's human bullshit going on, and if that isn't what this is, I don't know what would be. And I can't remember the last time I saw Erick."

"Kerry, it's human bullshit on *your* part, if you don't mind my saying so," Pam said. "He has a right to a private problem. You're the one going bugshit."

"I know. It's just really getting to me. Not the problem, but the way he's putting this distance between us."

"Well, remember what I told you before. Don't push him."

George was sitting there with Devin when we walked in. He must have dropped in looking for Pam and just stayed. We'd left all the packages in the trunk in case the kids were still up.

"Where are they?" I asked.

Devin exaggeratedly looked beyond Pam and me with a grin. "Never mind them. Where's the loot?"

"In the car. I'm afraid to tell you what it came to."

George and Devin exchanged amused glances.

"George, here," Devin said, "was just telling me what a big mistake I made sending two women out with charge cards."

"Well, it's too late now. You're going to have to guess the amount. I don't have the guts to tell you."

"Come on! *How much?*" George prompted, his surety that he'd been right showing in his smug grin. "A thousand dollars. That's my guess."

"Hundred and forty," Devin obliged with his own guess.

"Hundred thirty," I said.

"Okay, cool. The kids are in their room but I doubt they're sleeping. I'll help you unload the car. Come on."

For a while, it almost seemed like Devin was okay. He joked with George and teased the kids, telling them he knew where the toys were hidden and what they were. After they went to bed, he even went through the toys with a little genuine interest.

"Damn, look at all this stuff!" he said. "All the shit that Santa hauls around…oh, Kerry, I did talk to Michelle tonight about Santa Claus."

"Oh, you did?" I felt a mother's pang. "How did she take it?"

"Pretty good. She listened anyway. And Mandy helped by admitting that she's known for a while herself."

"Okay, good. I'm glad that's over with. And thanks for the charge cards, Devin."

"That's cool. I'm glad we could get them everything they wanted."

Pam and George went off into the den, and Devin went back to his dream world. I tried to engage him in conversation, but he only answered absently and continued to sit in his gold chair, lost in thought.

Completely disoriented, I wandered outside where the cold air was actually a refreshing relief from the hot house and hopscotch moods of Devin's.

The car sat silent and vacant in the driveway. I wandered over to it and hopped up on the hood, using the windshield as a backrest…actually loving my car tonight and the personal peace it afforded. Devin wasn't the only one who needed to think. Even if he did occasionally break into a kidding mood, that unknown something was still smoldering just beneath the surface. My nerves were beginning to go. I watched the burning red sun disappear into the horizon and lit a cigarette.

"This a private party?"

I looked up, surprised that Devin had bothered to come looking for me. I hadn't heard him approach. "No. Just sitting out here," I said, moving over. "Watching the sun set. Want to join me?"

"Might as well. It's a little warm in the house. I opened some windows." He eased himself up beside me, and I went back to my own reflective thinking, although now conscious of Devin's unhappy presence. His mood hadn't changed. I could feel it.

"I love you," I said, for all it was worth to him.

"Hey, I love you too, you know? What's wrong with you tonight? You should be happy. You got the kids all their toys and—"

"What's wrong with *me* ?" The words were out before I could stop them. "What's wrong with *you*, Devin?"

He didn't reply for a minute. As though I'd slapped him. Finally, he said, "Ain't nothing wrong, babe. Except the perspective you may be looking at things from." He lit a cigarette and fell silent again.

"Where are the kids?" I could hear the TV running in their bedroom from where the car was parked.

"They're asleep." There was another lengthy silence before he sighed, slid down from the hood and looked at me. "You coming in?"

"In a minute."

I remained outside for a few minutes longer, trying to pull myself out of the mood I was in. We didn't need a stalemate.

We spent the remainder of the evening in solitude, listening to the tapes. I didn't need them tonight with the way the lyrics had turned. I was depressed enough as it was, but the messages were relentless.

I tried one more time before we went to bed, and his answer indicated his weariness of the same tired question.

"I've already answered this, Kerry. Now, the last thing we need right now is to be at each other's throats. Right?"

"But everything has changed. Nothing is right anymore."

He rolled over and reached for me, crushing me against him. "I told you before, you're the only bright spot in the middle of all this. Please...let's not ruin that."

"Well, will you at least answer me this? You say it has nothing to do with me, and I can't believe that. You'd either talk to me about this or at least not ignore me like you've been doing. I think it *does* have something to do with me."

He sighed. "Yes, it does," he said finally. "What *else* could cause me such concern? But it's nothing you did, and you can't get involved. It's between me and..." His voice trailed away, and then he kissed me, long and hard and almost desperately. There was no way he was going to finish that sentence so I just let it go, let my grief and worry get buried in his passion. Afraid to question him further.

And, as usual, drifting in from the living room came those telltale lyrics from Devin's ten tapes.

The final song, before the machine shut itself off, was the worst. It was a song from Badfinger. He was going away...packing his bags...going home. It was over. He thanked the world but said it was just too much to stay. It was done now, and he was going home. He now felt fused...like he was one...and for that he thanked me.

It was over, and for that he thanked me.

5 When I awoke, I was alone.

  Puzzled, I searched the house, but there was no sign of him. The motorcycle was still in the den but the van was gone. There was no note explaining his absence.

Under normal circumstances, I would have just assumed he was at the store. But coffee hadn't been made, and the way things had been going I was pretty sure he'd taken off somewhere. This was Sunday. Where would he go on a Sunday?

I started some coffee and waited. Pam was still asleep although the way the kids were carrying on in there I didn't see how she could sleep through it. She didn't, for long.

"Good morning."

I was sitting on the couch, lost in dark thoughts and a heavy heart. "Oh, hi Pam."

I could see Pam's gaze sweeping the empty room.

"Don't ask," I said. "I couldn't tell you."

"On a Sunday? Are you sure you'ns aren't fighting?"

"I'm starting to wonder myself. Want some coffee?"

"Yeah, but I'll get it. Man, he just left? No note or nothing?"

"No note."

It was getting harder and harder to take Pam's advice to act like nothing was wrong and keep my mouth shut. Things seemed to be getting worse every day.

Devin still hadn't returned by lunchtime, nor had he called, but the laundry and grocery shopping had to be done so we herded the kids into the car and left. I did leave a note in case he returned, but when we came back, it was still there on the coffee table, untouched. Silently we put the groceries away. A dark cloud hung over the house.

When the phone rang I flew to it, sure it had to be Devin.

"Hello?"

"Hello, Kerry?" A soft female voice. "How are you?"

"Oh…Faye! Hi." I wondered if she could hear the disappointment in my voice.

"Am I interrupting anything?"

"Oh, no. We just came in from shopping."

"Is Devin around?"

"I was hoping he was down there. I guess not, huh?"

"No, he's not here. Did he say he was coming? He was just here yesterday."

"I know, but he was gone when I woke up, and I couldn't think of anywhere else he might go on a Sunday." I tried to sound light, as though it wasn't really a big deal.

"Gee, I wish I could help. Want me to ask Gerald?"

"No…I'm sure he'll be back soon. Probably went to Trevor's or Daniel's. Neither of them have phones so it's always a shot in the dark. Hey, Faye, how did Devin seem to you when he was there? How was he acting?"

"Well, he wasn't really in that hot of a mood, now that you mention it. Kind of quiet. Gerald thinks he's just trying to decide whether to quit that job or not. Maybe it's harder to quit because you're still working there?"

I hadn't thought of that, and if only it were true. I would have welcomed so simple an explanation, but according to both the tapes and Devin himself, I wasn't going to get off that easy. But at least this told me it was obvious to other people too. It wasn't just me blowing things out of proportion.

"Well," Faye went on, when I didn't comment, "I'm calling to see if you guys have made any plans for Christmas yet. Gerald wants to barbeque, and he asked me to call and invite you and your family, and also Pammy and…George, is that his name?"

"Yes. Thank you. That's really sweet of you guys to include them."

"Well, it would be kind of nice to have the family together. That is, if you haven't already made plans."

"No, we haven't. I'd love to come, but I'll have to check with Devin, of course."

"Well, let me know, okay?"

"Will do. Thanks for calling."

I hung up and looked at Pam. "He's obviously not there."

"Well, I'm going over to see Bonnie today. She really wants to meet Devin, especially after the card he sent over, but it's not looking like a good time is it? He told her Sunday when they talked on the phone, so she's been planning on it."

"Don't ask me, Pam. With Devin it changes from minute to minute."

By 3:00 I'd quit listening for the sound of the van. Too many false alarms had sent me flying to the window only to meet another letdown.

When the van did finally lumber up to the front of the house, I didn't even get up. I continued to read, not wanting him to know of my anxiety the past few hours. I watched through the window as he strode up to the house, his steps heavy, his black Greek fishing cap cocked on the back of his head.

"Hey." He nodded in my direction when he opened the door, then came over to sit beside me on the couch. It took everything in my power to hide the fact that I'd been so upset. I didn't dare hope that I could breathe a sigh of relief.

"Faye called."

"Yeah? What'd she want?" His tone reflected no interest. Nothing had changed.

"She invited us all down for Christmas."

No response.

"You can call her back. I didn't know what to tell her."

"Why don't you call her for me. I'm not much in the mood for bullshitting."

So I'd noticed.

"Okay, but what should I tell her? Yes? No? Maybe?"

"Whatever. What do *you* want to do? Christmas is just another day to me." He glanced at the tree and added, "In most respects."

"Well, either way is okay with me. If you don't feel up to parties, we can just stay here."

"No, might as well go down. We're not doing anything else. Maybe we can even plant the tree in their backyard. At least I could take care of it there. Water it, and make sure it grows okay. If we take it to the woods...I...well, I'd feel responsible, you know?"

"I know. It's a great idea, Devin, and I don't think Gerald will mind. Chris probably would, or we could plant it here."

"Okay. Call her back. Tell her—" He walked over to the tape recorder and turned it on. "Damn, so quiet in here. Hey, is this music getting on your nerves? I never thought to ask. I know you never were much up on rock and roll."

"No, it's fine, Devin." *Just what I needed. More ominous songs.* "I just don't mess with your stuff when you aren't here. What do I tell Faye?"

"Tell her we'll be there. Noon maybe? Is Trevor going?"

"I don't know, but I'll ask."

"Okay." He nodded. "Maybe Daniel and Julie will go, too. Unless she has to work."

"How *is* Daniel doing anyway?"

"He's okay. No job yet. I just came from there."

"Oh. Is that where you were?"

"Yeah, you were sleeping. I didn't want to wake you up."

He pulled the beanbag over to the stereo, sat facing it in that cross-legged position, the pose that indicated he would soon shut the whole world out, including me.

I tried to turn my attention back to the book I'd been reading. *Journeys.* The author had written about countless trips to other worlds, but the book still didn't tell me where Devin was now, sitting there transfixed with zero breathing. If anything, the book only reminded me of how much I didn't know.

After what seemed like an hour and probably was, Devin opened his eyes, got up, and headed for the bedroom.

Tears stung my eyes as they remained staring at that same meaningless print. I'd read the same paragraph three times. It seemed like Devin didn't even want to be in the same room with me.

When Pam arrived with Bonnie and their friend Lorry, my heart sank. What a time for introductions.

Devin was polite enough to join us long enough to meet the girls. He even flashed Lorry a fleeting smile when she proudly modeled her new Christmas necklace, a large silver inverted pentagram from her boyfriend.

Devin examined it and raised his eyebrows with that knowing smile. "Not the sort of thing one would wear on a Sunday afternoon," he said.

They didn't stay long, and somehow we managed to plug through Sunday evening without any real friction between us. It was hard to follow my sister's advice when I didn't know what to say, what to do, or even how to act. His silence unnerved me and made it difficult to even act cheerful.

Trevor and Mia dropped in at nine and stayed until eleven. If they were aware of the tension, they never let on. Trevor was Trevor...Devin's...brother. Maybe he could pull Devin back to the world of the living.

Even if he couldn't, I was glad to see them. At least Mia would talk to me.

The tapes had been shut down in favor of the radio. Devin was busy sketching something in the tablet when the commercials advertizing sales of last minute Christmas trees drove Trevor to turn the radio off. Devin paused in his sketching to switch the radio button to tape, and the reel-to-reel crawled to life. Moody Blues. *One more time to live*, they sang.

I glanced down at the tablet Devin had set aside to see what he'd been doing. At first glance, it looked like a giant horseshoe, but then I realized it was a giant word shaped like a horseshoe. The bottoms of the letters were wider than the tops, indicating that the letters stretched for miles. It was a weird way to print, and Devin had been working on this for some time tonight. The word printed was *US*.

At the top of the tablet were three more, one underneath the other, smaller but printed in that same s-t-r-e-t-c-h-y way.

Time
One
Last

I picked up the tablet and studied the page, trying to decipher its meaning. When Devin returned from the reel-to-reel, I tapped it with my finger.

"I don't understand."

"What's to understand?" he replied, picking up the pen.

It was like October all over again, and once again, I was overcome with a feeling of déjà vu…time running backwards. Every time I thought I'd caught on to whatever Devin meant, he pitched another curve. Now he was writing something to me on the tablet, just as he had when we first met. He wrote in swift strokes across the paper, then pitched the tablet lightly to the floor. It landed directly in front of me.

You Me Him Us Time One Last

I read the added words and looked up at him again, sitting in his gold chair but turned away from me, deliberately it seemed. When he turned back and saw that I still did not understand, he took the tablet from me and began to write again.

You seem to think that our relationship is confined to the boundaries of this material existence, and that it will end with the deterioration of our mortal bodies. Can you not see that Time *is nonexistent and that we have always been* One, *and that this physical trip, having brought to us eternal love, secures our future as the* Last?

I read what he'd written and shook my head. "What's this supposed to mean?"

He exchanged a look with Trevor, who couldn't possibly have read the tablet from where he was.

"Well, okay," Devin said finally. "It wouldn't make sense that war and hate and death and pain and sickness would be shown to you in your life's experiences *last*, would it?"

"Last?"

"Sure. The reward for learning the lessons of this world would be total and complete love, wouldn't it? No, if you've made it to love, you're on your way out of here forever. Love has to be the last physical trip."

"Hey, Devin," Trevor said, standing up. "We gotta go. When are you gonna come down and see *us?*"

"I was just down there Wednesday."

"Big deal. Once." Trevor laughed.

"Soon," Devin promised.

He and Trevor went to our bedroom where Trevor's girls had fallen asleep on our bed. Each took a sleeping child in his arms.

"I'll see them off," Devin whispered to me at the front door. "Mia's warming up the car, and it's too cold out there for you in your bare feet. Wait here for me."

Thankfully, I said my goodbyes, changed into a sleep shirt, and crawled into our bed. I didn't want any of them to see me cry. It was getting harder and harder to maintain my composure, and I didn't know how much patience Devin had left.

I didn't understand those words he'd written in the notebook.

Time—One—Last, or One Last Time...

Either way it sounded final.

6 Monday, December 23rd, was as dark and gray as I felt. Devin had left for work without bothering to wake me, and I rationalized that it was because he had to be there so much earlier than I did. Normally I awoke when he did, but the emotional thing was beginning to wear on me physically.

I stopped at Daniel's at seven, but Julie told me I'd just missed him. I wondered if he'd gone up to the coffee shop.

He never turned up there either. Disappointed, I left for work at 8:25, telling myself that the route itself made his meeting me difficult.

Kelly had called in sick, and I was relieved she wasn't there. I wasn't in the mood for her fooling around today. Work was slow and tedious. I couldn't keep my mind on what I was doing, and Lola was getting more and more irritated with my mistakes.

At 4:30, she called me in for the fourth time to point out yet another error, this one a little more costly than the others.

"This isn't like you, kid," she said with a patient smile. "What's the problem?"

I looked into her concerned eyes and felt a tug-of-war going on inside me. Lola was my friend. I wanted to talk, but how could I tell her any of this? She would think I'd gone completely around the bend.

"Nothing," I finally lied.

"Oh, come on, Kerry. You've never done work like this. What is it? Money? You're good for a loan, you know."

"No, Mama. We just did all our Christmas shopping. For the kids, I mean."

"Well, what is it then? Are you sick? Kelly is."

That wasn't too far off the mark. I was getting there. "No."

"Do you want to just go ahead home?"

I considered the offer. There was less than a half hour left of the day. I wasn't sure I even wanted to be home any sooner than I had to.

"No, it's okay, Mama. Really." I turned away so she wouldn't see the tears welling in my eyes. I had to get away from her. Without waiting to be dismissed, I turned for her doorway. "I'll be right back."

She nodded, confused, but was too much of a friend to pull rank on me.

Inside the lounge stalls I let the dam burst, all the emotions that had been building up since Wednesday. The mere thought of losing Devin threw me into a panic. Even the music confirmed that things were reversing themselves. It seemed to me that Devin had awoken from a dream and suddenly didn't have any feelings for me anymore. His actions showed it. His attitude. Was it only guilt that made him try to treat me patiently? He wasn't lashing out at me. Wasn't picking a fight. Wasn't doing anything.

That was just it. As though we had become overnight strangers. I was in the middle of a situation that I could neither understand nor deal with. And he was refusing to talk to me about it. The writing on the wall seemed pretty clear to me.

Devin simply didn't love me anymore. And didn't know how to get out of it.

"That is *ridiculous!*" Pam shot at me later when I poured out my frustration and grief. "Kerry, you're letting your imagination get to you. I mean it. Nobody can turn love on and off like that!"

"No?" I interrupted her. "Remember how long it took to get started?"

She fell silent, as if remembering.

"That's right, Pammy. Five days."

"Well, that was different. Look, you didn't *do* anything, Kerry. I don't know what's wrong with him either, but he *acts* like he's under pressure. Think about it. He's been the perfect boyfriend. He's always treated you like gold. Now he's acting like he's got some kind of a time limit to some kind of problem or decision he has to make and—"

"Pam, it's easy for you to tell me to ignore it. You don't have to live with it. It's a nightmare. He won't talk. Now he admits it has something to do with me, and how do you think that makes *me* feel?"

"Wow…you're freaking out." Pam went into the bathroom and came out with some toilet paper. "Here. Blow your nose. Look, Ker. I know it's easy for me to say, and I do know how I'd feel if the shoe were on my foot. But from an objective standpoint, if you say anything else to him…"

"Yeah, I know you're right, Pam, but my nerves are shot. I'm screwing up at work. I can't concentrate. I don't know how much longer I *can* hold out."

"It *will* blow over, Ker, I'm telling you. Look, go wash your face. Jump in the shower. Don't let him see you crying like this."

"Where is he anyway?" I said, sniffling.

"He's only up at the grocery store. He'll be here any minute."

"Is it Devin?" There were very few people that I could ask a question like that without sounding totally insane, but Pam didn't blink as she answered.

"No. It's *him*. It's *been* him. You never *see* any of the others anymore, except flashes of Devin once in a while. These last couple weeks…*he's* taken over. He's here *all* the time."

"I know. He says he's at home here and that it's the one place he can be himself. I *have* seen Devin once in a while, and he's a little strained too, but that could be because whatever decision *he* makes could affect Devin's life. *He's* the one with the big decision, and the rest of us just have to bide our time and wait. Probably Devin, too."

I went into the bathroom and heard the front door open as I was getting undressed.

Devin…*Devin, hell*… *HE* was involved with the tree when I came out, and talking to Pammy about something. I went straight into the bedroom to dress. I hoped he couldn't tell by looking that I'd been crying.

"Hey, lady!" His voice. Calling me.

"Kerry." Pam rapped on the bedroom door. "Devin's calling you." Like me, Pam used Devin's name, even if she knew it was *him*.

"I'll be right out."

I finished dressing and went out into the living room.

"Lady. Come here a minute." He pointed to the tape recorder, and I sat down near it in the beanbag.

"I've been wanting to play you this song. It's come on a couple times, but you've always been busy with the kids or something. I want you to hear the words to this. Maybe it'll help you feel better. At least, it may help you to understand my position. It's my song to you. Everyone else had one for you."

He smiled but I couldn't return it. What horrible song was I going to hear now? Another *no place like home* song?

He hit the play button, and it was no surprise that it was another Moody Blues single. This one was called *For My Lady*.

I tried to focus on the lyrics that were just now beginning after a beautiful flute and symphony lead-in. I could see that he had actually stopped the reel while I'd been in the other room. By now, I was willing to listen to anything that might help me understand what was really going on.

The song was another omen. The singer's boat was sailing on stormy seas. He was battling a sea of tears. But his port had come into view when he'd discovered me. But I had been sighing, bowing my head and crying. He mentioned words that I spoke when we were alone, but that my actions spoke louder than words. Still, he loved me and to say those words to me helped to drive away all the hurt he felt at my actions. In the end, though, he would give his life for me, his gentle lady.

I looked at him, and it was as though I could read his thoughts. He had come, found me, and thought he could make me remember the things that he continually assured me were true, and though I had said I believed him, my actions plainly indicated that I didn't.

And it was all true.

7 Not long after playing the song for me, Devin seemed restless. Apparently, the song had not produced the intended comfort he'd hoped for, and I was unable to fake a joy about a song that had said what it had. No matter how much I *wanted* to believe…how simple it could have been if I'd been able to…I just couldn't make myself accept something that seemed so unreal.

I knew he could sense all this, and it was evident that it was affecting him very deeply. After pacing the house for a while he mentioned that he felt he needed to get out and was thinking about driving to Daniel's. I was surprised that he asked if I wanted to come along. Usually he just assumed I would go with him, but tonight he was giving me a choice.

It might have been better if I *had* given him some space, but I went.

George stopped in as we were boarding the van and asked if he could come along. Devin had no objection.

There was no conversation during the ride to Daniel's. George must have picked up on the vibe that things were not all okay for even he did not attempt to engage Devin in any conversation. He may have wished he had not invited himself along.

It wasn't that Devin was mean or rude to me. If I made any comment at all, he answered me normally, the way he would anyone else. I couldn't think of any way to break the communication barrier and wouldn't have tried anyway since we weren't alone, so I finally fell silent too.

It was embarrassing to go in with the tension between us so obvious. At least when we were seated in Daniel's living room, Devin did sit beside me, but I noticed a sympathetic look from Julie that told me she sensed something. I wondered if Devin had said something to them during his last visit.

Julie went in to the kitchen to make coffee and beckoned me to follow. When we were out of earshot, she asked me the same question Pammy had earlier.

"Are you two fighting?"

"No." I mentally debated whether to polish it up and pretend everything was normal the way Devin seemed to be doing with Daniel, then decided against it. "I don't know what's wrong, Julie, but there hasn't been any fight."

She looked in at the guys. Daniel had handed the stash box to George who was busily rolling. Nobody could hear our conversation.

"So you can tell, huh?" I said.

"Yeah, it's pretty obvious. Do you think it's because of the baby? You know, that you weren't pregnant after all?"

"Well, it does seem to go back that far," I allowed, "but there were a few normal days between that news and the mood he's in now. A few days can make a big difference when we're talking about Devin. A lot can happen."

"I know." She smiled. "You two have a warped sense of time. Well, let's go out and see what they're doing."

Daniel was suggesting a trip down to see Devin's dad, and Devin didn't try to discourage it. Maybe he felt a need to keep moving. Julie wasn't interested and stayed home with the kids.

The ride to Gerald's house was the same as the ride to Daniel's only with another person. Cat Stevens's *Tea for the Tillerman* played over and over on the eight-track. Occasionally I glanced over at Devin as flashes from the streetlights fell on his face, but he was engrossed in the music, his fingers unconsciously tapping out the beat on the steering wheel. I could have stayed home for all my presence seemed to mean to Devin.

When we arrived at Gerald's house, all the men left for the backyard, but I was not invited. It was cold and black out there, and the stars glittered like jewels. As soon as Devin greeted his dad, they all trooped out, leaving me to sit alone in the living room.

Faye's awareness wasn't too far off tonight.

"Devin forget about you?" she asked, startling me out of my brooding thoughts as she handed me a steaming cup of coffee. There seemed to be a hidden understanding in her gentle smile.

"Oh. Thanks, Faye. Yes, I guess he did."

She sat down in Gerald's throne and picked up the stash box. "I just can't figure out what's eating him, Kerry. Have you?"

"Jeez, everyone seems to be aware of it, and before you ask, we aren't fighting."

"That probably would have been my next question," Faye said kindly. "But I'll take your word for it. He was like this the other day. Have you tried to talk to him?"

I almost laughed, but I restrained myself. "Yes. He admits something is on his mind but he won't talk about it."

"That's about all I could get out of him too," Faye said. She got up, went to the glass sliding door and listened for a minute. Then she returned to the throne.

"They're out there arguing about whether the constellation they're looking at is Scorpio or not." She sighed and began to roll a joint for us.

The sliding doors opened suddenly, and the four trooped in, followed by Thor, the latter at Devin's heels, just as George was. Devin didn't appear to notice either of them.

"Come on, guys. We're lighting a joint," Faye called.

Gerald came in first and sat down in the smaller matching throne beside his. Daniel and George took a seat on the couch. Devin strolled over to the easy chair by the window where he remained, oblivious to me or anyone else in the room. I watched him, worried, but said nothing.

"Here." A tap on my shoulder, the odor of grass, and a cold roach clip placed in my hand. Faye.

"I'd just leave him alone," she whispered. "He'll come out of this all right. I know Devin. He's got something to settle in his head, and that's just what he's doing right now."

The ride home was even quieter than the trip down. George asked to take the wheel, and Devin handed him the keys. There was no music playing and no Devin to speak of. Oh, his body was there all right, propped up against the back of the passenger seat where Daniel sat. And he *was* awake. At least his eyes were open, but they remained staring fixedly at some nothing in the air.

Nobody changed seats when Daniel was dropped off at his house. Devin made no motion to move up front. I remained huddled on the leather beanbag near the couch in the rear of the van.

I fought back panicky tears. I longed to go over and touch him…say something…but I didn't dare. Devin just wasn't there.

George was nobody's fool. When he coasted the van to a stop, he put it in park, cut the engine and left immediately. The slam of the van door in the engineless silence seemed to awaken some flicker of movement in Devin's eyes. The only sound in the van was the muffler ticking…cooling off.

I finally knelt down beside him. "Devin. We're home."

He nodded.

"Are you okay?"

He reached into his shirt pocket for a cigarette. I knew he'd smoked his last cigarette at Gerald's house. I'd seen him crumple up the pack.

"You're out. Here." I handed him one of mine. He took it and lit it.

"Why wouldn't I be?" he asked suddenly.

"Be what?"

"Okay. Isn't that what you asked? If I was okay?"

The coldness of his words and tone twisted my heart.

"Devin…I…I love you."

"That's good," he mumbled, opening the latch to the side door. "It'll help."

He dropped to the ground, and I followed and slid the side door shut.

"Should we lock the van?" I asked.

He didn't answer, just started up the walk, then stopped and looked up at the sky. I watched him from the gate. Finally, he turned back and looked at me.

"You coming?"

I hurried to catch up with him, and he wrapped an arm around my shoulder. My teeth were beginning to chatter.

"You're cold," he said.

I held my breath and squeezed my eyes shut, trying desperately to hold back the sobs. Devin was talking to me as he might talk to a stranger he'd run into on the street who'd forgotten his jacket on this cold night.

The house was dark except for one lone red bayberry candle flickering on the stereo boards.

"Go ahead in." He nodded towards the hall and bedroom. "I'll be there in a minute."

Without a word, I left for the bedroom.

"Hey, lady?"

His voice stopped me dead in my tracks. It was no longer Devin's voice, but when I turned back towards him, I saw the same anguished expression on *his* face.

"I love you," he said, his eyes pleading for me to believe him.

Bewildered, I nodded, my fist to my mouth to stop the sobs, and I hurried on down the hall to our room.

I don't know when he finally came in. I had cried myself to sleep into my pillow on the big empty bed as the reel-to-reel chided me with yet another slap in the face.

Floating in from the living room, it could not have been another coincidence. It just couldn't have been.

8 Christmas Eve day.

The weather was as dark and dreary and cold as my very soul. I just couldn't shake the lyrics to the song that had played last night. The Moody Blues again…singing about a melancholy man. Although his feet were on the ground, he was lonely, and this world astounded him. When things got to be at their worst, I was going to hear angry voices on the wind, and realization would hit me. I would see another man that *looked* like him, but he would somehow no longer feel or be the same. This man was going to be miserable. He wouldn't think like *him* and me because he wouldn't be able to see what *He* and *I* could.

All of this was running through my mind as I drove to the coffee shop. There could only be one of two things wrong with Devin that I could think of. Either he was tired of me and wanted out, which was the human explanation and easier for me to believe, or *he* was definitely trying to decide whether to leave Devin's body and return home. If I believed the lyrics of the most recent songs, it was the latter, but if Devin had recorded these tapes years before we met, how could he have known the future, that he would agree to a benign possession that would only last for a little while and that he would face the same future I did. A life and a world without *him*.

Of course, I chose to believe the former since it made perfect human sense.

He didn't show up at the restaurant, and I didn't stay long.

I trailed into the office at 8:35, not caring if I was late, my purse heavier than usual. It contained a huge astrology book for Kelly. It was my only Christmas present to anybody other than the kids. I'd meant to wrap it, but with everything so topsy-turvy I hadn't gotten around to it. It was a wonder I'd remembered to grab it on the way out the door. She had admired this book more than once so I'd decided to give it to her.

"Hi, Mama. Where's Kelly?"

Lola pointed toward the lounge. "Where else?"

I decided to wait until work was over to give it to her. It would be less embarrassing for both of us.

Kelly, having a mild case of the flu, went straight to work without her usual banter, but not before announcing to Lola that the only reason she'd come in was because of the heavy Christmas rush.

"Oh," Lola had said. "And the big company office party after work didn't influence your decision at all?" She smiled and added, "Kelly, if you're really that sick, you can go home."

"No, that's okay," Kelly said dramatically. "I need the paid holiday tomorrow. Maurice would dock the holiday pay if I'm out the day before or the day after."

"Now it comes out," Lola said with a smirk.

"Well, it ain't for no shitty Christmas party. What kind of a party can *this* place throw?"

"You mean besides free food, drinks and presents for everyone? Oh, come on, Kelly. They even invited the drivers."

"And champagne," Hannah piped up.

I pulled my head out of my files. The drivers were invited? That would include Devin.

"Are you staying for it?" Kelly asked me.

"I don't know. I guess it's up to Devin. Whether he wants to or not."

Kelly burst into cackles of laughter. "Oh, *sure*. I can just *see* Devin wanting to hang around for a dumb old Christmas party...hey, Kerr, don't you think that's funny—" Her laughter stopped short at my unamused expression. "Hey, kid! What's wrong?"

I shook my head and went back to work. Kelly didn't push it, but I knew it was only dropped temporarily.

At 11:30, Ethel came in and, after a breezy good morning, informed me that line 22 was holding for me. "It's *Devin*," she breathed dramatically.

I tried not to show my irritation with her. "Okay, Ethel."

"You know, you can *call* in here, Ethel," Lola reminded her.

I was glad Lola diverted her. I didn't want anyone listening in, as bad as things were right now.

"Hello, Devin?"

"Yeah, it's me. What's goin' down?"

"Down? Here?" I glanced around the office. Nobody was paying attention.

"Well, you know what I mean. Just an expression."

There was a long silence. Finally, I broke it. "You on a route?"

"Where else? Hey, babe. Are you sure there isn't something wrong that you're not telling me?"

I nearly dropped the phone. "With *me?*

"Yeah. I mean, you've been pretty moody this past week."

I could scarcely believe my ears. "You're kidding, right?"

"Why would I joke about something like that?"

I still wasn't sure he wasn't putting me on. "Look, Devin. The *only* thing wrong with me…the only thing that's *been* wrong with me, *at all*, is *you."*

Surely he was aware of how he'd been all week. How could he put this on *me* now?

"Well, excuse *me*," he replied, his tone a little miffed. "Should I even bother to come home tonight?"

More verification that he was looking for a way out?

"Devin." I stopped right there. If he was trying to pick a fight, I was not going to fuel it.

"What's the matter? Lose your sense of humor?"

My eyes were welling up again. "Devin, I have to hang up," I whispered, wiping my eyes, thankful the room was full of machine noise.

"Yeah, me too. Hey, you got any bread on you?"

"Five dollars. You need something?" Hope rose in me. He'd cut the sarcasm and almost sounded normal.

"Well, we need a few Christmas cards. I know, don't say it. For Pat and Tim. It's too late to mail any, and they both sent us one."

"Sure. I'll pick them up at lunch."

"Nothing too Christmassy. You know what to get. Better grab one for Gerald while you're at it."

"Holiday cards."

"Or *Peace*. Something like that. I'll be in early today. I'll stop back there."

"Okay, Dev. Thanks for calling."

"Damn. You're always thanking me for shit." I could almost hear a smile in his voice. "Like it's some big deal or something."

"Well, it is…to me," I said in a low voice.

"Well, then thanks for being there. I'll see you soon."

The phone went dead in my hand. No goodbye, no *I love you*, no *go to hell* even. Nothing. I hung up and went to the lounge.

How long was this craziness going to go on? Crying…it seemed like that was all I was doing these days.

I washed my face, and when I was pretty sure my emotional breakdown wasn't evident, I went in to find Kelly. Walgreens had the lunch area and a pretty good card rack, so I could kill both birds with one stone.

Back at the office, I threw myself into my posting, but my mind was going a hundred miles an hour, mulling over the mystery of what had gone wrong. I longed to be able to talk to somebody about it, but the only one who really knew what was going on was Pammy, and her advice was to ignore it.

How could I? It seemed to me that Devin had awoken last Thursday from some dream, wondering what the hell he was doing living with this chick…planning *marriage*, no less. It was as though all his love had evaporated on the border of the dream universe. Was it possible that Devin just didn't love me anymore?

There was nothing left to do but confront him with it.

Devin stopped in shortly after lunch to pick up the cards. He looked them over briefly, told me they were perfect, and left.

I almost forgot to give Kelly her present, as engrossed in my thoughts and plans as I was by 5:00. It was her "Look, I don't care if you *are* a witch…you have a merry Christmas anyway," that reminded me. I reached into my purse.

"Here, kid. Merry Christmas. I didn't wrap it, but—"

"Oh, no." She looked at me mournfully. "What'd you do that for? I…I didn't get you anything."

"What makes you think this is a Christmas present? I was going to give it to you anyway, just because you showed an interest in it."

"Gee…thanks, Ker." She thumbed through it with wide eyes. "Oh! I can do my own chart, huh?"

"Yeah. It's pretty accurate too. Well, see you Thursday. You have a good one."

I didn't want to think about the evening ahead or how it might turn out. Like the night I had confronted him about his various personalities, I was just going to take the plunge and see where it led.

Pam wasn't home when I got there, but Devin was. As usual, the house was clean, and the tape recorder was running. I found him in the bedroom, sketching with a pencil on a canvas. He smiled when he saw me.

"Hi. Oh, hey, uh…I didn't get the kids. It was way too early when I got off. We really need to put them in the school down the street."

"That's okay." I took my jacket off and sat down on the bed. "I'll go get them in a while. I thought we might be able to talk better if we were alone."

"Talk?" I could almost feel a defensive bristle at the word but he recovered instantly. "It really bothers you when you don't know something, doesn't it?"

"It does if it's messing things up. You know what I mean."

He continued sketching, not looking up. "So go ahead. Talk."

He wasn't going to make this easy for me.

"Devin, do you still love me?"

He dropped the pencil and stared at me as if he couldn't believe I'd asked such a question. Then, when he seemed to have adjusted to the idea of the topic we were about to discuss, he picked up the pencil again and said, "No."

After glancing at my stunned expression, he resumed his attention to the canvas. "I can't believe you just asked me that, Kerry. I really can't. What in the hell brought *that* on?"

I swallowed hard. "Devin…something's been wrong and you know it. Since Thursday. Since the day we were supposed to go to Thompson's station. Even since the day Steve brought the scorpion over. You've admitted something was wrong, and you admit it has to do with me. Other than that it's been silence and you treating me like I'm not even in the same room with you."

He set the pencil aside and looked at me. "Would you care to expound on that?"

"The *mood* you've been in, Devin," I almost screamed, not in volume but in tone. "You're like a total stranger. You treat me like…" The tears broke then and, as hard as I tried, I couldn't stop them. Nor did he make a move to comfort me. I struggled to regain composure knowing tears didn't work with Devin, even when they were genuine.

"Treating you like what? I thought I was treating you pretty damn good under the circumstances." He leaned back against the pillow. "But then, I guess you would know how you're being treated." He lit a cigarette and added quickly, "But since you feel that way, I'm sorry. Okay?"

His expression told me that I'd hurt *his* feelings. "Devin, I'm not looking for apologies."

"Then what *are* you looking for, Kerry? Christ!" He ran a hand through his curls and sighed loudly in frustration. "I clean the house to save you that trouble when you get home. I cook the meals. I try to give you everything you desire. Even Christmas and a tree. And sex? You can't possibly be unhappy there. I don't neglect you in that department, except for that one night. I'm home with you all the time. I don't run around or leave you here by yourself. Let's see. Have I missed something? Maybe *that's* it. I'm around too much. Am I getting on your nerves?"

"Devin, stop it, please."

"Well, what is it? If it's your privacy you need I can go out a couple of nights and give you that, too. At least I can stay out of your way. I can come back here…damn, Ker. I don't know what more I can do. I really don't."

I didn't reply. It was the most he'd said in the entire week of his brooding. All of it was an evasion of the truth. I knew Devin too well now to believe he wasn't aware of how he had been the past six days. He must have read my thoughts, for he sighed again and tried another approach. Maybe he realized how hollow it all sounded.

"Look, Kerry. All right. I realize I've shut you out this week. If that's what you want to call it. And I said I'm sorry. Damn. What more can I do? I'll try not to take it out on you from now on. I didn't realize it was putting such a strain on you."

He paused, and when I still didn't comment, he went on. "The most disappointing thing for me is that I really thought you understood, lady. I really did. But I guess that's asking a lot. A little much to expect. A pretty big order to fill, isn't it?"

"Understood *what*, Devin? You haven't explained anything."

"Understood what," he repeated. "That's a good question. What *is* there that you *don't* understand? Have you ever considered that you might be making a mountain out of a molehill?"

"Devin, six days of you barely speaking to me is no molehill. Everybody's noticed it. I'm tired of trying to explain that we're not fighting. My hands are shaking all the time. I'm a fucking nervous wreck trying to figure out what's wrong with you. You've shot down all the possibilities I can think of. It's not your wife, it's not your losing interest in me, it's not work and it's not money. I don't know about *you*, Devin, but I don't think I can take much more of this."

The worried expression on his face deepened for a minute, and I was instantly sorry I'd said that. That almost sounded like an ultimatum. He set the sketch aside, walked over to the dresser, and looked at me in the mirror's reflection. "I'm sorry," he said. "If I've really made you *that* unhappy, I'm really sorry. I was *never* trying to hurt you."

"Devin...I know that. I know you aren't doing any of this on purpose. It's just that whatever's been on your mind...whatever is wrong, just tell me. Let me help you. If it's something I'm doing, tell me so I can change it."

"I've told you already. You haven't done anything. How many times do I have to repeat that before it sinks in?" I could see his impatience returning.

I didn't care. If this was what needed to be done to bring the problem out in the open, then so be it. Before I could say another word, though, he began to talk again. His voice was calm, but filled with resignation.

"I'm surprised at you, lady. Stooping to this...human bullshit. That's all it is. I really thought we were above this."

"Evidently we aren't, Devin. Or at least I'm not. But you think about it for a minute." Now I was losing my patience, too. "How would *you* like it if *I* woke up one day...stopped getting *you* up in the mornings, stopped talking to you, stopped telling you I loved you or even showing it...gave *you* the silent treatment for a whole week, and every time *you* asked *me* what was wrong, my answer was 'Oh, no, Devin. You haven't done anything. Of course I have a problem and it concerns *you*, but it's really none of your business. Just trust me.' Now, *how* would *you* feel? Don't tell me that after a week of that, it wouldn't start affecting *you*."

He appraised me coolly, obviously surprised that I was capable of such anger, and blinked as if in disbelief. "It's been as bad as all that, lady? Damn. Why do you stay with me? I'm surprised you haven't thrown me out by now if it's been as bad as all that."

I couldn't believe my ears. "Devin, what are you trying to get me to do? Ask you to leave? Is *that* why you've been doing this? To push me to the edge so I just ask you to leave?"

He wheeled around, suddenly angry. "Hey...uh, I've got two legs and I know my way out of here, if that's what *you* want. In fact, *that* would solve the whole *problem!* There wouldn't *be* a fucking decision to make!" With that said, he walked out, shutting the bedroom door behind him.

I found him in the kitchen, leaning against the counter, waiting for a pot of water to boil on the stove. He wasn't even bothering with perked coffee.

"You keep saying decision. What do you mean by decision?"

"Never mind, Kerry," he said wearily. "I *will* not fight with you, if that's what you're trying to get me to do. If you *want* me to leave, just say the word. Of all things, I don't want you unhappy."

"Devin, is that what you *want* to do? I mean, if you're sorry you moved in—"

"I'm *not* sorry I moved in," he interrupted. "I was *never* sorry. *You're* the one who said that. Don't put words in my mouth."

"Then what *has* been wrong with you?"

No answer. He threw two cups of coffee together and then turned to me. "I'm beginning to think you *want* me out of here. The way you keep bringing it up. If you want your home back to yourself—"

"It isn't that at *all!*" I shot back, the sobs welling up in my chest again. "If you left, I wouldn't even *stay* here! This has nothing to do with me wanting my house back to myself."

"No? You wouldn't stay here, huh? Where, if you don't mind my asking, would you go?" He crossed his arms and looked at me. "Oh, Kerry." His features, though hollowed and fatigued, softened a little. "Kerry, this is so serious that this whole episode here is almost comical. If I didn't *love* you so fucking much, I'd laugh. Now. You'd just move out, huh? Just like that. Where to?"

My answer was swift. "Back up north. To Allentown. Right before I met you and we got together, I was considering going back. My mother was on me all the time, and most of my family is there." That actually wasn't completely untrue. My mother *had* badgered me weekly to move back, and though I'd never admitted it to her, I had considered it a few times.

"Oh. And now *I'd* be the reason you went up there, right?"

I lit a cigarette and looked at him. There was no anger in his face and no hint of a simmering, hidden temper. He was calm, but he did look concerned. And as worried as he'd looked all week.

"Devin, why are you pursuing this? I didn't say I was *going* to do this! I just said that if you *did* move out, I might, so obviously it has nothing to do with my wanting my house back."

"What for? Why? I don't understand you, Kerry. Why *Allentown?* What would you do? Quit your job? You're pretty well set up here. Why would you go anywhere? And you're the one who brought up *my* leaving. I don't recall ever saying I wanted to move out."

"Devin, please. Look at it from my point of view. You were *too* talking about leaving. Just recently!"

"I wasn't referring to moving out of this house," he said impatiently. "I thought you *at least* understood that! Damn, lady. And to think that I've been so sure that you were ready to know more. Just when I thought you could handle it...and now *this!* I thought you understood what I was saying that night, but evidently I was wrong. Obviously you didn't. I'm wondering now just what you *do* understand at *all.*"

I stared at him mutely. Before I could defend myself, he went on.

"When I said *home*," he said slowly, "I meant *home.* Not this fucking little dimension *you've* called home for twenty-five years. Yeah, can you believe it? *I* can't. You've been here so long, you actually think you're one of them. Don't you."

I didn't reply. It wouldn't be the answer he wanted. Not if I answered honestly.

"Well? Don't you? Aren't you going to tell me again that you *are* one of them, lady? Or do you at *least* know *that* much now? Did I, *at least*, get through to you on that?"

When I still didn't answer, he slumped down into the couch in defeat.

"All my talking," he said quietly, his eyes closed. "Everything we've done. Everything *you've* done. All our plans and all I thought was understood, and you *still* don't know for sure. *Do* you! Come on. Let's get the real cards out on the table. Just what *do* you believe?"

I buried my face in my hands, trying to find my voice and the right words to say. I was going to be honest no matter what the price. "Devin, I just can't sit here and truthfully say that I believe that I'm not one of them, as you put it. You tell me I'm not human and that I am the same as you, but I can only take that in blind faith. Because I don't know. I have no proof."

He sighed. "And how about *me*, lady? Or do you doubt that, too?"

"You mean do I believe that you *are* who you *say* you are?"

"Never mind. Don't answer," he said sharply. "I already know what your answer is. The doubt is engraved all over your face. All this time you've just been humoring me."

"But, Devin—"

"Yes?" He closed his eyes wearily.

"Devin, listen." I touched his hand softly. "I believe that…that you're *you*. I don't care what label you've put on yourself, and I don't believe that you're all those bad things that supposedly come from Hell, but I *do* know that you're *you* and that you're not Devin. I know that Devin isn't *you*. I *do* know that, even if parts of me are unsure of other things. I can't and don't deny the validity and reality of *you*."

"You even believe that much?" he asked skeptically. "With no proof? That's usually want you want. Just like them. The people. That's what *they* need. And how about *there…home?* Have you thought about how little you know of it consciously? I've been trying every way I can *think* of to get you to go, but you're not even close. Hey, I know it takes *time*, but I'm running out of *that.*"

His outburst had the effect of a bucket of ice water tossed in my face. For the first time it dawned on me that all his pressure and tension and…yes, even his decision, might be subject to a time limit. Just like Pam had said. A time limit.

"Devin, our whole problem seems to stem from what I *don't* know. You could help…even *speed* things up, if you'd quit making me guess what you think I should already know."

"I can't *do* that! There's too much to it. And you wouldn't understand."

"But Devin—"

"Believe me, you wouldn't, Kerry. Take my word for it. And besides that, there's the question of how much I *can* tell you. Don't you think I haven't been all *for* you knowing everything? Don't you suppose there could be a reason you *don't?* A reason just slightly beyond my influence and authority?"

"You mean…from back *there?* Where you come from?"

"I'm not referring to *here*, lady, that's for sure. And now you want to go to Allentown. Well, if you do that, then realize just how easy you'll be making it for me. You'll be deciding *for* me."

"You're saying that the whole entire reason you've been so deep in thought and worried this week is because of this *one* decision? And that you still can't tell me what it's about?"

"I thought you understood that."

"But you said it involved me. And that it was pretty much none of my business."

"Well, to be technical, it isn't. And I shouldn't even have to tell you *that.*"

I flinched at his stinging bluntness.

"It's true, lady. You *don't* have a right to know everything. Not until you've *earned* that right."

"Earned it? You mean as far as you're concerned?"

His eyes softened again. "You've already earned it with me. That was never the problem."

"Then someone else besides you is against my knowing."

"That's only part of it, lady. A small part. There are other issues besides *us* involved here. There's the earth, for instance. And all of the people."

That last sentence rendered me mute. I had not been prepared for any hint of a reason, but I somehow knew that what he'd just said was true. It was engraved in his anguished expression.

"Oh my God, Devin," I said, tears threatening again. "I had no idea it was anything this serious. I'm so sorry."

He pulled me into his arms. "So am I, lady. So am I."

"Devin, you know I don't want to leave you."

"You might want to think twice before making a statement like that, Kerry. Just a minute ago, you were ready to quit your job and move up north. Just leave the state. And me. I can't *have* that kind of a problem, lady. The one I've got now needs all the attention I can give it at the present. And I need *your* support. Your moral support. I *can't* have you working against me. Not now."

I felt like a fool. Here I'd searched every possibility and probable avenue of human reasoning trying to understand what his problem could be. I hadn't considered that *his* problems might not necessarily be Devin's problems, or even human ones.

He lifted my face to his and looked intently into my eyes. "Think about it on your way over to get the kids. Really think about it. Be sure. Or stay here, and I'll go get them if you want."

"No, that's okay." I felt immeasurably better. "Wow, it's so late. Kathy's probably wondering what happened to me."

"It's not that late. It's not even dark. If you go now, you'll be back before seven. Oh, and Ker…you've *got* a friend, you know." He nodded towards the bedroom. "In there. Same corner as usual. Why don't you take him with you?"

"Blue, you mean."

"Sure. He's been in there all afternoon. I swear that dude loves you. Well, I think he's concerned anyway. Invite him along. See what *he* tells you."

"I don't know how to talk to him, Devin."

"You *think* to him, you don't talk," he said with a smile. "And you *listen*. It won't be in *words* that he'll answer you, but he *will* answer you. In any case, you'd better get going."

I leaned over to kiss him. "I'm sorry I acted so stupid," I began.

"Don't be sorry," he said. "And think about taking Blue, would you? He'll go with you. See what he says." He kissed me tenderly on the cheek and then ruffled my hair. "It's your decision, lady."

I felt as though a hundred pounds had been lifted from my shoulders as I pulled out of the driveway. I could hear the tapes still playing as I started down the street. I switched on the radio, but I was too deep in thought and too relieved to worry about what the words were saying.

I should have. If things were really all right, the music would have reflected it. Instead, they continued their warnings.

Uriah Heep was singing about sweet freedom and asking if I liked what I saw when I looked around me. The singer asked if I was sure I'd be okay without him. He wanted me to be happy even if I wasn't with him.

I had been lulled into a false sense of security.

9 I could definitely sense a presence in the car on my drive over to pick up the kids.

While I hadn't issued a formal invitation to Blue, it felt like he'd picked up on Devin's suggestion and chosen to come along. According to Devin, my capital sin these days was chalking everything up to my imagination, so I decided to suspend my disbelief and really give it a chance.

"Well...hello," I said aloud to the seemingly empty space beside me, and goosebumps erupted when I immediately sensed a response. Not knowing how to relate to a presence, type unknown, I took Devin's advice and just drove, waiting for *it* to make the next move. Truthfully, my thoughts were really more on Devin.

Alien thoughts shot in and out, disrupting my own thinking, but I assumed all of them to be interruptions from my own disoriented mind. A dismal gray picture of Allentown came and went with a series of what-if thoughts, all having to do with Devin and my near loss of him. And all because of my own childish stupidity and...human behavior.

But it's not fair, my ego argued, *for him to have treated me that way.*

What way? A foreign thought countered, and I jolted back to reality.

Where had *that* argument come from?

You wouldn't be happy anywhere without him.

Again, a dreary flash of Allentown accompanied that thought, from my own ego this time. I saw a picture of my mother's living room crowded with its madhouse of children still living at home, and older children visiting with grandchildren. A blanket of pain and loneliness swept over me that was as real as if I had already returned.

This will blow over, but you alone have the power to destroy it now and forever.

Those definitely weren't my own thoughts. A crawly feeling trailed across my cheeks, like a living spider web. No, I was not alone in the car. Blue, I realized, was riding shotgun.

"Well, welcome aboard," I said aloud, wondering what Lola or Kelly would think if they knew I was doing this.

Isn't it time you stopped worrying about what other people might believe or think?

That thought came as a sharp realization. No words. Just a realization.

You're right, I thought back, as I coasted the car up to Kathy's curb. *You're so right.*

Mandy and Michelle were excited and full of elation and anticipation…and no wonder. Nobody was going to change the thrill of Christmas Eve for them. With the small headway I felt I'd made with Devin this afternoon, I was almost relieved enough to take my mind off the whole problem for the sake of the kids.

"Mommy?" Michelle said from the back seat. "Is Santa Claus going to bring us presents too? Or are they all going to be from you and Devin?"

"What?" I looked at her in the rearview mirror. "I thought Devin told you there wasn't any real Santa Claus."

"Uh-huh, he did, Mommy," she said smugly, patting my shoulder. "But don't worry. I didn't believe him."

Mandy and I both burst into laughter. I leaned back over the car seat to hug her, and Mandy moved in, still laughing, to be included in the hug. As I drove away, I had the uncanny sensation that somebody else was enjoying the happier vibrations as much as we were.

I found dinner on and Christian cooking when I came in. The kids were miles ahead of me and both dove affectionately for his legs, one apiece. The girls never questioned who or what Devin was. He was just plain *magic* as far as they were concerned.

Christian looked up with a grin at our arrival. "Hey la-dee…check it out."

He nodded toward a package wrapped in brown paper, his hands busy pounding hamburgers together. Devin's black hat sat perched at the back of his head the way *Devin* wore it, but Christian didn't even seem aware that he had it on. Had Devin been there to begin with? Had Devin replaced *him* while I was on my way to pick up the kids? Something must have happened during my absence to bring Christian on.

"You got a Chris'mas present. Yer sister picked it up at the post office today."

The sudden appearance of Christian, after so long an absence, was startling enough. The complete absence of Devin's now routine frown, though, was a breath of fresh air.

"Hey, man!" I threw my arms around him and hugged him happily.

"Hey, yerself, lad-ee!" He grinned sheepishly, holding the greasy spatula over the sink with one hand while returning the hug with the other. "Ah *dig* th' greetin', but ya jist left, y' know."

"Yeah," I agreed, releasing him and picking up the package. "But *you* just got here. Oh, this is from my mother? Where's Pammy?"

"She's in th' shower, but she said to go 'head and open it when you got home. Ah think she maht know what it is."

Pam came out just as I'd torn the paper off and was lifting the lid off a box that blazed the name of an expensive department store. In the box, to my shock, was a dark-blue, hooded robe. I gaped at it in astonishment. "Jeez…can you believe my *mother* sent me this?"

He whistled approvingly. "That's all *right*, lady. Hold it up! Damn, you can really use that."

Erick. Of course. It was so obvious. I smiled at his arrival and held up the flowing robe. "What do you think?"

"She has good taste."

"I knew about it," Pam confessed. "She told me the day she found it in the store. She thought it was the perfect witch robe. Wow...check it out. A hood and everything."

"Yeah, more like a dark-blue version of the Grim Reaper outfit. You know, I just can't figure her out. One minute she warns me that I'm being exploited, and the next minute she becomes an accomplice by buying me accessories for the rituals."

Erick laughed. "I'm sure she means well, Kerry, and it *is* a nice robe."

"It is," I agreed, impressed. "But it's just the principle of the thing. Back when Devin was out of town during Thanksgiving, she called me because she was worried about me. She'd heard I was involved in black magic or something and wanted to send me this book that she'd sent me once before, and that I never read. She said it was because of him that I'd better read it." I folded the robe back into the box.

Erick picked it up and held it so that it hung suspended from his hands to the floor. "What book was this?"

"Oh, that book I was reading...or *trying* to read when...you know...I told you."

He set the robe aside. "What book? Have *I* heard about this book?"

"Well, I told *him*...but that's the same thing. I might not have named the book, though. I was more focused on telling him what *happened* when I tried to read it, so I may not have said the title."

"Well, what *is* the title of the book?"

"It was a long name...*UFOs...colon...*"

"*Operation Trojan Horse*," Pam finished for me.

"UFOs? It's about *flying saucers*? What would *that* have had to do with what she was worried about? That black magic stuff she was referring to." Erick looked baffled.

"Well, it's not exactly about flying saucers," I said. "They're mentioned, of course, since they're the most commonly sighted and documented, but it didn't stay on that subject from what I remember from thumbing through the book. For some reason the book scares people, and I did have that experience of fear while I was trying to read it, but it had nothing to do with what I was reading. It was because of what *happened* while I was trying to read it. I told you about it. The flying magic carpet-like ride from wall to wall...the white mansion...the blue cloud in front of my car. I never picked it up after that experience, and when Pam went back for a visit, I gave her the book to return. Anything that has a history of instilling fear in people, I don't need to read."

"You have to know my mother," Pam added.

"Well, what *else* does it talk about besides UFOs?" Erick leaned back against the couch, his full attention on me.

"I'm not completely sure since I didn't really read it. I was so shook up after what happened that I never wanted to see it again."

"So that's how you handled it? Just put the book away?"

"Yeah. All I'd really read was a few pages of UFO history. I didn't want to find out what would happen when I got to the *really* scary stuff."

"I remember how she bugged you to send it back," Pam said. "So she could scare someone else, probably."

"Would you refuse to read it now?" Erick asked me.

"Oh, probably not now. I'm not alone now. It was creepy reading it with no one else in the house."

"I'll read it with you," Erick offered quietly. "It sounds like a challenge. Your mother has the book now?"

"Yeah, she's still got it, but she *does* lend it out if she can talk someone into reading it. Pam's right. Probably scaring some more of her friends."

"Hmm. That's interesting," Erick mused. "And other than those few pages you have *no idea* what else is in the book?"

"Oh, I got the gist of it. It's got something to do with the electromagnetic spectrum. About how the UFOs aren't really what they seem to be. You know, something about how UFOs are made of the same stuff as elves, vampires, werewolves, Bigfoot...whatever form the energy wants to take. Apparently it can take any shape it wants to."

"The electromagnetic spectrum?" Erick echoed. "And you set the book *aside* ?"

"Threw it, actually. There was something creepy about this invisible parallel world that—" I stopped. "Hey...that does sound a little familiar now. A parallel world that coexists with this one in the same space. Erick, that book was about other dimensions. Not outer space."

"I think I *would* like to see that book." He paused, his eyes focusing out the window. "Who's pulling up?" He raised up a little so he could make out the car outside. "Looks like...yep...Trevor."

The change of voice was immediate. I looked up to find Devin's face smiling at me. "Wouldn't you know it? Christmas Eve. Them suckers. I told them we'd be home, but I really didn't think they'd make it."

He went out to meet them in the yard, and I looked blankly at Pam. "Are you catching all this in and out stuff? First Christian, then Erick and now Devin."

"I know," she said softly. "It's blowing my head. Especially when we haven't seen much of those guys lately. At least *I* haven't. All I've seen around here lately is *him. Him,* and once in a great while, Devin. But things kind of seem better tonight. Did you'ns get a chance to talk?"

"Yeah, a little," I admitted. "He does seem better now. I'm afraid to hope it's over with...you know...like last week, but I'll tell you about it later."

She laughed. "I'm not sure I want to know. I gotta go anyways. I'm supposed to be at George's."

The front door banged open, and Devin came in talking a mile a minute to Trevor. He paused long enough to ask me to put coffee on, then they went in past us. I took the jackets and sweaters from Mia. Pam waved a general hi and goodbye to everyone and left.

"Should I say Merry Christmas?" I teased Mia, and she giggled.

"You can to *me*. I don't know about Trevor, but I still have a lot of the old Christmas punch in me. I really love your tree." Her cheeks were ruddy from the brisk air outside, and her eyes sparkled with seasonal excitement.

"Devin's tree," I corrected. "That's his baby."

"I'll bet."

"It is. He's going to plant her tomorrow. I sure am glad she survived through Christmas."

"Yeah, Devin's been worried about it," Mia agreed with her hoarse, throaty laugh. "The last time we saw him, every other word was about that tree. Now what are they doing? Jesus, you'd think they'd been separated for months."

I looked toward the den to see what she was referring to. Devin and Trevor clutched each other emotionally in a brotherly hug. Then Trevor pulled away and buried his face in his hands, from which dangled a set of silver keys.

"Hey, bro, don't be getting emotional on me, man," Devin was saying. "Now come *on*!" He led the way back to the living room and Trevor followed, heading straight to his wife. He then whispered something in her ear and held up the keys.

If it was a surprise to Mia, she didn't show it. "It's yours now, huh?" she said in her placid way, smiling over at Devin with warmth. "He's always loved that bike."

"Yeah, well, now it's his."

"We have a couple things for you guys, too," Mia said to me. "And I made some red felt stockings for the girls with their names on them."

Devin shook his head. "Now, I *told* you we don't celebrate Christmas. Damn. I didn't even get *Kerry* anything."

"We just focused on the kids," I admitted.

Trevor handed Devin a small, wrapped, elongated present. Mia gave me a smaller one wrapped in the same red and gold paper. I opened mine immediately. A tan suede wallet. Something I could really use.

"Thanks, Mia," I said.

She smiled and pointed to Devin and Trevor. Devin was staring dumbstruck at a carved wooden statue of the Grim Reaper. It held its scythe upright but peacefully at its side, and the robe hood was pulled up and over its face. Devin had admired it the night of Mickey's party just before all the confusion had erupted.

Devin's eyes shone. "He *gave* it to me, Kerr...It's *mine*!"

Trevor beamed at Mia and jerked a thumb at Devin, shaking his head at Devin's appreciation. She nodded back happily. They both knew how much he had admired the statue.

Myself, I wasn't so sure. It was a beautiful piece of art but the subject matter itself...another death symbol. Who or what was dying? Or *going* to die?

Meanwhile, Devin wasn't thinking about death symbols. "Here." He thrust the statue into my hands. "You're good at that Theban script, babe. Would you print something on it for me? I'll mix up the paint."

I was momentarily honored. "Sure. What do you want it to say?"

"The words...*from a brother*. It's redwood, so perhaps black paint, huh?"

Devin took the paint from the altar and began to mix it. It was so good to see him back to normal. It really did seem like the crisis had passed. With enthusiasm, I dismissed my first impression of the statue's symbol and set to work on the lettering. I was just finishing up when Devin emerged from the den with the canvas tire cover that I'd begun painting for him a week ago.

"Here, babe," he said. "Not that I expect you to do it now, but I'm setting it out here in case you get back in the mood."

"Oh, that reminds me," Mia said suddenly. "Trevor brought a camera."

"Really?" I was up instantly, the tire cover forgotten. "What kind?"

"Polaroid." She nodded at the camera beside her purse. "It's loaded and ready. We were hoping to get some pictures tonight, you know, of our first Christmas together."

"And some of you guys too," I said. "Hey, Mia, can you get a picture of Devin for me?"

"You ain't taking *mine*," Devin said, laughing as he ducked away from Trevor's aim. "I mean it. I don't want any pictures of me around."

"Oh, who wants your ugly mug anyway," Trevor said affectionately. "Let's get some of the tree and one of the dragon there."

Seven of the pictures went on just those things and one of him and Mia. The final picture, Trevor announced, was to "get" Devin with.

"No way…back off, Jack," Devin warned, sitting down on the edge of the gold-leather footstool. He turned away from the camera and patted the stool, inviting me to join him. When I did, he leaned over quietly and whispered in my ear. "I love you, lady."

I looked directly into his eyes, realizing at once who had taken Devin's place, and at the same time and for the very *first* time, feeling an equality with him. A peer, instead of a worshipper kneeling at the foot of the pedestal that both Devin and I put him up on.

"Hey, man!" Trevor's sharp call caused a natural reaction from both of us. We looked up, startled—to the blinding flash of the last shot in the camera. With no warning, Trevor had pulled it off.

Something flickered in *his* eyes for a split second. Maybe simply momentary surprise…possibly anger, but it melted into his Vulcan-like features almost immediately. "That's one picture you lose, bro," he said, rising from the stool. "Let's have it."

Trevor held the camera away from him with an outstretched arm, winked at Mia and looked at his watch. "Twelve…thirteen…fourteen…I got both of them, Mia, sixteen…seventeen…"

I looked over at *him* as Trevor counted down the necessary seconds before the picture would be ready. *He* didn't exactly look pleased with Trevor.

"Here it comes," Trevor announced with one last glance at his watch.

Mia and I moved in to look at the picture. *He* didn't move towards us at all. A hush had fallen over the room, and when I saw the picture, I gasped. What Trevor had captured in the photo was impossible.

Mia was the first to audibly comment. "Oh my God, Trevor! What happened?"

"Damn." Trevor stared at the photo, then held it out to Devin. "Check this out, bro."

"I don't have to see it," he said curtly. "That wasn't cool. I don't want any picture...*that* one especially, around."

"Devin, you ought to at least look at it," Mia said, frowning. "You look so...sinister."

"Yeah? Look at Kerry, too," Devin said, still not getting up to see.

I took the picture from Trevor's hand.

Trevor had caught the two of us dead center. His calling Devin had caused both of us to turn, totally unprepared for the flash. The result...his actual face. The face I'd seen on the night of the peyote...the face I'd seen on the porch of that mansion the night I'd tried reading the book...the flaming hair...the amber and black eyes. His features were pointed and sharp. Ears, nose, and chin. His eyes shone with a green cast, like a jackal's at night when caught in the headlights. The expression in them...they bored into the eyes of the person looking at the photo, burned deep into the brain. All this captured in a second. An unguarded second.

I didn't look any more human than he did. The flash had given my skin a pallid unearthly hue and had caught my eyes, turning them red. The expression on my face was as alien as his. I remembered that equality feeling I'd experienced a split second before the flash, and an odd feeling went through me as I stared at this photograph of both of us.

"You'd *better* look at it, Devin." I handed it to him.

He took the picture, glanced at it briefly, then up at Trevor. "Did you say I get to keep this one, bro?" he asked, starting to slip it into his pocket.

"If it means that much to you," Trevor said, shrugging indifferently. "But I'd put it up with the others till it dries. It'll get messed up in your pocket."

It was late when they finally rose to leave. After they were gone, we checked on the girls to make sure they were asleep. Devin then gestured towards the closet in our room.

"I guess it's time to get the presents under the tree."

We set to work, arranging them in some order, Mandy's wrapped in red paper, and Michelle's wrapped in green. Pam's idea. Saved on nametags, she'd said.

"What did you think of that picture?" I asked him as we worked with the gifts.

"I'm amazed it even took at all," he replied. "And I'm not sure what I'm going to do with it. We can't have it lying around." He set the last gift under the tree. "There. All set for the morning. You about ready to turn in?"

I yawned. "You bet." It had been a long day.

It was almost like old times again, before the horrible week of silence had begun, but if I thought that the afternoon's talk would go unmentioned I was in for a rude awakening. When the lovemaking had subsided and we were lying quietly in the dim bedroom, he brought it up.

"So. Did you think about what you're going to do?"

At first, I didn't even realize what he meant. Then it hit me.

"Devin, there really wasn't anything to think about. I wouldn't leave you. I *couldn't* leave you...for Allentown or anywhere."

"How about your friend, Blue? Did he have anything to say? Or didn't you take him along?"

"No, he went," I replied hesitantly. Ghosts, spirits, thought forms, or whatever Blue was had not been scientifically proven to exist, and yet here we were, not wondering if there *was* a Blue, but whether he had gone for a ride in the car-car. Like the family pet.

"So what'd he say?"

I drew a deep breath. "He said I didn't want to leave you, not for anywhere, and that this would all pass."

He nodded and pulled me closer to him. "So…you're going to stay, then?"

"Devin, I *wouldn't* have left. Really."

"Well, I had some time to think while you were gone, and I gave what *you* said a lot of thought." His expression was serious in the dim lamplight. "You were right. Just because I have something on my mind doesn't justify taking it out on you or ignoring you. Looking back over the past week, I guess I have been pretty distant. So I made up my mind that I'm going to act differently. I'm going to watch it from now on. I'll try not to…to take it out on you. I think I did pretty well tonight, right?"

My heart sank. Now I knew why Christian and the others had been around all evening. His way of not taking it out on me was to leave. So things were *not* back to normal. Tonight had just been a charade…a happy act I had forced him to put on. I opened my mouth to protest, to tell him that that wasn't the answer either, but closed it quickly. I'd already made too many mistakes this week.

"Want me to turn off the recorder?" he asked suddenly.

"No, why?"

"Okay." He adjusted the pillow and rolled over, away from me. "I just wanted to make sure you weren't getting tired of the music."

"Do *you* want it off?"

He shook his head. "It'll shut down by itself," he said, his voice muffled in his pillow. "Anyhow, we've got a heavy day tomorrow. What time do you want to go down to Gerald's?"

"Anytime after the kids open their presents is okay." I yawned. "If I know them, that will be early."

"Yeah. It looked like a lot of that stuff has to be assembled, huh?"

He didn't wait for my answer. Within seconds, I felt his breathing subside away to almost nothing. To that lifeless way he had of sleeping.

I rested my face against his back. Exhausted.

10

Christmas Day.

I awoke to an empty bed. A glance at the clock radio told me it was dawn, although the drawn curtains throughout the house and the soft light of the candles glowing from the living room gave the atmosphere a nighttime feeling. I heard low voices in the living room. The aroma of coffee and marijuana wafted into the bedroom.

No sound of the girls' excited voices. Groggily, I crawled out of bed, wondering why they were still asleep.

"Well, good morning," Pam greeted me. "You're as bad as the kids. What's wrong with them anyway? *All* kids are up at five on Christmas Day."

"Hey, that talk 'bout Santa Claus musta done the keeds some good." Christian smiled up at me from his cross-legged position on the floor, in the act of stringing my guitar. A box of new strings lay open on the coffee table. Both Puff and the tree flashed rainbows of color on his face, his expression set in concentration on the job at hand. I knelt down to kiss him good morning. Of *all* people to show up on Christmas Day.

"Hey!" He laughed, returning my hug and flashing me a wide grin. His black features were more prominent than I'd seen them since Halloween. Pam, just slightly out of his line of vision, pointed silently to him, eyebrows raised. *Christian* she mouthed and then smiled happily. Pammy loved Christian.

"Damn." I rubbed my eyes and looked around. "What time *is* it? Where did the strings come from? I didn't know you knew how to string a guitar, Devin."

"Watch that," Christian corrected, flipping the guitar to the opposite side, three strings already affixed. "Devin *can't* string a guitar, but Ah can." He winked and reached for another string. "An' the strings're compliments of yer sister. Ah tol' you, lady, Ah kin do anything."

I smiled at Pam. "Thanks."

"'s okay. I got two sets for Christmas. I only need one."

"Hope Ah'm doin' this raht," Christian muttered, examining the old strings that were still attached to the guitar. "Shee-it! Ain't much to it. Jist hope they was on right t' begin with." He fastened the fourth string. "Here, la-dee. You want to tune it before Ah go any further? Hey, what *is* it with them keeds. Ah know they got th' message about Santa, but shee-it...they didn' even bother t' git *up!*"

I laughed. "I'll go get them. This is a first, though. Usually they get *me* up on Christmas."

"Oh, Ker," Pam said. "There's coffee made for you on the counter. I don't know if it's still hot."

"Thanks, Pam. I can use it."

The coffee was still warm. "How long have you two been up?"

"*He* woke *me* up," Pam moaned, yawning. "A few minutes before *you* woke up."

"Well, this iz a *dead* house for Christmas morning," Christian said, pouting. "Well? Now what?"

"I'll get them." I went into the kids' room. It was gray outside, unusual for 7:30. The sun was usually up by now. Something had begun to needle at me, and when I saw Pam's pillow and blankets on the floor I realized what it was. He had awoken my sister but not me.

Stop it! I tried to shake the feeling. He probably had opened the door to see if the kids were up and saw her sleeping there. Better to put my energy into shaking the kids awake. I was *not* going to start this day looking for problems. I wondered just *when* Christian had arrived. He had a talent for taking over in uncomfortable situations.

My mind went back to a night when Christian had jumped to his own defense. It was during one of my late-night talks with Erick regarding Christian during the early days. I could still hear that black drawl as he'd emerged for a second, indignant at the comparison of Devin and himself from Erick's point of view.

"Jist who d' ya think loves *them keeds, huh?"* He'd demanded suddenly in the middle of Erick's statements. *"Ah'll tell ya who! Me. Christian! Tha's who!"*

In any case, as rarely as he was around these days, I was happy to see him.

It didn't take much to rouse the girls from the dead sleep they were in. They were alert in seconds.

"Come on, you guys! It's Christmas!"

The gift opening was a riot. I'd followed their lists to the letter, and the girls spent the morning guessing what was what by the shapes of the packages. It was all Barbie gear and every mode of transportation ever invented for the pint-sized teenager.

As each gift was opened, Christian happily set to assembling. Barbie had a mansion, roller skates, an airplane, a swimming pool, a motorcycle, a bicycle, a van, a surfboard, a skateboard, a sled, and finally, a sailboat. There was also a realistic set of ski gear.

"Damn, this chick's got it *made* !" Christian observed aloud as he struggled to piece the pool together. "When she gits tard of sleddin' an' skiing she kin hop on her airplane an' fly south t' her pool. Then she kin drive her van to th' grounds of that ridiculous mansion where she kin swim till she gits bored with *that*, then she kin roller-skate her ass down ta th' beach an' jump off her sailboat with her surfboard…shee-it! This chick's got more ways t' git around than *Ah* do!"

The girls giggled hysterically, and Christian looked up at me with stone-faced horror. "Wonder what th' payments'll run on all this shee-it. Hell, mah van's a couple hunert a month an' it's nowhere *near* as fancy as *hers* !"

Guiltily I thought of the charge bill I'd run up to get the things. Obviously, Christian didn't. He set the assembled pool aside, shook his hair out of his eyes and stood up to stretch. "Go to it, keeds. Ya got fahve minutes to play! Then we have t' go down to visit Gerald and Faye."

The kids gave him a dirty look, and Pam and I burst into laughter.

"Five *minutes* !" Michelle wailed.

"He's exaggerating," I assured her, "but we do have to eventually go down there to eat dinner."

"Come on, guys," Christian said, hugging both of them at once. "We still gotta git this livin' room picked up an' the tree ready ta go. We got a plantin' ta attend to."

He walked over to the tree and looked down at her reverently. "Okay if Ah start pullin' this shee-it off her?"

"Of course," I said. "Want some help?"

"No, I'll get it," he replied, turning toward me, and with those normal words in Devin's own voice, I saw the transformation take place before my very eyes. Christian's features melted into Devin's face, and when he continued the sentence, it was as if Christian had never been there at all. "I put the shit on her, and I know she'll be a little dry in spots. I want to get that angel hair off her without hurting her branches." He stooped down and touched the needles. "She *is* doing better than I thought. You can get the boxes for these balls, though."

Pam glanced at me and shook her head. She too had witnessed the change.

Devin had the tree stripped in minutes and carried her out into the front yard.

Outside, in the crisp December air, the little pine tree seemed to expand in happiness at the sudden exposure to the sun, which had finally come out. It was warming up rapidly.

The girls followed us out to watch, their toys momentarily forgotten, as Devin pulled the hose over to water the tree. It was unusually warm for Christmas day, and the girls giggled, screeched, and danced gleefully as Devin sprayed their toes playfully and then stooped to shoot the water straight up where it could fall naturally like rain on the branches.

The commotion brought Steve and Chris out from their side of the duplex, and they watched curiously for a few minutes. There were already several trees on the curbs awaiting the trash pickup, their life and usefulness to the planet—and their torture—finally over. I saw Devin's gaze take in the neighborhood scene, but he didn't comment. He didn't have to. I saw the look in his eyes.

Chris walked over to Devin and nodded at the tree. "It's still alive, huh?"

"Yep."

"How come? I mean, was it cheaper that way?"

"Yeah, really, man." Steve strode up alongside his roommate, beer already in hand.

I remembered the scorpion and decided not to hang around for Devin's probable remarks. His opinion of Steve had changed drastically since that awful night. "I'll get the kids ready to go," I said quickly. "Merry Christmas, you two, and all that shit." I herded the girls into the house.

"I'll get the tree in the van," Devin called after me.

George pulled up as Pammy and I stuffed the last of the paper and boxes into the garbage cans.

"How *is* he today?" Pam asked me as we watched George join the men in the front yard. I jammed the lid on the can, one of the few cans in the neighborhood that didn't have a dead tree beside it.

"Who, Devin?"

"Any of them. Did you'ns get it straightened out? Things seemed pretty cool before Trevor's family showed up. Did everything go all right from there?"

"It's hard to say right now, Pam. It seemed okay when we went to bed, and we did talk about it a little. He as much as said he'd watch it from now on so as not to take it out on me. The whole time Christian was here this morning it was like normal. But the minute Devin arrived, that mood seemed to arrive with him. He's barely smiled since he showed up, but he seems to be making an effort not to be as distant as he's been lately."

"It's amazing how they do that," Pam said. "I've been around them both a lot, but it's not often I actually *see* him change like that."

"Well, come on. Let's go get the kids and get out of here."

When Devin and George came into the house, I looked out and saw that the tree was no longer in the yard.

"You about ready?" Devin asked me, his expression and tone serious.

"Yes. The girls were just playing with the toys until it was time."

"Okay. We're ready. Oh, and Chris said to tell you…there's no rush…but he's got some stuff over there for the kids. I think his mother brought it over."

"Can it wait till we get back?"

"He said whenever you get time."

George emerged from the bathroom, the sound of the toilet flushing behind him. "I'm ready," he announced.

"Then, let's go."

Sunshine on Christmas. Pam remarked on the absence of seasonal snow as we all headed for the van. When Devin unlocked the sides, I went to climb up front like I always did. Just as I sat down, Devin opened his own door and boarded the driver's side. "Hey, Ker. You sit back there with Pam and let George sit up here."

I turned to find George casually waiting by the sliding van doors. "Everybody in now? Hands away from the doors. I'm slamming up."

It took a few seconds for Devin's command to register. I could hardly believe I'd heard right. Tears of humiliation stung my eyes, but my pride refused to let him see what a slap in the face that had been. Without looking at him, I rose and moved to the rear of the van where Pam and the kids were.

"You girls can surely find something to gossip about," George told us, taking my usual seat at Devin's right. I saw Pam's face go from surprise at Devin's order to stiffening anger at George's attempted joke.

"That sonofabitch," she murmured. "Just what does he think he's doing?"

"It was Devin's idea," I told her in a low voice, the sick feeling growing worse. Things were obviously not going to be any different today. I struggled to maintain control, aware of the flush in my face. Was it really such a big deal?

Devin started the van with a flick of the wrist and shoved a tape in. *Dark Side of the Moon.* George laughingly mentioned how much the van's engine almost sounded like a helicopter. Pam took advantage of the engine revving up front to talk to me.

"I think I'm seeing what you've been talking about. And George. Wait till I get my hands on *him!* I don't believe he went along with it."

I wiped my eyes roughly. I didn't want the girls, who had moved up behind Devin's seat, to see me on the verge of tears again. Not on Christmas Day. I was angry at myself for being so sensitive and tried to tell myself that this didn't mean anything.

"Let it go, Pam. Devin's the one who told me to move. What could George do?"

"I'm just blown away, Ker," Pam said. "I heard Devin's tone of voice. He ordered you to the rear like he would Titan. This is the first time I've actually *seen* why you've been so upset. Shit. I take all my advice back. I don't know what I'd do in this situation."

Devin and George, however, were oblivious to any reactions coming from the rear of the van. They had gone off on the subject of helicopters.

"Hey, them things are *neat*," George was saying. "They sell rides in 'em downtown. Ever go down there? I think for two bucks—"

"*Two bucks!*" In mock exaggeration, Christian was back, blinking dramatically at George. "*Two bucks?*"

"Well, maybe five bucks," George allowed sheepishly. "Hell, it's been so long—"

"*Fahve bucks!*"

We were on the road. I saw Pam's expression go from anger to affection. "Aw, look who's back," she whispered.

Christian caught my eye in the rearview mirror and winked. I tried to smile, but the sick feeling was too strong. Christian's attention, however, wasn't on me anyway.

"Fahve bucks, Jack…fer fahve bucks you maht git an' appointment to *see* the damn thing."

"No, it's *two* for the appointment," George joked back, "and five that they start it up. I think you get to hear it for five."

"Fahve fer the appointment," Christian insisted. "Fer another fahve they maht start it up. Maybe vibrate ya a little bit."

Both of them burst into laughter. Even Pam couldn't suppress a smile. I couldn't even pretend to. My mind was too preoccupied with Devin to care how much a fucking helicopter ride was.

My vibes must have finally made it up front. After carrying the joke to the extreme, they both fell silent, and nothing was heard but Pink Floyd, and eventually Grand Funk Railroad, for the remainder of the trip. Even George seemed to have sensed, somehow, that he'd made a big boo-boo and lapsed into his own silence. Pam didn't spare him any of her glares whenever he glanced behind him.

As the van rolled into Gerald's driveway, George turned around and addressed Pam. "Did you remember the camera?"

In response, she held it up, but her expression was cold and accusing.

"What's with *you* !" he snapped, possibly encouraged by Devin's seeming attitude towards me. Pam stood up, and Devin hopped out to open the door.

The girls raced for the backyard where Trevor's kids were already at play.

Pammy alit first. As George followed her up the walkway, Devin waited at the side of the van for me. "You coming in?" He lifted the tree and set it on the ground, keys in hand. When I stepped out, he slammed the sliding door shut and put a casual arm around me. "What's the matter?" His voice was indifferent with a slight edge.

"Women," George called back. "Ain't they a bust in the ass?"

It took everything in me not to show any emotions as I answered. "Nothing." I forced a smile.

George had caught up with Pammy as Faye opened the door for everyone.

"Come on in, you guys. Merry Christmas. Go ahead out back. That's where everyone is."

Devin took the tree along the side yard, not bothering to go through the house. I watched him disappear from view and then went on through the way Pam and George had.

For me, the whole visit was a nightmare. Devin seemed to forget I had come along and spent the next hour in the kitchen with Gerald and Brian, pulling out prepared side dishes from the refrigerator and stacking plates with silverware and napkins. Gerald came out to greet me with a fatherly hug and told me to dig in. The food was simmering on the barbeque. Chicken and ribs. Steaks.

When Devin wasn't talking to Trevor and Mia, he was wrestling with Thor in the yard or swinging the girls one by one in the hammock to their sheer delight. At least *they* were having a good time.

I had no appetite. I put a few items on my plate to be polite and went out in the sunny yard to sit in one of the lounge chairs.

Brian ceased his own romp with Thor to join me for a few minutes, glancing around first to make sure we weren't within earshot of anybody.

"What's wrong with my brother?"

"You noticed?"

"Hard to miss. You two fighting on Christmas?"

How tired I was of that question. "No. I don't know what's wrong. Maybe—" I stopped right there. Not only had I run out of maybes, but what business did I have crying on his younger brother's shoulder?

"Well, anyway, come on in. I think Faye might be rolling some joints."

The party had, by now, completely moved into the house. I found a chair across from Devin at the dining room table. He finally acknowledged my presence with a wink. I knew that face instantly and well. Erick. It came and went for only a second, and then Trevor called him. Devin answered, and Erick vanished as suddenly as he'd appeared. When Devin strolled over to talk to Trevor, Pammy came over and sat beside me.

"Hey, Ker, don't be all bummed out, huh? Look. I got a couple of pictures of Devin playing with the dog."

"Yeah? Thanks, Pam. I am trying to shake it off. It's just been going on for so long now. Even his brother asked me about it. Anyway, if you catch Erick or Christian around today, could you try to get one of each of them?" I didn't know what to make of all the switches Devin was doing, but it was not a usual thing. Especially in such mixed company. Before Pam could answer, Christian's black drawl came loudly from the couch. We looked over, and he was standing beside Trevor with his hands on his hips.

"What you *mean* yer splittin'?"

Mia was rounding up her kids, and Trevor stood patiently at the front door. "Man, Devin, we've *got* to get over to her parents yet. It's Christmas *Day!* You *dig?*"

"Shee-it. You ain't been here two hours. And Daniel ain't even showed *up* yet."

Pammy turned back to me. "I think I'm just going to take it," she whispered. "He'll never agree to it if I ask."

"No, don't, Pam. I don't know how he'll react. He's pretty down on getting his picture taken, so make sure it's okay."

"Okay. I will." Pam jumped up and followed Christian with her camera. "Hey! *You*, man!"

Christian smiled at her. "Don't give me that camera jive! You already *got* one of me."

"We'll see you later, guys." Trevor waved to the roomful of people and then gestured to Devin. "Come on, dude. Walk me out."

After they left, Pam resumed her relentless pursuit as soon as Christian emerged again. It was hard to pin him down because Devin was there as often as Christian, who gave momentary way to Erick, and back to Devin again. When Christian caught sight of her with her camera again, he turned away exaggeratedly. "Git tha' thing outta here."

"Not till I get *your* picture."

"You got it. Out in th' yard. I seen ya."

"No, that was *Devin* I got. I want *yours!*" Boldly she aimed the camera at him, attempting to look impatient and determined. "Come *on*, now. Just one."

"No way." Christian turned his head just as the flash went off and then turned back to Pam, laughing. "See that? Yer not *fast* enough." Christian was obviously enjoying this special attention from Pam, and he radiated nothing but warmth towards her throughout this interchange. Then he turned on his heels and headed for the kitchen.

Pammy looked after him, camera held limply at her side, frustrated, as he emerged from the kitchen and left to join George and the girls at the grill area. I watched him push the kids in the hammock for a few minutes, and then someone placed a joint in my hand. It was Pam.

"Did you ever get it?" I asked her, taking a toke and handing it back.

"No, damn him. He's too fast. I ain't givin' up, though."

She persisted with the camera, dogging his steps, picking up on the porch where she'd left off in the house, demanding that he stand still for one picture.

"Jis *who* do ya want?" Christian teased her, grinning, his black smile broader than ever.

"Man, I don't want *you* no more," she clowned back smugly. "I *got* you! Whether you know it or not. I want *him*, and you know *damn* well who I mean."

"Him?" Christian chuckled and rolled his eyes. "Lahk Ah got any control over *that*!" Then suddenly his expression melted. He placed a hand on his hip and leaned against the deck support beam. "Go ahead."

She wasn't quick enough, and Christian burst into laughter. "Man, you can't *do* it! His picture's don' take. *You* should know *that*!"

"Aw, come on, Devin." Pam glared at him, fixing her face into that impatient, indignant expression.

"Just for you, Pam," *he* said. He sighed heavily, and vanished.

This time she got it. For some reason he had let her do the unthinkable.

"Thank *you*," she said, and he tipped his black fishing cap with one finger. "It won't turn out. You'll see. He blacks them out." That statement from Devin himself.

I watched from the dining room, a little jealousy stirring within me at his easygoing friendliness with everyone, it seemed, but me.

At last, he signaled for me to round up the crew. I was only too happy to comply.

Pam and George, like Trevor, had another dinner to attend with George's family, so it made it easier to bow out early, just as Trevor had.

Gerald approached me and took both of my hands in his. "It was a pleasure seeing you again," he said in his deep rough voice. "And I personally want to apologize for not being able to take more time to visit with you today." He glanced at the other guests milling about in the room. "Maybe next time we can sit down and talk."

As far as I was concerned, Gerald had no obligation to entertain me. His focus on his guests was understandable and insignificant compared to the way Devin seemed to have abandoned me. In all the hours we'd spent at this house, he'd barely spoken directly to me, yet he had been his normal social and joking self with everyone else, including Pammy.

I thanked Gerald and Faye and ushered the girls out to the van, anxious to get home. And I would be damned if I would sit anywhere else *but* the back seat now. Even if I were invited.

The only invitation I *did* receive for the front seat was from George. Pam must have really raked him over the coals for his part in this morning's drive. He approached me sheepishly, just before Devin came out of the house.

"Hey, uh, Ker...I didn't mean to...well, you know. About the seat this morning. Really, I wasn't thinking."

"Forget it, George," I interrupted. "I'm sitting in the back, so you might as well sit up there. I wouldn't sit there now if Devin begged me."

It was childish, I knew, but I didn't care. I was at my wit's end and not thinking rationally.

Devin, however, having boarded up front, was hardly in a begging mood. After an odd glance back at me, he started the van and backed out of the driveway. Within minutes we were headed for the Interstate and home.

"I give up," I said to Pam once the music had begun, assuring us of private conversation. Pam observed my trembling hand as I attempted to light a cigarette.

"Calm down," she said soothingly. "You're freakin' out."

"I know. Wouldn't you be? I give up, Pam. I just can't live with this kind of pressure. I think he doesn't love me anymore and just can't face me with it. He's been like this for over a week, and I guess I'm the one who's going to break first. He obviously wants his freedom. Well, he doesn't have to go through all this. He can have it..." My voice started to break, but I forced myself back under control. The stirrings of anger helped.

"Wow. What're you going to do, Ker?"

"Get the hell away from him, like he wants," I said. "He hasn't got the heart to break it off, so his method apparently is to be like this until I can't stand it anymore, and then I break it off *for* him. He's forcing *me* to do it."

"Oh, I don't *think* so..." She glanced up front where Devin was talking to George as though I wasn't even in the van. "Look, I'd be upset too, Ker, but you can't just...I mean, where would you go? You've got a job and kids in school and—"

"I almost went back to Allentown last year. Remember? It was meeting Devin that made me change my mind."

"Well, I remember you *threatening* to," Pam said, "but I didn't think you were serious. You *know* you don't want to go back *there*. You *hated* Allentown."

"What else *can* I do? If he's trying to get me to throw *him* out, I'm not going to do it."

Pam made a serious attempt to look at it from my perspective. "Okay. Say you did move back. What about your stuff? All your furniture?"

I wiped my eyes with my jacket sleeve. "What stuff? We threw out the desk and the chair to make room for his things. Gave my stereo to Trevor. All that's left is the old couch, bedroom stuff and *his* furniture."

"But—come on, Ker. You've got to get *off* this kind of talk. You guys were getting *married* ! Everything you're feeling is justified, but you might be going too far with the solution. You've got to give this a little more time. I just know that whatever's wrong with him will blow over. If you can just stand it a little while longer. You wouldn't be happy without him. You'd be miserable and you know it."

"I…I can't stay here if he doesn't love me," I whispered. "And I'm afraid that's what's happening."

"Oh, Ker…you're *assuming* again. Before you do anything that drastic, *talk* to him…*ask* him."

"I've *done* that." I could no longer hold back the tears, and they were streaming freely now. "You know I have. After last night I thought at least the *tension* was going to be over with, even if he couldn't tell me exactly what he was worried about, but…you saw him today. He talked to everyone *except* me."

She had no answer for that. She knew it was true.

"He wants out. That's the only other explanation," I added.

Pam still shook her head. "I don't think so, Ker. I think it's something else. I'm not saying I wouldn't be as upset as you are, but if you tell him you're leaving…with that Scorpio pride…you know, he just might take you up on it. If you *do* tell him that, at least be sure that's what *you* want, 'cause you'll probably get it."

I couldn't see where I had any other choice. I wiped my tear-streaked face and looked up to see where we were. Just a few blocks from home. I knew I couldn't just pack up and leave. Not just like that. The thought of life without Devin…

But then, this was just as bad, if not worse.

When Devin pulled up to the gate, he didn't shut the engine off. George jumped out and unlatched the side door.

Pam stood up and nudged me. "Come on, Ker. We're home." There was sympathy in her eyes. I followed her mutely out of the van. The kids were already at the door. I wondered why Devin wasn't getting out too, but I found out quickly enough.

"You got the house key?"

I felt in my jacket pocket and nodded.

"Okay. Go ahead in. I'll be back."

With no further explanation, he pulled away. We watched until the van was out of sight.

"See what I mean?" I gave Pam a final look and turned toward the house.

I was glad the kids had those new toys to keep them occupied now. My day was ruined, but I didn't want theirs to be too.

"Wonder where he went," Pam said, sitting beside me on the couch. "Hey, Ker…aw, don't cry…"

I couldn't stop the tears. There was so much pent-up emotion in me from the whole week of tension that the dam had finally burst. I'd struggled to hold them in during Devin's presence, but it was now impossible to contain them any longer. "Go ahead over to George's," I told her. "He's waiting for you in the Jeep, and he probably feels bad. Please. You guys have got dinner, and I need to be alone. I need to think."

"I hate to leave you like this, Ker. You want me to stay here with you? I *will.*"

"No, Pam. Go ahead. I really need to be alone. I'm even glad *he* left."

"Well…you're *sure.*"

I nodded, not looking up.

"Don't do anything yet. Okay? Try to hold on, no matter what."

I nodded but didn't raise my head until I heard the front door shut. Then I went into the bedroom and sat down on the bed, thinking hard.

If I left, Devin wouldn't have to. All of those things he had said yesterday had to have been just fantastic evasions. The only decision that Devin really had to make was *how* to ease out of this relationship. He'd even admitted that his decision did concern me, and this made perfect sense. It was all coming together now, at least in my mind. This whole thing had been a game. A game he'd grown tired of playing.

Even as these suspicions lingered, I knew the events of the past three months challenged that conclusion. Nobody could pretend to read minds. Nobody could control the music the way he did. Nobody could put on that kind of an act without a hole showing up somewhere.

Nobody could pull the wool over the eyes of three damn dogs.

I looked at my reflection in the dresser mirror. Red blotched eyes and nose. Stringy uncombed hair. Frown furrowed in my forehead. What was the answer? What was I going to do? I wanted to follow Pam's advice, but I also knew I couldn't go on much longer like this either.

I went into the bathroom. I would take a bath, I decided. Wash my hair. Get changed. And if he *still* wasn't back, I would take a nap. But I wasn't going to cry anymore. No matter what happened, I wasn't going to cry.

I heard knocking at the front door as I was filling up the tub. I turned the water off, and called out to Mandy to see who was at the door. A few minutes later, she closed the front door and headed back to her room. "Chris said to come over," she said in passing.

"Okay." I'd forgotten about Chris's mom's gifts. I turned the water back on wishing I didn't have to go over there today. I was in no frame of mind, but I would have to go. The obligation was there. Devin had sure been right about Christmas.

Although the toys were mostly secondhand from Chris's own childhood, his mother had not gone halfway. It took me, both kids, and Chris to cart over all the bags and boxes of things she'd brought.

Among the assortment of toys was a child's record player.

I thanked Chris and asked him for his mom's phone number. He gave me a curious look as he scribbled it on a piece of paper.

"You been crying, Ker?"

"No," I lied. "I just got out of the tub."

He didn't comment further, just excused himself and left. Thankfully, he didn't ask where Devin was.

After we'd gotten the latest toys into the girls' room, I fished out some old country albums for their little record player. That and the Barbie stuff should keep them occupied for a while and give me some time to think.

Just as I was settling into bed for a nap, I heard Devin come in. No door slamming. Nothing out of the ordinary. I glanced at the clock radio. 6:30. He'd been gone a couple of hours.

"Kerry?"

"Back here." I forced myself to answer in as cheerful and normal a voice as I could muster. I was relieved to hear no antagonism in *his* voice. Relieved enough to completely forget the whole day's episode and try to start fresh. Anything to get things back to normal.

He appeared in the doorway, his silhouette blocking out the light from the living room. "Where's that black book? Have you seen it around?"

"Which one?" I got up and went into the living room, determined not to mention his absence for the past two hours. "The Journeys book?"

"No, the Huson Book. *Mastering Witchcraft.*"

"Oh, that's still in my purse." I found it and handed it to him.

"Thanks."

Without another word, he sat down and scanned through the table of contents with his finger, then flipped to the middle of the book. He seemed to know exactly what he was looking for.

Feeling dismissed, I returned to the bedroom. My determination to forget the whole thing was weakening, but I stuck to it, leaving him alone to his reading. I was grateful that the kids had hit the refrigerator throughout the afternoon. It eliminated the supper obligation.

I don't remember falling asleep. The poor kids must have put themselves to bed for when I awoke at nine that evening, they were in their nightclothes and asleep in their own beds, arms filled with Barbies.

On the floor, the little record player was still on, the arm at the end of the album clicking against the paper label area over and over. I turned it off, lifted the arm, removed the record, glanced at the artist and winced. Tammy Wynette. The title of the country album…D-I-V-O-R-C-E.

I shuddered, thinking of the reflective tapes on Devin's reels and wondered whatever controlled *them*. Did they corner the market on *any* music? Did every kind of music have to reflect our personal situation?

I jacketed the album, set it aside and went out in the living room.

I found Devin asleep on the couch. The book was on the floor beside him. A familiar mass of blue energy hovered over him, barely disconnected from his ultraviolet aura. It made me wonder if *he* hadn't had something there when he'd suggested that Blue might somehow be an extension of himself. I no longer felt any fear in Blue's presence, for whatever he was or wasn't, he had proven to be my friend.

The only light in the room was our red bayberry candle that Devin kept lit continually when he was home and replaced when it burned out. The candlelight made the living room look more eerie than ever, especially without the soft twinkle lights of the tree that no longer brightened that corner by the window.

The tree. Devin had not even bothered to plant it. How could he even hint that everything was normal? *HE* would not have left that tree to die in the already too-cramped pot. That was *hardly* normal for Devin, either.

When I looked back over at Devin, Blue was gone.

I tiptoed over to the couch and knelt beside him. Poor Devin. Even in his sleep, his face had that same anguished, worried frown. Just as it had been all week. What could be causing him so much grief?

I touched his shoulder gently, all hurt feelings of today dissipating. "Devin?"

He opened his eyes and looked at me, then around at the darkened room. "Hey, babe." He pulled himself up on one elbow. "What time is it?"

"After nine. You want to move into the bedroom?"

He covered his eyes for a minute and rubbed them. "Yeah. I guess we might as well. Put out the candle, will you?"

A wave of love washed over me for him. If only things could be this normal again.

I don't think he ever fully awakened, but when he took me in his arms that night he crushed me to him, and for the second time ever he didn't make any move to make love. Just fell asleep, his arms holding me tightly. Almost desperately.

It was also the first time I fell asleep to normal breathing from his chest, rising and falling like any mortal man's.

As though he never really did go back to sleep.

11

He was gone when I woke up.

It didn't really surprise me. Mechanically, I went through the motions of getting ready for work and driving the kids to the sitter's. I was so lost in my thoughts that I didn't even realize I'd driven from Kathy's house to the coffee shop until I was already there.

I had no recollection of driving past the plant to get here. No memory of passing his van.

I went in, not bothering to pick up a newspaper. What I didn't need today was a negative horoscope. The music was bad enough lately. Fortunately, the restaurant was crowded so, other than dropping my coffee off in passing, Jane had no time to stop and talk.

I thought about the book that Devin seemed so interested in recently, and wondered if he had put it back up on the shelf or taken it with him. I checked my purse and was astonished to find it there. Devin had put it back.

Speaking of Devin...

I didn't see him until he slid in across from me. Since I hadn't expected him, I had my back to the door.

"Hey."

"Devin!"

His physical appearance was shocking. Not a trace of color in his face, just that taut, gray expression. Eyes dark and hollow as though he hadn't slept in days. He looked far worse than in our first early days when neither of us had slept much. Just what had this week done to him? And for *what?* Why?

"You're losing weight," I said.

"Yeah?" He didn't sound surprised.

I nodded. "You don't look good at all, Devin. You haven't been sleeping, I know."

He reached across and squeezed my hand. "Looks like I blew it again last night, didn't I?"

I looked at him blankly, not understanding, just as Jane arrived with his coffee.

"Want any breakfast?" she asked.

"No, no thank you." To me he added, "Fell asleep."

I smiled. "You sure did. You even breathed normal last night. That's a first."

He didn't reply. He just released my hands and lit a cigarette while I proceeded to doctor his coffee with cream and sugar for him.

"It must really be bad, Devin," I said. "You've got dark circles under your eyes."

He ran a hand through his black curls. "Yeah? That bad, huh?"

We fell into an awkward silence. I wanted to ask him for the millionth time to tell me what was so wrong, but the words just choked up in my throat. It would only irritate him. He did have a question for me, though.

"You got that book on you?"

I took it out and pushed it over to him. "You put it back in my purse."

He didn't respond, just opened the book to the middle again, and scanned quickly what I was pretty sure he'd read last night. Then he closed it and pushed it back over to me.

Another long silence. We sure seemed to be becoming strangers lately.

"By the way," he said suddenly. "I'll probably be a little busy this full moon. I've been meaning to tell you. It's business." When I didn't comment he added, "I can't take you with me to Thompson's Station this time."

"Okay," I said. I hadn't been aware he'd been planning such a trip.

"Uh...nothing personal. I just have to settle a few things and, well, I just don't think it would be cool...or even safe...to have you with me."

"Okay. It's all right."

Another long silence.

Finally, I spoke. "Devin, can I ask you a question?"

He shook his head with a heavy sigh. "Kerry, if it's about us, I'm not in the mood for this right now."

"It's not that same question. It's not about...what your problem is either."

"Go ahead, then."

"Well, I was just wondering if...whatever this decision is...and I'm not asking *what* it is, but...will it come to an end sooner or later?"

"You mean will things ever get back to the way they were. That's what you mean, isn't it?"

"No, not exactly. Just...are we ever going to be happy again...like we were?"

He took a sip of his coffee. "I wasn't aware that I was *unhappy.* But then, you should know. You're getting pretty good at telling me how I feel anymore."

"Devin, you haven't seemed happy to me."

He set the spoon down, his laugh almost bitter. "No? Oh, okay. Like I said. You should know."

When I didn't comment he went on. "If I wasn't happy, all this wouldn't be down on me now. That goes to show you how off you are. Damn. I know what the next question has got to be. Do I still love you?"

I looked at him miserably. It probably would have been. "Okay, Devin. Let's just drop it. No more questions."

"What *is* there to *drop?*" he asked impatiently. "You had a pretty good day yesterday, didn't you? I didn't do anything wrong all day. I—"

"*Okay*, Devin. I'm not going to fight with you. Let's just *drop* it."

He sighed. "Details. Okay, you want details." He seemed to make a small decision and looked me directly in the eyes as he went on. "Lady, I've got business to take care of. It's with the old man and it's between him and me. It concerns a lot of things. One of them is the child we were going to have. That's on a personal level. On the global level, I'm sorry, but I just can't tell you. As far as our son goes, it seems there has been a little misunderstanding on my old man's part, and I've been trying to straighten it out from here. Going home, however, is starting to look more tempting every day." He paused and added, "I didn't mean that the way it sounded."

That last remark had been like a slap in the face. "Going home," I said. "You've actually, *really* been thinking about going *home* ! You've been thinking about whether you should *leave* or not? *That's* what this has been all about?"

He looked away.

"Devin, you mean to tell me that *that* has been the decision you've been trying to make? To leave here or not leave here?"

He grimaced. "Oh, that's what he would *like* me to do. And I have to admit, his insight was right on. I have to give him credit for that. For someone who's never been here, he sure seemed to know that this place isn't what I'd believed it would be. He was sure right about that. And he was right about *them*, too. But aside from what the old man thinks or wants, my decision goes a little deeper than whether or not I'm going to stay or go back. That's only been a small part of it."

"It sounds…serious." I didn't know where he was going with this, but I wanted to keep him talking.

"Oh, it's serious all right. Anything involving my future son is serious. My old man is weary of the weight he carries as the authority back home. When he told me he needed a son to carry on I just assumed he meant our son, the one we planned on bringing into this world. I told him I wouldn't turn my son over to him or anybody. Anyhow, it turned out that he wasn't even referring to that. Our son wasn't what he had in mind. All along he has been referring to me."

I stared at him dumbstruck. I had expected no further explanations from him.

"He's right about one thing, though," he continued after a pause. "Impossible odds and human bullshit. And lady, forgive me, but I don't think I can take the human bullshit in this world another week. At least, that's the way I feel right now."

"He must have been right about me, too." I looked down, unable to look him in the eyes. I didn't really know *who* this old man was that he continually referred to. I didn't know where *there* was, and I wasn't unhappy in *this* world as long as he was with me and things were normal. But he'd rarely discussed *there* in any detail. He'd always maintained that to talk about it would be to color my experience with expectations of what I'd been told. Devin seemed to be pondering my comment as he stirred his coffee.

"No, I still say he was wrong about that. He felt that you wouldn't recognize me or remember me. He was both wrong and right. If he'd been completely right, I don't think we could have come together at all here, no matter *what* I did. He never thought it was important that you remember where you came from, reasoning that you'd surely remember the instant you got out of here. I disagreed then, and I still do. I think you *need* to remember, or you will continue to doubt everything I ever say. Anyhow, I've said too much as it is." He picked up the check. "You're late, aren't you?"

"I don't care." I said. I was, and I didn't.

My apathy really produced a funny look from him. "Well, Devin still has a job there. Today, at least." He stared down at his coffee.

"Devin?"

He looked up.

"I love you."

Something like pain flickered in his eyes. Then he looked away. "Let's go, lady. You don't need Mama on you first thing this morning."

When we reached our vehicles, he made no move to kiss me goodbye, so I just kissed him lightly on the cheek and turned towards my car. He'd parked in front of it. I heard him start the truck and looked up to see the slight wave of his hand and his troubled eyes in the side mirror as the truck rolled out onto the boulevard.

It was later than I'd thought. The time clock area was deserted and people were all busy in their offices. I managed to get to mine without being seen or stopped, not caring if I was fired. Almost hoping I was so I could go home and process the things he'd told me this morning. I was in no frame of mind to work.

When I was dealing with *him*, there was never any conscious doubt or question of whether the things he said were fantasy or fact. There was something about the presence of *him* that forced doubts and suspicion totally out of the picture. But *he* wasn't always around. Sometimes I had to deal with Devin, and that was when I questioned both his sanity and my own.

As luck would have it, Lola wasn't at her desk, and Kelly and Hannah were already posting.

"Oh, so you decided to show up, huh?" Kelly greeted me. "Lola thought you weren't coming in."

"Why, am I fired?" I set my purse down by my machine. Checks were already set out on my tray. "Oh, thanks, Hannah."

"Oh, well, I was going to do yours next," she said with a smile, "but since you're here…"

"Hey, Kerry! What did you and Devin do yesterday?" Kelly asked. "Sacrifice a turkey?"

"Come on, Kelly," I said irritably. "Don't start, huh?"

"Oh, okay." She flinched, looking wounded, and turned back to her machine. "What's the matter? Don't you feel good?"

I seized on that. "No."

"Well, go home. Lola thinks you aren't coming in anyway."

"Can't afford to." Even though I wasn't physically sick, I wondered if nervous breakdowns counted. I went on posting, glad that Kelly had supplied the excuse for the way I was today. When Lola returned, Kelly went into her office, and a few minutes later she came back and Lola called me in.

"Hi." She smiled. "Kelly says you don't feel good. If you want to go home, I'll try to get you paid for the holiday. You've never taken a day off, and if you're really sick I can't see why that rule should apply to you."

How I wished later that I had taken her up on her offer right then and there. But I didn't. And unable to lie to her, even though I probably looked like I had the plague, I simply thanked her and turned to go back to work.

"You sure?"

I nodded and sat back down at my machine.

It was hard to concentrate on my work. My eyes kept blurring and filling up with tears. Each time I angrily pushed them back and kept posting. Lola left at 10:30 for another meeting, and after a long period of silence, commendable for Kelly, she finally stopped her machine and turned to me.

"Look, Ker. I had the flu just a few days ago. I'm still not completely over it, but I know what you must feel like. Or…does this have something to do with Devin?"

I shrugged, realizing that my eyes were too wet and red to pretend otherwise. I was glad that my back was to her.

"Oh. So *that's* what's wrong," she murmured. "Okay. We can talk at lunch."

Devin called at 11:30. It was the straw that broke the camel's back.

Once I picked up the phone, and after his initial hello, he seemed to have nothing to say. Trapped with an audience around me, there was little I could say either, especially with nothing to respond to. He finally told me that he didn't know why he'd called, and hung up. It had been *Devin,* and when I dealt with Devin, I had a hard time buying that story he had dropped on me early this morning. I guess, looking back now, I had never really believed it with my whole heart, although I had tried so hard to believe it with my mind.

After I replaced the receiver, I ran to the ladies' room, to the old familiar stalls where I could break down without anyone hearing or seeing me. I had finally cracked. I had reached the point where my ego could no longer handle any of it.

Why was he doing this? *Why?* What kind of story was he using to get out of this relationship with me? Why didn't he just tell the truth? Anything would have been better than this crazy story I couldn't really accept or believe, and if I did, I'd be as crazy as the story itself.

Out! I had to get out! Away from the office! Away from work! Away from prying eyes! Home, where I could try to think. Oh, why hadn't I taken Lola up on her offer? What could I tell her now?

Anything. Anything! That I was quitting...leaving...anything! Anything to get the hell out of here.

A numbness spread over me, and I was almost in a trance as I washed my face and prepared to do the insane. It was fitting, since I was almost there by now.

Later I would not recall the sequence of my actions. I barely recollected the walk back to my office.

It was almost twelve.

"Where's Lola?" I asked Kelly.

"She went to lunch," she replied without looking up.

Lunch. I couldn't wait that long to talk to her. Like a robot, I scribbled a note that I could barely see through the blur of tears. I had lost all tact, logic, sanity and reason.

Lola, I can't work here anymore, my note began. *Am going to Allentown...*

"What're you doing?" Kelly approached and tried to read over my shoulder, but I covered my tracks as I wrote. "Come on, Ker. Let's go."

How could the day be so normal for everyone else? I shook my head and continued to write. I don't remember exactly what I wrote or how I worded it. I'm sure I must have apologized for the way I was quitting, and hastily signed it. She'd be lucky she could even read it. I hoped she would somehow read between the lines because, God knew, I couldn't tell her the real truth.

"Come *on*," Kelly persisted gently. "Let's go out. We can talk when we get there."

"I'm going to the lounge first," I said abruptly. I sealed the note in an envelope and asked Kelly to put it on Lola's desk.

She said she would, and stared after me as I bolted from the office. When I reached the lounge I kept going...down the hall...out the exit...blinded by tears I ran and ran. I never looked back.

Not even when I reached my car.

12

I drove frantically from the plant to my duplex, hysterics mounting as I screeched around corners and charged through red lights and stop signs. All rational thought was gone now.

The car radio had burst on when I'd turned the ignition key, and what came out of that speaker was not the kind of music the teeny-bop AM stations played, but cuts from those goddamn reels of Devin's. It didn't seem to matter what medium *they* had to work with, they always managed to find an outlet to mirror-reflect the very exact thing that was happening. Or worse, they sang prophesies of what was to come. I started to reach for the knob to silence the lyrics but found that I couldn't...the very preciseness of the audio phenomenon held me in a hypnotic grip rendering me powerless to do anything but listen. A very unwilling prisoner of the radio waves.

Of course, it was Uriah Heep.

I cringed as the singer told me that he believed that I was trying, but he knew in his heart that I was really lying. He said it was the pain in my heart that made me afraid for my soul and my mind. Then he seemed to switch tracks, asking 'what's the use?' I'd turned him loose, and it was time to go. He had to find his dream and go on to live in his paradise.

The song segued into *The Spell*, one of the songs Devin had put on the eight-track tape for me in the beginning, and it did not end until I pulled into my driveway.

When I burst into the house, a startled Pam looked up from the couch.

"Kerry! You're home early! Kerry?"

I rushed past her, heading straight for the bedroom, bursting into sobs too long contained today, ripping from my insides in guttural despair.

She followed quickly, alarm in her voice. "Kerry! What's the matter?"

She touched my arm, and I shook her away from me. "If the phone rings, don't answer it."

"But I have to. I'm waiting for my boss to call. Kerr—what happened?"

"I quit...I quit my job."

"What? Why? Does Devin know? What the hell happened?"

I took a few minutes to try to get control of myself. Pam sat down across from me on the edge of the bed. "Take it easy...what started it? When did it start? Yesterday?"

Before I could answer, the phone rang. I looked at the clock. One o'clock. I knew who it was. "Don't answer it."

"Kerry, I have to. Look. I'll just tell—" The ringing stopped. "Okay. Wait. Let me go call my boss right now. Otherwise, he's going to call any minute. I'll find out what time he wants me in, and then I'll take the phone off the hook, okay?"

I nodded, and she left to make the call. By the time she returned I had calmed down considerably. I was still trembling, but I was able to talk.

"Okay, now...first of all, *who* might call? Devin?"

"Lola. Devin's on a route right now."

"Well, tell me what happened. Oh, I left the phone on. I had to. My boss wasn't there. Did Devin initiate all this? Oh...that's right. He's on a route."

I shook my head, the tears threatening again at the mention of Devin's name. I buried my face in my hands as I replied. "No...yeah, that's just it. He...he...he doesn't talk civilly to me for a we-we-week...and when he finally does this morning he tells me he's thinking about g-g-going ho-ho-home." My voice poured out my grief in hitches."

You don't mean back up *north?* Back to his *wife?"*

"No, Pammy, *home*. You know damn well where he's been saying he came from."

"You're saying he'd *die? Devin?"*

"No, *him*. I don't know what would happen to Devin, but, yeah, he probably *would* die." I was losing control again, crying so hard I could barely talk.

"Whoa! Jump *back,"* Pam exclaimed. "I don't understand." She got up, went into the bathroom, and returned with a roll of toilet paper which she handed to me. "He's *leaving? Him?* And Devin might *die?* Good grief! What brought *this* on?"

The phone rang again.

"No…don't…"

She had already dashed to the living room and lifted the receiver. She walked back down the hall with the phone base unit in one hand, the receiver to her ear. I knew who it was and violently shook my head. I would *not* talk to anybody.

"Oh, Lola?" Pam gestured helplessly to me. "Yeah, she's here…but I don't think she'll talk to anyone."

A long silence.

"I know, but she said *nobody*…no matter who it was."

I sat frozen on the bed. It was too late now to undo what I'd done. She apparently had the note in her hand.

"I'm *trying* to find out. Want me to have her call you later? Oh…okay. Bye, Lola."

She returned the phone to the living room and came back to the bed. "Wow. What'd you do? Just leave her a note?"

I nodded. "I guess she's pissed, huh?"

"Well, she is *now!* I don't think she was when she first called. I wish you'd have gotten on the phone and explained…" Our eyes met for a second, and then she looked away. "Oh, yeah. Right. How *can* you?"

"Sure, Pammy," I said. "I can just see it all now. Lola, I quit. It's very simple, really. My boyfriend is leaving for another dimension, and if I want to take the same train he has reservations on, I simply can't work anymore." It was as far as I got before the sobs started again.

"Kerry, look. I've *got* to go to work. I've been sitting here ready to walk out the door, just waiting for a call. Are you going to be okay? I don't want to leave you like this."

The phone rang again, and she looked at me expectantly. "Kerry, I *have* to answer it."

"I'm not here."

"What if it's Devin? Hurry up, before it quits."

"*No.*"

She raced to the phone. "Hello…oh, uh, Devin?" She glanced in warningly to me. *Don't do to him what you just did to Lola* her eyes seemed to say, and she pointed at the phone. "Just a minute…"

She was right.

With a sense of doom, I walked into the living room and reluctantly took the phone. "Hello?"

"What's the matter?" came the sarcastic greeting. "Is it too hot for you down here?"

I nearly dropped the receiver at his tone of voice. "What…what do you mean?"

"*You* know what I mean."

I didn't answer.

"Kerry?"

"Yeah?"

"So *talk.* What's on your mind?"

"Where are you?"

"Oh, I'm at Lola's desk, here. She just handed me this note." When I didn't respond, he added, "She's pretty upset."

"Tell her…I'm sorry."

"Yeah, well you should be. That's a hell of a way to quit a job…and a friend to boot."

Shame swept over me.

"Look, uh, you going to be there a while, or does your plane leave any minute?"

"No…I mean yes," I said, trying to ignore his sarcasm. "Where in the hell would I go?"

"Well, I just want to be sure. I don't want to come all the way up there for nothing."

"Devin, don't jeopardize your job. You'll—"

"Hey, I'm not jeopardizing *anything*. I'll be there in about twenty minutes. I hope you have an explanation for this." The phone went dead in my hand.

I returned to the bedroom in a daze. Pam, now dressed for work, was pulling on her shoes.

"Mad?"

"Yeah. Real mad."

"Well, I have to get outta here. You'ns'll be able to talk. I still don't understand what happened."

"He says he'll be here in about twenty minutes."

"He's on his way now?"

"Yeah. Twenty minutes. Knowing Devin, and it *is* Devin, it'll be *exactly* twenty minutes."

"Oh, man. It's Devin, huh? Oh boy. He's just going to leave work? He could end up getting fired, Ker."

I lay back against the propped-up pillows, a lump descending from my throat clear down to my stomach. I had really done it now.

"Kerry, what does Devin think?"

"I don't know."

"Well, what was in that note you left Lola?"

"That I was quitting. Leaving the state."

"Oh my God! What a way for Devin to get the news. No warning besides *that?* Was there a fight or something?"

I shook my head. "You know Devin. He won't fight."

She heaved a heavy sigh. "Well, for *your* sake, I hope he keeps that policy today. Look, I'll call you from work, okay?"

I sat alone in a stupor after she left, all emotion drained. If ever I wished for Erick or Christian, it was now. I wasn't sure I could deal with *this* Devin. I'd never heard such controlled fury in his voice. And he *was* furious.

I heard the van pull up to a dead stop from what appeared to be a speed of about fifty. I heard the crunch of gravel, then the slam of the van door and footsteps on the walk. The front door opened.

It wasn't Devin.

At first he said nothing. Just set his keys down on the stereo board and stared down at me, the same eyes and face that Trevor had captured in the Polaroid photo. I noticed that photo now, lying facedown on the table. Pam must have been looking at it when I'd burst in today.

"So. It's Allentown again."

I made no reply. Just returned his stare.

"Damn it, Kerry, don't look at me like that. I haven't done anything to deserve that defensive glare. Now, what's with this Allentown threat again?"

"Do you have to go back to work today?"

"No." He sat down in his gold leather chair and looked at me. "I left for the day."

"Was Tim mad?"

"Hey, I showed him the note. I didn't stick around to see how he felt about it."

I squinched my eyes shut. It would be all over the plant now. "I'm sorry," I said. "I wish she hadn't shown you that note. It was supposed to be a personal note to her."

"Oh. You were just going to leave, is that it? No goodbye? No explanation for *me*? Tell me something, lady. Do you have a plane reservation, or was this all just a big bluff...a scare tactic?"

I fought to hold in the swelling tears. "Devin, if you're going to be sarcastic..."

He slapped his hand over his eyes exasperatedly, and exhaled loudly. "All right. I'm sorry. But how in the hell do you *expect* me to react? I came in from the route, went in to your office expecting to see you, and instead Lola shoves *this* in my hand." His fist closed over the paper I'd left with Lola, crumpling it to a wad. The nauseated feeling swept over me again as I imagined how he must have felt. "So, I repeat," he went on, "and I am *not* being sarcastic, Kerry, really. Did you *plan* to leave without any word to me?"

"No. I was g-g-going to tell you my...self. Wh-when you g-got home tonight."

"So. Then you *are* going," he said. "Just like that."

I didn't answer.

"Well, then, I guess you've decided, right? Isn't that what you just said?"

"That's...how I felt at the time I wrote the note. I w-was in a p-pretty bad frame of mind." I took a deep breath to stop the hitches. "I don't feel that way now."

"Yeah? Well you must have felt that way pretty strongly to pull something like that. Answer me *this*, will you? What brought all this on? I saw you this morning at the coffee shop. You seemed okay. Well, maybe I overlooked something. I thought I had clarified matters for you a little, but I guess I didn't do too good of a job." He rose and walked over to the window, leaned on the sill, and turned around. "In fact, it looks like I just made them worse. So. It's Allentown again."

I just watched him, not knowing what to say, feeling sicker by the minute.

"What makes you think that *you* have to leave?"

"I'm...I wasn't going to tell you to go. It was...better if I...just left," I stammered.

"Oh?" The fury trembled in his voice, and I realized how my answer had been taken. "Well, allow me to spare you the trouble." He snatched the phone from the altar and dialed quickly. "Yeah, Gerald? You want to get Brian and bring a truck up here? Oh, at home."

I winced at the word home. Gerald had apparently asked him where he was.

"No, no violence. Nobody's hurt. Yeah…in about an hour? That's fine. Later." He replaced the receiver. "There. That's half your problem solved. Now *you* don't have to go anywhere."

My mouth hung open in shock. I was dumbfounded. He had *actually* made that call.

"Just like *that*, Devin?" I said, as quietly as he'd asked me the same question.

He wheeled on me. "Just like *what*? What's the matter now? You change your mind already?" He stalked into the bedroom. "I'll be out of your way in an hour."

I watched in horror as he began to pack, throwing shirts out on the bed from the closet and Levis from the drawers into a large army suitcase. Just like that, he was leaving.

I think that's when the reality of this nightmare actually hit me. He was *leaving*.

I bolted from the couch and tore into the bedroom. "I'm…I'm *sorry* Devin…I didn't *mean* it. I don't know what made me do it—"

He glanced at me briefly, coolly, unsympathetically, and went right on packing. "But you *did* it," he replied, without looking up again. "And I've told you before, don't be fucking *sorry*. It must be what you want, or it wouldn't be happening."

There were no tears in *his* eyes. He glanced around the room and then turned to me. "I'll get some help loading up. How about putting some coffee on, huh?"

His rage seemed to have dissolved into a weary resignation.

I left for the kitchen, still shaking, but finally realizing now just what he had already known. I had subconsciously pulled an emotional bluff, not deliberately, but a bluff just the same. A scare tactic, to use his words, that had backfired. I knew for sure now that I had never had any intention of going anywhere. I had unconsciously hoped to scare him into talking to me.

Mechanically I made the coffee and brought it into the living room where the planks and bricks supporting the stereo system were coming down, piece by piece. I knew then that I had better get control of myself if I had any hope of straightening this mess out before it went too far. If it hadn't already. Tears were not going to move him at this point.

"Here."

"Thanks." Devin took a sip and set it down. "I'll miss this shit, probably. It's funny, isn't it, the habits one can pick up in this human world in so short a time. I'll say this much. You sure made making my decision easier for me. I don't have to make it anymore. You made it for me." He lit a cigarette and added, "I'd thank you for that but you might think I'm being sarcastic."

"Like you are," I said.

"Yes," he said with a sigh. "I guess I am. Tell me, lady. Why Allentown? I think I understand your reasoning behind all this, but why *there*?"

"Well, I guess…because my family is there?"

"Oh, I see. Mother's there. So you were just going to go home and live with her?"

"No."

"What, then? Get your own place? A nice job in the coal mines? Lady, did you really think you could get away from me that easily if I didn't want to lose track of you? And I guarantee you, I will *never* lose track of you. I'll be watching your every move until the day you *die*."

It almost sounded like a threat, so positively did he make that statement. That irritated me a little. "If…if I didn't want you to…you wouldn't be able to find me," I countered defensively.

His eyes burned into mine. "You really think you could get away from me, don't you, lady. You know, it would be pretty simple to borrow another body in Allentown. Hell knows…Devin was easy enough."

"Keep Devin out of this."

"Why? Devin is as involved in this as you and me. He might as *well* come with me, and if he *wants* to, far be it from me to stop him. I don't doubt that *he* can."

"What do you mean? Where would you take him?"

"I don't see where that should make any difference to *you*," he replied. "You weren't leaving Devin. You were leaving *me.*"

"I wasn't really leaving *anyone*," I said. "So, you would take him with you when you go?"

"If he wants to go."

I swallowed a lump in my throat. "Then…you *are* going back. Home. For *sure*. There's no changing your mind."

"I guess I am."

"*You* had already decided *that*? And you're pissed off at *me*?"

He stubbed his cigarette out. "No, lady. *You* decided that." He got up and started towards the bathroom when he spotted the Polaroid photo Trevor had snapped. It was still facedown on the table. Trevor had taken the others with him, and it was the only Polaroid *in* the house. "Oh…and get rid of *that*, will you? I don't want any pictures left behind, especially that one." With that, he went into the bathroom and quietly shut the door. Clearing that room out of all his things, probably.

I looked around at the once organized living room…now destroyed. All the pictures were down off the walls and stacked. All the speakers unhooked from the unit. The only thing remaining operable was that damn reel-to-reel. Everything else was disengaged and awaiting the truck.

The books still remained on the bookshelf, however, and I was alone with it all. Chaos. The actual reflection of my very state of mind right there in front of my eyes. There were no tears left in me. I was all cried out. I sat quietly, thinking.

If his intent had been to push me to the point where I drove him to pack up and leave, he had succeeded. I picked up the photo from the coffee table and looked at it one last time. The only picture of him in existence. Get rid of it, he'd said.

Feeling completely beaten and burned out, I methodically tore it to pieces, first in half, then in half again. I didn't look at what I was doing, just continued until the picture was nothing but sixteen tiny squares, and then tossed them into a large, green, unused ashtray. Uncannily, all the little white squares landed, once again, as when it had been a whole photograph, facedown.

"Oh, and another thing, lady—" He stopped short on his way out of the bathroom as his glance fell on the ashtray. Something beyond recognition flared in his eyes.

"Why…did you do *that*?"

"You just said to," I replied, confused at his reaction and a little irritated. "You just told me to get rid of it."

"*Rid* of it?" He picked up a single little white square and shoved it in my face. "Do you really think you can get rid of *us* that way? *Do* you? Think it's that *easy?*"

I gasped. He hadn't even looked at *which* white square he had picked up, yet between his thumb and forefinger was the *only* square that contained both of our faces, and *nothing* else.

"Big shock, huh?" he said, dropping it into his shirt pocket, still not looking at it. "I thought you knew better than that. When I said get rid of it, I meant burn it. Not just rip it up. I guess now you're going to tell me that the *way* that picture happened to tear is a coincidence too, right, lady?"

He still hadn't looked at it.

I was too shocked to answer him. Just took a deep breath and looked at him.

He shook his head, grimaced, and left for the bedroom.

I got up, followed him in, and stopped in the doorway.

"Devin?"

He was emptying the drawers of his socks and underwear.

"Devin!"

He looked up. I had no idea what I was going to say. I just let the words come out.

"I'm…sorry. I *know* I did this. I know it's my fault. I *caused* all this. But Devin…I didn't *mean it.*"

He sat down wearily and shook his head. I could see he didn't want to go over it again.

"I didn't, Devin. I know I left the note, and I know it was stupid. Maybe it was an outlet for my hysterics, and maybe it was just a way to leave work that minute, but I *wouldn't* have gone anywhere. If Lola hadn't handed you that note, I would never have mentioned going *anywhere* to you because I had no intention of really leaving. I don't have any reservations, and I had no intention of making any. It was just the excuse I used for her because I couldn't tell her the truth. I was…mentally running away. And if you *do* move out, I still won't go anywhere."

"Is your mother expecting you?"

"No. I never called her. I wasn't going to."

He shook his head again. "It's no good, Kerry. It'll just happen again. This is just human bullshit. Games. And if there's anyone who should know better, it's you. I swear, sometimes you act just like *them*. If I didn't know better, I'd swear you *were* one of them."

I flinched. *Human* was an insult, coming from *him*.

"I said if I didn't know better," he added softly.

"I must be," I said in a low voice.

"Yeah, right," he retorted. "You *think* you are, so you *must* be. Well, I'll clue you, lady. As you *think* you are, so then you become."

"Well, if I take the word as an insult, that must be some kind of progress for you," I said quietly. "At one time I'd have considered it a compliment."

"Anything is an improvement, Kerry. It would be nice to at least see you face up to the fact that you're not human. Oh, but you can't just take *my* word for it. That would be blind faith."

"Devin, stop it, *please.*"

"Oh, I'm doing it again, huh? Tell me, is *this* what I did wrong yesterday, too?"

"Yesterday. Devin, you *know* what yesterday was. You're doing a lot of things you never did before last week."

"Like what?"

"Like telling me to sit in the rear of the van instead of beside you.

He stared at me. "I can't believe you're going to make something out of that."

"It was the *way* you did it, though," I countered, trying to keep my voice calm and even. "Like I was some dog or something. Come on. Don't act like you weren't aware that it upset me. The whole time we were at Gerald's you almost acted like I wasn't even there."

"Don't pin that one on me. *I'm* the one who wasn't even there."

"And then the minute we got home, you just took off."

The look on his face was genuine bafflement. "So this is about you being left alone for a couple hours?"

"No, it's not that. You know I've always told you to go when you ever feel like being alone. But you just drove off without any explanation."

"I wasn't aware that I had to report or punch a time clock."

"Devin, you're not letting me finish."

"What difference does it make? Apparently, I did it all wrong, but what does it matter now? I'll be out of your way very shortly. In fact, I'd like to know what's keeping them."

"So you're really going to go through with this."

"Hey, don't say that like it was *my* idea."

"I told you I didn't mean it."

He sighed. "Kerry, I'm not going to fight with you, okay? I really think it's better now that I *do* leave. I'm sorry if you were unhappy yesterday, really." His tone of voice had softened, impatience with me seemingly gone and in its place again, tired acceptance. "I tried. I really did. Sure, I took a run down to Daniel's, but I was only gone a couple hours."

"It wasn't *that* you went, Devin," I protested. "It was the *way* you did it. Before last week, you'd have said, 'Hey, Ker, I'm leaving, okay?' or something."

"All right. I'm not discounting your side of it," Devin said quietly. "I can't see where it's any reason to quit your job and leave town, but maybe from your perspective it is. And if I've been that hard to live with—"

"But you haven't been, Devin. It's just this past week or so...since this…decision you've been trying to make."

"Well, that's out of the way now, but you lived with it that long, you couldn't deal with it *one* more day? Or is it two days? When is the full moon anyway?"

"The twenty-ninth. Was *that* when all this really would have been settled?"

"Perhaps. I was working hard towards it. I thought you understood that. Didn't we just discuss it this morning?"

"We did, but you didn't really *tell* me anything. I don't even know what I'm supposed to understand. All I know is I just wanted us to be happy again."

"Well, this may come as a surprise, but I *was* happy. At least up till about one o'clock today. Oh, there were a couple bumps over Christmas, but I really thought all that was over with when we talked this morning. I thought wrong, apparently. It's actually gotten worse. That's okay, though. I can't deny that I was contemplating leaving anyway. I was very undecided. You were the only thing holding me here. The only reason to stay. But, well, everything happens for a reason, so I guess that's all taken care of now, isn't it?"

"God, Devin. You really are *going back* ?"

"I am. There isn't any reason to hang around anymore."

With that, he picked up the paintings and carried them out to the van. When he came back in, he walked over to the reel-to-reel and knelt down. It was the only thing left that was capable of playing any music. Its speakers were self-contained.

"Devin, what do you mean when you say hang around? Do you mean this house and me?"

He closed his eyes impatiently, and his lips tightened. "No, I did not mean this house and you, Kerry. You know what I meant." He plugged the recorder directly into the wall and turned to me with a let-bygones-be-bygones tone of voice. "Is it okay to put this on? Or will it get on your nerves?"

I shook my head. There was still a reel affixed. He gathered the other boxes of reels together and stacked them beside the albums. Then he switched on the recorder and turned the volume down low. "I've been through the albums and separated mine from yours, but you might want to go through them yourself in case I missed some."

I didn't move toward it. Just sat in shocked disbelief as he carried his personal things out to the van. His leather beanbag. The clothes. The pictures. The speakers, planks, candles, boards and cement blocks. The altar. My heart wrenched as he carefully unplugged Puff's flashing globe from the dragon's stomach area. That too went out to the van.

Panic was mounting inside me. Gerald was surely on his way up by now, and the house was pretty well emptied of his things except for the gold chair, the books and, of course, the reel-to-reel. It had ended as fast as it had begun. With no fight or argument, or even any apparent reason, it had taken almost as many exact days to end as it had taken to begin.

When he came in from the final load, he sat down in his gold throne to wait.

There was a long silence for a while, except for the music playing, volume low but running still, all the way to the end. I looked at Devin, still trying to find words to make him change his mind and stay, but apologies were out.

"Devin," I began. "I was wrong. I was hysterical when I left that note. I...please don't move out."

"I have to, Kerry." There was no anger at all in his voice now. Just that tone of deep resignation. "It's happened, not just once, but twice in the last three days. I don't think I could handle it a third time."

"But Devin...if I promised...promised you it won't ever happen again..."

"I can't chance it. I'm carrying a huge burden right now as it is. This...this human bullshit. I'm surprised at you, Kerry. I really thought you were above all this. I believed that. For that matter, I know you really *are*. It was just so surprising to see you behaving that way, the way you did today." He went over to the window and looked out, glanced back at the phone and then turned again to me. "Look, Devin would say that Kerry King is a 'nice chick.' Works in the accounting office. Anybody would be proud to be with a 'chick' like her. But 'nice chicks' are a dime a dozen, Kerry. I needed something deeper than a 'nice chick.' I thought that, given time, you'd become aware of who you are and who I am, but I see now that it was never going to happen. It's bad enough that you still think you're one of them. It's even worse that you think I am too."

I looked up quickly. "That's not true, Devin."

"No?"

"If there is *one* thing and *only* one thing I've come to believe, it's that *you* are *you*. I still don't know about me, that's true, but there's no doubt in my mind now that *you* are *you*. I told you that already, and I meant it."

At least I thought I meant it.

"Well, if that's true, then that's good. All this won't have been a complete failure. At least maybe I did get *something* across to you."

"Devin, please give me another chance."

"Lady, this episode today and the other day, all this has shown me is that as long as I *am* here in this world with you, you're never going to be convinced that anything I've tried to tell you is true. Those doubts, Kerry. Even as we sit here talking, I can see by the look on your face that you still don't believe. You still don't know."

I could feel my inner agony and desolation changing inside me as he talked. It sure hadn't taken *him* long to pack up everything and empty the house. It was as if he'd just been waiting for that moment when I would break first so that he could gratefully clear out. My thoughts were living proof that what he'd just said was true. I had not believed a lot of this.

"Okay, Devin," I said finally. "Evidently, this is what you really want. I've said and done everything I can think of to try to apologize, make it up, and stop you from leaving. I said I was wrong, and I was. But you could at least understand the frame of mind I was in by this morning. You could have at least taken that into consideration before you picked up that phone." I reached for my purse and pulled out the two books that belonged to him. "Here. Don't forget these." I tossed them on the coffee table.

He picked up the Huson book and went into the bedroom. I followed curiously and found him, book open in the middle again, open to that same chapter on psychic self-defense. When I walked in, he closed it and set it aside.

"I could say the same thing to you, you know, lady," he said wearily, leaning against the pillow, eyes closed.

My anger melted. Just looking at the dark shadows under his eyes and his pale face was enough to jolt me back to reality. It was apparent that he'd been through a great strain himself, mental or otherwise. It showed physically. Whatever his problem actually was, it seemed to be physically deteriorating him. Anyone else with such a problem would have *really* taken it out on me. Devin had merely tried to stay out of my way.

"Devin." I put my hand on his knee. "If…if you're dead set against changing your mind, well, okay. I can't make you stay. But I wish that you'd at least try to look at what I did today from my standpoint. At least try to understand what was going on in *my* mind."

"Tell me. What *was* going on in your mind?"

"Well…" At least he was willing to listen. "This all started about a week ago. Can we take it from there?"

He rubbed his eyes with his thumb and forefinger and then looked at me. "Yeah. I guess it *has* been about a week. Look, Kerry. I *do* realize it's been hard on you, all right? I'm not blind or stupid. And I *did* try not to take it out on you. I guess I just took it for granted that you did understand I was in a dilemma of great magnitude and needed the time and space to work it out."

"Devin…was it, or *is* it, so serious that if I *had* known, I wouldn't have understood?"

"Yes."

"But how do you *know* that? Have you ever told me anything that I couldn't accept before?"

He ignored that question. "This is different. A *lot* different."

"But regardless of what it *was*, was it a reason to be sullen and brooding and off in your own little world—"

"There's nothing fucking *little* about that world, lady," Devin interrupted, "but you don't seem to understand that. Much less believe it."

"See, Devin, there you go. You keep telling me what I wouldn't understand. What I *don't* understand is why you couldn't trust me with your confidence and talk to me about it. Bottling it up doesn't help. If this was the other way around, you'd be pretty upset if I did that to you."

"Maybe so, but then, I'd hardly expect *you* to come down with a problem like this one. And lady, I *know* you couldn't understand it, okay?"

"Devin, I don't think you're giving me any chance to show you that I could and would. Do you think I couldn't understand if, say, your wife suddenly turned up pregnant? Or that you just wanted to go back to her? Or you met a completely different girl and—"

"So you really think I'd add another *female* to my problems," he interrupted again with a wry laugh. "Listen to yourself, Kerry. You're just proving to me that I'm right. You *wouldn't* understand. Do you realize how many human reasons and problems you just spurted out? You're trying to rationalize this with *human* reasoning. All of those things you just mentioned…any of those I could roll off my back."

"Then what else could there be that I wouldn't understand? What else *is* there?"

"What *else*? Kerry, this…situation…is so serious." He paused and looked at me with anguished eyes, apparently weighing what he was about to say carefully. "It's so serious that it isn't *possible* for you to understand it. It's *not* a human problem, okay? Well, maybe, in a way, it is. It has to do with this entire planet *Earth* and every living thing on it, human or otherwise." He stopped, took a deep breath and continued slowly, watching me guardedly. "It has to do with something I could do…could influence…to stop what may be about to happen. I could do it *easier* from there. That doesn't mean I couldn't have done it from here, but I can do it better from *there*. The simple solution would have been to leave immediately…a week ago. Go home. Take care of business. With or without you. Since you don't know how to *get* there yet, and you aren't even completely convinced that it's even *there*, taking you with me was out of the question. Think back a week. I *did* approach the subject, but you didn't find it to your fancy. And you do have the kids, so you couldn't go back with me anyway. That's why I didn't push the issue. You *do* have responsibilities here. Maybe if I had left *then*, and left you here, you and Devin could have lived happily ever after like you thought you wanted in the first place. I knew you weren't ready or able to go with me. Perhaps that was my fault too, for not pushing you a little harder to try, so that you could at least come *see* me once in a while. But you won't learn to go there if you really don't believe it *is* there. But what the hell, lady, I'm pretty new at this too. I had no idea what this place would really be like before I got here. And I couldn't stand it with you here and me there. The separation. Watching you, headed the wrong way, studying primitive little religions and getting caught up in human bullshit…"

I stared at him incredulously. What had brought this rash of explanation on? Because he was leaving *anyway*?

"I figured it wouldn't be easy to get you to believe me, or remember, or even really understand," he went on. "Not unless I could get you to take that little trip in. But if you look back on that tablet that we…met…over, you'll see I was trying to tell you from that first night. That very *first* night. I thought then that by now you would be able to walk through those gates with me, but look at you. You still don't really know that world is *there*. And how do you think that looks to the old man? To make matters worse, there's a lot sitting on thin ice *anyway*. I was the one who was so sure you'd come around. All my talking and pleading for a chance to try…well, I guess he has a good right to be laughing at me now."

"So…this…this problem…it never *was* a human problem."

"I'll tell you just how much you could *not* understand it, Kerry. It's a problem that I *know* you are not even aware of existing on this planet right now, and since the worlds overlap, any problem here could be a problem *there*. Okay? Now, how can you understand a problem about something that doesn't even *exist* to you? Don't you think I've considered all this? That I've given deep thought to it? Every time you *asked*? And aside from the fact that I have no *business* telling you…completely aside from that, why burden you with something you couldn't possibly do anything about? You see what it's done to me. Now, you take it from there."

He got up and went back into the living room. I sat there trying to absorb some of what he'd said. With my little human perspective, I tried to fit his magnificent problem in with all this happening now and I couldn't. I followed him out and sat on the couch.

"Why couldn't you have told me all this to begin with?"

He stared at me, his expression a mixture of disbelief and hurt. "Would it have done any good? Would you really have believed me? Do you even believe me *now*?" He lit a cigarette, frustrated, and continued. "Don't you think I might be reading your thoughts right this instant? After all this, you surely must realize I can at least do *that*. I can *feel* your doubts, lady, even now. We're being watched right now, but you don't believe that either, do you? I just hope, for your sake, that my old man doesn't show up after I'm gone. I really don't think you could handle it. Look how it is with just Blue. You still don't really accept him, or it, or whatever it is. Hey, you think Blue scared you, lady? My old man is enough to turn you to stone. Don't get me wrong. He wouldn't hurt you. In spite of your ignorance, you're still one of us. And that holds true whether you accept it or not. Well, it looks like you need everything proved to you, and I can do that a lot better from *there*, assuming I can *still* get back. After all the static I've given him this week, he just might let me sit it out here and stew."

I didn't know what to say. If there was any truth to *any* of this, I had screwed things up even worse than I thought.

"I don't even *like* Blue that much," he said suddenly, "but then he never was all that friendly with me. But if I were *you*, I'd make friends with him pretty damn fast. He may be the only ally you've *got* right now, believe me."

"So, there's no changing your mind. You're definitely going to go. Back to…your world."

"There's no reason to stay. I can keep an eye on you from there, just as I always have since you left. Since your birth here. But whether you see me or hear me, or whether you look right *past* me, will depend entirely on you. Oh, you could *still* come with me. Right now, if you believed you could, but—"

"But I don't know how," I finished for him. "You keep saying I can go, and I just don't know how."

"That's because you don't really *want* to know." He picked up his black cap and slammed it on his head. "Just as I thought, you *still* don't really believe any of this. Oh, I can see that you *want* to, but that damn doubt…it's still there. You just don't know. You still aren't sure."

I knew there was no use in denying it. "What…what will happen to Devin?"

"Devin may *die*," he said bluntly and went out to the kitchen. "You want some more coffee?"

"I'll get it." I started to rise.

"No, sit down. I'm quite capable. By the way, I hope you don't think you will ever be able to settle for a human companion again after all this."

I was sure I'd heard wrong. "*What* did you say?"

"You couldn't possibly go back to living that way again, but I guess you'll find that out for yourself."

Anger flared up inside me. In the middle of this insane conversation, which was absurd enough as it was, *now* he was telling me how I was going to continue my life after he was gone? "Look, Devin," I said. "Assuming everything you've ever told me is true—"

"And that's a big assumption, isn't it?" he interrupted.

"Let me finish. If you and I are not human but *we're* here, I'm sure we can't be the only ones."

"Of course there are others," he said tiredly. "Hell, people are here from everywhere." He threw the coffee together and brought it in. "If I were you, Kerry, I'd start cramming. I mean it. You're going to need everything you've got and then some. If I can't stop what's scheduled to go down in seven days—"

"*What* did you say?"

"You heard me, lady. I realize you don't believe a word of this, but that doesn't change the facts. You wait it out. Seven days. You look in the paper. That's all. Seven fucking days."

"It will be in the *paper*? Even if you *can* stop...whatever you're talking about?"

"Whether I can or I can't. It'll make headlines. You'll see then. The proof you've been looking for. And maybe then, for once in your twenty-five years of physical existence, you'll begin to realize...just maybe get a glimmer of comprehension of all that I've been trying to tell you. Look what it's done to me, lady, just from trying to stop it. Look. Don't get me wrong. I still love you. I always will. If I didn't love you so fucking much I wouldn't even bother wasting these words." He took a deep breath and exhaled a heavy sigh. "As it is, they *are* pretty much wasted now. You're taking all this in, and I can see how much you really don't believe. And as for how it will all turn out, I still don't know. But when we meet again someday, if and when you've learned to go, Kerry, then you'll look back on all this and realize that I didn't *leave you*, and I *didn't* desert you. If anything, I'm doing this *for* you. I will always be at your side, whether you perceive me or not. I'll be there when you're trying to learn to go...that is, if you keep working towards that end. Oh, you may not see me at first, but if it's proof you need, I can more than guarantee that you'll get *that*."

"What do you mean?"

"I'm not leaving *you*, lady, that's what I mean. I'm leaving this body of Devin Drew's, but I'm not leaving *you*. This crazy world of time and space, matter, opposites, action...this dimension...*that's* what I'm leaving. Oh, but you can't *possibly* believe that right now, and you won't until after I'm gone. Then, well, you'll see. It will be a little hard to argue with your senses, and impossible to deny what's right in front of you."

"What...what will Devin think about all this...your leaving him?"

"Devin?" His tone was sharp. "Devin is going to be devastated."

A wave of bitterness swept through me as I wondered how he could do this to Devin. "What're you going to do? Put a gun to his head?"

"What, *suicide*? No. An accident, perhaps. Maybe on the truck. Pneumonia...who knows? Who cares how, really?"

"I care. I love Devin, and you have no right to take him."

"Hey, lady, I assure you, from what I know of Devin, and I know him well...inside and out, you could say...given a choice between there and *here*, there won't be one with Devin."

"And Erick and Christian?"

"They can either stay or go, depending on what Devin decides to do. They're pretty mobile. They've been with him longer than I have. I thought you understood that, too." As if an afterthought he added, "I keep assuming you understood a lot of things. Now? I don't know that this hasn't been one big game to you...that you haven't been humoring what you think is some psycho. Do you even believe that other realities are even *there*, lady?"

"I do believe they're there, Devin," I admitted. "There's too much evidence that's been documented for centuries, so that much isn't hard to believe. I just don't know how to get there, that's all. But I promise you, I *will*. I'll keep trying, even if it takes me the rest of my life."

He exhaled with obvious relief. "That's good, lady. At least we did get *that* far. You know who I am, and you have some idea of how to get...home. Perhaps we *will* see each other before you leave this physical system."

"Will you be able to help me from there?"

"Help you? I'll be able to fucking live *for* you if that's what you want. You won't have to do anything but *breathe*. If proof is what you need, you'll get all the proof your little ego can handle without blowing your mind to pieces."

"What do you mean by proof? What kind of proof?"

"What kind? How would it be to *know* that you never have to work again to survive here? To just get everything you need and every material thing you ask or wish for? No matter what it is. Things will fall into your lap. That much I can do blindfolded from there. I told you before...we don't have the time problem when it comes to materialization. Instant materialization is our specialty."

When I didn't comment he sat down on his gold footstool and continued. "You'll see what it's like to have to feel people's feelings and hear their thoughts screaming at you. And, oh, you'll learn to watch every destructive or negative thought that pops into your head, and watch carefully *how* you think. Things will happen as fast as you think them. No, you won't doubt me much longer. It's just a shame that it has to be proved to you at all. Well, that *is* what I was warned of before I came. And...once again, they were right."

"When is all this going to happen, Devin? When will you actually leave? How much time do I have to learn to go before *you* go?"

"A day, a week, a month. Who knows, Kerry? It won't be long. Not if I have anything to say about it, but I'll really have to do some talking *now*. After all my arguments to *stay* this week, I may get some static about doing an about-face. They *could* leave me here."

"Would they do that?"

"The old man *could*. Oh, but he won't. I wouldn't stand for it. He'll either let me come back, or I'll become the biggest renegade this world would ever have to deal with. Our world has a bad enough reputation as it is. Hell...demons...Satan...fear...pain...evil...all the bullshit. They don't need any more stories added to those. And I wouldn't stop until they let me in." He pulled his black cap down over his eyes and settled back in the chair. "Must be about time to go get the kids."

I looked at the clock. It was only 5:30. This had been going on for three-and-a-half hours. "I'll call Kathy. I don't really want to bring the kids home in the middle of this. Devin...I know it sounds hollow, but...I do love you."

"Well, you may not believe this, but I love you too. I may not have said it often, but…words aren't really my style. I do hate to see this happen to Devin. I don't think he's really going to understand. He's rather attached to me now…uh, no pun intended." He glanced out the window. It was twilight. "Maybe Gerald decided to wait for a second call."

I sat quietly while he dialed again.

"Faye? Devin. Hey, has Gerald left yet? Oh, yeah? About how long ago? Okay. Just checking. No, everything's cool. Nothing's changed." He replaced the receiver and turned back to me.

"I do hope you keep trying, Kerry. I know I've been trying to reach you for twenty-five years. You've shoved everything under religion, imagination, hallucination, coincidence…or just plain unexplainable… just like the humans do. I just hope that after I'm gone, that the first time you feel a wave of heat on your body, or a picture drops, or a song comes on the radio…I hope you take a few other possibilities into consideration. But don't worry. I will never give up on you. I'll get through to you no matter what drastic measures I have to take…but it would help if you would keep your eyes open."

"Are you…even going to say…goodbye?"

"I'm saying it now. Not goodbye…*later*. I don't know exactly when I can split, but it will be the first possible opportunity."

"How will I know when you're gone? If Devin isn't living here, how will I even know?"

"You'll be the very *first* to know. Even before Devin himself realizes it's happened. If you keep your channels open you'll hear from me the very second I'm there."

"And Devin…he's going to freak, isn't he."

"I'm afraid so. I'm afraid of how he's going to react when he finds out I'm actually going to *leave*. He's been aware of the possibility and, unfortunately, you've been getting the backlash from his realizing *that* this past week. But once he really *knows* it's going to happen…as you say, he *is* going to freak out. Lady, I understand you, and why you did what you did, but Devin…I just hope he doesn't blame you for my decision to leave. It may be a little different Devin Drew than what you've been accustomed to the past few months." He glanced at his watch. "Look, why don't you go get the girls?"

"Why?"

"Well, I'd kind of like to say goodbye to them."

"If I go now, will you be here when I get back?"

"It'll take some time to pack up all these books and load up. I'll wait."

I rose, dizzy and nauseated. He was really going to leave. Unlike me, he had not been bluffing.

As I pulled out of the driveway I could hear the tapes droning unmercifully on…appropriate to the immediate situation.

As usual.

13

It was raining when I left the house. I turned on the radio and was stunned to hear the exact same song as the one that had been playing on the reel a minute ago.

It was a Quicksilver song, one I'd heard before, but never

had it been so apropos to a current situation as it was now. The predominant theme of the song was that the singer had tried everything he knew to tell me the truth, that it appeared to him that I was only make-believing. He said every time he had tried to tell me what I was doing wrong I just hid my head and called him crazy, and that he knew I could do what I needed to if I just wasn't so lazy. He was frustrated. How could he convince me that everything was true?

What it didn't say, and maybe should have, was how selfish I was being. I was so lost in my own agony and grief that I never once considered how this was going to affect the kids.

When Kathy cut them loose at the door, jackets over their heads as they ran, I had the rear door open for them. I was glad for the rain. Not only was it fitting tonight, but it kept Kathy from following them out and holding me up. She waved to me from her doorway as I pulled the car door shut and put on the headlights. It was dark now, and the roads would be slippery.

Whether it was my lack of greeting to them or whether the girls saw the tears glistening in my raw, red eyes, they both stopped short in their chattering as they bolted into the car, and Michelle was the first to speak.

"Mommy…why are you crying?"

"What's wrong, Mom?" Mandy asked, leaning forward in her seat.

"Devin's moving out," I began, sure it was better to let them know before we drove up and they saw the stark empty nakedness of the house.

Michelle sat rigidly in the back seat, eyes wide with shock and beginning to brim with tears. "Devin's moving out? Right now? Why, Mommy…'cause you spent so much money on our Christmas toys?"

Suddenly Mandy burst into sobs, and she continued to sob all the way home. Michelle sat motionless, hands folded in her lap, tears streaming quietly. Their emotional reactions just made it worse for me. How could I possibly try to comfort them? I had to keep my eyes on the road and get us home safely.

When we pulled into the driveway, Gerald was already there. The bright porch light lit up the front yard, and Devin was visible in the doorway talking to Brian and Gerald. All three looked up when the car pulled in. Mandy and Michelle spotted Devin and looked at me hopefully.

"Mommy, he's *there*! He's *there*! Devin's there, he's there!" Michelle screeched, eyes wide and still wet with tears.

"He's leaving," I said quickly, not wanting them to get any false hopes and almost hating Devin at that moment. "He's packing the van up right now." I wiped my eyes and shut the ignition off. Mandy was still sobbing her heart out. I leaned over the seat and caressed her head which was bent over to her knees. "Come on, Mandy. We have to make a run for it…oh Mandy, please don't cry. I'm so sorry."

Mandy suddenly bolted from the car with Michelle right at her heels. The rain had slowed to a drizzle, but they ran like lightning was chasing them. I followed at a slower pace. When they reached the doorway Mandy kept right on going, straight towards her bedroom. She did not stop to even look at Devin. Michelle was right behind her.

Devin looked after her in surprise, and I looked desperately to him. He comprehended instantly.

"I'll go talk to them," he said and went immediately to their room.

Brian left for the van with another load of books, and I was left alone in the room with Gerald. Thankfully, he didn't ask what happened.

"These things are always harder on the kids, it seems," he commented kindly, looking towards their room. "How about you? Are you holding up okay?"

I nodded. There was nothing to say, and every time I opened my mouth, the tears started again. When Devin came out of their room some fifteen minutes later, he spoke to Gerald in private for a few seconds, and then Brian and Gerald boarded their truck.

After Devin waved them off, he returned to the house and looked around. It was stripped bare.

"I owe you a stereo," he said quietly.

"No, you don't. I owe you a hundred and thirty dollars for toys, so let's just call it even."

"No. I can't leave you without music."

"Forget it."

He looked at me for a long minute and then at the two bookshelves stacked one on top of the other. Once crammed with books, now only a few hardcovers lay on one shelf. Few of the books had been read while they'd been there. Now, all that remained were their outlines in a thin layer of dust. There were a few tablets on the bottom shelf. They'd been tucked there under the books when Devin had arrived. They, too, sat in the dust.

"I thought you had more books than that," Devin said suddenly, breaking the silence.

"No. Most of them were yours." A tomblike atmosphere had settled over the living room. "Are the kids all right?"

"Mandy's taking it extremely hard. I think Michelle might be a little young to really realize what's going on. I talked to them both for a long time and explained the best I could. I really love those kids. I told them I would stop back and see them."

"They're okay now?"

"Believe it or not, they're actually sleeping."

"Kathy probably fed them dinner since I picked them up so late." I refrained from suggesting that he'd used one of his magic tricks to put them out. "Thanks."

He shrugged. "Kids adjust to things fast. How about their mother?"

I looked at him and walked over to the bookshelf. "I don't know about their mother." I stooped and picked up the notebooks and dusted them off. There were three of them. One was the first journal tablet we'd first communicated with.

Devin recognized it. "I'm surprised you still have that," he said. "What else did you keep?"

"Everything. Everything you ever gave me. All the pictures you drew. All the cards from Devin, Erick, and Christian, with all the different handwritings." I started to cry, caught myself, and wiped my already raw eyes on my sleeve.

"Please don't do that," he said. "It evokes human emotion in me, and that's the last feeling I want to identify with right now."

"I'm trying *not* to."

"I know you are, lady."

I turned around and looked at him. He was half sitting on the arm of the couch, black hat on, jacket over his arm. "Devin, I love you so much."

He reached over and ruffled my hair. "I know you do, lady." He looked down at the tablet and the metal box beside the shelf which was now open, displaying everything I had saved. "You even have the napkin from Lums? With all that stuff about our son?"

I nodded. "You're not going to take them too, are you?"

He flinched. The living room was completely stripped except for my beanbag, the couch, coffee table and empty bookshelves. "You didn't have those bookshelves when I moved in, did you?"

"No. I had my books on the desk. The one we threw away. Uncle Joe gave us these, remember?"

"You sound muffled."

"It's hard to talk. I'm getting a sore throat or something." I sneezed, then sneezed again.

"You're getting sick."

"Yeah, well, that's confused thinking for you. That's all a cold is." I sneezed again. "You know that."

His eyes changed expression. "*You* know that?"

"Yeah, well, sure. I'm not entirely ignorant. You didn't teach me *everything* I know."

"That's right. You were pretty heavy into the occult when we got together, huh? I keep thinking this is all pretty new to you." He almost smiled. "What else do you know?"

I wiped my eyes and set the tablets aside. "How much time do you have? I'll tell you what I learned just tonight."

He crossed his arms. "What *have* you learned, lady? Tell me."

"Not to cry wolf, for one thing." I stood up, and he put his arms around me. "Damn, Devin, I love you so much."

He held me close for a minute, and I felt him sigh. "I love you too."

We stood like that for some time, and finally he nudged me gently. "Come on. I've got to go. If nothing else, tomorrow is a workday."

When I stepped back, he glanced again at the bottom shelf. "What *are* you going to do with all that stuff? We can't just have it lying around. Someone might get their hands on it."

"All the proof." I looked down at it and back at Devin. "Please let me keep it. It's all I have left of you and us…and everything. Please, Devin…"

He looked at me doubtfully. "Lady, I don't know if that's a good idea. I'm not saying you'd distribute it around, but it could fall into the wrong hands. You know, how about if you keep the one tablet, and I burn the rest."

I shook my head. "Please don't, Devin." I sneezed again. "I'll put it away somewhere."

"You'd better get some sleep," he said. "And I have to go. Come on…let's get some of these windows closed."

"I can keep the stuff?" I asked as he began pushing the windows down.

He took a deep breath and exhaled slowly. "Like I said, I don't know how they…at home…would feel about it, but…I guess it's okay with me."

The tape recorder, which had been left running in the corner, had been playing soft Moody Blues from the moment Gerald and Brian had left. Now, suddenly, a piano chord sounded, and Devin's eyes misted as he obviously recognized the song by the beginning note. "Oh, lady, I don't even believe this *myself*. Do you recognize this song?"

I shook my head against his shoulder, tears streaming.

"Listen to this song. If you ever doubted me, listen to this song.

I didn't know it at the time, but the group was Quicksilver Messenger Service, the same group that had chided me all through the drive to Kathy's tonight with the song saying that everything was true.

The title of this song was *Don't Cry My Lady Love,* the very first lyrics to the song, and they were clear and easy to understand. The words could have been penned by someone sitting outside my front door listening to our conversation this afternoon. I wondered how words like these could ever have been written to mean anything else.

The singer begged me, his lady love, not to cry. He said I knew how he couldn't stand to see me crying. He admitted that he knew how hard I'd been trying. He said someday I would remember that he'd been the sun in my window, but things like this happened all the time. It was the same old thing. One was always crying, and one was always easing the pain.

Then he told me to just say goodbye, that he didn't want any memories haunting me. He said I could look into his eyes and change his mind if I really wanted to, but someday I would see something in someone I had never cared for to begin with… that I'd remember the one I'd once shared my heart with.

But these things were happening, never right on time. One was always leaving, and one was always changing his mind.

These lyrics were blow enough to my fragile ego, but they continued even more bluntly. He said there had been another time and place when I knew that he really did love me. He told me to dry my eyes, that he would never place another world above me. He reminded me that I'd once tried to leave him and admitted that someday maybe I would know I really didn't need him. But, then again, these things happened all the time. It was always the same. One was always crying, and one was always taking the blame.

The song was beautiful. It was the final song I would ever hear on the reel-to-reel from his ten tapes playing in my house. He let it finish to the end as he held me. Then he unplugged the recorder and latched the lid. There was nothing else to say that the song hadn't already said.

He picked up the tape recorder and stepped out into the icy night air. I followed him and watched him place it carefully inside the van. It was still drizzling, and as I stood there shivering he started the engine and rolled the window down. "You're getting sick. Go inside."

"Devin…"

"Go ahead."

He pulled the van out, made a U-turn and parked in the gravel on the other side of the street. He was now facing south, in the direction of home. Home for him now, was Gerald's house. I saw him put his head down in the crook of his arm, and for the first time it occurred to me that he might be having second thoughts after all. I ran across the street, tears intermingling with the rain as it struck my face.

"Devin…" I reached in, touched his shoulder. "Please come back. I'm so sorry. I love you so much."

He looked up at the sky, and I saw that his eyes were glistening too. Then he looked down at me. "I love you too, lady. Go back in the house. Please." Thunder almost drowned out his last word.

"Will you at least think about it?" I pleaded, my last desperate effort. "Reconsider…"

He searched my face for a long minute and nodded. I hugged him through the window, heart bursting with hope, and then I finally stepped down from the running board so he could leave. As he pulled away it sounded like he said, 'I'll call you.'"

I didn't leave the glistening street until the van lights had disappeared in the distance. Then I turned, crossed the street, and went back into the house.

Seven days, he'd said. And then there was the question of what would happen to Devin when he left. He'd really gone out on a limb.

Seven days.

14 The phone rang. It was so soon after Devin had gone that I snatched it quickly, hoping it would be him calling the whole nightmare off. I refused to accept the arrangement as permanent.

"Hello?"

"Is Devin there?" The voice was crisp and metallic. Lola. And not sounding at all like the Lola I was used to.

"Lola? No, he's not." I didn't want the word to start moving so fast. In fact, deep down inside I hoped that, after sleeping on it, Devin and I would work the whole thing out tomorrow.

"Where is he? Do you know?"

"He might be at his father's," I said, trying to imply that he was just down there visiting. "Oh, Lola, I'm glad you called. I—"

"Don't bother," she said abruptly, cutting me off. "We have nothing to discuss."

"But Lola—"

"Goodbye, Kerry."

The phone went dead in my hand. I stared at the receiver in shock. Lola was one of my oldest friends. Since before she'd even hired me. The tears welled up again, but I wiped them away. She had a good right to be mad. She was going to need time to cool down.

I wasn't so eager to answer the next call, which came shortly after Lola's. True to her word, Pammy had grabbed the first conceivable break to check back on me. Pammy was the only one who had been involved from the beginning and who knew everything that had really happened the past few months. It was probably good therapy for my stunned mind to have to put into words exactly what had happened this afternoon. God knew, I wouldn't be able to do the same with anyone else.

"Well, he's gone, Pammy."

"He's *gone* ?" It stopped her short for a minute. "You mean he moved out?"

"Out. Everything. He's gone…" My voice broke as the tears choked up in my throat again. She waited quietly while I got my bearings. I guess she had a few bearings out of place now, too.

"Hey, Pam?"

"Yeah, I'm still here. Wow. I just can't believe it. You'ns are blowing my head. He moved *out* ? He just up and moved *out* ?"

"Yeah. Right away. Immediately."

"I knew you should have left him alone. Oh, Ker, I was afraid of this. That's why I kept saying to leave him be. Didn't you'ns talk about it at all?"

"Yes, me and *him* did. I'm not sure what the rest of himself thinks."

"Wait a minute. When you say you and him, you mean *Devin*, right?"

"No Devin, no Erick, no Christian. It was just *him*."

I tried to tell her some of the actual conversations that had taken place, the unrealistic-sounding facts that surrounded our personal situation. Devin had not left because of money or wife or girlfriend. He had left so he could prepare to go home. Home to that other dimension where he had come from.

Knowing as much as she did, that absurd explanation didn't really surprise Pammy. Like me, she was pretty much used to hearing this kind of talk. I ended my summery with an account of the phone call from Lola, and that was her first interruption. It was also, with all the talk of other dimensions, alternate realities, multiple personalities, and even the episode with Trevor's Polaroid picture, her first verbal register of surprise.

"Wait a minute. Lola hung up on you?"

"Yeah. I guess I can't blame her."

"Yeah, but still…wow, Kerry, you should call her back. Explain to her—"

"How can I, Pam? How in the fucking hell can I tell her any of this?"

She was quiet for a minute, then, "You know, Ker, I think you and Devin just hit your first real problem out here in the real world. Just what *are* you going to tell people?"

"I don't know. I guess Devin will run into that problem at work tomorrow."

"Well, did you tell Lola he moved out?"

"No, but I think that's what she was calling to find out. She asked for Devin, and she never calls Devin."

"Well, don't go jumping to conclusions. She could have had a work reason. I'll be home in a couple of hours. We'll talk more about it then."

After she hung up, I took the phone off the hook and went into the bedroom. It too looked like a vacant motel room. The closet where his clothes had hung, the partially opened drawers—now empty. A yellow legal tablet lying open on the bed with nothing written on it.

Afraid that I would miss a call from Devin, I put the phone back on the hook, and it rang instantly. This time it was Kelly, but I didn't even let her get to the question. I said I couldn't hold the phone and would call her back at work tomorrow. Deep down inside I hoped to reach Devin and get him to come home before the rumors hit work. Lola already had an idea that Devin wasn't around. If she called Gerald's house, Devin just might verify it.

The emptiness of the house was a constant slap in the face. Once so full that a path could barely be walked from the front door to the kitchen, it was now far emptier than it had ever been before Devin had moved in.

What was so different? I surveyed the room. My old stereo was gone. The armchair had been pitched, as had the pole lamp, to make way for Devin's fortress of stereo equipment and his gold chair and altar…and, of course, Puff. The desk that once had been in the kitchen. All these things had helped to make my apartment more like a home…now vanished. The paneling that had once displayed the tapestry and later all of his paintings…now obscenely bare. The only thing left hanging on any of the walls was the small Virgo plaque that Devin had given me.

I sat down on the couch and buried my face in my hands. Allentown. It didn't seem like such a hot solution now.

I sneezed again and went back into the bedroom. There was no question about it. I was actually getting sick. I brought the roll of toilet paper out and set it on the coffee table, then drew a blanket over me. There was no way I was going to sleep in that back bedroom, not because of Blue, but because of the happier memories associated with it.

By the time Pam came in from work, I was still awake and now running a fever. She was aghast at both the emptiness of the house and at my appearance. My eyes were red and swollen, my face white and raw from the tears. There must have been black circles under my eyes. She walked from the living room to the bedroom, and then to the kitchen, in stunned shock as she looked over the house that now resembled a very sparsely furnished vacancy. Then, because neither of us could sleep, she put some coffee on, and I told her the whole story, this time in detail.

It was good to talk to somebody, and I needed some feedback from someone who wouldn't be shocked at the things Devin had said. Pam couldn't believe that Devin could be capable of such harsh bluntness or of impulsiveness such as he'd displayed when he'd called Gerald.

"What're you going to do?" she asked finally. "It looks like it's really over. He's really gone."

"I don't know. I'm going to try to talk to him tomorrow. I just can't believe he really meant this. Maybe this is all just to teach me a lesson. He *can't* just stay at Gerald's. I just can't believe this is where we're ending. I just can't."

"Yeah. Maybe tomorrow he'll be in a little better frame of mind. I can't believe he left that quick either. What about your job? Are you really thinking about moving back to Allentown?"

"No, but there is no job. Lola is furious. Well, I guess I can always find another one. It's Devin that matters to me right now. I'll just have to wait and see what happens tomorrow."

I fell asleep really believing we could work it all out tomorrow. It was that hope that kept me going through the night, my only link with sanity.

The following morning, Friday, December 27ᵗʰ, I got a call from a girl I hadn't heard from in months. She had once worked in our department before she'd quit to have a baby. I hadn't seen or spoken to her for over a year, yet she was the first to call to ask about his moving out. I rudely cut her off, shocked that the rumors had spread so quickly in just the span of a few short hours, and to people who weren't even around when Devin had even moved in.

"How in the hell did you hear about anything?" I demanded.

She was only too happy to tell me. "Well, I was talking to Ethel, the phone girl," she said. "We're still friends, you know, and she told me that Devin called in this morning from the route, and Kelly supposedly asked him, and *he* told Kelly that you kicked him out. Let's see…his exact words were… 'and I left my wife for that bitch.'"

I knew Devin well enough to know that those weren't his words. The phone girls could sure spice up the truth if it wasn't spicy enough.

"Well, *did* you?" she asked when I didn't comment.

"What? Kick him out?"

"Uh-huh."

"Well, Mary, you know Devin is not a liar."

"What?"

"If he says I kicked him out, well, then I must have kicked him out. Goodbye, Mary."

It was *my* turn to hang up on somebody. If Mary was any indication of what was going around already, I shuddered for what Devin must be dealing with. Just what the hell *could* he tell these people? I had really put him in an awkward position.

I wondered how the kids were holding up and went into their room to see them. They were playing with their new Barbie things. Mandy looked up when I entered. "Mommy? Is Devin going to move back in?"

"We can take all these toys back, and then he'll come back." Michelle's voice conveyed both sincerity and a confidence I didn't believe she felt. It had wavered on the word toys.

"No, no, it's not the toys." I stooped down and kissed them both. "And maybe if I ask him today, he *will* move back in."

"Is he going to call you?"

"If he doesn't," I assured them, "I'll call him."

"Mommy, you don't have a stereo anymore," Mandy said. She knew how much time I had once spent with music before Devin had come into our lives.

"That's okay. I don't need one."

"Well, *here*. Use *this* one." Michelle unplugged the little record player that Chris's mom had included in the box of toys. "It works good…huh, Mandy?"

Mandy nodded. "Me and Michelle were playing it last night." She frowned. "Well, not last night because that's the day Devin moved out." Her face crumpled, and I gathered her in my arms.

"Come on, Mandy. He'll be up to see you. He said he would."

She wiped her eyes on her sleeve and attempted a smile. "He told us he would. Would you come get us if he comes?"

"You know I will. You sure you guys don't want this thing?"

"No, Mom. You take it. You don't have *any* toys." Michelle patted Mandy on the shoulder. "Don't worry, Mandy."

I took the record player out and plugged it in, then retrieved the box of country albums I'd left with the kids. All the old records I'd once spent hours with in the evenings. I hadn't played them in months. The record player worked all right. Oh, it wasn't loud, and the sound was a little tinny, but it was at least something.

As it turned out, so were the records. It only took one for me to realize just how much my taste in music had changed. Not only was the mournful hick-twanging irritating, but the songs brought back painful memories of the very early days of Devin before he'd moved in. How many hours of this music had I sat through, waiting for the sound of that van to drive up? How new Devin had been to me then.

After lunch, the kids went back to their Barbie fantasies in their room, and I stood by the stove, waiting for my coffee water to boil. Now that Devin was gone, I was back to my Sunrise instant coffee. Real coffee was too much trouble for just me.

I was staring at the label on the coffee jar…a red ocean and a yellow sun emerging from the horizon…when a knock sounded at the door. I looked up, half expecting to see Chris out there wanting to know what had happened with Devin. He hadn't been over with his questions yet, and I figured he was about due. I walked over to the window, peeked out the drapes, and was floored to see the familiar blue-and-white Sparklear truck parked on the side of the property.

Even knowing who was at the door, it was still a start to see Devin standing there. He looked like he'd been up all night.

The kids burst from the room shrieking his name. They'd apparently seen him from their window. He knelt down and took both of them in his arms, as they wrapped theirs around whatever hold they could find. Then they both led him into their room, and I didn't see him for about fifteen minutes. I was glad he'd kept his promise to them and that he'd given them first priority. He would never know just how much it meant to them.

Or maybe he did.

Eventually he returned to the living room, closing their room door quietly behind him. We were left to face each other.

"Want some coffee?" I asked, not knowing what else to say. "I made you some while you were in there."

"No…well, okay, if it's already made. Oh, I forgot. I've got some shit in the truck."

He went out and returned with two gaily wrapped boxes. "Compliments of the company," he said with a half smile. "From the big party we didn't stick around for. Everyone got the same thing. Camping gear, if you can believe that." He set them down and looked at me quietly. "So. Did you call your mother?"

I set his coffee in front of him. "Devin, please don't start with the sarcasm, okay? I was wrong. I know I was wrong. I'd do *anything* to make up for what I did, so please…" If this was what *he* was going to be like, I shuddered to think of the moment when I would have to deal with Devin. I wasn't worried about Erick or Christian. They never *had* seemed native to this realm. But Devin…Devin could…hell, Devin *was* going to freak out.

"I'm not being sarcastic," he said tolerantly, jolting me out of my thoughts. "I just want to know what you're doing so that I'll know you're going to be all right."

"You sound pretty final."

"Yes, well, I did think it over last night, like you asked me to. I've made the final decision to go home. The way everything went down yesterday, it seems like it was inevitable anyway."

"You mean, even if I hadn't pulled that stupid stunt yesterday you might still be leaving…telling me this anyway?"

"Perhaps. Well, I don't think I'd have decided to go. I was fighting in the other direction. To stay. I didn't want to leave without taking you with me somehow, but when all that happened, well, let's just say you may have speeded up things a little. Or maybe you just helped me decide. Staying may have been the wrong decision, and maybe you helped me make the right decision."

"And Devin? Does Devin consciously know yet?"

"I'm sure he does. He knew I was considering it. But I'm maintaining hold while I'm still here. I've got a lot of things to tie up myself, personally. One more tape to put on and—"

"Tape?"

"Yes, one more. You know…for the ten tapes?"

"The *ten* tapes?"

He looked at me as though I should know what he was talking about. "Yeah. The ones you've been listening to for the past month?"

"Oh, the reel-to-reels. I didn't realize there were ten of them."

"Well, there aren't yet. There are nine completed. I finished one last night. Those tapes have been one of my projects since before I came here. I was working with Devin on a subconscious level before I decided to come, but it became much easier to put them together after I arrived."

"So you were recording last night?"

"Yes, since I don't know how much time I have to finish them. And it gives me something to do while I'm waiting. I moved into Brian's room where the waterbed is already set up. He'd been using it. He moved into that room where I had all my stuff stored in November."

"That's funny. I never thought of those tapes as anything but a lot of mirror reflections of our life. And some great music, too. Oh, by the way. I got a call from Mary Berg today. Remember her?" Mary was well known for her love of gossip.

"Just what you needed." He shook his head with disgust. "Well, how bad *is* it?"

"Pretty bad if *she* called. She *never* calls me." I told him what she'd reported, and he laughed bitterly.

"Now does *that* sound like something *I* would say?"

"No, and I didn't believe you'd said it either. For that matter, I don't believe Kelly would even *repeat* something like that to that gang of hens, even if you *had* said it."

"I don't think she would either. She's pretty loyal to you. For the record, I stayed out of your office all day anyway. Never went in there and didn't call in either. Avoiding your office is pretty simple."

"What *are* you going to tell them, Devin?"

"Everything," he said, laughing again. "And nothing. If any two get together to compare stories they won't know which end is up."

"Well, I'm the one who put you in that position, and you're the one who has to face them, so whatever you want to tell them is fine with me. I'll go along with it."

"Yeah. It's funny how the truth would be the least believed of all."

I sighed. "So I guess this is it, huh? There's no chance of you changing your mind and coming back." It wasn't a question.

"What would be the point, lady? I'd just get settled in here again and then have to leave from here. I might as well just stay where I'm at."

I flinched. I kept forgetting what the real problem was. That *He* was leaving.

He picked up on my thought instantly. "I can't believe you're still looking at this in human terms, lady. I told you I've decided to go home. What sense would it make to move in just for a few days or a week?"

"It would at least be something," I said, tears welling up again.

"I will be in touch. Right up till the moment I leave."

"What about the drivers, Devin. It would help to know what they think happened so that—"

"I wouldn't waste your energy worrying about what people *think*, lady," he said wearily. "That's a good way to get hurt. All anyone knows is that I've moved out. From the mood they think Devin is in, I didn't get hassled too much for details."

"So you're staying in control, even at work."

"It postpones the Devin problem and, like I said, they think Devin is in a really bad mood."

"Don't you think they'll notice that Devin isn't exactly the same?"

"No. *Devin* hasn't got a whole lot to say to anybody, and they think Devin is reacting exactly like anyone would, given the same situation. They see a very preoccupied Devin, and they couldn't conceive of him being any other way."

"Yeah. I guess that's what they'd expect from Devin since…the bitch kicked him out."

We both smiled.

I refilled the coffee cups, still wishing I could find the words to make him change his mind and stay…to come home *here*, not the one *he* referred to. I couldn't ask him anymore. Every time I did, it just reinforced in his mind that I didn't believe he had any other world to go *to*. While I made the coffee and mulled over that one, Devin went back in to see the kids.

The coffee sat until it was lukewarm before he came back out.

"I'd kind of like to know what you're going to do, lady."

"I'm not going anywhere, if that's what you mean. Even if you never come back."

"That's not what I meant," he said. "I could be gone tomorrow. It would be nice to know whether I'll be yesterday's news by the time I get back there, or if you're going to keep trying to learn."

"How could I *not*, Devin? You say there's another world in there, one that isn't alien to either one of us. Well, if it's there, and especially if that's where you're going, I'll find it even if it takes me the rest of my life."

He looked relieved. "That's good. That's what I needed to hear. I'll help you, lady. Just remember, even if you don't see me at first, just know I'm there. In a way, it's almost better this way. I'll be there waiting at the other end instead of sending you in blind by yourself."

"And if I learn to do it before you leave, then I could really go with you when you leave? Even just once? You know I couldn't stay...I got those two little buggers in there to raise."

He smiled. "I've always been aware of that. But I'd like to see you learn to go before I leave. If you've got the desire...well, that's all you need, really. And until you do, you've got Blue. That sucker seems to be here to stay. He been around?"

I shrugged. I didn't want to talk about Blue. "I haven't seen him."

"I can believe you haven't seen him. I rather doubt that he hasn't been around, though."

That was a dig. Devin had always expected me to be more receptive to Blue than I was. "How many years do I have to find you? I mean, if I don't learn how to get there before you leave?"

"As many years as you live. Don't forget, you had a reason for coming here to begin with...and against the advice of everyone there. I was wrong to think I could bring you back but, there again, you can't just take my word on that either, can you."

I shook my head. "I have to find out that it's true by myself. And I will."

He smiled. "That's the way I like to hear you talk, lady. Now you *do* sound like my lady. I was a little worried there, yesterday. And once I get there, it will be like the blink of an eye for me. Even if you stay the rest of your natural life, it will go quick for me. For you, it won't go so quickly. Unfortunately, you have to experience it all as time. But one thing will be different than before I came. You'll know I'm in there. Before I came, you had no idea or recollection of me. Now, even though you still can't place me, you'll know who you're looking for. And you'll know to be *looking*, so this sojourn wasn't a total loss. It will be easier for me to keep an eye on you from there, and whenever you think of me, *please*, just know I'm there with you. My attention will never be far from you."

"I wish there was a book that could help me."

"I've never *seen* an accurate book on *us*. There are so many distortions."

"So I should maybe start with meditating."

"For starts, and the Journeys book isn't a bad one. At least it pounds home the many inner realities and worlds there are just in *that* author's experience. And then there are the Seth books, but I don't see how you could accept anything Seth says at this point in your development. If you could accept it, though, he takes the hocus-pocus out of alternate worlds. I'm just afraid you may have to experience some things yourself before you can take Seth on. Oh, and those visions and voices you get? You ought to start writing them down. See how accurate some of them are."

"Yeah, like that skull on your pillow that night. I should have known it meant the death of something to do with us. That's why it was on *your* pillow. And the scorpion incident, too. Well, I guess I'll just learn by hit-and-miss. I sure am going to miss *you.*"

"I'm going to miss your acknowledgment of my presence…for a while at least. You know, lady, this little setup has been nice. Sex…it's been a mindblower, especially for me, but you just weren't learning anything. We were both caught up in the physical aspects and, unfortunately, that just impeded your development. Retarded your growth."

I sighed and said halfheartedly, "So I guess getting down on my knees wouldn't change your mind." I wasn't really serious, but he obviously took it that way.

"Don't you *ever* get down on your knees for *anybody*. Especially not me. I'm going to tell you something, lady. You'd better realize who you are and remember it. Really remember it because you're going to *need* to in the next few months just to keep your sanity. For example, has your friend Lola called you yet?"

I looked away.

"Don't expect her to. She's going to hurt you pretty badly before this is all over. Far worse than you deserve."

I started to cry. "She…she called. Last night…for *you.*" I took a breath and regained control, wiped my eyes and told him what she'd said. He listened and then took me in his arms.

"Mama's human, lady. She's hurt, and she doesn't understand, but she will get over it eventually. She's just not rational right now. I'll try to talk to her in the morning."

"Devin, I'm so sorry I caused all this. Will you ever forgive me?"

"You're already forgiven, Kerry," he said gently. "What you did wasn't so bad. You've more than made up for it. To me, anyway. I just feel that it's time to go. That's all. Mama will come around in time. And if she doesn't…so what? Just remember who you are. That's all I ask." He looked into my eyes and sighed. "It's all you've got right now, lady. You may be fighting for your sanity, and you're going to need faith in yourself. Look…I'll try to call you tonight, okay? I'm going to go say goodbye to the girls now."

After he left, my pent-up emotions burst again. I couldn't seem to stop crying no matter how hard I tried. The world had simply come to an end for me.

When I pulled myself together again, I went back to the bookshelf. I didn't even *have* the Seth book now. Surely *one* of my books could tell me something about this invisible world his…father…ruled, where the air was cold and not belching with fire and brimstone…where the entrance, for me, was straight through a blue-and-purple hole in my mind. Surely, *someone* had accidently stumbled upon such a world and written about it.

I knelt down and picked up the white tablet. The very first one. Devin had mentioned how hard he'd tried to impress upon me, even back then, who he was. How really naïve I had been then. Would those carefully structured paragraphs read any differently to me now? Now that I had lost everything?

I opened it up and skipped past my own diary notes until I came to the first words Devin had written. His first attempts at trying to reason with my very human conditioning. As I read, I realized how right he'd been. Knowing what I knew now, there was no way he could have answered directly what I'd persisted in asking him to explain that night. It was the one paragraph close to the end that hit me the hardest.

To feel…to touch…to experience…the wants of need. There it is. Man's pathway of solving all…

The words had an entirely different meaning to me now. Experience. That was all he'd ever pushed. The hell with books…the hell with what you'd been taught. Experience. That was all he'd ever held any faith in.

Could play havoc of your mind. The doors being opened before their time. Ahead lies disturbing times.

How much had he known was ahead of us? And why had he bothered if he wasn't going to stay? Even now, he spoke in terms of maintaining my sanity. And here it was again, his proud words on a dusty shelf. Buried under the music books and occult magazines.

As I sat pondering the memories of those early days, a song came on the radio. It had been playing softly from atop the refrigerator. The band sounded like Uriah Heep. Those guys just wouldn't leave me alone. This sounded more like the keyboardist, Ken Hensley, with the band playing backup rather than a recording from the group. The message, however, remained right in line with my present.

Stand up and fight, he advised, or I would lose my right. Did I want to stand in a line trying to hold on to my sanity? If I searched, I would find proud words on a dusty shelf. I should keep on trying to help myself. The words that drummed home over and over were to *stand up and fight*.

And right there and then, I decided to take that advice.

I would not go down without a fight.

15 When I finally did call Allentown that afternoon it was not to make any going-home arrangements with my mother.

Maybe it was the song. Maybe it was those ironclad words in that tablet, and maybe it was the desperate will to earn Devin's approval. If he could not be persuaded to stay, then maybe it was the desire to go with him. As Pam had pointed out, seven-day predictions and inferences of Devin's possible death were too rash to make from someone who didn't positively know what he was talking about. Furthermore, too much in the way of proof had already gone down in the last few months. It was time I quit looking for rational explanations and just accepted what appeared to be true, just as he'd said all along.

Everything was true. Like the song said.

When my mother answered, I got right to the point.

"Mom, I need you to send me that book," I told her.

"Keel's book?"

"Yeah. You did say it was about an invisible world, didn't you?"

"Well, yes, but it will take over a week to get it to you if I mail it. I don't mind, but you might make faster headway with a library. It sounds like you're in a hurry."

"Okay, I'll try, but if I can't get it I'll be calling you right back."

The library search was fruitless. Of the eight libraries I called, four had never heard of it, two had loaned it out and the books had never returned, and two had somehow misplaced their copies. Nor could it be purchased through a bookstore. Long out of print, it could not even be ordered from the publisher.

"Nobody has it here," I told her when I called back at five. "Can you send it airmail?"

"Kerry, what *is* the hurry?"

"I need it *now*, Mom." I thought maybe if I filled her in on what had been happening the past few months that she'd see things from my angle, so I took the time to do just that. It backfired.

"Kerry, I think you need to come home…even just for a visit. I know you're upset, and I really do understand, but you should have listened to me back when I first asked you to read it. I don't doubt one bit that what you're mixed up in is interdimensional. That's what the book is *about*. But these entities *lie*, Kerry. You don't realize it but you're being exploited, and he's been exploiting you all along."

"Spare me the lecture, Mom. Just send the book, please?"

"It isn't going to be that easy or that fast, Kerry. I've loaned the book out again, and I don't know if they're finished with it." When I didn't say anything, she sighed and added, "All right. I'll see what I can do."

I put dinner on and went over to my own books again. Surely, *one* of them could be of some help in the meantime. I scanned the titles. They were all on the subject of religion or witchcraft and the occult. Although most were full of love spells and hexes and distorted legends, none of them went much into any reality but the physical. Any manifestations were passed off as light or dark forces. Nothing concrete, to say the least.

When Kelly called me at six o'clock, her tone of voice was accusing.

"You never called me back, Kerry. What the hell is going *on?* Did Devin really move out?"

"Yeah." I sighed. "How bad is it down there?"

"Pretty bad. It's all over the plant that you kicked Devin out. What's the real story?"

"Is that what Lola said?"

"No. Lola won't even mention your name. I can't even bring your name *up.*"

"Well, can't blame her. That reminds me. Mary called."

"Mary Berg? That fucking nosy bitch? What'd *she* want?"

I told her, taking care to include the quote Kelly was supposed to have made to the phone girls.

"I said *what* ? Kerry, honest to God, I haven't even *seen* Devin! He never called our department, not even once. I think he's avoiding everybody."

"Yeah, that's what *he* said. I knew you wouldn't spread something like that around anyway."

"Devin said *what* ? I thought you two weren't speaking."

"We're speaking, Kelly."

"Well…" Kelly sounded confused. "If you're not fighting, and you two are still talking, then what's wrong?"

"I can't tell you that, Kel. I'd like to but I just can't. There's a lot more going on than meets the eye. Let's just say…there's a third party involved in this that no one even knows exists."

"The line went quiet for a minute, then, "That sounds pretty heavy, Kerry. What is it? His wife?"

"No. This is someone that no one knows *exists*."

"Kerry, what is it? Mafia? Drugs? What? Are you in some kind of trouble?"

"I wish it were any one of those, Kel. Anyway, I can't stay on the line. He said he was going to call."

"But, Kerry. How could this happen? Devin *loves* you."

"I know, Kelly, and I love him. Believe me. Maybe that's why this *is* happening."

"Jesus, you've got me going in circles. But…okay, pal. Keep in touch, will you? Let me know if I can do anything to help. I'll let you know what's happening at work."

"Okay, Kelly, thanks. I appreciate that."

"I hope you two get it straightened out."

"Not half as much as I do, Kelly."

Another phone call immediately after I hung up and from an old friend. A friend I'd practically forgotten since October. Lola's son, Mark. His mom wasn't home yet, but he'd heard what happened at work yesterday. Was it okay to come over and spend the weekend like old times?

I almost refused, as depressed as I was, but his tone of voice stopped me.

"You know Devin's not here anymore, don't you Mark?"

"Yeah, I heard about that. That's okay. I can bring my Monopoly game over."

"In that case, buddy, I'd love to see you. But make sure it's okay.

"Oh, it'll be okay," he said happily. "I'll just ask my dad."

"No, you'd better clear it with your mother, Mark. She's pretty mad at me right now."

"Well, what's that got to do with *me?*" he asked, with eleven-year-old logic and indignity. "That's *her* problem."

What did that have to do with Mark? As it turned out, plenty. Pam was home when the call came through from a tearful Mark, choking on his own sobs.

"My mom said…my mom…said…" He paused and sniffed, then began again, more controlled. "She said if you can't talk to her…I…I…can't talk to y-y-you."

"Oh, no, Mark. I was afraid of this. I have tried to talk to her, but she cuts me off."

"W-well. It was worth a try," he said, sniffing again. I could almost see his head hanging. "I'll call you during the day when she's at work, okay? I sure hope you and Devin patch things up. Man, I really like him."

"Boy, how *childish*!" Pam exploded after I'd hung up. "Taking it out on her *kid*!"

"Not childish, Pammy. Human. Look at Mark. He's a child, but he's not holding anything against me."

When ten o'clock came and went with no word from Devin, I decided to call him.

"I've been busy with the reels," he explained. "Has Trevor been up to see you yet?"

"No. No one has. Not Daniel and Julie either…why? Is Trevor *supposed* to be coming up?"

"Well, it would be just like him to do that. You know, stop by and see how you are. I'm surprised that he hasn't. He may yet, though."

I told him about Mark's call and Lola's restriction.

"Human bullshit," he said. I could almost see him rolling his eyes. "I know she's upset, but I didn't think she'd go *that* far. Poor kid."

"He was really hurt and disappointed. There was a time when he was here almost every weekend. Maybe if I tried to call her again and—"

"Don't bother," he said quickly. "She won't listen, and you'll just get your feelings hurt again. You'd better give her a little more time." It sounded like he'd already tried to reason with her on my behalf.

It turned out he was right. Lola cut me off before I could even begin to explain.

"But Mark—"

"That goes for Mark too. Sorry."

I hung up, refusing to let it get to me. I'd been warned, but at least I'd tried.

Devin had mentioned that he'd try to stop by tonight, so on that hope I didn't go to bed. Just kept digging through the books. From drugs to psychiatry, philosophy, religion, *The Bible* and, of course, the occult.

Pam dug up a couple weird ones from her own collection and left them with me on her way out the door. "One's about Atlantis, but it barely mentions Atlantis, and it even gets into your invisible worlds a little."

"Thanks, Pam. I need all the help I can get. What's the other one?"

"Oh, that. It's called *Songs of the Open Road,* but it's not about any physical open road. I think the title's metaphorical, and from what I could see thumbing through it, the songs are metaphysical. I recognized a couple Moody Blues. It just made me think of those ten tapes of Devin's."

I set the Atlantis one aside for later and picked up the songbook. It was a pocketbook with a forward that explained the reasoning behind the selection of songs. The *road* was apparently a road to awareness and not a physical one as Pam had suspected. Some of the lyrics looked *very* familiar.

I was deep into that book when the van pulled up, and a very tired-looking Erick came to the door. This would be Erick's final physical appearance to me, but at the time I had no way of knowing that. For me, his smile of greeting was like water to someone dying in the desert.

If anyone could help me find that door out of this physical world, Erick could.

16 Erick turned out to be a far bigger help than I ever could have imagined, not just in helping to explain *the doors*, but also in healing my emotional wounds.

The first thing he did after putting water on for coffee was check out the cupboards.

"You got any food in this place?"

"Yeah, for all I feel like eating."

"Well, I was thinking about the kids. I see you're stocked up on coffee." He smiled and spooned the instant coffee into two cups. "Looks pretty empty in here."

"I know. You can hear the echo."

He brought the coffee in and set it on the coffee table. "That…uh, stereo." He chuckled. "Get any complaints on the volume?"

"Don't be smart. It's something, anyway. What's worse is those old records of mine. I just can't listen to country anymore."

He flipped through them quickly and extracted the Crosby, Stills, Nash and Young albums. "The stack isn't a total loss," he said optimistically. "And you still have *Harvest*, the Neil Young album." He placed the Déjà Vu album on the turntable and turned it on, probably curious to see how it sounded. When it began, we both burst into laughter. "I think we owe you a stereo," he said. "I'll get you one, Kerry. Maybe I'll go talk to Trevor about the one you gave him."

"No, please don't. We gave it to him. I don't want it back."

"How're the girls?"

"Sleeping now. Better since this afternoon. Seeing Devin really helped them a lot. But, boy do I ever need your help. I've been going through books like crazy. It doesn't seem like any of these writers have ever heard of this place *he* calls home."

"No?" He raised his brows. "Perhaps you are looking in the wrong books."

"Well, he *did* say there were no credible books on it."

"And there aren't, really. But…if you took a little of *The Bible's* Heaven and Hell, a snatch of Wonderland, looked into where the Yogis go when they're phased out all day, checked into the UFO phenomenon a little deeper than the surface…all that and you might touch on the truth. There's a clue in this love business, too. You may believe that love is an emotion and that *home* is a place, but actually, the combination of the two creates a condition he calls home. It's a state of mind, but then again, so is this world you live in now. I know that sounds confusing. Don't get me wrong, though. I'm not selling the validity of either world short. This *state of mind* that he refers to is a very real one, and while it is not tangible while you are *here*…this world you live in now is just as etheric when you are *there*. I have to keep comparing it to this world because this one is the only one you consciously *know*."

"So what you're saying is that while I live in this world, *his* world seems very dreamlike and unreal, but if I looked at *this* world from *there*, then *it* would be the solid tangible one, and *this one* would be like a dream."

"Exactly. There are scads of other realities, by the way, not just the one *he* identifies with. There *are* books that attempt to describe many of them, but humans tend to view things from their own personal frame of reference. A deeply religious person might touch on a world while praying and call it a vision from God. An ordinary human might hallucinate on a drug and think he saw Hell. Both are viewing a valid world, but the vision is colored by their own beliefs and couched in their own means of acceptance. Okay, take for example, an entity such as *him*. If Devin Drew had been obsessed with UFOs, then he might have believed that *he* was a creature from another planet. And *he*, needing to communicate with Devin, would become for a while Devin's man from space. By presenting himself this way, Devin wouldn't be afraid to deal with him."

"This reminds me of that old story about the blind men all touching different parts of the elephant and describing only the part he felt...like the trunk or the ears...and believing that that part represented the whole elephant."

"That's a good analogy. None of them are wrong. They just weren't getting the whole picture. You have to remember that the whole is actually more than the sum of its parts when you're talking about other realities. That's why you won't really find the answer in books. However, with the situation you're in, I can understand your searching frantically through the only source you think you have."

"You know of another way?"

"You do too." He turned off the record player. "That's pretty bad. You been playing this thing much?"

"No. Mostly reading and answering the phone. I do feel better, though. I guess I'm all cried out."

"You're learning. And, I guess, aren't we all." He patted the beanbag. "Come here, love."

I sat down beside him, and he wrapped his arms around me. "I hate that you have to go through this."

"Well, it's good to see you, Erick," I said. "It's been such a long time."

He nodded. "It has. I kind of figured you'd be in need of some company tonight, and I was afraid you might get the wrong kind. Whatever you do, Kerry, don't get hostile or resentful over this. You may invite problems you don't want or need. Just keep your focus on learning to go. It's your one hope right now. That is, if you're serious about finding that door."

"Is it really that final that he's going, Erick? There's no possible way he could change his mind?"

"It looks that way. Try to remember that he does love you. Everything he's done has been for you. Even leaving. There are things you don't know about."

My interest picked up sharply. "Do *you* know about them, Erick?"

"Oh, no you don't." He laughed, but then sobered when he saw how serious I was. "Oh, Kerry. I hate to use the expression that it's over your head."

"But what could it possibly have to do with? You *do* know, don't you? He said it would be in the newspaper."

"Oh, Kerry...love." He took a deep breath and exhaled. "Let me put it this way. Since you mention the news, let's look at that. The biggest thing going in the news since August...since you and he came together... has been political, but maybe there's something much worse than what the headlines are giving you…much more to the story. All year we've been hearing about the president…Nixon…and all the scandals associated with him. He steps down, and eventually a jury is impaneled for a cover-up trial. Do you know when that was?"

"No, I wouldn't know that. I don't pay attention to politics."

"Understandable. I can tell you, though, that the jury for the Watergate Cover-up trial was impaneled on October eleventh. Do you know what day Devin first brought that ring up to your house and gave it to you?"

"It was…October eleventh. I know because I remember thinking it was the same day as Crowley's birthday, which is the twelfth. It was the eleventh when Devin promised to bring the ring, but considering it was after midnight when he actually got there…" I was referring to Aleister Crowley, a notorious figure in the black magic cults. "But what's that got to do with it?"

"Do you know that the jury has been *sequestered* since the day of their empanelment? It's a pretty serious trial, but the president is not the one on trial. Five dangerous people who have come to believe they have the power of *God* are on trial."

"Wait a minute, Erick. Are you telling me that this decision of his is somehow related to the welfare of this country? Why would he *care?*"

"It's bigger than that. Even *I* don't know exactly what it is, but it seems to be related to that, and it feels like it extends far beyond what could happen to this country if these men are not stopped from moving forward with whatever agenda they have in mind. This is where his statement that it involved the whole world and everybody in it may come into play. And, love, that is honestly all I can tell you from what I've picked up from his thoughts."

I pressed my face against his shirt and exhaled. I hadn't realized I'd been holding my breath. "Wow, Erick. I never even considered it might have anything to do with the news going on now. But it's been going on for months, hasn't it, this trial? Why would it suddenly be so important now?"

"Maybe because the jury is about to come to a decision soon?"

"Is it?"

"I think so."

I pulled away from him and sat up. "If you're right, I'm more dead in the water than I realized. How could I fight something like that?" I got up to make more coffee. "Thanks for even that much, Erick. I still don't understand what it has to do with us and why he has to leave because of it."

When I brought the coffee in I returned to his side, still trying to digest what he'd told me. "God, Erick. It's so good to be with you. He's been so intense this past week. Christian hasn't really been around, and Devin…I don't think I *want* to see *him*. I guess I'm going to have to, eventually. At least you are the way you always have been, and you don't hate me."

"Nobody hates you, Kerry. As for me, and even Christian, we don't have anything to do with what's going on. Just bystanders, really. *He* has a reason for being so intense. As for Devin, well, now *there* is someone who stands to lose a great deal if *he* leaves. I'm just hoping he can handle it."

"What about all this stuff about his old man?"

"There again, that isn't my territory. The only one who has any connection with the old man is *him*."

"But when has *he* had the chance to go back and forth? He's always been here with me, especially this past week."

"Your waking hours, you mean," Erick corrected. "Think about all those nights you could have sworn he wasn't breathing. That's when he goes. See, he never even took any time away from you to do that."

"You make it sound like I've been sleeping with a corpse."

"You could put it that way, but only in a manner of speaking. What he's actually doing is slowing down the heart...the pulse...and the breathing. Then he goes. When he's gone, the body consciousness takes over. All the atoms composing the body are aware and alive. It's pretty complicated but, it's what you have to learn."

"I'm never going to figure it out."

"Love, try to absorb this. *You* leave your body every time you go to sleep. So does every human that falls asleep. For that matter you pulse on and off like a strobe every nanosecond of your existence here and you're also there every other pulse, although that might be a little heavy to lay on you right now."

"Erick, anything you can lay on me that would help, please do it. I don't want to lose him. I love him."

"Don't we all. But why are you still speaking in terms of loss? He isn't *leaving* you. Do you think you've lost *me* when I'm not in the flesh?"

"No, but I miss you all the same. And if Devin...dies...I'd miss him too."

Erick sighed. "Devin doesn't *have* to die. He can if he wants to, but that's going to be his own decision. And you're *still* looking at the grave as the end of it all instead of the beginning. Come on, Kerry. Let's see what we can do with you."

It was one of the most enlightening and comforting nights I was to ever spend. Talking, questioning, searching under every stone and leaving none unturned. Erick answered what he could and tried to explain the process of leaving the body.

"You've got to slow your heartbeat *down*," he said patiently when I asked him how to raise my vibrations. "Not speed it up. Concentrate on directing the energy to your head. When you hit that point, you'll go through a period of disorientation...a strangling feeling, even, for you are accustomed to breathing to stay alive. When you reach this point, and you *will* know when you've reached it, don't back down. I'm afraid that's where you'll stop and pull back. You see, once you've gone that far...once you leap that pulse, you'll be on your way and you'll be there, wondering how anything so beautiful and marvelous could have scared you at all. And you've even got that built-in entrance. I don't know why you don't use it. You've already been there, you know."

"That dream?"

"Love, I've told you. He's told you. *This* world is a dream from there."

As we talked, the radio continued to play softly in the background. At one point Erick nodded toward it, and we both stopped to listen. Moody Blues again. *Emily's Song*. I didn't know who Emily was, but once again the words reflected our conversation. The singer was asking someone to take him into 'your world' because he couldn't go alone. He'd been here so long he was being left behind. He asked that person to walk with him into his land of fairy tales and to help open up a book of pages in his mind. Erick smiled as the song concluded and then turned his attention back to me.

"Okay, now, where were we?"

He gave me enough instruction to start with and then turned the conversation back to my book search.

"It's not a *bad* idea to scope out what the humans think," he consoled me when I complained again that books were all I had to work with. "Read all you can, but don't accept any fear programs. Books are loaded with them. And spend an *equal* amount of time practicing what I've shown you. Keep practicing. You just might hit the right frequency by accident. Oh, and another thing. You'll run across every explanation for life on this planet from the Pulsating Universe Theory to the human-descended-from-the-ape evolution pitch." He smiled and pointed to a statue that Devin had left behind. A mocking lampoon of *The Thinker*. An ape was holding a human skull and scratching his head in puzzlement. "I see he left that for you."

"Either that or he forgot it."

"He also left you that statue of the meditating Buddha. Left you a couple hints, it looks like."

"He probably just forgot them," I repeated.

"I doubt it. He doesn't do things by accident." Erick stood up. "Come on. Walk me to the van. It's two o'clock in the morning."

When I hugged him goodbye I had no idea I would never hold him again. And I had no idea what was in store for me in the coming days ahead. Had I known, I doubt that I would have had the inner strength to keep up the search.

Blissfully ignorant, I was left feeling more positive, happy and confident than I'd felt in days. Pam came in from work at three, tired but anxious to know what was going on. Floored to find me in good spirits, she headed for the stove to make coffee.

"I'm keeping you *awake,* man," she said, laughing. "I leave you on the verge of suicide and…oh, hey! Is Devin moving back in? Is *that* it?"

"No, but Erick was here." I must have looked radiant.

"Oh, well, Erick always was a peaceful one to be around from what you've told me. But *him*, man. I *still* don't know what to make of him. He scares me sometimes."

"Welcome to the K-nine corps. Dogs seem to feel the same way."

"Yeah? Well, I'd pay more attention to a dog than a human judgment any day."

"You been talking to Mom? Why is it that dogs are loyal to murderers who own them? Dogs don't have judgment, but they do recognize what is unusual, and they *do* react to that, good or bad." I closed up the book I'd been reading and picked up the coffee she'd brought in. "Thanks. Hey, that book on Atlantis? It's *all right*. I was surprised."

"Oh, you started getting into it, huh? I'm glad I found that thing. I'd skim over the Atlantis stuff…who knows about that, but the rest of the chapters…There's some really weird shit in that book. Oh, and getting back to Erick—"

"Well, nothing's changed. *He's* still leaving, and I guess I have anywhere from a day to…who knows when…to learn to go where he's going. If I figure that out I could go with him."

"Whoa! Jump *back!* Didn't *he* say that Devin was going to die?"

I still flinched at the word. "Yeah, he did say he might but—"

"What are you'ns going to do? *Shoot* each other?"

I laughed. "No. It would be sickness or something. At least that's what *he* said. Or an accident or something."

"You…and Devin."

"If I were to learn how to go and if I wanted to leave with him. Of course, I couldn't go permanently because of the kids, but I could go with him when *he* leaves, and then be able to at least go see him once in a while."

She seemed to digest that for a minute and must have decided I had to be handled with kid gloves. "Look, Ker. How about this for an alternative. You take a few weeks off and read all those books. We can live off *my* salary. Shit, I lived off you when I first moved here. We can do this without you having to go *with him,* or back to Allentown."

"Oh, I'm not going *there.*"

"For sure?"

"For sure."

"What are you going to do, then? Look for a job?"

I rubbed my eyes sleepily. "Either that or write a book." I yawned.

"There you go, Ker!" Pam jumped up enthusiastically. "That's *it!* This story would make a *great* book."

I shook my head, realizing that Pam had taken me seriously. "I was kidding, Pam."

"No, seriously, just start writing, man…oh, wait a minute. Nah…if you published it as a true story they'd lock you up." She laughed and I joined her.

"There's something else, too. I have to wait and see how the story ends." We both stopped short in our laughter and looked at each other.

"Come to think of it, this isn't really funny," Pammy said. "But it *is* good to see you in a little better mood. I've really been worried about you, Kerry."

"Well, don't, Pam. I've given this all a lot of thought, and moping isn't going to bring Devin back. I know he still loves me so there's still hope. And just from the way Erick was tonight, I can't help thinking that just maybe…well, if *he* goes, I can't do anything about that. But if Devin Drew *doesn't* die…well, you know."

She looked at me hopefully. "You think you might get him to change his mind about leaving Devin?"

"I don't know about *that,* but Erick said that Devin doesn't *have* to die. And if he chooses to stay here—"

"You forget, Kerry. Dying isn't a bad thing to any of the Devins. And *he* doesn't look at it like he's *killing* Devin."

"I know. He talked like he'd be doing Devin a favor to allow him to go. Like Devin might not be able to cope with being just himself after *he* was gone."

"Man, this is crazy! I sure hope you'ns get this worked out."

"You know something, Pam? For the first time since he moved out, I feel like there *is* a little hope."

When Pammy went to bed, I went back to the Atlantis book and checked through the table of contents. Erick was right. The theory of ape evolution was one of the first chapters. There were also a chapters on UFOs, and angels and demons from other dimensions. From the scientists' theories to the madness of Charles Fort, it looked like Pammy had scored me a winner.

17 *Atlantis Rising.* Brad Steiger's exploration into the history of the lost continent devoted only a few short pages to the possibility of its existence, and many chapters to other stories that were similar to it. One chapter covered the legend of an undersea race of people and, like Atlantis, it was divided into the good guys and the bad guys.

As I moved through the chapters, I began to notice a trend. While backgrounds and geographical factors shifted from one time and place to another, from one set of beliefs to another, there remained that duality that ran like a common thread throughout the book. Atlantis had the good *Children of the Law of One* and their enemies, the evil *Sons of Belial. The Bible* had its Heaven and Hell, and the Buddhists had their own set of opposites. This persisted even as subjects changed from various religions to more scientific and modern explanations, all attempting to prove that Atlantis had really existed at one time. The UFOs had their benevolent aliens and their evil ones. For every theory mentioned, each had its group of good guys and bad guys within the stories.

The continuous duality behind all these schools of thought was exactly Steiger's intention. His conclusion was that no matter which story was right, there was always a good side and a bad side. I began to understand what Devin had meant by *the stories.* Everyone seemed to be aware that there *was* an invisible world, but nobody could agree on what or where it was.

All of the invisible worlds had inhabitants, but nobody could agree on who they were, only that they were superior to the human race in their own evolutions.

While the book did help me accept that Devin had been right about his invisible world, it only confused me as to where the hell *he* was going. Devin had practically *called* it Hell, yet he seemed more to me like a visitor from Heaven. Erick seemed to be as divine as an angel, and Christian…the worst he could be called was mischievous. I just couldn't accept that *he* had meant that literally. I thought what he really meant was that the *rumors* of Hell and the Devil had stemmed from man's misinterpretations of *his* reality.

On the other hand, I *had* been into the study of Wicca when we'd first gotten together, and so had Devin Drew. Maybe, as Erick had hinted, *he* had chosen that particular frame of reference because it fit with our interests at that time. Maybe, as Erick had suggested, if we'd been into something else…religion, for example, *he* might have chosen to call himself Michael, right hand man of God, instead of Lucifer's son. Or whatever demonic name he might have used.

Well, he hadn't left *yet,* so I could always ask him.

When he called from work the next morning, Saturday, December 28th, I was more sure than ever that I could talk him into staying. His visits and phone calls, regardless of which personality made them, told me that he still cared. Maybe he was just trying to teach me a lesson, or maybe the plan was to force me to speed up my education. If that was the case it was working, because after finishing Steiger's book my education was, for once, more in the forefront of my thoughts than our separation.

After briefing him on the nature of the book, I hit him point-blank with a string of questions. And with two words, he slowly chopped up question after question. When he was finished, he rolled them all into a confusing little ball.

"I'm still allowed to ask questions, right?" I'd begun before firing.

"That's always been the only requirement," he'd replied.

I refrained from asking just whose requirement it was and went down my list.

"Devin, does your world have anything to do with the stories of Atlantis?"

"A little."

"What about *The Bible?*"

"A little, and a little of all the major religions, so don't hit me with a gang of churches."

"Does it have anything to do with…well, listen. I'll read you something first." The paragraph dealt with some of the transmissions purportedly coming from spacecraft that existed in a "fourth dimension." It warned the earthlings that they would soon be "transmuted"…changed…converted. Transformed into the fourth-dimensional existence, whether they were ready for it or not.

Devin laughed, but when I asked him if there was a connection he admitted, "A little."

"Then you're saying it *is* directly connected with the so-called UFOs."

He sighed. "A little. Lady, try to remember there are a million schools of thought out there on *what* we are, but I'm trying to tell you—don't confine yourself to *any* of them. Your scientists, your physicists, your philosophers…your UFO investigators…they are *all* studying different aspects of the same *source.* The black magician taps the exact same source as the priest. The UFO contactees and the trance mediums are *both* communicating with the same source. I've told you over and over, it is *all one.*"

I sighed. "Then none of these stories are really a true picture of it. Not even the legend of the *watchers,* Devin? Your *Mastering Witchcraft* goes into these giants…fallen angels…who supposedly keep an eye on this universe. Is that all mixed up with this too?"

I could feel his smile. "A little. And I hope you're getting the point."

I closed the book. "I think you guys made sure nobody would ever get the real picture of you and your world."

He laughed. "Hey-hey-hey." So different from the way *Devin* said it. "So how are you coming on everything else?"

"You mean meditating?"

"Well, get rid of the labels if you can. Let's just call it taking a trip into yourself."

"Well, I've been reading that book all night and this morning, but I think I'll be spending some time on meditat—uh, trying to go, today. At least I'm going to try."

"You sound like you're anticipating failure already. That practically guarantees it."

"Well, I'm trying not to anticipate *anything*. What are you doing working on a Saturday anyway?"

"Only a half day. Due to our *day off* on Christmas, the routes are all behind."

"Will you be coming up later?"

"I don't know. It depends," he said. "I'll call you. Maybe tonight."

"What does it depend on?"

"Whether it would be wise or not."

When I didn't comment he added, "I didn't mean that the way it sounded. I'd just rather you put your time into other things, that's all. Besides that, I've got a lot on my mind. Full moon's tomorrow, remember?"

I'd forgotten. A sense of impending doom crept over me. Time was inching up on me rapidly. I wondered if, after his meeting, he might decide not to leave after all. And if he *did* stay, I couldn't see any reason why he couldn't just move back in. There was still a serious undertone in his voice, that *mood* that had started this whole thing, but I had to reluctantly admit that it had eased up a little since he'd decided to leave for his home stomping grounds.

I picked up the Atlantis book after we hung up and checked through the table of contents. A little, a little, a little. All I'd learned from Devin this morning was that I couldn't trust a book to enlighten me...except a little. I now wondered if it was even worth having my mother's book sent down. Wouldn't it also be intermingled with a bunch of bullshit? My mother hadn't thought so.

When I called her back to see if she'd reclaimed her book (and she had), I voiced my fears about jeopardizing such a rare book by sending it through the mail when it probably wouldn't help me anyway.

"Look," she said. "You've told me about this purple blob. Blue, you call him? Well, Keel mentions them in his book. And don't forget the car incident back in June. You've told me things that I've noticed all seem to occur around ten o'clock. Your experiment with this...Erick. And that airplane crash vision. You haven't noticed, but I have. Ten o'clock. And Keel mentions that ten o'clock is one of their most powerful times."

"Mom, clarify yourself, will you? Which *them* are you talking about?" I told her about the Steiger book and even gave her a multiple choice of *theys* and *thems* to choose from. Her answer nearly made me drop the phone.

"They are all different manifestations of the same energy source, according to Keel. At one time, before UFOs were even seen in the sky, huge airships flew over America. *Before* airships were invented. Planes hadn't been invented. We're talking late eighteen hundreds. These airships looked even more absurd than the modern saucer-shaped UFOs of today. It's the same intelligence projecting these tangible illusions. It just switches its projections to keep up with the times. They stay one step ahead of human technology. They conform to beliefs—individual and local—and are even responsible for the religious miracles that have occurred at places like Lourdes, France, and Fatima, Portugal. Both are places where kids have claimed to have seen and conversed with the Blessed Virgin. Keel says this intelligence is below the range of light in the electromagnetic spectrum. It can materialize and dematerialize by lowering or raising its vibrations, but technically it resides in the atmosphere in the same ranges as radio waves and heat waves."

"Whoa. Radio waves? Heat waves?" Both were Devin's specialties. He'd always been able to project heat and control the radio, or at least anticipate what record the station was going to play next. And then there was the issue of the Ten Tapes. Just how much *did* music play a part in all of this?

"Radio waves," she confirmed. "That's what Keel says. Lower frequencies. He says if you could slow down your own frequency you'd see all kinds of things that already exist there but are invisible to you now. They coexist *with* us, and whether they're good or bad, they're just using the human race for their own ends."

"Oh, bullshit!" That last line of hers blew the whole thing. "Mom, whatever Devin is, and wherever he is from, he is *not* exploiting me. He's been honest from the very beginning. Everything you've just told me, he already has."

"I can't believe that, Kerry. Keel started out as a skeptic, and he spent four years coming to these conclusions."

"Well, Devin's had an eternity of knowing already then, Mom, because if he was exploiting me he damn sure wouldn't tell me in one phone conversation what it took this Keel guy four years to figure out."

"Telephones, that's another thing he mentions. You make a long-distance call, you might as well get a megaphone and scream your conversation directly into their world, just as we are undoubtedly doing at this moment. The telephone company utilizes high-frequency radio for long-distance. You see microwave relay towers all over the country, and microwave is also in that same area as heat and radio. Keel says they can adjust beams of electromagnetic energy to any frequency they want to. They manipulate patterns of frequency to take form and become visible. They are pure energy. Kerry, I'm really worried about you. This thing that's happened with Devin is classically what always happens. They'll say anything to get you to listen. They use you and then dump you. There is case after case in this book of people who fell for their pitch, and they're all documented. Names, dates, everything. He proves every claim he makes."

"Yeah, but like I told you, Mom, Devin's already told me all that. He didn't say he was from Mars or Venus or some other galaxy. He admitted right off exactly what you just told me. He's got these reel-to-reels…tapes of recorded music, and he manipulates the radio as though he *were* the deejay."

"Oh, that's nice," she said sarcastically. "Now I *know* you're involved in the very thing I'm talking about. See how you defend him? Kerry, don't you realize that if they suddenly can't control *you* they will get to you in other ways? They'll attack Mandy and Michelle. Possession is no joke!" She paused, and her voice softened a little. "Kerry, please. Come home for a rest."

I couldn't let her worries deter me, and I didn't have the time to spend defending Devin. He could be gone tomorrow. "I can't, Mom. Not until I get to the bottom of this. Could you just send the book?"

"That's another thing, Kerry. Look how hard it is to get. You think that's an accident too? Keel lists page after page of famous people who got too close to the truth. As long as they were chasing lights in the sky, they were fine. The minute they put the electromagnetic connection to it, they either died or went insane. And all on that same range of dates, too. Just as the UFOs show up in what they call flaps...certain dates."

"Which dates, and who died? I want to *hear* this."

"Okay, you want specifics?" I could hear the rustle of pages, and I flashed on that night I had rustled those same pages and nearly went insane myself. "Just to cite a few," she went on. "Arthur Bryant was contacted in Devon Field, England, on June twenty-fourth. His contactors used the name Yamski. George Adamski, another famous contactee, had died on April twenty-fourth, sixty-five. Arthur Bryant died suddenly of a brain tumor on June twenty-fourth, in sixty-seven. That was the anniversary of the first official Ken Arnold sighting over Mount Rainier that spawned the term flying saucer from then on. Frank Edwards. You remember him. He wrote *Stranger than Science*. He died just a few hours before Bryant. Frank Scully...he wrote *Behind the Flying Saucers*. He died June twenty-fourth, sixty-four. You want more?"

The twenty-fourth. The very day Devin and I had had our first discussion of the terrible world situation. I was beginning to feel uneasy.

"Go ahead," I said. "I'm listening."

"Well, there's just too much to go into long-distance. It would be easier to just mail you the book. There are a couple more mentioned on this page. A Richard Church. Contactee again. A British UFO expert. Died June twenty-fourth. Willy Ley...pioneer rocket and space authority. Fatal heart attack on June twenty-fourth. Here's more. Remember Betty and Barney Hill? They're the couple who claimed to have been taken into a UFO for tests. Well, Barney suddenly became ill and died February twenty-fifth, sixty-nine. His dog died December twenty-fourth, the year before. Now, you can chalk all this up to coincidence but, well, you decide for yourself. I think you're mixed up in the same thing. Here's another one. Harry Price. He wrote a book on poltergeists. Died April twenty-fourth. Should I keep going?"

It was too close to my own personal dates. "Is that it? Just the twenty-fourth?"

"No, the dates seem to run from the eighteenth to the twenty-ninth, peaking on the twenty-second, twenty-third and twenty-fourth. Especially March and December. Keel chalked these dates up to electromagnetic conditions at certain times in our time-space continuum."

I glanced at the calendar on the refrigerator and mentally ran back through the dates when our problem had actually...and very suddenly...begun. The day after Mandy's birthday. The eighteenth of December had been the very first real indication that something was wrong. I didn't like the drift of it. "Look, Mom. I'll talk to you later. Like I said, I don't care what the UFOs are doing. I know him, and he is *not* evil."

"Suit yourself," she said. "I see there's no point in sending you the book. You're obviously going to defend him to the end."

"You're right," I said. "Mom, I appreciate your concern, but please try to understand. I love him. Whatever he is, I am too. That's why I have to get to the core of this whole thing."

I went back to the bookshelf. I had to find the truth, and books were all I had to work with. No matter what the truth was, I had to find it and find it fast. Whether this Keel guy was wrong or right, I'd have followed Devin anyway, anywhere. To Hell or Venus, it didn't matter. Not what any human said he was.

Whatever Devin was, I was too.

18 Saturday Evening, December 28, 1974

I had no sooner hung up the phone when I heard the familiar sound of a Jeep crunch into the graveled driveway. Pam and George.

Because I wanted to try the meditation and it was too early for the kids to go to bed, I talked Pam into hanging around until 8:30 or so to keep an eye on them.

"I'll just be in the back room for a while," I explained, "and the kids can't ignore a closed door. I don't want any interruptions."

"We were just heading out to the rock quarry," Pam said, "but we can go later. Is Devin coming up?"

"I hope so. If I'm still in here after the kids are in bed, you can go ahead and leave. But if you come by later and see that Devin's here, just keep going. We have a lot to discuss if he does come."

"You think he might move back in?" Pam asked.

"Oh, sure he will," George said. "Probably within a week. His pride's hurt, that's all." George, like Pam, had seen too much for us to suddenly start talking privately and excluding him. In fact, it was a matter of pride with George that he'd known Devin's secret even before Pam had.

"I hope you're right, George," I said. "Thanks for hanging around."

"Oh, that's okay," Pam said. "We'll feed the kids too, so take your time. Good luck."

It was with some apprehension that I entered the darkened bedroom. I really had no idea how to begin. Nor was I expecting company.

Blue.

The shimmering mass of purple was hovering in its usual corner. It was the first time I'd really been face-to-face with him, or it, alone, without at least Devin's presence in the house. Pam had said she'd never seen Blue and here he was now, more visible tonight than he'd ever been. I started for the door to get her, but something stopped me. This was not a circus.

"Okay, Blue, whatever you are," I whispered aloud to the mass that had descended lower to the bed. "It's me and you, I guess."

Hesitantly I sat down on the bed, not quite brave enough to move all the way to the corner. Blue had never shone so brightly. While I wasn't afraid of him...it...personally, my mother's warnings were too fresh in my mind and the *idea* of Blue produced a crawly feeling. So *this* was one of those purple blobs. Well, Blue or no Blue, I had to try to relax if I was ever going to get anywhere, no pun intended.

I leaned up against the wall, propping myself with two pillows. Blue moved over to the other side of the room. With a final glance at Blue, I closed my eyes.

Blackness. I was too nervous. I tried one eye instead of two, and that seemed to help. The bedroom was growing darker as the sun sank outside, and I could hear the TV running faintly in the kids' room. I was just finally starting to relax when I felt the weight of somebody suddenly sitting down on the bed. Startled, my eyes flew open, and I was stunned to see that it was not Pammy or somebody with some human weight. Blue had moved down to the bed where I felt the weight.

I knew what he...it...wanted to do. I just didn't know if I had the guts to carry it out. Then a memory of Devin's last remarks came to mind, and hesitantly I gave in. I had to overcome the fears and programs I'd been conditioned to all my life. I couldn't afford not to, and there was no time to get used to it gradually.

"*Go ahead, Blue*," I thought, closing my eyes tightly. I hoped that, whatever it was, it couldn't sense fear like animals did. The last thing I wanted to do was hurt his feelings, or worse, get him mad. Like Devin said, he might well be the only friend I had left.

I didn't have to be looking directly at Blue to track him. The closer he got, the cooler the emanations from him were. Unlike *him*, whose hands had trailed my body leaving waves of warmth and heat, Blue's waves of energy washed over me like a silent fan, over my legs and feet, leaving that coolness behind him as he moved. A flash of fear went through me as I realized how real Blue was, and I shuddered.

It stopped instantly. No movement. No cool air. Nothing.

I opened my eyes and looked around the room, then up at the ceiling. There he was. Considerate of my fright and feelings, he was waiting for me to relax again.

I closed my eyes again, took a deep breath. "Go ahead, Blue."

This time Blue started from the top, the coolness beginning on top of my head and spreading over my shoulders. He was enveloping me in his coolness. I sat frozen, unsure of what to do next. Blue, I realized, was not hurting me at all.

It was just too new to me. I opened one eye. The room was purple. I wondered if that was how Blue viewed things and then realized suddenly that the coolness was passing through my back and stomach, moving towards the bedroom door. The room returned to its normal darkened state. Blue had vanished.

Somewhat excited, and more than a little shaken, I bounded from the bed and out into the living room where the air conditioner had the room much colder than those waves of coolness that had radiated from Blue.

No sign of Pammy or George.

Quiet in the kids' room. No TV running. When had it gone off?

I looked at the clock. Exactly ten o'clock.

I had been in the room for over two hours, and it had seemed like only twenty minutes. Ten o'clock and no Devin.

I couldn't warm the living room up fast enough. I opened both doors, not that it was much warmer outside, and picked up the phone. I could wait outside on the swings and leave the phone by the back porch.

My mind went back to Blue as I sat on the small wooden seat, clutching the cold chains with both hands, heels planted firmly in the dirt. What the hell *was* Blue? Did Devin really *know?* I glanced over at the phone, gleaming white in the moonlight. Maybe I should call *him.*

The moon was almost full. Tomorrow was official, but tomorrow was in two hours…midnight. Had Devin already left for Thompson's Station? I didn't want to nag him. He said he'd *try* to come.

At eleven, I gave in and dialed the number. Gerald answered the phone.

"It's your dime."

"Gerald? Is Devin around?"

"Yes, he is. Just a minute, please." He set the phone down, and a minute later Devin picked it up. The ironic thing was that it *was* Devin. I had hoped *he* would remain in position until this was settled.

"H'lo?"

"Hello, Devin?"

There was an embarrassed silence at first. Then he said, "Oh, I never did make it out of here. Trevor's here." As if an afterthought, he added, "I'm pretty stoned." He almost sounded defiant.

"That's okay. I just didn't know whether to give up on your coming or not."

He sighed. "What time is it?"

"About eleven."

"You still have that book…Mastering Witchcraft?"

"Yes, I put them out for you, but you left them anyway."

"I don't need that Witches Bible. I just need the other one. I'll be up. Trevor's leaving anyway."

"Oh, then you *are* coming up?"

"Yeah, if I leave right now." He half laughed. "Later."

I replaced the receiver, not sure if I *did* want to see him now. He sounded…bitter.

The van barreled up about 11:30. I watched him from the open front door. His greeting was merely a tired nod. His eyes looked sunken in from lack of sleep, and his face was gaunt. He looked worse than he had the day he moved out.

For once, he refused coffee. And he had a hacking cough. He sat down in the beanbag and leaned back against the front of the couch. He'd looked like he'd been up for days.

"You're not feeling good, are you," I said.

He turned to look at me. "I feel all right."

"You want a backrub?"

He nodded gratefully and rolled over onto his stomach, bunching the beanbag up to form a pillow. As uncomfortable as I felt, I was glad my hands would be busy. Devin seemed like a total stranger, and I found myself floundering for something to say.

"I can't stay long," he said suddenly, "but don't stop what you're doing. It feels good."

"You look awful, Devin. Is it all right down at Gerald's?

A muffled half laugh, then a quiet, "no."

"Is he hassling you?"

"No. Nobody is. I just don't get into the vibe, you know? Gerald and Faye are off on their own trip. Brian…he's a kid brother. He's okay, you know? But—"

I felt his shoulders shrug beneath my hands. I thought about asking him again to move back in. He obviously wasn't happy at Gerald's. What did I have to lose?

"You're still welcome to move back here, at least until you know what *he's* going to do."

He opened his eyes and looked around at me coldly, a frozen accusing stare. "I already *know* what he's going to do."

I looked down at the floor and stopped the massage. He got up and went outside, shutting the door quietly behind him.

Well, I had dreaded the day I would have to face Devin. It looked like he'd just up and left without a goodbye. I had expected that he might inwardly blame me for the course of events, but I hadn't been prepared for the accusing tone of voice. I reminded myself that I had it coming and went outside.

He was leaning over the chain-link fence, smoking, gazing skyward, eyes misty and distant.

"Devin?"

"Pretty soon."

I reached for his shoulder and he jerked away.

"Devin?"

"I'll be *in* in a minute."

I returned to the house, determined to stay in control of my emotions. Dimly, I remembered a similar wall between us once before. Back on Halloween Night. Erick had stepped in then, when I could have let Devin drive away forever. Who would step in now, now that I couldn't?

He didn't stay out long. When he returned it was to the beanbag again, this time lying on his back, his arm slung over his eyes. "Can you kill that lamp?" he asked.

"Sure."

When the room plunged into darkness, he pulled his arm down. A small candle flickered on the floor beside the record player. He reached for me then, pulling me tightly against his chest, and closed his eyes. The tenseness had gone out of his body.

"I still love you, Devin."

In response, he patted my shoulder where his hand rested.

"Devin, I'm sorry…"

"Don't apologize," he said sharply. "I told you before. Don't be sorry. Okay?"

"But it's my fault that he's leaving."

"There's no fault to it. If he leaves, he leaves. That's all." He burst into another hacking cough, and I listened helplessly. Nothing I could do. Nothing I could say.

Five minutes passed. I sat up to see if he was asleep. He wasn't.

When he did speak, his voice was loud and sudden in the uncomfortable silence. "Guess who attacked me today. For no reason."

"Thor?"

He nodded. "I was giving him his fucking dog food. Dig that one."

"Did he hurt you?"

"That's not the point. I raised that dog. Dogs that you raise from puppyhood don't fucking bite the hand that feeds them." He lit a cigarette, drew on it and offered it to me.

I shook my head. "You don't know why he did it?"

"Yeah. I know why."

I didn't pursue it. Instead, I changed the subject. "Ever get the tree planted?"

"No." No explanation. Devin, who'd freaked out all through Christmas over the senseless murder of trees. Finally, he added, "I watered it today. It still has room in the pot."

He hadn't thought so on Christmas Day.

"I guess I'd better be going. The later it gets, the longer that drive seems." He sat up. "I guess maybe I will take that coffee now."

I breathed a sigh of relief. "You feeling better?"

He shrugged. "This is unusual for me to get sick. It's almost …embarrassing."

I remembered what *he'd* said about Devin's possible departure. An accident. Pneumonia. No, embarrassing wasn't the word. At least, not the one I had in mind. I felt a tug of irritation that *he* would let this happen to Devin, but I didn't dare voice it. Devin was touchy as hell tonight. I busied myself with the coffee, and when I brought it in, I saw that he'd once again rolled onto his stomach.

"Want me to keep rubbing your back?"

"Aren't your hands tired?"

"No, not at all."

This time it never became a full-fledged backrub. The urgency of sexual need, the desperation and the pent-up energy and emotions overtook him. In spite of everything, he *had* to still love me. He *had to* if he still wanted me after everything I had caused. He clung to me almost desperately after it was over. It seemed like tonight *he* was the one fighting back tears. He totally avoided my eyes as he sipped his now lukewarm coffee, his back to me as he lay facedown again.

"Seen Blue around lately?" he said finally.

"As a matter of fact, I made a little headway with him tonight." I brightened, thankful that he'd brought up something we could talk about.

"Yeah?" He lifted his head with interest. It was actually the first real interest he'd shown in anything all night. "What went down?"

I told him of my evening's experience, and he actually smiled.

"I figured that sucker would pull that shit once I was gone. Shit. I guess I should feel jealous."

"Well, it was *your* idea."

He gave me an affectionate look, one I hadn't seen in weeks. A ghost of the old teasing Devin. "Not *my* idea."

"Well…"

"But that's cool. I was just jiving you. I mean, I'm not wild about the dude myself, but still. I think that's pretty far out."

Another long silence. I guess he felt the need to keep changing subjects because he never stayed on one for any length of time.

"Oh, I've been painting again. Remember that one I started to sketch out…the Virgo-Scorpio? I've been painting that. But…I had to change it a little."

I knew that meant the Virgo was gone.

"And I finished that zodiac wheel you started. You know, the one for the spare tire on the van?"

Guilt rippled through me. He had asked me several times to finish it before he left.

Before I could comment, a dark shadow fell over us in the beanbag. With the candle illuminating most of the living room and part of the kitchen, this shape was noticeable. My first thought was that someone had come in without our hearing the door open, and I glanced up. Nobody stood over us, yet the shadow remained, casting darkness over our bodies. I felt a clammy fear, and goosebumps broke out on my arms.

"Devin."

"Hmm." His face was buried again.

"Devin. There's something in here."

It was not like Blue—light and airy—but dark and thick like a fog. I could feel my skin crawling. I knew the fear I felt now was nothing like it would have been had I been alone in the house. Was this the wrong kind of company Erick had warned of? Devin lifted his head, glanced up casually, then put his face down in the crook of his arm again. "Just ignore it. Lie here with me."

His tone of voice was enough to keep me from asking questions. I settled in closer to him, and he put his arm around me protectively.

"You know what it is?" I whispered.

"Not what. Who. The old man." He spoke in a normal tone of voice.

"Yours?"

"His. Fucking checking up on me, I guess. Probably doesn't like my being up here with you. Might screw up *his* plans. *He* might decide to stay after all. Don't look at him. That's what he wants."

I didn't like this at all. "You *know* him?"

He shrugged. "I know who he is, sure. That's all right. He can stand there all night if he wants to. Don't make a fucking bit of difference to me."

The black fog evaporated instantly. Unlike Blue's rounded form, this thing had height. I'd felt its presence and strength, even after I'd turned away from it at Devin's suggestion.

"Oh, *hey* ! Check *this* out," Devin said suddenly, rolling over on his back. "Looks like old Blue thinks he's gonna protect you. What a laugh."

I looked in the direction he was staring, and sure enough, there was Blue, heading for the corner where Christian's picture once hung, then floating over to the corner by the front door.

"What's that? Another door he uses?"

"I don't know," I replied, awed by what was happening right in front of us. I knew damn well how calm I'd be if Devin weren't here.

Devin didn't seem worried or afraid. If anything, he seemed bitter and sarcastic about the presences. "Well, you're the one who can see what's going on," he said impatiently.

Blue remained stationary right where he'd stopped. I resented Devin's sarcasm. Blue had every right to be there. As much right as anyone's old man.

"I guess Blue thinks he scared him away," Devin said.

I looked around. "Is it…gone?"

"Hardly. Check out the kitchen. Over by the fridge." Devin didn't bother to turn his head and look. I did, and just as he'd implied, the tall black cloud now cast a gray shadow over the white refrigerator. "Good thing we took that masking tape down."

It remained that way for several minutes. Blue in his corner and the black shrouded mist in the other.

"Looks like a real match," Devin commented dryly. "Maybe we should place bets." He pointed to Blue and said loudly, "And in *this* corner…"

"Devin!"

He fell silent.

"You've made your point."

Devin sighed. "Is he gone?"

I looked around us, behind and over us. "Yes. So is *your* friend."

He smirked. "You don't seriously think Blue is any match for the old man, do you?"

"We don't know who or what Blue really is," I said resentfully. "For all we know, Blue could be as much a father to me as—"

"As the old man?" he finished for me. "Okay. I can't argue the point, really. I don't know." He sat up. "But I do have to get going."

"What if…he comes back?" I didn't even try to hide my anxiety.

"He won't. He's been here once tonight. I'm glad it was while I was here. At least he knows, now. I'm going to do whatever the fuck I *want* to do."

"But what if he does? What should I do?"

He nodded in the direction of the front door corner. "Your watchdog's here, remember?" He glanced around the room, eyes searching for something. "You got that book?"

"Yeah. On the shelf." I got it for him, along with the Witches' Bible.

"I don't need that one," he said. "You keep it." He walked over to the front door. "Gonna walk me out?"

I followed him to the van. He paused just before he boarded. "I don't know if I'll be seeing you tomorrow."

"I know. The moon."

"I'll try to call you, though."

"Okay." I kissed him on the cheek. "Good luck, Devin. I hope it works out to whatever *you* want."

He got in, started the engine, then laid his head against the steering wheel.

"Damn, it's a long drive."

"You could stay here," I offered hopefully. "I'll get you up. Tomorrow *is* Sunday."

He seemed to consider it for a minute, then shook his head. "No. I'll just go to sleep when I get back to Gerald's. Might as well make the drive now. I'll have far enough to go tomorrow as it is."

"Thompson's Station."

He nodded.

"Okay. Then I guess I'll see you…whenever."

"I'd stay tonight, but—"

"It's okay. I understand. I just wish you still lived here."

"Well, let's see how tomorrow goes."

Once again, he'd left me with enough hope to get through another night. At the same time, I knew that he *could* have stayed tonight.

There was a final feeling in the air as his van disappeared into the distance.

He could have stayed.

19 Of course, the radio greeted me with a song when I walked in the door. Pink Floyd sang about midnight moons growing cold. Pink sang of my urging him to stay, and knew Devin have been surprised to find me by his side if he *had* stayed. He'd wrack his brain trying to remember my name, as he searched for the words to say goodbye.

I didn't let this dampen my spirits. Anything could change once his full moon deal went down. I could only wait and see.

"You're still *up*?" Pam greeted me at four o'clock when she came in.

I was still up all right. "Well, I got it over with."

"What? Devin was here?"

"Yup. *Devin*."

"Uh-oh. How bad was it? Wait. Let me put some coffee on before you start."

"I don't want any. Did you guys go down to the quarry?"

"Yeah. I love that place. At night, we build a fire, and it's banked all around so you can't see the neighborhood. It's almost like being on an island. Well, you can talk while I'm making the coffee. How was Devin? Is he blaming you for *him* leaving?"

"Right now he's kind of being a good sport about it."

I told her everything that had happened tonight, starting with my experience with Blue in the bedroom while they'd been watching the kids, and ending it with the last words spoken before Devin drove away. As usual, she didn't blink at my wild story and never interrupted until I was finished.

"So what do you think, Ker? That he might move back in? You don't sound too optimistic."

"I'm afraid to be, Pam. One day he seems okay, then boom. I never know what to expect. And how can I fight his reasons? Another girl I could deal with, but…another world? Shit. Not if that black thing tonight was any example of it."

"Watch that," she kidded me. "That's probably your uncle or something."

"Yeah, you can joke about it, but you weren't there. It was really scary with both that thing and Blue in the room at the same time."

"I still haven't seen Blue." She brought her coffee in and sat down on the couch.

"You will. I almost came out and got you. He shows up at the most unexpected times. When you *do* see him, you'll understand what I mean. It's unmistakable. You think your eyes are playing tricks on you. I can't even *imagine* how Lola or Kelly would react to something like this."

"I can't even imagine you trying to *tell* them about it."

"I can't either. Lola still hasn't called. I did try to call her but, well… I shouldn't bitch. I embarrassed her pretty badly, quitting the way I did. I'd be mad too."

"Oh, she'll get over it," Pam said. "It was just a shock, you know? She'd have never expected you to quit *her* that way. But then, she couldn't possibly understand what drove you to it." She laughed, then sobered apologetically. "I'm sorry, but I just keep flashing on you trying to explain any of this to her. No one at work has any idea, huh? Not even Kelly?"

"Are you kidding? Not from me."

"Well, I doubt that Devin would tell them anything. Shit, I've been living with this whole thing, watching it for the past three months, and even *I* have a hard time believing it's really happening."

"Yeah, imagine how it is for me. I've been dealing with it *directly*, not just watching it."

"You're right. No wonder you're not all there. Well, keep me posted if anything changes. This gets better by the day."

"Well, tomorrows D-day. Full moon."

"You mean *today*," she corrected. "It's almost five."

"Jeez! I'd *better* get to sleep. I've almost been up two days straight."

"Yeah," she agreed, pulling pillows and bedding from the closet in the hall. "I've got a feeling about tomorrow. You know what, Ker? I think he's going to come back. He still loves you, and anyways, didn't he say it all depended on what happened on the full moon?"

"Yes. That's what I'm afraid of, Pam. All kidding aside, Devin doesn't *want* him to leave."

"That's what I mean. He doesn't and you don't. Can't the two of you'ns convince him to stay?"

"What worries me more is if he does leave…what will *happen* to Devin? He's sick right now. Coughing…like he's got walking pneumonia."

"You don't really believe that Devin might *die!* I don't know…I'd have to *see* that!"

"I hate to say it, but you just might." I caught the pillow she tossed to me.

"Well, then at least you could tell Lola what happened, and she'd *have* to believe you." Pam yawned. "G' night."

It seemed to me that Pam was starting to wonder about the outrageous claims that *he* had made concerning Devin's fate. He had made some highly dubious predictions. Unlike Pam, though, I was taking them seriously. I had to. I had too much at stake.

When I finally did fall asleep, I slept until three in the afternoon.

I slept much longer than I should have, and I wondered how I could have with the kids zooming in and out of their room, still on vacation from school. Must have needed it, I thought.

The kitchen told its own story. Open jar of Miracle Whip, and lunchmeat still out on the counter. The kids had even let me sleep through their lunch. A note from Pam lay on the coffee table. Working today but home by six.

I made coffee and returned to the couch. Full moon tonight. Wasn't likely I'd see Devin, but he still might call. I picked up the Atlantis book and sighed. Back to the grind.

Funny twinges in my abdomen started up sporadically, a little like cramps, but not lingering long enough to alarm me. It crossed my mind that at this point pregnancy wasn't out of the question. I didn't seriously believe I was, so I continued with my research.

I was cooking dinner when Pam and George arrived a little after six. I looked up from the stove, watched through the window as they parked their vehicles, and reached for a dishtowel.

"You hear from Devin?" Pam greeted me. "Hey, what's cooking?"

"Just Italian sausage. There's plenty there for you two." I turned off the gas burner. "I didn't even get up till three. I guess I would have heard the phone if he *had* tried to call."

"I don't know," Pam said. "You've been up for days. You were pretty tired."

"I know. I'm not feeling so hot either. Maybe I'm getting what Devin has. Seems like I've been feeling sick off and on since the day he left."

"Oh, Ker. I have to talk to you about Bonnie and Jake."

"What about them? They finally break the news to the grandparents?"

"That's what I gotta talk to you about. Jake wants to tell his parents soon. Bonnie's due any day now, you know. Any day."

"I can't believe they've put it off this long, but what's that got to do with me?"

"I know. He's such a chicken. But anyways, he wants to bring Bonnie here and then bring his parents up."

"In the middle of all *this*?"

"I'm just relaying the message. They're going to stop up tonight and talk to you themselves. I think Jake is looking for neutral territory so there won't be too much yelling. I'm just warning you that they're coming, in case you want to turn off all the lights in the—hey, Kerry? What's the matter?" Pam's face went white as another cramp doubled me over. "What's wrong?"

"Man, I'm falling apart, huh," I said. "I told you I don't feel that great. I've been getting these cramps off and on since I woke up."

I didn't feel much better by the time Bonnie and Jake arrived. Bonnie was aghast at the change in the house compared to the last time she'd been here.

"I remember the dragon," she said, "and all the books. Jake, this place was *jammed*. Paintings, candles, stereo equipment that took up that whole wall. I wish you could have seen it. You could barely walk a path through the living room."

The stark nakedness of the house was all Jake had to work with visually. "Too bad I never met him," he said. "Is he moved out permanently?"

"I don't know," I said, exchanging glances with Pam. "I guess I just have to wait and see." I flinched suddenly at a searing pain that ripped through my belly. It was getting sharper.

"Kerry! Are you okay?" Pam asked again. "Is it that same pain?"

It came again on the heels of her question, and this time I seized my belly and bent over until it subsided.

Bonnie looked worriedly at Jake. "It could be appendicitis."

I managed to get up and make it to the bedroom where I could lie down.

"I think she should go to the emergency room," I heard Pam telling them. "This started this afternoon and seems to be getting worse."

The pain *was* getting worse, and now it wasn't subsiding. It felt as if something was literally sucking my intestines with tiny razor sharp teeth. Tears sprung to my clenched eyes, and I shoved a pillow into my stomach area and pulled my knees up. The pain was excruciating. An involuntary scream escaped.

Pam and Bonnie burst into the room, followed by Jake.

"Kerry, Jake's taking you to the hospital," Pam said.

"No!" My reply was muffled in another pillow.

"Come on, just to be sure it isn't—"

"No! It'll quit. It's probably just nerves or—" The pain gripped me again, and I felt Pam's hand on my shoulder.

"Kerry, please!" She sounded frightened.

"No...I can't...leave...what if...Devin...comes up..." My words came between gasps. Breathing made the pain worse. Exhaling was almost impossible, but if I held my breath there was at least suspension.

"Then let me call Devin."

I shook my head violently. "Full moon. Can't." Talking brought another one on, this one so agonizing that even holding my breath brought no relief.

"Kerry!" Pam sounded close to tears. "Come on. We'll help you up."

What happened next happened so fast and so simultaneously that I can't even put the events into any kind of order. It seemed to all happen at once.

First, that searing pain. Then my agonized scream. Jake's hands reaching for my shoulders and Pam's sudden sharp intake of breath as suddenly everything—stopped. The pain stopped. Bonnie and Pam stopped in mid-motion like statues. Even Jake stopped.

"Oh...wait," I whispered. "It's gone. It's gone! It quit...it...just...quit." My voice was the only sound in the room. A minute passed, seeming to last an eternity as I waited to see if it would start up again. Then I cautiously let my legs down a little.

Quit.

I opened my eyes and looked at their stunned expressions.

"It's...gone."

"Try to sit up." Jake, the practical one, extended a hand to hoist me with. I could sit up very easily.

"It *is* gone. Completely gone."

"Yeah, well, I *believe* it's gone," Pam said suddenly, her voice hushed with awe. "Just as you screamed that last time, I saw that...that blue thingie hovering over you. *Right* over you. I saw it, man. It came down on you, and your pain stopped. I don't believe it, but I saw it."

"Blue?" I looked around. There was nothing now. I smiled at Pam. "You saw Blue?"

She nodded reverently. "Devin's right, Ker. He must really love you."

Bonnie and Jake looked confused, having only seen the cessation of my pain. They exchanged looks but didn't ask any questions. They couldn't know what Pam was babbling about.

I stayed in the room fifteen minutes before daring to get up and walk, but it was unnecessary. The pain was gone, including that pinching cramp that had started it off.

Jake and Bonnie left about midnight. I told them to call ahead before they made any decisions about bringing Bonnie up for the parental faceoff in case the Devin situation changed.

I had survived the first weekend without Devin. Kelly would be at work tomorrow, and I still hadn't called her. If I called her at work, I could get an idea of what the vibes were at the plant. I fell asleep on the couch that night, the phone close to my ear, but it never rang.

I woke early, even before the kids were up. The Sunday newspaper was stacked on the floor, and empty Pepsi bottles spiked the living room. Jake always brought his own newspapers and snacks wherever he went. I glanced through the want ads just to see if anything was available. By the time Pammy got up, I already had an appointment at nine o'clock for a receptionist position.

Pam looked surprised that I'd even bothered. "Why?" she asked. "What you *need* is a damned vacation!"

"Well, maybe Devin will realize that I'm really going to stay here."

"You sure about this? Really, Ker, that pain could start up again. You don't know for sure if there isn't something wrong with you."

"Just my nerves, probably."

Pam raised her brows. "Well, I guess you know what you're doing."

I knew I had the job the minute I walked in. I left with company literature and a starting date of Thursday, January second. I felt so much more respectable that I put a call in to Devin at the plant. It was a good excuse to call, and maybe I'd find out what had happened during the full moon.

Pat answered, greeted me cheerfully, and handed the phone to Devin.

"What's up?" There was a definite formality in his voice that I was sure had to do with both Pat's presence in the room and his pride.

"I just wanted to tell you I got a job today."

"Yeah? Far out." His tone didn't convey much interest. "Doing what?"

"Office work. Hundred a week."

"Not bad." He yawned. "Man, I'm tired. I was out almost the whole night."

"The moon?"

"Yeah, hey, I hate to cut you short, but I gotta go. I'll call you—no…I'll *try* to call you later. I don't want to make any promises. I just don't want to put you into the position of waiting. You know me."

"How *did* it go last night, Devin?"

No response.

"Did…did you get anything settled?"

Another long silence before he spoke. "It went down, if that's what you mean."

"Then…then he's still leaving."

Another long pause. Then, "I guess so. The contract's signed, so to speak. It's all settled."

It was like a punch in the stomach. Deep inside I had really believed that somehow, someway, Devin would drive up and tell me that *he* had changed his mind and decided to stay after all. That he would be moving back in, and we could pick up where we had left off. I had not believed it would really be any other way. We loved each other too much…didn't we? And obviously, this was just more proof to myself that I wasn't swallowing this bizarre story. I swallowed and took a breath. "So…there's nothing you or I can do or say that would make him reconsider and stay here? Nothing at all?"

Devin scoffed with bitterness in his voice. "Are you kidding? You think after everything he went through to get permission to return…you think he'd just flip around and stay? The old man probably took him at his word that he'd become a fucking renegade. The place has a bad enough name as it is."

"Like Hell," I said quietly.

"Like Hell, yes."

"So this is it. There's no chance of changing his mind."

"Hey, if *I* can't do it, Kerry, you damn sure can't. I think you've done enough already, don't *you?*"

The words hung in the air and stung.

"Hey, are you still there?" he asked.

"Yes."

"Got quiet all of a sudden. I didn't want to think I was talking to an empty phone. Hey, uh… I didn't mean that last remark the way it sounded, Kerry. Kerry?"

"I'm still here, Devin. It's okay. I understand how you feel. It is my fault."

"Hey, he was thinking of going home before you did what you did. You know that. You just…clinched it, that's all. I have no right to make you feel like it was all your doing."

"Devin…" I hesitated, but I had to ask him. I had to know. "Look, besides all this with *him*, what about us? You and me? Do you love me at all?"

There was hesitation in his reply. "I don't know, Kerry. I wish I could say I do, but…I just don't know how I feel. I mean, I feel *something*, but I'm not sure what it is."

Tears began to swell in my throat, and I covered the mouthpiece.

"I'm…I'm not *him*, Ker…hey…please don't…don't cry. I don't know how the fuck I feel right now."

I took a deep breath, swallowed back the tears and made sure I could talk before I tried. "I understand the way you feel right now, Devin. *Especially* now. I've screwed up and I know it, but in the middle of all this mess, Devin, I know I still love you. If you don't feel the same way now, maybe it's because you never did—"

"I know what you're saying," he interrupted, "but I just don't know. I mean, sure I love you, but, well...it's not the same thing anymore. It's suddenly...changed. It's hard to explain, and I'm not sure I even understand, myself."

For a minute, I flashed on the original Devin. The *original* Devin. The one I hadn't cared for at one time. Was *this* the real Devin now? The flash came and went, but the voice was still there.

"I gotta go. Look, I'll try to call you, okay?"

Poor Devin. He sounded as confused and dismal as I felt, but then, we were both losing the same person, weren't we? Suddenly the new job didn't mean anything. Nothing did. For the first time since *he* had hinted that he might be leaving, the reality hit me, and it hit me hard. Devin wasn't ever going to move back in. Devin didn't even love me. For all I knew Devin was sitting in a stupor now wondering what the *hell* had happened. Where was his wife, and Kerry who? When Devin was finally *only* Devin, just how much would he remember? How much would he be aware of?

No secrets, they'd all told me. Everyone knows what's going on among us. It's all one. But something was becoming clear to me now. The existences of Erick and Christian...and even the Devin I loved...were not connected to *him* in any way at all. The arrangement had taken place between Devin Drew and *him*... one entity. *He* had been able to enter Devin because others were already there...had been there for seven years. If the original Devin Drew lived, he might be the Devin I had only seen in passing at work, one I had never cared much for. A loud, boisterous, ponytailed throwback to the sixties. Not the Devin I had fallen in love with. Just how deeply had he infiltrated Devin Drew, and which Devin would be left when *he* finally went home?

From the way Devin sounded now, I was the furthest thing from his mind. I was nowhere near as important to Devin as *he* was. Devin was in as much of a panic over *his* leaving as I was, maybe more, and if I had understood him correctly, Devin had good reason to panic. Was he only going to leave Devin, or was Devin going to choose to die? And which Devin? The one I knew and loved, or the legal body and personality of Devin Drew? I wondered if I had ever really known *this* Devin at all.

When I hung up, I rolled a joint and smoked it, then lay down on the couch. I didn't want to face reality the way it was so I slept. Slept well into the six o'clock supper hour when Pam's clattering dishes woke me up.

At first, my mind was a blank. Then it hit me all at once. Devin. The finality of the whole thing. And over what? Nothing any human could understand. Except Pammy.

"The kids ate," she said, setting a steaming cup of coffee before me. "What's going on? Have you heard from Devin?"

I sat up, still groggy and shaky and trying to pull myself out of it. "I called him." I sipped the coffee gratefully. "Thanks. I needed that."

She shut off the kitchen light and joined me on the couch. "There's…ugh…raviolis if you want some. Okay, first of all, did you get the job?"

"Forget the job. He's leaving."

"He is? For sure? That's it?"

"Yeah. For sure. He was out on the full moon thing last night, Pam, and you really don't want to hear what Devin sounds like right now. He's sarcastic and cold and…confused and…bitter. All mixed up. Not happy at all. I've never heard him so miserable and expressionless and—"

"You mean *Devin* Devin. He's different than usual?"

"Well, he's bitter for sure. Maybe that's all it is. But he did verify that *he's* leaving him, and it's definite. That's it."

"Can't you do something, Ker?"

I shook my head. "It's too late. To use his exact words…the contract's signed."

As if to put an exclamation point to my words, a song by Savoy Brown began on the radio. Hellbound Train. Savoy was on its track, and it was too late to turn back. The conductor had come to claim his soul, had his watch in his hand and was going to take him to his land. He had to get aboard. He said to take a last long and hard look, lady, as he was moving down now, could never look back and was going hand and hand with the devil.

I couldn't have said it better myself.

20 Talking to Pam was my only outlet and link with the sane world. We talked about the things that tied together the Atlantis book chapters, and how there seemed to be documentation of many intangible worlds that could very well be distortions, or versions, of the world where *he* claimed he'd come from. The worlds had so many names and backgrounds, yet they were all invisible worlds, just as *he* had claimed. And one of those invisible worlds was where both Devin Drew and I were losing him to. By the time I had caught Pam up to the way Devin had reacted to my call this afternoon, we were on our third cup of coffee.

"Man, Ker, if it weren't for what I saw with my own eyes while he was here, and that blue thingie last night, I'd swear you were making all this up. So, now what? Is Devin still supposed to up and die?"

Before I could answer, the phone rang and Pam answered it.

"House of laughs, what's your problem…oh…Devin? Hey, man! How're you doing?…hold on." With an *I give up on you'ns* look she handed the phone to me, threw her arms up in the air, and left for the shower.

"Hello?"

"Yeah, Ker. I only have a minute. I'm still at work. I just talked to Gerald. He and Faye have invited you, Pam, and George down to his place for a New Year's Eve party." His tone of voice was friendly, but formal. As though there was an audience there that he didn't want to feed.

"Oh. Okay, Devin, thanks."

"He was going to call you himself, but I told him I'd do it since it doesn't cost anything to call from here. So...what do I tell him? That you're going?"

If Devin had lost *all* feeling for me, he not only wouldn't have bothered to call, but he'd have done his best to discourage Gerald from even inviting us. "I don't think Pam and George have any plans for that night, so I think we'll be able to come."

"Far out. I guess I'll see you down there then."

"Okay. Thanks again, Devin."

He sighed at the thanks. "Later."

Friendly, but formal. A little like a stranger. Devin, but with his daily customer voice. As though that was all I had ever been to him.

Pammy came out of the bathroom and took one look at my face. "Now what?"

"Just him, Pam. The way he sounds. Like a passing acquaintance. We're invited to a New Year's party at Gerald's." Tears stung my eyes again but I forced them back.

"I wish I knew what to say, Ker. When I heard Devin on the phone, I thought, right on, man. But it changes every time I turn my back. Are you going to go?"

I nodded. "I love him, Pam. I can't help it. Even being there in the same room with him and a bunch of people is better than this."

Pam just shook her head. "Maybe you're right. Maybe you'ns will get a chance to talk at the party and get things back together again."

"That's what I'm hoping. It might be the last chance I'll have to try. It wasn't even Devin's idea to invite me. It was Gerald and Faye's. He was just being the messenger."

I refused to verbally express what my real belief had come to be. That there wasn't any chance at all. Devin didn't act or sound like he wanted to move back in or resume anything. It seemed to me like he really wanted to leave with *him*. Out of physical reality. Off the planet. Like *he* had predicted Devin would. Dead.

Dead to the people *here*, maybe, I had to remind myself. According to Erick and Christian and Him, dead was very much alive *there*. And *there* was where Devin Drew sounded like he wanted to be.

Of course, the radio had to put its two cents in. The Moody Blues singers were asking someone to ride their seesaw, to take their place on a trip. They offered their seat on the seesaw for free. Encouraged someone to come ride with them to find another place that was real.

It wasn't difficult to figure out what those lyrics meant.

I was afraid Devin was going to take them up on the offer.

21 Tuesday, New Year's Eve, was filled with apprehension. The thought of seeing Devin again set my heart to hammering. Afraid of how he might act, what he might be like now, and at the same time, starving just to look at him again. I tried to concentrate on the books I was pouring through until six o'clock when it

would be time to start getting ready. George's mother had agreed to keep the kids until morning. That gave me the freedom to stay out the whole night, and even stay with him if he invited me to.

During the confusion of getting ready came the one phone call I didn't need. My mother had reread her book again and was now fully convinced that I was either being controlled by *them* or mentally brainwashed by some devious scheme of *theirs*.

I had been through a rough week. There was no hope of Devin's returning, and no hope of *his* staying. It changed everything.

"Look, Mom," I began, trying to remain calm. "I'm sorry I ever mentioned any of this to you. You keep the book. I don't care what it says. Reading it now won't keep him from leaving."

Pam's eyes bulged. She knew how short my temper and nerves were at this moment and quickly intercepted the phone, urging me to finish getting ready. "I'll talk to her, Kerry. You don't have much time…hello? Mom? Yah, she's all right. She's just been through some crazy things, that's all. Believe me, Mom, she's got her head together. Will you quit worrying?"

When I came back out, dressed to go, she was off the phone. George had already left with the girls and was due back any minute to pick us up.

On the way down, nobody discussed the phone call, the party, or even Devin. I was glad for the wind and the noise of the Jeep, for it made any conversation impossible, especially at Interstate speeds. I needed the time to collect myself. The way things stood now, I wasn't even sure how to *greet* Devin.

As it turned out, I didn't have to worry about it.

He opened the door before we even knocked. When he stepped back to let us in, he didn't acknowledge me any differently than he did Pam or George. After everyone had taken a seat on the floor, he nodded in my direction, but other than that he returned to what we'd apparently interrupted. The stash box.

I watched him closely. Gerald, seated in his throne with Faye at his side, raised a stoned hand in greeting. Trevor and Mia nodded a greeting from the couch and smiled at us. Even Daniel and Julie were there. The room was fairly darkened, illuminated by a couple of candles and a no-volume television. No one appeared to be watching it.

Pam and Mia exchanged a few whispers, glancing at Devin on and off. I guessed that Mia was commenting on our split, but she didn't say much to me. Even Trevor acted awkward and uncomfortable, as if neither knew how to approach me or what to say now that *it* had happened. They weren't unfriendly. They just weren't *anything*, as if we'd all just been introduced.

I stayed glued to my spot on the carpet feeling like a fifth wheel. Everyone in the room was paired up. The only other solo person here was Devin, and moving between the record player and the stash, he didn't appear to mind his solitary status at all.

For that matter, he seemed to be there as host for everyone in general, not remaining with any one couple for any length of time. When he did talk, it was to jokingly argue with Gerald about the proper way to roll a joint, or to demand that the album he was playing over and over remain *on*. The album argument took precedence over the weed.

"Look," Gerald said gruffly. "I don't know what your problem is these days, but I don't have to listen to that noise over and over. I don't mind if you keep it moving, but this is the third time we've been subjected to that side."

"What *is* it, bro?" Trevor asked Devin.

Devin handed the cover to Trevor and grinned at Gerald. "You have to let our new arrivals hear it. *They* just got here."

"Well, play it in your room, damn it. At least turn it over."

"One more time," Devin insisted as Gerald reached over to shut it off. Devin turned it back on and nudged me with his elbow. *Listen*, his eyes told me. "Just this one song, Gerald, okay?"

Gerald exhaled loudly with exasperation. "My house," he complained, and Devin tossed him another joint.

"Here, Gerald. Shut up now, or I'll have to put it on again."

He looked at me again as the song began and it was then that I realized *who* had just arrived at this New Year's party.

Try to catch it, his eyes seemed to say as he took the album cover from Trevor and handed it to me.

The room fell silent under Dr. John's spell. The album: *The Sun, Moon, & Herbs.* The song: *Where Ya at, Mule?*

I could feel my face turn crimson in the semidarkness. Pam glanced at my expression as the words began, the meaning plain and clear to anyone sitting there who happened to understand the implications behind the song.

Dr. John asked the same question over and over, where ya at mule, and added that he was coming on home. He'd be so glad to get down there. And he knew that I knew he would be. He knew how much his old man cared. He was going home, back where he was better known. There was no place that he'd rather be. There was no place like home. He didn't know what he had until he was so far away. Home sweet home.

When the song ended, Gerald reached for the arm of the record player. Devin wrestled playfully for a minute and then agreed to the removal of the record, insisting, though, on the right to remove it himself.

Faye, bored with the arguments, left to get the buffet dishes ready. Most of the food was already set out in the dining room, spread over a linen tablecloth. No routine menu, and exquisitely prepared. As the guests were signaled to approach the table and line up with their plates, I saw Devin turn the record over.

No one noticed until it began its second wave of voodoo songs. Gerald, in the midst of eating, paused and glared stonily at the record player.

"I *thought* I heard that damn thing again."

"Oh, don't give me none of your shit, man," Devin said, laughing. Obviously the two of them spoke to each other this way all the time. "You're only just now noticing it."

Gerald set his plate aside. "You could think of the other guests for once, Devin." He removed the record completely. "Where's the jacket?"

I handed it to Gerald.

"You can play it back in your room anytime you want to," Gerald said.

"I'm sure Kerry's heard enough of it by now. Everyone *else* has."

Devin shrugged, smiled, took the album, and set it with a few others he'd brought out. "That's cool." He leaned back against the bookcase. "Put on whatever you want."

Someone turned the radio on, and Ringo Starr began his no-no song. Daniel, Julie and Pam wandered back to the buffet for seconds.

As the midnight hour approached, the group once again gathered in the circle of the darkened living room to watch the fireworks explode beyond the window, just past the long driveway, and the neighbors who were now out in the road.

Five minutes before 1975. Faye entered the room with a tray of champagne. "Anyone for a toast?"

Devin came out of his shell and stood up. "I'll take one of those," he said quietly. "Might as well get my…uh…final word in on seventy-four. My final contribution to the old year." He held up his glass, and everyone else followed suit, watching him.

"To us," he said.

The hour struck midnight just then, and it was the weirdest, quietest New Year's I had ever witnessed. Nobody moved. Nobody stood up and yelled.

Outside in the distance horns honked, and sirens and fireworks announced the end of the year, but inside it was like somebody had temporarily stopped the world. Trevor looked over at Devin intently, and *he* returned the look. Faye kissed Gerald on the cheek, the other couples kissed each other—including Pam and George—but Devin never even looked at me. Just drew the curtain aside and watched.

"There it goes," he said finally, then rose and went on down the hall to his room.

"Nineteen seventy-five," Trevor said quietly, shaking his head. "Listen to them nuts out there."

"Hope it's a better year than last year," George contributed. Daniel and Julie nodded in agreement.

When conversation started up again in the room, I looked around and, satisfied that no one was paying any attention, slipped out of my corner and tiptoed down the hall. I tapped cautiously at Devin's partially open door.

He was hooking up the tape recorder when I looked in. "Devin?"

"Yeah. Come on in." He flashed me a slight smile. "I forgot. I have to finish up this tape. The tenth one. Time's running out on me now. I can feel it."

At least it was *him*. Full moon or not, he was still here, and I was glad he hadn't disappeared already the way Devin had made it sound.

"You're still here," I said.

"Yes. It's just the waiting now. I don't know when, but soon."

I sat down on the carpet, not knowing what else to say.

"I'm going to miss the music," he said finally with a sigh. "Damn, lady, I'm going to miss you, too. But…I'll be with you all the time, then. What I'm really going to miss is your recognition of my existence. You'll probably forget about the whole thing in a couple of months."

"You really think so."

"Well, in time. It has to be that way, I guess."

"Look. I love you. I did then. I do now. And I loved Devin before you ever came into it."

"That's where you're wrong, lady," he replied gently, still threading the reel-to-reel. "The fact is that I've been around from the very beginning. From when you first took any notice of Devin that wasn't one of *distaste*. Who do you think *prompted* Devin to buy that damn ring that you're so enchanted with? Oh, you might argue with me until the split second I leave, and then it will all prove itself out to you. Even now, lady, it's pretty obvious to me that you still aren't sure...whether I am who I say I am, or whether Devin is a...how'd that go...a paranoid schizophrenic, after all. But like I said, things usually prove themselves out in the end. Sometimes after it's too late, but...they do. And...I'll see you *there*...in time."

"Then you do at least believe I'll make it there if I keep trying?"

"Well, I'd hoped that, by now, well...what's the use? Do I think you can? I *know* so. Whether or not you *will*...well, that's entirely up to you, lady. I have a lot of patience. And I've been *here* now, so I'll understand if you get caught up in the human bullshit." He snapped on the tape. "Did you hear the words to this side okay? There is one I'm putting on this tenth tape. I had to erase a couple, but that's cool. This fits better. I can't believe how this album just fell...into place." He tapped me affectionately on the nose. "I love you, lady."

I looked up at the gesture, feeling lower than I had all night. For sure, he hadn't changed his mind about leaving.

"Listen to it again now, lady. It's for *you*. Believe me, half of these songs are about us, but this one was written for you." He saw the tears welling up in my eyes, pulled me close to him, and held me for the duration of the song, letting me cry it all out of my system. I clung tightly to him, my face against his chest, feeling the helplessness and the hopelessness of it all. When the song was over, he gently moved me away from him, dried my eyes with his fingertips, hit the off button and kissed me lightly on the forehead. "I had to cut it off there," he said. "It's too bad. There were so many, and in the years to come after I leave there will be many, many more. But, well, it's finished anyway. The Ten Tapes. At least I did accomplish something while I was here in your world. The ten tapes are together. That was the last one." He stacked the boxes and looked at them.

"What are you going to do with them now? Just leave them here?"

"Oh, they'll be scattered. Along with everything else." He looked at me with defeat in his eyes. "That's too bad, too. They should be kept together. As a unit. Mass-produced just the way they are. It's too bad." He stood up and walked over to the waterbed. "Damn, I'm tired."

"Look, Devin. If you want us...me...to go home, just say the word. I can let Pam know. I know she won't suggest it herself."

"No, go get Pam and George. I'm pretty sure everyone else has left by now. You can stay awhile, can't you? Smoke a few numbers. And don't tell me it's that late. It can't be more than one or one-thirty."

"We've been in here that long?"

"Sure. I think Gerald and Faye might be getting ready to hit the rack, but go get your sister. She's another one I'm going to miss. At least go find out what they want to do."

They stayed. Why we did, I don't know. Devin fell asleep before two, his arm still around me. Pam and George did the same, lulled by the swishing warm water beneath us all.

At seven, I nudged George and Pam and motioned for them to follow me out to the living room. I hadn't slept at all. Devin had coughed himself awake several times but had gone right back to sleep. I had lain there listening to the rumble of congestion in his chest.

When we all boarded the Jeep, I remembered my jacket and went back to the room for it while they waited outside, the Jeep idling in the gray, misty dawn. I took one last look at him, still sleeping, and bent over to kiss his cheek. He never stirred.

No one spoke on the way home. Too noisy. Pam and George were still groggy with sleep and I sat on the heater in the rear, that last song now playing over and over in my head. I'd heard it so many times last night. The message had been pounded into me. Where ya at, mule? He was going home.

When we were just a few blocks from home I suddenly remembered what date it was. January first. The seventh day. Get the newspaper, he had said. Well, there was a 7-Eleven store coming up, so I yelled over the noise to pull in. George yelled back that he needed cigarettes anyway, so he pulled in and both of us got out.

Well, there it was. The Herald. The New Year's edition.

Even after I bought it, I didn't open it. It was just a few more minutes to the house. I couldn't get that empty, cold feeling out of my heart or that unmerciful song out of my head. Just playing over and over...

22 Nothing.

When I opened the paper, I don't know what I expected to see. World War III maybe? Or a flying saucer invasion...an assassination...even an earthquake...But I didn't expect to find nothing.

I went through the paper page by page and through the local news twice. Nowhere was there even a headline to wonder about. Oh, Nixon's inner circle...Haldeman, Ehrlichman and Mitchell...that bunch. They'd been found guilty today, and I was sure every paper in the country carried that same huge headline. Still, I couldn't see where *that* could have anything to do with what he had been talking about. Ironic, though, that Nixon had been involved in tapes too, and that the jury had been especially interested in *ten* tape-recorded conversations. But then, that was probably just another coincidence.

Just a regular old coincidence in a regular old newspaper.

When I closed it up, I counted the days forward from the day he'd made the prediction. December 26th. Seven days from that day was today, unless he hadn't been including the 26th itself. I wasn't sure.

Devin himself settled the matter by calling at eleven to apologize for falling asleep. And it *was* Devin. I told him apologies were unnecessary, that everyone had had a good time at the party, and that I'd been happy just to be there with *him* on New Year's Eve. Devin knew who I was referring to but chose to ignore it.

"It's almost embarrassing," he admitted. "I can't figure out why he's still here, or why *I'm* even here, for that matter."

"I'm glad you both are," I assured him. "How are *you* feeling anyway? You coughed all night."

"Yeah, not so hot. This being sick is a new one for me. I guess *he'll* be more comfortable when he gets out of this finally. Hey…did you ever pick up a newspaper? I was thinking about what he'd said…that seven days from now thing."

"I did, but I can't find anything in it."

"Got it nearby?"

"Yeah. It *has* been seven days, hasn't it?"

"Oh, it should be in there. Get the local section."

The local section? For a world event?

"Don't you want me to start on the first section and read you the headlines?"

"No, don't bother. Just get the local news, and read the highlights."

I ran through everything in the local section with no response from Devin except… "No, go on." I finally read him what was on the last page. "That's it."

"There's nothing else?" He sounded puzzled.

"That's it. You sure you don't want me to read you the national headlines?"

"No. If anything were in there, I'm sure it would have been in the local news. Maybe it just didn't make the papers, or hasn't yet. Must be on somebody's desk. Either that, or a decision was made not to publicize it."

"Could it be in tomorrow's paper, since he may not have been counting the day that he made the statement?"

"Could be. Wouldn't hurt to check. Damn, I just can't believe it didn't make the press. Well, okay. That's all I called about, really. I'm sure whatever it was, it's been done. Or something was averted that was *going* to happen."

"You don't think that Nixon crowd that all got convicted today had anything to do with it?"

"I don't see why it would."

"Okay, Devin." I wondered if Devin had any idea what *he* had meant or if Devin even knew what he was looking for.

"I'll keep in touch."

"Tell Faye it was a super party. The food was great."

"Right. I'll call you later."

I replaced the receiver and looked at Pammy.

"Well?" she demanded.

"Not in there, Devin says. Must be on somebody's desk."

"Could it be in tomorrow's paper? Are you gonna *look* tomorrow? When's the seven days up anyway?"

"Either today or tomorrow. I don't know."

"Well, now what?"

I don't know that either. Devin is surprised he's still alive."

"He's still talking like that? What do *you* think, Ker?"
"I don't know what to think. Devin *is* sick."

The newspaper was a huge letdown. When Pam left, I sat down with the little record player and rolled a joint, determined to numb myself out all day. Just sit there and listen to music. I hadn't been able to in so long. I'd been so wrapped up in this Devin thing, I hadn't even bothered to try and meditate.

Not that my mind was much on meditating. I needed to know. *Was* Devin who he claimed he was, or *wasn't* he? If he wasn't, was some force or thing tricking him like my mother believed? I'd put a lot of faith, hope and belief in that paper prediction, sure the news he'd predicted would explain everything with a thud. Instead, there was nothing. And Devin's attitude about it? *So what?* How was I supposed to know now what to think or believe? I squinched my eyes tightly shut and stared at that bluish-purple hole in my mind. I had never consciously crossed it, but it sat there silently…inviting.

"Well?" I mentally screamed up into the vastness of space beyond the hole. "Well, *is* he or *isn't he*?"

As if in reply, three small letters floated to the surface, becoming clearer as they approached, then dissipating like smoke rings into nothing again. But not before they'd registered an answer. In exactly the same way I had been told Blue's name.

Not a yes. Not a no. But the word *WAS*.

It jolted me back to reality. Blue? I looked around suspiciously, but I was definitely alone. I must have misread it or misunderstood. Burying my eyes in the heels of my hands, I tried again.

Is he who he says he is? Or is Devin being deceived?

Again, the same word surfaced. Clearer and faster than the first one. *WAS*.

Nothing else. Just that simple word and that purple sky in the background beyond the hole.

This was hopeless. What was *that* supposed to mean? I had just spoken to Devin. Devin had not sounded like he believed *he* had left yet.

Feeling dead inside, I gave up for the day. There was always tomorrow. I had finished the Atlantis book and went searching through my own collection for something else. It almost seemed a waste to bother now. For that matter, I was supposed to be starting a new job tomorrow, and it would be a wonder if I even got up at all. I made a mental note to call when they opened and tell them to just find somebody else. I was in no shape to be learning a new job.

The following morning I woke early and drove to the 7-Eleven for another paper. After yesterday's disappointment, I didn't expect any earth-shattering kabooms this time and I was right. After making a strong cup of coffee, I sat down to go through it, pretty much noting the same political and national headlines as yesterday.

The phone rang suddenly, and my heart jumped. Who would be calling me at this hour of the morning?

"Hello?"
"Yeah. It's me." It was almost a snarl.
"Devin?"

"Yeah, *Devin. Just* me. Guess who's gone."

I wasn't sure I was hearing right. "W-what?"

"You heard me. Guess who's gone." There was no describing the controlled anger, bitterness and misery he'd managed to integrate into his voice.

"Him?"

"Yeah, *him*. Gone. *Not* here. Completely gone." He wasn't even trying to hide the emotions in his voice.

"Devin, where are you?"

"At work. Where the fuck *else* would I be?"

"Are you *sure* he's gone?"

"No question about it. I felt his absence throughout the day yesterday, but that's not unusual. He does come and go. But this is different. He's not coming back now. I feel different, you know? Like I'm not all myself. Or maybe that's just the problem. That all I am is me. I tried to do certain things that I used to be able to do…it's not the same. I…I can't—" His voice broke, and it sounded like he'd covered the mouthpiece for a minute.

My heart ached for him. He was freaking out. This emotional breakdown was no act. His voice trembled as he attempted to get control of himself and continue on.

"I…can't control the radio anymore…can't even…what the fuck…I'm just me all of a sudden. I don't like it." Bitterness was again seeping into his voice. "I guess he's having himself a good laugh now."

"Devin, listen to me. After we hung up yesterday, I was having a lot of doubts myself. I could see that blue hole in my mind when I shut my eyes. It's always there now. So just like when I asked for Blue's name, I asked the most insulting question about whether he really was who he'd been saying he was. The word that floated up was WAS. I asked this twice. Same answer."

"And you think that word…that answer had to do with him? Or *was* him?"

"I don't know. I was looking for a yes or a no, not a was. If it *was* him answering me, maybe that was the instant he left here."

"Well, if that's the case, how come *I* didn't get some word from him?" he snapped. "I guess I don't count for much anymore now that he doesn't *need* me?"

"Devin!"

"Hey, well, what am I supposed to do *now*? Do *you* know, Kerry? I'm fucking sick. I cough myself awake all night long. I'm working with a fever, and it's getting harder to take a deep breath. This morning, on my way to work, I ran a red light. I stopped for it, but then continued on. I was halfway through the intersection before I realized it was a light, not a stop sign. I just missed a damn car. Me, running lights. Come on, Ker, you know I don't drive like that."

"I know." It was true. Driving was Devin's business, and he was good at it.

"Well, anyway, I just thought you'd want to know. I wasn't expecting you to have already…been informed. I am going to have to get moving, though. I guess you do too. Aren't you starting a new job today?"

"No, I'm getting ready to call them. I'm not going to take it. It's a new position they created, so they won't be any worse off than the day I went in.

They'll get someone else." Before he had a chance to ask why, I added, "Oh, Devin, I was wondering if you could do me a favor. Tomorrow's payday, and my last check should be there. Could you pick it up for me? It would be really uncomfortable going in there with Lola as mad as she is at me right now."

"They won't give me your paycheck, Ker."

"They will if I call Rita and ask her to."

"Okay. Make sure you call her, though. For that matter you might want to call and remind me."

"I will. Thanks, Dev."

It felt strange not to add that familiar 'I love you.' It was just as strange not to hear it from him either. My mistake had cost me my entire relationship with Devin, not to mention the loss of other relationships as well. Lola no longer spoke to me. Kelly was too busy with her own life to call. Daniel and Julie…even Trevor and Mia…none of them had bothered to drop by to see how I was. Mark wasn't allowed over, and my old friend Scotty was long gone. Even the old Friday night crowd of days past had drifted away. It was as though I was dead to the world, and the only one bothering to call this number at all was Devin. Now there was this lifeless bitterness in his voice. An edge to it that would flare into sarcasm at the slightest remark. Who *was* Devin now? Where had everything gone so abruptly?

Seven days, he'd predicted. Well, it was the seventh day that I received that answer to my question. On that seventh day, had he vanished, sparing Devin, but still leaving him to fend for himself? Hadn't he taken into consideration the wreck he would be leaving behind?

Even Devin's calls seemed to be an obligatory thing. As though he knew no one else would bother.

I sighed and picked up the telephone. I still had a job to quit.

Chris stopped in Friday morning, anxious for his rent. It was already 3 days late.

"Devin's picking up my check today," I told him. "I'll just sign it over to you. In fact, you'll owe *me* change, so stop worrying."

"Okay." He smiled. "Not trying to bug you, but I just didn't know. Now that Devin's moved out and you're not working…"

"Don't worry. Pam's working, and I will be soon. I'm just taking a little breather. We can handle this on just what Pam makes."

"Okay. Just bring it by when you get it."

Rita was at lunch when I called, so I left a message with phone girl Marianne to tell Rita to give my check to Devin. Marianne was silent for a minute, then, "Devin? She's supposed to give your check to *Devin Drew* ?"

"Well, what other Devin you got down there?"

"Oh, I'm sorry. None of my business…but…well, are you two talking?"

"No. We communicate by telepathy. Would you just make sure Rita gets that message?"

"Yeah, uh…sure, Ker." She sounded thoroughly confused. "Does…Devin know he's supposed to pick it up from her?"

I could hear new rumors flying around already. "Yes, Marianne. Jeez, you writing a book?"

"Sorry. But I am glad to hear your voice. We're all kind of worried about you. Devin hasn't been in here, so we can't ask him. In fact, he doesn't even call like he used to. Are you working?"

"No, just kicking back. Hey, is Kelly in the office right now?"

"I think so. She hasn't been going out for lunch. She didn't today either. She'll want to talk to you. Hold on."

"Okay, but don't announce to Lola that it's me. She's pretty mad at me."

"Oh. Okay, yeah, I won't." Apparently, everyone was up to speed on that one.

"Heeeey, kid!" Kelly's voice came on the line. "Sorry, I had a dehydrated, rasping, irate person on the line. Remember the d-r-i-ps? You haven't been gone *that* long. Oh, this damn place. I hate it. How are you anyway?"

"Kelly!" She was making me laugh, as usual. "Boy, you sound good. Don't tell anyone, but I really miss it down there. Not the drips, though."

"You're crazy. I'd trade places with you anytime. Hey, are you working?"

"Well, I had a job, but I quit before I started. Guess I'm getting good at that. I was actually thinking about meeting you down at the coffee shop for lunch. Obviously I didn't make it."

"I ordered a sub delivery anyway. It's no fun to go out alone."

"I probably didn't have the gas to make it anyway. Have you seen Devin at all?"

"No, matter of fact…" she lowered her voice to a conspiratorial whisper. "I think he's avoiding this department. He hasn't been in here since the day you left. I haven't even seen him hanging out at the exit. For all I know, he might have quit too."

"No, he's still there. He was yesterday, anyway. But he is pretty sick. Maybe he didn't come in this morning. I haven't talked to him since yesterday, but he was supposed to pick up my paycheck today."

Kelly was quiet for a minute, then, "Sounds like you two are still on speaking terms."

"Well, we have been. Nothing's changed about his moving back in, though."

"Ah, well, maybe he just needs time to think. I hope I *do* run into him today. He can't avoid me forever."

"You're lucky. I wish I was somewhere where I could run into him. If you do see him, will you remind him to pick up my check? I really don't want to call the route office."

"Sure thing. Oh, call me at home tonight, huh?"

"Okay. Hey, who took my job?"

"Nobody, but Lola has her daughter, Lana, working in here, at least for now."

"Are you *shitting* me?"

"No, oh, hey, that's right! You two are friends, aren't you? Oh, she's waving at me…said to tell you hi…spelled h-i-g-h."

I laughed. "I don't believe it. Lana working for her mother. How's it working out?"

"Oh, great! She's a blast. I didn't think I'd like her. Oh, her mom's glaring at me. It probably wouldn't be a good idea to put Lana on right now."

"Does Lola know it's me on the phone?"

"Yeah. Hannah told her. I was talking to that drip when your call came through."

"Okay, I hope I didn't get you in any trouble."

"Nah...hey, don't forget to call me tonight."

When I hung up, I was pretty sure the plant was thoroughly confused by now.

Devin called me at six, still at work. There was a problem with the check, he told me. Rita had given it to Brenda the receptionist, who had locked it in her desk and gone home for the weekend. How bad did I need the bread, he wanted to know, and could Chris wait until Monday?

"He'll just have to understand," I said. "It's out of my hands."

"Hey, uh, I'm *sorry*," he said, a little defensively. "I would have gotten it sooner, but I've been busy. And I've got a lot on my mind."

"It's all right, really, Devin. It wasn't your responsibility anyway."

"I'll get it Monday, for sure. Soon as Brenda comes in. So...did you ever go in for that new job?"

"No. I don't want to be cooped up in an office. I've been thinking about the racetrack down the road. I've heard you don't need experience to work in the barns, and it would be kind of cool to be around horses."

"Why don't you just take a break?... if you can afford to. He *did* tell you that you wouldn't *have* to work if you didn't want to, didn't he? Hell, I wouldn't mind a setup like that."

"He did say that, but I think I should be working. It'll keep my mind occupied."

"Okay. Well, Pat's waving at me. I guess Tim's looking for me. I'll talk to you later."

"Okay, Dev. And cheer up, huh? I still don't believe that this is permanent."

"Oh, you think he'll come back, do you?" That bitterness crept back into his voice. "I don't. At first I hoped so, but I'd say it's pretty obvious now that it's final."

"But, Devin—"

"Hey, the way I feel about it now, he can *shove* it. All I ever was to him was a puppet. Now that he don't need me anymore—"

"That's not true, Devin."

"Then where the fuck *is* he? *Huh?* How come he ain't dropped in on *me*?" His voice had raised to a hysterical pitch, then dropped back to a bitter low.

I took a deep breath, sorry I'd mentioned anything. There was no reasoning with him when he got on this track.

"You still there?" he demanded.

"Yeah, I'm here."

"Okay, look. I'll talk to you later."

Before I could reply, the phone went dead in my hand.

I tried not to let it get to me. He was upset, sure, but could I blame him? He was actually holding up better than I'd have expected, all things considered.

When Pam came in, I told her about the latest phone call. She seemed doubtful, even though she admitted it was really no stranger than anything else she'd seen over the past few months.

"It's hard to believe we're talking about the same Devins. Hanging up on you? Exploding every few minutes? I don't know, Ker. It just doesn't sound like Devin."

"That's because you and I haven't crossed paths much, Pam, and you haven't heard the whole story. It changes every day."

"I guess. Well, wait till I put some coffee on, and you can fill me in. Something tells me this is going to take a while."

"Yeah, okay. Did I tell you about asking that question on New Year's Day and getting the answer *was*?"

"On the phone, yeah." She was listening from the kitchen.

"Well, yesterday morning Devin called to tell me that *he* was gone."

Pam, on her way in, nearly dropped the coffee cups. "He's gone? *He* actually *did* leave, like he said?"

"That's what Devin said."

"I thought he also said that when he left, that Devin would die."

"Jeez, don't even put that thought in the air. Devin's really sick right now. He went to work, but he was running a fever."

"And you really believe *he's* gone permanently? Or do you still think there's any chance he might come back?"

"He never said he might come back. And Devin is so bitter right now, he doesn't *want* him back. You should hear him every time I mention any possibility that he might. So far Devin seems to be trying to deal with it without getting too emotional, but there are those flare-ups."

"How about you, Ker? You seem to be holding up pretty well. Better than it sounds like Devin is."

"Well, ever since that word…that answer *was*…along with the way Devin's been ever since, it seems to be proving that *he* was *him*, and that he *is* gone, and Devin is just himself now. And this Devin is not the Devin I fell in love with. *He* said he'd be there waiting for me if I ever learned to go, and that's all I really care about doing right now. Either being where *he* is now or having it back the way it was before he left. And with Devin's attitude about him right now, I don't see that happening."

"So are you saying you never did love *this* Devin?"

"This doesn't even seem to be the *same* Devin, Pam. It's taken me a while to put it together, but the one we called Devin the hippie, the Devin *we* knew, the one I do love along with Erick and Christian and *him*…that Devin is just as different from Devin Drew's personality as the others. This Devin seems to be the original Devin Drew. The Devin who worked as a route man while I was working in the office."

"Do you think *he* took the other Devin with him? Do you think that's what he meant about taking Devin with him?"

"I don't know. I don't know if any of them *but* him left. I just haven't seen any evidence of them right now, and that might be because Devin is so angry he isn't letting any of them through. And on top of that, he's sick. Maybe that's his body adjusting to the change, but he told me he ran a light on his way to work."

"That *doesn't* sound like Devin."

"You know, once I asked Devin if he'd ever been to the world that *he* called home, and he said no, but that *they* had, and he thought that was the same thing as if he'd been there himself. This was a while back, so I'm just as confused as you are about *any* of the Devins except *him*. *He* was always very clear about where he's from, but the other three have always been pretty vague. All I know is that with all the interactions with the four of them, I've never dealt with this Devin in a personal relationship."

"Do you think he's schizophrenic?"

"No, I don't think it's as simple as that, Pam."

"Okay, then let me get this straight. You're talking about a fourth Devin now?"

"Fourth, Fifth, hell I don't know. I've fucking lost track. I think that before *he* came, those three were already there in Devin Drew. At least that's what I've gathered from conversations with Erick and Christian. I just know they haven't been around since *he* left, so whether they all went with him, or whether they still might turn up, I just don't know." I paused to take a breath, feeling winded.

"Well, when *he* first told you that he was going home for sure, did he say goodbye? The day Devin moved out?"

"No. He said *later.*"

She sighed. "That could mean anything."

"Look, I know it sounds like I'm separating them into alter egos, but I'm not. I think they are all entirely independent agents, and I think that even though *he* left, that Devin might still have what he had to begin with. The other three. But you can't even suggest that to him right now. Devin feels like everyone has deserted him, and the only one he really seems to be bitter towards right now is *him*. He hasn't even mentioned the other three."

"So, you don't think the others are gone?"

"I don't think they're any further away than they've always been. And for that matter, *he* isn't really *gone* either, since none of them were physical anyway. He only left Devin's physical body and this world. But Devin was even irritated that I'd heard from him and he hadn't, so telling him about that word *WAS* just fueled the flames. I should have kept my mouth shut, but I thought he'd be happy to hear that *he* was home now and able to communicate…with both of us, probably."

"Good grief," Pam said. "Well, if they're still here, those other guys, how come they aren't helping Devin now like they used to?"

"This is just a stab in the dark, but I'll bet it's because Devin Drew won't grant them existence, at least right now. He identifies them with *him,* so in his mind, if *he* is gone, then they must be too. He's actually giving his perception mechanisms the license to tune them out. As far as he's concerned, they aren't there. If there was any chance at all that *he* might have come back, Devin is making sure that won't happen. Devin does have the right to say no, but I think all the trouble *he* had to go to…just to get back, it's probably not likely that he'd even want to, now."

Pam ran a hand through her hair. "Aw, poor Devin. Don't be too hard on him, Ker. Imagine how you'd feel if the shoe was on the other foot. Here he was, all used to being magic, and now, well, come on. It's no wonder he's freaking out."

"I do understand that, Pam. But it's still hard to talk to him. I don't know what to say anymore that won't set him off."

At ten o'clock, I sat down again, alone, to try to reach *him*. He was there, I told myself. That's what he'd promised. He would be aware that I was looking for him.

As hard as I tried, I couldn't find him. I asked questions and looked for words, but they never came. After a while, I just sat and watched the silent purple hole and the occasional dark silhouettes that appeared over the rim from time to time.

They didn't frighten me. They seemed too distant and non-approachable. It was like watching a tense movie, but knowing that it wasn't real, and therefore no threat. I always remained aware of the room I sat in and drew my boundaries so I'd never lose touch with my own familiar environment.

Eventually I began to daydream, bored by the monotony of the tunnel-like hole, and I allowed other thoughts to come and go for a while, forgetting that my whole intention was to try to get out of here.

That's when it happened.

It couldn't be called Astral Projection, for I could have gotten up and walked away at any time. As usual, I didn't lose touch with the room I sat in. But suddenly I wasn't looking at the same room.

My living room had become another room. A naggingly familiar one.

I couldn't see *me*. I knew I was sitting with full consciousness on my own carpet, yet I viewed this new room as if I were the mobile eye of a movie camera.

This room *should* have been familiar. With a sudden thud in my heart, I recognized it. The back bedroom of Gerald's house. Devin's room now. The waterbed had now come into view. Like watching a silent movie, my camera eyes turned to show Devin, hunched over the waterbed, as if in prayer. Protruding from his back was the clear hilt of a knife. There was no blood or similar evidence of physical violence. It had to be symbolic, but the sight of it shocked me out of the light trance state a little too quickly.

Blood throbbed to my head in what could have been the worst headache of my life, but I pressed my hands to my temples, and the blood seemed to drain away. The headache never came to be.

Miserably, I realized I'd failed again. Failed to establish that reunion that I knew I'd had on New Year's Day. I felt half together, and when I looked down at the carpet, I seemed to be looking down from a much higher viewpoint than it should have been. Gradually I felt a shifting, a settling in or descending sensation, until I finally felt whole and able to stand up.

When I did, the temporarily forgotten memory of what I'd seen hit me. Devin with a knife in his back. The memory of that scene made me shudder.

Was it symbolic of the way Devin felt? Or did it mean something more literal?

I decided not to mention it to him. He had enough to deal with right now. Adjustment to being himself was hard enough.

I was disappointed that I'd been unable to reach *him*. I hadn't been afraid, but still he hadn't been there. I wondered if I would have been so brave if he had magically appeared before me in my living room. Could I have handled that? I doubted it, especially with no Devin beside me to laugh it off or treat it like a natural thing as he'd done with Blue.

And then there was that black, shrouded mist. What would I do if it were to show up now?

Even if *he* were to materialize before me, how would I know if it were really him? What if it was something else disguising itself to look like him? Would I know the difference?

There were too many doubts and what-ifs still in me. Was I even ready to make that trip in yet? He hadn't stayed long enough to see that the doubts were completely gone.

I buried my face in my hands. What was the truth, anyway? The hole was still there, as clear as the day it had first appeared, but was that really the way home? Was that really a doorway? How come he'd never had to use it?

As I sat there discouraged, pondering these things, two things happened at once.

First, the word *was* floated up, and at the same time, a warm electric wave flooded my foot and crept all the way across my ankle. I recognized the sensation. When I was on the peyote, *he* had anticipated a chill coming on and had run his hands along the length of my body. That same heat had radiated from them.

Heat waves. Heat. They were beyond the range of light and in that same band of frequencies as radio waves. Those ten tapes and the radio had talked to me even when he hadn't. Many of those songs had sung of worlds beyond the range of light.

Heat and music. He had come after all. He was here, showing me in the most obvious and least frightening way of all, that he had kept his promise. He was still with me and probably even there for Devin Drew.

His thoughts seemed to pour into me through that flood of warmth which had begun creeping along the side of my leg. Devin still had the ability to communicate with him, as he always had done, even before *he* had come here. Erick and Christian and even warmhearted, pushover Devin were still there for him, unless he rejected them too.

In Devin's own personal despair, he was blocking all of them out.

In that instant, I wanted to call Devin, to tell him of this latest visit and what I had been told. But with the frame of mind Devin was in now, this message might well be the end of our speaking terms.

No, I couldn't call Devin and tell him any of this.

The heat and thoughts had only come for a few minutes, along with that reassuring word *was*, but peace and serenity settled over me, and there was a warm, contented glow in my heart. *He* had been exactly who he'd said he was all along. And while he might have been alien to the human race, he wasn't alien to me.

I was still in that state of ecstasy when Pam arrived home. She was relieved that nothing new had added itself to my already outrageous soap opera, she told me, as she plopped wearily onto the couch. "I don't think I could handle it tonight," she said, laughing. "You'ns are driving me crazy. I can't stand it from day to day, wondering what's going to happen next. How come you're in such a good mood anyway?"

I hadn't realized it showed. It was still too personal to share so I changed the subject.

"You know that racetrack we pass down on the county line road? I'm seriously thinking of getting up early tomorrow…maybe five or so… and try to get hired on there. You want to come with me?"

"Tomorrow morning? I don't know. That's pretty early."

"Okay, but I'm going to try for it. It would be something different."

She yawned. "I don't know. You'd have to get me up. You can try. And hey, wake me up if Devin shows his face up here. I'd like to see him."

"Yeah, you and the kids both. Don't count on it, though."

We were hauling out the blankets from the closet when Pam jolted me out of my serenity. "Wouldn't it be weird if you turned up pregnant now? *After* he was gone? Wow. What a rush that would be."

"Yeah, right. Ha-ha," I retorted sarcastically. "Then I *would* write a book. Seriously."

I knew she wasn't serious, but I did sit down that night and add up the days since my last pregnancy scare. I was okay. I wasn't even due until the ninth of this month. Now if I didn't start by then, I might have something to worry about.

Devin had suggested that I write down the visions and words I saw and heard, even occurrences and experiences that happened when I was trying to phase out. Keep a record, he'd said. Well, now, with no one to talk to except Pammy, and tonight I'd learned that some things were just too private to share with anyone, I could see the value of keeping a journal again. I had stopped writing when Devin moved in.

So on January 4th, 1975, I started recording everything, from the knife vision to my contact with *him* during that heat transference. After detailing all I could remember, I dipped into the past and also recorded the skull on Devin's pillow, the plane crash vision and the subsequent occurrence. Even Blue was recorded along with the event with the black shrouded mist.

It would seem that I should have been somewhat content with my progress, but when I went to bed that night I was alone with my logic and conscious misgivings. That maybe I'd wanted to believe in him so badly that I'd subconsciously manufactured everything that had transpired. That I saw Blue only because Devin said he was there.

In the midst of these inner mental conflicts, underneath the blanket, I felt the heat again circling and curling around my foot, spreading over my ankle again. Unmistakable heat. It lasted long enough to make me realize one thing. Regardless of whether I was losing my mind or not, that heat was real.

No wonder *he* had thrown in the towel in frustration with my human ways. Prove it. Show me. And then the scientific analysis. Yet, here was proof manifesting, just as he'd promised. And still I was trying to rationalize it.

No wonder he had shaken his head with doubt when I'd said I'd keep trying. I was no more ready to go 'home' than Devin Drew was.

We both had to learn to live with it.

Part Five

Pictures of Home

"But I am now inclined to accept the conclusion that the *phenomenon is mainly concerned with undefined (and indefinable) cosmic patterns and that mankind plays only a small role in those patterns.*

That "other world" seems to be a part of something larger and more infinite. The human race is also a part of that something—particularly those people who seem to possess psychic abilities and who seem to be tuned in to some signal far beyond our normal perception....

We are surrounded by energies we cannot see. It is possible that some of these energies form objects, entities, and even worlds that we can't see either.

Just because we can't see, hear, feel or taste them doesn't mean they aren't there."

John A. Keel
UFOs: Operation Trojan Horse
© 1970 John A. Keel
Originally published by G.P. Putnam's Sons

1 I was in a good mood when I awoke at 4:30, sure that I'd land something at the racetrack. I didn't expect to be hired within fifteen minutes, though, and that's what happened. I was beginning to wonder about the ease of my getting these jobs.

I was immediately catapulted into the world of the "backside of the track," where the racehorses lived and trained and waited their turns to race. Every day those horses galloped around the track and returned to the barn, hot and breathing hard, for a bath and a walk.

That's where my job came in. I was hired as a hotwalker. The trainer sent me to an office on the racetrack for a photo ID, and off track for a suitable pair of walking boots. I was to report back with both.

I wasn't used to walking. I wasn't used to horses either, and the barn people knew it. I'd admitted freely of my inexperience at the onset, so my first day was mercifully easy. They gave me the gentlest horses to walk, and I discovered that I had time to think as I walked these horses around and around the barn underneath the roof of the shedrow. I found myself observing the symbol of my new job. Going in circles was, indeed, reflective feedback on my personal life.

It was, however, just the kind of job I needed right now. It was seven days a week, but it didn't matter how I felt or what mood I was in. Nobody cared. As long as I showed up every day, I was told, the job was mine.

I had to admit I felt good when I returned home at 9:30 that first day, blood pumping and adrenalin rushing. The job would be good for me in time, but now I was tired and sore.

Pam was waiting when I stomped the last of the racetrack mud off my new boots outside, set them on the porch, and collapsed in the beanbag.

"Well? How was it?" She had a smirk on her face, probably because she had never known me to do anything other than office work.

"You wouldn't believe. God damn, my feet are sore. My legs, too. Shit. I hope I'm back to normal by tomorrow."

"You won't be," she said, "but I have some good news...I think. Devin called."

Instantly I forgot how sore and tired I was. "He did? What did he say?"

"Not much. He sounded like he was in a hurry. He just said to call him when you got home."

"It's Saturday, so he must mean call the house. He shouldn't be working today."

Devin wasn't there when I called. Gerald promised to give him the message when he returned.

When Devin still hadn't called by 8:00 that evening I decided to try again.

Devin answered this time, and he sounded terrible. Hoarse and coughing, he told me he hadn't gotten the message that I'd returned his call. Apparently, he and Gerald had not crossed paths.

"Pam said you're working again," he said. "You like it? Seems like it's kind of out of your realm of expertise."

"I do like it. It doesn't even feel like a job because I'm just walking horses, but I sure am sore. Why don't you come up? It would be nice to see you, and I've got something to tell you anyway." My mind flashed to the memory of that warmth and the word *was* that had appeared during the heat wave.

"Well, actually I was going to ask you to come down *here*. I've got some kind of chest virus, so I probably shouldn't be out running around, but it's not contagious or anything."

The invitation and hospitable tone nearly bowled me over. The last thing I'd expected to be doing tonight was driving 70 miles south, but here I was, at 9:30, nervously knocking on Gerald's front door.

Gerald greeted me with his usual dry welcome. Devin emerged from the hallway and beckoned me to follow him to the bedroom and didn't shut the door when I did.

"I see you brought your friend," he commented. "He follow you everywhere now, or is this a special occasion?"

I looked around the darkened room. "What? Who?"

"Blue." He nodded at the area by the open door. Sure enough, there it was, that quivering, shaking mass of purple.

"Well, I'll be damned. I didn't bring him. I mean, I don't think he travelled down *with* me."

"Yeah? Well, this is *my* house now, not his," Devin said with a smile. "He'd better not pull that snob shit on me *here*. I'll throw his ass out."

Blue wasn't the subject I had in mind. "How're you feeling?"

"Lousy. Running a fever again. Infection in my lungs. I probably won't be very good company tonight."

Then why had he invited me down?

I reached over and touched his forehead. He was burning up. He lay down on a cot that was set up near his closet. "This feels a lot better than that waterbed," he said. "My back's aching like hell from sleeping on it."

"You want a backrub?"

He glanced at me gratefully, and I went over to the cot. "You want to take your shirt off?"

"No. Too cold."

"Did you take any aspirins to get that fever down?"

His answer was a stony look. Devin didn't believe in medicine, but then, Devin wasn't usually sick. His mood was a little less sociable than it had been when he'd called, and I wondered if something had happened in the interim.

"I had something to tell you," I began, but he cut me off.

"If it has anything to do with what I think it is, forget it. I don't want to hear it."

"I wish you wouldn't be so bitter, Devin—" I began again, but he cut me off again.

"I'm *not* bitter." His reply was muffled and jerked as I massaged his knotted muscles, muscles as tight and tense as the feeling in the room was becoming.

"Okay, but at least try not to be so depressed."

This time he didn't reply at all, and the room lapsed into silence. Within minutes, he was asleep. It was one of those rare times when I would see his breathing deep and even while he slept. Goosebumps had formed on his arms, and he unconsciously drew them in protectively against his chest. I found a blanket, covered him, and gently stroked his hair. He never stirred.

I picked up my jacket quietly and slid into my sandals. There was no point in staying. He wasn't going to be waking up tonight, and I had to be up early for the racetrack.

I was disappointed that I hadn't been able to talk to him tonight. Even if he'd been well, it didn't seem like he was open to any conversations about *him*.

Overhead, I noticed, Blue hadn't gone very far. Still bobbing in and out in his customary fashion. A thought hit me. I couldn't talk to Devin right now, but with Devin in a deep sleep, Blue sure as hell might be able to. I knew enough about the levels of sleep to realize that something like whatever Blue was could get through to that mind much better than any words I could have used tonight.

"Get him, Blue," I whispered, and left the room, closing it quietly behind me.

Gerald looked up when I emerged from the room this early in the evening.

"So. He fell asleep on you, did he?" He laughed. "That's Devin for you."

"Well, he isn't feeling good."

"Hell, I knew *that* before you got here. So did he."

"So did I," I replied. "I'd rather see him sleeping. He sounds like he's got walking pneumonia."

"I suppose," Gerald retorted in his dry way.

Faye brought out some coffee, and it seemed rude to just leave without visiting for a few minutes. She asked about my new job, a safe subject, and I told her a little about the workings of the racetrack. That subject also gave me the opportunity to leave after I'd finished the coffee, as one of the things about it was the early rising hour. The stiffness was setting in from the morning's walking, and I knew it was going to be worse by morning.

Blue wasn't in the car with me on the return trip, but then, he hadn't come down with me either. I admired the little bugger's transporting abilities and hoped he did as well at delivering messages. Neither of us could define Blue, but if there was any chance that *he* might have been right, that Blue could somehow be a projection or extension of *him*, it might well be the only hope I had of anything getting through to Devin.

Pam had waited up, as usual, curious to hear how the evening had gone.

"It didn't," I said with a sigh, tossing my jacket over the arm of the couch. There weren't too many places to toss my jacket anymore. "He's really sick, and fell asleep not long after I got there. He seems to be making an effort to be friendly unless he even thinks I'm going to mention *him*. Oh, guess who was down there tonight. In his room."

"Just tell me."

"Blue. Devin noticed him right away, but made a comment that may have hurt Blue's feelings. Blue just hovered in the doorway. Devin always did make little comments about not getting along with Blue, but he forgot about him after a while and just went to sleep. I left Blue there. Like it or not, Devin's got him now."

"What'd ya do that for if Devin don't like him?"

"I'm hoping he'll thought-interject. He's done it to me."

"Well, let's hope he thinks the right things at him." Pam yawned and stood up. "Anyways, I'm going to bed. I stayed up to see if you came home with another wild tale, but I see nothing's changed."

Five o'clock came early enough. I'd set the alarm, but awoke a half hour before it went off. The track was only a few minutes from my house so I just went in early.

Like the day before, the horses I was assigned to walk were the most gentle in the barn, and by ten o'clock, I actually had a little confidence in myself and a certain sense of achievement. The job was turning out to be not as scary as I'd expected, got me home early, and allowed me to feel respectable again.

Now that I was working, it wouldn't be nearly as awkward to face Kelly and Lana for lunch on Monday. Maybe I'd even stop in at Daniel's and break the ice there. Their uneasiness was probably due to the fact that they just didn't know what to say to me. Maybe they just didn't know how to go about mentioning, or not mentioning, Devin.

I didn't hear from Devin until later that Sunday night. The call was unexpected, and he sounded a little better than he had last night. There was no denying the sincerity in his voice, as he apologized for falling asleep so rudely.

"I know I've got balls to ask, but if you want to come down again tonight, well, I guarantee I won't pass out on you this time." His voice was humble…sheepish, almost embarrassed.

"It's all right, Devin," I said, really meaning it. "I know you're sick. I was just glad to be there."

"You feel up to the drive down? I never did cash my check, and I don't know if I have enough gas—"

"Oh, I can come. You know Pam and her crazy hours. She's off tonight. But are you sure…"

"Hey, I wouldn't ask if I didn't want you to come," he assured me.

It was like a date. Almost as though he wanted me to give him a chance. As though he had never loved me or lived with me, and was only now just beginning to notice me. Maybe Blue had done some good after all.

As I made the long drive to his house, I hated to admit that hope was stirring in me again. Hope that at any minute Devin would tell me that *he* had miraculously returned with fresh news from *home* and was ready to try again.

I was having a hard time accepting our present relationship as final. There was just too much love at stake.

As I wheeled onto the ramp of the Interstate, I remembered the radio and switched it on. What burst out was a Moody Blues song, from the beginning as if just cued up, as usual. It was a wonder I didn't wreck the car right then and there. Not only was it a record that AM radio just didn't play, and not only were the words once again mirroring back to me what was happening in my life...

The song was from the Ten Tapes. The title... *You Can Never Go Home Anymore.*

2 The first thing I noticed about Devin was that he wasn't stoned or doped up on any medication. It was evident from the moment he opened the door and stepped back with a shy smile to let me in.

Gerald nodded politely, and Faye greeted me with a smile.

"You're limping," Faye observed. "Aren't you getting used to your new job?"

"No, not yet. Feet hurt worse today than yesterday. I've got a couple blisters now, too. The trainer says every greenhorn breaks down the first week, and that I can expect another five days of this soreness."

"Then it'll be five days for sure, if you accepted that," Gerald said.

Devin signaled me to follow him to his room. I did, and this time he shut the door. He then slid the stash box towards me and began threading the reel-to-reel. "Smoke. I wish I could. It makes me cough."

"I'd better not. I have to drive back."

"Well, it should be worn off by then. You can stay awhile, can't you?"

"Yes. Pam's with the kids."

His eyes softened. "How *are* the kids?"

"Oh, they're fine. They do ask about you, but I just tell them you have to work and live a long ways away."

He nodded. "And your sister?"

"The same. Still hasn't completely broken it off with George, though."

"She won't for a while. She's too softhearted." He lit a cigarette, coughed, and immediately put it out. "Damn, can't even smoke *those.*"

"Are you feeling *any* better?"

"Well, yes," he admitted. "That sleep did me some amazing good last night. I don't know why, since all I've *been* doing is sleeping since this started, but for some reason, after that sleep, I woke up not only feeling better, but happy and serene too. I can't tell you how good that finally felt. But it wasn't cool of me to nod out on you."

I waved that off indifferently. "When did you get up?"

"About eleven. When I saw that you were gone, I just fell back again." He switched on the reel and walked over to the waterbed. "Come on, get comfortable." He made room for me, patted the bed as the water swished beneath his sudden weight, stretched out on his stomach, and tucked his arms under a pillow.

I sat beside him and started to rub his back.

"Don't put me to sleep," he warned. "I'll never live it down." He reached back and patted my leg. "Hey, didn't you say you had something to tell me? Yesterday."

The possibility of jealousy ruining this mood thwarted any chance of Devin's hearing about my contact with *him.* "It was just about the depression you were in, that's all."

He fell silent, and I continued with the backrub, hoping he'd also lost that phenomenal ability to read minds. I could still sense that brooding sadness under the façade of lightness he seemed to be trying to put off.

"You're not much happier than you were yesterday, are you, Dev."

He shrugged. "I'm not *unhappy*." The words were toneless. "Anyway, I'm not taking it out on you." He paused and rubbed his face with both hands.

"Devin…he left you with…friends here," I blurted, unable to stop myself. "Erick and Christian and—"

He cut me off midsentence instantly. "Hey, no offense or anything, but I don't want to talk about *him*." The stress on the word *him* was anything but respectful.

"That's all I was going to say."

"He didn't leave *anything* here. He…took…everything." He reached over the side of the bed, extracted a cigarette from the pack, and rolled it across the floor to himself.

"You'll cough."

"You can smoke it." His tone had softened some. "I just want the first couple hits." He struck a match to it and added, "Oh, by the way. How do you stand period-wise?"

"Fine. I'm not due yet."

"Okay. I've been meaning to tell you…if you don't start, or if—"

"Nothing will go wrong." I didn't want him to start worrying about that. The possibility of my being pregnant was too distant and remote.

"All I'm saying is…I'd want to know."

"Why? If I *was* pregnant, Devin, it wouldn't be yours anyway. You know that."

"That's *why* I'd want to know. The thought hit me last night. Or maybe I dreamed it. Anyhow, it was on my mind the first time I woke up, and you were gone. I thought maybe that's what you wanted to tell me."

"I don't think I am, Devin. But if by some slim possibility I *did* turn up pregnant, just so you know, I'm not getting rid of it, and I wouldn't drag you into it."

"I just told you. I'd want to know."

"Well…okay." I was disturbed by the sudden twist of antagonism that flared up in him every few minutes. He was fine unless the subject touched…in any way…on *him*. I sighed. I hadn't come down here to rile him up like this.

"And you wouldn't *have* to get rid of it," he added, his voice barely audible in the darkened room. "They would never let it be born."

"What do you mean by that?" I stopped the backrub and peered down at him. His face was buried in his crossed arms.

"*They'd* abort it," he replied simply. "Do you really think *he* would let you raise that kid by yourself? Hey, not that you aren't a good mother, and I don't mean to hurt your feelings, Kerry, but you couldn't handle a kid like that."

The words stung, and my reaction was spontaneous. "What's *that* supposed to mean? He never had any doubts about my raising it before."

"That was *before*. He was *here* then. That was different. You read *Rosemary's Baby*. Don't you remember how that kid was described?"

I heaved a heavy sigh. "*Yes*, Devin," I said, trying to humor him. This was in no way anything like that silly horror movie.

"Remember her reaction to her own kid?"

"Oh, come *on*, Devin," I exploded. "Will you stop comparing this to that stupid movie?"

"It wouldn't be any different," he insisted stubbornly, and dropped back into that brooding mode.

There was no talking to him. I had to weigh every word before I said it. Trying to reason with this miserable Devin was as fruitless as trying to talk *him* into coming back. The more time I spent with this Devin, the more I realized how unlikely that was. Devin was too bitter. There didn't seem to be anything I could say that didn't provoke snappish comments. *He*, it seemed, had been our sole mutual interest. With *him* out of the picture, I didn't know what to say to this sullen stranger.

Devin apparently came up with the same conclusion and changed the subject. "How're things at work?"

"Sore, but okay." I breathed a sigh of relief. A human topic. What could go wrong with that? "I really do like it. There's such a weird feeling in the air at that hour of the morning. Everything's dark when I arrive, and I get to see the sun come up. The sky turns blood red...the place has a certain smell...hay and horseshit...and in spite of all the activity, there's a stillness, a quiet... where a horse's hoof clop in the dirt sounds so loud...you'd have to be there to see what I mean. Oh, and I'm thinking about taking a run down to the plant area tomorrow after I get off. For lunch. With Kelly and Lana."

"You're going to the *plant?*"

"No, just the area. Coffee shop."

"While you're down there you ought to stop in at Daniel's. They're not mad at you. They just don't know what to say. Just stop by and be yourself." He paused. "Well, I don't have to tell you what to say. You know."

"Well, it would help if I knew how much Daniel knows about all this...about me and you."

"About me and you? Nothing. I don't discuss it. They won't ask. I guess he thinks we had a fight or something."

"Well, what should I say if he *does* ask? I know I really put you on the spot, so I'll say whatever you want."

"I don't *care* what you tell Daniel."

"I can see that, but I can't tell him the truth and—"

"Daniel *knows*," Devin said. "*He* told Daniel he was leaving, so Daniel *knows*."

"He *did* tell Daniel? That he was *leaving?*" I frowned. "You mean Daniel is sitting over there waiting for you to kick the bucket now?"

"I don't know *what* Daniel's thinking," Devin snapped. "I'm not a mind reader."

"Look, Devin. If you're going to keep getting pissed off every time I try to talk to you, I might as well go home."

He didn't respond. I was instantly sorry I had reacted so quickly. I resumed rubbing his back, half expecting him to take me up on my threat and ask me to go. As I massaged, I watched his eyes stare mistily off into the dark reaches of the room, not focusing on anything, but glistening as though he were fighting off tears.

"Devin, I'm so sorry about all this."

He turned over on his back, reached for me, and crushed me to his chest.

Even sex wasn't the same that night. He seemed to feel that I expected it of him. After resignedly fulfilling the "obligation," unrequested no less, he resumed his lifeless, disinterested staring, eyes fogged with emotion in check.

I should have stayed home.

I stood up and began to dress. For the first time, he lifted his head and then sat up. "What's the matter?"

"Nothing. It just seems like you'd rather be alone."

"So you're leaving."

I drew in another deep breath before I answered. Dealing with Devin required a lot of patience these days. "Yes, Devin. There's no point in being here. I'm just getting you all riled up every five minutes. I keep saying all the wrong things and, well maybe I just remind you too much of *him* or something."

"I don't fucking *need* anybody to remind me of *him*." Devin bolted from the bed and pulled on his jeans, cinched up the belt, and then ran a hand through his thick curls. "Sorry if I've bored you."

Tears sprung to my eyes. Tears of anger. "Oh, Devin, you know damn *well* that's not it! How do you think *I* feel, huh? You act like you're the only one who lost him. Well, he loved *me* too, remember? I lost him just as much as *you* did. And I'm not holing up in my room, feeling sorry for myself…and whether you want to hear it or not, you still have Erick and Christian and possibly a Devin you aren't even aware *exists*, but *no*, you can't have an open mind and see what *they* might have to say!"

"He didn't leave *nobody*! I ain't seen or heard from *anybody*! Not *him*, not Christian, not—"

"See what I mean? Listen to yourself!" I lowered my voice so he would lower his. "You're so fucking bitter that *he* wouldn't come back through *you*, even if he *did* change his mind." I slipped into my sandals and stopped, suddenly realizing the dead quiet in the room. I might as well have slapped him.

"I'm…I didn't mean that, Devin."

"He ain't been *here*." Devin sat down on the cot, the picture of desolation.

"Have you *tried* to talk to him? To them? To anyone?"

He looked away. "Yes, Kerry. I've tried. I've pleaded. I've even threatened. I'm talking to an empty wall. So…fuck him."

"Devin, that attitude is what's probably blocking everything." No response, so I went on. At least he seemed to be listening. "Can't you see that? If you keep that attitude up you'll cement it. He *could* come back. He *might*. But if you keep this up—"

"Keep it up? He could have stopped in *here*. Given me five minutes of his precious time…fuck…it ain't time to *him* where *he's* at…I mean, I know he's *busy*, but—"

"There you go again, Devin."

"Yeah, well, he took enough of *my* time."

That did it. "I'll see you Devin." I turned to leave.

"At least *you've* heard from him. That's more courtesy than he's given *me.*"

I looked back, patience about run out. "I know how you feel, Devin. I could say the same thing, you know. Say he used me too, and then dropped me."

"He didn't *drop* you," Devin reminded me bitterly.

"Dammit, he didn't drop you either. Do you really think he'd come all this way just to stay a couple months and then say fuck it and leave? Put us two together just so he could blow it up in our faces now? Ever since this whole thing began, we never had a fight. Not even once. Remember? Or was that so long ago? We used to take that for granted, that there was no human bullshit between us. I'm talking about me and you, Devin. Not him. Now that he's gone, that's all you and I seem to do. Throw daggers at each other. Well, all right. I may have pushed him on his way...or helped. But *you're* bolting that door so he can never get through. Anyway...I'll see ya."

He didn't follow me to my car. I cried all the way home. When I walked in, Pammy just looked at me and shook her head.

"Now what?"

"It's hopeless," I said. "Just hopeless."

3 The following morning I tried to put the memory of last night's dismal failure out of my mind and keep my mind on the horses, but since the job was so mechanical I had nothing but time to think. Think, and fight the hopeless feelings of wanting Devin back. I knew we couldn't get along the way things were now. Devin didn't say it aloud, but I was sure he blamed me for everything. Deep down, I believed he was right.

I barely made it through the morning because of my feet. They were not just sore anymore. They were badly blistered, and I was relieved to turn in the last horse and head for home.

I wondered if Devin would even bother to pick up my check after the way things had gone last night. I supposed I could ask Kelly to get it for me and bring it with her when we met for lunch.

I put in a call to her at six o'clock.

"What happened last night?" she demanded accusingly. "You were supposed to call me."

"I would have, Kel, but I ended up down at Devin's."

"Oh. Oh! You think you guys might get back together?"

I opened my mouth and shut it again. Kelly was my friend. I couldn't tell her the truth, but I just didn't have it in me to pretend everything was hunky-dory. Kelly knew me too well. "Look, Kelly. I can't stick my neck out too far on this, but there's more to all this than I'm allowed to tell anyone. As I said, there's a third party involved, and that third party is kind of a problem right now."

"And you say it's not his wife. Well, is this a friend of yours or his?"

"Our friend. Then and now. Believe me, Kelly, I just don't quit good jobs, and especially not the way I did. Damn, you know I had to be half out of my mind that day."

I heard Kelly sigh. "I know that. Lola does too."

"She does?"

"Yeah. I tried to reason with her about you the other morning, but she refused to discuss you."

"Then how do you know—?"

"'Cause I told her your leaving that note wasn't like you, and she said she knew it wasn't. So...she knows."

"But she still won't let me try to explain."

"I doubt it, Ker. I'd give her a little more time. Lana's waiting to try to get a word in on your behalf."

"I'm glad *she's* not mad at me."

"Why should she be? Lana and Lola are two different people. Lana thinks her mom is being unreasonable."

"Has Devin come into the office yet?"

"Well, he finally did this afternoon. For some ticket reason. He was only in there for a minute, and he only talked to Lola. He never even stuck his head in. Shit. I thought he was my friend."

"Don't blame him, Kelly. He's got a lot on his mind."

"Yeah. The whole thing sounds pretty heavy."

"It is. More than you know. Well, look. I have to call him anyway to see if he picked up my check. If he didn't, maybe Debbie can give it to you. I was thinking about going down to the coffee shop for lunch...if you and Lana can break away."

"Tomorrow? Cool! It'll be great to see you. We've been talking about going to lunch together, so she'll definitely be with me."

"Right on! It'll be great to see her, too."

I had a lot of misgivings about calling Devin about the check, afraid for the mood he might be in after the way I'd left the night before, but when Chris came over, frantic for his rent money, I picked up the phone and dialed, Chris still standing there.

"Hello, Devin?" I hadn't expected him to answer, and, once again, he was wide awake and straight.

"You're not going to believe this," he said, as if last night had never happened.

"You forgot it."

"I forgot it. I meant to get it, but—"

I glanced at Chris. "He forgot it," I began, but Devin interrupted me.

"Who are you talking to?"

"Chris is here for the rent. Hold on."

I explained to Chris and again reassured him that the check was there, and just hadn't been picked up yet.

"Okay," he said, "But I *have* to have it tomorrow. My mortgage is due on the eighth."

"You'll have it."

He walked out, banging the door behind him.

"Chris is a little distressed," I told Devin, and he apologized again.

"Look," he suggested. "Why don't you come down tomorrow night? I'll remember the check if I have to...well, I *will* have it. Come down. You can stay a while. Smoke a joint. Whatever...that is, if you want to."

"I'd love to," I began, shocked at his complete lack of coldness after last night.

"Far out. I'll see you tomorrow then."

"You feeling better?"

"Yeah. A lot better. I got to thinking about what you said. Maybe it *is* me. I'm starting to get my bearings a little. I guess I've been making an ass out of myself."

It thawed me completely. "I love you, Devin," I blurted, before I could stop myself.

"I'll talk to you about that tomorrow, too."

It only took a sentence like that to start that old hope stirring in me. I had loved *him* with my whole heart and soul, but there was no question about it. I still loved Devin, too. Or so I thought.

Walking was agony on the fourth day. The blisters broke, and I could tell by the swelling of my feet that an infection had set in. On both ankles. I tried taping them at the barn, to the amusement of the lifers, and it worked all the way until quitting time.

"You sure you'll make it?" Nina, the tall, lanky assistant trainer, asked me when I limped up for the last horse.

"Yeah, I'm okay."

I walked those last twenty minutes like a martyr, and after I'd returned the horse to its stall, I went back to Nina. "You have anything I can soak these blisters in? Look." I peeled part of the tape off, exposing an ugly wound.

"I know. We've all been watching you limp. I thought there might be a swelling...let's see...yeah. Uh-huh. I have just the stuff."

She fixed me up with a bucket and some fluid to dump in the hot water I'd be soaking my feet in. By now, the blisters were both ripped open again.

"Soak them for about forty-five minutes. There's a drawing salve in there. It'll pull the infection out. If you still can't walk by tomorrow morning, stay home. Take the day off."

My mouth dropped open. Horse racing was seven days a week. Nobody got the day off. "Well...thank...thank you," I stammered. "That's really—"

"It's all right. I saw it coming all week. We call it breaking down. At least you didn't quit on us. We aren't that busy tomorrow. Not many horses going to the training track, and most of them will walk cold. We'll get by."

I thought about the unexplained kindness all the way home. What in hell could have prompted that?

"Boy, someone's looking out for you," Pammy observed aloud with a smile. "The day off. Right *on*."

"It just doesn't happen at the racetrack." I pulled my feet out of the bucket and let the cold air hit them, my lobster-red skin steaming. "Check it out, Pam.

That stuff's like a liquid Ben Gay. Smells great! My feet feel normal for the first time in four days. I was going to cancel my lunch with Kelly, but not now. There's no back strap on my sandals so it won't irritate the sores."

"Oh, yeah, man, go," Pam urged. "You can also stop in afterwards and see Daniel and Julie. Maybe Devin'll even drop in. For that matter, you could go pick up your own check."

"Oh, no. Daniel's house, maybe, but I'm not ready to get thrown out of Sparklear Water."

"They wouldn't do that."

"Still. Lola is there. It would be really uncomfortable. I'll just let Devin get it. He's probably already got it by now anyway, and he's out on a route."

"Have you talked to any of them since you quit?"

"Kelly. One phone girl. No one acts like they're mad at me. Except, of course, Lola. Kelly says they can't bring my name up with her. I feel awkward talking to the phone girls too, because I don't know what they think happened. Who knows? Maybe they *do* think I kicked Devin out." I gingerly slid into my sandals and picked up my keys. "Later, wild thing."

I was okay until I exited the freeway and headed toward the industrial neighborhood where the plant stood. I actually trembled as I neared the street by the stop sign, and a funny old feeling that I hadn't experienced in a long time swept through me.

The chest pain. That familiar old ache in my heart. That infallible alarm that told me when Devin's thoughts were in the area. The hardest part was passing the plant itself. The sight of it stirred up painful memories of our early days.

Devin's van was there. Over the spare tire in the rear was the zodiac cover. Finished. I flashed on Devin painting that wheel cover in the dreary darkness of Gerald's back room, and on the evening he'd first asked me to paint it for him. I was relieved to pass it by and make the turn at Daniel's corner.

Nobody appeared to be home at Daniel's, at least no cars were there, so I continued up the street to my old parking place. Across the boulevard was the coffee shop. It too stirred strong emotion in me. It was as if I'd been gone for months instead of a couple of weeks. Even the thought of seeing Kelly and Lana was a little frightening.

Did I look happy enough? Was the smile forced? It had to be just right. Nobody at Sparklear was going to know just how sad my life had really become.

I pulled my racetrack tam on, a new-job gift from Pammy. It was pink with a little visor and looked just like what the jockeys wore. Then I took a few deep breaths to slow down the shaking, and got out of the car.

Jane spotted me sitting in my usual booth, watching nervously out the window.

"Where have you been?" she demanded, setting a cup of coffee in front of me. "Well, I'll be...you just disappeared. What happened? Have you been sick?"

"I quit my job," I confessed. "I'm just visiting today."

"Oh. Slumming, huh? Why'd you quit?"

"It's a long story, Jane. Anyway, I'm working at the racetrack now." I told her a little about the track, and when duty called her I pulled out a book to read, only to be startled by Kelly's unexpected but welcome big mouth.

"What the *hell* are you reading now? Another witch book? Oh, that figures. The Golden Dawn. That's hocus-pocus, isn't it?"

"Kelly!" I looked up and slammed the book shut, all nervousness vanishing at the sight of her familiar face. "And Lana! Jeez, is it ever good to see you guys!"

"We still take our forty-five minute lunches," Kelly said, laughing. "They don't like it, but what are they going to do? Fire everyone? Shit! I've been *trying* to get fired." They both slid into the booth opposite me.

I laughed too. Kelly was the same. "How do *you* like it, Lana? I heard you were working there. I about *shit!* Of all the people to replace me."

"Oh, it's a blast working in there," Lana said, grinning. "I can't believe how much fun my mom is at work. I always imagined her real stiff and formal on the job. She hardly *ever* yells at me."

"She yells at *me,* instead," Kelly said teasingly. Jane came by to take their order, so they turned their attention to the menu, ordered the house special; ham barbeque sandwiches, fries, and slaw, and then Kelly turned back to me. "I see you still eat coffee for lunch."

"Some things never change, Kel. Anyway, Lana, I'm really glad you're working with Kelly. She always did need someone to play with. Someone to argue with over the radio stations."

"Yeah, she *does*, too," Lana said.

"Just like old times," I said, smiling. "Just like we used to."

"It's still not the same," Kelly said seriously, moving her arms so that Jane could put their plates in front of them. "The place is like a morgue now. I mean, even *without* you gone. Everyone's on edge in there. The drivers never come in and joke around anymore. Lola is touchy lately, and the fucking bigwigs from Chicago are always in town now, patrolling the halls, shit! It's really getting to be a drag. If it weren't for Lola, I probably *would* quit."

"Maurice is really queer," Lana put in, between mouthfuls. "He can joke around when *he* feels like it, but boy, if we try it, look out." Lana looked wistful for a minute. "Tim's bitchy as hell, you know, Devin's boss? Now he's starting a big fight with my mom. Stirring up the drivers against our department. And now they're all treating us like shit. You should see how smart-alecky they are now."

"Wow," I said, sipping my coffee. "All that in two weeks? Devin, too?"

Kelly and Lana exchanged glances. Apparently, Kelly decided to take this one.

"Kerry, Devin's not too friendly to anybody. I saw him this morning and I said hi, but he just turned his back on me and walked away. I know he heard me. He looked right at me. He acts like he doesn't even know me."

"I haven't seen him at *all*," Lana said. "She's doing better than me."

"Well, uh, *you've* seen him, Kerry," Kelly said. "Right?"

"A couple days ago," I admitted, wishing she hadn't asked. "He's supposed to have picked up my check, and I'm going down tonight to get it."

"That's pretty good," Kelly said to Lana. "Devin and *we* work here five days a week. Those two are over seventy miles apart, and we have to ask *her* how

Devin's doing. Doesn't that get expensive, Kerry? Why doesn't he just move back in?"

"You know, it's so weird," Lana interrupted. "Remember how you used to talk about how much fun he was in the office and how he was always turning up in the halls, the lobby, the exit? In and out of my mom's office all day long? Well, I have yet to see this. He must just go to work, do his job, and split."

"Maybe he's just pissed off because of what they did to him," Kelly offered. "That really was a dirty trick they pulled on him. I was surprised that Devin accepted the route at all."

"Well, still," Lana said. "That's no reason to take it out on *us.*"

"No, it isn't," Kelly agreed. "But Devin was never like this before." Kelly wasn't even talking to *me* now. "I've known him for years, and during *most* of that time, Devin was always a routeman. He only got promoted right before he and Kerry got together. It's not like he wasn't used to a route. Now he just does his work, punches out, and splits, and Lana, if you'd have known him before, you'd swear he traded places with an unsociable twin brother. Devin was always gregarious, outgoing and…an extravert. He used to be, anyway."

I hated to hear this kind of talk about Devin. "Well, for one thing, you guys, my quitting the way I did, leaving that note…you have to admit that it would be embarrassing to face anyone down there that saw the romance blossoming before their eyes. I pretty much humiliated him. And on top of that, he's not feeling good these days. I'm surprised that he's showing up for work at all. I think he's got pneumonia."

"Devin Drew? Sick?" Kelly scoffed. "Since *when?* Devin's not only never been sick a day I've known him, but he's never had any patience for people who *get* sick. He always said it's a reflection of your state of mind, and that people who get sick are sick mentally first."

Lana cleared her throat and changed the subject, asking what it was like to work on a racetrack. I was relieved to squirm out of the Devin discussion and gladly told her what a typical morning's work was for me.

When we finally parted, I headed straight for Daniel's, and this time they were home.

4 Julie's expression was a mixture of surprise and delight as she opened the door to me.

"Where have you *been* ?" she exclaimed. "Daniel, Kerry's here!"

Daniel emerged from the kitchen, drying his hands on a dishtowel, a wide grin on his face. "Hey, Kerry! Far out!"

"Where have *you* guys been?" I countered, relieved to have the openers over with. Nothing had changed.

"Sit down, sit down." Julie ushered me over to the dining room table. "We've got coffee on." She was literally beaming. "I'm so glad you came by. We don't have wheels right now. Hey, I love your hat!"

"It's my racetrack hat." I settled into one of the chairs.

"I *heard* you were working down there. What's it like anyway?"

"How'd *you* find out?"

"From Dev—" Julie stopped as if a forbidden word had slipped out.

"It's okay, Julie. It's not a sore subject. We're talking."

I still sensed her hesitation and had even expected it. I hoped to do away with any discomfort whenever Devin's name came up. Julie excused herself to get the coffee, and Daniel spoke quickly.

"Devin doesn't stop by here as often as he used to. He's changed, Kerry. It's almost like he doesn't want anything to do with us."

"Daniel, he probably feels really uncomfortable. I really put him in a bad spot. I'm sure you heard how I quit."

"Yeah, but…it's just…he comes and he goes, but he never stays. And while he's here…well, it's hard to talk to him. He just doesn't have much to say."

"Daniel, don't be too hard on him," I began, not sure just how much Daniel did know. Devin had told me that Daniel had been informed about everything, including *his* departure plans. What I wondered was if Daniel knew *he'd* already gone.

Daniel shook his head. "No, Kerry. He's changed. I know the difference. It's not that he's just in a bad mood or anything like that. It's just not the same Devin."

This was still too vague for me to assume anything. "Daniel, what do you mean he's not the same Devin?"

Daniel glanced up at the red velvet painting and back to me again. "You know who Devin was," he began hesitantly, as if unsure whether I knew that *he* knew. When I nodded he seemed to relax a little. "He just stares at that picture when he's here, Ker. That picture. It's *him*, Kerry." He glanced at it again, then back at me. "But Devin? Uh-uh. That's not the Devin I know. Don't get me wrong. Devin's been like a brother to me. I loved him…and you, too. You two were family…but…well, he's changed, Kerry. This isn't a Devin I'm familiar with."

I remembered that Daniel was a more recent addition to the plant and had never met the Devin who'd worked there all those years. I could see where that alone could be noticeable, but I still had to know. "Daniel, didn't *he* tell you *he* was leaving? Devin told me *he* did."

"Well, he did say…uh, that he…uh…didn't expect to be around much longer," Daniel faltered, as if aware of how insane these words must have sounded.

"Okay, then he *did* tell you. And do you also know that what he told you was going to happen *did* happen? He *did* leave."

"I know. Devin told me. But I didn't need Devin to tell me."

"Now, when you say Devin, you mean *our* Devin, the one who works at Sparklear?"

Daniel ignored my question. "He said…he said he wasn't…himself right now. No shit. I could see that before he said anything. You know what I mean?"

I looked up at the red velvet painting and sighed. "Yeah. I know exactly what you mean. I hadn't realized, though, that you would be this informed."

"Devin will get his head together," Daniel said, putting a gentle hand on my shoulder. "He's just…freaking out. I don't think Devin believed *he* meant it when he said he was going to go."

Julie walked in with the coffee at that moment, and with a silent nod at each other, Daniel and I dropped the subject.

"So tell me about this racetrack job!" Julie said as she poured the coffee.

It was a relief to change to that subject. Safe. I spent about an hour with them before I got up to leave, and as they walked me to my car, I knew we were all still friends. I promised to stop back in a day or two.

I was glad to have that out of the way. Now, the only thing left to blame those stomach flutterings on was my pending trip to Devin's house tonight.

Lately, any encounter with Devin was turning out to be a trip. The only thing consistent about Devin these days was his inconsistency.

Pam agreed to stay with the kids again, laughing that it would certainly be cheaper for Devin to move back in. It was true. I was going through a lot of gas. Since the gas crisis last year, gas prices had permanently changed from the 30-cents-per-gallon category to the 60-cents bracket. Although they had run out of the 30-cent gas, they'd apparently had plenty of the 60-cent stuff stored underground.

"I'm only doing this because of the wild stories you bring home every time," she teased me. "You lead such an exciting life now. I never know what you're coming home with next."

"Well, tonight it'll be the paycheck, I hope," I said. "Otherwise, Chris is going to drive down and get it himself."

"I think he's ready to," Pam agreed. "He's been here twice today."

"Oh, speaking of stories. I got one today. From Daniel. About who Devin *was*."

"Say, *what?*"

"Uh-huh. Devin told Daniel that *he* left. I guess he felt he needed to explain the way he is now."

"Why? How's he being to them?"

I did my best to explain everything Daniel had told me.

Pam looked down. "Poor Devin. I feel so sorry for him. Here he was all magic and then…nothing. I still don't think it was fair, him leaving Devin that way."

"I've been wondering if this has all just been a test. I hope not."

"Why?"

"'Cause if it has been, we're *both* flunking it. See ya later."

It was off to the classroom.

My lighthearted attitude was more of an act than I'd even admit to myself, but the drive to Devin's was fifty minutes of self-honesty. I wasn't happy the way things were, and it was pretty obvious that Devin wasn't happy where he was either. Even though I now knew that Devin and *him* were two separate individuals, I rationalized that so too were Erick and Christian, and we'd all managed to get along just fine when we were all living together. I decided to ask Devin again about moving back in. If he was unhappy enough or just plain uncomfortable living under his dad's roof, maybe, just maybe, he'd say yes.

Gerald answered the door and told me where to find Devin. He was sleeping in Brian's bedroom. Go ahead and wake him up," he told me. "I was supposed to a half hour ago."

"How's he feeling anyway?"

"He's alive."

The irony of his words rang in my ears as I opened the door to Brian's room. Sure enough, there was Devin's huddled figure visible in the darkened room, sleeping in Brian's bed and even breathing like a regular person. Breathing the way everyone does when they sleep. I could still hear that congestion in his chest, though. I tried to wake him as gently as I could.

I shook him slowly. "Devin…if you want to keep sleeping, don't wake up all the way. How're you feeling?" I sat on the edge of the bed. He opened his eyes and smiled.

"Pretty good."

"Really?"

"Really. I took some codeine a while ago…for the…" he thumped his chest with his fist and smiled again.

"Is that why you're sleeping?"

"Shit. That stuff is supposed to keep you awake. Got more caffeine in it than anything. That and aspirin. Oh, but I'll get up. Damn. What time is it anyway?"

"About ten."

"Shit. Brian must want his room back, huh? Come on. Let's move into mine. I've got your check."

When he closed the door to his room, he went straight to the waterbed to stretch out. I sat on the framed edge and waited until he was comfortable.

"Devin, can I ask you something?"

"Sure, go ahead."

"Would you consider moving back in? I understand how you feel…or don't feel about me, and that's all right. I know you aren't happy here and…well, I'd even sleep on the couch and you can have the bedroom."

He smiled again. It had been so long since I'd seen him smile like that, I almost dared to hope. I watched him light two cigarettes, and as he handed me one he bowled me over with his answer. "I'd consider it, yes, but you wouldn't have to sleep on the couch."

My heart all but stopped. I had come prepared with rehearsed protests and rationalizations for any argument he could possibly have had to the idea. "You…*will*?"

"I'd consider it," he repeated. "I've had a lot of time to think, and there's been a lot flying at me that I keep forgetting to tell you. For example, Blue and I finally made friends."

I looked up quickly. "You did? When?"

"The other day. I just forgot to tell you last night. I had so much going through my head that I needed to think about, but I meant to tell you yesterday. Remember he came in with you and then I nodded off on you? You brought him in, regardless of whether or not you meant to. I guess he just stayed."

"I *told* him to. And he didn't come back with me. In fact, I haven't seen him in a couple of days."

It was Devin's turn to be surprised. "You told him *what*?"

"To stay with you. While you were asleep. To try to get through to you. I was so worried about you, so I left him with you. He must have done some good, Devin. You're...happier now. You even told me you woke up after that night feeling happy and serene. But what happened with Blue? I didn't realize you were ever aware of him. Tell me."

"Well, I was lying there, and pretty bummed out if you remember. Then I fell asleep, and when I woke up I felt almost sedated, and you were already gone. Hey, are you sure Blue is a male?"

I laughed. "He'd better be. Damn, with those Russian hands and Roman fingers."

"Well, I got the distinct impression that it was female. Remember how *he* used to look into your eyes and tell you to *go inside*? Well, I had the definite feeling that she...it...that *that* was what it wanted *me* to do."

"And?"

"Well, at first I was a little nervous. But then I thought, whoa, Devin old boy. You never had that *fear* problem before. Anyway, it's kind of hard to explain, but it was like *it* went inside me. It was almost a sexual thing, but it was...well, beautiful. I guess I sound like some nut, huh?"

I hugged him. "No, and don't forget, Blue's done that to *me*, so if you're a nut, what does that make me?"

He smiled. "I'm really beginning to wonder about old Blue. It does seem like it has a thing about getting physical."

"Yes, he does. Now you'll have *me* wondering about him...or her."

"Or it. Maybe it's both. Or sexless," he mused. "Actually it would stand to reason. But then, we never really knew *what* it was. Who knows? Maybe *he* was right, and it is some kind of projection of *him*. It sure did help me, though, when I really needed help. I won't forget that."

"Are you sure it was Blue?"

"That's the only thing I *am* sure of. I've always been able to sense him. It feels a little strange putting any sex on it. The main thing is that I was losing it. I was so full of rage when *he* left that I almost *hated* him. I really felt stabbed in the back, but after this happened it forced me to reevaluate everything I was thinking and feeling. And it still took me a couple days to really digest it all."

That scene I'd seen with the black-hilted knife in his back crossed my mind. It must have been symbolic after all. Another "vision" had come to pass. Devin noticed the look on my face and frowned.

"What's wrong?"

I told him what I'd seen, and he listened quietly. Then he shrugged. "It *was* symbolic. It's exactly the way I have been feeling. I'm glad to hear you're working with that talent of yours. Are you writing anything down?"

"Everything. I just started the notebook. A few days ago. I even recorded that one."

"Cool. Oh, by the way, aren't you about due by now?"

"Due...oh. My period. No, tomorrow. Why, you're not worried about it, are you?"

He shrugged. "I guess not. Unless you're pregnant and it's *mine*. That could have happened, but then again, if it *was* mine, it would be okay anyway, so no,

I guess I'm not worried." He gave me such a long and serious look that I reminded him that I wasn't even late. Why even talk about it?

"You're right," he said. "I was just checking."

He didn't speak for a while, and I just lay there, happy to be next to him, surprised at the many references he had made about *him* without switching moods or blowing up, and elated at the possibility that he might consider moving back in. This was a complete about-face from the way he'd been. What had Blue actually done? Whatever it was, for me it was almost like being with the *old* Devin, the one I'd fallen in love with. There were no remnants of the unpleasant Devin that I'd been running into day after day. Maybe Blue had done more good than I ever could have hoped for. It was at this stage of my thoughts that Devin broke the silence.

He spoke quietly, as though he wasn't sure he should even mention it. "Guess who's coming to visit."

"Who?"

"My wife. She called today."

I sat up. "Your wife? She's coming to visit?"

"Yeah. Well, I was just as surprised. With her new single independence, she didn't even bother to ask. Just told me she had her plane ticket and had already cleared it with Gerald to stay here. She has friends and relatives she wants to see, and it's not my house, so I didn't have any say-so in it one way or the other."

"Is she moving *back* here?"

"Oh, hell, no. I laid that down immediately, and no, she'll only be here about a week. I have to give her credit for some consideration, though. She said the only way she would cancel the ticket is if I out-and-out forbade her to come. Which would be just a way of trying to make me responsible for her actions again, as if we were still together. I told her it didn't matter to me one way or the other, but that she was *not* staying, and she was fine with that."

His wife. I hadn't thought about his wife in so long that I'd forgotten he still *had* a wife. "Do you *want* her to come?"

He lifted his shoulders and reached for his cigarettes. "I don't care, Kerry. I don't even want the authority to tell her anything she can or can't do, one way or the other. I reminded her I was living my own life now and if she came, not to expect me to entertain her. She ran down a list of people she wanted to see. One of them was her grandmother, and who am I to tell her she can't visit the state? It *is* Gerald's house, so I wasn't even consulted. Anyhow, I don't care. I just thought you should know. It doesn't change anything between you and me."

His answer, attitude, and tone of voice set me at ease. His wife was the least of my worries. She could have been my worst.

"Would her coming to visit have anything to do with your decision on whether or not you'd move back in?"

"No, not at all. It's just a decision I'd really have to think on and make sure it's the right one. Whatever I decide, I'd want it to be permanent and final, you know? This sickness…it's clearing up. Oh, it took a while, but I can still do a thing or two. I guess I just gave *him* credit for everything. Anyhow, it looks like I'll be around a while, you know…living. I'm surprised but, well…there it is."

When he walked me to the doorway at 11:30, Gerald and Faye had already retired. Devin didn't speak until after he'd closed the heavy door behind him and we'd stepped out into the starry night.

"I hate you driving all this distance every night. I've done it, and I know what a trek it is. I'll give you some jing for the gas you've been going through when I cash my check. Oh, you got your check, didn't you?"

"Yes, it was on the dresser. And forget the gas. You went through enough of it visiting me in the early days."

We walked the long driveway to my car. He took me in his arms for a goodnight kiss, held me for a long time, and finally released me. It was so much like the early days when Devin had been so new to me. I was almost afraid to bring up the subject about his wife, but I had to know.

"When is she due in?"

"Friday. And truthfully, I really don't mind her coming. Everything's friendly, and I feel a little bad about how anxiously I pushed the dates forward to get her to leave sooner. But everything's cool. I'll call you Friday…well, no, I'll call you before that."

"Okay. And let me know about moving in…as soon as you decide."

"I will. And don't worry about my wife. It's nothing. Just bad timing."

I believed it was nothing. When I burst in that night with the check in hand, Pam was just hanging up the phone and, as late as it was, Chris was just leaving.

"Oh, there you are, Ker…I was just talking to Devin." Pam looked relieved. Chris must have been giving her a hard time about the rent.

"He called here?" I asked her.

"No, I called him. I think I woke him up. He said you were already gone."

I peeled off my jacket and tossed it on the couch. "Give me a damn pen." I couldn't have cared less about rent or checks.

The signature completed and Chris gone, I dropped into the beanbag with a happy smile. I had really brought home a whopper story for Pam tonight.

"All right, let's have it. What happened to put that smirk on your face? You get laid or something?"

"Devin might move back in."

"Oh, git *outta* here!"

I laughed, knowing she had to be astonished. I was.

"Spit that out again?" she said.

"You heard me."

"Devin might…man…you'ns are crazy…*crazy* !"

"Thanks a lot. You're supposed to be happy for me."

"Give me the details. Man, every night you go down there and come back with a completely different contradictory story from the time before that. I guess tonight will be the end of your book, huh?"

"What book?"

"You know. The one you're going to write."

"Oh…oh, the *book*." I laughed. She'd been teasing me about writing a book. "Yeah, if Devin moves back in, it would make a good ending."

"Yeah, well, don't kid yourself. This would sell just as good if he doesn't."

"Pam!"

"Okay, okay, I'm kidding. Anyways, what *happened*?"

I didn't know where to start. "Well, first of all, Devin's wife is coming to town."

"What?"

I buried my face in my hands. This was going to take all night. "Where did I leave you off?"

"Your lunch with the girls today and how everyone was ragging on Devin. Then your visit to Daniel's. Same thing. What the hell happened between then and now? And what's this shit about his wife coming? I just got off the phone with Devin. He was *fine*. Soft-spoken. Sounded just like Devin when you wake him out of a sound sleep. Not like *him*, I admit, but like Devin."

"Okay, I'm getting to that. When I got there tonight, that's exactly who *was* there. Not Devin Drew, but *our* Devin. Up till tonight, all I've seen is the original Devin Drew...ever since January First."

"And *this* time it really *was* Devin?"

"Yeah, but hopefully a more permanent kind of Devin. One that I wouldn't have to worry might get up and leave again."

"What brought all *this* on?"

"Shit, I don't know, Pam. I don't write these serials."

"The hell you *don't*. Man, it's so good to see you happy, though, Ker." She yawned and stretched. "Anything else before I hit the sack?"

"No. Hey, throw me a pillow and blanket, will you?"

"Sure thing." She opened the hall closet where the bedding was stored. "It'll probably make a good movie, too."

"What did you say?"

She threw me the bedding. "Nothing."

5 Wednesday, January 8, 1975

The following morning I began to consider the possibility that I really might be pregnant.

Ironically, the event that triggered the thought was the birth of Bonnie's baby. Two weeks late and the grandparents still uninformed, the baby had finally decided to take matters into its own hands.

Pam got the call in the middle of the night and told me about it over coffee. I had just come in from work.

"So, she finally had it, huh?" I was still wound up and elated from last night. "What'd she have?"

"A boy. They named him Adrian. I told her she should have saved that name for *your* baby."

"Pammy, I'm not having a baby. Don't be funny...anyway, why?"

"You know...*Rosemary's baby*? Anyways, I'm going to run over there and see the baby and Bonnie."

"*Now* what's Jake going to do?" The thought of him walking into his parents' home with both Bonnie and the baby sent me and Pam into peals of hysterical laughter. "Maybe Jake will just let the baby speak for himself. Adrian will probably be talking by the time they get around to the announcement."

"That coward. I wouldn't put it past him. Anyways, I'm going."

"Tell Bonnie I said congratulations."

After she left, I sat pondering the idea of a baby over a second cup of coffee. I remembered Devin's remarks about the possibility of my being pregnant. Other than that one time in December, I was usually pretty regular. But even *that* period had been unusual…very light. I was due today, but I didn't have any sign that it was going to start. No cramps. No bloating. Nothing.

The phone rang and I grabbed it, thinking it was Devin.

It was Kelly, calling on her lunch hour.

"Kerry, it's all over the plant that Devin's wife is back in town. Do you know anything about that?"

"Huh? Kelly, I was just at Devin's last night. I know she's *coming*, but she's not here yet."

There was a long silence before Kelly spoke, as if she were weighing her words carefully. "Kerry, whether she's here now or coming soon…don't you think that's a little weird?"

"Well, the way Devin put it, she didn't even ask if it was okay…other than Gerald, I mean. She just told Devin she had her ticket and was coming."

Another long silence, then, "Kerry, like I said, doesn't this all sound a little weird?"

"Kelly, what are you driving at?"

"His *wife* is coming and is going to stay at the same house *he* is? Maybe the same bedroom? Come on, Ker. Think."

"Look, he didn't even have to tell me. I think *that* says something."

"Yeah, maybe it says he knew it would be all over town and thought he'd better beat the rumors to the punch."

Now it was my turn to be silent. Could it be true? Could there be more to this than what Devin had told me?

"I'm not trying to upset you, Ker. I just think you should keep your eyes wide open. I'm sorry to be the bearer of bad news, but how do you think it got around so fast?"

I felt like all the air had gone out of my balloon. "Look, Kelly, I gotta go. Thanks for calling."

"Ker, I'm sorry if I up—"

"It's okay, Kelly, thanks. I know you're just being a friend. Look, I'll talk to you later, huh?"

As if in confirmation of Kelly's haunting warning, the phone did not ring again for the rest of the day. I made every excuse in the book for Devin's not calling. He was busy. He was working. He would surely call tonight.

It wasn't pride that kept me from calling *him*, either. I didn't have any left. If Devin was going to move back in, it had to be his decision. His *own* decision. I didn't want to ruin any small chance there was by pestering him. And if Devin *wanted* to talk to me, he would call *me*. I could only know if that was the case, or if there was something to Kelly's warning, by waiting.

And waiting.

I still hadn't heard from him when Pam came in that evening. She plopped herself into the beanbag.

"Well?"

"Well, what?" I was buried in my notebook, recording the day's events. I'd been keeping it up since I started it, but to read it back, I sounded like some nut. Pam was right about one thing. Things changed drastically every day.

"Well, is it safe to ask what's new?"

"I haven't heard from Devin all day, if that's what you mean. Oh, and guess what else?"

"I couldn't. You've exhausted every possibility."

"Wanna bet? Guess whose period didn't start today."

She fell facedown into the beanbag. "I don't want to *hear* it," her muffled reply came, mixed with hysterical laughter.

"Hey. It's not funny."

"Aw, come *on,* Ker. As screwed up as things have been since Christmas? You'll be lucky if you even *have* one this year. Shit, I wouldn't even worry about it."

"I'm not…really. Just thought I'd mention it. Hey, how's Bonnie's baby?"

"Oh, he's so cute. He looks just like a little spider monkey. Jake's arms and legs. And Jake is really freaking. He *has* to tell his parents now. You know our aunt and uncle. They're going to decapitate him when they find out. He'd have been better off telling them *before* he was born. I mean, Jake *did* get so far as to tell them he was going to marry Bonnie, and they reluctantly accepted *that.* So, now they've called all their family and friends, announcing this big *white* wedding. Can you just imagine their reaction if Jake strolls in there with Adrian?"

"I'm glad I won't be there for it."

Pam glanced at the notebook in front of me. "What're you doing there?"

"Oh, keeping track of this Devin shit. Last night I really believed he might move back in. Today…I don't know. Kelly called and told me Devin's wife was in town already. I told her I knew she was coming, but she wasn't here yet. But she made some insinuations that the rumors were telling a different story than the one Devin gave me."

"Well, that doesn't make any sense. Devin could have just said no when you asked him about moving back in. If his wife was coming so they could get back together, why would he agree to think about coming back?"

What Pam said did make sense. I wanted to believe that.

"So, next subject," Pam said. "Are you going to tell him your period didn't start?"

"No. I wouldn't say anything unless I was sure. And I really don't believe I am. It wouldn't be the first time I was late."

"Well, you've had two kids. You ought to know what pregnancy signs are by now."

"Yeah, and right now I don't feel anything either way. I don't feel like it's going to start any minute, and I don't feel pregnant either."

Pam raised her eyebrows. "Kerry, how do you get yourself into these things? Do you study?"

"I don't know." I sighed. "But I'm going to bed. I've had about enough for one day."

When I finally did hit the couch, I put the phone beside me on the floor. It mocked me silently, its gleaming whiteness mute in the dark living room. The radio was playing softly in the background. Just what I needed. It was *that* station again, and the Moody Blues chided me softly, voicing my fears, as usual.

The singer had decided that I really wasn't to blame and that our love was still the same as always. But the tide was turning, and he feared that the sunny day we'd been waiting for was going to turn to rain. When everything was over, he was sure that the curtain was going to fall. It was the story in my eyes.

Devin didn't call on Thursday either. I stubbornly stuck to my guns, not calling him and just waiting. Kelly's warning had added a whole new dimension to my assessment of the situation.

My feet were finally used to the new job, and the blisters were nearly healed. I wasn't as exhausted and sore when I came home as I had been in the beginning. The only soreness in me now was in my heart.

Friday was just as silent as the day before. Not a word from Devin. My period still hadn't started, and Devin's wife was due in today. I jumped every time the phone rang, but it was never Devin. When Pam and George left for the hospital to see Bonnie, I tried to get interested in a book, but my mind was down south in another county. I waited for a call that would never come.

We were out of weed. The record player sounded like shit. Kelly had laid the groundwork, and Devin's silence did the rest.

On top of that, I hadn't heard from or felt *his* presence since my last experience with the heat wave and the repetition of the word *was*. My patience and faith were running out.

By ten o'clock, I knew it was too late to expect any call from Devin. His wife was surely already there. My disappointment and depression were getting worse by the minute. Even Blue seemed to have deserted me. I reached for my notebook, turned off the tinny record player, and picked up the pen. After days and days of feeding myself false hope, I was finally, and for the first time, *angry*.

I'd tried to be patient. I had put up with Devin's moods, indifference, and self-pitying spurts. And now, it seemed, I was putting up with his *lies*. In my state of mind, another belief was coming to surface now.

It had all been an act. Devin had simply tired of the game and now wanted his cozy marriage back. It had all been a lie and a game, and I had been gullible enough to swallow it. With tears in my eyes, I pulled the notebook over and wrote in dark, angry, bold letters.

Devin is a liar…liar…LIAR!

A dark shadow crossed the page and sudden terror swept over me. With no warning, on the third word *LIAR*, something slammed me with a karate chop on the nape of my neck. A searing electrical charge jolted through my entire body. I went from heartsick fury, to fear of a sudden presence, to paralytic panic, horror, and unspeakable terror, all in the span of three seconds. I screamed, bolted upright in pain and fright, only to have it hit me again in the same place, this time harder…then another electrical shock. It was as if I stood, bare feet in water, screwing a fuse into the fuse box.

I looked around the room, eyes bulging in terror, more frightened than I'd ever been in my entire life. The black shadow was gone, but my terror wasn't. And, as if on cue, a third shock hit me, nearly knocking me over on my back.

I grabbed the phone, blood pounding in my head to the rhythm of my triphammering heart, fingers shaking so badly I almost couldn't dial.

Pam answered the phone at George's mother's house, and I could have screamed in relief. I doubt if any of my blubbering made any sense to her, but she knew I wasn't dramatizing. I begged her to come home, to bring George…immediately…please…to please hurry!

My urgency was too real. For fifteen minutes I waited in terror, anticipating another one, but it never came.

When Pam and George burst into the house, I was huddled in the middle of the room, still shaking and sobbing, expecting at any minute another electrocution. I had maintained my sanity while waiting for them by blotting the room from my mind and sight and repeating over and over the only names I'd ever held any faith in. Devin, Erick, Christian, *him*.

Those shocks had *hurt* ! Those thuds at the nape of my neck had been *real…real physical pain*. Whatever it had been, it had the ability to *hurt*. I was completely petrified.

Pam's very presence seemed to dissipate some of the electrical energy in the room. George lit up a joint, hoping it would calm me down, at least to the point where I could explain. I had interrupted their evening, and he expected an explanation.

I tried to tell them, in bits and pieces, with faltering halts between sobs and sentences, looking around fearfully for that black shadow. I expected another hit at any second, just for telling them. I refused the joint, knowing it would only make things worse and increase my paranoia.

Pam was looking at me, deeply concerned. "What the *hell* were you writing?" she asked. "Come on, calm down. We're going to stay here with you."

Unable to speak further, I shoved the notebook over to her. She scanned it, then closed her eyes as George read over her shoulder. Neither of them spoke.

For a long time I sat there thinking, going over my thoughts, backtracking to the time of the first appearance of the shadow that preceded the first shock. Was *this* what Devin had gone through back when he'd told me of his horrifying physical attack, back in those early days? Whatever it had been, then or now, it didn't appreciate my doubting the validity of *him*. Devin's imaginary "act" was capable of physical attack. It was impossible to continue doubting everything with that kind of proof. Had I needed this kind of drastic measure to turn my thinking back around? Hadn't the heat waves and words been enough?

The psychic energy that had filled the house while Devin had lived here— had always been all right with me. I'd never worried about anything hurting me as long as he'd been there. Now he was gone, and when he left, he'd left doors open behind him. I had no idea how to go about closing those doors now.

There was no physical *him* now, to steady or protect me. No *him* to hide behind now.

The last thing he had warned me of was my fears and doubts. Mostly my doubts. He'd even mentioned my persistent doubting and lack of faith that last day, the day Devin had moved…and how he knew I still didn't believe him. That I would *see* after he left.

Yet, I just couldn't believe that *this* was the kind of proof he'd promised me. He wouldn't hurt me just to prove a point. Nothing could make me believe that.

"Look, Ker," Pam said finally, with a sigh. "It's kind of late. Do you think you're going to be all right now?"

My eyes must have widened in fear. "You're not *leaving*, are you?"

"No. I'm going to stay here. George will be going, though. I'm going to go get some pillows, okay?"

"They're in the bedroom now. I was rearranging the closet today." I swallowed and added, "But I'm not getting them. I'm not moving from this spot."

"I'll get them. George, stay here with her, will you?"

She disappeared around the corner, and George held up another joint. "You *sure* you don't want to smoke this? It'll help you relax so you can fall asleep. It will at least calm your nerves—"

Pam's scream stopped him midsentence, and she came flying back as he bolted to his feet. "What the hell's the *matter* with you girls?" he exploded.

"Oh, man, Kerry must have *me* freaked. I went over to the bedroom door, tried to open it, and George, honest to God, something pulled back as hard as it could when I tried the knob."

"Oh, for *Christ's sake* ! I'll get the damn blankets. You two can sit here and freak each other out. And I'm leaving *you two alone with each other* ?" He stalked off down the hall, and we heard him stop dead at the bedroom door. Then cautiously the doorknob turned. Seconds later he bolted from the room, slamming the door behind him.

"You two even have *me* spooked," he grumbled. "I got to the doorway and the clammiest feeling came over me. I had to force myself to go in there. Jesus, look at the goosebumps on me. That room is *freezing*." He tossed the blankets onto the couch. "And I don't scare easy."

"Ker…" Pam's voice. "Kerry. George is going to go. I'm going to stay with you, okay? I'm just walking him out to the Jeep."

I nodded. It had been forty minutes since the last shock. It had all stopped when I reexamined my thinking. Then, even the fear, though not completely gone, had lightened somewhat. In its place was a deep sense of shame. I had to force myself to face something I had been reluctant to admit.

There was no longer any physical connection between *him* and Devin. Devin Drew had failed me, but I had included *him* in my doubts instead of placing the blame where it belonged. *Devin Drew* had promised to call and when he hadn't, I had blamed, not only Devin, but *him*, Blue, and anything else I had ever connected to Devin. In all this time, and with all the proof from the very beginning, I still had not severed in my mind the connection between *him* and Devin Drew.

I looked down at my trembling hands. I hadn't *really* been *hurt*. Oh, it *had* hurt, but I was still *unhurt*. I'd been knocked senseless for a minute…shocked three times…but I hadn't been physically damaged in any way. I had merely been painfully frightened out of my wits. And I still didn't believe *he'd* done it. Maybe the old man? Tired of my lack of backbone and faith? Maybe just my negative, hateful, doubting energy had manifested?

It proved something to me, and when I finally acknowledged it, a warm wave of rippling air spread over my foot and ankle.

Pam came back in, still looking worried. "Are you okay?"

I nodded. "Would you sleep on the couch? I'd feel better if I can look over and see you here in the room."

"You're going to stay in that beanbag?"

"Yeah. I don't know if I'll be able to sleep anyway."

"Man, you scared the *shit* out of us, Kerry!"

"I had the shit scared out of *me*, Pam. I don't know what I'd have done if you hadn't answered the phone and come over. I've never been so terrified…"

"I can't even imagine what you went through. If I were you, I'd call Devin tomorrow. You don't *need* these kinds of problems."

I didn't need a lot of the problems I had. If *this* was a sample of his *proof*…but no, I still didn't believe that. I didn't believe he was behind that attack in any way. He would never do that to me.

I closed my eyes and watched the purple hole phase in like it always did. It didn't frighten me. To see it now was somewhat of a comfort. Familiarity. Friends.

No, I decided. *He* would never go to such an extreme to prove he had nothing to do with what Devin was doing now.

The old man. With a shudder, I knew I couldn't rule that out. A black shadow *had* appeared right before the first shock.

Myself? Could I have brought the whole thing on, myself?

I wasn't sure. It had come unexpectedly. I hadn't been entertaining any possibility of physical attack. I had been entering an angry thought into that journal when it had happened. It had come fast and unexpected while my thoughts were steaming with hurt and anger over the things that Devin was not doing.

But then again, I'd seen that black shadow before. Devin had identified it. The old man, he'd called it.

I didn't *dare* call Devin Drew about this. Not tomorrow or any time in the next few days. His wife was in town, and not knowing what the real story was there, I was going to have to fend for myself. I wasn't equipped with any knowledge of psychic self-defense either, so if that attack had not come from him, I was in no way able to defend myself against wherever it *had* come from.

I didn't sleep that night. I lay there thinking until the clock read 4:30. I got up from the beanbag. Pam still slept peacefully on the couch. I decided to forego coffee and let her sleep without me clattering around in the kitchen.

After work, I decided as I dressed, I was going down to the occult shop.

There was one book I knew of that *did* have a chapter in psychic self-defense.

Mastering Witchcraft.

6 I was finished at the track by nine. After I pulled off my muddy boots and tossed them in the trunk, I headed towards the occult store. Pam got the kids off to school in the morning now that they were in the closer school, as Devin had once suggested. I was free to head out.

On the way, I stopped at the house where Bonnie was living. She was home from the hospital now, and I thought she might want to get out of the house. There were six kids and their mother living there, but with Bonnie and Jake and the new baby, that made a houseful of ten.

As I suspected, Bonnie jumped at the chance to pack Adrian up and come along for the ride. It wasn't until we were almost there that I told her where we were going and why. Needless to say, Bonnie had some reservations about coming home with me, but I convinced her that whatever *it* had been, it wasn't out to hurt her or the baby.

Pete, the store's owner, listened to my tale with quiet sky-blue eyes. I didn't go into any details about *him*, Blue, or Devin. Just the attack. Just exactly what had happened last night. Pete must have assumed I was yet another student of the occult who had gone one step too far with the magical arts and gotten myself into trouble.

"Have you ever had this sort of problem before?" he asked me, frowning.

"No, and I'm not going through it again, either," I said. "I know what book I need. It's by Paul Huson. *Mastering Witchcraft*."

This produced an even sterner frown. "You *don't* want *that* one," he said emphatically as he walked over to his shelves. "We carry it, but it's books like that one that let this stuff in to begin with. *This* is what you *need*."

He handed me a paperback entitled: *Helping Yourself with White Witchcraft*. "This has several chapters on psychic attack and what to do if it happens. It's not as rare as you might think. You have to get rid of whatever that thing is. You have any kids?" He glanced at Bonnie's baby.

"Yes."

"Yeah, then you don't want to fool around. Take this one, and I'll pack up some of the things you'll need. They're only small change items, so it won't cost much. First, you'll need white candles. How many rooms in your house?"

I told him, adding that there hadn't been any problems in the kids' room. The attack had happened in the living room, but I suspected the bedroom was part of the problem. I told him about the incident last night with the bedroom door.

"Sounds like you *do* have a problem. Would you like me to come up and check it out? I have a couple friends who are qualified to perform an exorcism. There wouldn't be any charge."

"Well, thanks, but let's see if these things work." I looked in the bag. Besides the book and white candles, there was some kind of incense and a bottle labeled *protection powder*. "What's all this?"

"You'll need to burn that incense. It'll keep any low negative energy out. And read this chapter…" he removed the book from the bag. "See, I have it marked…here." He showed me where to start reading and how far to read before I carried out the instructions. I paid him, thanked him, and we left for the car.

Bonnie had heard enough. "Kerry, are you sure it's safe to take Adrian in there? You heard what he said about kids."

"Well, Bonnie, with a name like Adrian, I don't think he has anything to worry about. You do know you named him after *Rosemary's baby?*"

"Oh, get outta here!"

"No, really. Pam told me. Anyway, look, seriously, nothing's happened since last night, and all I'm doing here is taking precautions. I don't even know if I believe in all this shit." I nodded at the bag on the seat between us. "It just sounds so primitive, but I guess it can't hurt. I don't want it happening again."

"Are you going to call Devin and tell him?"

"I can't. His wife is visiting there now. I'll just have to handle this myself."

In spite of the daylight, I didn't relish going back into that house alone. I finally convinced Bonnie to come back with me. She joked that the hell in my house couldn't be any worse than the hell she was living in now, what with the kids running in and out of the house at all hours and waking the baby. "I appreciate Lorry's mom taking us in, don't get me wrong, but she spoils Adrian so much. Look, he's only a couple days old and already he thinks he has to be held all the time."

I glanced down at Adrian, placidly lying in her lap, watching us with alert eyes. "He's a good baby, though, Bonnie," I pointed out. "He hasn't cried once."

"That's 'cause I'm holding him. Jake's no help either. Now he thinks I should be holding him all the time, just because Lorry's mother grabs him up at the first whimper."

I laughed. "Everyone spoils new babies, Bonnie. Didn't you know that?"

We'd arrived at my house. I hopped out and opened the door for her. "Come on in."

The house was dark and cool and as quiet as a church. The bayberry scent almost reinforced that church feeling. The atmosphere held none of the frightening vibes that had been present the night before. Still, I wasn't taking any chances. I took the three candles and placed them all separately on three white Melmac saucers. Bonnie tossed me a pack of matches and I lit the three, one after the other, all with one match.

"Looks like an assembly-line exorcism, doesn't it?" I smiled at Bonnie, trying to tease that frown off her face.

"Kerry, I don't know about this," she began. "Can we call Jake? He could come up here and get me when he gets off work." Jake worked at a dairy plant that had no respect for weekends. Like the track, now that I thought of it.

"Go ahead, call him. I have to put two of these candles in the bedrooms."

I set one on the kids' television and one on my own dresser. The house was closed up because of the air conditioner constantly running, but this morning it was shut off. The rooms were chilly enough by themselves. I shut both doors and returned to the living room.

"Well, I hope that works," I said. "Want some coffee, Bonnie?"

"Sure. Oh, and I did call Jake. He's getting off at one, and he'll come right up here and get me."

"Cool. Then you'll be here a while. Pam will be home soon too."

"Well, I thought about it while you were in the bedroom, and I guess I wouldn't want to be alone either. Adrian's sleeping, finally. I guess I can lay him down. Maybe in your room?"

"How about in the den? I don't know about that back bedroom right now."

By the time the coffee was ready, the candles in the living room had melted all over the saucer.

"Damn, that was fast," I observed aloud. "Look, Bonnie!"

"Wow. Are they supposed to burn away that fast?"

"I don't know. They'd sure be worthless as emergency candles. I think that's what they're supposed to be, but for what I wanted them for, I guess the sooner the better. I'll go see what the other two are doing." Using the small Tetragrammaton ring, I stamped the Seal of Solomon into the warm wax…couldn't hurt…and went into the kids' room.

That candle had also melted to nothing. I wondered about the reliability of exorcism candles that melted that fast, but stamped that one as well and went into my bedroom.

The air was oppressively heavy in this room, which hadn't been slept in since Devin's departure. I was startled to find the candle here intact and still in one long piece. The flame was going all right, but it was as if I had just lit it.

"Hey, Bonnie!" I went back to the living room. "See how this candle out here completely melted down? The kids' room candle did the same. Well, come check *this* out."

I led her into my bedroom. Upon sight of the candle, she stopped in her tracks.

"Oh my God." Her face paled.

"What do you make of it?" There wasn't even a drop of melted wax anywhere near the wick.

We just looked at each other in wonder.

Bonnie shuddered visibly. "I'm getting out of here."

The words were barely out of her mouth when a streak of black flashed upwards, visible even in this morning light. It looked nothing like our friend Blue, or even *his* friend, the shrouded black mist. Fear of another occurrence like last night gripped me, and I looked at Bonnie who had also witnessed it. She was frozen in place.

The room was obviously occupied. Had been since Devin had come. Or left. Remembering last night, I felt a stirring of anger.

"Get the *hell* out of here!" I demanded aloud.

The streak flashed again, this time spiraling upwards like a foggy black screw, then twisted into the ceiling, and vanished. The air seemed to lift, and I looked over at the candle.

It was burning now, beads of wax running down the sides like lava. I felt an uncomfortable guilt as we left the room, Bonnie just ahead of me. I didn't know if I'd thrown out friend or foe.

I called the occult shop immediately.

"Tell him one didn't burn right away," Bonnie said, just as Pete picked up.

"Hello Pete? Kerry again."

"Oh, hey! How'd that work out?"

I told him I hadn't read the book pages yet, but I had lit the candles. I asked if they were supposed to burn down that quickly.

He told me it didn't matter how long it took as long as I'd burned them in the rooms. When I told him about that black streaky thing, he sighed. "I wish you'd have read the pages before doing that. You might have just pissed it off. Are you sure you don't want me to call my friends?"

I felt another tug of guilt. "No, that's okay," I told him. "Thanks anyway, but I think I'll wait and see what happens now."

I didn't feel very good about the whole thing. When I rechecked the third candle, I was almost sorry to see that it too had gone the way of the others. It was now a flattened soft puddle of warm white wax. I didn't stamp the seal in this one, not wanting to add insult to injury.

When Jake came to pick Bonnie up, we told him the whole story. Jake came up with half a dozen logical explanations, such as the temperature from the shaded yard coupled with the overnight temperature in the room causing more pressure in my bedroom, which to me sounded fantastic enough to market if we could find a use for his theory.

"If it were as simple as all that," I said, "it would be more bizarre than the spirit theory. It would revolutionize air conditioning, for one thing, or make it obsolete. I'm not sure which, because I don't understand a word of what you just said."

A car door slammed outside. Pammy was home.

We repeated the story for Pam, with Jake rolling his eyes, jostling Adrian on his lap.

"What a bunch of hysterical women," he told Adrian, laughing.

"Oh, speaking of hysterical women, Jake," Pam interrupted. "Have you talked to your mother about Adrian yet?" Pam sure knew how to jab back.

"Well, no, as a matter of fact. I decided to talk to my dad first. Then *he* can tell Mom. Anyway, we do have to get going. Is it still okay if I leave Bonnie and Adrian here when I do go down?"

I smiled. "Sure."

"We'll call you before we do anything," Bonnie said with a sigh. "It may not be for years anyway."

"I'll walk you out," Pam offered, and left the house with them.

"Boy, it doesn't take much to get Jake nervous, does it?" I remarked to Pam when she came back in.

"I know. The big baby."

When the phone rang at seven that evening, I didn't race for it like I'd been doing for two days. When Pam told me it was Devin, I could feel my hands shaking even before I took the receiver. My nerves were not going to hold up through much more of this. Pam left for the den.

"Hello?"

"Hey…what's up?"

"Devin?"

"Yeah. Who else were you expecting?"

"God *damn*. Where've you been? Did your wife show up?"

"Oh, yeah. She's here, but she's not. That's why I called. You feel up to driving down here tonight?"

"Huh? What about *her*?"

"Oh, she's gone for the weekend. Visiting her grandmother."

This really gave me pause. I thought about what Kelly had said and decided that the best way to find out what was really going on was to take him up on his invitation. I told him I'd love to come.

"Far out. When can you make it? You got anyone to stay with the kids?"

"Yeah, guess."

He laughed. "Tell your sister I really appreciate it."

Once again, I found myself driving the seventy miles with the chest pain increasing as I drew closer. When I stopped at the light close to his turnoff, I glanced down at the ring and pentagram. Neither had been any help that night.

I decided to tell Devin about the attack. He'd been through one not so long ago.

He'd know what to do. He'd remember.

7 Pink Floyd entertained me all the way to Devin's, singing about shuffling gloom in sick rooms and talking to yourself as you die. I hoped that song was just reflecting what had already happened, and not a prediction of the future. I made a mental note to pick up that album, *Obscured By Clouds*, which the station was playing in its entirety, as I recognized a few of the songs from Devin's ten tapes.

Devin answered the door and ushered me down the hall to his room. It appeared that nobody else was home, but he still shut the bedroom door and then took me in his arms.

"How's it going?" I asked him, returning the hug. He kissed me before he replied.

"Not bad. Pretty good, in fact. My wife's been a jewel. She doesn't try to play the wife role, and we're getting along better as friends. She has her life, I have mine, and everybody's getting along."

I breathed a sigh of relief. I knew every word he had just spoken was the truth. I could hear it in his voice, and not only did he not have to bring it up at all, but wasn't my being here in his bedroom living testimony to each of them living separate lives? "That's great," I said. "How about *you?* How are you feeling?"

"Better. My chest is clearing up, so I guess I'm going to live." He smiled. "And I'm not as tired as I was either. Getting my old strength back."

"That's really good to hear. You should have heard the songs they were playing on the radio during my drive down here." I told him some of the lyrics and what I had wondered about them.

"They're still at it, huh? This was on AM radio?" For a minute I thought I saw a slight, almost imperceptible frown cross his face, as if remembering the source of these musical messages, but he recovered immediately. "Well, they're a little late with that one. I'm feeling great now. So anyway, how's that racetrack job of yours going?"

"It's okay. Pays the rent. Good exercise, fresh air. It's even kind of fun. A lot better than being holed up in an office. The only drag is it's every day. No days off, but the hours are short, and I'm usually home by ten."

"Far out." He sat on the edge of the waterbed and patted the space beside him. "Sit down. I'll roll us a number." He reached for the stash box.

"Don't do that on my account. I can't drive on the stuff." I sat where he'd indicated.

"I worked a half day today myself. Lola and her girls were working too. They're doing a lot of overtime lately."

"No kidding? Did you talk to them?"

"Nope. I stay completely out of there. Unless I *have* to go in."

Someone tapped lightly on the bedroom door. Apparently, someone *was* home.

It was only Brian, wanting to borrow the van. At first, he seemed surprised to see me sitting there, but then he smiled. "Oh…hi. Sorry if I'm disturbing anything."

I smiled back. "You aren't."

Devin told him there wasn't any gas in the van, and Brian promised to put some in, so Devin reached down on the floor, scooped up his keys and handed them to him. "Here. Hey, you're still going in to work with me Monday, aren't you?"

"Yeah, sure."

"Okay, but I get off pretty early now. You'll be there until at least six. How're you going to get home?"

"I'll get a ride. Gerald will pick me up. Be right back. Thanks."

"Brian is working down there now?" I asked after he'd left.

"Yeah. In the chemical division…you know, where they process the water."

"He's a good kid."

"Yes, he is. I used to just think of him as a punk kid brother, but I hardly knew him when he got here with Gerald. Lots of years of separation. Now, we're pretty close. Like real brothers should be, you know? Anyhow, no one's out there. Want some iced tea? Faye made a whole pitcher of it."

We took the tea out on the back deck where the hammock hung. It was built for two so we climbed in. I was so happy to be in Devin's company again. The Devin I knew and loved. The one who might have evaporated with *him*.

I asked him if he'd been to Daniel's. He said he'd been in and out of there.

"There's usually a crowd there from the plant, so I just don't stick around long."

Exactly what Daniel had said.

"How about Trevor?"

"Oh, he's stopped in here. I haven't been out visiting much. Been sick, you know? Oh, by the way…I've been wanting to ask you. Did your period ever start?"

I looked down at wooden deck. "Well, no, but don't worry about it. I'm pretty sure I'd feel it if I were pregnant."

"Well, other than that one other time, you're pretty regular, aren't you?"

"Yeah. But I *have* been pretty tense this past month. Where's everybody tonight?"

"Gerald and Faye?" He shrugged. "Who knows? They go out a lot. It's a little weird living with my father again, and I'm sure it's the same way for him. We pretty much stay out of each other's way."

I sighed. "I hope you'll move back in, Devin."

"Oh, I might. I'm waiting for my wife to go back. It's the least I can do since she's already here now. It would be pretty rude to start packing up while she's visiting."

I held my breath, afraid that any comment I made at all would cause him to rethink any decision he might make about coming back. I was relieved to know, though, that the rumors Kelly had warned me of had been just that…rumors.

The attack. Would it be wise to bring that up? I decided that I might as well. He'd been through it, and who knew, maybe back then he'd been doubting *him* just as I had.

"Oh, Devin?"

"Yeah?"

"I had a problem in the house last night. I would have called you right away, but—"

"What kind of a problem?"

I told him the whole story, and I was completely truthful about what I'd been thinking because he hadn't called…about the words I'd written in the tablet… to the attack, to the candles that I'd purchased and burned. I finished with the black twisty thing in my bedroom and what I had said to it. As I talked, his expression made me more and more uncomfortable. Finally, he spoke.

"You're telling me that it started the instant you wrote the word 'liar?'"

"On the third one. Yeah, that's as far as I got. I wasn't in my right mind. It wasn't just that your wife was here and that you hadn't called like you said you would. Kelly had called and told me it was all over the plant that your wife was in town. She wasn't even *here* yet, so I don't know how that rumor got started, but the implication was that she was here to get back together with you, not just to visit."

"Hold it. Kerry, *when* did I tell you I'd call? I don't remember saying anything like that."

"That night, out at my car, when I was leaving. You said you'd call before Friday, which was when she was due in."

"I don't remember that, but I probably did. There was a flurry of activity going on, fixing her up a room, rearranging things in the house for her visit, but I'd never expected you to completely freak out just because I didn't call. You could have called me, you know, and avoided all that bullshit."

"I probably would have, Devin, if it hadn't been for what Kelly said. It really sounded like you were getting back together with your wife, and I guess I was thinking that if you really wanted to call me, you would. And when you didn't…"

"You know, Brian's working there now. All he had to do was even mention we had a visitor coming and who it was." He sighed. "You see how that shit gets started? Anyhow, that's not important. About those candles...what did you do that for? I just don't understand why you didn't call *me*!"

"Because she was already here, Devin, and I was scared out of my wits! Terrified. Those shocks were like being electrocuted. They *hurt*. But still, I was so pissed off at you. So afraid that Kelly had been right."

"Yeah, I hear you," he said wearily. "I've been through it too. I don't remember thinking about anything except getting it to stop."

"And you were terrified too."

He stared at me. "Sure I was. But I didn't throw it *out*! I called it on. I challenged it. But I didn't kick it the hell *out*!"

I was alarmed at his reaction. Alarmed and confused. "What do you mean?"

"Look, Kerry. I don't know what the fuck you thought white candles were going to do. Damn. If that...whatever it was...didn't want to leave, white candles ain't gonna do *shit* for you. You don't even know what it was. And if it decides to come back...you're lucky it didn't...you're lucky you're here in your right mind to tell me about it. Don't you realize—?"

"Devin?" Brian was back.

"Out here," Devin called.

"Oh. Sorry. I keep disturbing you."

"It's cool. Want your hammock?"

"No, that's okay. Stay where you are. Here's your keys. Thanks, man."

Devin sat up. "Hey, it's *your* bed. We were going in anyway."

Brian protested politely, but we got up and went back to Devin's room.

Devin stretched across the bed wordlessly, obviously deep in thought. His mood had changed so drastically that I didn't know if I was invited or not. I perched on the cushioned frame.

"Devin...are you mad at me now?"

He shook his head. "I just don't fucking understand you, Kerry. That's all. Instead of calling me, you go run to some fucking...human...who fed you a lot of human bullshit, and which you swallowed. I thought you'd be...beyond that. Tell me something, Kerry. Did you try *talking* to it?" He raised his head, looked over at me, then looked away with frustration. "Oh, that's right. You sure did. You told it to *leave*."

I didn't know what to say. I was too numb and shocked by his reaction. I just sat there, miserable. I couldn't seem to do anything right by Devin's standards.

"I just don't understand you at all," he repeated quietly.

"What...what did you expect me to do? In the middle of an attack?"

"You called your sister. You could have called *me*. You *should* have called me! I've told you from the very beginning. *Nobody* intercepts my calls."

"But...she might have answered the phone."

"So you say, 'is Devin there?' just like you would with Gerald or Faye or Brian."

"But I thought...I believed...your wife..."

"And that's the other thing, Kerry. I *told* you she was just coming for a visit, but you couldn't believe me. You chose to believe the rumors. You have a hard time believing anything, don't you? You didn't believe *him*, and you don't believe me. Tell me, Kerry." He exhaled loudly. "Just what *do* you believe?"

He was the picture of disappointment.

"I'm sorry, Devin. I guess I wasn't thinking."

"Maybe you *were* thinking. Maybe that's the problem. Anyhow, it's too late now. You'd better hope like hell that it doesn't come back, whatever it was. White candles…" His voice trailed off, and he shook his head with resignation. "Never mind." He patted the bed beside him. "Come lie down with me."

I did, and he drew his arm around me. I lay against his chest, listening to his rapid heartbeat. He was so upset, and I had done this to him. I loved him so much. Why did I keep screwing up?

"It's not your fault, I guess," he said finally. "You just don't know any better."

"Devin, next time…"

"Kerry, for your sake, I hope there won't *be* a next time. You got somebody mad, probably. I just wish…you had called me. You don't know what you're fucking with. It doesn't look good, your reacting like that. Like he used to tell you, you keep forgetting who you *are.*"

"I wish I *knew* who I'm supposed to be," I said miserably. "And why he left, and why he won't come back."

We both lay there for a while, each of us lost in our own separate thoughts. Once Devin reached for me, then drew back sheepishly. "I keep forgetting. If you're not already pregnant, I could get you pregnant now."

I didn't push it. I was just feeling better that he seemed to be putting the attack incident behind us and wasn't going to hold it against me forever.

As the hour approached one, I reluctantly got up. He wasn't asleep, and my sudden movement stirred him.

"What's wrong?"

"I've got to go, Devin. I hate to, but I have to be at work by five."

"Oh, damn. I forgot. You work seven days a week. Okay, hang loose. I'll walk you out."

"You don't have to get up."

"I want to."

He walked me to the car, and when he kissed me goodbye I crushed him tightly to me, hating to let him go back in. "I…I…feel like I'm not going to see you anymore, Devin," I said, wiping tears from my eyes.

"You'll see me," he said. "I won't say when. It seems like my saying *when* causes a lot of trouble. But I will call you. It may not be until after she goes back."

"What day is she coming back *here?*"

"Tomorrow night. And she's leaving on Tuesday." He kissed me again. "I'll let you know."

"About moving back in…" I began.

"I'm considering all angles. I may not be at this job much longer and I won't move in if I can't help pay the expenses. I'll keep you posted. Anyway, I'm going back in. It's cold out here. I'll call you, okay? And if I don't, *you* call me. Anytime."

"Okay, Devin, thanks."

One final kiss and he stepped back so I could start the car and turn it around. He was still standing in the driveway when I headed down the road, so I flashed my headlights and he waved.

.

The drive home stretched ahead, long and lonely. I should feel *happy*, I thought. All in all, it had been a good night, except for that business about the attack, and I didn't blame him for reacting the way he had. Still, I didn't *feel* happy. I felt lonely. Like I had just lost my last friend.

I had no way of knowing that I would never see this Devin, the Devin I'd just spent the evening with, ever, ever again.

8 Devin didn't call on Sunday, but I didn't really expect him to. I went to bed early that night, knowing that his wife was probably back and the family was back to visiting.

Other than work, I'd remained at home all day, so it wasn't until Monday that I realized my sandals were missing. I always drove with my shoes off, so I hadn't missed them Sunday. The only other shoes I owned were the track boots, and when I took those off, I was in my bare feet. The last place I'd worn the sandals was at Devin's.

I put a call in to Devin at the plant, and at 4:30, he called me back. When I answered the phone, I didn't even recognize his voice.

"Devin?"

"It's me. Why do you always sound like you don't know me?"

"It...well, it didn't sound like your voice, that's all."

"Well, which one do you want?" he snapped. "I've got five of them."

The sarcasm and bitterness were back with a vengeance. But why? Where was the Devin I'd kissed goodbye so sweetly Saturday night? What had happened between Saturday and today?

"Anyway," he went on, in a more normal voice. "You left your shoes at the house. I guess you need them, huh?"

"Well, I didn't even miss them yesterday. I never went anywhere but the track. I'm really sorry. I hope it didn't cause any problems."

"Here you go again, implying that there's still something between my wife and me. Why should she care if I had someone over?"

Damn, talking to Devin today was like walking on eggs. "Sorry, I didn't mean to imply that. Did you bring them with you?"

"I meant to, but I forgot them. You think you can be in this neighborhood tomorrow?"

"Yes. I could have lunch with Kelly and meet you at Daniel's if you want."

"Okay."

"Did your wife make it back okay?"

"Yeah. She's packing up to leave right now. Look, I'm pretty busy here. I'll see you tomorrow at Daniel's."

"Okay, Devin."

The line went dead in my hand. Here we go again, I thought.

I called Kelly that evening, and she agreed to meet me at the coffee shop. She sounded anxious to catch up on the gossip.

After work Tuesday morning, I showered and headed down, slowing at Daniel's corner house. No one appeared to be there. I continued on up to the restaurant and slid, barefooted, into one of the back booths. Only in this town could you get away with bare feet in a restaurant, even though signs on the front door *did* clearly announce the necessity of shoes for entrance.

Kelly and Lana bounced in exactly at noon, announcing that Lola had released them early.

"Did she know you were meeting me?" I asked.

"Yes. We even invited her." Kelly snickered. "She just gave us a dirty look. Oh, have you seen Devin?"

"Saturday, why?"

"Well, after all the rumors about his wife being back, I was just curious. So, did he come to your house?"

"No. I went down there."

Kelly and Lana exchanged looks, but must have decided not to pursue the subject.

"He's hiding from us," Lana said. "And I don't think I like him anymore. I said hi to him, and he just walked right past me. What did *I* ever do to him? And I know he heard me. He looked right at me, but then he looked away real fast and tried to pretend he didn't."

"Again? That's what Kelly said the last time I saw you guys. When was this?"

"This morning. Pat's nice, though. He talks to us all the time."

"I see you're still wearing Devin's ring," Kelly observed aloud. "What's going on?"

I shrugged. "Can we talk about something else?"

"Oh, the big secret, huh."

"Kelly, please. I can't." Kelly and Lana were definitely down on Devin right now. I worked the conversation around to the racetrack, which fascinated them, and kept it there until it was time for them to leave. I promised Kelly that I'd call her.

"I'll be stopping by your house," Lana called over her shoulder. "When are you home?"

"I don't know. Call before you come."

There was a company truck parked at the curb when I drove into Daniel's driveway. I checked it out mentally, but it didn't feel like Devin's. I parked and went to the door.

Luke was the first to it, tail wagging. I'd never had any problem with Daniel's dog, and I gave him a pat on the head. Julie was right behind him and opened the door widely when she saw it was me.

"Well, look who's here!" she announced loudly, her hand clutching Luke's collar. Come on *in*, stranger!"

Ethan was sitting on the couch, his nose in a book. Daniel sat beside him, and Joey Burns was sprawled comfortably on the floor, toking loosely on a joint. Ethan looked up from his book and gave me a friendly wave. Daniel walked over and gave me a sisterly hug, and Joey looked up at me as though he hadn't seen me in years.

"Hey, Ker! Where ya been, girl?"

"Working. Is this the company hangout or a Sparklear former-employee convention?"

Ethan burst into laughter, and Joey passed the joint to me. "I beg your pardon, madam," he said with indignation. "I haven't quit, *yet*. What're you doing here anyway?"

"Visiting. How's things at the water hole?"

He made a face. "If you don't mind, I come here to get away from that place. Where're ya workin' at now?"

"Racetrack. Julie, has Devin been here yet?"

"This morning. He usually stops in after his route, though. Before he takes the truck in."

"Okay, good. I didn't miss him, then."

"Well, he doesn't *always* stop," Daniel began.

"He said he would today. He's supposed to drop my shoes off."

"Oh," Julie said, glancing at Daniel.

"That makes sense," Ethan put in, without looking up from his book. "Perfect sense to me."

I realized how confusing this must sound to them. "Well, I left them at his place," I explained uncomfortably, sorry I'd mentioned them.

Another company truck pulled in, and my heart jumped as I glanced up nervously.

"No," Daniel said, who had a better view than I did. "It's Mike...and...yeah, that looks like Whippet with him."

As the two alit from the truck, their joking comments could be heard as they approached the house. Daniel waved them in from the window, and the screen door opened. Mike swept the room with a collective wave. "So. This is where they go when the route is finished." Apparently, this was his first time. He recognized me and smiled. "How *are* you, Kerry?"

"Good," I lied, growing more uncomfortable by the minute.

"Well, come in," Daniel said. "Don't stand in the doorway."

"No, we're taking the truck in. We saw that one and figured Joey was here."

"Hey, I'm not ready to go back," Joey protested. "It's only one. Sit down and smoke a number."

Another truck pulled up onto the grass, and this time it was Devin.

I died and came back watching him slam up and stroll casually to the house. He was wearing that black cap of Christian's, and I could feel my pulse racing when he entered.

"Hey-hey-hey." His gaze swept the room. "Little crowded in here, ain't it?"

Luke bounded up to him, tail wagging furiously, and Devin stooped to engage him in a few seconds of playful roughhousing before he took a seat on the floor beside Joey.

"Hey, whadaya say, man?" Joey flashed him a peace sign and tossed him a joint. Devin's eyes met mine and he nodded slightly, then turned to Joey.

"Where were *you* today?"

Joey flicked his Zippo open and lit the joint Devin held. "Doing fucking specials."

"Oh, hey, them suckers were *my* problem before *you* got them." Devin laughed. "I'm almost glad I'm driving again. Don't need *those* headaches."

"Yeah, thanks a lot, bro. Man, I wish I had the route they gave you."

Devin lifted his shoulders and passed the joint to Daniel. "I may not be here much longer. You can have it if you want." He turned to me suddenly and snapped his fingers. "Oh…your shoes. They're in the van. I'll drop them off after I take the truck in. You in any hurry?"

"No." I wasn't exactly puzzled by Devin's formal coolness towards me. He obviously didn't care to show any feelings in front of his coworkers. I was probably an embarrassment to him.

Joey stood up and stretched. "Now, I'm ready."

The other two drivers rose.

Devin remained where he was. I breathed a sigh of relief. Maybe he'd loosen up after the room emptied.

He didn't. As soon as the floor was clear, Devin took advantage of the space and stretched out on his stomach, head buried in his crossed arms.

Ethan and Daniel had their heads together at the dining room table, counting money. Julie was getting ready for work.

Even when Daniel and Ethan left to drop Julie off, Devin didn't move. Alone together in the house, I had hoped we'd get a chance to talk, but he remained motionless for fifteen minutes. When he finally did raise his head, it was to ask for the time.

When I told him, he rose and stretched. "Hey, uh, tell Daniel I'll be back. I'm going to go check on Brian."

"Are you supposed to take him home?"

"If he's ready when I'm ready. There's no way I'm hanging out here for two hours."

A Sparklear truck pulled into the yard, and a driver I didn't know came to the door. "Is Devin here?" he asked, through the screen.

Devin looked up. "Over here. What's up?"

"Brian said to tell you to stop over. I think he's working some overtime."

"No fuckin' way. You tell that sucker…hell with it. I'll go tell him myself." He stopped and looked at me, as if an afterthought. "I'll probably call you."

Without another word, he slammed out of the house. The other driver looked after him, perplexed, then looked at me and shrugged. Then he too turned and left.

Not knowing what else to do, I wandered into the kitchen and started filling up the sink with soapy water. Devin had made a few contradictory statements. He'd said to tell Daniel he'd be back. He'd then said he'd call me. Since Daniel didn't have a phone, did that mean he wasn't coming back? He still had my shoes, but it didn't sound like he intended to drop them off.

"Hello? Anybody home?"

I recognized Brian's voice, dried my hands, and went out to let him in. He seemed surprised to see me there, especially when nobody else was.

"Hi," he said, looking around.

"Hi, Brian. Did Devin find you?"

"No. That's why I'm here. Isn't he—?"

"Uh-uh. He left to go find you. A driver came over with your message."

"Shit. I must have just missed him. Think he'll come back here?"

"Your guess is as good as mine. But you're welcome to wait here." I poured us both coffee and brought it into the dining room.

"Thanks." Brian looked anxious. "Was he mad? I mean, did he say anything about staying and waiting for me? I don't *have* to work the overtime, but it's a new job and I could use the money, too."

"He seems to be in a bad mood," I admitted. "You're lucky you missed him."

"Man, he's *been* in a bad mood. This whole fucking *month*. He seemed to be in a little better mood when I borrowed the van Saturday night, and I really thought hell month was over. But the next morning...Jesus Christ! I hate to say he came out of that room like a bat out of hell, but Jesus! How's he treating you?"

"Well, like I said… I wonder if it's because I forgot my shoes down there. He said it didn't matter, but maybe he thinks I did it on purpose, you know, because his wife was due back the next day."

Brian scratched his head. "No. He didn't even know the shoes were there until Monday morning. I'm the one who found them, out by the hammock. When I gave them to him, he didn't act like it was any big deal. But he was a pain all day Sunday, so it couldn't have been the shoes. That much I *can* tell you. I can't figure out how someone can go to sleep in a good mood and wake up like a bastard. I mean, what the fuck *could* have happened?"

"I wish I knew, Brian."

"Well, I wouldn't take it personal. He's even treating *me* like shit. And he's not getting along with Dad either. I hate to ask Faye to drive all the way down here and get me again. She would, but I hate to impose on her kindness." When I didn't comment, he added, "Don't worry. Whatever it is, he's taking it out on everybody. Including his wife." He stood up and drained his cup. "I'd better go, in case he's waiting over there for me. See ya later, huh?"

"Okay, Brian. Good luck."

"Thanks." He smiled. "I'll need it."

There was a heaviness to his gait as he crossed the yard and trudged around the corner towards the plant. I felt sorry for him. Of everybody, Brian had done nothing that I knew of to upset his brother.

Daniel and Ethan returned minutes later, with three fat bags of Columbian Gold. Daniel waved me over to the table while Ethan proceeded to roll an overstuffed joint. I joined them as they began to weigh the weed and bag them into ounces. Daniel asked where Devin was and I told him everything that had transpired since he'd left with Julie.

"Man, what's gotten *into* him? He never used to be this way. I just don't fucking understand it. He used to go out of his way to help everyone. Brian is his *brother*, for Chrissake!"

"Speaking of the devil," Ethan said, looking up. "Brian's back."

"Come on in," Daniel called out.

Brian entered, spotted the weed, and smiled. "What's going on?"

"Columbian," Ethan said proudly. It must have been his connection. "Did your brother find you?"

The smile vanished. "No. No, he wasn't there. I guess he just left. I should have just stayed and worked the overtime."

"He left you stuck here?"

"Well, I'm not stuck," Brian said. "Gerald is coming to get me. Okay if I wait here?"

"Sure. Does Gerald know where to come?"

"Yeah. I told him."

Daniel refilled the cups still sitting on the table. "Pretty mad, huh Brian?"

"So I heard. Wish I could figure out what's wrong with him. He's pretty much been like this since New Year's Day. Oh, we've had a couple good days, but all in all, I think that's when it started."

I wondered if those "couple days" had anything to do with the rare appearance of *our* Devin.

"Nobody can figure out what's wrong with him," Daniel said, "but everyone's trying to. Hey, I realize he's been through a lot, Brian, and I guess you would know more about that than I do. His job…Kerry…his wife being here, even. But Damn. He's treating all his friends like shit. You, his own brother…he's not too friendly with us—"

"And Kerry," Ethan threw in casually. I shot him a resentful look. I hadn't asked for his opinion of our relationship.

"It's a shame you two broke up," Ethan went on, sounding sincere. "You two made such a perfect couple."

"There's no shame about it," I replied, defending my position. "He's exactly where he wants to be, or he wouldn't be there."

Daniel looked at me intensely. "That right, Kerry? Did you *tell* him that?"

"Tell him? Daniel, I've all but gotten down on my knees and *begged* him to come back. I've tried everything I can *think* of. And I didn't throw him out, either. I don't know what else I can do."

"I didn't know that. I thought it was *you* who didn't want *him* back. Then I guess what I *thought* was behind all this isn't what's bothering him. I don't know, though, Kerry. He's got a lot of pride. A *lot* of pride."

"I know." I looked up at the velvet picture of *him*, and Daniel's eyes followed my gaze.

"*That*'s the whole problem, huh, Kerry?"

"Yeah. I think you've hit the nail on the head. It's not the Devin we knew, and most certainly not *him.*" I nodded at the painting.

Daniel sighed. "Devin's freaking out. I've tried to talk to him, but he won't listen. I've tried to tell him how he's losing it, but he just cuts me off."

"Oh, he won't listen to *anyone* right now," Brian said wearily, unaware of what Daniel and I were referring to. "Not now, anyway. Even his wife is staying out of his way."

"Oh, is she still there, Brian?" I asked.

"Yeah. She extended her visit another couple days." He laughed wryly. "Maybe *that's* what's wrong with my brother."

It was getting dark and late. Brian looked at his watch several times. "Wonder what's keeping my ride—" He stopped as Ethan craned his neck, watching headlights illuminate the curb outside. Brian went to the window and peered out. "Yep. It's the van. I guess Devin came after all." He drained his coffee and picked up his jacket. "Later."

Even though I was hidden by the wall that divided the living and dining rooms, I was picking up a strange uncomfortable vibe radiating through those walls. A vehicle door slammed outside, and I knew Devin was approaching the house. I looked at Daniel. "He's going to notice my car is still here," I said.

"Don't worry about it, Kerry. You're a friend of ours. You have every right to be here."

"Hey! Brian!" Devin's voice through the screen door.

Brian, who had a full view of the lighted yard from where he stood, motioned for me to stay out of sight.

"His wife must have come along for the ride," Daniel whispered.

A few words were exchanged between Devin, Daniel, and Brian, and minutes later I heard the engine start up and the front door close. Daniel returned to the table with a brown paper bag. "He brought your shoes. His wife was out there, so that's probably why he didn't come in."

I nodded. "I might as well go home. He sure was emitting some ugly feelings."

Daniel agreed. "I picked up on that too, but well, I've just about had enough of his negativity. I might try to talk to him one more time, but if he keeps this up, he's not going to have any friends left."

Ethan looked directly at me. "You're the one I feel sorry for." To Daniel, he added, "Devin was *my* friend, too. I know he's going through some shit right now, but that's no way to treat a lady."

"Ethan, stay out of it, will you," Daniel said tiredly. "You don't even know the half of it. Believe me, Devin ain't no friend of yours, and he never was. I'm beginning to wonder if he's even a friend of *mine*."

"Daniel," I began, but he went on anyway.

"Hey, Ker. This chip he's got on his shoulder. Yeah, I know what his fucking problem is, and I admit it wouldn't be easy for anyone to adjust to, but he's fucking blowing it. Take the way he's treating *you* for instance, as Ethan so aptly put it." Daniel stubbed his cigarette out angrily. "Anyway, don't go home just because he so obviously resents you being here with us."

Ethan laughed. "You gotta admit, though, Dan. It *does* look kinda bad. Julie *is* at work."

"Well, he told me he'd be back with my shoes," I said, getting up, "so it shouldn't have been any surprise I was still here. Anyway, I am going to go. I'm not in that great of a mood."

I had plenty to think about as I drove home. Devin's turn in attitude since Saturday when I last saw him was completely inexplicable. That night he'd talked optimistically of moving back in with me. Now, he wouldn't even look me in the eye.

By the time I reached home, a light rain had begun to fall. I took my time getting out of the car, feeling like I carried the weight of the world on my shoulders. The rain took me back to the night that seemed like ages ago. The first night with the tablet. The night we had called Myrna about the ring. Devin had been the one who'd been attacked back then. Now it was reversed, but I was coming home alone.

To add to my mounting depression, my period still hadn't started. With a sick feeling, I walked toward the house on the same sidewalk that Devin had once strode on that rainy night only three months ago.

Three months ago I had been a fairly contented, well-adjusted, steadily working posting clerk, secure in my reasonably well-paying job and not that unhappy with my life. Now, I realized as I turned the key in my door, that my whole world had been irreparably shattered, just as quickly as the entire thing had begun. I didn't even *know* Devin anymore.

I wondered if Devin even knew himself.

Everything and everyone had deserted me, it seemed. Like an episode straight out of *The Twilight Zone*, I had gone from routine existence, to indescribable joy, to *this*. I had no fairly well-paying office job, no stereo, and no furniture to speak of. No Devin. No close friendship with Lola and Mark. Like the *too-perfect* relationship with *him*, it had all vanished.

There was no security in my reality anymore.

Did Devin also look up at the sky, or into his mind, with these same abandoned feelings? Did he too look around at his once secure existence, now crumbled to a few paltry reel-to-reels, an argumentative father, and a lousy, meaningless job?

If I was having trouble looking at my empty walls and listening to my house echo back at me, was Devin also unable to adjust? Even more so than me?

I could still grasp tightly to the belief that, even in my seeming aloneness, *he* was still watching out for us. I just couldn't accept that *he* had abandoned us, as Devin believed. I had faith that I would see *him* again, even if it meant my learning to go *there* to do it. I still had hope.

I wondered if Devin could say the same.

9 Pam was up at five on Wednesday when my alarm went off. She asked how things had gone yesterday, and when I told her, she just shook her head in disbelief.

"He never did call last night, did he," I said.

"Nobody did."

"I knew he wouldn't. That's why I wasn't in any hurry to get home. He was already mad at me."

"But why? You haven't even talked to him since Saturday."

"I know, but I have a pretty good idea of what's wrong with Devin these days. Everyone's commented on what a rat they think Devin turned into. They think it's because we broke up, or because I threw him out, or…they just don't know what to think."

"But not Daniel."

"No. Daniel is the only one who even has an inkling, but I don't even think Daniel is really grasping the whole situation. What I think is that *he* finally kept his promise and took Devin with him…the Devin we know and love. What I believe we're dealing with now is the real, original Devin Drew. It's making it a lot easier for me to let go of the idea of Devin moving back in. There's just no similarity to the two Devins."

"Wow. Well, I'm afraid to ask, but did your period ever start?"

"No."

"How late are you?"

"A week. And if I don't get out of here, I'm going to be late for work, too. See ya."

Pam was gone when I got home at ten, tired, but glad I had a job that didn't consume too much of my time. The kids were in school so I lay down on the couch, exhausted both physically and mentally. I had finally reached the stage where I didn't know what to do next. Sleep was a welcome escape.

The phone startled me awake at 2:30, right out of a dead sleep.

It was Devin, and he sounded miserable.

"So, you got your shoes back," he said. "I was surprised you were still there when I dropped them off."

"Well, I didn't know if you were coming back or not. I ended up sitting around with Daniel while I waited, and just when I was about to leave, you showed up with them."

"It looked like you were sitting around with a lot more guys than Daniel."

"Well, one of them was your brother, who was also waiting for you, and the other two live there."

"It doesn't matter." There was a long silence, so I decided to try to reason with him.

"Devin, I really believe you still have access to Erick and Christian and Him…even Devin. Those guys could really help you right now. They know the position you were left in, and they know—"

"Nobody *fucking knows*!" he cut in. "*Nobody* knows!"

I didn't comment. This had been a bad idea.

"Look at *you*, Kerry! I'll never fucking understand you! You've got a spirit living with you, not just popping in and out…but *living* with you." He lowered his voice and added, "And you treat it like it's fucking nothing."

"Devin, how do you know how I'm treating Blue these days? You haven't bothered to come around here. You haven't been up to see the kids. I guess *they* don't count anymore with you either. Or their feelings, or their endless unceasing questions about you. You're just taking this all out on them, too…like you're doing with everyone else."

"Hey, I didn't call to fight with you," he interrupted. "You know, I'm kind of sorry I even called."

For once, I could say it and really mean it. "You know what, Devin? So am I."

The conversation terminated. My feelings were a mixture of anger and confusion. What in the *hell* had brought this whole thing on since Saturday? I retraced my steps over and over, and couldn't even come up with something he might have *heard* wrong.

Kelly called that Wednesday evening, wanting to know if I wanted to meet her for lunch the next day. That sounded better than staring at the walls and waiting for the phone to ring, so I agreed.

She met me at the Walgreens on Thursday. The same one where the baby had first been mentioned. Considering my lack of a period right now, I thought Kelly's restaurant suggestion was ironic, if nothing else. When I came to the red-light crossing, the memories came flooding back. To look at the Devin I was dealing with now, there was just no comparison. No resemblance.

Lana was home faking sick, Kelly declared when she found me at the table. And she hadn't seen Devin today, nor did she care to. The whole plant, though, was talking about Devin's wife's return. When I told Kelly that she was probably gone by now, she conceded a laugh.

"They're all saying he's back with his wife, and you're telling me she went home? I'll have to drop it around."

"No, Kelly, don't. Leave things alone. Let them think what they want, but don't go adding to any more rumors."

We parted at 12:30. I found myself magnetically drawn to Daniel's house, yet hesitant to stop because of the company crowd that gathered there every day. I didn't want it to look like I was only dropping by in hopes of running into Devin. I finally decided to do it anyway. It was early, and I could be sure to leave the place before the trucks started raining down on Daniel's yard.

Julie let me in, and I followed her to the dining room where a man I didn't know sat with Daniel and Ethan.

"This is Jerry, our brother-in-law," she explained.

"Can I get you some tea?" Daniel asked, rising. "We're out of coffee."

"Tea's fine. Okay if I sit here? Nice to meet you, Jerry."

Julie pulled the chair out for me. "Are you still at the track?" she asked.

"Yeah. It's finally getting routine now."

We actually talked for an hour without Devin's name even being mentioned. Julie had to get ready for work but wanted to know if I could come back tonight and hang out a little longer than I usually could. She even wanted me to bring the kids. She wasn't sure when her shift would end.

I hesitated, and reminded her I got up really early these days, but she wouldn't let up until I agreed to at least come by myself. I stood firm about bringing the girls because it was a school night, and I didn't want to keep them out as late as I might end up staying. I was a little hesitant about being there before she got off work, what with three guys being the only ones there until she was off her shift. She assured me that they didn't bite, and made me promise to wait for her to get home.

Pam was good with staying with the kids, and I tried to wait until it was a little closer to when Julie might be home, but I still ended up arriving a couple hours before her shift ended. I'd grabbed my Sunrise coffee on the way out the door.

Devin picked that same time frame to drop in on Daniel. He didn't come in. Obviously, my car was a dead giveaway that I was in there, so he just stood in the doorway talking to Daniel for a few minutes. Just before he left, he gave the room a sweeping appraisal, and his gaze came to rest on me for one brief nanosecond.

"You going to be home tonight?"

"Eventually. Why?"

"I'll call you later."

Like hell, he would. Even though not one trace of anger had flickered in his expression, I could feel the waves of fury radiating from him. I didn't know if it was because I was with *his* friends, or because *they* were spending the evening with *me*.

Julie had cooked a great dinner for us all, but after Devin left I had pretty much lost my appetite. The guys insisted that if I wouldn't eat, I should at least join them at the table with my coffee, and I couldn't think of a way to say no. This whole thing with Devin was unnerving and depressing, and I felt like we were bringing the whole vibe into Daniel's happy home.

After dinner, Ethan brought the stash box out, and I began to clear the table. Daniel ran into me when he came in to make coffee. He squeezed my shoulder gently and said, "Come on, Kerry, smile. Devin will get his head together."

Sympathy was the one thing I didn't need right now. "He's not going to call, Daniel."

He sighed. "I know. Do you want to go home now? Is that what's bothering you? That he said he'd call and there's that chance that he might?"

I shook my head. "He was furious from the minute he saw my car out there. You know that. He won't call for sure, now. Me sitting here with three men and Julie away at work? He could make a heyday out of that little scene."

"Oh, fuck what he thinks," Daniel said. "Julie's the one who insisted you come. Come on. I'll make you some coffee. She'll be home soon."

Once the joints started rolling, Jerry and Ethan began to discuss Devin. Ethan tried to fill Jerry in on the way he *used* to be. Jerry had never known Devin the way we had.

"Devin's okay," Jerry said. "I mean, I don't know him that well, but he seems to be a pretty cool dude."

"He used to be a lot cooler," Daniel said. "You'd have liked him better if you'd have met him a month ago. No...you'd have *loved* him."

Jerry shook his head. "Uh-uh. I know what's wrong with him. I can see the signs. He's moody. He don't talk to no one. That boy is in love. You can't tell me no different."

I almost laughed. Daniel answered for me. "He sure has a funny way of showing it."

Ethan cleared his throat. "Look. Maybe we shouldn't be sitting here talking about Devin."

"Yes," I agreed hastily. "Let's change the subject."

"No, let's not," Jerry argued. "There's a lot of tension in here since he was here. Lot of...bad vibes. Kerry's uptight. She thinks she has to go home because Devin's mad at her, and from what I can see, he won't give her the time of day when he *is* here."

"Jerry, *please*," I began.

"Oh *nooooo*..." Daniel suddenly covered his eyes and groaned. "I know what it *is* now!"

Everyone looked at him.

"With *Devin!* What's *bugging* him." He looked at me solemnly. "Those *candles,* remember? You were having problems last week, right? An attack or something?"

I stared at Daniel. "How'd *you* know?"

"Devin told me. He stopped over here on Sunday. And when he told me, he was *furious* about it! *Furious!* And I don't think he's been the same since that day. Not that he was Mister Terrific before that, but I swear it's been ten times worse since Sunday."

"Furious? Jeez, Daniel, I know he wasn't *happy* about the way I handled it, but furious is a pretty strong word."

"He thought you should have called him. He said that, instead, you went to a…human." He glanced at the others, then at the floor, as if embarrassed *for* me.

"But I had no *choice* !"I exploded. "His *wife* was there!"

"But if she hadn't been…*would* you have called him? Truthfully, Ker."

I thought about it. Would I have? The way things had been lately?

I considered it from all angles. "No, Daniel, truthfully, I guess not. It would have looked like a play for attention…like I was trying to create a reason to get him to come up to my house. So no, I probably wouldn't have, just for that reason. I don't know, though…I was terrified. If my sister hadn't come, who knows what I'd have been driven to do."

Jerry and Ethan were taking in this sudden private interchange with interest and bewilderment. "What are you two *talking* about?" Jerry finally asked.

Daniel looked at both men. "Look. I'm with Kerry, here. Let's drop the discussion of Devin entirely. First of all, Devin and Kerry aren't ordinary people. I'm not going to try to define that for you. Suffice it to say that they aren't like us. They're…different. Kerry had some kind of psychic attack last week, and Devin blew up because she didn't call him when she needed help."

Ethan looked genuinely interested. "What *did* you do? The book I'm reading right now is about that kind of thing. It's about sorcery and awareness from an American Indian's point of view. There's quite a bit of stuff about invisible worlds and realities and well, things that go bump in the night."

"What's the name of it?"

"It's called *A Separate Reality.* Ever hear of it? I believe it's the first in a series of continuing books, all written by Carlos Castaneda. Supposed to be all true accounts of his apprenticeship with this old Indian who was teaching him sorcery…magic…and awareness."

"And it has invisible worlds in it?" He had my attention.

"Yeah, supposed to be real. It's convincing. *I* believe it."

"I'd like to borrow that book when you're done with it."

Ethan smiled. "Sure. It sounds like it might be right up your alley. But what *did* you do after the attack? Why *didn't* you call Devin?"

I sighed. "Please…can we drop this?"

Daniel changed the subject to a more human topic—cars— and my mind drifted off into my own private world of daydreaming. It was dark outside now, and the living room drapes were open. I watched the street for a while, thinking of Devin's recent drop-in here. The red velvet picture of *him* was right in my line of vision.

Him. Where had he gone? Who was Devin now? Which way was I supposed to go? Tears began to well up, blurring my vision. I blinked and tried to think of something else…anything else, when suddenly the room changed.

I felt a physical drop and realized at once that my body was frozen in the position I sat. The whole room seemed to be "down there," and my head felt like it was protruding a foot above the height it should have been. I was, unbelievably, halfway out of my body. I felt invisible. I knew the guys could see me if they turned to look, but they were engrossed in *men* talk, and I was just another chair at the table to them.

The picture of *him* was doing funny things too. Wavering in and out, like the letters on the cupboard had done during my peyote trip. I wasn't on anything now, but sometimes the picture was visible, and other times it would totally vanish. I noticed one thing, though. The eyes in the painting remained visible even when the rest of the painting blurred completely away. Those eyes of flame locked with mine, and there was no way I could *not* watch because I was half out of my body, paralyzed a foot above my physical head. I felt as sedated as if I'd taken a load of Valium. I couldn't move, and I didn't *want* to.

Those hypnotic fiery eyes! They seemed to bore a hole through my brain, the way *his* eyes had done so many times when he was here. *Him.* I hadn't really thought about *him* because I'd been too wrapped up in the problems with Devin Drew.

Him. Warmth began to trail across my foot, and I knew at once that I had to get alone somewhere. Had to be alone where *he* could talk to me. I realized now that he was exactly where he'd said he'd be. *There,* but here with me now. Here and aware of every thought shooting in and out of my confused head.

Just as suddenly came the realization that Devin Drew didn't matter. Didn't have a damned thing to do with this presence that was trying so hard to get my attention. The flood of warmth flashed over my foot again, and I found that I was suddenly able to move again. With a painless snap, my ethereal body reconnected with my physical, and instead of looking down at the table and everything on it, I was eye level with the men again.

Without a word to anyone, I rose from my chair, heart pounding loudly in my ears, and walked into the kitchen and out the screen door that led to the backyard. Nobody called me or tried to follow me. I had the weird feeling that not one of them had even noticed me leave.

Outside, the chilly, crisp air brought a certain clarity back, sharply contrasting with the overheated boxed-in atmosphere in the house. I hadn't smoked any of the weed because I'd been too upset about Devin and afraid my paranoia and depression would be enhanced by the stuff. It was black out here, and I could barely distinguish the fruit trees and bushes silhouetted against the night. There was no full moon, but the stars gazed down like those eyes in that portrait of him. The grass was cold, damp, and prickly under my bare feet, but I made my way to the bushes that had once reflected a tragic survival group only a month ago. I shuddered, remembering, and went on past until I found a clearing in the yard, and immediately dropped to the ground.

That plunge I'd felt in the dining room came over me again, and I closed my eyes, steeling myself for the unbalanced sensation that I knew would follow. As I felt the world shifting, a coolness began to radiate over the top of my head. Cooler, even, than the night air outside. A dry ice kind of coolness. It wasn't uncomfortable. Then, simultaneously, that warmth, that wave of heat, blasting my foot, stronger than ever. Unmistakably there. Somewhere in my mind, beyond the hole at the top of the tunnel, I could see *him*, black hat cocked to one side, eyes watching me intently. I could feel his thoughts.

I love you, lady.

His voice, inaudible to my ears, but unmistakably clear in my mind.

Remember who you are.

I closed my eyes, more in rapture than trance, and watched him fade and reappear the way the painting had done. He didn't look like any devil or demon, but he didn't look like Devin Drew either, in spite of the landmark hat. He looked the way he had in the Polaroid photo that Trevor had snapped on Christmas Eve. Not human, but not like any devil.

Remember who you are.

Then he vanished, and once again I was alone with colors swirling and that bluish-purple hole. The so-called "gate." Did I dare cross it?

It was too late. If I had thought of it while *he* had been there, I might have at least tried to. Now it gaped, silent and dark, inviting me through, but I was alone.

Remember who you are.

Those words rang in my mind as I got up, the presence of him getting more and more faint, until I knew that whatever opening existed between our worlds was gone…that the veil had dropped again. Not forever, but for now.

I really was alone now, sharing the yard only with the crickets and frogs that occasionally strayed from the bay nearby. The peaceful serenity remained with me, though, as I made my way through the dark to the back door, into the lighted kitchen, and over to the coffee pot on the stove.

That heat was *real*. I'd felt it again. I hadn't *heard* with my ears the words he'd said to me, but I knew he'd spoken to me just the same. Spoken in whatever way he could from a world where there was no physical body necessary and no tongue needed to form the words.

The dining room had cleared. Daniel was bringing in the empty plates and cups. Ethan had moved to the living room to read, and I didn't see Jerry at all.

"Hey!" Daniel's voice, in a surprised tone. "There you are! Where'd ya go?"

Before I could reply, the front door opened, and Jerry came in calling, "She's not anywhere on the block."

"She's in here, Jer…Kerry, are you okay?"

"Sure. Fine. Just sitting in the backyard, getting some air, that's all."

"You had us worried. Jerry's been out looking for you. Nobody saw you leave."

"All you had to do was yell."

"Yeah? Kerry, we *did* yell. Jerry's been yelling his fool head off, all over the neighborhood."

Ethan looked up, marked his place in the book with a match pack cover, and smiled. "I told you she was all right. She just didn't want to be found."

"I didn't," I agreed. "I was…uh…thinking. I just needed to be alone. But I didn't hear anyone call me."

"Well, glad you're all right. I guess I'd better go pick up Julie. Jerry, do you want to come?"

"No," he said, sitting down. "I think I'll stay here."

"Okay, then I'll be right back. Roll us a few numbers, will you?"

"I'll do it," Ethan offered.

I made myself a cup of coffee and wandered out to the front yard. A short, white brick wall surrounded the house, enclosing the flower garden. I sat down on it with my coffee, feeling serene and totally at peace. I didn't want to lose the feeling and wished the others would go with Daniel, but they'd declined the offer, so I'd come outside. I just felt too good and didn't want to break the spell by talking to anyone.

As luck would have it, Jerry left the house a few minutes later with his own cup of coffee and joined me, uninvited, on the wall outside. I was still feeling too good for it to irritate me that much. I was just happy to sit there looking at the trees under streetlights that radiated bluish-yellow halos and streaming rays of color. Daniel came out, keys jangling, and glanced at us on his way to the car.

"You guys are going to get wet out here," he said. "There's rain in the air."

As if to confirm it, a large drop of water splattered on my wrist, and I wiped it away. Rain again. Another drop fell, this one hitting Jerry. Dark clouds were indeed rolling in around us. It was going to be a big one.

"Hey, he's right," Jerry said. "Come on, let's wait inside."

There was no wind to accompany the rain. Just the dark threatening clouds around us.

"Come *on* !" Jerry insisted. "Before it hits."

"You go ahead," I said. "I just want to sit here for a while."

Jerry had risen, but sat right back down again. "Then I'll sit with you. If you can take it, so can I."

Another large drop splattered on the wall between us.

"Listen, Ker. Can I talk to you?"

"It depends. If it's got anything to do with Devin, no."

He lit a cigarette and stared out at the streetlights. "It'll only take a minute. I'm not blind, you know. I can see what's happening. The both of you are miserable, and I know what you feel like too. I miss my wife. Like *crazy* !"

I suppressed a smile. He did look like the henpecked sort. He probably *did* miss her. "Where *is* your wife?"

"Oh, she's coming. She'll be here. Tuesday. I've been going nuts! And Devin's going through the same thing. I'm sure of it."

Another drop hit, this one right into my coffee cup. I laughed, feeling giddy, and Jerry took it as a sign to continue.

"I know what will get him back," he began.

"Jerry, I asked you to drop it. I didn't come out here to think about Devin, or to talk about him. He's a big boy now. He's made his decisions, obviously. So *please*, let's talk about your wife or something."

"Okay." He sighed. "Just trying to help." He'd crossed one leg over his knee, and his foot jiggled nervously.

"I don't need any help. Anyway, you say she'll be here Tuesday?"

"Yeah." He brightened. "Ann, her name is. She's really pretty. Want to see her picture?" Without waiting for an answer, he reached for his wallet and flipped to the picture section. "Here. See? Isn't she?"

"Uh-huh. Looks just like Daniel."

"Yes, she does." He fell silent again. Another drop of rain fell and he looked up. "Damn, this rain. It's really going to hit hard in a minute."

"You should go in."

"And leave you sitting out here?" He tucked the wallet back in his pocket.

I didn't want company, but Jerry didn't seem to understand that. He continued to talk about his own drive down from upstate, and mentioned that his wife would be flying. He confessed to a deep-rooted fear of planes and admitted that he was very anxious about the flight. Then he looked up as a couple more large drops hit him straight on the head.

"Hey, this rain is really picking up. Let's go in."

"I don't really feel like sitting in there. I'm going to hang out until Daniel and Julie get here."

"Yeah, but it's already starting now."

I laughed at him. "Well, would you prefer not to get wet?"

The rain really began to pelt down now, still large single drops making random wet spots on the sidewalk and exposed front steps.

"Yeah?" He looked up, and a large drop hit him square in the eye. "How're you going to manage *that?*"

As if in response, somebody hit the button that said *pour,* and with a large thunderclap, it hit. As it pelted down I realized, in awe and amazement, that although the rain could be seen pouring down in sheets under the streetlights and over the yard, and although the streets and sidewalks were instantly slicked and wet, not one other drop fell on us. Or *near* us.

Even the wall we sat on remained dry. The grass directly under our feet...bone dry. I looked up, expecting to see an awning, but there was nothing over our heads.

Jerry looked stunned. "How...how in the hell are you doing that?"

There wasn't a tree, roof or awning overhead, yet that invisible umbrella remained, even when Daniel drove up with Julie and they bolted from the car, coats over their heads, making a mad dash for the front door. When they reached cover under the porch roof Daniel looked over at us.

"What in blazes are you two doing still sitting out here in this...well...what the *hell?*"

I was actually pretty impressed myself. I knew I hadn't done it, and I also knew who had.

Daniel blinked again as if not believing his eyes. "Will you look at this, Julie?"

"She did it! She did it," Jerry exclaimed excitedly. "I swear to *God* !" He jumped up, and I followed them into the house, shaking my head as Jerry blubbered all the way in to Daniel, who'd gotten his bearings and was now laughing at Jerry's enthusiasm and winking at me.

"Now, you *see,* bro?" Daniel smiled. "I told you she was different. Devin's the same way." His smile fell. "Or, he *was,* anyway. So…how about those joints?"

I only stayed about an hour more. I was acutely aware of how early I needed to be up, and the memory of his contact with me in the backyard was still too fresh in my mind for me to want to engage in any social visiting.

That memory was still with me as I dropped off to sleep, confident now, that *he* was with me, even though Devin wasn't. And as far as I was concerned, Devin could just hack his way through this alone, the way he was doing, the way he seemed to want to. He was cutting himself off from friends, family and me. There wasn't anything I could do about that, but I was not going to let him affect my life any longer.

I was learning how to separate Devin Drew from *him.*

10 The next morning I methodically walked the horses, my body on autopilot. My mind was still serene with the memory of my contact with him the night before, and I had put Devin entirely out of my mind. He didn't matter anymore.

Devin, however, must have had other ideas about that. I was in no way prepared for his call that afternoon, and from his first words I knew that this wasn't going to be a very friendly call.

"So, did you have a good time last night?"

His very tone of voice made me wary. "Reasonably, why?"

"Well, I see you were hanging out with the guys again. And my brother wasn't there this time."

"So what? I can't hang out with my friends? Devin, why are you doing this? Why?"

"Actually, that's *my* question. Why are *you* suddenly so interested in hanging out at Daniel's? It wouldn't be because *I* might drop in there, would it?"

When I didn't respond, he went on. "You know, maybe you're just using them in the hopes that I might visit them while you're there. That's not very fair to Daniel or Julie, is it?"

"I was invited, Devin. Julie invited me. In fact, she insisted."

"That's not what I heard today. I stopped in there at lunchtime, and Daniel was pretty fed up…he said he's sick of the whole thing, and he's tired of his home being used as a battleground, and that his house has been declared neutral territory. Personally, I'm not going to be dropping by any more, and you might want to consider doing the same. It really *isn't* fair to them."

Apparently that was all he'd called about because he suddenly had to go, and I hung up feeling shocked and sick to my stomach. *Had* Daniel said those things? Why hadn't he said them to me last night? Would Devin lie about something like this?

Still, there might have been some merit in Devin's accusations. *Was* I only visiting because of whatever small chance there was that Devin would turn up at their door?

I thought about what Devin had said all day, and it was still on my mind when I went to bed Friday night. I just couldn't believe that Daniel had said those things, but Daniel didn't have a phone, so I couldn't call and ask.

After work on Saturday, I took a nap and awoke to someone hammering on my door. I looked out the window and was floored to see Jerry standing there. *Now* what?

He had his baseball cap in hand and appeared to be even more nervous than he'd been Thursday night. I wondered if he was here to deliver the same message that Devin had, to advise me not to stop at Daniel's anymore and to quit using them to get to Devin. Reluctantly I opened the door, braced for whatever was to come.

"I came up here to ask you a favor," he began, twisting his hat as he spoke. "I wanted to ask you the other night, but I couldn't think of how to do it, and then Devin stopped by yesterday. I told him what I was going to ask you, and he said you couldn't do it, that you're a fake, that you had everyone convinced you could do magical things."

Well, it wasn't the message I expected, so I invited him in and put on some coffee.

"What's this all about, Jerry?" I asked when we were seated in the living room.

"He's not going to show up here, is he? He told me to stay away from you, but I had to come. He made me promise not to tell you what he said, but Daniel said you'd know anyway. He said you have ways of finding out. He says you can look into a crystal ball and…see things." He sipped his coffee, glancing toward the window as if he expected Devin to come walking up to the door.

I told Jerry about Devin's phone call and what his message had been, and Jerry looked genuinely puzzled.

"What does Daniel have to do with any of this?" he asked. "He wasn't even there when Devin came, and I've never heard him declare his house neutral territory or say anyone wasn't welcome there. Devin lied to you. Damn…Maybe he lied to me, too."

"Well, I'm relieved to know that he was lying about what Daniel supposedly said, but how did he lie to you?"

"He said you couldn't do me this favor, and Daniel said you can. I don't know who to believe now." His foot was back on his knee, shaking again.

I buried my face in my hands. This was going nowhere. "Okay, Jerry, just what *is* the favor you wanted to ask. I'm the only one who can really tell you if I can do it or not."

"Well…you know my wife is coming in on Tuesday, right? I told you that. On a plane. And I told you how I feel about planes. Daniel told me you can tell about plane wrecks, and Devin says you can't. I don't know what to believe."

"So…you want me to…see…if the plane is going to come in on Tuesday with no problems? To see if she's going to get here okay?"

He looked embarrassed. "Uh…yeah. I guess you think that's stupid and I'm henpecked and—"

"No, Jerry, I don't think that, but in a way, Daniel and Devin are both right. I have no control over what I'm going to *see* if I do try to see anything.

The plane crash incident I saw at Daniel's was a fluke. I wasn't looking to see anything like that. It just happened. It's really not a pastime of mine, and I can't guarantee I'll see *anything.*"

"But would you at least try?"

I sighed. "I will since you drove all the way up here, but don't get your hopes up. I may not see anything."

"Oh, *would* you try?" Gratitude flashed in his eyes. "I'd appreciate it so much. I'd feel so much better."

The minute I closed my eyes and concentrated on Tuesday I saw police cars. All parked on Daniel's street. In front of his house and across the street too. I shook my head and pulled out of it.

"Hey, Jerry, on second thought, I don't think this is really a good idea."

His eyes widened. "There *is* something to worry about. I *knew* it! I've had this feeling ever since she made the goddamned reservations...the plane—"

"No, Jerry, Jesus...*nothing*. It was *not* any plane!"

He leapt to his feet. "Don't say it's nothing! Daniel told me the last time you saw a plane crash you said it was nothing. And my wife and kids...I've got to warn them. I've got to stop them from getting on that plane!"

"Jerry, it was no plane. It was just police cars, okay? You know, those black-and-white cars with the little red—"

His eyes bulged. "At Daniel's house? You saw police at Daniel's?"

"Yeah, but just on the street, Jerry. It doesn't mean they were at Daniel's. I mean, if you have drugs around, I wouldn't leave them lying out in the open, but hell, that's just good sense anyway. Just don't take any chances and keep it cool on Tuesday."

"A raid! I've got to warn Daniel!"

"Don't say *raid*, Jerry! Jesus Christ!"

"Well there's a deal pending...Ethan's. You don't know about it. It's supposed to go down on...ohmygod...Tuesday The same day my wife gets here. I've got to go tell Daniel. I'll see you later. Oh...you're sure you didn't see any planes going down?"

I smiled. What a character he was. "No planes, Jerry."

"Okay, later. And thanks!"

When Pam woke up, I told her the story and concluded with a question. What should I do now? Should I just stay away from Daniel's? Jerry didn't hear Daniel say any of the things Devin claimed he'd said. Pammy said something didn't sound right and advised me to go down and talk to Daniel directly.

"Daniel's your friend," she said. "He'll give you a straight story. Even if he *did* say that, you gotta admit, poor Daniel's gotta have a limit too."

She asked if my period had ever started. In all this chaos, I'd forgotten all about it.

"No, it didn't."

"How late are you?"

I counted up the days and looked at Pam in genuine horror. "Would you believe eleven days?"

"Wow. That is pretty late. Do you *feel* pregnant?"

"No. I mean, I don't feel anything either way."

"What are you going to do if you are? Tell Devin?"

"No. Not unless I was sure, and even then, Pam, I don't know if it would be Devin's baby or *his*. I might not know until it's born."

"Oh, that's *right*! It could be *his*!"

"Well, let's not add *that* to my problems. Jeez, that's all I need right now."

"Would you raise it if it was *his*? The way *he* would have raised it?"

"I hope I could. You remember what he said it would look like."

"Yeah, the eyes, he always said. Man, if that kid's eyes come out anything like *his* eyes were, man…he used to scare *me* sometimes…and *I* loved him." Pam's own eyes misted with recent memory.

"Well, let's not go counting our babies before they're verified," I said. "The way this past month's been, it's no wonder I'm late. By the way, speaking of *real* mothers, how's Bonnie doing?"

"Mad. Jake still hasn't told the parents."

"What's he waiting for?"

She shrugged. "The baptism, I guess."

"Why? Is he afraid they'll kill the *kid*? I think Jake better make sure that *he's* been baptized, not Adrian." According to Catholicism, you would be refused admittance to Heaven if you weren't baptized.

"Poor Bonnie. She's not holding up too well where they're staying. She's not used to kids, and those kids are wild."

"Damn. Maybe she *should* come up here and stay with us. I seriously doubt anything's going to change with Devin. Why don't you mention it to her."

"You'd do that? Oh, Kerry…but…what if Devin suddenly—"

"We'll cross that bridge if we come to it," I said, shrugging. "I'm not expecting anything like that to happen at this point."

I spent Sunday listening to the radio and trying to decide whether or not to continue visiting Daniel's house. I examined the situation from all angles, and the radio did the rest. By the end of the day, I had made the decision to stay away from there, at least for a while. The radio seemed to confirm this decision with every song it played.

Monday, January 20th went by with me sticking to my decision. Other than work, I stayed home and didn't even call anyone. Devin didn't contact me either, and by late Monday night, when Kelly called me about meeting her for lunch the next day, I relented and agreed. As Kelly pointed out, Devin was bound to think what he wanted to anyway, and why should I give up *all* my friends just because *he* thought I should.

Kelly and Lana were already at the coffee shop when I arrived at noon. Lola had released them early again, they said. Their office was being revamped and moved into the conference room clear on the other side of the lobby.

"You got out just in time," Kelly declared. "Hannah's late with her period, and she thinks she's pregnant."

"Now, she's a bitch all day," Lana added, slurping the dregs of her coke loudly. "My mom yells at us all day. Well, not *all* day, but a lot. Things are pretty tense around there lately."

"The other day," Kelly put in, "I told her she was being a bitch and to go home."

"Smiling, of course," Lana added, "but my mom didn't do anything when Kelly said it. She just asked if she was really that bad."

"I assume she still won't talk to me, huh?" I said.

"I still can't mention your name," Kelly said. "She just cuts me off midsentence and says she doesn't want to discuss it."

I sighed. "I wish she'd at least let Mark come over. Anyway, have you guys seen much of Devin lately?"

"I don't *want* to see him," Lana said, wrinkling her nose. "My mom told my dad last night that he's really changed."

"I haven't actually *seen* it yet," Kelly added, "but Ethel says he's got his hair in that ponytail again and is wearing that silver earring he used to wear. I guess he's going back to the way he used to be."

"He's wearing a *what?*"

"That earring. Don't you remember? That and the ponytail. He looks just exactly like he did before he ever got his hair cut and then changed his whole appearance. You know! Remember, right before you two got together? Remember when he switched from the routes to sales...cut and styled his hair? Shaved off the mustache...fancy clothes? Well, I hear the mustache is back, too."

"Yeah," I breathed, an eerie feeling creeping over me. "Right before he bought..." I glanced down at my hand..."this ring." The story of Algernon the mouse pricked at the back of my mind. The degeneration of the mouse once turned genius, going backwards until it was just a mouse, and then it had died. I shivered.

"Well, anyway, that's what the phone girls say, and they see him all the time."

"He doesn't come near our office, and he doesn't even call in to check account status anymore."

I changed the subject. It was too hard to accept that he had changed so much at work too, not just towards me and Daniel. With the topic turning to the two girls' social lives, we finished out the lunch with Devin forgotten, at least by them.

When I walked across the boulevard to my car, I thought about Daniel's house at the bottom of the hill, and when I passed it I saw that there were no trucks in the yard. On an impulse, I parked at the curb, planning on only staying a few minutes...long enough to see what Daniel really had to say.

Jerry opened the door, and upon seeing me, stomped back to his chair, pouting, arms crossed. "I haven't got a *thing* to say to *you* !" he lashed at me angrily.

I gaped at him, completely stunned. "Now what?"

"Oh, Jerry, *shuddup*," Daniel said irritably. "Come on in, Kerry. Don't mind him... He's on one of his tangents."

"Tangent, *hell* ! She made an ass...a goddamn *ass* out of me."

"What is he talking about, Daniel?"

"Jerry, I said shut *up* !" Daniel repeated. Then, more quietly, to me: "What's this about a raid today, Kerry?"

"A raid?"

"There! See?" Jerry jumped up, red-faced. "Now she's gonna tell you she never said that. Just like Devin *said* she would!"

"I see he's been talking to Devin," I observed aloud. "Well, I didn't *say* raid, Daniel."

"See? See?" Jerry pointed at me accusingly. "Don't lie about it. I heard ya!"

I looked at Daniel and rolled my eyes. "I didn't *say* raid," I repeated calmly. "If you want to know what I *did* say, if you can tone him down a minute, I'll tell you."

Daniel looked menacingly at Jerry. "Just keep your mouth shut, Jer. Kerry, I know you have the ability. If there's going to be a raid, I'd want to be prepared."

"Daniel, Jerry asked me to see what Tuesday looked like for his wife's plane coming in. I saw police cars, but I didn't say *raid*. That was Jerry's word. Shit, I don't even know if the cop cars were here for you or not. They were just all over the street out there." I jerked a thumb towards the picture window. "There was no flashing sign that said *raid at Daniel's.*"

"Cop cars, huh? How many?"

"Daniel, they were all over the street. One in front. One across the street. One two houses up. Two idling *in* the street, but you're not the only one who lives on this street!"

Daniel laughed and turned to Jerry. "That right, bro? Big raid, huh?"

Jerry, who had his back to the window, turned on Daniel then. "You can believe what you want!" I ain't hiding no dope! There ain't gonna be no raid!"

"Jerry, she just said that. She didn't say *raid* !"

"Look," he puffed. "I talked to Devin, and he told me everything she says is fake. He said she means well, but she can't see into no futures, and *he* oughta *know*. There ain't gonna be no raid, and furthermore, there ain't gonna be no cop cars…"

"Oh my *God,* Daniel. *Look!*" There was genuine alarm in Julie's voice as she craned her neck toward the picture window. A black-and-white city police car was pulling up to the curb and parking right behind my car.

"Hey, Jer!" Daniel pointed beyond Jerry's shoulder. Jerry turned and flinched visibly as another police car pulled up into the neighbor's driveway across the street. Two more pulled up, idling in the middle of the street, red flashers revolving while two uniformed officers walked up Daniel's sidewalk towards his front door.

By now, everyone in the room had ceased talking. Jerry wouldn't even look at me. Ethan and Daniel leapt to their feet and went out to meet the policemen before they reached the front door. We watched the silent drama as the uniformed men gestured and talked, while Daniel shrugged and pointed to the corner. When they returned to the house, they were laughing.

"Good thing we *did* get rid of the stuff," Daniel said, grinning. "It's a robbery across the street. They wanted to use our phone."

"We don't have one," Julie said.

"No *shit*. I sent them down to the pay phone on the corner. Still, it wouldn't have been cool to have the big deal spread out on our dining room table along with the scale when they came to the door. I guess we can thank Kerry for that." He gave Jerry a disgusted look. "No cops, huh?" Then he turned to me. "And Kerry, Jerry told me what Devin said to you. Since when aren't you welcome in this house?"

"Well, Devin said—"

"Aw, Jesus Christ! I never said you weren't welcome here, or that anything couldn't be discussed here, or that this house was neutral territory!" He sat down and rubbed his eyes with his fingertips. "So that's the kind of games Devin is playing, huh? I should have known."

"I can't understand it," Julie said. "This just isn't like Devin."

"I know," Daniel said. "I've been trying to bear with him, but if he keeps pushing things like this, the house *is* going to be off limits...to *him*. And Kerry, don't you go leaving if he ever shows up while you're here. I mean it. I've *had* it with him. He's trying to bust up friendships, kicking his friends in the teeth...lying. Man, his *voice* don't even sound like Devin. If I didn't see him speaking, I'd swear some jerk was talking *for* him."

"It *isn't* Devin, Dan," I reminded him, as Jerry stalked off to his room, still angry with me. "It's not the Devin we knew and loved." I could feel tears stinging my eyes, and I tried to wipe them away with my sleeve.

Daniel put a gentle arm around my shoulders and shook his head. "Don't you dare cry...not over him. You don't need him." He sighed and went on. "I might as well tell you. Devin...he doesn't refer to you very respectfully these days. Oh, not that he calls you any names or anything. He's too smart and careful to try to pull that around here. He just says that you and he are completely finished. You told us he was considering moving back in, and he tells us the opposite. Told us he never even considered it. I wouldn't even tell you this, but he's telling *you* things about us that aren't true. I never said the shit he claimed I did."

"And I wouldn't have stood by idle and kept my mouth shut," Julie added, "even if Daniel *had.*"

"Devin didn't exactly say anything *against* you, Ker," Daniel said. He just thinks you've gone back to your...human ways."

"The pot calling the kettle black," I said, wiping my eyes again. "Anyway, I guess I should get going. I just wanted to see what you had to say about...you know."

"Well, now you know, and stop in anytime. I mean it. You're always welcome here."

Later, back at home, I was still mulling over my decision to stay away from Daniel's house, and today had kind of proven it had been the right one. Now that I knew for sure that Daniel had not said those things, it made me wonder just what else Devin was saying to everyone else. There was no telling what was going around the plant. Sparklear Water was probably laughing its collective ass off at me, I was sure. Maybe it was time to pull the plug on visiting anywhere in the whole area.

Another thing on my mind was the incident with the police. I was really in awe over it myself. Things like this had never happened before *him*, had only seemed to really start after he'd left. He had promised to shower me with proof, and here it was, yet here *I* was, so meshed in the human bullshit that I rarely took the time to look "in there" to try to find him and his world. Even though I now knew the difference between *him* and Devin, it was hard to remember that Devin was just another guy on the street now, and even harder not to remember the good times we'd had when he had been someone other than just and only himself.

Well, at least everyone was, by some miracle, still friends. With me, anyway.

When Pam came in, I filled her in on the events of the day. She was as much in awe of the police incident as I was. She shook her head and said, "Man, I can just see it. One cop car at a time, just as you described, and all the while Jerry's spouting off that there wasn't going to *be* no cops!"

"Yeah, he turned purple. But, you know, he still wouldn't speak to me. I guess he was embarrassed. Boy, what a nut he is."

"It's funny, though," Pam mused aloud. "All these supposed coincidences. The rain the other day...the cops today. And all since *he* left. Wonder what the point was."

"What do you mean?"

"Well, there *was* no raid, and you weren't even *planning* to visit Daniel. Then today, you have a sudden impulse to stop in—"

"Yeah, but that was to ask Daniel if he'd said those things to Devin, really. I never even put it together that it was Tuesday."

"But still, if those cops weren't there for Daniel, what was the point of you seeing them at all?"

"I don't know. Two possibilities. One, the more obvious, is that maybe without Jerry playing Paul Revere and shouting *raid*, the dope deal *might* have been out in the open, and the cops might have made it to the door. Ever try to hide a bunch of weed in a couple minutes when it's weighed out in ounces all over the table? But the second thing is this. I was trying to tune in to Tuesday at Jerry's request, remember? Tuesday was a future at the time. I was shown an event, maybe not the one Jerry was worried about...but an actual happening, and then led there to watch it happen. In other words, maybe the event wasn't really as important as my seeing that I could draw in futures if I wanted to, period. No point in anyone getting busted just to make a point."

"Man, seems like someone's engineering this," Pam said. "And what about Devin? As you seem to be collecting yourself, it sounds like he's getting worse."

"I know. It's really sad, Pam. Devin's just really freaking out. And with good reason. This was a huge blow to him and he justifiably believes that I caused him to leave. He's right. I did. It *was* my fault, but now everybody has something to say about him, and none of it is good. He's so angry at me he's going to run off every friend he ever had. I feel like I have an obligation to try to help him. The way he is now, I don't think he's capable of helping himself."

"But what can you *do?*"

"Myself, not much. Devin sure wouldn't listen to anything I have to say. But I could appeal to *him*. You know, ask him to help Devin adjust. There's another reason I should try to contact *him*. Guess how late I am."

Pam's mouth dropped. "How late?"

"Fourteen days. Two weeks. According to the medical experts, after fifteen days you can safely assume you're pregnant. And with all the weird stuff going on since I *became* pregnant, if I am, that is, I think we can also safely assume it's *his*, not Devin's."

"You can't have that kid, Ker! What's he trying to *do* to you?"

"I had a talk with Devin about this possibility not too long ago. Back when I was going to his house a lot. Devin said he didn't think they'd let it be born. He said they'd abort it. That they wouldn't let me try to raise it alone without his father here to bring him up."

"Who's *they?* The old man *he* always referred to?"

"I think when he said *they* he was referring to that world of his in general."

Pam gulped. "Boy, this book's getting better and better. You realize that if you *are* pregnant, and with *his* child, you've got a best seller?"

"It's already been done, Pam." I attempted a laugh. "*Rosemary's Baby,* remember? Anyway, it's really not funny."

"Maybe *you're* joking," Pam mumbled, then added at my dirty look, "Okay, okay, I'm kidding. For your sake, I really hope you aren't. But if you *are*, and they *don't* abort it, then would that mean it was Devin's? Would they care about *that* baby?"

"Pam, what difference does it make? I'm going to keep it no matter whose baby it is."

"You mean if you *are* pregnant, you plan to *stay* that way?"

I nodded.

"Devin will kill you."

"He'll have to. Hey, that's one way to get *there*, huh? By the way, did you have a chance to talk to Bonnie?"

"Oh, yes! About moving in. I did, and she said to thank you a lot, and to tell you she may take you up on it. It wouldn't be until around the first, though. I guess they still have rent to live out that they paid to Lorry's mother. She said she'll call you about it."

"What about Jake's parents?"

She scoffed. "They still don't know."

Everything came to a dead stop after that. Other than work, I didn't go anywhere, and I didn't hear from anyone. Not Devin. Not Bonnie. Not Daniel or Julie. Not even Kelly.

On Saturday, I was laid off from the barn. My outfit was losing some horses and didn't need as many hotwalkers. After receiving my paycheck, I walked to the very next barn where I was promptly hired. I drove home at 9:30 that morning, still in shock that it had been so easy. More proof?

Pam and George were home, so I told them about my new barn. George was busy hooking up some large stereo speakers to the little toy record player while I talked, and Pam busied herself making coffee as she listened.

"I'm not all that surprised that you got hired right away," she said. "The last two jobs you got were the same way. Hired immediately. At least *he* seems to be keeping his word. He *is* taking care of you."

"I guess so. Hey! Where did *those* speakers come from?"

"My house," George said. "I'm not using them. Anything's better than the speakers in this thing. Go ahead. Put a record on."

We put a country album on and were all floored at the tone quality the larger speakers added.

"There ya go, Ker." George grinned. "Got yourself a stereo now. It looks ridiculous, but it sounds pretty good."

"That's amazing," I agreed. "Now what I need is some good old Uriah Heep. You know, like the ones he put on that eight-track he made me. I really miss the music."

"Well, why don't we take a run down to the flea market…where Devin got your ring? It'll get us out of the house for a while, and you never can tell. We might run across some used records."

"Yeah, I'd hate to buy a brand new album and ruin it with the shape that needle's probably in."

The first thing we saw after we entered the main doors was a table with a sign that announced albums marked down from fifty cents to twenty-five. There were only three albums left. The first one was an old, used Uriah Heep record entitled…*was I really seeing this?* "Demons and Wizards." The very first album Devin had taken cuts from, and introduced me to.

"Oh my God," Pam said. "I don't believe it! Would you check this out?"

For a quarter, we couldn't go wrong. The jacket was so beat up that we were sure the record would probably be the same, hissy with many scratches, but maybe even one song would be okay. Devin had scooped up the original eight-track he'd made for me on his way out the door, and I no longer had an eight-track player anyway, so I would be happy with even just one song.

Back at home, the three of us sat transfixed as we played both sides of the record. It never skipped once, and George insisted that was just flat impossible. That album cover was worn and torn and scribbled on with ink, and the surface of the album itself was covered with what looked like many accidental skids.

Later, when afternoon had given way to night and I had settled down to sleep, the miracles did not stop. At 2:30, someone pounded on the front door, and when I opened it, a very wretched-looking Devin stumbled in.

I rubbed my eyes and looked again, sure I was dreaming.

"I…I don't know what I'm doing up here," he said, his eyes red and raw and glazed as though he was in some kind of trance. He'd lost at least ten pounds. His cheekbones protruded beneath dark hollows below his eyes. It looked like he hadn't slept in days.

"Devin! My God…come in."

I couldn't have hidden my surprise at seeing him, or my shock at his appearance, even if somehow I'd been prepared for this.

He followed me back to the bedroom like a motorized zombie and fell onto the bed. "I have a lot of nerve waking you up like this," he mumbled.

All the anger I'd felt throughout the week melted as I looked down at him.

He looked so bad.

"I shouldn't be here." His voice was muffled in the pillow. "You need to sleep..."

"It's all right. You can stay here. I'll have to leave for work at five, but...come on...relax." I sat down at the edge of the bed and began massaging his back. He laid a hand on the calf of my leg gratefully but didn't speak again. He was still awake at five, still staring at some fixed point in the darkened room.

"I have to leave any minute," I told him. "Would you wait here till I get home?"

He shrugged. "I shouldn't."

"Please. I'll be back early. Nine or ten. Get some sleep. I'd stay home, but I just got this job, and I have to show up."

"I don't know. Maybe." There was no life or expression in his voice at all.

"Damn, Devin. I wish you were happy."

"I wish I could be," he said. "I'd do *anything*..." His voice broke, and he buried his face and his eyes in the pillow again. "Anything to be the way I was. The way I *used* to be. He just can't...can't leave me like this. He *can't* !" His shoulders shook, and he tightened the pillow against his face.

"Devin..."

He shook off my hand. "He can't. I won't let him! I'm going to call him down. This full moon. I'm going to *make* him come back."

I looked at the clock. Devin sat up, blotting his eyes with the heels of his hands. "I'm sorry," he said, attempting to get himself under control. "I'm going to cause you to be late. Go to work. I'll be all right."

"You sure?"

"Yeah."

He didn't sound like it. I gathered my clothes for work and then leaned over to kiss his cheek. "I'll get dressed in the other room. I...I hope you'll still be here when I get home."

There was no answer so I turned and quietly shut the door, more sure than ever that Devin needed help. Something needed to be done.

Before he completely lost his mind.

11 My new job terminated at the end of the week. Had I known that, I would have stayed with Devin that morning, tried to get him to talk, tried to help him work through this nightmare, but I'd gone to work, hoping he'd be there when I got home.

The Moody Blues were on the radio when I started the car, and chided me all the way to the racetrack. The singer had been searching for his dreams that he'd built up, and I just knocked them down like they were made of clay. The tide would rush in then and wash all his trouble away, but still he didn't know which side of the bed he should lay.

.

Devin was gone when I got home.

Pam told me that she'd seen him come in the middle of the night. She'd heard the knocking from her bed in the den, had caught a glimpse of what he looked like. She hadn't seen him leave, but he'd been gone when she woke up.

"It was like watching someone sleepwalking," she said. "You never told me he looked that bad." She poured me a cup of coffee and set it before me. "Did you mention the possibility that you might be pregnant?"

"No. That would have been real bad timing. But I don't think it's *might be* anymore. I'm twenty days late. Almost a full cycle."

"You'd better see a doctor."

"What for? If Devin's right, I'll lose it. If it's Devin's baby, well…there's no telling."

"Are you worried about it?"

"Not yet. I guess I keep hoping something will change. Something needs to. You saw what he looks like, Pam. Something is draining the hell out of his health, not to mention his mental state. I'm going to ask *him* for help. Maybe that's all Devin needs is to be in contact with *him* just once. He's just hurting so bad."

Later, when I was alone, I did try to contact him but never felt like I'd reached him. I put in the silent prayer to him, though, to do whatever he could to help Devin through this transition.

As the days went by it was pretty obvious that I wasn't going to hear from Devin again.

The morning of my layoff, the trainer gave me the name of another barn who might be needing help. Horses came and went at these barns, some sold, some put to pasture, and some claimed at the races. Evidently, this barn had added some, so I decided to walk over and give it a shot.

Again, I was hired on the spot.

The racetrack had definite advantages, not the least of which were the short hours. The job gave me plenty of time to think as I walked, and I did a lot of thinking about Devin and *him*.

Between horses, we were allowed to get coffee and sit on the tack boxes waiting for the next one to come in from the training track. Sometimes I felt like I had when I had taken that peyote. I remembered Devin's explanation of what happens to adrenalin after it decomposes, how its waste formed adrenochrome, the chemical almost identical to mescaline. It made sense that my visions and aura-reading abilities were picking up. I was certainly working up enough adrenalin as I walked these horses. It didn't occur to me at the time that there may have been a very different reason. That maybe carrying a special child might be the reason I was changing.

I found myself anticipating every thought the barn people entertained before they verbalized them. During those waits between horses, with my coffee warming my hands which were often frozen from the early morning winter air, I studied the barns across from the one I worked in. I'd get myself into such a state of altered consciousness that I could actually see *through* the barn to the other side where another barn stood. And always, no matter how thick the socks and boots, there would come that impossible wave of warmth, somehow having the ability to penetrate even the thickest footwear and circle my ankle as if I were barefooted. The heat wave usually came at moments of my worst doubts, but sometimes it came when I wasn't even thinking about

Devin or *him*.

Also, during those waiting periods, I found time to close my eyes and watch that ever-present hole, which had become even clearer since I'd begun this fast-paced walking for four straight hours every day. When I wondered if *he* had deserted me too, the warmth would come again. When I arrived home each morning I would find that my own natural mescaline production within my body was stepping up everything inside my mind and promising to aid me in my continual efforts to find *him* and his world.

One of the most astounding proofs of his invisible world, or one similar to it, took place at the actual track itself.

I was walking a particularly nervous, high-strung racehorse. As I turned the bend from the rear of the shedrow and approached the front of the barn again, I noticed that a small mare was hooked up to the hotwalking machine. The machine belonged to the barn across from us and was a mechanical way of walking hot horses when no hotwalker was available.

It resembled a circular clothesline and had straps hanging down with leads, which attached to the rings on the horses' halters. It revolved, pulling the horses along in a circle. Many trainers didn't like the machine, contending that the more high-strung horses could hurt themselves before anyone could get to them and remove them, but I recognized the horse and knew that she was anything but overactive. Her nickname was Sissie. I had, at times, gone over to her stall to pet her during my waiting periods. She was gentle and had never bitten or kicked like most of the other horses. She was a perfect candidate for the machine.

I was on the third round with my horse, my mind quite a distance from the routine circle I was walking, when Sissie began to act up.

At first, her own barn people paid no attention to her, but my trainer and several of the grooms had stopped their work to watch, apparently with amusement. Sissie walked a few feet, wheeled suddenly and snapped at the area over her shoulders, and then resumed walking in her slow easy gait. She was the only horse on the machine, even though it could accommodate four. I watched her until I reached the corner again and turned left, heading for the other side of the barn.

On the fourth round, all of the grooms at my barn had gathered at the shedrow row fence to watch. Sissie's activity had increased. Now she was bucking every other step, moving sideways, and lurching backwards as if to throw a rider off her back. She snapped frantically at the air in the same area where a jockey would crouch.

My own horse was reacting too. After he'd stopped short, reared and backed up, he began moving hesitantly forward again. I'd been well rehearsed on what to do if the horses backed up, and I went with him until he stopped. Then, without looking directly at him—they got nervous if you did—I led him over to the water bucket hanging on the rail and exhaled with relief. As he drank, I took a few minutes to watch Sissie. She was now putting on a full rodeo show for her spectators.

The "bleachers" were filled by now. The trainer, assistant trainer, and all loose hotwalkers were hanging over the rails, making my job of getting the horse past them even more difficult. My horse bolted again, and after calming him to a standstill, I stood to watch too.

"Go *get* it, Sissie!" One of our grooms called out eagerly. "*Bite* 'em, Sissie!"

"Hey, Mike!" I called over to the groom whose horse I was holding. "What the hell's going *on*? I can't hold this horse still, and I can't walk him past these people either."

As if to verify my words, my horse reared up as another encouraging call went out to Sissie from the rails.

By now, Sissie was not just snapping and wheeling every few feet. She bucked and kicked outward, then, with eyes bulging backward, she made another attempt to "throw" the invisible rider.

Mike dove in to grab his horse from me.

"What's wrong with Sissie?" I asked, glad to release my horse back to his groom, if only temporarily. I wasn't experienced enough to handle this behavior.

Mike settled his horse down and then handed the shank back to me. "Stay put. I don't know what's wrong with Sissie, but don't try to walk this maniac until she settles down. I'm going over to see what the problem is and let the trainer know." He looked down the shedrow at other horses and walkers coming up behind us. "Whoa back!" he called and the line stopped, each walker echoing the phrase to the walker behind him. All hotwalkers understood what it meant. The line was stopped up ahead.

By now, Sissie had everybody's attention.

"Go, Sissie!" another voice called out as the antics continued. Sissie wheeled again, snapped at the air behind her, and then reared up on her hind legs, almost falling over backwards. Her eyes revealed stark terror, and I knew everyone watching could see that, yet no one made a move to help her. Except for Mike who had stridden quickly across the yard and disappeared into the office of Sissie's trainer. It wasn't "our" horse so it wasn't "our problem," or so everyone seemed to think.

Sissie made a complete circle before attempting to continue her walk. She couldn't stop because the machine was motorized and would drag her along, regardless.

Mike returned to my side. "That can't be flies," he said, taking his horse from me again. "See how she's not actually snapping at her own flesh? Sissie sees something that the rest of us can't see. This isn't like that old mare at all. In all my years on the track, I've never seen a horse spook that way on a machine. It's not like it's her first time on it either. Hell, Sissie would be more apt to spook if someone hand-walked her, she's so used to the machine." There was genuine wonder in his eyes and voice. He handed me back the shank again. "Don't try to walk. You think you can hang onto him here for a couple minutes? I'm almost done with his stall."

I gripped the shank tightly, close to the halter, fear growing in me. This horse was not tame like Sissie. This was a stallion, not a gelding, and couldn't be trusted to behave any more than the line of skittish horses behind us. We weren't supposed to let them stop anyway, except for eight seconds of water, because they could tie up if they didn't keep moving until they cooled down. I didn't understand why our own trainer wasn't at least worried about that, but he seemed to be just as amused as everyone else watching.

He turned to the assistant trainer standing at his side. "*She* knows what she's after."

Sissie had become a maniacal bronco. Bets began circulating down the line behind me as to whether the machine would hold firm under the stress. The only ones in the entire crowd who didn't see any humor in the pathetic situation were Mike and me.

Even *I* could see that it wasn't a fly irritating her. When she bared her teeth, it was never at her own coat but at the air above her withers.

"This is holding up the fucking *line* !" I heard Mike shouting to the trainer. "I'm going back over there to see why those assholes haven't come out to get her off. They need to get her down before they don't have a machine to walk any of their horses on, or a Sissie to put up there again."

The machine was rocking and swaying from her rearing, bucking, and kicking. Then, suddenly someone emerged from Sissie's trainer's office carrying a shank. He turned off the machine and tried to approach her, but she was anything but cooperative. Her bulging eyes flitted from the groom she trusted to the invisible area above her withers. It wasn't going to be easy to get near her much less get hold of the halter so she could be cut loose. She wheeled around every time her groom attempted, kicking and snapping viciously at the same area. She nearly kicked the groom with her back legs as she continued to try to protect herself.

Up to this point, I hadn't attempted to watch her with anything except my physical eyes, but suddenly, as I stood there with my own skittish horse, a heavy wave of warmth penetrated my ankle. It occurred to me then that I could probably adjust my vision and actually *see* what was really antagonizing the horse.

Out at the machine, the groom suddenly quit trying to get hold of Sissie and returned to his own barn, presumably for help. As dangerous as I suspected it was to drop into any alternate state holding a horse, I chanced it, adjusting my vision the way I had during so many tack-box sittings and coffee breaks.

What I saw made my stomach lurch.

A "thing" resembling a monkey, purple in color similar to Blue, was hunched over the withers of the wild-eyed horse. It seemed to be having a maliciously gleeful joyride. Each time Sissie bucked, attempting to dislodge it, it raised itself like a helicopter until she stopped bucking. Then, when she settled down, although her eyes were still bulging backward, it floated back down to her withers and continued the harassment.

Other than the color, there was no similarity to the hazy, hovering Blue. This creature had definite form. Its bony monkey-like fingers were long and slender, as were its toes. It didn't appear to be solid. I could see through it to the barn across from ours. The outlines of its arms, legs, and facial features seemed to be *sketched* in a darker purple than its general color. Like an ink-drawn, living, monstrous cartoon. When Sissie wasn't wheeling around and snapping, she was attempting to pull the walking machine, her muscles twitching as if in hopes of shaking the *thing* off her.

My repulsion turned to fear for an instant, and then slow anger began to boil within me.

"Mike!"

But Mike had already left for the other barn. Sissie was now in hysterics, and the horses behind me were becoming more agitated as they pawed and fidgeted in place, anxious to get moving again. Most of the grooms had joined the hotwalkers, taking over their horses until the commotion in the yard was settled. Jokes, jeers, and catcalls from our barn abruptly ceased, and the racehorses were shanked to standstills by nervous grooms and hotwalkers. Even our own trainer seemed to have finally sensed the likelihood of injury to any of our own valuable stock.

"Someone had better get that horse off," our trainer growled, no longer amused. "Sissie isn't even a good runner. That mare should have been turned out years ago."

"This horse is getting harder to hold still," I called over to him. "Should I get him moving?"

"Yeah, go ahead. They're all better off on the other side of the barn where they can't see what's going on…whatever *that* is. Matter of fact, pull him up on that side until your groom gets back. I'll pass the word on down the line."

I began to walk nervously, slowly, my hand close to the halter in case the horse tried to bolt again. As I neared the bend, Mike returned and motioned for me to keep going and to come back around to the front again. The trainer from across the yard was now at the machine, the groom at his side, with not only the shank but a scarf of some kind. They obviously meant to blindfold the horse so they could lead her away.

As I completed the round and was coming up to the front, I saw that neither of them was having much success. Mike signaled me to pull up again, and I called the customary "whoa back," my eyes on the drama in the field.

The trainer had finally managed to grasp Sissie's halter and was talking to her gently. Our barn maintained their bleacher seats, but quietly. All of them knew how easy it was to get hurt.

As I stood there, I adjusted my vision again, blurring out everything physical in order to watch the *thing* clearly. The creature had floated upwards as the two humans approached, and I breathed a sigh of relief as the two worked together to first affix the blindfold, then snap the shank on and lead her away.

"Get those horses *moving* before they tie up!" our trainer bellowed.

Reluctantly, I continued on my circular route, still dazed by what I had witnessed. I had never seen anything like that thing in my entire life, but Pammy had given me a pretty accurate description of one like it the day she'd tried to sleep in my back room. It was frightening to think that this kind of thing could be loose in my house, yet invisible to physical eyesight. It bothered me that the general attitude of the onlookers had largely been one of amusement. No one had seemed to care what was wrong with the normally placid horse. My own horse had calmed down somewhat when he began walking again, other than occasional jumps and starts. There was an air of tension that had spread to the other horses and throughout the barn. Grooms could be heard jerking and shanking their own horses into submission.

Even when Sissie had been led away, in spite of the blindfold, she'd never stopped whipping her neck around until she'd been secured in her own safe stall.

I continued to walk, with Devin's invisible world more on my mind than ever.

Mike took his horse from me at long last, and I returned to the office for another cup of coffee. Across the way, another horse had been put on the machine, but it was faring no better. After walking a few steps, it also wheeled and slashed angrily at his flanks and withers. I knew this horse was no Sissie, and if it got riled up the way she had been, no one would be able to unhook it, much less lead it away. The trainer there must have come to the same conclusion, and that horse was taken down as well. The walking machine was shut down for the day. This time I didn't bother to drop into the state necessary to perceive the monkey-thing. I'd seen enough for one day.

When I arrived home that morning, my feelings were a mixture of anger at the barn people, pity for the poor horse, and stunned contemplation of the point that *he* had made to me. There *were* some things that humans did not perceive, yet I had been able to. I wondered if Pam would be as interested in *this* wild tale as she was in the Devin episodes.

"I'm not going back," I told her, concluding the story. "Not to that barn. Not because of the monkey thing, but because of the racetrackers' attitudes in general over what happened out there. It doesn't matter whether they could see the thing or not. The little horse was obviously in distress and torment, and all they did was laugh and jeer. Before I left, I told the trainer that his horses were too wild for me, and he sent me over to another barn…supposedly one that doesn't have near the amount of expensive and high-strung horses."

"Did you go?"

"Yeah. The people who work for this barn are okay, and that's what makes the job anyway. And yes, I was hired."

She laughed. "You're too much. You should have at least taken a day off before starting another seven-days-a-week stretcher."

"I can't. I'd feel like a sponge if you were the only one bringing in money, and I don't know if sitting around is a good idea. But, you know, that incident with Sissie, it really got me to thinking."

"I wonder if it was the same kind of monkey thing I had that bad experience with."

I sighed. "I couldn't even venture a guess."

Devin had said he was going to try to contact *him* this coming full moon, and I hoped that he would. Even though I'd never felt like I reached *him* when I'd tried, I still hoped that he'd somehow heard my prayers for his intervention in Devin's sad and desperate life and would do something to help. I watched the moon cycles with trepidation the next few days and planned on putting a casual call in to Devin when it was full, just to see if he sounded any better.

Meanwhile I was to see many changes take place over the next few days. I was getting tired of the track and considering taking a break from it, but during the few days I worked at the new barn, I did meet a young groom…a guy I thought might interest Pammy. I introduced Tank to her, and as I suspected, they hit it off immediately. I knew this was going to be a blow to George, who seemed to hope their breakup was only temporary, but I also knew that Pam really was finished with that level of their relationship, and that it was healthier for all parties to move on with their lives.

Just as I'd had to.

Bonnie and Jake stopped in to verify that they would be moving in with us on the first of February.

And Kelly was the first to hit me with the most shocking news of all.

Devin had a girlfriend.

It was all over the plant. Nobody knew who she was. Nobody had much of an opinion of her either. She wore low-cut, tight-fitting clothes and hung around the time-clock area flirting with the other drivers until Devin clocked out. Apparently, Devin had gotten rid of his van, and she was his ride back and forth to work.

I was to receive one more visit from Jerry too, to sheepishly apologize for his behavior and doubt, and to announce Devin's new girlfriend.

Hearing this news from two separate sources just took the last wind out of my sails. From that point on I threw in the towel as far as Devin was concerned. I didn't know if *this* was *his* way of helping Devin adjust to his new life of being himself or not. Maybe it was, but it sounded like Devin had attracted the type of girl who matched his present state of mind. I could only pray that she would somehow bring Devin back to the world of the living.

On February 1st, 1975, I had not had a period in almost two months.

After leaving the barn where I'd met Tank, I didn't bother to look for another job. I needed the time off.

On February 2nd Jake and Bonnie moved in with the new baby. I spent my days helping Bonnie with Adrian and nursing a mild depression. I wouldn't admit to myself that the news of Devin's new girlfriend was affecting me. Maybe it was just my pride and the humiliation of Devin flaunting her at my former workplace for all my friends to see, but it definitely had an effect on me for a few days.

Even though Pam was glad to see me taking any kind of break from working, her new boyfriend Tank stopped in often to try to coax me back to the track. He'd heard of a well-paying hotwalking job and hoped I would apply for it before it was taken. I knew that sitting around the house moping wasn't doing me any good, so I took down the barn number and applied for it.

Again, I was hired immediately.

"We're just about done here today," the trainer told me. "Come back tomorrow, ready to work. We've got forty horses and one hotwalking machine. Your job will be short walks and then putting the horses on the machine. If you can keep track of when they go on and come off, I'll pay you a hundred and fifty a week. Cash. No taxes."

This was more than I'd made at the water plant. I knew I needed to keep busy, and I thought, for the sake of my sanity, that I needed the job.

12 I threw myself into the new job and didn't call or even think about Devin after that. Neither did I bother to visit the plant neighborhood to see Daniel and Julie, or even Kelly and Lana.

As the days went by with no sign that my period was ever going to start, and despite Pam's advice and urging, I still refused to call Devin. My pride had been shattered, and I would not use this as an excuse to get in touch with him.

Meanwhile, Jake and Bonnie provided company for me during my off-hours, and with a little help from Pam, Bonnie was filled in on the entire Devin story. She was completely in agreement with Pam that the story deserved to be written into a book.

Their reasons were debatable.

"Look how weird the whole thing started," Bonnie said.

"And look how it turned out," Pam added.

"Yeah," I said bitterly. "Just look at the disaster that's left. So *what* if Lola isn't speaking to me. Or if I'm pregnant. So *what* if Devin has a new girlfriend. Jesus Christ, you guys, nobody's friends anymore. We never see Trevor and Mia, or Daniel and Julie. Mark's not allowed over. Kelly and Lana have almost dropped out of my life. Great ending, huh? And don't forget how worried he was about the written proof falling into the wrong hands."

"I still think he meant...say... Lola or Kelly. *Those* people finding out. You know... people at work. You can understand *that*. He didn't want *Devin* to be embarrassed."

"Yeah, really," Bonnie said, siding with Pam. "How would *you* feel if the whole company knew what happened, and *you* had to face everybody at work."

"Right. Another reason not to. Devin still works there, you know."

"But *he's* gone now, Ker. *He* wouldn't care *now*!"

"No, it's out of the question. First of all, if I wrote it as a true story, nobody would believe it. Secondly, the ending's terrible. And third...I can't see any point in writing it. Why? What would be the point?"

"Those ten tapes are one good reason right *there*," Pam said. "Who would ever dream that music was a medium for communication from another world? A world that supposedly *exists* in that radio and heat part of the spectrum within the same space here in *this* world. How many people have probably listened to those very songs that *he* put together and never had any inkling of what they were all about? A lot of them were hits, too. A lot of people heard them and didn't *get* it."

"And there's another reason you're forgetting," Bonnie put in. "Devin as much as claimed some sort of kinship with Hell and Satan. Yet he didn't believe in the devil, you know, the church creation. So what he must have meant was...who I am and who we are has been mistakenly *called* the Devil and Hell. But he never described this Hell as fire and flames, or ever inferred that there was anything evil about it. If anything, it sounds like he described a place somewhere that was invisible to the human world, but rumors of it were distorted until it was *called* these things. Heaven...Hell...or whatever other religions label this place...it's still *there*. And a lot of people, like Jake here..."

she punched him playfully… "don't believe in a god *or* a devil. If for no other reason, this book could clear *his* name, and his *world's* name. You see what I'm saying? Just because our parents, and their parents before them, swallowed that fire and flames bullshit, it doesn't mean it was a true picture of a world that's equally as valid as this one."

"I beg your pardon," Jake spoke up indignantly. "I *do* believe in a Supreme Being. It's all that astral shit and hocus-pocus I think you all have blown out of proportion."

"You'll have to excuse Jake," Bonnie said apologetically. "He's so human."

"Well?" I turned to Jake, who had not only been raised Catholic in the strictest terms but had spent a year in the seminary with intentions of becoming a priest. "Just what *do* you believe happens to you after you die?"

"I know you are put into a hole until you rot," he retorted teasingly.

"See?" Bonnie said pointedly. "He really *means* that! Now if you could just change *one* person who thinks like him…"

"I don't know, Bonnie," I said doubtfully. "Maybe in a couple of years."

"You'll forget *everything* by then," Pam argued. "Look, it's already written. You've been keeping those notebooks. You've got all the cards and notes from Devin, and even those beginning notebooks from the night it all really started."

"Yeah, right, Pam. Use the original stuff. Devin *would* kill me then. He's still pretty touchy about *him*, you know."

"Well, change the names. Change the descriptions. Don't mention the location. And how do you know that he'd even be upset? He might *welcome* a book that didn't degrade *him* like most of the occult literature does. For instance, if the Devil stands for evil, how come *he* was so *good*? All he ever did was *give!*"

I gave all their arguments a few minutes of serious consideration before I replied. "No," I said finally. "I just couldn't change Erick's name to anything but what it is…or Christian or Blue either, for that matter. Uh-uh. Forget it."

"But the ending's already *done*. In that journal of yours," Pam protested. "All you have to do is fill in the things that happened between the ring and that journal."

"What, and leave it hanging like this? Me pregnant with who-knows-whose child. Everyone thinking Devin is schizo. No way. Forget it. Devin's been through enough."

"Uh…to change the subject," Jake interrupted. "What *are* you going to do about Junior?" He glanced at my swollen belly.

"Call him Beelzebub, I guess." I smiled and Jake covered his eyes.

"You'd never get it baptized," he said.

The very idea of Baptism of *this* kid hit us all funny, including Jake, who, having only heard bits and pieces of the Devin saga, thought we were *all* a bit balmy.

"Oh, Jake," Bonnie said, laughing, "You're soooo Catholic. You're a living example of why Kerry should write this book."

"Well, while I'm *still* living, if we're ever going to go…uh…see my mother, let's get on with it."

I gaped at him. "You mean you're finally going to tell her?"

"Well, I've already broken the news to my dad," Jake said defensively.

Bonnie stuck her index finger in the air and made a circle. "Whoopi ding!" she said, without enthusiasm. "His dad was all happy...grandson and all that. His *mother's* the one I'm worried about."

"How *are* you going to break it to her, Jake?" I asked curiously.

Jake shrugged. "We'll just tell her he's yours until she gets attached to him."

"Jake!" Bonnie glared at him.

"I'm kidding, I'm kidding." He stood up and picked up the bundle of blankets and the diaper bag. Adrian was well obscured in his pink and blue camouflage. "I've got him hidden. Will this look too conspicuous when we walk in?"

The sight of Jake laden out like a new father was almost too much to bear. Everybody, including Bonnie, burst out laughing.

"You should come down later," Jake said as Bonnie rose.

"I don't know. I'd have to call first. Make sure you're still alive."

"Well, if you can't make it, send your astral bodies. Come on, Bonnie. Let's get this over with."

Adrian was almost six weeks old. Our aunt was going to explode.

Meanwhile, I was developing some extraordinary abilities, which I discovered that same evening. George had dropped over, depressed over Pam's new boyfriend and at a loss for something to do with himself. I was surprised to see him at my door, bored shitless and armed with a couple of joints.

"I figured you might want some company tonight too," he said glumly. "It sure looks like Pam and Tank are getting serious. Oh, I know...it's my own fault. I did it, slowly but surely. My temper. My bad moods. Too possessive. I guess I just didn't appreciate her, and I just pushed her too far."

I shut down the record player and pushed my journal aside. "Well, welcome to the club." It was the only condolence I could offer him.

He shrugged sadly, then caught sight of the notebook. "What were you doing?"

"According to Pam and Bonnie, writing my new book. Actually, just recording in the journal...everything that's happened since the year began. Wouldn't be much of a book with an ending like there is now."

"Oh, that's right. You might be pregnant, huh?"

"Don't think it's 'might be' anymore."

He glanced at my belly. "Yeah. Looks like you *do* have a problem, chick."

"Well, until a doctor *says* it's a problem, I'm trying to ignore it."

When I told George about the weird things that were happening lately, he came up with an interesting idea. One of the last things Pam had done for him was to introduce him to Transcendental Meditation. He had taken the classes and had been working on relaxing using the alpha state. He suggested some ESP experiments—just for the fun of it, of course—not that he believed in it. We decided to use the back bedroom where it was dark and quiet, and the lighting was adjustable with the dimmer switch. George's logic was that with his newly acquired meditation techniques and my natural ability to see auras, that together we might come up with something unusual. And if we didn't, at least it was something to do.

Our experiments added a whole new slant to the word unusual.

Pammy found us there, sitting on the bed cross-legged, projecting numbers and letters. George did the transmitting. He'd drop into alpha, and when I saw his normally greenish-yellow aura change to pale blue, I closed my eyes. George then touched my forehead, concentrating on first one number or letter, then moving to sets of two or three at a time. A few seconds after I closed my eyes, I actually saw the numbers and letters loom up in the same way as the word *was* had appeared. Seeing letters floating in my mind's eye wasn't new to me. It happened a lot when I was listening to music with my eyes closed. What was different about this was that I was receiving things that someone was thinking of and attempting to transmit to me. After three consecutive "guesses," all exactly correct, Pam had come in, tapping on the bedroom door first.

"Kerry?"

"Come on in, Pam."

"What are you'ns doing?"

"ESP," George said excitedly. "So far, she hasn't missed. And she's not *guessing* either. Look! I've been writing my numbers down first, so she knows I'm not bullshitting *her*. We're doing it in sets of three now. Do you know what the odds are of getting three correct?"

Pam must have had her fill of psychic phenomena. She'd been blasted with it ever since Devin had entered our lives, and she didn't seem impressed at all. "Well, I came back here to meditate. Will my presence bother your...experiments?"

"Not if we don't bother *you*," George said, then to me, "Try letters again this time, Ker. How about a three letter word...man, this is so *neat*!"

"Okay. Drop into alpha."

I waited until the yellow of concentration dropped abruptly to blue. "Okay, George, you're ready. Hit me."

"Okay, here goes. Three letters...and it's not a word either. That might be making it too easy to guess."

"I-T-A," I said, reading off what appeared as his fingers touched my forehead. Hold on...I'm sure of the I and T, but the third one is a little smoky..."

Pam jumped up from her lotus position and leapt to the floor. "I'm leaving," she muttered. "You guys are reading off my mantra, and that's supposed to be *my* secret word!"

We continued the experiments for another twenty minutes before it became boring. I began to wonder if George wasn't just a good transmitter, what with his training in meditation and mastery of the alpha state. Maybe he was being too quick to give me the credit.

"I've got to get another opinion," I told him, and left for the living room where I found Bonnie, back from the parent visit, who agreed to be a good, unbiased, willing transmitter. I explained what we were doing and how we were doing it and had her write down three numbers without showing them to me.

"Now just relax a minute, and then try it the way George was doing it."

"Kerry, I'd feel better just doing one number at a time," she said. "I don't know how to go into alpha the way George does."

"Whatever. Do the three you wrote down, one number at a time."

After the third accurate "hit" with the one number routine, we switched to two, and then tried two letters. To be honest, I was more amazed than either Bonnie or George. But also a little afraid.

"I don't fucking believe this," I groaned. "What's happening to me? I could never do this before."

"Do you think your pregnancy could have anything to do with it?" Bonnie asked casually. The idea of my being pregnant with the "Devil's" child didn't seem to worry her in the least. She'd come a long way since our exorcism of the house last month.

"I don't know, Bonnie, but you do realize this just isn't possible."

"Where's Jake?" Pam piped up. "He could use a demonstration like this."

"He's working," Bonnie said. "Night shift this week. I'd like to see that skeptic explain *this* away. Pammy, how come you don't seem surprised at this?"

"Are you kidding, man? If you'd have been around Devin as much as I was...or *him*, anyway...you wouldn't be either. It wouldn't surprise me if Kerry started levitating on the *delivery* table with *that* kid."

"Speaking of kids, Bonnie. How rude of me. How did the parent confrontation go?"

"Well, to give Jake courage, I had him stop at a phone booth, and I called my mother in Allentown first. You know, to show him how it's done. She was thrilled. Stunned at first, but then thrilled."

"But what about Jake's moth—"

"Well, his dad had already prepped her, but it was still a trip. She was really pissed at first. Wailed about the humiliation of the kid being so old before she found out...how she'd missed the first few weeks of his life. She was *really* mad at Jake because he hadn't thought she'd understand. Oh, but Adrian! She took *right* to him. I think it bothered her that she was going to have to call all those people she'd invited to the wedding and admit this *sin* in the family. She said she can't face them now, you know?"

"Yeah, I guess that would be tough for her," Pam agreed. "We did try to tell Jake to do this sooner...but look how cute Adrian is. How could anybody hate *him?*"

"Oh, she doesn't. Well, at first she tried to distance herself from him, but, well, he grows on people. And his dad made up for it. He really is elated. It's their first grandson."

Pam sighed. "So, all's well that ends well. In some cases, anyway. What about *you* Ker? When are you going to break the news to Devin?"

"When hell boils over," I said, and the two girls smiled. "No, I guess I might one of these days. Or maybe I won't. He has a new girlfriend now, remember? He'd just *love* me for an announcement like that."

"Are you sure about this girlfriend being real?"

"It's been verified by a couple sources. Kelly said everyone at the plant has seen her."

Maybe because of her, Devin was finally getting his head together. Our entire relationship seemed to have evaporated, as if it had never happened. Vanished into thin air. Just like *he* had.

Other problems began to arise that weren't as welcome as Blue or as harmless as the ESP experiments. Doors began to creak open by themselves from a tight close, and at times a presence besides Blue was obvious to all of us, though we couldn't determine whether it was any relationship to *him* or his world or if psychic doors were just open in the atmosphere.

Adrian was an unusually happy baby. Within another week, we had him "hey-hey-heying" in his crude baby sounds, just the way Devin used to. The only other words he attempted were mama and dada. I thought *any* words were pretty unusual for his age, but the hey-hey-hey was just plain comical.

Bonnie met Blue the hard way. She had put Adrian down to nap out in the den, the room that had once been a patio before walls had been added. The floor was still hard concrete under the linoleum, though. Pam, Bonnie and I were in the living room discussing the latest subject—the announcement of *it* to Devin—when Pam happened to glance out to where Adrian was sleeping.

The baby had somehow rolled over to the edge of the bed. Half his body was *off* the bed, one arm and one leg frantically flailing in the air as he suddenly burst into his baby cry. None of us could have made it out to the den in time to arrest the fall, and Adrian seemed to be as good as *on* that hard concrete floor.

Pam, first to spot him, sprang to her feet. Then, out of nowhere, the vibrating mist of purple appeared, enveloped the child for a second and then, before our disbelieving eyes, Adrian flipped back over on his stomach, cries ceasing abruptly. When Pam reached the bed, the baby lay panting, but quiet, watching the mass of Blue as it evaporated back into the corner.

"Oh, my God, my God!" Bonnie, right behind Pam, scooped up the baby and began rocking him. There was no need to. Adrian was as calm as if he'd been in her arms all along. "Oh, I don't believe it! I don't believe it! Did you see what happened? Am I going crazy in this house?"

"Well, Bonnie. Meet Blue." I smiled. "Or, I would have liked you to, but as usual, he's here one minute and gone the next."

Bonnie seemed more worked up than Adrian would have been if he had hit the floor. I lit a joint and handed it to her. "Here, Bon. Smoke this and calm down. The baby is all right."

"Yeah, but he'd be hurt or—"

"Maybe, but it didn't happen."

The joint did calm Bonnie down, and she eventually became one of Blue's staunchest defenders, especially to Jake who, upon hearing the story, chalked the whole thing up to coincidence and mass hysterics.

Morning sickness began at the end of the second week of February, and coffee, of all things, began to have a nauseous effect when I tried to drink it. This, in itself, settled the issue of whether I was actually pregnant or not. I simply could not drink coffee no matter how much I wanted to or how hard I tried. But I really didn't need that signal to point out the obvious. My slacks and jeans grew tighter, and I couldn't keep anything zipped for any length of time. Even though my job had trimmed at least fifteen pounds from my original weight, I was forced to start wearing the stretch pants that I'd worn to work at the office.

There was still no word from Devin, and I flatly refused to call him, baby or no baby.

"From the looks of you, Kerry," Pam said, "I don't think there's any doubt about it anymore."

"I know," I replied as I poured another full cup of cold coffee down the sink.

"And to think this all started with that *thing* you wear on your finger," Pam mused, shaking her head. "One week and you'ns were talking about getting married."

"And about that baby," Bonnie added.

"And a few weeks after that, he really did separate from his wife and move in. It was never a shack job, Kerry. Everyone could see that he loved you. *Him,* anyway. And while he was here, he treated you like gold. But from what you tell me, now look at Devin. Look at how unhappy he is. The miserable way he looks at the world now. His friends know something is really wrong, and so does the water plant, for that matter. Really, Kerry, how can you *not* write the book? How much more proof do you need?" Pam crossed her arms and looked at me.

"I don't know, Pam. Sometimes I get to thinking that maybe everything is a manifestation of what I *want* to believe. Even those warm flashes. How do I know what they really are?"

"Yeah? How about this kid you're carrying? Is that a figment of your belief, too? Come *on,* Ker. All the things going on around here? All the things you're doing that even *you* admit you never could do before? What about that word *was* right when he left?"

"And *I* saw Blue," Bonnie reminded me. "I believe *my* eyes, even if you don't believe *yours.*"

"And look how easy your life's become," Pam said. "Just like he promised you. You have to admit, job or no job, you haven't had to give money a second thought."

"How about those seven days he told us to wait out, and nothing happened?" I countered.

"That you *know* of," Pam shot back. "Kerry, how can you even say that? He had *told* you it was something you couldn't comprehend. He said it was something that you weren't even aware existed. That could mean anything from some arcane universal secret the world is totally blind to, to something politically sinister that the population at large isn't aware of. And how do you know that he didn't *stop* whatever it was by leaving. I mean, just on a small scale, you're forgetting what was splattered all over the headlines of every paper in the country, if not the world. That Watergate Cover-up trial came to a head the day he left. January first. How would we know what course the country might have taken if those creeps had gotten off? How do you know if he didn't have something to do with their being found guilty? And what about those *ten* tape-recorded conversations that the jury asked to hear before they made their final decision? Don't you think *that's* a little weird? Ten tapes, Ker. *Ten.* And you might want to look at the correlation of the *dates* of that whole Nixon scandal with Devin's…*his*… arrival and departure."

She paused to take a breath, thoroughly worked up. She seemed to have acquired more blind faith and loyalty for *him* through this experience than even *I* was demonstrating.

"Pam, those are all good points, but he had said to look in the local news. He wouldn't even *listen* to the headlines that morning I got the paper."

"And that was *Devin* who said that. Not *him*. I doubt that Devin even knew what he was looking for. And when Devin said that it must be on somebody's desk, well, maybe it *was*. It wouldn't be the first cover-up in history. Maybe it was suppressed by all the papers. And forgetting all these things, *he* left on that seventh day. Kerry, it sounds to me like you're starting to doubt the whole thing."

"Well, I just have this damn skeptical mind. I'm throwing at you what a reading public would throw at me if I really did write a book. There are lots of things that I, personally, can't doubt away, but only time will prove them out. I might just *quit* working and see if I really am provided for like he promised."

"Well, if I were you, Ker, I would do that anyway." Pam pulled a joint out of the stash and handed it to me. "We don't need the money, not with Jake making eleven dollars an hour, and the poor kids never see you anymore."

That much was true. My new job paid well, but the hours at this barn were outrageous. The local track had closed the racing meet for its season, and the horses were now transported to neighboring tracks for racing. Since I was the sole hotwalker for the barn, it meant my attending all races where we had a horse in, and walking them after the races. Sometimes this meant two or three horses an afternoon, and sometimes I didn't even get home until six-thirty at night. There were times when it was even later because the horses all had to be vanned back to the home stable, fed, and bedded down before I could even leave. The kids were usually dressed for bed and waiting up only to kiss me goodnight.

My day started at five in the morning, and there was no time in this schedule to try to meditate, phase out, or even try to "go." Human bullshit was simply taking up too much of my time. I was grateful for the combined efforts of Pam, Bonnie and Jake, and even Tank who had also moved into our house. All had become substitute parents while I was gone. Work had become too much a part of my waking life. I barely knew the kids anymore, even though they seemed to have made the adjustment.

Sleeping quarters were a little tight, to say the least. Bonnie, Jake, and Adrian shared the den. Pam and Tank squeezed themselves together on the living room couch, and I still slept in the beanbag. Nobody who'd tried to sleep in my back bedroom ever repeated it.

Bonnie and Jake had tried, at first. Jake felt it was ridiculous for a full private bedroom with a queen-sized bed to go to waste while everyone packed into the front of the house like sardines in a can. Bonnie was the first to complain because she couldn't sleep due to the sound of continual scratching sounds coming from the closet. Jake, of course, attributed this to mice, but when he received a sharp poke in the ribs and awoke to find both wife and child snuggled together on the other side of the bed, he removed the family from the private bedroom and set up quarters in the den.

Pam's previous experience with the "monkey" trying to smother her was the prime reason for her evacuation from the room, and no amount of coaxing from Tank could convince her otherwise.

Sometimes I wondered if the presence was only Blue playing his well-intentioned touch games, oblivious to the fright he was causing his unsuspecting victims, or whether we had another problem in the house. Devin had written in the original tablet, that the doors being opened before their time could wreak havoc on the mind. But regardless of everyone else's reasons, mine was simply that I couldn't sleep back in the room that was so full of memories of *him*. The back bedroom, with its privacy and closable door, remained empty.

Uncle Joe called one evening with a problem of his own. His wife was going to be hospitalized indefinitely, which left the three children in need of full-time supervision. He needed a live-in nanny. Pam and I were first choice on his list for both housekeeper and housemother. Pam, who was tired of her late hours at the photo lab, talked Tank into taking the live-in position with her. Tank kept his job at the track but returned each day to Uncle Joe's, and their move opened up a little more space in my overcrowded house. In the evenings, when Uncle Joe was home, they drifted back to my house where apparently life was more exciting.

In the meantime, I'd begun to practice some private experiments by myself. Tarot cards that I held to my forehead produced vividly colorful images of the pictures on the cards. When I looked to see which card I'd pulled from the deck, it was always the card with the image I'd seen. When I got bored with that, I threw numbers in a hat and found I could call them without looking at them first.

One afternoon Jake sat watching me, scoffing that only coincidence could explain so many accurate hits. I picked up the nearest thing to me, a saltine cracker box on the coffee table that Jake himself had placed there along with some cheese. The box contained both large capital letters and small ingredient print. Facing Bonnie and Jake, I held the box so that the small print was directly in front of their eyes. Then I ran my finger backward along the list of ingredients. When I called off letters which were words from end to front, Jake was finally convinced. He tested further by thinking his own letters and numbers and touching my forehead, and for once he had no explanation for the accuracy.

For that matter, neither did I. There was no hunch or guesswork involved. The characters simply appeared in front of my mind's eye.

"Just how far along *are* you?" Bonnie asked.

"How would I know?" I wasn't elated over these astonishing feats. I was just plain scared. "Guessing...maybe two and a half months?"

"Well, we'll save the bassinet for you. Adrian won't be able to fit in it by the time you need it. That is, if you intend to keep the baby."

You'd have thought that walking horses, mucking stalls, and raking heavy sand at the end of each day around the hotwalking machine, plus the long hours, would have caused a miscarriage. But as the time passed, I only seemed to grow stronger and bigger. There was no doubt that I was pregnant. The only doubts I harbored were those regarding the question of whether Devin Drew should even be told. I *had* promised to tell him if it happened, yet I still couldn't bring myself to call him.

On the 20th of February, I had put in one of those extremely long days. Four races and four horses to walk after they raced. Additional time to stall the four upon return to the home track. A couple of winners that day dragged the evening out even longer, for after the horses were stalled, a barn celebration party ensued. I was grateful to see Tank finally pull up at 9:30, a very welcome rescue squad. I was exhausted.

"We got tired of waiting for you to call," he said as I plopped into the passenger seat of my own car. "You've got company at home, but I ain't allowed to tell you who. It's supposed to be a surprise. There's more good news too, I think, anyway. Someone called you. That Devin guy."

My heart almost stopped. "Did he say what he wanted?"

"I don't know. You'll have to ask your sister."

The house was a mass of confusion when we walked in. Lana was sitting there with Mark, both of them grinning like the Cheshire Cat. Also seated in the living room were Bonnie and Adrian, Pam and George.

I grinned at Lana and gave Mark an enthusiastic but most embarrassing hug. He squirmed out of my grip with twelve-year-old indignity. Lana spoke for him.

"Mark's allowed to stay over this weekend," she announced, glancing at her beaming little brother. "He nagged her and nagged her."

"Far *out*, Mark!" I hugged him again, and this time he didn't fight it. "How ya been, buddy?"

"Oh, bored at home. I got a new girlfriend and a new game we can play, and I have a whole bunch of stuff to tell you."

"Wow, that's *great!* You'll be over Friday, then?"

"Yup!" He made a series of victorious hand gestures, clasping his fingers together and waving both hands over his head.

"Ahem," Pam said. "Do you want to hear about your phone call?"

"Yeah, I sure do." I turned to her. Before she could continue, the phone rang.

Pammy, closest to the phone, grabbed the receiver, held her hand to her other ear to block out the room noise, and then beckoned to me. "It's Devin," she whispered, handing me the receiver.

I snatched both pieces of the phone and numbly transported my body to the back bedroom. It had been almost a month.

"Hey, what's happening?" he greeted me.

"Devin!" was all I could say.

"What was all the noise in the background? Sounds like you've got a full house up there."

"Yeah, Lana's here visiting with Mark, and my house, these days, is a full house with *no* visitors."

"Mark? Lola's kid? I thought he wasn't allowed over."

"So did I. I didn't get any details yet, because I just walked in. There's a lot of confusion right now. Pam has a new boyfriend, and he lives here when they aren't down at my uncle's. That's a long story. Plus I have Bonnie, Jake and the baby living here, too."

"Oh, she had it finally, huh? What did the parents have to say?"

"Believe it or not, they just recently found out. They took it pretty much the way we expected them to."

"I'll bet. Oh, and speaking of babies…what's the story on you?"

I'd been hoping the idea wouldn't even cross his mind. "Well, Devin," I said finally. "I've been vacillating over whether or not to even tell you about it. I know you have a girlfriend, and the way things are—"

"Forget the girlfriend. That was a moment of temporary insanity. So…so you *are* pregnant."

"Well, there's been no medical verification. But if I miss the next period I'll be about three months along, I guess."

"Kerry, do you *think* you are? It's cool. You can tell me. I just want to know. I mean, if you are, we'll take it from there."

"Devin, I don't think you need to concern yourself about it. I don't think it's yours."

There was a long silence as Devin apparently digested this information. A statement such as the one I'd made would ordinarily be taken that another man was responsible. Devin didn't take it that way.

"I was afraid of that. You think it might be *his*, huh."

"There's no maybe to it. I can't explain on the phone. It's pretty involved, and I have company out there waiting for me."

I could hear his labored breathing over the wire. Finally, he said, "Kerry, we've been over this before. If it's *his*, and I don't see how it could be if you've carried it *this* far, but if it *is* his, you won't carry it to full term. Don't you understand that?"

"Why do you keep saying that? Don't you think I could raise *his* child?"

"Kerry, I really don't believe they'd allow it to enter this world. You know what that means? They won't let it be born. Not with *him* back there now."

"Well, I guess that remains to be seen, Devin, because it *is* his child. You wouldn't believe what's been going on around here."

"Like what?"

I told him. The ease of the jobs, the money flowing through the house, the doors opening by themselves and Blue's rescue of Adrian. The unnerving psychic ability I'd acquired almost overnight.

His reaction surprised me. "Well. I see you're kicking some dust in my face."

"What do you mean?"

"Never mind. That was uncalled for. Sounds like old Blue is having a field day with the houseful of humans you've taken in." I could feel his smile over the phone. "Are *you* still afraid of him?'"

"No, not at all," I assured him. "I've gotten rather attached to him. Anyway, how are *you* doing?"

"Oh, not bad. I've been slowly getting my head together. And you were right. I can still reach *him*. It's just back the way it was before he…came. I was just blowing my cool too much over his leaving to accept that. And blaming you for his leaving. I'm sorry about that. Anyhow, I'd appreciate it if you'd let me know how this pregnancy thing goes."

"Okay, but I am keeping it," I said emphatically. "You might as well understand that right now. Yours or his, I'm keeping it. You still want to know?"

"It's like I just told you. If it *is* his, it won't live to see the third dimension. And if it's mine, yes, I do still want to know. I'd want to contribute to the support and be a father to him."

"Even finances are no problem," I said. "I hope you don't think I'm looking for child support. That's not why I told you."

"I know you're not, but it will still be my child and my responsibility."

"Damn, Devin…I sure am happy to hear you sound so back together. I was so worried about you."

"Believe it or not, I was a little worried myself. Then, right after this past full moon, I don't know what happened. I never did reach him, but I woke up feeling more at peace with myself. It's been steadily uphill since that day. Anyhow, I know you have guests, so I'll let you go. Just keep me posted, okay?"

It was such a relief to know that he'd come through okay. He sounded so much like the old Devin that I could feel the emotions tugging at me again. But I had to put that aside and get out to see my latest visitors. I had been rude long enough.

"What the hell?" Lana smirked at me when I came back into the living room. "We've been sitting here since seven-thirty waiting for you to come home from work, and when you finally get here you get on the phone for a half hour?"

"I'm really, really sorry, you guys. That was Devin."

"Devin?" Her eyes narrowed. It was plain that she hadn't changed her opinion of him. "Well, really…we gotta go. I just wanted to bring him over and let you know. If you *want* this little monster—"

"Boy, do I ever. Hey, Mark. You could go to the races with me on Saturday. You can ride in the horse van with me. Not too many people ever see the backside of the track. Just the windows and window dressing up front. Here's your big opportunity to track in shit and roll in mud."

He laughed with delight. "All *right* ! Can I ride the horses?"

"Well, I don't know about *that*, but you can pet them and feed them."

"Hey!" Lana said. "Has Devin *been* calling you?"

"No. That was the first time in a month. And of all the times, it had to be Mark's first trip over here."

"Oh. I was going to *say*." She rose to go. " Because he sure doesn't have any friendly words for *us*."

"Really, Lana? Still? He sounded okay to me. Pretty good, actually."

"Do you think you two might get back together again?"

"No. So…okay. See you Friday, Mark? And Lana…thank your mom for me, will you? I really appreciate this."

"Well, okay, I will, but it's only fair to warn you. She only relented because of Mark. Not that I agree with her, but you know my mom. I really didn't think she'd hold a grudge this long."

"Well, still, it was nice of her. Tell your dad and brother I said hi."

"Will do! *They* aren't mad at you. My mom will come around eventually."

"I hope so. Thanks for bringing him by. See you Friday, Mark."

They had no sooner driven away when Uncle Joe came to the door, complete with kids, booze, ice, cokes and cigarettes. Scotty, my old friend, stopped by to introduce me to his new girlfriend. She was a sweetheart, and they were a very happy couple. Scotty thanked me for pushing him towards his future wife, even if I hadn't consciously meant to. I felt a relief that my friend had had a happy ending out of all this. Chris and Steve dropped in from the other side of the house, just to say hello. I looked around at the people packed into my small living room and counted heads, including Lana and Mark who had just left. All the people who'd practically evaporated from my life during the time Devin had lived here. It was almost as if I'd dreamed the whole thing. If it wasn't for the sparse furnishings, I could almost convince myself that I had. Well, that and the small embryo in my womb. That was a secret that only the immediate household knew.

And Devin. And probably *his* invisible world.

I discovered that I had changed. I no longer enjoyed the drinks Uncle Joe had brought with him, and the noise and chaos were starting to get to me. I just felt so different from all of them. I was actually relieved when everyone left, and glad to be alone when Pam took off with Tank, and Bonnie went to bed.

So much had happened since *he* had come and gone. As I sat contemplating the things still visibly here, including those marks on my arm which were as clear as they'd been the day they arrived, that familiar heat wave crossed my ankle and circled my foot. He had done this so many times when he was here that when it happened now, there was never any doubt that it was him trying to get my attention. I knew he was here now trying to tell me something. I was sure it had to do with the baby. These changes taking place in me were no accident.

On impulse, I pulled a Tarot card from the deck without looking at it and closed my eyes. A vivid image floated up in my mind. *Ace of Wands*. I hadn't even held it up to my forehead. I turned it over. Ace of Wands.

No, none of this was any accident. Something was happening to my mind, and it was getting stronger. Something or someone was trying hard to get my attention and keep it. I felt the flash of heat again and looked up at the digital clock radio on the refrigerator. *Ten o'clock*. I knew who it was.

I did try. I tried so hard to connect with him, but I just couldn't relax. I finally gave up and fell into a defeated rest, frustrated to tears. *He* had been here, I was sure of that. Why hadn't I been able to reach him?

As I started to drift off to sleep, a voice said something in my mind's ear. Not surprised by anything anymore, I groggily reached for the pen I kept near the journal. It had been a female voice, gentle and clear and…even familiar. Not a voice I knew from this world, but familiar just the same. It came and went so fast that it was over before I'd even realized I'd heard it.

Keep an eye on your nines

The message made no sense to me. Even when I awoke at five and sat pondering it before work, I couldn't come up with anything to connect its meaning to.

I thought about it all morning as I walked those horses until they finished drinking water and thought about it as I hooked them to the machine to continue their walk. I thought about the whole experience from beginning to end, from my first conversation with Devin in the office to the present. I just couldn't hide my head in the sand any longer. I was pregnant with a child that only my love for *him* and stubborn pride would have me keep.

I was a coward. I knew damn well the way home. It was there, beckoning to me every time I closed my eyes. I knew he was there, and I knew that door led to his world. If I could only overcome my terror and get there, *he* would set me straight on what to do about this child. I knew he was patiently waiting for me to work up the courage to find him.

That purple hole at the top of the volcano-like tunnel. The doorway between my reality and his. It had taken me there once by accident, just from staring at it. The night Devin had arrived back from his Thanksgiving trip. I'd even come back with the marks on my arm, as if to prove to me that it had been real.

He'd promised he'd be waiting if I ever managed to make it through that hole at the top.

Well, I knew now as I walked, that this was the end of the line. This was *it*. Indecision was over, and I had to take a step in some direction.

It was either shit, or get off the pot.

13 Bonnie was still sleeping when I walked into my house that Friday morning. February 21st, 1975. I had been wearing a tampon during my working hours just in case I got "surprised" at work. I was still wearing it when I turned on the radio to a low volume so that any other house noises wouldn't distract me from my mission.

I pulled the beanbag into a living room corner and sank into it, sitting the way Devin had shown me. I closed my eyes, let my muscles go limp, and then began taking some very deep breaths, holding them, and exhaling slowly.

The radio chose that moment to begin a series of songs having to do with *home*.

Quicksilver assured me that I was only three or four feet from home. Blind Faith couldn't find their way home. Ten Years After was going home. The Moody Blues would never be able to go home anymore. Deep Purple was seeing pictures of home but claiming no one was up there, that it was an illusion. Dr John assured me that there was no place like home, and Grand

Funk Railroad promised to be my captain, and get me closer to my home.

Then the Moody Blues told me to rise, to let them see me. Assured me that I would find my way. They were trying to find me, and I was supposed to leave this crazy life behind me. Don't doubt it, they said. Just do it.

I was acutely aware of these lyrics as I continued my deep breathing. Slowing myself down. Raising my vibrations. All the instructions *he* had ever given me came back in a flood of memories. And then, suddenly, there it was.

Straight up that bluish-purple funnel tunnel, and beyond that…that deep blue opening at the top.

My heart was in my throat. I still remembered the panic I'd felt the last time I'd almost gone through. My heart and pulse began to pound at a much slower pace. I was aware that I was still breathing, but the breaths were shallow and few.

I'd been this far on a conscious level so I wasn't afraid yet. I fixed my attention on the hole and watched it loom closer and larger with each passing second. In recent past attempts I'd learned that to actually pass through that opening at the top I had to try to descend, not ascend. Trying to float backward, away from it, always brought me even closer to the rim. Either time and space ran backward in this volcano-like tunnel, or the laws of the physical universe were in reverse. My success today was going to depend on my ability to fall backward.

I took my last conscious deliberate deep breath and then took the backward plunge, facing the hole and never taking my eyes off it. As the opening got further away, I suddenly found myself just beneath the rim but, it seemed like that was as far as I would be able to go. Then, unexpectedly, I plummeted *up* and through. I emerged in a colorless cloud of fog. No blue sky. No yellow sky. No yacht club. No anything.

Where am I?

I turned to look back through the hole and should have seen the bottom. Instead, the tunnel was level. Level with my vision, so level I could have walked across and through it to the other end until I came to a wall…*not the bottom of a well.* I was too absorbed in my mysterious surroundings to give any thought toward my body, still sitting in the room I'd left behind. I wasn't bodiless, though. I could see myself from the chest down, the same way I would if I was back *there* in *that* body.

The hole. I was on the other side of the hole. I had made it through, but where was *he?* Where was *anything?*

Where was the rest of this world that he'd urged me to find?

That thought had no sooner crossed my mind when I suddenly found myself up on a high ledge viewing a landscape that looked like it had been painted with neon pastels. The hole was gone. Before me stretched a vast terrain of chocolate-colored mountains peaking against a lemon-yellow sky.

It was breathtaking. Below, crystal-blue rivers gorged rust-colored rock and lime meadows. No view from any airplane back *there* could ever compare to this vista. My fear was completely gone, replaced by curiosity and awe. He had told me this would happen, that once I got there I would question how I ever could have been afraid.

The ledge I stood on was actually a foot-wide ridge that jutted out from a tall mountain and ran the length of it for as far as the eye could see. It was so narrow that the thought of falling crossed my mind, and I immediately lost my balance and tumbled off. Panic was short-lived, though. I remembered what he'd told me about how quickly thoughts manifested here, and I suddenly stopped in midair, weightless and calm. Then I fixed my eyes on the ledge and purposely floated back to it.

My entire being was filled with a sense of both wonder and nostalgia. Why had I been thinking like such a big coward? This fear thing was bullshit. I lived here too.

What *was* becoming vague and unfamiliar was the memory of the world I'd left behind. Was *that* really the dream, and was I just now waking up? And if so, *where* was *he*?

My car would sure beat walking all over hell's half acre looking for him, I thought, unsure of what to do next.

Instantly I found myself behind the wheel of a car very similar to my Rambler, driving down a dirt road somewhere in what I would call "the country." The brilliant scenery and sparkling colors of daylight were gone. Somehow, I had brought in the *night*.

A part of me was completely familiar with this road and the direction I was taking. A kind of déjà vu. After what seemed like only seconds, I pulled up to a luminous lawn that glowed the color of violet. Unlike my first visit back in June when it had been a luminous radio-dial green, I wondered what the color change meant. I parked the car, just as if I did this every day. I knew exactly where I was, and in that instant a feeling of apprehension rippled through me. The luminous lawn stretched upwards, leading to a bone-white mansion perched at the top of the swell. It too glowed like the glow-in-the-dark toys back in the third dimension, but it glowed pastel white, not eerie green.

He lived here.

When I got out of the car, I found the air refreshingly brisk, like dry ice, and not uncomfortably cold. *So much for the fire and flames.* My gaze swept over what appeared to be several acres of tall grass and then up to the mansion at the crest of the slope. Majestic pillars of gleaming white seemed to beckon me closer to the wide veranda. The mansion was at least three stories tall. Trees and shrubbery around it all glowed their own phosphorous illumination, as though everything was plugged in. A full moon was up there, also pastel white and the sky was a deep-purple blackboard speckled with glittering, winking, pinprick points of sparkling white light.

Was this for real? Or was this a reality I'd constructed when I'd passed through the opening at the top of the tunnel? Did it really matter? I was finally here.

As I stood there, momentarily unsure of what to do next, I saw *him*. He didn't even resemble Devin. *He* no longer wore the body of Devin Drew, but I knew that face. I'd seen it a few times before, once in a Walgreens parking lot, and once captured in the Polaroid picture I'd destroyed. Twice when he'd flashed it during the peyote night. Once on my first visit to this house back in June. Hesitantly, I waved.

He caught sight of me then and walked toward me as casually as he had in the lobby of the water plant. He didn't appear surprised to see me. There was no remark that I'd finally made it, no affectionate hugs in happy reunion.

Something seemed to be wrong. He wasn't even smiling. The serious edge became more apparent as he neared me.

"Hey, lady. You coming in?" he asked in the voice I'd grown so familiar with back there.

"Is it okay?" *What was wrong with him?*

"Why wouldn't it be?" He gave me an odd look, as though I *did* come here often, unconsciously as I slept. Maybe he was just used to seeing me in that unconscious state, but that didn't explain why something seemed to be wrong. "Go ahead in. I'll be along shortly."

As if I showed up here every day.

He didn't need to direct me to the usual entrance to the house. As he waved and left in a direction away from the house, I walked up the sloping hill, passed the wide veranda with its towering pillars, and proceeded along the side of the house towards the rear until I came to the side door.

I opened it and walked in, unannounced, also as if I did this all the time.

The first jolt I received, after the déjà vu effect of the interior, was the recognition of three males and an older man whose very air of authority permeated the room. He sat in a large throne-like chair, almost like Gerald's, but the velvet material was black, not red. The other three males sat on a couch-like apparatus, and all three turned when I walked in, nodded, and waved. One of the men was black and, with a second jolt, I realized I could call these three by name. They didn't even remotely resemble Devin Drew, but I recognized them by their features that had once molded into the face of the instrument they'd used now and then when mobility was required. I felt a wave of relief that they were here and longed to join them, but I knew I couldn't. I must not forget the serious purpose for which this trip had been made.

Nothing was unfamiliar. Nobody acted surprised to see me. The only person I not only recognized but felt an overwhelming affection for was the woman who had rescued us on the yacht.

She sat in a chair by a doorway that faced the side door I'd entered. When she held out her open arms to me, I ran to her and hugged her with relief. I knew that I loved this golden-haired lady very much. I knew that, in human terms, she was his maternal authority. My sense of relief deepened to a feeling of belonging. I was home now, and I was confident that everything would be resolved.

She released me gently and beckoned me to follow her into the hallway which was just outside of the doorway. It was as though she'd been both expecting me and patiently waiting.

"Come with me," she said in a musical voice that reminded me of chimes. "My son is waiting for us upstairs. Together we will do what must be done."

"What's wrong with him?" I asked, sure that she would straighten this whole mess out. "He barely spoke to me. And he looks so upset."

She didn't answer, just led me across the hall and up a staircase.

At the landing was a large old-fashioned bathroom with an spotless claw tub. We made a sharp left, and I stopped to look over the railing at the hallway below. My fingers trailed over the varnished banister, and I marveled at the solidity of this house. Then another sharp left and down the hallway, which led to the rear of the house. There were numerous doors, but she turned into the first one on the right. I followed her into an immaculate white room. The only furniture in it was a small white cot. The pure, brilliant whiteness of the room reminded me of a hospital. There was a huge picture window that overlooked the rolling front lawn, and the sky it reflected was daytime blue, robin's-egg blue... not yellow, or black and starry as it should have been. The room had an antiseptic, clinical aroma to it.

A black nurse in a crisp white uniform and cap sat on a chair beside the cot. She held a long, gleaming, silver hypodermic needle with a sharp point. She smiled sweetly at me and gestured that I sit down on the cot.

With a wave of shock, I suddenly comprehended why I had been brought up here. I looked at the smiling blond lady and saw only sympathy and warm concern in her eyes. She didn't appear to realize *why* I was frightened, but she did seem to know that I was afraid.

"There is no pain here," she said gently.

As she spoke, *he* walked in.

His expression was no different than it had been that final week of silence back on earth. For a moment, I thought it was because the problem he had carried then had not been resolved. He looked at the nurse, the blond lady, and the needle, and his eyes narrowed with seething anger. There was no question in my mind that he'd instantly understood what was about to take place.

"Devin!" I cried frantically. "Tell them! Tell them I'm *not!* Tell them I'm not *pregnant!*"

All three watched me silently as I backed away from them. Away from the cot and the smiling nurse. Away from the beautiful blond lady...even away from *him*. My fright must have been very obvious to them. My mind searched frantically for some excuse to get away from them. For the first time since I'd arrived, I was totally paralyzed with terror. They were going to take my baby, and *he* either wasn't going to stop them, or wasn't *able* to. I had to think fast.

"Wait a minute!" I cried desperately, my voice betraying my fear and panic. "I can prove it. *Please!* I can *prove* it! This is a terrible mistake!"

Without waiting for anyone's permission, I bolted from the room and tore into the bathroom. I yanked the tampon out and plunged it into the toilet.

No blood.

Then I gasped. The tampon was beginning to swell, swell to the size of a huge coiled snake. And then, before my eyes, I saw the beginnings of blood appear. First at the tip, then spreading halfway down the tampon.

How could they have injected that needle into me? Even as disjointed as the events were, how could I have not known if that needle had pierced my skin?

I could see no further solution for me and my baby than to run.

Down the staircase and through the door I'd entered, along the side of the house and across the huge lawn. Out to the road where I'd left my car.

Nobody tried to follow me. They'd remained behind as if a chase was completely unnecessary. As if they'd accomplished their purpose somehow, before I'd bolted from the room.

The car sat where I left it, but even in my panic, I knew it would not take me where I needed to go. I needed to find that tunnel.

No sooner had that decision flashed through my mind, I found myself back on that high, narrow ledge, this time with no fear whatsoever of falling. I heard someone call my name and turned toward the sound. *He* was stepping quickly towards me on the same ledge. Coming for me. Was he going to take me back?

"Lady! Wait!"

I couldn't wait. I couldn't take the chance. Without the slightest hesitation, I jumped.

Jumped into the air.

14

A scream welcomed me splat back into the third dimension. Back to my safe beanbag. Back to my living room. Like ice water thrown in my face I realized, with a chill, that the scream had been my own.

"Kerry?"

I looked over, dazed and in a mild shock. Bonnie was watching me intently. The radio was playing softly in the background. Quicksilver singing about trying to find a sign on the mountainside, and finally realizing that home was a frame of mind.

"Kerry, what happened? You screamed! You were just sitting there like you were dead one minute, and the next minute you screamed."

As disconnected as that world seemed to have been, I was sure there were no gaps in my memory as to what had happened. At no time had I been asleep from the moment I closed my eyes. Yet, here I sat, fully alert, looking at Bonnie who sat nervously on the end of the couch, patting Adrian to keep him calm.

"Oh, Bonnie! Oh my God!" I shot to my feet. "They're going to take the baby!" I dashed into the bathroom and yanked out the real tampon and threw it in the toilet. My toilet. No blood. Not a sign of it.

I began to breathe easier. There was no blood. I waited a minute to make sure it didn't suddenly appear the way it had back *there,* but nothing happened. No blood. No swelling. No cramps. No reason to fear what I had escaped from. I had gotten out of there in time.

I pulled up my sleeve. No marks. No bruises and no puncture holes in my arm. No additional "tattoos." With a deep sigh of relief and more than a little trembling, I raced back out to Bonnie. There was one other test I had to attempt.

"Bonnie! Think of any two numbers. Any two."

"You mean from one to ten?" She seemed confused by my behavior.

"Any two!" I nearly screamed.

She concentrated and I closed my eyes. Two clear ones floated up in the black spaces of my mind.

"Is it…eleven?" I asked hesitantly.

She nodded. "Jesus Christ, Kerry. I can't figure out how you—"

"Never mind. Oh, Christ! Thank God! Thank *God* I got away in time."

Bonnie half laughed, a nervous titter. "Kerry, you're not making a whole lot of sense. Away from *where* ?"

I was too shaken *not* to talk about it. They were going to take that kid!

There was no doubt in my mind that that had been their sole intention. And *he* had done nothing to try to stop them. I told her the whole story, and she listened, wide-eyed.

"Kerry, is it possible that this was a dream?"

"No way! No fucking way. Bonnie, I had my hand on that banister and it was cold and slippery and *real.* Solid. I was wide awake the whole time. Devin was right. *He* was right! They *did* try! They *did!*"

"Damn." Bonnie looked down at the carpet, still jostling Adrian who lay placidly across her knees. "I guess this isn't a good time to tell you about *my* dream, then." She sighed. "But it definitely *was* a dream."

"Aw, Jesus, Bonnie, what? Tell me!"

"Well, it was probably nothing. I'm sure there isn't any connection to what happened to you. But I was sleeping out there in the den with Adrian. I know this sounds weird, but in my *dream* I was also sleeping out there with him. In the dream, I woke up suddenly, and there were three men standing at the foot of my bed. They looked oriental...slanted eyes, olive skin...and they were looking at Adrian. I knew right then and there that my baby was what they'd come for. Adrian. Then as I was sitting up, still asleep, I woke up and they weren't standing there anymore. So I know it was a dream."

"Bonnie, this third dimension *is* a dream. I found that out about thirty minutes ago. Do you know that while I was there, I could only recall fragments of *this* world?"

Bonnie got up and switched off the radio, paused for a second and then turned back to me. "These songs are really getting on my nerves. Could we get out of here for a while? There's such a weird feeling in this house right now. I'd...I'd feel better if we could just go for a ride or something."

"Sure. Sure, we can. Pam asked me to pick her up at Uncle Joe's house later. We could just go do that now. He should be home from the fire station by now."

"Okay...anything." She seemed relieved.

I was still pretty shook up myself, and even getting into my car produced electric flashes of that too-real trip home. It had *not* been a dream. No more of a dream than this reality I was living in now. I had never lost consciousness. I had made the trip because of the baby, and they had acted like they were going to relieve me of...a burden. Except for *him.* He had looked royally pissed off, but I thought I knew why. It hadn't only been *my* child who was in danger of extinguishment. I still believed that he'd had no choice in their decision.

When we picked up Pammy, we headed directly for the local Burger King where I could talk freely to the only two who really understood what was going on.

I related the story to Pam, who listened soberly and intently. Then, Bonnie added *her* dream, insisting that there was some kind of parallel in that both instances were connected to some form of kidnapping. Baby kidnapping. Pam was far more interested in my sojourn.

"Well, if they *do* take it," she said finally, "you'd be better off, wouldn't you, Ker?" She stirred her iced tea with her straw and looked up to me. "You *can't* raise that kid *human.* And you might not be able to handle him anyway."

"Devin said they would take it," I reminded her, still trembling from the experience. "I think they can do that from *there*. God, what if it was just a flat-out warning that they *are* going to take it? Why did he look so upset, and why couldn't he stop them? Pam, he was upset when I first saw him there, and he seemed kind of abrupt, but he really wasn't directing his anger at me. It was like his hands were tied and like he didn't have the last word, and definitely like he was pissed off about it."

"Maybe he did fight for it...and lost. He always spoke of some superior over him. That old man he always referred to."

"Yeah. His old man. I believe I saw him, but you know what, Pam? I've got the weirdest feeling that the things I saw and heard there were not really the way it was. This is going to be hard to explain, but I got the strangest impression that whatever is beyond the rim of that hole is so nonphysical that my own mind could only translate what was there into physical terms. Symbols. Real, tangible houses and cars and scenery. I'm not taking away from the reality of them but, like an interpreter, my mind was taking a nonphysical event and creating symbols that were earth-oriented so that I'd understand what was happening. I was seeing things from a third-dimensional perspective. What I saw and believed to be the old man seemed like a very regal figure, but I don't think he *has* any permanent form, and I don't think *he, him,* does either. As if they wore costumes I could relate to."

"How did the old man treat you?"

"Like a daughter or daughter-in-law who had just been out at the local supermarket for a few minutes. He looked up and smiled when I walked in, and so did those three guys that I strongly suspect were Erick, Christian and Devin. Not Devin Drew. The Devin *we* knew. They were watching some tube that I seriously doubt was a television. Probably watch this world all the time, and God only knows, they probably don't need any device to do it. And that blond-haired lady. She didn't act like she was going to do anything to hurt me. She acted like she was doing me a favor. Well, it would be like if *you* were pregnant and went to a doctor for an abortion. You'd be scared, and the nurse would be gentle and treat you like she understood your fear, but she'd assure you that it would all be over very soon, and that you'd be very relieved for the assistance."

"Yeah." Pam looked at Bonnie and then back at me. "Like you should have been overflowing with gratitude."

"But I don't *want* to be relieved of a burden."

"Well, maybe they're right, Ker. How are you going to raise a kid like this? You can't send him to a school for humans. You just can't. He'd kill you for sure."

"He'd blow his stack, all right," Bonnie put in. "But how about one of those freedom schools? You know, like in *Billy Jack*? He might fit in there."

"No *humans*," Pam repeated emphatically. "Freedom schools are full of humans, too. Without *him* here to raise his kid *his* way, we're talking, second choice, a private school for nonhumans...and quite frankly, I don't know of one. At best, some kind of tutor, and no human could teach this kind of kid. For Pete's sake, Ker, look what *you* are able to do, just because you're *carrying* it."

Bonnie suddenly kicked Pam under the table, and we looked up to see a woman taking in the whole conversation. She sat at the next table, chomping on her Whopper with no expression, but she was watching us intently, all ears.

"Good grief," Pam groaned. "Check her out! Wonder how much of this she's heard."

"Oh, fuck her," Bonnie retorted. "She's taking it all in like Burger King staged it for customer entertainment. Come on." She lifted Adrian up and over her shoulder. "Let's get out of here."

Later that night, when Pam and I were alone, she asked me again about my trip. Had it verified anything for me one way or the other?

"I know it wasn't a dream, Pam. I went through that hole wide awake. I remember all of it."

"Well, if you made it through consciously, which you obviously did, what did it do for the doubts you were having?"

"It's real, Pam," I said slowly. "It's there. It's exactly as he said, and more. Cold. Beautiful…oh, Pam, before all that stuff started in the mansion, I was never so dumbstruck with the beauty and color of a scenic view. And what he said about thoughts…you wouldn't believe how fast something will happen the minute the thought pops into your head. It happens instantly. But it *is* there. And it's real. I don't have any more doubts. Everything he said turned out to be true. I knew those people there, and they obviously knew me. They acted like I'd been away at a class on physical existence and had just come in from school. He was there, and there was real. So I guess what he said about my belonging to that world…I guess there is something to that."

The radio, which had been playing softly in the background as we talked, started a song from the Moody Blues. Pam and I just stared at each other as the singer's first words were…*Now you know that you are real*, and went on to tell me to show my friends that he and I belonged to the same world. And now that I was free from the doubts, they said, I could live the rest of my life in ease and know that eternity was waiting for me. There were doorways that could lead me there.

These lyrics, considering what Pam and I had been discussing, were completely outside any realm of coincidence. It was from an album entitled *On the Threshold of a Dream.*

15 Working with the horses the following morning, I had not forgotten the world I'd plunged into yesterday. I doubted I would ever forget it. I was glad for an especially busy morning. It meant that I could walk the fifth horse constantly while four were hooked to the machine for twenty to forty minutes. I needed to keep moving, and I needed to walk. I was looking forward to getting off and picking up Mark. It would be a welcome change of pace to have his company again.

While four horses occupied the machine, I had to keep track of the time, remove one horse from the machine, and attach the one I was currently walking. The grooms were a big help with the switches since I could only handle one horse at a time. When that process was completed, I would return to the front of the barn for the next horse.

It was easy to lose track of the times each horse was to come off, especially with the things I had on my mind. As I held the last horse in from the track, the groom squeezed the big yellow coral sponge between the horse's ears and began to wash the horse's face and head. These daily baths generally took five to ten minutes, and this horse was one of the easier ones to handle. My mind drifted out to the hotwalking machine, and I tried to remember what time I had hooked up the last horse.

"This one only walks thirty minutes," the groom told me, tossing the sponge into the bucket and picking up the sweat scraper. He began scraping the horse in wide strokes. "He may drink for ten minutes, so don't leave him on that ring for more than another twenty. You'll be walking him, of course, until he's finished drinking."

I took the horse and began to walk, still trying to remember when I had hooked up that last horse. Just my luck, the trainer came around the corner to find at least two of the horses dry enough to take off. I stopped my horse at his water bucket that was hanging on the rail, and he bent to drink thirstily.

"How long has McCally been on that ring?" Mr. Lopez bellowed.

My mind fished weakly for an approximate time.

McCally's groom appeared with shank in hand. "He can come off now. I'll get him since she's got her hands full. He paused and looked intently at me. "She put him on about nine."

I smiled at him, grateful for the rescue.

Another groom appeared. "And mine comes off ten minutes after yours. He went on at ten after nine."

Mr. Lopez shrugged, accepting their made-up timetable. "Then the third one went on about twenty after nine."

I was grateful to both grooms for saving my neck. I had no idea what time the other horses were put on, much less which horse was which. Walking in that endless circle, they all looked the same to me.

"Get McCally off," the trainer told the groom gruffly. "And if the second one went on at ten after, he's been walking thirty minutes already."

"But I didn't put him *on!*" I protested. "I've been walking this one, and I'm not the only one hooking these horses up there."

"That one's done drinking," Mr. Lopez growled. "Frank. Get your horse off so she can put this one on. Juan! Get your last horse out here. I want him walked this morning. The shedrow still needs raked, and I'd like to get out of here at a decent hour." He stalked off down the shedrow.

Frank made an obscene gesture at the trainer's back, gave me a sympathetic pat on the shoulder, and went out to retrieve his horse.

I snapped the one I'd been walking onto the machine, in no mood for grouchy trainers, and sick and tired of the whole job in general. Gloomily, I started back towards the barn.

"We need another hotwalker," I grumbled to Frank as I passed his stalls. "I'm supposed to be finished, and did you hear Lopez hollering at Juan? Juan's horse didn't even *go* to the track, so he waits until now to decide he needs to be walked anyway? I can't keep track of the times these horses are on the ring and still be out front taking new horses."

"Just round it off to fifteen minutes the next time you find yourself in that predicament. I'll keep track of my own four horses and so will Juan. If you get mixed up, just ask one of us."

"Okay, thanks."

I walked down the shedrow to get Juan's horse, and I heard Frank call to me: "Just keep an eye on your nines! They've only got a few minutes left."

"Okay, okay," I muttered. I reached Juan's stalls where he had the cold horse haltered and waiting. He took the shank from me and attached it to the halter.

"If I'm out front holding these bathing beauties, how am I supposed to know what time the grooms put horses on the ring?" I demanded, feeling a bit sorry for myself.

Juan shrugged, and I continued on down the shedrow with his horse. Keep an eye on your nines, Frank had called to me. The wording sounded so familiar. Where had I heard that before?

The answer came suddenly and without warning. A searing cramp ripped through my abdomen, and I doubled over, paralyzed with agony. I was lucky that most of the horses in this barn had never been sold, claimed or traded. They'd had the same affectionate grooms for years, and most were gentle and well trained. The horse stopped as I hit the ground and waited for me to get up and resume his walk. I kept a tight grip on the shank and remained in a crouch until the pain passed. When I stood up, I leaned against the barn, fighting a wave of nausea and the beginnings of a complete blackout. As I stood there, knees trembling, a warm wave passed over my foot, underneath my socks and shoes, and then the searing pain came again. A hot liquid broke in my stretch pants, and the pain seized me again. I screamed to the groom. "Juan! Come take this horse!"

The horse reared when I screamed, and Juan rushed out and snatched the shank from my hand. I dashed for the bathroom, which, miraculously, was only steps away from the corner I had been about to turn. Once inside, I pulled my slacks down to my knees and sat down on the toilet. My legs were streaked with blood, my inner thighs crimson. A flood of blood poured out of me, expelling the tampon. The pain was agony and I sat, doubled over on the toilet, for almost fifteen minutes.

Keep an eye on your nines. Had that been a warning of when the miscarriage would take place? Frank had said it just before the pain came. Something inside me had cut loose, and I was afraid to look and see what it was. When I was finally able to stand up, I stared down in horror at a huge clot of jellylike substance the size of my fist. It floated in a pool of blood while even more blood streamed down my leg. I grabbed a wad of brown paper hand towels from the rack on the wall and stuffed them between my legs. In seconds, they were drenched. I shoved them in the wastebasket and snatched another stack. I stared at the floating mass, streaked with what looked like veins. The fringes of it looked milky. Then the pain came again.

I sat back on the toilet waiting for the outpour of blood to subside. It was a half hour before I finally wadded up another batch of paper towels, stuffed them into my pants, and looked down at that bloody, vein-streaked clot. The beginning of life that had come to this end.

My eyes filled with tears. "I'm sorry," I whispered, then closed my eyes and flushed the toilet.

Conscious of my blood-soaked pants, I stepped out into the air and made my way back to the corner where Juan's stalls were. I hoped I wouldn't have to explain.

Juan had already stalled his horse and was sitting on the tack box waiting for me to return. He had a steaming Styrofoam cup of coffee sitting there for me beside his own, both cooling on the rail. He didn't speak great English, but he wasn't blind. He took one look at my pants and my belly and then looked into my eyes.

"Bambino." I pointed to my stomach and the obvious blood on my pants. His eyes widened with instant understanding.

"You go home," he said. "I tell Lopez." He rocked his arms to show he understood and then pointed to my stomach. "Hospital. You drive car?"

"Yes, but—"

"I finish up." Juan gestured toward the shedrow and the sand around the hotwalking machine. "I tell Lopez. You go."

Bonnie had a carton of extra Kotex pads from her post-delivery days. After showering and changing to a third pad, I tearfully told Bonnie what had happened at the track. Bonnie listened, her eyes a mixture of fear and worry.

"Do you want me to drive you to the hospital?"

"No...shit...it's overflowing again. Excuse me. Could you call Mark? I can't pick him up today."

The pads were drenching in a matter of minutes between changes. There were only four left, so Bonnie ran up to the 7-Eleven for more boxes.

Each trip to the bathroom resulted in another stream of watery blood into the toilet. When Pammy came in at five, Bonnie filled her in as I sat on the toilet, sick with pain and even sicker at the loss of the special child. The loss that Devin had predicted. Sick, in fact, at the loss of everything. I was running a fever and spent the rest of the day and night under blankets, teeth chattering and drenched in sweat.

There could be no coincidence to this. It had happened just two days after I'd admitted to Devin that I was pregnant, and one day after my journey "home."

Did Devin have that kind of communication with *them*? Had *they* caused the termination of this baby? Or had *they* already known and merely tried to prepare me for the fact that it would have to be taken... that it simply *had* to be.

The bleeding lasted eleven days, and even after the heavy gushing had subsided, the watery discharge continued through the month that followed.

Keep an eye on your nines, the female voice had whispered so clearly the night before. The miscarriage had erupted only seconds after Frank had called that same sentence out to me.

On Saturday, February 22nd, the evening of the miscarriage, I made the final entry into my journal, and it contained only three words. They seemed somehow appropriate.

It is finished.

16 It was only then that I began to give serious thought to writing this story down. An event like this with a beginning, a middle and an abrupt tragic ending must have happened for a reason. The minute details of the past few months were branded into my memory. Had this drama only been enacted…staged…in order for me to realize where I was from? So I would know beyond the shadow of a doubt that there really was such a place? A place among scads of others that overlapped the physical dimension here? So that I would know that other forms of consciousness could enter this world here under the right conditions?

I now knew that his world existed. That he really did come from a place beyond the time-space continuum here. He'd told me that *his* world had more names and legends than the legendary Hell. Someone should put this story on paper, but I wasn't sure I could remember every sequence of events exactly as each had happened, or even if I had the talent to tie them together into book form. I wasn't a writer.

At ten o'clock the following evening I put the radio on and sat down for the guidance I needed, guidance only *he* could give. Well, him and the radio.

Fear of phasing out, as I had come to call it, was gone—had vanished with the child—but going *home* was still not as simple as walking into the next room. Not that I was in any hurry to go back there now. I had, however, become an expert at dropping into alpha for a starting point, so I began the process of slowing my body rhythms down and raising my vibrations. When I knew I was in the right receptive state I waited for a sign.

A song by Ken Hensley, member of Uriah Heep, came on the radio. He told how he had finally started thinking, and his hands began to write, and his dreams answered his calls. He wondered if he'd been wasting his mind. He said when visions opened up for him he grew cold. Restraints of time had burst, so he gathered everything he had and looked at everything that had happened. It made him sad.

Was this a message from him?

Thoughts began to hit me, simultaneously with that heat wave of air I'd grown to associate with his absolute presence. *The Bible* had its version of God's story. Where was the book that told the other side of the story? Where was the book that truthfully explained the nature of the reality that people here erroneously called Hell?

He had tried to do it with music. Those ten tapes were vital. Not only had he managed to complete them before he left, but he had firmly believed that mass production of them as a unit would actually make people sit up and listen. Ponder the meaning of the lyrics. These thoughts, combined with the warmth that flooded my body as I sat in trance, could only be coming from one source.

Could it really be that he *wanted* this book to be written?

At midnight, I went back to the September notebooks, back to when the whole thing had begun. After viewing the entire event as a whole, and with the bleeding still pouring from my swollen womb and the pain still burning inside, I picked up a new tablet and a pen.

Chapter 1

It had all started the day that book had arrived. *UFOs: Operation Trojan Horse.* So that was where I began the story. My hand never stopped writing as the memory of that day reenacted before my mind's eye like a miniature movie. The steady wave of warm air increased as I wrote, and I knew that what I was doing was okay with *him.*

I needed to record it exactly the way it had happened. No exaggerations and nothing omitted. Once I started, I felt driven to write it all down. I was the only one qualified to do it. The only one who knew the whole story.

Two days after the bleeding began, just three days after my conversation with Devin Drew, Kelly called me.

"Guess who quit his job."

I didn't have to guess. When I didn't respond, she went on.

"That's not all. He split for Mexico without a goodbye to anyone. It's the major rumor all over the plant."

"Are you sure?"

"Well, sure as Tim Lipton announcing it to everyone."

I hung up feeling dazed. Mexico. He had always talked about going, at least back in the early days before we had gotten together. Trevor had been included in those plans back then. They had planned to live in the wild and off the land. Then Mia had come along and the plans had ended. I picked up my journal and recorded the date. I didn't know why it even mattered to me. Maybe because it put the blanket of finality over everything. I was on my own for sure now.

As that thought hit me, the heat came again, not just to my foot or ankle but spreading over my entire body.

Well, not quite on my own.

A song came on the radio, and I recognized Grace Slick's voice singing about corners in time and advising listeners that "anyone can go."

I looked up to the top of the corner where Blue quivered and flashed, seeming to beckon me to follow him with his very brilliance. I watched him vanish into the triangular point where the two walls met the ceiling.

Never mind Devin Drew, he seemed to be saying. Come with me. Don't be afraid. Follow me.

I moved up to the corner and sat facing it, my face almost touching the cold walls. Grace continued to wail. Anyone can go. A feeling of indifference to Devin Drew swept over me, coupled with a sense of peace and serenity. Through my closed eyes, I saw the hole, and Blue, further away now, hovering at the rim.

After only a few seconds of hesitation, I followed him.

17 To say that psychic phenomena picked up in the house during the months that followed would be the understatement of the century.

I didn't go back to the track. *He* had promised me that I would not have to work, and that was now proving to be true. When I wasn't phasing out, I was putting full time into writing. It would be interesting to see how I was going to continually manage without an income. My rent and utilities alone came to more than four hundred a month, but for some reason I just wasn't worried about it.

In March, an income tax refund arrived, and my bills were covered as if I were still working. I even had a few extra bucks to pick up some books that *he* had loosely recommended.

While browsing through books at the occult shop, I found a page of so-called demonic signatures which had supposedly appeared throughout recorded history at one time or another. I remembered what Devin had said about those marks on my arm being similar to something he had seen in one of his books, so I scanned the page, looking them over. The book was Huson's *Mastering Witchcraft*, the same book Devin had asked for during the last days and had gone straight to the chapters on psychic self-defense when handed the book. My finger paused at one of the signatures, and my heart almost stopped.

There, before my eyes, was the mark on my arm that was still as clear as it had been the day it arrived. The name printed under the demonic signature was *Asmodeus*.

I wondered what Devin Drew would have to say if he saw this. Now I wished we *had* looked it up back when this very book had been in the house. Since I was already in the bookshop, I did some checking into the legends behind this demon. Keeping in mind the distortions *he* had warned me about, I was almost amused to see so many conflicting statements about him, but all the books agreed that he was best known for his help in constructing Solomon's temple.

Apparently, he'd been summoned by King Solomon, who was able to invoke him with a ring given to him by Saint Michael, a ring with a powerful pentacle. Using this ring, Solomon was able to hold Asmodeus in bondage and force him to help build the temple. Solomon then taunted him because he, a mortal man, was able to control a demon. Asmodeus told the king to give him the magic ring, and he would prove how powerful he actually was. The minute the ring touched the demon's hand he was able to fling the king far away from Jerusalem and take over as ruler of Israel, masquerading as King Solomon for some time. He was often depicted with three heads, and one medieval writer described meeting Asmodeus in Egypt, a country that supposedly adored him.

In spite of the obvious distortions and fabrications, there were some things that struck home. Devin had worn the ring of Solomon, and Trevor's daughter had given Michelle a smaller version. St. Michael… Erick?…had given the ring to King Solomon, which enabled him to *summon* Asmodeus and enlist his help. Using the ring, Devin had summoned Asmodeus, who then turned the tables and enlisted *Devin's* help. Asmodeus was able to use the ring to take over the life of King Solomon for a while. *He* was able to use the ring to take over Devin's life for a while. Then there was the depiction of the demon having three heads. Devin had three personalities, not counting *him*. Finally, the mention of Asmodeus and Egypt, which seemed to tie the jackal's eye ring to the supposed demon as well. Jackals were associated with the god Anubis who stood guard over the dead pharaohs and guided them across to the other side.

Yes, what *would* Devin have to say about all this?

Material necessities, and even some luxuries began to roll in.

A neighbor gave the girls bicycles that looked new. I had never been able to afford bikes on my salary at work. When I found myself with no gas in the car, I received a call from an old friend—someone I had once worked for as a secretary at his towing garage. I mentioned my predicament, not just the gas, but a leaking radiator. He told me he'd called because he wanted to pay me a visit, that he had some things I might be able to use. He promised to bring welding equipment so he could fix my radiator while he was there.

Bruce arrived at seven with the repair equipment and a five-gallon can of gas. He was also carrying a large cardboard box full of frozen meats and vegetables.

"A friend of mine loaded me up from a deal he'd gotten from one of those places you get things in bulk. Too much for his freezer and too much for mine. I don't know why I thought of you, but I'm glad I did. Now, where's that heap of yours?"

Chris and Steve peered out their window as he went to work. He'd brought portable lights that lit up the area where he was working. I watched from my front steps in awe, contemplating this miracle.

Steve, on his way out to the trashcan, passed me and shook his head. "You're the only chick I know that gets house calls from mechanics, and after hours to boot. How do you rate?"

Bruce was finished with the welding in an hour. After emptying the gas into my tank, he asked if I could use a couple eight-track tapes he had in his glove box. Both were Moody Blues, and I recognized the titles from Devin's ten tapes. When I told him I had nothing to play them on, he smiled and assured me that that would change soon.

Two days later, I received a call from a groom who'd worked at the racetrack with me. His barn was leaving for a meet in another state, and he was trying to lighten his travel load. Could I use a good stereo? Practically brand new. Had a great radio, record player, and even an eight-track player.

Could I use it? I could have kissed him. I didn't even have to pick it up. He delivered it.

April produced *another* income tax refund, a back payment from a shortage in the first one. I had figured my income tax incorrectly, and the government had corrected my return. I paid the bills, stocked the house with more food, and put the rest in checking.

Furniture began to arrive. Word must have gotten out at the racetrack that my house was pretty bare, and the phone started ringing. There were others leaving for that same meet as my friend with the stereo, and none of them could take their furniture with them for the permanent relocation. Mandy and Michelle received a brand new set of bunk beds. My living room completely refurnished itself. I now had a beautiful gold velvet couch with high throne-like backs behind each seating area. Matching chairs and lamps filled the room. The house was beginning to take shape.

Juan, my savior the day of the miscarriage, stopped up to see how I was doing and noted that the walls could use a fresh coat of paint. He left and came back with enough paint for all the rooms and proceeded to pull out and cover the new furniture. He wouldn't even let me help.

He even painted my bookshelves with red and black enamel and, at my request, placed a pentagram on each corner. I now had almost as many books as Devin had taken when he left.

The interior of my home had been completely transformed.

Juan left enough red enamel paint to give me an idea. I had always wanted to paint something on that heavy desktop we had saved when we got rid of the desk. I decided that the Tarot card, The Magician, would be perfect. I had always associated that card with *him*.

I used the red paint to completely cover the wood. After it dried, I brought out my oils and added the rest of the image. I had never been good at faces, so I screwed it up enough times that I turned the paintbrush around and, using the wooden tip, sketched the outline of the head and face into the wet paint. Then I picked up another brush.

With no warning, I dropped into a trance state, and my hand took off, shaking though it was, until *his* face began to take shape. My hand didn't stop until the black fishing cap was placed on his head, completing the image.

Then I dropped the brush and sat back in shock, staring at it. *How?*

The door opened and the girls burst in, excited from their day at school.

"Mommy! You painted *Devin*!" Michelle squealed.

"How did you do that?" Mandy asked from behind Michelle, her expression reflecting the wonder that I felt.

George's reaction was the same.

"Pretty good likeness of Devin," he said, staring at the five-foot painting.

I knew that it looked no more like Devin Drew than I did. Oh, maybe a little like Devin, a little bit of Erick and a little like Christian. All in all, it seemed to represent the combined unit of *him*.

It was time to put some new pictures on these walls. In no time at all, the house was covered in paintings. It was really looking like a home now, albeit a strange home. There was no resemblance to the vacancy Devin had created when he'd moved out.

I continued to write, and when I wasn't bent over the tablet, I was entranced in the shadowy half-world of the hole, basking in the glow of his presence as yet another chapter would be shown to me like a tiny movie.

Actually getting *through* the hole was not as simple. It only took the slightest doubt to send me reeling backwards, away from the entrance at the top, which somehow brought me up to the rim. Sometimes hours would go by before I'd come to, unable to remember what, if anything, had taken place.

I didn't always return with no memory. Once he took me to a bookstore and showed me the completed book that I had put so many hours into each day. I removed it from the shelf and thumbed through it. None of the names had been changed. I wondered why the real names were printed. Wasn't it customary to change names for publication?

On another occasion, I had the opportunity to sit down with him *there*, in that big white mansion, while he explained to me the reason he'd had to leave, why he'd been so distraught, and why he couldn't have told me these things at that time.

His revelations rendered me mute. As he talked, I completely understood why he had been so withdrawn and silent that last week. I hugged him and thanked him for the explanation. I was so grateful to finally know what had really been on his mind. I told him I would never forget what he'd told me.

He had sighed. "You will. I'm only telling you now while you're here, so you'll understand, but when you go back, there will be no memory of anything I've said. I hope you understand, but you just can't take it back with you."

Sure enough, when I returned to this reality, I did remember the visit with him and the entire conversation...minus those forbidden facts. It was just as well. I doubted I would even have understood them in my usual world.

The trips in and out taught me that this world I called earth was nothing more than a classroom, and that I had a far richer, greater homeland that I also existed in. I began to understand the nature of time and space here and the total absence of it there. I also began to understand that I'd come here for a reason, and I was spending far too much time phasing out instead of living life here in this world. Somewhat akin to enrolling in college, and then spending your entire school day calling home instead of learning the lessons you signed up for.

My experiences pushed me further into books, no longer on possession and demonology, but of consciousness and awareness. Jane Robert's book, *Seth Speaks*...well, Seth's book, actually, finally shed some light on what I'd been doing, where I'd been going, and how I'd been getting there. His sequel, *The Nature of Personal Reality*, was a handbook for physical existence.

When I wasn't reading, I continued to write, plugging away at this book day after day. The only mar in my blissful existence was an infection that had developed since my miscarriage. I couldn't bring myself to go to a doctor. I hoped it would heal in time by itself.

Pam joined the racetrack world with Tank in March, and Bonnie and Jake found their own apartment. I was left with only Blue and the kids, my sole house companions.

The manifestations and miracles are far too outrageous to list here. Physical commodities appeared out of nowhere. If I needed shampoo, it arrived as a free sample in the mailbox. Everything I listed on my needs list manifested in one way or another. When I wanted to take the girls to a movie, someone gave me tickets. Books continually were donated by friends and even from strangers, through friends.

Ethan stopped by one day to drop off the book he'd been so wrapped up in while he lived at Daniel's. *A Separate Reality*. This book was a lot wilder than the one *I* was writing, and I didn't wonder about my sanity after I read *it*. If Carlos Castaneda could write a book like this, why couldn't I? Mine was tame in comparison.

The message in all of these books was the same. There *is* life in other worlds. Invisible worlds.

What had happened to the ten tapes?

Pam suggested a trip to Trevor's house. If *anyone* had them, she was sure it would be Trevor, or he'd at least know who did. Rumor had it that Devin had disbanded everything he owned when he'd left.

We hadn't seen Trevor since Christmas, and I was surprised I was able to even find his house. On March 26th, a few days before Pam and Tank's racetrack outfit shipped out for the out-of-state meet, we paid Trevor and Mia a visit.

Their attitudes were strained, as though my very presence was a painful reminder of their once close friend. Yes, Devin was living in Mexico, Trevor confirmed. Just got a postcard from him. Used a general delivery address. Didn't want anyone to know exactly where he was. Including Trevor.

The ten tapes? Scattered like everything else. Gerald's in all probability. He'd bought all the musical equipment. The paintings, books…Puff…all scattered. Given away. The decision had been reached on one of Devin's full moon meetings.

Had he seemed okay before he left? Well, as okay as could be expected under the circumstances.

Would they stop by sometime? Oh, sure. One of these days.

The visit had been a dismal failure. Either Trevor blamed me for his brother's departure, or he couldn't talk freely in front of Mia. Or maybe he just wasn't talking, period.

Gerald also made his position clear when Pammy called him to ask about possibly purchasing the ten tapes. The phone went dead in her ear. No doubt, I was the enemy here, too.

Shortly after our attempts to locate the original ten tapes, it soon became evident that I didn't need human sources to recreate them. By accident or design, they began to assemble themselves. Bonnie went through her album collection and turned up quite a few that I recognized when she played samples from them. She donated those to the cause.

I browsed record shops, new and used, and found myself drawn to certain album covers that looked like they *could* be part of the ten tapes, and I recognized the songs the instant I put the albums on at home.

Moody Blues, Uriah Heep and Pink Floyd were all a given. It didn't matter which album I purchased. All the groups had many albums, and all the albums had songs I recognized from those reels. Not only was the house looking like he was still around, it was beginning to *sound* like it too.

As the stack of albums and tapes grew, so too did this book. Uncannily, the albums seemed to arrive about the time I was at a certain chapter or event in the book, as if providing a soundtrack to my words.

As I continued to "phase out" for the next chapter and return to put the vision on paper, I was often amazed at the memories I'd been shown. Events and conversations I'd forgotten. The most insignificant details were replayed before my mind's eye in those little movie memories. As I wrote, I was often suspicious that even the words were not coming from me. The deeper I delved into the story, books would present themselves with scientific and metaphysical explanations as backup research tools.

In my research, I discovered that, just as he'd told me, all frames of references seemed to originate from the same source. Whether I was reading about religious miracles, UFOs, mediums in trance states, prophetic dreams, or messages from God delivered to nuns and priests during prayer, the messages all seemed to be coming from the same source. It seemed that the only difference between what certain UFO contactees had been told and the messages delivered to trance mediums was the frame of reference these people were using. Devin had not been deep into UFO research, or he might have contacted an "alien from space," but the contact would still have been *him*.

He'd told me all of this once, but I had refused to believe. He had told me the truth all the way down the line.

With continual contact with him during my ten o'clock appointments, I made it through the creation of this book with no job and no income. My wants and needs were always met in one way or another.

Pam's outfit left in April, and Uncle Joe implored me to take over as housekeeper and temporary mother for his children. Because he was a fireman, it would only require one twenty-four-hour period every third day. He promised to cover my rent, utilities, and necessities and assured me that it would still be cheaper for him than hiring a stranger to take the position. I agreed to help, and for the next five months I lived in peace and ease, purchasing tapes, albums and books, and still had plenty of free time to continue my research, appointments with him, and the book.

By July, when even Chris ceased to question the arrival of the monthly rent, I received a visit from Trevor. He was alone.

His stay was brief. Not even long enough for coffee. He only wanted to apologize for his silence and seeming rudeness the day Pam and I had stopped by. He wanted to explain.

Mia grew very distressed when the subject of Devin was mentioned. She had watched his personality change after *he* had left and was horrified by what had happened. Trevor wanted to assure me that he and Mia had had nothing to do with the way things had turned out. When I asked him if he had been aware of all the facets of Devin, he paused and looked down at the floor. Then he cautiously admitted that he had been completely aware of exactly what had been going on. Remembering how he'd gone with the flow every time a different personality had emerged when we were all together, I knew the question had really been unnecessary.

By mid-July, I knew that the infection caused by the miscarriage was not going to heal by itself. The bleeding had never completely stopped so I finally, reluctantly, made an appointment with a doctor.

After the exam, the doctor asked me if I had recently lost a child. I admitted that I had and that I had not had a D&C. He gave me a strong penicillin shot and some backup pills, advised douching with Betadine, and also with vinegar and water twice a day. If this treatment did not clear up the problem, I was to come back to schedule the procedure.

Well, at least I'd finally gotten a doctor's verification that I had been pregnant. Not that I'd needed it. The shot and pills did clear everything up, and I was relieved that I wouldn't have to return.

I sorely missed Puff, that little flashing dragon lamp. When the kids brought home a paper mâché project from school, it gave me an idea.

It only took five minutes and several wire hangers to bend the dragon's body into shape. I secured the joints with Band-Aids to hold it all in place. It took another few hours to cover it completely with strips of occult and horoscope magazine pages dipped in flour paste. Uncle Joe found a white plastic globe exactly like the original Puff globe while frequenting a garage sale and dropped it off for me. George jumped in on the wiring of the board Puff would frolic on and put a layer of decoupage on it to make it shine.

Puff was taking shape.

Kelly kept me informed of the Sparklear gossip weekly and one day, toward the end of July, she called to announce Devin's return. Not only was he back in town, but he was working at the plant again. Delivering specials.

It was with an achingly familiar chest pain that I dialed the company's number, hoping to be able to say hello and welcome him back.

Pat took the call and told me Devin was out on the truck. He promised to give him the message when he came in.

When Devin called, I couldn't believe the change in his voice. Older, more resigned, and slightly impersonal. Yes, he was back at the plant, he said, but he didn't plan to stay long, even though Tim had offered him his old supervisor job back. It wasn't the same, he assured me, and I was lucky to have gotten out when I did.

Even though he sounded more serious than the original Devin I remembered from the early days at the plant, he still sounded even more together than he had the last time I'd talked to him. I asked him if he would stop up to visit. He said he would try, but that he was getting ready to leave the state again. Heading north. He wasn't sure when, but he would try to come by before he left.

When he asked how I was doing, I told him the truth. I said he ought to stop by just to see the house, that he wouldn't recognize it. Again, he promised to try, but from the sound of his voice, I doubted that he would.

Mark visited often on weekends, and one day, in the process of dropping him off, Lola and I bumped into each other. Her attitude had changed. She wasn't mad at me anymore, but she admitted she still felt hurt at the way I had quit. She simply couldn't understand what could have been so bad that I couldn't have explained it to her. She felt we'd been friends too long for me to have pulled a stunt like that.

I presented her with the first twenty chapters of my book and told her to see if she had an idea by the time she was finished reading them what I'd been dealing with. Maybe she would realize the state of mind I'd been in that day.

The next time I saw her, again in transporting Mark, she handed the notebooks back.

"Kerry, I finally have an idea what you were going through, and I must say it certainly is a strange story. But how in God's name could you possibly have remembered all that stuff? I read parts of the office segments to Kelly, and she said you must have had a tape recorder in your purse to be able to detail our conversations so exactly. Reading this was like watching a movie of the past. Even *I* didn't remember that stuff until I read it, and then it all came back to me. It was so accurate."

I promised to deliver her the full story when it was finished.

I received an unexpected visit one evening from Charlie, the general manager of the plant. The bookkeeper, Maurice—Mussolini to us at one time—was with him. I was startled to see them standing at the door when I opened it. It was after 9 o'clock, and my appointment with *him* was at ten.

They only had a few questions for me. Would I tell them what had happened to Devin? They recounted the early days, the changes in his physical appearance back then, and how he'd seemed to become someone else completely different. They brought up Devin's amazing healing of the sixteen stitches over that three-day period and wanted to know how he'd been able to do that. They noted that I still wore the ring and pentagram and that I appeared to be at some kind of peace with myself. Surely, I could answer these questions for them.

I told them I couldn't.

They said they'd heard I was writing a book.

I said yes, I'd heard that rumor, too.

Always searching for knowledge and answers, I signed up for two mind-control seminars. One at the Psychic Science Institute and one at Silva Mind Control. After a month and a half of their training, I realized it had all been a waste of money. They had nothing to teach me that I didn't already know. I continued the meetings only because the idea of an alternate reality didn't faze the instructors one bit, and I felt more comfortable among the kind of people who were even attracted to these types of classes. Eventually the instructors of both institutions asked me to assist in teaching the classes.

The house was filled with music again, and the Moody Blues were singing about how lovely it was to see their friend again when the knock came at the door. When I glanced out the window, I saw a very serious Devin standing there in company uniform. The blue-and-white truck was parked outside the gate in the dirt.

18

I was on the phone with the aura teacher from PSI, making arrangements for the class, when I heard the knock.

"Hold on, someone's at the door," I told Woody, "and I might have to call you back."

When I opened the door, I was eye level with the white uniform shirt and the Sparklear logo. Looking up, I met Devin's eyes, nervous, so completely unprepared for this.

He smiled. "You going to invite me in?" He seemed a little uncomfortable too, but he looked great. Healthy. Rested.

"Of course," I said, opening the door wide for him. "I have someone on the phone, but I can call him back."

For all the self-control and confidence I'd acquired at PSI, it had only taken this moment to throw me back to stuttering and self-consciousness. While I concluded the call, Devin was walking around the living room examining the house wordlessly, staring at the new paint, furniture, stereo system, books, albums and paintings. When I finally replaced the receiver to give my full attention to him, he was transfixed in front of the magician I'd painted on the desktop.

"Who was that on the phone?" he asked, his eyes still on the painting.

"Oh, some psychic training place. PSI."

"PSI? What's that stand for?"

"Psychic Science Institute."

Devin walked over to the table I kept in the corner for my writing. "Incorporated?" he asked.

"Well, yeah, I guess it is. But…it's something to do. Somewhere to go and a way to be useful. There are a lot of people out there that are as confused as I once was."

He frowned. "Incorporated. Shit. Some worthy cause. I suppose they charge people. I'm surprised you got mixed up with something like that."

"At least I'm around conscious people, Devin, or people learning to be. I can't live in that human world out there."

He smiled. "Yeah. Tell me about it."

He walked back over to the magician painting and looked at it searchingly. I knew what he was wondering, and I half smiled myself. At one time, this kind of mind reading was actually magic to me.

"I didn't have anything to do with the head," I offered. "I had a little unasked-for help."

He nodded, as though he knew exactly what kind of help I'd had. "I was going to *say* ! Why didn't you finish it though? It needs an eternity sign over the…uh…cap here."

That black Greek fishing cap wasn't part of the original Tarot card and he knew it. "I haven't touched it since that day. I will, though, one of these days."

"What's this?" He nodded at the new Puff, all boarded and wired and almost ready for painting. The head was still incomplete.

"Oh, I just really missed yours, so I decided to make my own. I'm kind of glad you dropped by. I've been racking my brain, and I just can't remember what Puff's head looked like. "How did they put the eyes in?"

He turned and looked at me. "Ping-pong balls cut in half. You just form the paper mâche mix around them, and they come out like lizard's eyes. They actually have a mix on the market for detail work like facial features and muscle tone." He looked back at Puff and smiled again. "Pretty good likeness. Pretty good memory. You'd better get some ears on that sucker, though."

"Oh, he *did* have ears, huh? I wasn't sure."

Devin raised both index fingers to his temples. "Doberman ears. Like this."

He stooped down to examine my album and tape collection and began flipping through them. He didn't comment on the difference in my musical taste from when he'd first met me.

Then suddenly it hit me. Who else but Devin himself would be able to give me the missing albums—the ones I needed to complete the Ten Tapes. "Devin, I've been trying to reassemble those ten tapes again. I hope you can help me. Do you think you could go through my collection and tell me which albums I *don't* have?"

He squinted, then looked at me curiously. "Ten? There were only three reels."

Now I was the one who squinted. "Uh-uh, Devin. He always referred to the collection as the Ten Tapes. Even when there were only eight or nine. I saw them with my own eyes, stacked up by the recorder that last day and on New Year's Eve."

He shrugged. "Maybe so."

Why didn't he remember?

"If you could just take what's here and separate the albums you recognize from the ones you don't...it would really be helpful."

"Well, I can try."

He began to separate the tapes and albums into two piles, and I was stunned to see him put Uriah Heep's *Demons and Wizards* in the "no" pile. I simply could not believe it. If there was one album and *only* one album I could swear to, it was that one. He *couldn't* have ruled it out, but he did.

My hopes fell. I was so sure he'd be able to supply all the missing albums and artists. "Never mind, Devin. But maybe you'd remember that last one. The one played over and over on New Year's Eve. You remember? You and Gerald got into a hassle over how many times you played it, and even later that night, back in your room, *he* was adding it to the reel."

He rubbed his eyes with thumb and forefinger. "That was...Dr. John...I'm sure of that. It was a title something like...*The Moon, the Stars and the Sun*...or...no...*The Sun, the Moon, and the Herbs*. That's it, I think. The album cover has the words *The Night Tripper* on it."

"You're positive?"

He gave me a look that dared me to contradict the memory of that album...and that last final night.

"Okay, are there any more you're positive of? Please...it's very important."

"Got a tablet? I'll write down what I can remember."

I couldn't move fast enough. "Here."

He sat there contemplating, and then wrote in Devin Drew's own ticket print:

Moody Blues: Seventh Sojourn. Threshold of a Dream.

Deep Purple: ?
Dr. John: Sun, Moon, and Herbs

Then he laid the pen and tablet down. "Those are the ones I'm positive of. The Deep Purple...I can't remember anything about the album cover or title. You'll figure it out."

"Thanks, Devin. Especially for that New Year's Eve one."

He rose and looked at the wall paintings for a while. I watched him go from picture to picture, then return to The Magician again. As if trying to remember something. He raised his eyebrows at me, a questioning look, then moved to another painting.

"How about this one? The demon riding the horse of fire? Black background. I see you have a full moon here."

I smiled. "You know who that is, Devin."

He nodded. "Yeah. I know."

I felt a sudden impulse to give it to him. He was gazing at it so longingly. "Devin, you can have that one if you want."

He took one last look at it. "No, you keep it. It would only get ruined as transient as I am. I just hope you appreciate that one."

"It was an accident, how it came out. Oh, not like The Magician. I didn't receive any help, but it was still pure accident. I was putting fire on the horse's mane and tail, and the brush slipped. The rider came out like the entity on the big picture we gave to Daniel and Julie."

He walked over to the bookshelf and scanned more books than he'd ever had. "Got a new batch, I see."

"Yeah, I needed them, as confused as I was in January. Reading helped me keep my sanity." When he didn't comment, I decided to change the subject to something he was more comfortable with. "Want some coffee?"

He smiled as if remembering, and accepted.

When I came in with it I sat down on the floor beside my new chair that he'd chosen to sit in. "So, how do you like working at the water hole again after all this time?"

He laughed. "They actually want to make me a supervisor again. I don't know, though. It's kind of lost its charm after everything that went down. I don't want the job, and I won't be staying at the company. Like I said, I'm getting ready to go up north."

"I could probably get my old job back if I really wanted it," I said. "Lola is speaking to me again, and I hear they need help."

"You probably could. I've heard those rumors too, but you don't want to go back there, Kerry. Fuck, I'm getting out. It's never the same. You can never go back."

I knew he wasn't just talking about the job. "You're probably right. When are you planning to go?"

"It depends on some friends of mine. When they get here. I'll be going with them."

It crossed my mind that Devin was finally going back to his wife. She was up north. He had taken her there last Thanksgiving. Before he'd moved in with me. A wave of relief swept over me. Devin's life was going back to what it had been back then, and it was probably just what he needed.

"How about old Blue?" he asked, snapping me out of my thoughts. "Ever see him? I see him once in a while, when I least expect to."

"I'm not surprised. He was always a friend of both of ours."

"You still write?"

I had to smile. I pulled out four journals and tossed them on the coffee table.

"I still write too," he said. "But not like I used to." He paused for a long moment as if wondering if he should ask the next question. Finally, "How about *him*?"

I pondered over whether I should tell him. Finally, I chose a neutral way of putting it. "He's always here, Devin."

"You're telling me you go out on full moons?"

"No, I don't need to do that. I just sit down at ten o'clock like I always did."

For a minute, Devin looked upset. "How did you…man, I just can't believe that *he's* what you're communicating with, Kerry." He glanced around the room skeptically. "I mean, there's no *doubt* that *something* is taking care of you. You're not even working! So that's pretty obvious. But *him*? I just can't see how it can be *him*. Shit! *I* can't even contact him without the rituals and candles and incantations. You know, you just don't call someone like him like you do with a telephone."

"Devin, you don't need to go through all that to connect with him. You just think you do. And as for who's taking care of me, I know it's him. He has ways of showing me who he is."

"Does he look anything like me?"

I almost laughed. "No."

His expression changed somewhat.

"And by the way," I added, "I was pregnant but I lost it, just like you predicted."

He looked at me with a frown. Apparently, he hadn't received this news.

"Back in February," I added, "so…"

"I knew they'd never let you keep it."

He looked up at the *horse and demon* painting again. "Well, I'm not convinced it's him, but it can't be dangerous…whoever you're dealing with, I mean. If it was going to hurt you, it would have done it by now. You're obviously being taken care of by someone who loves you. That's pretty obvious."

"Why do you think it isn't him?"

"I just don't think it is. Because of what I have to do, just to talk to him. Maybe I'm wrong. But, well, there is one way to find out. One thing that would convince me. Do me a favor, will you? Drop a name on *him* for me. Drop the name *Asmodeus*. I'd like to hear his reaction to that."

Asmodeus. The name of the so-called demon whose mark was on my arm.

"Why would that convince you?" I asked.

"That would prove to me whether or not it's really *him*."

I considered, then rejected the idea of telling him about what I'd learned about the mark on my arm. Devin had just answered his own question to me.

A Quicksilver song began on the radio, *Just for Love,* and while I'd heard this song before, it had new meaning today. I would hear every word of the songs he would sing to me, they sang. Someone would touch me softly, and it would be him. Someone would call my name, and I was to go to *him*, free as the wind. These things could only happen once in someone's life and would only matter if I had the time. Just when the song seemed to be over, it started again, saying almost as an afterthought…that all the songs had been sung, and our love had won over all masquerades. Charades were over. He said he loved me three times in succession before the song ended. I had chills as the song played out. I don't think Devin even noticed, but it was all I needed to hear to put a period to this whole event.

When I walked him to the truck, I studied him with scrutiny. I had some feeling for him, but exactly what, I wasn't sure. Maybe it was a feeling of bond at what we'd both gone through together.

When Devin stepped into his truck, he made one more promise to try to stop up before he left the state.

"Devin," I began as he started the engine and put the truck in gear.

"Yes?" He looked down at me expectantly.

"Devin…what happened to you…to us…I never had the chance to thank you for…what happened. For the part you played. For the agreement you made so that it could happen. The role you agreed to, whether consciously or not, that made it possible for him to come."

He nodded and gave me a long searching look. "Yeah," he said with a soft sigh. Sadly. "It was pretty heavy for me, too."

I never saw Devin again.

Music Bibliography by Chapter

<u>Part 1</u>

<u>Title</u> & <u>Album</u>	<u>Artist</u>	<u>Year</u>
1) *Time* Dark Side of the Moon	Pink Floyd	1973
2) *Lovely to see you Again* On the Threshold of a Dream	Moody Blues	1969
Sally Simpson Tommy	The Who	1969
3) *Money* Dark Side of the Moon	Pink Floyd	1973
4) *Dear Diary* On The Threshold of a Dream	Moody Blues	1969
5) *Dark Side of the Moon* Dark Side of the Moon	Pink Floyd	1973
6) *Tales* Magician's Birthday	Uriah Heep	1973
7) *Tubular Bells* Tubular Bells	Mike Oldfield	1973
9) *Easy livin'* Demons and Wizards	Uriah Heep	1972
10) *Eyes of a Child* To Our Children's Children's Children	Moody Blues	1969
11) *Sunrise* Magician's Birthday	Uriah Heep	1973
15) *Lost in a Lost World* Seventh Sojourn	Moody Blues	1972
Paradise/The Spell Demons and Wizards	Uriah Heep	1973

16) *Watching and Waiting* To Our Children's Children's Children	Moody Blues	1969
17) *Miles from Nowhere* Tea for the Tillerman	Cat Stevens	1970
On the Road to Find Out Tea for the Tillerman	Cat Stevens	1970
18) *Sun is Still Shining* To Our Children's Children's Children	Moody Blues	1969
19) *No Fair at All* Greatest Hits Album	The Association	1968
20) *Out of My Mind* Quicksilver	Quicksilver	1971
21) *Breathe* Dark Side of the Moon	Pink Floyd	1973

<u>Part 2</u>

1) *Dark Side of the Moon* Dark Side of the Moon	Pink Floyd	1973
The Word/ Om In Search of the Lost Chord	Moody Blues	1968
Never Comes the Day On the Threshold of a Dream	Moody Blues	1969
3) *None of Your Doing* The Second	Steppenwolf	1968
7) *Sweet Freedom* Sweet Freedom	Uriah Heep	1973
8) *Teach Your Children* Déjà Vu	Crosby, Stills, Nash &Young	1970
9) *Sweet Lorraine* Magician's Birthday	Uriah Heep	1973

10) *Stairway to Heaven* Led Zeppelin IV	Led Zeppelin	1971
12) *Born to be Wild* Steppenwolf	Steppenwolf	1968
14) *Traveler in Time* Demons and Wizards	Uriah Heep	1972
16) *Witchy Woman* Eagles	Eagles	1972
On the Way Home Four Way Street	Crosby, Stills, Nash &Young	1971
19) *You Need Love* Styx II	Styx	1973
Look at Yourself Look at Yourself	Uriah Heep	1971

Part 3

1) *Our House* 4 Way Street	Crosby, Stills, Nash &Young	1971
Beware of Darkness Everything Must Pass	George Harrison	1970
Lady Styx II	Styx	1973
I'm Just a Singer in a R&R Band Seventh Sojourn	Moody Blues	1972
2) *War of the Gods* War of the Gods	Billy Paul	1973
3) *New Horizons* Seventh Sojourn	Moody Blues	1972
The Spell Demons and Wizards	Uriah Heep	1972

4) *The Wizard* Demons and Wizards	Uriah Heep	1972
Easy Livin' Demons and Wizards	Uriah Heep	1972
Traveler in Time Demons and Wizards	Uriah Heep	1972
5) *King Without a Throne* Proud Words on a Dusty Shelf	Ken Hensley	1973
White Rabbit Surrealistic Pillow	Jefferson Airplane	1967
Magic Carpet Ride The Second	Steppenwolf	1968
6) *Can't Find My Way Home* Blind Faith	Blind Faith	1969
7) *Never Comes the Day* On the Threshold of a Dream	Moody Blues	1969
Legend of a Mind In Search of the Lost Chord	Moody Blues	1968
9) *Baby Blue* Straight Up	Badfinger	1971
Candle of Life To Our Children's Children's Children	Moody Blues	1969
11) *A Job like Mine* Tea for The Tillerman	Cat Stevens	1970
12) *Out and In* To Our Children's Children's Children	Moody Blues	1969
14) *Childhood's End* Obscured By Clouds	Pink Floyd	1972
Bad Moon Rising Green River	Creedence Clearwater Revival	1969
15) *Magician's Birthday* Magician's Birthday	Uriah Heep	1973

The Easy Road Wonderworld	Uriah Heep	1974
16) *Om* In Search of the Lost Chord	Moody Blues	1968
Thinking is the Best Way to Travel In Search of the Lost Chord	Moody Blues	1968
17) *Voices in the Sky* In Search of the Lost Chord	Moody Blues	1968
Visions of Paradise In Search of the Lost Chord	Moody Blues	1968
18) *I'm just a Singer in a R&R Band* In Search of the Lost Chord	Moody Blues	1968
20) *Are you sitting Comfortably* On the Threshold of a Dream	Moody Blues	1969
21) *I Wanna Be Free* Look at Yourself	Uriah Heep	1971

Part 4

1) *It's all over now Baby Blue* Bringing It All Back Home	Bob Dylan	1965
2) *It's all over now Baby Blue* Bringing It All Back Home	Bob Dylan	1965
3) *Procession* Every Good Boy Deserves Favor	Moody Blues	1971
4) *Gypsy* To Our Children's Children's Children	Moody Blues	1969
It's Over Straight Up	Badfinger	1971
5) *Story in Your Eyes* Every Good Boy Deserves Favor	Moody Blues	1971
One More Time to Live Every Good Boy Deserves Favor	Moody Blues	1971

6) *For My Lady* Seventh Sojourn	Moody Blues	1972
7) *Melancholy Man* A Question of Balance	Moody Blues	1970
8) *Sweet Freedom* Sweet Freedom	Uriah Heep	1973
10) *Closer to Home* Closer to Home	Grand Funk Railroad	1970
12) *Paradise/The Spell* Demons and Wizards	Uriah Heep	1972
13) *The Truth* Quicksilver	Quicksilver	1971
14) *Proud Words* Proud Words on a Dusty Shelf	Ken Hensley	1973
16) *Emily's Song* Every Good Boy Deserves Favor	Moody Blues	1971
19) *Stay* Obscured By Clouds	Pink Floyd	1972
Hellbound Train Hellbound Train	Savoy Brown	1972
20) *Ride My See-saw* In Search of the Lost Chord	Moody Blues	1968
21) *Where you at Mule* Sun, Moon and Herbs	Dr. John	1971

Part 5

1) *You Can Never Go Home Anymore* Every Good Boy Deserves Favor	Moody Blues	1971
5) *The Story in Your Eyes* Every Good Boy Deserves Favor	Moody Blues	1971

www.ingramcontent.com/pod-product-compliance
Lightning Source LLC
Chambersburg PA
CBHW052337020726
47503CB00001B/7